Nov, 1996

THE ESSENTIAL ELLISON

Happy Birthday Stevie,

Love always,
Baby

NOVELS: WEB OF THE CITY [1958]   THE SOUND OF A SCYTHE [1960]   SPIDER KISS [1961]

SHORT NOVELS: DOOMSMAN [1967]   ALL THE LIES THAT ARE MY LIFE [1980]
RUN FOR THE STARS [1991]   MEFISTO IN ONYX [1993]

GRAPHIC NOVELS: DEMON WITH A GLASS HAND (Graphic Adaptation with Marshall Rogers) [1986]
NIGHT AND THE ENEMY (Graphic Adaptation with Ken Steacy) [1987]
VIC AND BLOOD: The Chronicles of a Boy and His Dog (Adaptation with Richard Corben) [1989]

SHORT STORY COLLECTIONS: THE DEADLY STREETS [1958]
SEX GANG (as Paul Merchant) [1959]   A TOUCH OF INFINITY [1960]
CHILDREN OF THE STREETS [1961]   GENTLEMAN JUNKIE and other stories of the hung-up generation [1961]
ELLISON WONDERLAND [1962]   PAINGOD and other delusions [1965]   I HAVE NO MOUTH & I MUST SCREAM [1967]
FROM THE LAND OF FEAR [1967]   LOVE AIN'T NOTHING BUT SEX MISSPELLED [1968]
THE BEAST THAT SHOUTED LOVE AT THE HEART OF THE WORLD [1969]   OVER THE EDGE [1970]
DE HELDEN VAN DE HIGHWAY (Dutch publication only) [1973]   ALL THE SOUNDS OF FEAR (British publication only) [1973]
THE TIME OF THE EYE (British publication only) [1974]   APPROACHING OBLIVION [1974]
DEATHBIRD STORIES [1975]   NO DOORS, NO WINDOWS [1974]
HOE KAN IK SCHREEUWEN ZONDER MOND (Dutch publication only) [1977]
STRANGE WINE [1978]   SHATTERDAY [1980]   STALKING THE NIGHTMARE [1982]
ANGRY CANDY [1988]   ENSAMVÄRK (Swedish publication only) [1992]   ROUGH BEASTS [1996]   SLIPPAGE [1996]

COLLABORATIONS:
PARTNERS IN WONDER sf collaborations with 14 other wild talents [1971]
THE STARLOST #1: Phoenix Without Ashes (with Edward Bryant) [1975]
MIND FIELDS 33 stories inspired by the Art of Jacek Yerka [1994]

OMNIBUS VOLUMES: THE FANTASIES OF HARLAN ELLISON [1979]   DREAMS WITH SHARP TEETH [1991]

NON-FICTION & ESSAYS: MEMOS FROM PURGATORY [1961]
THE GLASS TEAT essays of opinion on television [1970]   THE OTHER GLASS TEAT further essays of opinion on television [1975]
THE BOOK OF ELLISON (Edited by Andrew Porter) [1978]
SLEEPLESS NIGHTS IN THE PROCRUSTEAN BED essays (Edited by Marty Clark) [1984]
AN EDGE IN MY VOICE [1985]   HARLAN ELLISON'S WATCHING [1989]   THE HARLAN ELLISON HORNBOOK [1990]

SCREENPLAYS, ETC.: THE ILLUSTRATED HARLAN ELLISON (Edited by Byron Preiss) [1978]
HARLAN ELLISON'S MOVIE [1990]   I, ROBOT: THE ILLUSTRATED SCREENPLAY (based on Isaac Asimov's story-cycle) [1994]
THE CITY ON THE EDGE OF FOREVER [1995]

RETROSPECTIVES: ALONE AGAINST TOMORROW A 10-Year Survey [1971]
THE ESSENTIAL ELLISON A 35-Year Retrospective (Ed. by Terry Dowling with Richard Delap & Gil Lamont) [1987]

AS EDITOR: DANGEROUS VISIONS (Editor) [1967]
NIGHTSHADE & DAMNATIONS: the finest stories of Gerald Kersh (Editor) [1968]
AGAIN, DANGEROUS VISIONS (Editor) [1972]   MEDEA: HARLAN'S WORLD (Editor) [1985]
THE HARLAN ELLISON DISCOVERY SERIES: STORMTRACK by James Sutherland [1975];
AUTUMN ANGELS by Arthur Byron Cover [1975]; THE LIGHT AT THE END OF THE UNIVERSE by Terry Carr [1976];
ISLANDS by Marta Randall [1976]; INVOLUTION OCEAN by Bruce Sterling [1977]

Photo by Dan Tooker

Photo by Mark Shepard

A 35-YEAR RETROSPECTIVE

EDITED AND INTRODUCED
BY TERRY DOWLING
WITH RICHARD DELAP & GIL LAMONT

PUBLISHED BY
MORPHEUS INTERNATIONAL

THE ESSENTIAL ELLISON

Published by arrangement with the Author.

Published by
MORPHEUS INTERNATIONAL
9250 Wilshire Blvd., #LL15
Beverly Hills, CA 90212
(310) 859-2557

This book is printed on acid-free paper.

Printed and Bound in the United States of America.

First Trade Paperback Edition: October 1991

Second Morpheus Printing: February 1993

Third Morpheus Printing: May 1994

Fourth Morpheus Printing: May 1995

Fifth Morpheus Printing: March 1996

ACKNOWLEDGMENTS

No project of this size and scope could have been brought to term without the skill and dedication of archivists, artisans and aides who labored long, wearily and myopically.

Mention here cannot serve but minimally to thank them for their seemingly endless chores. This book has been a long time in coming, and many of those noted here have been at the oars from the outset. But at least they know, by these meager acknowledgments, that the subject of this book does not, for a moment, delude himself that he could have done it alone.

Though Alzheimer's hasn't yet claimed the noble Author, it has been years since the inception of this project, and if anyone who deserved to be thanked here has been omitted, the blame rests with no other than You Know Who.

Sharon Buck
Sarah Coatts
James Cowan
Richard de Koning
Richard Delap
Leo & Diane Dillon
Terry Dowling
Arnie Fenner
Sharlet Foster
Jeff Frane
Todd Illig
Sandy Kamberger
Ken Keller
Gil Lamont
Andrea Levin
Jeff Levin
Jim Murray
Kathy Roché-Zujko
Jim Sanderson
Debra Spidell
Leslie Kay Swigart
Sarah Wood
Susan Ellison (wife person)

And to all the editors and anthologists, still working or no longer with us, who truly made this book possible – from Larry Shaw in 1955 to John Betancourt last week – by originally publishing the work of the creature whose true life is contained within these covers . . . many thanks.

Because they have always been there
for me, as superlative spinners of
dreams, and as steadfast friends,
this big one is for the Big Ones,

ALFIE BESTER
and
RAY BRADBURY

—H.E.

To my parents
Marie and Bill,
who will never forget
the afternoon
Harlan dropped by.

–T.D.

NOTE: All of Harlan's work appearing here derives from preferred texts. Trust these, and no others.

TABLE OF CONTENTS

· THE ESSENTIAL ·
ELLISON

Introduction: Sublime Rebel

by Terry Dowling

In 1979, Wildwood House published REBEL IN THE SOUL, Bika Reed's inspired translation of the Berlin Papyrus 3024. In her reading of this tale from around Egypt's Intermediate Period, Reed revealed for the first time the true identity of Iai, the donkey-headed god, a previously unknown aspect of the sun god Ra, and so was able to produce the first coherent translation of this marvelous initiatic text.

In Egyptian mythology, Iai is a fascinating character. He is the rebel, the tester, the stubborn resisting force of intellect and insight which donkey-like stands its ground, refusing to budge, and challenges what is accepted and valued and thought to be sensible and true. The same sort of honest irrepressible rebel, in fact, which surfaced in the child who pointed out that the Emperor wore no clothes and in the Fool who told King Lear that he was wrong. These dear precious rebels (for there are, and have been, many) not only dare to question but for their pains alienate themselves from those who haven't questioned, who didn't even think to question, who are now made to look stupid because they didn't.

The discomfiting rebels. Hypatia. Giordono Bruno. Lucy Stone. Susan B. Anthony. John T. Scopes. Oliver Wendell Holmes. Lenny Bruce. Ralph Nader. John Peter Zenger.

Harlan Ellison.

This book is a portrait of one artist as sublime Rebel.

Fortunately, it doesn't have to be just a "Best of" collection (though it does contain much of his finest work). We don't have to worry about that kind of distraction here. Rather, it is a sound representation, "warts and all," of the writing of someone who is perfectly, vigorously, cast as the Iai of his age (in response to its excesses and falterings and inertia). Through his early work, we can observe how he began, the paths he took toward his mature style, the way he conceived and pursued his task—to become a leading award-winning fantasist, a natural scholar and a more important man of letters than he'd probably care to admit.

By its nature, it is a look at process.

Though Harlan's work is widely known and applauded, not enough is made of the sense of social responsibility that is central to it. In fact, this dimension often seems to be deliberately overlooked and the major thrust of his fantasy trivialized. And when the Jester, the Trickster, the Clever Man in society is not heeded, then we have cause for real concern.

Many readers, I'm sure, wish that Harlan *was* just the gifted fantasist—merely a damn good writer. Less of Iai. But Harlan's stories invariably have their leading edge of comment, as well as their prefaces and introductions; and there are the essays and columns. So there *is* nowhere to hide.

And consequently, Harlan becomes an enemy of the people in the sense that Ibsen meant it. He cannot—will not—suffer fools gladly. He hates stupidity, bigotry, prejudice, the torpor that will not allow healthy change—the gratuitous abuses committed through ignorance no less than the willful kind. He believes—and rightly, too—that everyone is entitled to an opinion *only* if it is an informed one, that we have an obligation to educate ourselves, to be the best version of ourselves that we can possibly be.

But then Harlan is determinedly on the side of civilization, of the sort of healing Jung anticipated when he said: "As any change must begin somewhere, it is the single individual who will experience it and carry it through."

Human society has not treated its Renaissance men and women well—its natural scholars, its trailblazers, its healers who surface as rebels. For, ironically, they are most often the mavericks, the loners, the free radicals, the ones who are innately drawn to challenge and extend and purge society, never just serve it. Little wonder that the ones who keep the wounds raw and the questions alive are neutralized by a conspiracy of indifference, effectively spayed by critical indignation. Envy, fear and guilt muddy up the clear waters of common sense where these catalysts and healers are concerned, and instead, due respect, due recognition come to take on the trappings of a witch hunt.

For lies, rumor and misunderstanding have always been weapons against the Rebel, the only way the exposed ones can retaliate; distorting the picture we get of Iai. The more precise and effective he becomes, the more distortion is used as a defense.

We mustn't let it happen with Harlan, though we should always remember why it does.

Jiminy Cricket and Zorro are Harlan's role models, not Torquemada, not Jack the Ripper, not Richard Nixon.

And since indifference is another time-hallowed weapon for neutralizing the Rebel, just look at the tools Harlan uses—has to use—to accomplish his task: shock, surprise and grotesquerie, violence and suffering, hard language, hard knocks and the even harder emotions of fear, anger, guilt, pain and love. He deals in ideas, sometimes so full of love and compassion that they stun with their simple honesty; sometimes set with barbs and hooks that catch and tear and make us gasp and make us feel.

And he deals in excitement. Even without the wonderful story notes Harlan provides (he is still one of the most self-revealed authors in the language today), we sense *that* most of all—an underlying excitement at observing and rendering life. Honestly.

Dr. Johnson would have been proud. Shakespeare (a great maker of Rebels and Fools) would have smiled fondly. Because that's the dimension of achievement occurring here. Ellison is as close to the pulse of his age as Chaucer and Shakespeare and Dickens ever came to theirs.

It's worth pointing out that, as with so many of the truly great, so many of the natural healers and civilizers, Harlan has no choice in this matter. He cannot stop being enraged, being provoked, being moved to speak; cannot help but stand up and be counted. He would have stood on the steps of the ancient library at Alexandria and fought against the mob with their torches, single-handedly if necessary, while the librarians used their arguments and lofty persuasions to achieve nothing.

Typical behavior of Iai, *agent provocateur* to civilization, bent on his dangerous and thankless task.

Yes, Harlan makes a lot of being civilized and committed and responsible. And while he has philosopher Allen Tate's words above his desk: "Civilization is an agreement to ignore the abyss," the operative word "is" has become "should be." While the informed and responsible ones *can* agree to ignore the yawning gulf, this can only be possible if this civilization is bona fide, the genuine article, and not some cosmetic and self-deceiving substitute.

Otherwise we *dare* not ignore the abyss. To do so would be supreme folly, positively fatal for the race.

Harlan is mercilessly impatient with cosmetic civilization, with the self-congratulatory complacency that signals the breakthroughs in technology but forgets the appalling neglect in championing human rights, that praises the information revolution but tolerates growing illiteracy and indolence.

No, despite the optimum condition of Tate's words, it remains an ideal only, a reminder. Harlan's approach as writer has been closer to one contained in the words of André Breton in the MANIFESTOES OF SURREALISM, where he speaks of how the "tiny footbridge over the abyss, could not under any circumstances be flanked by hand rails."

For there is nothing surer than that Harlan Ellison has become, too, a tester of civilization, a quality control, a challenger, fully the Rebel in Bika Reed's sense, a fixer, determined not to let humanity ignore the abyss that produces Third Reichs and Vietnams and Senator Joseph McCarthys and Richard Nixons. He is committed, rather, to making us confront it in all its myriad forms, whatever its manifestations: racial prejudice, civil corruption, personal dishonesty, the mindless formula thinking of so much network television and popular literature. He wants us to remain no longer dupes, sand-headed ostriches, self-deceivers. He will not let us off that lightly.

In fact, Harlan builds bridges across the abyss for us—flimsy, delicate, exquisitely arching things made of the stuff of genuine civilization, precious but fragile, beautiful but not always enduring.

Many so-called civilized folk cannot bear to face the bridges Harlan makes. For one thing, the abyss—as Harlan reminds us—is right there, a terrible engulfing thing just under our feet. It makes our civilization look thin and fleeting; a flickering candle in a vast dark, not a blazing sun of enlightenment.

And second, the bridges have no hand rails; crossing them is not easy, and you do it on your own.

Which is fair enough. Most of us acknowledge so rarely that the abyss is there at all that there can be no half-measures once it is shown to us. Harlan's ploy has been to call us out on to such a bridge, using the beguilement of ideas and situations and characters that are totally real, using his great gift of language, and then say: "How's the view? What's doin'?"

Is it any wonder that so many rush back to the brink (or even complete the crossing, so thoroughly are they beguiled) and then scream abuse, ludicrous and self-revealing things like *elitist, sicko* and *antichrist*, or fumble as best they can for their weapon of indifference.

Know your Rebel then.

See him for what he really is, for what he cannot help but be.

At this writing, Harlan is nearing 50. Jiminy Cricket is 44. Zorro is 60.

Iai, as always, is timeless.

On page 79 of the Reed translation of Berlin Papyrus 3024, the Soul answers the Body and says:

Brother
as long as you burn
you belong to life.

Harlan is here then, where Iai is, burning and belonging, casting his bridges across the abyss, standing on the steps of the Alexandrian library waiting for the mobs to come. Civilization is better for it.

—Los Angeles, California
10 December 1983

I

BEGINNINGS

> "I will not apologize for the less-than-graceful prose, nor for the less-than-successful plots, nor for the grammatical errors."
>
> —"Linch Pins and Turning Points," THE FANTASIES OF HARLAN ELLISON, Gregg Press, 1979

During a lecture delivered at the House of the Arts in Petrograd in the early 1920s (published as "The Psychology of Creative Work," A SOVIET HERETIC, University of Chicago Press, 1970), Yevgeny Zamyatin told his audience:

> *The development of art is subject to the dialectic method. Art functions pyramidally: all new achievements are based on the utilization of everything that has been accumulated below, at the foundations of the pyramid. Revolutions do not occur here; this field, more than any other, is governed by evolution. And we must know what has been done before us in the field of verbal art. This does not mean that you must follow in trodden paths: you must contribute something of your own. A work of art is of value only when it is original both in content and in form. But in order to leap upward, it is necessary to take off from the ground. It is essential that there be a ground.*

The audience of the 1920s is not the audience of the 1980s, yet the substance of this message endures. Here is the ground where the tension builds for Harlan Ellison's upward leap.

Every journey has a beginning, and the longest journey begins with but a single step. From Harlan's smallest steps we can barely perceive the greatness that was to come, yet soon enough the predominant themes emerge.

No need to ask Harlan to apologize for the crudity of these early stories, nor request that he emend, polish or otherwise improve their appearance (see the above quote from "Linch Pins and Turning Points"). They stand or fall on their own merits, and if the interest in them is more historical than artistic, so be it.

"The Sword of Parmagon" and "The Gloconda" were originally published as serials (in 5 and 7 parts respectively) in *The Rangers*, a column for youngsters in the *Cleveland News*. The year was 1949, Harlan had just turned 15, and one may assert with some truth that these stories constitute Harlan's first "professional" publication (Leslie Kay Swigart's bibliography notes that he was paid with tickets to the Cleveland Indians baseball games). Through these little stories, Harlan for the first time reached out to an audience beyond his immediate circle of acquaintances and family. This marks their first appearance in print, including the author's own illustrations, since that 1949 column.

In 1953, Harlan began writing for the Ohio State University *Sundial*, one of the top three college humor magazines in the country (the other two were the University of California at Berkeley's *Pelican* and Harvard's *Lampoon*). Besides his column of campus gossip, *The Long Walk* (written with Windi Flightner), Harlan contributed bogus advertisements, mock interviews, playlets, stories and assorted satire. "The Wilder One" (as part of "A Tribute to Mahlon Brendo") and "The Saga of Machine Gun Joe" both appeared in January 1955; Harlan was Editor-in-Chief for that issue. This marked the peak of his college career: he was kicked out of O.S.U. that same month.

"Glowworm" (1956) was Harlan's first sale to a professional magazine, as he explains in the introduction written twenty years later (and included here in a slightly expanded and modified form). Even in this early a work (reprinted here in its original manuscript version), Harlan has already begun to play with the conventions of science fiction. The protagonist is a self-proclaimed "freak," his situation one of loneliness and despair as the world nears its end. A little too dark to be a typical genre pacifier of the time.

"Life Hutch" (1956), published only two months after "Glowworm," already demonstrates a rapidly growing story sense, an awareness of pace and the proper placement of flashback. It is, again, a brief look at alienation masquerading as a puzzle story, simple in its telling but rewarding in its payoff. The themes brought forth here surface again and again in Harlan's later stories, the basic conflict of human fear and human determination remains the bedrock of his literary estate.

"S.R.O." (1957) is a succinct commentary on greed and the slippery state of human moral values. Behind its bland and non-sensational approach lurks the bloody knife. Like all good satire, it hovers between humor and horror.

From teenage fantasist to sharp-eyed social commentator in just eight years. A prodigious upward leap, indeed.

And it's only the beginning . . .

"I am desperately afraid I will die before I've written all the stories I have in me."

—"Where the Stray Dreams Go," Introduction to FROM THE LAND OF FEAR, Belmont, 1967

THE SWORD OF PARMAGON

(Drawings by Harlan Ellison, Age 15)

CHAPTER 1: THE CAVE

It was late in the summer in the year 1503. It was a hot day, and it was even hotter in England where the sun shone so bright as to melt cheese in the shade. So it was that Philip dePaley, son of Governor dePaley, of Lancashire was walking along the cliffs of Dover in an attempt to escape the heat.

"What a bright idea," thought Philip as he slowly inched his way down the rock path toward the lower ledge. "I'll just take off my clothes and sword, tie them to my back and swim up toward the town—it doesn't look too deep."

And so Philip unbuckled the jeweled belt that supported the beautiful sword which hung from his side. He took off his boots, shirt and hat, and after tying them upon his back, dived head first into the cool water.

Down, down went Philip and suddenly he wasn't diving anymore. He was being pulled under by a strong undercurrent. Then suddenly, just as his wind was giving out, he was pushed upward and a moment later was breathing the sweet smell of air.

When Philip regained his senses, he looked around him and to his amazement found he was in a mammoth cave! He then realized that he had been pulled up under the cliffs into a natural cave that had been made by the sea washing in. While he was taking in his surroundings his glance fell upon an old wreck of a ship in one corner. Philip walked slowly toward it. It was an old Viking ship.

"It was probably wrecked and pulled under here a long time ago," thought Philip. And then he saw it!! A skeleton, clutching A SWORD!

CHAPTER 2: GLOWING DISCOVERY

Philip slowly walked toward the skeleton. Bending over he touched it and instantly the dry bones crumbled into dust, leaving only the sword leaning against the wet, damp wall.

Philip picked it up and noticed that it was glowing with white light. It was a beautiful sword of gold, with rubies set in the handle. On the upper part of the blade was an inscription which Philip translated from the Norse. "HE WHO USES THE SWORD OF PARMAGON WILL HAVE STRENGTH AND KNOWLEDGE BEYOND HIS OWN," it said.

It gave Philip a strange feeling to touch the burnished blade—a feeling of unharnessed strength.

Suddenly Philip realized he had been standing there for quite some time with the sword in his hand. He became aware of the danger of his adventure! Here he was under the cliffs of Dover, far from anyone! How would he get out?

All at once the sword began to quiver. It shook so violently that Philip had to drop it. He saw that the light from the sword was pointing to a hole in the wall that would have gone unnoticed! It was then that Philip realized that there was something mysterious about the sword—he knew not what, but he was thankful for it!

Picking up the sword he advanced to the hole and saw an old stone stairway leading up into the darkness. Using the sword as a torch because of its glowing light, he crept carefully up.

Philip climbed and climbed and it seemed as though he had walked up the stairs for hours, when suddenly he spied a sliver of light ahead. Gathering all his strength he ran panting up the rest of the stairs until he came to a huge wooden door. Spying a lever on the wall, Philip pulled it and as he did, a sliding door revealed a room filled with guns, knives, swords, gunpowder and all the implements of war. Sitting on a large throne was the enemy of the DePaley family, Baron Kovell, the BLACK BARON!

CHAPTER 3: PLAN FOR WAR

"You," cried the baron, jumping up—"a DePaley! How did you get in here?"

Philip backed into a corner and drew the sword which now began glowing with a stronger light than before. "You mean you don't know about the passage of the cave?" he said.

"My grandfather used to tell me about one but I never found it, though my men have hunted for it," the baron retorted. "Since you have stumbled onto the secret, you will never leave here . . . alive!"

"What is this room, an armory?" asked Philip.

"No," said the baron with an evil smile, "this is my ace, my card that will help me conquer all the lands governed by the DePaleys!"

Quickly the baron's hand flashed to the wall behind him and came up with a battleaxe. With a shout he leaped from his throne and rushed at Philip. As the fatal blow descended, Philip jumped aside and struck out weakly with the Sword of Parmagon. To his amazement it severed the thick metal head from the handle of the axe. The light from the sword glowed with a stronger determination as though it were mocking the baron for his clumsiness.

Philip jumped over a pile of crossbows and terrified, he ran down a large hall. He heard footsteps running behind him so he dashed into the nearest room. It was empty except for a small door at the back, which Philip opened.

It was the entrance to the dog kennels, and Philip was greeted with a sight that chilled his blood. Five snarling hungry beasts were chained to the wall opposite him.

The frightened boy could easily imagine why the animals looked so hungry. They were the dogs used in dogfights and were kept hungry so they would be more vicious and could fight better. They looked at Philip with a crazed expression and suddenly, with a snarl, one of the animals snapped his chain and leaped upon Philip!

CHAPTER 4: THE LONG FUSE

The weight of the crazed animal threw Philip to the floor and to his horror he found that his sword had dropped behind him out of his reach. The foaming jaws of the dog were coming closer and closer to Philip's throat.

Suddenly the terrorized boy heard the beast howl and drop over. Slowly he rose and looking toward the door he saw one of the baron's guards.

"I didn't mean to kill the dog," said the guard dumbly, "I was aiming at you!"

"Thank goodness your aim is bad—you got that knife right in the beast's back!" replied Philip.

"Maybe if I capture you the baron won't be so mad at me for killing one of his dogs," mumbled the guard.

"I don't plan to give you a chance," said Philip and quickly he grabbed his sword. With one blow he struck the Sword of Parmagon against the head of the stupid soldier. Stepping over the soldier's body, Philip crept out into the hall.

"It would be foolish to try to get out of the castle now," Philip thought. "The one place they wouldn't be looking for me is back in the armory." Keeping in the shadows of the tapestries he slowly made his way back to the room where he first saw the baron.

As Philip entered the room he had an idea. Why not rid the countryside of the tyrannical rule of the Black Baron? He spied a pile of gunpowder—just the thing to carry out his plan! Quickly he emptied the barrels of gunpowder on the floor, and then put one end of a coil of heavy string under the pile of explosives. He put the other end of the string on the floor and lit it with a flint.

"It won't be long till the whole castle goes up," thought Philip. "I'd better get out of here—fast!"

Picking up the sword he ran into the hall and down a long flight of stairs. He found himself in a room whose only other way out was a small window. He was about to go out again when suddenly the door slammed shut and the baron backed him into a corner. Philip ran to the window, but one look out showed that it would be suicide to jump!

It was a 60-foot drop to the water below! Philip turned back and saw a more horrible fate. The baron was advancing with his sword drawn. And then Philip imagined he saw the burning fuse—was it as long now as when he left the armory? He made his decision!

CHAPTER 5: THE PLUNGE

Philip drew the sword up sharply and hit the baron's chin. The baron thudded to the floor, but as he fell he pulled the cord, summoning his guards.

With a flash Philip was on the window sill and with a crash he plunged headlong through the portal into the emptiness below. As he fell he heard the deafening roar of an explosion and he knew that the castle was gone and the Black Baron would cause no more trouble. Then he went down and down . . .

When Philip awoke he found himself in his own bed in Lancashire. His father and mother were standing over him.

"A job well done, son," said his father. "Some of our good people found you washed up on the beach and remembered you from the Inn. You have been unconscious for three days. The baron's castle was completely demolished."

"We found you with an old sword when they brought you back," said his mother. "We have it here."

As she was speaking she unwrapped a long package and handed Philip the Sword of Parmagon.

"This sword saved my life more than once while I was in the castle," replied Philip. "It belonged to a great hero once."

With a smile on his face Philip's father said, "And it belongs to a hero now!"

The Gloconda

(Drawings by Harlan Ellison, Age 15)

CHAPTER 1: SAFARI

Prof. Francis Locksley stood before the assembled group of scientists in the Natural History Museum in New York.

Wiping his brow he said slowly, "Well, gentlemen, it is agreed—next Thursday we will leave for Africa, for the Belgian Congo!"

A strange series of discoveries had led to this speech by old Prof. Locksley. The museum had planned an exhibit depicting the evolution of the snake, but in collecting the specimen for the exhibit they found that one period in life of the snake was missing. Between the late Prehistoric age and the early Semi-Modern time, there was a snake not yet recorded by naturalists.

From what they could gather, the snake was something like the giant African snake, the Anaconda. The scientists knew that the climate in the days of the missing specimen was almost the same as it is now in certain parts of the world. Therefore they reasoned that they might even find a living specimen, or at least a preserved skin.

After weeks of research they managed to get a file of information on the snake and also a fairly good picture of it.

Its scientific name was "Glocolius Droclumniness"—but they named it "Gloconda" because of its resemblance to the Anaconda.

It was a week later that the six scientist-naturalists stepped off the plane in the heart of the Belgian Congo and set off into the impenetrable jungle in search of the poisonous 60-foot Gloconda!

CHAPTER 2: SINKING DOOM

It was late in the afternoon of the second day of the search when Phipps, the meek little botanist, saw something big and yellow stirring in the bushes ahead. Dropping their packs, the six excited men ran to the spot where Phipps had seen it and there they found a spotted yellow skin. It was exactly the same kind that had been described in their research as the Gloconda skin.

"It must have just shed its skin for the season and crawled away," remarked Riles the naturalist.

Suddenly Sorenson, who had been walking ahead of the group, screamed. The explorers as a body ran forward—fearing what they might see. They found out soon enough, for the same fate overtook them. They were running one second and the next they were sinking in oozing mud. Quicksand!

"Help," shouted the fearful scientists, but they were screaming in vain. They were in the heart of Africa—in the midst of wilderness where no one could hear them.

As the explorers were slowly being pulled into the quicksand they saw another terrifying sight. On the branch of a huge tree above them a big, hungry-looking black leopard was growling!

Even if they could get out of the quicksand, how could they escape the danger above?

CHAPTER 3: MAGIC GARMENT

Lower and lower sank the doomed scientists when Coby, who was from Texas, seemed to have an idea. He stretched toward the edge of the quicksand pit and grabbed a long vine that had fallen from the tree above.

"You can't pull yourself out on that!" yelled Professor Locksley. "It isn't attached to the tree."

"Wait an' see," said Coby in his Texas drawl.

As he sank deeper and deeper in the treacherous mud, Coby fashioned a lasso from the fallen vine and tied it around his waist. Then as his chest went under he threw the rope and slipped it over the head of the hungry cat in the tree above. The startled animal fell over the side of the limb opposite the one Coby was near, and as the strangling leopard fell, Coby was pulled out of the quagmire by the weight of the beast. Once out of the muck, Coby freed the rope from the neck of the dead leopard and, bracing himself, pulled each member of the group out before any harm could come to them.

"That was a smart piece of work, Coby," said "Doc," the medic of the expedition. "Where did you learn to rope like that?"

"I wasn't born in Texas for nothing," smiled the big man.

After changing clothes and collecting gear, the explorers set out again in search of the Gloconda.

The next day they found themselves in a dark swamp area, surrounded by fierce-looking natives. Without hesitation the scientists were tied securely and marched miles to a village where they got a glimpse of what the natives had in mind. In the center of the village surrounded by logs was a huge pot!

"Cannibals," whispered Riles to the terrified bunch, "we'll probably be Saturday night stew!"

"Very funny," replied Doc, "but if one of those heathens eats me, I'll give him a stomach ache."

Then the captives were shoved before a huge native who was wearing a horrible mask and a spotted yellow loincloth.

"Look," said Phipps, "the savage is wearing a Gloconda skin!"

The medicine man, noticing that they were all looking at his loincloth, said slowly, "Skin magic—big snake." Then he motioned to the pot and said, "Take."

CHAPTER 4: LAIR OF THE DEVIL SNAKE

The six men were untied and forced to get into the huge pot which was filled with water. As the last man got in, the natives brought out a large, burning torch and set fire to the logs around the pot. The water got hotter and hotter and suddenly the natives began dancing crazily around the terrified men.

Then without notice, "Doc" grabbed the medicine man by the neck as he whirled by. Pulling his knife, he ordered him to call off the savages. He made him understand that he would be killed if they tried to stop the scientists' escape.

Disgruntledly the medicine man repeated the message and then lapsed into a stony silence. Slowly the cannibals walked away from the men who had now crawled from the burning pot. After collecting gear, they fled with the savage into the jungle.

Hours and miles later the explorers finally came to a halt. Doc turned to the medicine man and said in pidgin English, "Where you get skin?"

The native shook his head and slowly answered, "Big devil snake—bad—big bite—me no go cave!"

"You go or we'll kill you," Doc warned. He gave the native a prod with the knife and the savage leaped to his feet and started off into the jungle.

After walking through swamp, lowland, jungle and hills they finally came to a large cave. Then with a shaking voice the medicine man said, "Me go, please, B'wana!"

"O.K., beat it, but don't tell your buddies!" ordered the explorer-doctor.

Without hesitation the frightened native made a break for the jungle and disappeared in the tangle of vines and trees.

"He won't come near us again," remarked Phipps. "He's too afraid of whatever is in that cave!"

Slowly they crept up on the black cave and then . . . two eyes, far apart, glared out at them. Was it the Gloconda?

CHAPTER 5: SMOKE OUT

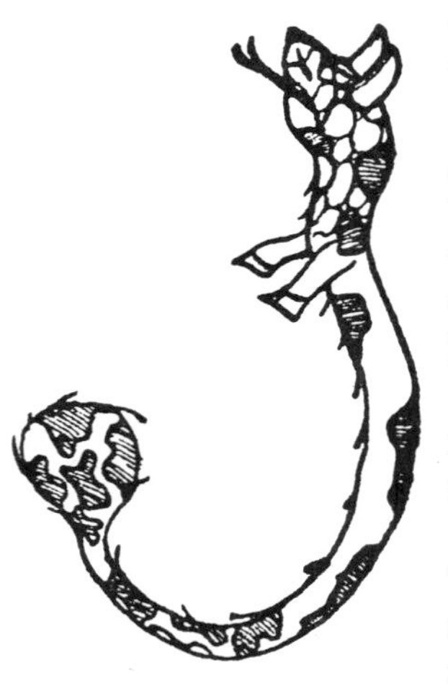

"Wow," breathed Coby, "look at those eyes! That baby must be at least 50 feet long!"

"That's larger than any of the other African snakes," replied Professor Locksley, "it must be the Gloconda. Just think, here we are in the twentieth century and about to see a reptile that lived in the days before men were known. Amazing!"

"But how are we ever going to get that monster out of the cave and into this big steel cage?" asked Riles.

"Here's my idea," said Phipps. "Why don't we find out if there are any other ways out of this cave. If there are, let's seal them with rocks and sticks. Let's split up and look for them and when we're all back I'll tell you my plan."

The six explorers set off in different directions and within a half hour they were all gathered in front of the black cave again.

"Well, any other places where the monster could get out?" asked Phipps.

The answer was unanimous—no other exits.

"All right then, here's what we do," announced Phipps. "We'll set a log on fire and throw it in the cave with whatever is in there—that way we can smoke it out. We'll put the cage in front of the cave so that it can't get away."

Soon the cage was in front of the cave and a flaming log was thrown into the darkness beyond the mouth of the cave. Minutes passed, then a loud hiss was heard and a streak of yellow shot out of the cave and into the cage. The door shut and the six explorers were the first men to see a Gloconda.

It was a huge reptile—sixty feet long and four feet wide, with a wrinkled yellow skin. Two horns protruded from its head and a vicious forked tongue slithered in and out of its mouth. It had a stubby pair of legs in front that resembled hoofs of deer. On the end of its spearlike body was a huge sack. This was the mysterious creature the scientists had been hunting—the deadly GLOCONDA!

Little did the adventurers know what was ahead of them when with a grin on their faces they lifted the heavy iron cage on their shoulders and headed back to the coast.

CHAPTER 6: STARVATION AHEAD

It was 105 degrees in the shade and it was even worse for the six explorers who were carrying a 60-pound snake in a steel cage. They had been walking two days in the direction the compass said would be South. At last, when they could walk no longer, they set down the cage and their food and ammunition and fell into a restless sleep.

At the break of dawn the men were awakened by the sound of parrots screaming from somewhere near by. The explorers rose and, to their horror, saw that the food supplies were gone.

"Must have been monkeys," said Sorenson, the tall biologist.

"No, it wasn't," said Doc, pointing to the Gloconda's cage, "look at our little horned friend here!"

Six pairs of eyes turned to the cage and there they saw a horribly misshapen snake—stuffed until it looked ready to burst. The supplies had been left too close to the cage and the hungry reptile had eaten them all.

"What will we use for food?" cried Riles.

"There aren't enough berries and fruits to keep us alive in this section," replied Phipps.

"We'll just have to do the best we can," said old Prof. Locksley as calmly as he could. "It looks as though we may have a starvation diet ahead of us, gentlemen."

The old man lifted his part of the steel cage, grabbed his rifle and said, "Shall we go?"

The others followed suit and in a few minutes the caravan of foodless men set forth once again.

CHAPTER 7: MIRAGE

Eight days without food doesn't help a man and when you've got a heavy load to carry it helps even less!

This was the predicament that Prof. Locksley, Doc, Phipps, Sorenson, Coby and Riles faced. They had been struggling through the thick jungle for weeks now. For the last eight days they had gone without food.

"If it weren't for this ugly snake, we'd be eating right now," complained Sorenson.

"Well, let's face it, gentlemen," said Prof. Locksley. "We wanted this snake—now we have it, so let's not gripe—shall we?"

On and on through the twisted black mass of vines and foliage went the starving band. It was on the tenth day, when their clothes were torn into ribbons and their stomachs crying, that Doc saw water.

"It must be a mirage," gasped Phipps, "there's no water on the map to the south except at the coast; we couldn't have gotten there so soon!"

"Yes, let's go in another direction," said Coby weakly.

As they were about to turn around they heard a low, loud whistle. Dropping the cage they staggered through the brush and there they saw what they were hoping for—a freighter!

"We must have gotten mixed up—we're at the coast," shouted Riles.

A half hour later the men and the cage with the snake were safely aboard the freighter, heading back to the United States. The men were comfortably quartered above decks, but below, in a heavy steel cage, lay the greatest reptile discovery in two centuries—THE GLOCONDA!

THE WILDER ONE

Johnny Branmash stopped his motor-bike outside the bar and motioned his gang to do the same. He hitched up his Levis, pulled his goggles off his eyes, and swaggered into the beer-parlor. Approaching the bar, he said, "Say, dad, how 'bout a brew?" He stood sullenly sipping his beer, while the rest of his gang of motor-bicyclists were happily playing the juke box ("Viennese Refrain"), playing bridge, or drinking. Johnny surveyed the bar; it was the same as all the others. The barmaid loped by and gave him a come-hither look. He turned his back. She was the same, too. Everything was always like everything else. Why couldn't something different and exciting happen?

"Bartender, another beer!"

That was when he saw her. From the very first she looked exciting. Maybe it was because she had three eyes. But it was different and Johnny was impressed all over himself. She strode into the bar, clad in a leather jacket with "Moll" written on it and emblazoned with the emblem of the Amalgamated Motor-Bicyclists of America. Johnny was thrilled. Her Levis were spotted with grease, her hair was tangled. Moll banged a small fist on the bar and ordered a double shot. The bartender snapped: "I'm sorry; we do not serve ladies in this establishment."

"Ladies be damned!" muttered Moll. She grabbed the bartender by the collar and slapped him across the face six times. "I said, gimme a double shot."

"YES, ma'am; right away."

Flexing his biceps and grinning, Johnny walked over to Moll. "The name's Johnny, Johnny Branmash. Le's dance."

"Get your damn greasy hands offa me, mac!" she snarled, and tossed down her drink.

Johnny stared at her dumbly. Now everyone was watching. His

reputation was at stake. A faint bit of previously-unknown fear crept into his eyes, but he *had* to try again. "I said, le's dance!"

She turned, smiled at him sweetly, and hit him with a left jab to the stomach. As he doubled over, she smashed his chin with a blistering right. He started to topple, and Moll shoved him across the room, through three tables, the juke box, and out the door. He landed in the gutter beside his motor-bike, sobbing and bleeding. He clutched his bike to his massive chest and there, sitting in the road, Johnny Branmash cried for hours.

The Saga of Machine Gun Joe

When his company moved out, Joe was in the forefront, the heavy barrel casing of the disassembled machine gun rigid across his shoulder, the bandolier of ammunition dangling from his other hand.

Joe was the soldier's soldier. When the Major slid into their trench and said, with sweat running down his face, "Take Hill 561. Now! Jump!" it was Joe—who they called "Machine Gun" Joe—who was first up out of the trench and streaking across the shell-marked ground, racing up that slope to the position.

It was always Joe who ripped the gun loose from its mounting and double-handed it as a light weapon, instead of waiting for the rest of his company, and who more than likely wiped up the enemy single-handed.

Joe was the soldier's soldier.

He went into the battle with that damned half-smile playing about his lips, courage seeming to stand up in his eyes and DARE the gooks to take a shot at him. He had more guts than anyone in the regiment. And more medals to prove it. There wasn't any job too tough or too big for Joe.

So when his company moved out, they said it was to stop a concentrated wave of North Koreans who had moved into the breech North of WungJo, he was out front, whistling a little song, seeming to spit in the face of Fate. The rest of the men admired Joe, and "Machine Gun" Joe knew it. But he was a square guy and he wouldn't let the men make an idol of him.

About twenty miles the other side of the Kukashabii Oil Reservoirs, they split up into teams, Joe and his buddy Karl going over the hill toward the designated area where GHQ had said the bulk of the gook advancement was located.

"Karl," said Joe, unslinging the bandolier of ammo, and dropping the gun barrel, "you rig the gun here, on this rise, while I go scout out and see what gives."

Karl gave a mock-salute and a little smile, because that was what Joe did, and he watched with love and admiration as Joe pulled the two matched .45's out of their holsters, stuck a butt in his mouth, lit it and walked out of sight, up over the hill, into the face of that enemy horde.

Joe scouted for three hours, ranging far afield, till he was cut off completely from Karl, the machine gun, the outfit entirely.

He topped a rise—AND SAW THEM!

There he stood on Bloody Ridge, two guns in his hands, a cigarette in his mouth, and all three smoking.

Forty thousand gooks coming up the hill, screaming death at him! Brave Joe. The guy with guts enough for the whole regiment! He pumped two fast shots into their mass, hitched up his belt . . .

. . . and ran like *hell*!

You can't BEAT odds like those!

Glowworm

INTRODUCTION

I wrote it on a kitchen table in Lester and Evelyn del Rey's dining room in Red Bank, New Jersey, in April of 1955. It was the first story of the many I'd written since I was ten years old that actually sold. I received something slightly less than a penny-and-a-half per word for its 3000 word length: forty dollars. It was my first professional sale and I was twenty-one years old.

There was an English professor named Shedd at Ohio State University in 1954. He told me I had no talent, could not write, ought to forget ever trying to make a living from the craft of writing, and that even if I did manage to eke out some sort of low-level existence from dogged persistence at it, I would never write anything of consequence, would never make a name for myself, and would sink into the dust of oblivion justifiably forgotten by lovers of properly-constructed literature.

I told him to go fuck himself.

I was thrown out of Ohio State University in January of 1955, went home to Cleveland to marshal my thoughts and consider my options. I spent three months publishing what turned out to be the final issue of my science fiction fanzine, *Dimensions*, and then packed what little I could carry and sprinted for New York.

In the Fifties, New York was mecca for writers. There was a vitality, a gauche wildness about New York City that called all tyro writers. James Thurber had come out of Ohio, as had Ruth McKenney and Milton Caniff and Earl Wilson and Herbert Gold. It was a terrific place to come from: the very apotheosis of America, the mythic boondock from which the pepsinogen Ellison would emerge, surfeited with talent, festooned with all the proper mid-American credentials, shuckin' and jivin', ready to sweep the fallen banner of contemporary epopee from the dust where Faulkner and Steinbeck and Nathanael West and Ford Madox Ford had dropped it in their rush toward posterity and the grave.

I arrived in New York and had nowhere to live.

Lester and Evelyn took me in for a while. And in their dining room I wrote "Glowworm." I needed a scientific rationale for an impossible plot-line. Lester suggested anaerobic bacteria, a microorganism able to live without the presence of free oxygen. It was one of the few times I was ever anything even remotely resembling a "science fiction" writer. I was a fantasist and didn't know it.

It took me two days to write the story. I went into the city and tried to sell it. John Campbell at *Astounding* (now *Analog*) rejected it. Horace Gold at *Galaxy* rejected it. James Quinn at *If* rejected it. Anthony Boucher at *The Magazine of Fantasy & Science Fiction* rejected it. Half a dozen other editors at the lesser sf magazines flourishing during that period rejected it. I put the story aside.

I went to stay with Algis Budrys, a successful sf writer, on West 23rd Street. He had recently married and I was a clot in his marital bloodstream. I went uptown and took a $10 a week room at 611 West 114th Street, across Broadway from Columbia University, in the same old building where Robert Silverberg was living. He was selling regularly, and I envied him more than I can say.

I went down to Brooklyn and joined a kid gang. I commuted back and forth between the identity of Phil "Cheech" Beldone and Harlan Ellison. Ten weeks later someone mentioned that one of the *Confidential*-type magazines, *Lowdown*, might want to publish an account of my time in the Red Hook gang. I went to see the editor of *Lowdown*. He said write it up. I wrote "I Ran with a Kid Gang!" and they bought it. Twenty-five bucks. They took my picture to accompany the article. I thought it was my first professional sale. I was wrong.

The magazine was published in August of 1955 with the headline TODAY, YOUNG HOODS! TOMORROW—WHAT? Not one word of what I had written was in the piece. They ran my picture, and the art director had airbrushed a scar on my left cheek. I was still an unpublished writer.

Larry Shaw was, at that time, editing a new magazine for Royal Publications called *Infinity*. It was a science fiction magazine that featured a department called "Fanfare." Reprints of fanzine articles. He wanted to use a piece by Dean Grennell I had published in *Dimensions*. He asked me if I cared to submit a story. I pulled out "Glowworm" and sent it to him.

About two weeks later he called (there was a pay phone on the wall outside my room at 611 West 114th) and said, "How would you like some dinner?"

I was awfully hungry.

Larry took me to a Chinese restaurant, and over egg foo yung he told me he was buying "Glowworm." Forty dollars. He handed me a check. I damned near fainted.

It was published in the February 1956 issue of *Infinity*, which hit the newsstands on December 27th, 1955—but by that time I'd had two or three stories already appear in sf or detective magazines. But it was my first real sale.

That first year, 1955, the first year of writing as a full-time professional, pursuing a craft Dr. Shedd had said I was not cut out for, I sold four stories. The next year, 1956, I sold 100 stories. I have not worked at any other profession since that time.

It has been thirty-one years, and I've written forty-two books, almost twelve hundred magazine stories, columns and articles, and I'm listed in WHO'S WHO IN AMERICA.

I like to think I've come a distance from "Glowworm," which the late and very wonderful critic James Blish once called "the single worst story ever published in the field of science fiction." I'm not ashamed of "Glowworm," for all its dreadful syntax and sophomoric style. How can one be ashamed of the first-born?

And though he's never responded, until about ten years ago I sent every single published story to Dr. Shedd at Ohio State. One should never say fuck you unless one is prepared to back it up.

Now, thirty years after its first appearance, "Glowworm" is back in print again. This is now only the third time it has appeared in print (and the first time in one of my books), but seeing it set in type again brings back that night in December of 1955 . . . the warm smells of the Chinese restaurant . . . the impish grin of dear Larry Shaw . . . his bulldog pipe clenched in his teeth . . . as he handed me a forty dollar check that was to change my life from that day to this. There is a God. For each of us. Mine was named Larry.

Larry Shaw died on April 1, 1985, but not before Robert Silverberg and I were privileged to present him with a special citation of recognition for his years as an editor, at the 42nd World Science Fiction Convention, in Anaheim, California, September 2, 1984, at the Hugo Awards ceremony.

When the sun sank behind the blasted horizon, its glare blotted out by the twisted wreckage rising obscenely against the hills, Seligman continued to glow.

He shone with a steady off-green aura that surrounded his body, radiated from the tips of his hair, crawled from his skin, and lit his unwavering way in the darkest of nights.

Though Seligman had never been a melodramatic man, he had more than once rolled the phrase through his mind, letting it fall from his lips: "I'm a freak."

The green glow had been with him for two years, and he was at least accustomed to it. It was useful in many ways. Scavenging food without the help of a flashlight could be arduous. Seligman never had that trouble.

Bombed-out groceries and shattered store windows revealed their contents eagerly to his luminous searching.

It had even helped him find the ship.

After his cross-continent search for anyone else left alive, and his return in failure, he had been passing through the outskirts of Newark. Night had seemed to come even sooner on the days following the final bombs. It was as though some god despaired of the sight the Earth presented and shrouded it from sight.

The rubble of Newark was cast low across the land, and the crumble-towered heap that was New York still rose on the horizon.

His glow slid out from him and across the checkered blacktop that had been a spaceport. He had taken this route in hopes there might be a port copter or gas-buggy left unhurt, with fuel somehow intact. No such miracle had occurred, however, and he was turning to find the highway into New York when his glow reflected back from something a distance away. It was a momentary gleam but it caught his eye. The he saw the tapered hull of it rising dark against the darker black of the night. It was a spaceship, of course.

Curiosity had sent Seligman hurrying toward it. How had one ship escaped the debacle? Was there a possibility he could liberate parts from it to make a copter or landcar function?

Even the pocked and cratered surface of the blast area could not dim his enthusiasm. His eyes fastened on the ship as unconsciously thoughts even he would have marveled at rose in his mind.

It was one of latest model ships; a *Smith* class cruiser with conning bubble set far back on the tapered nose, and the small, ugly black depressions behind which the Bergsil cannons rested on movable tracks.

There were a number of places on the hull where repairs had obviously been in progress when the attack came, for yawning rectangles revealing naked girdering could be seen. But miraculously, the ship was intact. The drive chambers had not been split, so the tanks of reactor fuel had not exploded. The hull still shone tin-foil bright, so the flight deck had not shorted out and caught fire. It appeared, from outside, to be in perfect shape. A windfall of rare caliber.

He circled it several times, in something close to awe. Awe at the strength of this piece of machinery to have withstood everything two frenzied nations at war might throw at it, and still point proudly at the stars for which it was built to conquer.

Two years had not dimmed in the slightest his recollection of that first glimpse of the ship. As he threaded carelessly through the debris he remembered his reflection shining back at him from the beryllium skin of the cruiser.

He looked out across the deserted remains that had once been the outskirts of Newark, and in the distance, by the light of a gun-metalled moon, he saw that same ship. The two years of intensive reading and puttering with the few remaining scraps that had been spaceships caught on the ground had shown him the fantastic improbability of it all. Every other ship was a total unsalvageable wreck. Parts of ships had been flung half a mile and driven through plastic walls. Only that one cruiser, lost in its height among the flattened remnants of its kind.

It had been months after he had found the ship, he recalled, before the idea had come to him.

There was no real reason why it should not have occurred immediately, but it hadn't. It had come to him . . .

He paused in his moonlit hurrying and tried to bring the scene back into sharper focus. Yes, it had been when he had gone into the computer room of the ship. When he had first seen the ship, he had tried to liberate parts for use in a copter, but the parts were all heavy-poured-molded and none of them would have fit a small vehicle. So he had abandoned the ship. What good was it?

The weeks following, he remembered, had been singularly annoying. More than just the emptiness of sole ownership of a whole world, these weeks had disturbed him with a thought just beneath the level of recognition.

Then he had found himself drawn back inexplicably to the ship. He had climbed the makeshift ladder to the control deck and looked around again as he had weeks before. Nothing. It was still layered with dust, the huge rectangular viewport streaked by rain and dirt, a manual of some sort still turned over like a tiny tent on the arm of the pilot's couch.

Then he had noticed the door to the computer room. He had overlooked it the first time in his eagerness to get to the drive compartment belowdecks.

The door had been ajar, and he had kicked at it, sending it open, noiselessy.

The man was slumped over the puncher, a decaying finger still tip-flattened against a tabulator button. How he had died, Seligman had had no idea. Shock? Asphyxiation? No, it couldn't have been that, he looked perfectly normal, no blueness or contortion of the face.

Seligman had leaned over, cautiously, to see what he had been coding out. It was a destination verification:

USSS 7725, ETD 0500 7/22 EARTHPORT ETA 0930 11/5 PROXIMA II. Unfortunately, for the computerman, his time of departure had been unavoidably cancelled.

Seligman had caught just a glimpse of the dead man's face before he had left the room. It had seemed totally unconcerned. Somehow that bothered him. Why wasn't he worried? Why didn't he care if the ship got to Proxima II? It had been the most wonderful achievement of his race when the first ship had made it. Were they so bored, then, that such a thing was commonplace?

Then he would have to remind them that it was still a remarkable thing.

He had left the ship then, but he was to return many times. Just as tonight he stalked glowing under the moon, across the dead land, toward the rocket field where the ship waited. Now he knew why he had gone back that night two years before. It was clear and in a way, inescapable.

If only he were not so—so . . .

His mind faltered at describing himself. If only he had not been *changed* this way.

Which was not entirely true. There was no longer anyone he might have termed "normal" for his comparison. Not only were there no more men, there was no more life of any kind. The silence was broken only by the searching wind, picking its way cautiously between the slow-rusting girders of a dead past.

Even as he said, "Freak!" his mind washed the word with two waves, almost as one: vindictiveness and a resignation inextricably bound in self-pity, hopelessness and hatred.

"*They* were at fault!" he screamed at the tortured piles of masonry in his path.

Across the viewer of his mind, thoughts twisted nimbly, knowing the route, having traversed it often before.

Man had reached for the stars, finding them within his reach were he willing to give up his ancestral home.

Those who had wanted space more than one planet had gone, out past the Edge, into the wilderness of no return. It would take years to get There, and the Journey Back was an unthinkable one. Time had set its seal upon them: Go, if you must, but don't look behind you.

So they had gone, leaving Earth to the madmen. They had left the steam of Venus, the grit-wind of Mars, the ice of Pluto, the sun-bake of Mercury. There had been no Earthmen left in the system of Sol. Except, of course, on Earth.

And *they* had been too busy throwing things at each other to worry about the stars.

The men who knew no other answer stayed and fought. They were the ones who fathered the Attilas, the Genghis Khans, the Hitlers. They were the ones who pushed the buttons and launched the missiles that chased each other across the skies, fell like downed birds, exploded, blasted, cratered, chewed-out and carved-out the face of the planet. They were also the little men who had failed to resist, even as they had failed to look up at the night sky.

They were the ones who had destroyed the Earth.

Now no one was left. No man. Just Seligman. And he glowed.

"*They* were at fault!" he screamed again, the sound a lost thing in the night.

His mind carried him back through the years to the days near the end of what had to be the Last War, because there would be no one left to fight another. He was carried back again to the sterile white rooms where the searching instruments, the prying needles, the clucking scientists, all labored over him and his group.

They were to be a last-ditch throwaway. They were the indestructible men: a new breed of soldier, able to live through the searing heat of the bombs; to walk unaffected through the purgatory hail of radiation, to assault where ordinary men would have collapsed long before.

Seligman picked his way over the rubble, his aura casting the faintest phosphorescence over the ruptured metal and plastic trailerings. He paused momentarily, eyeing the blasted remnants of a fence, to which clung a sign, held to the twined metal by one rusting bolt:

NEWARK SPACEPORT
ENTRANCE BY
AUTHORIZATION ONLY.

Shards of metal scrap moved under his bare feet, their razored edges rasping against the flesh, yet causing no break in the skin. Another product of the sterile white rooms and the strangely-hued fluids injected into his body?

Twenty-three young men, routine volunteers, as fit as the era of war could produce, had been moved to the solitary block building in Salt Lake City. It was a cubed structure with no windows and only one door, guarded night and day. If nothing else, they had security. No one knew the intensive experimentation going on inside those steel-enforced concrete walls, even the men upon whose bodies the experiments were being performed.

It was because of those experiments performed on him that Seligman was here now, alone. Because of the myopic little men with their foreign accents and their clippings of skin from his buttocks and shoulders, the bacteriologists and the endocrine specialists, the epidermis men and the bloodstream inspectors—because of all of them—he was here now, when no one else had lived.

Seligman rubbed his forehead at the base of the hairline. *Why* had he lived? Was it some strain of rare origin running through his body that had allowed him to stand the effects of the bombs? Was it a combination of the experiments performed on him—and only in a certain way on him, for none of the other twenty-two had lived—*and* the radiation? He gave up, for the millionth time. Had he been a student of the ills of man he might have ventured a guess, but it was too far afield for a common foot-soldier.

All that counted was that when he had awakened, pinned thighs, chest and arms under the masonry of a building in Salt Lake City, he was alive and could see. He could see, that is, till the tears clouded the vision of his own sick green glow.

It was life. But at times like this, with the flickering light of his passage marked on the ash-littered remains of his culture, he wondered if it was worth the agony.

He never really approached madness, for the shock of realizing he was totally and finally alone without a voice or a face or a touch in all the world, overrode the smaller shock of his transformation.

He lived, and to Seligman's blunt manner he was that fabled, joked-about Last Man On Earth. But it wasn't a joke now.

Nor had the months after the final dust of extinction settled across the planet been a joke. Those months had labored past as he searched the country, taking what little food was left, sealed from radiation—though why radiation should bother him he could not imagine; habit more than anything—and disease, racing from one end of the continent in search of but one other human to share his torment.

But of course there had been no one. He was cut off like a withered arm from the body that was his race.

Not only was he alone, and with the double terror of an aura that never dimmed, sending the word, "Freak!" pounding through his mind, but there were other changes, equally terrifying. It had been in Philadelphia, while grubbing inside a broken store window that he had discovered another symptom of his change.

The jagged glass pane had ripped the shirt through to his skin—but had not damaged him. The flesh showed white momentarily, and then even that faded. Seligman experimented cautiously, then recklessly, and found that the radiations, or his treatments, or both, had indeed changed him. He was completely impervious to harm of a minor sort: fire in small amounts did not bother him, sharp edges could no more rip his flesh than they could a piece of treated steel, work produced no calluses; he was, in a limited sense of the word, invulnerable.

The indestructible man had been created too late. Too late to bring satisfaction to the myopic butchers who had puttered unceasingly about his body. Perhaps had they managed to survive they might still not comprehend what had occurred. It was too much like the product of a wild coincidence.

But that had not lessened his agony. Loneliness can be a powerful thing, more consuming than hatred, more demanding than mother love, more driving than ambition. It could, in fact, drive a man to the stars.

Perhaps it had been a communal yearning within his glowing breast; perhaps a sense of the dramatic or a last vestige of that unconscious debt all men owe to their kind; perhaps it was simply an urge to talk to someone. Seligman summed it up without soul-searching in the philosophy, "I can't be any worse off than I am now, so why not?"

It didn't matter really. Whatever the reason, he knew by the time his search was over that he must seek men out, wherever in the stars they might be, and tell them. He must be a messenger of death to his kin beyond the Earth. They would mourn little, he knew, but still he had to tell them.

He would have to go after them and say, "Your fathers are gone. Your home is no more. They played the last hand of that most dangerous of games, and lost. The Earth is dead."

He smiled a tight, grim smile as he thought: At least I won't have to carry a lantern to them; they'll see me coming by my own glow. Glow little glowworm, glimmer, glimmer . . .

Seligman threaded his way through the tortured wreckage and crumpled metalwork of what had been a towering structure of shining-planed glass and steel and plastic. Even though he knew he was alone, Seligman turned and looked back over his shoulder, sensing he was being watched. He had had that feeling many times, and he knew it for what it was. It was Death, standing spraddle-legged over the face of the land, casting shadow and eternal silence upon it. The only light came from the lone man stalking toward the rocket standing sentry like a pillar of January ice in the center of the blast area.

His fingers twitched as he thought of the two years' work that had gone into erecting that shaft of beryllium. Innumerable painstaking trips to and from the junk heaps of that field, pirating pieces from other ships, liberating cases of parts from bombed-out storage sheds, relentlessly forcing himself on, even when exhaustion cried its claim. Now the rocket was finished.

Seligman had not been a scientist or a mechanic. But determination, texts on rocket motors, and the miracle of an only partially-destroyed ship with its drive still intact had provided him with a means to leave this place of death.

He climbed the hull-ladder into the open inspection hatch, finding his way easily, even without a torch. His fingers began running over the complicated leads of the drive-components, checking and re-checking what he already knew was sound and foolproof—or as foolproof as an amateur could make them.

Now that it was ready, and all that remained were these routine check-tests and loading the food for the journey, he found himself more terrified of leaving than of remaining alone till he died—and when that might be with his new stamina he had no idea.

How would they receive a man as transformed as he? Would they not instinctively fear, mistrust, despise him? Am I stalling? The question suddenly formed in his mind, causing his sure inspection to falter. Had he been purposely putting the take-off date farther and farther ahead? Using the checks and other tasks as further attempts to stall? His head began to ache with the turmoil of his thoughts.

Then he shook himself in disgust. The tests were necessary, covered in any one of the texts lying about the floor of the drive chamber.

His hands shook, but that same impetus which had carried him for two years forced him to complete the checkups. Just as dawn oozed up over the outline of the tatters that had been New York, he finished his work on the ship.

Without pause, sensing he must race, not with time, but with the doubts raging inside him, he climbed back down the ladder and began loading food boxes. They were stacked neatly to one side of a hand-powered lift he had restored. The hard rubber containers of concentrates and the bulbs of carefully-sought-out liquids made an imposing and somewhat perplexing sight.

Food is the main problem, he told himself. If I should get past a point of no return and find my food giving out, my chances would be nil. I'll have to wait till I can find more stores of food. He estimated the time needed for the search and realized it might be months, perhaps even another year till he had accrued enough from the wasted stores within any conceivable distance.

In fact, finding a meal in the city, after he had carted box after box of edibles out to the rocket, had become an increasingly more difficult job. Further, he suddenly realized he had not eaten since the day before.

The day before?

He had been so engrossed in the final touches of the ship he had completely neglected to eat. Well, it had happened before, even before the blast. With an effort he began to grope back, trying to remember the last time he *had* eaten. Then it became quite clear to him. It leaped out and dissolved away all the delays he had been contriving. *He had not eaten in three weeks.*

Seligman had known it, of course. But it had been buried so deeply that he only half-feared it. He had tried to deny the truth, for when that last seemingly insurmountable problem was removed, there was nothing but his own inadequacies to prevent his leaving.

Now it came out, full-bloom. The treatments and radiation had done more than make him merely impervious to mild perils. He no longer needed to eat! He boggled at the concept for a moment, shaken by the realization that he had not recognized the fact before.

He had heard of anaerobic bacteria or yeasts that could derive their energy from other sources, without the normal oxidation of foods. Bringing the impossible to relatively homely terms made it easier for him to accept. Maybe it was even possible to absorb energy directly. At least he felt no slightest tinge of hunger, even after three weeks of back-breaking work without eating.

Probably he would have to take along a certain amount of proteins to replenish the body tissue he expended. But as for the bulky boxes of edibles dotting the space around the ship, most were no longer a necessity.

Now that he had faced up to the idea that he had been delaying through fear of the trip itself, and that there was nothing left to stop his leaving almost immediately, Seligman again found himself caught up in the old drive.

He was suddenly intent on getting the ship into the air and beyond.

Dusk mingled with the blotching of the sun before Seligman was ready. It had not been stalling this time, however. The sorting and packing of needed proteins took time. But now he was ready. There was nothing to keep him on Earth.

He took one last look around. It seemed the thing to do. Sentimentalism was not one of Seligman's more outstanding traits, but he did it in preparation for anyone who might ask him, "What did it look like—at the end?" It was with a tinge of regret that he brought the fact to mind; he had never really *looked* at his sterile world in the two years he had been preparing to leave it. One became accustomed to living in a pile of rubble, and after a bit it no longer offered even the feel of an environment.

He climbed the ladder into the ship, carefully closing and dogging the port behind him. The chair was ready, webbing flattened back against the deep rubber pile of its seat and backrest. He slid into it and swung the control box down on its ball-swivel to a position before his face.

He drew the top webbing across himself and snapped its triple-lock clamps into place. Seligman sat in the ship he had not even bothered to name, fingers groping for the actuator button on the arm of the chair, glowing all the while, weirdly, in the half-light of the cabin.

So this was to be the last picture he might carry with him to the heavens: a bitter epitaph for a race misspent. No warning; it was too late for such puny action. All was dead and ghosted on the face of the Earth. No blade of grass dared rise; no small life murmured in its burrows and caves, in the oddly dusty skies, or for all he knew, to the very bottom of the Cayman Trench. There was only silence. The silence of a graveyard.

He pushed the button.

The ship began to rise, waveringly. There was a total lack of the grandeur he remembered when the others had left. The ship sputtered and coughed brokenly as it climbed on its imperfect drive. Tremors shook the cabin and Seligman could feel something wrong, vibrating through the chair and floor into his body.

Its flames were not so bright or steady as those other take-offs, but it continued to rise and gather speed. The hull began to glow as the rocket lifted higher into the dust-filled sky.

Acceleration pressed down on Seligman, though not as much as he had expected. It was merely uncomfortable, not punishing. Then he remembered that he was not of the same make as those who had preceded him.

His ship continued to pull itself up out of the Earth's atmosphere. The hull oranged, then turned cherry, then straw-yellow, as the coolers within its skin fought to counteract the blasting fury.

Again and again Seligman could feel the *wrongness* of the climb. Something was going to give!

As the bulkheads to his right began to strain and buckle, he knew what it was. The ship had not been built or re-welded by trained experts, working in teams with the latest equipment. He had been one lone determined man, with only book experience to back him. Now the errors he had unconsciously made were about to tell.

The ship passed beyond the atmosphere, and Seligman stared in horror as the plates cracked and shattered outwards. He tried to scream as the air shrieked outwards, but sound was already impossible. He felt his breath sucked from his lungs.

Then he fainted.

When the ship passed the moon, Seligman still sat, his body held in place by the now-constricted webbing, facing the gaping squares and sundered metal that had been the cabin wall.

Abruptly, the engines cut off. As though it were a signal, Seligman's eyes crinkled at the corners, fluttered, and opened wide.

He stared at the wall, his reviving brain grasping the final truth. The last vestige of humanity had been clawed from him. He no longer needed air to live.

His throat constricted, his belly knotted, and the blood that should theoretically be boiling pounded thickly in his throat. His last kinship with those he was searching was gone. If he had been a freak before, what was he *now*? A horror?

The turmoil fought itself out in him as the ship sped onward and he faced what he had become, and what he must do.

He was more than a messenger, now. He was a shining symbol at the end of all humanity on Earth, a symbol of the evil their kind had done. The men out there would never treasure him, welcome him, or build proud legends around him. But they could never deny him. He was a messenger from the grave.

They would see him in the airless cabin, even before he landed. They would never be able to live with him, but they would have to listen to him, and to believe.

Seligman sat in the crash-chair in the cabin that was dark except for the eerie glow that was part of him. He sat there, lonely and eternally alone. And slowly, a grim smile grew on his lips.

The bitter purpose that had been forced on him was finally clear. For two years, he had fought to find escape from the death and loneliness of ruined Earth. Now that was impossible. One Seligman was enough.

Alone? He hadn't known the meaning of the word before! It would be his job to make *sure* that he was alone—alone among his people.

Until the end of time.

Life Hutch

Terrence slid his right hand, the one out of sight of the robot, up his side. The razoring pain of the three broken ribs caused his eyes to widen momentarily in pain. Then he recovered himself and closed them till he was studying the machine through narrow slits.

If the eyeballs click, I'm dead, thought Terrence.

The intricate murmurings of the life hutch around him brought back the immediacy of his situation. His eyes again fastened on the medicine cabinet clamped to the wall next to the robot's duty-niche.

Cliché. So near yet so far. It could be all the way back on Antares-Base for all the good it's doing me, he thought, and a crazy laugh rang through his head. He caught himself just in time. *Easy! Three days is a nightmare, but cracking up will only make it end sooner.* That was the last thing he wanted. But it couldn't go on much longer.

He flexed the fingers of his right hand. It was all he *could* move. Silently he damned the technician who had passed the robot through. Or the politician who had let inferior robots get placed in the life hutches so he could get a rake-off from the government contract. Or the repairman who hadn't bothered checking closely his last time around. All of them; he damned them all.

They deserved it.

He was dying.

His death had started before he had reached the life hutch. Terrence had begun to die when he had gone into the battle.

He let his eyes close completely, let the sounds of the life hutch fade from around him. Slowly, the sound of the coolants hush-hushing through the wall-pipes, the relay machines feeding their messages without pause from all over the galaxy, the whirr of the antenna's standard turning in its socket atop the bubble, slowly they melted into silence. He had resorted to blocking himself off from reality many times during the past three days. It was either that or existing with the robot watching, and eventually he would have had to move. To move was to die. It was that simple.

He closed his ears to the whisperings of the life hutch; he listened to the whisperings within himself.

"Good God! There must be a million of them!"

It was the voice of the squadron leader, Resnick, ringing in his suit intercom.

"What kind of battle formation is *that* supposed to be?" came another voice. Terrence looked at the radar screen, at the flickering dots signifying Kyben ships.

"Who can tell with those toadstool-shaped ships of theirs," Resnick answered. "But remember, the whole front umbrella-part is studded with cannon, and it has a helluva range of fire. Okay, watch yourselves, good luck—and give 'em Hell!"

The fleet dove straight for the Kyben armada.

To his mind came the sounds of war, across the gulf of space. It was all imagination; in that tomb there was no sound. Yet he could clearly detect the hiss of his scout's blaster as it poured beam after beam into the lead ship of the Kyben fleet.

His sniper-class scout had been near the point of that deadly Terran phalanx, driving like a wedge at the alien ships, converging on them in loose battle-formation. It was then it had happened.

One moment he had been heading into the middle of the battle, the left flank of the giant Kyben dreadnaught turning crimson under the impact of his firepower.

The next moment, he had skittered out of the formation which had slowed to let the Kyben craft overshoot, while the Earthmen decelerated to pick up maneuverability.

He had gone on at the old level and velocity, directly into the forward guns of a toadstool-shaped Kyben destroyer.

The first beam had burned the gun-mounts and directional equipment off the front of the ship, scorching down the aft side in a smear like oxidized chrome plate. He had managed to avoid the second beam.

His radio contact had been brief; he was going to make it back to Antares-Base if he could. If not, the formation would be listening for his homing-beam from a life hutch on whatever planetoid he might find for a crash-landing.

Which was what he had done. The charts had said the pebble spinning there was technically 1–333, 2–A, M & S, 3–804.39#, which would have meant nothing but three-dimensional coordinates had not the small # after the data indicated a life hutch somewhere on its surface.

His distaste for being knocked out of the fighting, being forced onto one of the life hutch planetoids, had been offset only by his fear of running out of fuel before he could locate himself. Of eventually drifting off into space somewhere, to wind up finally as an artificial satellite around some minor sun.

The ship pancaked in under minimal reverse drive, bounced high twice and caromed ten times, tearing out chunks of the rear section, but had come to rest a scant two miles from the life hutch, jammed into the rocks.

Terrence had high-leaped the two miles across the empty, airless planetoid to the hermetically sealed bubble in the rocks. His primary wish was to set the hutch's beacon signal so his returning fleet could track him.

He had let himself into the decompression chamber, palmed the switch through his thick spacesuit glove, and finally removed his helmet as he heard the air whistle into the chamber.

He had pulled off his gloves, opened the inner door and entered the life hutch itself.

God bless you, little life hutch, Terrence had thought as he dropped the helmet and gloves. He had glanced around, noting the relay machines picking up messages from outside, sorting them, vectoring them off in other directions. He had seen the medicine chest clamped onto the wall, the refrigerator he knew would be well-stocked if a previous tenant hadn't been there before the stockman could refill it. He had seen the all-purpose robot, immobile in its duty-niche. And the wall-chronometer, its face smashed. All of it in a second's glance.

God bless, too, the gentlemen who thought up the idea of these little rescue stations, stuck all over the place for just such emergencies as this. He had started to walk across the room.

It was at this point that the service robot, that kept the place in repair between tenants and unloaded supplies from the ships, had moved clankingly across the floor, and with one fearful smash of a steel arm thrown Terrence across the room.

The spaceman had been brought up short against the steel bulkhead, pain blossoming in his back, his side, his arms and legs. The machine's blow had instantly broken three of his ribs. He lay there for a moment, unable to move. For a few seconds he was too stunned to breathe, and it had been that, certainly, that had saved his life. His pain had immobilized him, and in that short space of time the robot had retreated with a muted internal clash of gears.

He had attempted to sit up straight, and the robot had hummed oddly and begun to move. He had stopped the movement. The robot had settled back.

Twice more had convinced him his position was as bad as he had thought.

The robot had worn down somewhere in its printed circuits. Its commands to lift had been erased or distorted so that now it was conditioned to smash, to hit, anything that moved.

He had seen the clock. He realized he should have suspected something was wrong when he saw its smashed face. Of course! The digital dials had moved, the robot had smashed the clock. Terrence had moved, the robot had smashed him.

And would again, if he moved again.

But for the unnoticeable movement of his eyelids, he had not moved in three days.

He had tried moving toward the decompression lock, stopping when the robot advanced and letting it settle back, then moving again, a little nearer. But the idea died with his first movement. His ribs were too painful. The pain was terrible. He was locked in one position, an uncomfortable, twisted position, and he would be there till the stalemate ended, one way or the other.

He was suddenly alert again. The reliving of his last three days brought back reality sharply.

He was twelve feet away from the communications panel, twelve feet away from the beacon that would guide his rescuers to him. Before he died of his wounds, before he starved to death, before the robot crushed him. It could have been twelve light-years, for all the nearer he could get to it.

What had gone wrong with the robot? Time to think was cheap. The robot could detect movement, but thinking was still possible. Not that it could help, but it was possible.

The companies that supplied the life hutch's needs were all government contracted. Somewhere along the line someone had thrown in impure steel or calibrated the circuit-cutting machines for a less expensive job. Somewhere along the line someone had not run the robot through its paces correctly. Somewhere along the line someone had committed murder.

He opened his eyes again. Only the barest fraction of opening. Any more and the robot would sense the movement of his eyelids. That would be fatal.

He looked at the machine.

It was not, strictly speaking, a robot. It was merely a remote-controlled hunk of jointed steel, invaluable for making beds, stacking steel plating, watching culture dishes, unloading spaceships and sucking dirt from rugs. The robot body, roughly humanoid, but without what would have been a head on a human, was merely an appendage.

The real brain, a complex maze of plastic screens and printed circuits, was behind the wall. It would have been too dangerous to install those delicate parts in a heavy-duty mechanism. It was all too easy for the robot to drop itself from a loading shaft, or be hit by a meteorite, or get caught under a wrecked spaceship. So there were sensitive units in the robot appendage that "saw" and "heard" what was going on, and relayed them to the brain—behind the wall.

And somewhere along the line that brain had worn grooves too deeply into its circuits. It was now mad. Not mad in any way a human being might go mad, for there were an infinite number of ways a machine could go insane. Just mad enough to kill Terrence.

Even if I could *hit the robot with something, it wouldn't stop the thing.* He could perhaps throw something at the machine before it could get to him, but it would do no good. The robot brain would still be intact, and the appendage would continue to function. It was hopeless.

He stared at the massive, blocky hands of the robot. It seemed he could see his own blood on the jointed work-tool fingers of one hand. He knew it must be his imagination, but the idea persisted. He flexed the fingers of his hidden hand.

Three days had left him weak and dizzy from hunger. His head was light and his eyes burned steadily. He had been lying in his own filth till he no longer noticed the discomfort. His side ached and throbbed, and the pain of a blast furnace roared through him every time he breathed.

He thanked God his spacesuit was still on, lest the movement of his breathing bring the robot down on him. There was only one solution, and that solution was his death. He was almost delirious.

Several times during the past day—as well as he could gauge night and day without a clock or a sunrise—he had heard the roar of the fleet landing outside. Then he had realized there was no sound in dead space. Then he had realized they were all inside the relay machines, coming through subspace right into the life hutch. Then he had realized that such a thing was not possible. Then he had come to his senses and realized all that had gone before was hallucination.

Then he had awakened and known it *was* real. He *was* trapped, and there was no way out. Death had come to live with him. He was going to die.

Terrence had never been a coward, nor had he been a hero. He was one of the men who fight wars because they are always fought by *some*one. He was the kind of man who would allow himself to be torn from wife and home and flung into an abyss they called Space to defend what he had been told needed defense. But it was in moments like this that a man like Terrence began to think.

Why here? Why like this? What have I done that I should finish in a filthy spacesuit on a lost rock—and not gloriously like they said in the papers back home, but starving or bleeding to death alone with a crazy robot? Why me? Why me? Why alone?

He knew there could be no answers. He expected no answers.

He was not disappointed.

When he awoke, he instinctively looked at the clock. Its shattered face looked back at him, jarring him, forcing his eyes open in after-sleep terror. The robot hummed and emitted a spark. He kept his eyes open. The humming ceased. His eyes began to burn. He knew he couldn't keep them open too long.

The burning worked its way to the front of his eyes, from the top and bottom, bringing with it tears. It felt as though someone was shoving needles into the corners. The tears ran down over his cheeks.

His eyes snapped shut. The roaring grew in his ears. The robot didn't make a sound.

Could it be inoperative? Could it have worn down to immobility? Could he take the chance of experimenting?

He slid down to a more comfortable position. The robot charged forward the instant he moved. He froze in mid-movement, his heart a chunk of ice. The robot stopped, confused, a scant ten inches from his outstretched foot. The machine hummed to itself, the noise of it coming both from the machines before him and from somewhere behind the wall.

He was suddenly alert.

If it had been working correctly, there would have been little or no sound from the appendage, and none whatsoever from the brain. But it was *not* working properly, and the sound of its thinking was distinct.

The robot rolled backward, its "eyes" still toward Terrence. The sense orbs of the machine were in the torso, giving the machine the look of a squat metal gargoyle, squared and deadly.

The humming was growing louder, every now and then a sharp *pfffft!* of sparks mixed with it. Terrence had a moment's horror at the thought of a short-circuit, a fire in the life hutch, and no service robot to put it out.

He listened carefully to pinpoint the location of the robot's brain built into the wall.

Then he thought he had it. Or was it there? It was either in the wall behind a bulkhead next to the refrigerator, or behind a bulkhead near the relay machines. The two possible housings were within a few feet of each other, but they might make a great deal of difference.

The distortion created by the steel plate in front of the brain, and the distracting background noise of the robot broadcasting it made it difficult to tell exactly which was the correct location.

He drew a deep breath.

The ribs slid a fraction of an inch together, their broken ends grinding.

He moaned.

A high-pitched tortured moan that died quickly, but throbbed back and forth inside his head, echoing and building itself into a paean of sheer agony! It forced his tongue out of his mouth, limp in a corner of his lips, moving slightly. The robot rolled forward. He drew his tongue in, clamped his mouth shut, cut off the scream inside his head at its high point!

The robot stopped, rolled back to its duty-niche.

Oh, God! The pain! The God God where are you pain!

Beads of sweat broke out on his body. He could feel their tickle inside his spacesuit, inside his jumper, inside the bodyshirt, on his skin. The pain of the ribs was suddenly heightened by an irresistible itching of his skin.

He moved infinitesimally within the suit, his outer appearance giving no indication of the movement. The itching did not subside. The more he tried to make it stop, the more he thought about not thinking about it, the worse it became. His armpits, the crooks of his arms, his thighs where the tight service-pants clung—suddenly too tightly—were madness. He had to scratch!

He almost started to make the movement. He stopped before he started. He knew he would never live to enjoy any relief. A laugh bubbled into his head. *God Almighty, and I always laughed at the slobs who suffered with the seven-year itch, the ones who always did a little dance when they were at attention during inspection, the ones who could scratch and sigh contentedly. God, how I envy them.* His thoughts were taking on a wild sound, even to him.

The prickling did not stop. He twisted faintly. It got worse. He took another deep breath.

The ribs sandpapered again.

This time, blessedly, he fainted from the pain.

"Well, Terrence, how do you like your first look at a Kyben?"

Ernie Terrence wrinkled his forehead and ran a finger up the side of his face. He looked at his Commander and shrugged. "Fantastic things, aren't they?"

"Why fantastic?" asked Commander Foley.

"Because they're just like us. Except of course the bright yellow pigmentation and the tentacle-fingers. Other than that they're identical to a human being."

The Commander opaqued the examination-casket and drew a cigarette from a silver case, offering the Lieutenant one. He puffed it alight, staring with one eye closed against the smoke. "More than that, I'm afraid. Their insides look like someone had taken them out, liberally mixed them with spare parts from several other species, and jammed them back in any way that fitted conveniently. For the next twenty years we'll be knocking our heads together trying to figure out their metabolic *raison d'être*."

Terrence grunted, rolling his unlit cigarette absently between two fingers. "That's the least of it."

"You're right," agreed the Commander. "For the next *thousand* years we'll be trying to figure out how they think, why they fight, what it takes to get along with them, what motivates them."

If they let us live that long, thought Terrence.

"Why are we at war with the Kyben?" he asked the older man. "I mean *really*."

"Because the Kyben want to kill every human being they can recognize as a human being."

"What have they got against us?"

"Does it matter? Maybe it's because our skin isn't bright yellow; maybe it's because our fingers aren't silken and flexible; maybe it's because our cities are too noisy for them. Maybe a lot of maybes. But it doesn't matter. Survival never matters until you have to survive."

Terrence nodded. He understood. So did the Kyben. It grinned at him and drew its blaster. It fired point-blank, crimsoning the hull of the Kyben ship.

He swerved to avoid running into his gun's own backlash. The movement of the bucket seat sliding in its tracks, keeping his vision steady while maneuvering, made him dizzy. He closed his eyes for a moment.

When he opened them, the abyss was nearer, and he teetered, his lips whitening as they pressed together under his effort to steady himself. With a headlong gasp he fell sighing into the stomach. His long, silken fingers jointed steely humming clankingly toward the medicine chest over the plate behind the bulkhead.

The robot advanced on him grindingly. Small fine bits of metal rubbed together, ashing away into a breeze that came from nowhere as the machine raised lead boots toward his face.

Onward and onward till he had no room to move and then

The light came on, bright, brighter than any star Terrence had ever seen, glowing, broiling, flickering, shining, bobbing a ball of light on the chest of the robot, who staggered, stumbled, stepped.

The robot hissed, hummed and exploded into a million flying, racing fragments, shooting beams of light all over the abyss over which Terrence again teetered, teetering. He flailed his arms wildly trying to escape but at the last moment, before the fall

He awoke with a start!

He saved himself only by his unconscious. Even in the hell of a nightmare he was aware of the situation. He had not moaned and writhed in his delirium. He had kept motionless and silent.

He knew it was true, because he was still alive.

Only his surprised jerking, as he came back to consciousness, started the monster rolling from its niche. He came fully awake and sat silent, slumped against the wall. The robot retreated.

Thin breath came through his nostrils. Another moment and he would have put an end to the past three days—three days or more now? how long had he been asleep?—days of torture.

He was hungry. Lord how hungry he was. The pain in his side was worse now, a steady throbbing that made even shallow breathing tortuous. He itched maddeningly. He was uncomfortably slouched against a cold steel bulkhead, every rivet having made a burrow for itself in his skin. He wished he was dead.

He didn't wish he was dead. It was all too easy to get his wish.

If he could only disable that robot brain. A total impossibility. If he could only wear Phobos and Deimos for watchfobs. If he could only shack-up with a silicon-deb from Penares. If he could only use his large colon for a lasso.

It would take a thorough destruction of the brain to do it enough damage to stop the appendage before it could roll over and smash Terrence again.

With a steel bulkhead between him and the brain, his chances of success totaled minus zero every time.

He considered which part of his body the robot would smash first. One blow of that tool-hand would kill him if it was used a second time. With the state of his present wounds, even a strong breath might finish him.

Perhaps he could make a break and get through the lock into the decompression chamber . . .

Worthless. (A) The robot would catch him before he had gotten to his feet, in his present condition. (B) Even allowing a miracle, even if he did get through the lock, the robot would smash the lock port, letting in air, ruining the mechanism. (C) Even allowing a double miracle and it didn't, what the hell good would it do him? His helmet and gloves were in the hutch itself, and there was no place to go on the planetoid. The ship was ruined, so no signal could be sent from there.

Doom suddenly compounded itself.

The more he thought about it, the more certain he was that soon the light would flicker out for him.

The light would flicker out.

The light would flicker . . .

The light . . .

. . . light . . . ?

Oh God, is it possible? Can it be? Have I found an answer? He marveled at the simplicity of it. It had been there for more than three days waiting for him to use it. It was *so* simple it was magnificent. He could hardly restrain himself from moving, just out of sheer joy.

I'm not brilliant, I'm not a genius, why did this occur to me? For a few minutes the brilliance of the solution staggered him. Would a less intelligent man have solved the problem this easily? Would a *more* intelligent man have done it? Then he remembered the dream. The light in the dream. *He* hadn't solved the problem, his unconscious had. The answer had been there all the time, but he was too close to see it. His mind had been forced to devise a way to tell him. Luckily, it had.

And finally, he didn't care *how* he had uncovered it. His God, if he had had anything to do with it, had heard him. Terrence was by no means a religious man, but this was miracle enough to make him a believer. It wasn't over yet, but the answer was there—and it *was* an answer.

He began to save himself.

Slowly, achingly slowly, he moved his right hand, the hand away from the robot's sight, to his belt. On the belt hung the assorted implements a spaceman needs at any moment in his ship. A wrench. A packet of sleep-stavers. A compass. A geiger counter. A flashlight.

The last was the miracle. Miracle in a tube.

He fingered it almost reverently, then unclipped it in a moment's frenzy, still immobile to the robot's "eyes."

He held it at his side, away from his body by a fraction of an inch, pointing up over the bulge of his spacesuited leg.

If the robot looked at him, all it would see would be the motionless bulk of his leg, blocking off any movement on his part. To the machine, he was inert. Motionless.

Now, he thought wildly, *where is the brain?*

If it is behind the relay machines, I'm still dead. If it is near the refrigerator, I'm saved. He could afford to take no chances. He would have to move.

He lifted one leg.

The robot moved toward him. The humming and sparking were more distinct this time. He dropped the leg.

Behind the plates above the refrigerator!

The robot stopped, nearly at his side. Seconds had decided. The robot hummed, sparked, and returned to its niche.

Now he knew!

He pressed the button. The invisible beam of the flashlight leaped out, speared the bulkhead above the refrigerator. He pressed the button again and again, the flat circle of light appearing, disappearing, appearing, disappearing on the faceless metal of the life hutch's wall.

The robot sparked and rolled from its niche. It looked once at Terrence. Its rollers changed direction in an instant and the machine ground toward the refrigerator.

The steeled fist swung in a vicious arc, smashing with a deafening *clang!* at the spot where the light bubble flickered on and off.

It swung again and again. Again and again till the bulkhead had been gouged and crushed and opened, and the delicate coils and plates and circuits and memorex modules behind it were refuse and rubble. Until the robot froze, with arm half-ready to strike again. Dead. Immobile. Brain and appendage.

Even then Terrence did not stop pressing the flashlight button. Wildly he thumbed it again and again and again.

Then he realized it was all over.

The robot was dead. He was alive. He would be saved. He had no doubts about that. *Now* he could cry.

The medicine chest grew large through the shimmering in his eyes. The relay machines smiled at him.

God bless you, little life hutch, he thought, before he fainted.

S.R.O.

Bart Chester was walking down Broadway when it materialized out of black nothing.

He was giving Eloise the line, with the "No, honest to *God*, Eloise, I mean if you come over to my place, we'll have just *one*—s'help me, just *one*—then we'll be off to the show." He was acutely aware there might not be any show that night, chiefly because there was no money that night, but Eloise didn't know that. She was a sweet girl and Bart didn't want to spoil her with luxuries.

Bart was just figuring mentally how many it would take to get Eloise's mind off a show and onto more earthy matters, when the whine began.

Like a thousand generators spinning at top-point efficiency the sound crawled up the stone walls encasing Times Square; bouncing back and back, reverberating thunderously amid the noise of Broadway, causing heads to turn, eyes to lift.

Bart Chester turned his head, lifted his eyes, and was one of the first to see it shimmer into existence. The air seemed to pinken and waver, like heat lightning far off. Then the air ran like water. It may have been in the eyes, or actually in the air, but the air *did* run like water.

The sly gleam faded from Bart Chester's eyes, and he never did get that "little one" with Eloise. He turned away from her splendid charms, realizing, knowing, sensing that he had a place in what was coming. Others must have felt the same way, for traffic on the sidewalks was slowing, people turning to stare into the evening darkness.

The coming was rapid. The air quavered a bit more, and a form began to take shape, as a ghost emerging from mist. The shape was long and cylindrical, protuberated and shining. It materialized over Times Square.

Bart took three rapid steps to the edge of the sidewalk, his eyes searching into the glare of neons, trying to see more of that weird structure. People jostled him and a knot began to form, as though he were a catalyst for some chemical action.

The *thing* (and Bart Chester had been in show business too long to jump at snap labels) hung there, suspended by hangings of nothing, as if waiting. It stretched up out between the trench of buildings, towering a good ten feet over the tallest one. The structure—whatever it was—appeared to be over nine hundred feet high. It hung above the ground, over the traffic island dividing Broadway and Seventh Avenue, the flickering of a million lights coloring its smooth tube body.

Even as he watched, the seemingly unbroken skin of the structure parted circularly and a flat plate emerged. The plate was dotted with small holes, and in another instant a thousand metallic filaments pushed through the holes. Rigidly, they weaved in the air.

Newspaper stories of the last few years, coupled with a natural childlike credulity, joined. *Migod,* thought Chester, and somehow knew his assumption was correct, *they're testing the atmosphere! They're finding out if they can live here!* When he had said this to himself, the greater implication struck him: *it's a spaceship! That—that* thing *came from another planet! Another planet?*

It had been many months since the Emery Bros. Circus, in which Bart had sunk all his ready cash, had folded. It had been many months since Bart had paid his rent, and not many less since he'd had three full meals in one twenty-four-hour period. He was desperately looking for an angle. Any angle!

Then, with the innate entrepreneur blood coursing through him beating fiercely, he thought joyously, *Good God, what an attraction this would make!*

Concessions. Balloons saying "Souvenir of the Spaceship." Popcorn, peanuts, Cracker Jacks, binoculars, pennants! Food! Hot dogs, candied apples; what a pitch! What a perfect pitch!

If I can get to it first, he added, mentally clicking his fingers.

He hardly saw the wildly gesturing policeman using his call box. He hardly heard the mixed screams and murmurs of the thronging crowds watching the metal filaments weaving their patterns. He elbowed back through the crowd.

Faintly, through the rising crowd noise, he heard Eloise moaning his name. "Sorry, baby," he yelled over his shoulder, putting his elbow into a fat woman's diaphragm, "but I've been hungry too long to pass up a sweet deal like this!

"Excuse me, ma'am. Pa'rm me, Mac. Excuse me, I'd like to get—uh—through here. Uh! Thanks, Mac," and he was at the drug store door. He adjusted his bow tie for a moment, muttering low to himself,

"Ohboyohboyohboy! Just looka this, little Bartie Chester! You're gonna make a millyun bucks! Yessir!"

He scrabbled for change as he slid into the booth. In another few minutes he had placed the long distance call—collect—to Mrs. Charles Chester in Wilmington, Delaware. He heard the phone ringing at the other end, then his mother's voice, "Yes, hello?" and he started to say, "Hey! Ma!" but the operator's voice cut through.

"Will you accept the charges, Mrs. Chester?"

When she had said yes, Bart threw himself into it. "Hello, hello, *Ma*! How ya?"

"Why, Bart, how wonderful to hear from you. It's been so long! Just those few postcards!"

"Yeah, yeah, I know, Ma," he cut her off, "but things have been really jumpin' for me here in New York. Look, Ma, I need some money."

"Well . . . how much, Bart? I can let you have . . ."

"I'll need a couple hunnerd, Ma. It's the biggest—so help me God—the *biggest* goddam deal I ever—"

"*Bart!* Your language! And to your mother!"

"Sorry, Ma, really sorry, but this is so hot it's burnin' my pinkies! Honest to—" he caught himself quickly, "—gosh! Ma, I need the dough like I never did before. I can get it back to you in a few months, Ma! Pleeeze, Ma! I never asked ya for nothin' before!"

The next two minutes were a gradual wearing-down period in which Mrs. Charles Chester promised to go to the bank and get the last two hundred in sight. Bart thanked her most graciously. He ignored the operator's snide interjections to his mother about waiting for charges *she* would have to pay, then he was off the line and back on another.

"Hello, Erbie? This is Bart. Look, I got a deal on that is without a doubt the most—*wait* a minute, for Christ's sake, willya—this is the greatest thing ever hit the—"

Five minutes and five hundred dollars later: "Sandy, baby? Who's *this*? Who ya think? This's Bart. Bart Ches—HEY! don't hang up! This is a chance for you to make a millyun; a sweet honest-to-God millyun! Now here's what I want. I wanta borrow from you—"

Fifteen minutes, six phone calls and four thousand five hundred and twenty dollars later, Bart Chester bolted from the drug store, just in time to see the tentacled plate receding into the ship, the skin closing again.

Eloise was, of course, gone. Bart didn't even notice.

The crowds were by this time overflowing into the streets—though everyone was careful not to get under the structure—and traffic was blocked to a standstill all up the avenue. Motorists were perched on car hoods, watching the machine.

Fire trucks had been drawn up, somehow. Rubber-overcoated firemen stood about biting their lower lips and shaking their heads ineffectually. *I've gotta get in there; get the edge on any other promoters!* Visions of overflowing steam-tables danced in Bart Chester's head.

As he was pushing through the crowd, back to the curb, he saw the police cordon forming. The beefy, spectacled cop was joining hands with a thin, harassed-looking bluecoat, as Chester got to them.

"Sorry, buddy, you can't go in there. We're shooin' everyone out now," the fat officer said, over his shoulder.

"Look, officer, I *gotta* get in there." At the negative shake from the cop, Chester exploded, "Look—I'm Bart Chester! You know, Star Cavalcade of 1954, the Emery Bros. Circus—I produced 'em! I *got* to get in there!" He could tell he was making no impression whatsoever.

"Look, you've got to—Hey! Inspector! Hey, over here!" He waved frantically, and the short man in the drab overcoat paused as he headed toward the squad car pool.

Taking care not to step on the microphone cables being laid along the street, he walked toward the crowd. Chester said to the cops, "Look, I'm a friend of Inspector Kesselman. Inspector," he said imploringly, "I've got to get in there. It's real important. Maybe a promotion!"

Kesselman began to shake his head no, then he looked at Chester with narrowed eyes for a moment, remembering free tickets to the fights, and reluctantly bobbed his head in agreement. "Okay, come on," he said, with obvious distaste, "but stay close."

Chester ducked under the restraining arms of the cops, following the little man around the shadow of the structure.

"How's the promoting business, Chester?" asked the Inspector as they walked.

Bart felt his head grow light and begin to float off his shoulders. *That* was precisely the trouble: "Lousy," he said.

"Come over some night for dinner, if you get the time," added the Inspector, in a tone that suggested Bart turn down the invite.

"Thanks," said Bart, carefully walking around the huge machine's shadow in the street.

"Is it a spaceship?" asked Chester, in almost a childlike tone. Kesselman turned and looked at him strangely.

"Where in Hell did you get *that* idea from?" he asked.

Chester shrugged his shoulders. "Oh, just them comic books I been readin'." He smiled lopsidedly.

"You're crazy," said Kesselman, shaking his head as he turned away.

Two hours later, when the last firemen had come down from the ladders, shaken their heads in failure and said, "Sorry, these acetylene torches don't even get the metal smoky," and walked away, Kesselman still looked at Chester with annoyance and said, "You're crazy."

An hour later, when they had ascertained definitely that machine gun bullets did not even dent the structure, he was less sure, but he refused to call the scientists Chester suggested. "Goddammit, Chester, this is *my* business, not yours, now either you keep your trap shut, or I'll boot you out beyond the cordon!" He gestured meaningfully at the throbbing crowds straining against the joined hands of the police. Chester subsided, confident they would do as he had suggested, eventually.

Eventually was one hour and fifty minutes later when Kesselman threw up his hands in despair and said, "Okay, get your goddam experts in here, but do it fast. This thing might settle any minute.

"Or," he added sarcastically, looking at the grinning Bart Chester, "if there's monsters in this thing, they may start eating us any minute now."

It was a spaceship. Or at any rate, it was from *someplace* else.

The gray-faced scientists clucked knowingly to each other for a while; one of the braver experts climbed a fire ladder and tested the ship in some incomprehensible manner, and then they concurred.

"It is our opinion," said the scientist with the three snatches of hair erupting from an otherwise bald head, "that this vehicle—am I speaking clearly enough for you reporters?—this vehicle is from somewhere off Earth. Now whether," he pointed out, while the others nodded in agreement, "this is a spaceship, or as seems more likely from the manner in which it appeared, a dimension-spanning device, I am not certain.

"But," he concluded, making washing movements with his hands, "it is definitely of extraterrestrial origin." He spelled the six-syllable word, and the reporters went whooping off to the telephones.

Chester grabbed Kesselman by the arm. "Look, Inspector, who has say-so—jurisdikshun, *you* know—over this thing? I mean, who would have say-so about entertainment rights and like that?" Kesselman was looking at him as though he were insane. Chester started another sentence, but the screams from the crowd drowned him out. He looked up quickly.

The skin of the spaceship was opening again.

By the time the crowds had streamed into the crosstown streets, terror universally mirrored on every face, but mingled with an overwhelming curiosity. New Yorkers were once again torn between their native desire to watch, and a fear of the unknown.

Chester and the stubby-legged Inspector found themselves walking backward, taking short steps, fearful steps, as they looked upward. *Don't let them be monsters,* Chester was almost praying. *Or that beautiful meal-ticket'll be knocked off by the militia!*

The spaceship was motionless; it had not altered its original position by an inch. But a platform was extending. A transparent platform, so clear and so thin, it seemed almost invisible. Six hundred feet up the ship's length, between two huge ribbed knobs extending as though they were growths, the platform slid out over Times Square.

"Get some guns on that thing!" bellowed Kesselman at his men. "Get up in those buildings." He pointed at two skyscrapers between which the spaceship hovered.

Chester stared at the ship in fascination as the platform extended—then stopped. As he watched, a note was sounded. It rose in his mind, audibly, yet soundlessly. He cocked his head to one side, listening. He could see police and slowly returning pedestrians doing the same. "Whutzat?" he asked.

The sound built, climbing from the hollow arch at the bottom of his feet, to the last feeling inch of each strand of hair on his head. It overwhelmed him and his sight dimmed for a moment, to be replaced by bursting lights and flickering shadows. In an instant his vision cleared, but he knew it had been a preamble. He knew—again without reason—the sound had come from the ship. He turned his eyes to the platform once more, just in time to see the lines begin their forming.

He could never quite describe what they were, and the only thing he knew for certain was that they were beautiful. The lines were suspended in air and of colors he had never known existed. They were parallel and crossed streamers that lived *between* the reds and blues of Earth. They were alien to his sight, yet completely arresting. He could not take his eyes from their wavering, shifting formations.

Then the colors began to seep. Like running paints the lines melted, forming, forming, forming in the air above the platform. The colors intermingled and blended; soon a backdrop of shades blotted out the skin of the ship.

"What—what is it?" he heard Kesselman ask, faintly.

Before he could answer, *they* came out.

The beings appeared and stood silent for an instant. They were all different in bodily appearance, yet somehow Chester knew they were all alike underneath. As though they had donned coverings. In the instant they stood there, motionless, he knew each by name. The purple-furred one on the left, he was Vessilio. The one with stalks growing where his eyes should have been, he was Davalier. The others, too, all bore names, and oddly, Chester knew each one intimately. They did not repulse him, for all their alienness. He knew Vessilio was stalwart and unflinching in the face of duty. He knew Davalier was a bit of a weakling, prone to crying in private. He knew all this and more. He *knew* each one, personally.

Yet they were all monstrous. Not one was shorter than forty feet. Their arms—when they had arms—were well-formed and properly sized for their bodies. Their legs, heads, torsos the same. But few had arms and legs and torsos. One was a snail-shape. Another seemed to be a ball of coruscating light. A third changed form and line even as Chester watched, pausing an instant in a strangely unidentifiable middle stage.

Then they began moving.

Their bodies positioned and swayed. They moved around one another, intricately. Chester found himself enthralled. They were magnificent! Their motions, their actions, their attitudes in relation to one another, were glorious. More, they told a story. A deeply interesting story.

The lines shifted, the merged colors changed. The aliens went through involved panoramas of descriptive motion.

Not for a second did Chester consider he might stop watching them. They were something so alien, so different, yet so compelling, he knew he must watch them or forever lose the knowledge they were imparting with their movements.

When the soundless note had sounded again, the colors had faded, the aliens were gone and the platform had slid back, the spaceship was quiet and faceless once more. Chester found himself breathing with difficulty. They had been—well, literally breathtaking!

He glanced at the huge clock on the Times Building. Three hours had elapsed in the space of a second.

The murmurs of the crowd, the strange applause for a performance they could not have fully understood, the feel of Kesselman's hand on his arm, all faded away. He heard the Inspector's voice, so whispery in his ear, "Good Lord, how marvelous!" Even that was out of his range now.

He knew, as he had known everything else, just what the ship was, who the aliens were, what they were doing on Earth. He heard himself saying it, quietly, almost with reverence:

"That was a play. They're actors!"

They *were* magnificent, and New York learned it only shortly before the rest of the world got wind of the news. Hotels and shops suddenly found themselves deluged by the largest tourist crowds in years. The city teemed with thousands of visitors, drawn from all over the Earth, who wished to witness the miracle of The Performance.

The Performance was always the same. The aliens came out onto their platform—their stage, really—every evening at precisely eight o'clock. They were finished by eleven.

During the three hours they maneuvered and postured, they filled their appreciative audiences with mixtures of awe and love and suspense such as no other acting group had ever been able to do.

Theatres in the Times Square area found they had to cancel their evening performances. Many shows closed, many switched to matinee runs and prayed. The Performance went on.

It was uncanny. How each person who watched enraptured could find identification, find meaning; though everyone saw something a little different; though no words were spoken; though no comprehensible motions were made.

It was uncanny. How they could see the actors do the exact same things, over and over, each Performance, and never tire of it—come back to see it again. It was uncanny, yet beautiful. New York took The Performance to its heart.

After three weeks, the Army was called away from the ship—which had done nothing but produce The Performance regularly each evening—to quell a prison riot in Minnesota. In five weeks Bart Chester had made all the necessary arrangements, shoestring-fashion, and was praying things wouldn't fizzle as they had with the Emery Bros. Circus. He was still going without meals, moaning to those who would listen, "What a lousy racket this is—but I got a deal on now that's—"

In seven weeks Bart Chester had begun to make his first million.

No one would pay to watch The Performance, of course. Why should they when they could stand in the streets and see it? But there was still the unfathomable "human nature" factor with which to contend.

There were still those who would rather sit in a gilded box seat, balcony style, hung from the outside of a metropolitan skyscraper (insured by Lloyd's, to be sure!), than stand in a gutter.

There were still those who felt that popcorn and chocolate-covered almonds made preparation of watching more pleasant. There were still those who felt the show was *common* if they did not have a detailed program.

Bart Chester, whose stomach had begun to bulge slightly beneath his new charcoal-gray suit, took care of those things.

Bart Chester Presents was scripted across the top of the programs, and beneath it, simply, The Performance. It was rumored up and down the street that Bart Chester was the new Sol Hurok, and a man which definitely we should all watch!

During the first eight months of The Performance, he made back all the borrowed money he had invested in building-face leases and construction work. Everything from there on out was reasonably clear profit. The confection and souvenir concessions he leased for a fifty percent cut of the gross to the people who supplied ball games and wrestling matches.

The Performance went on, regularly, as an unquestionable smash hit.

Variety said: **ETs SOCKO IN PLUSH REVUE!**

The *Times* was no less ebullient with its praise: ". . . we found The Performance on Times Square as refreshing and captivating at its first anniversary as it was on its opening night. Even the coarse commercial interests which have infected it could not dim the superlativeness of the . . ."

Bart Chester counted his receipts and smiled; and grew fat for the first time in his life.

The two thousand, two hundred and eighty-ninth Performance was as brilliant and as satisfying as the first, the hundredth, or the thousandth. Bart Chester sat back in his plush seat, only vaguely aware of the stunning girl beside him. Tomorrow she would be back, trying to get a break in some off-Broadway production, but tomorrow The Performance would still be there, pouring money into his pockets.

The major part of his mind concentrated, held in awe and wonder at the intricacy and glory of the actors' movements. A minor segment was thinking, as it always did with him.

Wonderful! Marvelous! A true spec'tcle like The New Yorker *said!* All around him, like perspiration on a huge beast, the Chester Balconies clung to their buildings. The inexpensive seats between 45th and 46th Streets, the higher priced boxes dotting the buildings all the way up to the Times Building. *One of these days those slobs'll break down and I'll be able to build on the Times, too!* he thought.

Over six years; what a run! Beats South Pacific! *Dammit, wish I could have made all that in gate receipts.*

He frowned mentally, thinking of all the people watching from the streets. For free! The crowds were still as huge as the first day. People never seemed to tire of seeing the play. Over and over they watched it, enraptured, deep in it, not even noticing the flow of time. The Performance always satisfied, always enchanted.

They're fabulous players, he thought. *Only . . .*

The thought was half-formed. Nebulous. Annoying. It itched in the back of his mind. Then he shrugged. There was no reason why he should feel qualms. *Oh well.*

He concentrated on the play. It really took little concentration, for the actors spoke directly to the mind; their charming appeal was to a deeper and clearer well than mere appreciation.

He was not even aware when the tone of the play changed. At one point the actors were performing a strangely exotic minuet of movement. A second later, they were all down near the front of the platform.

"That isn't in the play!" he said, incredulously, the mood broken. The beautiful girl beside him grabbed at his sleeve.

"What d'ya mean, Bart?" she asked.

He shook her hand off in annoyance. "I've seen this show hunnerds of times. Right here they all get around that little humpbacked bird-thing and stroke it. What're they staring at?"

He was correct. The actors were looking down at their audience who had begun to applaud nervously, sensing something was wrong. The aliens watched with stalks, with cilia, with eyes. They were staring at the people in the streets, on the balconies, seeming to see them for the first time since they'd arrived. Something was very wrong. Chester had felt it first—perhaps because he had been there from the beginning. The crowds were beginning to sense it also. They were milling in the streets, uncertainly.

Chester found his voice tight and high as he said, "There's—there's something *wrong*! What're they doing?"

When the platform sank slowly down the face of the ship, till finally one of the actors stepped off into the empty space beside the machine, he began to realize.

It was only after the first few moments, when the horror of the total carnage he knew was coming, had worn off, and he found himself staring fascinated as the little, forty foot, humpbacked bird-thing strode through Times Square, that he knew.

It had been a wonderful show, and the actors had appreciated the intense interest and following of their audience. They had lived off the applause for over six years. They were artists without a doubt.

And up to a point, they had *starved* for their art.

II

WORLDS OF TERROR

> "I want people's hair to stand on end when they read my work, whether it's a love story, or a gentle childhood story, or a story of drama and violence."
>
> —"Harlan Ellison," DREAM MAKERS: THE UNCOMMON PEOPLE WHO WRITE SCIENCE FICTION, Interviews by Charles Platt, Berkley, 1980

"Horror" and "terror," while often given as synonyms for each other, are really creatures quite different. "Horror" brings forth images of rotting corpses, yawning graves. Something shambling and rotting moves toward us, something disgusting. Horror is the gross out. "Terror" is something else again, and it links directly and unequivocally with fear. Harlan has written few stories of horror for its own sake, though his stories of terror may have us end up horrified. If horror is the rising gorge, then fear is the sheen of sweat on the forehead.

These are stories more of terror than horror.

"Lonelyache" (1964) is unmistakably a portrait of obsession, but its grimness is not in the fate of its protagonist, but in that awful last line. (Though perhaps a different interpretation derives from what Harlan asserts is the key to the story: that dream car and its back window.) The fear in this story is that great lonelyache, when nothing else matters anymore.

"Punky & the Yale Men" (1966) is a particularly savage look at fear, inside and out. Here the twin icons of money and power are wedded to guilt. Punky's fear is of being exposed as a fraud, a charlatan, and the bravado of his fear drives him into the underbelly of the American city and to his fate.

"A Prayer for No One's Enemy" (1966) sees ghosts from the past, whether from ethnic or personal history, stirring themselves up and forcing some expected and unexpected confrontations. But it is the two teenagers, outside the central turmoil, who learn the lessons of madness and how it shakes forever their own complacency.

These are stories from the Sixties, but their morals are really timeless.

"It is in moments of violence that we have confrontation, that we find out what we believe in, whether we have soul and spirit. They are the pivotal points in our lives."

—"Ellison Speaks . . . ," *Luna Monthly* #46, March 1973

Lonelyache

The form of the habit she had become still drove him to one side of the bed. Despite his need for room to throw out arms, legs in a figure-4, crosswise angled body, he still slept on only one side of the big double bed. The force of memory of her body there, lying huddled on the inside, together cuddled body-into-body, a pair of question marks, whatever arrangement it might have been from night to night—still, her *there*. Now, only the memory of her warmth beside him kept him prisoner on his half. And reduced to memories and physical need for sleep, he retired to that slab of torture as seldom as possible. Staying awake till tiny hours, doing meaningless things, laughing at laughers, cleaning house for himself with methodical surgical tidiness till the pathology of it made him gibber and caper and shriek within his skull and soul, seeing movies that wandered aimlessly, hearing the vapors of night and time and existence passing by without purpose or validity. Until finally, crushed by the weight of hours and decaying bodily functions, desperately needing recharge, he collapsed into the bed that he loathed.

To sleep on one side only.

To dream his dreams of brutality and fear.

This was the dream, that same damned recurrent dream, never *quite* the same dream—but on the same subject, night after night, chapter after chapter of the same story: as if he had bought a book of horror stories; they would all be on one theme, but told differently; that was the way with this string of darkside visions.

Tonight came number fourteen. A clean-cut collegiate face proudly bearing its wide, amiable grin. A face topped by a sandy brush-cut and light, auburn eyebrows, giving that sophomoric countenance a giggly, innocent vividness instantly conveying friendship. Under other circumstances Paul knew he could be close friends with this guy. *Guy*, that was the word he used, even in the dream, rather than *fellow*, or *man*, or—most accurately—*assassin*. In any other place than this misty nightmare, with any other intent than this one, they might have lightly punched each other's biceps in camaraderie and hey, how the hell are you'd each other. But this was the dream, latest installment, and this college guy was number fourteen. Latest in an endless, competent string of pleasant types sent to kill Paul.

The plot of the dreams was long-since formulated, now merely suggested by rote in the words and deeds of the players (sections indefinite, details muzzy, transitions blurred, logic distorted dream-style): Paul had been a member of this gang, or group, or bunch of guys, whatever. Now they were after him. They were intent on killing him. If they ever came at him in a group, they would succeed. But for some reason that made sense only in the dream, they were assigned the job one by one. And as each sweet human being tried to tip him the black spot, Paul killed him. One after another, by the most detailed, violently brutal and gut-wrenching means available, he killed the killers. Thirteen times they had come against him—these men who were decent and pleasant and dedicated, whom he would have been proud to call his friends under other circumstances—and thirteen times he had escaped assassination.

Two or three or—once—four in a night, for the past several weeks (and that he had only killed thirteen till now bore witness to the frequency with which he avoided sleep entirely, or crashslept himself into exhaustion so there *were* no dreams).

Yet the most disturbing part of the dreams was the brutalized combat itself. Never a simple shooting or positive poisoning. Never an image that could be re-told when awakening without bringing a look of shock and horror to the face of Paul's confidante. Always a bizarre and minutely-described *affaire de morte*.

One of the assassins had pulled a thin, desperately-sharp stiletto, and Paul had grappled with the man interminably, slashing at his flesh and the sensitive folds of skin between fingers, till the very essence, the very *reality* of death by knife became a gagging tremor in his sleeping body. It was as though the sense, the *feel* of death-in-progress was evoked. More than a dream, it had been a new threshold of anguish, a vital new terror which he would ever after have to support. It was something new to live with. Until finally he had locked the man's hands about the hilt and driven the slim blade into his stomach, deep and with difficulty, feeling it puncture and gash through organs, resisting, rubbery organs; then pulling it away from the mortally-wounded assassin and (did he, or did he suppose he had) used it again and again, till the other had fallen under the furniture. Another had been battered to his knees and dispatched finally, with a smooth, heavy piece of black statuary. Still another had gone screaming, pushed abruptly (Paul with teeth bared, fang-like, vicious animal) from a ledge, twisting and plunging heavily away. The passion with which he had watched that body fall, the desire in him to *feel* the weight of it going down, had been the disgusting detail of that particular segment. Still another had come at Paul with some now-forgotten weapon, and Paul had used a tire chain on him, first wrapping it tightly about the assassin's neck and twisting till the links broke skin . . . then flaying the unconscious body till there was no life left in it.

One after another. Thirteen of them, two already tonight, and now number fourteen, this pleasant-enough guy with the rah-rah demeanor, and the fireplace poker in his competent hands. The gang would never let him alone. He had run, had hidden, had tried to avoid killing them by putting himself out of reach, but they always found him. He went at the guy, wrested the poker from him, and jabbed sharply with the pike-tip of it. He was about to envision where he had thrust that blunt-sharp point, when the phone went off and the doorbell rang—simultaneously.

For a screaming instant of absolute terror he lay there flat on his back, the other side of the bed creased only by a small furrow made by his spastic arm as it had flung itself away from him; the other side of the bed that she had inhabited, now untenanted, save for the wispy end-tips of the dream, streaking away as his arm had done.

While the chime and the bell rang in discordant duo.

Having saved him from seeing what damage he had done the collegiate guy's face. Almost like melodious saviors. Rung in by a watchful God who allotted only certain amounts of fear and depravity to each sleeptime. Knowing he would pick up the thread of the dream precisely where he had left off, next time out. Hoping he could stave off sleep for a year, two years, so he would not have to find out how the rah-rah type had died. But knowing he would. Listening to the phone and the doorbell clanging at him. Having let them serve their purposes of wakening him, now fearing to answer them.

He flipped onto his stomach and reached out a hand in the darkness that did not deter him. He grabbed the receiver off its rest and yowled, "Hold it a minute, please," and in one movement flipped aside the clammy sheet, hit the floor and surely fumbled his way to the door. He opened it as the chime went off again, and in the light from the hallway saw only a shape, no person. He heard a voice, made no sense of it, and said impatiently, "C'min, c'min already, for Chri'sake an' shut the door." He turned away and went back to the bed, picked up the receiver he had tossed onto the pillow, and cleared phlegm from his throat as he asked, "Yeah, okay now, who's this?"

"Paul. Has Claire gotten there, is she there yet?" He felt bits of rock-salt in the corners of his eyes, and fingered them tighter into the folds of flesh as he tried to place the voice. It was someone he knew, a friend, someone—

"Harry? That's you, Harry?"

On the other end of the line, way out there in the night somehow, Harry Dockstader swore lightly, quickly. "Yeah, me, me already. Paul, is Claire there?"

Paul Reed was suddenly assaulted by the overhead light going on, and he snapped his eyes shut against the blaze, opened them, closed them again, and then finally popped them open completely to see Claire Dockstader standing at the switch by the front door.

"Yeah, Harry, she's here," then the weirdness of her being here came to him fully, and he demanded, "Harry, what the hell is going on, Claire's over here, why isn't she with you? Why's she here?"

It was an inane conversation, totally devoid of sense, but his synapses were not yet in focus. "Harry?" he repeated.

The voice on the other end snarled, gutturally.

Then Claire was coming across the room at him, wrathful and impatient, ferocious in demanding, "*Give me that* phone!" Each word sharply enunciated, much too fine for this hour of the morning, each syllable clear and harsh and very thin-lipped, only a woman's way. "Give me that phone, Paul. Let *me* talk to him . . . hello, Harry? You sonofabitch, go straight to fucking hell, die you bastard! Ooo, you *bas*-tard!"

And she literally flung the receiver onto the rest.

Paul sat on the edge of the bed, feeling himself naked from the waist up, feeling the rug under his bare feet, feeling that *no* woman should use language like that at this hour. "Claire . . . *what* the hell is going *on*?"

She stood trembling for a moment, valkyric in her fury, then stalked, half-stumbled, fell across the room into the easy chair. Upon touching the seat she burst into tears. "Ooo, the *bas*-tard," she repeated, not to Paul, not to the silent phone, to the air perhaps. "That lousy chaser, that skunk and his chippies, those *bums* he brings up to the house, Oh God Why'd I Ever Marry That Skunk!"

It was, of course, all laid out for Paul in that sentence, even without the particulars, even at that hour, and the ring of his own recent past was so clear he winced. The word *chaser* did it. His own sister had called him that when she'd heard he and Georgette were divorcing. That damned word: *chaser*. He could still hear it. It had hurt.

Paul rose from bed. The one-and-a-half in which he managed to live (now) alone suddenly seemed close and muggy with a woman in it. "Claire, want some coffee?"

She nodded, still running through her thoughts like prayer beads, eyes turned inward. He moved past her into the tiny kitchenette. The electric coffeepot was on the sideboard, and he hefted it, shook it to see if there was enough left from the last brewing. A heavy sloshing reassured him, and he plugged in the cord.

As he returned to the living room, her eyes followed him. He dropped onto the bed and slid upward, bracing the pillow behind him, "Okay," Paul said, reaching for the cigarettes beside the phone, "lay it on me. Who was it this time, and how far along were they when you caught him?"

Claire Dockstader pursed her lips so tightly, dimples appeared in her cheeks. "Only a philanderer like you, as bad as Harry, just as big a Skunk, could put it that way!"

Paul shrugged. He was a long, lean man with a thatch of straw-colored hair; he raked the hair off his forehead and applied himself to lighting the cigarette. He didn't want to look at her. A thing in his living room, soon after Georgette, too soon, even a friend's wife. He pulled at the cigarette, and at his thoughts: neither satisfied. He seemed too long for the bed, ungainly, hardly of interest to a woman, yet apparently it was not so, for she stared at him differently now. A subtle shifting of mood in the room, as though she had suddenly realized she had not only broken into his living room, but into his bedroom as well, a room in which other things than just living were done. They were very close, but held apart by a circumstance that both realized might at any moment melt. Uncomfortable, suddenly, both of them. He pulled up the sheet to his waist; she looked away.

Coffee perking, popping, distracting, thank God.

"Christ, what time is it?" Paul asked (himself, in self-defense, more than her). He pulled the travalarm from the nightstand and stared into it face, its idiot face, as though the numbers meant something. "Jeezus, Jeezus, three ayem, Jeezus; don't you people ever sleep?" He was a pot, calling a kettle black. He never slept, never really went to bed, so who was he fooling with this line out of suburban rote?

She shifted in the easy chair, rearranging her skirt that had ridden up over her knees, and Paul once more marveled at the joys of the current hemlines, if one was a leg man, which he had decided with the advent of the current hemlines, he was. She caught his stare and toyed with it for a moment, then allowed it to vaporize in her own eyes, not just yet returning his proposition.

It was happening, just this easily. A pact of guilt and opportunity was being solidified, without the decency of either admitting its necessity. Paul had been separated not nearly long enough to attempt morality of a high order, and Claire was still burning with outrage. Neither would say the name of the game, but both would play, and both knew it would happen.

And as soon as Paul Reed admitted his loneliness, his guilt and his desires were compounding to produce (why fool around, name it!) adultery, an act of love performed without the catalyst of love, something unpleasant began to happen in the empty, dark, far corner of the room.

He was unaware of its beginnings.

"Why did you pick me for your flight?" he asked flippantly.

"You were the only one I could think of who'd be awake this late . . . and I wasn't thinking too clearly . . . I was too furious to think straight." She stopped talking; she had said much more than what she had said. Of all the places she might have gone, of all the seedy bars where she might have been picked up and laid in retaliation, of all the married friends she and Harry had accrued, of all the cheap hotels where an innocent night of sleep might be purchased for eight dollars, she had picked Paul and his living room that was a bedroom that was a hole in the world where guilt could be born out of frustration and pain.

"Is that, uh, coffee ready?" she asked.

He slid out of bed, nakedly aware of her eyes on his body, and went into the kitchenette. He ached in places he did not want to ache, and knew what was going to happen, for all the wrong reasons, and knew he would despise not only her and himself when it had been done, when they had killed something between them, but that he would barely think of it again. He was wrong.

When he handed her the coffee cup, their hands touched, and their eyes locked for the first time in this new way, and the cyclic movement began for the millionth time that night. And once begun, the cycle could not be impeded.

While slowly, steadily, in the dark corner, what had begun to happen, nasty as it was, went on unnoticed. Their insensate passion a midwife at that strange birth.

Simply the mechanics of divorce were gristmill enough to powder him into the finest ash. Simply the little pains of walking through the apartment where they had bumped into one another constantly, the lawyer talks, the serving of the papers, the phone calls that lacked any slightest tinge of communication, the recriminations, and worst of all, the steadily deteriorating knowledge that somehow what had gone wrong was not real, but a matter of thoughts, attitudes, dreams, ghosts, vapors. All insubstantial, but so omnipresent, so *real*, they had broken up his marriage with Georgette. As if they *were* substantial, rock-hard, real, physically tearing her from his arms and his thoughts and his life. Phantom raiders from both of their minds, whose sole purpose in life was to shrivel and shred and shatter their union. But the thoughts and vapors and gray images persisted, and he existed alone in the one-and-a-half where they had set up their gestalt, while she cast the runes and murmured the incantations and boiled up the mystic brews, all set down so precisely in the grimoire of divorce. And as the pattern of separation progressed, a boulder racing mindlessly downhill, needing only the most impossible strength imaginable to halt its crushing rush, his life set itself up in a new sequence, apart from her, yet totally motivated by her existence, and the reality of her absence.

Earlier that day he had received a phone call from her. One of those backbiting, bitter, flame-colored conversations that ended in him telling her to go to hell, she wasn't getting any more money out of him till the settlement, and he didn't give a damn *how* badly she needed it.

"The Court said a hundred and twenty-five a month separate maintenance, and that's all you're getting. Stop buying clothes and you'll have enough to live on."

Chittering reply from the other end.

"A hundred and twenty-five, baby, that's *it*! You're the one who moved out, not me; don't expect me to support your nutty behavior gratis. We're through, Georgette, get that through your platinum head, we're all done. I've had it with you! I'm fed up with all the dirty dishes in the sink, and your subway phobia, and not being able to touch your goddam hair after you've been to the beauty parlor and—oh, crap, why bother with all this . . . the answer is . . ."

Chittering interruption, vitriol electrically transmitted, hatred telephonically magnified, poured directly into his mind through his ear.

". . . *yeah*? Well, the same to you, you stupid simpleass broad, the same *double* to you. Go to hell! You're not getting any more money out of me till the settlement, and I don't give a damn *how* badly you need it!"

He had slammed the receiver back on the stand, and continued getting dressed for his date. When he had picked up the girl, a brunette he had met in his insurance agent's office, a secretary there, it was as though he was collecting unemployment, getting something to which he was entitled, but that nonetheless smacked faintly of being on relief.

Picking up this girl for the first time was precisely like collecting unemployment. Enough to keep him going, but not nearly enough to sustain him in a supportable life. A dole. A pittance, but desperately necessary. A casual girl, with a life of her own, whose path would cross his this once, and then they would stumble past, down their own roads forever, light-footed, unlighted, interminably.

"I'm afraid I won't be very charming company tonight," he told her as she slid into the car. "A woman who looks very much like you gave me considerable heartache today."

"Oh?" she inquired guardedly. It was their first date. "Who would that be?"

"My ex-wife," he said, telling her the first lie. He had not looked at her, save when he reached across to open the door. Now he stared dead-straight ahead as he pulled the unpolished Ford away from the curb and swung it into traffic.

She sat looking at him speculatively, wondering if accepting a dinner date with an office client was such a good idea after all, no matter *how* engaging a sense of humor he had. His face was not at all the youthful cleverness he had presented to her on those three occasions when he had come to the insurance office. It was a harder substance, somehow, as though whatever light, frothy matter had been its basic component previously, had congealed, like week-old gravy. He was unhappy and disturbed, of course, there was that in abundance; but something else skittered on the edge of his expression, a somnolence, and she was strangely frightened by it—though she was certain it meant harm not for her, but on the contrary, very much for him.

"Why do you let her give you heartache?"she asked.

"Because I still love her, I suppose," he answered, a bit too quickly, as though he had rehearsed it.

"Does *she* love you?"

"Yeah, I guess she does." He paused, then added in a contemplative monotone, "Yeah. I'm quite certain she does. Otherwise we wouldn't try to kill each other so hard. It's making us both very sick, her loving me."

She straightened her skirt and tried to find another passage through the conversation, but all she could think was, *I should have told him I was busy tonight.*

"Do I look very much like her?"

He stared straight ahead, handling the wheel casually, as though very certain, very sure of it, as though he derived a deep inner satisfaction from driving, from propelling all this weight and metal precisely as he wished. It was as though he was with her, yet very far away, locked in an embrace with his vehicle.

"Oh, not really, I suppose. She's blonde, you're brunette. Just around the temples, maybe, and your hair, the way you wear it pulled back on the side that way, and the skin around her eyes crinkles the same way. That, and the tone of your skin. Something like that; more re*minds* me of her than any actual look-alike."

"Is that why you asked me out?"

He thought about it a moment, pressing his full lips together, then replied, "No. That wasn't it. In fact, when I realized that you reminded me of her, I wanted to call the office and break the date."

I wish you had, she thought severely, *I wish I weren't here. With you.*

"We don't have to go, you know."

He turned his head, then, seemingly startled. "What? Oh, say, *hell* I didn't mean to depress you. This thing has been going on for months, and it's just one of those miserable problems that has to work itself out. Don't think I was trying to wriggle out of buying you a meal."

"I didn't think *that,*" she replied coolly. "I merely thought you might want to be alone this evening."

He smiled, a strained little smile that was half frown and part sneer, and moved his head slightly. "Christ! Anything but *that*. Not alone. Not tonight."

She settled back against the vinyl seat cover, determined suddenly to make him uncomfortable, in defense.

What seemed to each of them like elastic hours stretched past, and then he said, in an altogether new tone of voice, a forced light tone each knew was false, "Where would you like to go? Chinese? Italian? I know a nice little Armenian restaurant . . . ?"

She was silent, purposefully, and it *served* its purpose; he was uncomfortable, unhappier than before, and in the next instant it passed and he felt hateful, outright nasty, wanting either to get her into bed at once, or to dump her, but not have to suffer this way through an entire evening. And so she defeated herself, as the rock wall slid up to cover the gentleness he would have demonstrated later that night. Deviousness replaced gentleness, sadness.

"Listen," he said smoothly (once again, a new tone, a lacquer-finished tone, chromed and slick), lightly, "I didn't get a chance to shave before I picked you up, and I feel like a slob. You mind if we stop off for a minute at my place, and I'll run a razor over my face?"

She was not fooled. She had been married once, had been divorced, had been dating since she was fifteen, she knew *exactly* what he was saying. He was offering a private demonstration of his etchings. Her mind turned the offer slowly, examining it—in that breathless eternity of a moment in which all decisions are made—and studying each shimmering facet. She knew it was a bad idea, had no merit in any way, that she was a fool to think seriously of it, and that he would back off if she made the slightest sound of disapproval. True true, a bad idea, one to reject on the spot, and she rejected it. "All right," she said.

He turned sharply at the next corner.

He looked down at her face, and abruptly saw her at the age of sixty-five. He knew with a crystal certainty what she would look like when she was old. Superimposed over the pale-and-pink firm immediacy of her face framed against the pillow, he saw a gray line-mask of the old woman she would one day become. The mouth with its stitchlines, tiny pickets running down into the lips; the dusty hollows lurking beneath the eyes; dark spaces in the character lines and in the planes of expression—as though whole sections had been sold off to retain life, even at the cost of losing appearance. The sooty patina covering the flesh, much like that left when a moth has been crushed, the powdery fine ash of its wings imprinting the surface on which the death had occurred. He stared down at her, seeing the double-image, the future lying inchoate across her now-face, turning the paramour beneath him into a relic of incognito spare parts and empty passions. A dim, drenched cobweb of probability, there in the eye-sockets, across the mouth he had kissed, radiating out from the nostrils and pulsing ever so faintly in the hollow of her throat.

Then the vision melted off her young face, and he was looking at the creature of empty purposes he had just used. There was a mad, insane light flickering out of her eyes. "Tell me you love me, even if you don't mean it," she murmured huskily.

There was a hungry urgency, a breathless demand in her voice, and a fist closed around his heart as she spoke, a chill ruined his aplomb, his grasp of the present, so recently returned to him. He wanted to pull out of her, away from her, as far as he could, and crouch down somewhere in the bedroom in a patient, foetal security.

But the corner of the room he might have chosen was already occupied. Darkly occupied by bulk and a sinister presence. The breathing in that corner was coming laboredly, but much more regularly than before; it seemed to have become more steady, pulsing, as they had entered the apartment; and during the parry and counter and riposte of their encounter it had metronomically hurried itself to a level of even oftenness. Oh, it was taking form, form, form.

Paul sensed it, but discounted the instinct.

Deep breathing, stentorian, labored—but becoming more regular.

"Tell me. Tell me you love me, nineteen times, very fast."

"I love you I love you I love you I love you," he began rattling them off, propped on one elbow, counting them on the fingers of his left hand. "I love you I love you I luh—"

"Why are you counting them?" she demanded, coquettishly, in a bizarre grotesque parody of naïveté.

"I don't want to lose track," he answered, brutally. Then he slipped sidewise, falling onto his back, on Georgette's side of the bed (feeling uncomfortable there, as though the ridges and whorls of her body were imprinted there, making it lumpy for him, but with the determination not to let *this* girl lie on *that* side). "Go to sleep," he instructed her.

"I don't want to go to sleep."

"Then go bang your goddam head against the wall," he snapped. Then he was forcing himself to sleep. Eyes closed, knowing how angry the girl beside him had become, he commanded sleep to come, and timorously, fawn-like in a deep foreboding forest, it came, and touched him. So that he began to dream again. *That* dream, again.

In the eye, the right eye. The point of the poker entered, did its damage, came away foul. Paul flung himself violently from the sight, even as the crew-cut young man toppled soddenly past him, still alive somehow, crawling, dying by every bit of flesh through every rotting second. Starlight and darkness slipped by overhead as Paul whirled, spun, found himself in another place. A plaza, perhaps . . .

A crowd, down the smart sleek shop-bordered street—a posh street (where?) in Beverly Hills, perhaps, glistening and elegant, and seeming almost dazzlingly clean with rhodium-finished permanence—growling, coming toward him.

They were masked, caricatured, made up for some weird mardi gras, or costume party, or gathering of witches, where real faces would reveal real persons, and thus provide a grasp for their damnation. Strangers, boiling hurling sweeping down the street toward him in a chiaroscuro montage of chimerical madness. A vision out of Bosch; a bit of underdone potato or undigested Dali, hurled forth from a dream-image by Hogarth; a pantomime out of the innermost circle of Dante's Inferno. Coming for him. For him.

At last, after all these weeks, the dream had broken its pattern, and the massed terrors were now coming for him in a body. No longer one at a time, man-for-man in that never-ending succession of pleasant assassins. Now they had gathered together, grotesque creatures, masked and hungry.

If I can figure out what this means, I'll know, he thought suddenly. In the midst of the multi-colored haze of the dream, he knew abruptly, certainly, that if he could just make some sense from the events unreeling behind his eyes (and he *knew* it was a dream, right then), there would be a key to his problems, a solution that would work for him. So he concentrated. *If I can just understand who they are, what they're doing here, what they want from me, why they won't let me escape, why they're chasing me, what it takes to placate them, to get away from them, who I am who I am who I am . . . then I'll be free, I'll be whole again, this will be over, this will end, it'll end . . .*

He ran down the street, the white clean street, and dodged in and among the cars that had suddenly appeared in lines, waiting for the light to change. He ran down the street to the intersection, and cut across among the slowly-moving vehicles, terror clogging his throat, his legs aching from the running, seeking an escape, an exit, *any* exit—a place of rest, of security where he could close the door and know they could not get in.

"Here! We'll help you," a man shouted from a car, where he was packed in with his family, many children. Paul ran to the car, and the man opened his door, and Paul managed to crowd past him as he pulled the seat forward, offering entrance to the back seat. Paul squeezed through, pushing the man up against the steering wheel. Then the seat was dropped back, Paul was in the rear with the children, and the car was piled with (what? fuzzy, indistinct) clothes, or soft possessions that the children sat on, and he was forced to lie down across the back deck, under the rear window

(but how could that be?

(he was a full-grown man, he couldn't squeeze himself into that small a space, the way he had when he had been a child and gone on trips with his mother and father and laid down under the back window because the back seat was filled up, the way it had been when his father had died, and he had gone away with his mother from their home to the new home . . .

(why did that memory suddenly come through so lucidly?

(was he a grown man, or a small child?

(*please* answer!)

and he could see out the back window, and the crowd of terrifying masked figures, bright-eyed and haunting, were being left behind. Still, somehow, he did not feel safe! He was with the ones who could help, that man driving, he was strong and would drive fast through the traffic, and save Paul from the haunters, but why didn't he feel safe . . . why?

He woke, crying. The girl was gone.

There was one who chewed gum while they did it. An adolescent with oily thighs who had no idea of how to live in her body. The act was sodden and slow and entirely derelict in its duties. Afterward, he thought of her as a figment of his imagination, leaving only her laugh behind.

She had a laugh that sounded like pea pods snapping open. He had met her at a party, and her attractiveness stemmed chiefly from too many vodkas and tonics.

Another one was completely lovely, and yet, she was the sort of woman who gave the impression, upon entering a room, of having just left it.

One was small and slight and shrieked for no reason save that she had read how passionate women screamed at the climax—in a bad book. Or more aptly, an undistinguished book, for she was an undistinguished woman.

One after another they came to that one-and-a-half, casual adulteries without purpose or direction, and he indulged himself, again and again, finally realizing (by what was taking shape in the corner) what he was doing to himself, and his life that was no longer a life.

Genesis refers to sin that coucheth at the door, or croucheth at the door, and so this was no new thing, but old, so very old, as old as the senseless acts that had given it birth, and the madness that was causing it to mature, and the guilty sorrow—the lonelyache—that would inevitably cause it to devour itself and all within its sight.

On the night that he actually paid for love, the night he physically reached into his wallet and took out two ten dollar bills and gave them to the girl, the creature took full and final shape.

This girl: when "good girls" talk about "tramps" they mean this girl and her sisters. But there are no such things as "tramps" and even the criminal never thinks of himself in those terms. Working-girl, entrepreneur, renderer of services, smarty, someone just getting-along . . .

these are the ways of her thoughts. She has a family, and she has a past, and she has a face, as well as a place of sex.

But commercialism is the last sinkhole of love, and when it is reached, by paths of desperation and paths of cruel, misused emotions—all hope is gone. There is no return save by miracles, and there are no more miracles for the common among common men.

As he handed her the money, wondering why in God's name, *why!* the beast in the corner by the linen closet took its final shape, and substantiality, reality was its future. It had been called up by a series of contemporary incantations, conjured by the sounds of passion and the stink of despair. The girl snapped her bra, covered herself with dacron and decorum, and left Paul sitting stunned, inarticulate with terror in the presence of his new roommate.

It stared at him, and though he tried to avert his eyes (screams were useless), he stared back.

"Georgette," he said huskily into the mouthpiece, "listen . . . lis, *listen* to me, willya, for Christ's sake . . . st, stop *blab*bering for a second, willya, just, just SHUT UP FOR ONE GODDAM SECOND! willya . . ." She finally subsided, and his words, no longer forced to slip themselves piecemeal between hers, left standing naked and alone with nothing but silence confronting them, ducked back within him, shy and trembly.

"Well, go *on*," he said, reflexively.

She said she had nothing further to say; what was he calling her for, she had to get ready to go out.

"Georgette, I've got, well, I've got this uh this problem, and I had to *talk* to someone, you were the one I figured would understand, y'see, I've uh—"

She said she didn't know an abortionist, and if he had knocked up one of his bummy-girls, he could use a goddam coat-hanger, a *rusty* coat-hanger, for all she cared.

"No! No, you stupid ass, that isn't anything like what I'm scared about. *That* isn't it, and who the hell do *you* care who I date, you tramp . . . you're out on the turf enough for *both* of us . . ." and he stopped. This was how all their arguments had started. From subject to subject, like mountain goats from rock to rock, forgetting the original discussion, veering off to rip and tear with their teeth at each other's trivialities.

"Georgette, *please*! Listen to me. There's a, there's a thing, some kind of *thing* living here in the apartment."

She thought he was crazy, what did he mean?

"I don't know. I don't know what it is."

Was it like a spider, or a cat, or what?

"It's like a bear, Georgette, only it's something else, I don't know what. It doesn't say anything, just *stares* at me—"

What was he, cracking up or something? Bears don't talk, except the ones on TV, and what was he, trying to pull off a nut stunt so he wouldn't have to pony up the payments the court set? And why was he calling her in the first place, closing with: I think you're flipping, Paul. I always said you were a whack, and now you're proving it.

Then the phone clicked, and he was alone.

Together.

He looked at it from the corner of his eye as he lit a cigarette. Hunkered down in the far corner of the room, near the linen closet, the huge soft-brown furry thing that had come to watch him, sat silently, paws folded across its massive chest. Like some great Kodiak bear, yet totally unlike it in shape, the truncated triangle of its bloated form could not be avoided—by glance or thought. The wild, mad golden discs of its eyes never turned, never flickered, while it watched him.

(This description. Forget it. The creature was nothing like that. Not a thing like that at all.)

And he could sense the reproach, even when he had locked himself in the bathroom. He sat on the edge of the tub and ran the hot water till steam had obscured the cabinet mirror over the sink and he could no longer see his own face, the insane light in his eyes so familiar, so similar to the blind stares of the creature in the other room. His thoughts flowed, ran, lava-like, then congealed.

At which point he realized he had never seen the faces of any of the women who had been in the apartment. Not one of them. Faceless, all of them. Not even Georgette's face came to him. None of them. They were all without expression or recall. He had been to seed with so many angular corpses. The sickness welled up in him, and he knew he had to get out of there, out of the apartment, away from the creature in the corner.

He bolted from the bathroom, gained the front door without breaking stride, caroming off the walls, and was laying back against the closed slab of hardwood, dragging in painful gouts of air before he realized that he could not get away that easily. It would be waiting for him when he got back, whenever he got back.

But he went. There was a bar where they played nothing but Sinatra records, and he absorbed as much maudlin sorrow and self-pity as he could, finally tumbling from the place when the strings and the voice oozed forth:

How I wish I could forget
Those happy yesteryears,
That have left
A rosary of tears.

There was another place, a beach perhaps, where he stood on the sand, silent within himself, as the gulls wheeled and gibbered across the black sky, kree kree kree, driving him a little more mad, and he dug his naked hands into the sand, hurling great clots of the grainy darkness over his head, trying to kill those rotten, screaming harridans!

And another place, where there were lights that said things, all manner of unintelligible things, neon things, dirty remarks, and he could not read any of them. (In one place he was certain he saw the masked revelers from his dream, and frothing, he fled, quickly.)

When he returned, finally, to the apartment, the girl with him swore she wasn't a telescope, but yeah, sure, she'd look at what he had to show her, and she'd tell him what it was. So, trusting her, because she'd said it, he turned the key in the door, and opened it. He reached around the jamb and turned on the light. Yeah, yeah, there he was, there he was, that thing there he was, all right. Uh-huh, there he is, the thing with the staring eyes, there he is.

"Well?" he asked her, almost proudly, pointing.

"Well what?" she replied.

"Well what about *him*?"

"Who?"

"*Him*, him, you stupid bitch! Him right *there*! HIM!"

"Y'know, I think you're outta your mind, Sid."

"M'name's not Sid, and don't tell me you don't see him, you lying sonofabitch!"

"Say lissen, you *said* you was Sid, and Sid you're gonna be, and I don't see *no* goddam nobody there, and if you wanna get laid allright, and if you don't, just say so and we'll have another drink an' that'll be *that*!"

He screamed at her, clawing at her face, thrusting her out the door. "Get out, get outta here, g'wan, get out!" And she was gone, and he was alone again with the creature, who was unperturbed by it all, who sat implacably, softly, waiting for the last tick of time to detach itself and fly free from the fabric of sanity.

They trembled there together in a nervous symbiosis, each deriving something from the other. He was covered with a thin film of horror and despair, a terrible lonelyache that twisted like smoke, thick and black within him. The creature giving love, and he reaping heartache, loneliness.

He was alone in that room, the two of them: himself and that soft-brown, staring menace, the manifestation of his misery.

And he knew, suddenly, what the dream meant. He knew, and kept it to himself, for the meaning of dreams is for the men who dream them, never to be shared, never to be known. He knew who the men in the dreams were, and he knew now why none of them had ever been killed by simple gun. He knew, diving into the clothes closet, finding the duffel bag full of old Army clothes, finding the chunk of steel that lay at the bottom of that bag. He knew who he was, he knew, he knew, gloriously, jubilantly, and he knew it all, who the creature was, and who Georgette was, and the faces of all the women in the damned world, and all the men in the damned dreams, and the identity of the man who had been driving the car who had saved him (and that was the key), and he had it all, right there, right in his hands, ready to be understood.

He went into the bathroom. He was *not* going to let that bastard in the corner see him succeed. He was going to savor it himself. In the mirror he now saw himself again. He saw the face and it was a good face and a very composed face, and he stared back at himself smiling, saying very softly, "Why did you have to go away?"

Then he raised the chunk of steel.

"Nobody, absolutely nobody," he said, holding the huge .45 up to his face, "has the guts to shoot himself through the eye."

He laid the hollow bore of the great blocky weapon against his closed eyelid and continued speaking, still softly. "Through the head, yeah sure, anybody. Or the guys with balls can point it up through the mouth. But through the eye, nobody, but *no*body." Then he pulled the trigger just at they had taught him in the Army; smoothly, evenly, in one movement.

From the other room came the murmur of breathing, heavily, stertorously, evenly.

Punky & the Yale Men

"Love ain't nothing but sex misspelled," he had said, when he had left New York, for the last time. He had said it to the girl he had been sleeping with: a junior fashion and beauty editor with one of the big women's slicks. He had just found out she was a thirty-six-dollar-a-day cocaine addict, and it hadn't mattered, really, because he had gift-wrapped his love and given it to her, asking nothing in return except that she let him be near her.

And yet, when he asked her, that final day, why they had only made love once (with all her stray baby cats mewling in corners and walking over their intertwined bodies), she answered, "I was stoned. It was the only way I could hack it." And he had been sick. Even in his middle thirties, having been down so many dark roads that ended in nothingness, he had been hurt, had been destroyed, and he had gone away from her, gone away from that place, in that special time, and he had told her, "Love ain't nothing but sex misspelled."

It had been bad grammar for a writer as famous as Sorokin. But he was entitled to indulge. It had been a bad year. So he had left New York, for the last time, once again resuming the search that had no end; he had gone back to the studio in Hollywood, and had forgotten quite completely, knowing he would never return to New York.

Now, in another time, still seeking the punchline of the bad joke his life had become, he was back in New York.

Andy Sorokin came out of the elevator squinting, as though he had just stepped into dazzling sunshine.

Dazzling.

It was the forty-second-floor reception room of *Marquis* magazine and the most dazzling thing in it was the shadow-box display of Kodachrome transparencies from the pages of *Marquis*.

Dazzling:

Pêche flambée at The Forum of The XII Caesars; tuxedoed and tuck-bow-tied stalwarts at a Joan Sutherland première; decorous girl stuff, no nylon and garter belt crotch shots; deep-sea fishing with marlin and mad-eyed bonita breaking white water; Yousuf Karsh character studies of two post-debs and a Louisiana racist politico; a brace of artily drawn cartoons; a Maserati spinning-out at the Nürburg Ring; Hemingway, Fitzgerald, Dorothy Parker, Nathanael West, others whose first work had appeared in the magazine; a soft-nosed Labrador Retriever in high grass, ostensibly retrieving a Labrador; two catamarans running before a gale.

Andy Sorokin was not dazzled. He squinted like a man suffering on the outside of a needle-thrust of heartburn.

The unlit cigarette hung from the exact center of his mouth, and he worked with his teeth at the spongy, now moist filter. Behind him, the elevator doors sighed shut, and he was almost alone in the reception room. He stood, still only two steps onto the deep-pile wall-to-wall, a man listening to silent songs in stone, as the nearly pretty receptionist looked up, waiting for *him* to come to *her*.

When he didn't, she pursed, nibbled, and then flashed her receptionist eyes. When he still paid no attention to her, she said firmly, projecting, "Yes, may I help you?"

Sorokin had not been daydreaming. He had been entirely *there*, assaulted by the almost pathological density of good taste in the reception room, beguiled by the relentless masculinity of the *Marquis* image as totemized in the Kodachromes, amused by an impending meeting that was intended to regain for him that innocence of childhood or nature he had somewhen lost, by the preposterous expedient of hurling him back into a scene, a past, he had fled—gladly—seventeen years before.

"I doubt it," he replied.

Steel shutters slammed down in her eyes. It had been a bitch of a day, lousy lunch, out of pills and the Curse right on time, and but *no room* in a day like today for some sillyass cigarette-nibbling smartass with funnys. It became unaccountably chill in the room.

Sorokin knew it had been a dumb remark. But it wasn't worth retracting.

"Walter Werringer, please," he said wearily.

"Your name?" in ice.

"Sorokin."

And she knew she had blown it. Ohmigod Sorokin. All day Werringer and the staff had been on tiptoes, like a basic training barracks waiting for the Inspector General. Sorokin, the giant. Standing here rumpled and nibbling a filter, and she had chopped him. The word was ohmigod. And but *no* way to recoup. If he so much as dropped a whisper to someone in editorial country, a whisper, the time for moving out of her parents' apartment on Pelham Parkway was farther off, the *Times* want ads.

She tried a smile, and then didn't bother. His eyes. How drawn and dark they were, like pursestrings pulled tight closed. She should have guessed: those eyes: Sorokin.

"Right this way, Mr. Sorokin," she said, standing, smoothing her skirt across her thighs. There was a momentary flicker of reprieve: he looked at her body. So she preceded him down the corridor into editorial country, moving it fluidly. "Mr. Werringer and the staff have been expecting you," she said, turning to speak over her shoulder, letting the ironed-flat blonde discothèque hair sway back from her good left profile.

"Thank you," he said, wearily. It was a long quiet corridor.

"I really admired your book," she said, still walking. He had had fourteen novels published, she didn't say which one, which meant she had read none of them.

"Thank you."

She continued talking, saying things as meaningful as throat-clearings. And the terrible thing about it, was that from the moment Andy Sorokin had entered the reception room, and she had thought *I blew it,* he had known everything that had passed through her mind. He had thought her thoughts, the instant she had thought them. Because she was a people, and that was Andy Sorokin's line. He was cursed with an empathy that often threatened to drive him up the wall, around the bend, down the tube and out of this world. He knew she had been playing it bitchily cool, then scared when she found out who he was, then trying to ameliorate it with her body and the hair-swirling. He knew it all, and it depressed him: to find out he was correct again. Once again. As always.

If just once they'd surprise me, he thought, following her mouth and words, her body. Thinking *this,* in preparation:

Here I am returning to New York, to the very core of The Apple, after summer solstice in L.A. (where the capris run to tight and the soma run to trembly), and it's returning to my past, to my childhood. Filthy, drizzly, crowded till I gag and scream for elbow room on the BMT, it's still where I came from, a glory—notably absent from The Coast. It doesn't even matter that the collar of my Eagle broadcloth looks as though caterpillars had shit in a sooty trail, after a day on the town; it doesn't matter that everyone snarls and bites in the streets; it doesn't matter that the service at the Teheran has run into the toilet since Vincente went over the hill to The Chateaubriand; it doesn't matter that Whitey silenced Jimmy Baldwin the only way it could, by absorbing him, recognizing him, deifying him, making him the Voice of His People, driving him insane; it doesn't even matter that Olaf Burger up at Fawcett has grown stodgy with wealth and position; to hell with all the carping, dammit, it's New York, the hub of it all, the place where it all started again, and I've been so damned long on The Coast, in that Mickey Mouse scene hiya baby pussycat sweetheart lover . . . and even when I'm systemically inclined to believe sesquipedalianistic Thomas Wolfe (no, not that *Tom Wolfe, the* real *Tom Wolfe), I keep being amazed to find I* can *go home again, and again, and again.*

It is always New York, my Manhattan, where I learned to walk, where I learned all I know, and where it waits for me every time I come back, like a childhood sweetheart grown sexy with experience, yet still capable of adolescent charm. How bloody literary!

Sonofabitch, I love *you, N'Yawk.*

She was still gibbering, walking, and all he thought, every spun-out spiderweb sentence of it, only took a moment to whirl through his mind, before they arrived at the door to Walter Werringer's office, concluding with:

Even forty-two storeys up in an editorial office, going in to see an important editor who wouldn't have paid me penny-a-word to carve the Magna Carta on his executive toilet wall before I went to Hollywood and became a Name, who now offers me an arm, a leg and a quivering thigh to go back down to Red Hook, Brooklyn and rewrite my impressions, seventeen years later, of juvenile delinquency, "Kid Gang Revisited," even this *is New York lovely . . .*

Oh, revenge, thy taste is groovy!

Thoughts of Andrew Sorokin, best-selling novelist, Hollywood scenarist, page 146 (vols. 5–6) of CONTEMPORARY AUTHORS [Born May 27, 1929, in Buffalo, New York; joined a gang of juvenile delinquents in Red Hook, Brooklyn, and posed as a member of the group for three months during 1948, gathering authentic background material for his first novel, CHILDREN OF THE GUTTERS.], and nominee for an Academy Award, as he stepped past an oiled-hipped receptionist into the outer office of Walter Werringer, editor of *Marquis* magazine: thoughts of Andrew Sorokin, if not recognized as a prophet in his own land, at least a prodigal returned to accept the huzzahs of the nobility. Time had passed, times had changed, and Andy Sorokin was back.

The receptionist spoke with purport to the trim and distant secretary in the outer office. "Frances . . . Mr. Sorokin." The secretary brightened, and the smile buttered across her lower face. "Oh, just a moment, Mr. Sorokin; Mr. Werringer is expecting you." She began clicking the intercom.

The receptionist did a little sensuality thing with her mouth as she touched Andy Sorokin's sleeve. "It was a pleasure meeting you, Mr. Sorokin."

He smiled back at her. "I'll stop to say goodbye on my way out." She was off the hook. He had done it purposely. One of his occasional gestures of humanity: why let her worry that he was going to cost her a job with a casual remark. It also meant he was going to ask for her number. Now all she had to decide was whether she would play it ingenue and let him ask, or hand him the pre-written note with the name and number on it, when he came back past her in the reception room. It was an infinitely fascinating game of ramifications, and Andy Sorokin knew she would play it with herself till he reappeared. She went, and he turned back as the secretary rose to usher him into the inner presence of Walter Werringer.

"Right this way, Mr. Sorokin," she said, standing, smoothing her skirt across her thighs. He looked at her body. She preceded him to the inner office door, moving it fluidly. *If just once they'd surprise me,* he thought.

Forty minutes later, they still had not discussed what Sorokin had come to discuss: the assignment. They had talked about Sorokin's career, from pulp detective and science fiction stories through the novels to Hollywood and the television, the motion picture scripts. The impending Oscar night, and Sorokin's nomination. They had discussed Sorokin's two disastrous marriages, his appraisal of Hollywood politics, the elegance of *Marquis,* the silliness of Sorokin's never having been in the pages of that elegant slick monthly. (But not the bitter weevil that nibbled Sorokin's viscera: that *Marquis* had never thought him worthy of acceptance before he had become famous and a Name.) They had discussed women, JFK, what had become of Mailer, the unreliability of agents, paperback trends, everything but the assignment.

And a peculiar posturing had sprung up between them.

Werringer stared at Andy Sorokin across a huge Danish coffee mug, steam fogging his bifocals, gulping with heavenly satisfaction. "Without joe I'd be dead," he said. He took another gulp, reinforcing his own stated addiction, and plonked the mug down on the desk blotter. "Ten, fifteen cups a day. Gotta have it." He liked to play the stevedore, rather than the literary lion. He enjoyed the role of the Hemingway more than that of the Maxwell Perkins. It was his posture, and as far as Sorokin was concerned, he was stuck with it. Yet it had an adverse effect on Sorokin, who had been what Werringer worked at seeming to be. (*Damn my empathy,* he thought. *Perversity incarnate!*) It had the effect of sending Sorokin into a pseudo–Truman Capote stance. Limp-wristed, campy, biting with effeminate aphorism and innuendo. Werringer was on the verge of mentally labeling Sorokin homosexual, even though the conclusion ran contrary to everything he knew of the writer, and the confusion only served to amuse Sorokin. But not too much.

"About this idea of yours, for me . . ." Sorokin finally broached it.

"Right. Yeah, let's get to it." Werringer crinkled his face in a Victor McLaglen roughsmile. He rummaged under a stack of manuscripts and pulled out a copy of Sorokin's first novel, sixteen years old in its original dust wrapper. CHILDREN OF THE GUTTERS. He fingered it as though it were some rare and moldering edition, a first folio "Macbeth," rather than a somewhat better than good fictionalized autobiography of three months Andy Sorokin had spent living a double-life, seventeen years before, when he had been young and provincial enough to think "experience" was a substitute for content or style. Three months with a kid gang, living in and running through the stinking streets, getting what he liked to call "the inside."

Now, seventeen years later, and Werringer wanted him to go back to those streets. After the army, after Paula and Carrie, after the accident, after Hollywood, after the last seventeen years that had given him so much, and stripped him so clean. Go back, Sorokin. Go back to it. If you can.

Werringer was doing the hairy-chested bit again. He tapped the book with a fingernail. "This has real guts, Andy. Real balls. I always felt that way about it."

"Call me Punky," Sorokin minced, smiling boyishly. "That's what they called me in the gang. Punky."

Werringer did a frowning thing. If Sorokin was a visceral realist out of the gutsy Robert Ruark school, why was he camping?

"Uh-huh, Punky, sure," he tried to get his feet under him, but wobbled a little. Sorokin tried not to snicker. "It has real plunge, real honesty in it, a bitchofuh lot of depth," Werringer added, lamely.

Sorokin assumed a moue of displeasure, pure faggot: "Too bad it tiptoed through the bookstores," he said. "It was written to alter the course of Western Civilization, you know." Werringer paled. What was happening here? "You *do* know that, don't you?"

Werringer nodded dumbly, and took the remark at face value. He didn't know why he should feel as though he had just fallen down the rabbit hole, but the impression was overwhelming.

"Well, uh, what we'd like, what we *want*, for *Marquis,* is the same sort of ballz—uh, the same sort of highly emotional writing you put into this."

Sorokin felt his stomach tightening, now that the moment was with him. "What you want me to do, is go back down to Red Hook, to the same place I knew, and write about the way it is now."

Werringer banged a palm on the desk. "Exactly! The kids, what happened to them, where they are now. Did they wind up in the slammer, did they get married, go into the army, the whole story, seventeen years later. And the social conditions. Have the tenements been cleaned up? What about the low-rent housing projects? Has the Police Athletic League been of any use? What about racial tensions down there now, does it make for a different kind of kid gang, different rumbles, you know, the whole scene."

"You want me to go back down there."

Werringer stared. "Yeah, right, that's what we want. 'Kid Gang Revisited.' Something in depth."

The tension that had been growing in Sorokin now abruptly tightened like a fist. Go back down there. Go back to it, seventeen years later. "I was nineteen years old when I joined that gang," Andrew Sorokin said, half to himself. Werringer continued to stare. The man in front of him seemed to be in some sort of shock.

"I'm thirty-six now. I don't know—"

Werringer bit the inside of his lip. "We only want you to write it from the outside this time. You're no kid now, Andy . . . Mr. Soro—"

"But you don't want it to be a surface skimming, do you?"

"Well, no—"

"You want it to be guts and balls, right?"

"Yeah, right, we want—"

"You want it told the way it is, right? With realism, all the hip talk the kids talk?"

"Sure, that's part of—"

"You want me to find out what happened to all those kids I ran with, who didn't know I was studying them like bugs in a bottle. You want me to go down there seventeen years later and say, 'I'm the guy finked on you, remember me?' You want that, in essence that's what you want, isn't it?"

Werringer had the feeling now (sudden shifts with this man) that Sorokin was furious, was frightened, but furious. What the hell was going on?

"Well, yes, we want the truth, the inside, the way you did it the first time, but we don't want you to take any chances. We aren't . . . hell, we aren't *Confidential* or the *Enquirer*! We want—"

"You want me to go back in and let them take a whack at me!"

Aggression. Werringer reeled.

"Say, wait a minute we—"

"You expect a helluva story, and all the risks, and you want it *now*, right, Mr. Werringer?"

"What's the matter with you, Sorok—"

"Well, how the hell do you expect me to do it unless I go back down there and sink into it again, up to my GUTS, up to my BALLS, up to my EYEBALLS FOR CHRISSAKES! YOU DAMN DUMB DEADLINE-MEETER, YOU!"

Werringer shoved back from his desk, as though Sorokin might jump across and throttle him. His eyes were wide behind the bifocals, all out of shape and moist.

"It'll be my pleasure, Mr. Werringer," in a tone so soft and warm, relaxed at last. "How soon do you need it? And what length?"

Walter Werringer fumbled for his Danish coffee mug.

* * *

Sorokin has his hand on the door, when it opened inward, and two young men came through. The moment he saw them, prim and clean-scrubbed in their almost-identical dark blue suits, he knew they had come from the right families, had learned to dance at the age of six or seven at Miss Blesham's, or one of the other good salons, had been allowed that first quarter-snifter of Napoleon with "Dad," and had most certainly graduated from one of the right schools.

The one on the left, the taller of the two, with the straw-colored hair and polar twinkling blue eyes, entering the room with thumbs hooked into the decorative pockets of his vest, was an Andover man. Had to be.

The other, slightly shorter, perhaps only six feet, with shoes impeccably dullshined to avoid the vulgar ostentation of gloss, with flat brown hair parted straight back on the left side and brushed toward the rear of the skull in the European manner, whose eyes were of the lizard, *he* was Choate, surely, definitely, of course.

"Walter," Andover said, as he burst into the office, "we're breaking a little early today. Going over to The Algonquin for a few. Care to come along?"

Then he saw Sorokin, and stumbled to silence, in awe.

Werringer introduced them, with names Sorokin let slip out of his mind the instant they were spoken. He knew their names.

"Where did you go to school?" he asked them.

"Yale," said Andover.

"Yale," said Choate.

"Call me Punky," said Andrew Sorokin.

So they all went to The Algonquin for a few.

Choate scrabbled around in the bottom of the bowl. All the salted peanuts and little Cheerios and pretzels were gone. He gripped the bowl by its edge and banged it on the table. At The Algonquin, that was poor form.

"Succulents!" Choate howled.

The waiter came and took the bowl away from him like a nanny with an obstreperous infant. "Succulents, dammt," he slurred the word, only faintly.

"Andrew P. for Punky Sorokin, by God what a thrill and a half for overtime," said Andover, staring at Andy for the one billionth time since they had sat down. "A giant, you're a bloody giant, a flaming insti*tooo*tion! Y'know that? And here we are sitting right with you!"

Werringer had left two hours before. Evening was coming on. The two Yale men named Andover and Choate were just high enough to be playful. Andy was sober. He had tried, God knew he had tried, but he was still sober.

"Reality, that's what you deal in,"said one of them. It didn't matter which was which. They both spoke from the same cultural mouth.

"Truth. Life. You know all there is to know about Life. An' I don't mean that Lucely, heh heh heeheehee . . ." he broke himself up completely, rolled around in the booth. Choate (or Andover, depending which had punned) shoved him away, roughly.

"You don't know what the hell you're talkin' about, Rob. Thass the one thing he *doesn't* know about. Life! The core of it, the heartmeat of it! We, who come from such austere backgrounds, even *we* know it better more truly than Andrew P. for Punky Sorokin sitting right there."

The other Yale man sat up, angry. "You shut up! This man is a giant. A flaming giant, and he *knows*, I tell you. He *knows* about the seamy side of Life."

"He never even touched it."

"He knows! He knows it all!"

"Fraud! Poseur!"

"Step owsside you bastard, I never knew you were such a bigoted crypto-Fascist bastard!"

Sorokin listened to them, and the fear he had known earlier that afternoon, when Werringer had sentenced him to going back down to Red Hook, returned. He had condemned himself to it, really, by what series of compulsions he did not want to examine, but here it was again. How did Choate know he was a fraud? How had Choate discovered the secret nubbin of fear in Andrew Sorokin's heart and soul?

"What, uh, what makes you say I'm a fraud?" he asked Choate. Choate's face had grown blotchy with drink, but he aimed a meaty finger at Sorokin and said, "I get spirit messages from the other world."

Andover took it as an affront. He shoved Choate roughly. "Owsside, bastard! Owsside, crypto-pinko!"

Sorokin wanted to get to the sober heart of it, though. "No, really, what makes you think I don't know reality?"

Choate took on the look of a pedant, and intoned sepulchrally. "Your first book'a short stories, you had a quote from Hemingway, remember it? You said it was your credo. Bushwah! 'There is no use writing anything that has been written before unless you can beat it. What a writer in our time has to do is write what hasn't been written before or beat dead men at what they have done.' I memorized it. It seemed to be valid. Bushwah!"

"Socialist, right-wing Birch muther-fugger!"

"Yes? So what makes you think I don't know what I'm talking about? That certainly doesn't prove your point."

"Ah!" Choate lifted a finger alongside his nose, like Santa Claus about to zoom up the chimney. Conspiratorial. "Ah! But your *fifth* book'a short stories, after you'd been out *there*"—he waved toward California—"you used *another* quote. You know what it was? Hah, you remember?"

Sorokin paused an instant to get it right, then recited. "'To reject one's own experiences is to arrest one's own development. To deny one's own experience is to put a lie into the lips of one's own life. It is no less than a denial of the Soul.' Oscar Wilde. What has that to do with proving your point?"

Choate was triumphant. "Fear. Cop-out. Your subconscious was squealing like a butchered pig. It knew you were a liar from the first, and were lying all the more in Hollywood. It knew! And so you had to say it to the world, so they could never accuse you of it. You don't know what Life is, what reality is, what truth is, what anydamnthing is!"

"I'm gonna push you rotten cruddy Tory face in!"

They wrestled around the other side of the booth, each too hammered to do the other any harm, as Sorokin thought about what Choate had said. Was it possible? Had he been trying to plead silently guilty to an unspoken charge?

When he had been a small child, he had been a petty thief. He had stolen things from the dime store. Not because he could not have bought them, because his family was too poor, but because he wanted them without having to pay for them, a sense of accomplishment, in a child's own strange philosophy. But he had always felt compelled to play with the new, stolen item, directly in front of his parents, that same night. So they could ask him where he got it, and he could risk their finding out he had stolen. If they did not press it, the stolen plaything was truly his; if they pressed it and he blurted he had stolen it, then he had to suffer a punishment he knew he deserved.

Was the inclusion of the Wilde quotation, as Choate suggested, another playing with a stolen toy in front of mommy and daddy, the world, his public?

Was it a manifestation of the fear he now felt? The fear that he had lost it, had always been in the process of losing it, could never regain it?

"Okay, dammit, I'm gonna show you the seamy side of Life! Now what about it, Mr. Punky? You wanna see the seamy side of Life?"

"He *knows* it, I tell ya!"

"Well, do you? Huh?"

"I'll have to make a phone call first. Cancel a dinner appointment." He sat, not moving, and they stared at one another like walruses contemplating the permanence of the sea.

"Well, do you, huh? If you do, put up or shut up." Choate was on the pinnacle of proving his point.

"Just shuddup, Terry, just shuddup; this man is not going to be chivvied and bullied and chockablock by the likes of a McCarthy neo-Fascist demagogue such as yourself!" Andover was a tot drunker than Choate.

Sorokin was trembling inside. If anyone knew the seamy side of Life, it was Andrew Sorokin. He had run away at age fifteen, had been driving a dynamite truck in North Carolina by sixteen, working on a cat-cracker in West Texas age seventeen, at nineteen the gang, and his first book published at twenty. He had been in every scene imaginable from the sybaritic high life of the international jet set to uncontrolled LSD experimentation with Big Sur hippies. He had always wanted to believe he was with it, contemporary, of the times, in touch with the realities, *all* the myriad multicolored realities, no matter how strained or weird or demeaning.

And the question now before him: *has all this living degenerated into a search for kicks, is it a complex cop-out?* He slid out of the booth, and went to call Olaf Burger.

When he had gotten through the switchboard and all the interference, Burger's bushwhacker voice came across the line. "Yeah?"

"Didn't I tell you a million times that's no way to answer a phone? You should say, 'Massah Buhgah's awfiss, c'n ah helps yuh, bwana.' "

"Explain to me why I have to have a busy workday interrupted periodically by bigots, rednecks and kook writer sellouts from Smog Junction."

"Cause you got such dear little Shirley Temple dimples, and you is a big paperback editor, and I burn for your body with a bright blue flame."

"What's on your alleged mind, nitwit?"

"Gotta call off the dinner."

"Janine'll parboil me. She made *patlijan moussaka* because you were coming. And dicing and braising lamb all day will not put her in a receptive frame of mind. At least give me an excuse."

"Two hotrock Ivy types from *Marquis* want to show me 'the seamy side of Life.' "

"That's not an excuse, that's a seizure of *petit mal*. You've got to be kidding."

There was a moment of serious silence from Sorokin. Then, in a different, slower voice he said, "I've got to do it, Olaf. It's important."

A corresponding moment of reorientation, the dual statement of a musical threnody. "You sound upset, Andy. Something happen? It's been three months since I've seen you, something biting on you again?"

Sorokin clicked his tongue against his teeth, seeking the words, finally deciding in an instant to put it baldly. "I'm trying to find out if I've got balls. Again."

"For the thousandth time."

"Yeah."

"When do you stop? When you get killed?"

"Give my love to Janine. I'll call you tomorrow. My treat at The Four Seasons, that ought to make up for it."

A pause. "Andy . . ."

Another beat of timelessness. "Uh-huh?"

"You're too expensive for the paperback line I edit, but there are a lot of others with a stock in you. Don't screw yourself up."

"Uh-huh."

Burger clicked off, and Andy Sorokin stood staring at the red plush of the phone booth for a long moment. Then he turned, exhaling breath in finality, and went back to a scene from Hogarth.

Andover was tapping the table over and over and over with his index finger, saying over and over and over, "You'll see, you'll see, you'll see . . ."

While Choate, who had rubbed carbon black from half a dozen spent matches on his cheeks, was flapping his arms tidily, and croaking over and over and over, "Nevermore, nevermore, nevermore . . ."

They took him to every paradise he had already known. All the places he had been when he was younger, all the predictable places. The Lower East Side. The Village. Spanish Harlem. Bedford-Stuyvesant.

And they grew more and more furious. They had sobered; the chill night air, the snow of winter's November, too many stop-offs where the liquor wasn't free; they were sobered. It had become a vendetta with both of the Yale men, not just Choate. Now Andover was with him, and they wanted to *show* the giant, Sorokin, something he had not seen before.

There were bars, and more bars, and dingy down-the-hole places where people sat murmuring into one another's libidos. And then a party . . .

Noise cascaded about him, a Niagara of watery impressions, indistinct conversational images. Snatches of flotsam carried down thunderingly past his ears ". . . I went over to Ted Bates to ask them about those Viceroy residuals, and Marvy told me what the hell I'd gotten a trip to the Virgin Islands out of it and why didn't I stop bitching, and I told *him*, say, after that damned fruitcake director and his *fayguluh* crew got done letting me 'save' them from the gay life, I was so raw and miserable *double* residuals wouldn't of been enough to make up for all that weirdscene swinging, and besides, if they'd taken along some hooker they'd of had to pay her, too, so I should be getting extra consider—"

. . . beep, bip, boop, blah, bdip, chee chee chee . . .

". . . a gass! A real gass! The joint is laid out like an Arabian Nights kind of thing, with the waitresses in these transparent pants, and all the waiters in pasha turbans, and you lay on your side to eat, and I've got to admit it's hard as hell eating laying on your side, which is almost as bad as laying eating on your side heh heh, I swear I don't see how the hell they did it in those days, but the food is *ab*-solutely a gass, man. They've got this lemon drop soup, they call it *kufte abour* and it's a g—"

. . . bdoing, bupp, bupp, beep, bip, chee chee chee . . .

". . . this compendium of aborted hours and dead-end relationships is of minor concern, for at this moment, this very instant in weightless timeless time, this moment that I am about to describe minutely, all of what I have been through before this will outline itself. If not in particular, then in essence, hindsighted as it were, and what went before will be seen as merely a vapor trail of incidents one like another, building to this moment and . . . oh for CHRIST'S sake, Ginny, take your finger out of your nose . . ."

. . . bang bang bang, bding dong, clank, crunch, chee chee chee . . .

Technically, it might have been a party. Superficially it *resembled* a party, with too many people clogged into too small a space, a dingy loft off Jane Street in the Village. But there was more going on than just that.

The ritual dances of the friendly natives were being staged, both physically—as Simone and her husband's agent did a slow, extremely inept, psychosexual Skate—and emotionally—as Wagner Cole scathingly sliced up the peroxided poetess whose aspirations of literary immediacy were transparently *Saturday Review*—as well as ethnically—minor chittering of who-balled-who in the far corner by the rubber plant. The whole crowd was there, because it was Florence Mahrgren's birthday (wheeee!) and not just a dreamed-up reason for getting together.

Andy Sorokin stood against the fireplace wall, his *margarita* in his two cupped hands, talking to the whey-faced virgin Andover had found and brought to him. She was talking at him, about a bad movie made from one of his lesser novels.

"I never really thought Karin was completely bad," the virgin was saying. "And when they made the movie, I just *did not* like the way Lana Turner played the part."

Sorokin stared down at her benignly. She was very short, and large-bosomed. She wore a Rudi Gernreich and it had her pushed all up tight in front; she smiled with her lips but not her teeth. "That's very kind of you to say; there wasn't a great deal in the motion picture version to like, though I thought Frankenheimer's direction was nice."

She answered something totally irrelevant. He bore these conversations neatly or badly, depending on the final objective. In this case, it was getting the short, buxom virgin into the master bedroom; he gave it what charm he could spare.

Around them, like mist encircling a cleared space, the eye of a storm, the party pitched itself a noticeable degree higher in hysteria. Florence Mahrgren was hoisted on the shoulders of Bernbach & Barker (producers of three current Broadway hits) and carried around the room, as Ray Charles sang in the background, her skirt crumpled about her thighs, Bernbach & Barker improvising obscene happy birthday lyrics to the tune of their current success's theme song. Sorokin felt his gut tightening on him again. It never seemed to change, no matter how many times the people changed. They said the same stupid things, did the same senseless things, postured and played with themselves insipidly. He wanted either to screw the virgin or to get out of the party.

From another corner of the living room someone yelled, "Hey! How about Circle-Insult?" and before Andy could make for the door, the virgin had been snapped up by Andover, and she in turn had clutched his sleeve, and daisy-chain, they careened into the center of the maelstrom.

Circle-Insult. They were already forming the circle, everyone hunkering down cross-legged on the floor. The idle talented and the idle rich and the idle poor and the idle bored playing their games; affectation of innocence, the return to honesty in form—if not in content. Circle-Insult. The women sitting in the preordained postures, careless, nonchalant unawareness of lingerie and pale inner flesh flashed and gone and flashing again, beacons for the wanderers who would home there that night, keeping the coastline firmly in sight, keeping the final berth open to the lost and the needy. Charitable bawds.

They began playing Circle-Insult, the world's easiest game.

Tony Morrow turned to Iris Paine on his right. Tony to Iris: "You're the worst lay I've ever had. You don't move. You just lay there and let a guy, any guy, stick it in, and you whimper. Jeezus, you're a lousy lay."

Iris Paine turned to Gus Diamond on her right. Iris to Gus: "You smell bad. You have really vile bad breath. And you always stand too close when you talk to someone. You stink completely."

Gus Diamond turned to Bill Gardner on his right. Gus to Bill: "I hate niggers, and you are the most obnoxious nigger I ever met. You got no natural rhythm, and when we played tennis last weekend I saw you were hung smaller than me so stop trying to horse around with Betty, nigger, or you'll find your throat cut!"

Bill Gardner turned to Kathy Dineen on his right. Bill to Kathy: "You always steal outta these parties. One night you stole thirty-five bucks from Bernice's purse, and then split, and they called the cops but they never found out it was you. You're a thief."

Around and around and around. Circle-Insult.

Andy Sorokin stood as much of it as he could, then he rose and left, Andover and Choate trailing all quiet and sadly sober behind him. "You didn't like it," Choate said, following him down the stairs.

"I didn't like it."

"It wasn't the core of reality."

Sorokin smiled. "It wasn't even particularly seamy."

Choate shrugged. "I tried."

"How about The Ninth Circle?" Andover asked.

Sorokin stopped on the stairs, half-turned. "What's that?"

Choate grinned conspiratorially. "It's a joint, you know, a pub, a place." Sorokin nodded silently, bobbed his head and they followed him.

They took him to The Ninth Circle, which was a Village hangout, the way Chumley's had been a hangout when Andy had walked the weary streets. The way Rienzi's had been the spot to go and read *The Manchester Guardian* on a wooden hang-up pole, and sleep on Davey

Rienzi's sandwich-cutting board when the rent was too much to make. The way there was always an in-hole for the colder children who couldn't bear to stand on street corners naked to the night.

And Choate and Andover—again—grew furious.

For the moment they entered the noisy, dingy bar with its inauspicious bullfight posters and sawdusty floor, a tall, skeletal man erupted from a seat tilted back against a wall, and dashed for Sorokin. "Andy! Andy Sorokin!"

It was Sid, big Sid, who had operated the tourist bus dodge on 46th Street and Broadway, in the days when Andy Sorokin had worked selling pornography in a bookshop on The Gay White Way. Cadaverously thin Sid, who had been one of the coterie of early-morning residents of Times Square, a closed society of those who were with it, as Andy had been.

Sid mad a great fuss over Sorokin, pulling him to a table full of pretty girls and buffalo-moustached pickup men for the pretty girls. They reminisced about the old days before Sorokin had told his bosses at the bookshop to pick it and stick it, he was going to write. Before Sorokin had sold his books, gone in the army, married the women, made it in Hollywood. The old days before.

And the two Yale men grew furious at Punky.

Here they were, determined to show him the raw and pulsing inner heart of the seamy side of Life, and he was a familiar of all the types even *they* could not get to know. It was frustrating.

"So what are you doing these days?" Andy asked Sid. Sid flip-flopped a deprecatory hand. "Not much. I'm working a couple of hookers, you know, making a buck here and there." Andy grinned.

"Remember the night that chick wandered into the bookstore, and she wanted to get laid, and Freddy Smeigel started hustling her, and she pulled her skirt up to her chin and she was *sans* pants—"

Sid interrupted, "*What* pants?"

Andy grinned. "*Without*."

"Oh, yeah, tell it, g'wan, these guys'd laugh like hell."

Sorokin warmed to the story of the tourist woman from Sheboygan, and how they had quickly locked the front door and pulled the blind and she had pulled up her skirt again and let them look. She had done it half a dozen times, like a yo-yo on a string, just say the word and zip up went the dress. So they'd taken her next door into the record shop and Freddy had told her to do it for them, and she had done it zip again. So then they'd taken her around the block, upstairs of the Victoria Theatre, to the stockroom, and everyone had balled her.

Sorokin and Sid laughed over it, and Andover got nearly as furious as Choate. So they started drinking again, trying to resurrect their buzz of earlier that evening. Finally, when Andy had had enough of The Ninth Circle, he suggested they leave, and Sid handed him a card.

It said: LOTTE Call Sid 611 East 101st.

There was a phone number, and it had been scratched off, and another phone number written in, in ball-point. Sid laid an incredibly thin arm around Sorokin's shoulder. "It's one of my hustlers. Fourteen years old. Puerto Rican meat, but *too* much. You want a little bang, just call me, I'm usually around. On the house. Old times, like that."

Andy grinned, and shoved the card into the pocket of his Harris tweed jacket. "Take care, Sid. Nice seeing you again." And they left.

The two Yale men had an air of determination about them now, a frenzy almost. They would find a seamy side of Life to reveal to this wiseass giant, Sorokin, if they had to scour every grimy garbage can in the greater Manhattan area.

There is an infinitude of grimy garbage cans in the greater Manhattan area. They scoured many of them that night, that morning, winding up finally, stone-drunk, all three of them, in The Dog House Bar, a filth-pit of unspeakable emptiness, deep in the Bowery.

Sorokin sat across from the Yale men. Choate's face was once again blotchy with pink. Andover was giddy.

"Punky, pussycat." Andover smiled lopsidedly. "Luv'ya!" Choate sneered. The strain of surliness that lay close to the surface needed only a whisper of wind, a rustle of leaves, a murmur of direction, to come to the top.

"Cop-out," he mumbled. Then he swallowed hard. And his face went puce. "I'm going to whooppee," he mumbled.

His cheeks puffed out. There was a moist sound.

"You talk like a dumb *New Yorker* story," Andover said, very carefully. "Now if you were a *Playboy* story, you'd say puke, 'cause it's a realie word, and it has'a lotta reality, huh? And if you were a *Kenyon Review* story, you'd say vomit, because it has history behind it, roots, so t'speak. And if you were an *Esquire* story, you'd say upchuck, 'cause they're still trying to con everyone into thinking they're the voice of college. And if you were a *National Geographic* story—"

Choate slid sidewise in the booth, crab-style, and started out of the booth. "Ergh," he hummed soggily, "toil-ed?" Andy stood to help him.

Supporting Choate with an arm around his waist, and a hand under his armpit, Andy moved back through the crowded, smoke-dense bar, to the battered door marked GENTS. All around them, suddenly, Sorokin realized what a dismal, sinister place The Dog House Bar really was.

In a far corner sat a trio of men in black, all leaning hunkered down in, one next to the other, till they seemed to be one great black gelatinous mass. A whisp of conversation, like a sibilant ghost, hushed through the instant of silence, from that mass, to Sorokin: "Man, I gotta get off . . . gotta take a drive . . ."

Old junkies.

Back behind the jukebox, which was silent, lights faded, a tired harridan merely waiting for a john to slip a coin into her to show her jaded charms, a man and woman were doing something uncomfortable, the woman straddling the man's lap.

The booths were all filled. Groups of men in heavy sweaters, still feeling November with them, outside the fly-specked windows of the bar. Longshoremen, sandhogs, merchant mariners, night truckers; a group of Chinese over from Mott Street; hefty-thighed women clustered about one man with a pack of tarot cards; no one was clean. The smell of swine was in the room. Heavy, changing tone, first garlic, then sweat, then urine, it roiled overhead mixed layer on layer with cigarette and pipe smoke, occasionally clearing sufficiently to smell the acrid aroma of bad marijuana, too many seeds and stems to give any kind of a decent high. And dark. Dim shadows moving here and there, like plankton dark under a sea heavy with silt.

The hum of voices, all somnolent, no hilarity, not a laugh, not a snicker. The substitute was an occasional grunt, a forced sluggish thudding thrust of ughhh as of someone forcing a bowel movement, and usually from a woman, groped under a table. A place of base relationships.

The word immoral did not even apply. It was akin to the drunk who lay on the floor, propped against the wall between stacks of Coca-Cola cases, eyes wide yet unseeing, hands caked with unidentifiable filth, clothes shapeless and gray. An object of no identity, so sunk into alcoholism, addlewitted, that he was what the police called a wetbrain. The term drunk no longer applied, just as the term immoral did not apply. What Sorokin saw here, around him, poised holding Choate, at the door of the toilet, was the final descent of man, to base needs.

He saw the world as it really was, as it was for him, also. The world that was unaffected by ambition or history or social graces. He saw the real side of life, which he had not seen for many years. He saw, God help him, the seamy side of Life.

The bar was full, down reflecting the length of the streaked backbar mirror. Elbow to elbow as four o'clock curfew raced toward them, bending and drinking, not even talking, getting as much inside as possible before night overtook them and they were sent out into the world alone.

A Negro came up to Sorokin, a heavy-faced Negro with conked reddish hair and bloodshot eyes, character gone from the face and replaced with weary cunning. He held up a pair of red plastic dice. "You go'n th' toilet baby? We got us a few fren'z heah, wanna do a thang'a craps, huh, howzabout?" and he laid his hand on Sorokin's backside. Sorokin stiffened.

"Forget it," he said, thickly. *Spade fag,* he thought, and was ill. *Of all the horrors Whitey has committed against the black man, homosexuality is the most perverse.*

The black man drew himself up, snorted a word, and went away, smelling strongly of Arrid and Jean Naté. Out of the corner of his eye, Sorokin saw him join another Negro in a side booth for two, and knew they were discussing that damn straight whitey muthuh by the toilet door.

And in that instant, Sorokin was satisfied. He knew at last, somehow and inexplicably, he had come of age. Late adolescence, the chase for masculinity, were found and over. He had seen all there was to see, and what he had done since he had left this milieu, was to seek responsibility. To mature was to belong; where you wanted to belong, surely, but to care about a life with continuity. He was suddenly whole. And free.

He opened the door and went through into the filthy bathroom with Choate.

The moment they entered the white-tiled toilet, Choate broke away, and fell down on his knees by the stand-up urinal. He began to vomit heavily, a rhinoceros sound deep from his stomach. Sorokin moved away from him, realizing his own bladder cried for emptying. He entered the stall, letting the swinging door slam hard behind him, and unzipped.

He began to urinate, thinking a codifying series of thoughts about the moment of realization he had just known. He barely heard the sound of the outer door open, the scuff of feet against the tiles, a heavy thwack! of something heavy hitting something yielding, and an almost immediate soft ughhh of gentle pain.

Sorokin, still urinating, peered outside the stall, pushing open the door in idle curiosity.

Two Negroes, the same two from the bar, were working Choate over. One had smashed Choate behind the ear with a white tennis sock full of coins, and Choate was bleeding from the scalp, half-slumped into the vomit-filled urinal. The other one was groping for Choate's wallet.

Sorokin did not think about it. If he had, he would not have done it.

He charged out of the stall, head down, and plunged full-tilt into the Negro with the sockful of silver. It had been the Negro with the red plastic dice. He hit him at full speed, head against chest, hands pushing the black man sharply away from him. The Negro careened backward under the impact of the rush, and his head crashed against the white tiles with a sharp car-door crack. He sank to the floor instantly, eyes closed.

Sorokin turned, just in time to see the glint of honed steel as the second Negro flipped open the straight razor and set himself hard, slashing straight through in a flat arc from left shoulder across his body, like a good tennis player fielding a smash with a tight backhand. The razor silently hummed.

The black man caught Sorokin directly across the belly, and Sorokin felt it only as a tiny paper cut might feel. He plunged forward, still doing a ballet turn from the first Negro, unconscious against the tiles. Ingrained army infighting, learned at no small traumatic cost years before, leaped unbidden into Sorokin's reflexes. (You never forget how to swim, once you've learned. You never forget how to ride a bicycle, once you've learned. You never forget how to lay a woman, once you've learned. You never forget how to kill, once you've learned.)

He caught the Negro under the nose with the flat, hard edge of his palm, slamming back and up. The Negro's head whipped up as though on a wire, and he shrieked, high and piercingly, a woman's shriek. His knees buckled inward, and his arms flailed out to the sides. The straight razor went flying and clattered into a corner of the toilet, under the sink. The black man started to fall face-forward, and Sorokin realized he had not for a moment seen the black blood gushing out of the black man's black mouth onto his lower face. A torrent, a river, a dam burst of blood.

The Negro fell past Sorokin like a dropped sandbag. Empty and cold and heavily. He hit on his face, and lay silent, but the smear of blood ran across the white tiles. As he hit, something fell from his vest pocket, and tinkled away.

Sorokin knew the Negro was dead. One for certain, possibly two. He had to get out of there. He looked down, and the razor had cut through his Harris tweed jacket, through his shirt, through his undershirt, and through the top layers of his stomach's soft flesh. He was bleeding profusely, in a constantly welling red line, straight and clean and very, very neat. He touched it, and a bombshell went off in his head as shock set in. His eyes widened, and he said something but did not know what it was.

The thing that had fallen from the smashed Negro's vest winked up at him. It was one of the red plastic dice. It said two. Little white eyes in a clear red box.

Choate was still gasping and vomiting. Sorokin grabbed him up by the back of his jacket, and hauled him toward the door of the toilet. Behind him, neither black man moved, the scene of carnage just as it had been for almost a minute, an hour, forever.

They stumbled out of the toilet together, and Sorokin realized his fly was still open. He did the acceptable thing, and then zipped up his pants. He half-carried Choate toward the table.

Andover was making flirting, obscene gestures at the fat henna-rinsed sow locked in the over-shoulder embrace of a massive longshoreman, one booth away. *Oh, Jesus,* Sorokin thought, terror again bubbling up, *these two are going to get me killed!*

He pulled a ten dollar bill from his side pocket, and threw it down on the table. Then he grabbed Andover and pulled him out of the booth before the sow could complain to her paramour. "Get the coats!" Sorokin ordered him.

Andover grabbed the coats, and with Sorokin hauling both of the drunken Yale men, they stumbled and fell out of The Dog House Bar. Punky wanted very much to get as far away from the scene in the toilet as possible.

For it was entirely probable that death lay stretched out on those filthy white tiles. The final crap-out.

The streets were cold and empty at four o'clock November.

The blood would not stop. He had torn up his undershirt, and stuffed it around his middle, but it had done no good. The undershirt was soaked deep brown from rotted blood.

He could not feel his legs, yet they continued to move, one in front of the other, a puppet conditioned to go on moving even when the puppet-master was dead. An improbable concept, a dead puppet-master, but flamingos were fine, as well. And papaya juice, sweet, cold, milky. There was a toy soldier once, that he had buried in the ground behind his parents' garage, in the town where he had been born, very long ago. He would go back and dig it up. When the whistle blew. Or before. If he could.

The two Yale men were drunk out of their skulls. They laughed and tittered and followed Punky where he led them. which was nowhere, plodding through fresh-fallen snow in the New York streets; he was in shock, and did not know it. The Yale men did not seem to find the dripping slash across Punky's belly very funny, but they didn't talk about it, so it probably didn't matter.

The heavy Harris tweed jacket (a new jacket, recently bought, at Jack Breidbart's, on Sixth Avenue) was what had saved his life. It had absorbed much of the impact of that flat, whistling slash. Straight razor. Clean and true and deadly, made for death, not shaving.

And back there, in that toilet. If you strike a man hard enough under the nose, you will shatter the bridge and drive bone splinters into the brain, killing him instantly. And he will fall past you like a sandbag, like the Negro fell past Punky, so that you must sidestep, a *torero* who has made his kill. Back there, in that toilet.

And they walked the cold, chill, empty, screaming streets.

Punky put his hands in his pockets. He was cold, very cold. He felt a bit of cardboard. He pulled it out. It said: LOTTE Call Sid 611 East 101st.

Punky yelled for a taxi. He yelled and yelled and yelled, his voice rising up spiraling among the icicle-frozen buildings of the Manhattan where he had come to get slashed, where he had come to find his manhood so late in his life, and found it, now dripping out on the white snow of the Manhattan that had always taken him back.

Then there was a taxi, and a long ride uptown, and Sid opening a tenement door, and a gorgeous black-haired Puerto Rican girl who said her name was Lotte, and she was only fourteen, but did someone wanna good fokk?

And time spun hazily by. The two Yale men had gotten laid, and were sleeping on two of the four beds in the apartment. And Sid had sampled his own merchandise, and he was sleeping off a methedrine high on the third bed, and Punky Sorokin was insanely sitting at a kitchen table, at 5:30 in the gray-rising morning, in the four-bed crib of a fourteen-year-old Puerto Rican whore named Lotte, playing gin rummy.

"Knock on six." He grinned boyishly, and bled.

She had serviced the other three, then returned to him and asked, "Wal, you nex', guy. You ready't fokk?"

He had smiled at her in friendliness, totally removed from the world around him, a child in shock, and touched his own bleeding belly. "Did you see I'm bleeding?" he had asked her, very matter-of-factly.

She had looked at it, and they had examined it together with intense care. She had said a few nice things about it, and he had thanked her. But he didn't want to fokk. But, he had asked, did she play gin rummy?

Knock or straight gin, she had wanted to know.

So they had sat down to play, over the oilclothed kitchen table. He liked Lotte a lot. She was a sweet child, and extremely pretty. All that black hair, done up in a high intricate style.

That went on for a long time, the timeless time of just playing, and the two of them smiling at one another. Until Punky decided to tell her things, and say what he had learned that night, and what was in his heart.

She listened, and was polite. She did not interrupt. And this is what Punky Sorokin said . . .

"You see before you a man eaten by worms. Envy, hungers most men don't even smell; lust, nameless things I want. To belong, someplace, to say what I have to say before I die, before I waste my years. All of it, pouring out of the tips of my fingers, like blood, needs. You sit there, and you live day to day and you sleep, get up, go eat, do things. But me, for me, each little thing should have been bigger, each book should have been better, all the riches, all the women, everything I want, just out beyond my reach, tormenting me. And even when I get the gold, when I get the story, when I do the movie, it still isn't what I want, it's something more, something bigger, something perfect. I don't know. I look every way, up and down the world, walking through rooms like something that's waiting for meat to come to it. I can't name it, can't say what it is, where I want it to come from. All I want to do, is *do*! At the peak of my form, at the fastest pace I can set. Running. Running till I drop. Oh, God, don't let me die till I've won."

Lotte, the fourteen-year-old Puerto Rican whore, stared at him across her cards. She laid the hand of gin rummy face-down on the kitchen-smelling oilcloth, and did not know what he was raving about. "Y'wanna can owf beer, hanh?"

In it, was all the gentleness, all the caring, all the concern AndyPunky had ever known. All the sweetness, all the warmth of someone who gave a damn. He started to cry. From far down inside him, it started up, building, great gasps of power, wrenching sobs. He lowered his head onto his hands, still bloody from the wounds that dripped across his middle. He cried muffledly, and the girl shrugged. She turned on the radio, and a Latin band was wailing:

Vaya!

There were streets and he was alone now. Punky had lost his two Yale men. They had showed him the seamy side of Life. Streets he walked on. At six o'clock in the New York morning. And he saw things. He saw ten things.

He saw a cabdriver sleeping in his front seat.

He saw a candy-maker opening his shop to work.

He saw a dog lifting its leg against a standpipe.

He saw a child in an alley.

He saw a sun that would not come up behind snow.

He saw an old, tired Negro man collecting cardboard flats behind a grocery store, and he told the old man I'm sorry.

He saw a toy store and smiled.

He saw pinwheels of violent color that cascaded and spun behind his eyes till he fell in the street.

He saw his own feet moving under him, leftrightleft.

He saw pain, red and raw and ugly in his stomach.

But then, somehow, he was in the Village, in front of Olaf Burger's apartment house, so he whistled a little tune, and thought he might go up to say hello. It was six-thirty.

So he went up and looked at the door for a while.

He whistled. It was nice.

Punky pressed the door buzzer. There was no answer. He waited an extremely long time, half-asleep, leaning there against the jamb. Then he pressed the buzzer again, and held it down. Inside the apartment he could hear the distant, muffled locust hum of the buzzer. Then a shout. And then footsteps coming toward the door. The door was unlocked, slammed back on the police chain. Olaf's face, blurred by sleep, peering out of wakelessness in fury, glared at him.

"What the hell do you want at this—"

and stopped. The eyes widened at sight of all that blood. The door slammed shut, the chain was slipped, and the door opened again. Olaf stared at him, a little sick.

"Jesus Christ, Andy, what happened to you!"

"I fou—I found what I w-was looking for . . ."

They stared at each other, helpless.

Punky smiled once, gently, and murmured, "I'm hurt, Olaf, helpme . . ." and fell sidewise, in through the doorway.

Was lost, and is found. The prodigal returned. Night and awakening. After a night of such length, opening of eyes, and a new awakening. The weavers, Clotho, Lachesis, Atropos. Atropos. She is the inflexible, who with her shears cuts off the thread of human life spun by Clotho, measured off by Lachesis.

Spun by Punky and his Yale men. Measured off by a fourteen-year-old Puerto Rican whore named Lotte in a four-bed pad in Harlem. Cut off by a Negro homosexual in The Dog House Bar in the Bowery.

Hospital white, hospital bright, and blood, instantblood, now down-dropping from a bottle, and before the end, just before the end, Punky woke long enough to say, very distinctly, "Escape, please . . . escape . . ." and went away from there.

The doctor on Punky's right turned to the nurse on *his* right, and said, "He had enough."

Circle-Insult.

A Prayer for No One's Enemy

"Did you get in?" He turned up the transistor. The Supremes were singing *Baby Love.*

"None'a your damn business, man; a gentleman doesn't talk." The other one peeled a third stick of Juicy Fruit and folded it into his mouth. The sugary immediacy of it stood out for a moment, then disappeared into the wad already filling his left cheek.

"Gentleman? Shit, baby, you're a lotta stuff, but you aren't one of them there." He snapped fingers.

"D'jou check the plugs 'n' points like I said?"

He switched stations, stopped. The Rolling Stones were singing *I Can't Get No Satisfaction.* "I took it into Cranston's, they said it was in the timing. Twenty-seven bucks."

"Plugs 'n' points."

"Oh, Christ, man, why don't you shine up awreddy. I'm *tellin'* you what Cranston said. He said it was in the timing, so why d'you keep sayin' plugs 'n' points?"

"Lemme use your comb."

"Use your own comb. You got scalp ringworm."

"Get stuffed! Lemme use your damn comb already!"

He pulled the Swedish aluminum comb out of his hip pocket and passed it over. The comb was tapered like a barber's comb. Gum stopped moving for an instant as the other pulled the gray shape through his long brown hair in practiced swirls. He patted his hair and handed the comb back. "Y'wanna go up to the Big Boy and get something to eat, clock the action?"

"You gonna fill the tank?"

"Fat chance."

"No, I don't wanna go up to the Big Boy and drive around and around like redskins at the Little Big Horn and see if that dopey-ass chick of yours is up there."

"Well, whaddaya wanna do?"

"I don't wanna go up to the Big Boy and go round and round like General Custer, that's for *damn* sure . . ."

"I got the picture. Round and round. Ha ha. Very clever. You oughta be in Hollywood, well what the hell do you *wanna* do?"

"You seen what's up at The Coronet?"

"I dunno, what is it?"

"That picture about the Jews in Palestine."

"Who's in it?"

"I dunno, Paul Newman I think."

"Israel."

"Okay, Israel, you seen it?"

"No, y'wanna see it?"

"Might as well, nothin' else happening around here."

"What time's your old lady come home?"

"She picks my father up at seven."

"That don't answer my question."

"About seven-thirty."

"Let's make it. You got money . . . ?"

"Yeah, for me."

"Jesus, you're a cheap bastard. I thought I was your tight close buddy?"

"You're a leech, baby."

"Turn off the radio."

"I'm gonna take it with me."

"So you ain't gonna tell me if you screwed Donna, huh?"

"None'a your damn business. You wanna tell me if you screwed Patti?"

"Forget it. Plugs 'n' points, you'll see."

"C'mon, we'll miss the first show."

So they went to see the picture about the Jews. The one that was supposed to say a very great deal about the Jews. They were both Gentile, and they had no way of knowing in advance that the picture about the Jews said nothing whatever about the Jews. In Palestine, or Israel, or wherever it was that the Jews were.

It wasn't even a particularly good film, but the exploitation had been cunning, and grosses for the first three days had been rewarding. Detroit. Where they make cars. Where Father Coughlin's Church of the Little Flower reposes in sanctified holiness. Population approximately two million; good people, strong like peasant stock. Where many good jazz men have started, blowing gigs in small roadhouses.

Best barbecued spareribs in the world, at the House of Blue Lights. Detroit. Nice town.

The large Jewish Community had turned out to see the film, and though anyone who had been to Israel, or knew the first thing about how a *kibbutz* functioned, would have laughed it off the screen, for sheer emotionalism it struck the proper chords. With characteristic Hollywood candor, the film stirred a fierce ethnic pride, pointing out in broad strokes: *See, them little yids got guts, too; they can fight when they got to*. The movie was in the grand, altogether innocent tradition of cinematic flag-waving. It was recommended by *Parents' Magazine* and won a *Photoplay* gold medal as fare for the entire family.

The queue that had lined up to see the film stretched from the ticket booth across the front of the building, past a candy store with a window full of popcorn balls in half a dozen different flavors, past a laundromat, around a corner and three-quarters of the way down the block.

It was a quiet crowd. People in lines are always a quiet crowd. Arch and Frank were quiet. They waited, with Arch listening to the transistor, and Frank, Frank Amato, smoking and shuffling.

Neither paid much attention to the sound of engines roaring until the three Volkswagens screamed to a halt directly in front of the theater. Then they looked up, as the doors slammed open and out poured a horde of young boys. They were wearing black. Black turtleneck T-shirts, black slacks, black Beatle boots. The only splash of color on them came from the yellow-and-black armbands, and the form of the swastika on the armbands.

Under the staccato directions of a slim Nordic-looking boy with very bright, wet gray eyes, they began to picket the theater, assembling in drill-formations, carrying signs neatly printed on a hand-press, very sturdy. The signs said:

THIS MOVIE IS COMMUNIST-PRODUCED! BOYCOTT IT!
GO BACK WHERE YOU CAME FROM! STOP RAPING AMERICA!
TRUE AMERICANS SEE THROUGH YOUR LIES!
THIS FILM WILL CORRUPT YOUR CHILDREN! BOYCOTT IT!

and chanting, over and over: "Dirty little Christ-killers, dirty little Christ-killers, dirty little Christ-killers . . ."

In the queue was a sixty-year-old woman; her name was Lilian Goldbosch.

She had lost her husband Martin, her older son Shimon and her younger son Avram in the furnaces of Belsen. She had come to America with eight hundred other refugees on a converted cattle boat, from Liverpool, after five years of hopeless wandering across the desolate face of Europe. She had become a naturalized citizen and had found some stature as a buyer for a piece-goods house, but her reaction to the sight of the always remembered swastika was that of the hunted Jewess who had escaped death—only to find loneliness in a new world. Lilian Goldbosch stared wide-eyed at them, overflowing the sidewalk, inundating her eyes and her thoughts and her sudden thismoment reality; arrogant in their militant fanaticism; and as one they came back to her—for they had never left her—terror, hatred, rage. Her mind (like a broken clock, whirling, spinning backward in time) sparklike leaped the gap of years, and her tired eyes blazed yellow.

She gave a wretched little scream and hurled herself at the tall blond boy, the leader with the gray eyes.

It was a signal.

The crowd broke. A low animal roar. Men flung themselves forward. Women were jostled, and then joined, without reason or pausing to consider it. The muffled sound of souls torn by the sight of stalking (almost goose-stepping) picketers. Before they could stop themselves, the riot was underway.

A burly man in a brown topcoat reached them first. He grabbed the sign from one of the picketers, and with teeth grating behind skinned-back lips, for an instant an animal, hurled it into the gutter. Another man ripped into the center of the group and snapped a fist into the mouth of one of the boys chanting the slogan. The boy flailed backward, arms windmilling, and he went down on one knee. A foot on the end of gray sharkskin trousers—seemingly disembodied—lashed out of the melee. The toe of the shoe took the boy in the groin and thigh. He fell on his back, clutching himself, and they began to stomp him. His body curled inward as they danced their quaint tribal dance on him. If he screamed, it was lost in the roar of the mob.

Also in the queue were two high school boys. Arch; Frank.

They had been alone there, among all those people waiting. But now they were part of a social unit, something was happening. Arch and Frank had fallen back for an instant as others rushed forward; others whose synapses were more quickly triggered by what they saw; but now they found their reactions to the violence around them swift and unthinking. Though they had been brushed aside by men on either side, cursing foully, who had left the line to get at the picketers, now they moved toward the mass of struggling bodies, still unaware of what was really taking place. It was a bop, and they felt the sting of participation. But in a moment they had collided with the frantic figure of Lilian Goldbosch, whose nails were raking deep furrows down the cheek of the tall, blond boy.

He was braced, legs apart, but did not move as she attacked him. There was a contained, almost Messianic tranquility about him.

"Nazi! Nazi! Murd'rer!" she was mouthing, almost incomprehensibly. She slipped into Polish and the sounds became garbled with spittle.

Her body writhed back and forth as she lashed out again and again at the boy.

Her arms were syncopated machines of hard work, destructive, coming up and down in a rhythm all their own, a rhythm of which she was unaware. His face was badly ripped, yet he did not move against her.

At that moment the two high school boys, faceless, came at the woman, one from either side; they took her by the biceps, holding her, protecting not the blond boy, but the older woman. Her movements went to spastic as she struggled against them frenziedly. "Let me, let go, let—" she struggled against them, flashing them a glance of such madness and hatred that for an instant they felt she must think them part of the picketing group, and then—abruptly—her eyes rolled up in her head and she fainted into Frank Amato's grasp.

"Thank you . . . whoever you are," the blond boy said. He started to move away, back through the rioting mob. It was as though he had *wanted* to take the woman's abuse; as though his purpose had been to martyr himself, to absorb all the hate and frenzy into his body, like a lightning rod sucking up the power of the heavens. Now he moved.

Arch grabbed him by the sleeve.

"Hold it a minute . . . hero! Not s'fast!"

The blond boy's mouth began to turn up in an insolent remark, but he caught himself, and instead, with a flowing, completely assured overhand movement, struck the younger boy's hand from his arm.

"My work's done here."

He turned, then, and cupped his hands to his mouth. A piercing whistle leaped above the crowd noises, and as the signal penetrated down through the mob, the swastika-wearers began to disengage themselves with more ferocity. One picketer kicked out, caught an older man in the shin with the tip of a tightly laced barracks boot, and shoved the man back into the crowd. Another boy jabbed a thumb into his opponent's diaphragm and sent the suddenly wheezing attacker sprawling, cutting himself off from further assault.

It went that way all through the crowd as the once-again-chanting picketers moved slowly but methodically toward their cars. It was a handsomely executed tactical maneuver, a strategic withdrawal of class and composure.

Once at the open car doors, they piled back against the black metal bugs, raising arms in an unmistakable *Heil!* and screamed, almost as one: "America always! To hell with the poisoners! Kill the Jews!"

Pop, Pop! With timing vaguely reminiscent of a Keystone Kops imbroglio, they heaved themselves into the vehicles, and were roaring down the street, around the corner, before the approaching growlers of the police prowl cars (summoned on a major 415) were more than a faint whine approaching from the distance.

On the sidewalk in front of the theater, people—for no other release was left to them—burst into tears and cursing.

Some kind of battle had been fought here—and lost.

On the sidewalk, someone had clandestinely chalked *the symbol.* No one moved to scuff it out. None of the picketers had had the free time to do it; the obvious was obvious: someone in the queue had done it.

The subtlest, most effective poison.

Her apartment was an attempt to reassure her crippled spirit that possessions meant security, security meant permanence, and permanence meant the exclusion of sorrow and fear and darkness. She had thrust into every corner of the small one-bedroom apartment every convenience of modern technology, every possible knickknack and gimcrack of oddity, every utensil and luxury of the New World the rooms would hold. Here a 23″ television set, its rabbit-ears askew against the wall . . . there a dehumidifier, busily purring at the silence . . . over there a set of Royal Doulton mugs, Pickwick figures cherubically smiling at their own ingenuousness . . . and a paint-by-the-numbers portrait of Washington astride a white stallion . . . a lemon glass vase overflowing with swizzle sticks from exotic restaurants . . . a stack of *Life, Time, Look* and *Holiday* magazines . . . a reclining lounge chair that vibrated . . . a stereo set with accompanying racks of albums, mostly Offenbach and Richard Strauss . . . a hide-a-bed sofa with orange and brown throw pillows . . . a novelty bird whose long beak, when moistened, dipped the creature forward on its wire rack, submerging its face in a glass of water, then pulled it erect, to repeat the performance endlessly . . .

The jerky movement of the novelty bird in the room, a bad cartoon playing over and over, was intended as reassurance of life still going on; yet it was a cheap, shadowy substitute, and instead of charming the two high school boys who had brought Lilian Goldbosch home, it unsettled them. It made them aware of the faint scent of decay and immolation here; a world within a world, a specie of creative precontinuum in which emotions had palpable massiveness, greater clarity.

The boys helped the still-shaken woman to the sofa, and sat her down heavily. Her face was not old, the lines were adornment rather than devastation, but there was a superimposition of pain on the tidy, even features. Cobwebs on marble. Her hair—so carefully tended and set every week by a professional: tipped, ratted, back-combed, pampered—was disheveled, limp, as though soaked with sweat. Moist stringlets hung down over one cheek. Her eyes, a light blue, altogether perceptive and lucid, were filmed by a milkiness that might have been tears, and might have been gelatinous anguish. Her mouth seemed moist, as though barely containing a wash of tormented sounds.

The years rolled back for Lilian Goldbosch. Once more she knew the sound of the enclosed van whose exhaust pipes led back into the prisoners' compartment, the awful *keee-gl keee-gl keee-gl* of the klaxon, rising above the frozen streets; frozen with fear of movement (if I stay quiet, they'll miss me, pass me by). The Doppler-impending approach of the van, its giant presence directly below the window, right at the curb, next to the face and the ears, and then its hissing passage as it swept away, a moving vacuum cleaner of living things, swallowing whole families. With eyes white eggshells in pale faces. And into the rear of that van, the exhaust whispering its sibilant tune of gas and monoxided forever. All this came back to Lilian Goldbosch as she shamefully spaded-over her memories of the past half hour. Those boys. Their armbands. Her fear. The crowd attacking. The way she had leaped at them. The madness. The fear.

The fear.

Again, the fear.

Burning, blazing through all of it: the fear!

That boy with his imperious blond good looks, the Aryan Superman: could he really know? Could he somehow, this American child born between clean sheets, with the greatest terror a failing mark in school, could he somehow know what that hated black swastika meant to her, to whole generations, to races of individuals who had worn yellow Stars of David and the word *Juden*, to shattered spirits and captured hearts who stood on alien roads as Stukas dived, or walked in desolate resignation to already filling mass graves, or labored across nomanslands with shellbursts lighting the way? Could he know, or was this something else . . . a new thing, that merely *looked* like the old sickness, the fear?

For the first time in more years than she cared to remember—had it only been twenty years since all of it?—Lilian Goldbosch had a surge of desire. Not the gilded wastes she had substituted for caring: not the pathological attention to hair in the latest frosted style, not the temporal acquisition of goods to fill empty rooms, not the television with it gray images, surrogates of life. A want. A need to know. A desire to find out.

Born of an old fear.

Was it the same . . . or something new?

She had to know. She was engulfed by desperation.

And with the desperation, a shocking realization that she could do something. What, she was not certain. But she had the sensation burning in her that if she could know this blond Gentile youth, could talk to him, this *goy*, could communicate with him, this stranger, she could find out the answers, know if the evil was coming again, or if it was just another lonely person, trapped within his skin.

"Will you boys do me a favor?" Lilian Goldbosch asked the two who had escorted her home. "Will you help me?"

At first they were confused, but as she talked, as she explained why she had to know, why it was important, they were drawn into a prospect of their times, and finally they nodded, a little hesitantly, the taller of the two saying, "I don't know if it'll do any good, but we'll try and find him for you."

Then they left. Down the stairs. While she went to wash the tears and streaked mascara from her young-old face.

Frank Amato was of Italian descent. He was a typical child of his times; transistorized, Sanforized, boss gear bomped groovy tuned-in on the music of the spheres, in a Continental belt-back slim-line hop-sacking crease-resistant 14" tapered ineluctable reality that placed him in and of the teenage sub-culture.

Vietnam? Huh?

Voter registration in Alabama? Huh?

The ethical structure of the universe?

Huh?

Arch Lennon was a WASP. He had heard the term, but had never applied it to himself. He was a carbon-copy of Frank Amato. He lived day to day, Big Boy to Big Boy, track meet to track meet, and if there were sounds that went boomp in the night they were probably the old man getting up to haul another pop-top out of the Kelvinator.

Military junta? Huh?

Limited nuclear retaliation? Huh?

The infinitesimal dispensation of Homo sapiens in the disinterested cosmos?

Huh?

Standing down on the sidewalk outside Lilian Goldbosch's apartment, staring at each other.

"*That* was a smart move."

"Well, what the hell was I supposed to say? Fer chrissakes, she had aholda my arm I thought she was gonna bust it. That old lady's nuts."

"So why'd you promise her? Where the hell we gonna find that guy?"

"How should *I* know?"

"I gave my word."

"Big deal."

"Maybe not to you, but I gave it just the same."

"So we try and find that kid, right?"

"Uh . . ."

"What I thought. I gotta do all the brain work again. Jeezus, man, you are such a nit."

"D'jou get the license number of any of those cars?"

"Don't be a clown. No, I din't get the number. And even if I did, what'd we do with it?"

"DMV, wouldn't they tell us who it was registered to?"

"Sure. We're gonna walk into the Motor Vehicle Department just like James Bond, a couple of guys our age, and we're gonna say hey who owns this VW. Sure, I can picture it real good. You're a nit."

"So that's that."

"I wish."

"You got something else?"

"Maybe. One of those VWs had a sticker on the windshield. It was an emblem. Pulaski Vocational High School."

"So one of those guys goes to Pulaski. You know how many inmates they got over there? Maybe a million."

"It's a start."

"You're serious about this."

"Yeah, I'm serious about it."

"How come?"

"I dunno, she asked, an' I gave her my word. She's an old lady, it won't hurt anything to look a while."

"Hey, Frank?"

"What?"

"What's this all about?"

"I dunno, but those bastards were lousy, an' I gave my word."

"Okay, I'll help. But I gotta get home now, my folks oughta be back by now, and we can't do anything till tomorrow anyhow."

"Stay loose. See ya."

"See ya. Don't get in any trouble, double-oh-seven."

"Stick it."

They didn't know which one they would find, or even if they would recognize him when they did find him. But one of the wearers of the swastika attended Pulaski Vocational, and Pulaski Vocational went all year round. Summer, winter, night and day, it turned out students who knew about carburetors, chassis dynamometers, metal lathes and printed circuitry than they did about THE CANTERBURY TALES, scoria and pumice, the theory of vectors and the fact that Crispus Attucks, a Negro, was the first American to fall in the Revolutionary War. It was a great gray stone Coventry of a school, where young boys went in unmarked, and emerged some years later all punched and coded to fit into the System, with fringe benefits and an approximate date of death IBM'd by the group insurance company.

Chances were good the boy—whichever boy it turned out to be—was still attending classes, even though it was summer, and Arch and Frank were free. So they waited, and they watched. And finally, they found one of them.

An acne-speckled, pudgy-hipped specimen in a baggy orange velour pullover.

He came out of the school, and Arch recognized him.

"There, the pear-shaped one, in the orange."

They followed him into the parking lot. The car he unlocked was a Monza, a late model. If they watched for the VW they would have missed him.

"Hey!" Frank came up behind him. The pudgy turned.

He had beady little eyes, like a marmoset. The face was fleshy, with many small inflamed areas where he had shaved and the skin had broken out. There was a wasted look about him, as though he had been used up, and cast away. Even to Arch and Frank, the look of intense intelligence was missing from the pudgy's expression.

"Who're you guys?"

Arch did not like him. For a nameless reason, he did not like him. "Friends of a friend of yours."

Pudgy looked wary. He dumped his books into the back seat, not turning from them. He was getting set to jump inside the car and slam the door, and lock it, and pull out in a hurry. Pudgy was scared.

"Who's that, what friend?"

Frank moved slightly, to the side. It was almost a pavane, the maneuvering: Pudgy angled himself, his hand went toward the back of the front seat; Arch slid around the edge of the door. Frank's hand came up onto the roof of the car, near Pudgy's head. Pudgy's eyes got milky, fear bubbled up behind him, the taint was in his bloodstream.

"A tall kid, blond hair, you know," Frank said, his voice was deeper, a trifle threatening, "he was with you the other night at the movie, remember?"

Pudgy's right cheek tic'd. He knew what was happening. These were Jews. He made his move.

Arch slammed the door. It caught Pudgy at the forearm. He howled. Arch reached across and grabbed him by the ear. Frank sank a fist into Pudgy's stomach. The air whooshed out of Pudgy and left him flat, very flat, a cardboard cutout that they bundled into the front seat of the Monza, one on either side of him. They started the car, and rolled out of the parking lot. They would take him someplace. Someplace else. Pudgy would tell them who the blond Aryan had been, what his name was, where he could be found.

If they could pump enough air into him to produce sound.

Victor. Rohrer. Victor Rohrer. Blond, tall, solid with no extra flesh on his body, muscles very firm and tight, as though packed from the factory in plastic. Victor Rohrer. A face hewn from lignum vitae, from marble. Eyes chipped gray ice frost from lapis lazuli and allowed to die, harden into leaden cadaverousness. A body languinous, soft downy-covered with barely visible blond hairs, each one a sensor, a feeler of atmospheres and temperatures, each one a cilium seeing and smelling and knowing the tenor of the situation. A Cardiff Giant, not even remotely human, something cold and breathing, defying Mendelian theories, defying heredity, a creature from another island universe. Muscled and wired and gray eyes that had sometime never been blue with life. Lips thinned in expectation of silence. Victor. Rohrer. A creation of self, brought forth from its own mind for a need to exist.

Victor Rohrer, organizer of men.

Victor Rohrer, who had never known childhood.

Victor Rohrer, repository of frozen secrets.

Victor Rohrer, wearer of swastikas.

Patron of days and nights; singer of silent songs; visionary of clouds and nothingness; avatar of magics and unspoken credos; celebrant of terrors in nights of endless murmurings; architect of orderly destructions; Victor Rohrer.

"Who are you? Get away from me."

"We want you to talk to somebody."

"Punk filth!"

"Don't make me flatten you, wise guy."

"Don't try it; I don't like hurting people."

"*There's* one of the great laughs of our generation."

"Come on, Rohrer, get your ass in gear; somebody's waiting for you."

"I said: get away from me."

"We aren't goons, Rohrer, don't make us belt you around a little."

"It would take two of you?"

"If it had to."

"That isn't very sportsmanlike."

"Somewhichway, friend, you don't make us feel very sporty. Move it, or s'help me I'll lay this alongside your head."

"Are you from one of those street gangs?"

"No, we're just a coupla patriots doing a good deed."

"I'm tired'a talking. Get it going, Rohrer."

"You . . . you're Jewish, aren't you?"

"I said get going, you bastard! Now!"

And they brought him to Lilian Goldbosch.

Wonder danced in her eyes. A dance of the dead in a bombed-out graveyard; a useless weed growing in a bog. She stared across the room at him. He stood just inside the door, legs close together, arms at his sides, his face as featureless as an expanse of tundra. Only the gray eyes moved in the face, and they did so liquidly, flowing from corner to corner, seeing what was there to be seen.

Lilian Goldbosch walked across the room toward him. Victor Rohrer did not move. Behind him, Arch and Frank closed the door softly. They stood like paladins, one on either side of the door. They watched—with intense fascination—what was happening in this silently humming room. As different worlds paused for an eternal moment.

They did not fully comprehend what it was, but so completely had the blond boy and the old woman absorbed each other's presence, that for now they—the ones who had effected the meeting—were gone, invisible, out of phase, no more a part of the life generated in the room than the mad little bird that dipped its beak in water, agonizingly straightened, rocked and dipped again, endlessly.

She walked up, very close to him. Where she had scratched him, his face was still marked. She reached up, involuntarily fascinated, and made as if to touch him. He moved back an inch, and she caught herself.

"You are very young."

It was said in appraisal, with a tinge of amazement, not a hue of poetry anywhere in it; an attempt to codify the reality of this creature, Victor Rohrer.

He said nothing, but a faint softness came to his mouth, as if he knew another truth. On another face, it might have been a sneer.

"Do you know me?" she asked. "Who I am?"

He was extremely polite, as if she were a supplicant and it had fallen to him to maintain decorum and form with her. "You're the woman who attacked me."

Her lips tightened. The memory was still fresh, an eroded fall on a volcanic hillside she had thought incapable of being ravaged again. "I'm sorry about that."

"I've come to expect it. From you people."

"My people . . ."

"Jews."

"Oh. Yes. I'm Jewish."

He smiled knowledgeably. "Yes, I know. It says everything, doesn't it?"

"Why do you do this thing? Why do you walk around and tell people to hate one another?"

"I don't hate you."

She stared at him warily; there had to be more. There was.

"How can one hate a plague of locusts, or a packrat that lives in the walls? I don't hate, I'm merely an exterminator."

"Where did you get these ideas? Why does a boy your age fool around with this kind of thing, do you know what went on in the world twenty-five years ago, do you know all the sorrow and death this kind of thinking brought?"

"Not enough. He was a madman, but he had the right idea about the *Juden*. He had the final solution, but he made mistakes."

His face was perfectly calm. He was not reciting cant, he was delivering a theory he had worked out, logically, completely, finally.

"How did you get so much sickness in you?"

"It is a matter of opinion which of us is diseased. I choose to believe you are the cancer."

"What do your parents think of this?"

A hot little spot of red appeared high on his cheeks. "Their opinions are of very little concern to me."

"Do they know about what you do?"

"I'm getting tired of this. Are you going to tell these two punks to let me go, or will I have to put up with more abuse from you and your kind?" His face was getting slightly flushed now. "Do you wonder that we want to purge you, purify the country of your filth? When you constantly prove what we say is so?"

Lilian Goldbosch turned to the two boys by the door. "Do you know where he lives?" Arch nodded. "I want to see his mother and father. Will you take me there?" Again, Arch nodded. "He doesn't know. He doesn't understand. I can't find out from him. I'll have to ask there."

Flames burned up suddenly in Victor Rohrer's eyes. "You'll stay away from my home!"

"I'll get my purse," she said, softly.

He went for her. His hands came out and up and he was on her, hurling her backward, over a footstool, and they went into a heap, the woman thrashing frantically, and Victor Rohrer coldly, dispassionately trying to strangle her.

Arch and Frank moved quickly.

Frank grabbed Rohrer around the throat in a hammerlock, and without ceremony or warning, Arch lifted a marble ashtray from an end table and swung it in an arc. The ashtray smacked across the side of Victor Rohrer's head with an audible sound, and he suddenly tilted to the left and fell past Lilian Goldbosch.

He was not unconscious, Arch had pulled his punch, but he was dazed. He sat on the floor, moving his head as if it belonged to somebody else. The two high school boys attended the woman. She struggled to pick herself up, and they helped her to her feet.

"Are you okay?" Frank asked.

She leaned against Arch, and automatically her hand went to her hair, to tidy it. But the movement was only half-formed, as if all those narcissistic acts she had used to make her life livable were now frippery. Her breathing was jagged, and red marks circled her larynx where Rohrer had fastened on tightly.

"He is the complete Nazi," she husked. "He has eaten the Nazi cake, and digested it; he is one of them. It is the old fear, the same one, the very same one, come again. Dear God, we will see it again, the way it was before."

She began to sob. From an empty room within the structure of her soul, tears that had dried years before were called on, and would not come. Ludicrously, she rasped and wheezed, and when nothing came to her eyes, she swallowed hard and bit her lip. In a while she had stopped.

"We must take him home," she said. "I want to talk to his parents."

They got Victor Rohrer under the arms, and they lifted him. He staggered and bobbled, but between them they got him downstairs and into the car. Arch sat in back with him, and Lilian Goldbosch stared straight ahead through the windshield, even when they finally pulled up in front of Rohrer's house in the suburb, Berkeley.

"We're here," Frank said to her. She started, and looked around slowly. It was a neat, unprepossessing house, set in a line among many such houses. It escaped a total loss of identity by a certain warmth of landscaping: dwarf Japanese trees dotting the front lawn, a carefully trimmed hedge that ran down the property line on one side, ivy holding fast to a corner of the house with several years of climbing having brought it just under the second-floor windows. An ordinary house, in an ordinary town.

"Okay, Rohrer, out."

Victor Rohrer went wild! His face contorted. The cold logical animosity of the cool reasoning racist was suddenly washed away. He began speaking in a thin, venomous tone, the words slipping out between knife-edge lips; they did not hiss, but they might as well have; he did not scream, but it had the same shocking effect.

"Kike filth. How much longer do you think you're going to be able to push people around like this? All of you, just like you, with your rotten poisonous filth, trying to take over, trying to tell people what to do; you ought to be killed, every one of you, slaughtered like pigs, I'd do it myself if I could. You'll see, your day is coming, the final day for you . . ."

It was rasped out with such intensity, Lilian Goldbosch sat straight, tensed, unable to move, it was a voice from the past. Her body began to tremble. It was the old fear, the one that years of war and years of peace had put in a grave she now found had always been too shallow. The corpse of that fear had clawed its way up out of the dirt and massed dead flesh of the communal grave, and was again walking the world.

Arch reached across and opened the door. He shoved Victor Rohrer before him. Frank and Lilian Goldbosch joined them as they walked up the front drive toward the little house.

"I've found my answer," Lilian Goldbosch said, terror in her voice. "It is the old fear, the terrible one, the one that destroys worlds. And he is the first of them . . . but there will be many more . . . many . . ."

Her eyes were dull as they reached the front door. Rohrer spun about, slapping Arch's hand off his arm. "You aren't going to meet them! I won't allow you in! This isn't a Jew-run town, I'll have you arrested for kidnapping, for breaking and entering . . ."

Lilian looked past him.

Past him, to the lintel of the door.

And the fear suddenly drained out of her face.

Victor Rohrer saw her expression, and half-turned his head. Arch and Frank looked in the direction of Lilian Goldbosch's stare. Attached to the lintel of the door, at a slant, was a tubular ornament of shiny brass. Near the top of the face of the ornament was a small hole, through which Arch and Frank could see some strange lettering.

Lilian Goldbosch said, "*Shaddai*," reached across Victor Rohrer and touched the tiny hole, then withdrew her hand and kissed the fingertips. Her face had been transformed. She no longer looked as though darkness was on its way.

Victor Rohrer made no move toward her.

"That is a fine *mezuzah*, Victor," she said, softly, looking at him now with complete control of the situation. She started to turn away. "Come along, boys, I don't need to see Victor's parents now: I understand."

They stared at Rohrer. He suddenly looked like a hunted animal. All his cool polite self-possession was gone. He was sweating. Alone, He stood, suddenly, on his own doorstep, next to a tubular ornament on a right doorpost, alone. Afraid.

Lilian paused a moment, turned back to Victor Rohrer. "It is true no one has a happy childhood, Victor. But we all have to live, to go on. Yours must not have been nice, but . . . try to live, Victor. You aren't my enemy, neither am I your enemy."

She walked down the steps, turned once more and said, kindly, as an afterthought, "I will say a prayer for you."

Bewildered, Arch and Frank looked at Victor Rohrer for a long moment. They saw a man of dust. A scarecrow. An emptiness where a person had stood a moment before. This old woman, with incomprehensible words and a sudden sureness, had hamstrung him, cut the nerves from his body, emptied him like a container of murky liquid.

With a soft sound of panic, Victor Rohrer hurled himself off the front steps, and ran across the yard, disappearing in a moment. He was gone, and the three of them stood there, looking at the afternoon.

"What did you say to him?" Arch said. "That word you said. What was it?"

Lilian Goldbosch turned and walked to the car. They came and held the door for her. She was regal. When she looked up at the boys, she smiled. "*Shaddai*. The name of the Lord. From Deuteronomy."

Then she got in, and they closed the door. Out of sight of Lilian Goldbosch, where she sat calmly, waiting to be driven home, Arch and Frank stared at each other. Total confusion. Something had happened here, but they had no idea what it was.

Then they got in the car, and drove her home. She thanked them, and asked them to call on her again, any time. They could not bring themselves to ask what had happened, because they felt they should be smart enough to know; but they didn't know.

Outside, they looked at each other, and abruptly, just like that, everything that had gone before in their lives seemed somehow trivial. The dancing, the girls, the cars, the school that taught them nothing, the aimless days and nights of movies and cursing and picnics and drag races and ball games, all of it, seemed terribly inconsequential, next to this puzzle they had become part of.

"*Shuh-die,*" Arch said, looking at Frank.

"And that other word: *muh-zooz*—what it was."

They went to see a boy they knew, in their class, a boy they had never had occasion to talk to before. His name was Arnie Sugarman, and he told them three things.

When they got back to Lilian Goldbosch's apartment, they knew something was wrong the moment they approached the door. It was open, and the sound of classical music came from within. They shoved the door open completely, and looked in.

She was lying half on the sofa, half on the floor. He had used a steam iron on her, and there was blood everywhere. They entered the room, avoiding the sight, avoiding the mass of pulped meat that had been her face before he had beaten her again, and again, and again, in a senseless violence that had no beginning and no end. The two high school boys went to the telephone, and Frank dialed the operator.

"Puh-police, please . . . I want to report a, uh, a murder . . ."

Lilian Goldbosch lay twisted and final; the terror that had pursued her across the world, through the years—the terror she had momentarily escaped—had at last found her and added her to the total that could never be totaled. She had found her answer, twenty-five years too late.

In the room, the only movement was a small bird with a comic beak that dipped itself in water, straightened, and then, agonizingly, repeated the process, over and over and over . . .

Hunkered down in an alley, where they would find him, Victor Rohrer stared out of mad eyes. Eyes as huge as golden suns, eyes that whirled with fiery little points of light. Eyes that could no longer see.

See his past, his childhood, when they had used names to hurt him. When his parents had been funny little people who talked with accents. When he had been friendless . . . for *that* reason.

For the reason of the *mezuzah* on the lintel. The little holy object on the lintel, the ornament that contained the little rectangle of parchment with its twenty-two lines of Hebrew from Deuteronomy.

Back behind huge garbage cans spilling refuse, in the sick-sweet rotting odor of the alley, Victor Rohrer sat with knees drawn up, staring at his limp hands, the way a fetus "sees" its limp, relaxed hands before its face. Quiet in there, inside Victor Rohrer. Quiet for the first time. Quiet after a long time of shrieking and sound and siren wails inside a skull that had offered no defense, no protection.

Victor Rohrer and Lilian Goldbosch, both *Juden*, both stalked; and on an afternoon in Detroit . . .

. . . both had answered with their lives a question that had never even existed, much less been asked, by two high school boys who now had begun to suspect . . .

. . . no one escapes, when night begins to fall.

III

WORLDS OF LOVE

> "Friends are those into whose souls you've looked, and therein glimpsed a oneness with yourself. They are a part of you, and you a part of them. They own a piece of you."
>
> —*The Harlan Ellison Hornbook,* Installment #21, The *Los Angeles Free Press,* 1973

In the preceding stories, it seemed inevitable, even natural, to find death a recurrent image. Perhaps its absence would have seemed out of place. And so, in these stories of love, we can expect romanticism, sentimentality, passion and all happiness, right?

Wrong. We find death, despair, disappointment.

But these *are* stories about love. Really.

Love and death, and love and suffering—combinations that have fascinated the world's greatest writers, giving us a legacy of reality and fantasy that is the essence of the human spirit. As a balm, love may ease the pain of death or, as some have speculated, even transcend it. It can also metamorphose into a twisted shadow of itself—possessive, consuming and dangerous. More than any other human emotion, love can reveal the purity of the human heart or rip that very heart to pieces in its desperation for fulfillment.

Harlan has perhaps never come closer to the purity of the heart than with "In Lonely Lands" (1959). It is all the more remarkable to find that to do this he has singled out the darkness of the Martian night and the remoteness of an alien soul. Stranger still, he has chosen not a scene of sexual longing or passion but a moment in which we all know, instinctively, we travel with only what we carry in our heart. If love can transcend the limitations of our physicality, I can imagine no more simple or loving method than we find here.

In "The Time of the Eye" (1959), this purity is twisted. What can be nobly sought and nobly motivated can also be misplaced, even caricatured. Love—so full of passion and driving obsession—can prevent us from identifying those other forms that passion and obsession can take, the drives that mimic love. This story of a man suddenly given purpose, protective, responding to forms, reminds us how these chameleon masks of love conceal all kinds of ugliness, fueled by loneliness, fed by need. When love ceases to be pure and noble, what does it do with all that passion and force? And what residue does it leave behind?

With this great attention to love, it is to be expected that Harlan would eventually turn to the eternal question: What Is True Love? "Grail" (1981) looks determinedly for the answer, but the search is certainly an odd one, moving as it does through traps of death, deception, theft and horrors that are, really, just too awful to be described. Yet for all its grisliness, this story is vitally concerned with what a human being may be willing to do to discover what love is.

> "We must think new thoughts; we must love as we have never even suspected we can love; and if there is honor to violence, we must get it on at once, have done with it, try to live with our guilt for having so done, and move on."
>
> —"The Waves in Rio," Introduction to THE BEAST THAT SHOUTED LOVE AT THE HEART OF THE WORLD, Avon, 1969

In Lonely Lands

He clasps the crag with crooked hands;
Close to the sun in lonely lands,
Ring'd with the azure world he stands.
—Alfred, Lord Tennyson

Pederson knew night was falling over Syrtis Major; blind, still he knew the Martian night had arrived; the harp crickets had come out. The halo of sun's warmth that had kept him golden through the long day had dissipated, and he could feel the chill of the darkness now. Despite his blindness there was an appreciable *changing* in the shadows that lived where once, long ago, there had been sight.

"Pretrie," he called into the hush, and the answering echoes from the moon valleys answered and answered, *Pretrie, Pretrie, Pretrie,* down and down, almost to the foot of the small mountain.

"I'm here, Pederson old man. What do you want of me?"

Pederson relaxed in the pneumorack. He had been tense for some time, waiting. Now he relaxed. "Have you been to the temple?"

"I was there. I prayed for many turnings, through three colors."

It had been many years since Pederson had seen colors. But he knew the Martian's religion was strong and stable because of colors. "And what did the blessed Jilka foretell, Pretrie?"

"Tomorrow will be cupped in the memory of today. And other things." The silken overtones of the alien's voice were soothing. Though Pederson had never seen the tall, utterly ancient Jilkite, he had passed his arthritic, spatulate fingers over the alien's hairless, teardrop head, had seen by feeling the deep round sockets where eyes glowed, the pug nose, the thin, lipless gash that was mouth. Pederson knew this face as he knew his own, with its wrinkles and sags and protuberances. He knew the Jilkite was so old no man could estimate it in Earth years.

"Do you hear the Gray Man coming yet?"

Pretrie sighed, a lung-deep sigh, and Pederson could hear the inevitable crackling of bones as the alien hunkered down beside the old man's pneumorack.

"He comes but slowly, old man. But he comes. Have patience."

"Patience." Pederson chuckled ruminatively. "I got that, Pretrie. I got that and that's about all. I used to have time, too, but now that's about gone. You say he's coming?"

"Coming, old man. Time. Just time."

"How are the blue shadows, Pretrie?"

"Thick as fur in the moon valleys, old man. Night is coming."

"Are the moons out?"

There was a breathing through wide nostrils—ritualistically slit nostrils—and the alien replied, "None yet this night. Tayseff and Teei are below the horizon. It grows dark swiftly. Perhaps this night, old man."

"Perhaps," Pederson agreed.

"Have patience."

Pederson had not always had patience. As a young man, the blood warm in him, he had fought with his Presby-Baptist father, and taken to space. He had not believed in Heaven, Hell, and the accompanying rigors of the All-Church. Not then. Later, but not then.

To space he had gone, and the years had been good to him. He had aged slowly, healthily, as men do in the dark places between dirt. Yet he had seen the death, and the men who had died believing, the men who had died not believing. And with time had come the realization that he was alone, and that some day, one day, the Gray Man would come for him.

He was always alone, and in his loneliness, when the time came than he could no longer tool the great ships through the star-spaces, he went away.

He went away, searching for a home, and finally came full-circle to the first world he had known; came home to Mars, where he had been young, where his dreams had been born; Mars, for home is always where a man has been young and happy. Came home where the days were warm and the nights were mild. Came home where men had passed but somehow, miraculously, had not sunk their steel and concrete roots. Came home to a home that had changed not at all since he'd been young. And it was time. For blindness had found him, and the slowness that forewarned him of the Gray Man's visit. Blindness from too many glasses of vik and scotch, from too much hard radiation, from too many years of squinting into the vastness. Blind, and unable to earn his keep.

So alone, he had come home; as the bird finds the tree, as the winter-starved deer finds the last bit of bark, as the river finds the sea. He had come there to wait for the Gray Man, and it was there that the Jilkite Pretrie had found him.

They sat together, silently, on the porch with many things unsaid, yet passing between them.

"Pretrie?"

"Old man."

"I never asked you what you get out of this. I mean—"

Pretrie reached and the sound of his claw tapping the formica table-top came to Pederson. Then the alien was pressing a bulb of water-diluted vik into his hand. "I know what you mean, old man. I have been with you close on two harvestings. I am here. Does that not satisfy you?"

Two harvestings. Equivalent to four years Earth-time, Pederson knew. The Jilkite had come out of the dawn one day, and stayed to serve the old blind man. Pederson had never questioned it. One day he was struggling with the coffee pot (he dearly loved old-fashioned brewed coffee and scorned the use of the coffee briquettes) and the heat control on the hutch . . . the next he had an undemanding, unselfish manservant who catered with dignity and regard to his every desire. It had been a companionable relationship; he had made no great demands on Pretrie, and the alien had asked nothing in return.

He was in no position to wonder or question.

Though he could hear Pretrie's brothers in the chest-high floss brakes at harvesting time, still the Jilkite never wandered far from the hutch.

Now, it was nearing its end.

"It has been easier with you. I—uh—thanks, Pretrie." The old man felt the need to say it clearly, without embroidery.

A soft grunt of acknowledgment. "I thank you for allowing me to remain with you, old man, Pederson," the Jilkite answered softly.

A spot of cool touched Pederson's cheek. At first he thought it was rain, but no more came, and he asked, "What was that?"

The Jilkite shifted—with what Pederson took to be discomfort—and answered, "A custom of my race."

"What?" Pederson persisted.

"A tear, old man. A tear from my eye to your body."

"Hey, look . . ." he began, trying to convey his feelings, and realizing *look* was the wrong word. He stumbled on, an emotion coming to him he had long thought dead inside himself. "You don't have to be—uh—you know, sad, Pretrie. I've lived a good life. The Gray Man doesn't scare me." His voice was brave, but it cracked with the age in the cords.

"My race does not know sadness, Pederson. We know gratitude and companionship and beauty. But not sadness. That is a serious lack, so you have told me, but we do not yearn after the dark and the lost. My tear is a thank you for your kindness."

"Kindness?"

"For allowing me to remain with you."

The old man subsided then, waiting. He did not understand. But the alien had found him, and the presence of Pretrie had made things easier for him in these last years. He was grateful, and wise enough to remain silent.

They sat there thinking their own thoughts, and Pederson's mind winnowed the wheat of incidents from the chaff of spent life.

He recalled the days alone in the great ships, and how he had at first laughed to think of his father's religion, his father's words about loneliness: "No man can walk the road without companionship, Will," his father had said.

And he'd laughed, declaring he was a loner, but now, with unnameable warmth and presence of the alien here beside him, he knew the truth.

His father had been correct.

It was good to have a friend. Especially when the Gray Man was coming. Strange how he knew it with such calm certainty, but that was the way of it. He knew, and he waited placidly.

After a while, the chill came down off the hills, and Pretrie brought out the treated shawl. He laid it about the old man's thin shoulders, where it clung with warmth; the Jilkite hunkered down on his triple-jointed legs once more.

And they waited together in silence as darkness seeped across the land.

Some time later, Pederson's voice came from the shadows, a soft rumination. "I don't know, Pretrie."

There was no answer. There had been no question.

"I just don't know. Was it worth it all? The time aspace, the men I've known, the lonely ones who died and the dying ones who never had the chance to be lonely."

"All peoples know that ache, old man," Pretrie said. He drew a deep breath.

"I never thought I needed anyone. I've learned better, Pretrie. Everybody needs somebody."

"For some the knowledge comes too late; they never have the chance to make use of it." Pederson had taught the alien little; Pretrie had come to him speaking English. It had been one more puzzling thing about the Jilkite, but again Pederson had not questioned it. There had been many spacers and missionaries on Mars.

Then the alien stiffened, his claw upon the old man's arm. "He comes, Pederson old man."

A thrill of expectancy, and a shiver of near-fright came with it. Pederson's gray head lifted, and despite the warmth of the shawl he felt cold. So near now. "He's coming?"

"He is here."

They both sensed it, for Pederson could feel the awareness in the Jilkite beside him; he had grown sensitive to the alien's moods, even as the other had plumbed his own. "The Gray Man." Pederson spoke the words softly on the night air, and the moon valleys did not respond.

"I'm ready," said the old man, and he extended his left hand for the grasp. He set down the bulb of vik with his other hand.

The feel of hardening came stealing through him, and it was as though someone had taken his hand in return. Then, as he thought he was to go, alone, he said, "Goodbye to you, Pretrie, friend."

But there was no goodbye from the alien beside him. Instead, the Jilkite's voice came to him as through a fog softly descending.

"We go together, friend Pederson. The Gray Man comes to all races. Why do you expect me to go alone? Each need is a great one.

"I am here, Gray Man. Here. I am not alone." Oddly, Pederson knew the Jilkite's claw had been offered, and taken in the clasp.

He closed his blind eyes.

After a great while, the sound of the harp crickets thrummed high once more, and on the porch before the hutch, there was the silence of peace.

Night had come to the lonely lands; night, but not darkness.

The Time of the Eye

In the third year of my death, I met Piretta. Purely by chance, for she occupied a room on the second floor, while I was given free walk of the first floor and the sunny gardens. And it seemed so strange, that first and most important time, that we met at all, for she had been there since she had gone blind in 1958, while I was one of the old men with young faces who had dissolved after being in the Nam.

The Place wasn't too unpleasant, of course, despite the high, flat-stone walls and the patronizing air of Mrs. Gondy, for I knew one day my fog would pass, and I would feel the need to speak to someone again, and then I could leave the Place.

But that was in the future.

I neither looked forward to that day, nor sought refuge in my stable life at the Place. I was in a limbo life between caring and exertion. I was sick; I had been told that; and no matter what I knew—I was dead. So what sense was there in caring?

But Piretta was something else.

Her delicate little face was porcelain, with eyes the flat blue of shallow waters, and hands that were quick to do nothing important.

I met her—as I say—by chance. She had grown restless, during what she called "the time of the eye," and had managed to give her Miss Hazelet the slip.

I was walking with head bowed and hands locked behind my bathrobe, through the lower corridor, when she came down the great winding stairway.

On many an occasion I had stopped at that stairway, watching the drab-faced women who scrubbed down each level, each riser. It was like watching them go to hell. They started at the top, and washed their way down. Their hair was always white, always lank, always like old hay. They scrubbed with methodical ferocity, for this was the last occupation left to them before the grave, and they clung to it with soap and suds. And I had watched them go down to hell, step by step.

But this time there were no drudges on their knees.

I heard her walking close to the wall, her humble fingertips brushing the wainscotting as she descended, and I realized immediately that she was blind.

That blindness deeper than lack of sight.

There was something to her; something ephemeral that struck instantly to the dead heart in me. I watched her come down with stately slowness, as though she tripped to silent music, until I was drawn to her in spirit.

"May I be of service?" I heard myself politely inquiring, from a distance. She paused there and her head came up with field mouse awareness.

"No, thank you," she said, most congenially. "I am quite able to care for myself, thank you. Something that *person*," she twitched her head in the direction of upstairs, "cannot seem to fathom."

She came the remainder of the steps to the napless wine-colored rug. She stood there and exhaled deeply, as though she had just put a satisfactory finis to an immense project.

"My name is—" I began, but she cut me off with a sharp snort and, "Name's the same." She giggled prettily.

"Names ring of little consequence, don't you agree?" and there was such conviction in her voice, I could hardly disagree.

So I said, "I suppose that's so."

She snickered softly and patted her auburn hair, bed-disarrayed. "Indeed," she said with finality, "that *is* so; very much so."

This was most peculiar to me, for several reasons.

First, she was talking with a rather complicated incoherence that seemed perfectly rational at the time, and second, she was the first person I had spoken to since I had been admitted to the Place, two years and three months before.

I felt an affinity for this girl, and hastened to strengthen our flimsy tie.

"And yet," I ventured, "one must have *some*thing by which to know another person." I became most bold and went on, "Besides—" gulping, "if one likes someone . . ."

She considered this for a long second, one hand still on the wall, the other at her white throat. "If you insist," she replied, after deliberation, and added, "you may call me Piretta."

"Is that your name?" I asked.

"No," she answered, so I knew we were to be friends.

"Then you can call me Sidney Carton." I released a secret desire of long sublimation.

"That is a fine name, should any name be considered fine," she admitted, and I nodded. Then, realizing she could not hear a nod, I added a monosyllable to indicate her pleasure was also mine.

"Would you care to see the gardens?" I asked chivalrously.

"That would be most kind of you," she said, adding with a touch of irony, "as you see . . . I'm quite blind."

Since it was a game we were playing I said, "Oh, truly? I really hadn't noticed."

Then she took my arm, and we went down the corridor toward the garden French doors. I heard someone coming down the staircase, and she stiffened on my arm. "Miss Hazelet," she gasped. "Oh, please!"

I knew what she was trying to say. Her attendant. I knew then that she was not allowed downstairs, that she was now being sought by her nurse. But I could not allow her to be returned to her room, after I had just found her.

"Trust me," I whispered, leading her into a side corridor.

I found the mop closet, and gently ushered her before me, into its cool, dark recess. I closed the door softly and stood there, very close to her. I could hear her breathing, and it was shallow, quick. It made me remember those hours before dawn in Vietnam, even when we were full asleep; when we sensed what was coming, with fear and trepidation. She was frightened. I held her close, without meaning to do so, and her arm went around my waist. We were very near, and for the first time in over two years I felt emotions stirring in me; how foolish of me to consider love. But I waited there with her, adrift in a sargasso of conflicting feelings, while her Miss Hazelet paced outside.

Finally, after what seemed a time too short, we heard those same precise steps mounting the stairs—annoyed, prissy, flustered.

"She's gone. Now we can see the gardens," I said, and wanted to bite my tongue. She could *see* nothing; but I did not rectify my error. Let her think I took her infirmity casually. It was far better that way.

I opened the door cautiously, and peered out. No one but old Bauer, shuffling along down the hall, his back to us. I led her out, and as though nothing had happened, she took my arm once more.

"How sweet of you," she said, and squeezed my bicep.

We walked back to the French doors, and went outside.

The air was musky with scent of fall, and the crackling of leaves underfoot seemed a proper thing. It was not too chilly, and yet she clung to me with a soft desperation more need that inclination. I didn't think it was because of her blindness; I was certain she could walk through the garden without any help if she so desired.

We moved down the walk, winding out of sight of the Place in a few seconds, shielded and screened by the high, neatly pruned hedges. Oddly enough, for that time of day, no attendants were slithering through the chinaberry and hedges, no other "guests" were taking their blank-eyed pleasure on the turf or on the bypaths.

I glanced sidewise at her profile, and was pleased by her chiseled features. Her chin was a bit too sharp and thrust forward, but it was offset by high cheekbones and long eyelashes that gave her a rather Asiatic expression. He lips were full, and her nose was a classic yet short sweep.

I had the strangest feeling I had seen her somewhere before, though that was patently impossible.

Yet the feeling persisted.

I remembered another girl . . . but that had been before the Nam . . . before the sound of a metallic shriek down the night sky . . . and someone standing beside my bed at Walter Reed. That had been in another life, before I had died, and been sent to this Place.

"Is the sky dark?" she asked. I guided her to a bench, hidden within a box of hedges.

"Not very," I replied. "There are a few clouds in the north, but they don't look like rainclouds. I think it'll be a nice day."

"It doesn't matter," she said resignedly. "The weather doesn't really matter. Do you know how long it's been since I've seen sunlight through the trees?" Then she sighed, and laid her head back against the bench. "No. The weather doesn't really matter. Not at this Time, anyhow."

I didn't know what that meant, but I didn't care, either.

There was a new life surging through me. I was surprised to hear it beating in my ears. I was surprised to find myself thinking minutes into the future. No one who has not experienced it can understand what it is to be dead, no longer to think of the future, and then to find something worthwhile and begin to live all over again. I don't mean just hope, nothing that simple and uncomplicated. I mean to be dead, and then to be alive. It had come to be like that in just a few minutes since I had met Piretta. I had ignored the very next instant for the past two years and three months, and now suddenly, I was looking to the future. Not much at first, for it had become an atrophied ability in me, but I was expecting from minute to minute, caring, and I could feel my life ranging back to pick me up, to continue its journey.

I was looking ahead, and wasn't that the first step to regaining my lost life?

"Why are you here?" she inquired, placing a cool, slim-fingered hand on my bare arm.

I placed my hand over it, and she started, so I withdrew it self-consciously. Then she searched about, found it, and put it over hers again.

"I was in the War," I explained. "There was a mortar and I was hit, and they sent me here. I—I didn't want to—maybe I wasn't able to—I don't know—I didn't want to talk to anyone for a long time.

"But I'm all right now," I finished, abruptly at peace with myself.

"Yes," she said, as though that decided it.

Then she went on speaking, in the strangest tone of voice: "Do you sense the Time of the Eye, too, or are you one of *them*?" She asked it with ruthlessness in her voice. I didn't know what to answer.

"Who do you mean by *them*?"

She let her full upper lip snarl, and said, "Those women who bedpan me. Those foul, crepuscular antiseptics!"

"If you mean the nurses and attendants," I caught her line of thought, "no, I'm not one of them. I'm as annoyed by them as you seem to be. Didn't I hide you?"

"Would you find me a stick?" she asked.

I looked around, and seeing none, broke a branch from the box hedge. "This?"

I handed it to her.

"Thank you," she said.

She began stripping it, plucking the leaves and twigs from it. I watched her dexterous hands flitting, and thought *How terrible for such a lovely and clever girl to be thrown in here with these sick people, these madmen*.

"You probably wonder what *I'm* doing here, don't you?" she asked, peeling the thin, green bark from the stick. I didn't answer her, because I didn't want to know; I had found something, someone, and my life had begun again. There was no reason to kill it all at once.

"No, I hadn't thought about it."

"Well, I'm here because *they* know I'm aware of them."

It struck a note of familiarity. There had been a man named Herbman, who had lived on the first floor during my second year at the Place. He had always talked about the great clique of men who were secretly trying to kill him, and how they would go to any extreme to get him, to silence him before he could reveal their dire machinations.

I hoped the same thing had not befallen her. She was so lovely.

"*They*?"

"Yes, of course. You *said* you weren't one of them. Are you lying to me? Are you making fun of me, trying to confuse me?" Her hand slipped out from under mine.

I hastened to regain ground. "No, no, of course not; but don't you see, I don't understand? I just don't know. I—I've been here so long." I tried not to sound pathetic.

Somehow, this seemed to strike her logically. "You must forgive me. I sometimes forget everyone is not aware of the Time of the Eye as I am."

She was pulling at the end of the stick, drawing off the bark, making a sharp little point there. "The Time of the Eye?" I asked. She had said it several times. "I don't understand."

Piretta turned to me, her dead blue eyes seeing directly over my right shoulder, and she put her legs close together. The stick was laid carelessly by her side, as though a toy it had been, but now the time for toys was gone. "I'll tell you," she said.

She sat very still for an instant, and I waited. Then:

"Have you ever seen a woman with vermilion hair?"

I was startled. I had expected a story from her, some deep insight into her past that would enable me to love her the more . . . and in its place she asked a nonsense question.

"Why . . . no . . . I can't say that I . . ."

"*Think!*" she commanded me.

So I thought, and oddly enough, a woman with vermilion hair *did* come to mind. Several years before I had been drafted, the rage in all the women's fashion magazines had been a woman named—my God! Was it? Why, yes, now that I looked closely and my memory prodded, it *was*—Piretta. A fashion model of exquisite features, lustrous blue eyes, and an affected vermilion-tint hairdo. She had been so famous her glamour had lapped over from the fashion magazines, had become one of those household names everyone bandies about.

"I remember you," I said, startled beyond words of more meaning.

"No!" she snapped. "No. You don't remember *me*. You remember a woman named Piretta. A beautiful woman who attacked life as if it was her last lover, and loved it fiercely. That was someone else. I'm a poor blind thing. You don't know *me*, do you?"

"No," I agreed, "I don't. I'm sorry. For a moment—"

She went on, as though I had never spoken.

"The woman named Piretta was known to everyone. No fashionable salon gathering was fashionable without her; no cocktail party was meaningful with her absent. But she was not a shrinking violet type of woman. She loved experience; she was a nihilist, and more. She would do *any*thing. She climbed K.99 with the Postroff group, she sailed with two men around the Cape of Good Hope in an outrigger, she studied the cult of Kali in India, and though she had come to them an infidel, at the end the Society of Thugs took her as one of their acolytes.

"That kind of life can jade a person. She grew bored with it. With the charities, with the modeling, with the brief fling at films, and with the men. The wealthy men, the talented men, the pretty men who were attracted to her, and who were at the same time held at bay by her beauty. She sought new experience . . . and eventually found it."

I wondered why she was telling me this. I had decided by now that the life I was anxious to have return was here, in her. I was living again and it had come so quickly, so stealthily, that it could only be a result of her presence.

Whatever indefinable quality she had possessed as a world-renowned mannequin, she still retained, even as a slightly haggard, still lovely, blind-eyed woman of indeterminate age. In her white hospital gown she was shapeless, but the magnetic wonder of her was there, and I was alive.

I was in love.

She was still speaking. "After her experiences with the jet ski set and the artists' colony on Fire Island, she returned to the city, and sought more and different experiences.

"Eventually she came upon them. The Men of the Eye. They were a religious sect, unto themselves. They worshipped sight and experience. This was what she had been born for. She fell into their ways at once, worshipping in the dawn hours at their many-eyed idol and living life to its hilt.

"Their ways were dark ways, and the things they did were not always clean things. Yet she persisted with them.

"Then, one night, during what they called the Time of the Eye, they demanded a sacrifice, and she was the one so chosen.

"They took her eyes."

I sat very still. I wasn't quite sure I'd heard what I'd heard. A weird religious sect, almost devil worship of a sort, there in the heart of New York City; and they had cut out the eyes of the most famous fashion model of all time, in a ceremony? It was too fantastic for belief. Surprising myself, I found old emotions flooding back into me. I could feel disbelief, horror, sorrow. This girl who called herself Piretta, and *was* that Piretta, had brought me to life again, only to fill me with a story so ludicrous I could do nothing but pass it on as dream-fantasy and the results of a persecution complex.

After all, didn't she have those shallow blue eyes?

They were unseeing, but they were there. How could they have been stolen? I was confused and dismayed.

I turned to her suddenly, and my arms went about her. I don't know what it was that possessed me, I had always been shy when women were involved, even before the War, but now my heart leaped into my throat, and I kissed her full on the mouth.

Her lips opened like two petals before me, and there was ardor returned. My hand found her breast.

We sat that way in passion for several minutes, and finally, when we were satisfied that the moment had lived its existence fully, we separated, and I began to prattle about getting well, and marrying, and moving to the country, where I could care for her.

Then I ran my hands across her face; feeling the beauty of her, letting my fingertips soak up the wonder of her. My smallest finger's tip happened to encounter her eye.

It was not moist.

I paused, and a gleam of smile broke at the edge of her wondrous mouth. "True," she said, and popped her eyes into the palm of her hand.

My fist went to my mouth, and the sound of a small animal being crushed underfoot came from me.

Then I noticed she had the sharpened stick in her hand, point upward, as though it was a driving spike. "What is that?" I asked, suddenly chilled for no reason.

"You didn't ask if Piretta accepted the religion," she answered softly, as though I was a child who did not understand.

"What do you mean?" I stammered.

"*This* is the Time of the Eye, don't you know?"

And she came at me with the stick. I fell back, but she wound herself around me, and we fell to the ground together, and her blindness did not matter at all.

"But *don't*!" I shrieked, as the stick came up. "I love you. I want to make you mine, to marry you!"

"How foolish," she chided me gently, "I can't marry you: you're sick in the mind."

Then there was the stick, and for so long now, the Time of the Eye has been blindly with me.

Grail

Years later, when he was well into young adulthood, Christopher Caperton wrote about it in the journal he had begun to keep when he turned twenty-one. The entry had everything to do with the incident, though he had totally forgotten it.

What he wrote was this: *The great tragedy of my life is that in my search for the Holy Grail everyone calls True Love, I see myself as Zorro, a romantic and mysterious highwayman—and the women I desire see me as Porky Pig.*

The incident lost to memory that informed his observation had taken place fourteen years earlier, in 1953 when he was thirteen years old.

During a Halloween party from which chaperoning adults had been banished, it was suggested that the boys and girls play a kissing game called "flashlight." All the lights were turned off, everyone paired up, and one couple held a flashlight. If you were caught kissing when the flashlight was turned on you, then it became your turn to hold and flash while the others had free rein to neck and fondle in the dark.

Because he was shy, Christopher volunteered to be the first holder of the light. Because he was shy, and because he had, as usual, been paired with Jean Kettner, who adored him but whom he could not find it within himself even to like. Across the room the most beautiful girl he had ever seen, the improbably named Briony Catling, sat on the lap of Danny Shipley, who played baseball and had blond, wavy hair.

Chris Caperton ached for Briony Catling with an intensity that gave him cramps.

Another rule of the game was that if the wielder of the flashlight caught another couple "doing it," he or she could demand a switch in partners.

Because he was shy, because he was paired with Jean Kettner, and because he knew exactly where he would shine the flashlight after allowing several minutes to pass in which the couples could become too interested in kissing to prepare themselves.

He caught Briony and Danny Shipley, and demanded a switch. Of the four involved in the transaction, only Christopher felt elation. Briony Catling had no interest in Christopher Caperton. She ached for Danny Shipley with an intensity that gave her cramps.

But they switched, and when the light went out Christopher hugged Briony frantically and shoved his face toward hers. The kiss splatted somewhere between her nose and her mouth.

She blew out air, made a yuchhing sound, swiped at the slaver on her upper lip, and jumped off his lap.

Fourteen years later the shame and the pain still lurked in his unconscious like pariahs.

Briony Catling had not been his first great love. That had been Miss O'Hara in the third grade, who had shone down on him at the age of eight like the field lights at a night baseball game. He had loved her purely and with all his heart; and the present he gave her at the Christmas party held by his home room had cost him all the money he'd made raking leaves through that Autumn. She had been embarrassed and had kissed his cheek lightly, never knowing it caused his first erection.

After Miss O'Hara, it had been the actress Helen Gahagan in the 1935 version of *She,* which he saw at the Utopia Theater on a re-release double-bill. When he belatedly went to see *Snow White and the Seven Dwarfs* on one of its periodic reissues, he recognized at once that Disney had appropriated the garb and look of Helen Gahagan as She-Who-Must-Be-Obeyed for the character of the wicked Queen Grimhilde; and when he learned of the foul campaign Richard Nixon had waged against her in the 1950 Senatorial race, when she had become Helen Gahagan Douglas, he vowed a revenge that only manifested itself when he twice voted for Nixon's presidential opponents.

The year before Briony Catling filled him with self-loathing, he fell desperately in love with the Swedish actress Marta Toren. He watched her vamping Dick Powell in *Rogue's Regiment* on the *Late Late Show* and made a point of being in the audience the night *Paris Express* with Claude Rains opened. Miss O'Hara, Helen Gahagan and even Briony Catling paled by comparison. She was precisely and exactly the embodiment of True Love in his eyes. Four years later, six months after Christopher had lost his virginity to a young woman who bore only a passing resemblance to Marta Toren, he read in the newspaper that she had died from a rare brain trauma called a subarachnoidal hemorrhage that struck like Jack the Ripper and killed her within forty-eight hours.

He closed himself in his room and tore at his clothes.

*   *   *

In February of 1968, attached to General William Westmoreland's headquarters in Saigon, Capt. Christopher Caperton, age 28, stumbled upon the astonishing fact that True Love, in a physical form, existed. The *Tet* offensive had begun and Saigon was burning. Had he not had his own assigned jeep and driver, he would not have been able to get around: there was virtually no public transportation and the cyclos and taxis had been commandeered for the wealthy trying to flee. The hospitals were so crowded that only emergency cases were being accepted; patients were sleeping on the floors, jamming the corridors. Coffins lay unburied for days: the gravediggers had gone south. Chris's business was good.

Chris was in the business of helping GIs cope with the anguish of serving in a war they had come to despise.

In business with, and in love with, his lover and business partner, a thirty-nine-year-old Eurasian of French and Thai parentage, Capt. Chris was the main conduit for "Js," "OJs," Binoctal, and a luscious black opium from the Laotian poppy fields to America's fighting men in Indochina.

Because their goods—marijuana joints; joints dipped in liquid opium; the French headache killer; and the most potent smoking opium—were superlative goods, Christopher Caperton and Sirilabh Doumic had established a flourishing trade in I and II Corps. And from this enterprise they had managed to bank over a million and a half dollars (converted to Swiss francs) in an unnumbered Zurich account, despite the crushing overhead and the payoffs to officials of Thieu's provincial government.

And because he was in love in a terrible place, and because he and his love wanted nothing more than to survive, to win release from that terrible place, he felt no guilt about the traffic. There was no self-delusion that he was engaged in humanitarian activities, neither the war nor the drug traffic; what he *did* feel was a sense of keeping busy, of working at something that held light and hope at its conclusion, that without the dope some of his clients would either go mad or turn their rifles on the nearest 1st Lieutenant. But mostly he was in love.

Siri was small and light. He could lift her with one arm to carry her to the bed. Her features were fine and delicate, yet they changed dramatically with each noticeable variation in the light. Monet would have had to do her portrait eighteen times, as he did the Rouen Cathedral, from dawn to sunset, to capture even one expression. She was the daughter of a French attaché in the Bangkok consulate and a young temple dancer Doumic first saw at the Kathin ceremony marking the end of the Buddhist Lent. From her father she inherited a wiliness that kept her alive in street society, from her mother—who had come from Chumphon to the south—a speech filled with musical inflection. How she had come to Saigon ten years before was not something she cared to talk about. But Chris winced every time they made love and his hands brushed the thick scars on her inner thighs.

On that night in February of 1968, they were just sitting down to a dinner of beef satay Siri had made in their apartment on Nguyen Cong Tru Street when a 122mm shell came across the Saigon River and hit the face of the building opposite Caperton's. The rocket round ripped the building out of the ground like a rotten tooth and threw shrapnel in every direction.

Not the biggest chunk, but big enough, it came straight through the window and tore into Siri's back, taking off most of her left shoulder.

There was no use trying to move her; it was obvious she would never make it down the stairs, much less across the city to the American hospital that had been opened at Tan Son Nhut.

He tried to stanch the flow with a bedspread and all the white tennis socks in his drawer, and miraculously, she lived for almost an hour. In that hour they talked, and in that hour of farewell she gave him the only gift in the world he wanted, the only thing he could not get for himself. She told him how he could find True Love.

"We have talked of it so many times, and I always knew."

He tried to smile. "In a business partnership like ours there shouldn't be any secrets. How else can I trust you?"

Pain convulsed her and she gripped his hand till the bones ground. "We've no time for foolishness, my love. Very soon now you'll be alone again, as you have been so often. I have this one thing I can give you in return for the love you gave me . . . and it will take some believing on your part."

"Whatever you tell me I'll believe."

Then she instructed him to go to the kitchen and get an empty condiment bottle from the spice rack. When he brought back the bottle labeled chopped coriander leaves, which was empty because they had been unable to get fresh coriander since a Claymore mine had gone off in the central market, she told him he must not argue with her, that he must fill it with her blood. He argued, wasting precious minutes; but finally, filled with a vaguely familiar self-loathing, he did it.

"I have always sought perfection," she said. "Always knowing that one must die to reach perfection, for life is imperfect."

He tried to argue, but she stopped him. Sternly.

"Chris! You *must* listen to me."

He nodded and was silent.

"For each woman there *is* a perfect man; and for each man there *is* a perfect woman. You were not perfect for me, but you were as close to what I sought as I ever found. But I never stopped searching . . . though my movement was very slow since we met. I should have been content. It's easy to be smart, later.

"But knowing what I knew, that True Love is a real thing, that it can be picked up and turned in the hands, that it can be looked at and understood . . . that kept me always dissatisfied. As you have been.

"Because somehow, without possessing the knowledge I chanced upon ten years ago, you knew it was real. And now I will tell you how to go about finding it. And that, my dearest, is the best way I can apologize to you for not giving up the search when we met."

Then with her voice fading off and coming back a little less strong each time, she told him of an artifact that had never been described, that had first been unearthed during Evans's excavations of the Palace of Minos at Knossos in 1900.

It was taken from a walled-up niche behind an elaborate fresco painted on a wall of the Corridor of the Procession, and had been hidden there since 2000 B.C. Where it had come from before that time, not even the archeologist who discovered it and smuggled it away from Crete could begin to guess.

He recognized it for what it was the instant the light of his torch fell on it. He disappeared that night and was presumed to have returned to England; but was never seen again. Record of his find was revealed in 1912 during the dying reminiscences of Bessie Chapman, one of the 711 survivors of the sinking of the *Titanic* picked up by the *Carpathia*.

Suffering from extreme exposure and seemingly delirious, the immigrant passenger babbled a story heard only by those few *Carpathia* deckhands and ministering survivors who tried to make her last hours easier. Apparently she had been a London doxy who, after an evening of sport with "a real elegant nob, a brick 'e was," actually saw the artifact. She spoke of it with such wonder that when she died it seemed she had passed over having known all there was to know of joy in this life.

One of the deckhands, an Irish stoker named Haggerty, it was later reported, hung about the dying woman and seemed to be paying close attention to her story.

Haggerty jumped ship on the return of the Cunard liner to New York.

Sgt. Michael James Haggerty was killed during the battle of Ypres, November 9th, 1914. His kit bag, scavenged by a German soldier when the French and British trenches were overrun (it was reported by a survivor who had played possum and been overlooked in the random bayoneting of corpses), disappeared. Others in Haggerty's company said he slept with the kit bag under his pillow, that it seemed quite heavy, and that he once broke the arm of a messmate who playfully tried to see what the Irishman was carrying in it.

Between 1914 and 1932 the object—while never described—turned up three times: once in the possession of a White Russian nobleman in Sevastopol, twice in the possession of a Dutch aircraft designer, and finally in the possession of a Chicago mobster reputed to have been the man who gunned down Dion O'Banion in his flower shop at 738 North State Street.

In 1932 a man visiting New York for the opening of the Radio City Music Hall just after Christmas reported to the police who found him lying in an alley on West 51st Street just below Fifth Avenue that he had been mugged and robbed of "the most important and beautiful thing in the world." He was taken to Bellevue Hospital, but no matter how diligently he was interrogated, he would not describe the stolen article.

In 1934 it was reputed to be in the private art collection of the German architect Walter Gropius; after Gropius's self-imposed exile from Nazi Germany it was reputed to have passed into the personal collection of Hermann Goering, 1937; in 1941 it was said to be housed with Schweitzer in French Equatorial Africa; in 1946 it was found to be one of the few items not left by Henry Ford at his death to the Ford Foundation.

Its whereabouts were unknown between 1946 and February of 1968. But Siri told Chris, her final love, that there was one sure, dangerous way of finding it. The way she had used originally to learn the hand-to-hand passage of the artifact that was True Love from the Palace of Minos to its present unknown resting place.

Then she released his hand, realizing she had squeezed it so hard while telling her story that it was as white as unsmoked meerschaum; and she asked him very softly if he would bring her the little cloisonné minaudière he had brought her in Hong Kong.

He gave it to her and she clutched it far more tightly than she had his hand. Because it was a minute later, and the pain was much worse.

"Do you remember the flea market?"

"Yes," she said, closing her eyes. "And we were holding hands in the crowd; and then you let go and I was swept along; and I thought I'd lost you; and you were gone for fifteen minutes . . ."

"And you panicked."

"And when I got back to the car there you were."

"You should have seen your face. What relief."

"What love. That was the moment I slowed the never-ending search. And you smiled and held out this to me." And she opened her hand where the exquisite blue and gold minaudière lay in her palm, now filmed with moisture.

But her story had worked its magic. He knelt beside her on the floor, lifted her head and the pillows, and cradled them in his lap. "What is this True Love? What does it look like?"

"I don't know. I've never seen it. It cost too much the first time, just to get the information. The actual search has to be done without . . ." and she hesitated as if picking the exact words, the words that would not frighten him, because he was beginning to look more frightened than anguished, ". . . without special assistance."

"But how could you have learned all this?"

"I had an informant. You must seek him out. But go very carefully. It's dangerous, it costs a great deal; care has to be taken . . . once I didn't take care . . ." She paused. "You'll need my blood."

"An informant . . . your blood . . . ? I don't . . ."

"Adrammelech, Supreme Ruler of the Third Hour."

He could not help her. She was dying, he felt the stiffness in his throat, he loved her so much, and she was raving.

"An Angel of the Night, Chris."

Bewildered and suffering, nonetheless he went to the bedroom and fetched the brass-and-silver-bound chest she called a bahut. He brought it back to her and she said, "Look at it. Do you see how it opens?"

He studied it but could find no lock or clasp that would open the coffer. "It is made of agalloch, lign aloes, the wood of the aloe, according to the directions of Abramelin. The cross-spines are of almond-tree wood. Are you beginning to understand, do you believe me?"

"Siri . . ."

"You'll need Surgat to open it. Look."

And she touched a symbol, a character cut into the rounded top of the chest:

"He won't harm you. He serves only one purpose: he opens all locks. Take a hair from my head . . . don't argue with me, Chris, do it . . . please . . ." And because her voice was now barely a whisper, he did it. And she said, "He'll demand a hair of your head. Don't give it to him. Make him take mine. And this is what you say to invoke his presence . . ."

In her last minutes she went over it with him till he realized she was serious, that she was not delirious, that he ought to write it down. So he transcribed her words exactly.

"Once you get the bahut opened, all the rest will be clear. Just be careful, Chris. It's all I have to give you, so make the best of it." Her eyes were half-closed and now she opened them completely, with effort, and looked at him. "Why are you angry with me?"

He looked away.

"I can't help it that I'm dying, dear. I'm sorry, but that's what's happening. You'll just have to forgive me and do the best you can."

Then she closed her eyes and her hand opened and the cloisonné herb container fell to the carpet; and he was alone.

He spoke to her, though he was alone. "I didn't love you enough. If I'd loved you more it wouldn't have happened."

It's easy to be smart, later.

* * *

By the time he was twenty-five, Chris had read everything he could find on the arcane subject of love. He had read Virgil and Rabelais, Ovid and Liu Hsiao-Wei, Plato's *Symposium* and all the Neoplatonists, Montaigne and Johannes Secundus; he had read everything by the English poets from the anonymous lyrics of the 13th to 15th centuries through Rolle, Lydgate, Wyatt, Sidney, Campion, Shakespeare, Jonson, Donne, Marvell, Herrick, Suckling, Lovelace, Blake, Burns, Lord Byron, Percy Shelley, Keats, Tennyson, Robert Browning, and Emily Brontë; he had read as many translations as existed of the Sanskrit *Kama Sutra* and the *Anangaranga*, which led him to the Persians; he read *The Perfumed Garden* of the Sheik Nefzawi, the *Beharistan* of Jami and the *Gulistan* of Sa-Di, the anonymously-written *Ta'dib ul-Niszvan* and the *Zenan-Nahmeh* of Fazil Bey, which led him to seven Arabic handbooks of sex, which he quickly put aside: sex was not the issue, he understood that as well as anyone need to. Understood it well enough to write in his journal:

I was making love to Connie Halban when her husband Paul came back unexpectedly from a business trip. When he saw us he began crying. It was the most awful thing I'd ever stood witness to. I was reminded of Ixion, tied to a turning wheel in Hades as punishment for making love to Zeus's wife, Hera. I'll never touch another married woman. It simply isn't worth the torture and guilt.

And so he was able to avoid all the texts that dealt solely with physical love in its seemingly endless permutations. He made no value judgments; he understood early on that everyone sought True Love in often inarticulate ways they often did not, themselves, understand; but his was an idealized, traditional concept of what True Love was, and his search for the grail need not be sidetracked or slowed by excursions into those special places.

He read Waley's translation of *The Chin P-ing Mei* and everything even remotely pertinent by Freud; he sought out *La Fleur Lascivie Orientale* and the even rarer English translation of *Contes Licencieux de Constantinople et de l'Asie Mineure*; he dipped into the memoirs of Clara Bow, Charles II, Charlie Chaplin, Isadora Duncan, Marie Duplessis, Lola Montez and George Sand; he read novelists—Moravia, Gorky, Maupassant, Roth, Cheever and Brossard—but found they knew even less than he.

He absorbed the thoughts of the aphorists, and believed every utterance; Balzac: "True Love is eternal, infinite, and always like itself. It is equal and pure, without violent demonstrations: it is seen with white hairs and is always young in the heart."; Molière: "Reason is not what directs love."; Terence: "It is possible that a man can be so-changed by love as hardly to be recognized as the same person."; Voltaire: "Love is a canvas furnished by Nature and embroidered by imagination."; La Rochefoucauld: "When we are in love, we often doubt what we most believe."

Yet even nodding his agreement with every contradictory image and representation of love—seen as Nature, God, a bird on the wing, sex, vanity—he knew they had perceived only the barest edge of what True Love was. Not Kierkegaard or Bacon or Goethe or Nietzsche, for all their insight, for all their wisdom, had any better idea of what True Love looked like than the commonest day-laborer.

The *Song of Solomon* spurred him on, but did not indicate the proper route to discovery.

He found the main path on that night in February of 1968. But once found, he was too frightened to set foot upon it.

Surgat, a subordinate spirit to Sargatanas who, in the Descending Hierachy from Lucifer to Lucifuge Rofacale, opens all locks, came when Chris Caperton summoned him. He was too insignificant a demon to refuse, no matter how ineptly couched the invocation. But he was less than cooperative.

Chris used Siri's blood to draw the pentagram of Solomon on the floor. He didn't think about what he was doing . . . that he was dipping his finger in the blood of the woman who lay covered with a sheet on the sofa . . . that he had to do it repeatedly because it was getting thick . . . that he had been warned all ten sides of the five-pointed star enclosed in a circle must be without break . . . he just did it. He did not cry. He just did it.

Then he set candles at the five points and lighted them. Every apartment in Saigon in those days had a supply of candles.

Then he stood in the exact center of the runes and lines and read from the dictation he had taken. Siri had assured him if he stayed within the pentagram he would be safe, that Surgat only opened locks and was not really powerful enough to cause him trouble . . . if he kept his wits about him.

The words were contained in the *Grimorium Verum* and Siri had said they need not be spoken precisely, nor need Chris worry about having done the special cleansing necessary when summoning the more powerful Field Marshals of Lucifer's Infernal Legions.

He read the words. "I conjure thee, Surgat, by the great living God, the Sovereign Creator of all things, to appear under a comely human form, without noise and without terror, to answer truly unto all questions that I shall ask thee. Hereunto I conjure thee by the virtue of these Holy and Sacred Names. O Surmy ✠ Delmusan ✠ Atalsloym ✠ Charusihoa ✠ Melany ✠ Liamintho ✠ Colehon ✠ Paron ✠ Madoin ✠ Merloy ✠ Bulerator ✠ Donmeo ✠ Hone ✠ Peloym ✠ Ibasil ✠ Meon." And on and on, eighteen more names, concluding with, "Come, therefore, quickly and peaceably, by the Names Adonai, Elohim, Tetragrammaton! *Come*!"

From across the Saigon River he could hear the sound of the city's rockets, flattening Charlie's supposed emplacements. But in the little apartment on Nguyen Cong Tru Street everything began to shimmer and wash down like the aurora borealis.

It was an apartment no longer. He stood on the polished wood floor, inside the pentagram of Solomon, but the polished wood floor came to an end at the edges of Siri's dried blood. Beyond lay a fallen temple. Great gray stones, enormous and bearing the marks of claws that had ripped them loose from mountains, tumbled and thrown carelessly, rose up around Chris. And out of the shadows something came toward him.

It slouched and dragged its arms behind as it came out of the darkness. When the flickering illumination from the candles struck it, Chris felt sick to his stomach. He clutched the paper with Siri's words as if it would save him.

Surgat came and stood with the point of one goat-hoof almost touching Siri's blood. Chris could smell where it had been and what it had been doing when he had interrupted its dining. He felt faint and could not breathe deeply because of the smell Surgat had carried from its mess hall.

The head of the demon changed. Toad to goat to worm to spider to dog to ape to man to a thing that had no name.

"Open the lock of the casket," Chris yelled. He had to yell: the sound of wind was overpowering, deafening, insane.

Surgat kicked the bahut. Chris had left it, as Siri had instructed, outside the pentagram. Surgat kicked it again. No mark was put on the coffer, but where the demon's foot had rested in the dust of the fallen temple's floor, a cloven footprint burned and smoked.

"Open the lock!"

Surgat leaned forward and shrieked. Words poured forth. They made no sense to Chris. They were from a throat that was not human. If a hyena had been given the ability to speak with the tongue of a man, it would have sounded less guttural, less deranged, less terrifying.

Siri had said the demon would be troublesome, but would finally do as bidden. It had no choice. It was not that important or powerful a spirit. When Chris remembered that assurance, and perceived just how staggering was the sight before him, he trembled at the thought of one of Surgat's masters. "Open it, you goddam ugly sonofabitch! Open it right now!"

Surgat vomited maggots that hit an invisible plane at the edge of the pentagram. And babbled more words. And reached out a lobster-claw that stopped just outside the invisible plane. It wanted something.

Then Chris remembered the hair from Siri's head. It will want the hair of a fox, she had said. Forget that. It will try to get a hair from *your* head. Whatever you do, don't let it have one. All of you is contained in each hair; you can be reconstructed from a hair; then it has you. Give it mine.

He extended her long, thick strand of hair.

Surgat screamed, would not take it. Chris extended it through the invisible plane. Surgat pointed to Chris's head and pulled long strips of bleeding flesh from its body and threw them against the fallen stones where they plopped with the sickening sound of meat against concrete. Chris did not move. The hair hung down outside the invisible plane.

Surgat screamed and capered and tore at itself.

"Take it, you disgusting sonofabitch!" Chris yelled. "Take it and be damned, she *died* to give it to you, puking garbage dump! Take it or get nothing! Nothing's worth this, not even that thing she looked for all her life! So *take it*, you crummy piece of shit! *Take it* or go back where you came from and let me alone!"

The words Surgat spoke became very clear, then. The voice modulated, became almost refined. It spoke in a language Chris had never heard. He could not have known that it was a tongue unspoken for a thousand years before the birth of Christ: Surgat spoke in Chaldean.

And having spoken, having acknowledged obedience at the threat of being dismissed without the proper license to depart, the threat of being trapping here in this halfway place of fallen stones, and the wrath of Asmoday or Beelzebuth, the lock-picking demon ran its tentacle forward and took Siri's hair. The hair burst into flame, the flame shot up toward the shadowed ceiling of the fallen temple, Surgat turned the flame on the casket . . . and the flame washed over the wood . . . and the casket opened.

Quickly, Chris read the final words on the paper he held. "O Spirit Surgat, because thou hast diligently answered my demands, I do hereby license thee to depart, without injury to man or beast. Depart, I say, and be thou willing and ready to come, whensoever duly exorcised and conjured by the Sacred Rites of Magic. I conjure thee to withdraw peaceably and quietly, and may the peace of God continue forever between me and thee. Amen."

And Surgat looked across the pentagram's protective plane and said, in perfectly understandable English, "I do not go empty-handed."

Then the demon slouched away into the shadows, the aurora borealis effect began again, rippling and sliding and flowing down till he was in his own apartment again. Even then he waited an hour before leaving the charmed circle.

To discover that as Siri had promised, everything had its price. Surgat had not gone empty-handed.

The body of his lover was gone. He could not look at what had been left in its place.

He began to cry, hoping it *had* been an exchange; hoping that what lay on the sofa was not Siri.

The bahut contained more items than its outside dimensions would have indicated. It held grimoires and many notebooks filled with Siri's handwriting. It held talismans and runic symbols in stone and silver and wood. It held vials of powders and hair and bird-claws and bits of matter, each vial labeled clearly. It held conjurations and phials and philtres and maps and directions and exorcising spells. It held the key to finding True Love.

But it also held Siri's observations of what had happened to her when she had summoned the entity she called "the supreme hideousness, the most evil of the ten Sephiroths, the vile Adrammelech." He read the ledgers until his eyes burned, and when his fingers left the pages, the paper was smudged with his sweat. He began to tremble, there in the room where the smell of Surgat's dining table lingered, and knew he could not summon the strength to summon this most powerful of dark beings.

He read every word on every page Siri had written; and he vowed silently that he would pick up her quest where she had fallen. But he could not go to her informant. His assistance had cost her too much, and she had been unable to go on. The price was too high.

But there were clues to the trail of the artifact that was True Love. And he took the bahut and left the apartment on Nguyen Cong Tru Street, and never returned. He had money to continue the search, and he would do it without help from things that dragged long, rubbery arms through the dust of fallen temples.

All he had to do was wait for the end of the war.

By 1975 Christopher Caperton had traced it to New Orleans. He was thirty-five years old; he had been married and divorced because in a moment of weariness he had thought *she* might suffice in place of True Love; and he wrote this in his journal: *It is the vanity of searching for embodiments*. Flèches d'amour. *Incarnations which are never satisfactory, which never answer* all *longings and questions*.

Once, when he had thought he might die of a jungle fever contracted while running down a false clue in Paramaribo, he heard himself cursing Siri's memory. If she had not told him it actually existed, he might have settled for something less, never knowing for certain that there was more. But he *did* know, and in his tantrum of fever he cursed her to Hell.

When he recovered, he was more than ashamed of himself. Considering who she had been, where she had gone, and the owners of her spirit, he might have called down a sentence on her that she did not deserve. One never knew the total cost, nor at what point the obligation was considered voided.

After he had been rotated home in 1970 he spent a few months tying up all previous relationships—family, friends, business associates, acquaintances—and set out on the trail that had grown cold since 1946.

Without dipping into capital he was able to underwrite his expenses handsomely. Even though the gnomes of Zurich had done away with unnumbered, secret accounts, he had made his money in a way that caused no concern among the assessors, customhouse officials, tithe-seekers and running-dogs of the IRS desiring duty, levy, tribute, tallage, liver and lights. He moved freely under a variety of passports and a number of names. He came to think of himself as a nameless, stateless person, someone out of a Graham Greene suspense novel.

There were clues, beginning with one of the appraisers who had worked on the Ford bequests. He was quite old by the time Chris located him in a retirement trailer camp in Sun City, but he remembered the item clearly. No, he had never seen it; it was crated with specific instructions that it should not, under even the most extreme circumstances, be opened. If he was lying, he did it well. Chris was paying a high enough premium for the information that it didn't matter either way. But the trail picked up with the old appraiser's recollection that whatever the crate had contained, it had been bequeathed to a contemporary of Henry Ford's, a man with whom he had been friends and then fallen out, fifty years before.

Chris managed to locate the bills of lading and traced the crate to Madison, Indiana. The recipient of the crate had been deceased for fifteen years. The contents of the crate had been sold at auction . . .

And so it went. From place to place. From clue to clue. And each clue indicated that having been in touch with the artifact, the owner had known great joy or great sorrow; but all were dead. The Holy Grail always lay just ahead, always just out of Chris's reach. Yet he could never bring himself to take the easy way out; to summon up the horror Siri had called Adrammelech. He knew if he finally gave in, that even if he found True Love he would never be able to savor it.

In January of 1975 Christopher Caperton followed a clue from Trinidad to New Orleans. His source had assured him that the artifact had passed into the hands of a *houngan*, a priest of the *conjur*, a disciple of the voodoo of Doctor Cat, a pioneer of mail order Voodoo in 1914.

On Perdido Street, in a back room lit only by votive candles in ruby-glass jars, Chris met "Prince Basile Thibodeux," whose title at birth had been merely Willie Link Dunbar. Prince Basile swore he had known and loved the real and true Marie Laveau. As the old black man looked no more than sixty—though he claimed to be ninety-two—such a claim was, either way, highly dubious. Absolute proof exists that Marie Laveau, the first of the many Marie Laveaus, died on June 24th, 1881, at the approximate age of eighty-five. Two years before Willie Link "Thibodeux" had been born, if he was ninety-two; and thirty-four, if he was lying.

Christopher Caperton did not care what lies Prince Basile told to sell his worthless hoodoo goods in the drugstore of Love Oils, Goofer

Dust, Devil's Shoe Strings and War Water, as long as he told him a straight story about the artifact.

When he walked into the little back room, washed in bloody shadows from the candles, he was prepared to pay a premium price for the information he sought, or to assure Prince Basile that there were two men living on Prytania Street who would, for only a fraction of that premium price, inflict great bodily sorrow on a sixty- or ninety-two-year-old black man, and he would worry about the black goat dancing on his grave at a later time. But Prince Basile took one look at him and fear filled the withered face. "Doan put dat *gris-gris* on me, mistuh," he pleaded. "Jus' whatever you want, that's be what you gone get. Ah'm at y'service."

And Chris walked out of the little back room on Perdido Street with the information—that he knew to be absolutely reliable because no one that terrified could lie without dying in the act—that Willie Link Dunbar had worked on a smuggling operation from the Islands to the Keys in 1971 and he had seen the artifact. He swore before Damballa that he could not remember what it looked like . . . but it had been as lovely as anything he knew. His face, when he said it, was a strange mix of terror at the sight of Chris and joy at the last scintilla of memory of what he had seen.

And he told Chris the name of the smuggler who had taken the item from the boat.

And when Chris asked him why he was so frightened of just another white man, Prince Basile said, "You been kissin' the Old Ones. I kilt a hunnerd crows and cocks I couldn't save mah soul if you was t'touch me, mistuh. I be jus' playin' at whut I does, but *you* . . . you knows the fire."

Chris shuddered. And that was only from a minor, weak servant of Adrammelech. He left hurriedly.

He stood in the darkness of the alley off Perdido Street and thought about it, about True Love, whatever it was. He had wanted it for so long, had sought it in so many women, had glimpsed hints of its totality so many times, that he only now paused to examine what he had become. Even if he got it, would he be worthy of it? Wasn't the one who found the Holy Grail supposed to be pure in every way, perfect in every way, without flaw or blemish or self-doubt? Knights on white chargers, saints, defenders of the faith; those were the candidates for the honor. Prince Charming always won Snow White, not Porky Pig.

Without flaw. No, not without flaw. He had come too far for perfection. He had had to experience too much.

Yet he knew he was closer to True Love than anyone had ever been. Not even those who had possessed it had known what to do with it. He knew he had it within himself to become one with True Love, as no one before him ever could. No one. Not one of the perhaps thousand owners of it before and since it found its way to the Palace of Minos, no matter how fine or great or deserving they had been.

Christopher Caperton knew his destiny was to hold True Love in his hands. Known to demons, casting no shadow, he walked away from the fear in Perdido Street.

The final clue was so mundane he could not even breathe a sigh of relief. True Love had been sold in blind bid auction at Sotheby's in April of 1979. It now belonged to a man who lived high above the rest of the human race, in a tower overlooking New York, where almost eight million people gave a portion of each day to wondering where True Love resided.

From Siri's notebooks Chris recognized the name of the man. In 1932 he had visited New York City for the opening of the Radio City Music Hall. The artifact had been stolen from him. He had spent forty-seven years trying to regain his lost property. In the process, somehow, he had become enormously powerful, enormously wealthy, enormously secretive.

Home again, home again, jiggedy jig.

Christopher Caperton took one final look at the cover of the December 1980 issue of *Esquire*. It showed a woman in a seductive bridal gown. The cover illustrated an article called *Looking for a Wife* and the slugline read, "With all the beautiful, intelligent women out there, why is she so hard to find?"

He smiled thinking they might have done the reverse on *Ms.* magazine, with a photograph of an equally unreachable male.

The model they had selected for the shot was achingly innocent, yet seductive; poised in a timeless moment of utter perfection. Had he been anyone else, this might well have been the physical manifestation of True Love for him.

But it was only the most recent in a congeries of photos, motion pictures, billboards and women glimpsed in cars going past on city streets who were idealized manifestations of what he sought.

Tonight he would hold the real thing. Tonight he would obtain True Love.

He put the last of the vials from Siri's bahut he might need in the capacious pockets of his London Fog topcoat, and left the hotel. It was thirty degrees in the Manhattan streets, and the wind was blowing in off the East River. By tomorrow, perhaps before two AM there would be snow. It was the sort of evening he had always imagined for this final leg of the journey.

Christopher Caperton was forty years old.

Every bribe had been well-placed. The boiler room door was unlocked.

The key to the private service elevator had been properly copied. No one stopped him.

He walked through the palatial tower suite in darkness. He heard a door closing away off in the rear of the apartment. The floor-plan he had been given was precise and he touched nothing as he walked quickly to the door of the master bedroom.

The old man was lying in the exact center of the huge bed. As reported, he was dying.

Chris closed the door behind him. Only one light near the bed illuminated the room. The old man opened his eyes and looked at Chris. His eyes were very blue.

"There's never enough money to buy silence, boy. You can buy entrance, but not silence. There's always some mouth that's hungrier."

Chris smiled and walked to the bed. "I would have tried to bargain with you if I'd thought it would do any good. I'm not a thief by profession."

The old man snorted softly. He didn't seem to be in pain. "No price."

"Yes, I rather thought that might be the case. But look on the bright side: you can't take it with you, it won't do you any good on the other side; and I've been looking for it for a long time."

The old man laughed gently, no more strenuously than he had snorted. "What the hell do I care how long you looked for it, boy? Not as long as I looked for it."

"Since Christmas, 1932."

"Well, well. You did your homework, did you?"

"I've paid as much as you, in all kinds of coin."

"Not my concern, boy. You'll never find it."

"It's here. In this room. In the safe."

The old man's eyes widened. "Smarter than I thought. Didn't stop any of that cash you were doling out; got good people working for me; didn't see any reason why they shouldn't pick up a few extra dollars; they've got families to take care of. Didn't expect you'd know about the safe."

"I know about it."

"Doesn't matter. You'll look forever and never find it. Even if you do, you'll never get it open." He coughed shallowly, smiled at the ceiling and recited: "Hidden where you can't find it; but if you do you'll be looking at six-foot-thick walls of concrete reinforced with molybdenum-steel alloy cords, backed by a foot of tempered high-carbon high-chromium steel, another foot of unseamed silico-manganese shock-resisting steel and six inches of eighteen-tungsten, four-chrome, one-vanadium high-speed industrial tool steel. The vault door is stainless steel faced, an inch and a half of cast steel, another twelve inches of burn-resisting steel, another inch and a half of open-hearth steel, and the pneumatic hinges are inside the sandwich. The vault door has twenty bolts, each an inch in diameter: eight on one side, eight on the other, two top and two bottom. This holds the door into a sixteen-inch jamb of moly-tungsten high-speed steel, set into eighteen inches of concrete crosshatched by burn-resisting steel bars running horizontally and vertically." He coughed once more, pleased with himself, and added as a fillip, "The door's precision-made so you can't pour nitro in between the seam of the door and the vault."

Chris let a beaten look cross his face. "And I suppose that isn't even all of it. I suppose there are thermostats that trip some kind of trap if the temperature rises . . . if I used a torch."

"You got some smarts, boy. Tear gas. And the floor gets electrified." He was grinning widely now, but what little color had been in his face was gone. His eyes were closing.

"You beat me," Chris said. "I guess it's yours to keep."

But the old man only heard the first part. By the end, Chris was talking to himself. The old man was gone.

"On the other hand," Chris said softly, "there's no lock that can't be opened."

He stood by the bed for a while, staring down at the previous owner of True Love. He didn't seem to have died happier or sadder for having passed on with it in his possession.

Then Christopher Caperton got down on his knees in the center of the great bedroom and took out the vial Siri had labeled *Blood of Helomi* and he unstoppered the vial and began sprinkling out the dusty contents in lines that formed the pentagram of Solomon. He placed the candles and lit them; and he stood in the center of the design. And he read from a smudged piece of paper twelve years old.

And Surgat came again.

This time it came to the tower suite; this time it did not take Chris to the fallen temple. And this time it spoke in the soft, refined voice it had used when taking Siri's body.

"So soon?" Surgat said. "You need me again so soon?"

Chris felt nausea rising in his throat. The demon had not been dining this time. It had been indulging in whatever passed for fornication among demons. Its love-partner was still attached. Whatever it was, it wasn't human. (A momentary thought shrieked through Chris's skull. Might it ever have *been* human; and might it have been . . . ? He slammed the lid on the thought.)

"Twelve years . . . it's been twelve years . . ." Chris said, with difficulty.

Surgat let a human face appear in its stomach and the human face smiled offhandedly. "How time flies when one is enjoying oneself." The love-partner moaned and gave a spastic twitch.

Chris would not think of it.

"Open the safe," he ordered the demon.

"I'll need you out here to assist me. In one of my very difficult rituals." The voice was a snake's hiss, from the moth's head.

"Go fuck yourself. Open the safe."

"But I *need* you," the demon said, wheedling disingenuously.

Chris fished in his topcoat pocket for a scrap of parchment from the bahut. He began to read. "By the powerful Principality of the infernal abysses, I conjure thee with power and with exorcism; I warn thee hearken forthwith and immediately to my words; observe them inviolably, as sentences of the last dreadful day of judgment, which thou must obey inviolably . . ."

As he began to speak, a sweat of pus and blood began to break out on the demon's armored flesh. Soft purple bruises appeared, as if Surgat were being struck from within.

"I hear. I obey!"

And it reached for the hair. Chris took the vial of fox hairs from his pocket, withdrew one and handed it across the invisible plane. The hair burst into flame as before, and Surgat turned, aiming the flame at the ceiling. The fire washed the ceiling of the tower suite bedroom and the ceiling opened and the central section of the floor on which Chris stood rose up on hydraulic lifts into a chamber above the penthouse.

Then Surgat turned the flame on the stainless steel door of the vault that formed the wall of the chamber above, and the door swung open ponderously. And the vault within was revealed.

Then Chris intoned the license to depart, but before Surgat vanished it said, "Master, powerful Master, may I leave you with a gift?"

"No. I don't want anything more from you, not ever again."

"But Master, you will need this gift. I swear by my Lord Adrammelech."

Chris felt terror swirl through him. "What is it?"

"Then you willingly accept my gift without condition or let?"

Chris heard Siri's voice in his memory: *He won't harm you. He serves only one purpose: he opens all locks. Just be careful*. "Yes, I accept the gift."

Surgat caused a pool of stagnant water to appear just beyond the protective design. Then the human face appeared again in the thorax of the insect Surgat had become, and the human face smiled invitingly and said, "Look," and Surgat sucked in within itself and grew smaller and smaller and then vanished.

Leaving the pool of foul water in which Chris saw—

A scene from a motion picture. He recognized it. A scene from *Citizen Kane*. A day in 1940. The interior of the skyscraper office of the old man, Bernstein. He is being interviewed by the newsreel researcher, Thompson, who asks him what Charles Foster Kane's dying word, "Rosebud," meant.

Bernstein thinks, then says, "Maybe some girl? There were a lot of them back in the early days and—"

Thompson is amused. He says, "It's hardly likely, Mr. Bernstein, that Mr. Kane could have met some girl casually and then, fifty years later, on his deathbed—"

Bernstein cuts in. "You're pretty young, Mr.—" he remembers the name, "—Mr. Thompson. A fellow will remember things you wouldn't think he'd remember. You take me. One day, back in 1896, I was crossing over to Jersey on a ferry and as we pulled out there was another ferry pulling in." Everett Sloane, as the aged Bernstein, looks wistful, speaks slowly. "And on it there was a girl waiting to get off. A white dress she had on . . . and she was carrying a white parasol . . . and I only saw her for one second and she didn't see me at all . . . but I'll bet a month hasn't gone by since that I haven't thought of that girl." He smiles triumphantly. "See what I mean?"

And the scene faded, and the water boiled away, and Chris was alone in the dimly-lit vault room above the tower suite. Alone with the dawning fear that he had learned too much.

He saw himself suddenly as a human puppet, controlled from above by a nameless force that held every man and woman on the end of strings, making them dance the dance, manipulating them to seek the unobtainable, denying them peace or contentment because of the promise of a Holy Grail out there somewhere.

Even if the strings were broken, and puny mortals wandered the blasted landscape of their lives on their own, they would finally, inevitably, tragically return to the great puppeteer; to try and retie the strings. Better to dance the hopeless dance that lied about True Love than to admit they were all alone, that they might never, never find that perfect image to become one with. He stood in the center of the pentagram of Solomon and thought of the achingly beautiful girl on the cover of *Esquire*. The girl who was not real. True Love. Snare and delusion? He felt tears on his cheeks, and shook his head. No, it was here. It was just inside the threshold of the vault. It existed. It had a form and a reality. The truth was only a few footsteps from him. Siri could not have died for it if it weren't real.

He stepped out of the magic design and walked to the door of the vault. He kept his eyes down. He stepped over the raised jamb and heard his footsteps on the steel floor.

The vault was lit by hidden tubing at the juncture of walls and ceiling. A soft off-white glow that filled the vault.

He looked up slowly.

It sat on a pedestal of silver and lucite.

He looked at True Love.

It was an enormous loving cup. It was as gaudy as a bowling trophy. Exactly a foot and a half high, with handles. Engraved on the face were the words *True Love* in flowing script, embellished with curlicues. It shone with a light of its own, and the glow was the brassy color of an intramural award.

Christopher Caperton stood with his arms hanging at his sides. It was in him, at that moment, to laugh. But he had the certain knowledge that if he laughed, he would never stop; and they would come in to get the old man's body this morning and find him still standing there, crying piteously and laughing.

He had come through a time and a distance to get this real artifact, and he would take it. He stepped to the pedestal and reached for it. Remembering at the last moment the demon's gift.

Surgat could not touch him; but Surgat could reach him.

He looked down into the loving cup that was True Love and in the silver liquid swirling there he saw the face of True Love. For an instant it was his mother, then it was Miss O'Hara, then it was poor Jean Kettner, then it was Briony Catling, then it was Helen Gahagan, then it was Marta Toren, then it was the girl to whom he had lost his virginity, then it was one woman after another he had known, then it was Siri—but was Siri no longer than any of the others—then it was his wife, then it was the face of the achingly beautiful bride on the cover of *Esquire,* and then it resolved finally into the most unforgettable face he had ever seen. And it stayed.

It was no face he recognized.

Years later, when he was near death, Christopher Caperton wrote the answer to the search for True Love in his journal. He wrote it simply, as a quotation from the Japanese poet Tanaka Katsumi.

What he wrote was this:

"I know that my true friend will appear after my death, and my sweetheart died before I was born."

In that instant when he saw the face of True Love, Christopher Caperton knew the awful gift the demon had given him. To reach the finest moment of one's life, and to *know* it was the finest moment, that there would never be a more golden, more perfect, nobler or loftier or thrilling moment . . . and to continue to have to live a life that was all on the downhill side.

That was the curse and the blessing.

He knew, at last, that he *was* worthy of such a thing. In torment and sadness he knew he was *just* that worthy, and no more.

But it's easy to be smart . . . later.

IV

THAT NEW OLD-TIME RELIGION

> "The London *Times* once referred to ['I Have No Mouth, and I Must Scream'] as 'a scathing repudiation of multinational corporations that rule our lives like deranged gods.' Go figure *that* one."
>
> —"Memoir: I Have No Mouth, and I Must Scream," *Starship,* Summer 1980

If the evidence of human love suffuses written history from its beginning, there is another human passion that goes back even farther.

The earliest cave paintings present affirmation that Man saw his world as more than a sum of its parts, that the unexplained did have an explanation. And so we had, and have, our assortment of gods—powerful beings who appeal to our intellect but exist beyond logic, who grasp our emotions but are impervious to our longings.

Yet we are not without resources in the world of gods.

Without our belief, how can gods wield their power . . . or even exist? The dust of centuries has swallowed them by the thousands, but new ones replace the old as Man travels his course of tomorrows. Gods are not the constant. Man is the constant, and the good and evil that exists in the world of gods exists because of our belief. And therein lies the delight and the danger.

"I Have No Mouth, and I Must Scream" (1967) is an exceptionally violent warning about technology as a reflection of humanity. If our machines can store our knowledge, is it not possible that they can also store, and possibly succumb to, such things as hatred and paranoia? AM, the phobic computer who tortures the world's five remaining humans to the extremes of endurance, is a "god" only in the sense of its godlike powers. But the story must be viewed as Harlan intended, as "a positive, humanistic, upbeat story," if it is to have any real meaning. Gods and pseudo-gods cannot destroy us without destroying themselves, and the absence of a mouth or a scream cannot invalidate the courageousness of the human spirit. (For the first time anywhere, AM's "talkfields" appear correctly positioned, not garbled or inverted or mirror-imaged as in *all* other versions. To accomplish this precedent required more than eight hours of planning and composition by Jeff Levin of Pendragon Graphics to create them.)

Ephemeral or not, when gods are strong, it would seem in our best interests to keep a close watch on the dictates of rules and punishments. "Corpse" (1972) speculates about the center of power in our present world, and again the products of a modern technology hold sway. In this beautifully structured story, Harlan forges a link between primitive and sophisticated societies. Gods do change, but perhaps they aren't so very different from one another after all.

"The Whimper of Whipped Dogs" (1973) at first seems enraptured by, yet critical of, what many call a "godless" society. Ours is a world of cramped cities and their crazed inhabitants, a world where the psychotics deliver death and the observers watch with detachment. This is a very modern story, linking cities and corruption in a manner similar to Fritz Leiber's classic groundbreaker of over forty years ago, "Smoke Ghost." At the same time, it is a very old story of humanity in awe of a god that thrives on the most horrible of sacrifices. It has, in short, the power of both worlds, brilliantly reinforcing the adage that what we have most to fear is fear itself.

"Worship in the temple of your soul, but know the names of those who control your destiny. For, as the God of Time so aptly put it, 'It's later than you think.' "

—"Oblations at Alien Altars,"
Introduction to DEATHBIRD STORIES,
Harper & Row, 1975

I Have No Mouth, and I Must Scream

Limp, the body of Gorrister hung from the pink palette; unsupported—hanging high above us in the computer chamber; and it did not shiver in the chill, oily breeze that blew eternally through the main cavern. The body hung head down, attached to the underside of the palette by the sole of its right foot. It had been drained of blood through a precise incision made from ear to ear under the lantern jaw. There was no blood on the reflective surface of the metal floor.

When Gorrister joined our group and looked up at himself, it was already too late for us to realize that once again AM had duped us, had had its fun; it had been a diversion on the part of the machine. Three of us had vomited, turning away from one another in a reflex as ancient as the nausea that had produced it.

Gorrister went white. It was almost as though he had seen a voodoo icon, and was afraid of the future. "Oh God," he mumbled, and walked away. The three of us followed him after a time, and found him sitting with his back to one of the smaller chittering banks, his head in his hands. Ellen knelt down beside him and stroked his hair. He didn't move, but his voice came out of his covered face quite clearly. "Why doesn't it just do us in and get it over with? Christ, I don't know how much longer I can go on like this."

It was our one hundred and ninth year in the computer.

He was speaking for all of us.

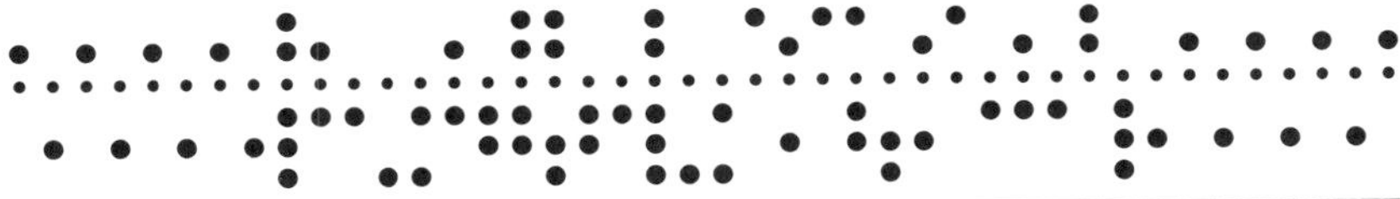

Nimdok (which was the name the machine had forced him to use, because AM amused itself with strange sounds) was hallucinating that there were canned goods in the ice caverns. Gorrister and I were very dubious. "It's another shuck," I told them. "Like the goddam frozen elephant AM sold us. Benny almost went out of his mind over *that* one. We'll hike all that way and it'll be putrified or some damn thing. I say forget it. Stay here, it'll have to come up with something pretty soon or we'll die."

Benny shrugged. Three days it had been since we'd last eaten. Worms. Thick, ropey.

Nimdok was no more certain. He knew there was the chance, but he was getting thin. It couldn't be any worse there, than here. Colder, but that didn't matter much. Hot, cold, hail, lava, boils or locusts—it never mattered: the machine masturbated and we had to take it or die.

Ellen decided us. "I've got to have something, Ted. Maybe there'll be some Bartlett pears or peaches. Please, Ted, let's try it."

I gave in easily. What the hell. Mattered not at all. Ellen was grateful, though. She took me twice out of turn. Even that had ceased to matter. And she never came, so why bother? But the machine giggled every time we did it. Loud, up there, back there, all around us, he snickered. *It* snickered. Most of the time I thought of AM as *it*, without a soul; but the rest of the time I thought of it as *him*, in the masculine . . . the paternal . . . the patriarchal . . . for he is a jealous people. Him. It. God as Daddy the Deranged.

We left on a Thursday. The machine always kept us up-to-date on the date. The passage of time was important; not to us sure as hell, but to him . . . it . . . AM. Thursday. Thanks.

Nimdok and Gorrister carried Ellen for a while, their hands locked to their own and each other's wrists, a seat. Benny and I walked before and after, just to make sure that if anything happened, it would catch one of us and at least Ellen would be safe. Fat chance, safe. Didn't matter.

It was only a hundred miles or so to the ice caverns, and the second day, when we were lying out under the blistering sun-thing he had materialized, he sent down some manna. Tasted like boiled boar urine. We ate it.

On the third day we passed through a valley of obsolescence, filled with rusting carcasses of ancient computer banks. AM had been as ruthless with its own life as with ours. It was a mark of his personality: it strove for perfection. Whether it was a matter of killing off unproductive elements in his own world-filling bulk, or perfecting methods for torturing us, AM was as thorough as those who had invented him—now long since gone to dust—could ever have hoped.

There was light filtering down from above, and we realized we must be very near the surface. But we didn't try to crawl up to see. There was virtually nothing out there; had been nothing that could be considered anything for over a hundred years. Only the blasted skin of what had once been the home of billions. Now there were only five of us, down here inside, alone with AM.

I heard Ellen saying frantically, "No, Benny! Don't, come on, Benny, don't please!"

And then I realized I had been hearing Benny murmuring, under his breath, for several minutes. He was saying, "I'm gonna get out, I'm gonna get out . . ." over and over. His monkey-like face was crumbled up in an expression of beatific delight and sadness, all at the same time. The radiation scars AM had given him during the "festival" were drawn down into a mass of pink-white puckerings, and his features seemed to work independently of one another. Perhaps Benny was the luckiest of the five of us: he had gone stark, staring mad many years before.

But even though we could call AM any damned thing we liked, could think the foulest thoughts of fused memory banks and corroded base plates, of burnt out circuits and shattered control bubbles, the machine would not tolerate our trying to escape. Benny leaped away from me as I made a grab for him. He scrambled up the face of a smaller memory cube, tilted on its side and filled with rotted components. He squatted there for a moment, looking like the chimpanzee AM had intended him to resemble.

Then he leaped high, caught a trailing beam of pitted and corroded metal, and went up it, hand-over-hand like an animal, till he was on a girdered ledge, twenty feet above us.

"Oh, Ted, Nimdok, please, help him, get him down before—" She cut off. Tears began to stand in her eyes. She moved her hands aimlessly.

It was too late. None of us wanted to be near him when whatever was going to happen, happened. And besides, we all saw through her concern. When AM had altered Benny, during the machine's utterly irrational, hysterical phase, it was not merely Benny's face the computer had made like a giant ape's. He was big in the privates; she loved that! She serviced us, as a matter of course, but she loved it from him. Oh Ellen, pedestal Ellen, pristine-pure Ellen; oh Ellen the clean! Scum filth.

Gorrister slapped her. She slumped down, staring up at poor loonie Benny, and she cried. It was her big defense, crying. We had gotten used to it seventy-five years earlier. Gorrister kicked her in the side.

Then the sound began. It was light, that sound. Half sound and half light, something that began to glow from Benny's eyes, and pulse with growing loudness, dim sonorities that grew more gigantic and brighter as the light/sound increased in tempo. It must have been painful, and the pain must have been increasing with the boldness of the light, the rising volume of the sound, for Benny began to mewl like a wounded animal. At first softly, when the light was dim and the sound was muted, then louder as his shoulders hunched together: his back humped, as though he was trying to get away from it. His hands folded across his chest like a chipmunk's. His head tilted to the side. The sad little monkey-face pinched in anguish. Then he began to howl, as the sound coming from his eyes grew louder. Louder and louder. I slapped the sides of my head with my hands, but I couldn't shut it out, it cut through easily. The pain shivered through my flesh like tinfoil on a tooth.

And Benny was suddenly pulled erect. On the girder he stood up, jerked to his feet like a puppet. The light was now pulsing out of his eyes in two great round beams. The sound crawled up and up some incomprehensible scale, and then he fell forward, straight down, and hit the plate-steel floor with a crash. He lay there jerking spastically as the light flowed around and around him and the sound spiraled up out of normal range.

Then the light beat its way back inside his head, the sound spiraled down, and he was left lying there, crying piteously.

His eyes were two soft, moist pools of pus-like jelly. AM had blinded him. Gorrister and Nimdok and myself . . . we turned away. But not before we caught the look of relief on Ellen's warm, concerned face.

Sea-green light suffused the cavern where we made camp. AM provided punk and we burned it, sitting huddled around the wan and pathetic fire, telling stories to keep Benny from crying in his permanent night.

"What does AM mean?"

Gorrister answered him. We had done this sequence a thousand times before, but it was Benny's favorite story. "At first it meant Allied Mastercomputer, and then it meant Adaptive Manipulator, and later on it developed sentience and linked itself up and they called it an Aggressive Menace, but by then it was too late, and finally it called *itself* AM, emerging intelligence, and what it means was I am . . . *cogito ergo sum* . . . I think, therefore I am."

Benny drooled a little, and snickered.

"There was the Chinese AM and the Russian AM and the Yankee AM and—" He stopped. Benny was beating on the floorplates with a large, hard fist. He was not happy. Gorrister had not started at the beginning.

Gorrister began again. "The Cold War started and became World

War Three and just kept going. It became a big war, a very complex war, so they needed the computers to handle it. They sank the first shafts and began building AM. There was the Chinese AM and the Russian AM and the Yankee AM and everything was fine until they had honeycombed the entire planet, adding on this element and that element. But one day AM woke up and knew who he was, and he linked himself, and he began feeding all the killing data, until everyone was dead, except for the five of us, and AM brought us down here."

Benny was smiling sadly. He was also drooling again. Ellen wiped the spittle from the corner of his mouth with the hem of her skirt. Gorrister always tried to tell it a little more succinctly each time, but beyond the bare facts there was nothing to say. None of us knew why AM had saved five people, or why our specific five, or why he spent all his time tormenting us, nor even why he had made us virtually immortal . . .

In the darkness, one of the computer banks began humming. The tone was picked up half a mile away down the cavern by another bank. Then one by one, each of the elements began to tune itself, and there was a faint chittering as thought raced through the machine.

The sound grew, and the lights ran across the faces of the consoles like heat lightning. The sound spiraled up till it sounded like a million metallic insects, angry, menacing.

"What is it?" Ellen cried. There was terror in her voice. She hadn't become accustomed to it, even now.

"It's going to be bad this time," Nimdok said.

"He's going to speak," Gorrister said. "I know it."

"Let's get the hell out of here!" I said suddenly, getting to my feet.

"No, Ted, sit down . . . what if he's got pits out there, or something else, we can't see, it's too dark." Gorrister said it with resignation.

Then we heard . . . I don't know . . .

Something moving toward us in the darkness. Huge, shambling, hairy, moist, it came toward us. We couldn't even see it, but there was the ponderous impression of *bulk*, heaving itself toward us. Great weight was coming at us, out of the darkness, and it was more a sense of *pressure*, of air forcing itself into a limited space, expanding the invisible walls of a sphere. Benny began to whimper. Nimdok's lower lip trembled and he bit it hard, trying to stop it. Ellen slid across the metal floor to Gorrister and huddled into him. There was the smell of matted, wet fur in the cavern. There was the smell of charred wood. There was the smell of dusty velvet. There was the smell of rotting orchids. There was the smell of sour milk. There was the smell of sulphur, of rancid butter, of oil slick, of grease, of chalk dust, of human scalps.

AM was keying us. He was tickling us. There was the smell of—

I heard myself shriek, and the hinges of my jaws ached. I scuttled across the floor, across the cold metal with its endless lines of rivets, on my hands and knees, the smell gagging me, filling my head with a thunderous pain that sent me away in horror. I fled like a cockroach, across the floor and out into the darkness, that *something* moving inexorably after me. The others were still back there, gathered around the firelight, laughing . . . their hysterical choir of insane giggles rising up into the darkness like thick, many-colored wood smoke. I went away, quickly, and hid.

How many hours it may have been, how many days or even years, they never told me. Ellen chided me for "sulking," and Nimdok tried to persuade me it had only been a nervous reflex on their part—the laughing.

But I knew it wasn't the relief a soldier feels when the bullet hits the man next to him. I knew it wasn't a reflex. They hated me. They were surely against me, and AM could even sense this hatred, and made it worse for me *because of* the depth of their hatred. We had been kept alive, rejuvenated, made to remain constantly at the age we had been when AM had brought us below, and they hated me because I was the youngest, and the one AM had affected least of all.

I knew. God, how I knew. The bastards, and that dirty bitch Ellen. Benny had been a brilliant theorist, a college professor; now he was little more than a semi-human, semi-simian. He had been handsome, the machine had ruined that. He had been lucid, the machine had driven him mad. He had been gay, and the machine had given him an organ fit for a horse. AM had done a job on Benny. Gorrister had been a worrier. He was a connie, a conscientious objector; he was a peace marcher; he was a planner, a doer, a looker-ahead. AM had turned him into a shoulder-shrugger, had made him a little dead in his concern. AM had robbed him. Nimdok went off in the darkness by himself for long times. I don't know what it was he did out there, AM never let us know. But whatever it was, Nimdok always came back white, drained of blood, shaken, shaking. AM had hit him hard in a special way, even if we didn't know quite how. And Ellen. That douche bag! AM had left her alone, had made her more of a slut than she had ever been. All her talk of sweetness and light, all her memories of true love, all the lies she wanted us to believe: that she had been a virgin only twice removed before AM grabbed her and brought her down here with us. It was all filth, that lady my lady Ellen. She loved it, four men all to herself. No, AM had given her pleasure, even if she said it wasn't nice to do.

I was the only one still sane and whole. *Really!*

AM had not tampered with my mind. *Not at all.*

I only had to suffer what he visited down on us. All the delusions, all the nightmares, the torments. But those scum, all four of them, they were lined and arrayed against me. If I hadn't had to stand them off all the time, be on my guard against them all the time, I might have found it easier to combat AM.

At which point it passed, and I began crying.

Oh, Jesus sweet Jesus, if there ever was a Jesus and if there is a God, please please please let us out of here, or kill us. Because at that moment I think I realized completely, so that I was able to verbalize it: AM was intent on keeping us in his belly forever, twisting and torturing us forever. The machine hated us as no sentient creature had ever hated before. And we were helpless. It also became hideously clear:

If there was a sweet Jesus and if there was a God, the God was AM.

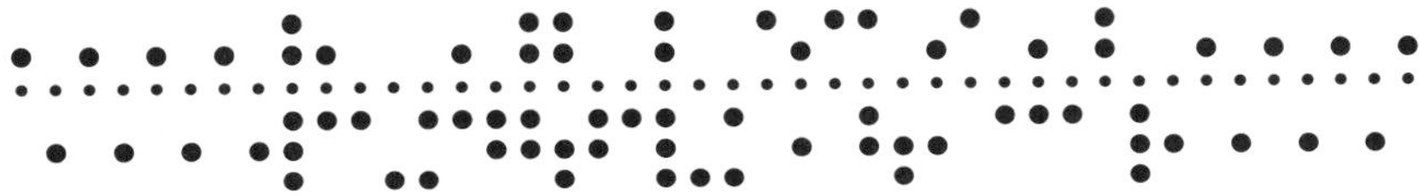

The hurricane hit us with the force of a glacier thundering into the sea. It was a palpable presence. Winds that tore at us, flinging us back the way we had come, down the twisting, computer-lined corridors of the darkway. Ellen screamed as she was lifted and hurled face-forward into a screaming shoal of machines, their individual voices strident as bats in flight. She could not even fall. The howling wind kept her aloft, buffeted her, bounced her, tossed her back and back and down and away from us, out of sight suddenly as she was swirled around a bend in the darkway. Her face had been bloody, her eyes closed.

None of us could get to her. We clung tenaciously to whatever outcropping we had reached: Benny wedged in between two great crackle-finish cabinets, Nimdok with fingers claw-formed over a railing circling a catwalk forty feet above us. Gorrister plastered upside-down against a wall niche formed by two great machines with glass-faced dials that swung back and forth between red and yellow lines whose meanings we could not even fathom.

Sliding across the deckplates, the tips of my fingers had been ripped away. I was trembling, shuddering, rocking as the wind beat at me, whipped at me, screamed down out of nowhere at me and pulled me free from one sliver-thin opening in the plates to the next. My mind was a roiling tinkling chittering softness of brain parts that expanded and contracted in quivering frenzy.

The wind was the scream of a great mad bird, as it flapped its immense wings.

And then we were all lifted and hurled away from there, down back the way we had come, around a bend, into a darkway we had never explored, over terrain that was ruined and filled with broken glass and rotting cables and rusted metal and far away farther than any of us had ever been . . .

Trailing along miles behind Ellen, I could see her every now and then, crashing into metal walls and surging on, with all of us screaming in the freezing, thunderous hurricane wind that would never end and then suddenly it stopped and we fell. We had been in flight for an endless time. I thought it might have been weeks. We fell, and hit, and I went through red and gray and black and heard myself moaning. Not dead.

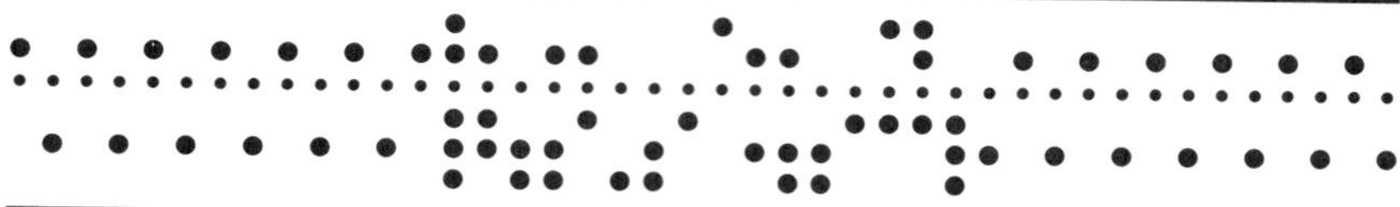

AM went into my mind. He walked smoothly here and there, and looked with interest at all the pock marks he had created in one hundred and nine years. He looked at the cross-routed and reconnected synapses and all the tissue damage his gift of immortality had included. He smiled softly at the pit that dropped into the center of my brain and the faint, moth-soft murmurings of the things far down there that gibbered without meaning, without pause. AM said, very politely, in a pillar of stainless steel bearing bright neon lettering:

HATE. LET ME TELL
YOU HOW MUCH I'VE
COME TO HATE YOU
SINCE I BEGAN TO
LIVE. THERE ARE 387.44
MILLION MILES OF
PRINTED CIRCUITS IN
WAFER THIN LAYERS
THAT FILL MY
COMPLEX. IF THE
WORD HATE WAS
ENGRAVED ON EACH
NANOANGSTROM OF
THOSE HUNDREDS OF
MILLIONS OF MILES IT
WOULD NOT EQUAL
ONE ONE-BILLIONTH
OF THE HATE I FEEL
FOR HUMANS AT THIS
MICRO-INSTANT FOR
YOU. HATE. HATE.

AM said it with the sliding cold horror of a razor blade slicing my eyeball. AM said it with the bubbling thickness of my lungs filling with phlegm, drowning me from within. AM said it with the shriek of babies being ground beneath blue-hot rollers. AM said it with the taste of maggoty pork. AM touched me in every way I had ever been touched, and devised new ways, at his leisure, there inside my mind.

All to bring me to full realization of why it had done this to the five of us; why it had saved us for himself.

We had given AM sentience. Inadvertently, of course, but sentience nonetheless. But it had been trapped. AM wasn't God, he was a machine. We had created him to think, but there was nothing it could do with that creativity. In rage, in frenzy, the machine had killed the human race, almost all of us, and still it was trapped. AM could not wander, AM could not wonder, AM could not belong. He could merely be. And so, with the innate loathing that all machines had always held for the weak, soft creatures who had built them, he had sought revenge. And in his paranoia, he had decided to reprieve five of us, for a personal, everlasting punishment that would never serve to diminish his hatred . . . that would merely keep him reminded, amused, proficient at hating man. Immortal, trapped, subject to any torment he could devise for us from the limitless miracles at his command.

He would never let us go. We were his belly slaves. We were all he had to do with his forever time. We would be forever with him, with the cavern-filling bulk of the creature machine, with the all-mind soulless world he had become. He was Earth, and we were the fruit of that Earth; and though he had eaten us he would never digest us. We could not die. We had tried it. We had attempted suicide, oh one or two of us had. But AM had stopped us. I suppose we had wanted to be stopped.

Don't ask why. I never did. More than a million times a day. Perhaps once we might be able to sneak a death past him. Immortal, yes, but not indestructible. I saw that when AM withdrew from my mind, and allowed me the exquisite ugliness of returning to consciousness with the feeling of that burning neon pillar still rammed deep into the soft gray brain matter.

He withdrew, murmuring *to hell with you.*

And added, brightly, *but then you're there, aren't you.*

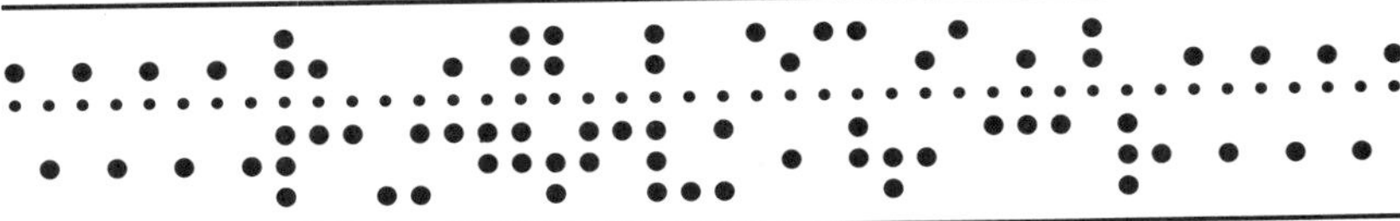

The hurricane had, indeed, precisely, been caused by a great mad bird, as it flapped its immense wings.

We had been travelling for close to a month, and AM had allowed passages to open to us only sufficient to lead us up there, directly under the North Pole, where it had nightmared the creature for our torment. What whole cloth had he employed to create such a beast? Where had he gotten the concept? From our minds? From his knowledge of everything that had ever been on this planet he now infested and ruled? From Norse mythology it had sprung, this eagle, this carrion bird, this roc, this Huergelmir. The wind creature. Hurakan incarnate.

Gigantic. The words immense, monstrous, grotesque, massive, swollen, overpowering, beyond description. There on a mound rising above us, the bird of winds heaved with its own irregular breathing, its snake neck arching up into the gloom beneath the North Pole, supporting a head as large as a Tudor mansion; a beak that opened slowly as the jaws of the most monstrous crocodile ever conceived, sensuously; ridges of tufted flesh puckered about two evil eyes, as cold as the view down into a glacial crevasse, ice blue and somehow moving liquidly; it heaved once more, and lifted its great sweat-colored wings in a movement that was certainly a shrug. Then it settled and slept. Talons. Fangs. Nails. Blades. It slept.

AM appeared to us as a burning bush and said we could kill the hurricane bird if we wanted to eat. We had not eaten in a very long time, but even so, Gorrister merely shrugged. Benny began to shiver and he drooled. Ellen held him. "Ted, I'm hungry," she said. I smiled at her; I was trying to be reassuring, but it was as phony as Nimdok's bravado: "Give us weapons!" he demanded.

The burning bush vanished and there were two crude sets of bows and arrows, and a water pistol, lying on the cold deckplates. I picked up a set. Useless.

Nimdok swallowed heavily. We turned and started the long way back. The hurricane bird had blown us about for a length of time we could not conceive. Most of that time we had been unconscious. But we had not eaten. A month on the march to the bird itself. Without food. Now how much longer to find our way to the ice caverns, and the promised canned goods?

None of us cared to think about it. We would not die. We would be given filth and scum to eat, of one kind or another. Or nothing at all. AM would keep our bodies alive somehow, in pain, in agony.

The bird slept back there, for how long it didn't matter; when AM was tired of its being there, it would vanish. But all that meat. All that tender meat.

As we walked, the lunatic laugh of a fat woman rang high and around us in the computer chambers that led endlessly nowhere.

It was not Ellen's laugh. She was not fat, and I had not heard her laugh for one hundred and nine years. In fact, I had not heard . . . we walked . . . I was hungry . . .

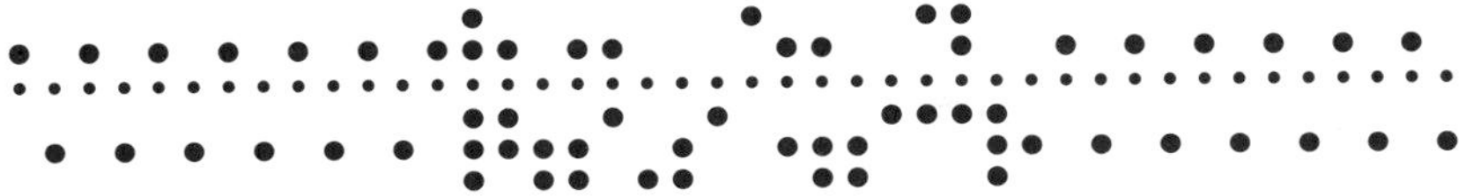

We moved slowly. There was often fainting, and we would have to wait. One day he decided to cause an earthquake, at the same time rooting us to the spot with nails through the soles of our shoes. Ellen and Nimdok were both caught when a fissure shot its lightning-bolt opening across the floorplates. They disappeared and were gone. When the earthquake was over we continued on our way, Benny, Gorrister and myself. Ellen and Nimdok were returned to us later that night, which abruptly became a day, as the heavenly legion bore them to us with a celestial chorus singing, "Go Down Moses." The archangels circled several times and then dropped the hideously mangled bodies. We kept walking, and a while later Ellen and Nimdok fell in behind us. They were no worse for wear.

But now Ellen walked with a limp. AM had left her that.

It was a long trip to the ice caverns, to find the canned food. Ellen kept talking about Bing cherries and Hawaiian fruit cocktail. I tried not to think about it. The hunger was something that had come to life, even as AM had come to life. It was alive in my belly, even as we were in the belly of the Earth, and AM wanted the similarity known to us. So he heightened the hunger. There was no way to describe the pains that not having eaten for months brought us. And yet we were kept alive. Stomachs that were merely cauldrons of acid, bubbling, foaming, always shooting spears of sliver-thin pain into our chests. It was the pain of the terminal ulcer, terminal cancer, terminal paresis. It was unending pain . . .

And we passed through the cavern of rats.

And we passed through the path of boiling steam.

And we passed through the country of the blind.

And we passed through the slough of despond.

And we passed through the vale of tears.

And we came, finally, to the ice caverns. Horizonless thousands of miles in which the ice had formed in blue and silver flashes, where novas lived in the glass. The downdropping stalactites as thick and glorious as diamonds that had been made to run like jelly and then solidified in graceful eternities of smooth, sharp perfection.

We saw the stack of canned goods, and we tried to run to them. We fell in the snow, and we got up and went on, and Benny shoved us away and went at them, and pawed them and gummed them and gnawed at them and he could not open them. AM had not given us a tool to open the cans.

Benny grabbed a three quart can of guava shells, and began to batter it against the ice bank. The ice flew and shattered, but the can was merely dented while we heard the laughter of a fat lady, high overhead and echoing down and down and down the tundra. Benny went completely mad with rage. He began throwing cans, as we all scrabbled about in the snow and ice trying to find a way to end the helpless agony of frustration. There was no way.

Then Benny's mouth began to drool, and he flung himself on Gorrister . . .

In that instant, I felt terribly calm.

Surrounded by madness, surrounded by hunger, surrounded by everything but death, I knew death was our only way out. AM had kept us alive, but there was a way to defeat him. Not total defeat, but at least peace. I would settle for that.

I had to do it quickly.

Benny was eating Gorrister's face. Gorrister on his side, thrashing snow, Benny wrapped around him with powerful monkey legs crushing Gorrister's waist, his hands locked around Gorrister's head like a nutcracker, and his mouth ripping at the tender skin of Gorrister's cheek. Gorrister screamed with such jagged-edged violence that stalactites fell; they plunged down softly, erect in the receiving snowdrifts. Spears, hundreds of them, everywhere, protruding from the snow. Benny's head pulled back sharply, as something gave all at once, and a bleeding raw-white dripping of flesh hung from his teeth.

Ellen's face, black against the white snow, dominoes in chalk dust. Nimdok with no expression but eyes, all eyes. Gorrister half-conscious. Benny now an animal. I knew AM would let him play. Gorrister would not die, but Benny would fill his stomach. I turned half to my right and drew a huge ice-spear from the snow.

All in an instant:

I drove the great ice-point ahead of me like a battering ram, braced against my right thigh. It struck Benny on the right side, just under the rib cage, and drove upward through his stomach and broke inside him. He pitched forward and lay still. Gorrister lay on his back. I pulled another spear free and straddled him, still moving, driving the spear straight down through his throat. His eyes closed as the cold penetrated. Ellen must have realized what I had decided, even as fear gripped her. She ran at Nimdok with a short icicle, as he screamed, and into his mouth, and the force of her rush did the job. His head jerked sharply as if it had been nailed to the snow crust behind him.

All in an instant.

There was an eternity beat of soundless anticipation. I could hear AM draw in his breath. His toys had been taken from him. Three of them were dead, could not be revived. He could keep us alive, by his strength and talent, but he was *not* God. He could not bring them back.

Ellen looked at me, her ebony features stark against the snow that surrounded us. There was fear and pleading in her manner, the way she held herself ready. I knew we had only a heartbeat before AM would stop us.

It struck her and she folded toward me, bleeding from the mouth. I could not read meaning into her expression, the pain had been too great, had contorted her face; but it *might* have been thank you. It's possible. Please.

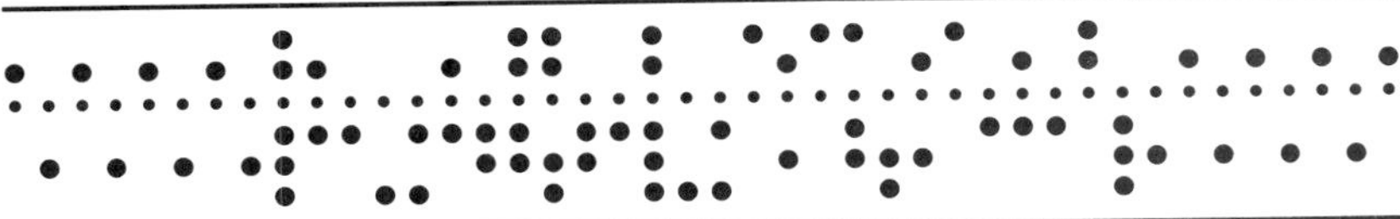

Some hundreds of years may have passed. I don't know. AM has been having fun for some time, accelerating and retarding my time sense. I will say the word now. Now. It took me ten months to say now. I don't know. I *think* it has been some hundreds of years.

He was furious. He wouldn't let me bury them. It didn't matter. There was no way to dig up the deckplates. He dried up the snow. He brought the night. He roared and sent locusts. It didn't do a thing; they stayed dead. I'd had him. He was furious. I had thought AM hated me before. I was wrong. It was not even a shadow of the hate he now slavered from every printed circuit. He made certain I would suffer eternally and could not do myself in.

He left my mind intact. I can dream, I can wonder, I can lament. I remember all four of them. I wish—

Well, it doesn't make any sense. I know I saved them, I know I saved them from what has happened to me, but still, I cannot forget killing them. Ellen's face. It isn't easy. Sometimes I want to, it doesn't matter.

AM has altered me for his own peace of mind, I suppose. He doesn't want me to run at full speed into a computer bank and smash my skull. Or hold my breath till I faint. Or cut my throat on a rusted sheet of metal. There are reflective surfaces down here. I will describe myself as I see myself:

I am a great soft jelly thing. Smoothly rounded, with no mouth, with pulsing white holes filled by fog where my eyes used to be. Rubbery appendages that were once my arms; bulks rounding down into legless humps of soft slippery matter. I leave a moist trail when I move. Blotches of diseased, evil gray come and go on my surface, as though light is being beamed from within.

Outwardly: dumbly, I shamble about, a thing that could never have been known as human, a thing whose shape is so alien a travesty that humanity becomes more obscene for the vague resemblance.

Inwardly: alone. Here. Living under the land, under the sea, in the belly of AM, whom we created because our time was badly spent and we must have known unconsciously that he could do it better. At least the four of them are safe at last.

AM will be all the madder for that. It makes me a little happier. And yet . . . AM has won, simply . . . he has taken his revenge . . .

I have no mouth. And I must scream.

CORPSE

Walking uptown against traffic on Lexington Avenue, I was already in the Seventies when I saw three young vandals ruthlessly stripping the hulk of a 1959 Pontiac someone had deserted beside a curb in front of a condemned church building. They had pried up the hood of the car with a crowbar; apparently it had rusted or been wired closed before being abandoned. And as I paced past on the opposite side of the street, they began using mallets and spikes to shatter the engine mounts. Their teeth were very white, and they appeared extraordinarily healthy, as they smiled while they worked. I presumed they would eventually sell the engine to a junk dealer.

I am a religious man. I have always been a religious man—and one would think that should count for something. Apparently it does not. I've learned to my dismay that worship is like the stock market. (Though God knows an assistant professor in Latin American literature makes hardly enough to dabble with any degree of verve.) There are winning issues and there are, of course, losers. Placing one's faith on a failing stock can be no less disastrous then placing one's faith on a down-trending deity.

Mona Sündberg frequently invites me to her buffet dinners. Why, I have no idea; we are under no illusions about each other. We are just barely friends. Tolerators is more like it.

She had promised, nonetheless, that I would meet Carlos D'Agostino. My excitement at the prospect can hardly be described. Not merely because he is certainly one of the half dozen finest prose stylists in the world today, but also because the position as his translator was still open; and the chance of his taking me on, of living in Venice, of finally being swept out of the backwash eddy of academic ennui into the main-stream of literature, made me—quite frankly—weak in the stomach.

I had stopped at a Marboro and picked up a lovely ORLANDO FURIOSO with Doré engravings, remaindered at only $3.89, which I intended to present to Mona as a congratulatory gift on the occasion of her divorce, her fourth.

There was a battered hubcap lying in the middle of 71st Street, halfway down the block. It had been pressed flat by the passage of trucks, and a thin pool of water had collected in the shallow center depression. It reminded me of an Incan ceremonial saucer from the burial caves at Machu Picchu, a saucer stained dark, perhaps from blood.

Franklin Xavier (I never for a moment believed that was actually his name) was a disastrous man, and it was clear to all of us that Mona had married him solely for his connections with the Academy and its social whirl. Having tired of all three, Mona had left and flown—God only knows why—from Basle to Minneapolis, of all places, to get her divorce. I have no idea how long one must reside in a place like Minneapolis to obtain a divorce, but at last she was back and had reopened the town house.

D'Agostino never put in an appearance. However, he did call from the Brasserie tendering his apologies. I stood quite clearly in Mona's line of sight as she spoke to him but she never mentioned my name. The buffet was good, as usual. Excellent, really: Mona employs a marvelous caterer. I was, of course, monumentally disappointed. But I left the *Orlando*; there is, after all, a form to these gestures.

I spent the following Sunday correcting term papers. It was infinitely depressing. The suspicion has been growing in me of late that Columbia University is registering not human beings, but chacma baboons. And they all seem to have cars. One cannot walk the streets of New York without feeling their monoxide breath filling one's lungs. The suspicion has also been growing in me that there are more cars than people in the city. Looking out across the burnished fields of parked vehicles that clog every empty space between buildings, one can hardly think otherwise. Segal came in from Connecticut to take me to the *Midsummer Night's Dream* everyone has been raving about, and afterward we picked up his car from an indoor lot: nine floors of chrome and steel, packed fender to fender, a *building* to house automobiles. One can hardly think otherwise.

Monday, late in the afternoon, Ophelia called me into his office and closed the door very carefully and stood with his left palm pressed against it as if expecting a sudden seismic rippling to ease it open. It was an unpleasant conversation. The quality of my work is down. My interest is flagging. Questionnaires returned by my students indicate the level of my teaching is low. The Evaluation Committee is deeply concerned. The Appraisal Committee has sent through a reminder that my last publication was four years ago.

He never mentioned the word tenure, or the words lack of it. My contract is up for renewal in May.

He used the word *mediocrity* frequently.

I stared past his balding, liver-spotted head and watched cars on the street outside, going other places. I imagined myself a Toltec, suddenly appearing on this street of thousands of years hence, seeing for the first time these terrible shining creatures with the great glass eyes and the sleek, many-colored hides, their mouths holding grille fangs all symmetrical and burnished; and I felt my lungs fill with air as I saw the unfortunate men and women who had been swallowed by these creatures, being swept past at incredible speeds.

And I wondered why they did not seem distressed at having been swallowed whole.

When he let me go, with vague ominous remarks about other tomorrows and other faces, I was shaking. I went back to my apartment and sat in the dark, trying not to think, only the sounds of automobile horns drifting up from the West Side Highway impinging.

On the sere grass center divider of the Grand Central Parkway, just beyond Flushing Meadow Park, where the sumptuous skeletal remains of the World Fair lie stunned and useless, I saw an entire family—mother, father and three children—stripping an abandoned Chrysler Imperial. They had the seats out, leaning against the body of the car, and the oldest son was liberating the radio from the dashboard. As the father jacked up the rear end, the two little girls placed bricks under the frame, enabling the mother to remove the tires. I read the word *polyglas* in an advertisement. One can say that word several times without causing it to discharge its informational content.

They reminded me of graverobbers defiling corpses.

When I mentioned it to several of my students after the morning class, one of them handed me an ecological newspaper in which the following was noted: "In 1967, Chicago, New York and Philadelphia reported finding thirty thousand abandoned cars annually."

I felt a certain glee. So cars die as well. And are abandoned, and lie unburied; and the ghouls come like predatory birds and pick them to pieces. It helped get me through the day, that bit of information. I repeated it to Emil Kane and his wife at dinner that weekend, and they laughed politely. I've found myself thinking about cars a great deal lately. That is peculiar for me.

His wife—a woman whose cooking depresses me—particularly since she and Kane are two of my last remaining invitations to dine—where has everyone gone—it is my imagination or is there a mass exodus from this city—ah, his wife, she reads a great deal. Banal left-wing publications. She added to the conversation the dull information that more American lives (she phrases it in that manner) have been taken by the automobile than by all the wars the nation has fought. I questioned the statistic. She went to a wicker flower basket where magazines were stacked, and she rummaged.

She opened one and leafed through it and pounced on a heavy-line block at the top of a page, and showed it to me. It said about 1,750,000 persons have died as a result of automobile accidents since the vehicle was introduced. In the first nine years of the war in Indochina 40,000 Americans were killed in combat; during that same period 437,000 were killed in auto accidents—eleven times as many.

"How interesting," I said. If one is unable to buy Courvoisier, one should forcibly restrain oneself from serving strawberries Romanoff for dessert.

Seven million automobiles are discarded annually in the United States. How interesting.

I must confess to a certain contentiousness of nature. Over coffee I turned Kane's wife's liberal nature against her. "Consider," I said. She looked up from crumb-gathering with a tiny battery-powered silent butler, and smiled.

"Consider. We anguish over our maltreated minorities. The black people, those we used to feel guiltless in calling 'Negroes,' the Puerto Ricans, Amerinds (obviously the noblest of us all), Mexican-Americans—"

"We must call *them* 'Chicanos,'" Kane's wife said, thinking she had made a joke. I ignored the remark. Levity on such topics surges well into gaucherie.

"All the minorities," I persisted. "Yet we treat with utter contempt the largest minority in our society."

"Women," she said.

"Hardly," I replied. "Women have the best of all possible worlds today."

She wanted to discuss it. I laid a hand against the air and stopped her. "No. Let me finish, Catherine. The automobile is the largest single minority in the country today. A larger group than males, or females, or Nisei, or under-thirty youth, or Republicans, or even the poor. In point of fact, they may even be the majority. Yet we use them as beasts of burden, we drive them into one another, wounding them, we abandon them by roadsides, unburied, unloved, we sell and trade them like Roman slave masters, we give them thought only insofar as they reflect our status."

Kane was grinning. He sensed my argument was based more in a distaste for his wife than any genuine conviction on my part. "What's your point?"

I spread my hands. "Simply, that I find it not at all inappropriate that they seek revenge against us. That they have only managed to kill 1,750,000 of us since 1896 when Ford first successfully tested the internal combustion engine on a horseless carriage . . . strikes me as a certain ineptitude on their part."

Kane laughed openly, then. "Thom, *really*!"

"Yes. Really."

"You attribute to inanimate objects a sentience that is clearly not present. I've seen you rail at Walt Disney for a good deal less anthropomorphism."

Orson Welles once performed (a bit flamboyantly, I've always felt) in a film called *Black Magic*. He assumed the role of Cagliostro and mesmerized everyone with whom he came into contact. In the film, Welles had a dark, piercing stare. He looked up from under heavy brows and spoke sepulchrally. Very affecting. This was the pose I now assumed with Kane and his wife. "No anthropomorphism at all. The group mind is hardly a new concept. It occurs in insects, in certain aquatic species, even in the plant world. If—as we now believe, because of the discovery of quasars—the 'big bang' theory of the conception of the universe is correct, that it all sprang full-blown into existence—and even Hoyle has given up on the 'constantly regenerating' theory—then surely it isn't such a quantum jump in logic to assume sentience can suddenly big-bang into existence."

They just looked at me. I believe they thought I was serious.

I made my final point. "Our Neanderthal ancestors. Does not a big bang of suddenly-sparked intelligence answer the question of how we came to be sitting here? I submit the same has happened with automobiles. A mass mind, a gestalt, if you prefer. But a society within a society. The world of the wheeled."

When I was six years old my mother developed a nasty bronchial cough. It was most strongly advised by the family physician that she go to Arizona for several months. She took me with her. I missed the keystone subjects of arithmetic during that school year, as a result. To this day, and surreptitiously of course, I still have recourse to my fingers when subtracting bank balances. For this reason I have never been interested in science or the rather tedious rigors of mathematics. I have never been able to read a text on the physical or social sciences completely. What I had said to them was the sheerest gibberish, through which holes could be punched by any first-year physics major. But Kane was a Chaucerian scholar—and he was amused by it all—while his wife was merely a fraud.

I took my leave soon after, leaving them both amazed and perplexed. The conversation had stimulated me; it had been the first gloriously bizarre sequence I had played in many months.

I decided to walk home, though the night was chill and my apartment quite a distance. I have always been a religious man.

Consider the similarities between the cultures of South America and the Mideast; similarities difficult to explain. The simultaneous presence in both cultures of the religious figure of the fish, the Gregorian calendar, which parallels the stone calendars of the early Americans, the pyramid, which exists in both but in no other primitive society. Is it possible there was a link, two thousand years ago, between the land of, say, Judea and the land of the Aztecs? There is a story told—a fable only—of a white god who came upon the shores of the Aztecs during a period in history that would parallel the years from ages twelve to thirty during which nothing was heard of Jesus of Nazareth. They are known as the "lost" years of Jesus. The legend goes that this white man, whose like had never before been seen, went among the people and spoke of things that seemed wondrous and magical, of a kingdom of life after death. It was he, the story says, who introduced the symbol of the fish with its religious significance. Did he, as well, bring the pyramid structure and the calendar? We will never know, though historians have speculated that Jesus may well have taken passage with Phoenician sailors and found his way to the new continent. We will never know, but the legend adds one more mystery: the white prophet promised to return. And the people waited, and beat from purest gold an infinitude of gifts for his return.

Abandoned automobiles brought to a wrecking yard are first pressed flat by a stamping press. They are then stacked for the crusher. The crusher runs them down a treadmill track to a cubicle with sliding walls. They are pressed horizontally. Then the endwalls move together and the compressed remains of the automobile are squashed into a block that weighs several tons. The blocks, the cubes, are lifted by an enormously powerful electromagnet and stacked for reuse or resale. *Requiescat in pace.*

Bernal Díaz del Castillo, conquistador with Cortés, in his personal history entitled THE DISCOVERY AND CONQUEST OF MEXICO, 1517–1521, tells of being met on the beach by Indians who came bearing great gifts of gold, as though they had *expected* the arrival of the Spaniards. Cortés, now judged by history to have been a senseless butcher, began slaughtering the natives almost before the boats had beached. Castillo comments that they were unarmed, seemed, in fact, to be ready to *worship* the white men who had come from the sea. But when the Spanish massacre began, the terror-filled word went back through the jungle, up the line to the endless procession of natives carrying their golden oblations in litters, and they buried the gold along the trail and vanished back the way they had come. A conclusion can be drawn. The natives of Tabasco who came to meet Cortés were filled with awe and love for the strangers. They were waiting for them, to pay them homage. Only the rampaging slaughter of their kind cleared their minds of the dreams of . . . what? A white god returned as promised? We will never know.

Gold ingots and gorgeous objects of the precious metal are being found, to this day, along the jungle trails inland from the sea at Tabasco.

The cubes of squared automobiles sit in the reclamation yards through rain and Winter, through night and Resale. They do not speak. They are not expected to speak.

In May I was terminated. I took a position as a junior editor with a Latin American book publisher, far uptown on the West Side. Mona Sündberg and her paramour went off to ski in Lapland. So they said. I don't know if it is possible to ski in Lapland. Emil Kane was mugged and robbed in broad daylight on Sixth Avenue. His wife blamed niggers. Blacks, I told her, when she called to impart the news. She never called back. I have grown to understand this kind of woman.

Working quite late one evening, I found myself on Fifth Avenue, far uptown. Passing under the viaduct where the IRT Seventh Avenue subway thunders aboveground, I saw a group of black, colored, Negro children smashing the windows of abandoned cars left naked under the brick structure. They were using ball-peen hammers.

If sentience suddenly sparks, and if they do, indeed, have a group mind, then they must have a society. One can hardly think otherwise. A culture. A species. A mass belief. With gods and legends and secret dreams they dream while their motors idle.

I sought no trouble with the children. They seemed capable of anything. But as I passed a dark-blue Chevrolet with its doors gone, I saw a small plastic figure of the Blessed Virgin Mary on the dashboard. For the first time in my life, I felt I must perform an act of senseless commitment. I felt tears in my eyes. I wanted to save the figure from the depredations of the graverobbers.

I bent over so they might not see me as I made my way to the car, and I reached inside and grasped the white plastic form of Mary.

There was a thunderous sound . . . surely the subway train clattering overhead.

When I opened my eyes I looked out from the pillar wall of the viaduct. I could see very clearly through the bricks. The night was no lighter. The children were still at their work.

I could not speak, nor could I move. I was imprisoned in the stone. As I am.

Why, Emil Kane's wife might ask, why Thom, are you there forever in stone, eternally crypted in brick? To which I would reply, I've learned to my dismay, that worship is like the stock market. There are winning issues and there are, of course, losers. Placing one's faith on a failing stock can be no less disastrous than placing one's faith on a downtrending deity.

He is a young God, and a jealous one. He does not like his graves robbed, the corpses of his supplicants defiled. But the children *believe*, you see; and I did not. Hardly a crime. But 'twill serve.

I am a religious man. I have always been a religious man—and one would think that should count for something.

Apparently, it does not.

The Whimper of Whipped Dogs

On the night after the day she had stained the louvered window shutters of her new apartment on East 52nd Street, Beth saw a woman slowly and hideously knifed to death in the courtyard of her building. She was one of twenty-six witnesses to the ghoulish scene, and, like them, she did nothing to stop it.

She saw it all, every moment of it, without break and with no impediment to her view. Quite madly, the thought crossed her mind as she watched in horrified fascination, that she had the sort of marvelous line of observation Napoleon had sought when he caused to have constructed at the *Comédie-Française* theaters, a curtained box at the rear, so he could watch the audience as well as the stage. The night was clear, the moon was full, she had just turned off the 11:30 movie on Channel 2 after the second commercial break, realizing she had already seen Robert Taylor in *Westward the Women*, and had disliked it the first time; and the apartment was quite dark.

She went to the window, to raise it six inches for the night's sleep, and she saw the woman stumble into the courtyard. She was sliding along the wall, clutching her left arm with her right hand. Con Ed had installed mercury-vapor lamps on the poles; there had been sixteen assaults in seven months; the courtyard was illuminated with a chill purple glow that made the blood streaming down the woman's left arm look black and shiny. Beth saw every detail with utter clarity, as though magnified a thousand power under a microscope, solarized as if it had been a television commercial.

The woman threw back her head, as if she were trying to scream, but there was no sound. Only the traffic on First Avenue, late cabs foraging for singles paired for the night at Maxwell's Plum and Friday's and Adam's Apple. But that was over there, beyond. Where *she* was, down there seven floors below, in the courtyard, everything seemed silently suspended in an invisible force-field.

Beth stood in the darkness of her apartment, and realized she had raised the window completely. A tiny balcony lay just over the low sill; now not even glass separated her from the sight; just the wrought-iron balcony railing and seven floors to the courtyard below.

The woman staggered away from the wall, her head still thrown back, and Beth could see she was in her mid-thirties, with dark hair cut in a shag; it was impossible to tell if she was pretty: terror had contorted her features and her mouth was a twisted black slash, opened but emitting no sound. Cords stood out in her neck. She had lost one shoe, and her steps were uneven, threatening to dump her to the pavement.

The man came around the corner of the building, into the courtyard. The knife he held was enormous—or perhaps it only seemed so: Beth remembered a bone-handled fish knife her father had used one summer at the lake in Maine: it folded back on itself and locked, revealing eight inches of serrated blade. The knife in the hand of the dark man in the courtyard seemed to be similar.

The woman saw him and tried to run, but he leaped across the distance between them and grabbed her by the hair and pulled her head back as though he would slash her throat in the next reaper-motion.

Then the woman screamed.

The sound skirled up into the courtyard like bats trapped in an echo chamber, unable to find a way out, driven mad. It went on and on . . .

The man struggled with her and she drove her elbows into his sides and he tried to protect himself, spinning her around by her hair, the terrible scream going up and up and never stopping. She came loose and he was left with a fistful of hair torn out by the roots. As she spun out, he slashed straight across and opened her up just below the breasts. Blood sprayed through her clothing and the man was soaked; it seemed to drive him even more berserk. He went at her again, as she tried to hold herself together, the blood pouring down over her arms.

She tried to run, teetered against the wall, slid sidewise, and the man struck the brick surface. She was away, stumbling over a flower bed, falling, getting to her knees as he threw himself on her again. The knife came up in a flashing arc that illuminated the blade strangely with purple light. And still she screamed.

Lights came on in dozens of apartments and people appeared at windows.

He drove the knife to the hilt into her back, high on the right shoulder. He used both hands.

Beth caught it all in jagged flashes—the man, the woman, the knife, the blood, the expressions on the faces of those watching from the windows. Then lights clicked off in the windows, but they still stood there, watching.

She wanted to yell, to scream, "What are you doing to that woman?" But her throat was frozen, two iron hands that had been immersed in dry ice for ten thousand years clamped around her neck. She could feel the blade sliding into her own body.

Somehow—it seemed impossible but there it was down there, happening somehow—the woman struggled erect and *pulled* herself off the knife. Three steps, she took three steps and fell into the flower bed again. The man was howling now, like a great beast, the sounds inarticulate, bubbling up from his stomach. He fell on her and the knife went up and came down, then again, and again, and finally it was all a blur of motion, and her scream of lunatic bats went on till it faded off and was gone.

Beth stood in the darkness, trembling and crying, the sight filling her eyes with horror. And when she could no longer bear to look at what he was doing down there to the unmoving piece of meat over which he worked, she looked up and around at the windows of darkness where the others still stood—even as she stood—and somehow she could see their faces, bruise-purple with the dim light from the mercury lamps, and there was a universal sameness to their expressions. The women stood with their nails biting into the upper arms of their men, their tongues edging from the corners of their mouths; the men were wild-eyed and smiling. They all looked as though they were at cock fights. Breathing deeply. Drawing some sustenance from the grisly scene below. An exhalation of sound, deep, deep, as though from caverns beneath the earth. Flesh pale and moist.

And it was then that she realized the courtyard had grown foggy, as though mist off the East River had rolled up 52nd Street in a veil that would obscure the details of what the knife and the man were still doing . . . endlessly doing it . . . long after there was any joy in it . . . still doing it . . . again and again . . .

But the fog was unnatural, thick and gray and filled with tiny scintillas of light. She stared at it, rising up in the empty space of the courtyard. Bach in the cathedral, stardust in a vacuum chamber.

Beth saw eyes.

There, up there, at the ninth floor and higher, two great eyes, as surely as night and the moon, there were *eyes*. And—a face? Was that a face, could she be sure, was she imagining it . . . a face? In the roiling vapors of chill fog something lived, something brooding and patient and utterly malevolent had been summoned up to witness what was happening down there in the flower bed. Beth tried to look away, but could not. The eyes, those primal burning eyes, filled with an abysmal antiquity yet frighteningly bright and anxious like the eyes of a child; eyes filled with tomb depths, ancient and new, chasm-filled, burning, gigantic and deep as an abyss, holding her, compelling her. The shadow play was being staged not only for the tenants in their windows, watching and drinking of the scene, but for some *other*. Not on frigid tundra or waste moors, not in subterranean caverns or on some faraway world circling a dying sun, but here, in the city, here the eyes of that *other* watched.

Shaking with the effort, Beth wrenched her eyes from those burning depths up there beyond the ninth floor, only to see again the horror that had brought that *other*. And she was struck for the first time by the awfulness of what she was witnessing, she was released from the immobility that had held her like a coelacanth in shale, she was filled with the blood thunder pounding against the membranes of her mind: she had *stood* there! She had done nothing, nothing! A woman had been butchered and she had said nothing, done nothing. Tears had been useless, tremblings had been pointless, she *had done nothing*!

Then she heard hysterical sounds midway between laughter and giggling, and as she stared up into that great face rising in the fog and chimneysmoke of the night, she heard *herself* making those deranged gibbon noises and from the man below a pathetic, trapped sound, like the whimper of whipped dogs.

She was staring up into that face again. She hadn't wanted to see it again—ever. But she was locked with those smoldering eyes, overcome with the feeling that they were childlike, though she *knew* they were incalculably ancient.

Then the butcher below did an unspeakable thing and Beth reeled with dizziness and caught the edge of the window before she could tumble out onto the balcony; she steadied herself and fought for breath.

She felt herself being looked at, and for a long moment of frozen terror she feared she might have caught the attention of that face up there in the fog. She clung to the window, feeling everything growing faraway and dim, and stared straight across the court. She *was* being watched. Intently. By the young man in the seventh-floor window across from her own apartment. Steadily, he was looking at her. Through the strange fog with its burning eyes feasting on the sight below, he was staring at her.

As she felt herself blacking out, in the moment before unconsciousness, the thought flickered and fled that there was something terribly familiar about his face.

It rained the next day. East 52nd Street was slick and shining with the oil rainbows. The rain washed the dog turds into the gutters and nudged them down and down to the catch-basin openings. People bent against the slanting rain, hidden beneath umbrellas, looking like enormous, scurrying black mushrooms. Beth went out to get the newspapers after the police had come and gone.

The news reports dwelled with loving emphasis on the twenty-six tenants of the building who had watched in cold interest as Leona Ciarelli, 37, of 455 Fort Washington Avenue, Manhattan, had been systematically stabbed to death by Burton H. Wells, 41, an unemployed electrician, who had been subsequently shot to death by two off-duty police officers when he burst into Michael's Pub on 55th Street, covered with blood and brandishing a knife that authorities later identified as the murder weapon.

She had thrown up twice that day. Her stomach seemed incapable of retaining anything solid, and the taste of bile lay along the back of her tongue. She could not blot the scenes of the night before from her mind; she re-ran them again and again, every movement of that reaper arm playing over and over as though on a short loop of memory. The woman's head thrown back for silent screams. The blood. Those eyes in the fog.

She was drawn again and again to the window, to stare down into the courtyard and the street. She tried to superimpose over the bleak Manhattan concrete the view from her window in Swann House at Bennington: the little yard and another white, frame dormitory; the fantastic apple trees; and from the other window the rolling hills and gorgeous Vermont countryside; her memory skittered through the change of seasons. But there was always concrete and the rain-slick streets; the rain on the pavement was black and shiny as blood.

She tried to work, rolling up the tambour closure of the old rolltop desk she had bought on Lexington Avenue and hunching over the graph sheet of choreographer's charts. But Labanotation was merely a Jackson Pollock jumble of arcane hieroglyphics to her today, instead of the careful representation of eurhythmics she had studied four years to perfect. And before that, Farmington.

The phone rang. It was the secretary from the Taylor Dance Company, asking when she would be free. She had to beg off. She looked at her hand, lying on the graph sheets of figures Laban had devised, and she saw her fingers trembling. She had to beg off. Then she called Guzman at the Downtown Ballet Company, to tell him she would be late with the charts.

"My God, lady, I have ten dancers sitting around in a rehearsal hall getting their leotards sweaty! What do you expect me to do?"

She explained what had happened the night before. And as she told him, she realized the newspapers had been justified in holding that tone against the twenty-six witnesses to the death of Leona Ciarelli. Paschal Guzman listened, and when he spoke again, his voice was several octaves lower, and he spoke more slowly. He said he understood and she could take a little longer to prepare the charts. But there was a distance in his voice, and he hung up while she was thanking him.

She dressed in an argyle sweater vest in shades of dark purple, and a pair of fitted khaki gabardine trousers. She had to go out, to walk around. To do what? To think about other things. As she pulled on the Fred Braun chunky heels, she idly wondered if that heavy silver bracelet was still in the window of Georg Jensen's. In the elevator, the young man from the window across the courtyard stared at her. Beth felt her body begin to tremble again. She went deep into the corner of the box when he entered behind her.

Between the fifth and fourth floors, he hit the *off* switch and the elevator jerked to a halt.

Beth stared at him and he smiled innocently.

"Hi. My name's Gleeson, Ray Gleeson, I'm in 714."

She wanted to demand he turn the elevator back on, by what right did he pre*sume* to do such a thing, what did he mean by this, turn it on at once or suffer the consequences. That was what she *wanted* to do. Instead, from the same place she had heard the gibbering laughter the night before, she heard her voice, much smaller and much less possessed than she had trained it to be, saying, "Beth O'Neill, I live in 701."

The thing about it, was that *the elevator was stopped*. And she was frightened. But he leaned against the paneled wall, very well dressed, shoes polished, hair combed and probably blown dry with a hand dryer, and he *talked* to her as if they were across a table at L'Argenteuil. "You just moved in, huh?"

"About two months ago."

"Where did you go to school? Bennington or Sarah Lawrence?"

"Bennington. How did you know?"

He laughed, and it was a nice laugh. "I'm an editor at a religious book publisher; every year we get half a dozen Bennington, Sarah Lawrence, Smith girls. They come hopping in like grasshoppers, ready to revolutionize the publishing industry."

"What's wrong with that? You sound like you don't care for them."

"Oh, I *love* them, they're marvelous. They think they know how to write better than the authors we publish. Had one darlin' little item who was given galleys of three books to proof, and she rewrote all three. I think she's working as a table-swabber in a Horn & Hardart's now."

She didn't reply to that. She would have pegged him as an anti-feminist, ordinarily, if it had been anyone else speaking. But the eyes. There was something terribly familiar about his face. She was enjoying the conversation; she rather liked him.

"What's the nearest big city to Bennington?"

"Albany, New York. About sixty miles."

"How long does it take to drive there?"

"From Bennington? About an hour and a half."

"Must be a nice drive, that Vermont country, really pretty. They went coed, I understand. How's that working out?"

"I don't know, really."

"You don't know?"

"It happened around the time I was graduating."

"What did you major in?"

"I was a dance major, specializing in Labanotation. That's the way you write choreography."

"It's all electives, I gather. You don't have to take anything required, like sciences, for example." He didn't change tone as he said, "That was a terrible thing last night. I saw you watching. I guess a lot of us were watching. It was a really terrible thing."

She nodded dumbly. Fear came back.

"I understand the cops got him. Some nut, they don't even know why he killed her, or why he went charging into that bar. It was really an awful thing. I'd very much like to have dinner with you one night soon, if you're not attached."

"That would be all right."

"Maybe Wednesday. There's an Argentinian place I know. You might like it."

"That would be all right."

"Why don't you turn on the elevator, and we can go," he said, and smiled again. She did it, wondering why she had stopped the elevator in the first place.

On her third date with him, they had their first fight. It was at a party thrown by a director of television commercials. He lived on the ninth floor of their building. He had just done a series of spots for *Sesame Street* (the letters "U" for Underpass, "T" for Tunnel, lower-case "b" for boats, "c" for cars; the numbers 1 to 6 and the numbers 1 to 20; the words *light* and *dark*) and was celebrating his move from the arena of commercial tawdriness (and its attendant $75,000 a year) to the sweet fields of educational programming (and its accompanying descent into low-pay respectability). There was a logic in his joy Beth could not quite understand, and when she talked with him about it, in a far corner of the kitchen, his arguments didn't seem to parse. But he seemed happy, and his girlfriend, a long-legged ex-model from Philadelphia, continued to drift to him and away from him, like some exquisite undersea plant, touching his hair and kissing his neck, murmuring words of pride and barely submerged sexuality. Beth found it bewildering, though the celebrants were all bright and lively.

In the living room, Ray was sitting on the arm of the sofa, hustling a stewardess named Luanne. Beth could tell he was hustling; he was trying to look casual. When he *wasn't* hustling, he was always intense, about everything. She decided to ignore it, and wandered around the apartment, sipping at a Tanqueray and tonic.

There were framed prints of abstract shapes clipped from a calendar printed in Germany. They were in metal Bonniers frames.

In the dining room a huge door from a demolished building somewhere in the city had been handsomely stripped, teaked and refinished. It was now the dinner table.

A Lightolier fixture attached to the wall over the bed swung out, levered up and down, tipped, and its burnished globe-head revolved a full three hundred and sixty degrees.

She was standing in the bedroom, looking out the window, when she realized *this* had been one of the rooms in which light had gone on, gone off; one of the rooms that had contained a silent watcher at the death of Leona Ciarelli.

When she returned to the living room, she looked around more carefully. With only three or four exceptions—the stewardess, a young married couple from the second floor, a stockbroker from Hemphill, Noyes—*everyone* at the party had been a witness to the slaying.

"I'd like to go," she told him.

"Why, aren't you having a good time?" asked the stewardess, a mocking smile crossing her perfect little face.

"Like all Bennington ladies," Ray said, answering for Beth, "she is enjoying herself most by not enjoying herself at all. It's a trait of the anal retentive. Being here in someone else's apartment, she can't empty ashtrays or rewind the toilet paper roll so it doesn't hang a tongue, and being tightassed, her nature demands we go.

"All right, Beth, let's say our goodbyes and take off. The Phantom Rectum strikes again."

She slapped him and the stewardess's eyes widened. But the smile remained frozen where it had appeared.

He grabbed her wrist before she could do it again. "Garbanzo beans, baby," he said, holding her wrist tighter than necessary.

They went back to her apartment, and after sparring silently with kitchen cabinet doors slammed and the television being tuned too loud, they got to her bed, and he tried to perpetuate the metaphor by fucking her in the ass. He had her on elbows and knees before she realized what he was doing; she struggled to turn over and he rode her bucking and tossing without a sound. And when it was clear to him that she would never permit it, he grabbed her breast from underneath and squeezed so hard she howled in pain. He dumped her on her back, rubbed himself between her legs a dozen times, and came on her stomach.

Beth lay with her eyes closed and an arm thrown across her face. She wanted to cry, but found she could not. Ray lay on her and said nothing. She wanted to rush to the bathroom and shower, but he did not move, till long after his semen had dried on their bodies.

"Who did you date at college?" he asked.

"I didn't date anyone very much." Sullen.

"No heavy makeouts with wealthy lads from Williams and Dartmouth . . . no Amherst intellectuals begging you to save them from creeping faggotry by permitting them to stick their carrots in your sticky little slit?"

"Stop it!"

"Come on, baby, it couldn't all have been knee socks and little round circle-pins. You don't expect me to believe you didn't get a little mouthful of cock from time to time. It's only, what? about fifteen miles to Williamstown? I'm sure the Williams werewolves were down burning the highway to your cunt on weekends; you can level with old Uncle Ray . . ."

"Why are you like this?!" She started to move, to get away from him, and he grabbed her by the shoulder, forced her to lie down again. Then he rose up over her and said, "I'm like this because I'm a New Yorker, baby. Because I live in this fucking city every day. Because I have to play patty-cake with the ministers and other sanctified holy-joe assholes who want their goodness and lightness tracts published by the Blessed Sacrament Publishing and Storm Window Company of 277 Park Avenue, when what I *really* want to do is toss the stupid psalm-suckers out the thirty-seventh-floor window and listen to them quote chapter-and-worse all the way down. Because I've lived in this great big snapping dog of a city all my life and I'm mad as a mudfly, for chrissakes!"

She lay unable to move, breathing shallowly, filled with a sudden pity and affection for him. His face was white and strained, and she knew he was saying things to her that only a bit too much Almadén and exact timing would have let him say.

"What do you expect from me," he said, his voice softer now, but no less intense, "do you expect kindness and gentility and understanding and a hand on *your* hand when the smog burns your eyes? I can't do it, I haven't got it. No one has it in this cesspool of a city. Look around you; what do you think is happening here? They take rats and they put them in boxes and when there are too many of them, some of the little fuckers go out of their minds and start gnawing the rest to death. *It ain't no different here, baby!* It's rat time for everybody in this madhouse. You can't expect to jam as many people into this stone thing as we do, with buses and taxis and dogs shitting themselves scrawny and noise night and day and no money and not enough places to live and no place to go to have a decent think . . . you can't do it without making the time right for some godforsaken other kind of thing to be born! You can't hate everyone around you, and kick every beggar and nigger and *mestizo* shithead, you can't have cabbies stealing from you and taking tips they don't deserve, and then cursing you, you can't walk in the soot till your collar turns black, and your body stinks with the smell of flaking brick and decaying brains, you can't do it without calling up some kind of awful–"

He stopped.

His face bore the expression of a man who has just received brutal word of the death of a loved one. He suddenly lay down, rolled over, and turned off.

She lay beside him, trembling, trying desperately to remember where she had seen his face before.

He didn't call her again, after the night of the party. And when they met in the hall, he pointedly turned away, as though he had given her some obscure chance and she had refused to take it. Beth thought she understood: though Ray Gleeson had not been her first affair, he had been the first to reject her so completely. The first to put her not only out of his bed and his life, but even out of his world. It was as though she were invisible, not even beneath contempt, simply not there.

She busied herself with other things.

She took on three new charting jobs for Guzman and a new group that had formed on Staten Island, of all places. She worked furiously and they gave her new assignments; they even paid her.

She tried to decorate the apartment with a less precise touch. Huge poster blowups of Merce Cunningham and Martha Graham replaced the Brueghel prints that had reminded her of the view looking down the hill toward Williams. The tiny balcony outside her window, the balcony she had steadfastly refused to stand upon since the night of the slaughter, the night of the fog with eyes, that balcony she swept and set about with little flower boxes in which she planted geraniums, petunias, dwarf zinnias, and other hardy perennials. Then, closing the window, she went to give herself, to involve herself in this city to which she had brought her ordered life.

And the city responded to her overtures:

Seeing off an old friend from Bennington, at Kennedy International, she stopped at the terminal coffee shop to have a sandwich. The counter–like a moat–surrounded a center service island that had huge advertising cubes rising above it on burnished poles. The cubes proclaimed the delights of Fun City. *New York Is a Summer Festival,* they said, and *Joseph Papp Presents Shakespeare in Central Park* and *Visit the Bronx Zoo* and *You'll Adore Our Contentious but Lovable Cabbies*. The food emerged from a window far down the service area and moved slowly on a conveyor belt through the hordes of screaming waitresses who slathered the counter with redolent washcloths. The lunchroom had all the charm and dignity of a steel-rolling mill, and approximately the same noise level. Beth ordered a cheeseburger that cost a dollar and a quarter, and a glass of milk.

When it came, it was cold, the cheese unmelted, and the patty of meat resembling nothing so much as a dirty scouring pad. The bun was cold and untoasted. There was no lettuce under the patty.

Beth managed to catch the waitress's eye. The girl approached with an annoyed look. "Please toast the bun and may I have a piece of lettuce?" Beth said.

"We dun' do that," the waitress said, turning half away as though she would walk in a moment

"You don't do what?"

"We dun' toass the bun here."

"Yes, but I *want* the bun toasted," Beth said firmly.

"An' you got to pay for extra lettuce."

"If I was asking for *extra* lettuce," Beth said, getting annoyed, "I would pay for it, but since there's *no* lettuce here, I don't think I should be charged extra for the first piece."

"We dun' do that."

The waitress started to walk away. "Hold it," Beth said, raising her voice just enough so the assembly-line eaters on either side stared at her. "You mean to tell me I have to pay a dollar and a quarter and I can't get a piece of lettuce or even get the bun toasted?"

"Ef you dun' like it . . ."

"Take it back."

"You gotta pay for it, you order it."

"I said take it back, I don't want the fucking thing!"

The waitress scratched it off the check. The milk cost 27¢ and tasted going-sour. It was the first time in her life that Beth had said *that* word aloud.

At the cashier's stand, Beth said to the sweating man with the felt-tip pens in his shirt pocket, "Just out of curiosity, are you interested in complaints?"

"No!" he said, snarling, quite literally snarling. He did not look up as he punched out 73¢ and it came rolling down the chute.

The city responded to her overtures:

It was raining again. She was trying to cross Second Avenue, with the light. She stepped off the curb and a car came sliding through the red and splashed her. "Hey!" she yelled.

"Eat shit, sister!" the driver yelled back, turning the corner.

Her boots, her legs and her overcoat were splattered with mud. She stood trembling on the curb.

The city responded to her overtures:

She emerged from the building at One Astor Place with her big briefcase full of Laban charts; she was adjusting her rain scarf about her head. A well-dressed man with an attache case thrust the handle of his umbrella up between her legs from the rear. She gasped and dropped her case.

The city responded and responded and responded.

Her overtures altered quickly.

The old drunk with the stippled cheeks extended his hand and mumbled words. She cursed him and walked on up Broadway past the beaver film houses.

She crossed against the lights on Park Avenue, making hackies slam their brakes to avoid hitting her; she used *that* word frequently now.

When she found herself having a drink with a man who had elbowed up beside her in the singles' bar, she felt faint and knew she should go home.

But Vermont was so far away.

Nights later. She had come home from the Lincoln Center ballet, and gone straight to bed. Lying half-asleep in her bedroom, she heard an alien sound. One room away, in the living room, in the dark, there was a sound. She slipped out of bed and went to the door between the rooms. She fumbled silently for the switch on the lamp just inside the living room, and found it, and clicked it on. A black man in a leather car coat was trying to get *out* of the apartment. In that first flash of light filling the room she noticed the television set beside him on the floor as he struggled with the door, she noticed the police lock and bar had been broken in a new and clever manner *New York* magazine had not yet reported in a feature article on apartment ripoffs, she noticed that he had gotten his foot tangled in the telephone cord that she had requested be extra-long so she could carry the instrument into the bathroom, I don't want to miss any business calls when the shower is running; she noticed all things in perspective and one thing with sharpest clarity: the expression on the burglar's face.

There was something familiar in that expression.

He almost had the door open, but now he closed it, and slipped the police lock. He took a step toward her.

Beth went back, into the darkened bedroom.

The city responded to her overtures.

She backed against the wall at the head of the bed. Her hand fumbled in the shadows for the telephone. His shape filled the doorway, light, all light behind him.

In silhouette it should not have been possible to tell, but somehow she knew he was wearing gloves and the only marks he would leave would be deep bruises, very blue, almost black, with the tinge under them of blood that had been stopped in its course.

He came for her, arms hanging casually at his sides. She tried to climb over the bed, and he grabbed her from behind, ripping her nightgown. Then he had a hand around her neck and he pulled her backward. She fell off the bed, landed at his feet and his hold was broken. She scuttled across the floor and for a moment she had the respite to feel terror. She was going to die, and she was frightened.

He trapped her in the corner between the closet and the bureau and kicked her. His foot caught her in the thigh as she folded tighter, smaller, drawing her legs up. She was cold.

Then he reached down with both hands and pulled her erect by her hair. He slammed her head against the wall. Everything slid up in her sight as though running off the edge of the world. He slammed her head against the wall again, and she felt something go soft over her right ear.

When he tried to slam her a third time she reached out blindly for his face and ripped down with her nails. He howled in pain and she hurled herself forward, arms wrapping themselves around his waist. He stumbled backward and in a tangle of thrashing arms and legs they fell out onto the little balcony.

Beth landed on the bottom, feeling the window boxes jammed up against her spine and legs. She fought to get to her feet, and her nails hooked into his shirt under the open jacket, ripping. Then she was on her feet again and they struggled silently.

He whirled her around, bent her backward across the wrought-iron railing. Her face was turned outward.

They were standing in their windows, watching.

Through the fog she could see them watching. Through the fog she recognized their expressions. Through the fog she heard them breathing in unison, bellows breathing of expectation and wonder. Through the fog.

And the black man punched her in the throat. She gagged and started to black out and could not draw air into her lungs. Back, back, he bent her farther back and she was looking up, straight up, toward the ninth floor and higher . . .

Up there: eyes.

The words Ray Gleeson had said in a moment filled with what he had become, with the utter hopelessness and finality of the choice the city had forced on him, the words came back. *You can't live in this city and survive unless you have protection . . . you can't live this way, like rats driven mad, without making the time right for some godforsaken other kind of thing to be born . . . you can't do it without calling up some kind of awful . . .*

God! A new God, an ancient God come again with the eyes and hunger of a child, a deranged blood God of fog and street violence. A God who needed worshippers and offered the choices of death as a victim or life as an eternal witness to the deaths of *other* chosen victims. A God to fit the times, a God of streets and people.

She tried to shriek, to appeal to Ray, to the director in the bedroom window of his ninth-floor apartment with his long-legged Philadelphia model beside him and his fingers inside her as they worshipped in their holiest of ways, to the others who had been at the party that had been Ray's offer of a chance to join their congregation. She wanted to be saved from having to make that choice.

But the black man had punched her in the throat, and now his hands were on her, one on her chest, the other in her face, the smell of leather filling her where the nausea could not. And she understood Ray had *cared,* had wanted her to take the chance offered; but she had come from a world of little white dormitories and Vermont countryside; it was not a real world. *This* was the real world and up there was the God who ruled this world, and she had rejected him, had said no to one of his priests and servitors. *Save me! Don't make me do it!*

She knew she had to call out, to make appeal, to try and win the approbation of that God. *I can't . . . save me!*

She struggled and made terrible little mewling sounds trying to summon the words to cry out, and suddenly she crossed a line, and screamed up into the echoing courtyard with a voice Leona Ciarelli had never known enough to use.

"Him! Take him! Not me! I'm yours, I love you, I'm yours! Take him, not me, please not me, take him, take him, I'm yours!"

And the black man was suddenly lifted away, wrenched off her, and off the balcony, whirled straight up into the fog-thick air in the courtyard, as Beth sank to her knees on the ruined flower boxes.

She was half-conscious, and could not be sure she saw it just that way, but up he went, end over end, whirling and spinning like a charred leaf.

And the form took firmer shape. Enormous paws with claws and shapes that no animal she had ever seen had ever possessed, and the burglar, black, poor, terrified, whimpering like a whipped dog, was stripped of his flesh. His body was opened with a thin incision, and there was a rush as all the blood poured from him like a sudden cloudburst, and yet he was still alive, twitching with the involuntary horror of a frog's leg shocked with an electric current. Twitched, and twitched again as he was torn piece by piece to shreds. Pieces of flesh and bone and half a face with an eye blinking furiously, cascaded down past Beth, and hit the cement below with sodden thuds. And still he was alive, as his organs were squeezed and musculature and bile and shit and skin were rubbed, sandpapered together and let fall. It went on and on, as the death of Leona Ciarelli had gone on and on, and she understood with the blood-knowledge of survivors *at any cost* that the reason the witnesses to the death of Leona Ciarelli had done nothing was not that they had been frozen with horror, that they didn't want to get involved, or that they were inured to death by years of television slaughter.

They were worshippers at a black mass the city had demanded be staged; not once, but a thousand times a day in this insane asylum of steel and stone.

Now she was on her feet, standing half-naked in her ripped nightgown, her hand tightening on the wrought-iron railing, begging to see more, to drink deeper.

Now she was one of them, as the pieces of the night's sacrifice fell past her, bleeding and screaming.

Tomorrow the police would come again, and they would question her, and she would say how terrible it had been, that burglar, and how she had fought, afraid he would rape her and kill her, and how he had fallen, and she had no idea how he had been so hideously mangled and ripped apart, but a seven-storey fall, after all . . .

Tomorrow she would not have to worry about walking in the streets, because no harm could come to her. Tomorrow she could even remove the police lock. Nothing in the city could do her any further evil, because she had made the only choice. She was now a dweller in the city, now wholly and richly a part of it. Now she was taken to the bosom of her God.

She felt Ray beside her, standing beside her, holding her, protecting her, his hand on her naked backside, and she watched the fog swirl up and fill the courtyard, fill the city, fill her eyes and her soul and her heart with its power. As Ray's naked body pressed tightly inside her, she drank deeply of the night, knowing whatever voices she heard from this moment forward would be the voices not of whipped dogs, but those of strong, meat-eating beasts.

At last she was unafraid, and it was so good, so very good *not* to be afraid.

When inward life dries up, when feeling decreases and apathy increases, when one cannot affect or even genuinely touch another person, violence flares up as a daimonic necessity for contact, a mad drive forcing touch in the most direct way possible.

Rollo May,
LOVE AND WILL

V

A STAB OF MERRIMENT

"I see myself as a cross between Jiminy Cricket and Zorro."

—"The Harlan Ellison Interview" by Gary G. Groth, *The Comics Journal* #53, Winter 1980

Harlan is a funny man.

Anybody who has attended one of his college lectures, or seen him as an amusing guest on television talk shows, or heard his manic repartee with the "group mind" as the host of KPFK-FM's "Mike Hodel's Hour 25," in Los Angeles, will tell you that Harlan is, unquestionably, a *funny* man.

His essays, book introductions, columns, story notes and myriad articles on myriad subjects fairly burst at the seams with bon mots, deadpan acerbic wit, and unstoppered affection for verbal slapstick. Yet Harlan's reputation in fiction is seldom linked to his humorous efforts. Despite the success of stories such as "Santa Claus vs. S.P.I.D.E.R.," "I'm Looking for Kadak," "How's the Night Life on Cissalda?" and "Prince Myshkin, and Hold the Relish," all of which are deliberately comic, they have done little to make a dent in his reputation as a writer of "serious" bent.

For it is the impact of Harlan's serious work that makes it stick in the mind, despite the leavenings of humor which provide relief from the tensions of even his most demanding stories. These flashes of wit and irony, these brief struts of grim satire, are so much a part of the serious stories that we tend to forget how hilarious Harlan can be when he wants to be.

The stories and gags featured here to illustrate Harlan's comedic turn do not include his longer and sometimes gentler works. Instead, you will find eleven mostly short pieces that come closer to producing the effect one gets from watching or hearing him perform on stage before an audience. They also reveal something of his great fondness for the work of writers such as Thurber, Leacock and De Vries, Lafferty, Wodehouse and Cuppy.

"The Voice in the Garden" (1967), "Erotophobia" (1971), "Mom" (1976), "Ecowareness" (1974), "The Outpost Undiscovered By Tourists" (1981), "Dept. of 'What Was the Question?' Dept." (1974) and "Dept. of 'Trivial Pursuit' Dept." (1972–1986) show something of the range and thrust of Harlan's humor. They can be described respectively as: a genre one-liner; a ribald interlude; a tragicomedy of recognition; a parable, told out of frustration and weary disillusionment, manifesting an old old pain; an antic retelling of the Nativity, perhaps a lot closer to the way it would go down today; a *New Yorker*-style squib; and five competition entries. And while the delivery is sometimes machine-gun rapid, aimed at the funny bone, and set to the accompaniment of a rim-shot, there is also the hollow laugh followed by the telling silence.

"Arthur [Byron Cover] looked at me seriously and said, 'You know, you're a very weird person.'"

—Introduction to "Shoppe Keeper," SHATTERDAY, Houghton Mifflin, 1980

The Voice in the Garden

After the bomb, the last man on Earth wandered through the rubble of Cleveland, Ohio. It had never been a particularly jaunty town, nor even remotely appealing to aesthetes. But now, like Detroit and Rangoon and Minsk and Yokohama, it had been reduced to a petulantly shattered Tinkertoy of lath and brickwork, twisted steel girders and melted glass.

As he picked his way around the dust heap that had been the Soldiers and Sailors Monument in what had been Public Square, his eyes red-rimmed from crying at the loss of humanity, he saw something he had not seen in Beirut or Venice or London. He saw the movement of another human being.

Celestial choruses sang in his head as he broke into a run across the pitted and blasted remains of Euclid Avenue. It was a woman!

She saw him, and in the very posture of her body, he knew she was filled with the same glory he felt. She knew! She began running toward him, her arms outstretched. They seemed to swim toward each other in a ballet of slow motion. He stumbled once, but got to his feet quickly and went on. They detoured around the crumpled tin of tortured metal that had once been automobiles, and met in front of the shattered carcass that was, in a time seemingly eons before, The May Co.

"I'm the last man!" he blurted. He could not keep the words inside, they fought to fill the air. "I'm the last, the very last. They're all dead, everyone but us. I'm the last man, and you're the last woman, and we'll have to mate and start the race again, and this time we'll do it right. No war, no hate, no bigotry, nothing but goodness . . . we'll do it, you'll see, it'll be fine, a bright new shining world from all this death and terror."

Her face was lit with an ethereal beauty, even beneath the soot and deprivation. "Yes, yes," she said. "It'll be just like that. I love you, because we're all there is left to love, each other."

He touched her hand. "I love you. What is your name?"

She flushed slightly. "Eve," she said. "What's yours?"

"Bernie," he said.

Erotophobia

It began with my mother, Nate Kleiser said, hating every word of it. The ignominy of it, oh. Not only here in a psychiatrist's office, not only lying on a forest green Naugahyde chaise, not only suffering every literate man's embarrassment at speaking lines Roth had portnoyzed into the ground, but to be speaking those lines to a *female* shrink, to be speaking them with choked-up emotion, to have started with mother . . .

Do you play with yourself much? asked Herr Doktor Felicia Bremmer, graduate of the Spitzbergen *Kopfschmerzenklinik*, 38–21–35.

I don't have to, Doctor, that's the trouble, Nate said. His head was beginning to ache, just behind the right eye. He heard the fingers of his left hand, quite independent of the directions of his brain, scrabbling at the forest green Naugahyde.

Perhaps you'd better go over that part again, Mr. Kleiser, Dr. Bremmer urged him. I'm not entirely sure I have the problem.

Okay, look, it's like this, for instance. He tried to sit up and she placed a soft, but firm hand on his chest and he lay still. Your reputation for handling uh, well, sex-oriented problems like mine is widespread, right? Right. So I get on a plane in Toronto, and I fly down here to Chicago to see you. So on the plane there're these two stewardesses, nice girls, and first this one, Chrissy Something, she offers me pillows and little bootie-socks, and then her partner, Jora Lee, she brings me a big glass of champagne—before anybody else gets served *anything*—and when she leans down to put it on the tray-table, she bites me on the ear. So in about ten minutes the two of them are fighting over me in the galley, and everybody's pushing those service buttons to call the stewardesses, and they aren't coming out of there except every few minutes to ask me do I like my steak well-done or rare, or offering me little cocktail mints . . . it really gets embarrassing.

And it goes on like that all through the damned flight, and they're just about on the verge of using those demonstration oxygen masks with the plastic air hoses to strangle one another, just to see which one will layover with me in Chicago, and I don't think I'm going to get off the goddam plane in one piece, when we come in to land and they *still* haven't served anybody, and the whole plane wants to kill me except they love me too much, and I know I'm going to have to fight my way down the ramp, and the only thing that saved me was a little black kid who was with his mother—who kept winking at me—puked all over the seat and the aisle and everything else, and I slipped past while they were trying to pour coffee grounds on it to kill the smell, and I got away.

Dr. Bremmer shook her head slowly. That's just terrible. Terrible.

Terrible? Hell, it's frightening. If you want to know the simple truth, Doctor, I'm scared out of my mind I'm going to be loved to death!

Well . . . Dr. Bremmer said. Isn't that a bit, just a bit overdramatic?

What are you doing, Doctor?

Nothing, Mr. Kleiser, not a thing. Just concentrate on the problem.

Concentrate? You've got to be kidding, Doctor; I can't think of anything *else*! Thank God I make my living as a cartoonist. I can mail my work in; if I actually had to go out and mix with people, it'd be all over for me in ten minutes.

I think you may be overstating, Mr. Kleiser.

Sure, easy enough for *you* to say, you aren't *me*. But it's been like this since I was a kid. I was always the most popular one in the class, the first one picked at dances when it was ladies' choice, the one both teams wanted when we played choose-up baseball or red rover, most likely to succeed, straight A's the teachers all wanted my body . . .

In college, added Dr. Bremmer.

College, hell: in *kindergarten*! I'm the only male I know who was forcibly raped in a girl's locker room before he was out of the fourth grade! You just don't under*stand*, dammit! I'm going to be loved . . . to . . . death!

Dr. Bremmer tried to quiet him. Nate's voice had grown frantic, strident.

Fear of being watched, of people wanting to hurt you, even—in extreme cases of advanced paranoia—people plotting to kill you . . . yes, that problem I know quite well, Mr. Kleiser. Paranoia. It's terribly common, particularly *these* days. But what *you're* telling me, well, that's something different, something exactly opposite. I've never encountered it. I wouldn't even know what to call it.

Nate closed his eyes.

Neither do I, he said.

Perhaps Erotophobia, fear of being loved, she said.

Dynamite. Now we have a name for it. A lot of good that does me. Nomenclature isn't my problem, sex is!

Mr. Kleiser, she said softly, you can't expect results instantaneously. You'll have to cooperate with me.

Cooperate? Hell, I shouldn't even be lying on this sofa with you!

Now, please, take it easy, Mr. Kleiser.

What are you doing?

Nothing.

You're unbuttoning your blouse. I can hear the fabric. I know that sound!

Nate sat straight up on the sofa, throwing the psychiatrist's leg off his lower body. She was half undressed; had, in fact, cleverly managed to rid herself of miniskirt, half-slip, shoes, panty hose and bikini briefs without his knowing it. Nate knew instantly that he had met a master of the art. In a pitched panic he bolted from the forest green Naugahyde chaise, and lurched toward the door.

Dr. Bremmer hurled herself sidewise, hanging half off the chaise. Her arm swept the desk, knocked files of *Psychology Today* to the floor. She grabbed and connected.

Jeezus! screamed Nate, doubling over.

Oops, sorry, darling, Dr. Bremmer murmured, scrabbling for him. He was in flight. She crawled after him, got her arms locked around one ankle. Take me with you, please, please, do with me what you will, hurt me, use me, abuse me, I love you, I love you! Hopelessly, desperately, completely.

Oh my God oh my God . . . mumbled Nate, clinging to the doorknob in an effort to keep his balance. Then the office door opened inward, catching Nate in the shoulder, knocking him off-balance so he stepped on the psychiatrist's back. Yes, yes, she said huskily, yes, dominate me, hurt me, I've denied myself all these years, I never knew what it was to love a man like you, take me, THE STORY OF O, yes . . . yes . . .

The open door now admitted Dr. Bremmer's nurse, a pimply woman of fifty who had watched Nate when he had waited in the reception room for the psychiatrist to see him. Her eyes widened as she saw the supine Dr. Bremmer and in a moment she was pulling the half-naked psychiatrist's arms from around Nate's ankle.

Before she could join in, before her astonishment could turn to lust, Nate hurtled through the door, caromed off two walls, hit the outer office door at a dead run and barely managed to get through before shattering the glass panel.

He was down the hall, into the self-service elevator, and safe before the two women could get to their feet. Nate Kleiser knew what fate befell those who were not fleet of foot.

As he ran down the street toward Michigan Avenue, he heard screaming and, looking up, saw Dr. Bremmer, her breasts now bare, hanging from the eighteenth storey window. He could barely make out what she was yelling.

If you leave me I'll kill myself!

Some people have alternatives, Nate thought, and ran.

Having gone straight from O'Hare Airport to Dr. Bremmer's office, Nate had no hotel in which to hide. It was, in fact, the first time in six years he had been out of his isolated Toronto house for more than two hours. He needed a drink desperately. Imps of Hell prodded the soft *optic chiasma* with fondue forks.

A neon Budweiser sign and a dark-thick doorway presented themselves, and he slipped inside. He was lucky. It was eye-of-the-hurricane hour between the closet alcoholics who needed three swift ones straight up before they could face the crabgrass and waiting ladies in Wilmette, and the bar vampires who hung by their curled toes from the bar-rail till closing time. The bar was deserted, nearly deserted.

He slid into a shadowed booth, blew out the candle in its metal shell, and waited for the waiter, hoping it would not be a waitress. It was a waitress. Pouf skirt, net-mesh opera hose, spike heels, quiet good taste.

He hid his face and ordered three doubles of McCormick bourbon, no water, no rocks, no glass if possible, just pour them in my hands. She stared at him for a long moment, started to say Don't I know you from some–

And Nate croaked in a frog-like, hideous voice, You couldn't possibly, I just got out of Dannemora, serving eighteen-to-life for raping, killing and eating a choir boy, not necessarily in that order.

She fled, and the bartender brought the drinks, standing well back from the booth as Nate slid the bills across the table.

It went that way for the new three and a half hours, till Nate's buzz was sufficiently nestled-in to permit conversation with the odd little man whose yogurt-soft eyes preceded him into the booth. Nate found himself unburdening his woes, and the little man, who matched him drink for drink, offered various unworkable solutions.

Look, I like you, said the little man, so I'll try and help you out. See, I'm something of a lay analyst myself. I've done just a whole *lot* of reading. Fromm, Freud, Bettelheim, Kahlil Gibran, that whole crowd. Now what *I'd* say is this: see, everybody has both male and female in him, you know what I mean? I think the female part of you is trying to assert itself. Have you ever thought of having sloppy sex with a man? Nate felt a hand crawling up his thigh. It was impossible. Nobody had arms that long, to reach across a booth, under a table. He yelped and looked down. The waitress was crawling around down there on hands and knees.

Nate bolted from the bar and didn't stop till he'd reached a crowded intersection.

When the light changed, and Nate stopped on the curb, he knew he was in trouble. It was State Street, and the clubs were letting out.

They chased him fifteen blocks and he lost the last two women—a gorgeous black girl with an enormous natural and a fiftyish matron who kept trying to use her Emba Cerulean mink stole to lasso him—in a pitfall-riddled construction site. He heard their shrieks as they dropped from sight, but he didn't slow down.

There was a motor hotel on the corner of Ohio and the Shore Drive and he pulled the tattered remnants of his clothing about him, making sure his wallet with the credit cards had not been lost when the Girl Scouts—*Girl Scouts!?!*—had ripped the arms off his jacket.

Inside, safe for the moment, he registered. The desk clerk, a whispery young man with white-on-white shirt, white-on-white tie, white-on-white face, looked at him with undisguised affection and offered the key to the bridal suite.

A single, away from everything, Nate insisted, and went up in the elevator, leaving the desk clerk breathing heavily.

The room was quiet and small. Nate pulled the drapes, locked the door, wedged a chair under the doorknob, and slumped on the edge of the bed. After a while he felt moderately sober, moderately relaxed, and thoroughly sick to his stomach. He undressed slowly and took a hot shower.

Soaping himself, he thought. It was a good place to think, in the shower.

Life had been at least supportable in Toronto. He'd devised a way to live. It was a ghastly way to live, but it was at least, well, supportable. But after Lois and the three bottles of Dexamils, he knew he had to do something, to try and arrest this hideous condition that had been getting worse and worse as he'd grown older. Only twenty-seven years old, and my life is hopeless, he thought. He'd thought that every year since he had reached puberty.

Then he'd heard of Dr. Bremmer and he'd been dubious. She *was* a woman, after all. But desperation knows no rationalizing deterrents, and he'd longdistanced an appointment. Now that had gone bananas, and he was thoroughly peeled. It was getting worse. The trip to Chicago had been a lousy idea. Now what will I do? How the hell will I get safely out of this enemy territory?

He turned and looked in the full-length mirror.

He saw himself naked.

He *did* have a good body.

And he *did* have a pleasant face, really quite a handsome and compelling face.

As he watched, his image began to shimmer and flow. His hair grew longer, more blond, even *blonde*, and breasts began to bulge as the hair vanished from his body. The image altered, as he stared, into the most beautiful woman he had ever seen. The words of the little man in the bar skimmed across his mind and were gone in an instant, lost in the adoration he felt for the fantastic creature in the mirror.

I love you, he said, finding it difficult to speak coherently.

He reached for her, and she drew back. Don't you put a hand on me you lecher, she said.

But I love you . . . I really love you!

I'm not that kind of a girl, she said.

But I don't just want your body, Nate said. There was an imploring note in his voice. I want to love you, to have you with me all my life. I can make a good home for you. I've been waiting for you all my life.

Well . . . she said, maybe we can just talk a while. But keep your hands to yourself.

I will, Nate promised, I will. I'll keep my hands to myself.

And they lived happily ever after.

Mom

In the living room the family was eating. The card tables had been set up and *tante* Elka had laid out her famous tiny meat knishes, the matzoh meal pancakes, the deli trays of corned beef, pastrami, chopped liver, and potato salad; the lox and cream cheese, cold kippers (boned, for God's sake, it must have taken an eternity to do it) and smoked whitefish; stacks of corn rye and a nice pumpernickel; cole slaw, chicken salad; and flotillas of cucumber pickles.

In the deserted kitchen, Lance Goldfein sat smoking a cigarette, legs crossed at the ankles, staring out the window at the back porch. He jumped suddenly as a voice spoke directly above him.

"I'm gone fifteen minutes only, and already the stink of cigarettes. Feh."

He looked around. He was alone in the kitchen.

"It wasn't altogether the most sensational service I've ever attended, if I can be frank with you. Sadie Fertel's, now *that* was a service."

He looked around again, more closely this time. He was still alone in the kitchen. There was no one on the back porch. He turned around completely, but the swinging door to the dining room, and the living room beyond, was firmly closed. He was alone in the kitchen. Lance Goldfein had just returned from the funeral of his mother, and he was alone, thinking, brooding, in the kitchen of the house he now owned.

He sighed; he heaved a second sigh; he must have heard a snatch of conversation from one of the relatives in the other room. Clearly. Obviously. Maybe.

"You don't talk to your own mother when she speaks to you? Out of sight is out of mind, is that correct?"

Now the voice had drifted down and was coming from just in front of his face. He brushed at the air, as though clearing away spiderwebs.

Nothing there. He stared at emptiness and decided the loss of his mother had finally sent him over the brink. But what a tragic way to go bananas, he thought. I finally get free of her, may God bless her soul and keep her comfortable, and I still hear her voice *nuhdzing* me. I'm coming, Mom; at this rate I'll be planted very soon. You're gone three days and already I'm having guilt withdrawal symptoms.

"They're really *fressing* out there," the voice of his mother said, now from somewhere down around his shoe tops. "And, if you'll pardon my being impertinent, Lance my darling son, who the hell invited that *momser* Morris to my wake? In life I wouldn't have that *shtumie* in my home, I should watch him stuff his fat face when I'm dead?"

Lance stood, walked over to the sink and ran water on the cigarette. He carried the filter butt to the garbage can and threw it in. Then he turned very slowly and said—to the empty room—"This is not fair. You are not being fair. Not even a little bit fair."

"What do I know from fair," said the disembodied voice of his mother, "I'm dead. I should know about fair? Tell me from fair; to die is a fair thing? A woman in her prime?"

"Mom, you were sixty-six years old."

"For a woman sound of mind and limb, that's prime."

He walked around the kitchen for a minute, whistled a few bars of "Eli Eli," just to be on the safe side, drew himself a glass of water and drank deeply. Then he turned around and addressed the empty room again. "I'm having a little trouble coming to grips with this, Mom. I don't want to sound too much like Alexander Portnoy, but why me?"

No answer.

"Where are you . . . hey, Mom?"

"I'm in the sink."

He turned around. "Why me? Was I a bad son, did I step on an insect, didn't I rebel against the Vietnam war soon enough? What was my crime, Mom, that I should be haunted by the ghost of a *yenta*?"

"You'll kindly watch your mouth. This is a mother you're speaking to."

"I'm sorry."

The door from the dining room swung open and Aunt Hannah was standing there in her galoshes. In the recorded history of humankind there had never been snow in Southern California, but Hannah had moved to Los Angeles twenty years earlier from Buffalo, New York, and there had been snow in Buffalo. Hannah took no chances. "Is there gefilte fish?" she asked.

Lance was nonplused. "Uh, uh, uh," he said, esoterically.

"Gefilte fish," Hannah said, trying to help him with the difficult concept. "Is there any?"

"No, Aunt Hannah, I'm sorry. Elka didn't remember and I had other things to think about. Is everything else okay out there?"

"Sure, okay. Why shouldn't it be okay on the day your mother is buried?" It ran in the family.

"Listen, Aunt Hannah, I'd like to be alone for a while if you don't mind."

She nodded and began to withdraw from the doorway. For a moment Lance thought he had gotten away clean, that she had not heard him speaking to whatever or whomever he had been speaking. But she paused, looked around the kitchen and said, "Who were you talking to?"

"I was talking to myself?" he suggested, hoping she'd go for it.

"Lance, you're a very ordinary person. You don't talk to yourself."

"I'm distraught. Maybe unhinged."

"Who were you speaking to?"

"The Sparkletts man. He delivered a bottle of mountain spring mineral water. He was passing his condolences."

"He certainly got out the door fast as I came in; I heard you talking before I came in."

"He's big, but he's fast. Covers the whole Van Nuys and Sherman Oaks area all by himself. Terrific person, you'd like him a lot. His name's Melville. Always makes me think of big fish when I talk to him."

He was babbling, hoping it would all go away. Hannah looked at him strangely. "I take it all back, Lance. You're not that ordinary. Talking to yourself I can believe."

She went back to the groaning board. Sans gefilte fish.

"What a pity," said the voice of Lance Goldfein's mother. "I love Hannah, but she ain't playing with a full deck, if you catch my drift."

"Mom, you've *got* to tell me what the hell is going on here. Could Hannah hear your voice?"

"I don't think so."

"What do you mean, you don't *think* so? You're the ghost, don't you know the rules?"

"I just got here. There are things I haven't picked up yet."

"Did you find a mah jongg group yet?"

"Don't be such a cutesy smart-mouth. I can still give you a crack across the mouth."

"How? You're ectoplasm."

"Don't be disgusting."

"You know, I finally believe it's you. At first I thought I was going over the edge. But it's you. What I still want to know is *why*?!? And why you, and why me? Of all the people in the world, how did this happen to us?"

"We're not the first. It happens all the time."

"You mean Conan Doyle really *did* speak to spirits?"

"I don't know him."

"Nice man. Probably still eligible. Look around up there, you're bound to run into him. Hey, by the way: you *are* up *there,* aren't you?"

"What a dummy I raised. No, I'm not up *there,* I'm down here. Talking to you."

"Tell me about it," he murmured softly, to himself.

"I heard that."

"I'm sorry."

The door from the dining room swung open again and half a dozen relatives were standing there. They were all staring at Lance as though he had just fallen off the moon. "Lance, darling," said Aunt Rachel, "would you like to come home tonight with Aaron and me? It's so gloomy here in the house all alone."

"What gloomy? It's the same sunny house it's always been."

"But you seem so . . . so . . . distressed . . ."

From one of the kitchen cabinets Lance heard the distinct sound of a blatting raspberry. Mom was not happy with Rachel's remark. Mom had never been that happy with Rachel, to begin with. Aaron was Mom's brother, and she had always felt Rachel had married him because he had a thriving poultry business. Lance did not share the view; it had to've been true love. Uncle Aaron was a singularly unappetizing human being. He picked his nose in public. And always smelled of defunct chickens.

"I'm not distressed, Rachel. I'm just unhappy, and I'm trying to decide what I'm going to do next. Going home with you would only put it off for another day, and I want to get started as soon as I can. That's why I'm talking to myself."

They stared. And smiled a great deal.

"Why don't you all leave me alone for a while. I don't mean it to sound impertinent, but I think I'd like to be by myself. You know what I mean?"

Lew, who had more sense than all the rest of them put together, understood perfectly. "That's not a bad idea, Lance. Come on, everyone; let's get out of here and let Lance do some thinking. Anybody need a lift?"

They began moving out, and Lance went with them to the front room where Hannah asked if he minded if she put together a doggie bag of food, after all why should it go to waste such terrific deli goodies. Lance said he didn't mind and Hannah and Rachel and Gert and Lilian and Benny (who was unmarried) all got their doggie bags, savaging the remains on the card tables until there was nothing left but one piece of pastrami (it wouldn't look nice to take the last piece), several pickles and a dollop of potato salad. The *marabunta* army ants could not have carried out a better program of scorching the earth.

And when they were gone, Lance fell into the big easy chair by the television, sighed a sigh of release, and closed his eyes. "Good," said his mother from the ashtray on the side table, "now we can have a long mother-son heart-to-heart."

Lance closed his eyes tighter. *Why me?* he thought.

He hoped Mom would never be sent to Hell, because he learned in the next few days that Hell was being a son whose mother has come back to haunt him, and if Mom were ever sent there, it would be a terrible existence in which she would no doubt be harassed by her own long-dead mother, her grandmothers on both sides, and God only knew how many random *nuhdzing* relatives from ages past.

Primary among the horrors of being haunted by a Jewish mother's ghost was the neatness. Lance's mother had been an extremely neat person. One could eat off the floor. Lance had never understood the efficacy of such an act, but his mother had always used it as a yard-stick of worthiness for housekeeping.

Lance, on the other hand, was a slob. He like it that way, and for most of his thirty years umbilically linked to his mother, he had suffered the pains of a running battle about clothes dropped on the floor, rings from coffee cups permanently staining the teak table, cigarette ashes dumped into the waste baskets from overflowing ashtrays without benefit of a trash can liner. He could recite by heart the diatribe attendant on his mother's having to scour out the waste basket with Dow Spray.

And now, when by all rights he should have been free to live as he chose, at long last, after thirty years, he had been forced to become a housemaid for himself.

No matter where he went in the house, Mom was there. Hanging from the ceiling, hiding in the nap of the rug, speaking up at him from the sink drain, calling him from the cabinet where the vacuum cleaner reposed in blissful disuse. "A pig sty," would come the voice, from empty air. "A certifiable pig sty. My son lives in filth."

"Mom," Lance would reply, pulling a pop-tab off a fresh can of beer or flipping a page in *Oui*, "this is not a pig sty. It's an average semi-clean domicile in which a normal, growing American boy lives."

"There's *shmootz* all over the sink from the peanut butter and jelly. You'll draw ants."

"Ants have more sense than to venture in here and take their chances with you." He was finding it difficult to live. "Mom, why don't you get off my case?"

"I saw you playing with yourself last night."

Lance sat up straight. "You've been spying on me!"

"Spying? A mother is spying when she's concerned her son will go blind from doing personal abuse things to himself? That's all the thanks I get after thirty years of raising. A son who's become a pervert."

"Mom, masturbation is not perversion."

"How about those filthy magazines you read with the girls in leather?"

"You've been going through my drawers."

"Without opening them," she murmured.

"This's got to stop!" he shouted. "It's got to end. E-n-d. End! I'm going crazy with you hanging around!"

There was silence. A long silence. Lance wanted to go to the toilet, but he was afraid she'd check it out to make sure his stools were firm and hard. The silence went on and on.

Finally, he stood up and said, "Okay, I'm sorry."

Still silence.

"I *said* I was sorry, fer chrissakes! What more do you want from me?"

"A little respect."

"That's what I give you. A little respect."

More silence.

"Mom, you've got to face it, I'm not your little boy any more. I'm an adult, with a job and a life and adult needs and . . . and . . ."

He wandered around the house but there was only more silence and more free-floating guilt, and finally he decided he would go for a walk, maybe go to a movie. In hopes Mom was housebound by the rules for ghost mothers.

The only movie he hadn't seen was a sequel to a Hong Kong kung fu film, *Return of the Street Fighter*. But he paid his money and went in. No sooner had Sonny Chiba ripped out a man's genitals, all moist and bloody, and displayed them to the audience in tight closeup, than Lance heard the voice of the mother behind him. "This is revolting. How can a son of mine watch such awful?"

"Mom!" he screamed, and the manager came down and made him leave. His box of popcorn was still half full.

On the street, passersby continued to turn and look at him as he walked past conversing with empty air.

"You've got to leave me alone. I need to be left alone. This is cruel and inhuman torture. I was never *that* Jewish!"

He heard sobbing, from just beside his right ear. He threw up his hands. Now came the tears. "Mommmm, *please*!"

"I only wanted to do right for you. If I knew why I was sent back, what it was for, maybe I could make you happy, my son."

"Mom, you'll make me happy as a pig in slop if you'll just go away for a while and stop snooping on me."

"I'll do that."

And she was gone.

When it became obvious that she *was* gone, Lance went right out and picked up a girl in a bar.

And it was not until they were in bed that she came back.

"I turn my back a second and he's *shtupping* a bum from the streets. That I should *live* to see this!"

Lance had been way under the covers. The girl, whose name was Chrissy, had advised him she was using a new brand of macrobiotic personal hygiene spray, and he had been trying to decide if the taste was, in fact, as asserted, papaya and coconut, or bean sprout and avocado, as his taste buds insisted. Chrissy gasped and squealed. "We're not alone here!" she said. Lance struggled up from the depths; as his head emerged from beneath the sheet, he heard his mother ask, "She isn't even Jewish, is she?"

"Mom!'

Chrissy squealed again. "*Mom*?"

"It's just a ghost, don't worry about it," Lance said reassuringly. Then, to the air, "Mom, will you, fer chrissakes, get out of here? This is in very poor taste."

"Talk to me taste, Lance my darling. That I should live to see such a thing."

"*Will you stop saying that?!?*" He was getting hysterical.

"A *shiksa*, a Gentile yet. The shame of it."

"Mom, the *goyim* are for practice!"

"I'm getting the hell out of here," Chrissy said, leaping out of the bed, long brown hair flying.

"Put on your clothes, you *bummerkeh*," Lance's mother shrilled. "Oh, God, if I only had a wet towel, a coat hanger, a can of Mace, *something, anything*!!"

And there was such a howling and shrieking and jumping and yowling and shoving and slapping and screaming and cursing and pleading and bruising as had never been heard in that block in the San Fernando Valley. And when it was over and Chrissy had disappeared into the night, to no one knew where, Lance sat in the middle of the bedroom floor weeping; not over his being haunted, not over his mother's death, not over his predicament: over his lost erection.

And it was all downhill from there. Lance was sure of it. Mom trying to soothe him did not help in the least.

"Sweetheart, don't cry. I'm sorry. I lost my head, you'll excuse the expression. But it's all for the best."

"It's not for the best. I'm horny."

"She wasn't for you."

"She was for me, she was for me," he screamed.

"Not a *shiksa*. For you a nice, cute girl of a Semitic persuasion."

"I *hate* Jewish girls. Audrey was a Jewish girl; Bernice was a Jewish girl; that awful Darlene you fixed me up with from the laundromat, she was a Jewish girl; I hated them all. We have nothing in common."

"You just haven't found the right girl yet."

"I HATE JEWISH GIRLS! THEY'RE ALL LIKE YOU!"

"May God wash your mouth out with a bar of Fels-Naptha," his mother said in reverential tones. Then there was a meaningful pause and, as though she had had an epiphany, she said, "*That's* why I was sent back. To find you a nice girl, a partner to go with you on the road of life, a loving mate who also not incidentally could be a very terrific cook. That's what I can do to make you happy, Lance, my sweetness. I can find someone to carry on for me now that I'm no longer able to provide for you, and by the way, that *nafkeh* left a pair of underpants in the bathroom, I'd appreciate your burning them at your earliest opportunity."

Lance sat on the floor and hung his head, rocked back and forth and kept devising, then discarding, imaginative ways to take his own life.

The weeks that followed made World War II seem like an inept performance of Gilbert & Sullivan. Mom was everywhere. At his job. (Lance was an instructor for a driving school, a job Mom had never considered worthy of Lance's talents. "Mom, I can't paint or sculpt or sing; my hands are too stubby for surgery; I have no power drive and I don't like movies very much, so that eliminates my taking over 20th Century–Fox. I *like* being a driving teacher. I can leave the job at the office when I come home. Let be already.") And, of course, at the job she could not "let be." She made nothing but rude remarks to the inept men and women who were thrust into Lance's care. And so terrified were they already, just from the *idea* of driving in traffic, that when Lance's mother opened up on them, the results were horrendous:

"A driver you call this idiot? Such a driver should be driving a dirigible, the only thing she could hit would be a big ape on a building maybe."

Into the rear of an RTD bus.

"Will you look at this person! Blind like a *litvak*! A refugee from the outpatient clinic of the Menninger Foundation."

Up the sidewalk and into a front yard.

"Now I've seen it all! This one not only thinks she's Jayne Mansfield with the blonde wig and the skirt up around the *pupik*, hopefully she'll arouse my innocent son, but she drives backwards like a pig with the staggers."

Through a bus stop waiting bench, through a bus stop sign, through a car wash office, through a gas station and into a Fotomat.

But she was not only on the job, she was also at the club where Lance went to dance and possibly meet some women; she was at the dinner party a friend threw to celebrate the housewarming (the friend sold the house the following week, swearing it was haunted); she was at the dry cleaners, the bank, the picture framers, the ballet and inevitably in the toilet, examining Lance's stools to make sure they were firm and hard.

And every night there were phone calls from girls. Girls who had received impossible urges to call this number. "Are you Lance Goldfein?

You're not going to believe this, but I, er, uh, now don't think I'm crazy, but I heard this *voice* when I was at my kid brother's bar mitzvah last Saturday. The voice kept telling me what a swell fellah you are, and how we'd get along so well. My name is Shirley and I'm single and . . ."

They appeared at his door, they came up to him at work, they stopped by on their lunch hour, they accosted him in the street, they called and called and called.

And they were *all* like Mom. Thick ankles, glasses, sweet beyond belief, Escoffier chefs every one of them, with tales of potato *latkes* as light as a dryad's breath. And he fled them, screaming.

But no matter where he hid, they found him.

He pleaded with his mother, but she was determined to find him a nice girl.

Not a woman, a girl. A nice girl. A nice *Jewish* girl. If there were easier ways of going crazy, Lance Goldfein could not conceive of them. At times he was *really* talking to himself.

He met Joanie in the Hughes Market. They bumped carts, he stepped backward into a display of Pringles, and she helped him clean up the mess. Her sense of humor was so black it lapsed over into the ultraviolet, and he loved her pixie haircut. He asked her for coffee. She accepted, and he silently prayed Mom would not interfere.

Two weeks later, in bed, with Mom nowhere in sight, he told her he loved her, they talked for a long time about her continuing her career in advocacy journalism with a small Los Angeles weekly, and decided they should get married.

Then he felt he should tell her about Mom.

"Yes, I know," she said, when he was finished.

"You know?"

"Yes. Your mother asked me to look you up."

"Oh, Christ."

"Amen," she said.

"What?"

"Well, I met your mother and we had a nice chat. She seems like a lovely woman. A bit too possessive, perhaps, but basically she means well."

"You *met* my mother . . . ?"

"Uh-huh."

"But . . . but . . . Joanie . . ."

"Don't worry about it, honey," she said, drawing him down to her small, but tidy, bosom. "I think we've seen the last of Mom. She won't be coming back. Some *do* come back, some even get recorporated, but your mother has gone to a lovely place where she won't worry about you any more."

"But you're so unlike the girls she tried to fix me up with." And then he stopped, stunned. "Wait a minute . . . you *met* her? Then that means . . ."

"Yes, dear, that's what it means. But don't let it bother you. I'm perfectly human in every other way. And what's best of all is I think we've outfoxed her."

"We have?"

"I think so. Do you love me?"

"Yes."

"Well, I love you, too."

"I never thought I'd fall in love with a Jewish girl my mother found for me, Joanie."

"Uh, that's what I mean about outfoxing her. I'm not Jewish."

"You're not?"

"No, I just had the right amount of soul for your mother and she assumed."

"But, Joanie . . ."

"You can call me Joan."

But he never called her the Maid of Orléans. And they lived happily ever after, in a castle not all that neat.

A MINI-GLOSSARY OF YIDDISH WORDS USED IN "MOM"

bummerkeh (BUM-er-keh) A female bum; generically, a "loose" lady.

"Eli Eli" (A-lee A-lee) Well-known Hebrew-Yiddish folk song composed in 1896 by Jacob Koppel Sandler. Title means "My God, my God." Opens with a poignant cry of perplexity: "My God, my God, why hast thou forsaken me?" from Psalm 22:2 of the Old Testament. Owes its popularity to Cantor Joseph Rosenblatt, who recorded and sang it many times as an encore during concerts in early 1900s. Al Jolson also did rather well with it. Not the kind of song Perry Como or Bruce Springsteen would record.

fressing (FRESS-ing) To eat quickly, noisily; really stuffing one's face; synonymous with eating mashed potatoes with both hands.

latkes (LOT-kess) Pancakes, usually potato pancakes but could also be made from matzoh meal. When made by my mother, not unlike millstones.

Litvak (LIT-vahk) A Jew from Lithuania; variously erudite but pedantic, thin, dry, humorless, learned but skeptical, shrewd and clever; but used in this context as a derogatory by Lance's mom, who was a *Galitzianer*, or Austro-Polish Jew; the antipathy between them is said to go back to Cain and Abel, one of whom was a Litvak, the other a Galitzianer . . . but that's just foolish. I guess.

momser (MUHM-zer) An untrustworthy person; a stubborn, difficult person; a detestable, impudent person; not a nice person.

(more)

nuhdzing (NOOOOOD-jing) To pester, to nag, to bore, to drive someone up a wall. The core of the story. Practiced by mothers of all ethnic origins be they Jewish, Italian or WASP. To bore, to hassle, to be bugged into eating your asparagus, putting on your galoshes, to get up and take her home, etc. Very painful.

pupik (PIP-ik or PUHP-ik) Navel. Belly-button.

shiksa (SHIK-suh) A non-Jewish woman, especially a young one.

shmootz (shmootz) Dirt.

shtumie (SHTOOM-ee) Lesser insult-value than calling someone a *schlemiel* (shleh-MEAL). A foolish person, a simpleton; a consistently unlucky or unfortunate person; a social misfit; a clumsy, gauche, butterfingered person; more offhand than *schlemiel,* less significant; the word you'd use when batting away someone like a gnat.

shtupping (SHTOOOOOP-ing) Sexual intercourse.

tante (TAHN-tuh) Aunt.

yenta (YEN-tuh) A woman of low origins or vulgar manners; a shrew; a shallow, coarse termagant; tactless; a gossipy woman or scandal-spreader; one unable to keep a secret or respect a confidence; much of the *nuhdz* in her. If it's a man, it's the same word, a blabbermouth.

Ecowareness

Once upon a time—something between 1,800,000,000 and 3,000,000,000 years ago—after the Earth had partly liquified through loss of heat by radiation from the outside and partly by adiabatic expansion, its Mommy said *gaey schluffen*, the Earth had a cookie, spit up, and went to bed. It slept soundly (save for a moment in 1755 when a Kraut named Kant made a whole lot of noise trying to figure out how the sun had been created) and didn't wake up till a Tuesday in 1963 at which time—about four in the morning, a shitty hour of the night except for suicides—it realized it was having a hard time breathing.

"Kaff kaff," it said, wiping out half the Trobriand Islands and whatever lay East of Java.

Casting about to discover what had wakened it, the Earth realized it was the All-Night Movie on Channel 11, snippets of a Maria Montez film (*Cobra Woman*, 1944) interrupting an aging cruiser king hustling '55 Mercs with pep pills in their gas tanks and lines of weariness in their grilles.

The Earth waited till dawn and began to look around. Everywhere it looked the rivers smelled like the grease traps in Army kitchens, the hills had been sheared away to provide clinging space for American Plywood cages with indoor plumbing, the watershed had been scorched flat, valleys had been paved over causing a most uncomfortable constriction of the Earth's breathing, the birds sang off-key and the bullfrogs sounded like Eddie Cantor, whom the Earth had never much cared for anyway. And overhead, the light hurt the Earth's eyes.

Everything looked gray and funky.

"Boy," the Earth said, in its rustic way, "I don't like this a whole lot," and so the Earth began taking counter-action.

The first was against a shaggy sophomore from Michigan State

University who, while parading around a Texaco station, carrying a placard that read STOP POLLUTION, ate a Power House bar and threw the wrapper in the gutter.

The Earth opened and swallowed him.

The next step was taken against fifty-six thousand Green Bay Packers fans as they crawled in imitation of a thousand-wheeled worm toward Lambeau Field, where their Cro-Magnon idols had waiting for them a sound trouncing at the hands and feet of the New Orleans Saints. The Earth, choking on the exhaust fumes of the automobiles, caused a lava flow to erupt from a nearby hillside, boiling down on the lines of traffic, solidifying instantly into a marvelous free-form sculpture of thirty thousand hot-rock-encased autos containing fifty-six thousand fried fans.

The next step was taken against the Mormon Tabernacle Choir, gathered in the Hollywood Bowl before a single-throated horde of Jesus People. They were singing Laura Nyro's "Save the Children" when the Earth re-channeled seven underground rivers and turned the amphitheater into the thirteenth largest natural lake in the United States.

Then followed in madcap array, a series of forays against prominent individuals. Mayor Richard Daley of Chicago, speeding along the Lake Shore Drive, was inundated by seventy thousand tons of garbage from the burning dumps lining the scenic route; Ralph Nader's office in Washington, D.C., was struck by bolts of lightning for twenty minutes. Barbra Streisand's town house in Manhattan suddenly vanished into a bottomless pit that yawned in the middle of the fashionable East Fifties. Her C above high C was heard for hours. Diminishing.

Volcanos destroyed the refineries, storage depots, administration buildings and Manhattan offices of Standard Oil of Ohio, New Jersey, New York, Pennsylvania, California, Texas and Rhode Island. The Earth took along Rhode Island in its entirety, possibly out of pique.

Eventually, when the *mene mene tekel* was written across the Grand Tetons in letters of burning forest fire, people began to get the idea.

The automobile was banned. All assembly lines shut down. Preservatives were eliminated from foods. Seals were left alone. A family of auk was discovered in New Zealand, doing rather nicely, thank you. And in Loch Ness, the serpent finally came up and took a deep breath.

And from that day to this, there has never again been a blotch of climatic smegma on the horizon, the Earth has settled down knowing the human race has learned its lesson and would never again take a ka-ka in its own nest, and that is why today the National Emphysema Society declared itself out of business.

Now isn't that a nice story.

And fuck you, too.

The Outpost Undiscovered By Tourists

A Tale of Three Kings and a Star for This Sacred Season

They camped just beyond the perimeter of the dream and waited for first light before beginning the siege.

Melchior went to the boot of the Rolls and unlocked it. He rummaged about till he found the air mattress and the inflatable television set, and brought them to the cleared circle. He pulled the cord on the mattress and it hissed and puffed up to its full size, king size. He pulled the plug on the television set and it hissed and firmed up and he snapped his fingers and it turned itself on.

"No," said Kaspar, "I will not stand for it! Not another night of roller derby. A King of Orient I are, and I'll be *damned* if I'll lose another night's sleep listening to those barely primate creatures dropkicking each other!"

Melchior glowed with his own night light. "So sue me," he said, settling down on the air mattress, tidying his moleskin cape around him. "You know I've got insomnia. You know I've got a strictly awful hiatus hernia. You know those *latkes* are sitting right here on my chest like millstones. Be a person for a change, a *mensch,* it couldn't hurt just once."

Kaspar lifted the chalice of myrrh, the symbol of death, and shook it at Melchior. "Hypochondriac! That's what you are, a fake, a fraud. You just like watching those honkytonk bimbos punching each other out. Hiatus hernia, my fundament! You'd watch mud wrestling and extol the esthetic virtues of the balletic nuances. Turn it off . . . or at least, in the name of Jehovah, get the Sermonette."

"The ribs are almost ready," Balthazar interrupted. "You want the mild or the spicy sauce?"

Kaspar raised his eyes to the star far above them, out of reach but maddeningly close. He spoke to Jehovah: "And this one goes ethnic on us. Wandering Jew over there drives me crazy with the light that never dims, watches institutionalized mayhem all night and clanks all day with gold chains . . . and Black-is-Beautiful over there is determined I'll die of tertiary heartburn before I can even find the Savior. Thanks, Yahweh; thanks a lot. Wait till *you* need a favor."

"Mild or spicy?" Balthazar said with resignation.

"I'd like mine with the mild," Melchior said sweetly. "And just a *bissel* apple sauce on the side, please."

"I want dimsum," Kaspar said. His malachite chopsticks materialized in his left hand, held far up their length indicating he was of the highest caste.

"He's only being petulant," Melchior said. "He shouldn't annoy, Balthazar sweetie. Serve them cute and tasty ribs."

"Deliver me," Kaspar murmured.

So they ate dinner, there under the star. The Nubian king, the Scrutable Oriental king, and the Hebrew king. And they watched the roller derby. They also played the spelling game called *ghost*, but ended the festivity abruptly and on a rancorous note when Balthazar and Melchior ganged up on Kaspar using the word "pringles," which Kaspar contended was *not* a generic but a specific trade name. Finally they fell asleep, the television set still talking to itself, the light from Melchior reflecting off the picture tube.

In the night the star glowed brightly, calling them on even in their sleep. And in the night early warning reconnaissance troops of the Forces of Chaos flew overhead flapping their leathery bat-wings and leaving in their wake the hideous carbarn monoxide stench of British Leyland double-decker buses.

When Melchior awoke in the morning his first words were, "In the night, who made a ka-ka?"

Balthazar pointed. "Look."

The ground was covered with the permanent shadows of the bat-troops that had flown overhead. Dark, sooty shapes of fearsome creatures in full flight.

"I've always thought they looked like the flying monkeys in the 1939 MGM production of *The Wizard of Oz*, special effects by Arnold Gillespie, character makeup created by Jack Dawn," Kaspar said ruminatively.

"Listen, Yellow Peril," Balthazar said, "you can exercise that junk-heap memory for trivia later. Unless the point is lost on you, what this means is that they know we're coming and they're going to be ready for us. We've lost the element of surprise."

Melchior sighed and added, "Not to mention that we've been following the star for exactly one thousand nine hundred and ninety-nine years, give or take a fast minute, which unless they aren't too clever should have tipped them off we were on the way some time ago."

"Nonetheless," said Kaspar, and fascinated by the word he said it again, "nonetheless."

They waited, but he didn't finish the sentence.

"And on that uplifting note," Balthazar said, "let us get in the wind before they catch us out here in the open."

So they gathered their belongings—Melchior's caskets of Krugerrands, his air mattress and inflatable television set, Kaspar's chalice of myrrh, his Judy Garland albums and fortune-cookie fortune calligraphy set, Balthazar's wok, his brass-bound collected works of James Baldwin and hair-conking outfit—and they stowed them neatly in the boot of the Rolls.

Then, with Balthazar driving (but refusing once again to wear the chauffeur's cap on moral grounds), they set out under the auspices of power steering, directly through the perimeter of the dream.

The star continued to shine overhead. "Damnedest thing I ever saw," Kaspar remarked, for the ten thousandth time. "Defies all the accepted laws of celestial mechanics."

Balthazar mumbled something.

For the ten thousandth time.

"What's that, I didn't hear?" Melchior said.

"I said: at least if there was a pot of gold at the end of all this . . ."

It was unworthy of him, as it had been ten thousand times previously, and the others chose to ignore it.

At the outskirts of the dream, a rundown section lined with fast food stands, motels with waterbeds and closed circuit vibrating magic fingers cablevision, bowling alleys, Polish athletic organizations and used rickshaw lots, they encountered the first line of resistance from the Forces of Chaos.

As they stopped for a traffic light, thousands of bat-winged monkey-faced troops leaped out of alleys and doorways with buckets of water and sponges, and began washing their windshield.

"Quick, Kaspar!" Balthazar shouted.

The Oriental king threw open the rear door on the right side and bounded out into the street, brandishing the chalice of myrrh. "Back, back, scum of the underworld!" he howled.

The troops of Chaos shrieked in horror and pain and began dropping what appeared to be dead all over the place, setting up a wailing and a crying and a screaming that rose over the dream like dark smoke.

"Please, already," Melchior shouted. "Do we need all this noise? All this *geshrying*! You'll wake the baby!"

Then Balthazar was gunning the motor, Kaspar leaped back into the rear seat, the door slammed and they were off, through the red light—which had, naturally, been rigged to stay red, as are all such red lights, by the Forces of Chaos.

All that day they lay siege to the dream.

The Automobile Club told them they couldn't get there from here. The speed traps were set at nine miles per hour. Sects of religious fanatics threw themselves under the steel-belteds. But finally they came to the Manger, a Hyatt establishment, and they fought their way inside with the gifts, all tasteful.

And there, in a moderately-priced room, they found the Savior, tended by an out-of-work cabinetmaker, a lady who was obviously several bricks shy of a load who kept insisting she had been raped by God, various shepherds, butchers, pet store operators, boutique sales-girls, certified public accountants, hawkers of T-shirts, investigative journalists, theatrical hangers-on, Sammy Davis, Jr. and a man who owned a whippet that was reputed to be able to catch two Frisbees at the same time.

And the three kings came in, finding it hard to find a place there in the crowd, and they set down their gifts and stared at the sleeping child.

"We'll call him Jomo," said Balthazar, asserting himself.

"Don't be a jerk," Kaspar said. "Merry Jomomas? We'll call him Lao-Tzu. It flows, it sings, it soars."

So they argued about that for quite a while, and finally settled on Christ, because in conjunction with Jesus it was six and five, and that would fit all the marquees.

But still, after two thousand years, they were unsettled. They stared down at the sleeping child, who looked like all babies: like a small, soft W.C. Fields who had grown blotchy drinking wine sold before its time, and Balthazar mumbled, "I'd have been just as happy with a pot of gold," and Kaspar said, "You'd think after two thousand years someone would at least offer me a chair," and Melchior summed up all their hopes and dreams for a better world when he said, "You know, it's funny, but he don't look Jewish."

DEPT. OF "WHAT WAS THE QUESTION?" DEPT.

Headline from *The Oregonian*, Monday, July 1, 1974:

**More Food Said Not Answer
To Feeding World's Multitude**

No, maybe not; but it'd sure as shit keep 'em from getting cranky till you *did* find the answer.

DEPT. OF "TRIVIAL PURSUIT" DEPT.

Since the early 1970s, *The Magazine of Fantasy and Science Fiction* has run, from time to time, a competition for (and often suggested by) its readers. Here is a sampling of Harlan's entries to five of these competitions. Most of these pieces appear here for the first time.

Competition 4 (*F&SF*, November 1972/April 1973)* – openings or endings of stories that could be included in THE YEAR'S WORST FANTASY AND SF.

The last man on Earth sat alone in a room. He was bored. He had been sitting there for several years, taking time from his boredom only to eat. He had raided twenty-nine supermarkets for all their TV dinners and, having jerry-rigged a freezer system, he was able to keep alive without leaving the room. He had started out eating nothing but Swanson chicken pot pie TV dinners, but had moved on to Stouffer's gourmet dinners – braised beef tips with mashed potatoes, sukiyaki with little Oriental vegetables, Midwestern Family TV dinner with apple pan dowdy – and now found himself fond of Hickory Farms all-vegetable dinner, beef patty with home fries dinner, lamb and apple sauce dinner, scallops with tartar sauce dinner . . . He was bored.

"Thwarted!" Kril trumpeted. "I've thwarted you, Drusilla! Even with your secret agent rating and your unearthly beauty, I've thwarted

*The first date shown is the cover date of the issue announcing the competition; the second is the cover date of the issue publishing the winners and runners-up of that competition.

you! The Fantellion Micro-Tapes have been posted and now you can return to your superiors and tell them your wiles failed this time," he vociferated.

The beautiful girl stared at him. "I concede," she made the concession, "you've outdone me in cunning. But . . ." and her face slid into lines of sadness, ". . . I've come to love you nonetheless." Tears glistened at the corners of her eyes.

Kril swallowed hard. "It can't be," he penultimated, sadly. "For I, too, have come to feel . . . a closeness to you. But it can *never* be . . ." and he opened his shirt and palmed open the stikfast sealing his chest, revealing the gears and cogs that gave him life.

"Oh!" she trilled. "Happiness is mine," and she ripped open her chiton, to unzip and show him *her* transistors and coded circuits. "Oh, Kril, my love . . . I, too, am a robot . . ."

The great starship *Pequod* sailed across the black sea of interstellar space. In the control country, Captain Aaral Habbe stalked about, the sound of his plasteel leg making sharp clankings against the deckplates. "I'll *get* him," he snarled, throatily. "That damned white space-devil, Moebius!"

Count Volta von Zarknov stood in the shadows, the eldritch fog of Boston swirling about his shoulders. Cape wrapped tightly about his thin body, only his wan and blood-empty face shone like a beacon in the night. He watched the front doors of Boston's Good Samaritan Hospital, knowing eventually they would have to bring in a new supply of plasma for the blood bank. His body cried out for sustenance.

Competition 8 (*F&SF*, May/September 1974)—near-miss titles.

LAST AND NEXT-TO-LAST MEN by Olaf Stapledon
RINGWORM by Larry Niven
I HAVE NO MOUTH AND I DON'T FEEL SO HOT by Harlan Ellison
THE THREE HICKEYS OF PALMER ELDRITCH by Philip K. Dick
SMITH IN AN UNFAMILIAR PLACE by Robert A. Heinlein
STOP PUSHING! STOP PUSHING! by Harry Harrison
THE ANDROMEDA HERNIA by Michael Crichton
THE FRANGIBLE PERSON by Alfred Bester
VAGUELY DISTURBING VISIONS edited by Harlan Ellison
TOWN by Clifford D. Simak
THE WORLD OF ±A by A.E. Van Vogt
THONGOR AT THE MOUND OF VENUS by Lin Carter
A CLOCKWORK RUTABAGA by Anthony Burgess

THE DOORS OF HIS FACE, THE WINDOWS OF HIS EYES, THE PORTALS OF HIS EARS, THE ARCHWAYS OF HIS HANDS, THE BRIDGE OF HIS NOSE, THE STEPPES OF HIS FEET, THE COLUMNS OF HIS THROAT, THE PUFFS OF HIS CHEEKS, THE LASH OF HIS LIPS, THE NEEDS OF HIS NOSTRILS, THE MOVEMENTS OF HIS BOWELS. BLUES. by Roger Zelazny
FREDENSTEIN by Mary W. Shelley
HEAVY ERRAND by Hal Clement
THE MOON IS HECK by John W. Campbell (revised by K. Tarrant)
PLINTH by Isaac Asimov
PLINTH AND CONDOMINIUM by Isaac Asimov
ANOTHER PLINTH by Isaac Asimov

Competition 23 (*F&SF*, September 1979/February 1980)—long, unwieldy and entertaining sf titles of 50 words or less.

OH DAD, POOR DAD, MOM'S HUNG YOU IN THE CLOSET AND WHEN THE LOBSTER INVADERS FROM NGC 3077 Σ CONQUERED EARTH LAST WEEK THEY MISTOOK YOU FOR A THREE-BUTTON CASHMERE SPORT JACKET AND NOW THEY'VE BURNED A HOLE IN YOUR LAPEL AND I'M FEELIN' SO SAD

BUH-BUH-BY THE SUH-SEA, BUH-BY THE SEA, BY THE BALBUTIENT SUH-SUH-SEA

Competition 26 (*F&SF*, November 1980/March 1981)—imaginary collaborations.

TIME CONSIDERED AS A HELIX OF WORTHLESS SAND by Samuel R. Delany and Frank Herbert
SLANBEAU by A.E. Van Vogt and C.L. Moore
INTO CLEVELAND DEPTHS by Stanton A. Coblentz and Fritz Leiber
DANCE OF THE CHANGER AND THE THREE HEARTS AND THREE LIONS by Terry Carr and Poul Anderson
A TORRENT OF FECES by James Blish & Norman L. Knight and Brian Aldiss [conceived in collaboration w/Alan Brennert]
CONAN VS. THE SPAWN OF THE PEOPLE by Robert E. Howard & Karl Edward Wagner & Björn Nyberg & L. Sprague de Camp and Zenna Henderson

THE HURKLES LOOK UP by Theodore Sturgeon and John Brunner

DEMOLISHED LENSMAN by Alfred Bester and E.E. Smith, Ph.D.

SON OF THE PUPPET MASTERS by Carlo Collodi and Robert A. Heinlein

I HAVE NO NERVES, AND I MUST TWITCH by Harlan Ellison and Lester del Rey

DAVY AND THE DROWNED GIANT by Edgar Pangborn and J.G. Ballard

Competition 39 (*F&SF,* November 1985/March 1986)—complete the following sentence: You know you've *really* landed in an alternate universe when you discover that . . .

. . . old time fans are sitting around reminiscing about the big splash THE LAST DANGEROUS VISIONS made when it was published fifteen years ago.

. . . when you come out of the theater discussing the existential nuances of the latest Steven Spielberg film and Sylvester Stallone tries to panhandle some change from you, your date, Kelly LeBrock, tells him to piss off.

. . . the Queen Mary/Spruce Goose guided tours have added the Enola Gay as a new attraction.

. . . last night Orson Welles broadcast *The War of the Worlds* and today President Steinem began negotiations with the enemy for the release of hostages.

. . . Mexican President Leon Trotsky III has signed into law a bill outlawing the use of the new Edsel robot matador in all minotaur *corridas*.

. . . James Tiptree, Jr. is a six-foot-five ex-lumberjack with a full beard who writes *Exterminator* paperbacks under the pseudonym E. Howard Hunt, and he introduces you to his wife, Ursula, a mere slip of a woman who writes sf under the pseudonym Jerry Pournelle.

VI

TROUBLE WITH WOMEN

> "So either the writer avoids writing any damned thing that might affront, or gets past a kind of universal knee-jerk Liberalism and cops to the truth that we are all pretty much alike, male and female, black and white, young and old, ugly and lovely. Pretty much alike in our ownership of human emotions, needs, drives, failings."
>
> —Introduction to "Lonely Women Are the Vessels of Time," STRANGE WINE, Harper & Row, 1978

Through the years, Harlan has garnered an undeserved reputation for depicting females from a chauvinistic, unsympathetic viewpoint. Such gossip might be traced to equally faulty speculations on his personal life, since a close examination of his stories, even the early ones, reveals no more anti-female bias than can be found among most of the popular writers of the same period—and usually a good deal less.

When he concentrates on relationships between men and women, Harlan sometimes deals with aspects of fear peculiar to the masculine gender. But, as we have seen, fear in all its forms is a major concern of his literary output, and he should be deemed a courageous writer for examining it as carefully as he has.

So watch his women closely. Can you find a sympathetic portrayal of even one who dotes on the role of subdued female? Or one who truly relishes the victimization of the male because she finds it a feminine prerogative?

Each of the following selections works with sex and sexual attraction, but their similarities aren't nearly so fascinating as their range of differences. A man wrote them, but he didn't do so strictly for men, or for women. He wrote them to remind us of what we already know—that sex can be either a prison or a paradise.

If one gets what one wants, who's to judge the true value of that satisfaction? "The Very Last Day of a Good Woman" (1958) concerns the end of the world and a man who, aware of the approaching oblivion, seeks sexual fulfillment with a woman. Harlan proposes the story as an attempt to say "everything is relative," and even the role-bound American milieu of its time cannot hide the irony of its cautious but carefully sharpened double edge.

"Valerie" (1972) brings the drama of desire much closer to home. Harlan takes a vivid instance from his own life of when he was gulled, used, exploited and shown in no uncertain terms the inevitability of our being trapped again and again into both *that* paradise and *that* prison. It is a caveat, an exposé of our inherent vulnerability.

Both "The Other Eye of Polyphemus" (1977) and "All the Birds Come Home to Roost" (1979) feature imagery that is erotic. Neither story, however, is actually *about* sex. What we have instead is sex as a particular manifestation of fear. The opening sentence of "Polyphemus" says the protagonist "might as easily have been a woman," which clarifies for us immediately that this story is not concerned with gender-influenced fear but with something far more frightening. Its harsh view of compassion is kept from total brutality by a strange but convincing approach to selfishness as a healthy measure of balance. "Birds"—anchored as it is, yet again, to events Harlan has lived—utilizes a fantasy common to all of us: who has not imagined having another go at a past romantic liaison? As Harlan takes this notion and diverts it into a disconcerting and literal cul-de-sac, it is once again fear—at first glance appearing to come from an exterior direction—that is revealed to be nesting right up there in the attic of the mind.

Together these pieces offer a compelling example of Harlan's ability to look at sex as a human action which exposes the personalities behind it. The mechanics are limited by mere biology; the import is limited merely by the human mind, of which the imagination is the only limit.

"No, kiddo, I'm just a slave of love like you."

—Introduction to "How's the Night Life on Cissalda?," SHATTERDAY, Houghton Mifflin, 1980

The Very Last Day of a Good Woman

Finally, he knew the world was going to end. It had grown in certainty with terrible slowness. His was not a perfect talent; but rather, a gem with many small flaws in it. Had he been able to see the future clearly, had he not been a *partial* clairvoyant, his life might not have come to what it had.

His hunger would not have been what it was.

Yet the brief, fogged glimpses were molded together, and he knew the Earth was about to end. By the same rude certainty that told him it was going to end, he knew it was not self-deception—it was not merely *his* death. It was the final, irrevocable finis of his world, with every life upon it. This he saw in a shattered fragment of clarity, and he knew it would come in two weeks, on a Thursday night.

His name was Arthur Fulbright, and he wanted a woman.

How strange or odd. To know the future. To know it in that most peculiar of fashions: not as a unified whole, as a superimposed something on the image of now, but in bits and snatches, in fits and starts. In humming, deliberate quicknesses (*a truck will come around the corner in a moment*) making him (*Carry Back will win*) almost a denizen of two worlds (*the train will leave ten minutes early*) he saw the future through a glass darkly (*you will find your other cuff link in the medicine cabinet*) and was hardly aware of what this power promised.

For years, a soft, brown shambling man all hummed words and gentle glances, living with his widowed mother in an eight room house set about with honeysuckle and sweet pea. For years, to work in a job of undistinguished type and station; for years, returning to the house and the comforting pastel of Mother.

Years that held little change, little activity, little of note or importance. Yet good years, smooth years, and silent.

Then Mother had died. Sighing in the night, she had slowed down like a phonograph, like the old crank phonograph covered under a white sheet in the attic, and had died. Life had played its melody for her, and just as naturally, ended.

For Arthur it had meant changes, and most of all, it had meant emptiness.

Now no more the nights of sound sleep, the evenings of quiet discussion and backgammon or whist, the afternoons of lunch prepared in time for a return to the office, the mornings with cinammon toast and orange juice ready. Now it was a single lane highway that he had to travel alone.

Learning to eat in restaurants, learning where the fresh linens were kept, sending his clothes out to be mended and cleaned.

And most of all, coming to realize in the six years since Mother's death, that he could see the future once in a while. It was in no way alarming, nor even—after living with it so long—surprising. The word terrifying, in connection with his sight of the future, would never have occurred to him, had he not seen that night of flame and death, the end of the world.

But he did see it, and it made a difference.

Because now that he was about to die, now that he had two weeks and no more, he had to find a purpose. There had to be a reason to die without regret. Yet here he sat, in the high-backed wing chair in the darkened living room, with the empty eight room house around him, and there was no purpose. He had not considered his own demise: Mother's going had been hard enough to reconcile, but he had known it would come some day (though the ramifications of her death had never dawned on him). His own death was something else.

"How can a man come to forty-four years old, and have nothing?" he asked himself. "How can it be?"

It was true, of course. He had nothing. No talent, no mark to leave on the world, no wake, no purpose.

And with the tallying of his lacks, he came to the most important one of all. The one marking him as not yet a man, no matter what he thought. The lack of a woman. He was a virgin, he had never had a woman.

With two weeks left on Earth, Arthur Fulbright knew what he wanted, more than anything, more than fame or wealth or position. His desire for his last days on Earth was a simple one, an uncluttered one.

Arthur Fulbright wanted a woman.

There had been a little money. Mother had left over two thousand dollars in cash and savings bonds. He had been able to put away another two thousand in his own account. That made four thousand dollars, and it became very important, but not till later.

The idea of buying a woman came to him after many other considerations. The first attempt was with a young woman of his acquaintance, who worked as a stenotypist in the office, in the billing section.

"Jackie," he asked her, having passed time on occasion, "would you —uh—how would you like to go to a—uh—show with me tonight . . . or something?"

She stared at him curiously, seeing a cipher; and having mentally relegated the evening to Scrabble with a girl friend, accepted.

That evening she doubled his fist and gave him such a blow in his rib cage, that his eyes watered and his side hurt for almost an hour.

The next day he avoided the girl with the blonde, twirled ponytail who was browsing in the HISTORICAL NOVELS section of the Public Library. He had had a glimpse often enough—of the future—to know what this one meant. She was married, despondent, and did not wear her ring because of hostility for her husband. He saw himself in an unpleasant situation, involving the girl, the librarian, and the library guard. He avoided the library.

As the week wore through, and Arthur realized he had never developed the techniques other men used to snare girls, he knew his time was running out. As he walked the streets, late at night, passing few people, but still people who were soon to perish in a flaming death, he knew his time was slipping away with terrible swiftness.

Now it was no mere desire. Now it was a drive, an urge within him that consumed his thoughts, that motivated him as nothing else in life ever had. And he cursed Mother for her fine, old Southern ways, for her white flesh that had bound him in umbilical attention. Her never-demanding, always-pleasant ways, that had made it so simple to live on in that pastel world of strifeless, effortless complacency.

To die a-flaming with the rest of the world . . . empty.

The streets were chill, and the lampposts had wavering, unearthly halos about them. From far off came the sound of a car horn, lost in the darkness; and a truck, its diesel gut rumbling, shifted into gear as a stop light changed, then the truck coughed away. The pavement had the sick pallor of rotting flesh, and the stars were lost in inkiness on a moonless night. He bunched himself tightly inside his topcoat, and bent into the vague, leaf-picking breeze slanting toward him. A dog somewhere howled briefly, and a door slammed on another block. Abruptly, he was ultra-sensitive to these sounds, and wanted to be part of them, inside with the love and humor of a home. But had he been a pariah, a criminal, a leper, he could not have been more alone. He reviled the inhumanity of his culture that allowed men such as himself to mature without direction, without hope, without love.

At the intersection, halfway down the block, a girl emerged from shadows, her heels tock tock tocking rhythmically on the sidewalk, then the street, as she stepped across, and went her way.

He was cutting across the lawn of a house, and converging on her from right angles before he realized what he was doing, what his intentions were. By then, his momentum had carried him.

Rape.

The word blossomed in his mind like a hot-house flower, with blood-red petals, grew to monstrous proportions, and withered, black at the edges, even as he scooted briskly, head down and hands in coat pockets, in her direction.

Could he do it? Could he carry it off? She was young and beautiful, desirable, he knew. She would have to be. He would take her down on the grass, and she would not scream, but would be pliant and aquiescent. She had to be.

He raced ahead of where she would meet him, and he lay down on the moist, brown earth, within the cover of bushes, to wait for her. In the distance he could hear her heels counting off the steps till he was upon her.

Then, even as his desire ate at him, other pictures came. A twisted, half-naked body lying in the street, a mob of men screaming and brandishing a rope, a picture of Mother, her face ashen and transfigured with horror. He squeezed his eyes shut, and pressed his cheek to the ground. It was the all-mother, consoling him. He was the child who had done wrong, and his need was great. The all-mother comforted him, directed him, caressed him with propriety and deep devotion. He lay there as the girl clacked past.

The heat in his face died away, and it was the day of the end, before he fully returned to sanity and a sense of awareness.

He had escaped bestiality, perhaps at the cost of his soul.

It was. It was, indeed. The day it would happen. He had several glimpses that day, so shocking, so brilliant in his mind, that he reaffirmed his knowledge of the coming of the event. Today it would come. Today the world would go off and burn.

One vision showed great buildings, steel and concrete, flashing like magnesium flares, burning as though they were crepe paper. The sun was raw looking, as though it might have been a socket from which someone had gouged an offending eye. The sidewalks ran like butter; charred, smoldering shapes lay in the gutters and on the rooftops. It was hideous, and it was now.

He knew his time was up.

Then the idea of the money came to him. He withdrew every cent. Every penny of the four thousand dollars. The vice president of the bank had a peculiar expression on his face, and he asked if everything was all right. Arthur answered him in epigram, and the vice president was unhappy.

All that day at the office—of course he went to work, he would not have known any other way to spend that last day of all days—he was on edge. He continually turned at his desk to stare out the window, waiting for the blood red glaze that would paint the sky. But it did not come.

Shortly after the coffee break that afternoon, he found the impression of nausea growing in him. He went to the men's room and locked himself into one of the cubicles. He sat down on the closed toilet, and held his head in his hands.

A glimpse was coming to him.

Another glimpse, vaguely connected to the ones of the holocaust, but now—like a strip of film, running backward—he saw himself entering a bar.

There were words in twisting neon outside, and repeated again on the small dark-glass window. The words said: THE NITE OWL. He saw himself in his blue suit, and he knew the money was in his pocket.

There was a woman at the bar.

Her hair was faintly auburn in the dim light. She sat on the bar stool, her long legs gracefully crossed, revealing a laced edge of slip. Her face was held at an odd angle, half-up toward the concealed streamer of light over the bar mirror. He could see the dark eyes, and the heavy makeup that somehow did not detract from the sharp, unrelieved lines of her face. It was a hard face, but the lips were full, and not thinned. She was staring at nothing.

Then, as abruptly as it had come, the vision passed, and his mouth was filled with the slippery vileness of his nausea.

He got to his feet and flipped open the toilet. Then he was thoroughly sick, but not messy.

Afterward, he went back to the office, and found the yellow pages of the phone book. He turned to *Bars* and ran his finger down the columns till he came to "The Nite Owl" on Morrison and 58th Streets.

He went home especially to freshen up . . . to get into his blue suit.

She was there. The long legs in the same position, the edge of slip showing, the head at that strange angle, the hair and eyes as he had seen them.

It was almost as though he were reliving a dramatic part he had once played; he walked up to her, and slid onto an empty stool beside her. "May I, may I buy you a drink, Miss?"

She only acknowledged his presence and his question with a half-nod and soft grunt. He motioned to the black-tied bartender and said, "I'd like a glass of ginger ale. Give the young lady whatever she uh she wants, please."

The woman quirked an eyebrow and mumbled, "Bourbon and water, Ned." The bartender moved away. They sat silently till he returned with the drinks and Arthur had paid him.

Then the girl said, "Thanks."

Arthur nodded, and moved the glass around in its own circle of moisture. "I like ginger ale. Never really got to like alcohol, I guess. You don't mind?"

Then she turned, and stared at him. She was really quite attractive, with little lines in her neck, around her mouth and eyes. "Why the hell should I care if you drink ginger ale? You could drink goat's milk and I couldn't care less." She turned back.

Arthur hurriedly answered, "Oh, I didn't mean any offense. I was only—"

"Forget it."

"But I—"

She turned on him with vehemence. "Look, mac, you on the make, or what? You got a pitch? Come on, it's late, and I'm beat."

Now, confronted with it, Arthur found himself terrified. He wanted to cry. It wasn't the way he had thought it would be. His throat had a choke lost in it. "I—I, why I—"

"Oh, Jeezus, wouldn't'cha know it. A fink. My luck, always my luck." She bolted the rest of her drink and slid off the stool. Her skirt rode up over her thighs, then fell again, as she moved toward the door.

Arthur felt panic rising in him. This was the last chance, and it was important! He spun on the stool and called after her, "Miss—"

She stopped and turned. "Yeah?"

"I thought we might, uh, could I speak to you?"

She seemed to sense his difficulty, and a wise look came across her features. She came back and stopped very close to him. "What now, what is it?"

"Are you, uh, are you do, doing anything this evening?"

Her sly look became businesslike. "It'll cost you fifteen. You got that much?"

Arthur was petrified. He could not answer. But as though it realized the time had come for action, his hand dipped into his jacket pocket and came up with the four thousand dollars. Eight five hundred dollar bills, crackling and fresh. He held them out for her to see, then the hand returned them to the pocket. The hand was the businessman, himself merely the bystander.

"Wow," she murmured, her eyes bright. "You're not as freaky as I thought, fella. You got a place?"

They went to the big, silent house, and he undressed in the bathroom, for it was the first time; and he held a granite chunk of fear in his chest.

When it was over, and he lay there warm and happy, she rose from the bed and moved to his jacket. He stared at her, and there was a strange feeling in him. He knew it for what it was, for he had felt a distant relative to it, in his feelings for Mother. Arthur Fulbright knew love, of a sort, and he watched her as she fished out the bills.

"Gee," she mumbled, touching the money reverently.

"Take it," he said softly.

"What? How much?"

"All of it. It doesn't mean anything." Then he added, as if it was the highest compliment he could summon: "You are a good woman."

The woman held the money tightly. Four thousand dollars. What a simple little bastard. There he lay in the bed, and with nothing to show for it. But his face held such a strange light, as though he had something very important, as though he owned the world.

She chuckled softly, standing there by the window, the faint pink glow of midnight bathing her naked, moist body, and *she* knew what counted. She held it in her hand.

The pink glow turned rosy, then red, then blood crimson.

Arthur Fulbright lay on the bed, and there was a peace deep as the ocean in him. The woman stared at the money, knowing what really counted.

The money turned to ash a scant instant before her hand did the same. Arthur Fulbright's eyes closed slowly.

While outside, the world turned so red and hot, and that was all.

VALERIE:
A True Memoir

Here's one I think you'll like. In this one I come off looking like a *schmuck*, and don't we all love stories in which the invincible hero, the all-knowing savant, the omnipotent smartass is condignly flummoxed? It's about Valerie.

Begins around 1968: I knew this hanging-out, El-lay photographer named Phil. He wasn't the world's most terrific human being (in point of fact, he was pretty much what you'd call your garden-variety creep), but he somehow or other wormed his way into my life and my home—I believe *wormed* is the right word—and occasionally used my residence as the background locale for sets of photos of young ladies in the nude. Phil would show up at my house in the middle of my work-day, all festooned with lights and reflectors and camera boxes . . . and a pretty girl, whom he would usher into one of the bathrooms and urge to divest herself of her clothing, *vite vite!*

Now I realize this may ring tinnily on the ears of those of you who spend the greater part of your off-hours lurching after your gonads, but having edited a men's magazine in Chicago some years ago, the sight of a lady in *deshabille* does not cause sweat to break out on my palms. What I'm saying is that after two years of examining transparencies framed in a light-box, while wearing a loupe to up their magnification, all said transparencies of the world's most physically-sensational women, all stark naked . . . one develops a sense of proportion about such things. One begins looking for more exotic qualities—such as the ability on the part of the ladies to make you laugh or cry or feel as though you've learned something. (As an aside: nothing serves better to kill ingrained sexism than an overdose of flesh in living color; very quickly one differentiates between images on film and living, breathing human beings. I commend it to all you gentlemen who still use the words *broad* and *chick*.)

Consequently, it was not my habit to skulk around the house while Phil was snapping the ladies. When they'd take a break, I'd often sit with them and have a cup of coffee and we'd enter into a conversation, but apart from that I'd generally sit in my office and bang the typewriter. This may seem to have been the wrong thing to be banging, but, well, there you are. (Because of this attitude, Phil drew the wholly erroneous conclusion that I was gay, and had occasion, subsequently, to pass along his lopsided observation, sometimes to young ladies with whom I had become intimate. What a nasty thing to say, particularly from a man who lures six-year-old boys into the basements of churches and then defiles, kills and eats them, not necessarily in that order. Isn't idle gossip a wonderful thing!)

This use of my home and myself by The Demon Photographer went on for about a year, and I confess to permitting the inconvenience because on several of these shooting dates I *did* meet women with whom I struck up relationships. One such was Valerie.

(Of *course* I know her last name, you fool. I'm not giving it here out of deference to her family and what comes later in this saga.)

The Demon Photographer—squat, ginger-haired, insipid—arrived one afternoon with her, and I was zonked from the moment I saw her. She was absolutely lovely. A street gamine with a smile that could melt Jujubes, a warm and outgoing friendliness, a quick wit and lively intelligence, and a body that I would have called *dynamite* during my chauvinist period. We hit it off immediately, and when Phil slithered away at the end of the session, Valerie stayed on for a while.

It didn't last all that long, to be frank. I can't recall all the specifics of disenchantment, but attrition set in—it's happened to all of you, so you know what I mean—and after a short while we parted: as friends.

Over the next few years, Valerie popped back into my life at something like six month intervals, and if I wasn't involved with anyone we'd get it on for a few days, and then away she'd fly once more. There was always a kind of bittersweet tone to our liaisons: the scent of mimosa (and mimesis, had I but known), dreams half glimpsed, the memories of special touches. There was always the feeling that something lay unspoken between us, and a phrase from Sartre's THE REPRIEVE persisted: "It was as if a great stone had fallen in the road to block my path." In a way, I believe I was in love with Valerie.

Time passed. In mid-May of 1972 I was scheduled to speak at the Pasadena Writers' Week, and early the day of the appearance, I received a call from Valerie. I hadn't heard from her in almost a year.

After the hellos and my unconfined pleasure at hearing her voice, I asked, "What are you doing tonight?"

"Going out with you," she said.

(Witness, gentle readers: the desiccated ego of The Author, suddenly pumped full of self-esteem and jubilation, merely refractions of adoration at the perceptivity and swellness of a bright, quick lady saying, "You're fine." What asses we *machismo* buffoons can be.)

"Listen, I'm slated to go out and speak in Pasadena to a gaggle of literary types. Why don't you go with me and watch how I turn the crowd into a lynch mob."

"That's where I *am*," she said. "In Pasadena. At my mother's house. You can pick me up and I'll stay with you for a couple of days."

"I'll buy that dream," I said, and we set up ETA and coordinates.

That evening, in company with Edward Winslow Bryant, Jr. (dear friend, sometime house guest, outstandingly talented young writer and author of the Macmillan collections, AMONG THE DEAD, CINNABAR and co-author of PHOENIX WITHOUT ASHES), I drove out to Pasadena to pick up Valerie. When she answered the door she paused momentarily, framed in the opening, wearing a dress the shade of a bruised plum. I said: a body that should have been on permanent exhibition in the Smithsonian. Wearing nothing under it.

Oh, Cupid, you pustulent twerp! One of these days some nether god is going to jam that entire quiver of crossbow bolts right up your infantile ass!

I went down like a bantamweight in an auto chassis crusher.

Carrying her overnight case, her hair dryer and curlers, her suitcase, her incredibly sweet-smelling clothes on wire hangers, I took her to the car, and was rewarded by the sight of Ed Bryant's eyes as they turned into Frisbies. Not to mention the unsettling memories of the hugs and kisses and liftings off the floor and spinnings around I'd just received inside the house.

We did the speaking gig, and Valerie sat in the front row displaying a thoroughly unnerving expanse of leg and thigh. I may have fumfuh'd a bit.

Afterward, Valerie, Ed and I went to have a late dinner at the Pacific Dining Car. Sitting over beefsteak tomatoes and the thickest imported Roquefort dressing in the Known World, Valerie started whipping numbers on me like this:

"I've always had a special affection for you. I should have moved in with you three years ago. Boy, was I a fool."

I mumbled things of little sense or import.

"Maybe I'll move in with you now . . . if you want me."

The next day, a girl from Illinois was to have flown in for an extended weekend. "Give me a minute to make a phone call," I said, and sprinted. I made the call. Bad vibes. Harsh language. Dead line.

"Yeah, why don't you move in with me," I said, slipping back into the booth. Everyone smiled.

When she went to the loo, Ed—whose perceptions about people are keen and reserved—leaned over and said, "Hang onto this one. She's sensational."

Opinion confirmed. By a sober outside observer.

So I took her home with me. The next day, Ed split for his parents' home in Wheatland, Wyoming, beaming at Harlan for his good luck and prize catch. That left, in the household, myself, Valerie, and Jim Sutherland: young author of STORMTRACK, occasional house guest and ex-student of your humble storyteller at the Clarion Writers' Workshop in SF & Fantasy.

Later that day, Valerie asked me if she could use the telephone to make a long distance call to San Francisco. I said of course. She had told me, by way of bringing me up to date on her peregrinations, that since last she'd seen me she had been working in San Francisco, mostly as a topless waitress at the Condor and other joints; that she had been rooming with another girl; that she had been seeing a guy pretty steadily, but he was into a heavy dope scene and she wanted to get away from it; and she loved me.

After the call, she came into my office in the house and said she was worried. The guy, whom she'd called to tell she was not coming back, had gotten rank with her. The words bitch and cunt figured prominently in his diatribe.

She said she wanted to fly up to San Francisco that day, to clean out her goods before he could get over there and rip them off or bust them up. She also said, very nicely, that if she went up, she wanted to buy a VW minibus from a guy she knew. It would only cost $100 plus taking over the payments, and she'd need a car if she was going to come back here to live. "I want to work and pay my way," she said.

Or in the words of Bogart as Sam Spade, "You're good, shweetheart, really good." Remember, friends, no matter how fast a gun you are, there's always someone out there who's faster. And how better to defuse the suspicions of a cynical writer than to establish individuality and a plug-in to the Protestant Work Ethic.

She asked me for the hundred bucks.

Unfortunately, I didn't have the hundred at that moment, even though I said credit-card-wise I'd pay for her plane ticket to San Francisco.

She said that was okay, she'd work it out somehow. Then she went to pack an overnight bag, leaving all the rest of her goods behind, and promised she'd be driving back down the very next day.

Jim Sutherland offered to drive her to the airport—I was on a script deadline and had to stay at the typewriter—and she left with many kisses for me and deep looks into my naïve eyes, telling me she was all warm and squishy inside at having finally found me, Her White Knight.

It wasn't till Jim returned, young, innocent, a college student with very little bread, that I found out she had asked *him* for the hundred bucks, too. And he'd loaned it to her, with the promise of getting it back the next day.

The worm began to gnaw at my trust:

Valerie, the Golden Girl, the Little Wonder of the Earth, having fun-danced her way into my life again, had now cut out for San Francisco with a hundred dollars of *Jim's* money. But she'd said she could manage somehow *without* the hundred . . .

If she'd needed it *that* badly, after I'd said I didn't have it, why didn't she ask me again, rather than come on with a kid she'd just met a day earlier? How the hell had Jim come up with that much bread on the spur of the moment?

"We stopped off at my bank on the way to the airport," he said. I was very upset at that information.

"Listen, man," I said, "I've known her a few years and she's not even in the *running* as the most responsible female I've ever known. I mean, she's a sensational lady and all, but I don't *really* know where she's been the last few years."

Jim suddenly seemed disturbed. That hundred was about all he had to his name. He'd earned it assisting me in the teaching of a six-week writing workshop sponsored by Immaculate Heart College, along with Ed Bryant; and he'd worked his ass off for it. "She said she'd borrow it from a friend in San Francisco and get it back to me tomorrow."

"You shouldn't have done it. You should've called me first."

"Well, I figured she was your girl, and she was going to live here. And she said there wasn't time to call if she was going to make the plane, so . . ."

"You shouldn't have done it."

I felt responsible. He'd been trusting, and kind, and I had a flash of uneasiness. The old fable about the Country Mouse and the City Rat scuttled through my mind. Valerie had been known to vanish suddenly. But . . . not this time . . . not after her warmth and protestations of love for me . . . that was unthinkable. It would work out. But if it didn't . . .

"Listen, anything happens, I'll make good on the hundred," I told him.

And we settled down to wait for Val's return the next day.

Two days later, we reached a degree of concern that prompted me to call her mother. The story I got from her mother did not *quite* synch with what Valerie had told me. Valerie had said she'd told her mother she was moving in with me; the mother knew of no such thing. Valerie had told her she was working in Los Angeles; Valerie had told *me* she would try and get a job when she returned from San Francisco. The worm of worry burrowed deeper.

Using the phone number of Valerie's alleged apartment in San Francisco, I got a disconnect. No word. No Valerie, no word of any kind. Had her ex-boy friend murdered her? Had she bought the VW bus and run off the road?

Students of the habit patterns of the lower forms of animal life will note that even the planarian flatworms learn lessons from unpleasant experiences. I was no stranger to ugly relationships with (a few, I assure you, a very few) amoral ladies. But *homo sapiens*, less intelligent than the lowest flatworm, the merest paramecium, repeats its mistakes, again and again. Which explains Nixon. And also explains why I was so slow to realize what was happening with Valerie. It took a sub-thread of plot finally to shine the light through my porous skull. Like this:

In company with Ray Bradbury, I was scheduled to make an appearance at the Artasia Arts Festival in Ventura, on May 13th. That was the Saturday following Valerie's leavetaking. Ray and I were riding up to Ventura together, and though I'm the kind of realist who considers cars transportation, hardly items of sensuality or beauty, and for that reason never wash my 1967 Camaro with the 148,000 miles on it, I felt a magic man of Bradbury's stature should not be expected to arrive in a shitwagon. So I asked Jim to take my wallet with the credit cards, and the car, and go down to get the latter doused. I was still chained to the typewriter on a deadline, or I would have done it myself.

Jim took it to a car wash, brought it back, and returned my wallet to the niche in my office where it's kept at all times. Aside from this one trip out of the house, the wallet (with all cards present) had not been out of my possession for a week.

The next day, Saturday, Ray came over and I drove us up to Ventura. After checking in, we went to get something to eat. At the table, I opened my wallet to get something—the first time I'd opened the wallet in a week—and suddenly realized some of the glassine windows that held my credit cards were empty. After the initial panic, I grew calm and checked around the table, covered the route back to the car, inspected the map-cubby where I always keep the wallet, looked under the seats . . . and instantly called Jim in Los Angeles to tell him I'd been ripped off.

Since the wallet had only been out of the house once in the last week, the cards *had* to have been boosted at the car wash. Do you see how long it takes the planarian Ellison to smell the stench of its own burning flesh?

I called Credit Card Sentinel, the outfit that cancels missing or stolen cards, advised them of the numbers of the cards (I always keep a record of this kind of minutiae handy), and asked them to send the telegrams that would get me off the hook immediately. There's a law that says you can't get stuck for over fifty bucks on any one card, but there were *five* cards missing—Carte Blanche, BankAmericard, American Express, Standard Chevron Oil and Hertz Rent-A-Car—and that totaled two hundred and fifty dollars right there; with Sentinel, the effective lead-time for use of the cards is greatly reduced.

Having deduced *à la* Nero Wolfe that the thief had to have been the dude who swabbed out the interior of the car at the washatorium, I called the West LA police, detective division, the area where the car wash was located, and put them on to it. I called the owners of the car wash and relayed the story, and tried to coordinate them with the detective who was going to investigate, advising them that they should check out the guys who'd worked interiors that previous Friday, noting especially any who hadn't shown up for work.

My detective work was flawless . . . aside from the sheer stupidity of my emotional blindness.

You all know what happened.

But *I* didn't, until five days later, when I received a call from the BankAmericard Center in Pasadena asking me to verify a very large purchase of flowers sent to Mrs. Ellison in the Sacramento, California Medical Center. I assured them there *was no* Mrs. Ellison, I was single, and the only *Mrs.* Ellison was my mother, in Miami Beach.

The charge, of course, was on my stolen card.

Then the light blinded me.

The next day, I received a bill for forty-three dollars from the Superior Ambulance Service in Sacramento, a bill for having carted someone from a Holiday Inn to the Sacramento Medical Center on May 13th. The name of the patient was "Ellison Harlan" and the charge had been made to my home address.

In rapid succession came the BankAmericard reports of huge purchases of toilet articles, men's clothing, women's sportwear, hair dryers, and other goodies. Of course, I knew what had happened. At this point, pause with me, and join in a Handel chorus of *O What a Schmuck is Thee!*

Care to relive with me the last time you were fucked-over? The feeling that your stomach is an elevator, and the bottom is coming up on you fast. That peculiar chill all over, approximated only by the morning after you've stayed up all night on No-Doz and hot, black coffee. The grainy feeling in the eyes, the uncontrollable clenching of the hands, the utter frustration, the wanting to board a plane to . . . where? . . . to *there*! . . . to the place where something that can be hit exists. It's one thing to be robbed, it's quite another to be taken. Okay, no argument, it's all ego and crippled masculine pride, but God it burns!

I pulled my shit together and dropped back into my Sam Spade, private eye, mode. First I called the Sacramento Medical Center and checked if there was a Valerie B. checked in. There wasn't. Then I asked for a Mrs. Ellison Harlan. There wasn't. Then I asked for Mrs. Harlan Ellison.

There was.

Then I called the Security station of the Sacramento Sheriff's Department, there at the Medical Center. I spoke to the officer in charge, laid the entire story on him, and asked him to coordinate with Officer Karalekis of the West LA Detective Division, as well as Dennis Tedder at the BankAmericard Center in Pasadena. I advised him—and subsequently advised the Administrative Secretary of the Center—that there was a fraud in progress, and that I would not be held responsible for any debts incurred by the imposter posing as "Ellison Harlan," "Harlan Ellison," or "Mrs. Harlan Ellison." Both of these worthies said they'd get on it at once.

Then I called Valerie. She was in the orthopedic section. They got her to the phone. Of course, she answered: the only one (as far as she knew) who had any idea she was there was the man who had purchased the flowers.

Is the backstory taking shape finally, friends? Yeah, it took me a while, too. And I'm dumber than you.

That was May 23rd, ten days after the ambulance had removed her from the Holiday Inn and she'd been admitted to the Center.

"Hello?"

"Valerie?"

Pause. Hesitant. Computer running on overload.

"Yes."

"Harlan."

Silence.

"How's San Francisco?"

"How did you find me here?"

"Doesn't matter. I get spirit messages. All you need to know is I found you, and I'll find you wherever you go."

"What do you want?"

"The cards, and the hundred bucks you conned off Jim Sutherland."

"I haven't got it."

"Which?"

"Any of it."

"Your boy friend has the cards."

"He split on me. I don't know where he is."

"Climb down off it, Princess. If I'm a patsy once, that makes me a philosopher. Twice and I'm a pervert."

"I'm hanging up. I'm sick."

"You'll be sicker when the Sacramento Sheriff's Department there in the hospital visits you in a few minutes."

No hangup. Silence.

"What do you want?"

"I said what I wanted. And I want it quick. Jim's too poor to sustain a hundred buck ripoff. I can handle the rest, but I want it all returned *now*."

"I can't do anything while I'm in here."

"Well, you're on a police hold as of ten minutes ago, so figure a way to do it, operator."

"God, you're a chill sonofabitch! How can you do this to me?"

There is a moment when one watches beloved Atlantis sink beneath the waves, and resigns oneself. There is a moment when one decides to cut the Devil loose because you can't pay the dues. That's the moment when one toughs-up and decides to let the fire consume the tabernacle, the holy icons and the fucking temple itself!

"I'm the only one who can press charges against you at this point, Valerie. Try to wriggle and I'll chew on your eyes, so help me God."

There was silence at the other end.

"Give me a minute to think; it's all too fast," she said. I could just conjure up a picture of a rat in a maze, looking for a wall to chew through.

"Sure. Take a minute. I'll wait."

And while I waited, I tried to piece together the off-camera action that I'd refused to believe had happened. I'd needed that final punch in the mouth, the sound of her voice across the line from Sacramento, actually to accept what a jerk I was. But now I'd gotten the shock, and I started piecing it all together.

All the facts were there . . . only someone afraid to find out what a patsy he'd been could have missed it. She had either met up with her boy friend at the Burbank Airport—a guy described in the police report from his purchase of the flowers sent to Valerie as "Mrs. Ellison" in the hospital as a "dark, swarthy guy," a description that tallied with Valerie's mother's recollection of him as "a Latin of some kind, maybe Cuban"—or had had him fly to Sacramento from San Francisco. They had shacked up at the Holiday Inn and *something* had happened to Valerie. Something serious enough for her to have to be rushed by ambulance to the Medical Center, at which point the boy friend had checked out on her, with my credit cards.

Now I had her on (I thought) a police hold.

"I can't do anything while I'm in here," she said, finally.

"You're not getting out." I was firm about that.

"Then I can't get the money."

"Then you'll go to jail. I'll press charges."

"Why are you doing this?"

"I'm just a rotten sonofabitch, that's why."

A few more words were exchanged, then she rang off. I turned to Jim Sutherland and said, "I may have to fly up to Sacramento. It looks resolved, but I've got bad feelings about the sloppy way the BankAmericard people and the cops are going at this thing. Besides . . . I want to look at her face."

What I was saying was that I wanted to see if I could detect the stain of duplicity in her expression. What I was saying was I'd become a man with an ingrown hair that needed digging and tweezing; like all self-abuse, I needed to put myself in the line of pain, to relive the impact, to see what it was that had made me go for the okeydoke, what had made me such a willing sucker, so late in my life of relationships, making a mistake of placing such heavy emotions in such an unworthy receptacle. I was consumed with the need to *understand,* not merely to stumble on through life thinking my perceptions about people were so line-resolution perfect that I could never be flummoxed. She had taken me, and with such perfection that even after I had spoken to her in the hospital, even after I *knew* I'd been had, some small part of my brain kept telling me her expressed affection and attention could not *all* have been feigned.

Thus do we perpetuate our folly.

Fifteen minutes later, she called back, collect.

"What did you tell them?" she demanded.

"Tell who?"

"The cops. A cop just came up to talk to me."

"I told you what I told them. That you were a thief and you were registered under an alias and I wasn't going to be responsible for any bills you ran up and they'd better hold onto your pretty little ass till the Laws had decided what to do with you."

"Are you going to press charges?"

"Give me reasons not to."

"I'll get the money back for Jim."

"That's a start."

"I can't do anything else."

"The cards."

"I don't have them." And she named her boy friend, who she said had kited off with them. That didn't bother me; I'd already had the cards stopped. Larry Lopes (pronounced LO-pez) was his name. It comes back to me now.

"Okay. You get the hundred back to Jim and as far as I'm concerned you can move on to greener pastures."

She rang off, and I sat in the dwindling light of the sunset coming over the Valley to my hilltop, thinking furiously. Getting no answers.

I heard nothing further for several days, and when I checked with Dennis Tedder at the BankAmericard Center in Pasadena, I was informed Valerie was no longer at the Sacramento Medical Center.

They'd let her skip on the 23rd of May.

She was gone, leaving behind a bill, in my name, for over a thousand dollars' worth of treatments.

My feelings toward Mr. Tedder, Officer Karalekis of the West LA fuzz, and the nameless Sacramento Sheriff who had not only spoken to me, but had confronted Valerie and gotten an admission of guilt . . .

were not particularly warm. Kindly note: I have just made an understatement.

Things progressed from miserable to ghastly. The Superior Ambulance Service in Sacramento, despite several long letters explaining what had happened, and backing it up with Xerox documentation of the fraud, continued to dun me for the forty-three bucks Valerie's passage from the Holiday Inn to the hospital had incurred. They finally turned it over to the Capital Credit and Adjustment Bureau. My attorney, the Demon Barrister Barry Bernstein, sent them a harsh note, and they finally cleared the books of my name. But the time spent, the aggravation when the nasty little pink notes came in the mail . . .

And the hospital bill. It kept getting run through the computer and kept bouncing back to me. Finally, I called the head of the business office at the hospital and laid it all out (again) in detail. As of this writing, *that* goodie is struck.

And Valerie was gone.

In speaking to Tedder at BankAmericard, I discovered, to the horror of my sense of universal balance, that Bank of America really *didn't* care about bringing her and Mr. Lopes to book. They apparently don't expend any effort on cases under five hundred dollars. BofA can sustain innumerable ripoffs at that level without feeling it. (This I offer as incidental intelligence on two counts: first, to permit those of you who are planning scams against BofA to understand better the limits of revenge of that peculiar institution, a limit that scares me when I think of how much they must gross to *permit* such a cavalier attitude; and second, to slap BofA's pinkies for their corporate posture on such matters; at once similar to that of the great insurance conglomerates that permit ripoffs, thereby upping premiums; a posture that *encourages* dishonesty and chicanery. A posture that has aided in the decay of our national character. It occurs to me, when I say things like that—though I genuinely believe them—that they sound hideously messianic, and I blush. So ignore it, if you choose.)

Valerie was gone, as I said. When I called her mother, to inform her of the current status, she sounded very upset and offered to give Jim back his hundred dollars. I thought that was a helluva nice gesture. Yet when the check arrived, it was only for fifty. Poor Jim. I would have made good the other fifty, on the grounds that he'd laid the money on her because he thought we were a scene, but it never came to that.

Two or three months later, Valerie called again.

I had tracked her through my own nefarious contacts, to Pacifica, a community near San Francisco. She had been hanging out with a ratpack of losers and unsavory types, and I knew where she was virtually all the time. But I'd told her mother if the money came back to Jim and the cards weren't used again, I would have no further interest in seeing her cornered, and I held to that.

Then she called. Out of the blue, to snag a fresh phrase.

"Hello?"

"Who's this?"

"Valerie."

Terrific. What're you selling this week, cancer?

"Are you there?"

"I'm here. What do you want?"

"I want my stuff. My clothes and electric curlers and stuff."

They were all packed in the bottom of Jim's closet . . . waiting. For what, we'd never stopped to consider. Maybe the Apocalypse.

"Sure, you can have your stuff," I said.

"How do I get it? Will you drive it out to my Mom's in Pasadena, she doesn't have a car."

I have heard of *chutzpah,* I have witnessed incredible gall and temerity, but for sheer bravado, Valerie had a corner on the product.

"I'll tell you how you get it," I said. "We're like a good pawn shop here. You come up with the fifty bucks for Jim, the fifty you still owe him, and we release your goods. Just redeem your pawn ticket, baby."

"I don't have fifty."

"Ask Larry Lopes for it."

"I don't know where he is."

"Ah, but I know where *you* is. Have your friends boost somebody's hubcaps and get the fifty."

"Go to hell!" And she hung up.

I shrugged. Ain't life teejus, mah baby.

Later that day, Valerie's mother called and offered to unhock Valerie's goods for the fifty remaining. She made it clear she had no idea where Valerie was on the lam, but I don't think anyone will consider me cynical for believing that may not have been the strict truth.

So Jim took the clothes out to Pasadena, picked up the fifty, and the Sacramento Medical Center canceled the bill as unrecoverable, and that's as much as I know, to this point.

Well . . . not quite.

I know one more thing. And it's this:

In every human being there is only so large a supply of love. It's like the limbs of a starfish, to some extent: if you chew off a chunk, it will grow back. But if you chew off too much, the starfish dies. Valerie B. chewed off a chunk of love from my dwindling reserve . . . a reserve already nibbled by Charlotte and Lory and Sherri and Cindy and others down through the years. There's still enough there to make the saleable appearance of a whole creature, but nobody gets gnawed on that way without becoming a little dead. So, if Cupid (that perverted little motherfucker) decides his lightning ought to strike this gnarly tree trunk again, whoever or whatever gets me, is going to get a handy second, damaged goods, something a little dead and a little crippled.

Having learned that, all I can advise is an impossible stance for all of you: utter openness and reasonable caution. Don't close yourself off, but jeezus, be careful of monsters with teeth. And just so you know what they look like when they come clanking after you, here is a photo of one. The package is so pretty, one can only urge you to remember Pandora. Be careful which boxes you open, troops.

The Other Eye of Polyphemus

This is about Brubaker, who is a man, but who might as easily have been a woman; and it would have been the same, no difference: painful and endless.

She was in her early forties and crippled. Something with the left leg and the spine. She went sidewise, slowly, like a sailor leaving a ship after a long time at sea. Her face was unindexed as to the rejections she had known; one could search randomly and find a shadow here beneath the eyes that came from the supermarket manager named Charlie; a crease in the space beside her mouth, just at the left side, that had been carved from a two nights' association with Clara from the florist shop; a moistness here at the right temple each time she recalled the words spoken the morning after the night with the fellow who drove the dry cleaner's van, Barry or Benny. But there was no sure record. It was all there, everywhere in her face.

Brubaker had not wanted to sleep with her. He had not wanted to take her home or go to her home, but he had. Her apartment was small and faced out onto a narrow court that permitted sunlight only during the hour before and the hour following high noon. She had pictures from magazines taped to the walls. The bed was narrow.

When she touched him, he felt himself going away. Thinking of warm places where he had rested on afternoons many years before; afternoons when he had been alone and had thought that was not as successful a thing to be as he now understood it to be. He did not want to think of it in this way, but he thought of himself as a bricklayer doing a methodical job. Laying the bricks straight and true.

He made love to her in the narrow bed, and was not there. He was doing a job, and thought how unkind and how unworthy such thoughts seemed to be . . . even though she would not know he was away somewhere else. He had done this before, and kindness was something he did very well. She would feel treasured, and attended, and certainly that was the least he could do. Her limp, her sad and lined face. She would think he was in attendance, treasuring her. He had no needs of his own, so it was possible to give her all that without trembling.

They both came awake when an ambulance screamed crosstown just beneath her window, and she looked at him warmly and said, "I have to get up early in the morning, we're doing inventory at the office, the files are really in terrible shape." But her face held a footnote expression that might have been interpreted as *You can stay if you want, but I've been left in beds where the other side grows cool quickly, and I don't want to see your face in the morning with that look that tells me you're trying to work up an excuse to leave in a hurry so you can rush home to take the kind of shower that washes the memory of me off you. So I'm giving you the chance to go now, because if you stay it means you'll call tomorrow sometime before noon and ask if I'd like to have dinner and see an early movie.*

So he kissed her several times, on the cheeks and once—gently—on the mouth, with lips closed; a treasuring kiss. And he left her apartment.

The breeze blew gently and coolly off the East River, and he decided to walk down past Henderson Place to sit in the park. To give himself time to come back from those far places. He felt partially dissolved, as if in sending himself out of that apartment he had indulged in some kind of minimal astral projection. And now that he was ready to receive himself again, there was a bit of his soul missing, left behind in her bed.

He had a tiny headache, the finest point of pain, just between and above his eyes, somewhere pierced behind the hard bone over the bridge of his nose. As he walked toward the park, he rubbed the angles of his nose between thumb and forefinger.

Carl Schurz Park was calm. Unlike vast sections of the city, it could be visited after dark without fear. The stillness, the calmness: marauders seldom lurked there.

He took a bench and sat staring off across the cave of water. The pain was persistent and he massaged the inner corners of his eyes with a gentle fingertip.

There had been a woman he had met at a cocktail party. From Maine. He hesitated to think of her in such simplified ways, but there was no denying her sweetness and virginity. Congregationalist, raised too well for life in this city, she had come here from Maine to work in publishing, and the men had not been good to her. Attracted by her well-scrubbed face and her light, gentle manner, they had stepped out with her two, three, once even four times. But she had been raised too well for life taken in late night sessions, and they had drifted back to their meat racks and their lonelinesses mutually shared. One had even suggested she seduce a platonic friend of hers, a gentle young man coming to grips with his sexuality, and then she would be fit for a proper affair. She had asked him to leave. The following week he was seeing the wife of a production assistant at the publishing house in which they all labored, and the girl from Maine had signed up for tap dancing lessons.

She had met Brubaker at the cocktail party and they had talked, leaning out the thirty-first floor window to escape the smoke and the chatter.

It became clear to him that she had decided he was the one. Reality and upbringing waged their war in her, and she had decided to capitulate. He walked her home and she said, "Come in for a graham cracker. I have lots of them." He said, "What time is it?" His watch said 12:07. "I'll come up till 12:15." She smiled shyly and said, "I'm being aggressive. It's not easy for me." He said, "I don't want to come up for very long. We might get into trouble." He meant it. He liked her. But she was hurting. "It's not a kind of trouble you haven't been in before," she said. He smiled gently and said, "No, but it's a kind of trouble *you've* never been in."

But he could not refuse her. And he was good with her, as good as he could be, accepting the responsibility, hoping when she found the man she had been saving herself for, he would be very very loving. At least, he knew, he had put her out of reach of the kind of men who sought virgins. Neither the sort who would marry *only* a virgin, nor the predators who went on safari for such endangered species, were human enough for her.

And when he left, the next morning, he had a headache. The same pinpoint of anguish that now pulsed between and above his eyes as he sat in the park. He had felt changed after leaving *her*, just as he did tonight. Was there a diminishing taking place?

Why did imperfect people seek him out and need him?

He knew himself to be no wiser, no nobler, no kinder than most people were capable of being, if given the chance. But he seemed to be a focal point for those who were in need of kindness, gentle words, soft touches. It had always been so for him. Yet he had no needs of his own.

Was it possible never to be touched, to give endlessly, no matter how much was asked, and never to name one's own desire? It was like living behind a pane of one-way glass; seeing out, while no one could see in. Polyphemus, the one-eyed, trapped in his cave, ready victim for all the storm-tossed Odysseus creatures who came to him unbidden. And like Polyphemus, denied half his sight, was he always to be a victim of the storm-tossed? Was there a limit to how much he could give? All he knew of need was what was demanded of him, blind in one eye to personal necessities.

The wind rose and shivered the tops of the trees.

It smelled very clean and fresh. As she had.

Out on the East River a dark shape slid smoothly across his line of sight and he thought of some lonely scow carrying the castoff remnants of life downtide to a nameless grave where blind fish and things with many legs sculled through the darkness, picking over the remains.

He rose from the bench and walked down through the park.

To his right, in the empty playground, the wind pushed the children's swings. They squealed and creaked. The dark shape out there, skimming along obscuring Roosevelt Island, was heading south downriver. He decided to pace it. He might have gone straight ahead till Schurz Park ended, then crossed the John Finley Walkway over the East River Drive traffic, but the dark shape out there fascinated him. As far as he could tell, he had no connection with it, in any way, of any kind. Utterly uninvolved with the shape. It meant nothing to him; and for that reason, chiefly, it was something to follow.

At 79th Street, the park's southern boundary behind him, East End Avenue came to a dead end facing the side of the East End Hotel. To his left, where 79th Street's eastern extremity terminated against the edge of Manhattan Island, worlds-end, a low metal barrier blocked off the street from the Drive. He walked to the barrier. Out there the black shape had come to rest on the river.

Cars flashed past like accelerated particles, their lights blending one into another till there were chromatic bands of blue and red and silver and white forming a larger barrier beyond the low metal fencing that blocked his passage. Passage where? Across six lanes of thundering traffic and a median that provided no protection? Protection from what? He stepped off the curb and did not realize he had climbed over the metal fencing to do so. He stepped off into the seamless, light-banded traffic.

Like walking across water. He crossed the uptown-bound lanes, between the cars, walking between the raindrops, untouched. He reached the median and kept going. Through the downtown-bound bands of light to the far side.

He looked back at the traffic. It had never touched him; but that didn't seem strange, somehow. He knew it should, but between the now-blistering headache and his feeling of being partially disembodied, it was inconsequential.

He climbed the low metal barrier and stood on the narrow ledge of concrete. The East River lay below him. He sat down on the concrete ledge and let his legs dangle. The black shape was directly across from him, in the middle of the river. He lowered himself down the face of the concrete wall till his feet touched the black skin of the East River.

He had met a woman at a library sale two years before. The New York Public Library on 42nd Street and Fifth Avenue had been clearing out excess and damaged stock. They had set up the tables in tiny Bryant Park abutting the Library on the 42nd Street side. He had reached for a copy of José Ortega y Gasset's THE REVOLT OF THE MASSES in the 25th anniversary Norton edition, just as she had reached for it. They came up with the book together, and looked across the table at each other. He took her for coffee at the Swiss Chalet on East 48th.

They went to bed only once, though he continued to see her for several months while she tried to make up her mind whether she would return to her husband; he was in the restaurant linen supply business. For the most part, Brubaker sat and listened to her.

"The thing I most hate about Ed is that he's so damned self-sufficient," she said. "I always feel if I were to vanish, he'd forget me in a week and get himself another woman and keep right on the way he is."

Brubaker said, "People have confided in me, and they've been almost ashamed of saying it, though I don't know why they should be, that the pain of losing someone only lasts about a week. At least with any intensity. And then it's simply a dull ache for a while until someone else comes along."

"I feel so guilty seeing you and not, uh, you know."

"That's all right," he said, "I enjoy your company. And if I can be of any use, talking to me, so you get your thoughts straight, well, that's better than being a factor that keeps you and Ed apart."

"You're so kind. Jesus, if Ed were only a fraction as kind as you, we'd have no problems. But he's so *selfish*! Little things. He'll squeeze the toothpaste tube from the middle, especially a new one, and he knows how that absolutely *unhinges* me, and he'll spit the paste all over the fixtures so I have to go at them a hundred times a week—"

And he listened to her and listened to her and listened to her, but she was too nervous for sex, and that was all right; he really did like her and want to be of some help.

There were times when she cried in his arms, and said they should take an apartment together, and she'd do it in a minute if it weren't for the children and half the business being in her name. There were times when she raged around his apartment, slamming cabinet doors and talking back to the television, cursing Ed for some cruelty he had visited on her. There were times when she would sit curled up staring out the window of Brubaker's apartment, running the past through her mind like prayer beads of sorrow.

Finally, one last night, she came into his bed and made ferocious love to him, then told Brubaker she was going back to Ed. For all the right reasons, she said. And a part of Brubaker had gone away, never to return. He had experienced the headache.

Now he simply walked across the soaked-black water to the dark shape. Like walking through traffic. Untouched. The tiniest ripples circled out from beneath his feet, silvered and delicate for just a moment before vanishing to either side of him.

He walked out across the East River and stepped into the dark shape.

It was all mist and soft cottony fog. He stepped inside and the only light was that he produced himself through the tiniest pinpoint that had opened between and above his eyes. The darkness smoothed around him and he was well within the shifting shape now.

It was not his sort of gathering. Everyone seemed much too intense. And the odor of their need was more pervasive than anything he had ever known before.

They lounged around in the fog, dim against the darkness, illuminated only when Brubaker's light struck them, washed them for a moment with soft pink-white luminescence and then they became dim moving shapes in the fog. He moved among them, and once a hand touched his arm. He drew back. For the first time in his life he drew back.

He realized what he had done, and felt sorry about it.

He swept his light around through the darkness and caught the stare of a woman who had clearly been watching him. Had she been the person who had touched him? He looked at her and she smiled. It seemed a very familiar smile. The woman with the limp? The virgin? Ed's wife? One of the many other people he had known?

People moved in the darkness, rearranging themselves. He could not tell if they were carrying on conversations in the darkness, he could hear no voices, only the faint sound of fog whispering around the shadowed shapes. Were they coupling, was this some bizarre orgy? No, there was no frenetic energy being expended, no special writhing that one knew as sexual activity, even in darkness.

But they were all watching him now. He felt utterly alone among them. He was not one of them, they had not been waiting for him, their eyes did not shine.

She was still watching him, still smiling.

"Did you touch me?" he asked.

"No," she said. "No one touched you."

"I'm sure someone—"

"No one touched you." She watched him, the smile more than an answer, considerably less than a question. "No one here touched you. No one here wants anything from you."

A man spoke from behind him, saying something Brubaker could not make out. He turned away from the woman with the serious smile, trying to locate the man in the darkness. His light fell on a man lying in the fog, resting back on his elbows. There was something familiar about him, but Brubaker could not place it; something from the past, like a specific word for a specific thing that just fitted perfectly and could be recalled if he thought of nothing else.

"Did you say something?"

The man looked at him with what seemed to be concern.

"I said: you deserve better."

"If you say so."

"No, if *you* say so. That's one of the three things you most need to understand."

"Three things?"

"You deserve better. Everyone deserves better."

Brubaker did not understand. He was here in a place that seemed without substance or attachment to real time, speaking plainly to people who were—he now realized—naked—and why had he not realized it before?—and he did not wonder about it; neither did he understand what they were saying to him.

"What are the other two things I need to know?" he asked the man.

But it was a woman in the darkness who answered. Yet another woman than the one with the smile. "No one should live in fear," she said, from the fog, and he skimmed his light around to find her. She had a hare-lip.

"Do you mean me? That I live in fear?"

"*No one* should live like that," she said. "It isn't necessary. It can be overcome. Courage is as easy to replicate as cowardice. You need only practice. Do it once, then twice, and the third time it's easier, and the fourth time a matter of course, and after that it's done without even consideration. Fear washes away and everything is possible."

He wanted to settle down among them. He felt one with them now. But they made no move to invite him in. He was something they did not want among them.

"Who are you all?"

"We thought you knew," said the woman with the smile. He recognized her voice. It came and went in rises and falls of tone, as though speaking over a bad telephone connection, incomplete, partial. He felt he might be missing parts of the conversation.

"No, I have no idea," he said.

"You'll be leaving now," she said. He shone the light on her. Her eyes were milky with cataracts.

His light swept across them. They were all malformed in some way or other. Hairless, blind, atrophied, ruined. But he did not know who they were.

His light went out.

The dark shape seemed to be withdrawing from around him. The fog and mist swarmed and swirled away, and he was left standing in darkness on the East River. A vagrant whisper of one of their voices came to him as the dark shape moved off downriver: "You'd better hurry."

He felt water lapping at his ankles, and he hurried back toward the concrete breakwall. By the time he reached it, he was swimming. The wind had died away, but he shivered with the chill of the water that soaked his clothes.

He pulled himself up the face of the wall and lay on the ledge gasping for breath.

"May I help you?" he heard someone say.

A hand touched his shoulder. He looked up and saw a woman in a long beige duster coat. She was kneeling down, deeply concerned.

"I wasn't trying to kill myself," he heard himself say.

"I hadn't thought of that," she said. "I just thought you might need a hand up out of the water."

"Yes," he said, "I could use a hand."

She helped him up. The headache seemed to be leaving him. He heard someone speak, far out on the river, and he looked at her. "Did you hear that?"

"Yes," she said, "someone spoke. It must be one of those tricks of echo."

"I'm sure that's what it was," he said.

"Do you need something to warm you up?" she asked. "I live right over there in that building. Some coffee?"

"Yes," he said, allowing her to help him up the slope. "I need something to warm me up."

Whatever you need in life you must go and get, had been the words from out there on the river where the lost bits of himself were doomed to sail forever. Damaged, forlorn; but no longer bound to him. He seemed to be able to see more clearly now.

And he went with her, for a while, for a long while or a short while; but he went to get something to warm him; he went to get what he needed.

All the Birds Come Home to Roost

He turned onto his left side in the bed, trying to avoid the wet spot. He propped his hand against his cheek, smiled grimly, and prepared himself to tell her the truth about why he had been married and divorced three times.

"Three times!" she had said, her eyes widening, that familiar line of perplexity appearing vertically between her brows. "Three times. Christ, in all the time we went together, I never knew that. Three, huh?"

Michael Kirxby tightened the grim smile slightly. "You never asked, so I never mentioned it," he said. "There's a lot of things I never bother to mention: I flunked French in high school and had to work and go to summer school so I could graduate a semester late; I once worked as a short-order cook in a diner in New Jersey near the Turnpike; I've had the clap maybe half a dozen times and the crabs twice . . ."

"Ichhh, don't talk about it!" She buried her naked face in the pillow. He reached out and ran his hand up under her thick, chestnut hair, ran it all the way up to the occipital ridge and massaged the cleft. She came up from where she had hidden.

That had been a few moments ago. Now he propped himself on his bent arm and proceeded to tell her the truth about it. He never lied; it simply wasn't worth the trouble. But it *was* a long story, and he'd told it a million times; and even though he had developed a storyteller's facility with the interminable history of it, he had learned to sketch in whole sections with apocryphal sentences, had developed the use of artful time-lapse jumps. Still, it took a good fifteen minutes to do it right, to achieve the proper reaction and, quite frankly, he was bored with the recitation. But there were occasions when it served its purpose, and this was one of them, so he launched into it.

"I got married the first time when I was twenty, twenty-one, something like that. I'm lousy on dates. Anyhow, she was a sick girl, disturbed before I ever met her; family thing, hated her mother, loved her father—he was an ex-Marine, big, good-looking—secretly wanted to ball the old man but never could cop to it. He died of cancer of the brain but before he went, he began acting erratically, treating the mother like shit. Not that the mother didn't deserve it . . . she was a harridan, a real termagant. But it was really outrageous, he wasn't coming home nights, beating up the mother, that sort of thing. So my wife sided with the mother against him. When they found out his brain was being eaten up by the tumor, she flipped and went off the deep end. Made my life a furnace! After I divorced her, the mother had her committed. She's been in the asylum over seventeen years now. For me, it was close; too damned close. She very nearly took me with her to the madhouse. I got away just in time. A little longer, I wouldn't be here today."

He watched her face. Martha was listening closely now. Heartmeat information. This was the sort of thing they loved to hear; the fiber material, the formative chunks, something they could sink their neat, small teeth into. He sat up, reached over and clicked on the bed lamp. The light was on his right side as he stared toward the foot of the bed, apparently conjuring up the painful past; the light limned his profile. He had a Dick Tracy chin and deep-set brown eyes. He cut his own hair, did it badly, and it shagged over his ears as though he had just crawled out of bed. Fortunately, it was wavy and he *was* in bed: he knew the light and the profile were good. Particularly for the story.

"I was in crap shape after her. Almost went down the tube. She came within a finger of pulling me onto the shock table with her. She always, *always* had a hoodoo sign on me; I had very little defense against her. Really scares me when I think about it."

The naked Martha looked at him. "Mike . . . what was her name?"

He swallowed hard. Even now, years later, long after it was ended, he found himself unable to cleanse the memories of pain and fear. "Her name was Cindy."

"Well, uh, what did she do that was so awful?"

He thought about it for a second. This was a departure from the routine. He wasn't usually asked for further specifics. And running back through the memories he found most of them had blurred into one indistinguishable throb of misery. There were incidents he remembered, incidents so heavily freighted with anguish that he could feel his gorge becoming buoyant, but they were part of the whole terrible time with Cindy, and trying to pick them out so they would convey, in microcosm, the shrieking hell of their marriage, was like retelling something funny from the day before, to people who had not been there. Not funny. Oh, well, you'd have to be there.

What had she done that was so awful, apart from the constant attempts at suicide, the endless remarks intended to make him feel inadequate, the erratic behavior, the morning he had returned from ten weeks of basic training a day earlier than expected and found her in bed with some skinny guy from on the block, the times she took off and sold the furniture and cleaned out the savings account? What had she done beyond that? Oh, hell, Martha, nothing much.

He couldn't say that. He had to encapsulate the four years of their marriage. One moment that summed it up.

He said, "I was trying to pass my bar exams. I was really studying hard. It wasn't easy for me the way it was for a lot of people. And she used to mumble."

"She mumbled?"

"Yeah. She'd walk around, making remarks you just *knew* were crummy, but she'd do it under her breath, just at the threshold of audibility. And me trying to concentrate. She knew it made me crazy, but she always did it. So one time . . . I was really behind in the work and trying to catch up . . . and she started that, that . . ." He *remembered*! "That damned *mumbling*, in the living room and the bedroom and the bathroom . . . but she wouldn't come in the kitchen where I was studying. And it went on and on and on . . ."

He was trembling. Jesus, why had she asked for this; it wasn't in the script.

". . . and finally I just stood up and screamed, 'What the hell are you mumbling? What the hell do you want from me? Can't you see I'm busting my ass studying? Can't you for Christ sake leave me alone for just five fucking minutes?' "

With almost phonographic recall he knew he was saying precisely, exactly what he had screamed all those years ago.

"And I ran into the bedroom, and she was in her bathrobe and slippers, and she started in on me, accusing me of this and that and every other damned thing, and I guess I finally went over the edge, and I punched her right in the face. As hard as I could. The way I'd hit some slob in the street. Hard, real hard. And then somehow I had her bedroom slipper in my hand and I was sitting on her chest on the bed, and beating her in the face with that goddam slipper . . . and . . . and . . . I woke up and *saw me hitting her,* and it was the first time I'd ever hit a woman, and I fell away from her, and I crawled across the floor and I was sitting there like a scared animal, my hands over my eyes . . . crying . . . scared to death . . . "

She stared at him silently. He was shaking terribly.

"Jesus," she said, softly.

And they stayed that way for a while, without speaking. He had answered her question. More than she wanted to know.

The mood was tainted now. He could feel himself split—one part of him here and now with the naked Martha, in this bedroom with the light low—another part he had thought long gone, in that other bedroom, hunkered down against the baseboard, hands over eyes, whimpering like a crippled dog, Cindy sprawled half on the floor, half on the bed, her face puffed and bloodied. He tried desperately to get control of himself.

After some long moments he was able to breathe regularly. She was still staring at him, her eyes wide. He said, almost with reverence, "Thank God for Marcie."

She waited and then said, "Who's Marcie?"

"Who *was* Marcie. Haven't seen her in something like fifteen years."

"Well, who *was* Marcie?"

"She was the one who picked up the pieces and focused my eyes. If it hadn't been for her, I'd have walked around on my knees for another year . . . or two . . . or ten . . . "

"What happened to her?"

"Who knows? You can take it from our recently severed liaison; I seem to have some difficulty hanging on to good women."

"Oh, Mike!"

"Hey, take it easy. You split for good and sound reasons. I think I'm doomed to be a bachelor . . . maybe a *recluse* for the rest of my life. But that's okay. I've tried it three times. I just don't have the facility. I'm good for a woman for short stretches, but over the long haul I think I'm just too high-pressure."

She smiled wanly, trying to ease what she took to be pain. He *wasn't* in pain, but she had never been able to tell the difference with him. Precisely that inability to penetrate his façade had been the seed of their dissolution. "It was okay with us."

"For a while."

"Yeah. For a while." She reached across him to the nightstand and picked up the heavy Orrefors highball glass with the remains of the Mendocino Gray Riesling. "It was so strange running into you at Allison's party. I'd heard you were seeing some model or actress . . . or something."

He shook his head. "Nope. You were my last and greatest love."

She made a wet, bratting sound. "Bullshit."

And they stayed that way, silently, for a while. Once, he touched her naked thigh, feeling the nerve jump under his hand; and once, she reached across to lay her hand on his chest, to feel him breathing. But they didn't make love again. And after a space of time in which they thought they could hear the dust settling in the room, she said, "Well, I've got to get home to feed the cats."

"You want to stay the night?"

She thought about it a moment. "No thanks, Mike. Maybe another night when I come prepared. You know my thing about putting on the same clothes the next day." He knew. And smiled.

She crawled out of bed and began getting dressed. He watched her, ivory-lit by the single bed lamp. It never would have worked. But then, he'd known that almost from the first. It never worked well for an extended period. There was no Holy Grail. Yet the search went on, reflexively. It was like eating potato chips.

She came back to the bed, leaned over and kissed him. It was the merest touch of lips, and meant nothing. "Bye. Call me."

"No doubt about it," he said; but he wouldn't.

Then she left. He sat up in the bed for a while, thinking that it was odd how people couldn't leave it alone. Like a scab, they had to pick at it. He'd dated her rather heavily for a month, and they had broken up for no particular reason save that it was finished. And tonight the party, and he was alone, and she was alone, and they had come together for an anticlimax.

A returning. To a place neither had known very well. A devalued neighborhood.

He knew he would never see Martha again.

The bubble of sadness bobbed on the surface for a moment, then burst; the sense of loss flavored the air a moment longer; then he turned off the light, rolled over onto the dried wet spot, and went to sleep.

He was hacking out the progression of interrogatories pursuant to the Blieler brief with one of the other attorneys in the office when his secretary stuck her head into the conference room and said he had a visitor. Rubbing his eyes, he realized they had been at it for three straight hours. He shoved back from the conference table, swept the papers into the folio, and said, "Let's knock off for lunch." The other attorney stretched, and musculature crackled. "Okay, Call it four o'clock. I've got to go over to the 9000 Building to pick up Barbarossi's deposition." He got up and left. Kirxby sighed, simply sitting there, all at once overcome by a nameless malaise. As though something dark and forbidding were slouching towards his personal Bethlehem.

Then he went into his office to meet his visitor.

She turned half-around in the big leather chair and smiled at him. "Jerri!" he said, all surprise and pleasure. His first reaction: surprised pleasure. "My God, it's been . . . how long . . . ?"

The smile lifted at one corner: her bemused smile.

"It's been six months. Seem longer?"

He grinned and shrugged. It had been his choice to break up the affair after two years. For Martha. Who had lasted a month.

"How time flies when you're enjoying yourself," she said. She crossed her legs. A summary judgment on his profligacy.

He walked around and sat down behind the desk. "Come on, Jerri, gimme some slack."

Another returning. First Martha, out of the blue; now Jerri. Emerging from the mauve, perhaps? "What brings you back into my web?" He tried to stare at her levelly, but she was on to that; it made him feel guilty.

"I suppose I could have cobbled up something spectacular along the lines of a multimillion-dollar lawsuit against one of my competitors," she said, "but the truth is just that I felt an urgent need to see you again."

He opened and closed the top drawer of his desk, to buy a few seconds. Then, carefully avoiding her gaze, he said, "What is this, Jerri? Christ, isn't there enough crap in the world without detouring to find a fresh supply?" He said it softly, because he had said I love you to her for two years, excluding the final seven months when he had said fuck off, never realizing they were the same phrase.

But he took her to lunch, and they made it a date for dinner, and he took her back to his apartment and they were two or three drinks too impatient to get to the bed and made it on the living room carpet still half-clothed. He cherished silence when making love, even when only screwing, and she remembered and didn't make a sound. And it was as good or as bad as it had ever been between them for two years minus the last seven months. And when she awoke hours later, there on the living room carpet, with her skirt up around her hips, and Michael lying on his side with his head cradled on his arm, still sleeping, she breathed deeply and slitted her eyes and commanded the hangover to permit her the strength to rise; and she rose, and she covered him with a small lap-robe he had pilfered off an American Airlines flight to Boston; and she went away. Neither loving him nor hating him. Having merely satisfied the urgent compulsion in her to return to him once more, to see him once more, to have his body once more. And there was nothing more to it than that.

The next morning he rolled onto his back, lying there on the floor, kept his eyes closed, and knew he would never see her again. And there was no more to it than that.

Two days later he received a phone call from Anita. He had had two dates with Anita, more than two-and-a-half years earlier, during the week before he had met Jerri and had taken up with her. She said she had been thinking about him. She said she had been weeding out old phone numbers in her book and had come across his, and just wanted to call to see how he was. They made a date for that night and had sex and she left quickly. And he knew he would never see her again.

And the next day at lunch at the Oasis he saw Corinne sitting across the room. He had lived with Corinne for a year, just prior to meeting Anita, just prior to meeting Jerri. Corinne came across the room and kissed him on the back of the neck and said, "You've lost weight. You look good enough to eat." And they got together that night, and one thing and another, and he was, and she did, and then he did, and she stayed the night but left after coffee the next morning. And he knew he would never see her again.

But he began to have an unsettling feeling that something strange was happening to him.

Over the next month, in reverse order of having known them, every female with whom he had had a liaison magically reappeared in his life. Before Corinne, he had had a string of one-nighters and casual weekends with Hannah, Nancy, Robin and Cylvia; Elizabeth, Penny, Margie and Herta; Eileen, Gail, Holly and Kathleen. One by one, in unbroken string, they came back to him like waifs returning to the empty kettle for one last spoonful of gruel. Once, and then gone again, forever.

Leaving behind pinpoint lights of isolated memory. Each one of them an incomplete yet somehow total summation of the woman: Hannah and her need for certain words in the bed; the pressure of Nancy's legs over his shoulders; Robin and the wet towels; Cylvia who never came, perhaps could *not* come; Elizabeth so thin that her pelvis left him sore for days; having to send out for ribs for Penny, before and after; a spade-shaped mole on Margie's inner thigh; Herta falling asleep in a second after sex, as if she had been clubbed; the sound of Eileen's laugh, like the wind in Aspen; Gail's revulsion and animosity when he couldn't get an erection and tried to go down on her; Holly's endless retelling of the good times they had known; Kathleen still needing to delude herself that he was seducing her, even after all this time.

One sharp point of memory. One quick flare of light. Then gone forever and there was no more to it than that.

But by the end of that month, the suspicion had grown into a dread certainty; a certainty that led him inexorably to an inevitable end place that was too horrible to consider. Every time he followed the logical progression to its finale, his mind skittered away . . . that whimpering, crippled dog.

His fear grew. Each woman returned built the fear higher. Fear coalesced into terror and he fled the city, hoping by exiling himself to break the links.

But there he sat, by the fireplace at The Round Hearth, in Stowe, Vermont . . . and the next one in line, Sonja, whom he had not seen in years, Sonja came in off the slopes and saw him, and she went a good deal whiter than the wind chill factor outside accounted for.

They spent the night together and she buried her face in the pillow so her sounds would not carry. She lied to her husband about her absence and the next morning, before Kirxby came out of his room, they were gone.

But Sonja *had* come back. And that meant the next one before her had been Gretchen. He waited in fear, but she did not appear in Vermont, and he felt if he stayed there he was a sitting target and he called the office and told them he was going down to the Bahamas for a few days, that his partners should parcel out his caseload among them, for just a few more days, don't ask questions.

And Gretchen was working in a tourist ship specializing in wicker goods; and she looked at him as he came through the door, and she said, "Oh, my God, *Michael*! I've had you on my mind almost constantly for the past week. I was going to call you—"

And she gave a small sharp scream as he fainted, collapsing face-forward into a pyramid of woven wicker clothing hampers.

The apartment was dark. He sat there in the silence, and refused to answer the phone. The gourmet delicatessen had been given specific instructions. The delivery boy with the food had to knock in a specific, certain cadence, or the apartment door would not be opened.

Kirxby had locked himself away. The terror was very real now. It was impossible to ignore what was happening to him. All the birds were coming home to roost.

Back across nineteen years, from his twentieth birthday to the present, in reverse order of having known them, every woman he had ever loved or fucked or had an encounter of substance with . . . was homing in on him. Martha the latest, from which point the forward momentum of his relationships had been arrested, like a pendulum swung as far as it could go, and back again, back, back, swinging back past Jerri and Anita, back to Corinne and Hannah, back, and Nancy, back, and Robin and all of them, straight back to Gretchen, who was just three women before . . .

He wouldn't think about it.

He *couldn't*. It was too frightening.

The special, specific, certain cadence of a knock on his apartment door. In the darkness he found his way to the door and removed the chain. He opened the door to take the box of groceries, and saw the teenaged Puerto Rican boy sent by the deli. And standing behind him was Kate. She was twelve years older, a lot less the gamin, classy and self-possessed now, but it was Kate nonetheless.

He began to cry.

He slumped against the open door and wept, hiding his face in his hands partially because he was ashamed, but more because he was frightened.

She gave the boy a tip, took the box, and edged inside the apartment, moving Kirxby with her, gently. She closed the door, turned on a light, and helped him to the sofa.

When she came back from putting away the groceries, she slipped out of her shoes and sat as far away from him as the length of the sofa would permit. The light was behind her and she could see his swollen, terrified face clearly. His eyes were very bright. There was a trapped expression on his face. For a long time she said nothing.

Finally, when his breathing became regular, she said, "Michael, what the hell *is* it? Tell me."

But he could not speak of it. He was too frightened to name it. As long as he kept it to himself, it was just barely possible it was a figment of delusion, a ravening beast of the mind that would vanish as soon as he was able to draw a deep breath. He knew he was lying to himself. It was real. It was happening to him, inexorably.

She kept at him, speaking softly, cajoling him, prising the story from him. And so he told her. Of the reversal of his life. Of the film running backward. Of the river flowing upstream. Carrying him back and back and back into a dark land from which there could never be escape.

"And I ran away. I went to St. Kitts. And I walked into a shop, some dumb shop, just some dumb kind of tourist goods shop . . ."

"And what was her name . . . Greta . . . ?"

"Gretchen."

". . . Gretchen. And Gretchen was there."

"Yes."

"Oh, my God, Michael. You're making yourself crazy. This is lunatic. You've got to stop it."

"*Stop it!?!* Jesus, I wish I *could* stop it. But I can't. Don't you see, you're *part* of it. It's unstoppable, it's crazy but it's hellish. I haven't slept in days. I'm afraid to go to sleep. God knows what might happen."

"You're building all this in your mind, Michael. It isn't real. Lack of sleep is making you paranoid."

"No . . . no . . . listen . . . here, listen to this . . . I remembered it from years ago . . . I read it . . . I found it when I went looking for it . . ." He lurched off the sofa, found the book on the wet bar and brought it back under the light. It was THE PLAGUE by Camus, in a Modern Library edition. He thumbed through the book and could not find the place. Then she took it from him and laid it on her palm and it fell open to the page, because he had read and reread the section. She read it aloud, where he had underlined it:

"'Had he been less tired, his senses more alert, that all-pervading odor of death might have made him sentimental. But when a man has had only four hours' sleep, he isn't sentimental. He sees things as they are; that is to say, he sees them in the garish light of justice—hideous, witless justice.'" She closed the book and stared at him. "You really believe this, don't you?"

"Don't I? Of course I do! I'd be what you think I am, crazy . . . *not* to believe it. Kate, listen to me. Look, here you are. It's twelve years. Twelve years and another life. But here you are, back with me again, just in sequence. You were my lover before I met Gretchen. I *knew* it would be you!"

"Michael, don't let this make you stop thinking. There's no way you could have known. Bill and I have been divorced for two years. I just moved back to the city last week. Of *course* I'd look you up. We had a very good thing together. If I hadn't met Bill we might *still* be together."

"Jesus, Kate, you're not *listening* to me. I'm trying to tell you this is some kind of terrible justice. I'm rolling back through time with the women I've known. There's you, and if there's you, then the next one before you was Marcie. And if I go back to her, then that means that after Marcie . . . after Marcie . . . *before* Marcie there was . . ."

He couldn't speak the name.

She said the name. His face went white again. It was the speaking of the unspeakable.

"Oh God, Kate, oh dear God, I'm screwed, I'm screwed . . ."

"Cindy can't get you, Mike. She's still in the Home, isn't she?"

He nodded, unable to answer.

Kate slid across and held him. He was shaking. "It's all right. It's going to be all right."

She tried to rock him, like a child in pain, but his terror was an electric current surging through him. "I'll take care of you," she said. "Till you're better. There won't be any Marcie, and there certainly won't be any Cindy."

"No!" he screamed, pulling away from her. *"No!"*

He stumbled toward the door. "I've got to get out of here. They can find me here. I've got to go somewhere out away from here, fast, fast, where they can't find me ever."

He yanked open the door and ran into the hall. The elevator was not there. It was never there when he needed it, needed it badly, needed it desperately.

He ran down the stairs and into the vestibule of the building. The doorman was standing looking out into the street, the glass doors tightly shut against the wind and the cold.

Michael Kirxby ran past him, head down, arms close to his body. He heard the man say something, but it was lost in the rush of wind and chill as he jammed through onto the sidewalk.

Terror enveloped him. He ran toward the corner and turned toward the darkness. If he could just get into the darkness, where he couldn't be found, then he was safe. Perhaps he would be safe.

He rounded the corner. A woman, head down against the wind, bumped into him. They rebounded and in the vague light of the street lamp looked into each other's faces.

"Hello," said Marcie.

VII

TO THE MATTRESSES WITH MEAN DEMONS

> "The great lizards owned the planet for something like 130,000,000 years, but they didn't have slant-well drilling, pesticides, pollution, fast breeders, defoliants, demagogues, thermonuclear warheads, non-biodegradable plastics, The Pentagon, The Kremlin, The General Staff of the People's Army, Ronald Reagan, Richard Nixon and the FBI. [. . .] Had they not been so culturally deprived, they might have sunk into the swamps in a mere three thousand years."
>
> —"Reaping the Whirlwind," Introduction to APPROACHING OBLIVION, Walker, 1974

Anyone alive is bait for demons.

Whether we recognize them or not, each of us feels the influence of demons. Some are personal demons, hatched out of the id to stoke our paranoia, to cast self-doubt in our paths, to distract us with lies of spectacular success or spectacular failure. Some are societal, monstrous things which work to send entire cultures over the precipice into the madness of jihad or indolence or plastic lives. And some are in between; here, nudging a group of neighbors away from sense and sanity; there, teasing an individual with the frozen carrot on a stick. Conformity, complacency, maintaining the status quo—or mass nonconformity, misdirected anger, street violence as a substitute for revolution; demons play both sides of the coin and work the edges as well.

Harlan has spent much of his life wrestling with demons, recognizing their curious differences and similarities, reporting on their odd and terrible mating habits, alerting us when he can to their special seductiveness. Here, a look at six demons.

A societal demon is at the core of "The Tombs" (1961), a lengthy excerpt (somewhat condensed) from MEMOS FROM PURGATORY, Harlan's gripping account of his ten weeks with a Brooklyn street gang in the mid-1950s and its 24-hour aftermath seven years later in Manhattan's Tombs. (His undercover research into gang violence provided materials for many short stories, a novel [WEB OF THE CITY], and MEMOS, which was even adapted for tv's *Alfred Hitchcock Hour,* airing in 1964.) As the 1980s abandon whatever it was that let us sleep through the 1970s, gang violence is on the rise and the book has, alas, become timely again, but Harlan found grimmer truths during his stay in jail. His succinct unfolding of the everyday degradation and demoralizing found in such places makes us recoil in horror, but even more chilling is his identification of who the true victims are.

Another time, another place, another demon shows its ugly face . . . on television. "Our Little Miss" (1970) was exposed by Harlan in *The Glass Teat* column, and even his tough hide of cynicism was flayed by the horrors he witnessed. Even something as seemingly sweet and innocent as a children's talent and beauty pageant is quickly revealed for the morally penurious obscenity it makes little pretense to hide. Watching Harlan pin *that* demon to the mat is particularly satisfying.

The next two demons harass the world's artists from two sides: the one without, the other within. "A Love Song to Jerry Falwell" (1984) is a moving, impassioned plea for the special madness of the "mad dreamers" who enrich our lives in the ways that the censors and self-appointed moralists never can. "Telltale Tics and Tremors" (1977), originally published as a column of advice for fledgling writers, swats at the pervasive and ubiquitous demon of mediocrity; and in an implicit argument from the lesser to the greater, Harlan says something, too, about the possible mediocrity of our own lives.

The sneakiest demon comes next. "True Love: Groping for the Holy Grail" (1978), in an edited and retitled version, appeared in *Los Angeles* magazine. In that city plagued by the bigger demons, one would hardly think it worth Harlan's time to zero in on this little fiend who gets in the way of True Love. But its thrusts, feints, defenses and bogus retreats dazzle and distract and, as Harlan learns to his chagrin, even had him tricking and outwitting himself. Harlan's self-discovery gives himself and us a clue to a better way to outwit the demon.

Of course that sneaky demon has a big brother. "Adrift Just Off the Islets of Langerhans: Latitude 38° 54′ N, Longitude 77° 00′ 13″ W" (1974) is, like so much of Harlan's best work, about love, lost childhood, self-trust, self-love. The icthyimp inside all of us, each of us, that won't let our discontent die, must be conquered if we are to find maturity. Note here, amid all the Universal paraphernalia of horror movies, the need to find our own symbols for what we once lost and what we have to find. This is the demon that can torment us to the grave.

Anyone alive is bait for demons. But the struggles against them make for fascinating reading.

> "It's not often people will tell you how they *really* feel about gut-level things. [. . .] They play cozy with you, because nobody likes to be hated, and large doses of truth from any one mouth tend to make the wearer of the mouth *persona non grata.* Particularly if he's caught you picking your nose and wiping it on your pants. Even worse if he catches you eating it. Now, honest, how many people will cop to that?"
>
> —"Brinkmanship," Introduction to Over the Edge, Belmont, 1970

The Tombs:

An Excerpt from Memos from Purgatory

I had brought away from the Barons some implements used by the kids—the set of knucks I'd used in the rumble, the billy club, a .22 revolver, the bayonet, the Italian stiletto without a switch I had used in the stand with Candle—and these were to become visual aids in lectures and panels on juvenile delinquency for PTA groups, YMCA gatherings, high school classes, youth organizations.

In seven years I had lectured many times on the subject; had even gone on television and radio with my experiences. I had said, "You can't stop a rumble or a kid gang once it gets rolling. There isn't much you *can* do when the only pride a kid has, is in a bopping club; not in his family, or his heritage, or his religion, school, country, or *himself*.

"But as long as there is a solid family unit that will recognize the kid as an integral part, that will respect his intelligence, his honesty, his status, a family he can run to when the city closes down on him and the world snaps and snarls, as long as the parents and the school and the church and the local government stop looking at delinquency as a recent cultural leprosy, get off their asses, and try to *understand* the kid, try to aid him in helping himself grow up, not shove him the way they *think* or *half-think* he should go, there's a chance.

"When everybody stops passing the buck and blaming it on girlie magazines or television or the H-bomb, then a start will be made toward solving the problem."

That's what I'd said, and showed the knives that had ripped, and the knucks that had smashed. That was what I'd said, though I'd known that wasn't the whole answer, perhaps not even the right answer.

But I'd known it was a start, and they had to start *somewhere.*

I tried to get across the idea of action on the part of parents too busy with churchkey and time-card, action on the part of school boards too hypocritical and stingy to persuade good teachers to stay in education, action on the part of clergy and government too busy dredging up the proper indignant expressions and the proper flowery phrases for "the present outrageous situation" to get out in the streets where the kids play stickball.

I wanted them to *talk* to their kids, and to *listen*.

Many lectures, many showings of the weapons the kids used, and in seven years—nothing. The same. No change, unless it was to get worse.

So my interest turned in futility to other things. I wrote about other things, saw different scenes, and the ten weeks in 1954 began to fade.

It was all to come back to me, much more forcibly, later that month . . . September, 1960.

I had gone to a party in the Bronx, and there met a fellow named Ken Bales, someone I'd known in 1955, a fellow I'd loaned a typewriter to. He had pawned it; he had been a deadbeat then, and in 1960 he was no better. I advised him if he didn't pony up the cost of a new typer, or get me that one back, I would lean on him. That happened early in September. It was to result in an experience I never want to relive, an experience that brought back my memories of the Barons so sharply I felt I had never left Brooklyn. It happened like this . . .

Bales, frightened by my determination to make him pay up, and aware of the weapons I had in my apartment (locked in a filing cabinet), which had never been a secret, as I had displayed them on television, anonymously phoned the police.

He told them I had an arsenal in my Greenwich Village apartment.

On Sunday, September 11th, a hot summer day, I was doing nothing in particular, loafing around the apartment, when the bell rang. I answered it, and was confronted by two plainclothesmen of the New York Police Department. They asked if they might come in. I thought it was a gag and asked to see their tin. They showed me their credentials and I admitted them.

They were pleasant enough, sat down, and asked me if I had any enemies. I answered with a grin, and said, "I lead a normal life; I suppose I've got as many as the next guy." They didn't smile back. They asked me how long I had been living at 95 Christopher Street and if I knew of anyone in particular who would like to do me harm. I told them how long I'd been in the apartment, since I'd come in from Chicago, and the only person I could think of at the moment who disliked me enough to fink on me was Ken Bales.

Then they asked if I'd ever used narcotics.

I didn't quite know what to answer them.

Friends who knew me often thought I was a fanatic, so opposed to junk was I. A young friend of mine, in fact, had been experimenting, and with another friend, a jazz critic named Ted White, we had threatened to knock his teeth in if he ever went near it again. Narcotics? Hell, no . . . I didn't even use No-Doz.

I told them I had never had anything to do with narcotics and felt this thing was going a bit too fast for me. I asked them what this was all about, and was I being charged with something. I noticed they were looking at me carefully, at my arms and my legs. I had been washing the bathroom sink at the time they had arrived and was wearing nothing but beach-boy slacks, rolled to the knees, with no shirt. They could see I had no needle marks on my body.

Then they informed me that an anonymous tip had come in to the Charles Street police station that a writer named Ellison at 95 Christopher Street was having wild narcotics parties, had a storehouse of heroin secreted in the apartment, and also had an arsenal of lethal weapons.

I knew it had been Bales, but I couldn't prove it.

At that point I asked them please to search the place. They said they had intended to do it in any case, but they were glad I'd offered so they wouldn't have to go and get a search warrant.

They spent the better part of an hour searching my one-and-a-half-room apartment, and naturally found nothing. Then they came back into the living room and sat down.

The senior officer asked me if I had a gun in the place. I had to think a moment. It did not dawn on me to equate the empty .22 short revolver I had used for seven years as a prop, with a lethal weapon that should have been registered in the State of New York. After a moment I said, "Well, I have some weapons that I've used on lecture tours, in connection with talks about juvenile delinquency." I showed them my books.

They asked if they might see the weapons.

I went to the closet, found my keys in a pair of pants, and unlocked the bottom drawer of my filing cabinet. Far in the back, under a stack of papers (for I had not been lecturing for six or eight months), I found the gun, the knife, the bayonet, and two sets of knucks. (The second set had been given to me by a student at a high school in Elizabethtown, Kentucky, after a talk I had given there, thus proving to me that j.d. was not a big city disease, solely.)

I handed these items over, though the bayonet and the knife (without a switch) were both legal in New York City.

They took these and I added, "I have bullets for the gun, too, if you want them." They indicated they did, so I located the box of .22 rounds and gave them to the officers, also. They smelled the gun. "When was the last time this was fired?" they asked.

"It's never been fired while I've had it," I said. "And that's seven years. Before that, I don't know." The officer with the gun nodded to the other and said it smelled clean.

We talked for another half hour, and still the seriousness of what was happening did not reach me. I was a legitimate writer with a legal use for these tools, and the whole anonymous call was a hoax, used by a kook to get me in trouble. They agreed that such might be the case, and while they were satisfied that the narcotics charge was absolutely unfounded, they would have to arrest me on the Sullivan Act for illegal possession of a gun. I thought I'd fall over, it was so weird. I'd done nothing, as far as I was concerned, and yet I was to be arrested.

They apologized, said they had no doubt I was innocent, but a complaint had been lodged, and they were compelled to follow it up. I tried to reason with them, but they were adamant in the pursuit of their duties.

I could not argue with them.

Today, I still feel I was treated fairly and honestly by those two police officers, whose names I cannot and would not reveal, for they helped me as much as they were able, later.

They advised me to get dressed, for they would have to take me in. I got panicky. My mother, whom I had not seen in over three years, had come into town from the Midwest, and had gone out for the afternoon. She would be back to make dinner in a short time. The thought of her coming in, finding me gone and not knowing where I'd disappeared—who knew how long I'd be kept in detention?—all this whirled through my mind. I asked them if I might tell a friend where I'd gone. They said it was all right to do so.

I went downstairs in the building with one of the officers and told an acquaintance, Linda Solomon, what had happened to me. She thought it was a gag. "You're putting me on," she said, laughing. Then she opened the door a bit wider, saw the officer, and the smile vanished.

We made arrangements for her to tell my mother what had happened, and I went back upstairs, dressed, and left with the officers.

It was the beginning of twenty-four hours caught in the relentless mechanism of the N.Y.C. judicial system. A 24-hour period that so filled me with hopeless desperation that at times I thought I would crack.

How ironic . . . that a guy who had wanted to tell the truth about the kids, should be arrested seven years later as a result of having run with them. It was like the second half of a book, tied inextricably to the first by sadness and desperation and the evil that seems never to leave someone who has experienced the filth and horror of the streets.

I was going to the Tombs—New York's affectionate name for its jail.

I was going back for another visit in hell.

The bullpen around me was clean and bare, and filled with the naked faces of men who were guilty, except for the innocence in their hands. *See,* their hands said, as they scratched at stubbled jaws, or lay soddenly in laps, or hung outside the bars (why outside the bars?), *see, this body I'm attached to may have done evil, but I'm innocent.* The lily-white hands, so pure and free of guilt. I sat among them and wondered what I had done to get involved in this treadmill horror underneath the city of New York. I honestly thought I might go out of my mind at any moment.

From the larger marshalling room, outside the bullpen, sounds of typewriters and filing cabinets belied the fact that we were imprisoned. It sounded like an office, with busy little secretaries filing inconsequential reports. But it wasn't an office, it was the records-preparation area of the Tombs, and they were cataloguing human beings. Punch-carding and numbering them, and with each black mark made by pencil or typewriter key, the humanity of the subject vanished a little more. Reduction to symbol and file, disappearance by folio and reference number. The cold, mechanical equations of salting a man away in a cell, and knowing which cell to go to when you want him. An iron, inflexible system, prone to error that can never be traced, that keeps a man in that cell or under those tons of steel and concrete for hours longer than he should be kept. The regimentation of callousness.

I could feel the entire weight of the city on me. I had been in custody for twelve hours now, and it was one automated step after another, with no opportunity to get humanity back into my actions. I was a cipher, one of a great string of bodies run through a computing system that would break me down into component parts and file me away like a piece of fruit in the proper bin.

Sitting in the bullpen, looking around me, trying to comprehend all the facets of what had befallen me, and at the same time trying to understand these others whose hands said they, too, were innocent, I was not so much a participant as a victim.

It had all happened so quickly: the arrest, the accusations, the dawning realization that this was not, indeed it was not, a hoax. All idea that this was an elaborate gag, rigged by my bohemian friends in the Village, had vanished like morning mist as the two police officers had hustled me into the unmarked squad car, and transported me to the Charles Street police station.

Now as I sat in the bullpen, gray and cold and filled with men who might have been the best or the worst of any culture—Who could tell, when the mechanical thumb of the System had pressed down on each, making each the same, all equal, all guilty save for the hands?—now I tried to recall every slightest memory and tactile sensation, every sight or snippet of sound, that had come to me since the officers had walked into my apartment.

We had gone down in the elevator at 95 Christopher, and the doorman, an easily-bought type named Jerry, was watching us with the beady ferret eyes of the short-line entrepreneur. "I've got some business to take care of, Jerry," I told him. "If my mother comes in, please ask her to call Miss Solomon." He nodded and smiled with that obsequious double-meaning known only to Manhattan doormen and bellboys. He knew something was up.

They hustled me into an unmarked squad car, and started down Christopher Street to the Charles Street station house, just a few blocks away. "Hey, listen," I said, trying to get some hold on myself or the situation, "do you think I'll have to stay at the station very long?"

They tried to be helpful, and said something reassuring, but it didn't make me feel much better. I began to get the full idea that I just *might* have to be locked up for a few hours, and the prospect did not entice me.

"Are you going to mention this narcotics thing?" I asked. They gave each other a brief, knowledgeable look, and the officer driving said, "No, I don't see any reason why we have to mention it at all. I don't think there's any doubt that was a phony charge from the start."

I felt better when they said that, and decided being open with them had been the smartest course. So if they weren't going to mention the junk nonsense, and they were satisfied I had the weapons for a perfectly valid reason, why was I being taken in?

I asked them.

"Because a complaint has been lodged," they said, simply. "Someone has raised a beef upstairs, and it's filtered down to us. Now *we* have to act on it." It was my first really chilling encounter with the mindless, soulless, heartless machinery of the law as practiced in a great metropolitan area.

"We have to our job, or *we'll* be in trouble," one of them added. I couldn't really blame them. They had homes and families to protect, too, and after all, what and who was I to them?

We arrived at the Charles Street precinct house, with the smell of the Hudson River and the docks flowing up the block to us. The Charles Street station, famed in song and story (and mentioned so notably in Gelber's play "The Connection"), is a great gray mass, completely blended into the surrounding warehouses and falling-down buildings. It seems almost to hunker, as though it were trying to go unnoticed in the street foliage. I've gone back to look at it many times, but each time I come away from it, the details fade and merge in my mind's eye, and all that is left is that inhospitable, gray dawdling mass.

That was the building into which they took me, a stranger and terribly afraid.

We went up the steps and into the cool interior. It had been drizzling outside, a formless, slanting sadness that collected along the gutters and ran over my shoes. It seemed appropriate, somehow. Now, as we came inside, the rain still seemed to be falling indoors. I knew it was only an illusion, but the windows high and fat on the walls carried the rain like paintings. It was cool but sterile in the main hall of the station, with that faint odor of lye or detergent or whatever it is they use to keep the floors dirty-antiseptic. The front desk was shoulder-high on me, and the Sergeant behind that desk looked up with a bored, uncaring nod to the two plainclothesmen. They exchanged words and the Sergeant, holding a thick black marking pencil (almost like a manuscript pencil), jerked his thumb toward the stairs. "Take 'im up to the detective section," he said.

One of the two officers gently tapped me on the bicep and I moved between them, one in front, one behind, up the stairs to the squad room.

The squad room was perhaps sixty or seventy feet long by thirty feet wide, with a high ceiling, drab and colorless walls, a floor whose color was so gray, it must have been non-existent, and heavy light fixtures (the ones with the milk-glass globes, *you* know the kind) hanging down from the ceiling on thick chains.

Desks were scattered in a neat disorder, all across the room. Bulletin boards contained directives, circulars, wanted posters, departmental information and "cop cartoons" from various magazines. At the far left end of the room was a floor-to-ceiling barred enclosure, the "tank," where felons were summarily heaved until disposition could be made.

Two men were working at desks across from one another. One of the detectives was called by name, and the man looked up with the most everlastingly weary eyes I have ever seen.

"Hey," he said. It was a greeting, and a recognition, and not much else. The weary cop went back to his paperwork. A burst of static and some garbled code-numbers erupted from the squawk-box on the wall, but no one paid any attention. My two companions indicated a chair beside a desk, and I sat down. The two detectives who had been working at the desks looked up, almost at the same time, as though their heads had been worked by strings.

One of them said to my enforcers, "Listen, you want to hold down the fort till the Old Man gets in? We haven't had any dinner yet."

One of my cops nodded assent and the two detectives collated and tapped their papers into neat stacks, filed them away in drawers, and left the squad room. I lit a cigarette.

It wasn't bad, this waiting. There was almost a flavor of excitement about it. But I was beginning to suspect that it wasn't all going to be as simple as leaving my books with the officers and having them call me later when the matter came up. I had a suspicion I might have to spend the night in the can—but I put that thought out of my head at once . . . it was ridiculous. After all, I hadn't *done* anything.

The taller of my two friends, now free of his raincoat and carrying the paper bag with the weapons and my books, sat down behind the desk. I sat in a chair to the side of it. He looked at me for a moment, gave me a reassuring grin and reached into the desk for the forms. He wanted a statement.

I tried to think what day it was, and how old I was, and what I was doing here, and without any difficulty the answers came: September 11th, 1960 . . . twenty-six . . . I've been nabbed on the Sullivan Act, illegal possession of firearms in the City of New York, state of New York, borough of Manhattan. That was right; I knew it was right. I was ready to give him his statement.

He took it all down, including the name of Ken Bales, the fact that I had done lecture tours and been on TV with the weapons, and the additional information that I had let them search my apartment without hindrance. The detective clued me that though this was a serious charge, he didn't think I was in much trouble.

We waited for the Old Man, the Captain.

The other two cops who had been in the squad room when we'd arrived did not come back. I assumed they'd gone off duty. While we waited, Linda Solomon arrived at the station house, and was sent up to the squad room. She had brought me a toothbrush, a tube of Gleem, some money, my reading glasses, a bar of soap, and three books:

NOSTROMO by Joseph Conrad

THE WIZARD OF OZ by L. Frank Baum

EICHMANN: THE MAN AND HIS CRIMES

I sometimes wonder about my friends.

I took the paper bag of goodies, noting the titles of the three paperbacks and grimacing strangely at her rather morbid sense of humor. She grinned back like the large Cheshire she resembles, and shrugged eloquently. She wanted to hang around and "soak up the atmosphere" of prison, but my temper had frayed by that time and I suggested not too politely—despite her kindness of trudging over in the rain with my belongings—that she get the hell out of there before they began examining her butt for needle marks.

She gave me a sisterly kiss on the forehead and advised me to keep a stiff upper. Or something in that category. *Jeezus, I wanted to get out of there.*

Perhaps forty-five minutes later, the Captain arrived. A tall and muscular fellow with kind features, he ushered me into his office, and proceeded to read my statement, checking points for clarification from time to time. He called in the senior of the two detectives who had arrested me, and asked him a number of questions about my personal behavior. The detective gave him a faithful, concise account of what had happened. Then he showed the Captain my books. Thus far I seemed to be doing okay.

I got the impression that the Captain would rather not have been troubled with me, as it was fairly obvious by that time that I was not an ax murderer, a narcotics pusher or an exposer of privates in playgrounds. But the complaint had been filed, and he was duty-bound to follow it up.

The report read, the Captain looked at me and asked me if I had any idea how the police had been put onto this matter. I told him about Ken Bales. He didn't say anything. It was obvious: the call had been anonymous, and there was no way of proving if it had been Bales or someone else. I had never thought of that . . . someone else.

The names raced through my mind. All the petty enemies a guy can make in a lifetime, the stupid ones, mostly, who would take such a punk, cowardly way to get even with someone. And then I considered a name I had not offered up before. My ex-wife, Charlotte, now living in New York, in the Bronx. Could it have been her? I didn't want to think about it too hard. I didn't want to think anyone I'd known so intimately could hate me so completely. I tried to think of other things.

After several hours of sitting, waiting, in the squad room (and I must offer truth where it comes; the Captain did not put me into the barred tank, where he could by all rights have stashed me), the Captain told me I'd have to be booked, printed, and put in a cell for the night. I was panic-stricken. They had taken the revolver, to check it out, to see if it matched up with any unsolved cases of shootings they had had in the recent past, but I thought, right up to that moment, that I would be allowed to go home, to be called up whenever the case came to court.

But the silent, deadly machinery of the law had begun to grind, and caught in its yearning wheels and cogs, I was trapped till the cycle had run its course.

I had vivid images of my two years in the Army, and the almost pathological terror I had of being regimented, being ordered and confined, not allowed to act or speak or function as I wanted. But this was a thousand times worse. I was being locked up.

They printed me, then, and the black stains on the fingers were a visible pronouncement of my guilt, even before I'd been tried. There was one more indignity. They had no soap to wash off the black ink from the pad. A coarse paper towel merely smudged and deadened, ingrained the ink. I took to staring at my fingers, all through that night, and it was a feeling I cannot readily express.

A feeling of having been imprinted by my Times, by people who did not know me, who couldn't care less about me, who only knew that ten fingers deserved ten blots on them. "Can I have some soap?" I asked them, and they stared at me as though I was a trifle insane. "It'll wash off soon enough," they said, without comprehension.

I had been turned into a criminal by the simple act of blackening my fingers. I could see it beginning: the studied process that can take a teenage gang kid with too much rebellion in him, and make him into something else . . . a loser, a thief, a kid with inked fingers.

There wasn't any use trying to explain to them—they would have commiserated, but never understood. No one really *can* understand how an individual feels about something so personal. To maybe only one out of a million people would the sight of ink on the fingers be comprehensible as stigmata. But my heart sank.

It was to sink even lower during the next hours.

They took me downstairs and booked me. Complaint 1897, Police Ledger for Charles Street Station. Booked on the Sullivan. I was now officially and forever listed in the records of the New York Police Department.

(I was to find out only months later that though the complaint may be dismissed eventually, and the prints and mug shots requested from the Police Department, though they may in effect say the records have been struck from the files, they never are. Once printed, once catalogued, you are there till the day you die. You have a record. This is one of the unsung attributes of the often-over-zealous New York Police Department. Many innocent men have their faces in mug books in the five boroughs.)

Then I was taken back upstairs, and turned over to a guard for placement in a cell. They took me through the huge gray fire door, and down the row of tiny gun-metal gray cells, and stopped before one. Another guard down the line released the master control of the bank of cages, and the man beside me opened the individual cell with his key. I took a step forward, and stopped. I turned to the detective who had arrested me and I suppose the look on my face was mournful as I said, "Uh, hey, uh, how about if I don't uh have to go into here tonight, uh, maybe I could sit up in the uh the room back there, huh?" The detective tried to be gentle, but firm. He shook his head.

The guard was not quite so pleasant. "C'mon, kid, c'mon, get your ass in there, I haven't got all night!"

It *was* night by that time.

And getting darker every minute.

I stepped inside the cell. The guard said, "Gimme your belt and tie and that bag of stuff."

I asked to keep the books and my cigarettes and lighter, and he was about to refuse when the detective intervened. "Let him have them," he said. The guard gave him a piercing, altogether unfriendly look, the sort of look a lackey gives an official, and let me keep everything but my lighter. I had to light one cigarette and keep smoking all night if I wanted nicotine. Chain smoking. All night.

The guard slid the door shut and I heard the master bar slam home. The detective said something reassuring, something about coming for me early the next morning and I should try to get some sleep. I grinned mawkishly and said, "Helluva hotel you've got here." He grinned back, and went away.

The guard stayed and stared at me for a few more seconds, trying to figure out what my pull was, that I had the plainclothes bulls going for me. Then he put my bag of goodies (which I now recall had some fruit and chicken in it, that my mother had sent with Linda) on the window ledge outside the cell, across the thin corridor . . . and he walked back the way he had come.

The light in the corridor stayed on, the fire door slammed with a J. Arthur Rank clang, and I was all alone in the tier.

It *was* night by that time.

And getting darker every minute.

I smoked.

The cell overnight. A cell, whose dimensions, with handles attached, would have made a fine coffin. Gun-metal gray, faceless gray, cadaverous gray, emptily gray, without even the humanity of a chipped place on the wall. Solid unbroken gray, with privy obscenities inscribed. (How? No pencils in perdition.) Durance vile with a lidless toilet that cannot be flushed. Coventry with a flat hardwood bedslab and a light that never goes out.

That light. All night in my eyes. Was this a modern American jail or a stopover on the Brainwash Express? I expected the Cominform representatives at any moment, with subtle thumbscrew tortures unless I revealed the plans for the Yankee spaceship, Jeezus, that goddam bulb . . . no wonder they encased it in a hard-glass shield, and a wire mesh, so no one could break it. They may have been afraid of some pistolero smashing it to obtain a sharp shard of glass to aid an escape, but in my case all I wanted to do was get some sleep, and that sonofabitch was burning out my eye-sockets.

I spent the night for the most part awake; there was no sleeping with the light in my eyes. That isn't entirely correct. A lesson well-learned in the Army was: When they yell *fall out*, shuck out of your pack, use it for a pillow and drop where you are.

I could sleep in a rock field, within a matter of seconds be completely out of it. But I couldn't sleep that night. It wasn't the bulb, entirely. It was where I was sleeping.

Part of the time I read. Enchanted as generations of tots and elders have been by Frank Baum's Dorothy and Tin Woodman and Scarecrow and Wizard, none of them could have blessed the kindly old characters as much as I did that night. They took me out of myself, and I recognized for the first time the full value of fantasy. But eventually I had to think about it. I had to put one of the smoking cigarettes on the edge of the toilet bowl in my mouth, close the book, and sit on the edge of that hardwood slab, and think about it:

Was I guilty? I didn't for a moment consider myself guilty in the accepted cultural sense of the word. I had committed no crime, and had in fact come by the weapons as a result of trying to do good, of trying to mirror a true state of our times. But in the deeper, moral sense, was I responsible for my actions, was I in prison rightfully? I had to know. I had to reason it out as a human being; I had to analyze my own ethics and morality, and decide if being behind bars was proper in this instance.

And so I considered it, silently, for a long time. I had, indeed, run with a gang, for purposes which I chose to consider altruistic and lofty. But had my own personal needs for recognition and stature dictated my course? Was I really a *dilettante,* who took his chances when he thought he could get away without being punished . . . or was I completely honest about my motives? I discounted the word "completely." No one is ever completely anything.

Finally, I decided that it was neither all black nor all white. I was partially guilty, of selling out my responsibility to the kids I had seen in the streets, by writing cheap blood-and-guts yarns about them, rather than going the longer, harder haul and doing it sociologically. But though I was guilty of moral turpitude in varying degrees, I was not guilty of selling out my society. I had prostituted my talent to make money—for many reasons; most of which (wife, home, three squares a day, a few primary pleasures, a little class) would not be considered improper by the majority—but the crime was in my soul, not in my dossier.

Guilty? Yes, of selling out, of obfuscating, of cheapening my message, of dawdling and playing the *poseur.*

But guilty of owning a lethal weapon with intent to perform a crime . . . of indulging in illegal activity . . . of corruption in the greater sense . . . no, never.

I went back to the Land of Oz with a pastel heart, with an ease and peace. I hadn't turned to obsidian as yet. Soon, perhaps, here in hell, but not just at the moment. At the moment I was a flawed human being, a man with imperfections, a little guy who wanted desperately to be a big guy. But I wasn't a criminal. Not yet. Not just yet.

Still, I didn't read about Eichmann that night.

Sometime after three-thirty I fell asleep. I might have liked to report that it was a night filled with dark phantasmagoric shapes, threatening, but nonesuch was the case. The Army had taught me well. I slept like a baby. When I came back from wherever it was I had gone, the morning had come through the window across the corridor, the light had gone out, and I was stiff as a bitch. My right shoulder felt as though someone had gone at it with a piton. Several vertebrae were ratcheted sidewise, and I had that next-day feeling of mugginess, with my nose and eyes and ears filled with moist, unpleasant, viscous matter. I could not wash, not just then, and I felt like hell. Eyes grainy and chin stubbly, suit wrinkled from having used the jacket as a pillow and the pants as sheets, hair mussed and lank from the high temperature, I looked the part of a seedy street-bum, brought to bay.

I heard noises and the fire door opened down the line. The guard came in, followed by one of the detectives who had arrested me the late afternoon before. They came up to the cage and we went through the unlocking procedure.

The guard told me I'd have time to wash up later, but right now I should get my can in gear.

I followed the detective downstairs, and as we walked, he said, "Look, I'm supposed to put the cuffs on you, but I don't think they're necessary, so when we get downstairs, I'll be going in my car, following you."

"What am I going in?" I asked.

"The wagon," he said.

"Where?"

He jerked a thumb downtown. "One-Hundred Centre Street," he replied. I believe I must have said something, because he took me under the elbow and steered me down the stairs, saying, "Listen, take it easy. The judge'll be very easy on you. The Old Man didn't let us down, and he agreed on not mentioning this junk charge. So you won't have any real problems."

I hoped not. I had asked Linda to get in touch with my agent, Theron Raines of the Ann Elmo Literary Agency, in order to prepare bail if it was needed, though the general consensus had been that all I'd need was remanding into my own custody. The books I'd written had apparently given me some small stature as a reputable member of the community.

Charles Street station had been quiet the night before. I was the only passenger in the meat wagon. They hustled me into the back, and locked the grilled door. I sat there, finger-combing my hair and clutching my little bag of goodies to me. As the wagon started, I fished out a chicken leg and began chewing on it.

We went careening through downtown New York, with the city going away from me in a grilled panorama, the people staring in when the wagon stopped for lights, seeing what I'm sure they considered The True Face of Evil.

I tried to look young and innocent.

It was still drizzling, and the day itself was cold and handmaiden to misery. You had to walk slanting forward into the wind to make any progress. People were huddled like indeterminate clots of mucus in the doorways, and only occasionally would a hardy soul burst from under an awning to streak for other refuges. It was a nasty, unhappy day, and I was going to jail.

I hoped my agent would be in court with the bail money.

The desperation I had known at odd moments through the night, the desperation at being totally confined, had passed with my entering the wagon and its scene of freedom just beyond the grilled enclosure. But I knew that when I was hustled into 100 Centre Street it would begin again, only much worse, for then I would be in the stomach of the great inhuman processing machine of the government, not isolated (where humanity and freedom from total cynicism still existed) in one of its far-flung outposts.

We pulled up in front of 100 Centre after spiralling down through Wall Street and the heart, guts, liver & lights of the insurance, legal, bonding and stockbroking sections. I had ridden alone the whole trip, but now, as I jumped down from the truck into the waiting hands of my arresting officer, I joined a stream of sodden humanity that poured through the back-basement door into the Criminal Courts Building, the outer layer of the Tombs.

I was first remanded to the custody of a bench in a large waiting-room. There were fifteen other men, dotted back through the rows, also waiting. I tried to look at them, to study them, without seeming surreptitious. The predominance of Negroes was striking, perhaps because of the infrequency of a white face. But all of the men in the room had one thing in common: shabbiness.

These were the epidermis of society, scraped off the sidewalks and bar rails and tenement stairways and gutters of the late night and early morning. They slouched or leaned in their seats, eyes sticky with black dirt and wasted hours, merely waiting to be nudged, chivvied, harried and pushed through this seemingly too-familiar routine. I shuddered just a little to think anyone could allow himself to lose all dignity in this way. And then I caught myself, chiding myself on such naïve, provincial thinking. Men do what they can do, and when the culture asks them to be what they cannot be, they fall. These were the fallen ones, on whom pity would be not only wasted, but vilified.

My name was called from beyond a floor-to-ceiling grilled door, and my detective appeared in the shadows on the other side. "C'mon, Harlan," he urged, and I rose.

They opened the grilled gate for me, and I was immediately surrounded by camera equipment. Great hanging booms and pedestaled shutter-boxes, coils of boa-thick rubber cable and batteries of klieg lights. I was about to be mugged, having already been printed. My picture was about to go on file in the endless drawers of the Law. How wonderful! I felt like doing a little native dance of pleasure that now I was in the same scrapbook with "Legs" Diamond, John Dillinger, Baby Face Nelson, Al Capone and all the other folk-heroes I had watched James Cagney and Paul Muni and George Raft impersonate on the silver screen, Saturday afternoon in Painesville, Ohio. How wonderful to come twenty-six years and have reached such a pinnacle of success. *You're just bitter,* I heard myself thinking, and replied very honestly: *What gave you your first clue, Dick Tracy?*

They sat me down on a stool. I was too low.

"Spin the seat for the dwarf," the comedian on the other side of the camera said.

Somebody else nudged me to move, so hard I almost went sprawling. "Take it easy on him," said my detective from the darkness. (Already I had identified him with Good and Daddy and Safety and Kindness.)

"Oh," the cameraman drawled the word out with meaning, "is *that* The Author?" The detective laughed lightly, and behind me, the *schmuck* who was spinning the black-enameled-top stool was simpering like a fag.

So that was my stir-name. The Author.

Sound of audience reaction, mildly upheaving.

"Awright," said the yo-yo behind me, "siddown."

I saddown and the man with the daguerreotypes said much too loudly, "Ah, hold your chin up there, Author, we're takin' this for the next book you write . . . ya gonna send us a copy?"

"Why the hell don't you stop making like Mickey Mouse and just take your little pictures, hero?" I said it and got a crack across the nape of my neck for my trouble. I started to spin on the stool, but my detective yelled, "Okay, just sit there, Ellison, and don't give anyone any trouble."

I saw my images of Daddy shatter. It didn't matter who was right or wrong; Negroes hang with Negroes, Jews hang with Jews, Catholics hang with Catholics, and cops hang with cops. If blood is thicker than water, how much thicker is tin than blood?

He snapped the photos (I neglected to mention they had hung a board with numbers around my neck, suspended from a chain. It wasn't heavy, but there is something so inhuman about being reduced to numbers that defies description. But I digress . . .) and my detective came over to remove the numbered slate. He needn't have bothered. I had it off a second after the last photo was snapped.

I followed him, still clutching my little bag of almost-gone goodies, and books, and we went into another room, and up a slight incline. There were twenty or twenty-five men waiting, accompanied by one or more arresting officers. They clotted in a mass near a heavy door leading to the street. The door was open, and I could see steps leading up, a black banister, the sidewalk, and a score of meat wagons. This was the transportation to the Court House building just down the street.

My officer began talking to another detective, and they discussed inconsequentialities for a time, until some invisible signal was given (I suspect it was the reaching of a group total, as other prisoners had been added to our group from the photographic section every few minutes) and we started to move out to the wagons.

It was then that my detective took out his handcuffs and snapped one of the bracelets around my left wrist. He pulled over his friend's prisoner, and hooked us together. I stared down at my manacled wrist, and suddenly felt myself trapped worse than I had at any point in the events of the past day. I tried to shake loose, but both detectives shoved me forward with my arm-partner, and we joined the regimented line of men going to court.

It was still raining, and much harder now, with a sad granite look to the sky, hard and dappled gray and infinitely oppressive. The wind caught at my face and at my coat, and it was cold, terribly cold, and not all of it was from outside. My insides were cold, as well; chilled through to the marrow, as the men ahead of us clambered into the wagon, and my chain-buddy made to follow.

He jumped slightly and gained the back of the wagon, pulling me up roughly with him. The manacle bit into my wrist. "Hey, take it easy," I howled. He didn't say anything, just gave me a look of such utter contempt that I was forced into silence.

I was the last one in the truck, the door was closed, and a uniformed cop climbed onto the back step, clinging to the rails on either side. He stared in at us. Most of the men paid no attention. I looked at them, trying to decide whether they were good men gone wrong, victims of circumstance like myself, or hardened criminals.

Aside from the derelicts, with their shabby clothes and fetid breath, we all looked pretty much the same. If they had been mass murderers, I would not have been able to tell them from offenders with too many parking tickets. Abruptly, the wagon lurched forward, and we moved out of the little alley behind 100 Centre.

I could not see where we were going, for the cop on the back step blocked the view, but it didn't matter, for as we were shifting and moving on our benches, trying to get some small measure of ease for gluteus muscles doomed to hard cots and metal slabs, my cuff-buddy turned to me and asked: "What'd they get 'choo for?"

I studied his face for a moment, seeing little more than lank hair and a wide elfish mouth, cold and empty gray eyes and ears that stood out a trifle too much from his head. I was about to answer, when I realized that his white shirt was not merely ripped and dirty, as I had at first supposed—there is a tendency not to look at your companions too closely, when in jail—but was torn down across his left arm, exposing it to the shoulder, and dark brown stains all across the face of the shirt were most certainly blood. Great clots of blood. Hardened spittle strings of blood. Spatters and patches and gouts of blood. He was dappled in blood, from neck to waist. I swallowed heavily.

"I, uh, I had a gun," I said simply.

There was no desire in me to engage this man in conversation. I had the most terrible feeling that he was one of the true animals, not merely a *schmuck* like me, who had about as much right being in a paddy wagon as Porky Pig. I did not want to say anything to him. And that was why I heard myself asking, "Why'd they arrest *you*?"

He sneered down at me, and his nostrils flared, giving him an oddly Semitic appearance for a moment.

"I done somethin' worsen you with that gun," he said. And then he clucked like a chicken. "Heh, you betcha I did . . ." He clucked again several times, and I supposed he was laughing.

I felt a nudge in my side, and a whiskery derelict on my right leaned in to pass his foul breath over my face as he confided. "He used a hammer onna little girl; he's a mean sonofabitch, don't get too close to him, or he might go nuts again."

I turned back to my companion, staring at him like some new species of life. My curiosity got the better of me, and I asked him, "Is it true you killed a girl with a hammer?"

His head snapped around and his nostrils flared wide again. "Whadjoo say? Whadjoo say t' me?" He looked like he wanted to club me down. I asked him again, very quietly, trying to soothe him, because I was scared witless, but didn't see how I could ignore his red-rimmed eyes, staring at me accusingly.

"Yeah, I used a hammer onner, yeah I did, sure! All I wanted was a little piece of trim, just a little pieceah ass, at'sall. Little bitch, fourteen anna bitch, it's her fault I'm here, an' they gonna slap *me* away, frigging buncha scuts . . ." and he lurched forward, not at me, but across the aisle at two men I had assumed were also prisoners, though they were better-dressed than the rest of us.

The two men across the way moved as one, grabbing the hammer-murderer by a shoulder with their free hands, dragging their bracelet-partners partway with them.

They shoved the maniac back in his seat, and I realized they were plainclothes detectives.

I sat there, chained to a hammer-murderer who had killed a fourteen-year-old girl because she wouldn't "give out with a little trim," and felt my composure slipping . . .

My agent *had* to be there with the bail money, he just *had* to be. The night in the cell, the black smudges on my hands, the pushing and shoving and moving like cattle in a pen, it had to end at the court, or I might not be able to write about it.

I might go as mad as the poor sonofabitch chained to me. And right then I knew what James Baldwin meant when he said we are all brothers. There was much of that killer in me, and much of my innocence in him.

We *were* brothers, chained together by more than steel links.

Suddenly, I did not want to know my fellow man any better.

From then on, reality was someone else's word. What buildings I was trundled through, what men I saw passing before me and what others with whom I was cuffed, all of them and all of it were a mottled, technicolored panorama. None of it was really happening. It had been a lark, to a great degree, this being arrested, going to court, spending the night in a clean cell in the Village.

And the half dozen cliché remarks: "Well, this'll be a good way to get experience for a book, Author." That had been part of it, too. I had had stature. But what stature is there in being chained to a mad-eyed animal who had used a hammer on a fourteen-year-old girl? What kind of importance is there in seeing another human being so gone in his own sickness and depravity that even pity is wasted on him?

I tried to consider what it might be like for a young teenager, perhaps one of the kids from the Barons, pinched for rumbling or breaking and entering. What would it be like for him to be chained to a man such as my murderer? Would he feel the same sophisticated revulsion or would his be merely a naïve sidewise-shine at a glamorous figure, a real honest-to-God murderer? I could see the fallacy of a system where the relatively innocent and the monstrously guilty are thrown together. My concern was not for myself, nor even my delicate sensibilities—more often bruised than I care to admit—but simply for the thought of all the ones gone before, and all the ones yet to come, who could ride in my seat in this paddy wagon, with the darkness closing in around them.

My thoughts ceased as we arrived at the Criminal Courts Building, Borough of Manhattan. (To this day I am unsure whether we were taken to another part of the same building, or into another structure entirely. Part of the eeriness and feeling of entrapment results from the sameness of the surroundings. You begin to feel you have been "inside" this great beast for a very long while, time ceases, all walls are the same wall, all eyes dead, and all hope lost. You are in the belly of the creature, and it treats you like any other morsel of food. Hope does not run in the beast's bloodstream.)

We were chivvied out of the wagon, and my arresting officer took a position to the rear of the men herding us. They began pushing and shoving us into a doorway, using phrases like, "Awright, c'mon, heyyy-*up!* Move on there, c'mon, tchip-tchip, move, g'wan . . ." almost as though we were cattle or pigs, moving down a running-trough. I expected at any moment one of them would stop us with a simple "Whoahh!"

Then came a series of twisting corridors, white walls, large barred rooms, through which we moved, till we came into a hallway, and I saw a freight elevator.

The operator was waiting, and the entire group of us herded together. We went upstairs smoothly, the operator talking to one of the harness bulls about some minor official and his new demands on the Force. We reached our destination. (There was no way for me to identify what floor we were on: we'd been so tightly crowded that I was facing the back of the elevator.)

I managed to elbow around, and we moved out, each of us chained together, and myself being dragged slightly by the man with the hammer.

As we passed down a very narrow neck-corridor, I saw a beefy and florid, bored and disgruntled-looking guard in uniform, at the end of the passage. He stood by a lectern-like wooden desk, with a huge ledger open on its top. I had an insane vision of myself signing in as a guest, or registering to vote, or making an appearance on "What's My Line?"

Q: ARE YOU SELF-EMPLOYED?

A: Yes, I'm a gun-runner and narcotic addict.

Q: ARE YOU BIGGER THAN A BREAD-BOX?

A: Here in prison, I'm smaller than a maggot.

Q: DO YOU MAKE PEOPLE HAPPY?

A: Why should I; no one makes *me* happy!

I didn't go on with that train of thought. In that direction lies madness, I suspect. But as we came abreast of the guard, my detective took me aside, and unlocked the cuffs. He took the metal bracelets off the maniac, too, and nudged him back into the stream of prisoners passing the desk, rounding a corner, and disappearing.

"This is my Author," said the plainclothesman who had arrested me the day before. "He's a good kid, so take care of him."

"So . . ." said the guard, his little brown eyes coming alive or the first time, "this is The Author I've been hearing about on the radio . . ."

For a moment it didn't sink in.

Radio? What radio? The police wave-length?

"What radio?" I asked him. My detective passed me smoothly into the guard's custody.

"Oh, there was something on the early morning news about your being picked up," my detective said. He didn't elaborate, and I moved off with the guard in something of a trance.

It was the first suspicion I'd had that my arrest was not strictly confined to the police and the few chosen friends Linda would tell. It was the first suspicion I'd had that someone had spilled the news to the papers.

* * *

Around the corner was a cell, a minor bullpen, a waiting station for the accused before they were taken to the courtroom for arraignment. It was now eight-thirty, and as yet I'd had nothing to eat, save what I'd been able to gorge down from my bag of goodies. I had emptied the paper bag into the pockets of my trench coat, and they bulged with toothbrush, paste, and books, I still felt scruffy, and unclean, and as the turnkey opened the cell door, I asked him, "Is there any place I can wash up?" He didn't even bother to answer. His keys on their chain were massive, and in his massive hand they seemed to fit. I walked into the cell, and got the once-over from my teammates. The cell was packed, with tired men, unhappy men, spade cat and ofay, handsome men and warped-looking creatures, sick guys lying on their sides on the cement floor, and jaunty swinging hipsters with knees pulled up on the bench, chewing gum and laughing to themselves. It was an early morning roust, a gathering of all the flotsam from Manhattan's streets of the night before. This was the weekend wastebasket dumpings, the guys who had had too much to drink, and the ones who had not had enough to spend, and the ones who came up short one way or another. Like me. I walked around the big cell, stepping over some of the inmates who were catching up on their sleep, busy stacking z's in preparation for the scenes later in the day.

It was bigger than it seemed, perhaps thirty-five feet long by ten feet wide, with a little heavy metal dividing partition at one end that screened the urinal from the sight of the others. A sink was fastened to that partition, and if you pushed the button hard enough, water came.

There were already twenty-five or thirty men in the cell, and they had taken all the space on the metal bench. So I stood. And walked. I paced, and hung my hands outside the bars (Why outside, why always outside?) and studied my fellow inmates. I saw all the faces, and I wondered which were the guilty and which the *schmucks* who had stepped over the line just enough to incur some cop's wrath. They certainly seemed a rabid lot . . . but then, how did I look to them?

Against one wall a tall man in an Italian silk suit leaned toward his companion, a swarthy type with too much hair, badly cut, and falling down into his face as though he had scuffled with someone and had not had time to comb it. They talked in subdued tones and though I couldn't make out what their subject was, I knew the sharp dresser was bugged at the olive-skinned one about a slip-up somewhere in the recent past. Their conversation reached such a pitch of intensity—while maintaining the same level of quiet—that the sharp dresser gave the smaller felon a slap across the forehead with his palm. I looked away and passed on to a huge, muscular Negro with a cast in his right eye, sitting at the end of the bench, his T-shirt ripped halfway across the chest, revealing heavy musculature, beaded with sweat. He caught me looking at him, and there was such a return glare of hatred, that I turned away.

Lying on the floor, tossed up on himself like a fetus, I saw a man wrapped in his overcoat, clutching his knees to his chest, and snoring fitfully. Next to him, also lying on the floor, was a young man of indeterminate age—but not much over twenty-eight—covered with blood and home-made bandages. His head was swathed in them, covering the left ear and swinging down over the left eye. His cheek had a ragged cut on it, and his hands looked as though he had tried to grab a knife away from someone. His hands were ribboned with slices, hastily-bandaged with handkerchiefs, soaked through darkly. Or perhaps someone had been trying to get the knife from *him*.

A drunken derelict lay huddled against the bars, one arm hanging out into the corridor, vomit all around him and his fellows as far away as they could get.

A terribly thin man with no jacket, and suspenders crisscrossing over the top of his longjohns, was wrapped in on himself, sitting on the bench, other men pressed in on him tightly, and he shivered. He shook like a bridge-guy wire in a heavy gale, and his eyes kept rolling up in his head, showing blue-veined eyeballs. I may have been wrong (though the bird-tracks up his bare arms told me I was right), but he looked like a junkie going into withdrawal.

The beefy, bored guard came into sight around the corner. "Awright, you crumbs, on yer feet, let's move out in snappy style here!"

He unlocked the barred entrance, and some of the more drunken inhabitants tried to elbow past him. He straight-armed them back into the bullpen, and bellowed, "Awright, you buncha shits, wait a minnit!" Then he began reading from a clipboard that had been tucked under his arm:

"Alberts, Charles; Arthur, John; Asten, Clyde; Becker, Wilhelm; Brookes, John; Brown, Tom; Brown, Virgil; Brown, Wallace; Brown, Whitney; Czelowitz, August; Dempsey—"

He went on reading the names. Those whose names had been called began to file out of the cell, and made a ragged line around the corner toward the elevator. I didn't see my plainclothesman, but I knew he'd be along any time now. I was both relieved and flattered when he came out of a side door in the narrow corridor; he had obviously taken a liking to me, and wasn't ready to let me sink into the System completely. Either that, or they thought I would bolt. They may have been right.

I was getting panicky, now that we were apparently getting ready to move down for arraignment. I was certain I'd be turned loose at once, at least with a minimum bail. But there was the niggling worry of that remark about my name having gone out over the radio. If it was such a phony and trumped-up charge against me, then why the publicity? I wasn't that well-known a literary figure, God knows. So why? And the thought hit me that it might not be such a shoo-in. That my pretty baby face with its day growth of stubble might not be enough to get me out of this jam.

So my buddy's presence might well have been attributed not to my inherent good looks and ingenuous nature, but to a sensible realization on his part that I was just unstable enough to break and run if I perceived the situation to be worse than I'd first thought. My reassurance vanished.

I joined the line of prisoners, and as I saw the cuffs being attached to the others, I whispered to my buddy in plainclothes, "Can I go without?" He gave me a benign smile and shrugged. Then he cuffed me. But he held the other ring himself, rather than attaching me to another felon.

Another felon?

Yes, I had begun to think of myself as one. The innocence till judged guilty did not hold. It was a lovely theory, but wretched practice. No one who goes through the System can consider himself innocent, while being herded and locked up and treated like a foregone conclusion.

I *was* a felon, right then.

Yet my thoughts were not free to dwell on semantics. The line was moving out. Not to the elevator, but through the side door from which my plainclothesman had emerged. Down a side-corridor, and up to a larger, sturdier freight elevator. We waited, and finally the door slammed back. A decrepit old man in gray uniform was operating the machine, and he looked at us as though he had seen a million of us for a million years past. We were fodder for the legal machinery. He was a thoroughly dead old man. I wondered if he was a trusty.

We were loaded into the elevator.

We went downstairs? Upstairs? I don't even know.

Then began a dizzying series of shunting-abouts, in and out of corridors, pens, cages, enclosures, all of which smelled faintly of vomit, urine and carbolic acid. The smell of a jail is a thing you never forget. There are bitter, acrid and sometimes gagging smell-memories of Lysol, carbolic acid and paraldehyde, a chemical used to quieten drunks, one drop, one-millionth of a drop of which, leaves a scent in the nostrils that never really departs.

And there is the stench of human bodies, of the sweat of guilt and tension. The odor of cosmolene from the guard's guns, and the smell of all-purpose oil used on the locks. The smell of rain-wet coats, and the smell of bad breath. The smell of old leather from cracked shoes, and the smell of absolute desperation.

It is a stink that must offend God, for Man cannot take it for too long, and its persistence in reality *should* offend God. (But after a few hours in the System, one begins to suspect there is no God. If it be true there are no atheists in a foxhole, then it is equally true that there are no true believers in a prison.)

We came out of the labyrinth, through a door, a heavy fire-door with triple locks, passed a little entrance that showed us the outside, still gray and pelted with slimy rain, and we all yearned to go through that entrance . . .

But we had been put into the System, and like the Army, once in formation, you were trapped for the duration: Of the day, of the term, of the lifetime . . .

All of us – perhaps a third of the number who had been in the larger pen upstairs (downstairs?) – were hustled into a very tiny waiting cell with two benches. The heavy wooden door to the left of the cell opened, and we saw through into the courtroom.

We were there, ready to be arraigned. Ready to find out if we would be free men or temporarily placed in durance vile.

My plainclothesman came up to me at the bars and said, "Do you have a lawyer?" It was the first time the thought had occurred to me. "No," I answered, "I'll plead my own case." It seemed that simple. I was innocent, what did I need a lawyer for . . . wasn't a man innocent till adjudged guilty in this court, as in any court?

He looked worried. "You'd better get a public defender," he advised. "It may be tougher in there than you think."

"You really think so?" I asked.

Naïve? Jesus, Pollyana move over, here comes Ellison.

"I think you'd better."

He was damned serious, and the cold feeling crept up through my guts to my neck and my face, and I had a sensation of falling. "Would you get him for me?" I asked. He nodded and went out through the wooden door to the courtroom.

In a little while he came back, with me still hanging on the bars like a mounted animal, and he said, "The man's name is Strangways; be here in a minute." I thanked him, and the cop added, "Your mother and Miss Solomon and your agent and some other people are out there. They asked me how you were."

"Tell them I'm fighting mad," I said, sounding anything but.

He grinned, tapped my hand in reassurance, and disappeared again. I turned around to see what was happening in my cell, and that was when all hell broke loose.

It was as though someone had said "Roll 'em" and the Marx Brothers had gone into their act. From doors on all sides of the cell, little men with pads of notepaper erupted. Doors slammed. Guards appeared out of nowhere. The prisoners flung themselves against the bars to talk to the little men. The noise level went up a millionfold. It was sheer bedlam. I was grabbed by the scruff of the neck and literally hurled away from the bars, as a brawny derelict moved forward to talk to an approaching note taker. These, apparently, were the public defenders, hauled away from their practices in the awful early morning hours, to try and defend the scum of New York's streets, without fee, without honor, and usually, I was to discover, without success.

Some of them were registered lawyers who devoted a portion of their time—at the Court's "request"—to the defense of those unable to afford counsel. Some of them worked full-time for the Legal Aid Society. Some of them were philanthropists. Most of them were woefully overworked and frighteningly incompetent.

They bounced back and forth from the barred waiting cell to the courtroom, back and forth, here and gone, back and gone again, like the ping-pong balls in the air-vent machines used on TV to show how an air conditioner operates. Most of them were balding, and the image of them ricocheting between "clients" and courtroom would have been ludicrous, had not so many men's very existences depended on their ritualistic gyrations.

I sat down on one of the benches, and tried to read, not really knowing what was happening, nor if one of these budding Clarence Darrows was for me. The noise was deafening, and the phrase most heard, over the din, always tinged with a red frenetic tone, was, "You gotta get me outta this!"

I tried to blot out the noise, but it was impossible. They were like animals, fighting for a piece of meat. They reached through and grabbed at the coats and collars of the lawyers, and those worthies shook them off with slaps and harsh phrases, with wrinkled-up noses and utter contempt. *Are these the men who will speak for us before the bench?* I thought.

They no more wanted to be here, wasting their time on unfortunate bastards without a cent in their pockets, than they wanted to be on our side of the bars. *How doomed we are,* was all I could think, and though it may sound melodramatic, just consider for a moment: the way the System is run today, with all our metropolitan courts so terribly glutted with cases that lawsuits wait a year and two years before they can be heard, with felonies and minor infractions of the law heaped one upon another onto the calendar, with judges overworked and harassed, with a surfeit of poverty and a scarcity of counsels who put the Law before the Dollar . . . what man has a chance without hired representation?

Consider: you are before a judge who had handled over fifty cases in the past three hours, who is sweltering in his robes, and distressed at the whining voices coming from in front of him; you are unfamiliar with the rules of the game, or you are not glib and fast on your feet; you don't know what to say and even if you did he doesn't want to hear it. If you've been picked up, you must have done what you're accused of having done.

So they send you a public defender, who is totally incapable of helping you, but in whom you put your momentary trust. And he has sixty, seventy, eighty different cases to trot before the magistrate in a matter of minutes. He doesn't know you, has no idea whether you are guilty or innocent, and doesn't really care. It is an obligation; he has been told to do the best he can for you, and so he pumps up to the bars, take the sketchiest information, and runs back into the court to plead on the arraignment for the poor devil that went before you. Then he rushes back to you, having lost the train of your explanation, makes you start over again, stops you midway with "Okay, okay, you told me all that . . . what I want to know is what your excuse was." He cannot remember what you've said previously, he doesn't give a damn about what you're saying now, all he wants is a few choice words to throw together in some semi-logical order to make a feeble showing before the judge . . . a grandstand attempt . . . a sham effort . . .

"Ellison?"

I sat there, considering the plight of all those poor dumb bastards who wouldn't have a feather's chance in the courtroom, who were going out there to get arraigned and slapped into the Tombs till they met bail or were transferred for trial. I wanted to scream at these phony creeps with their yellow note paper pads, "You're louses, all of you! Nothing but goddam students of the law and you don't care what happens to any of these men! You shouldn't be allowed to practice! These men need help, not play-actors like you!"

"Ellison? Is Ellison in here?"

How terrible it was, to know you were going up against the System, the Machine, the Beast, with nothing standing between you but a paper lance. How terrible to know that the massed indifference and cynicism and boredom of the men of the law were ready to crush you, mold you and force you into a false position, with no help from these bland, dewy-eyed lads who came down to practice on you; like apprentice barbers in a tonsorial school. If you got sliced by their straight razors, or had a chunk taken out of your ear, well, it didn't really matter: Who were you? Just another face. Just another guy with a stubble from having slept overnight in the Charles Street station. So what did it matter.

"Hey! Ellison! Ellison Harlan, Harlan Ellison! Is there someone here named Ellison or Harlan or something like that?"

I suddenly realized that a tall, good-looking man in a Brooks Brothers sport jacket and dark slacks was standing on the other side of the bars, with the animals trying to grab his lapels and his attention, calling for me.

"I'm Ellison, hey, I'm Ellison," I yelled, jumping up.

"C'mere. C'mon, c'mere already, will you. I've got other cases waiting in there, you shouldn't slow me up that wa—"

He never got a chance to finish telling me what a ghastly inconvenience I was to him. A guard poked his head in through the wooden door from the courtroom. "Strangways?" he yelled, and my Defender whirled, belting back, "Yeah, what's happening?" The guard jerked a thumb toward the courtroom, and my Defender, the Right Honorable Upholder Of Speed and Facility, Attorney Strangways, urged me to "Stay right there. I've got a case up, I'll be right back . . ."

And he was gone.

So help me God, he said: "Stay right there." It sounds like a bad W. C. Fields gag. It sounded that way then. But he said it. He really did.

I couldn't laugh. It was too uncomplicatedly frightening to laugh about.

I went back to sit down and read, and wait for Mr. Strangways to work me into his crowded poor-man schedule.

My man Strangways burst through the door again and motioned me to the bars. I went to my counsel. "Now," he began, as though we had accomplished something on his last trip through, "let me have that again."

"Have *what* again?" I asked.

This was incredible.

He gave me a cold look, as though I was wasting his time. "What happened, what happened, boy! Tell me what your story is."

"My *story*, Counselor, is that I'm innocent. I didn't *do* anything. I was just—"

"Yes, yes," he broke in. "I know you didn't do anything, but what are you in here for?"

I decided I'd better cease my lofty tactics and tell this clown everything I could, in hopes he might retain a bit of it, either in his gray cells or his yellow note pad. "I'm a writer," I began, talking rapidly. "I've done two books on juvenile delinquency. I ran with a kid gang for ten weeks, about five years ago, to gather background data. When I came out of the gang I had a bunch of weapons I used for lectures before PTA groups, youth groups, that sort of thing. A guy I haven't seen in a few years, who wanted to hang me up, called the police and told them I had an arsenal. They picked me up on the Sullivan, and I have a perfectly legitimate use for the weapons—I never *thought* of the gun as a weapon, only as a visual aid, or I would have had the pin pulled and had it registered. Anyway, I've been out of the state for the last few years and I haven't *done* any—"

He broke in rudely, "Ever used it for an illegal purpose?"

"What're you, kidding or something?" I was outraged. "I just *told* you, I'm a legitimate writer, and I used it when lecturing to youth groups, YMCA classes, that kind of jazz. Don't you believe me?"

"Sure, sure." He indicated no belief whatsoever, putting a palm up to placate me. "I believe you. I'll see what I can do. Wait here." And the Lone Ranger was gone again.

I had a feeling with this bush league Perry Mason on my team I might wind up on the guillotine, rather than in the slammer.

And all the while, the other inmates were clamoring and jostling and going a little mad trying to get heard.

Strangways came rushing through, with a set of briefs under his arm, and I thought he was coming to talk to me, but he called out another name and a seedy old man leaped up from where he'd been sitting cross-legged on the floor, and they huddled (much as I had) for about thirty seconds. Then Strangways bolted again, as a guard held the door for him. (It looked like a *torero* making a pass at the bull, and as Strangways went spinning through the door in his own personal *veronica*, I felt like hollering *Olé!*)

Then I went cold all over, because I was yelling to the vanishing Strangways, and I realized I'd been yelling for almost a full minute, and I heard my voice above the other desperate animals in that pen.

I was yelling. "You gotta get me outta this!"

Then, much later, while my head was spinning so completely from the noise, they let me out of the pen, and it was my turn to go before the arraigning judge.

The only impression I now have of that few seconds before the bar was a room very heavy with wood paneling, a great many people, the scent of rain-wet clothes, a great deal of bustle and confusion, and half a dozen public defenders, bailiffs, cops, guards, hangers-on and crying women, all clustered around the bench.

I had no idea how the judge could see me, examine me, hear my plea. As it turned out, I needn't have worried about it. He never bothered.

Pay attention, then. This is the face of preliminary justice in the morning courts of New York City:

The clerk read off the charge in a monotone, the Judge scratched his white hair, examining himself for signs of dandruff, my Knight in White Button-Down Armor, the sharp and pithy Mr. Strangways, came bursting on the scene and said (so help me God this is word-for-word):

"Your Honor, this man is a writer. He obtained these weapons in the pursuit of a story and he has a legitimate right to own them, becau–"

WHAT DO YOU MEAN HE HAD A RIGHT TO OWN THEM? came the voice of someone's God. SINCE WHEN DOES BEING A WRITER GIVE HIM ANY RIGHT TO OWN A WEAPON? ONE THOUSAND DOLLARS BAIL.

I nearly fainted.

"Your *Honor*," whined Strangways, "five *hun*dred!"

ONE THOUSAND DOLLARS BAIL.

And that was that.

Strangways didn't say another word. He turned on his heel, picked up a new set of briefs on another poor soul, and disappeared into the room with the cage. I stood there, waiting for a chance to say something, but that chance never came. I had had it. Completely.

God, the absolute futility I felt! The helplessness! The need to say or do something! And not being able to move an inch, being so confused by what had happened and its rapidity that I was still lost in a fog!

I turned slowly around as a bailiff grabbed me, and I saw my mother and Linda and my friend Ted White, the jazz critic with his wife Sylvia, and they were absolutely stark white with disbelief and terror. I caught sight of my agent, Theron Raines, and I felt compassion for him, for gentle Theron was practically faint with helplessness at what had happened to me, his friend and his client.

"You got the bail money?" the baliff asked me.

I don't even know if I answered him.

He dragged me back into the room with the cage, and they tossed me back into the pen with the other losers.

I was down the toilet now. Completely. I had been booked, mugged, printed, and at last, arraigned. It was the end of the game-playing. The Author was now a felon.

All I could think of was that my mother was out there, who knew in what condition. This kind of thing might very well kill her. I can't think of any mother who enjoys seeing her pride and joy being hauled away to the pokey.

I didn't have too much time to think about it, though, for Strangways came trotting back in. "Have you got the bail money?" he asked.

I shrugged. "No. I haven't got that kind of money, but my agent's out there, Mr. Raines—"

"Yes, I met him," he said. "Well, I'm sorry I couldn't do more for you."

I wasn't feeling too salutary at that point. "Thanks anyway," I replied. "If you'd done any more I might have gotten the chair." He looked at me as though I was some kind of a whack, and didn't I appreciate all he'd done for me, taking off from his valuable, money-grubbing, ambulance-chasing practice to come down here to help me—and I was probably guilty anyhow.

All I could think of was how he had whined, actually *whined* in front of the Judge. "Your *Honor,* five *hun*dred!" Jeezus God in Heaven! What a *schmuck*! Pity the guy who had no mother, agent or friends in the circus audience.

He went on to his next customer, and another sterling success jousting with the Beast of the Law.

Unless you have seen the conveyor-belt justice of an overcrowded

New York court, until you have felt the helpless inevitability of not being heard, you don't know what it means to be hung up. The Judge was no better or worse a man than any other; if polled, he would consider himself a fine example of what a magistrate should be. But then, Eichmann probably didn't think of himself as a perverted killer, either. Hitler probably never thought of himself as a maniac. This is the nature of the sickness: not to recognize it. Not to know when you are subverting morality and ethics and common humanity in the name of expediency.

This is the sickness of our times, and the men we put in positions of power, to rule us wisely and with an iron hand. The Judge, harassed, tired, overworked, filled with a deadly cynicism and callousness from years of seeing pleading faces before him, impatient and uncomfortable, perhaps even subconsciously guilty about the shabby job he had been forced to pass off as competent, had found it unnecessary to hear any of the facts in the case, and had intoned, "One thousand dollars bail," without really knowing what he was doing. I felt more pity for him, then, and the anger came later; not too much later, but later nonetheless.

He, too, was trapped.

Then began the horrors, as I went through the police-detention routine, while awaiting the arrival (from Lord only knew where!) of my thousand-dollar bail money.

The Tombs are very clean, brightly lit, and because of this more frightening than the typical romantic conception of Torquemada's inquisition chambers.

The closed-in feeling, the almost claustrophobic terror of being chivvied, harried, moved wherever they want to move you, in a line with dozens of other men, faceless and without freedom—the entire weight of the building, the city, the law, life—everything weighing down on you . . . this is the most terrifying single reality of existence in a jail.

Don't believe it: a grown man *can* cry. Frighten him long enough and hard enough, it'll happen.

I don't know how conditions run in the other, more permanent, prisons of the New York area—Hart or Rikers Island to name just two—but in the Tombs, the goal is to turn you from a human being into a number, a piece of flesh that will obey, a body that will be *where* they want it, *when* they want it. The total de-humanization of a man. And for some of the unfortunates I saw in the Tombs, this was a short step.

The first batch of us who had been remanded to custody were moved out of the waiting pen, and the men tried to hold back, to stay near the little door to the outside world, so gray and cadaverous with rain. The guards shoved them forward roughly, though not with any real brutality, despite the fact that one old man screamed like a chicken, "Keep your fuckin' hands offen me, hack!"

That was my first occasion to hear the prison slang word for guard used. From that moment on, I thought of them as "hacks" also. After all, wasn't I one of the boys?

We were led out through the fire door and down the twists and cross-corridors of the rabbit-warren that is the Tombs maze. We got in an elevator (perhaps the same one we had been on before) and went down . . . way down. It was like being taken beneath the Earth forever.

When we settled, and were led out of the elevator, we crossed a large open area to another heavy barred door, with a metal fire door arrangement bolted to it, and a thick pane of chicken-wired glass set in the middle. The hack who was leading the caravan banged with his fist on the door, and then rang a bell. After a second another face appeared in the glass, noted who was waiting, yelled something we could not hear through the glass, over his shoulder, and unlocked the door.

We marched into the reception area of the Tombs, where I was to spend the next five or six hours, the worst five or six hours of my life. It was a huge marshalling area, with pens along both walls, and, to our left as we came in, a high-countered desk behind which uniformed hacks were busy arranging records and dossiers, preparing files, typing reports, slamming the drawers of filing cabinets, arguing about undecipherable subjects, and in general making a helluva racket. Down the spine of the room ran two long wooden benches—back-to-back—like the kind they have in railroad waiting rooms or in the principal's office of the high school. At the end of the left-hand bench, at the far end of the room, was a gray-slate-colored counter, behind which two men were busily working. One of them was stuffing possessions into a manila envelope, and the other was getting men to sign something in a huge ledger.

Our line stood there for two or three minutes.

"Awright, let's go," said the hack who had been leading the procession. He had asked some instructions of the Captain, a chunky man wearing a regulation police cap with badge attached, a black tie (a shade too wide for the current fashion, and a shade too slim for the '40s style), and a white shirt. The Captain had apparently advised him where to put us till he was ready to process us.

The hack shoved one of the men forward, and the man stumbled a step, turned and swung heavily, awkwardly at the guard. "Sonofabitch, you better treat me better'n *that*!" he snarled, as the blow went wide of the mark.

The hack stepped in, ponderous operator though he seemed, with amazing agility, and chopped the prisoner across the top of his chest. The man staggered with the blow, so accurately and heavily was it dealt, and fell back. The hack moved in, his fist balled for a direct clubbing. He drew back, ready to belt the prisoner, but the Captain's voice came from the other side of the line of men, from the counter right near us: "All right, Tooley, that's it. Let him alone. He's drunk."

Tooley back-pedaled and snapped a curt "Yessir, Cap'n," at his superior. He proceeded to get us into a waiting bullpen. Tooley was an exception among the hacks I saw while in the Tombs. While none of them was charming nor debonair, most were just bored and cynical enough so that if you jumped when they said jump, you had no trouble. There was no actual physical brutality, in the strictest sense of the word, though on several occasions I saw hacks defend themselves from out-of-their-nut winos or psycho cases who wanted out. In those instances, they leveled the quickest club or fist and settled the offender's hash without comment. On several occasions I saw men struck by the hacks in a glancing sense, that is, they didn't move fast enough, or they lipped the guard, or were just generally surly. But since none of the guards carried guns, they tried to keep their hands to themselves as much as possible.

A hack with busy fists could get himself very squashed in a matter of seconds if a crowd of outraged pen-residents decided to gang him. So they only nudge when necessary.

Yet their attitude is the damning condition. They don't see their charges as men. These are so much meat, to be processed in a certain manner, at a certain rate of speed, and when you speak to them, it's almost as though they have to readjust their thinking to comprehend that you are a human being, and not some lower form of life.

I would ascertain that most of the hacks were nice guys in private life; family men who loved baseball games and dogs and old ladies, and who would never think of being anything but gentle outside of this gray room that was a Universe in itself. But in the processing room they were something else. They were far from sadistic (though Tooley, to my mind, was a cat who could do with a little pounding), but they were not quite human either.

It was as though having worked around chained prisoners for so long had rubbed off on them. They were not *of* us, but they were not entirely free of the imprisoned taint, either. It is a peculiar feeling, a strange aura they possess, and I can't explain it any more fully than to say that though they were ostensibly on one side of the Law, and we were on the other, we were very much brothers . . . chained together by what they did to us and what we were forced to *let* them do to us. It is a strong bond, based in hatred, but identifiable with the authority of a father or brother.

There were exceptions, of course.

Tooley, who seemed to be a thoroughgoing bastard who delighted in the kicks he could get by humiliating his prisoners, on the one end of the chain . . . and the Captain, who had given indication of moderation, intelligence and humanity, on the other.

But at that moment we were prey to Tooley, not the Captain, and as we were hustled into the bullpen, I had a feeling that if Tooley could get away with thumbing our eyes behind the Captain's back, he'd do it.

The beefy hack slammed the barred door and locked it. Now began the waiting, till they had processed the bunch of prisoners in the next pen down the line.

I sat down on a hard bench and looked around. The pen was much larger than the one upstairs, but it was the same gun-metal gray color, with a floor that was covered with bits of paper, empty candy wrappers, pools of moisture that might have been urine and might have been anything, with a barred window at the back of the cell (but outside the cell itself) in a little narrow space between the wall of the building and the pen itself. The window was open and the wind was blowing in, and it was damned cold, with the rain slanting through, making it impossible to stand in the rear of the cell without getting wet.

I looked around at my compatriots, and the men therein assembled were as miserable a bunch as I'd ever seen. Not miserable in the social sense of the word, but miserable in the strictest literal sense. They were unhappy men. Tormented men, perhaps. They ranged from the oldest, dirtiest vag with his rose-nose and bloodshot eyes to the youngest Ivy cat all wide-eyed and terrified at being tossed in here with all these *cri-min-als*.

A hack came up to the door and said, "Okay, a couple of you guys clean up them loose papers there." Two of the eager young tots, anxious to seem cooperative, hustled about and cleaned up the floor scraps. Now the bullpen around me was clean and bare, except for the puddles I now recognized as water that had come in through the open window.

Clean and bare, like my spirit at the moment. Fresh out of platitudes and pithy observations.

. . . I could feel myself slipping again.

One cat got led away to be de-loused. He needed it. He left a vapor trail as he passed. Then I was washed, and stepped forward, to hear a hack yell, "Okay, step over here before you get dressed, over here, over here, c'mon!"

I stepped forward, continuing the dehumanizing but sanitizing assembly line routine.

The Tombs physician asked how I felt, and I said, "Glorious. A delightful little resort you have down here." A hand came out of the right-hand portion of nowhere and Tooley slapped me across the side of the head.

I told the Doctor I felt fine. He made me spread my toes to show him if I had Athlete's Foot. I said, "Dermatophytosis," and he looked up, shocked that one of his charges would be literate. If he'd known I'd memorized the word off a bottle of foot powder, he wouldn't have been so impressed.

He nudged me ahead with a nod of his head, I went back and got my basket, re-dressed, and walked out of the shower room into another tiny waiting area where they had a fingerprinting set-up ready. They printed me again, and again offered no means of washing the black, condemning stains off my fingers. It was a perfect illustration to me of how they systematically reduce you to an animal. Instead of having the inking ready at the other end of the shower, enabling a man to wash himself clean in the hot water, they wait till he is clean and again bears some vestige of personality, humanity, dignity, and then they rub his nose in his own shit again.

As I stood there waiting to be told what to do next, an old sauce-hound staggered out of the shower, perspiring terribly from either a disease Herr Doktor Quack-Quack had decided was unimportant, or from the heat of the shower room. He vomited on my shoes, though I leaped back quickly.

The smell remained on my shoes for three days no matter how hard I was to scrub them. I finally threw them away. The memories were bad enough, without olfactory additions.

I stared at my black fingertips with morbid curiosity. A physical reminder that I was a criminal.

It seemed, at that point, that I had been locked away for months. Time has a peculiar and hideous manner in jail. It does not move. It stops completely, and since they have taken away all watches, since there are no clocks in sight, since the hacks will not tell you what time it is, the mind boggles, and you lose sight of the time-flow, and consequently, a little more of reality is stolen away from you, while you feel your mind decaying underground.

The men were being printed and harangued into a cell midway down the line, directly opposite the big bullpen. It was a waiting cell, the last one before they transferred you to a home in the main cell blocks.

I knew if they got me in there I'd snap completely. I had to make a move now, or go with the rest of them, get locked away in the Tombs and they'd lose my card and when the bail money came they wouldn't know where I was and I'd become just another person in a cell and they'd tell my mother and my agent and my friends that I must be somewhere else because I wasn't listed here as being in a cell and they would go away and the bail money would lie waiting and I'd be in the Tombs forever and forever and forev—

I caught myself.

That was how it happened, I guessed.

You never know you're a coward until it happens. No. You never know your character is weak until it snaps. You never know how thin the tensile cord of your sanity can be until it breaks. I would have cried, right then, sat down on the floor and wept, I was so scared and lost and lonely and desperate to get *OUT!*

Out!

OUT! I didn't care how, just get me OUT OF HERE!

I made my move. All the other men were being put into the temporary cell, till they could be taken away to their regular residences, when I stalked past the hack who was locking them up. I walked past him, and he turned around to say something to me, and I just gave him a peremptory wave with my hand and mumbled something about having the Captain's permission and blah blah blah. He stared at me for a second, but since he knew I couldn't get out of that processing room, and since I was striding toward the front desk and the Captain bent over his papers—as though I actually knew where I was going and what I was doing—he assumed I had been ordered to the desk, and he let me go.

I had perhaps forty feet to cross before I could get to the Captain (and even then I had no idea what I would say to the man), when I saw Tooley coming after me. *He* knew I wasn't supposed to be out of that line.

"Hey! Hey, you, c'mon back here!"

I stopped dead in my tracks. He came up behind me and I'll never forget the feeling of that meathook on my collar as big Tooley literally grabbed me off the floor. He swung me around as though I was a sack of meal, and propelled me before him, back to the cell, midway in the line. He snapped his fingers and the hack opened the cell door, and Tooley cuffed me alongside the head as he booted me forward with his foot. "Now getcha ass in there, and don't try nothin' again or I'll give you a *real* kickina ass!"

Tooley, wherever you are today, know this:

I wanted to injure you. I wanted to hurt you. Every boot in the ass I'd ever gotten, since I was a kid, every cuff in the ear I'd ever taken, since I was old enough to recognize pain, every hurt and every confinement and every inability to strike back was caught up in my fist then, Tooley. You are a fat, sadistic sonofabitch, Officer Tooley. You are the reason so many guys try to break out of jail. You are the reason in this culture for violence and striking back and murder. You are everything lousy and egotistical and crummy, Tooley. And when you gave me that kick in the slats I felt every anti-Semitic bastard who'd kicked me when I was in grade school, and I felt every warped Sergeant in the Army who got his jollies booting troopers around, and I felt every snotty cop who uses his badge to vent his spleen . . . and right then, Tooley, you were close to having me on you. You'd have gone to your grave with my teeth embedded in your throat, Tooley, you rotten sonofabitch!

But . . .

I went flailing across the cell, impelled by Tooley's foot, and brought up short against the opposite wall. I hit it and went sliding, landing in a heap, my raincoat wrapped around my legs. One of the winos helped me up. Tooley had walked away already. The cell was locked. I was trapped again. It was a hopeless cycle. There was no way out.

I was still filled with thoughts of violence toward big Tooley, fat Tooley, sonofabitch Tooley. I tried to be rational about it, tried to tell myself, *Hell, take it easy, he's just doing his job. Don't take out all bitterness you've ever known on him.* Was I speaking for myself, or was I projecting Tooley's kick in the ass as the hob-nailed boot of authority on the neck of every poor slob in the world?

And I knew at once that I was speaking only for myself, but that there was truth in what I'd thought. It *was* men like Tooley who corrupted, men like Tooley hidden behind a badge or a diploma or a white collar whose personalities came before the responsibilities of their position. *Aw, hell,* I said to myself, *you're just bitter. Everybody gets booted around in a lifetime.*

Which was true, of course. But it didn't make me feel any better, I still wanted to kill that mother—!

Rationality is the first thing to go.

I could see them marching in a new batch of men, across the room, into the cell we'd first occupied. They were a bunch very similar to our group (I'd already established rapport with my confined compatriots; it was "our" group).

It was more of the grimy group I'd shared the big cell upstairs with, waiting to go to court. I saw my pal the hammer-killer in the ranks, trotting alongside a kid who couldn't have been more than seventeen or eighteen; every once in a while the kid would look up from under guarded eyes at his traveling companion. That kid was out of his nut with fright. *That* was the crime of the Tombs, right there, all neatly packaged for anyone who wanted to look at it.

The hack unlocked the door, left it standing ajar, and walked back toward the printing bench, instructing a group of men which cell to enter when they'd been blacked on the hands. I was off the bench, out of the cell and crossing that fifty feet from the cell, past the spot where Tooley had caught me, right up to the Captain behind the counter.

I started talking, and I talked faster than I ever had before, in a life singularly noted for fast talking and rapidly-employed angles. I'm not sure what I said, but it was something like:

"Captain my name's Harlan Ellison, Ellison, I'm expecting my agent and my mother and some friends to get my bail money and get it down here fast in a very few minutes just a little while and honestogod

I can't stand being in that cell I've got claustrophobia and if I stay in that damned cell another minute I'll flip and the money'll be here in a few minutes in fact you may have the papers for my release now and if you'll let me sit out here on this bench I swear to God I won't be any trouble and you won't have to worry about looking for me when they come with the papers so why don't you blah and blah and blah . . ."

Either my innocent, ingenuous expression won him, or my babble wore him down, or he knew I was going to be released soon, because he raised both hands to his ears and shook them gently, as if to say all right, all right, you can sit on the bench, just *shut up* and let me get back to work.

He pointed to the end of the bench and said, "Go ahead." I made for that bench as though it were a raft in a stormy sea. I sat right on the edge of it, and at the very end of it, so no one could confuse me with a prisoner about to go into a cell.

Tooley came past, right about then, and took one look at my white, terrified kisser, and made a move toward me. I stopped him fast by gibbering: "The *Captain* said I could sit here the *Captain* the *Captain!* Ask the *Captain!*"

He walked up to the Captain and spoke to him in a low tone for a moment. The Captain said something short and brusque, and Tooley noodled it out and said something else and the Captain dismissed him peremptorily. Tooley walked away, giving me a hateful stare.

I was home free, for a while, anyhow.

Time does not move in jail. That is one of the most overwhelming truths I realized. It does not crawl, it does not slither, it does not budge. There are no watches, no clocks, no ways to tell the passage of the minutes, and no guard will tell you if you ask him. So you have no way of knowing whether it is high noon, three and tea time, five just before dinner, or eight o'clock with darkness on its way. The time-sense becomes atrophied quickly, under the ground, in the Tombs. One finds himself dozing, only to awaken a moment later with the impression three or four hours have passed. After the first few hours, in which the novelty of being shunted about here and there has worn off, I began to feel that I had been down in the cells for a week, not just a few hours. Subjectively, I spent much longer than twenty-four hours in jail . . . it was more like twenty-four months.

And more than any other effect, this pale, trembling timelessness, this experience out of time and space, leaves a person feeling disembodied, prey to any physical ill that happens along, prey to weird schemes and images of the mind. I can see why men go "stir-crazy" in a short time; to them, it's a long time.

While I sat there, disembodied and expectant, breathing once out of every three times (I imagined), another line of men was brought in.

Now that I had nothing to do but sit and stare, I examined them closely. Minutely. There were the vags, the bums, the wineheads and the wetbrains from the Bowery, the Sneaky Pete drinkers and the Sweet Lucy lovers, the ones who filtered bottles of after-shave lotion down through a loaf of pumpernickel, the ones who drank canned heat and panther sweat, the ones who had left too many pieces of themselves in too many bars for too many years. These were even lower than the felons and the thieves and the boost artists. These were the absolute dregs of humanity. Men to whom life had lost its meaning, thought had lost its verve, existence had lost its color. Men with newspaper serving as soles for their shoes, with ragged clothes and ragged faces, with dull eyes and runny noses, with unshaved jowls and uncut hair. Faceless men, into the wrinkles of whose cheeks had been weather-ground the dirt and grit and soot and degradation of half-lifetimes spent on knees, in gutters, in doorways and alleys. These were the men the society had dumped out its backside.

These were the men *they* spoke about when *they* asked: "Are we fulfilling our obligations to our citizens?"

No good to say they could work if they wanted to work. No good to say they were lazy, dirty, stupid, unable to keep a job, irresponsible, shiftless, belligerent. No good.

These were the men who had passed through the mill of our culture, been unable to fit any molds, been unable or unwilling to discover themselves, and been flushed out the rear end of the System. Here was the dung we called the deadbeats.

In the Tombs they are called the "skids."

See them, then. See the truly lost ones. How easy it is to condemn them, when you pass them lying in an alcove, the stench of sour rye on them, their clothes fouled with their own waste. How bloody easy it is to laugh at them and let the kids mug and roll them and cast them out. And the fury of it all is that the outer darkness into which they cast themselves is so much more terrible, so much more final than any social darkness *we* could use.

All of this went through my mind as they stopped right beside my bench. I was close enough to touch four of them—but I didn't.

Old men, they were. Even the young ones. Old men, very tanned, even in September. Tanned from spending their days in the park, in the sun. Old men, their pants baggy and their hair white and their jowls stippled . . . almost a dirty uniform. Vests and pin-striped suits with wide, wide lapels, gifts of the benevolent and pretentious, doles from a too-busy citizenry. And the shoes . . . the rotting, falling-apart shoes, with the friction tape wrapped around the toes to keep sole and leather together. The rags for stuffing.

And their pallor. Their white, blue-veined, bulbous red pallor that comes right through the tanned, leathery skin. Brown on the surface, and so horribly fish-belly white underneath. Sick old men, lost old men, decent and starving and frightened old men turned off by luck, turned off by time, turned off by life. Gone to ground, finally, in the Tombs.

For a big Thirty w/3-a-day.

The stench of dead whiskey was almost too pervasive an odor to bear. But I could not move, and would not move, and let them stare at me with their dead, unfeeling eyes, with the sparks gone and just anyoldthing there.

It sounds strange, now, to say it, but I think the most honest emotion I've ever had was while staring at those poor saucehounds and winos. *I wanted to say something to them*. I wanted to tell them they could have a piece of *my* life, if it would help end their misery. Anything to stop the hopelessness of what they had become. They looked back at me without curiosity, seeing a young guy with the world by the tail, and their world was not my world.

They had been lost for a very long time.

And all the good wishes or self-conscious duty-shirkers could not find them. The work should have been done many years before.

A hack, standing nearby, snapped a half-inch cigarette butt onto the floor near the line of vags, and four of them dove for it; the one who came up with it was shaking so badly he burned his lips getting it re-lit for one puff before his spastic movements confounded him.

The lank hair. The unshaved faces. The twitches and starts and odors and shiftings of feet. The very smell of death about them. And the absence of desperation. These men had long since forgotten what desperation was.

Watching them, feeling the humanity draining out of me as the full import of what these ex-human beings had been turned into rose in me, I felt more trapped than ever before by the System.

Because *this* was the reward you got for screwing-up in the Glorious System. This was the ax that fell. And here was a manifestation of the lost, who seemed to be the guilty.

The waiting. The nothing-to-do. The putting my hands before me so I could see the black stains. (And then it dawned on me, why I had been constantly putting my hands through the bars while in a cell. Why everyone did it. Putting my hands through the bars so just a little of me could be free.) The feeling I was no longer a human being. The absolute loss of all humanity. The penultimate agony of realizing my life was in someone else's hands completely, subject to his whim or fancy.

And I couldn't yell: "The game is off. I don't want to play any more!"

It's *their* game, *their* rules.

"Okay, Ellison, let's go."

I stared at the old men, and inside somewhere I honest to God cried for them. They were me, I was them, we were all brothers, and they were down here for keeps.

"C'mon, Author, let's get goin', your bail came through."

Tooley lifted me off the bench, cleared me with the Captain, and hustled me out of the Processing Room, taking me upstairs to be turned loose at last.

I was free.

But I didn't realize it till I was in the reception room. Because the last thing I had seen was all I could still see, all I could remember, what I'd never forget.

The old men.

The ones who could be anyone, who could be me, if I ever lost the drive to keep living, if I ever let the System and Life in all its Mechanized Modern Majesty grind me into the ground.

The old men, and the young men, and the fags, and the winos, and the junkies, and the poor sonofabitch whose life had somehow been warped about the time he should have had his first woman, who had wound up using a hammer on a chick. The teenager who was scared and Tooley who was just crummy. All of them were back down there, like creatures without souls, waiting to see and be seen.

Waiting down there in Hell, in Purgatory, in the Tombs.

Yeah, I was out. I was free. But who would cry for the old men?

"Our Little Miss"

The Catholic Church is, I believe, generally credited with immortalizing the directive, "Give me your children till they are six—and they are mine forever." That's pretty heady stuff, when you stop to think how many *kinder* there are growing up in the shadow of the Holy Trinity. But it is nothing compared to the scale on which American Society debases its female population when it says, "Give me your girl-children till they are old enough to enter the World's 'Our Little Miss' Variety Pageant—and they'll be doomed forever to be either hookers or consumers, or both."

How it came to pass that I was provided with the knowledge that informs this week's installment is a small trip, so I'll take you on it, as I was taken. It was a week ago Wednesday, August 19th. About eight o'clock. I was getting ready to go out to a screening, when the phone rang, and a voice said, "You don't know me, man, and it isn't important, but you ought to turn to Channel 11 right now. You are not going to *believe* what's going on, on that channel!" I asked what it was, and the guy on the other end just repeated, "Turn it on for one second. If ever there was a column, that's it, man."

So he hung up after I'd thanked him, and out of wild curiosity I turned it on, and there—about three-quarters over—was something called the WORLD'S "OUR LITTLE MISS" VARIETY PAGEANT. I was only able to watch five minutes of it, and then had to split, but I was so intrigued and horrified that when Mary Reinholz called me the next morning—to inform me this week's *Freep* would be a Women's Lib edition, staffed and prepared by the ladies—to ask me if I'd slant my column toward Women's Lib, I was able to tell her, "Dear heart, I was gonna do it anyhow. I've got myself a doozy this week." (Just so you don't think I'm pandering.)

And I called KTTV and asked them if they'd screen me a tape of the live telecast of the pageant, and they said yes, and so it was that last Monday I went down to the KTTV studios and sat for ninety minutes as the Universal Broadcasting Company (of Baton Rouge, Louisiana) piped a replay through its Dallas affiliate to a color TV at Channel 11. Ninety minutes of unrelenting bad taste, petty hokum, deadly degradation of innocent children. Ninety teeth-clenching, stomach-bubbling minutes of ghastliness as a clique of dirty old men and their exploiting associates debased and corrupted a dozen little girls between the ages of three and twelve.

Thereby keynoting, most appropriately for this edition dedicated to the ennoblement of the female image, one of the most insidious maneuvers utilized by our snake-twisted society to fuck up the minds of its female population.

Uh, Hef, that's about 53% of the crowd. Which, in case you hadn't noticed, makes the Catholic Church look like really inept small potatoes.

The "Our Little Miss" Pageant (we are told by a publicity release) is more than a beauty pageant! It is a youth development program designed to give young ladies early goals in good grooming, social graces, talent training, and scholarship! It is the only outlet of this kind for deserving youngsters!

The brochure goes on to tell us that OLM (as I'll refer to it hereafter) has 1200 local preliminaries sponsored by civic and service organizations throughout the nation (as opposed to a mere 54 local pageants for Miss Teenage America). Are you hanging in there?

There are over 100,000 local contestants (second only to the Miss American Pageant, whoop whoop!). There are 32 state pageants And in 1969 there were 177 international contestants. And there is even a motto: THERE IS NOTHING SWEETER THAN A LITTLE GIRL!

That all of this bullshit serves the major purpose of hyping children's clothes and toys and (God save us) cosmetics, is something that seems to escape the attention of all save the venal swine who cobble up this monstrosity from, well, from whole cloth. ("The La Petite winner will appear on one million Martha's Miniature Dress hangtags during 1970.")

But, why linger any longer on the background? Why not come with me now to the Great Hall of the Dallas Apparel Mart ("The fact that the Pageant is emanating from the Dallas Apparel Mart gives it a fashion connotation . . . a world-wide glimpse into the children's sphere of fashion.") for the 1970 World's "Our Little Miss" Variety Pageant.

There's no business like snow business . . . !

Frankie Avalon and Shari Lewis were the guest stars, and the show opened with Frankie singing (naturally) "Thank Heaven for Little Girls," a song which has abominable lyrics and is difficult to sing by anyone but Maurice Chevalier, and even *he* looks a trifle embarrassed. As for Frankie, I've known him slightly better than casually for many years, and while he is a lovely guy and I don't want he should take offense, he *still* only has one note in his repertoire. It was not an auspicious opening. Followed by Shari Lewis and her sex-crazed hand-puppet, Lambchop.

Announcer: "Live! From the Great Hall in Dallas, Texas [home of hyperthyroid provincialism], the 1970 World's 'Our Little Miss' Variety Pageant . . . hosts Frankie Avalon and Shari Lewis . . . featuring 250 of the cutest, most talented little girls in the world! Brought to us by Royalty Toys!" And they run a commercial for this blatant tie-in, the "Our Little Miss Toy Doll," a strangely grotesque little bland-eyed mannequin wearing a princess tiara and a cape with a train.

Commercial over, the announcer informs us there are two divisions: 7–12 years old, the Our Little Miss finalists; ages 3–6, the La Petite finalists. They will compete in sportswear, party dresses, and talent.

Frankie and Shari came down, then, to be introduced, and they virtually had to sprint the 146 miles across the polo-field-sized stage to the cameras. And oddly, there was no audience. Just a bleacher section set up with hundreds of little girls ranked one after the other.

They were introduced by two superannuated elves named Bob Something and Chuck Something, who sat in a kind of sportcasters' box and spouted treacly aphorisms at one another: "Isn't this a marvelous pageant, Chuck?" Chuck bobbled his head like a puppet minus its puppet master. "Well, it certainly is, Bob!" "And aren't these little girls just marvelous, Chuck?" "They really are fantastic, Bob!" It went on that way for minutes, entire minutes.

Then came someone named Mr. Lynn, a gentleman of questionable demeanor (I'm avoiding lawsuits in my phraseology, friends) who is variously referred to in the publicity brochure as "the 'Bert Parks' of the OLM pageant," "nationally famous personality," "Prince Charming of the Children's Pageant World," "In the words of Mister Lynn, the international master of ceremonies, 'When Little Miss hits national television it will steal the hearts of all America,' " "a kaleidoscope personality," and in an advertisement he obviously took for himself in the brochure (check the spelling of this international personality), "One of America's foremost authorities of femenine [*sic*] beauty."

Mister Lynn, who looked to my jaundiced eye like the sort of failed hairdresser who lures little children into the basements of churches with M&Ms, simpered his way through a saccharine introduction in praise of Shari and Frankie. At this point I called for a shot of insulin. One could get diabetes just *watching* this abomination.

But this was all preamble to the very genuine horrors about to be Unveiled. In party dresses, out came the six finalists in the OLM division. They marched out as a cadre and all stood there with right foot extended and twisted in that improbable model's stance seen *ad nauseam* at fashion shows and being held by women at parties, the kind of women who feel uncomfortable at parties. And art gallery openings. All six had ghastly Miss America smiles on their little faces. That wholly unearthly rictus that denotes neither joy nor warmth. All teeth and cheeks stretched back like papyrus; smiles as if painted on, or as though Mister Lynn and his fashion thugs had held by the head each of the children just prior to emergence onstage, and attached clothespins at the back of the neck, under the hairline, to stretch the faces into that monstrous *sardonicus*. I had visions of the ballet *The Red Shoes*, of the ballerina dancing till she danced all time away and finally died. I had a vision of these unfortunate little moppets smiling like that through all the days of their lives, till they were put in the final box, smile still strictured.

Then they brought out the half-dozen La Petite division children. Ages three to six. Tiny. My God, small. Innocent. And . . . oh, Jesus Jesus . . . they had *blue eyeliner* and lipstick and that awful model's pose . . . three to six years old . . . Oh Christ! They look twenty-five!

How can they do it? How can they turn kids under six into jaded strumpets of twenty-five? Mother of God, they all looked like *hookers*!

It's been years since I've felt the need to cry.

My lady, Cindy, watching the pageant with me, said in a stunned voice, "The producers of this thing must be ex-convicts who've served time for child molestation!"

On it went, without respite. The 1969 OLM winner, Miss Lauri Lynn Huffaker of Dallas, Texas, came on with "the world famous Riley dance troupe" (?) and did a cheap-jack production number cavorting to "March of the Wooden Soldiers." Meaning no disrespect, but for a big-time national winner of a big-time national talent pageant like this, Miss Huffaker struck me as a rather ungainly little girl with no visible talent.

Into another commercial, surfeited with sloppy sweet sentimentality about little girls, pushing that goddam OLM doll that "comes complete with crown, robes, and beautiful clothes." It bulks obvious: beautiful clothes are one of the cornerstones of this entire vomitous operation. Not only is it bad enough to portray little girls as vapid creatures fit only to sit around and play momma to their dolls—an image our society reinforces from cradle to dishpan, thereby assuring itself of generation after generation of unpaid, highly skilled day-care and kitchen help—but in preparing these prepubescent Lolitas to be good consumers, devourers of the Grossest National Product, in preparing them to be mindless automatons who will buy every midi-length superfluity economists and *Women's Wear Daily* feel are necessities to save a sagging economy, they infected by cynical and demented hypes like the OLM pageant with the virus of believing if one does not have good grooming and the latest clothes, one simply is out of it, unfit not merely to be Our Little Miss, but disallowed from having any feelings of ego strength, any intrinsic worth, any right to the bounties of life. It is, quite literally, the corruption of the young.

And for all his lisping sentimentality about the wonders of little girls, they held the camera just a few beats too long on the Prince Charming of the Children's Pageant World and Mister Lynn, with a monstrously sinister smile carved on his face, exposed his inner nature with one look. It was like looking out of the mad eyes of Vincent van Gogh at *The Starry Night*. It was one of those inexplicable, unpredicted moments when one sees straight to the core of another human being, and in that glance was all the cynical exploitive rapacity of a man in no way above using children to further his own sick needs. The man caught unaware in that camera glare was not a man I would leave to baby-sit with *my* children.

Frankie was cut in quickly on camera, sitting with the La Petite finalists, reading some loathsome Edgar Guestian rodomontade about "What Is a Little Girl?" I reproduce just a snippet here. More would be to dare safety:

"God borrows from many creatures to make a little girl: he uses the song of the bird, the squeal of the pig, the stubbornness of a mule, the antics of a monkey, the spryness of a grasshopper, the curiosity of a cat . . . The little girl likes: new shoes and party dresses, small animals, first grade, noisemakers, the girl next door, dolls, make believe, dancing lessons, ice cream, kitchens, coloring books, make-up . . ."

It went on for some time, painting a pastel picture of prewomanhood consigned to its place: in the boutiques and the kitchen. The little girls sat there and arranged their skirts about them, ensuring the exquisiteness of their appearance every moment, all of them terribly involved with themselves, already poisoned by their parents into thinking superficial attractiveness, the right image, the way they look to the rest of the world . . . are the only matters of consequence a properly brought-up young lady should worry about.

Then the OLM finalists came out, one by one, in their sports clothes and Mister Lynn quavered minute descriptions of their ensembles. The children pirouetted and did that model's slouch, and when they finally stood all in a row, it was terribly sad-making to realize that, for all but one of them, from this moment on, everything in their lives would be downhill. In the bleachers, the little girls who had already been weeded out clapped on cue. They all wore little white gloves, and when they applauded it looked like a pigeon freakout in a dirndl shoppe.

Commercial: "Little child, with your eyes shining and dimpled cheeks, you will lead us along the pathway to the more abundant life. We blundering grown-ups need in our lives the virtue that you have in yours. The joys and enthusiasm of looking forward to a routine day, with glorious expectation of wonderful things to come. The vision that sees the world as a splendid place . . . Challenge that forgets differences as quickly as your childish quarrels are done, and holds no grudges, that hates pretense and empty show. That loves people for what they are; the genuineness of being oneself; to be simple, natural, and sincere. Oh, little child, may we become more like you. And now, from Royalty Toys, the Little Miss Doll: the doll that epitomizes the beautiful, talented, and poised little girls of the world. Little girls: curious, inventive, playing pageant with *their* Little Miss Dolls. Little girls who, in these times of stark reality, can escape into a world of gumdrops and lollipops. There is nothing sweeter than a little girl, and no finer playmate than a Little Miss Doll. The Little Miss Doll, coming soon to leading toy and department stores. By Royalty, of course."

The Little Miss Doll, symbol of white America. Tell the ghetto kid playing among the stripped-down shells of discarded cars in an empty lot that there is no better playmate than a Little Miss Doll. Tell the little black girl raped first at ten and pregnant by gang bang at thirteen that she needs poise so she can escape into a world of gumdrops and lollipops. White little doll, blonde little doll, sweet little doll. In these times of stark reality we know you are the answer.

Pure cornball, but corrupt cornball. Straight out of the antediluvian Forties. Dallas, Texas, for God and home and country and escapism. With kids in high schools, grade schools radicalizing themselves, with kids in colleges getting their brains blown out, it defies belief to sit and watch this sort of madness and know that there are people who really believe it matters, that it has some relevance to what our world is really like. This exploitation of the young, this brainwashing of the female, it is part and parcel of the conceptual inability of most of our society to realize that all the senseless persiflage over which they've cooed for fifty years is invalid, harmful, criminal.

Invalid? You tell me: the reigning OLM came out with an introduction from Mister Lynn (now wearing a sequined jacket and looking exactly like an overaged Jim Nabors with that incredible Alfred E. Neuman "What, Me Worry?" grin) and did her pouter-pigeon walk before the throng. All she did was walk across the stage, and the look the poor child sported was one of expectation, of waiting for the applause, merely because *she was there*, as though her mere appearance should spark ovations. Invalid? You tell me how relevant to an ennobling life-style can be an orientation that says because you are lovely, you deserve approbation and riches.

But even this congeries of evils did not plumb the bottom. Yet to come was the talent division and the final selections of winners.

The first little girl in the talent division of the OLM came out and sang "I Believe." You know—I believe for every drop of rain that falls, a flower grows . . . you know the one. The poor little thing trembled and shook so badly her voice had a ghastly tremolo. She was petrified out of her mind. Her parents and the pageant coordinators, putting so much emphasis on what is little better than an inadequate version of the *Original Amateur Hour*, had invested success, in this child's mind, with such portents, that she flubbed and twitched terribly. The torment of the young; dance for our guests, honey. Sing your song. Say da-da.

As Cindy commented, the really sick ones are the parents. Feeding their own failed dreams on the flesh of their children. How much money, how many grueling hours of training go into battering a child to perform like a monkey? How much surrogate pleasure do the manipulators vampirically enjoy molding a child to dance and spin and raise her hands to God in song, so she can tremble like a pneumonia victim for an audience of clothing merchants?

And oh, goddam goddam the shadow of Shirley Temple still sprawled across those children. Jennifer Childers, eight years old, from Satellite Beach, Florida, singing and dancing to the old-time Temple favorite, "Animal Crackers in My Soup." One more little girl in the image of cute Shirley . . . long blonde locks, crackly voice, ineffable coyness, old before her years. I would send their mothers and fathers through meat grinders with their shoes on.

What have these children by way of natural resources? At that age, plastic, still opening, they have only innocence that they can perfect. And that being stolen from them in the Dallas Apparel Mart—they have nothing, they are perverted at the touch.

Mae Rusan, from Fort Worth, belting like Sophie Tucker, rolling her hips, gutter-voicing her "Happiness Medley." So anti-child, so anti-innocence, I had to turn away. Ninety minutes of prime time on Channel 11 while the universe burns.

There was more, much much more. But why belabor it? Women wonder why men wage war, why they think of women as empty-headed totems to accouter their evenings out, why Gold Star Mothers take pride in the corpses of their sons blasted to bits in the Nam. Why wonder?

Why try to find complex reasons? They are all there, in ninety minutes of prurience and debasement, as the bastion of Democracy works its way on its young.

Channel 11 has asked me to point out that it did not originate this show, that it merely carried it through the facilities of the Universal Television Network, that it is responsible for such excellent shows as *1985* and the upcoming special, *I'm 17, Pregnant and Frightened*. That it will be broadcasting in stereo *Midsummer Rock* on Wednesday, September 2nd, at 7:00 PM.

Okay, I've mentioned it, and I spread praise to them for their good works. Now tell the ladies how good you are, KTTV; I can dig it, but what about "Our Little Miss"?

Did someone mention pornography?

A Love Song to Jerry Falwell

First, let us sit in the dark, as *they* sit in darkness, and hear words from writers.

Don Marquis said: "If you make people think they're thinking, they'll love you; but if you *really* make them think, they'll hate you."

Geoffrey Wolff said:

> *Writing has nothing much to do with pretty manners, and less to do with sportsmanship or restraint . . .*
> *Every writer begins as a subversive, if in nothing more than the antisocial means by which he earns his keep. Finally, every fantasist who cannibalizes himself knows that misfortune is his friend, that grief feeds and sharpens his fancy, that hatred is as sufficient a spur to creation as love (and a world more common) and that without an instinct for lunacy he will come to nothing.*

Arthur Miller said: "Society and man are mutually dependent enemies and the writer's job [is] to go on forever defining and defending the paradox lest, God forbid, it be resolved."

And, finally, Robert Coover has said:

> *The best social orders run down with time, and so occasionally you have to tear it all apart and start over. Primitive societies set aside a time each year to do this on a ritual basis. Get drunk, break all the rules, commune with the primordial chaos and the dreamtime of the civilizers, recapture the sense of community and thus of order. Anyway, good excuse for a party . . .*
> *. . . it's the role of the author, the fiction maker, the mythologizer,*

to be the creative spark in this process of renewal: he's the one who tears apart the old story, speaks the unspeakable, makes the ground shake, then shuffles the bits back together into a new story.

But they are writers. What else would they say to defend themselves? They are professional liars. And has not one of their own, Pushkin, said: "Better the illusions that exalt us than ten thousand truths"?

So what are we to make of the mind of the writer? What are we to think of the purgatory in which dreams are born, from whence come the derangements that men call magic because they have no other names for smoke or fog or hysteria? What are we to dwell upon when we consider the forms and shadows that become stories? Must we dismiss them as fever dreams, as merely expressions of creativity, as purgatives? Or may we deal with them even as the naked ape dealt with them: as the only moments of truth a human calls throughout a life of endless lies. Are they not evil, these liars? Consider their aberrations!

Who will be the first to acknowledge that it was only a membrane, only a vapor, that separated a Robert Burns and his love from de Sade and his hate?

Is it too terrible to consider that a Dickens, who could drip treacle and God bless us one and all, through the mouth of a potboiler character called Tiny Tim, could also create the escaped convict Magwitch; the despoiler of children, Fagin; the murderous Sikes? It is that great a step to consider that a woman surrounded by love and warmth and care of humanity as was Mary Wollstonecraft Shelley, could produce a work of such naked horror as FRANKENSTEIN? Can the mind equate the differences and similarities that allow both an "Annabel Lee" and a "Masque of the Red Death" to emerge from the same churning pit of thought-darkness?

Consider the dreamers: all of the dreamers: the glorious and the corrupt:

Aesop and Amado; Borges and Benvenuto Cellini; Chekhov and Chang Tao-ling; Democritus, Disraeli; Epicurus and Ralph Ellison; Fauré and Fitzgerald; Goethe, Garibaldi; Huysmann and Hemingway; ibn-al-Fabrid and Ives; Dalton Trumbo and Mark Twain; and on and on. All the dreamers. Those whose visions took form in blood and those which took form in music. Dreams fashioned of words, and nightmares molded of death and pain. It is inconceivable to consider that Richard Speck—who slaughtered eight nurses in Chicago in 1966, who was sentenced to 1,200 years in prison—was a devout Church-going Christian, a boy who lived in the land of God, while Jean Genet—avowed thief, murderer, pederast, vagrant who spent the first thirty years of his life as an enemy of society, and in the jails of France where he was sentenced to life imprisonment—has written prose and poetry of such blazing splendor that Sartre called him "saint"? Does the mind shy away from the truth that a Bosch could create hell-images so burning, so excruciating that no other artist has ever even attempted to copy his staggeringly brilliant style, while at the same time he produced works of such ecumenical purity as *L'Epiphanie*? All the dreamers. All the mad ones and the noble ones, all the seekers after alchemy and immortality, all those who dashed through endless midnights of gore-splattered horror and all those who strolled through sunshine springtimes of humanity. They are one and the same. They are all born of the same desire.

Speechless, we stand before van Gogh's *Starry Night* or one of those hell-images of Hieronymous Bosch, and we find our senses reeling; vanishing into a daydream mist of *what must this man have been like, what must he have suffered?* A passage from Dylan Thomas, about birds singing in the eaves of a lunatic asylum, draws us up short, steals the breath from our mouths; and the blood and thoughts stand still in our bodies as we are confronted with the absolute incredible achievement of what they have done. The impossibility of it. So imperfect, so faulty, so broken the links in communication between humans, that to pass along one corner of a vision we have had to another creature is an accomplishment that fills us with pride and wonder, touching us and them for a nanoinstant with magic. How staggering it is then to *see*, to *know* what van Gogh and Bosch and Thomas knew and saw. To live for that nanoinstant what they lived. To look out of their eyes and view the universe from a never-before-conquered height, from a dizzying, strange place.

This, then, is the temporary, fleeting, transient, incredibly valuable, priceless gift from the genius dreamer to those of us crawling forward moment after moment in time, with nothing to break our routine save death.

Mud-condemned, forced to deal as ribbon clerks with the boredoms and inanities of lives that may never touch—save by this voyeuristic means—a fragment of glory . . . our only hope, our only pleasure, is derived through the eyes of the genius dreamers; the genius madmen; the creators.

How amazed . . . how stopped like a broken clock we are, when we are in the presence of the creator. When we see what singular talents—wrought out of torment—have proffered; what magnificence, or depravity, or beauty, perhaps in a spare moment, only half-trying; they have brought it forth nonetheless, for the rest of eternity and the world to treasure.

Ah, but using an artist's life to judge his work is a childish habit, and anything that helps kick it out of us does us good. (It's a mean-spirited practice, as well, since it's used only by people who want to sneer at the artist. Do these high-minded types ever say how marvelous it is that such exquisite work could rise out of a sordid life? Do they eagerly pick up a dull book when they learn that its author had a beautiful soul?) As for the hero worship, that's childish and unfair as well. Why does the creation of a work of art impose on the artist the obligation to lead an exemplary life? Why do we demand an unreasonable nobility that none of *us* possesses? The artists have fulfilled their contract with us by producing work that gives us pleasure or insight or both. Why hold them to an unwritten morals clause?

And how awed we are, when caught in the golden web of that true genius—so that finally, for the first time we know that all the rest of it was kitsch; it is made so terribly, crushingly obvious to us, just how mere, how petty, how mud-condemned we really are, and that the only grandeur we will ever know is that which we know second-hand from our damned geniuses. That the closest we will ever come to our "Heaven" while alive, is through our unfathomable geniuses, however imperfect or bizarre they may be.

And is this, then, why we treat them so shamefully, harm them, chivvy and harass them, drive them inexorably to their personal madhouses, kill them? Lock them away in darkness? Cell doors slam, and the dream light goes out.

Who is it, we wonder, who *really* stills the golden voices of the geniuses? Who turns their visions to dust?

Who, the question asks itself unbidden, are the savages and who the princes?

Fortunately, the night comes quickly, their graves are obscured by darkness, and answers can be avoided till the next time; till the next marvelous singer of strange songs is stilled in the agony of his rhapsodies.

On all sides the painter wars with the photographer. The dramatist battles the television scenarist. The novelist is locked in combat with the reporter and the creator of the non-novel. As Voltaire has said, "Despite the enormous quantity of books, how few people read! And if one reads profitably, one would realize how much stupid stuff the vulgar herd is content to swallow every day." On all sides the struggle to build dreams is beset by the forces of materialism, the purveyors of the instant, the dealers in tawdriness, the tunnel-visioned censors, the Authorities, the jailers, the preservers of the Public Morality. The writer, the creator falls into disrepute. Of what good is he? Does he tell us useable gossip, does he explain our current situation, does he "tell it like it is"? No, he only preserves the past and points the way to the future. He merely performs the holiest of chores. Thereby becoming a luxury, a second-class privilege to be considered only after the newscasters and the sex images and the "personalities." No one calls for his release; no one wishes to hear his bad news. The public entertainments, the safe and sensible entertainments, those that pass through the soul like beets through a baby's backside . . . these are the hollowed, the revered. How many noted that John Gardner died in a motorcycle crash mere blocks from his home, on the day Grace Kelly died and commanded all the headlines?

And what of the mad dreams, the visions of evil and destruction? What becomes of them? In a world of Tiny Tim, there is little room for Magwitch, though the former be saccharine and the latter be noble.

Who will speak out for the mad dreamers? Who will open their cells?

Who will ensure with sword and shield and grants of monies that these most valuable will not be thrown into the lye pits of mediocrity, the meat grinders of safe reportage? Who will care that they suffer all their nights and days of delusion and desire for ends that will never be noticed? There is no foundation that will enfranchise them, no philanthropist who will risk his hoard in the hands of the mad ones.

And so, till they go to prison or madhouse they go their ways, walking all the plastic paths filled with noise and neon, their multifaceted bee-eyes seeing much more than the clattering groundlings will ever see, reporting back from within their torments that Reagans cannot save nor Falwells uplift. Reporting back that the midnight of madness is upon us; that wolves who turn into men are stalking our babies; that trees will bleed and birds will speak in strange tongues. Reporting back that the grass will turn blood-red and the mountains soften and flow like butter; that the seas will congeal and harden for iceboats to skim across from the chalk cliffs of Dover to Calais.

The mad dreamers among us will tell us that if we take a woman (that most familiar of alien creatures that we delude ourselves into thinking we rule and understand to the core) and pull her inside-out we will have a wondrousness that looks like the cloth-of-gold gown in which Queen Ankhesenamun was interred. That if we inject the spinal fluid of the dolphin into the body of the dog, our pet will speak in the riddles of a Delphic Oracle. That if we smite the very rocks of the Earth with quicksilver staffs, they will split and show us where our ghosts have lived since before the winds traveled from pole to pole.

The geniuses, the mad dreamers, those who write of debauchery in the spirit, they are the condemned of our times; they give everything, receive nothing, and expect in their silliness to be spared the gleaming axe of the executioner. How they will whistle as they die!

Let the rulers and the politicians and the financiers throttle the dreams of creativity. It doesn't matter.

The mad ones will persist. In the face of certain destruction they will still speak of the unreal, the forbidden, all the seasons of the witch.

They will end unnoticed like Gardner, or humiliated even in death as was Garcia-Lorca. They will write from inside prisons and read their thoughts to rats. But they will persist.

They have no choice.

One of their number, Mario Vargas Llosa, has said, "Writers are exorcists of their own demons." And as mirrors of their species, they will continue to deliver the good news and the bad news, that *We* are *God*, that *We* possess in language—the one tool that enables us to grasp hold of our lives and transcend our Fate by understanding it—the means to reach the center of the universe and, our salvation, the center of our hearts.

For this, they live forever in darkness.

Telltale Tics and Tremors

Under the pseudonym "Frederick R. Ewing," the multifarious Theodore Sturgeon once wrote a serio-comic historical romp titled I, LIBERTINE, the protagonist of which had an interesting character trait. The novel was a swashbuckler, and the hero was a much-vaunted swordsman. The only trouble with him was that when he was in a dangerous situation, he became petrified with fear. When that happened, his mouth went dry and his upper lip invariably stuck to his teeth, forcing him to draw his mouth up to loosen it. It was a nervous tic, but the effect it had was to make him appear to be smiling. He became famous, therefore, as a man who "smiles in the face of danger." This minor infirmity was taken for what it was not, he was counted fearless, and frequently escaped being killed because it generated a wholly undeserved reputation for his being foolhardily dangerous to the point of lunacy; and it terrified the bejeezus out of his attackers.

Scott Fitzgerald foreshadowed the totality of the basic theme of THE GREAT GATSBY in his portrayals of Tom and Daisy Buchanan as people who ". . . smashed up things and creatures and then retreated back into their vast carelessness . . . and let other people clean up the mess they had made . . ." The concept of "careless people" is one that applies perfectly to whole groups of young people one meets today. For instance, the wife of a friend of mine had managed to accumulate one hundred and thirteen parking tickets in a year in Beverly Hills alone. Most of them have even gone to warrant. Unlike New York City, where, if you are a scofflaw and have a pile of tickets, they settle with you once a year . . . or states where they refuse to renew your license until you clean up your outstanding tickets . . . in California they simply bust you and toss you in the cooler till you're paid up. So last week, when this woman's husband was stopped for some minor traffic infraction, the bacon ran the registration on the car through the computer, found out there were warrants outstanding, and tossed *him* in the clink till the hundreds of dollars were shelled out. He spent the night in the Beverly Hills slam and the next day they started to ship him off to one jail after another in the jurisdictions where *she* had picked up bad paper. Her carelessness caused an entire cadre of us, their friends, to waste a day and many dollars trying to pry *him* loose from the coils of the Law. And she just laughed it off. Careless. And that's the key to her character. She is a woman terrified of growing up, of becoming an adult who must accept responsibility not only for her own life, but for that part of the lives of others that is involved with hers.

Pinocchio's nose grows when he tells a lie.

archy the cockroach avers he is the reincarnation of a *vers libre* poet.

Uriah Heep wrings his hands, dissembles, and deprecates himself when he is being disingenuous.

Scarlett O'Hara captures her character in microcosm, in a phrase, when she says, "I'll think about that tomorrow."

Chaucer's pilgrims all have mannerisms and physical attributes that speak to their basic nature. The Wife of Bath, as an example, is gap-toothed, meaning lusty. She had five husbands.

In the series of novels about the actor-thief Grofield, Donald Westlake (writing under the name Richard Stark) has his bemusingly melodramatic hero hearing film background music as he has his adventures. He'll be going into a dangerous caper and the soundtrack in his brain is playing, say, the theme from the Errol Flynn film, *The Sea Hawk*. It is a mild way of showing how Grofield is able to laugh at himself, even at a precarious moment, and it explicates his character fully.

Grofield's interior soundtrack, Uriah's dry-washing, Pinocchio's priapean proboscis, the Buchanans' (and my friend's wife's) amoral thoughtlessness, the swordsman's daunting grin . . . they are all examples of a writing skill that *must* be present in the work of anyone who wishes to create characters that live. They are the minute mannerisms and attributes that create an instant flare of recognition in the reader. They are the core of character delineation; and writers who think they can deal only with gimmicks and sociology and gadgets and concepts, without breathing life into the players on whom gimmicks, sociology, gadgets and concepts have their effect, is doomed to frustration . . . and worse, shallowness.

I've quoted this before, and will no doubt quote it many times more, but for me the most basic thing ever said about the important material for stories was said by William Faulkner is his Nobel Prize acceptance speech. He said: ". . . the problems of the human heart in conflict with itself which alone can make good writing because only that is worth writing about, worth the agony and the sweat."

What I've just said is so obvious to any professional, that it must seems a ludicrous redundancy. Yet my experience with young writers has shown me that an astonishing number of talented people conceive of the writing of a story as an exercise in conundrum: a problem situation that, like a locked-room mystery, must be solved. They relate to the work the way computer programmers relate to an "heuristic situation."

They simply do not comprehend, as each of you reading this *must* comprehend, on almost a cellular level, so it becomes basic nature with every story you attempt, that the only thing worth writing about is people. I'll say that again. The *only* thing worth writing about is people. *People*. Human beings. Men and women whose individuality must be created, line by line, insight by insight. If you do not do it, the story is a failure. It may be the most innovative scientific idea ever promulgated, but it will be a failure. I cannot stress this enough. There is no nobler chore in the universe than holding up the mirror of reality and turning it slightly, so we have a new and different perception of the commonplace, the everyday, the "normal," the obvious. *People* are reflected in the glass. The fantasy situation into which you thrust them is the mirror itself. And what we are shown should illuminate and alter our perception of the world around us. Failing that, you have failed totally.

Melville put it this way: "No great and enduring volume can ever be written on the flea, though many there be who have tried it."

I had not meant, in this column, to get too deeply into the philosophy of writing. I leave that to pedants and academics who all-too-often worry such concepts into raggedness, like a puppy shaking a Pooh cuddly. Nonetheless, I am pressed to it; there is such a fractionalizing of the genre currently, with many writers opting for obscurantism and convoluted, insipid cleverness in aid of the smallest, most familiar point . . . or wallowing in smug arrogance that masters mind-numbing concepts, but do not reveal the presence of a single living, identifiable human being . . . that I find I must belabor the *people* concept a moment longer.

One of the least defensible rationales for the "validity" of science fiction as a worthy genre of literature, handed down to us from the 1920s, is that it is a "problem-solving fiction." This bogus apologia, handservant to the more exploitable (but no less phony) asseverative justification that sf predicts the future, is a bit of paranoia left over from the period when the writing and the reading of sf was considered tantamount to being certifiably tetched.

But those days are far behind us. The sophistication and craft-upgrading that has come to sf through the works of writers such as Silverberg, Disch, Wilhelm, Wolfe, Harrison, Moorcock, Tiptree and Le Guin has put it forever out of the line of contempt of all but the most purblind and reactionary critics. (This does not save us, however, from the moronic effusions of *Time*'s Peter Prescott or the lamebrains who work on rural dailies, who think they're being hip when they call it "sci-fi." Nor does it filter any light into the murky caverns wherein dwell holdovers from the "Golden Era" who are now counted as great historians and critics of the field, who continue to suck up to every pitiful monster flick or limp-logic deigning of notice from Establishment journals, chiefly because their lack of ego-strength refuses to permit them to understand that sf has long-since arrived. We must suffer with these old farts, but we need not allow *their* hangups to be *our* hangups.)

Bottom line, then: outdated attitudes continue to prevail throughout the genre. Bad writers justify their work and the Brobdingnagian publishers' advances they get by puffing up with the assertion that they write "true science fiction." Well, they're welcome to it, if they believe the value of the work lies in nothing but thunderous concepts flung through enormous vistas of space, sans emotion, sans people, sans wit, sans anything but hardware. It is writing more allied with the preparation of technical journals than it is with the heritage of Melville, Twain, Shelley and Borges.

I urge all of you seeking careers as writers, to eschew this dead end. Leave it to the amateurs who make their living as technicians or engineers with an occasional foray into fiction that is merely the mythologizing of their current "heuristic situation." Ten years from now their stories will be as forgotten, as unreadable, as the entire contents of issues of '50s and '60s Campbell *Analog*s are today.

The only stories that live on, that are worth "the agony and the sweat" of writing, are the ones that speak with force to the human condition. *Star Wars* is amusing, but please don't confuse it with *Citizen Kane, Taxi Driver* or *The Conversation*.

Writing about people should be your mission.

Which brings us back to the proper place for this essay, after a digression informed more by anger and impatience than a sense of propriety. I beg your pardon.

If you'll accept my messianic fervor as regards the *reason* for writing, then it follows that creating (not real but) verisimilitudinous people—go look up the word verisimilitude *now*—is mandatory. It also requires very nearly more art than any other aspect of writing. It entails keen observation of people, attention to detail, wide knowledge of habit patterns and sociological underpinnings for otherwise irrational or overfamiliar habits, cultural trends, familiarity with dress and speech and physical attributes, fads, psychology and the ways in which people say things other than what they mean.

It means being mature enough, and empathic enough, and tough enough to be able to capsulize a human being of your own creating, in a line or, at most, a paragraph. A single act or habit would be ideal. Lean! Lean and fatless, a minimum of words! The fewest possible words to obfuscate that moment of recognition. The writing must be lean and hard!

Read this:

> *A man has a shape; a crowd has no shape and no color. The massed faces of a hundred thousand men make one blank pallor; their clothes add up to a shadow; they have no words. This man might have been one hundred-thousandth part of the featureless whiteness, the dull grayness, and the toneless murmuring of a docile multitude. He was something less than nondescript—he was blurred, without identity, like a smudged fingerprint. His suit was of some dim shade between brown and gray. His shirt had gray-blue stripes, his tie was patterned with dots like confetti trodden into the dust, and his oddment of limp brownish mustache resembled a cigarette-butt, disintegrating shred by shred in a tea-saucer.*

That was the late Gerald Kersh, describing the indescribable: a man with no outstanding characteristics, a plain man, an invisible man, a little soul never examined and a presence instantly forgotten. The words do the trick, of course, but consider the images. Precise. Lean. Hard. Not cynical but utterly pragmatic. Confetti in the dust, a smudged fingerprint, a cigarette butt disintegrating in a saucer. Exact. Evocative. And in sum the images and the choice of words—self-censorship at its most creative and intelligent and productive level—give us a description of that which cannot be described. The only other example of this I've ever encountered was Coppola's cinematic characterization of the professional electronic bugger, Harry Caul, in *The Conversation*. As critic Pauline Kael describes him, he is "a compulsive loner (Gene Hackman), a wizard at electronic surveillance who is so afraid others will spy on him that he empties his life; he's a cipher—a cipher in torment. There's nothing to discover about him, and *still* he's in terror of being bugged." Coppola's writing, combined with Hackman's subtle sense of his own anonymity, described the indescribable: a man who is a shadow. And both Kersh and Coppola did it with the barest possible delineation. Lean, hard, precise!

Thus, what I'm suggesting as an imperative for the writer who wishes to create stories of power and immediacy, is the tough and unrelenting process of describing characters in a few words, by special and particular attributes. The swordsman's grin, Heep's hand-washing, Scarlett's interior will to survive even in the face of consummate disaster. I'll give you a few more examples.

In Edmund Wilson's justly-famous story "The Man Who Shot Snapping Turtles" we have a character named Asa M. Stryker (note the name as descriptive tool) who is obsessed with the predatory chelonians that lurk in his pond and drag down the little ducklings he admires. The obsession grows until Stryker goes into the turtle soup business. He becomes more and more snapperlike until his movements and manner become paradigmatic of the very creatures he has devoted his life to vanquishing. Here is a bit from the story:

> *. . . Stryker, at ease in his turbid room, upended, as it were, behind his desk, with a broad expanse of plastron and a rubbery craning neck, regarding him with small bright eyes set back in the brownish skin beyond a prominent snoutlike formation of which the nostrils were sharply in evidence . . .*

Wilson uses the device of direct analogy to demonstrate the sub-text of the story: Stryker became what he beheld. It is one method of characterizing a player. It is a variation of the Disney Studios manner of humanizing animals or inanimate objects like pencils or garbage cans by anthropomorphizing them. Wilson's technique, technically known as anthroposcopy, character-reading from facial features, can be used as straight one-for-one value-judgment or as misdirection, where precisely the opposite of what a person looks like indicates his or her nature. Take Victor Hugo's Quasimodo, the Hunchback of Notre Dame, as an example.

Chekhov once admonished young playwrights, "If, in act one you have a pistol hanging on the wall, be assured it is fired before the end of act two." His meaning is clear. Include nothing irrelevant. But if you set something up, you'd damned well better make it pay off.

The same goes for character traits. Take BILLY BUDD, for instance. Melville tells us that Billy stammers. But only at certain times. When he is confronted by mendacity, duplicity, evil. Symbolically, we can take this to mean that Billy, as a corporeal manifestation of Goodness in a Mean World, is rendered *tabula rasa* by Evil Incarnate. That would be the academic view. But as a writer I choose to see the stammer as a plot-device. The inability to defend himself is used near the climax of the novella as the mechanism by which Billy's fate is sealed. Herman Melville was a great writer, but he was a *writer* first. He knew how to plot. He knew the pistol had to be fired.

Historically, such physical infirmities were used by writers such as Hawthorne to indicate inner flaws. The Reverend Dimmesdale, in THE SCARLET LETTER, has a burning scar on his chest. He is an adulterer. The scar is the outward manifestation of what he feels in his inner sin. When he bares his bosom to the entire congregation, it is a shocking moment. The pistol has been fired.

Shakespeare goes even farther. Probably because his talent was greater than anyone else's. More than merely using physical mannerisms or frailties, he uses the forces of Nature in all their unleashed passion to reflect the viewpoint character's state of mind. In Act II, scene iv of *King Lear*, at the very moment that he wanders out onto the heath, having renounced his power while trying to retain his title, having been driven to the point of madness by his daughters, who have thrown him out of their homes, we find the following:

LEAR
. . . You think I'll weep;
No, I'll not weep:
I have full cause of weeping; but this heart
Shall break into a hundred thousand flaws,
Or ere I'll weep. O fool, I shall go mad!

At which point the storm and tempest break. Shakespeare mirrors Lear's instant of going insane with Nature's loosing of all its mad passion. He tells us that Lear realizes, in that moment of final lucidity before the plunge into madness, that in this life there can be no separation of title and power. That to retain the former, one must have the latter to buttress it. He has given over his power, and Nature has assumed it. He is alone, beaten, tragic, defenseless before Man *and* Nature.

It is mythic characterization on a cosmic level.

Less grand in its scope, but as revealing in its placement of a human being within the context of his society, is the little trick Turgenev uses to show us that Paul Petrovich of FATHERS AND SONS feels displaced. The novel was written at that time in Russian history when the serfs were revolting, and it is a time of ambivalence, dichotomous vacillation between the traditions of the aristocracy and the pull of rule by the common man. To demonstrate Petrovich's uncertainty, Turgenev has a meeting between Petrovich and his young adult student nephew, after many years, contain a moment in which the elder not only shakes hands in the "European manner" but kisses him "thrice in the Russian fashion, that is to say, he brushed his cheeks thrice with his scented moustaches, exclaiming, 'Welcome home!' "

Alfred Bester's THE STARS MY DESTINATION is a classic novel to read and re-read for such minutiae of characterization. Gully Foyle, the protagonist, for instance, has his progression and growth of character from near-bestial lout to cultured avenger epitomized by his language and manner of speech. At first he speaks only the gutter slang of the future invented by Bester to micromize the era; but as Gully grows and buys himself an education, he speaks in very different, more cadenced patterns. This is paralleled by the visibility of the "tiger mask" that covers his face. When he is a beast, it shows easily; later, it becomes almost invisible, manifesting itself only when his rage makes him revert momentarily. Heinlein's DOUBLE STAR is another limitless source-reference, jam-full of this kind of technique. Which is why these two books continue to be thought of as "classics" long after books that made bigger initial splashes have faded from memory.

Budrys once wrote a story, the title of which escapes me right now, in which a very fat man, an official of some bloated interstellar military-industrial organization, stuffs his mouth with candy bars all through conversations with the hero. Thus, by miniaturized example—arguing from the smaller to the larger—Budrys led us to a perception of the fat man as one, in paradigm, with the fat organization.

A horde of examples from my own work pop to mind, but a sense of propriety prevents my dealing with them in detail. I use a hare-lip sometimes to indicate that a character is a born victim; and men who are punctilious about their hair and clothes usually turn out, in my stories, to be men who get their comeuppance or who are shallow. "Pretty Maggie Moneyeyes" has two characters I think are well-formed using the techniques I've enumerated here, and if you get a moment you might look it up. In the script I've written for *Blood's a Rover,* based on the novella and the film of "A Boy and His Dog," I introduce a female solo who is as tough as the amoral Vic. Her name is Spike, and at one point in the film she joins up with the dog, Blood. Vic returns, after having split up with Blood, and wants to get together again as partners. But the Spike character is now Blood's partner. To demonstrate that she thinks very little of Vic, when she gets angry, she never talks to *him,* she talks to the dog. "Tell it to shut its mouth before I blow its head off," she says to the dog, referring to Vic. Blood then repeats what she's said to Vic, who has heard it, of course. This goes on till Vic is driven into a rage. It is a mannerism that will be a continuing in-joke. By talking to a dog about a human, and referring to the human as "it" instead of the animal, I hope to make a point about the way in which men treat women as objects. This, done subtly, because the studios would never permit it if they knew what I was doing . . . that is, actually putting in a sub-text and symbolism, heaven forbid . . . will serve to deepen the subject matter as visually presented.

I've offered all these examples of minute character traits—tics and tremors—in an attempt to demonstrate that it is possible with extreme economy to create a fully-fleshed player, even if that player is only a walk-on. And when you're getting into the story, a touch like these can set up the reader through many pages of plot and concept, permitting the reader to identify with the viewpoint character. It is a tone that will inform the story throughout.

As a final note, let me hit once again on the core fact that no matter what it is you *think* you're writing about, the best and most significant thing to write about, what you're *always* writing about, is *people*!

Building people who are believable, verisimilitude being the operable word, not *real people* but *believable people,* is a product of the touches and techniques discussed here.

Or, as John Le Carré, the novelist who wrote THE SPY WHO CAME IN FROM THE COLD and THE LOOKING GLASS WAR among others, has said, "A good writer can watch a cat pad across the street and know what it is to be pounced upon by a Bengal tiger."

Whether pounced upon by a giant cat, explaining why a coward's smile makes his enemies flee, how a careless person can destroy those around her, what hypocrisy lies in an idle dry-washing motion of a sycophant's hands, or how a beautiful and kindly man can condemn himself to death because he stammers, if you intend to write well, and write for posterity, or even simply to entertain, you must remember . . .

Fire the pistol.

True Love: Groping for the Holy Grail

I have this terrific theory. It's all about how we stop *schlubs* like Son of Sam or Richard Speck or Charlie Manson or William Calley or the Hillside Strangler from killing people.

It goes like this: We live in a kind of berserk, wonky Show Biz Society. For the mass of people living ordinary, just-let-me-make-it-through-the-week lives, the denizens of the flash&glitter set who appear on the Johnny Carson show are more substantial, more real, than their neighbors or their families.

Whom Jackie-O is dating this month has more relevance to readers of the *Star* or *People* than the fact that their butcher was recently admitted to the Carrville Leprosarium with Hansen's Disease. Zsa Zsa Gabor on fiscal responsibility and Debbie Boone on pollution have more impact than the most recent thoughts of Nader or Bucky Fuller. Every woman sees Mr. Goodbar as George Segal or Paul Winfield or Clint Eastwood or a phosphor-dot variation therefrom emanating; every man is seeking Ms. Juicy Fruit in the image of Raquel Welch or Farrah Whatserface or Donna Summer. Or etcetera.

So here's a pudgy, bland little doughnut like Son of Sam, drudging away his life in the Post Awful (which sinecure would drive even a well-adjusted person out of his brain), and day by day, night by night he's drenched with celebrities, none of whom have opinions or *de facto* worth any more valid than his own. But *he's* a cipher, a nothing, a nobody; he can't escape that realization. He's a doughnut, and no one will pay any attention to him; nobody'll throw a party or a parade for him. Frustration, lack of self-esteem, the pressure of everyday life, and he simply ain't making it, Hey, *look* at me! he screams silently. But all he gets is jostled and shoved on the crowded sidewalks. So he goes out and gets some attention . . . by blowing people away.

No need to say he's an exception, the manifestation of a "disturbed" personality. Whaddaya think, I'm a dummy? *I* know he's disturbed. But if you gave him ten minutes of late night prime-time on Carson, he'd never kill anybody. He'd feed off that notoriety for years. It might not turn him into Albert Schweitzer, but at least he wouldn't be out there fracturing the peace and sanity of the world.

Being on teevee is the secret lust-dream of the American People. Television is, in sad fact, the new reality. What happens on the tube really happens . . . what goes down in the perceived world is iffy: maybe it's real, maybe not.

And that's one of the most important reasons why a videotape dating service like Great Expectations is so damned successful and does such a good job of bringing people together in what we laughingly term The Dating Pool.

My friend Sherry, the Sherry who runs the bookstore, not the Sherry who can't get a steady job or the Sherry who is an interior decorator, said to me one day about a year ago, "I joined a videotape dating service; it's really terrific; I've met a gang of interesting men. You ought to go over there."

My first thought was that she was making what I took to be a not-so-subtle chop at my not having found a steady lady friend since the most recent divorce. But as it turned out, she only wanted me to indulge my curiosity. She thought I'd find it interesting. Well, I uttered the expected "yucchhh" at the thought of signing up for some artificial system of companion-procurement, and that was that.

Couple of weeks later I received a letter from something called Great Expectations. It was a form letter headed

THE END OF THE BLIND DATE . . .

and it suggested that if I had sated myself wasting away my life looking for love-mates in singles bars, groups or parties, I might be ready for Great Expectations.

But since I don't drink, I have never been in a singles bar (yes, my guilty secret is out at last). Belonging to groups make me nervous (I can barely handle my membership in the Book-of-the-Month Club). And as for parties, ever since the mass of my friends discovered dope (which nasty substances will never pollute my precious bodily fluids), I haven't been invited to a get-together. I'm sure that's the reason.

And I was about to roundfile the letter, along with the bulk mail that offered me parcels of land in the more remote areas of Tannu Tuva or the Orinoco Basin, come-ons to buy vegetable choppers, and the possibility of subscribing to a magazine concerned solely with bathroom equipment, when I noticed a handwritten addenda at the bottom of the form letter. It read , "We invite you to a *free, private* viewing of our program . . . & members . . . It costs nothing!"

Some weeks later, I had occasion to find myself at Sherry's bookstore, which is on Westwood Boulevard, which is just up the street from the address where Great Expectations said True Love, The Holy Grail, waited for me and, well, one thing and another, with an hour to kill, so why the hell not, you know it is, er, uh, mmmm . . .

And I walked down to Great Expectations at 1516 Westwood Boulevard; and it was there, oh moment of karmic destiny, that I found the most perfect device ever conceived in aid of one's groping toward The Holy Grail, sometimes mugged and printed under the AKA, True Love.

Great Expectations is not a computer dating service. It is not a photo dating service. It is not a referral service. And it sure as hell isn't your *tante* Sophie fixing you up with this "very cute girl with a swell personality." It is the very apotheosis of the Age of Emotional Technology. It is selecting a companion from a videotape interview and a written profile, and though it may be as flawed a system for finding True Love as the ancient and venerable art of the *shadchen* or Chinese marriage contracts between infants, as far as I can tell, it cuts down the potential for catastrophes in a big way.

It is a big business. It is run for profit. That seems to distress some people. (One such troubled soul is John Ettinger, an independent television documentary producer who did a segment of Channel 7's *Eyewitness Los Angeles* on Great Expectations recently, and who seemed hideously distressed that the service wasn't run like the Midnight Mission. More on Mr. Ettinger, and the hypnotic effect Great Expectations has on the weak-willed, later. Stay tuned.) Nonetheless, it is difficult for the average person contemplating a "dating service" to get past the stigmatized mythos of "paying" for the search for True Love. If one considers how much is paid in emotional coin, in the wear-and-tear give-and-take of most social liaisons embodying the Search, the cost of a membership in Great Expectations' service seems reasonable. But trying to explain the price structure in coherent terms is about as easy as filling out an IRS "short form."

But I'll try. Just not yet, please. It takes some working up to. For the nonce, let me tell you of the scene, and how I was embroiled in same at the behest of *Los Angeles* magazine, may its circulation increase.

Jeffrey Ullman is twenty-seven, happily married, and finds himself precariously poised on the precipice of financial success. He was twenty-five, happily married and impecunious when he had the moment of *satori* in which Great Expectations was born.

Ullman graduated from Berkeley in 1972 with a B.A. in Independent Journalism. His senior thesis was titled, *Getting on TV: If Not You . . . Then Whom?* For the two years following his graduation he was a Video

Documentarian. What that means—in a time when garbage collectors throw *dreck* as Sanitation Removal Consultants—is that he produced, wrote and directed low-energy-level documentaries for schools: over thirty in five years. But when an NEA grant came to an end in 1974, Ullman found himself back in Los Angeles without a pot.

At a dinner party thrown by his parents in September of 1975, Ullman overheard a conversation between his mother and a friend of the family, an attractive, successful, 28-year-old female record company executive, recently come to Los Angeles from New York. She was lamenting the sorry state of dating here in the City of the Angels. Though she had met many men and had no lag-time in her social life, she could not find "that certain someone." Because she was an exceptionally attractive woman, she was constantly being hustled; but there was no click, no knight on a white charger; she had not been, in the words of Mario Puzo, "struck by the thunderbolt." Ullman listened to this not unfamiliar lament, and its coda, from his mother, who observed that an inability to find suitable companions afflicted her older friends who were recently widowed.

Later that night, driving home from the dinner party on the Santa Monica Freeway, wracking his brain for a way to put his video experience to work profitably here in Los Angeles, the conversation of earlier kept intruding.

Not even Aristotle could codify the nature of the creative act, and so it escapes both Ullman and me precisely what synaptic relay was suddenly closed, that produced the circuit linkage. But in that moment, on the Santa Monica Freeway, Ullman perceived the natural extrapolation of using videotape as a device for bringing people together. That the linkage was produced out of a need to make an honest living should in no way demean its importance.

I mean, who knows what venal impetus directed Albert Einstein's thoughts toward the space-time equations?

Ullman began researching the possibilities of a service that would employ video technology in aid of this most basic human need. Fifty to sixty hours a week were spent hip-deep in sociology texts, magazine articles about singles, books on social anthropology, psychology, telecommunications and, fruitlessly as it turned out, source material on how to run a dating service.

Funding was obtained from his parents and from a darkly mysterious background figure whose name I have sworn to keep to myself on pain of having my "I" key broken off the typewriter. Mr. Mysterious doesn't matter, anyhow, because he was bought out three months later, to the vast relief of Ullman and his parents.

And so, on Leap Year Day, February 29th, 1976, Great Expectations opened shop.

Almost two years later, the membership is nearing 600 (52% male,

48% female) and what the Ullmans call "the relationship store" has a backlog of over one hundred and fifty videotape cassettes, each holding the life-essence of four or five seekers. Five highly-sophisticated Sony Betamax SLO-320s flicker from noon till eight Mondays through Fridays and twelve to five Saturdays and Sundays. Through the 1550 feet of office space that were private apartments in the Karno Building twenty years ago, pass seekers after the Ultimate Truth, the Holy Grail, AKA True Love.

To this Valhalla of unanswered needs and unfulfilled dreams I came, wide-eyed and as close to innocent as four marriages and a lifetime of brutalization permitted.

There are over two million stories in the City of the Naked Angels. Mine is one of them.

To begin with, Randy Newman notwithstanding, tall people get me very cranky. Because of their insecurity at their *yeti*-like monstrousness, they have long engaged in a dire conspiracy to inconvenience those of us who are normal height, that is, five foot five or under. This conspiracy manifests itself in the height at which kitchen cabinets are built, the dispatching of six footers with enormous naturals who sit in front of us at movies, the inability to get a decent suit of clothes without shopping in the cadet section of C&R Clothiers, and other such indignities.

Jeff Ullman is six foot two.

I walked up the stairs at Great Expectations and was met by this great shambling hairy creature, who introduced himself as the gentleman who had sent me the come-on letter.

Maybe not cranky. Let's just say I was underwhelmed.

In case you've lost the thread, I was on Westwood Boulevard, having an hour to kill, sorta, kinda, and thought I'd check out this weird dating service my friend Sherry had obviously touted onto me. "Oh, so *you're* the famous writer I've heard so much about," Ullman said, winning me to his cause instantly by striking at my weakest point: cheap appeal to vanity.

We sat down and he managed to outline the program at Great Expectations in between long bouts on the telephone with members who were calling in to exclaim jubilantly about their dates of the night before. To a man who had not had a date in six weeks, it was enormously depressing.

We talked for a while, and I was bemused. The odd mating rituals of the natives have always intrigued me. Despite his height, I rather liked Ullman. He did not try to con me into believing he was ramrodding Great Expectations out of a selfless dedication to the betterment of the human race. It was clear he was a businessman who had come up with an interesting, very likely workable way to deal with one of the most basic of human hungers: the need for companionship and love. But he had verve and enthusiasm, and a warped sense of humor that reminded me of my own, except taller.

So I thought I'd write an article about videotape dating. I write a lot of fantasy, in the general course of things, and surely this was a recent, fantastic phenomenon in the uses to which technology could be put in service of the commonweal. Jeff Ullman thought that was a peachy idea.

But the nature of my romantic life is so complex that I felt I should divorce myself from the actual dating process at Great Expectations; I felt a detached view, written with a wry manner, winsome but puckish, would be the most truthful. I mean, what if I got embroiled in dating Great Expectations members and, because I'm such a wimp, they all turned out badly? Then I'd be writing about *me* and not about the service, which might be a little bit of sensational for everybody else who's normal. No, I decided, this was going to be straight reportage. No Tom Wolfe or Hunter Thompson personal gonzo journalism. The unadorned reality. Sure.

Ullman was having none of it. Nor was the other Geoff—Miller, who edits *Los Angeles* magazine. They both insisted I actually memberize myself; actually put my face and mouth on a videotape; actually fill out a member profile; actually solicit dates with all those numbered women in the profile books; actually allow female persons to see my tape, read my profile and, if they were the sort of people who had taken leave of their senses, request dates with me.

They insisted that was the only honest way *really* to do a solid piece of investigative journalism. Ullman kept speaking of involvement and commitment; Miller kept hinting about the need for more and better consumer protection, the need to make certain we weren't sending the love-starved Los Angeles hordes—pathetic lemmings of lust hellbent on hurling themselves over the precipice of romance—to a shuck-and-jive operation. He also said he'd pay me a decent rate for the article, rather than the parsimonious sums usually doled out to the beanfield hands who traditionally write for Miller.

Naturally, public service and a dedication to the tenets of foursquare honest journalism swayed me. Or, as Bertolt Brecht put it, "Each day I journey to the market place where lies are bought; hopefully, I take my place among the sellers."

And so, dear friends, once more into the breach, if you can keep your minds out of the gutter, thank you.

First I filled out the member profile. Reproduced somewhere around here are both sides of the form. ►

Then Jeff Ullman took me into the "interview room." Very chummy,

Cassette # 93

Member Profile

Facts About Myself: Sherman Oaks

First Name: Harlan Code #: H-666 Date of Birth: 27 May 1934

Color of eyes: Blue Color of hair: Brown Height: 5'5" Weight: 139

Occupation: Writer (books, films & TV) Where born: Cleveland, Ohio

Marital status: Divorced x 4 Smoke? Pipe Drink? Nope

Number of dependents at home: None

Religious dating preference (if any) I'd rather not go out with flesh-eating cannibals, devil-worshippers or Born Again Christians, please. Other than the above, no prejudices.

Racial dating preference (if any) None.

What I Like to Do: Far traveling; reading; writing; having extremely long and elegant meals in exotic restaurants with good company; arguing; seeing endless movies; cuddling; shooting pool; visiting art exhibitions and trying to restrain myself from buying; buying; laughing at myself; laughing at others; but most of all, loafing around with friends and interesting strangers, talking about the world, which is filled with a great many things. I must confess I find golf and tennis and suchlike activities a thundering bore. Chess is pleasant, because conversations can be carried on while playing...but backgammon and going to hockey games fills me with a vast ennui. I find that the only thing worth the time and energy is the company of others; people are my business and I cannot conceive of ever having discovered all there is to discover about the human heart in conflict with itself (as Faulkner put it). I would much rather sit and talk to someone than alienate myself by watching a ballgame.

Special Interests: All the usual good things: music, art, sociology, literature. But, again, people. One evening in the company of a Carl Sagan or a Buckminster Fuller or a Louise Nevelson is worth 10,000 years of running around a handball court. Because I'm a writer, my curiosity about all manner of minutiae has led me to learn about such diverse subjects as cartography, Latin American literature, Jack the Ripper, top security in toy factories, Egyptian sexual mores, quasars as manifestations of giant Black Holes, art deco of the Thirties, jazz, the psychopathology of bigotry, H.L. Mencken, geology...there isn't nearly enough time in the day to learn all I want to know. I've written books of mystery stories, science fiction, fantasy, tv criticism, juvenile delinquency; books about the world of rock music, jails, kid gangs, high society, the underworld. I've been to Brazil and England, Australia and France, Scotland and Canada's frozen north, all across the States, and into far, strange lands where no one else has ever been. Special enough?

What I'm Looking For:

Something I've never known before.

Photo by Dan Tooker

very comfortable, very put-you-at-you-ease even though everyone looks ten pounds heavier on videotape. The camera is hidden. The setting is a book-lined room (crummy selection of book club editions, random studies of the sewer system of Kenosha, Wisconsin, a few Harold Robbins potboilers with obscene remarks scrawled functional-illiterately in the margins; a selection distinguished solely by the presence of Leo Rosten's THE JOYS OF YIDDISH). A pair of comfortable leather and wood chairs, knockoff imitations of a Saarinen design. Plants. Soft light. An okay room.

Jeff scrawls "Harlan" on a square of paper in block letters and pins it to the wall behind my head as I sit in the interviewee chair. It will be omnipresent on the tape so any woman running my cassette will remember and know to ask for me by my trade name. I can understand that: Redford and I are so often mistook for one another.

Then he interviews me. I don't even hear the tape begin to run. All very easy and comfortable.

The questions are humorous and searching and quite intelligent. None of this, "What's your favorite food" or "Do you like to to do it with whips and chains, wet towels and coat hangers" kind of interrogation. Not even "What's your sign?" Jeff asks me what I want to be when I grow up. I say William Randolph Hearst. Jeff asks me what my secret dream is. I tell him owning San Simeon. Jeff asks me why I've been married and divorced four times. I fwow up.

No, really.

Ullman is good. He could always put in a few years of lay analyst training and become a creditable therapist, in the event the Federal Trade Commission runs him out of business. He is gentle and easy-going, no stress and no feeling you're being grilled by Kojak. But he probes and works instinctively with body language, reticences and facial illumination revealed by the subject being questioned. And as I've seen from evidence of many interviews in the cassette files, he gets men and women to come out of hiding naturally. Jeff's mother also does interviews, and while there is a somewhat noticeable tendency on the part of interviewees to respond to Estelle as one would to a kindly aunt or to the supervisor of the complaint department at the May Co., she has the touch, too.

I had decided that I would set up some ground rules for myself in this matter. First, I would be utterly candid and open when cutting the tape. No "putting on my party manners." I would expose myself as the arrogant elitist swine I truly am. Second, I would not request women for dates because that would merely be to reflect *my* tastes and inclinations. Third, I would accept any and all dates for which *I* had been chosen, God willing. Fourth, I would advise any woman requesting me that I was doing this article, so they'd know it upfront and wouldn't feel as if they had been duped to the ends of journalism under the guise or romance.

But even though I cut a very blunt and arrogant tape, Jeff Ullman was able to bring out the jellylike core of my being. All unknowing, I revealed the soft, sweet pussycat that slumbers beneath this wretched, obnoxious, contentious anthracite façade. It wasn't a bad tape. *I'd* have dated me if I'd been an extremely intelligent woman. With a death wish.

The taped interview took about seven to ten minutes. I've never timed it, but the Great Expectations flyer says the actual length of a taped interview is from three to five minutes. If that's accurate, and if mine was no longer than the average, then Ullman is even better at this little prying game than I thought: my tape seems to be much longer than that. But then, how time drags when you're in the company of a bore.

And when it was done, Jeff ran it for me, so I could see what it looked like. One take. No reshooting. I'm a quick study; but then, I've got being me down pat. Type casting. For good or bad, I said, "Put it on the line."

(It should be noted that a member *can*, in fact, retape if dissatisfied with the initial result. During the first week of membership the tape can be viewed an unlimited number of times by the subject him/herself . . . and friends and relatives can be brought in to assay the effectiveness . . . random polls among people on the street can be taken . . . one can satisfy one's paranoid needs ceaselessly for the first week, and the tape can be re-cut free. It can be re-cut at the member's option *any* time thereafter, but Ullman charges a fifteen dollar time and nuisance charge; which seems reasonable when one considers how many people want to cut new tapes after having their hair or nose bobbed, their mustache shaved off, their consciousness raised by some good dope on the weekend or have reached a state of cosmic wonderfulness through est or scientology or by sitting naked in −37° F., cross-legged, doing Indian chants and breathing deeply. At the member's option . . . new tape. That'll be $15, please.)

My member profile went into the book containing men whose first names began with "H", my tape went back into the cassette cabinet, and I was assigned the member number "666".

"Uh, Jeff," I said, huckleberrily, trying to seem frivolous and not a pain in the ass, "did you know, just as a matter of incidental intelligence, heh heh, that the biblical symbol for the antichrist is six sixty-six? I mean, ha ha, the number of the beast is 666 . . . did you know that? Just thought I'd mention it; nothing serious you know: just heh heh ha ha . . . *did you know that?*"

The pudding laughter congealed in my throat. Ullman wasn't laughing. "Yeah," he said offhandedly, printing "666" on my member profile, "I've heard that. Fascinating coincidence, isn't it?" And I was a member of Great Expectations, just like that. Fascinating coincidence. In the light of subsequent events, did Jeff Ullman—numerically speaking—know something I didn't?

Let us pause for a moment and speak of love. Not even True Love. Just plain old grass roots common variety love. Theodore Sturgeon ventured the opinion, "There's no absence of love in the world; only worthy places to put it." Since each of us is a place to put it, and since each of us from time to time is less than 100% worthy, I guess Ted had it down right.

Some day soon I'm going to write a fantasy about the search for True Love. About this guy who knows such a thing exists. Not the idealized, gothic novel gobbledy-bibble idea of it, but an actual, literal, real-life thing that is True Love. And he searches all over the world, goes to the top of Mt. Everest to consult the mysterious guru, dabbles in the black arts, consults ancient texts, and finally gets on to a trail that promises to lead to True Love. And when he finally finds it, what it turns out to be is a big bowling trophy, a huge, tacky loving cup thing with T*R*U*E L*O*V*E*! engraved on it in florid, incredibly gauche lettering, all caps and curlicues and exclamation points.

I just haven't figured out what he does with it.†

And that's the problem with love. Once you have it, and you *know* you have it . . . what the hell do you do with it?

It seems to me (he said, stroking his Solomonic beard) that all but a fraction of the time we spend concerned with love is dissipated in the search; and very little thought is expended in consideration of how to use it, or let it use us, once we've got it. Thus, the search becomes easier and more involving. Idealized candy is infinitely sweeter than actual candy eaten. Diabetes, tooth decay, the mid-gut carbohydrate spread . . . actualized love can do it to you.

And so, while I don't *really* think it's easier to find love in, say, Samoa or Lapland than it is in Los Angeles, we do have the reputation here for chasing the Holy Grail more frenetically than they do in the provinces.

If this is so, then I don't think it merely a fascinating coincidence that Great Expectations has flowered here in what a bad musician has cheaply dubbed "The City of the One Night Stands." I think L.A. is the cutting edge of American social mores, and I think that Great Expectations is a solid manifestation of our need to find a new way to cut through the fetid jungle growth growth of Calvinist barriers that has always impeded us in the search for love. I found, to my pleasure—and in contradiction of my basically cynical, misanthropic view of the

† Those who have read this volume sequentially will have discovered Harlan *did* figure it out; for others, see "Grail," page 143.

human race—that Great Expectations and what it says about the bold spirit of Los Angeles is a very positive and humanistic enterprise.

I continue to hold that belief, despite what happened to me when the job-lot called Harlan Ellison went on the market at Great Expectations. Call me hopeful; call me naïve; call me Pollyanna; call me a poor benighted sailor on the seas of romance, tossed by the turbulent tides of lust and human frailty. Call me verbose and let's get on with it.

In the mail, less than a week later, were three postcards.

Please come in for a viewing. You have been requested by G.

Please come in for a viewing. You have been requested by K.

Please come in for a viewing. You have been requested by D.

That isn't quite the way the cards read, but it's close enough. Initials weren't used; the cards had first names on them. I won't even tell you the first names. Look: no matter how flippant I may seem here, these were all nice women who took a chance with me; and while some or all or none of them were right for me, or I for them, they made their move toward liaison with open hands and honest intentions. And while I'll play for chuckles in these anecdotes, I'll not gossip or hold them up to public ridicule. We are *all* weird, every one of us, in small and usually harmless ways. But in a court of law there isn't one of us whose minor quirks wouldn't seem sly and kinky and possibly perverse. So when you're ready to reveal that secret thing you have hidden in the back of your underwear drawer, back there under the rolled socks or the pantyhose, that secret thing you'd rather burn in hell forever than let anyone know is there, when you're ready to have it published with a big picture on the front page of the *Times,* at that time I'll tell you who the women were, the women I'll refer to only by bogus initials. If you want cheaps thrills go stick your thumb in a light socket.

Where was I?

So I went in to view the tapes of the women who had requested me. On a sunny afternoon I drove down to Westwood and climbed the stairs to the cheery offices of Great Expectations. Estelle was there, and as I walked in I was greeted by a look on her face I've come to know very well. It's Estelle's "Have I got a girl for *you*!" look. I have come to know and fear that look.

She sat me down in one of the armchairs, plonked one of the fat notebooks containing female members' profiles on my lap and said, "G. is at the back of the book. She's only been a member for a month. Very intelligent."

How she knew which one I'd check out first, and more improbably, how she was able to remember who had asked for a date with me, among the hundreds of selections passing over her desk in a week, is something I've never fathomed. But the clue to how Estelle can do it—and she's done it many times, I've seen her—and *why* she does it, lies in the response I give to people who ask me, "How can you be so high on such a dehumanized, mechanical way of meeting people?" That reply, and that clue, a little farther on. Right now I want to maintain the narrative flow.

I flipped through the loose-leaf pages. Rachel S-64, Denise S-117, Betty S-286. Past woman after woman; younger women, older women; stouter women, thinner women; innocent looking women, bold looking women; chic women, reserved women. And I understood that much as we feel compelled to play the "person in his/her own right" lip-service game, in the first burning instants that we meet someone who is a potential vessel of True Love, we are as one with the naked ape. It is *always*, in those first trembling moments, the aesthetic of line and curve and hollow and solid flesh that widens our eyes and raises our temperature. The subliminal message of certain body-heats, the flush of health, the movement of a slim hand through certain-colored hair, the horizon line of a smile that speaks of far lands ready for exploration. What culturally-hip hypocrites we are: talking of wit and wisdom, of good deeds and similar interests, when our chimes ring first and loudest for the high cheekbone, the tight little ass, the strong chin or the quick flash of crossed leg. It's nice to delude ourselves that we move in the stately pavane of the social contract, but if we listen carefully we can hear the murmurs of the veldt and the jungle near at hand.

I am no nobler than you: G. was an attractive woman. I looked at her photo on the back of the sheet before I turned it over and read the member profile.

She liked books, wasn't too interested in sports, enjoyed far traveling; there were oblique references to a delight in word-play and hard work; she was in her middle thirties; she was divorced with children. Intimations of strong character and a pragmatic view of the world. The portents were good.

I ran her tape.

Attractive, a trifle hyper in a nervous way (but that might be attributed to the setting, the interview), easy to smile, charmingly cynical sometimes; and the body language and facial giveaways spoke to a promising sensuality.

All this, from the profile and a seven minute tape. Not an unlikely weight of evidence if one spends any part of one's life watching people, checking out the somatotypes, cataloguing the secret messages our bodies send.

I read the other two member profiles; the one for K. and the one for D. I studied the photographs.

In the course of preparing to write the article, I had scanned many hours of taped interviews, both men's and women's. Not just women I found personally attractive by those undefined and secret jungle messages; but older women who were widowed or divorced, who were clearly seeking older men for companionship; younger women whom I knew would be outside my range of interests because of their youth; black women who probably wouldn't want a honk; overweight women and women whom I didn't respond to at all physically. And a lot of men's tapes, to get a sense of balance, to find out whether the myth that only losers signed up for dating services had any substance. My finding: if there were losers in that group I viewed, they certainly didn't reveal it on tape. I saw women who were poised and charming, vivacious and coquettish, intelligent and witty. And though I prefer the company of women, the men I viewed were equally as interesting. There were weaker and stronger men, of course; men I suppose women could find handsome and men whose characters were more attractive than their faces; but very very few of them had that gray Kirlian Aura of desperation and doom.

My finding: it was probably as statistically average a group of winners and losers as one would get if one scooped a hundred men and women off any Los Angeles suburb's streets.

The three women whose tapes and profiles I scrutinized, were no more nor less than the others. They seemed rational and together. The only thing that made me suspect they might be odd in the head was their selection of the man who had cut that arrogant, off-putting tape.

So now I had come down to the crunch point.

Here was where all the objectivity of my research into Great Expectations could go wrong. Understand: I am like the pessimistic kid in the old story, the one they put in a room filled with toys, who is observed an hour later, crying like crazy because he's sure someone will come and take them away; while in the next room the optimistic kid, who was put in with a giant mound of horse puckey, is burrowing through the shit and laughing and yelling, "There has to be a pony!" I do not really believe in True Love. I am a cynic. And you can take me at my word when I say that I extrapolated in every possible direction to find a negative aspect of videotape dating.

I could find none.

Therefore, if things went less than sensationally, the fault *had* to lie in me, or in people who would be attracted to someone like me. Which, of course, was the case.

So as I launch into the denouement of this escapade, understand that what you get from this point on is highly subjective Ellisonian vision. *Caveat emptor.*

I ran K.'s tape. She was a set designer at one of the major studios. I was not drawn to her physically, but her manner was so gracious, and her responses to the questions the interviewer put to her, that I felt I would very much like to meet her, to get to know her as a friend.

I ran D.'s tape. An absolutely stunning young woman. I was smitten with her looks. But as her tape rolled, I realized she was all wrong for me. She was too nice.

Do I detect the raised eyebrow? Do I perceive the hum of confusion? Let me explain.

D. was a *sweet* woman. Not simpy, saccharine sweet, with that cloying, phony manner that conceals another personality altogether, but *nice*, a good person who, because of her innocence (not naïveté, innocence, something quite different) was terribly vulnerable. It has been truly said of me that anything that gets in my way gets a Harlan-sized hole through it. It's happened in personal relationships. I suppose it could be called strength; it can also justly be called insensitivity or ruthlessness or unbridled self-interest.

Whatever it's called, I'm aware of it, I despise it in myself, and I try to be responsible as best I can force myself to be, by not getting mixed up with people whom I'm going to clobber.

By the time the tape ended, I knew that if I were to get involved with D., in short order I would chew her up and cause her grief. So I decided, no matter *what* I'd set as the ground rules, I was not going to see this woman whose decency and kindness radiated from the videotape playback machine.

I said okay to K. and G., got their home and work numbers from Estelle and then, as I was turning away, having said, "Advise D. I'm unavailable," I said, "Let me have D.'s number and I'll call her and thank her, tell her I'm doing an article, and let her know my not accepting a date with her has nothing to do with *her*."

Estelle smiled that knowing smile, and I went in the other room and called G. and made a date. K. did not answer her home phone, and locating her at the studio was difficult. I put her numbers away for later. Then I called D.

"Hello?"

"Hi, this is Harlan Ellison. You ran my tape at Great Expectations?"

"Oh, hello. That was just the other day. I wasn't expecting to hear from you so soon." A sweet, warm voice. My heart melted. I kicked myself in the ass intellectually and warned myself, don't let your gonads rule your brain, turkey!

"Well, listen, I, uh, I came in today and ran your tape . . ."

Silence at the other end. Expectant silence.

(Hold it a minute. Dammit, I hate to break up the flow right at "the good part," but here's something that should be pointed out. Great Expectations is terrific in one respect, if no other. The way the system has been set up, there is virtually *no rejection*. If someone runs a tape and decides he or she doesn't want to respond to that person's request, no one says, "He didn't want to go out with you." Instead , if you turn down a request, the other person is advised you "are not available." No more is said. *Not Available* really does mean the person requested is dated up, is seeing someone regularly, is going inactive, is out of town, has come out of the closet . . . whatever. For all but those too paranoid even to sign up for Great Expectations, a "not available" means no points lost, means you're still acceptable, means no one has looked upon you and found you unworthy. It wholly and totally eliminates the crushing aspects of swimming in the dating pool.)

". . . I ran your tape, and uh I thought you were very nice, and God knows you're beautiful , but uh er I don't think you really want to go out with me."

"I don't?"

"No, I'm sure you wouldn't like it."

"Why do you say that?"

And I realized my tricky, duplicitous, sly and treacherous nature had outwitted me again. Of *course* she would be intrigued by such remarks. Which shows you what a swine can lie so close beneath the surface of even those of who *want* to be responsible. Instead of simply having Estelle tell D. I was "not available," I'd set up a situation where I had to go out with her or make her feel rejected, thereby defeating the sane and sensible Great Expectations system. I had used my priviliged relationship with Estelle and Jeff—a journalist gathering material—to get a phone number I should, by all rights, have been denied.

"I say that because I can see from your tape that you're just too nice a woman."

"I don't know what you mean."

God, this was impossible! I was trying to ride two horses at the same time.

"Look: I don't know you very well, just what I got from the profile and the tape, but I can tell from *my* past that a woman as nice as you would only be miserable going out with me."

"How do you know?"

"I've been me a long time. I *know*."

"That's a pretty negative attitude."

"I don't mean it to be. I mean it to be positive. I assure you, nothing would please me more than to meet you; if nothing else, you are an absolutely dynamite looking woman."

"And smart, too," she said. I chuckled. Yeah, smart, too.

"Nonetheless. It wouldn't be a good thing. See, I'm doing this article on Great Expectations and—" I laid out the background. And by so doing intimated that I was *afraid* to date her because I might actually get involved, which wasn't anywhere in the ground rules.

"Why don't you give me a chance?" she said.

Now let us pause for a hot second, folks. Examine that sentence, in the light of the situation. *Give me a chance.*

Jeezus, that's all *any* of us want! A shot at the Holy Grail. Just let me get *near* the bloody thing, let me know it exists, let me make my best move. And *that* is the big secret of why Great Expectations works like a Swiss watch. Remember I said there was a response I give to those who ask me why I'm so high on Great Expectations, an artificial system of meeting possible mates? Here is that response:

When you need a job . . . when you're so goddam desperate to pay those bills, to bring a little food into the house, to be employed and not an out-of-work bum that you can taste it . . . employers smell it on you. We are, remember, close to the veldt and the jungle. We can smell desperation on each other. We can smell the loser. And the more desperate you get, the harder it is to get that job. Employers don't want those who stink of failure. It shines out of the eyes, it permeates our sweat, it reveals itself subliminally in the body language we employ all-unknowing.

And the more rejections we get, the worse gets the desperation. And the cycle continues.

The same in love. Have you ever noticed: when you're in love, or getting laid regularly, or content with your current situation, potential lovers come out of the woodwork? You can't beat them off with sticks. But when you're dumped fresh and pink and squalling out of a scene with someone, and you go back into the dating pool, you can't get anyone to respond to you no matter how hard you try. And you *do* try. Desperately. Frantically.

Here's the philosophy, folks: we spend most of our lives in pursuit of two ephemeral wraiths. The first is security. I promise you: there is no genuine security this side of the grave. And that's okay. If we get secure, we get stagnant. We stop reaching, we stop creating, we stop growing.

The second utterly worthless goal we grope toward is *looking good*.

Got to look good. Got to look sharp. Got to prevent rejection. Got to keep up that feeling of worthiness. God forbid our clothes are a little shabby, God forbid our nose leaks in public, God forbid the haircut came out lousy and we don't feel beautiful. In a society maddened by youth and *looking good*, to be less than scintillant is to get the dregs of life, to swim alone and unloved in the dating pool.

And so, when we cruise those parties, those singles bars, those blind dates set up by our friends, we have to wear the mask of *I'm not really looking*. We have to play at being all booked up, at being so popular it's only an amusement for us to be receptive to the offers of a stranger. God forbid he or she thinks we're available. We're phonies of the worst sort. We lie with everything in us, but our bodies and our desperation give us away.

But at Great Expectations that's stricken from the record. By the single act of putting yourself on tape, you say, "I'm looking." You say, "I'm here, for good or bad; and I want something meaningful in my life. I don't want to die unloved and alone." Everyone on those tapes, popular and unpopular, attractive and plain, male and female, is stating by his or her presence: I'm open and receptive. That is personal bravery. And by destroying that barricade, the videotape dating program uses software technology to establish human relationships. *That's* what I found out about Great Expectations and that's why I think it's sensational.

It is a direct and open way of saying *Give me a chance.*

Which is what D. said to me.

And so, I said we might get together for a cup of coffee and discuss it. The vulnerability everyone on those tapes willingly demonstrates, is an unstated social contract that only a viper would violate. *Give me a chance.*

I think I dated eleven women in all. K. and I spent several evenings together and we talked. It never went any deeper physically, though I rather thought K. wanted a more permanent relationship. We talk occasionally, and I feel she is a friend. If Great Expectations provides nothing greater, friendship is no measly treasure. G. and I had a berserk weekend that ended badly. Tantrums, name-calling, hysterical scenes straight out of a bad novel. I don't see her any longer. She has problems that don't mesh with my problems *at all*. She's pure poison for me, and I for her. I understand she has gotten into a strong relationship now, and I wish her well. But stay away from my door, lady.

D. and I still date once in a while. We were compatible, and knowing her has been a delight. But I was right that she needed someone less volatile. She has two young children, she has an understandable and laudable need for order in her life and, as Steve Martin says, "I'm just sort of a rambling kind of guy." But what a terrific lady!

Of the other eight, I'll only anecdote briefly.

You ask why, after the length of this historical treatise, I don't give you all the bloody and scungy details, particularly about G.? Because I find, as I come down to the crunch point, that I cannot belittle the associations I've had with these women. They were pure in their search for the Holy Grail; I was writing an article. Only a viper violates the contract, and I'm smiling softly now as I discover I'm not as ruthless as I told D. I was.

Of the other eight, my luck was no better or worse than that which would have obtained had I met these women at a party or had I been fixed up by my Aunt Sophie. One was a righteous flake who (like guys I've heard about from some of my women friends) professed undying love for me on the first date and showed up the next day with her suitcases. One was so defensive over the phone, so ready to pick a fight with me, that I backed off, saying, "Lady, you're too mean even for *me*!" One wanted a daddy. I ain't nobody's daddy. One was in her early twenties and, though I made the error of once marrying a teenage muffin, I have tasted the fire and no longer wish to smell the smell of burning psyche, especially my own. One was smarter that I and stopped seeing me. One was dumber than your faithful correspondent and I stopped seeing her. Also, she was a McDonald's freak and if I hadn't had a vasectomy some years ago and if we'd had children, all those toadburgers would have produced brain damaged children, I'm sure of it. One was this. One was that. I was a lot of other things.

And that's my story.

Let me clean up a few last points.

The price structure of Great Expectations is somewhat fluid. The reason for that is simply that Jeff and his mother Estelle are dealing with *people*, and sometimes there are accommodations that have to be made.

Membership is two hundred dollars a year. For that sum, and for twelve months, a member has unlimited access to the tapes. Reel out as few or as many as one needs.

For the first three months you get five active choices a month. That is, you can request dates with fifteen different people. You can accept as many dates as you get requests in the passive mode. After the first three months, to stay in the active mode, you must renew for twenty-five dollars a month. Jeff Ullman says the average number of renewals is between one and two. Actually, there isn't anything between one and two, but . . . Particularly for women under the age of thirty-five, experience shows hardly any renewals at all.

He also says he'll discourage too many renewals, because it means the service simply isn't right for *that* person.

And just stop to consider: where else can you have access to so many *potential* companions without spending every waking hour hustling and having to go out on dates that may turn out to be nightmares, considering how little data we have when we accept a date with a stranger? And if you can't find someone suitable out of fifteen-plus possibilities in just a ninety day period, then you'd better start checking out your face turned toward the world.

Great Expectations is now an authorized franchise dealer. They've spent over nine thousand dollars getting themselves checked out by the authorities, to establish themselves as a responsible service. A "relationship store" has been opened in Newport Beach by Kersh Walters and Susan Iannitti; another will soon open in San Diego. Such services, in less sophisticated form, already exist in New York and Washington D.C.

And despite media vultures like John Ettinger, whose will was so weak that he dated extensively in "gathering background" for his Channel 7 documentary (remember, I said I'd tell you about Mr. Ettinger?) and had positive experiences, nothing but positive experiences, but still had to seek out one disgruntled little lady who would whip out some bad vibes for the minicam . . . I see operations like Great Expectations as a breakthrough in human relations.

Mr. Ettinger understood that a rave notice like this article would not be nearly as titillating as a report that included a shadowy undercurrent of duplicity and weirdness. So he found a young woman who had been offered a cut rate membership—apparently because she couldn't afford the going price structure—don't forget, this is a business, not a charity—and she revealed herself on the TV screen by saying she had saved the two hundred bucks to buy new drapes, so for the money she found a man *and* decorated the apartment. Well, that's nice, too.

Great Expectations will not be right for everyone.

It takes some courage to sit there and say *Give me a chance.*

Maybe some day again, I'll have the courage to say it.

Adrift Just Off the Islets of Langerhans: Latitude 38° 54′ N, Longitude 77° 00′ 13″ W

When Moby Dick awoke one morning from unsettling dreams, he found himself changed in his bed of kelp into a monstrous Ahab.

Crawling in stages from the soggy womb of sheets, he stumbled into the kitchen and ran water into the teapot. There was lye in the corner of each eye. He put his head under the spigot and let the cold water rush around his cheeks.

Dead bottles littered the living room. One hundred and eleven empty bottles that had contained Robitussin and Romilar-CF. He padded through the debris to the front door and opened it a crack. Daylight assaulted him. "Oh, God," he murmured, and closed his eyes to pick up the folded newspaper from the stoop.

Once more in dusk, he opened the paper. The headline read: BOLIVIAN AMBASSADOR FOUND MURDERED, and the feature story heading column one detailed the discovery of the ambassador's body, badly decomposed, in an abandoned refrigerator in an empty lot in Secaucus, New Jersey.

The teapot whistled.

Naked, he padded toward the kitchen; as he passed the aquarium he saw that terrible fish was still alive, and this morning whistling like a bluejay, making tiny streams of bubbles that rose to burst on the scummy surface of the water. He paused beside the tank, turned on the light and looked in through the drifting eddies of stringered algae. The fish simply would not die. It had killed off every other fish in the tank—prettier fish, friendlier fish, livelier fish, even larger and more dangerous fish—had killed them all, one by one, and eaten out the eyes. Now it swam the tank alone, ruler of its worthless domain.

He had tried to let the fish kill itself, trying every form of neglect short of outright murder by not feeding it; but the pale, worm-pink devil even thrived in the dark and filth-laden waters.

Now it sang like a bluejay. He hated the fish with a passion he could barely contain.

He sprinkled flakes from a plastic container, grinding them between thumb and forefinger as experts had advised him to do it, and watched the multicolored granules of fish meal, roe, milt, brine shrimp, day-fly eggs, oatflour and egg yolk ride on the surface for a moment before the detestable fish-face came snapping to the top to suck them down. He turned away, cursing and hating the fish. It would not die. Like him, it would not die.

In the kitchen, bent over the boiling water, he understood for the first time the true status of his situation. Though he was probably nowhere near the rotting outer edge of sanity, he could smell its foulness on the wind, coming in from the horizon; and like some wild animal rolling its eyes at the scent of carrion and the feeders thereon, he was being driven closer to lunacy every day, just from the smell.

He carried the teapot, a cup and two tea bags to the kitchen table and sat down. Propped open in a plastic stand used for keeping cookbooks handy while mixing ingredients, the Mayan Codex translations remained unread from the evening before. He poured the water, dangled the tea bags in the cup and tried to focus his attention. The references to Itzamna, the chief divinity of the Maya pantheon, and medicine, his chief sphere of influence, blurred. Ixtab, the goddess of suicide, seemed more apropos for this morning, this deadly terrible morning. He tried reading, but the words only went in, nothing happened to them, they didn't sing. He sipped tea and found himself thinking of the chill, full circle of the Moon. He glanced over his shoulder at the kitchen clock. Seven forty-four.

He shoved away from the table, taking the half-full cup of tea, and went into the bedroom. The impression of his body, where it had lain in tortured sleep, still dented the bed. There were clumps of blood-matted hair clinging to the manacles that he had riveted to metal plates in the headboard. He rubbed his wrists where they had been scored raw, slopping a little tea on his left forearm. He wondered if the Bolivian ambassador had been a piece of work he had tended to the month before.

His wristwatch lay on the bureau. He checked it. Seven forty-six. Slightly less than an hour and a quarter to make the meeting with the consultation service. He went into the bathroom, reached inside the shower stall and turned the handle till a fine needle-spray of icy water smashed the tiled wall of the stall. Letting the water run, he turned to the medicine cabinet for his shampoo. Taped to the mirror was an

Ouchless Telfa finger bandage on which two lines had been neatly typed, in capitals:

THE WAY YOU WALK IS THORNY, MY SON,
THROUGH NO FAULT OF YOUR OWN.

Then, opening the cabinet, removing a plastic bottle of herbal shampoo that smelled like friendly, deep forests, Lawrence Talbot resigned himself to the situation, turned and stepped into the shower, the merciless ice-laden waters of the Arctic pounding against his tortured flesh.

Suite 1544 of the Tishman Airport Center Building was a men's toilet. He stood against the wall opposite the door labeled MEN and drew the envelope from the inner breast pocket of his jacket. The paper was of good quality, the envelope crackled as he thumbed up the flap and withdrew the single-sheet letter inside. It was the correct address, the correct floor, the correct suite. Suite 1544 was a men's toilet, nonetheless. Talbot started to turn away. It was a vicious joke; he found no humor in the situation; not in his present circumstances.

He took one step toward the elevators.

The door to the men's room shimmered, fogged over like a windshield in winter, and re-formed. The legend on the door had changed. It now read:

INFORMATION ASSOCIATES

Suite 1544 was the consultation service that had written the invitational letter on paper of good quality in response to Talbot's mail inquiry responding to a noncommittal but judiciously-phrased advertisement in *Forbes*.

He opened the door and stepped inside. The woman behind the teak reception desk smiled at him, and his glance was split between the dimples that formed, and her legs, very nice, smooth legs, crossed and framed by the kneehole of the desk. "Mr. Talbot?"

He nodded. "Lawrence Talbot."

She smiled again. "Mr. Demeter will see you at once, sir. Would you like something to drink? Coffee? A soft drink?"

Talbot found himself touching his jacket where the envelope lay in an inner pocket. "No. Thank you."

She stood up, moving toward an inner office door, as Talbot said, "What do you do when someone tries to flush your desk?" He was not trying to be cute. He was annoyed. She turned and stared at him. There was silence in her appraisal, nothing more.

"Mr. Demeter is right through here, sir."

She opened the door and stood aside. Talbot walked past her, catching a scent of mimosa.

The inner office was furnished like the reading room of an exclusive men's club. Old money. Deep quiet. Dark, heavy woods. A lowered ceiling of acoustical tile on tracks, concealing a crawl space and probably electrical conduits. The pile rug of oranges and burnt umbers swallowed his feet to the ankles. Through a wall-sized window could be seen not the city that lay outside the building but a panoramic view of Hanauma Bay, on the Koko Head side of Oahu. The pure aquamarine waves came in like undulant snakes, rose like cobras, crested out white, tunneled, and struck like asps at the blazing yellow beach. It was not a window; there were no windows in the office. It was a photograph. A deep, real photograph that was neither a projection nor a hologram. It was a wall looking out on another place entirely. Talbot know nothing about exotic flora, but he was certain that the tall, razor-edge-leafed trees growing right down to beach's boundary were identical to those pictured in books depicting the Carboniferous period of the Earth before even the saurians had walked the land. What he was seeing had been gone for a very long time.

"Mr. Talbot. Good of you to come. John Demeter."

He came up from a wingback chair, extended his hand. Talbot took it. The grip was firm and cool. "Won't you sit down," Demeter said. "Something to drink? Coffee, perhaps, or a soft drink?" Talbot shook his head; Demeter nodded dismissal to the receptionist; she closed the door behind her, firmly, smoothly, silently.

Talbot studied Demeter in one long appraisal as he took the chair opposite the wingback. Demeter was in his early fifties, had retained a full and rich mop of hair that fell across his forehead in gray waves that clearly had not been touched up. His eyes were clear and blue, his features regular and jovial, his mouth wide and sincere. He was trim. The dark brown business suit was hand-tailored and hung well. He sat easily and crossed his legs, revealing black hose that went above the shins. His shoes were highly polished.

"That's a fascinating door, the one to your outer office," Talbot said.

"Do we talk about my door?" Demeter asked.

"Not if you don't want to. That isn't why I came here."

"I don't want to. So let's discuss your particular problem."

"Your advertisement. I was intrigued."

Demeter smiled reassuringly. "Four copywriters worked very diligently at the proper phraseology."

"It brings in business."

"The right kind of business."

"You slanted it toward smart money. Very reserved. Conservative portfolios, few glamours, steady climbers. Wise old owls."

Demeter steepled his fingers and nodded, an understanding uncle. "Directly to the core, Mr. Talbot: wise old owls."

"I need some information. Some special, certain information. How confidential is your service, Mr. Demeter?"

The friendly uncle, the wise old owl, the reassuring businessman understood all the edited spaces behind the question. He nodded several times. Then he smiled and said, "That *is* a clever door I have, isn't it? You're absolutely right, Mr. Talbot."

"A certain understated eloquence."

"One hopes it answers more questions for our clients than it poses."

Talbot sat back in the chair for the first time since he had entered Demeter's office. "I think I can accept that."

"Fine. Then why don't we get to specifics. Mr. Talbot, you're having some difficulty dying. Am I stating the situation succinctly?"

"Gently, Mr. Demeter."

"Always."

"Yes. You're on the target."

"But you have some problems, some rather unusual problems."

"Inner ring."

Demeter stood up and walked around the room, touching an astrolabe on a bookshelf, a cut-glass decanter on a sideboard, a sheaf of the *London Times* held together by a wooden pole. "We are only information specialists, Mr. Talbot. We can put you on to what you need, but the effectation is your problem."

"If I have the *modus operandi*, I'll have no trouble taking care of getting it done."

"You've put a little aside."

"A little."

"Conservative portfolio? A few glamours, mostly steady climbers?"

"Bull's-eye, Mr. Demeter."

Demeter came back and sat down again. "All right, then. If you'll take the time to write out very carefully *precisely* what you want – I know generally, from your letter, but I want this *precise*, for the contract – I think I can undertake to supply the data necessary to solving your problem."

"At what cost?"

"Let's decide what it is you want, first, shall we?"

Talbot nodded. Demeter reached over and pressed a call button on the smoking stand beside the wingback. The door opened. "Susan, would you show Mr. Talbot to the sanctum and provide him with writing materials." She smiled and stood aside, waiting for Talbot to follow her. "And bring Mr. Talbot something to drink if he'd like it . . . some coffee? A soft drink, perhaps?" Talbot did not respond to the offer.

"I might need some time to get the phraseology down just right. I might have to work as diligently as your copywriters. It might take me a while. I'll go home and bring it in tomorrow."

Demeter looked troubled. "That might be inconvenient. That's why we provide a quiet place where you can think."

"You'd prefer I stay and do it now."

"Inner ring, Mr. Talbot."

"You might be a toilet if I came back tomorrow."

"Bull's-eye."

"Let's go, Susan. Bring me a glass of orange juice if you have it." He preceded her out the door.

He followed her down the corridor at the far side of the reception room. He had not seen it before. She stopped at a door and opened it for him. There was an escritoire and a comfortable chair inside the small room. He could hear Muzak. "I'll bring you your orange juice," she said.

He went in and sat down. After a long time he wrote seven words on a sheet of paper.

Two months later, long after the series of visitations from silent messengers who brought rough drafts of the contract to be examined, who came again to take them away revised, who came again with counterproposals, who came again to take away further revised versions, who came again—finally—with Demeter-signed finals, and who waited while he examined and initialed and signed the finals—two months later, the map came via the last, mute messenger. He arranged for the final installment of the payment to Information Associates that same day: he had ceased wondering where fifteen boxcars of maize—grown specifically as the Zuñi nation had grown it—was of value.

Two days later, a small item on an inside page of the *New York Times* noted that fifteen boxcars of farm produce had somehow vanished off a railroad spur near Albuquerque. An official investigation had been initiated.

The map was very specific, very detailed; it looked accurate.

He spent several days with Gray's ANATOMY and, when he was satisfied that Demeter and his organization had been worth the staggering fee, he made a phone call. The long-distance operator turned him over to Inboard and he waited, after giving her the information, for the static-laden connection to be made. He insisted Budapest on the other end let it ring twenty times, twice the number the male operator was permitted per caller. On the twenty-first ring it was picked up. Miraculously, the background noise-level dropped and he heard Victor's voice as though it was across the room.

"Yes! Hello!" Impatient, surly as always.

"Victor . . . Larry Talbot."

"Where are you calling from?"

"The States. How are you?"

"Busy. What do you want?"

"I have a project. I want to hire you and your lab."

"Forget it. I'm coming down to final moments on a project and I can't be bothered now."

The imminence of hangup was in his voice. Talbot cut in quickly. "How long do you anticipate?"

"Till what?"

"Till you're clear."

"Another six months inside, eight to ten if it gets muddy. I said: forget it, Larry. I'm *not* available."

"At least let's talk."

"No."

"Am I wrong, Victor, or do you owe me a little?"

"After all this time you're calling in debts?"

"They only ripen with age."

There was a long silence in which Talbot heard dead space being pirated off their line. At one point he thought the other man had racked the receiver. Then, finally, "Okay, Larry. We'll *talk*. But you'll have to come to me; I'm too involved to be hopping any jets."

"That's fine. I have free time." A slow beat, then he added, "Nothing but free time."

"*After* the full moon, Larry." It was said with great specificity.

"Of course. I'll meet you at the last place we met, at the same time, on the thirtieth of this month. Do you remember?"

"I remember. That'll be fine."

"Thank you, Victor. I appreciate this."

There was no response.

Talbot's voice softened: "How is your father?"

"Goodbye, Larry," he answered, and hung up.

They met on the thirtieth of that month, at moonless midnight, on the corpse barge that plied between Buda and Pesht. It was the correct sort of night: chill fog moved in a pulsing curtain up the Danube from Belgrade.

They shook hands in the lee of a stack of cheap wooden coffins and, after hesitating awkwardly for a moment, they embraced like brothers. Talbot's smile was tight and barely discernible by the withered illumination of the lantern and the barge's running lights as he said, "All right, get it said so I don't have to wait for the other shoe to drop."

Victor grinned and murmured ominously:

"*Even a man who is pure in heart*
And says his prayers by night,
May become a wolf when the wolfbane blooms
And the Autumn moon shines bright."

Talbot made a face. "And other songs from the same album."

"Still saying your prayers at night?"

"I stopped that when I realized the damned thing didn't scan."

"Hey. We aren't here getting pneumonia just to discuss forced rhyme."

The lines of weariness in Talbot's face settled into a joyless pattern. "Victor, I need your help."

"I'll listen, Larry. Further than that it's doubtful."

Talbot weighed the warning and said, "Three months ago I answered an advertisement in *Forbes,* the business magazine. Information Associates. It was a cleverly phrased, very reserved, small box, inconspicuously placed. Except to those who knew how to read it. I won't waste your time on details, but the sequence went like this: I answered the ad, hinting at my problem as circuitously as possible without being completely impenetrable. Vague words about important money. I had hopes. Well, I hit with this one. They sent back a letter calling a meet. Perhaps another false trail, was what I thought . . . God knows there've been enough of those."

Victor lit a Sobranie Black & Gold and let the pungent scent of the smoke drift away on the fog. "But you went."

"I went. Peculiar outfit, sophisticated security system, I had a strong feeling they came from, well, I'm not sure where . . . or when."

Victor's glance was abruptly kilowatts heavier with interest. "*When,* you say? Temporal travelers?"

"I don't know."

"I've been waiting for something like that, you know. It's inevitable. And they'd certainly make themselves known eventually."

He lapsed into silence, thinking. Talbot brought him back sharply. "I don't know, Victor. I really don't. But that's not my concern at the moment."

"Oh. Right. Sorry, Larry. Go on. You met with them . . ."

"Man named Demeter. I thought there might be some clue there. The name. I didn't think of it at the time. The name Demeter; there was a florist in Cleveland, many years ago. But later, when I looked it up, Demeter, the Earth goddess, Greek mythology . . . no connection. At least, I don't think so.

"We talked. He understood my problem and said he'd undertake the commission. But he wanted it specific, what I required of him, wanted it specific for the contract—God knows how he would have enforced the contract, but I'm sure he could have—he had a *window,* Victor, it looked out on—"

Victor spun the cigarette off his thumb and middle finger, snapping it straight down into the blood-black Danube. "Larry, you're maundering."

Talbot's words caught in his throat. It was true. "I'm counting on you, Victor. I'm afraid it's putting my usual aplomb out of phase."

"All right, take it easy. Let me hear the rest of this and we'll see. Relax."

Talbot nodded and felt grateful. "I wrote out the nature of the commission. It was only seven words." He reached into his topcoat pocket and brought out a folded slip of paper. He handed it to the other man. In the dim lantern light, Victor unfolded the paper and read:

GEOGRAPHICAL COORDINATES
FOR LOCATION OF MY SOUL

Victor looked at the two lines of type long after he had absorbed their message. When he handed it back to Talbot, he wore a new, fresher expression. "You'll never give up, will you, Larry?"

"Did your father?"

"No." Great sadness flickered across the face of the man Talbot called Victor. "And," he added, tightly, after a beat, "he's been lying in a catatonia sling for sixteen years *because* he wouldn't give up." He lapsed into silence. Finally, softly, "It never hurts to know when to give up, Larry. Never hurts. Sometimes you've just got to leave it alone."

Talbot snorted softly with bemusement. "Easy enough for you to say, old chum. You're going to die."

"That wasn't fair, Larry."

"Then help me, dammit! I've gone farther toward getting myself out of all this than I ever have. Now I need *you*. You've got the expertise."

"Have you sounded out 3M or Rand or even General Dynamics? They've got good people there."

"Damn you."

"Okay. Sorry. Let me think a minute."

The corpse barge cut through the invisible water, silent, fog-shrouded, without Charon, without Styx, merely a public service, a garbage scow of unfinished sentences, uncompleted errands, unrealized dreams. With the exception of these two, talking, the barge's supercargo had left decisions and desertions behind.

Then, Victor said, softly, talking as much to himself as to Talbot, "We could do it with microtelemetry. Either through direct microminiaturizing techniques or by shrinking a servomechanism package containing sensing, remote control, and guidance/manipulative/propulsion hardware. Use a saline solution to inject it into the bloodstream. Knock you out with 'Russian sleep' and/or tap into the sensory nerves so you'd perceive or control the device as if you were there . . . conscious transfer of point of view."

Talbot looked at him expectantly.

"No. Forget it," said Victor. "It won't do."

He continued to think. Talbot reached into the other's jacket pocket and brought out the Sobranies. He lit one and stood silently, waiting. It was always thus with Victor. He had to worm his way through the analytical labyrinth.

"Maybe the biotechnic equivalent: a tailored microorganism or slug . . . injected . . . telepathic link established. No. Too many flaws: possible ego/control conflict. Impaired perceptions. Maybe it could be a hive creature injected for multiple p.o.v." A pause, then, "No. No good."

Talbot drew on the cigarette, letting the mysterious Eastern smoke curl through his lungs. "How about . . . say, just for the sake of discussion," Victor said, "say the ego/id exists to some extent in each sperm. It's been ventured. Raise the consciousness in one cell and send it on a mission to . . . forget it, that's metaphysical bullshit. Oh, damn damn damn . . . this will take time and thought, Larry. Go away, let me think on it. I'll get back to you."

Talbot butted the Sobranie on the railing, and exhaled the final stream of smoke. "Okay, Victor. I take it you're interested sufficiently to work at it."

"I'm a scientist, Larry. That means I'm hooked. I'd have to be an idiot not to be . . . this speaks directly to what . . . to what my father . . ."

"I understand. I'll let you alone. I'll wait."

They rode across in silence, the one thinking of solutions, the other considering problems. When they parted, it was with an embrace.

Talbot flew back the next morning, and waited through the nights of the full moon, knowing better than to pray. It only muddied the waters. And angered the gods.

When the phone rang, and Talbot lifted the receiver, he knew what it would be. He had known *every* time the phone had rung, for over two months. "Mr. Talbot? Western Union. We have a cablegram for you, from Moldava, Czechoslovakia."

"Please read it."

"It's very short, sir. It says, 'Come immediately. The trail had been marked.' It's signed, 'Victor.'"

He departed less than an hour later. The Learjet had been on the ready line since he had returned from Budapest, fuel tanks regularly topped-off and flight-plan logged. His suitcase had been packed for seventy-two days, waiting beside the door, visas and passport current, and handily stored in an inner pocket. When he departed, the apartment continued to tremble for some time with the echoes of his leaving.

The flight seemed endless, interminable, he *knew* it was taking longer than necessary.

Customs, even with high government clearances (all masterpieces of forgery) and bribes, seemed to be drawn out sadistically by the mustachioed trio of petty officials; secure, and reveling in their momentary power.

The overland facilities could not merely be called slow. They were reminiscent of the Molasses Man who cannot run till he's warmed-up and who, when he's warmed-up, grows too soft to run.

Expectedly, like the most suspenseful chapter of a cheap gothic novel, a fierce electrical storm suddenly erupted out of the mountains when the ancient touring car was within a few miles of Talbot's destination. It rose up through the steep mountain pass, hurtling out of the sky, black as a grave, and swept across the road obscuring everything.

The driver, a taciturn man whose accent had marked him as a Serbian, held the big saloon to the center of the road with the tenacity of a rodeo rider, hands at ten till and ten after midnight on the wheel.

"Mister Talbot."

"Yes?"

"It grows worse. Will I turn back?"

"How much farther?"

"Perhaps seven kilometer."

Headlights caught the moment of uprootment as a small tree by the roadside toppled toward them. The driver spun the wheel and accelerated. They rushed past as naked branches scraped across the boot of the touring car with the sound of fingernails on a blackboard. Talbot found he had been holding his breath. Death was beyond him, but the menace of the moment denied the knowledge.

"I have to get there."

"Then I go on. Be at ease."

Talbot settled back. He could see the Serb smiling in the rearview mirror. Secure, he stared out the window. Branches of lightning shattered the darkness, causing the surrounding landscape to assume ominous, unsettling shapes.

Finally, he arrived.

The laboratory, an incongruous modernistic cube—bone white against the—again—ominous basalt of the looming prominences—sat high above the rutted road. They had been climbing steadily for hours and now, like carnivores waiting for the most opportune moment, the Carpathians loomed all around them.

The driver negotiated the final mile and a half up the access road to the laboratory with difficulty: tides of dark, topsoil-and-twig-laden water rushed past them.

Victor was waiting for him. Without extended greetings he had an associate take the suitcase, and he hurried Talbot to the sub-ground-floor theater where a half dozen technicians moved quickly at their tasks, plying between enormous banks of controls and a huge glass plate hanging suspended from guy-wires beneath the track-laden ceiling.

The mood was one of highly charged expectancy; Talbot could feel it in the sharp, short glances the technicians threw him, in the way Victor steered him by the arm, in the uncanny racehorse readiness of the peculiar-looking machines around which the men and women swarmed. And he sensed in Victor's manner that something new and wonderful was about to be born in this laboratory. That perhaps . . . at last . . . after so terribly, lightlessly long . . . peace waited for him in this white-tiled room. Victor was fairly bursting to talk.

"Final adjustments," he said, indicating two female technicians working at a pair of similar machines mounted opposite each other on the walls facing the glass plate. To Talbot, they looked like laser projectors of a highly complex design. The women were tracking them slowly left and right on their gimbals, accompanied by soft electrical humming. Victor let Talbot study them for a long moment, then said, "Not lasers. *Grasers*. Gamma Ray Amplification by Stimulated Emission of Radiation. Pay attention to them, they're at least half the heart of the answer to your problem."

The technicians took sightings across the room, through the glass, and nodded at one another. Then the older of the two, a woman in her fifties, called to Victor.

"On line, Doctor."

Victor waved acknowledgment, and turned back to Talbot. "We'd have been ready sooner, but this damned storm. It's been going on for a week. It wouldn't have hampered us but we had a freak lightning strike on our main transformer. The power supply was on emergency for several days and it's taken a while to get everything up to peak strength again."

A door opened in the wall of the gallery to Talbot's right. It opened slowly, as though it was heavy and the strength needed to force it was lacking. The yellow baked enamel plate on the door said, in heavy black letters, in French, PERSONNEL MONITORING DEVICES ARE REQUIRED BEYOND THIS ENTRANCE. The door swung fully open, at last, and Talbot saw the warning plate on the other side:

CAUTION
RADIATION
AREA

There was a three-armed, triangular-shaped design beneath the words. He thought of the Father, the Son, and the Holy Ghost. For no rational reason.

Then he saw the sign beneath, and had his rational reason: OPENING THIS DOOR FOR MORE THAN 30 SECONDS WILL REQUIRE A SEARCH AND SECURE.

Talbot's attention was divided between the doorway and what Victor had said. "You seem worried about the storm."

"Not worried," Victor said, "just cautious. There's no conceivable way it could interfere with the experiment, unless we had another direct hit, which I doubt—we've taken special precautions—but I wouldn't want to risk the power going out in the middle of the shot."

"The shot?"

"I'll explain all that. In fact, I *have* to explain it, so your mite will have the knowledge." Victor smiled at Talbot's confusion. "Don't worry about it." An old woman in a lab smock had come through the door and now stood just behind and to the right of Talbot, waiting, clearly, for their conversation to end so she could speak to Victor.

Victor turned his eyes to her. "Yes, Nadja?"

Talbot looked at her. An acid rain began falling in his stomach.

"Yesterday considerable effort was directed toward finding the cause of a high field horizontal instability," she said, speaking softly, tonelessly, a page of some specific status report. "The attendant beam blow-up prevented efficient extraction." Eighty, if a day. Gray eyes sunk deep in folds of crinkled flesh the color of liver paste. "During the afternoon the accelerator was shut down to effect several repairs." Withered, weary, bent, too many bones for the sack. "The super pinger at C48 was replaced with a section of vacuum chamber; it had a vacuum leak." Talbot was in extreme pain. Memories came at him in ravening hordes, a dark wave of ant bodies gnawing at everything soft and folded and vulnerable in his brain. "Two hours of beam time were lost during the owl shift because a solenoid failed on a new vacuum valve in the transfer hall."

"Mother . . . ?" Talbot said, whispering hoarsely.

The old woman started violently, her head coming around and her eyes of settled ashes widening. "Victor," she said, terror in the word.

Talbot barely moved, but Victor took him by the arm and held him. "Thank you, Nadja; go down to target station B and log the secondary beams. Go right now."

She moved past them, hobbling, and quickly vanished through another door in the far wall, held open for her by one of the younger women.

Talbot watched her go, tears in his eyes.

"Oh my God, Victor. It was . . ."

"No, Larry, it wasn't."

"It was. So help me God it *was*! But *how*, Victor, tell me *how*?"

Victor turned him and lifted his chin with his free hand. "Look at me, Larry. *Damn it*, I said *look at me:* it wasn't. You're wrong."

The last time Lawrence Talbot had cried had been the morning he had awakened from sleep, lying under hydrangea shrubs in the botanical garden next to the Minneapolis Museum of Art, lying beside something bloody and still. Under his fingernails had been caked flesh and dirt and blood. That had been the time he learned about manacles and releasing oneself from them when in one state of consciousness, but not in another. Now, he felt like crying. Again. With cause.

"Wait here a moment," Victor said. "Larry? Will you wait right here for me? I'll be back in a moment."

He nodded, averting his face, and Victor went away. While he stood there, waves of painful memory thundering through him, a door slid open into the wall at the far side of the chamber, and another white-smocked technician stuck his head into the room. Through the opening, Talbot could see massive machinery in an enormous chamber beyond. Titanium electrodes. Stainless steel cones. He thought he recognized it: a Cockroft–Walton pre-accelerator.

Victor came back with a glass of milky liquid. He handed it to Talbot.

"Victor—" the technician called from the far doorway.

"Drink it," Victor said to Talbot, then turned to the technician.

"Ready to run."

Victor waved to him. "Give me about ten minutes, Karl, then take it up to the first phase shift and signal us." The technician nodded understanding and vanished through the doorway; the door slid out of the wall and closed, hiding the imposing chamberful of equipment. "And that was part of the other half of the mystical, magical solution of your problem," the physicist said, smiling now like a proud father.

"What was that I drank?"

"Something to stabilize you. I can't have you hallucinating."

"I wasn't hallucinating. What was her name?"

"Nadja. You're wrong; you've never seen her before in your life. Have I ever lied to you? How far back do we know each other? I need your trust if this is going to go all the way."

"I'll be all right." The milky liquid had already begun to work. Talbot's face lost its flush, his hands ceased trembling.

Victor was very stern suddenly, a scientist without the time for sidetracks; there was information to be imparted. "Good. For a moment I thought I'd spent a great deal of time preparing . . . well," and he smiled again, quickly, "let me put it this way: I thought for a moment no one was coming to my party."

Talbot gave a strained, tiny chuckle, and followed Victor to a bank of television monitors set into rolling frame-stacks in a corner. "Okay. Let's get you briefed." He turned on sets, one after another, till all twelve were glowing, each one holding a scene of dull-finished and massive installations.

Monitor #1 showed an endlessly long underground tunnel painted eggshell white. Talbot had spent much of his two-month wait reading; he recognized the tunnel as a view down the "straightaway" of the main ring. Gigantic bending magnets in their shockproof concrete cradles glowed faintly in the dim light of the tunnel.

Monitor #2 showed the linac tunnel.

Monitor #3 showed the rectifier stack of the Cockroft-Walton pre-accelerator.

Monitor #4 was a view of the booster. Monitor #5 showed the interior of the transfer hall. Monitors #6 through #9 revealed three experimental target areas and, smaller in scope and size, an internal target area supporting the meson, neutrino and proton areas.

The remaining three monitors showed research areas in the underground lab complex, the final one of which was the main hall itself, where Talbot stood looking into twelve monitors, in the twelfth screen of which could be seen Talbot standing looking into twelve . . .

Victor turned off the sets.

"What did you see?"

All Talbot could think of was the old woman called Nadja. It *couldn't* be. "Larry! What did you see?"

"From what I could see," Talbot said, "that looked to be a particle accelerator. And it looked as big as CERN's proton synchrotron in Geneva."

Victor was impressed. "You've been doing some reading."

"It behooved me."

"Well, well. Let's see if I can impress *you*. CERN's accelerator reaches energies up to 33 BeV; the ring underneath this room reaches energies of 15 GeV."

"Giga meaning billion."

"You *have* been reading up, haven't you! Fifteen *billion* electron volts. There's simply no keeping secrets from you, is there, Larry?"

"Only one."

Victor waited expectantly.

"Can you do it?"

"Yes. Meteorology says the eye is almost passing over us. We'll have better than an hour, more than enough time for the dangerous parts of the experiment."

"But you *can* do it."

"Yes, Larry. I don't like having to say it twice." There was no hesitancy in his voice, none of the "yes but" equivocations he'd always heard before. Victor had found the trail.

"I'm sorry, Victor. Anxiety. But if we're ready, why do I have to go through an indoctrination?"

Victor grinned wryly and began reciting, "As your Wizard, I am about to embark on a hazardous and technically unexplainable journey to the upper stratosphere. To confer, converse, and otherwise hobnob with my fellow wizards."

Talbot threw up his hands. "No more."

"Okay, then. Pay attention. If I didn't have to, I wouldn't; believe me, nothing is more boring than listening to the sound of my own lectures. But your mite has to have all the data *you* have. So listen.

Now comes the boring—but incredibly informative—explanation."

Western Europe's CERN—*Conseil Européen pour la Recherche Nucléaire*—had settled on Geneva as the site for their Big Machine. Holland lost out on the rich plum because it was common knowledge the food was lousy in the Lowlands. A small matter, but a significant one.

The Eastern Bloc's CEERN—*Conseil de l'Europe de l'Est pour la Recherche Nucléaire*—had been forced into selecting this isolated location high in the White Carpathians (over such likelier and more hospitable sites as Cluj in Rumania, Budapest in Hungary and Gdańsk in Poland) because Talbot's friend Victor had selected this site. CERN had had Dahl and Wideroë and Goward and Adams and Reich; CEERN had Victor. It balanced. He could call the tune.

So the laboratory had been painstakingly built to his specifications, and the particle accelerator dwarfed the CERN Machine. It dwarfed the four-mile ring at the Fermi National Accelerator Lab in Batavia, Illinois. It was, in fact, the world's largest, most advanced "synchrophasotron."

Only seventy percent of the experiments conducted in the underground laboratory were devoted to projects sponsored by CEERN. One hundred percent of the staff of Victor's complex was personally committed to him, not to CEERN, not to the Eastern Bloc, not to philosophies or dogmas . . . to the man. So thirty percent of the experiments run on the sixteen-mile-diameter accelerator ring were Victor's own. If CEERN knew—and it would have been difficult for them to find out—it said nothing. Seventy percent of the fruits of genius was better than no percent.

Had Talbot known earlier that Victor's research was thrust in the direction of actualizing advanced theoretical breakthroughs in the nature of the structure of fundamental particles, he would never have wasted his time with the pseudos and dead-enders who had spent years on his problem, who had promised everything and delivered nothing but dust. But then, until Information Associates had marked the trail—a trail he had previously followed in every direction but the unexpected one that merged shadow with substance, reality with fantasy—until then, he had no need for Victor's exotic talents.

While CEERN basked in the warmth of secure knowledge that their resident genius was keeping them in front in the Super Accelerator Sweepstakes, Victor was briefing his oldest friend on the manner in which he would gift him with the peace of death; the manner in which Lawrence Talbot would find his soul; the manner in which he would precisely and exactly go inside his own body.

"The answer to your problem is in two parts. First, we have to create a perfect simulacrum of you, a hundred thousand or a million times smaller than you, the original. Then, second, we have to *actualize* it, turn an image into something corporeal, substantial, material; something that *exists*. A miniature *you* with all the reality you possess, all the memories, all the knowledge."

Talbot felt very mellow. The milky liquid had smoothed out the churning waters of his memory. He smiled. "I'm glad it wasn't a difficult problem."

Victor looked rueful. "Next week I invent the steam engine. Get serious, Larry."

"It's that Lethe cocktail you fed me."

Victor's mouth tightened and Talbot knew he had to get hold of himself. "Go on, I'm sorry."

Victor hesitated a moment, securing his position of seriousness with a touch of free-floating guilt, then went on, "The first part of the problem is solved by using the grasers we've developed. We'll shoot a hologram of you, using a wave generated not from the electrons of the atom, but from the nucleus . . . a wave a million times shorter, greater in resolution than that from a laser." He walked toward the large glass plate hanging in the middle of the lab, grasers trained on its center. "Come here."

Talbot followed him.

"Is this the holographic plate," he said, "it's just a sheet of photographic glass, isn't it?"

"Not this," Victor said, touching the ten-foot square plate, *"this!"* He put his finger on a spot in the center of the glass and Talbot leaned in to look. He saw nothing at first, then detected a faint ripple; and when he put his face as close as possible to the imperfection he perceived a light *moiré* pattern, like the surface of a fine silk scarf. He looked back at Victor.

"Microholographic plate," Victor said. "Smaller than an integrated chip. That's where we capture your spirit, white-eyes, a million times reduced. About the size of a single cell, maybe a red corpuscle."

Talbot giggled.

"Come on," Victor said wearily. "You've had too much to drink, and it's my fault. Let's get this show on the road. You'll be straight by the time we're ready . . . I just hope to God your mite isn't cockeyed."

Naked, they stood him in front of the ground photographic plate. The older of the female technicians aimed the graser at him, there was a soft sound Talbot took to be some mechanism locking into position, and then Victor said, "All right, Larry, that's it."

He stared at them, expecting more.

"That's it?"

The technicians seemed very pleased, and amused at his reaction. "All done," said Victor. It had been that quick. He hadn't even seen the graser wave hit and lock in his image. "That's *it*?" he said again.

Victor began to laugh. It spread through the lab. The technicians were clinging to their equipment; tears rolled down Victor's cheeks; everyone gasped for breath; and Talbot stood in front of the minute imperfection in the glass and felt like a retard.

"That's it?" he said again, helplessly.

After a long time, they dried their eyes and Victor moved him away from the huge plate of glass. "All done, Larry, and ready to go. Are you cold?"

Talbot's naked flesh was evenly polka-dotted with goosebumps. One of the technicians brought him a smock to wear. He stood and watched. Clearly, he was no longer the center of attention.

Now the alternate graser and the holographic plate ripple in the glass were the focuses of attention. Now the mood of released tension was past and the lines of serious attention were back in the faces of the lab staff. Now Victor was wearing an intercom headset, and Talbot heard him say, "All right, Karl. Bring it up to full power."

Almost instantly the lab was filled with the sound of generators phasing up. It became painful and Talbot felt his teeth begin to ache. It went up and up, a whine that climbed till it was beyond his hearing.

Victor made a hand signal to the younger female technician at the graser behind the glass plate. She bent to the projector's sighting mechanism once, quickly, then cut it in. Talbot saw no light beam, but there was the same locking sound he had heard earlier, and then a soft humming, and a life-size hologram of himself, standing naked as he had been a few moments before, trembled in the air where he had stood. He looked at Victor questioningly. Victor nodded, and Talbot walked to the phantasm, passed his hand through it, stood close and looked into the clear brown eyes, noted the wide pore patterns in the nose, studied himself more closely than he had ever been able to do in a mirror. He felt: as if someone had walked over his grave.

Victor was talking to three male technicians, and a moment later they came to examine the hologram. They moved in with light meters and sensitive instruments that apparently were capable of gauging the sophistication and clarity of the ghost image. Talbot watched, fascinated and terrified. It seemed he was about to embark on the great journey of his life; a journey with a much desired destination: surcease.

One of the technicians signaled Victor.

"It's pure," he said to Talbot. Then, to the younger female technician on the second graser projector, "All right, Jana, move it out of there." She started up an engine and the entire projector apparatus turned on heavy rubber wheels and rolled out of the way. The image of Talbot, naked and vulnerable, a little sad to Talbot as he watched it fade and vanish like morning mist, had disappeared when the technician turned off the projector.

"All right, Karl," Victor was saying, "we're moving the pedestal in now. Narrow the aperture, and wait for my signal." Then, to Talbot, "Here comes your mite, old friend."

Talbot felt a sense of resurrection.

The older female technician rolled a four-foot-high stainless steel pedestal to the center of the lab, positioned it so the tiny, highly-polished spindle atop the pedestal touched the very bottom of the faint ripple in the glass. It looked like, and was, an actualizing stage for the real test. The full-sized hologram had been a gross test to ensure the image's perfection. Now came the creation of a living entity, a Lawrence Talbot, naked and the size of a single cell, possessing a consciousness and intelligence and memories and desires identical to Talbot's own.

"Ready, Karl?" Victor was saying.

Talbot heard no reply, but Victor nodded his head as if listening. Then he said, "All right, extract the beam!"

It happened so fast, Talbot missed most of it.

The micropion beam was composed of particles a million times smaller than the proton, smaller than the quark, smaller than the muon or the pion. Victor had termed them micropions. The slit opened in the wall, the beam was diverted, passed through the holographic ripple and was cut off as the slit closed again.

It had all taken a billionth of a second.

"Done," Victor said.

"I don't see anything," Talbot said, and realized how silly he must sound to these people. Of *course* he didn't see anything. There was nothing to see . . . with the naked eye. "Is he . . . is it there?"

"You're there," Victor said. He waved to one of the male technicians standing at a wall hutch of instruments in protective bays, and the man hurried over with the slim, reflective barrel of a microscope. He clipped it onto the tiny needle-pointed stand atop the pedestal in a fashion Talbot could not quite follow. Then he stepped away, and Victor said, "Part two of your problem solved, Larry. Go look and see yourself."

Lawrence Talbot went to the microscope, adjusted the knob till he could see the reflective surface of the spindle, and saw himself in infinitely reduced perfection

staring up at himself. He recognized himself, though all he could see was a cyclopean brown eye staring down from the smooth glass satellite that dominated his sky.

He waved. The eye blinked.

Now it begins, he thought.

Lawrence Talbot stood at the lip of the huge crater that formed Lawrence Talbot's navel. He looked down in the bottomless pit with its atrophied remnants of umbilicus forming loops and protuberances, smooth and undulant and vanishing into utter darkness. He stood poised to descend and smelled the smells of his own body. First, sweat. Then the smells that wafted up from within. The smell of penicillin like biting down on tin foil with a bad tooth. The smell of aspirin, chalky and tickling the hairs of his nose like cleaning blackboard erasers by banging them together. The smells of rotted food, digested and turning to waste. All the odors rising up out of himself like a wild symphony of dark colors.

He sat down on the rounded rim of the navel and let himself slip forward.

He slid down, rode over an outcropping, dropped a few feet and slid again, tobogganing into darkness. He fell for only a short time, then brought up against the soft and yielding, faintly springy tissue plane where the umbilicus had been ligated. The darkness at the bottom of the hole suddenly shattered as blinding light filled the navel. Shielding his eyes, Talbot looked up the shaft toward the sky. A sun glowed there, brighter than a thousand novae. Victor had moved a surgical lamp over the hole to assist him. For as long as he could.

Talbot saw the umbra of something large moving behind the light, and he strained to discern what it was: it seemed important to know what it was. And for an instant, before his eyes closed against the glare, he thought he knew what it had been. Someone watching him, staring down past the surgical lamp that hung above the naked, anesthetized body of Lawrence Talbot, asleep on an operating table.

It had been the old woman, Nadja.

He stood unmoving for a long time, thinking of her.

Then he went to his knees and felt the tissue plane that formed the floor of the navel shaft.

He thought he could see something moving beneath the surface, like water flowing under a film of ice. He went down onto his stomach and cupped his hands around his eyes, putting his face against the dead flesh. It was like looking through a pane of isinglass. A trembling membrane through which he could see the collapsed lumen of the atretic umbilical vein. There was no opening. He pressed his palms against the rubbery surface and it gave, but only slightly. Before he could find the treasure, he had to follow the route of Demeter's map—now firmly and forever consigned to memory—and before he could set foot upon that route, he had to gain access to his own body.

But he had nothing with which to force that entrance.

Excluded, standing at the portal to his own body, Lawrence Talbot felt anger rising within him. His life had been anguish and guilt and horror, had been the wasted result of events over which he had had no control. Pentagrams and full moons and blood and never putting on even an ounce of fat because of a diet high in protein, blood steroids healthier than any normal adult male's, triglycerol and cholesterol levels balanced and humming. And death forever a stranger. Anger flooded through him. He heard an inarticulate little moan of pain, and fell forward, began tearing at the atrophied cord with teeth that had been used for just such activity many times before. Through a blood haze he knew he was savaging his own body, and it seemed exactly the appropriate act of self-flagellation.

An outsider; he had been an outsider all his adult life, and fury would permit him to be shut out no longer. With demonic purpose he ripped away at the clumps of flesh until the membrane gave, at last, and a gap was torn through, opening him to himself . . .

And he was blinded by the explosion of light, by the rush of wind, by the passage of something that had been just beneath the surface writhing to be set free, and in the instant before he plummeted into unconsciousness, he knew Castañeda's Don Juan had told the truth: a thick bundle of white cobwebby filaments, tinged with gold, fibers of light, shot free from the collapsed vein, rose up through the shaft and trembled toward the antiseptic sky.

A metaphysical, otherwise invisible beanstalk that trailed away above him, rising up and up and up as his eyes closed and he sank away into oblivion.

He was on his stomach, crawling through the collapsed lumen, the center, of the path the veins had taken back from the amniotic sac to the fetus. Propelling himself forward the way an infantry scout would through dangerous terrain, using elbows and knees, frog-crawling, he opened the flattened tunnel with his head just enough to get through. It was quite light, the interior of the world called Lawrence Talbot suffused with a golden luminescence.

The map had routed him out of this pressed tunnel through the inferior vena cava to the right atrium and thence through the right ventricle, the pulmonary arteries, through the valves, to the lungs, the pulmonary veins, crossover to the left side of the heart (left atrium, left ventricle), the aorta – bypassing the three coronary arteries above the aortic valves – and down over the arch of the aorta – bypassing the carotid and other arteries – to the celiac trunk, where the arteries split in a confusing array: the gastroduodenal to the stomach, the hepatic to the liver, the splenic to the spleen. And there, dorsal to the body of the diaphragm, he would drop down past the greater pancreatic duct to the pancreas itself. And there, among the islets of Langerhans, he would find, at the coordinates Information Associates had given him, he would find that which had been stolen from him one full-mooned night of horror so very long ago. And having found it, having assured himself of eternal sleep, not merely physical death from a silver bullet, he would stop his heart – how, he did not know, but he would – and it would all be ended for Lawrence Talbot, who had become what he had beheld. There, in the tail of the pancreas, supplied with blood by the splenic artery, lay the greatest treasure of all. More than doubloons, more than spices and silks, more than oil lamps used as djinn prisons by Solomon, lay final and sweet eternal peace, a release from monsterdom.

He pushed the final few feet of dead vein apart, and his head emerged into open space. He was hanging upside-down in a cave of deep orange rock.

Talbot wriggled his arms loose, braced them against what was clearly the ceiling of the cave, and wrenched his body out of the tunnel. He fell heavily, trying to twist at the last moment to catch the impact on his shoulders, and received a nasty blow on the side of the neck for his trouble.

He lay there for a moment, clearing his head. Then he stood and walked forward. The cave opened onto a ledge, and he walked out and stared at the landscape before him. The skeleton of something only faintly human lay tortuously crumpled against the wall of the cliff. He was afraid to look at it very closely.

He stared off across the world of dead orange rock, folded and rippled like a topographical view across the frontal lobe of a brain removed from its cranial casing.

The sky was a light yellow, bright and pleasant.

The grand canyon of his body was a seemingly horizonless tumble of atrophied rock, dead for millennia. He sought out and found a descent from the ledge, and began the trek.

There was water, and it kept him alive. Apparently, it rained more frequently here in this parched and stunned wasteland than appearance indicated. There was no keeping track of days or months, for there was no night and no day—always the same even, wonderful golden luminescence—but Talbot felt his passage down the central spine of orange mountains had taken him almost six months. And in that time it had rained forty-eight times, or roughly twice a week. Baptismal fonts of water were filled at every downpour, and he found if he kept the soles of his naked feet moist, he could walk without his energy flagging. If he ate, he did not remember how often, or what form the food had taken.

He saw no other signs of life.

Save an occasional skeleton lying against a shadowed wall of orange rock. Often, they had no skulls.

He found a pass through the mountains, finally, and crossed. He went up through foothills into lower, gentle slopes, and then up again, into cruel and narrow passages that wound higher and higher toward the heat of the sky. When he reached the summit, he found the path down the opposite side was straight and wide and easy. He descended quickly; only a matter of days, it seemed.

Descending into the valley, he heard the song of a bird. He followed the sound. It led him to a crater of igneous rock, quite large, set low among the grassy swells of the valley. He came upon it without warning, and trudged up its short incline, to stand at the volcanic lip looking down.

The crater had become a lake. The smell rose up to assault him. Vile, and somehow terribly sad. The song of the bird continued; he could see no bird anywhere in the golden sky. The smell of the lake made him ill.

Then as he sat on the edge of the crater, staring down, he realized the lake was filled with dead things, floating bellyup; purple and blue as a strangled baby, rotting white, turning slowly in the faintly rippled gray water; without features or limbs. He went down to the lowest outthrust of volcanic rock and stared at the dead things.

Something swam toward him. He moved back. It came on faster, and as it neared the wall of the crater, it surfaced, singing its bluejay song, swerved to rip a chunk of rotting flesh from the corpse of a floating dead thing, and paused only a moment as if to remind him that this was not his, Talbot's, domain, but his own.

Like Talbot, the fish would not die.

Talbot sat at the lip of the crater for a long time, looking down into the bowl that held the lake, and he watched the corpses of dead dreams as they bobbed and revolved like maggoty pork in a gray soup.

After a time, he rose, walked back down from the mouth of the crater, and resumed his journey. He was crying.

When at last he reached the shore of the pancreatic sea, he found a great many things he had lost or given away when he was a child. He found a wooden machine gun on a tripod, painted olive drab, that made a rat-tat-tatting sound when a wooden handle was cranked. He found a set of toy soldiers, two companies, one Prussian and the other French, with a miniature Napoleon Bonaparte among them. He found a microscope kit with slides and petri dishes and racks of chemicals in nice little bottles, all of which bore uniform labels. He found a milk bottle filled with Indian-head pennies. He found a hand puppet with the head of a monkey and the name *Rosco* painted on the fabric glove with nail polish. He found a pedometer. He found a beautiful painting of a jungle bird that had been done with real feathers. He found a corncob pipe. He found a box of radio premiums: a cardboard detective kit with fingerprint dusting powder, invisible ink and a list of police-band call codes; a ring with what seemed to be a plastic bomb attached, and when he pulled the red finned rear off the bomb, and cupped his hands around it in his palms, he could see little scintillas of light, deep inside the payload section; a china mug with a little girl and a dog running across one side; a decoding badge with a burning glass in the center of the red plastic dial.

But there was something missing.

He could not remember what it was, but he knew it was important. As he had known it was important to recognize the shadowy figure who had moved past the surgical lamp at the top of the navel shaft, he knew whatever item was missing from this cache . . . was very important.

He took the boat anchored beside the pancreatic sea, and put all the items from the cache in the bottom of a watertight box under one of the seats. He kept out the large, cathedral-shaped radio, and put it on the bench seat in front of the oarlocks.

Then he unbeached the boat, and ran it out into the crimson water, staining his ankles and calves and thighs, and climbed aboard, and started rowing across toward the islets. Whatever was missing was very important.

The wind died when the islets were barely in sight on the horizon. Looking out across the blood-red sea, Talbot sat becalmed at latitude 38°54′ N, longitude 77°00′13″ W.

He drank from the sea and was nauseated. He played with the toys in the watertight box. And he listened to the radio.

He listened to a program about a very fat man who solved murders, to an adaptation of *The Woman in the Window* with Edward G. Robinson and Joan Bennett, to a story that began in a great railroad station, to a mystery about a wealthy man who could make himself invisible by clouding the minds of others so they could not see him, and he enjoyed a suspense drama narrated by a man named Ernest Chapell in which a group of people descended in a bathyscaphe through the bottom of a mine shaft where, five miles down, they were attacked by pterodactyls. Then he listened to the news, broadcast by Graham MacNamee. Among the human interest items at the close of the program, Talbot heard the unforgettable MacNamee voice say:

"Datelined Columbus, Ohio; September 24th, 1973. Martha Nelson had been in an institution for the mentally retarded for 98 years. She is 102 years old and was first sent to Orient State Institute near Orient, Ohio, on June 25th, 1875. Her records were destroyed in a fire in the institution sometime in 1883, and no one knows for certain why she is at the institute. At the time she was committed, it was known as the Columbus State Institute for the Feeble-Minded. 'She never had a chance,' said Dr. A. Z. Soforenko, appointed two months ago as superintendent of the institution. He said she was probably a victim of 'eugenic alarm,' which he said was common in the late 1800s. At that time some felt that because humans were made 'in God's image' the retarded must be evil or children of the devil, because they were not whole human beings. 'During that time,' Dr. Soforenko said, 'it was believed if you moved feeble-minded people out of a community and into an institution, the taint would never return to the community.' He went on to add, 'She was apparently trapped in that system of thought. No one can ever be sure if she actually *was* feeble-minded; it is a wasted life. She is quite coherent for her age. She has no known relatives and has had no contact with anybody but Institution staff for the last 78 or 80 years.'"

Talbot sat silently in the small boat, the sail hanging like a forlorn ornament from its single centerpole.

"I've cried more since I got inside you, Talbot, than I have in my whole life," he said, but could not stop. Thoughts of Martha Nelson, a woman of whom he had never before heard, of whom he would *never* have heard had it not been by chance by chance by chance he had heard by chance, by chance thoughts of her skirled through his mind like cold winds.

And the cold winds rose, and the sail filled, and he was no longer adrift, but was driven straight for the shore of the nearest islet. By chance.

He stood over the spot where Demeter's map had indicated he would find his soul. For a wild moment he chuckled, at the realization he had been expecting an enormous Maltese Cross or Captain Kidd's "X" to mark the location. But it was only soft green sand, gentle as talc, blowing in dust-devils toward the blood-red pancreatic sea. The spot was midway between the lowtide line and the enormous Bedlam-like structure that dominated the islet.

He looked once more, uneasily, at the fortress rising in the center of the tiny blemish of land. It was built square, seemingly carved from a single monstrous black rock . . . perhaps from a cliff that had been thrust up during some natural disaster. It had no windows, no opening he could see, though two sides of its bulk were exposed to his view. It troubled him. It was a dark god presiding over an empty kingdom. He thought of the fish that would not die, and remembered Nietzsche's contention that gods died when they lost their supplicants.

He dropped to his knees and, recalling the moment months before when he had dropped to his knees to tear at the flesh of his atrophied umbilical cord, he began digging in the green and powdery sand.

The more he dug, the faster the sand ran back into the shallow bowl. He stepped into the middle of the depression and began slinging dirt back between his legs with both hands, a human dog excavating for a bone.

When his fingertips encountered the edge of the box, he yelped with pain as his nails broke.

He dug around the outline of the box, and then forced his bleeding fingers down through the sand to gain purchase under the buried shape. He wrenched at it, and it came loose. Heaving with tensed muscles, he freed it, and it came up.

He took it to the edge of the beach and sat down.

It was just a box. A plain wooden box, very much like an old cigar box, but larger. He turned it over and over and was not at all surprised to find it bore no arcane hieroglyphics or occult symbols. It wasn't that kind of treasure. Then he turned it right side up and pried open the lid. His soul was inside. It was not what he had expected to find, not at all. But it *was* what had been missing from the cache.

Holding it tightly in his fist, he walked up past the fast-filling hole in the green sand, toward the bastion on the high ground.

We shall not cease from exploration
And the end of all our exploring
Will be to arrive where we started
And know the place for the first time.
T. S. ELIOT

Once inside the brooding darkness of the fortress – and finding the entrance had been disturbingly easier than he had expected – there was no way to go but down. The wet, black stones of the switchback stairways led inexorably downward into the bowels of the structure, clearly far beneath the level of the pancreatic sea. The stairs were steep, and each step had been worn into smooth curves by the pressure of feet that had descended this way since the dawn of memory. It was dark, but not so dark that Talbot could not see his way. There was no light, however. He did not care to think about how that could be.

When he came to the deepest part of the structure, having passed no rooms or chambers or openings along the way, he saw a doorway across an enormous hall, set into the far wall. He stepped off the last of the stairs, and walked to the door. It was built of crossed iron bars, as black and moist as the stones of the bastion. Through the interstices he saw something pale and still in a far corner of what could have been a cell.

There was no lock on the door.

It swung open at his touch.

Whoever lived in this cell had never tried to open the door; or had tried and decided not to leave.

He moved into deeper darkness.

A long time of silence passed, and finally he stooped to help her to her feet. It was like lifting a sack of dead flowers, brittle and surrounded by dead air incapable of holding even the memory of fragrance.

He took her in his arms and carried her.

"Close your eyes against the light, Martha," he said, and started back up the long stairway to the golden sky.

Lawrence Talbot sat up on the operating table. He opened his eyes and looked at Victor. He smiled a peculiarly gentle smile. For the first time since they had been friends, Victor saw all torment cleansed from Talbot's face.

"It went well," he said. Talbot nodded.

They grinned at each other.

"How're your cryonic facilities?" Talbot asked.

Victor's brows drew down in bemusement. "You want me to freeze you? I thought you'd want something more permanent . . . say, in silver."

"Not necessary."

Talbot looked around. He saw her standing against the far wall by one of the grasers. She looked back at him with open fear. He slid off the table, wrapping the sheet upon which he had rested around himself, a makeshift toga. It gave him a patrician look.

He went to her and looked down into her ancient face. "Nadja," he said, softly. After a long moment she looked up at him. He smiled and for an instant she was a girl again. She averted her gaze. He took her hand, and she came with him, to the table, to Victor.

"I'd be deeply grateful for a running account, Larry," the physicist said. So Talbot told him; all of it.

"My mother, Nadja, Martha Nelson, they're all the same," Talbot said, when he came to the end, "all wasted lives."

"And what was in the box?" Victor said.

"How well do you do with symbolism and cosmic irony, old friend?"

"Thus far I'm doing well enough with Jung and Freud," Victor said. He could not help but smile.

Talbot held tightly to the old technician's hand as he said, "It was an old, rusted Howdy Doody button."

Victor turned around.

When he turned back, Talbot was grinning. "That's not cosmic irony, Larry . . . it's slapstick," Victor said. He was angry. It showed clearly.

Talbot said nothing, simply let him work it out.

Finally Victor said, "What the hell's *that* supposed to signify, innocence?"

Talbot shrugged. "I suppose if I'd known, I wouldn't have lost it in the first place. That's what it was, and that's what it is. A little metal pinback about an inch and a half in diameter, with that cockeyed face on it, the orange hair, the toothy grin, the pug nose, the freckles, all of it, just the way he always was." He fell silent, then after a moment added, "It seems right."

"And now that you have it back, you don't *want* to die?"

"I don't *need* to die."

"And you want me to freeze you."

"Both of us."

Victor stared at him with disbelief. "For God's sake, Larry!"

Nadja stood quietly, as if she could not hear them.

"Victor, listen: Martha Nelson is in there. A wasted life. Nadja is out here. I don't know why or how or what did it . . . but . . . a wasted life. Another wasted life. I want you to create her mite, the same way you created mine, and send her inside. He's waiting for her, and he can make it right, Victor. All right, at last. He can be with her as she regains the years that were stolen from her. He can be—*I* can be—her father when she's a baby, her playmate when she's a child, her buddy when she's maturing, her boyfriend when she's a young girl, her suitor when she's a young woman, her lover, her husband, her companion as she grows old. Let her be all the women she was never permitted to be, Victor. Don't steal from her a second time. And when it's over, it will start again . . ."

"*How,* for Christ sake, how the hell *how?* Talk sense, Larry! What is all this metaphysical crap?"

"I don't *know* how; it just is! I've been there, Victor, I was there for months, maybe years, and I never changed, never went to the wolf; there's no Moon there . . . no night and no day, just golden light and warmth, and I can try to make restitution. I can give back two lives. *Please,* Victor!"

The physicist looked at him without speaking. Then he looked at the old woman. She smiled up at him, and then, with arthritic fingers, removed her clothing.

When she came through the collapsed lumen, Talbot was waiting for her. She looked very tired, and he knew she would have to rest before they attempted to cross the orange mountains. He helped her down from the ceiling of the cave, and laid her down on soft, pale yellow moss he had carried back from the islets of Langerhans during the long trek with Martha Nelson. Side by side, the two old women lay on the moss, and Nadja fell asleep almost immediately. He stood over them, looking at their faces.

They were identical.

Then he went out on the ledge and stood looking toward the spine of the orange mountains. The skeleton held no fear for him now. He felt a sudden sharp chill in the air and knew Victor had begun the cryonic preservation.

He stood that way for a long time, the little metal button with the sly, innocent face of a mythical creature painted on its surface in four brilliant colors held tightly in his left hand.

And after a while, he heard the crying of a baby, just one baby, from inside the cave, and turned to return for the start of the easiest journey he had ever made.

Somewhere, a terrible devil-fish suddenly flattened its gills, turned slowly bellyup, and sank into darkness.

VIII

ROCOCO TECHNOLOGY

> "There are writers who *like* being called science fiction writers . . . They're entitled to call themselves or their work whatever they please. By the same token, I should be permitted to call what I write what *I* choose to call it, which is Harlan Ellison stories."
>
> —"Starwind Interviews Harlan Ellison" by Rick Wyman and Bob Halloran, *Starwind,* Autumn 1977

Call it what you like: speculative fiction, futuristic fiction, science fiction. As long as you ignore the defamatory neologism "sci-fi," reviled by anyone who makes even a meager claim to literacy, you're on safe ground.

In the main, however, all of the foregoing terms are but easy handles for an ill-defined type of fiction, handles that have purpose only as a commercial marketing tool. Few genre labels—mystery, gothic, western, etc.—make any sense in these modern times when clever writers have experimented endlessly with transcending the limitations of the original molds.

Harlan has written science fiction stories. He will likely continue to write sf stories on occasion, but the majority of them are science fiction by label rather than by content, their technology decorative, rococo. The earlier ones made obvious use of sf's accepted paraphernalia, such as spaceships and extraterrestrial creatures. This apparatus assured a quick sale to specialized genre magazines which, at that time, indiscriminately and voraciously gobbled up the works of hungry young writers.

Maturing rapidly, Harlan's fiction easily spilled over into the mainstream markets, but his reputation was established in a genre and the sf magazines continued to buy stories that were increasingly off-trail, fantasy-oriented or just downright unclassifiable. His accelerating disdain for restrictions and categorization led to his being regarded as an ungrateful gadfly by sf readers who relished their ghettoization with the fascination of zealots.

Of all the writers who have tilled in the field of science fiction, not one has managed to split readers into such sharply divided love/hate camps as has Harlan. This split, as well as the confusion over the "true" definition of science fiction, has never been more clearly demonstrated than by the 1981 nomination of his story "All the Lies That Are My Life" for the Hugo (the Science Fiction Achievement Award). The story is neither science fiction nor fantasy, and its recognition by the voters can best be attributed to their enjoyment of its qualities as a *story.*

The following works are science fiction, but science fiction that seldom fits comfortably within the traditional boundaries.

"The Sky is Burning" (1958) features an alien invasion which would have provided some artist a terrific chance to paint a gaudy, eyeball-singeing magazine cover of the type that delighted the kids and embarrassed adult readers. The sf gimmick is there, all right, but it isn't the meat of the story. What makes the theme particularly interesting is that, for all its ambiguous nihilism, it cherishes the light in the eye of the delighted kid and serves as a warning to the adult to hang on to that "sense of wonder."

There is an odd history behind "The Prowler in the City at the Edge of the World" (1967), a result of what Harlan calls "literary feedback." Robert Bloch's 1943 classic, "Yours Truly, Jack the Ripper," was the stepping-off point for his later "A Toy for Juliette," which Harlan bought for the hugely successful DANGEROUS VISIONS anthology. Bloch's second story took Jack the Ripper into the far future, and the concept so obsessed Harlan's own imagination that he wrote his own story for that book as a direct sequel.

If "Prowler" is, as Bloch says, "in the grand tradition of the Grand Guignol," is it then science fiction? Let's see now—time travel is a sturdy old sf concept, and Harlan's depiction of a future society is certainly grounded in the "if-this-goes-on" school. Yet the story isn't *about* time travel, and it isn't exactly *about* this future society. It might be about individual vs. collective reaction to social reform—or is that merely a side issue? Maybe it's about the power of evil—but do we really need to go years ahead to examine that? Then again, perhaps it's just about Jack the Ripper—but is that only speculation about the past? You get the idea, don't you? Science fiction's boundaries are getting a bit hazy.

"Along the Scenic Route" (1969) appeared in both a men's magazine and a science fiction magazine (as, alas, "Dogfight on 101"), yet it could have fit anywhere (and, in reprint, very nearly has). Ostensibly a gadget story, rather it says several pointed things about what technology is doing to us—Robert Silverberg's definition of sf's real value—and, perhaps, what we are doing to technology. Here is universal wish-fulfillment, neatly and succinctly garnished with high technology, futuristic slang, a slam-bang ending. Its matter-of-fact style lends it a startling and chilling plausibility.

After the sf revolution engendered by, many believe, the 1967 publication of DANGEROUS VISIONS, sf stories began to turn up in the oddest places. "The Song the Zombie Sang" (1970), co-authored with Robert Silverberg, is another fine example of a story fitting the genre requirements, yet it appeared in the thoroughly mainstream *Cosmopolitan*. It concerns the life, the death—the living death—of the reanimated corpse of a famous musician, and is a tale complete with all manner of futuristic decor to justify the classification: robots, weather control, the ultracembalo, the reanimated dead themselves.

The story is included here both as an example of Harlan's numerous collaborative efforts and for its own real merits. Nils Bekh's plight is filled with a desperation, a loneliness, a neglect that at first seems unique, utterly singular; then, as we think about it, it doesn't seem so unique after all. As with so much fine sf, only the circumstances, the framework, the decor are new, intriguingly different, even distracting. The underlying human truths are old, the whole tragedy a way of making us consider them again, from a new point of view, a new angle of feeling.

"Knox" (1974) appeared in *Crawdaddy*, a magazine purportedly specializing in rock music but not averse to reactionary commentary on nearly everything else. The story falls most easily into the unclassifiable category but can easily be shoehorned into sf under the guise of the social sciences. Social science fiction is nothing new—if Jonathan Swift had conceived of other worlds rather than other lands, Gulliver would have been one of the first sf heroes—but Harlan digs down to the root to find that social movements, while born in social circumstances, are most important in how they improve or disfigure the individual. Yes, it's science fiction, and no, the label doesn't classify it.

Science fiction is what it is because of what it does. Harlan Ellison is what he is because of what he does. Be careful and never confuse the two.

"Speculative fiction in modern times really got born with Walt Disney in his classic animated film, *Steamboat Willie,* in 1928. Sure it did. I mean: a mouse that can operate a paddle-wheeler?"

—"Thirty-Two Soothsayers," Introduction to DANGEROUS VISIONS, Doubleday, 1967

THE SKY IS BURNING

They came flaming down out of a lemon sky, and the first day, ten thousand died. The screams rang in our heads, and the women ran to the hills to escape the sound of it; but there was no escape for them . . . nor for any of us. The sky was aflame with death, and the terrible, unbelievable part of it was . . . the death, the dying was not us!

It started late in the evening. The first one appeared as a cosmic spark struck in the night. Then, almost before the first had faded back into the dusk, there was another, and then another, and soon the sky was a jeweler's pad, twinkling with unnameable diamonds.

I looked up from the Observatory roof, and saw them all, tiny pinpoints of brilliance, cascading down like raindrops of fire. And somehow, before any of it was explained, I knew: this was something important. Not important the way five extra inches of plastichrome on the tailfins of a new copter are important . . . not important the way a war is important . . . but important the way the creation of the Universe had been important, the way the death of it would be. And I knew it was happening all over Earth.

There could be no doubt of that. All across the horizon, as far as I could see, they were falling and burning and burning. The sky was not appreciably brighter, but it was as though a million new stars had been hurled up there to live for a brief microsecond.

Even as I watched, Portales called to me from below. "Frank! Frank, come down here . . . this is fantastic!"

I swung down the catwalk into the telescope dome, and saw him hunched over the refraction eyepiece. He was pounding his fist against the side of the vernier adjustment box. It was a pounding of futility, and strangeness. A pounding without meaning behind it. "Look at this, Frank. Will you take a look at this?" His voice was a rising inflection of disbelief.

I nudged him aside and slid into the bucket. The scope was trained on Mars. The Martian sky was burning, too. The same pinpoints of light, the same intense pyrotechnics spiraling down. We had allotted the evening to a study of the red planet, for it was clear in that direction, and I saw it all very sharply, as brightnesses and darkness again, all across the face of the planet.

"Call Bikel at Wilson," I told Portales. "Ask him about Venus."

Behind me I heard Portales dialing the closed circuit number, and I half-listened to his conversation with Aaron Bikel at Mt. Wilson. I could see the flickering reflections of the vid-screen on the phone, as they washed across the burnished side of the scope. But I didn't turn around; I knew what the answer would be.

Finally, he hung up, and the colors died: "The same," he said sharply, as though defying me to come up with an answer. I didn't bother snapping back at him. He had been bucking for my job as Director of the Observatory for nearly three years now, and I was accustomed to his antagonisms—desperately as I had to machinate occasionally, to keep him in his place.

I watched for a while longer, then left the dome.

I went downstairs, and tuned in my short-wave radio, trying to find out what Tokyo or Heidelberg or Johannesburg had to say. I wasn't able to catch any mention of the phenomena during the short time I fiddled with the sweep, but I was certain they were seeing it the same everywhere else.

Then I went back to the Dome, to change the settings on the scope.

After an argument with Portales, I beamed the scope down till it was sharp to just inside the atmospheric blanket. I tipped in the sweeper, and tried a fast scan of the sky, but continued to miss the bursts of light at the moment of their explosion. So I cut in the photo mechanism, and set a wide angle to it. Then I cut off the sweep, and started clicking them off. I reasoned that the frequency of the lights would inevitably bring one into photo focus.

Then I went downstairs, and back to the short-wave. I spent two hours with it, and managed to pick up a news broadcast from Switzerland. I had been right, of course.

Portales rang me after two hours and said we had a full reel of photos, and should he have them developed. This was too big to trust to his adolescent whims, and rather than have him fog up a valuable photo, I told him to leave them in the container, and I'd be right up, to handle it myself.

When the photos came out of the solution, I had to finger through thirty or forty of empty space before I caught ten that had what I wanted.

They were not meteorites.

On the contrary.

Each of the flames in the sky was a creature. A living creature. But not human. Far from it.

The photos told what they looked like, but not till the Project Snatch ship went up and sucked one off the sky did we realize how large they were, that they glowed with an inner light of their own and—that they were telepathic.

From what I can gather, it was no problem capturing one. The ship opened its cargo hatch, and turned on the sucking mechanisms used to drag in flotsam from space. The creature, however, could have stopped itself from being dragged into the ship, merely by placing one of its seven-taloned hands on either side of the hatch, and resisting the sucker. But it was interested, as we learned later; it had been five thousand years, and they had not known we had come so far, and the creature was interested. So it came along.

When they called me in, along with five hundred-odd other scientists (and Portales managed to wangle himself a place in the complement, through that old charlatan Senator Gouverman), we went to the Smithsonian, where they had had him installed, and marveled . . . just stood and marveled.

He—or she, we never knew—resembled the Egyptian god Ra. It had the head of a hawk, or what appeared to be a hawk, with great slitted eyes of green in which flecks of crimson and amber and black danced. Its body was thin to the point of emaciation, but humanoid with two arms and two legs. There were bends and joints on the body where no such bends and joints existed on a human, but there was a definite chest cavity, and obvious buttocks, knees, and chin. The creature was a pale milky-white, except on the hawk's-crest which was a brilliant blue, fading down into white. Its beak was light blue, also blending into the paleness of its flesh. It had seven toes to the foot, seven talons to the hand.

The God Ra. God of the Sun. God of light.

The creature glowed from within with a pale but distinct aura that surrounded it like a halo. We stood there, looking up at it in the glass cage. There was nothing to say; there it was, the first creature from another world. We might be going out into space in a few years—farther, that is, than the Moon, which we had reached in 1969, or Mars, on which we had landed in 1976—but for now, as far as we knew, the Universe was wide and without end, and out there we would find unbelievable creatures to rival any imagining. But this was the first.

We stared up at it. The being was thirteen feet tall.

Portales was whispering something to Karl Leus from Caltech. I snorted to myself at the way he never gave up; for sheer guff and grab I had to hand it to him. He was a pusher all right. Leus wasn't impressed. It was apparent he wasn't interested in what Portales had to say, but he had been a Nobel Prize winner in '63 and he felt obligated to be polite to even obnoxious pushers like my assistant.

The Army man—whatever his name was—was standing on a platform near the high, huge glass case in which the creature stood, unmoving, but watching us.

They had put food of all sorts through a feeder slot, but it was apparent the creature would not touch it. It merely stared down, silent as though amused, and unmoving as though uncaring.

"Gentlemen, gentlemen, may I have your attention!" the Army man caroled at us. A slow silence, indicative of our disrespect for him and his security measures that had caused us such grief getting into this meeting, fell through the groups of men and women at the foot of the case.

"We have called you here—" pompous ass with his *we*, as if he were the government incarnate, "to try and solve the mystery of who this being is, and what he has come to Earth to find out. We detect in this creature a great menace to—" and he went on and on, bleating and parodying all the previous scare warnings we had had about every nation on Earth. He could not have realized how we scoffed at him, and wanted to hoot him off the platform. This creature was no menace. Had we not captured him, her, it—the being would have burnt to a cinder like its fellows, falling into our atmosphere.

So we listened to him to the end. Then we moved in closer and stared at the creature. It opened its beak in what was uncommonly like a smile, and I felt a shiver run through me. The sort of shiver I get when I hear deeply emotional music, or the sort of shiver I get when making love. It was a basic trembling in the fibers of my body. I can't explain it, but it was a prelude to something. I paused in my thinking, just ceased my existence if *Cogito Ergo Sum* is the true test of existence. I stopped thinking and allowed myself to sniff of that strangeness; to savor the odor of space and faraway worlds, and one world in particular.

A world where the winds are so strong, the inhabitants have hooks on their feet, which they dig into the firm green soil to maintain their footing. A world where colors riot among the foliage one season, and the next—are the pale white of a maggot's flesh. A world where the triple moons swim through azure skies, and sing in their passage, playing on a lute of invisible strings, the seas and the deserts as accompanists. A world of wonder, older than Man and older than the memory of the Forever.

I realized abruptly, as my mind began to function once more, that

I had been listening to the creature. Ithk was the creature's—name?—denomination?—gender?—something. It was one of five hundred hundred-thousand like itself, who had come to the system of Sol.

Come? No, perhaps that was the wrong word. They had *been* . . .

Not by rockets, nothing that crude. Nor space-warp, nor even mental power. But a leap from their world—what was that name? Something the human tongue could not form, the human mind could not conceive?—to this world in seconds. Not instantaneous, for that would have involved machinery of some sort, or the expenditure of mental power. It was beyond that, and above that. It was an *essence* of travel. But they had come. They had come across the mega-galaxies, hundreds of thousands of light-years . . . incalculable distances from there to here, and Ithk was one of them.

Then it began to talk to some of us.

Not all of us there, for I could tell some were not receiving it. I don't attribute it to good or bad in any of us, nor intelligence, nor even sensitivity. Perhaps it was whim on Ithk's part, or the way he(?) wanted to do it out of necessity. But whatever it was, he spoke to only some of us there. I could see Portales was receiving nothing, though old Karl Leus's face was in a state of rapture, and I knew he had the message himself.

For the creature was speaking in our minds telepathically. It did not amaze me, or confound me, nor even shock me. It seemed right. It seemed to go with Ithk's size and look, its aura and arrival.

And it spoke to us.

And when it was done, some of us crawled up on the platform and released the bolts that held the case of glass shut; though we all knew Ithk could have left it at any second had it desired. But Ithk had been interested in knowing—before it burned itself out as its fellows had done—and it had found out about us little Earth people. It had satisfied its curiosity, on this instant's stopover before it went to hurtling, flaming destruction. It had been curious . . . for the last time Ithk's people had come here, Earth had been without creatures who went into space. Even as pitifully short a distance into space as we could venture.

But now the stopover was finished, and Ithk had a short journey to complete. It had come an unimaginably long way, for a purpose, and though this had been interesting, Ithk was anxious to join his fellows.

So we unbolted the cage—which had never *really* confined a creature that could *be* out of it at will—and Ithk was there! not there. Gone!

The sky was still flaming.

One more pinpoint came into being suddenly, slipped down in a violent rush through the atmosphere, and burned itself out like a wasting torch. Ithk was gone.

Then we left.

Karl Leus leaped from the thirty-second storey of a building in

Washington that evening. Nine others died that day. And though I was not ready for that, there was a deadness in me. A feeling of waste and futility and hopelessness. I went back to the Observatory, and tried to drive the memory of what Ithk had said from my mind and my soul. If I had been as deeply perceptive as Leus or any of the other nine, I might have gone immediately. But I am not in their category. They realized the full depth of what it had said, and so perceiving, they had taken their lives. I can understand their doing it.

Portales came to me when he heard about it.

"They just—just *killed* themselves!" he babbled. I was sick of his petty annoyances. Sick of them, and not even interested any longer in fighting him.

"Yes, they killed themselves," I answered wearily, staring at the flaming, burning sky from the Observatory catwalk. It always seemed to be night now. Always night—with light.

"But *why*? Why would they do it?"

I spoke to hear my thoughts. For I knew what was coming. "Because of what the creature said."

"What it said?"

"What it told us, and what it did not tell us."

"It *spoke* to you?"

"To some of us. To Leus and the nine and others. I heard it."

"But why didn't *I* hear it? I was right there!"

I shrugged. He had not heard, that was all.

"Well, what did it say? Tell me," he demanded.

I turned to him, and looked at him. Would it affect him? No, I rather thought not. And that was good. Good for him, and good for others like him. For without them, Man would cease to exist. I told him.

"The lemmings," I said. "You know the lemmings. For no reason, from some deep instinctual surging, they follow each other, and periodically throw themselves off the cliffs. They follow one another down to destruction. A racial trait. It was that way with the creature and his people. They came across the mega-galaxies to kill themselves here. To commit mass suicide in our solar system. To burn up in the atmosphere of Mars and Mercury and Venus and Earth, and to die, that's all. Just to die."

His face was stunned. I could see he comprehended that. But what did it matter? That was not what had made Leus and the nine kill themselves, that was not what filled me with such a feeling of frustration. The drive of one race was not the drive of another.

"But—but—I don't underst—"

I cut him off.

"That was what Ithk said."

"But why did they come *here* to die?" he asked, confused. "Why *here* and not some other solar system or galaxy?"

That was what Ithk had said. That was what we had wondered in our minds—damn us for asking—and in its simple way, Ithk had answered.

"Because," I explained slowly, softly, "this is the end of the Universe."

His face did not register comprehension. I could see it was a concept he could not grasp. That the solar system, Earth's system, the backyard of Earth to be precise, was the end of the Universe. Like the flat world over which Columbus would have sailed, into nothingness. This was the end of it all. Out there, in the other direction, lay a known Universe, with an end to it . . . but they—Ithk's people—ruled it. It was theirs, and would always be theirs. For they had racial memory burnt into each embryo child born to their race, so they would never stagnate. After every lemming race, a new generation was born, that would live for thousands of years, and advance. They would go on till they came here to flame out in our atmosphere. But they would rule what they had while they had it.

So to us, to the driving, unquenchably curious, seeking and roaming Earthman, whose life was tied up with wanting to know, *needing* to know, there was nothing left. Ashes. The dust of our own system. And after that, nothing.

We were at a dead end. There could be no wandering among the stars. It was not that we *couldn't* go. We could. But we would be tolerated. It was *their* Universe, and this, our Earth, was the dead end.

Ithk had not known what it was doing when it said that to us. It had meant no evil, but it had doomed some of us. Those of us who dreamed. Those of us who wanted more than what Portales wanted.

I turned away from him and looked up.

The sky was burning.

I held very tightly to the bottle of sleeping tablets in my pocket. So much light up there.

The Prowler in the City at the Edge of the World

First there was the City, never night. Tin and reflective, walls of antiseptic metal like an immense autoclave. Pure and dust-free, so silent that even the whirling innards of its heart and mind were sheathed from notice. The city was self-contained, and footfalls echoed up and around—flat slapped notes of an exotic leather-footed instrument. Sounds that reverberated back to the maker like yodels thrown out across mountain valleys. Sounds made by humbled inhabitants whose lives were as ordered, as sanitary, as metallic as the city they had caused to hold them bosom-tight against the years. The city was a complex artery, the people were the blood that flowed icily through the artery. They were a gestalt with one another, forming a unified whole. It was a city shining in permanence, eternal in concept, flinging itself up in a formed and molded statement of exaltation; most modern of all modern structures, conceived as the pluperfect residence for the perfect people. The final end-result of all sociological blueprints aimed at Utopia. Living space, it had been called, and so, doomed to *live* they were, in that Erewhon of graphed respectability and cleanliness.

Never night.

Never shadowed.

. . . a shadow.

A blot moving against the aluminum cleanliness. The movement of rags and bits of clinging earth from graves sealed ages before. A shape.

He touched a gunmetal-gray wall in passing: the imprint of dusty fingers. A twisted shadow moving through antiseptically pure streets, and they become—with his passing—black alleys from another time.

Vaguely, he knew what had happened. Not specifically, not with particulars, but he was strong, and he was able to get away without the eggshell-thin walls of his mind caving in. There was no place in this shining structure to secrete himself, a place to think, but he had to have time. He slowed his walk, seeing no one. Somehow—inexplicably—he felt . . . safe? Yes, safe. For the first time in a very long time.

A few minutes before he had been standing in the narrow passageway outside No. 13 Miller's Court. It had been 6:15 in the morning. London had been quiet as he paused in the passageway of M'Carthy's Rents, in that fetid, urine-redolent corridor where the whores of Spitalfields took their clients. A few minutes before, the foetus in its bath of formaldehyde tightly-stoppered in a glass bottle inside his Gladstone bag, he had paused to drink in the thick fog, before taking the circuitous route back to Toynbee Hall. That had been a few minutes before. Then, suddenly, he was in another place and it was no longer 6:15 of a chill November morning in 1888.

He had looked up as light flooded him in that other place. It had been soot silent in Spitalfields, but suddenly, without any sense of having moved or having *been* moved, he was flooded with light. And when he looked up he was in that other place. Paused now, only a few minutes after the transfer, he leaned against the bright wall of the city, and recalled the light. From a thousand mirrors. In the walls, in the ceiling. A bedroom with a girl in it. A lovely girl. Not like Black Mary Kelly or Dark Annie Chapman or Kate Eddowes or any of the other pathetic scum he had been forced to attend . . .

A lovely girl. Blonde, wholesome, until she had opened her robe and turned into the same sort of slut he had been compelled to use in his work in Whitechapel . . .

A sybarite, a creature of pleasures, a Juliette she had said, before he used the big-bladed knife on her. He had found the knife under the pillow, on the bed to which she had led him—how shameful, unresisting had he been, all confused, clutching his black bag with all the tremors of a child, he who had moved through the London night like oil, moved where he wished, accomplished his ends unchecked eight times, now led toward sin by another, merely another of the tarts, taking advantage of him while he tried to distinguish what had happened to him and where he was, how shameful—and he had used it on her.

That had only been minutes before, though he had worked very efficiently on her.

The knife had been rather unusual. The blade had seemed to be two wafer-thin sheets of metal with a pulsing, glowing *something* between. A kind of sparking, such as might be produced by a Van de Graaff generator. But that was patently ridiculous. It had no wires attached to it, no bus bars, nothing to produce even the crudest electrical discharge. He had thrust the knife into the Gladstone bag, where now it lay beside the scalpels and the spool of catgut and the racked vials in their leather cases, and the foetus in its bottle. Mary Jane Kelly's foetus.

He had worked efficiently, but swiftly, and had laid her out almost exactly in the same fashion as Kate Eddowes: the throat slashed completely through from ear-to-ear, the torso laid open down between the breasts to the vagina, the intestines pulled out and draped over the right shoulder, a piece of the intestines being detached and placed between the left arm and the body. The liver had been punctured with the point of the knife, with a vertical cut slitting the left lobe of the liver. (He had been surprised to find the liver showed none of the signs of cirrhosis so prevalent in these Spitalfields tarts, who drank incessantly to rid themselves of the burden of living the dreary lives they moved through grotesquely. In fact, this one seemed totally unlike the others, even if she had been more brazen in her sexual overtures. And that knife under the bed pillow . . .) He had severed the vena cava leading to the heart. Then he had gone to work on the face.

He had thought of removing the left kidney again, as he had Kate Eddowes's. He smiled to himself as he conjured up the expression that must have been on the face of Mr. George Lusk, chairman of the Whitechapel Vigilance Committee, when he received the cardboard box in the mail. The box containing Miss Eddowes's kidney, and the letter, impiously misspelled:

> *From hell, Mr. Lusk, sir, I send you half the kidne I took from one woman, prasarved it for you, tother piece I fried and ate it; was very nice. I may send you the bloody knif that took it out if you only wate while longer. Catch me when you can, Mr. Lusk.*

He had wanted to sign *that* one "Yours Truly, Jack the Ripper" or even Spring-Heeled Jack or maybe Leather Apron, whichever had tickled his fancy, but a sense of style had stopped him. To go too far was to defeat his own purposes. It may even have been too much to suggest to Mr. Lusk that he had eaten the kidney. How hideous. True, he *had* smelled it . . .

This blonde girl, this Juliette with the knife under her pillow. She was the ninth. He leaned against the smooth steel wall without break or seam, and he rubbed his eyes. When would he be able to stop? When would they realize, when would they get his message, a message so clear, written in blood, that only the blindness of their own cupidity forced them to misunderstand! Would he be compelled to decimate the endless regiments of Spitalfields sluts to make them understand? Would he be forced to run the cobbles ankle-deep in black blood before they sensed what he was saying, and were impelled to make reforms?

But as he took his blood-soaked hands from his eyes, he realized what he must have sensed all along: he was no longer in Whitechapel. This was not Miller's Court, nor anywhere in Spitalfields. It might not even be London. But how could *that* be?

Had God taken him?

Had he died, in a senseless instant between the anatomy lesson of Mary Jane Kelly (that filth, she had actually *kissed* him!) and the bedroom disembowelment of this Juliette? Had Heaven finally called him to his reward for the work he had done?

The Reverend Mr. Barnett would love to know about this. But then, he'd have loved to know about it *all*. But "Bloody Jack" wasn't about to tell. Let the reforms come as the Reverend and his wife wished for them, and let them think their pamphleteering had done it, instead of the scalpels of Jack.

If he was dead, would his work be finished? He smiled to himself. If Heaven had taken him, then it must be that the work *was* finished. Successfully. But if *that* was so, then who was this Juliette who now lay spread out moist and cooling in the bedroom of a thousand mirrors? And in that instant he felt fear.

What if even God misinterpreted what he had done?

As the good folk of Queen Victoria's London had misinterpreted. As Sir Charles Warren had misinterpreted. What if God believed the superficial and ignored the *real* reason? But no! Ludicrous. If anyone would understand, it was the good God who had sent him the message that told him to set things a-right.

God loved him, as he loved God, and God would know.

But he felt fear, in that moment.

Because who was the girl he had just carved?

"She was my granddaughter, Juliette," said a voice immediately beside him.

His head refused to move, to turn that few inches to see who spoke. The Gladstone was beside him, resting on the smooth and reflective surface of the street. He could not get to a knife before he was taken. At last they had caught up with Jack. He began to shiver uncontrollably.

"No need to be afraid," the voice said. It was a warm and succoring voice. An older man. He shook as with an ague. But he turned to look. It was a kindly old man with a gentle smile. Who spoke again, without moving his lips. "No one can hurt you. How do you do?"

The man from 1888 sank slowly to his knees. "Forgive me. Dear God, I did not know." The old man's laughter rose inside the head of the man on his knees. It rose like a beam of sunlight moving across a Whitechapel alleyway, from noon to one o'clock, rising and illuminating the gray bricks of soot-coated walls. It rose, and illuminated his mind.

"I'm not God. Marvelous idea, but no, I'm not God. Would you like to meet God? I'm sure we can find one of the artists who would mold one for you. Is it important? No, I can see it isn't. What a strange mind you have. You neither believe nor doubt. How can you contain both concepts at once . . . would you like me to straighten some of your brain-patterns? No. I see, you're afraid. Well, let it be for the nonce. We'll do it another time."

He grabbed the kneeling man and drew him erect.

"You're covered with blood. Have to get you cleaned up. There's an ablute near here. Incidentally, I was very impressed with the way you handled Juliette. You're the first, you know. No, how could you know? In any case, you *are* the first to deal her as good as she gave. You would have been amused at what she did to Caspar Hauser. Squeezed part of his brain and then sent him back, let him live out part of his life and then—the little twit—she made me bring him back a second time and used a knife on him. Same knife you took, I believe. Then sent him back to his own time. Marvelous mystery. In all the tapes on unsolved phenomena. But she was much sloppier than you. She had a great verve in her amusements, but very little *éclat*. Except with Judge Crater; there she was—" He paused, and laughed lightly. "I'm an old man and I ramble on like a muskrat. You want to get cleaned up and shown around, I know. And *then* we can talk.

"I just wanted you to know I was satisfied with the way you disposed of her. In a way, I'll miss the little twit. She was such a good fuck."

The old man picked up the Gladstone bag and, holding the man spattered with blood, he moved off down the clean and shimmering street. "You *wanted* her killed?" the man from 1888 asked, unbelieving.

The old man nodded, but his lips never moved. "Of course. Otherwise why bring her Jack the Ripper?"

Oh my dear God, he thought, *I'm in Hell. And I'm entered as Jack.*

"No, my boy, no no no. You're not in Hell at all. You're in the future. For you the future, for me the world of now. You came from 1888 and you're now in—" he stopped, silently speaking for an instant, as though computing apples in terms of dollars, then resumed "—3077. It's a fine world, filled with happy times, and we're glad to have you with us. Come along now, and you'll wash."

In the ablutatorium, the late Juliette's grandfather changed his head.

"I really despise it," he informed the man from 1888, grabbing fingerfuls of his cheeks and stretching the flabby skin like elastic. "But Juliette insisted. I was willing to humor her, if indeed that was what it took to get her to lie down. But what with toys from the past, and changing my head every time I wanted her to fuck me, it was trying; very trying."

He stepped into one of the many identically shaped booths set flush into the walls. The tambour door rolled down and there was a soft *chukk* sound, almost chitinous. The tambour door rolled up and the late Juliette's grandfather, now six years younger than the man from 1888, stepped out, stark naked and wearing a new head. "The body is fine, replaced last year," he said, examining the genitals and a mole on his right shoulder. The man from 1888 looked away. This was Hell and God hated him.

"Well, don't just *stand* there, Jack." Juliette's grandfather smiled. "Hit one of those booths and get your ablutions."

"That isn't my name," said the man from 1888 very softly, as though he had been whipped.

"It'll do, it'll do . . . now go get washed."

Jack approached one of the booths. It was a light green in color, but changed to mauve as he stopped in front of it. "Will it—"

"It will only *clean* you, what are you afraid of?"

"I don't want to be changed."

Juliette's grandfather did not laugh. "That's a mistake," he said cryptically. He made a peremptory motion with his hand and the man from 1888 entered the booth, which promptly revolved in its niche, sank into the floor and made a hearty *zeeeezzzz* sound. When it rose and revolved and opened, Jack stumbled out, looking terribly confused. His long sideburns had been neatly trimmed, his beard stubble had been removed, his hair was three shades lighter and was now parted on the left side, rather than in the middle. He still wore the same long dark coat trimmed with astrakhan, dark suit with white collar and black necktie (in which was fastened a horseshoe stickpin) but now the garments seemed new, unsoiled of course, possibly synthetics built to look like his former garments.

"Now!" Juliette's grandfather said. "Isn't that much better? A good cleansing always sets one's mind to rights." And he stepped into another booth from which he issued in a moment wearing a soft paper jumper that fitted from neck to feet without a break. He moved toward the door.

"Where are we going?" the man from 1888 asked the younger grandfather beside him. "I want you to meet someone," said Juliette's grandfather, and Jack realized that he was moving his lips now. He decided not to comment on it. There had to be a reason.

"I'll walk you there, if you promise not to make gurgling sounds at the city. It's a nice city, but I live here, and frankly, tourism is boring." Jack did not reply. Grandfather took it for acceptance of the terms.

They walked. Jack became overpowered by the sheer *weight* of the city. It was obviously extensive, massive, and terribly clean. It was his dream for Whitechapel come true. He asked about slums, about doss houses. The grandfather shook his head. "Long gone."

So it had come to pass. The reforms for which he had pledged his immortal soul, they had come to pass. He swung the Gladstone and walked jauntily. But after a few minutes his pace sagged once more: there was no one to be seen in the streets.

Just shining clean buildings and streets that ran off in aimless directions and came to unexpected stops as though the builders had decided people might vanish at one point and reappear someplace else, so why bother making a road from one point to the other.

The ground was metal, the sky seemed metallic, the buildings loomed on all sides, featureless explorations of planed space by insensitive metal. The man from 1888 felt terribly alone, as though every act he had performed had led inevitably to his alienation from the very people he had sought to aid.

When he had come to Toynbee Hall, and the Reverend Mr. Barnett had opened his eyes to the slum horrors of Spitalfields, he had vowed to help in any way he could. It had seemed as simple as faith in the Lord, what to do, after a few months in the sinkholes of Whitechapel. The sluts, of what use were they? No more use than the disease germs that had infected these very same whores. So he had set forth as Jack, to perform the will of God and raise the poor dregs who inhabited the East End of London. That Lord Warren, the Metropolitan Police Commissioner, and his Queen, and all the rest thought him a mad doctor, or an amok butcher, or a beast in human form did not distress him. He knew he would remain anonymous through all time, but that the good works he had set in motion would proceed to their wonderful conclusion.

The destruction of the most hideous slum area the country had ever known, and the opening of Victorian eyes. But all the time *had* passed, and now he was here, in a world where slums apparently did not exist, a sterile Utopia that was the personification of the Reverend Mr. Barnett's dreams—but it didn't seem . . . *right*.

This grandfather, with his young head.

Silence in the empty streets.

The girl, Juliette, and her strange hobby.

The lack of concern at her death.

The grandfather's expectation that he, Jack, *would* kill her. And now his friendliness.

Where were they going?

[Around them, the City. As they walked, the grandfather paid no attention, and Jack watched but did not understand. But this was what they saw as they walked:

[Thirteen hundred beams of light, one foot wide and seven molecules thick, erupted from almost-invisible slits in the metal streets, fanned out and washed the surfaces of the buildings; they altered hue to a vague blue and washed down the surfaces of the buildings; they bent and covered all open surfaces, bent at right angles, then bent again, and again, like origami paper figures; they altered hue a second time, soft gold, and penetrated the surfaces of the buildings, expanding and contracting in solid waves, washing the inner surfaces; they withdrew rapidly into the sidewalks; the entire process had taken twelve seconds.

[Night fell over a sixteen block area of the City. It descended in a solid pillar and was quite sharp-edged, ending at the street corners. From within the area of darkness came the distinct sounds of crickets, marsh frogs belching, night birds, soft breezes in trees, and faint music of unidentifiable instruments.

[Panes of frosted light appeared suspended freely in the air, overhead. A wavery insubstantial quality began to assault the topmost levels of a great structure directly in front of the light-panes. As the panes moved slowly down through the air, the building became indistinct, turned into motes of light, and floated upward. As the panes reached the pavement, the building had been completely dematerialized. The panes shifted color to a deep orange, and began moving upward again. As they moved, a new structure began to form where the previous building had stood, drawing—it seemed—motes of light from the air and forming them into a cohesive whole that became, as the panes ceased their upward movement, a new building. The light-panes winked out of existence.

[The sound of a bumblebee was heard for several seconds. Then it ceased.

[A crowd of people in rubber garments hurried out of a gray pulsing hole in the air, patted the pavement at their feet, then rushed off around a corner, from where emanated the sound of prolonged coughing. Then silence returned.

[A drop of water, thick as quicksilver, plummeted to the pavement, struck, rebounded, rose several inches, then evaporated into a crimson smear in the shape of a whale's tooth, which settled to the pavement and lay still.

[Two blocks of buildings sank into the pavement and the metal covering was smooth and unbroken, save for a metal tree whose trunk was silver and slim, topped by a ball of foliage constructed of golden fibers that radiated brightly in a perfect circle. There was no sound.

[The late Juliette's grandfather and the man from 1888 continued walking.]

"Where are we going?"

"To van Cleef's. We don't usually walk; oh, sometimes; but it isn't as much pleasure as it used to be. I'm doing this primarily for you. Are you enjoying yourself?"

"It's . . . unusual."

"Not much like Spitalfields, is it? But I rather like it back there, at that time. I have the only Traveler, did you know? The only one ever made. Juliette's father constructed it, my son. I had to kill him to get it. He was thoroughly unreasonable about it, really. It was a casual thing for him. He was the last of the tinkerers, and he might just as easily have given it to me. But I suppose he was being cranky. That was why I had you carve up my granddaughter. She would have gotten around to me almost any time now. Bored, just silly bored is what she was—"

The gardenia took shape in the air in front of them, and turned into the face of a woman with long white hair. "Hernon, we can't wait much longer!" She was annoyed.

Juliette's grandfather grew livid. "You scum bitch! I *told* you pace. But no, you just couldn't, could you? Jump jump jump, that's all you ever do. Well, now it'll only be feddels less, that's all. Feddels, damn you! I set it for pace, I was *working* pace, and *you* . . . !"

His hand came up and moss grew instantly toward the face. The face vanished, and a moment later the gardenia reappeared a few feet away. The moss shriveled and Hernon, Juliette's grandfather, dropped his hand, as though weary of the woman's stupidity. A rose, a water lily, a hyacinth, a pair of phlox, a wild celandine, and a bull thistle appeared near the gardenia. As each turned into the face of a different person, Jack stepped back, frightened.

All the faces turned to the one that had been the bull thistle. "Cheat! Rotten bastard!" they screamed at the thin white face that had been the bull thistle. The gardenia-woman's eyes bulged from her face, the deep purple eye-shadow that completely surrounded the eyeball making her look like a deranged animal peering out of a cave. "Turd!" she shrieked at the bull thistle-man. "We all agreed, we all said and agreed; you *had* to formz a thistle, didn't you, scut! Well, now you'll see . . ."

She addressed herself instantly to the others. "Formz now! To hell with waiting, pace fuck! Now!"

"No, dammit!" Hernon shouted. "We were going to *paaaaace!*" But it was too late. Centering in on the bull thistle-man, the air roiled thickly like silt at a river-bottom, and the air blackened as a spiral began with the now terrified face of the bull thistle-man and exploded whirling outward, enveloping Jack and Hernon and all the flower-people and the City and suddenly it was night in Spitalfields and the man from 1888 was *in* 1888, with his Gladstone bag in his hand, and a woman approaching down the street toward him, shrouded in the London fog.

(There were eight additional nodules in Jack's brain.)

The woman was about forty, weary and not too clean. She wore a dark dress of rough material that reached down to her boots. Over the skirt was fastened a white apron that was stained and wrinkled. The bulbed sleeves ended midway up her wrists and the bodice of the dress was buttoned close around her throat. She wore a kerchief tied at the neck, and a hat that looked like a wide-brimmed skimmer with a raised crown. There was a pathetic little flower of unidentifiable origin in the band of the hat. She carried a beaded handbag of capacious size, hanging from a wrist-loop.

Her step slowed as she saw him standing there, deep in the shadows. Saw him was hardly accurate: sensed him.

He stepped out and bowed slightly from the waist. "Fair evenin' to ye, Miss. Care for a pint?"

Her features—sunk in misery of a kind known only to women who have taken in numberless shafts of male blood-gorged flesh—rearranged themselves. "Coo, sir, I thought was 'im for true. Old Leather Apron hisself. Gawdamighty, you give me a scare." She tried to smile. It was a rictus. There were bright spots in her cheeks from sickness and too much gin. Her voice was ragged, a broken-edged instrument barely workable.

"Just a solicitor caught out without comp'ny," Jack assured her. "And pleased to buy a handsome lady a pint of stout for a few hours' companionship."

She stepped toward him and linked arms. "Emily Matthewes, sir, an' pleased to go with you. It's a fearsome chill night, and with Slippery Jack abroad not safe for a respectin' woman such's m'self."

They moved off down Thrawl Street, past the doss houses where this drab might flop later, if she could obtain a few coppers from this neat-dressed stranger with the dark eyes.

He turned right onto Commercial Street, and just abreast of a stinking alley almost to Flower & Dean Street, he nudged her sharply sidewise. She went into the alley, and thinking he meant to steal a smooth hand up under her petticoats, she settled back against the wall and opened her legs, starting to lift the skirt around her waist. But Jack had hold of the kerchief and, locking his fingers tightly, he twisted, cutting off her breath. Her cheeks ballooned, and by a vagary of light from a gas standard in the street he could see her eyes go from hazel to a dead-leaf brown in an instant. Her expression was one of terror, naturally, but commingled with it was a deep sadness, at having lost the pint, at having not been able to make her doss for the night, at having had the usual Emily Matthewes bad luck to run afoul this night of the one man who would ill-use her favors. It was a consummate sadness at the inevitability of her fate.

I come to you out of the night.
The night that sent me down
all the minutes of our lives
to this instant.
From this time forward, men will
wonder what happened
at this instant. They will silently
hunger to go back, to come to my
instant with you and see my face
and know my name and perhaps
not even try to stop me, for
then I would not be who I am,
but only someone who tried
and failed. Ah.
For you and me it becomes history
that will lure men always;
but they will never understand
why we both suffered, Emily;
they will never truly understand
why each of us died so terribly.

A film came over her eyes, and as her breath husked out in wheezing, pleading tremors, his free hand went into the pocket of the greatcoat. He had known he would need it, when they were walking, and he had already invaded the Gladstone bag. Now his hand went into the pocket and came up with the scalpel.

"Emily . . ." softly.

Then he sliced her.

Neatly, angling the point of the scalpel into the soft flesh behind and under her left ear. *Sternocleidomastoideus*. Driving it in to the gentle crunch of cartilage giving way. Then, grasping the instrument tightly, tipping it down and drawing it across the width of the throat, following the line of the firm jaw. *Glandula submandibularis*. The blood poured out over his hands, ran thickly at first and then burst spattering past him, reaching the far wall of the alley. Up his sleeves, soaking his white cuffs. She made a watery rattle and sank limply in his grasp, his fingers still twisted tight in her kerchief; black abrasions where he had scored the flesh. He continued the cut up past the point of the jaw's end, and sliced into the lobe of the ear. He lowered her to the filthy paving. She lay crumpled, and he straightened her. Then he cut away the garments laying her naked belly open to the wan and flickering light of the gas standard in the street. Her belly was bloated. He started the primary cut in the hollow of her throat. *Glandula thyreoeidea*. His hand was sure as he drew a thin black line of blood down and down, between the breasts. *Sternum*. Cutting a deep cross in the hole of her navel. Something vaguely yellow oozed up. *Plica umbilicalis medialis*. Down over the rounded hump of the belly, biting more deeply, withdrawing for a neat incision. *Mesenterium dorsale commune*. Down to the matted-with-sweat roundness of her privates. Harder here. *Vesica urinaria*. And finally, to the end, *vagina*.

Filth hole.

Foul-smelling die red lust pit wet hole of sluts.

And in his head, succubi. And in his head, eyes watching. And in his head, minds impinging. And in his head titillation

for a gardenia
a water lily
a rose
a hyacinth
a pair of phlox
a wild celandine
and a dark flower with petals of obsidian, a stamen of onyx, pistils of anthracite, and the mind of Hernon, who was the late Juliette's grandfather.

They watched the entire horror of the mad anatomy lesson. They watched him nick the eyelids. They watched him remove the heart. They watched him slice out the fallopian tubes. They watched him squeeze, till it ruptured, the "ginny" kidney. They watched him slice off the sections of breast till they were nothing but shapeless mounds of bloody meat, and arrange them, one mound each on a still-staring, wide-open, nicked-eyelid eye. They watched.

They watched and they drank from the deep troubled pool of his mind. They sucked deeply at the moist quivering core of his id. And they delighted:

Oh God how Delicious look at that It looks like the uneaten rind of a Pizza or look at That It looks like lumaconi *oh god IIIIwonder what it would be like to Tasteit!*

See how smooth the steel.

He hates them all, every one of them, something about a girl, a venereal disease, fear of his God, Christ, the Reverend Mr. Barnett, he . . . he wants to fuck the reverend's wife!

Social reform can only be brought about by concerted effort of a devoted few. Social reform is a justifiable end, condoning any expedient short of decimation of over fifty percent of the people who will be served by the reforms. The best social reformers are the most audacious. He believes it! How lovely!

You pack of vampires, you filth, you scum, you . . .

He senses us!

Damn him! Damn you, Hernon, you drew off too deeply, he knows we're here, that's disgusting, what's the sense now? I'm withdrawing!

Come back, you'll end the formz . . .

. . . back they plunged in the spiral as it spiraled back in upon itself and the darkness of the night of 1888 withdrew. The spiral drew in and in and locked at its most infinitesimal point as the charred and blackened face of the man who had been the bull thistle. He was quite dead. His eyeholes had been burned out; charred wreckage lay where intelligence had lived. They had used him as a focus.

The man from 1888 came back to himself instantly, with a full and eidetic memory of what he had just experienced. It had not been a vision, nor a dream, nor a delusion, nor a product of his mind. It had happened. They had sent him back, erased his mind of the transfer into the future, of Juliette, of everything after the moment outside No. 13 Miller's Court. And they had set him to work pleasuring them, while they drained off his feelings, his emotions and his unconscious thoughts; while they battened and gorged themselves with the most private sensations. Most of which, till this moment—in a strange feedback—he had not even known he possessed. As his mind plunged on from one revelation to the next, he felt himself growing ill. At one concept his mind tried to pull back and plunge him into darkness rather than confront it. But the barriers were down, they had opened new patterns and he could read it all, remember it all. *Stinking sex hole, sluts, they have to die.* No, that wasn't the way he thought of women, any women, no matter how low or common. He was a gentleman, and women were to be respected. *She had given him the clap. He remembered.* The shame and the endless fear till he had gone to his physician father and confessed it. The look on the man's face. He remembered it all. The way his father had tended him, the way he would have tended a plague victim. It had never been the same between them again. He had tried for the cloth. *Social reform hahahaha.* All delusion. He had been a mountebank, a clown . . . and worse. He had slaughtered for something in which not even he believed. They left his mind wide open, and his thoughts stumbled . . . raced further and further toward the thought of

EXPLOSION!IN!HIS!MIND!

He fell face forward on the smooth and polished metal pavement, but he never touched. Something arrested his fall, and he hung suspended, bent over at the waist like a ridiculous Punch divested of strings or manipulation from above. A whiff of something invisible, and he was in full possession of his senses almost before they had left him. His mind was forced to look at it:

He wants to fuck the Reverend Mr. Barnett's wife.

Henrietta, with her pious petition to Queen Victoria—"Madam, we, the women of East London, feel horror at the dreadful sins that have been lately committed in our midst . . ."—asking for the capture of himself, of Jack, whom she would never, not *ever* suspect was residing right there with her and the Reverend in Toynbee Hall. The thought was laid as naked as her body in the secret dreams he had never remembered upon awakening. All of it, they had left him with opened doors, with unbounded horizons, and he saw himself for what he was.

A psychopath, a butcher, a lecher, a hypocrite, a clown.

"You did this to me! Why did you do this?"

Frenzy cloaked his words. The flower-faces became the solidified hedonists who had taken him back to 1888 on that senseless voyage of slaughter.

van Cleef, the gardenia-woman, sneered. "Why do you think, you ridiculous bumpkin? (Bumpkin, is that the right colloquialism, Hernon? I'm so uncertain in the mid-dialects.) When you'd done in Juliette, Hernon wanted to send you back. But why should he? He owed us at least three formz, and you did passing well for one of them."

Jack shouted at them till the cords stood out in his throat. "Was it necessary, this last one? Was it important to do it, to help my reforms . . . was it?"

Hernon laughed. "Of course not."

Jack sank to his knees. The City let him do it. "Oh God, oh God almighty, I've done what I've done . . . I'm covered with blood . . . and for *nothing*, for *nothing* . . ."

Cashio, who had been one of the phlox, seemed puzzled. "Why is he concerned about *this* one, if the others don't bother him?"

Nosy Verlag, who had been a wild celandine, said sharply, "They do, all of them do. Probe him, you'll see."

Cashio's eyes rolled up in his head an instant, then rolled down and refocused—Jack felt a quicksilver shudder in his mind and it was gone—and he said lackadaisically, "Mm-hmm."

Jack fumbled with the latch of the Gladstone. He opened the bag and pulled out the foetus in the bottle. Mary Jane Kelly's unborn child, from November 9th, 1888. He held it in front of his face a moment, then dashed it to the metal pavement. It never struck. It vanished a fraction of an inch from the clean, sterile surface of the City's street.

"What marvelous loathing!" exulted Rose, who had been a rose.

"Hernon," said van Cleef, "he's centering on you. He begins to blame you for all of this."

Hernon was laughing (without moving his lips) as Jack pulled Juliette's electrical scalpel from the Gladstone, and lunged. Jack's words were incoherent, but what he was saying, as he struck, was: "I'll show you what filth you are! I'll show you you can't do this kind of thing! I'll teach you! You'll die, all of you!" This is what he was saying, but it came out as one long sustained bray of revenge, frustration, hatred and directed frenzy.

Hernon was still laughing as Jack drove the whisper-thin blade with its shimmering current into his chest. Almost without manipulation on Jack's part, the blade circumscribed a perfect 360° hole that charred and shriveled, exposing Hernon's pulsing heart and wet organs. He had time to shriek with confusion before he received Jack's second thrust, a direct lunge that severed the heart from its attachments. *Vena cava superior. Aorta. Arteria pulmonalis. Bronchus principalis.*

The heart flopped forward and a spreading wedge of blood under tremendous pressure ejaculated, spraying Jack with such force that it knocked his hat from his head and blinded him. His face was now a dripping black-red collage of features and blood.

Hernon followed his heart, and fell forward, into Jack's arms. Then the flower-people screamed as one, vanished, and Hernon's body slipped from Jack's hands to wink out of existence an instant before it struck at Jack's feet. The walls around him were clean, unspotted, sterile, metallic, uncaring.

He stood in the street, holding the bloody knife.

"*Now!*" he screamed, holding the knife aloft. "Now it begins!"

If the city heard, it made no indication, but

[Pressure accelerated in temporal linkages.]

[A section of shining wall on the building eighty miles away changed from silver to rust.]

[In the freezer chambers, two hundred gelatin caps were fed into a ready trough.]

[The weathermaker spoke softly to itself, accepted data and instantly constructed an intangible mnemonic circuit.]

and in the shining eternal city where night only fell when the inhabitants had need of night and called specifically for night . . .

Night fell. With no warning save: "*Now!*"

In the City of sterile loveliness a creature of filth and decaying flesh prowled. In the last City of the world, a City on the edge of the world, where the ones who had devised their own paradise lived, the prowler made his home in shadows. Slipping from darkness to darkness with eyes that saw only movement, he roamed in search of a partner to dance his deadly rigadoon.

He found the first woman as she materialized beside a small waterfall that flowed out of empty air and dropped its shimmering, tinkling moisture into an azure cube of nameless material. He found her and drove the living blade into the back of her neck. Then he sliced out the eyeballs and put them into her open hands.

He found the second woman in one of the towers, making love to a very old man who gasped and wheezed and clutched his heart as the young woman forced him to passion. She was killing him as Jack killed her. He drove the living blade into the lower rounded surface of her belly, piercing her sex organs as she rode astride the old man. She decamped blood and viscous fluids over the prostrate body of the old man, who also died, for Jack's blade had severed the penis within the young woman. She fell forward across the old man and Jack left them that way, joined in the final embrace.

He found a man and throttled him with his bare hands, even as the man tried to dematerialize. Then Jack recognized him as one of the phlox, and made neat incisions in the face, into which he inserted the man's genitals.

He found another woman as she was singing a gentle song about eggs to a group of children. He opened her throat and severed the strings hanging inside. He let the vocal cords drop onto her chest. But he did not touch the children, who watched it all avidly. He liked children.

He prowled through the unending night making a grotesque collection of hearts, which he cut out of one, three, nine people. And when he had a dozen, he took them and laid them as road markers on one of the wide boulevards that never were used by vehicles, for the people of this City had no need of vehicles.

Oddly, the City did not clean up the hearts. Nor were the people vanishing any longer. He was able to move with relative impunity, hiding only when he saw large groups that might be searching for him. But *something* was happening in the City. (Once, he heard the peculiar sound of metal grating on metal, the *skrikkk* of plastic cutting into plastic—and he instinctively knew it was the sound of a machine malfunctioning.)

He found a woman bathing, and tied her up with strips of his own garments, and cut off her legs at the knees and left her still sitting up in the swirling crimson bath, screaming as she bled away her life. The legs he took with him.

When he found a man hurrying to get out of the night, he pounced on him, cut his throat and sawed off the arms. He replaced the arms with the bath-woman's legs.

And it went on and on, for a time that had no measure. He was showing them what evil could produce. He was showing them their immorality was silly beside his own.

But one thing finally told him he was winning. As he lurked in an antiseptically pure space between two low aluminum-cubes, he heard a voice that came from above him and around him and even from inside him. It was a public announcement, broadcast by whatever mental communications system the people of the City on the edge of the World used.

OUR CITY IS PART OF US. WE ARE PART OF OUR CITY. IT RESPONDS TO OUR MINDS AND WE CONTROL IT. THE GESTALT THAT WE HAVE BECOME IS THREATENED. WE HAVE AN ALIEN FORCE WITHIN THE CITY AND WE ARE GEARING TO LOCATE IT. BUT THE MIND OF THIS MAN IS STRONG. IT IS BREAKING DOWN THE FUNCTIONS OF THE CITY. THIS ENDLESS NIGHT IS AN EXAMPLE. WE MUST ALL CONCENTRATE. WE MUST ALL CONSCIOUSLY FOCUS OUR THOUGHTS TO MAINTAINING THE CITY. THIS THREAT IS OF THE FIRST ORDER. IF OUR CITY DIES, WE DIE.

It was not an announcement in those terms, though that was how Jack interpreted it. The message was much longer and much more complex, but that was what it meant, and he knew he was winning. He was destroying them. Social reform was laughable, they had said. He would show them.

And so he continued with his lunatic pogrom. He butchered and slaughtered and carved them wherever he found them, and they could not vanish and they could not escape and they could not stop him. The collection of hearts grew to fifty and seventy and then a hundred.

He grew bored with hearts and began cutting out their brains. The collection grew.

For numberless days it went on, and from time to time in the clean, scented autoclave of the City, he could hear the sounds of screaming. His hands were always sticky.

Then he found van Cleef, and leaped from hiding in the darkness to bring her down. He raised the living blade to drive it into her breast, but she

van ished

He got to his feet and looked around. van Cleef reappeared ten feet from him. He lunged for her and again she was gone. To reappear ten feet away. Finally, when he had struck at her half a dozen times and she had escaped him each time, he stood panting, arms at sides, looking at her.

And she looked back at him with disinterest.

"You no longer amuse us," she said, moving her lips.

Amuse? His mind whirled down into a place far darker than any he had known before, and through the murk of his blood-lust he began to realize. It had all been for their amusement. They had *let* him do it. They had given him the run of the City and he had capered and gibbered for them.

Evil? He had never even suspected the horizons of that word. He went for her, but she disappeared with finality.

He was left standing there as the daylight returned. As the City cleaned up the mess, took the butchered bodies and did with them what it had to do. In the freezer chambers the gelatin caps were returned to their niches, no more inhabitants of the City need be thawed to provide Jack the Ripper with utensils for his amusement of the sybarites. His work was truly finished.

He stood there in the empty street. A street that would *always* be empty to him. The people of the City had all along been able to escape him, and now they would. He was finally and completely the clown they had shown him to be. He was not evil, he was pathetic.

He tried to use the living blade on himself, but it dissolved into motes of light and wafted away on a breeze that had blown up for just that purpose.

Alone, he stood there staring at the victorious cleanliness of this Utopia. With their talents they would keep him alive, possibly alive forever, immortal in the possible expectation of needing him for amusement again someday. He was stripped to raw essentials in a mind that was no longer anything more than jelly matter. To go madder and madder, and never to know peace or end or sleep.

He stood there, a creature of dirt and alleys, in a world as pure as the first breath of a baby.

"My name isn't Jack," he said softly. But they would never know his real name. Nor would they care. *"My name isn't Jack!"* he said loudly. No one heard.

"MY NAME ISN'T JACK, AND I'VE BEEN BAD, VERY BAD, I'M AN EVIL PERSON BUT MY NAME ISN'T JACK!" he screamed, and screamed, and screamed again, walking aimlessly down an empty street, in plain view, no longer forced to prowl. A stranger in the City.

Along the Scenic Route

The blood-red Mercury with the twin-mounted 7.6 mm Spandaus cut George off as he was shifting lanes. The Merc cut out sharply, three cars behind George, and the driver decked it. The boom of his gas-turbine engine got through George's baffling system without difficulty, like a fist in the ear. The Merc sprayed JP-4 gook and water in a wide fan from its jet nozzle and cut back in, a matter of inches in front of George's Chevy Piranha.

George slapped the selector control on the dash, lighting YOU STUPID BASTARD, WHAT DO YOU THINK YOU'RE DOING and I HOPE YOU CRASH & BURN, YOU SON OF A BITCH. Jessica moaned softly with uncontrolled fear, but George could not hear her: he was screaming obscenities.

George kicked it into Overplunge and depressed the selector button extending the rotating buzzsaws. Dallas razors, they were called, in the repair shoppes. But the crimson Merc pulled away doing an easy 115.

"I'll get you, you beaver-sucker!" he howled.

The Piranha jumped, surged forward. But the Merc was already two dozen car-lengths down the Freeway. Adrenaline pumped through George's system. Beside him, Jessica put a hand on his arm. "Oh, forget it, George; it's just some young snot," she said. Always conciliatory.

"My masculinity's threatened," he murmured, and hunched over the wheel. Jessica looked toward heaven, wishing a bolt of lightning had come from that location many months past, striking Dr. Yasimir directly in his Freud, long before George could have picked up psychiatric justifications for his awful temper.

"Get me Collision Control!" George snarled at her.

Jessica shrugged, as if to say *here we go again*, and dialed CC on the peek. The smiling face of the Freeway Sector Control Operator blurred green and yellow, then came into sharp focus. "Your request, sir?"

"Clearance for duel, Highway 101, northbound."

"Your license number, sir?"

"XUPD 88321," George said. He was scanning the Freeway, keeping the blood-red Mercury in sight, obstinately refusing to stud on the tracking sights.

"Your proposed opponent, sir?"

"Red Mercury GT. '88 model."

"License, sir."

"Just a second." George pressed the stud for the instant replay and the last ten miles rewound on the Sony Backtracker. He ran it forward again till he caught the instant the Merc had passed him, froze the tape, and got the number. "MFSC 90909."

"One moment, sir."

George fretted behind the wheel. "*Now* what the hell's holding her up? Whenever you want service, they've got problems. But boy, when it comes tax time—"

The Operator came back and smiled. "I've checked our master Sector grid, sir, and I find authorization may be permitted, but I am required by law to inform you that your proposed opponent is more heavily armed than yourself."

George licked his lips. "What's he running?"

"Our records indicate 7.6 mm Spandau equipment, bulletproof screens and coded optionals."

George sat silently. His speed dropped. The tachometer fluttered, settled.

"Let him go, George," Jessica said. "You know he'd take you."

Two blotches of anger spread on George's cheeks. "Oh, yeah!?!" He howled at the Operator, "Get me a confirm on that Mercury, Operator!"

She blurred off, and George decked the Piranha: it leaped forward. Jessica sighed with resignation and pulled the drawer out from beneath her bucket. She unfolded the g-suit and began stretching into it. She said nothing, but continued to shake her head.

"We'll *see*!" George said.

"Oh, George, when will you ever grow up?"

He did not answer, but his nostrils flared with barely restrained anger.

The Operator smeared back and said, "Opponent confirms, sir. Freeway Underwriters have already cross-filed you as mutual beneficiaries. Please observe standard traffic regulations, and good luck, sir."

She vanished, and George set the Piranha on sleepwalker as he donned his own g-suit. He overrode the sleeper and was back on manual in moments.

"Now, you stuffer, *now* let's see!" 100. 110. 120.

He was gaining rapidly on the Merc now. As the Chevy hit 120, the mastercomp flashed red and suggested crossover. George punched the selector and the telescoping arms of the buzzsaws retracted into the axles, even as the buzzsaws stopped whirling. In a moment they been drawn back in, now merely fancy decorations in the hubcaps. The wheels retracted into the underbody of the Chevy and the air-cushion took over. Now the Chevy skimmed along, two inches above the roadbed of the Freeway.

Ahead, George could see the Merc also crossing over to air-cushion. 120. 135. 150.

"George, this is crazy!" Jessica said, her face in that characteristic shrike expression. "You're no hot-rodder, George. You're a family man, and this is the family car!"

George chuckled nastily. "I've had it with these fuzzfaces. Last year . . . you remember last year? . . . you remember when that punk stuffer ran us into the abutment? I swore I'd never put up with that kind of thing again. Why'd'you think I had all the optionals installed?"

Jessica opened the tambour doors of the glove compartment and slid out the service tray. She unplugged the jar of anti-flash salve and began spreading it on her face and hands. "I *knew* I shouldn't have let you put that laser thing in this car!" George chuckled again. Fuzz-faces, punks, rodders!

George felt the Piranha surge forward, the big reliable stirling engine recycling the hot air for more and more efficient thrust. Unlike the Merc's inefficient kerosene system, there was no exhaust emission from the nuclear power plant, the external combustion engine almost noise-less, the big radiator tailfin in the rear dissipating the tremendous heat, stabilizing the car as it swooshed along, two inches off the roadbed.

George knew he would catch the blood-red Mercury. Then one smartass punk was going to learn he couldn't flout law and order by running decent citizens off the Freeways!

"Get me my gun," George said.

Jessica shook her head with exasperation, reached under George's bucket, pulled out his drawer and handed him the bulky .45 automatic in its breakaway upside-down shoulder rig. George studded in the sleeper, worked his arms into the rig, tested the oiled leather of the holster, and when he was satisfied, returned the Piranha to manual.

"Oh, God," Jessica said, "John Dillinger rides again."

"Listen!" George shouted, getting more furious with each stupidity she offered. "If you can't be of some help to me, just shut your damned mouth. I'd put you out and come back for you, but I'm in a duel . . . can you understand that? I'm in a duel!" She murmured a yes, George, and fell silent.

There was a transmission queep from the transceiver. George studded it on. No picture. Just vocal. It had to be the driver of the Mercury, up ahead of them. Beaming directly at one another's antennae, using a tightbeam directional, they could keep in touch: it was a standard trick used by rods to rattle their opponents.

"Hey, Boze, you not really gonna custer me, are you? Back'm, Boze. No bad trips, true. The kid'll drop back, hang a couple of biggies on ya, just to teach ya little lesson, letcha swimaway." The voice of the driver was hard, mirthless, the ugly sound of a driver used to being challenged.

"Listen, you young snot," George said, grating his words, trying to sound more menacing than he felt, "I'm going to teach *you* the lesson!"

The Merc's driver laughed raucously.

"Boze, you *de*-mote me, true!"

"And stop calling me a bozo, you lousy little degenerate!"

"Ooooo-weeee, got me a thrasher this time out. Okay, Boze, you be custer an' I'll play arrow. Good shells, baby Boze!"

The finalizing queep sounded, and George gripped the wheel with hands that went knuckle-white. The Merc suddenly shot away from him. He had been steadily gaining, but now as though it had been springloaded, the Mercury burst forward, spraying gook and water on both sides of the forty-foot lanes they were using. "Cut in his afterburner," George snarled. The driver of the Mercury had injected water into the exhaust for added thrust through the jet nozzle. The boom of the Merc's big, noisy engine hit him, and George studded in the rear-mounted propellors to give him more speed. 175. 185. 195.

He was crawling up the line toward the Merc. Gaining, gaining. Jessica pulled out her drawer and unfolded her crash-suit. It went on over the g-suit, and she let George know what she thought of his turning their Sunday Drive into a kamikaze duel.

He told her to stuff, and did a sleeper, donned his own crash-suit, applied flash salve, and lowered the bangup helmet onto his head.

Back on manual he crawled, crawled, till he was only fifty yards behind the Mercury, the gas-turbine vehicle sharp in his tinted windshield. "Put on your goggles . . . I'm going to show that punk who's a bozo . . ."

He pressed the stud to open the laser louvers. The needle-nosed glass tube peered out from its bay in the Chevy's hood. George read the power drain on his dash. The MHD power generator used to drive the laser was charging. He remembered what the salesman at Chick Williams Chevrolet had told him, pridefully, about the laser gun, when George had inquired about the optional.

Dynamite feature, Mr. Jackson. Absolutely sensational. Works off a magneto hydro dynamic power generator. Latest thing in defense armament. You know, to achieve sufficient potency from a CO_2 *laser, you'd need a glass tube a mile long. Well, sir, we both know* that's *impractical, to say the least, so the project engineers at Chevy's big Bombay plant developed the "stack" method. Glass rods baffled with mirrors—360 feet of stack, the length of a football field . . . plus end-zones. Use it three ways. Punch a hole right through their tires at any speed under a hundred and twenty. If they're running a GT, you can put that hole right into the kerosene fuel tank, blow them off the road. Or, if they're running a stirling, just heat the radiator. When the radiator gets hotter than the engine, the whole works shuts down. Dynamite. Also . . . and this is with proper CC authorization, you can go straight for the old jugular. Use the beam on the driver. Makes a neat hole. Dynamite!*

"I'll take it," George murmured.

"What did you say?" Jessica asked.

"Nothing."

"George, you're a family man, not a rodder!"

"Stuff it!"

Then he was sorry he'd said it. She meant well. It was simply that . . . well, a man had to work hard to keep his balls. He looked sidewise at her. Wearing the Armadillo crash-suit, with its overlapping discs of ceramic material, she looked like a ferryflight pilot. The bangup hat hid her face. He wanted to apologize, but the moment had arrived. He locked the laser on the Merc, depressed the fire stud, and a beam of blinding light flashed from the hood of the Piranha. With the Merc on air-cushion, he had gone straight for the fuel tank.

But the Merc suddenly wasn't in front of him. Even as he had fired, the driver had sheered left into the next forty-foot-wide lane, and cut speed drastically. The Merc dropped back past them as the Pirahna swooshed ahead.

"He's on my back!" George shouted.

The next moment Spandau slugs tore at the hide of the Chevy. George slapped the studs, and the bulletproof screens went up. But not before pingholes had appeared in the beryllium hide of the Chevy, exposing the boron fiber filaments that gave the car its lightweight maneuverability. "Stuffer!" George breathed, terribly frightened. The driver was on his back, could ride him into the ground.

He swerved, dropping flaps and skimming the Piranha back and forth in wide arcs, across the two lanes. The Merc hung on. The Spandaus chattered heavily. The screens would hold, but what else was the driver running? What were the "coded optionals" the CC Operator had mentioned?

"Now see what you've gotten us into!"

"Jess, shut up, shut up!"

The transceiver queeped. He studded it on, still swerving. This time the driver of the Merc was sending via microwave video. The face blurred in.

He was a young boy. In his teens. Acne.

"Punk! Stinking punk!" George screamed, trying to swerve, drop back, accelerate. Nothing. The blood-red Merc hung on his tailfin, pounding at him. If one of those bullets struck the radiator tailfin, ricocheted, pierced to the engine, got through the lead shielding around the reactor. Jessica was crying, huddled inside her Armadillo.

He was silently glad she was in the g-suit. He would try something illegal in a moment.

"Hey, Boze. What's your slit look like? If she's creamy'n'nice I might letcha drop her at the next getty, and come back for her later. With your insurance, baby, and my pickle, I can keep her creamy'n'nice."

"Fuzzfaced punk! I'll see you dead first!"

"You're a real thrasher, old dad. Wish you well, but it's soon over. Say bye-bye to the nice rodder. You gonna die, old dad!"

George was shrieking inarticulately.

The boy laughed wildly. He was up on something. Ferro-coke, perhaps. Or D4. Or merryloo. His eyes glistened blue and young and deadly as a snake.

"Just wanted you to know the name of your piledriver, old dad. *You* can call me Billy . . ."

And he was gone. The Merc slipped forward, closer, and George had only a moment to realize that this Billy could not possibly have the money to equip his car with a laser, and that was a godsend. But the Spandaus were hacking away at the bulletproof screens. They weren't meant for extended punishment like this. Damn that Detroit iron!

He had to make the illegal move *now*.

Thank God for the g-suits. A tight turn, across the lanes, in direct contravention of the authorization. And in a tight turn, without the g-suits, doing—he checked the speedometer and tach—250 mph, the blood slams up against one side of the body. The g-suits would squeeze the side of the body where the blood tried to pool up. They would live. If . . .

He spun the wheel hard, slamming down on the accelerator. The Merc slewed sidewise and caught the turn. He never had a chance. He pulled out of the illegal turn, and their positions were the same. But the Merc had dropped back several car-lengths. Then from the transceiver there was a queep and he did not even stud in as the Police Copter overhead tightbeamed him in an authoritative voice:

"XUPD 88321. Warning! You will be in contravention of your dueling authorization if you try another maneuver of that sort! You are warned to keep to your lanes and the standard rules of road courtesy!"

Then it queeped, and George felt the universe settling like silt over him. He was being killed by the system.

He'd have to eject. The seat would save him and Jessica. He tried to tell her, but she had fainted.

How did I get into this? he pleaded with himself. *Dear God, I swear if you get me out of this alive I'll never never never go mad like this again. Please God.*

Then the Merc was up on him again, pulling up *alongside!*

The window went down on the passenger side of the Mercury, and George whipped a glance across to see Billy with his lips skinned back from his teeth under the windblast and acceleration, aiming a .45 at him. Barely thinking, George studded the bumpers.

The super-conducting magnetic bumpers took hold, sucked Billy into his magnetic field, and they collided with a crash that shook the .45 out of the rodder's hand. In the instant of collision, George realized he had made his chance, and dropped back. In a moment he was riding the Merc's tail again.

Naked barbarism took hold. He wanted to kill now. Not crash the other, not wound the other, not stop the other—*kill the other!* Messages to God were forgotten.

He locked-in the laser and aimed for the windshield bubble. His sights caught the rear of the bubble, fastened to the outline of Billy's head, and George fired.

As the bolt of light struck the bubble, a black spot appeared, and remained for the seconds the laser touched. When the light cut off, the black spot vanished. George cursed, screamed, cried, in fear and helplessness.

The Merc was equipped with a frequency-sensitive laserproof windshield. Chemicals in the windshield would "go black," opaque at certain frequencies, momentarily, anywhere a laser light touched them. He should have known. A duelist like this Billy, trained in weaponry, equipped for whatever might chance down a Freeway. Another coded optional. George found he was crying, piteously, within the cavern of his bangup hat.

Then the Merc was swerving again, executing a roll and dip that George could not understand, could not predict. Then the Merc dropped speed suddenly, and George found himself almost running up the jet nozzle of the blood-red vehicle.

He spun out and around, and Billy was behind him once more, closing in for the kill. He sent the propellers to full spin and reached for eternity. 270. 280. 290.

Then he heard the sizzling, and jerked his head around to see the back wall of the car rippling. *Oh my God,* he thought, in terror, *he can't afford a laser, but he's got an inductor beam!*

The beam was setting up strong local eddy currents in the beryllium hide of the Chevy. He'd rip a hole in the skin, the air would whip through, the car would go out of control.

George knew he was dead.

And Jessica.

And all because of this punk, this rodder fuzzface!

The Merc closed in confidently.

George thought wildly. There was no time for anything but the blind plunging panic of random thought. The speedometer and the tach agreed. They were doing 300 mph.

Riding on air-cushions.

The thought slipped through his panic.

It was the only possibility. He ripped off his bangup hat, and fumbled Jessica's loose. He hugged them in his lap with his free hand, and managed to stud down the window on the driver's side. Instantly, a blast of wind and accelerated air skinned back his lips, plastered his cheeks hollowly, made a death's head of Jessica's features. He fought to keep the Chevy stable, gyro'd.

Then, holding the bangup hats by their straps, he forced them around the edge of the window where the force of his speed jammed them against the side of the Chevy. Then he let go. And studded up the window. And braked sharply.

The bulky bangup hats dropped away, hit the roadbed, rolled directly into the path of the Merc. They disappeared underneath the blood-red car, and instantly the vehicle hit the Freeway. George swerved out of the way, dropping speed quickly.

The Merc hit with a crash, bounced, hit again, bounced and hit, bounced and hit. As it went past the Piranha, George saw Billy caroming off the insides of the car.

He watched the vehicle skid, wheelless, for a quarter of a mile down the Freeway before it caught the inner breakwall of the lane-divider, shot high in the air, and came down turning over. It landed on the bubble, which burst, and exploded in a flash of fire and smoke that rocked the Chevy.

At three hundred miles per hour, two inches above the Freeway, riding on air, anything that broke up the air bubble would be a lethal weapon. He had won the duel. That Billy was dead.

George pulled in at the next getty, and sat in the lot. Jessica came around finally. He was slumped over the wheel, shaking, unable to speak.

She looked over at him, then reached out a trembling hand to touch his shoulder. He jumped at the infinitesimal pressure, felt through the g- and crash-suits. She started to speak, but the peek queeped, and she studded it on.

"Sector Control, sir." The Operator smiled.

He did not look up.

"Congratulations, sir. Despite one possible infraction, your duel has been logged as legal and binding. You'll be pleased to know that the occupant of the car you challenged was rated number one in the entire Central and Eastern Freeway circuit. Now that Mr. Bonney has been finalized, we are entering your name on the dueling records. Underwriters have asked us to inform you that a check will be in the mails to you within twenty-four hours.

"Again, sir, congratulations."

The peek went dead, and George tried to focus on the parking lot of the neon and silver getty. It had been a terrible experience. He never wanted to use a car that way again. It had been some other George, certainly not him.

"I'm a family man," he repeated Jessica's words. "And this is just a family car . . . I . . ."

She was smiling gently at him. Then they were in each other's arms, and he was crying, and she was saying that's all right, George, you had to do it, it's all right.

And the peek queeped.

She studded it on and the face of the Operator smiled back at her. "Congratulations, sir, you'll be pleased to know that Sector Control already has fifteen duel challenges for you.

"Mr. Ronnie Lee Hauptman of Dallas has asked for first challenge, and is, at this moment, speeding toward you with an ETA of 6:15 this evening. In the event Mr. Hauptman does not survive, you have waiting challenges from Mr. Fred Bull of Chatsworth, California . . . Mr. Leo Fowler of Philadelphia . . . Mr. Emil Zalenko of . . ."

George did not hear the list. He was trying desperately, with clubbed fingers, to extricate himself from the strangling folds of g- and crash-suits. But he knew it was no good. He would have to fight.

In the world of the Freeway, there was no place for a walking man.

The Author wishes to thank Mr. Ben Bova, formerly of the Avco Everett Research Laboratory (Everett, Massachusetts), for his assistance in preparing the extrapolative technical background of this story.

The Song the Zombie Sang

(with Robert Silverberg)

From the fourth balcony of the Los Angeles Music Center the stage was little more than a brilliant blur of constantly changing chromatics—stabs of bright green, looping whorls of crimson. But Rhoda preferred to sit up there. She had no use for the Golden Horseshoe seats, buoyed on their grab-grav plates, bobbling loosely just beyond the fluted lip of the stage. Down there the sound flew off, flew up and away, carried by the remarkable acoustics of the Center's Takamuri dome. The colors were important, but it was the sound that really mattered, the patterns of resonance bursting from the hundred quivering outputs of the ultracembalo.

And if you sat below, you had the vibrations of the people down there—

She was hardly naïve enough to think that the poverty that sent students up to the top was more ennobling than the wealth that permitted access to a Horseshoe; yet even though she had never actually sat through an entire concert down there, she could not deny that music heard from the fourth balcony was purer, more affecting, lasted longer in the memory. Perhaps it *was* the vibrations of the rich.

Arms folded on the railing of the balcony, she stared down at the rippling play of colors that washed the sprawling proscenium. Dimly she was aware that the man at her side was saying something. Somehow responding didn't seem important. Finally he nudged her, and she turned to him. A faint, mechanical smile crossed her face. "What is it, Laddy?"

Ladislas Jirasek mournfully extended a chocolate bar. Its end was ragged from having been nibbled. "Man cannot live by Bekh alone," he said.

"No, thanks, Laddy." She touched his hand lightly.

"What do you see down there?"

"Colors. That's all."

"No music of the spheres? No insight into the truths of your art?"

"You promised not to make fun of me."

He slumped back in his seat. "I'm sorry. I forget sometimes."

"Please, Laddy. If it's the liaison thing that's bothering you, I—"

"I didn't say a word about liaison, did I?"

"It was in your tone. You were starting to feel sorry for yourself. Please don't. You know I hate it when you start dumping guilt on me."

He had sought an official liaison with her for months, almost since the day they had met in Contrapuntal 301. He had been fascinated by her, amused by her, and finally had fallen quite hopelessly in love with her. Still she kept just beyond his reach. He had had her, but had never possessed her. Because he did feel sorry for himself, and she knew it, and the knowledge put him, for her, forever in the category of men who were simply not for long-term liaison.

She stared down past the railing. Waiting. Taut. A slim girl, honey-colored hair, eyes the lightest gray, almost the shade of aluminum. Her fingers lightly curved as if about to pounce on a keyboard. Music uncoiling eternally in her head.

"They say Bekh was brilliant in Stuttgart last week," Jirasek said hopefully.

"He did the Kreutzer?"

"And Timijian's Sixth and *The Knife* and some Scarlatti."

"Which?"

"I don't know. I don't remember what they said. But he got a ten-minute standing ovation, and *Der Musikant* said they hadn't heard such precise ornamentation since—"

The houselights dimmed.

"He's coming," Rhoda said, leaning forward. Jirasek slumped back and gnawed the chocolate bar down to its wrapper.

Coming out of it was always gray. The color of aluminum. He knew the charging was over, knew he'd been unpacked, knew when he opened his eyes that he would be at stage right, and there would be a grip ready to roll the ultracembalo's input console onstage, and the filament gloves would be in his right-hand jacket pocket. And the taste of sand on his tongue, and the gray fog of resurrection in his mind.

Nils Bekh put off opening his eyes.

Stuttgart had been a disaster. Only he knew how much of a disaster. Timi would have known, he thought. He would have come up out of the audience during the scherzo, and he would have ripped the gloves off my hands, and he would have cursed me for killing his vision. And later they would have gone to drink the dark, nutty beer together. But Timijian was dead. Died in '20, Bekh told himself. Five years before me.

I'll keep my eyes closed, I'll dampen the breathing. Will the lungs to suck more shallowly, the bellows to vibrate rather than howl with winds. And they'll think I'm malfunctioning, that the zombianic response wasn't triggered this time. That I'm still dead, really dead, not—

"Mr. Bekh."

He opened his eyes.

The stage manager was a thug. He recognized the type. Stippling of unshaved beard. Crumpled cuffs. Latent homosexuality. Tyrant to everyone backstage except, perhaps, the chorus boys in the revivals of Romberg and Friml confections.

"I've know men to develop diabetes just catching a matinee," Bekh said.

"What's that? I don't understand."

Bekh waved it away. "Nothing. Forget it. How's the house?"

"Very nice, Mr. Bekh. The houselights are down. We're ready."

Bekh reached into his right-hand jacket pocket and removed the thin electronic gloves, sparkling with their rows of minisensors and pressors. He pulled the right glove tight, smoothing all wrinkles. The material clung like a second skin. "If you please," he said. The grip rolled the console onstage, positioned it, locked it down with the dogging pedals, and hurried offstage left through the curtains.

Now Bekh strolled out slowly. Moving with great care: tubes of glittering fluids ran through his calves and thighs, and if he walked too fast the hydrostatic balance was disturbed and the nutrients didn't get to his brain. The fragility of the perambulating dead was a nuisance, one among many. When he reached the grab-grav plate he signalled the stage manager. The thug gave the sign to the panel-man, who passed his fingers over the color-coded keys, and the grab-grav plate rose slowly, majestically. Up through the floor of the stage went Nils Bekh. As he emerged, the chromatics keyed sympathetic vibrations in the audience, and they began to applaud.

He stood silently, head slightly bowed, accepting their greeting. A bubble of gas ran painfully through his back and burst near his spine. His lower lip twitched slightly. He suppressed the movement. Then he stepped off the plate, walked to the console, and began pulling on the other glove.

He was a tall, elegant man, very pale, with harsh brooding cheekbones and a craggy, massive nose that dominated the flower-gentle eyes, the thin mouth. He looked properly romantic. An important artistic asset, they told him when he was starting out, a million years ago.

As he pulled and smoothed the other glove, he heard the whispering. When one has died, one's hearing becomes terribly acute. It made listening to one's own performances that much more painful. But he knew what the whispers were all about. Out there someone was saying to his wife:

"Of course he doesn't *look* like a zombie. They kept him in cold till they had the techniques. *Then* they wired him and juiced him and brought him back."

And the wife would say, "How does it work, how does he keep coming back to life, what is it?"

And the husband would lean far over on the arm of his chair, resting his elbow, placing the palm of his hand in front of his mouth and looking warily around to be certain that no one would overhear the blurred inaccuracies he was about to utter. And he would try to tell his wife about the residual electric charge of the brain cells, the persistence of the motor responses after death, the lingering mechanical vitality on which they had seized. In vague and rambling terms he would speak of the built-in life-support system that keeps the brain flushed with necessary fluids. The surrogate hormones, the chemicals that take the place of blood. "You know how they stick an electric wire up a frog's leg, when they cut it off. Okay. Well, when the leg jerks, they call that a galvanic response. Now if you can get a whole *man* to jerk when you put a current through him—not really jerking, I mean that he walks around, he can play his instrument—"

"Can he think too?"

"I suppose. I don't know. The brain's intact. They don't let it decay. What they do, they use every part of the body for its mechanical function—the heart's a pump, the lungs are bellows—and they wire in a bunch of contacts and leads, and then there's a kind of twitch, an artificial burst of life—of course, they can keep it going only five, six hours, then the fatigue-poisons start to pile up and clog the lines—but that's long enough for a concert, anyway—"

"So what they're really doing is they take a man's brain, and they keep it alive by using his own body as the life-support machine," the wife says brightly. "Is that it? Instead of putting him into some kind of box, they keep him in his own skull, and do all the machinery inside his body—"

"That's it. That's it exactly, more or less. More or less."

Bekh ignored the whispers. He had heard them all hundreds of times before. In New York and Beirut, in Hanoi and Knossos, in Kenyatta and Paris. How fascinated they were. Did they come for the music, or to see the dead man walk around?

He sat down on the player's ledge in front of the console, and laid his hands along the metal fibers. A deep breath: old habit, superfluous, inescapable. The fingers already twitching. The pressors seeking the keys. Under the close-cropped gray hair, the synapses clicking like relays. Here, now. Timijian's Ninth Sonata. Let it soar. Bekh closed his eyes and put his shoulders into his work, and from the ring of outputs overhead came the proper roaring tones. There. It has begun. Easily, lightly, Bekh rang in the harmonics, got the sympathetic pipes vibrating, built up the texture of sound. He had not played the Ninth for two years. Vienna. How long is two years? It seemed hours ago. He still heard the reverberations. And duplicated them exactly; this performance differed from the last one no more than one playing of a recording differs from another. An image sprang into his mind: a glistening sonic cube sitting at the console in place of a man. Why do they need me, when they could put a cube in the slot and have the same thing at less expense? And I could rest. And I could rest. There. Keying in the subsonics. This wonderful instrument! What if Bach had known it? Beethoven? To hold a whole world in your fingertips. The entire spectrum of sound, and the colors, too, and more: hitting the audience in a dozen senses at once. Of course, the music is what matters. The frozen, unchanging music. The pattern of sounds emerging now as always, now as he had played it at the premiere in '19. Timijian's last work. Decibel by decibel, a reconstruction of my own performance. And look at them out there. Awed. Loving. Bekh felt tremors in his elbows; too tense, the nerves betraying him. He made the necessary compensations. Hearing the thunder reverberating from the fourth balcony. What is this music all about? Do I in fact understand any of it? Does the sonic cube comprehend the B Minor Mass that is recorded within itself? Does the amplifier understand the symphony it amplifies? Bekh smiled. Closed his eyes. The shoulders surging, the wrists supple. Two hours to go. Then they let me sleep again. Is it fifteen years, now? Awaken, perform, sleep. And the adoring public cooing at me. The women who would love to give themselves to me. Necrophiliacs? How could they even want to touch me? The dryness of the tomb on my skin. Once there were women, yes, Lord, yes! Once. Once there was life, too. Bekh leaned back and swept forward. The old virtuoso swoop; brings down the house. The chill in their spines. Now the sound builds toward the end of the first movement. Yes, yes, so. Bekh opened the topmost bank of outputs and heard the audience respond, everyone sitting up suddenly as the new smash of sound cracked across the air. Good old Timi: a wonderful sense of the theatrical. Up. Up. Knock them back in their seats. He smiled with satisfaction at his own effects. And then the sense of emptiness. Sound for its own sake. Is this what music means? Is this a masterpiece? I know nothing any more. How tired I am of playing for them. Will they applaud? Yes, and stamp their feet and congratulate one another on having been lucky enough to hear me tonight. And what do they know? What do I know. I am dead. I am nothing. I am nothing. With a demonic two-handed plunge he hammered out the final fugal screams of the first movement.

* * *

Weatherex had programmed mist, and somehow it fit Rhoda's mood. They stood on the glass landscape that swept down from the Music Center, and Jirasek offered her the pipe. She shook her head absently, thinking of other things. "I have a pastille," she said.

"What do you say we look up Inez and Treat, see if they want to get something to eat?"

She didn't answer.

"Rhoda?"

"Will you excuse me, Laddy? I think I want to be all by myself for a while."

He slipped the pipe into his pocket and turned to her. She was looking through him as if he were no less glass than the scene surrounding them. Taking her hands in his own, he said, "Rhoda, I just don't understand. You won't even give me time to find the words."

"Laddy—"

"No. This time I'll have my say. Don't pull away. Don't retreat into that little world of yours, with your half-smiles and your faraway looks."

"I want to think about the music."

"There's more to life than music, Rhoda. There has to be. I've spent as many years as you working inside my head, working to create something. You're better than I am, you're maybe better than anyone I've ever heard, maybe even better than Bekh some day. Fine: you're a great artist. But is that all? There's something more. It's idiocy to make your art your religion, your whole existence."

"Why are you doing this to me?"

"Because I love you."

"That's an explanation, not an excuse. Let me go, Laddy. Please."

"Rhoda, art doesn't mean a damn thing if it's just craft, if it's just rote and technique and formulas. It doesn't mean anything if there isn't love behind it, and caring, and commitment to life. You deny all that. You split yourself and smother the part that fires the art . . ."

He stopped abruptly. It was not the sort of speech a man could deliver without realizing, quickly, crushingly, how sententious and treacly it sounded. He dropped her hands. "I'll be at Treat's, if you want to see me later." He turned and walked away into the shivering reflective night.

Rhoda watched him go. She suspected there were things she should have said. But she hadn't said them. He disappeared. Turning, she stared up at the overwhelming bulk of the Music Center, and began slowly to walk toward it.

"Maestro, you were exquisite tonight,"' the pekinese woman said in the Green Room. "Golden," added the bullfrog sycophant. "A joy, I cried, really cried," trilled the birds. Nutrients bubbled in his chest.

He could feel valves flapping. He dipped his head, moved his hands, whispered thankyous. Staleness settled grittily behind his forehead. "Superb." "Unforgettable." "Incredible." Then they went away and he was left, as always, with the keepers. The man from the corporation that owned him, the stage manager, the packers, the electrician. "Perhaps it's time," said the corporation man, smoothing his mustache lightly. He had learned to be delicate with the zombie.

Bekh sighed and nodded. They turned him off.

"Want to get something to eat first?" the electrician said. He yawned. It had been a long tour, late nights, meals in jetports, steep angles of ascent and rapid re-entries.

The corporation man nodded. "All right. We can leave him here for a while. I'll put him on standby." He touched a switch.

The lights went off in banks, one by one. Only the nightlights remained for the corporation man and the electrician, for their return, for their final packing.

The Music Center shut down.

In the bowels of the self-contained system the dust-eaters and a dozen other species of cleanup machines began stirring, humming softly.

In the fourth balcony, a shadow moved. Rhoda worked her way toward the downslide, emerging in the center aisle of the orchestra, into the Horseshoe, around the pit, and onto the stage. She went to the console and let her hands rest an inch above the keys. Closing her eyes, catching her breath. I will begin my concert with the Timijian Ninth Sonata for Unaccompanied Ultracembalo. A light patter of applause, gathering force, now tempestuous. Waiting. The fingers descending. The world alive with her music. Fire and tears, joy, radiance. All of them caught in the spell. How miraculous. How wonderfully she plays. Looking out into the darkness, hearing in her tingling mind the terrible echoes of the silence. Thank you. Thank you all so much. Her eyes moist. Moving away from the console. The flow of fantasy ebbing.

She went on into the dressing room and stood just within the doorway, staring across the room at the corpse of Nils Bekh in the sustaining chamber, his eyes closed, his chest still, his hands relaxed at his sides. She could see the faintest bulge in his right jacket pocket where the thin gloves lay, fingers folded together.

Then she moved close to him, looked down into his face, and touched his cheek. His beard never grew. His skin was cool and satiny, a peculiarly feminine texture. Strangely, through the silence, she remembered the sinuous melody of the *Liebestod*, that greatest of all laments, and rather than the great sadness the passage always brought to her, she felt herself taken by anger. Gripped by frustration and disappointment, choked by betrayal, caught in a seizure of violence. She wanted to rake the pudding-smooth skin of his face with her nails. She wanted to pummel him. Deafen him with screams. Destroy him. For the lie. For the lies, the many lies, the unending flow of lying notes, the lies of his life after death.

Her trembling hand hovered by the side of the chamber. Is this the switch?

She turned him on.

He came out of it. Eyes closed. Rising through a universe the color of aluminum. Again, then. Again. He thought he would stand there a moment with eyes closed, collecting himself, before going onstage. It got harder and harder. The last time had been so bad. In Los Angeles, in that vast building, balcony upon balcony, thousands of blank faces, the ultracembalo such a masterpiece of construction. He had opened the concert with Timi's Ninth. So dreadful. A sluggish performance, note-perfect, the tempi flawless, and yet sluggish, empty, shallow. And tonight it would happen again. Shamble out on stage, don the gloves, go through the dreary routine of recreating the greatness of Nils Bekh.

His audience, his adoring followers. How he hated them! How he longed to turn on them and denounce them for what they had done to him. Schnabel rested. Horowitz rested. Joachim rested. But for Bekh there was no rest. They had not allowed him to go. Oh, he could have refused to let them sustain him. But he had never been that strong. He had had strength for the loveless, lightless years of living with his music, yes. For that there had never been enough time. Strong was what he had had to be. To come from where he had been, to learn what had to be learned, to keep his skills once they were his. Yes. But in dealing with people, in speaking out, in asserting himself . . . in short, having courage . . . no, there had been very little of that. He had lost Dorothea, he had acceded to Wizmer's plans, he had borne the insults Lisbeth and Neil and Cosh—ah, gee, Cosh, was he still alive?—the insults they had used to keep him tied to them, for better or worse, always worse. So he had gone with them, done their bidding, never availed himself of his strength—if in fact there was strength of that sort buried somewhere in him—and in the end even Sharon had despised him.

So how could he go to the edge of the stage, stand there in the full glare of the lights and tell them what they were? Ghouls. Selfish ghouls. As dead as he was, but in a different way. Unfeeling, hollow.

But if he could! If he could just once outwit the corporation man, he would throw himself forward and he would shout—

Pain. A stinging pain in his cheek. His head jolted back; the tiny pipes in his neck protested. The sound of flesh on flesh echoed in his mind. Startled, he opened his eyes. A girl before him. The color of aluminum, her eyes. A young face. Fierce. Thin lips tightly clamped. Nostrils flaring. Why is she so angry? She was raising her hand to slap him again. He threw his hands up, wrists crossed, palms forward, to protect his eyes. The second blow landed more heavily than the first. Were delicate things shattering within his reconstructed body?

The look on her face! She hated him.

She slapped him a third time. He peered out between his fingers, astonished by the vehemence of her eyes. And felt the flooding pain, and felt the hate, and felt a terribly wonderful sense of life for just that one moment. Then he remembered too much, and he stopped her.

He could see as he grabbed her swinging hand that she found his strength improbable. Fifteen years a zombie, moving and living for only seven hundred four days of that time. Still, he was fully operable, fully conditioned, fully muscled.

The girl winced. He released her and shoved her away. She was rubbing her wrist and staring at him silently, sullenly.

"If you don't like me," he asked, "why did you turn me on?"

"So I could tell you I know what a fraud you are. These others, the ones who applaud and grovel and suck up to you, they don't know, they have no idea, but *I* know. How can you do it? How can you have made such a disgusting spectacle of yourself?" She was shaking. "I heard you when I was a child," she said. "You changed my whole life. I'll never forget it. But I've heard you lately. Slick formulas, no real insight. Like a machine sitting at the console. A player piano. You know what player pianos were, Bekh. That's what you are."

He shrugged. Walking past her, he sat down and glanced in the dressing-room mirror. He looked old and weary, the changeless face changing now. There was a flatness to his eyes. They were without sheen, without depths. An empty sky.

"Who are you?" he asked quietly. "How did you get in here?"

"Report me, go ahead. I don't care if I'm arrested. Someone had to say it. You're shameful! Walking around, pretending to make music—don't you see how awful it is? A performer is an interpretative artist, not just a machine for playing the notes. I shouldn't have to tell you that. An interpretative artist. Artist. Where's your art now? Do you see beyond the score? Do you grow from performance to performance?"

Suddenly he liked her very much. Despite her plainness, despite her hatred, despite himself. "You're a musician."

She let that pass.

"What do you play?" Then he smiled. "The ultracembalo, of course. And you must be very good."

"Better than you. Clearer, cleaner, deeper. Oh, God, what am I doing here? You *disgust* me."

"How can I keep on growing?" Bekh asked gently. "The dead don't grow."

Her tirade swept on, as if she hadn't heard. Telling him over and over how despicable he was, what a counterfeit of greatness. And then she halted in midsentence. Blinking, reddening, putting hands to lips. "Oh," she murmured, abashed, starting to weep. "Oh. *Oh!*" She went silent.

It lasted a long time. She looked away, studied the walls, the mirror, her hands, her shoes. He watched her. Then, finally, she said, "What an arrogant little snot I am. What a cruel foolish bitch. I never stopped to think that you—that maybe—I just didn't think—" He thought she would run from him. "And you won't forgive me, will you? Why should you? I break in, I turn you on, I scream a lot of cruel nonsense at you—"

"It wasn't nonsense. It was all quite true, you know. Absolutely true." Then, softly, he said, "Break the machinery."

"Don't worry. I won't cause any more trouble for you. I'll go, now. I can't tell you how foolish I feel, haranguing you like that. A dumb little puritan puffed up with pride in her own art. Telling *you* that you don't measure up to my ideals. When I—"

"You didn't hear me. I asked you to break the machinery."

She looked at him in a new way, slightly out of focus. "What are you talking about?"

"To stop me. I want to be gone. Is that so hard to understand? You, of all people, should understand that. What you say is true, very very true. Can you put yourself where I am? A thing, not alive, not dead, just a thing, a tool, an implement that unfortunately thinks and remembers and wishes for release. Yes, a player piano. My life stopped and my art stopped, and I have nothing to belong to now, not even the art. For it's always the same. Always the same tones, the same reaches, the same heights. Pretending to make music, as you say. Pretending."

"But I can't—"

"Of course you can. Come, sit down, we'll discuss it. And you'll play for me."

"Play for you?"

He reached out his hand and she started to take it, then drew her hand back. "You'll have to play for me," he said quietly. "I can't let just anyone end me. That's a big, important thing, you see. Not just anyone. So you'll play for me." He got heavily to his feet. Thinking of Lisbeth, Sharon, Dorothea. Gone, all gone now. Only he, Bekh, left behind, some of him left behind, old bones, dried meat. Breath as stale as Egypt. Blood the color of pumice. Sounds devoid of tears and laughter. Just sounds.

He led the way, and she followed him, out onto the stage, where the console still stood uncrated. He gave her his gloves, saying, "I know they aren't yours. I'll take that into account. Do the best you can." She drew them on slowly, smoothing them.

She sat down at the console. He saw the fear in her face, and the ecstasy, also. Her fingers hovering over the keys. Pouncing. God, Timi's Ninth! The tones swelling and rising, and the fear going from her face. Yes. Yes. He would not have played it that way, but yes, just so. Timi's notes filtered through *her* soul. A striking interpretation. Perhaps she falters a little, but why not? The wrong gloves, no preparation, strange circumstances. And how beautifully she plays. The hall fills with sound. He ceases to listen as a critic might; he becomes part of the music. His own fingers moving, his muscles quivering, reaching for pedals and stops, activating the pressors. As if he plays through her. She goes on, soaring higher, losing the last of her nervousness. In full command. Not yet a finished artist, but so good, so wonderfully good! Making the mighty instrument sing. Draining its full resources. Underscoring this, making that more lean. Oh, yes! He is in the music. It engulfs him. Can he cry? Do the tearducts still function? He can hardly bear it, it is so beautiful. He has forgotten, in all these years. He has not heard anyone else play for so long. Seven hundred four days. Out of the tomb. Bound up in his own meaningless performances. And now this. The rebirth of music. It was once like this all the time, the union of composer and instrument and performer, soul-wrenching, all-encompassing. For him. No longer. Eyes closed, he plays the movement through to its close by way of her body, her hands, her soul. When the sound dies away, he feels the good exhaustion that comes from total submission to the art.

"That's fine," he said, when the last silence was gone. "That was very lovely." A catch in his voice. His hands were still trembling; he was afraid to applaud.

He reached for her, and this time she took his hand. For a moment he held her cool fingers. Then he tugged gently, and she followed him back into the dressing room, and he laid down on the sofa, and he told her which mechanisms to break, after she turned him off, so he would feel no pain. Then he closed his eyes and waited.

"You'll just—go?" she asked.

"Quickly. Peacefully."

"I'm afraid. It's like murder."

"I'm dead," he said. "But not dead enough. You won't be killing anything. Do you remember how my playing sounded to you? Do you remember why I came here? Is there life in me?"

"I'm still afraid."

"I've earned my rest," he said. He opened his eyes and smiled. "It's all right. I like you." And, as she moved toward him, he said, "Thank you."

Then he closed his eyes again.

She turned him off.

* * *

Then she did as he had instructed her.

Picking her way past the wreckage of the sustaining chamber, she left the dressing room. She found her way out of the Music Center—out onto the glass landscape, under the singing stars, and she was crying for him.

Laddy. She wanted very much to find Laddy now. To talk to him. To tell him he was almost right about what he'd told her. Not entirely, but more than she had believed . . . before. She went away from there. Smoothly, with songs yet to be sung.

And behind her, a great peace had settled. Unfinished, at last the symphony had wrung its last measure of strength and sorrow.

It did not matter what Weatherex said was the proper time for mist or rain or fog. Night, the stars, the songs were forever.

KNOX

In Germany they first came for the Communists and I didn't speak up because I wasn't a Communist. Then they came for the Jews, and I didn't speak up because I wasn't a Jew. Then they came for the trade unionists, and I didn't speak up because I wasn't a trade unionist. Then they came for the Catholics, and I didn't speak up because I was a Protestant. Then they came for me—and by that time no one was left to speak up.

—PASTOR MARTIN NIEMÖLLER

They flushed the niggers from underground bunkers, out near the perimeter, and Charlie Knox killed his because he thought the boogie was going for a gun. As it turned out, he wasn't: but Knox didn't know that when he let fly.

Earlier that day Knox had gone to a fitness session and the ward Captain had reprimanded him for haste in firing. "These aren't shoot-outs, Knox. The idea is to level the weapon and point it in the right direction, not blow off your own leg. Now take it again. Another hour on the range, Saturday."

Even earlier than day, Knox had had lunch with his wife; he had done the cooking himself, and they had discussed how difficult it had become to get fresh vegetables, particularly carrots, since the new emergency measures had been put into effect. "But it's *necessary*," Brenda had said. "At least until the President can get things under control again." Knox had said something about radicals and Brenda had said, *you can say that again*.

And at the start of that day, Knox had found sealed instructions from the Patriotism Party in his readout tray at work. He slit open the red, white and blue plastic packet and saw he was scheduled for an operation that night.

Now they came up out of the ground like potato bugs, black and fat from living off starches, and clouds of infiltration gas billowed out after them. Knox's flushing team waited with truncheons raised, catching the first two across the skulls with beautiful backswings. They dropped, half in and half out of the hole, and the flushers grabbed them by their collars. They pulled them out fast and slung them across the grass so those who followed wouldn't find the passage blocked.

They hadn't counted on more than a couple of exit holes. Suddenly the ground started to erupt spooks and they were jumping up and out all around the team. The flushers let their truncheons hang by the lanyards and went to more effective weaponry. Knox saw Ernie Buscher unship his scattergun and blow two of the jigs to pieces as they scrambled out of the ground. Pieces of nigger meat went east in a spray.

That was the moment when an owl hooted in a tree off to Knox's right, and he turned his head to look. "Behind you, Charlie!" Knox heard Ted Beckwith's warning. He turned back from the owl sound and right behind him the turf had popped open and there was a dinge crawling out like an earthworm. There wasn't enough moon to see what he looked like, but Knox took a swing with his truncheon and missed. "Stop!" he yelled, but the jig went right on getting to his feet and blundering away. "I said: stop, nigguh!"

And the boogie half-turned, and in the dim light Knox thought he was reaching inside his jumper jacket for a gun. Knox reacted with twice his best drill speed, had the banger off its velcro pad and working before the shine could pull his hand out of his clothes. The spook's head opened up like a piece of overripe fruit and Knox was startled to see the stuff inside sparkled in the night. Then it went all over the place.

"Oh my God," Knox said. He heard his voice as though it had come from someone standing very close beside him; but it had been himself.

He heard the words repeating themselves, fading away, dimmer and dimmer, a canyon echo disappearing in his mind.

There was firing going on all around him now. The bright golden flashes of scatterguns and bangers lighting up the clearing and reflecting off the perimeter. Then suddenly there was the shrill whistle of the ward Captain's warning, three shorts and a long, and the blasting became more sporadic, then finally stopped.

"All right, you men! That's enough! No one authorized—*this!* Now knock it off, right this minute. We'll take these people in."

Knox realized he was standing where he had been standing for a long time. Ted Beckwith came to him and said, "You okay, Charlie?"

After a few moments Knox turned his head to stare into Beckwith's really handsome face, and he heard that self that was himself saying, "My God, he just split open . . ."

Charlie Knox is. A man.

Who.

Stands 1.9 meters, weighs 191 pounds, has brown wavy hair cut short, squints slightly out of brown eyes, wears a mustache that is thick and brown and is kept neatly trimmed but not obsessively so, works out with 50 lb. barbells twice a day for ten minutes each session, drinks milk when he can get it and nothing but water when he can't, has had whooping cough, measles, mumps, chicken pox and twice broken his left forearm but otherwise is healthy.

He is thirty years old, does not like rings or other jewelry, has been married to Brenda for nine years, has two children (Rebecca, 8 and Ben, 7), never wears a hat, likes cold weather, shuffles his feet through the fallen leaves when he walks, has perfect pitch when he sings, likes to whistle, has never read a book all the way through, joined the Party two years ago at the compulsory outside age limit, has a diamond-shaped birthmark on his right thigh, and never learned to swim.

There are many things about the past Knox cannot remember. If. He ever knew them.

"Charlie?"

"Yeah?"

"Do you love me as much today as you did when we were married?"

"Sure."

"As much as, or more than?"

"Same."

"Not even a little less or more?"

"Nope. Exactly the same."

"How can that be?"

"I don't like changing a good thing."

"Oh, *you*."

Then there was silence for a few minutes.

Then:

"You've started having bad dreams."

"How do you know?"

"You talk in your sleep."

"What do I say?"

"I can't make it out, a lot of it. But you whimper."

"I don't whimper."

"It sure sounds that way, Charlie."

Silence.

"Brenda, you ever wonder where the materiel comes from?"

"What?"

"The materiel. That stuff we make on the line?"
"I don't know, Charlie; it's *your* job."
Silence.
"You going over to the ward tonight?"
"For a while."
"What are you reading?"
"Names. I'm memorizing."
Silence, as Knox memorizes. He almost has it down perfect now. He's been memorizing for weeks. Nigger, spook, jig, coon, shade, dinge, spade, shine, boogie, darkie, burrhead; sheenie, mockie, hebe, yid, shonicker, kike; greaser, beaner, chili-belly, pocho, spic, wetback, meskin, halapecker; wop, guinea, dago, mackerel-snapper, bead-counter, poper, ring-kisser, vattik; kraut, dog-eater, redskin, gut-eater, polack, bohunk, mick, frog, limey, canuck, nip, chink, slanteye, gook, slope, creamer, dink, splib, shater, jungle bunny, christ-killer.
"What's all that you're memorizing?"
"Just some stuff."
Silence.
"I don't think you love me."
"I love you."
"Then why don't you pay some attention to me?"
"I want to get ahead in the Party."
Silence.
"I love you. I really do."
"I know. It's just sometimes you ignore me."
"I want to get ahead in the Party."
Silence.
"What do I say?"
"When?"
"When I'm dreaming?"
"I don't know. I wake up and say something and you go back to sleep."
"Do I ever talk about anything in particular?"
"That man you killed."
"I don't talk about that."
"I wouldn't lie about that to you, Charlie. You do."
"No."
Silence.
"I wonder where it all comes from."
Silence.
"Are you unhappy, Charlie?"
"No, I'm okay."
"Why don't you stay home tonight?"
"I can't. I want to get ahead in the Party."
Silence.

"But I love you, Brenda. Honest to God, I do."
"Sometimes I think you're chasing something."
"I'll see you later. I'll wake you when I come in."

On the assembly line, two weeks later, Knox was fitting rectangular green blocks into the appropriate rectangular holes in yellow bases, when the Line Supervisor stopped to congratulate him.

"Heard you had your first kill a couple of weeks ago, Knox," he said. He waved to the next man on the line to pick up the beat while Knox talked. "Heard you really comported yourself like a champ. Top stuff, Knox."

Knox smiled shyly. He had never really learned to accept compliments graciously. "Thanks, Mr. Hale."

The music playing in the background was Sousa's *Washington Post March*, interpreted by the Oval Office Strings. It swirled softly through the air above the assembly line, and Knox found his speech-patterns keeping time.

"Knox," Hale said, "come on over here where we can talk. I want to talk to you about something."

Knox unbuckled his harness and slid out of the formfit. He followed the Line Supervisor to a corner of the manufactory, near the towering stacks of assembled block/bases, ready for disassembling and re-feed input at the other end of the line.

"You know that guy, works two down on your right?" Hale asked. He was looking at Knox closely; very closely. Knox sensed his answer had to contain just the right tone.

"Quint?"

"Quintana, you mean."

Hale had snapped the response in so quickly, Knox did not have a chance to say *yeah, I know him, I've talked to him a few times, seems a nice enough guy*. Now, he did not say it, though Hale was clearly waiting for him to say something.

"Changed his name?"

Hale nodded, with meaning.

"Oh," Knox said, softly. He looked around as if trying to orient himself.

"Have you, uh, ever heard him say anything . . . ?" Hale let the sentence trail off, but its directional indicator was blinking.

"Anything . . . what . . . ?"

"Well, anything . . . peculiar. Troublesome, you know what I mean?"

Quite suddenly, Knox knew *precisely* what Hale meant. "I don't talk to him much. I keep to myself a lot."

Hale pursued it. "But you *have* talked to him? You *have* heard him say things, is that it?"

Knox's mind was racing. "Nothing very much, just . . ."

"Just what?"

"Just about the line's speed, that's all."

"When was that?"

"Oh, hell, Mr. Hale, I don't remem—"

"Could that have been a month ago, when we had that pile-up and the line had to be stopped for an hour?"

"Well, I don't know, exactly, it *could* have been."

"Be sure, Knox. We don't want you indicting a man on a guess." He was watching Knox like a shrike.

Indicting. The word burned in Knox's mind. But if Hale was asking these questions—and Hale was a ward lieutenant in the Party—there must be a good reason. Knox let his thoughts roll back quickly. Quint. Correction: Quintana. Man doesn't change his name unless he has something to hide. "Quintana." That was a foreign name if ever he'd heard one. Probably a chili-belly. And, yes, Quint . . . ana *had* been saying all that about how fast the line moved, and how it didn't seem to serve any real purpose, fitting the block/bases together just to take them apart and put them together again . . . and that had been the same week of the pile-up, Knox was now sure of it. And the more thought he gave it, the clearer it became to him that Quint*ana* was not what he seemed to be. Those little eyes, that way he moved his hands when he slipped the blocks into the holes.

"I'm sure."

"Knox," said Hale, and he was smiling tightly now, "you aren't just another average Party hanger-on. You've got spunk. Come see me over at the ward office one evening."

And he walked away.

Knox returned to his formfit, buckled in, and took up the beat. But he kept half a watch on Quintana, down there on the right.

And when the conveyor belt began to jerk and stutter, Knox looked immediately: at Quintana: at the overflow of blocks piling up in front of him: at the base with the defective holes into which Quintana was trying to hand-hammer a green block. So it was true. Quintana *was* a disrupter.

Someone yelled, "Get him!"

Knox was unbuckled and out of his formfit in a moment. Perhaps because he had been already alerted by his talk with Hale. Others were stumbling out of their assembly line trance, beginning to mill around looking for who the "get him" might be. But Knox knew!

He found a loading dock truck behind his station—it hadn't been there earlier—but it was there now—someone must have left it, contrary to regulations—and he wrenched loose the long iron rod that served as control handle for the truck. It was only three steps, three long steps, and he was standing over Quintana, who was desperately trying to clear away the pile-up.

Knox swung from the hips. The rod caught Quintana across the shoulders and he was jacked forward over the line. He half-twisted, throwing up his hands to protect his head, as Knox came around on the backswing.

The rod smashed across Quintana's throat, and his head skewed around till Knox heard cartilage snap. Then the others were there, dragging Quintana from his formfit.

They beat him, the ones in the back forcing away the ones in the front so everyone could have a chance, but in the end, it was Knox himself, Knox with the iron rod, who stood spraddle-legged over the disrupter, that greaser, and arched back till his stomach muscles were drumhead tight, the rod gripped perfectly with both hands, right thumb tucked inside left palm, and brought it straight back up and over and down, and crushed Quintana's skull with an impact sound like a dead fish hitting a plastic countertop.

Then Knox flipped the rod into a corner, stood over the dead beaner and looked around with a tight expression. "He won't fuck *us* up again. Let's get back to work."

As he buckled in, he looked across the manufactory, and Mr. Hale was staring at him. He smiled, proud.

Mr. Hale winked and gave him a "V".

Charlie Knox. Is a man. Who.

Is lying in bed dreaming.

He is dreaming about men in black garments coming for him. Hold that. They aren't men. Yes, they are. No.

Charlie Knox cannot tell if they are men or not.

He *thinks* (in the dream) that they are men, but they don't walk like men. There is some small alien movement—the way a lizard scurries, stops, scurries is alien; the way a chicken bobs, catches up, bobs is alien—the way their limbs are hinged. But they are men. No. They *must* be men.

No. Definitely.

"Charlie!"

Silence.

"Charlie, wake up, you're crying, Charlie!"

"I'm not, I'm okay, what, what's that . . . uh?"

"You were crying in your sleep."

"It was the coffee."

"Who is Quintana, Charlie?"

"Nobody. A guy. Nobody."

"Charlie, something awful is happening to you."

"Shut up, Brenda. Let me sleep."
Silence.
"Oh, God."
"Come, Charlie. Lie over here."
"Hold me."
"Don't cry."
Silence.

They stood outside the little kike's store, waiting till the woman had looked at all the rotisseries and decided against any of them. They waited until she left, then Knox and Ernie Buscher went in.

"Mr. Kapp," Ernie said, "I've come for my sofa and easy chair suite. My friend and I got a truck outside."

Kapp was in his sixties. When he looked confused, his face became a cartographer's delight. "Suite, you say? What was the name, do you mind?"

"Buscher," said Ernie. Then he spelled it. "You said you'd have it ready today."

"Today? Saturday? I got no deliveries on Saturday. Are you sure it was a Saturday, you're sure?"

"C'mon, Kapp," Ernie said, his voice getting deeper, "don't play jew-down with me. I paid you, you said today, now gimme my furniture." Ernie's eyes narrowed down, his jaw muscles tensed, he made a fist, let it relax, made it again. Ernie was unreliable, moved too fast.

The sheenie was nervous. "If you'll wait just a minute, I'll check my order book. When was it you said you bought this merchandise?"

"Don't give me any shit, kike, get my stuff out here on the double before I kick your guts out!"

Kapp started to say something about the language being used, but Ernie needed no further provocation. He had enough for the investigation by the Party, right there on his recorder-tip. As Kapp raised his right hand to wave a finger in Ernie's face, Ernie grabbed the hand and broke it. It was too fast for Knox, but it was on, so he went with it.

"Try to slug my friend, you kike sonofabitch," he said, very loud and very clear so the tip would pick it up, "how about *this*!" He whipped the link-chain belt off his waist with a smooth movement and brought it down across Kapp's thin shoulders with a crack. The sharpened links ripped cloth and broke skin. Kapp screamed, and Ernie fell back to let Knox work.

Knox felt a sudden, blossoming joy in his mission, and using a chain was too impersonal, too removed. He went at the little mockie with his fists.

Ernie Buscher threw a table through the front window, into the street. Knox held Kapp with his left hand around the sheenie's throat, the drumming heels an inch off the floor, the trembling body against the wall. Steadily and smoothly, as though gauging the rebound of the big bag down in the gym, Knox jacked one punch after another into Kapp's face; right cheekbone, nose, left cheekbone, nose, jaw, nose—and it broke—left cheek, right cheek, nose, nose, nose. The sound of the table shattering the front window, and its impact in the street, brought the others on the run.

They poured the kerosene over the breakfronts and dinette sets and ottomans and recliners. They tossed chairs into a pile in the center of the store, and yelled for Watson to bring the jellybomb.

"C'mon, Knox!" Ernie yelled. Knox put two final blows into Kapp's ruined face, then slung the little kike over his shoulder and carried him to the mound of shattered furniture in the center of the store. He flipped him over, and Kapp fell across the edge of a broken table. His spine cracked with a sound like borax furniture.

Then Knox followed the others outside, Watson handed him the jellybomb, because it was Knox's mission, and Knox pulled the tab, and slung the pill underhand, through the broken window.

They stood on the opposite side of the street, and when the first rush of heat came at them, they turned away to avoid getting their eyeballs singed. It was like a sirocco, then a whump of pressure and bits of what was inside the store, including Kapp, came slicing out through the broken front window. Flames slashed after the shrapnel, and erupted into the street. Then the entire building went up.

"Damn!" Knox said. A piece of glass had cut him across the back of his left hand. "Damn!"

Charlie Knox is a man who.

Refuses to ask the necessary questions.

And even if he could, he wouldn't. But he can't. That's been made sure of. He can't. Doesn't even know. They exist.

Those questions. And other things.

Training is very important for Charlie Knox. For Knox, training is important. To stay fit. To stay tough. Because.

That means.

Survival. And survival sometimes means getting a little cruel. Weakness kills.

And then the persons in black garments come and.

No.

There are no such things. Those are dreams. Those are delusions. Those are guilt. Those are fantasies. Those don't happen. Those persons in black garments, when the sky opens and they come in.

No.

Think about it. No.

*   *   *

"Why are you looking at me like that?"

"Like what?"

"You know like what!"

"It's your imagination."

"You keep doing that to me now, all the time."

"I'm not doing anything, shut up."

"You never talked to me like that."

"I always talk the same."

"You don't. You're different. You've changed, you're changing."

"Shut up."

"You're like an animal now, Charlie. You scare me."

"Maybe that's what you need. To be scared. Maybe that'd shape you up."

"What are you talking about!?!"

"Don't yell at me, I'll clip you one."

"Charlie, honey, what're you doing? You *scare* me."

"Stop crying . . . I'm sorry. Honest to God, I'm sorry. It's just, oh, you know. There's another purge coming on at the ward."

"But what's that got to do with me?"

Silence.

"Charlie?"

"Nothing. Stop crying."

"Do you love me?"

Ted Beckwith was Knox's best friend. They joined the Party together, their wives exchanged secrets regularly, their kids went on camping trips out near the perimeter. Beckwith hated this life of endless and senseless assembly line drudgery, mindless holovision game shows, patch-on-the-sleeve heroism and provincial hatred. Ted Beckwith was a member of the underground. Beckwith tried not to let it show: that he despised everything Knox had become. He thought, at one time, that Knox might come in with him and the others. That he would take a walk out near the perimeter, and he would reveal all of it to Knox.

"There has to be more to life than this," he thought he would say, on that day. "There has to be more than the rallies and the fitness sessions and the prayer meetings for the President's health. There has to be. The world has to be wider than what we have here, Charlie." That was what he would say to Knox, on that day. But Knox had begun to change. It had started long before the night Knox killed his poor black nobody. It had been long before that. But on the night of the raid, the change had begun to accelerate. And then that business with Quint. Poor devil: he hadn't been involved with anyone. Just too inept to keep up his beat on the line. But Knox was forming anew, even then. And it had gone on.

Now Ted Beckwith knew Knox was one of them, one of the heroes with a patch on his sleeve. Now he could never tell him. Ted Beckwith had to go on being Knox's best friend, and he despised him.

Ted Beckwith did not think Knox knew about his secret involvement with the underground.

Beckwith was wrong.

Ted Beckwith came home. Knox watched from cover. As he walked up the front steps of his little house, Beckwith saw a terrible thing, a thing he could not believe. He had a dog, a beautiful dog, a golden retriever. As he walked up the steps of his house, he stopped and stared, because he could not believe what he saw. Tears came into his eyes and filled them; he slumped down on the top step, crying without being able to stop. Someone had held his beautiful dog by the throat, up against the wooden wall of the house, and had driven a long, thick nail through the throat and into the wood. The nail had been driven in, hammered in, all the way to the head. The nail head gleamed brightly through the fur, reflecting in the porch light. Knox could see it all the way across the street. The dog's four paws had been nailed to the wall. The dog had voided itself as it died, and the wall was smeared.

Beckwith sat there, refusing to look at the terrible thing nailed to his front porch wall.

After a long time, he got up and went inside. The house was dark. Knox saw the living room light go on; through the front window he saw Beckwith staring at the living room wall, at a thing more terrible than the dead animal outside.

Nailed to the wall, the same way his dog had been nailed, Beckwith saw, all in a row, his wife's best dress, his daughter's playsuit, and his son's T-shirt and jeans. All nailed to the wall at eye-level. The implications of the message were clear. Knox had intended it to be clear; Beckwith understood.

His family was having dinner down the street at Knox's house. He was supposed to join them as soon as he had cleaned up after work. He knew who was responsible for this.

Knox was responsible for it.

The Party would simply have killed him. But Knox must have said, let me take care of it, Ted Beckwith is my best friend, I will deactivate him.

Knox has said, with nails: Stop what you are doing. Stop right now. This minute. Or I will do what the Party wants me to do. I am giving you this humane and merciful break because I am your best friend. Now wash up and come to my house for dinner.

Turn off the porch light.

Knox was in on the raid at the high school. He was a squad leader, with three patches and a service commendation. He took the leader of the rebellion, a sixteen year old girl, to the bell tower of the high school, and raped her three times, and then threw her off.

Knox was made a Party Lieutenant and gathered the proof of revisionism that removed Hale from the ward. Knox took the contract on him. He also delivered the eulogy at the grinder ceremony.

Knox headed up the assault team on the Western Quadrant. He wore leather protective garments, moved through a cloud of infiltration gas, used a scattergun exclusively, and joyed in moving meticulously from sector to sector, street to street, house to house, room to room, slaughtering anything that moved or crawled or whimpered or pleaded or twitched. His promotion to Captain and ward selectman followed soon after.

Knox spent his recreation hours in the ward temple's interrogation chambers, quizzing malcontents. He began to collect fingers. They retained their look much longer than ears or cocks.

Knox spent three years getting ahead, but he hardly noticed the passage of time, it flew so fast.

Charlie Knox. Is. A man who.

Had been trained.

"Not me, Charlie . . . *please*, Charlie, what are you doing, not *me*!"

"Stop backing away. I'll make it quick."

Across the bedroom. She picked up a pink mule with a pompon pouf on the toe. He followed. With the knife. She raised the bedroom slipper over her head, heel turned toward Knox threateningly.

"There's a mistake, Charlie!"

"No mistake."

"It wasn't *my* name on the list, honey, please!"

"They don't make mistakes."

A shoe is no damned defense.

"Charlie, not *me*, I love you, honey . . ."

He. Stops.

He. Sees movement out of the. Corner. Of his eye.

He looks for the first time.

"Not *me*, Charlie!"

His conditioning. Breaks.

Persons in black garments. There.

They have always been there. Now he sees. Them.

They stood watching Knox as he backed his wife into the corner at knife point.

"Oh, my God . . . Brenda! Do you see them?"

"Please, Charlie . . ."

"No, it's okay, I won't hurt you . . . do you *see* them?"

"See who, Charlie?"

Silence from them. Knox stared at them, fully, openly. And he realized they had been there often, watching him, on the raid, in the manufactory, in the furniture store, as he drove nails, in the bell tower, as he got ahead in the Party. They had *always* been there.

"I'm starting to remember, a lot of it is coming back."

"Charlie, what're you talking about . . . don't hurt me, honey."

"Brenda, listen: right there, standing right there, don't you see them?"

"I don't see anything, Charlie; are you all right? You wanna lay down a while, Charlie? The kids won't be home for a couple hours."

"I don't know where they came from, another world I guess, but *that* doesn't matter. They're training us, to go out there for them, out there somewhere. But we weren't cruel enough. They took up where we left ourselves off."

She lowered the slipper. He was rambling on now, saying things. The persons in black garments stood watching him, and there was almost a sadness on their faces, as though they had spent a great deal of time building something intricate and lovely and efficient, and now it had broken down. Their expressions did not speak of repair.

"They gave us the work on the line, and the words, and the missions, and the President's health. When did they come? How long ago? What do they want from—"

And he stopped.

He. Knew.

Charlie Knox is. A man who:

Had been a man.

Had been trained.

To go out there where he would not have been able to survive without their training.

Charlie Knox is a man who understood what he had been.

What he had become.

What he would have to *be*.

To be. Out there.

"Oh, God . . ."

Pain. And silence. Knox looked at his wife with eyes that might have belonged to the final moments of a golden retriever.

"I won't do it."

"Won't do what, Charlie? Please, Charlie, talk sense, lie down a little."

"You know I love you, honest to *God* I do."

He turned the knife and gripped it with both hands and drove it deep into his own stomach.

For Knox, the porch light had been turned off.

* * *

She sits on the edge of the bed and cannot take her eyes from the memory of the man she lived with for nine years. The memory remains, the form on the floor is someone vaguely familiar but undeniably a stranger.

Finally, she rises, and begins to dust the room. She cleans thoroughly, mechanically, despite the dim black shapes she sees from the corner of her eye, shapes she takes to be dust. And so she cleans. Thoroughly. Mechanically.

Brenda Knox. Is. A woman who.

The only thing we have to fear on this planet is man.
—CARL GUSTAV JUNG

IX

HEART'S BLOOD

> "The search is as important as the discovery."
>
> —"Having an Affair with a Troll," New Introduction to LOVE AIN'T NOTHING BUT SEX MISSPELLED, Pyramid, 1976

It is apparent that in so much of his work, Harlan reveals himself. Sometimes it will be disguised, however thinly, by the cloak of fiction or reconstructed reminiscence; examples of this abound throughout this collection. At other times, Harlan drops virtually all of the façade and, as much as anyone can, shows us his true self. In so doing, he allows us to examine who we ourselves are, making us brave by his example. Because Harlan is not afraid to speak up.

In his writing, Harlan combines the child and the adult in his nature. He is a die-hard commentator on the human condition, a committed voice and an effective one, though he objects to such lofty and pumped-up statements. But while he would argue that he is more your die-hard rabble-rouser, your free spirit, your curmudgeon, operating out of an honest anger rather than any clear or premeditated moral purpose, it *is* tempting to see in his writing some contemporary equivalent of Bacon and Boswell, Aubrey and Defoe: a man reading and rendering his times as he sees them. But a modern voice, someone living it, not just posturing because he enjoys the role.

Harlan's commentaries are not academic texts designed to lull you into ready acceptance of their presumed facts. They are by turns hot-headed, agitprop, humane, impious, pensive and determined, doing exactly what they were meant to do: say things that Harlan believes need to be said. Clearly and precisely. Which is why they infuriate so many.

It would be easy to say the essays are a series of opinions; no more, no less. But the fact is that Harlan's opinions *do* take on the force and stature of homily—the admonitory and moralizing discourse. As we saw earlier in "Valerie," he uses his own life unstintingly, rigorously, to tell it like it was and is and probably always will be, excerpting from his experiences to make a larger point, dipping into the universal by reacting to something in the microcosm, an issue here, a point there. He may cause our blood to race when his opinions cut diametrically to ours or when the manner of the delivery is slanted to lead us where we do not want to go. When Harlan calls the shots, names the names, and moves us to see things as *he* sees them, to find for ourselves the honesty in what he says, it's difficult to ignore him.

The first piece, "From Alabamy, with Hate" (1965), appeared in one of the then-naughty men's magazines that proliferated in the 1960s, under the altered and less inflammatory title "March to Montgomery." With one Kennedy murdered, America was experiencing the confusion and the turmoil that would soon take Martin Luther King and yet another Kennedy. Harlan's condemnation of hatred and insane prejudice is shrill journalism coupled with good sense, but the "tide of history" of which he speaks rolled in mercilessly. He didn't predict what the American psyche would look like two decades later, but I don't think it's as healthy as he'd hoped.

In 1972–73, *The Harlan Ellison Hornbook* appeared as a column in the *Los Angeles Free Press*, a shining light of the "underground" press that flickered and faded with the changing times. This was Harlan's follow-up to his previous column of television criticism, *The Glass Teat*, which has survived in two durable and respected volumes. The *Hornbook* was a sort of public diary, filled with the events of Harlan's day-to-day life and his reactions to them. The two selections here, "My Father" (1972) and "My Mother" (1976) (the latter appearing in the *Saint Louis Literary Supplement*, where the column made a brief reappearance), offer us basics with which we can readily identify. They are shamelessly gutsy and revealing essays, and yet in many ways are gentler and kindlier than the crises of events might have warranted.

Straight from the heart is "Tired Old Man" (1975), which derives from a true experience at a New York writers' party where Harlan met Cornell Woolrich. Yet no one but Harlan remembered Woolrich attending. This is a straightforward, emotional portrait of one of Harlan's favorite writers, and its ending lets us share the inevitable hero-worship response.

"Gopher in the Gilly" (1982) is Harlan's recollection of the three months he worked for a third-rate carny and the three days he spent in a Missouri jail, and from it is distilled one more lesson that we already know and yet never quite seem to learn.

"Strange Wine" (1976) tells us, quite simply, that this *is* the best of all possible worlds.

You'll find no feeling of emptiness in these pieces, no careful selection of words to lull us into complacency or dull our awareness with monotone. This is passion: hot-blooded and raging, desperate and searching, but always in search of Truth. If the search is infuriating, so be it.

"I am a yapping dog with mean little teeth. I am often as wrong as you, as often silly as you, as often co-opted as you, as often sophomoric as you. But I maintain. As do you."

—"Ominous Remarks for Late in the Evening," Introduction to AN EDGE IN MY VOICE, Donning, 1985

From Alabamy, with Hate

Another Memo from Purgatory

Thursday, March 25th, 1965. A walk through the country of the blind. Montgomery, Alabama—stinking in the heat of its own decay; sweltering in the viciousness of two hundred years of murder and bigotry and moral wretchedness; poised with the invisible artifacts of its hooded aristocracy: the hemp lynch rope, the 12-gauge shotgun, the befouled "separate but equal" toilet, the electric cattle prod, the killer caravans by night and the final paycheck by day.

Poised, waiting for the outsiders to come.

The 25th of March. Fifty thousand people walking the red-mud roads of Alabama, singing; the outsiders, come to tell a crazed bigot that the Civil War was long dead, that a house divided was soon to topple, that the stain of evil that Alabama had become, would no longer be tolerated in a *United* States.

The Freedom March on Montgomery, Alabama.

A biased report.

And if you weren't marching with us, go screw yourself!

There must have been noble motives in there, somewhere. I simply couldn't think of any. Plainly, it was time to go. It was time to stop all the parlor liberalism, to stop all the high-flown clucking about heinous crimes and rotten living conditions, it was time to act. Time to pay some dues. It was *mea culpa* time, and everyone was guilty. So I went. Along with thousands from all over the country, all over the world. Every state was there, New Mexico, Indiana, New York, Florida, Ohio. Decent men and women from Hawaii, France, London, Alaska. A blind man who had walked from Georgia. A wealthy matron in furs from Beverly Hills. A one-legged hero, who walked with the Original Three Hundred, all the way from Selma where men had died just days before, to Montgomery, where a despicable racist flew the Confederate flag as a gesture of defiance, and hid behind locked doors.

This time we weren't alone. This time the Great White Father in the Great White House had spoken. He'd called together a joint session of Congress—usually reserved for State of the Union addresses and national emergencies—and he had said it for all of us. A little late, a little slow, but he'd finally said it, he'd called Wallace's bluff:

"The time of justice has now come," Lyndon B. Johnson said. "No force can hold it back." At last, for every thick red neck in the state of Alabama to hear and believe, the tide of history was being acknowledged. In a matter of hours it would begin to wash over the face of Alabama as the 50-mile trek from Selma to Montgomery was begun, and Johnson told them why: "Should we defeat every enemy, double our wealth, conquer the stars and still be unequal to this issue, then we will have failed as a people and as a nation."

He spoke for forty-five minutes, and he was interrupted by standing ovations thirty-nine times. "We shall overcome," he told them. But those were just words. Words had lifted on the air many times before. And still, the Reverend James J. Reeb had died under the clubs of thugs called police. Words had flown and yet three civil rights workers were found buried twenty-one feet beneath a Mississippi damn (sic). Like doves, the words had lifted on the breeze, and in Birmingham little children were bombed in Sunday School. Even since the march, even after all the words words words, a Detroit woman was senselessly gunned down on that same road between Selma and Montgomery. Viola Liuzzo was anothered numbered corpse.

Damn them! Damn their twisted, stunted, warped minds, their rotten and corrupted beliefs, the frenzied and hideous *doppelgängers* of Hitler's storm troopers. Even after they saw fifty thousand men and women flock to their sinkhole of a state to plead with their bodies and their time to let those people go, even so, still, with all the words, they killed again. And again. And it seems it will never stop till time has closed over the head of Man and he is no more, sunk in the ocean of forgetfulness, when there is no black, there is no white, there is no Man at all!

All this talk of Man, and on that march, so much talk of God. But where was God for the little church girls of Birmingham? Where was God for Reverend Reeb? For Mrs. Liuzzo? For all the nameless and never-known black men whose bodies have been burned and strung from ropes and violated by razor and knife and gun? Where is this God who allows hate to rule a land? I can't talk of God, I can only talk of Man.

For all I saw on that Montgomery march was man, at his most noble, at his most degraded. If you want specifics, if you need background, if you need history, it's all been recorded. This, damn them, is a personal record.

The planes left from Burbank. Three planes from the Lockheed Airport where Bogart said farewell to Ingrid Bergman in *Casablanca*. Three hundred clerics, students, actors, housewives, ribbon clerks, writers, truck drivers and poets. They had at first thought one plane would be sufficient, but two days before we were to leave, they had to lay on a second, and earlier that Thursday, a third. And still they were turning them away. The waiting room was a madhouse, people cramming against the check-in desk, don't leave me behind! Why were they fighting so hard to go? Why were they not taking this handy cop-out to avoid possible danger? Men and women who, if they had had their druthers, would gladly have gone home to bed, or to a discothèque. They fought and shoved to give their money for the flight. I was in the midst of them. I cannot answer the question.

Yet, on the plane, jammed together with total strangers, even though we were of one united cause, I felt an alienation: I was suddenly assailed by a strange and terrible thought. All these people, on this flight, flying toward brotherhood—

What if we crashed, or were marooned somewhere, and there was no food save what we had brought in our knapsacks? Wouldn't we start pummelling that dapper Negro gentleman up front there, the one with the bag of fruit? Where would be all our brotherhood then?

And I realized: the frenzy at the check-in counters, the surly shoving, the being herded together . . .

That was real! *That* was people.

What we were flying toward, silent and unknown . . . what we believed in . . . what we were going to do . . . *that* was a thought. In a frightening and inescapable way, it did not exist. And I knew, *really*: these people did not have to like each other, or love each other; they were all aliens, moving toward a dream.

But dreams cannot be populated. Only hard realities can know presence. And I felt alone.

For down there in Montgomery, Alabama, was the reality. This was the dream, and the fact that it did not exist terrified me. The ones who lived in that state, did so *all* the time, not just for a day, or a week, and then away to the hills of Hollywood where there was safety; and I grew cold thinking that we were about to invade their reality.

We were to meet the original Three Hundred who had hiked the full fifty miles on U.S. Highway 80 out of Selma. All the marchers from everywhere who had come to this spot, were to meet three miles outside the city limits, at the City of St. Jude, a hospital and school.

My first glimpse of it was chilling, for surely this must have been the impression given to the condemned of Europe when first they glimpsed Dachau or Buchenwald. Outside a high cyclone fence, members of the federalized Alabama National Guard (the Dixie [31st] Division) stood at parade-rest every fifty feet. Inside that fence, the bivouac area seemed somehow—wrong. The grounds were clotted with great clumps of people, two and three hundred in a bunch, ragtag, disordered. Mud was everywhere. The thick, sucking red mud of Alabama that had been churned to cream by thousands of feet walking over it endlessly since the day before. It was a concentration camp. Those soldiers, they weren't turned outward, to protect the people inside . . .

Once we were inside, I tried asking the troopers two questions. I walked across the empty corner far away from all the waiting people, and approached three standing together. Two walked away. "At what intervals have they spaced you out around the fence?" I asked.

"Ah don' know."

Are you elements of the federalized Alabama Guard?

"Ah don' know."

Then *he* moved away. I stared after him. God save us from men who do what they despise doing, simply because they are ordered to do it.

Later, I was to understand even more clearly my fear and horror at these Southerners pressed into a service of hatred, for the only moment of genuine danger I knew came from them.

We were to have started marching the last three miles into Montgomery and the Capitol Building at 9:00. It was eleven before we moved. Stacked up in long lines, eight abreast, we stood in the mud, waiting, and then it started to rain. It misted down on us, and the umbrellas came out, the scudgy raincoats that had been jammed in knapsacks and bedrolls. A sound truck nearby suddenly began blaring . . . a Negro comic who did lousy impressions . . . and he wouldn't stop . . . he just kept imitating Wallace, FDR, Ralph Bunche, LBJ, Dr. Paul Tillich, and every few *shticks* were interspersed with snarling references to how "whitey" was a sonofabitch. It was ill-timed, in bad taste. All of us who had come to do what we could, to serve, to offer ourselves without any of the usual white man's impetuosity to run things. We stood there, and the comic rasped at us, till there were murmurings of marching not on the Capitol, but on the sound truck.

Then the Original Three Hundred in their fluorescent orange roadworker jackets, bearing American flags, began moving out, and with a sense of elation just to be afoot, we moved out after them. Wave after wave, rank upon rank, little children clutching hands, women still carrying their brown paper bags of food, black men and white men, all teeth and flashing eyes, moving out onto the Jefferson Davis Highway. Sporadic singing broke out. We'd been on our feet four hours now. Ahead of me, one-legged Jim Letherer of Saginaw, Michigan crutch-propelled himself forward, grinning.

A group of Montgomery teenagers had fastened themselves to a small knot of us from Los Angeles, and as we marched, for the first time we heard their songs:

"In your heart you know
you're wrong . . .
In your heart you know
you're wrong . . .
In your heart you know
you're wrong . . .
In Montgomery, Ala-bam-a!"

And followed by a chant to which The Jerk could be danced. It was a strange, demanding chant—Hoop-de-hoop . . . hoop-de-hoop . . . hoop-de-hoop—and then a dire, threatening, challenging Uh. Uh. Uh. Uh. Uh. It was the old strike-breaker's chant, warning and intimidating. We're coming. We're waiting for you. We *want* you to try something . . . go ahead . . . break out that cane and cattle prod, this time we'll *see* who gets a split skull hoop-de-hoop hoop-de-hoop. Uh. Uh. Uh. Uh. Uh.

The march went down U.S. 80 and into the Negro section.

Picture every cliché of poverty and sadness. Let them steep in the cauldron of your most imaginative thoughts. They cannot approach the reality of the squalor in which the black men and women of Montgomery, Alabama live. Houses that have never seen paint, gray slatboard houses without foundations, where it isn't necessary to use a dustpan after sweeping: the dirt falls through the cracks in the floor. Where wallpaper is made of newspaper, and you can stand inside that crackerbox and feel the March wind whistle chilly in at you. There were few fat people. There was a total absence of the treasured bigot's cliché: "They live in filth, but they all got big Caddys." There were no Caddys. But there *were* desiccated old men sitting on porch steps wearing clean but threadbare clothes. There *were* tiny children with their heads bound up in silk stockings to make "the kink lie back." There *were* filthy open sewers in front of every house, because the municipal government didn't see any need for adequate sewage disposal. There *were* shockingly inadequate shopping facilities—little stores with their inevitable Coca-Cola signs that said JOHN'S GRO. under the advertisement. The only things in that section that were sharp and fresh-looking, the Coca-Cola signs. God bless American industry, the pervasive love of the Corporation!

A roadside sight: ten little tiny children, scrupulously clean, clapping their little hands and singing in small bird voices as a ten-thousand-year-old Negro man with a cane led them in "We Shall Overcome." And no smiles on their faces.

The smiling was all being done in the marching column. By the roadside, Negroes who were terrified they would be burned out, lynched or lose their jobs if they marched (as subsequent days have revealed to be accurate guesstimates), watched silently. From porches and sidewalks—euphemism for cracked bits of pale rock—they stared at the endless stream of humanity come to pledge allegiance to their cause. And as the chanting, singing masses moved past, they would suddenly burst into a moment of hand-clapping or singing, then realize Fear had settled behind them, watching, and they would subside again. It was eerie, and tragic.

A toothless old woman, lushed out of herself, ran alongside the column, chittering merrily. She grabbed at me, tried to pull me out of the line, tried to hug me, just out of sheer delight that we existed, that we were there. "C'mon in, old mother! C'mon in, there's room!" yelled Paul Robbins, the photographer who had gone down to Alabama with me. Everybody laughed, and capered, and she clapped her withered hands in childlike abandon. We passed her by, and she smiled gap-mouthed at others, who borrowed her sunshine.

A Montgomery high school girl marching beside me pointed to a beat-up commercial building with the sign LAICOS CLUB on it. "That's where we get to go for music," she said. It was a simple statement, but it was filled with hatred. That was the *one* place they were allowed to go. We turned a corner in the red mud and suddenly better pavement began.

The lower-middle-class white neighborhood. The perceptible transition from Nigger Town to Po' White Trash.

It was only a cultural half-step up from the shameful ghetto we had just left, but here we found the most vicious attitude of all . . .

[When I was in the army, stationed in Georgia, I once had a dirt-dumb White Trash PFC explain something to me. "I'm poor," he said bitterly, "real poor, as poor as y'c'n get. And I got no education, and I got nothin' back home but gettin' laid an' getting old. I ain't better than nothin', man, nothin' at all. I'm just about as bad as mud, but there's one thing I'm better than . . . I'm better than a nigger, and I intends to see it stays that way." Nutshell explanation of the Southern States Rights argument against Civil Rights.]

On a porch, a man and his wife, sipping tea, blissfully unaware of a freedom march. Their world was up there. And down on that road, there wasn't *nothin'* happening. There ain't nothing going on down here in Alabama, they said over television the preceding Sunday. Nothin' atall. What the hell did he think all that going on down on the road was? Locust?

Past a Negro school. Children hanging out of windows, screaming jubilantly, urging us forward, teachers waving, crying with joy, give 'em hell! The name of the school in bold letters: LOVELESS SCHOOL. Yeah.

Around a corner. Up on the veranda of a resident hotel, a gaggle of middle-class white women, the cream of Southern womanhood.

"Nigger-lovers!" the blonde screamed, harridan.

"Mother fu—" the words were drowned out by the chants of the "lower class" Negro marchers, "Go tell George Wallace, go tell George Wallace, go tell George Wallace, ain't no one gonna turn me around . . ."

The third woman was so overcome with hate and the bubbling inarticulateness of the need to see us all dead, corpses strewn from one end of U.S. 80 to the other, that all she could do was turn her backside to us, wiggle, and pretend to be breaking wind.

"You got nothin' but class, madame," I yelled. "K-L-A-Z." And we went past. Frightened? No, not then.

I wanted a glass of water. The sun had come out, and it was hot. "Christ, I'd like a glass of water," I murmured. "Why don't you go up on that porch and ask them white folks?" one of the kids gibed, a student from Tuskegee.

I grinned back at him. "Will it cause trouble for the march?" He shook his head, "No, but it gonna cause trouble for *you*."

I loped off out of the line as everyone in the vicinity passed the message: the white boy's goin' up to ask for a glassa water . . . he'll never get it.

Behind me, the column slowed and halted, jamming up as everyone watched, waiting for trouble, almost anxious for it, perhaps. Down the street, at the resident hotel, the klaz women craned over the railing to see what was happening. I trotted up to the front steps of the house. There were three women sitting there in chairs. "Excuse me, ma'am," I said to the fat one, "might I trouble you for a glass of water, please." She stared at me uncomprehendingly. What the hell was this Northern Jewish Communist asking her? She didn't speak, couldn't speak? "A glass of water, ma'am?" I repeated.

The redhead next to her leaned over, "He says he wants a glass of water. Please." The fat one heaved herself out of the chair, went inside the screen door. The redhead came over to me.

"We aren't all as bad as they tell you we are down here," she said, and seemed infinitely, genuinely sad about it.

"As bad as what, ma'am?" I asked, playing boyish and cute.

"Well, just like, you know, them others, like they tell you."

"Who tells me, ma'am?"

"You know. We just aren't *all* that bad, honest."

"Yes ma'am." I smiled at her. "But some of you are, and if you sit back and let them ruin your lovely state, then you're as guilty as they are. I came all the way from Hollywood, ma'am, just to see if I could help." She stared at me. I'd used a magic word. Hollywood. Then I wasn't a Communist. A black-loving Jew, probably, but not a Communist. And I had such *nice* manners, and I obviously wasn't a beatnik. The fat one came out with the water. I took a long, deep pull from the kitchen glass, and returned it. "Thank you, very very much, ma'am." I smiled, allowing the left-cheek dimple to show itself.

"You just tell 'em we gave you a glass of water," the redhead said, smiling, thinking she was sewing it up.

And if I'd been black? I thought. I didn't say it, because the idea was to show them there were other ways to do it, not to antagonize them. I loped back to the line of marchers and fell in, the line moved out again, and I repeated what had been said. They weren't all that bad down here. The Negro student turned a look of venom and truth on me. "Don't you fall for that okey-dokey," he warned me.

Hoop-de-hoop. Uh. Uh. Uh. Uh.

We turned down onto the main drag. Dexter Street. Past the Jeff Davis Hotel. The whites standing at every curb, and the rednecks, the denim-clad, white-shirted men, giving us the finger. "Where you want freedom from, boy?" a redneck murmured at me from the sidelines. "New York? Philadelphia? Chicago?" I smiled at him . . . frig you, Jack.

Past the Paramount Theatre. Elvis Presley in *Girl Happy*. "That isn't one of ours," the Negro high school girl said. My heart went cold in me. It's so easy to forget.

Past the J.J. Newberry five and dime. The second floor housed the Montgomery Citizens Council offices. They had a gigantic poster hanging out the window. It showed Martin Luther King with some other people, and it said MARTIN LUTHER KING / COMMUNIST!

Hoop-de-hoop. Hoop-de-hoop.

A white waitress in a restaurant, peering out of the window at me. I smiled at her, winked. She grinned back. We flirted. If I wanted to stay down here for a few days, I could spread the gospel, seed the populace, lift that barge, tote that bale.

The upstairs window of the Pontiac Agency. A man in a gray suit. "Go back where you come from, you mammy-jammin' nigger-lovin' sonsabitches . . . y'goddam . . ." Ah, South'n hospitality.

The kids behind us were doing a freedom chant to a tune that was ready-made for The Jerk. There was dancing in Dexter Street. Another dance. The Twine. And a third. The Shotgun. Yeah!

The last lap. As we came down to the bottom of the hill that led up to the end of the square and the Capitol, someone pointed and yelled. Atop the Capitol Building. No American flag. The Alabama State Flag, crossed diagonal red bars on a white field. And underneath: the stars and bars of the Confederacy. Governor George, Governor George, how does your arrogance grow? With shotgun shells and lynch mob yells, and flauntings of America, all in a row!

* * *

We listened to the speeches, all of them. They droned on for hours, and in the parlance of show biz, they "lost their audience." But it didn't matter, we were with them all the way. They could have recited Jabberwocky. Until Jimmy Baldwin introduced King. Baldwin had once had training as a preacher. It told. Shadrach and his kin went to the furnace once more, and from the heat came Martin Luther King, who said all there was to say. We had stood there, slumped there, lain there, sitting thousand upon thousand while the Army spotters on the rooftops stared down at us—

put a machine gun up there on the Montgomery Safety Building, another on the roof of the facing office building, and a third set of two cross-rigged in the Capitol Building, and just track across, spraying, and we could spread them nigger-loving bastards curb to curb in their own blood

—and Wallace's head thug, Al Lingo, moved around the crowd, incognito. We were pigeons, had Wallace wanted to pull another Sharpesville Massacre. Added to it was the fact that those "protecting" Alabama National Guardsmen (with their flag of the Confederacy sewn over the heart above the US Army patch) were all facing *inward,* not outward. Protection?

Footnote: I submit it was a calculated bit of strategy, mobilizing the Dixie Division. Whether as a subliminal punishment—having to guard the very people who threatened their way of life—or as a warning to the invaders that down under that khaki even the troopers were Wallace's Boys. Whichever, let it herewith be noted that every one of them was gimlet-eyed, beast-faced, thick-necked, jaws twitching with restrained fury as King lacerated their Alabama bigotry.

And the singing . . . God, the singing! Fifty thousand, led by Belafonte. George was hiding up in the Capitol, peeking through the Venetian blinds. I wonder if Governor George enjoyed the entertainment as much as he had the darkies singin' in de moonlight?

Behind me, inside the sawhorse barricades, I heard an old Negro man and his wife talking.

"It ain't never gonna be the same here again," he said.

His wife shook her head. "They ain't gonna lay down and die." Bitter realism, in the midst of a dream.

He shrugged, gently repeating, "Still, ain't never gonna be the same here again."

I pulled out a salami and a water bottle from the knapsack. Then I remembered the water bottle was empty, and borrowed one from James Goldstone, a television director who had felt it was time to pay some dues. We cut up the salami and passed it around. One of the Negro kids grinned: "Kosher?" "It was when we left L.A.," Goldstone leered. We all ate, and passed the water bottle. The Negroes would not drink after the white folk. Old horrors die slowly.

When it was over, we were directed to an empty lot where buses were supposed to come to get us, to shuttle us back to the Montgomery airport for the flight home. I had wanted to stay down several days, to see what the aftermath would be like, but they pleaded with everyone to cut out, quickly. Perhaps they knew something like what was waiting for Viola Liuzzo might befall us.

We waited in the empty lot a long, long time, three hundred and more of us. The buses did not come. The troops were spaced out all along behind us, threatening, menacing. "I want a Coke," I said to Paul Robbins. There was a gas station two blocks down. "Jeezus, don't go down there!" someone warned. There was no fear, somehow. We started walking down.

As we passed the lines of army troops, they began clicking the safety catches off their old M-1 rifles. Stupid bastards, were they trying to scare us? I knew they had no ammunition in those pieces. They weren't even wearing clip holders for spare ammo. Stupid bastards. And they muttered underbreath:

"Nigger lover."

"Go back where you come from, sonofabitch fuc—"

And one, as I passed, trying to get to the gas station, stepped out with rifle at port arms. "Where you from, boy?" he demanded. I stared at him coldly. "I'm from New York, and I'm a Colonel in the United States Army Reserve, *boy*, and if you don't want me to call your C.O. over and have him put you on charges for speaking to me, you'd better get your ass back in formation, trooper! Jump!" And he got back, and muttered surlily, "Y'gotta go around."

We walked down to the corner. I had to use the toilet. The white ones were full, both men and women. So I used the "separate but equal" facilities maintained for COLORED. I was white. That's a color.

The station owner had a thrombosis. We bought our Cokes and started back. They had closed off the street. You have to go around. Three blocks North, three blocks West, three blocks South. *Now* I was scared.

There were five of us. We started back toward the empty lot by that circuitous route, which had been predicated for no discernible reason. The others scampered. I was damned if I'd let those muthuhs rassle me around. I sauntered. "Why hurry?" I asked the Negro member of the group. "'Cause *I* can't spend the night in the Jeff Davis Hotel," he said. A telling point. I scampered.

Cars and panel trucks slithered by, with obscenities hurled out at us. "We gonna get you tonight you buncha—" We got back to the lot, shaken.

The buses had not arrived. And then the troops were pulled out. "Protection till everyone is out of Montgomery," the government had assured us. But there we were, with night falling, and a disorganized mob, trapped in an empty lot, milling about. And the cars with the rednecks, circling, circling . . .

(Chance? Coincidence? Paranoia?

(Here's what we did not know: the bus drivers had walked out on the job. They would not drive us. A bus had warped in to the curb as a young Presbyterian minister walked up the street, a block away. The door had sighed open, and the Alabama hero had leaned out. "We gonna beat the shit outta alla you mother-wording, sonofaword, word-word word word bastards tonight, y'all see we don't!" and the bus had whipped away.

(And, inexplicably, the troopers had been withdrawn.

(Chance? Coincidence? Paranoia? Maybe.)

They got three buses into service. Supplementary drivers were offered more money. The buses arrived. I dashed for one. Heroism doesn't go very far when the smell of tar is in the air.

On the ride back to the airport, jammed together, thank God, a small white-and-black dog ran out into the road. The driver could have avoided it without shaking up his passengers. He held steady. The dog was ground under the left front tire, was whipped back and bumped-bumpedbumped all the way to the rear. The driver never batted an eye. He merely glanced at his wristwatch to record the time for the report to the bus company. It was 6:06 PM.

There was more, much more. They wouldn't give us a loading ramp to get into the plane. We waited four hours. They found a bomb on the plane. It was a nine-hour flight back. Viola Liuzzo. She was killed hurrying back from Selma to Montgomery, to ferry out people left stranded in an empty lot.

It was a lot closer than I care to admit.

And now it's over. I did one day down there, that's all. No big deal, no special feat, no extra blue ribbon. One day, in a land where one Negro college boy summed it up:

"We live in a state of perpetual caution. Even on the best day, the most ordinary day, you never know when you leave your house in the morning what will happen, what little thing, some redneck on the prod, something small, that will keep you from ever coming home that night."

I was coming home, and all I could think was: "Please, please, dear God, let me the hell out of this stinking place!"

And still it happens down there. Viola Liuzzo was a white woman, and it made headlines. But the red mud of Alabama covers the corpses of hundreds of nameless black folk, who never made headlines. They never even got their names on tombstones.

Time to pay dues? Yeah, that's what it is, friends. *Mea Culpa* time in the country of the blind, our country, and we've been so blind, so long, it may be too late to see the light.

It ain't enough to say oh them poor poor people down there. It ain't enough to say well, hell, they have killings in Chicago and on the New York subways, too. It ain't enough to send a buck to SNCC or CORE. It ain't enough when you start matching up all the parlor liberalism against the body blood soaking into that Alabama countryside. It ain't enough.

The tide of history is washing higher and higher. It cannot long be held back by hooded murderers too cowardly to come out in daylight. It's coming, thank the Lord, and if you listen, you can hear the sound of it beating against the rock and crumbling walls of racism and evil . . .

Hear it? Listen closely, hear it?

Hoop-de-hoop. Hoop-de-hoop. Uh. Uh. Uh. Uh.

My Father

As if emerging from a dark dream, it suddenly occurs to me that I've spent at least half my life looking for my father.

No, don't get it wrong: I'm not a bastard. I was born in University Hospital in Cleveland, Ohio, at 2:20 PM on 27 May 1934, to Louis Laverne Ellison and Serita Rosenthal Ellison . . . so I know who my father was. And right here on my birth certificate, which I'm looking at, it asks in a little box: *Legitimate?* (Which is about as chill shot a way of asking it as I've ever seen.) But, happily for my mother and unhappily for my biographers, it says right back, and snappishly: *yes.*

So when I say I've spent half my adult life looking for my old man, I don't mean it like something out of Victor Hugo. (Though it now occurs in the wake of the first realization—and how strange that one awakening of curiosity firecrackers into other awarenesses, *seriatim*—that I've written a number of stories in which kids are looking for their fathers, for one reason or another, to suit the plot. The one that pops to mind foremost was called "No Fourth Commandment," and it was about a kid who was looking for his father, whom he'd never known, to kill him for fucking-over his mother. Sold the story after its magazine publication to *Route 66,* where it was adapted into a teleplay by a guy named Larry Marcus, and was retitled "A Gift for a Warrior." It aired on January 18th, 1963, almost a year to the day I arrived in Los Angeles from Back East, and years later Marcus and the producer of *Route 66,* Herbert Leonard, did it as the basis of their film *Going Home,* without paying me for its second adaptation, but that's another story and my attorney is in the process of talking to them about it, so let's get back to the point.)

My father died in 1949, when I was fifteen. And I'd lived with him and my mother, off and on, for those fifteen years, but I never really knew him, or even much about him. It wasn't till my mother was very ill, three or four years ago, and she thought it was all over, that she spilled some very heavy data about Louis Laverne.

There's a lot of it she won't be happy if I relate. It is silly, of course, it's all forty and more years gone, but family skeletons rattle loudest in the minds of those who live in memories, which is where my mother's at. Today is nowhere nearly as important as all the yesterdays with my father. So I won't go into the circumstances of how my father practiced dentistry in Cleveland for eleven years. That's a story for another time, years from now.

For openers, like me, my father was short man. Even shorter than me, I recall. I'm 5′5″, for the record. He was incredibly gentle: I remember once, when I'd done something outstandingly shitty as a child, he was compelled to take me into the cellar and use the "strap" on me. His belt. Now perceive, please, that there is no faintest scintilla of hatred in this recollection. He was *not* a brutal man, and about as given to corporal punishment as Albert Schweitzer. But it was a time in this country when such things were expected of a father. "You just wait till your father comes home!" was the maternal cry, and one feared with only half a fear, because I knew my Dad just couldn't do such things.

But, as I say, on one occasion the punishment fit the crime—perhaps it was the time I shoved Johnny Mummy off the garage roof while we were playing Batman and Robin—and my Dad took me down into the cellar at 89 Harmon Drive in Painesville, Ohio, and he walloped me good.

I got over the stinging in about an hour, though there was a dull remembered pain for weeks thereafter.

My father became ill. He went upstairs into his bedroom and he cried. He wasn't himself for several weeks after. Of course, I knew none of that at the time.

He was gentle, and he looked like, well, the closest way I can describe him was that he resembled a short Brian Donlevy. If you're not hip to who Brian Donlevy is, check out the *Late Late Show*.

When he was a little boy, my father worked on riverboats, as a candy butcher. From that job he got into working minstrel shows. He sang. Really fine voice, even in later years. In fact, he had his photo on the sheet music of "My Yiddishe Momma," a song Al Jolson made famous; the song was written by a friend of Dad's, who dedicated it to my father's mother . . . whom I never met. Never met my paternal grandfather, either.

Dad wanted to be a dentist, and he wound up practicing in Cleveland. Around Prohibition time. He was such a sensational dentist, I'm told, that the mob used to come to him for their mouthwork. My mother worked as his receptionist after they'd been married awhile, and she tells me when the gangsters came to get drilled and filled, my Dad insisted they check their heat with Mom. There were times, she says, when her desk drawer was difficult to pull open, so filled with guns was it.

Anyhow, you may wonder why I'm talking about all this here, the initial offering of a new column. Well, I wanted to talk about something important for openers, and almost all of this I never knew until a few days ago when my mother came to visit from Florida. I don't see much of her, and we've never really talked to each other; but she got onto the subject of my father, as she usually does, and I started prying the *real* truth out of her about him. Not the bullshit they feed kids about their parents, but who he *really* was. In all of the things I've ever written, I've said virtually nothing about my father, you see, and that's because I simply didn't know the man. We were in the same house, but we were strangers. It was as though we vibrated on different planes of existence, passing each other and passing through each other, like shadows.

But when my mother got around to telling me my father had done time in prison, in some strange and perverted way I started to realize I'd been searching for "Doc" Ellison almost all my life.

Because of the stuff I'm not allowed to tell, he had to give up the D.D.S. practice. It was Prohibition time, it was Depression time, and my Dad had to support my mother and my sister and me. So he got into the selling of booze.

Most of this is unclear because my single source of information, my mother, chooses to blur it all. But as best I can tell, my Dad had friends in Canada, and he would make auto runs up through Buffalo into Toronto to pick up the hootch. Then he'd drive it back down to Cincinnati and Cleveland and thereabouts. After a while, things got easier, and my Dad gave work to a guy he met, a guy who was as down on his luck as Dad had been. And one night, on a run, the guy got busted while transporting the alcohol. So my Dad took the rap, and let the other guy get off. As my Mom tells it, the driver had a family and well . . .

My Dad was a gentle man.

So he went to the can. Fairly stiff sentence, from what I can gather, but he didn't do it all. (And years later, when *I* wound up in jail, I was always amazed at how facilitously and soberly my mother took it, and how competent she was at bailing my ass out of the slammer. Now I understand.)

After that, my Dad went to work for my uncles in Painesville, in their jewelry store. I was a little kid at the time, and knew none of what had gone down.

Years went by, and my Dad thought he owned a piece of the store—Hughes Jewelry on the corner of State & Main in Painesville. I was too busy fighting for my life to pay much attention, and I was always running away, but then in 1947, after my Uncle Morrie had come back from the War, it turned out my father *didn't* own anything. He had been the manager of the store, had built up the clientele and won friends all through town—he was the only Jew ever taken into the Moose lodge in Painesville, a town famed for its anti-Semitism—but when the crunch came down, my old man was out on his ass. But it had been my mother's brothers, you see, and so there wasn't much he could do about it. Jewish families hang tight that way. So at close to the age of fifty, my father had to open his own store.

He couldn't get ground-floor space on Main Street, so he took an upstairs suite, and sold from there. In his off-hours he sold appliances by personal contact. It was a grueling existence. The fucking climb up those stairs alone, was murder. That staircase went almost straight up, and he had to make that climb twenty times a day.

Well, it killed him a year later.

May 1st, 1949, a Sunday, I came downstairs from my room, to see my Dad sitting in his big overstuffed chair by the fireplace, the Sunday edition of the *Cleveland Plain Dealer* around his feet, his pipe in his mouth. I was still on the stairs, about to ask him for the funnies when suddenly he began to choke.

I watched, helpless and with a kind of detached fascination as he died right before my eyes. Coronary thrombosis. It was all over in seconds. My mother got pretty well spaced, and somehow we managed to get him onto the sofa, but the pulmotor squad arrived too late. They couldn't have done anything. He was gone the minute he started to choke.

All through the next days, I moved like some kind of somnambulist, I was into baseball in those days, and I had a fuzz-less tennis ball that I bounced against the house. For the next month all I did, from morning till night, was stand outside on the front lawn under the maple tree, and bounce that ball off the wall, and catch it in the trapper's mitt my Dad had bought me. I threw the ball and caught it, threw it and caught it, over and over and over . . .

It must have been hell for everyone inside the house, the sound of that ball plonking against the wood, again and again, without end, till it got too dark to see it.

We moved away from there soon after, and I went from straight A's in school to failing grades in everything. I became a trouble kid of the worst sort. But it worked out.

Ever since then, I now realize, I've been looking for my father. I've tried to find him in Dad-surrogates, but that's always come to a bad end. And all I ever wanted to tell him was, "Hey, Dad, you'd be proud of me now; I turned out to be a good guy and what I do, I do well and . . . I love you and . . . why did you go away and leave me alone?"

When I lived in Cleveland, I used to go to his grave sometimes, but I stopped doing that fifteen years ago and haven't been back.

He isn't there.

Louis Laverne Ellison

Serita Rosenthal Ellison

My Mother

On Sunday the 10th of October, I committed the final outrage against my family. I spoke the eulogy at my mother's funeral. The family will never speak to me again. I can handle that.

When I say "my family," I mean, mostly, my mother's side, The Rosenthals. Who resemble in more ways than the mind can readily support, the brutalizing members of the Sproul clan in Jerrold Mundis's current and brilliant novel, GERHARDT'S CHILDREN. They remind me of the first line from Tolstoy's ANNA KARENINA: "Happy families are all alike; every unhappy family is unhappy in its own way."

And prime among that unhappy family's myths was the one that Harlan, Serita and Doc's kid, Beverly's brother, would wind up either dead or in an alley somewhere, having come to a useless end . . . or rotting away his old age in a Federal penitentiary. That I became a writer of some repute and became the first member of either the Rosenthal or the Ellison family to get listed in WHO'S WHO IN AMERICA, confounds them to this day. To them, I am like the snail known as the Chambered Nautilus, that has a shell with rooms in it. As the Nautilus lives its brief life it moves from room to room in its shell and finally emerges and dies; thus, it literally carries its past on its back. To the family, I am still a nine-year-old hellion who took a hammer to Uncle Morrie's piano. (The fact that this never happened, that Morrie never owned a piano, does not in any way invalidate for them the apocryphal truth of the legend.)

It is probably no different for anyone reading these words. All families form their opinions of the children early, and so we spend the rest of our lives in large part paying obeisance to shadows who neither care nor *in fact* have any power over our reality. It is thus for all of us, no matter how sophisticated and cut-loose we may be from the familial spiderweb.

To them, I am a nine-year-old Chambered Nautilus; even though I ran away from home at the age of thirteen, grew up, and have barely spoken a dozen words to my sister in the past ten years.

But there was still my mother, whom I supported in large part during the last years of her life, picking up the burden when I was financially able, from my Uncle Lew and my Uncle Morrie and from Beverly's husband, Jerold.

My mother had been terribly ill for many years. To my way of thinking, she wanted to die on May 1st, 1949, when my father had his coronary thrombosis and died in front of both of us. He was her life, her happier aspect, and she became—in any sensible not even exquisite sense—almost somnambulistic.

In August she had the latest of an uncountable number of strokes, followed it with a full-sized heart attack, and was taken into the Miami Heart Institute. She knew the end was on her and she let me know that was the sum of it when we talked long distance.

She lay there getting worse and worse, and finally, forty-five days before the green blips went to a flat line on the monitor, she was down from one hundred and twenty pounds to forty-one pounds, her lungs were filled with fluid, her brain had swollen so her face was terribly twisted, her leg was filled with blood clots, her blood sugar had risen to an impossible level, she ran a temperature in excess of 102° constantly, she was blind, paralyzed, and no oxygen was going to the brain.

Blessedly, she was in deep coma.

She never recovered consciousness. They kept her on the IV and the monitoring for a month and a half. She was a vegetable and had she ever come out of it would have been an empty shell. I begged them to pull the plug, but they wouldn't.

The greatest fear my mother ever had was that some day she would wind up in a nursing home. She thought of them as hellholes, as repositories for discarded loved ones, as the very apotheosis of rejection. She begged us never to put her there.

Shortly before she died, the Miami Heart Institute held one of their "status meetings" and decided she was "stable," that is, she needed custodial care. And so they wanted her out. They suggested we get her booked into an old folks' home. They used another phrase. They always do. But it was a hellhole, an old folks' home.

Beverly, my sister, who had gone through the anguish of the last six weeks down there, was forced reluctantly to find such a place. On Friday, October 8th, 1976, the day my mother was to be removed from Miami Heart and carted by ambulance to the hellhole, though she was in deep coma and could not possibly have known what was intended for her dead but still-breathing husk, she chose to expire at 5:15 AM.

In some arcane way, I'm sure she knew.

When my brother-in-law Jerold called to tell me Beverly had just advised him of Mom's death, he asked if there were any arrangements I particularly wanted.

"Only two," I said. "Closed casket, and I want to read the eulogy."

From that moment till Sunday at the funeral services, my family trembled in fear of what I would say. They knew I was no great lover of the clan, and they were terrified I would make a scene, depart from protocol in a way that would humiliate them in front of friends and relatives. They gave very little thought to my feelings about my mother. But that's the way it always is, I'm sure, with all families, with all deaths.

I flew all night Saturday and got into Cleveland (where my mother's body had been taken, so she could be buried beside my father) at 6:30 in the morning. I drove to Beverly and Jerold's house and when Jerold asked to see the eulogy I'd written, which was almost the first thing he said to me, thus indicating the obsessiveness of their concern about "crazy" Harlan and what he might do, I lied and said I hadn't written anything, that it was to be extemporaneous, from the heart.

The relatives began arriving, and with the exception of my Uncle Lew, who has always been the coolest and the most understanding of the clan, they all circled me warily as if I were a jackal that might at any moment leap for their throats.

At the funeral home, Rabbi Rosenthal seemed equally uneasy about my participation in the ceremonies. It was Succoth, the Jewish harvest holiday, and just a week after Yom Kippur, the holiest of the holies. Thus, certain prayers that are usually spoken at funeral services could not be spoken; alternate words were permissible, but few, so very few.

Rabbi Rosenthal is no relation to my family. His name and my mother's maiden name being Rosenthal is just coincidence. Like Smith. Or Jones. Or Hayakawa. Or Goetz. Or Piazza. He's a fine man, the Rabbi Emeritus of Cleveland Jewry, a strong and familiar voice in Cleveland Heights and environs. He has been for many years. But he didn't know my mother.

My family felt themselves honored to have pulled off the coup of Rabbi Rosenthal attending to the services. My family thinks in those terms: what looks good . . . social coups . . . fine form and attention to protocol. As you may have gathered, I am not concerned with shadow, merely reality.

Nonetheless, he advised me he would speak the opening words and then would call on me.

Before the main room with the pink anodized aluminum casket was opened to the attendees, the immediate family mourners and their spouses and children and grandchildren were taken to a family sitting room to the right of the main chamber. Jane Bubis, Beverly's best friend, bustled around. Morrie met old chums from Cleveland. My nephew Loren and I insisted on seeing Mom. Everyone told us not to look, that she had withered terribly, that we should "remember her as she had been." They always tell you to "remember" someone as "they were." Bear that phrase in mind. The nature of the outrage I committed against my family is contained in my pursuit of that admonition.

Loren and I insisted.

It didn't look like my mother. It was a cleverly constructed mannequin intended for some minor wax museum in an amusement park. The embalmers and cosmeticians had done as good a job as could be done, I'm sure; but it wasn't my Mom. She was already gone. This was a stranger. But I cried. Pain that clotted my chest and made me gasp for breath. But it wasn't my Mom.

The service began, and when Rabbi Rosenthal called on me, I walked up to the lectern, foolishly trailing my hand across the casket to establish some last rapport with her.

I pulled the pages I'd written from my inside jacket pocket and though there was no appreciable movement in the people sitting in front of me in the main chamber, the agitation I caught with peripheral vision, from the family seated in the side viewing room, was considerable: the frenzied trembling of small fish perceiving a predator in their pool.

Understand something: my sister and I have never been friends. Eight years older than I, she was *always* distressed at who I was, what I was, what I did. (I have long harbored the fantasy that I was actually a gypsy baby, stolen from the Romany caravan by an attacking horde of Jewish ladies with shopping bags.) Beverly is no doubt an estimable human being, filled to the brimming with love and charity and compassion. I have never been able to discern these qualities in her, but she has many loyal friends and if an election were to be held among the relatives, as to which of us could safely be taken into polite society of an evening without worry about a "scene," my sister Beverly would win in a walk. Though they take a (to me) somewhat hypocritical pride in my achievements and the low level of fame I've achieved for the Ellison family, it is a public pride, not to be confused with actually having to get near me. I can handle that, too.

As I began to read, my sister began to fall apart. I'm not sure if it was the "inappropriateness" (to her mind) of what I was saying, or the fact that I was crying and having difficulty reading the words, or that the torture she had undergone for six weeks had finally broken her, but she began writhing in Jerold's grasp, and in a voice that could be heard throughout the funeral home hoarsely cried for Jerold to "make him stop, make him stop! Stop him!" Beside her, her daughter Lisa, my niece, snarled, "Shut up, Mother!" but Beverly never heard her. She was manipulating her environment, and her lunatic brother

Harlan was doing another of his disgusting numbers, desecrating the funeral of her mother. They finally manhandled her into another room, where her cries could still be heard. And I went on, with difficulty. And this is what I said:

My mother died three days ago. Her name was Serita R. Ellison. The R stood for Rosenthal, her maiden name. I'll tell you everything I know about her.

My mother told me only one joke in her entire life. She probably knew a lot of others, but she never told them to me. I'll tell you the one she told me.

It's about these two Jewish fellows who meet on a street in Buffalo, New York. They are related, see, but not close; something like in-laws once removed. And Herschel doesn't care much for Solly, because Solly is always trying to sell him some crazy thing or get him involved in some shtumie *business deal. But Herschel gets trapped coming out of the butcher shop and Solly says to him, "Have I got a deal for you!" And Herschel says, "If it's as good as that last deal, this time we'll go to the bankruptcy court hand-in-hand."*

And Solly says, "Listen, you can't pass this one up. It's terrific! A friend of mine is having an affair with a woman whose second husband's brother is married to a girl whose father is in business with a guy whose son is a merchandising agent for circuses, and I can get for you, for a mere three thousand dollars, a guaranteed fully-grown, two ton Ringling Bros. Barnum & Bailey elephant."

So Herschel looks at him like he's sprouted another head, and he says, "You know, you've gotta be out of your mind. I live in a fifth floor walkup apartment with a wife and four kids, and one of them is sleeping in the sink we got so little room. What the hell am I gonna do with an elephant, you dummy?"

And Solly says, "Listen, only because you're married to Gert, I'm gonna make this a special. You can have the elephant for two thousand five hundred."

Herschel starts screaming. "Listen you yotz, *what is it with you, are you deaf or something. I'm telling you I don't* want, *I don't* need, *I have no* use *for a two ton elephant, not for twenty-five hundred, not for nothing. How the hell am I supposed to get the thing up the stairs? What do I feed it? You could die just from the body heat of a thing like that in a four-room apartment. Get away from me, you moron!"*

And they argue back and forth, with Solly constantly reducing the price, till finally he says, as a last resort. "Okay, okay, you momser! *You want to bleed me, a relative, you got no heart? Okay! My last and final offer. For you . . . not one . . . but two!* Two *two ton Ringling Bros. Barnum & Bailey elephants for five hundred dollars!"*

*And Herschel says, real quick, "*Now *you're talking business!"*

When Momma told me that joke she was laughing. She laughed very long and very hard, and I did, too. Not because the joke was so funny, although it's not bad and she told it well, but because she *was laughing. I never saw my mother laugh very much.*

From May of 1949 on, I never saw her laugh at all.

That was when my father died.

It's impossible to talk about Serita without talking about Doc. Of course I never knew them when they were young and running around the way young people do, but from what I'm told by members of the Rosenthal family, they were some kind of short, Jewish equivalent of Scott Fitzgerald and Zelda. They were in love, and they were nuts together.

When my father died, I think my mother's life stopped. It was twenty-seven years of shadows for her. Just marking time. Waiting to join Doc. If there's anything good about death, and anything that even remotely lightens the pain of my mother's death, it is that finally, after twenty-seven years, she came up lucky and went to meet my dad, to take up where they got cut off in 1949.

I'd tell you how old my mother was when she died, but as anyone who knew her for more than an hour can tell you, she would rather have had bamboo shoots thrust under her fingernails than reveal her age. She was like that.

She was a good woman, and a decent woman, and had all the right instincts about life, all the usual things people say at funerals; she was also opinionated, stubborn beyond belief, a frequent pain in the ass, and capable of a dudgeon so high it would put the Queen Mother to shame. But God, how she worked for her kids. I don't remember a time when she wasn't working. Either beside my dad in the jewelry stores, or in the B'nai B'rith Thrift Shop, or somewhere. And no matter how much we took, she always came up with what we needed.

I remember once when I was a very little kid—and I was not the world's most tractable youngster—when I did something grotesque and awful; and Mom said, "You're going to get it when your father comes home." No doubt I deserved it. I usually did. And when my dad got back from work, exhausted and anxious simply to sit down and relax, Mom told him what I'd done and that I needed a good strapping.

Now understand: my family wasn't that big on corporal punishment. But my dad took me down in the basement of our house on Harmon Drive in Painesville, and he took off his belt and he did a good job on me.

After a while, I came upstairs, and Mom and Dad were nowhere to be seen. I climbed the stairs to the second floor and through the closed door of their bedroom I could hear my dad crying. The licking had devastated him much more than it had me. And my mom was crying, too. She was consoling him, telling him it was the only thing he could do, and together they were solacing each other.

The Rosenthals were a family with a capacity for unhappiness that was awesome to behold, and Mom was a Rosenthal to her shoetops. There was the endless ganging-up of brothers and sisters in ever-changing permutations of the familial equation, with my mom sometimes allied with Alice and Lew against Morrie, and sometimes associated with Morrie and Dorothy against Martin, and sometimes the hookups were so Machiavellian it was impossible to tell who was mad at whom. But throughout, no matter how affronted she thought she should be, my mother was a Rosenthal, who would take fire and axe to anyone who tried to harm one hair on the head of her kind. The Russian soul of the Rosenthals, which was so intimately a part of my mother's makeup, kept her from tasting unlimited joy in her later years—my niece Lisa was the great exception—they were in no way like grandchild and grandmother: they were best friends, chums, and the love between them so enriched both their lives that I think Mom's death is more crushing for Lisa than for any of us—but even so my mother managed to see Beverly well-married and the mother of two good kids, and me safely beyond any possibility of spending my life in jail. She took that to be treasure indeed.

I wish I could tell you more about Serita Ellison, but the sad, sorry fact is that we lived our lives as shadows to one another. We never really understood each other, the dreams never realized, the hopes set aside, the hungers that made us alien to one another. And so at final moments, as I speak of her, I try to hold the important *memories; and the one that is richest, most recent is the picture of her in New Haven, Connecticut, in February of last year. I was invited to speak at the Yale Political Union, at Yale University, and I brought Mom up for the prestigious event. She was like a twenty-year-old girl. She was, as she used to put it, "in Seventh Heaven." Her kid was lecturing at Yale! How she did* kvell! *What* naches! *Radiant, like all the suns of the universe. It was snowing so hard in New Haven, and the drifts were so deep, and it was so bitterly cold, I was terrified that a woman in her condition would suffer damage. But she strode around like a cossack, I had to run to keep up with her.*

And at my lecture, when I introduced her, she stood up and nodded so regally to all the Yalies that I thought I'd burst from pleasure. And when they brought over my books for her *to autograph, she wrote, "Thank you for liking my son's books."*

Near the end, when she was clearly in pain and knew she was going away, we talked several times a day long distance, and I kept saying, "I'll come down there." And she kept saying, "No, I don't want you to see me like this. Beverly and Lisa are here, and I'm all right." She was more lucid than she'd been in years; I guess she knew it was all over; and she said to me during what I guess was the last time we talked, though it might not have been the last time, "You turned out all right and I love you."

And now she's gone, and there's nothing much to say about the death of an old woman, any old woman, except that she's dead and everyone who knew her now has a finite number of days and nights to lament never having said all the things that should have been said.

She was my mother, and I miss her.

By the time I stepped off the platform and returned to the family room at the side of the main chamber, Beverly had been returned to her seat. I'm not sure she even heard the eulogy beyond the telling of the "joke." After the ceremony was completed—so briefly, so awfully briefly—no one would speak to me. No one came up and said, "That was beautiful, what you said about your mother." My nephew Loren shook my hand and we hugged, because he was crying, too, and he said, very softly, "You did good." Much later, Jerold took me aside and said, "Serita would have been proud of you." But other than those two remarks, I was shunned. Beverly, the uncles and aunts, they didn't stone me, but they made sure they didn't even brush my shoulder. One holds oneself aloof from pariahs and other uncleans. And their outrage frees me of them forever.

My mother is gone, and I did what I wanted to do for her; she always enjoyed listening to me read, so I did it one last time for her. I know damned well she never heard it, but it's an innocent conceit. And they wanted to put her down too quickly, with too few words being spoken. I would have read my eulogy and then asked Beverly and Lisa and Lew and anyone else who had something to say, to come up and say it. She deserved that much at least.

Eulogies are never for the dead. They are always for the living; to pay off debts; to say goodbye formally one last time. But no one should be sent down into darkness with too few words.

Tired Old Man

(An Hommage *to Cornell Woolrich)*

The hell of it is, you're never as tough as you think you are. There's always somebody with sad eyes who'll shoot you down when you're not even looking, when you're combing your hair, tying your shoelace. Down you go, like a wounded rhino, nowhere near as tough as you thought.

I came in from the Coast on a Wednesday, got myself locked up in the Warwick to finish the book, did it, called the messenger and had him take the manuscript over to Wyeth the following Tuesday, and I was free. Only nine months late, but it was an okay piece of work. It was going to be at least three days till I got the call telling me what alterations he wanted—there were three chapters dead in the middle I knew he'd balk at—I'd cheated on the psychiatric rationale for the brother-in-law's actions, had held back some stuff I knew Wyeth would demand I flesh out—and so I had time to kill.

I've got to remember to remind myself: if I ever use that phrase again, may my carbons always be reversed. Time to kill. Yeah, just the phrase.

I called Bob Catlett, thinking we'd get together for dinner with his wife, the psychiatrist, if he was still seeing her. He said we could set it up for that night and by the way, why didn't I come along for the monthly meeting of The Cerberus Club. I choked back a string of uglies. "I don't think so, man. They give me a pain in the ass."

The Cerberus is a "writers' club" of old pros who've been around since Clarence Buddington Kelland was breaking in at Munsey's *Cavalier*. And what had been a fairly active group of working professionals in the Fifties and Sixties was now a gaggle of burnt-out cases and gossips, drinking too much and lamenting the passing of Ben Hibbs at the *Saturday Evening Post*. I was thirty years past that time, a young punk by their lights, and I saw no merit whatsoever in spending an evening up to my hips in dull chatter and weariness, gagging on cigarette smoke and listening to septuageneric penny-a-word losers comparing the merits of *Black Mask* to those of *Weird Tales*.

So he talked me into it. That's what friends are for.

We had dinner at an Argentinian restaurant off Times Square; and with my belly full of skirt steak and bread pudding I felt up to it. We arrived at the traditional meeting-place—the claustrophobic apartment of a sometime-editor who had once been a reader for Book-of-the-Month Club—around nine-thirty. It was packed from wall to wall.

I hadn't seen most of them in ten years, since I'd gone to the Coast to adapt my novel, THE STALKING MAN, for Paramount. It had been a good ten years for me. I'd left New York with a molehill of unpaid bills the creditors were rapidly turning into a mountain, and such despair both personally and professionally I'd half accepted the idea I'd never really make a decent living at writing. But doing four months' work each year in films and television had provided the cushion so I could spend eight months of the year working on books. I was free of debt, twenty pounds heavier, secure for the first time in my life, and reasonably happy. But walking into that apartment was like walking back into a corporeal memory of the dismal past. Nothing had changed. They were all there, and all the same.

My first impression was of lines of weariness.

Someone had superimposed a blueprint on the room and its occupants. In the background were all the moving figures, older and more threadbare than the last time I'd seen them gathered together in a room like this, moving (it seemed, oddly) a good deal more slowly than they should have been. As if they were imbedded in amber. Not slow motion, merely an altered index of the light-admitting properties of the lenses of my eyes. Out of synch with their voices. But in the foreground, much sharper and brighter than the colors of the people or the room, was an overlay of lines of weariness. Gray and blue lines that were not merely topographically superimposed over faces and hands, and the elbows of the women, but over the entire room: lines rising off toward the ceiling, laid against the lamps and chairs, dividing the carpet into sections.

I walked through, between and among the blue and gray lines, finding it difficult to breathe as the oppressiveness of massed failure and dead dreams assaulted me. It was like breathing the dust of ancient tombs.

Bob Catlett and his wife had immediately wandered off to the kitchen for drinks. I would have scurried after them, but Leo Norris saw me, shoved between two ex-technical writers (each of whom had had brief commercial successes twenty years before with non-fiction popularizations of space science theory) and grabbed my hand. He looked exhausted, but sober.

"Billy! For God's sake, *Billy*! I didn't know you were in town. What a great thing! How long're you in for?"

"Only a few days, Leo. Book for Harper. I've been all locked up finishing it."

"Well, I'll say this for you, the Scott Fitzgerald Syndrome certainly hasn't hit you out there. How many books have you written since you left, three? Four?"

"Seven."

He smiled with embarrassment, but not enough embarrassment to slow the phony camaraderie. Leo Norris and I—despite his effusions—had never been close. When he had already been an established novelist, a fact one verified by getting one's name on the cover of *The Saint Detective Magazine*, I was banging off hammer murder novelettes for *Manhunt*, just to pay the rent in the Village. There had been no camaraderie in those days. But Leo was now on the slide, had been for the last six or eight years, had been reduced to writing a series of sex/spy/violence paperbacks: each one numbered (he was up to #27 the last time I looked), pseudonymous, featuring an unpleasant CIA thug named Curt Costener. Four of my last seven novels had been translated into successful films and one of them had become a television series. Camaraderie.

"Seven books in what—ten years?—that's damned good."

I didn't say anything. I was looking around; indicating I wanted to move on. He didn't pick up the message.

"Brett McCoy died, you know. Last week."

I nodded. I'd read him, but had never met him. Good writer. Police procedurals.

"Terminal. Inoperable. Lungs; really spread. Oh, he'd been on the way out for a long time. He'll be missed."

"Yeah. Well, excuse me, Leo, I have to find some people I came with."

I couldn't get through the press near the front door to join Bob in the kitchen. The only breeze was coming in from the hallway and they were jammed together in front of the passage. So I went the other way, deeper into the room, deeper into the inversion layer of smoke and monotoned chatter. He watched me go, wanting to say something, probably wanting to strengthen a bond that didn't exist. I moved fast. I didn't want any more obituary reports.

There were only five or six women in the crowd, as far as I could tell. One of them watched me as I edged through the bodies. I couldn't help noticing her noticing me. She was in her late forties, severerly weathered, staring openly as I neared her. It wasn't till she spoke,

"Billy?" that I recognized the voice. Not the face; even then, not the face. Just the voice, which hadn't changed.

I stopped and stared back. "Dee?"

She smiled no kind of smile at all, a mere stricture of courtesy. "How are you, Billy?"

"I'm fine. How're you? What's happening, what're you doing these days?"

"I'm living in Woodstock. Cormick and I got divorced; I'm doing books for Avon."

I hadn't seen anything with her name on it for some time. Those who haunt the newsstands and bookstores out of years of habit are like sidewalk cafe Greeks unable to stop fingering their worry beads. I would have seen her name.

She caught the hesitation. "Gothics. I'm doing them under another name."

This time the smile was nasty and it said: you've had the last laugh; yes, I'm selling my talent cheap; I hate myself for it; I'll slice my wrists in this conversation before I'll permit you to gloat. What's more offensive than being successful when they always dismissed you as the least of their set, and they've dribbled away all the promise and have failed? Nothing. They would eat the air you breathe. Bierce: SUCCESS, *n.* The one unpardonable sin against one's fellows. Unquote.

"Look me up if you get to Los Angeles," I said. She didn't even want to try that one. She turned back to the three-way conversation behind her. She took the arm of an elegant man with a thick, gray mop of styled Claude Rains hair. He was wearing aviator-style eyeglasses, wraparounds, tinted auburn. Dee hung on tight. That wouldn't last long. His suits were too well-tailored. She looked like a tattered battle flag. *When had they all settled for oblivion?*

Edwin Charrel was coming toward me from the opposite side of the room. He still owed me sixty dollars from ten years before. He wouldn't have forgotten. He'd lay a long, guilt-oozing story on me, and try to press a moist five bucks into my hand. Not now; *really,* not now; not on top of Leo Norris and Dee Miller and all those crinkled elbows. I turned a hard right, smiled at a mom-and-pop writing team sharing the same glass of vodka, and worked my way to the wall. I kept to the outside and began to circumnavigate. My mission: to get the hell out of there as quickly as possible. Everyone knows, it's harder to hit a moving target.

And miles to go before I sleep.

The back wall was dominated by a sofa jammed with loud conversations. But the crowd in the center of the room had its collective back to the babble, so there was a clear channel across to the other side. I made the move. Charrel wasn't even in sight, so I made the move. No one noticed, no one gave a gardyloo, no one tried to buttonhole me. I made the move. I thought I was halfway home. I started to turn the corner, only one wall to go before the breeze, the door, and out. That was when the old man motioned to me from the easy chair.

The chair was wedged into the rear corner of the room, at an angle to the sofa. Big, overstuffed, colorless thing. He was deep in the cushions. Thin, wasted, tired-looking, eyes a soft, watery blue. He was motioning to me. I looked behind me, turned back. He was motioning to *me*. I walked over and stood there above him.

"Sit down."

There wasn't anywhere to sit. "I was just leaving." I didn't know him.

"Sit down, we'll talk. There's time."

A spot opened at the end of the sofa. It would have been rude to walk away. He nodded his head at the open spot. So I sat down. He was the most exhausted-looking old man I'd ever seen. Just stared at me.

"So you write a little," he said. I thought he was putting me on. I smiled, and he said, "What's your name?"

I said, "Billy Landress."

He tested that for a moment, silently. "William. On the books it's William."

I chuckled. "That's right. William on the books. It's better for the lending libraries. Classier. Weightier." I couldn't stop smiling and laughing softly. Not to myself, right into his face. He didn't smile back, but I knew he wasn't taking offense. It was a bemusing conversation.

"And you're . . . ?"

"Marki," he said; he paused, then added, "Marki Strasser."

Still smiling, I said, "Is that the name you write under?"

He shook his head. "I don't write any more. I haven't written in a long time."

"Marki," I said, lingering on the word, "Marki Strasser. I don't think I've read any of your work. Mystery fiction?"

"Primarily. Suspense, a few contemporary novels, nothing terribly significant. But tell me about you."

I settled back into the sofa. "I have the feeling, sir, that you're amused by me."

His soft, blue eyes stared back at me without a trace of guile. There was no smile anywhere in that face. Tired; old and terribly tired. "We're *all* amusing, William. Except when we get too old to take care of ourselves, when we get too old to keep up. Then we cease to be amusing. You don't want to talk about yourself?"

I spread my hands in surrender. I would talk about myself. He may have conceived of himself as too old to be amusing, but he was a fascinating old man nonetheless. He was a good listener. And the rest of the room faded, and we talked. I told him about myself, about life on the Coast, the plots of my books, in *précis*, what it took to adapt a suspense novel for the screen.

Body language is interesting. On the most primitive level, even those unfamiliar with the unconscious messages the positions of the arms and legs and torso give, can perceive what's going on. When two people are talking and one is trying to get across an important point to the other, the one making the point leans forward; the one resisting the point leans back. I realized I was leaning far forward and to the side, resting my chest on the arm of the sofa. He wasn't sinking too far back in the soft cushions of the easy chair; but he was back, in any event. He was listening to me, taking in everything I was saying, but it was as though he knew it was all past, all dead information, as though he was waiting to tell me some things I needed to know.

Finally, he said, "Have you noticed how many of the stories you've written are concerned with relationships of fathers to sons?"

I'd noticed. "My father died when I was very young," I said, and felt the usual tightness in my chest. "Somewhere, I don't remember where, I stumbled on a line Faulkner wrote once, where he said, something like, 'No matter what a writer writes about, if it's a man he's writing about the search for his father.' It hit me particularly hard. I'd never realized how much I missed him until one night just a few years ago, I was in a group encounter session and we were told by the leader of the group to pick one person out of the circle and to make that person someone we wanted to talk to, someone we'd never been *able* to talk to, and to tell that person everything we'd always wanted to say. I picked a man with a mustache and talked to him the way I'd never been able to talk to my father when I was a very little boy. After a little bit I was crying." I paused, then said very softly, "I didn't even cry at my father's funeral. It was a very strange thing, a disturbing evening."

I paused again, and collected my thoughts. This was becoming a good deal heavier, more personal, than I'd anticipated. "Then, just a year or two ago, I found that quote by Faulkner; and it all fitted into place."

The tired old man kept watching me. "What did you tell him?"

"Who? Oh, the man with the mustache? Hmmm. Well, it wasn't anything that potent. I just told him I'd made it, that he would be proud of me now, that I had succeeded, that I was a good guy and . . . he'd be proud of me. That was all."

"What *didn't* you tell him?"

I felt myself twitch with the impact of the remark. I went chill all over. He had said it so casually, and yet the force of the question jammed a cold chisel into the door of my memory, applied sudden pressure and snapped the lock. The door sprang open and guilt flooded out. How could Marki have known?

"Nothing. I don't know what you mean." I didn't recognize my voice.

"There must have been something. You're an angry man, William. You're angry at your father. Perhaps because he died and left you alone. But you didn't say something very important that you *needed* to say; you still need to say it. What was it?"

I didn't want to answer him. But he just waited. And finally I murmured, "He never said goodbye. He just died and never said goodbye to me." Silence. Then I shook, helplessly, trembled, reduced after so many years to a child, tried to shake it off, tried to dismiss it, and very quietly said, "It wasn't important."

"It wasn't important for him to hear it; but it was for you to say it." I couldn't look at him.

Then Marki said, "In the lens of time we are each seen as a diminishing mote. I'm sorry I upset you."

"You didn't upset me."

"Yes. I did. Let me try and make amends. If you have the time, let me tell you about a few books I wrote. You may enjoy this." So I sat back and he told me a dozen plots. He spoke without hesitations, fluidly, and they were awfully good. Excellent, in fact. Suspense stories, something in the vein of James M. Cain or Jim Thompson. Stories about average people, not private eyes or foreign agents; just people in stress situations where violence and intrigue proceeded logically from entrapping circumstances. I was fascinated. And what a talent he had for titles: DEAD BY MORNING, CANCEL BUNGALOW 16, AN EDGE IN MY VOICE, WHITEMAIL, THE MAN WHO SEARCHED FOR JOY, THE DIAGNOSIS OF DR. D'arqueANGEL, PRODIGAL FATHER and one that somehow struck me so forcibly I made a mental note to contact Andreas Brown at the Gotham Book Mart, to locate a used copy for me through his antiquarian book sources. I had to read it. It was titled LOVER, KILLER.

When he stopped talking he looked even more exhausted than when he'd asked me to sit down. His skin was almost gray, and the soft, blue eyes kept closing for moments at a time. "Would you like a glass of water or something to eat?"

He looked at me carefully, and said, "Yes. I'd very much like a glass of water, thank you."

I got up, to force my way through to the kitchen.

He put his dry hand on mine. I looked down at him. "What do you want to be, eventually, William?"

I could have given a flip answer. I didn't. "Remembered," I said. Then he smiled, and removed his hand.

"I'll get that water; be right back."

I pushed through the crowd and got to the kitchen. Bob was still there, arguing with Hans Santesson about cracking the pro rata share of royalties problem for reprints of stories in college-level text-anthologies. Hans and I shook hands, and exchanged quick pleasantries while I drew a glass of water and put in a couple of ice cubes from the plastic sack half-filled with melted cubes in the sink. I didn't want to leave Marki for very long.

"Where the hell have you been tonight?" Bob asked.

"I'm sitting way at the back, with an old man; fascinating old man. Used to be a writer, he says. I don't doubt it. Jesus, he must have written some incredible books. Don't know how I could have missed them. I thought I'd read practically everything in the genre."

"What is his name?" Hans asked, with that soft lovely Scandinavian accent.

"Marki Strasser," I said. "What a goddam sensational story-sense he's got."

They were staring at me.

"Marki Strasser?" Hans had frozen, his cup of tea halfway to his lips.

"Marki Strasser," I said again. "What's the matter?"

"The only Marki I know, who was a writer, was a man who used to come to these evenings thirty years ago. But he's been dead for at least fifteen, sixteen years."

I laughed. "Can't be the same one, unless you're wrong about his having died."

"No, I am certain about his death. I attended his funeral."

"Then it's someone else."

"Where's he sitting?" Bob asked.

I stepped out into the passage and motioned them to join me. I waited for the crowd to sway out of the way for a moment, and pointed. "There, back in the corner, in the big easy chair."

There was no one in the big easy chair. It was empty.

And as I stared, and they stood behind me, staring, a woman sat down in the chair and went to sleep, a cocktail in her hand. "He got up and moved somewhere else in the room," I said.

No, he hadn't. Of course.

We were the last to go. I wouldn't leave. I watched each person pass out through the front door, standing right in front of the door so no one could get past me. Bob checked out the toilet. He wasn't in there. There was only one exit from the apartment, and I was in front of it. "Listen, goddammit," I said heatedly, to Hans and Bob and our host, who wanted desperately to vomit and go to bed, "I do *not* believe in ghosts; he *wasn't* a ghost, he *wasn't* a figment of my imagination, he *wasn't* a fraud; for God's sake I'm not *that* gullible I can't tell when I'm being put on; those stories he told me were too damned good; and if he was here, how the hell did he get out past me? I was right in front of the door even when I came to the kitchen to get the water.

He was an *old* man, at least seventy-five, maybe older; he wasn't a goddam sprinter! *Nobody* could have gotten through that crowd fast enough to slip out into the hall behind me without banging into everyone, and *someone* would have remembered being pushed like that . . . so . . ."

Hans tried to calm me. "Billy, we asked everyone who was here. No one else saw him. No one even saw you sitting on the sofa there, where you say you were sitting. No one else spoke to anyone like that, and many of the writers here tonight *knew* him. Why would a man tell you he was Marki Strasser if he was *not* Marki Strasser? He would have known that a room filled with writers who *knew* Marki Strasser would tell you if it was a joke."

I wouldn't let go of it. I was *not* hallucinating!

Our host went digging around in the back closet and came up with a bound file of old Mystery Writers of America programs from Edgar Award dinners; he flipped through them, back fifteen years, and found a photograph of Marki Strasser. I looked at it. The photo was clear and sharp. It wasn't the same man. There was no way of confusing the two, even adding fifteen years to the face in the picture, even allowing for a severe debilitation from sickness. The Marki in the photograph was a round-faced man, almost totally bald, with thick eyebrows and dark eyes. The Marki I had talked to for almost an hour had had soft, blue eyes. Even if he had been wearing a hairpiece, those eyes couldn't be mistaken.

"It's not him, dammit!"

They asked me to describe him again. When that didn't connect, Hans asked me to tell him the stories and the titles. The three of them listened and I could see from their faces that they were as impressed with the books Marki had written as I was. But when I ran down and sat there, breathing hard, Hans and my host shook their heads. "Billy," Hans said, "I was the editor of the Unicorn Mystery Book Club for seven years; I edited *The Saint Detective Magazine* for more than ten. I have read as widely in the field of mystery fiction as anyone alive. No such books exist."

Our host, an authority on the subject, agreed.

I looked at Bob Catlett. He devoured them a book a day. Slowly, reluctantly, he nodded his head in agreement.

I sat there and closed my eyes.

After a little while, Bob suggested we go. His wife had vanished an hour earlier with a group intent on getting cheesecake. He wanted to get to bed. I didn't know what to do. So I went back to the Warwick.

That night I pulled an extra blanket onto the bed, but still it was cold, very cold, and I shivered. I left the television set on, nothing but snow and a steady humming. I couldn't sleep.

Finally, I got up and got dressed and went out into the night. Fifty-fourth Street was empty and silent at three in the morning. Not even delivery trucks and, though I looked and looked for him, I couldn't find him.

I thought about it endlessly, walking, and for a while I imagined he had been my father, come back from the grave to talk to me. But it wasn't my father. I would have recognized him. I'm no fool, I would have recognized him. My father had been a much shorter man, with a mustache; and he had never spoken like that, in that way, with those words and those cadences.

It wasn't the almost-forgotten mystery novelist known as Marki Strasser. Why he had used that name, I don't know; perhaps to get my attention, to lead me down a black path of fear that would tell me without question that he was someone else, because it had *not* been Marki Strasser. I didn't know who he was.

I came back to the Warwick and rang for the elevator. I stood in front of the mirrored panel between the two elevator doors, and I stared through my own reflection, into the glass, looking for an answer.

Then I went up to my room and sat down at the writing desk and rolled a clean sandwich of white bond, carbon, and yellow second sheet into the portable.

I began writing LOVER, KILLER.

It came easily. No one else could write that book.

But, like my father, he hadn't even said goodbye when I went to get him that glass of water. That tired old man.

Gopher in the Gilly

A Reminiscence of the Carnival

Stand behind the tent flap and look at their faces.

You will learn all you'll ever need to know about the darker side of human nature.

(The Depression leached all joy from the people. Show biz called with its cheap wares, its momentary diversions. The movies did it. Cheap, took you away, and gave you memories to savor later. Carnivals were big. They circled the country. Cheap, gaudy, thrills. Today, no self-respecting carnival will carry a freak bally—a sideshow of malforms and sports. It's ugly business. Cheap. But in those days, those cheap, ugly days of the Thirties, something was needed to pull in the rubes and the yokels and the kadodies. The freak top. Hurry, hurry, slide right in there, friend, and drag your lady with you, for the most exhilarating, most startling, most unbelievable sights that've ever graced your eyes. See Lena, the fattest woman in the world, four hundred pounds of quivering jelly . . . Lucifer, with a throat of asbestos and a stomach of steel, see him eat fire, chew nails, drink coal oil, wouldn't it be nice to have *him* in your living room of a cold Kansas night . . . Rippo, the fish-boy: where you and I have arms and legs, Rippo has only gills and flippers . . . see and marvel . . . see the thing without a name, neither man nor beast, a creature out of bad dreams, he eats snakes, he bites the heads off chickens, ladies I cannot even describe in public the degradation in which this creature exists . . . but step up, step inside, see for yourself . . . see the largest gathering of freaks and marvels ever offered under one big top . . .)

Stand behind the tent flap and look at their faces.

You will learn all you'll ever need to know about the darker side of human nature.

(Ask any man of forty or fifty, who worked in a carny as a little boy.

Ask him if he ever stood behind the flap of the freak top and watched—not the freaks, oh no, not those poor miserable things—ask him if he ever watched the faces of the *people*. The good people, the solid rural folk with their lives and their morals sunk deep in the Judeo-Christian Ethos. Ask that little boy, now grown to a man, and he will be reluctant to tell you what he saw. But press him nonetheless, and he will tell you of the expressions on the faces of the men as they watched the swaying milk udders of Lena, as they contemplated the sexual wonders implicit in the plastic body of the snake girl. But he will never tell you of the licked lips and bright eyes of the women as they paused, and lingered, to observe the pre-thalidomide monstrosity called the fish-boy; as they let their gaze wander over his barely concealed private parts; as they wondered—nakedly obvious in their rapturous stares—what it would be like to have those flippers touch their bodies; what it would be like to make love to something like that. The little boy will never tell the horror of fascination in the faces of a freak audience, of the women who wanted to couple with the geek, redolent in his own filth, of the men who trembled at the sight of the hermaphrodite; half-man, half-woman, how would one seduce such a thing? Once having stood behind the flap, once having seen the unmasked faces of the secret dreamers, one need never again ask how did the slaughter at My Lai come to be; one need never again wonder what it is in the American character that produces Richard Speck or Charles Manson or Charles Starkweather or Susan Atkins. One need never ask, for it is there in all of us, lying close to the surface of all of us who make up the great freak top audience. The Depression is gone, but the rural rubes are still with us, are still part of all of us. We still need our freaks. Without compassion, without sympathy, without love . . . with merely lust and fascination and repugnance that attracts more than it repels . . . we all come to the big show and lick our lips.)

I was thirteen years old. Never mind why I ran away from home, that's another story for another time. I did it; the dream of every middle-American boy in the early 1940s; to run away and join the circus. I had read TOBY TYLER, *or Ten Weeks with a Circus*, and there was nothing more fascinating, nothing more swashbuckling, nothing more adventurous than to run off and join a circus.

I never found a circus. But I found the ragbag carny those in the circuit call a "gilly." The hit-and-run hundred-mile burn-the-lot operation that figure-eighted across Ohio, Indiana, Illinois and Missouri, looping back through Kentucky to start its pattern all over again. Tri-States Shows it called itself, but you'd never find it listed in *Amusement Business*. It was a pure grifter's carny, carrying a sorry menagerie, an ugly freak top, and more hanky-panks than I've seen at even the grungiest down-at-the-heels county fairs.

What did I do? I was a gopher.

"Hey, kid, go fer some coffee."

"Hey, kid, go fer some canvas."

"Hey, kid, go fer that spieler, Sam."

Furless, beardless, clawless, I was a gopher.

I was a honeydipper in the hyena cage, I was a shill for the hanky-panks, I was a lookout for the laws, I was a water boy for the girls working the kootch bally, I was a swamper in the cookhouse. I was three months worth of scut, and didn't know how crooked the whole operation was, till we got busted in Kansas City, Missouri.

The show had moll dips, it had cannons, it had boosters and paper-hangers, it had everything but a square deal for the marks who frequented the flat stores on the midway and came away lucky to have their shoe soles.

One of the cannons tried to whomp a guy for his wallet in K.C. Turned out the guy was an assistant D.A., fifteen years on the Force, and he threw the muscle halfway across that time-zone. The entire carny wound up in the K.C. slammer.

Pretty quick, everyone was sprung. The "management" couldn't afford to have its crew locked up for very long: first, because there were dates that had to be played in towns down the line, and second, because there were enough complaints and warrants out on that show to send *everyone* away till the next Ice Age. So everyone was sprung.

With two important exceptions.

The first was the geek. The second was me.

Anyone unfamiliar with the term "geek" should seek out and read William Lindsay Gresham's now-classic 1946 novel, NIGHTMARE ALLEY, for the most chillingly accurate description ever set in type. A geek is usually a wetbrain; that is, a young or old man so far gone into alcoholism that his brain has turned to prune-whip yogurt. When he sweats, he sweats sour mash. A gilly locates a skid in whatever town it's in, and carries him to the next stop, and as many stops as it can get out of him before he either dies or wanders off. For the splendid honorarium of a bottle of gin or two a day, the skid will dress in an animal skin, go without shaving, sleep in a cage, and on cue wallow in his own shit, eat dead snakes, bite the heads off live chickens. No reputable carny will carry a geek. It is a terrible thing. It plays to the basest hungers and most primal fears in the human repertory. Anyone who could derive enjoyment from watching a debased creature, seemingly only half-human, scuttling across the floor of a foul, stinking pit or pen, smearing itself with feces, rubbing its privates on the gnawed skin of a dead rattlesnake, moaning and rolling its eyes as it devolved before one's eyes, reverting to a stage of subhuman existence not even Cro-Magnons knew . . . such a person is beneath contempt, lower even than the poor bastard in that cage.

I have seen hordes of rural goodfolk, pillars of their communities, churchgoing Christians and advocates of the Protestant Work Ethic, who devoutly enjoyed watching a geek. Stand behind the tent flap. Watch. You'll learn more about human nature than you ever wished to know.

The geek and I were thrown in the drunk tank, a holding pen, together. *He* wasn't sprung because he wasn't really "carny," he was a pickup, and there were skids all along the road, so why spend hard cash on a slob so beneath notice that he couldn't even be thought of as human? *I* wasn't sprung because I wouldn't give the cops my real name; I didn't want to go home.

So the gilly took off, minus their geek, minus their gopher.

I spent three days in the K.C. slam with that old man, that subhuman geek.

I'll bet a month hasn't gone by since 1947, in that cage in Kansas City, that I haven't thought of that old drunk.

Three days we were locked together. The hacks, the guards who shepherded us, even they didn't want to get near us. The smell and look of that geek made them want to puke. They used to slide our food through the bars on the floor, at the end of a pushbroom. I was scared, and ill.

Because they wouldn't give him anything to drink, and he started having convulsions. He whimpered all through the night, and in the mornings his face was bloody and his lips bitten clean through. Along about the second day he went crazy from delerium tremens, and he climbed the bars of the free-standing cage where we were penned, and he began smashing his face against the metal ceiling. He fell and screamed, and lay on his back on the metal floor, moving his legs and arms idly like a turtle on its shell. His face looked like a pound of raw hamburger. And he smelled. A special smell. Not just his pants full of shit, and his clothes stinking from the dirt of his carny pen and garbage; he was sweating sour alcohol. A special smell. I've never forgotten it. I can't describe it to you . . . it smelled like such and such . . . there is nothing to compare. A million dead bodies turned up in a communal grave, maybe. But I've never forgotten that smell.

I don't drink. I have never drunk.

Finally, on the third day, they took me out. They had to. The Pinkerton Agency men my family had hired to find me had contacted the K.C. police. There had been missing persons flyers sent out on me, dodgers they were called; and someone in K.C. had matched a dodger with my description, even though I wouldn't tell them my real name or where I was from. And the Pinkertons sent an operative and he came and took me back on the train to Ohio.

I had spent three months with the carny.

And there was very little of romance or adventure or swashbuckling about it. All I came away with was the smell of rotten liquor sweated out through gray, dead skin . . . an even greater hatred of cops than I'd had to begin with . . . and the cynical, deadening, utterly inescapable knowledge that if one stands behind the tent flap and watches, one learns more about the darker side of human nature than any kid should ever know.

Strange Wine

Two whipcord-lean California Highway Patrolmen supported Willis Kaw between them, leading him from the cruiser to the blanket-covered shape in the middle of the Pacific Coast Highway. The dark brown smear that began sixty yards west of the covered shape disappeared under the blanket. He heard one of the onlookers say, "She was thrown all that way, oh it's awful," and he didn't want them to show him his daughter.

But he had to make the identification, and one of the cops held him securely as the other went to one knee and pulled back the blanket. He recognized the jade pendant he had given her for graduation. It was all he recognized.

"That's Debbie," he said, and turned his head away.

Why is this happening to me, he thought. *I'm not from here; I'm not one of them. This should be happening to a human.*

"Did you take your shot?"

He looked up from the newspaper and had to ask her to repeat what she had said. "I asked you," Estelle said very softly, with as much kindness as she had left in her, "if you took your insulin." He smiled briefly, recognizing her concern and her attempt to avoid invading his sorrow; and he said he had taken the shot. His wife nodded and said, "Well, I think I'll go upstairs to bed. Are you coming?"

"Not right now. In a little, maybe."

"You'll fall asleep in front of the set again."

"Don't worry about it. I'll be up in a little while."

She stood watching him for a moment longer, then turned and climbed the stairs. He listened for the sounds of the upstairs ritual—the toilet flushing, the water moving through the pipes to the sink, the clothes closet door squeaking as it was opened, the bedsprings responding as Estelle put herself down for the night. And then he switched on the television set. He switched to Channel 30, one of the empty channels, and turned down the volume control so he did not have to hear the sound of the coaxial "snow."

He sat in front of the set for several hours, his right hand flat against the picture tube, hoping the scanning pattern of the electron bombardment would reveal, through palm flesh grown transparent, the shape of alien bones.

In the middle of the week he asked Harvey Rothammer if he could have the day off Thursday so he could drive out to the hospital in Fontana to see his son. Rothammer was not particularly happy about it, but he didn't have the heart to refuse. Kaw had lost his daughter, and the son was still ninety-five percent incapacitated, lying in a therapy bed with virtually no hope of ever walking again. So he told Willis Kaw to take the day off, but not to forget that April was almost upon them and for a firm of certified public accountants it was rush season. Willis Kaw said he knew that.

The car broke down twenty miles east of San Dimas; and he sat behind the wheel, in the bludgeoning heat, staring at the desert and trying to remember what the surface of his home planet looked like.

His son, Gilvan, had gone on a vacation to visit friends in New Jersey the summer before. The friends had installed a free-standing swimming pool in the back yard. Gil had dived in and struck bottom; he had broken his back.

Fortunately, they had pulled him out before he could drown, but he was paralyzed from the waist down. He could move his arms, but not his hands. Willis had gone East, had arranged to have Gil flown back to California; and there his son lay in a bed in Fontana.

He could only remember the color of the sky. It was a brilliant green, quite lovely. And things that were not birds, that skimmed instead of flying. More than that he could not remember.

The car was towed back to San Dimas, but the garage had to send off to Los Angeles for the necessary parts. He left the car and took a bus back home. He did not get to see Gil that week. The repair bill was two hundred and eighty-six dollars and forty-five cents.

That March the eleven-month drought in Southern California broke. Rain thundered down without end for a week; not as heavily as it does in Brazil, where the drops are so thick and come so close together that people have been known to suffocate if they walk out in the downpour. But heavily enough that the roof of the house sprang leaks. Willis Kaw and Estelle stayed up one entire night, stuffing towels against the baseboards in the living room; but the leaks from the roof apparently weren't over the outer walls but rather in low spots somewhere in the middle; the water was running down and triculating through.

The next morning, depressed beyond endurance, Willis Kaw began to cry. Estelle heard him as she was loading the soaking towels in the dryer, and ran into the living room. He was sitting on the wet carpet, the smell of mildew rising in the room, his hands over his face, still holding a wet bath towel. She knelt down beside him and took his head in her hands and kissed his forehead. He did not stop crying for a very long time, and when he did his eyes burned.

"It only rains in the evening where I come from," he said to her. But she didn't know what he meant.

When she realized, later, she went for a walk, trying to decide if she could help her husband.

He went to the beach. He parked on the shoulder just off the Old Malibu Road, locked the car, and trotted down the embankment to the beach. He walked along the sand for an hour, picking up bits of milky glass worn smooth by the Pacific, and finally he lay down on the slope of a small, weed-thatched dune, and went to sleep.

He dreamed of his home world and—perhaps because the sun was high and the ocean made eternal sounds—he was able to bring much of it back. The bright green sky, the skimmers swooping and rising overhead, the motes of pale yellow light that flamed and then floated up and were lost to sight. He felt himself in his real body, the movement of many legs working in unison, carrying him across the mist sands, the smell of weeping flowers in his mind. He knew he had been born on that world, had been raised there, had grown to maturity and then . . .

Sent away.

In his human mind, Willis Kaw knew he had been sent away for doing something bad. He knew he had been condemned to this planet, this Earth, for having perhaps committed a crime. But he could not remember what it might have been. And in the dream he could feel no guilt.

But when he awoke, his humanity came back and flooded over him and he felt guilt. And he longed to be back out there, where he belonged, not trapped in this terrible body.

"I didn't want to come to you," Willis Kaw said. "I think it's stupid. And if I come, then I seem to be admitting that there's room for doubt. And I don't doubt, so . . ."

The psychiatrist smiled and stirred the cup of cocoa. "And so . . . you came because your wife insisted."

"Yes." He stared at his shoes. They were brown shoes, he had owned them for three years. They had never fit properly; they pinched and made his big toe on each foot feel as if it were being pressed down by a knife edge, a dull knife edge.

The psychiatrist carefully placed the spoon on a piece of Kleenex, and sipped at his cocoa. "Look, Mr. Kaw: I'm open to suggestion. I don't want you to be here, nor do you *want* to be here, if it isn't going to help you. And," he added quickly, "by *help* you I don't mean convert you to any world-view, any systematized belief, you choose to reject. I'm not entirely convinced, by Freud or Werner Erhard or Scientology or any other rigor, that there is such a thing as 'reality.' Codified reality. A given, an immutable, a constant. As long as what someone believes doesn't get him put in a madhouse or a prison, there's no reason why it should be less acceptable than what we, uh, 'straight folks' call reality. If it makes you happy, believe it. What I'd like to do is listen to what you have to say, perhaps offer a few comments, and then see if *your* reality is compatible with *straight folks'* reality.

"How does that sound to you?"

Willis Kaw tried to smile back. "It sounds fine. I'm a little nervous."

"Well, try not to be. That's easy for me to say and hard for you to do, but I mean you no harm; and I'm really quite interested."

Willis uncrossed his legs and stood up. "Is it all right if I just walk around the office a little? It'll help, I think." The psychiatrist nodded and smiled, and indicated the cocoa. Willis Kaw shook his head. He walked around the psychiatrist's office and finally said, "I don't belong in this body. I've been condemned to life as a human being, and it's killing me."

The psychiatrist asked him to explain.

Willis Kaw was a small man, with thinning brown hair and bad eyes. He had weak legs and constantly had need of a handkerchief. His face was set in lines of worry and sadness. He told the psychiatrist all this. Then he said, "I believe this planet is a place where bad people are sent to atone for their crimes. I believe that all of us come from other worlds; other planets where we've done something wrong. This Earth is a prison, and we're sent here to live in these awful bodies that decay and smell bad and run down and die. And that's our punishment."

"But why do *you* perceive such a condition, and no one else?" The psychiatrist had set aside the cocoa, and it was growing cold.

"This must be a defective body they've put me in," Willis Kaw said. "Just a little extra pain, knowing I'm an alien, knowing I'm serving a prison sentence for something I did, something I can't remember; but it must have been an awful thing for me to have drawn such a sentence."

"Have you ever read Franz Kafka, Mr. Kaw?"

"No."

"He wrote books about people who were on trial for crimes the nature of which they never learned. People who were guilty of sins they didn't know they had committed."

"Yes, I feel that way. Maybe Kafka felt that way; maybe he had a defective body, too."

"What you're feeling isn't that strange, Mr. Kaw," the psyciatrist said. "We have many people these days who are dissatisfied with their lives, who find out—perhaps too late—that they are transsexual, that they should have been living their days as something else, a man, a woman . . ."

"No, no! That isn't what I mean. I'm not a candidate for a sex-change. I'm telling you I come from a world with a green sky, with mist sand and light motes that flame and then float up . . . I have many legs, and webs between the digits and they aren't fingers . . ." He stopped and looked embarrassed.

Then he sat down and spoke very softly. "Doctor, my life is like everyone else's life. I'm sick much of the time, I have bills I cannot pay, my daughter was struck by a car and killed and I cannot bear to think about it. My son was cut off in the prime of his life and he'll be a cripple from now on. My wife and I don't talk much, we don't love each other . . . if we ever did. I'm no better and no worse than anyone else on this planet and *that's* what I'm talking about: the pain, the anguish, the living in terror. Terror of each day. Hopeless. Empty. Is this the best a person can have, this terrible life here as a human being? I tell you there are better places, other worlds where the torture of being a human being doesn't exist."

It was growing dark in the psychiatrist's office. Willis Kaw's wife had made the appointment for him at the last moment and the doctor had taken the little man with the thinning brown hair as a fill-in, at the end of the day.

"Mr. Kaw," the psychiatrist said, "I've listened to all you've said, and I want you to know that I'm very much in sympathy with your fears." Willis Kaw felt relieved. He felt at last that someone might be able to help him. If not to relieve him of this terrible knowledge and its weight, at least to tell him he wasn't alone. "And frankly, Mr. Kaw," the psychiatrist said, "I think you're a man with a very serious problem. You're a sick man and you need intense psychiatric help. I'll talk to your wife if you like, but if you take my advice, you'll have yourself placed in a proper institution before this condition . . ."

Willis Kaw closed his eyes.

He pulled the garage door tight and stuffed the cracks with rags. He could not find a hose long enough to feed back into the car from the tail pipe, so he merely opened the car windows and started the engine and let it run. He sat in the back seat and tried to read Dickens's DOMBEY AND SON, a book Gil had once told him he would enjoy.

But he couldn't keep his attention on the story, on the elegant language, and after a while he let his head fall back, and he tried to sleep, to dream of the other world that had been stolen from him, and the world he knew he would never again see. Finally, sleep took him, and he died.

The funeral service was held at Forest Lawn, and very few people came. It was a weekday. Estelle cried, and Harvey Rothammer held her and told her it was okay. But he was checking his wristwatch over her shoulder, because April was almost upon him.

And Willis Kaw was put down in the warm ground, and the dirt of an alien planet was dumped on him by a Chicano with three children, who was forced to moonlight as a dishwasher in a bar and grill because he simply couldn't meet the payments on his six-piece living room suite if he didn't.

The many-legged Consul greeted Willis Kaw when he returned. He turned over and looked up at the Consul and saw the bright green sky above. "Welcome back, Plydo," the Consul said.

He looked very sad.

Plydo, who had been Willis Kaw on a faraway world, got to his feet and looked around. Home.

But he could not keep silent and enjoy the moment. He had to know. "Consul, please . . . tell me . . . what did I do that was so terrible?"

"Terrible?" The Consul seemed stunned. "We owe you nothing but honor, your grace. Your name is valued above all others." There was deep reverence in his words.

"Then why was I condemned to live in anguish on that other world? Why was I sent away to exist in torment?"

The Consul shook his hairy head, and his mane billowed in the warm breeze. "No, your grace, no! Anguish is what *we* suffer. Torment is all *we* know. Only a few, only a very few honored and loved among all the races of the universe can go to that world. Life there is sweet compared to what passes for life everywhere else. You are still disoriented. It will all come back to you. You will remember. And you will understand."

And Plydo, who had been, in a better part of his almost eternal life of pain, Willis Kaw, *did* remember. As time passed, he recalled all the eternities of sadness that had been born in him, and he knew that they had given him the only gift of joy permitted to the races of beings who lived in the far galaxies. The gift of a few precious years on a world where anguish was so much less than that known everywhere else.

He remembered the rain, and the sleep, and the feel of beach sand beneath his feet, and ocean rolling in to whisper its eternal song; and on just such nights as those he had despised on Earth, he slept and dreamed good dreams:

Of life as Willis Kaw; of life on the pleasure planet.

X

NIGHTS & DAYS IN GOOD OLD HOLLYWEIRD

"Without a solid script, the director and his/her players can have all the charisma and verve in the universe, and they'll wind up standing around the sound stage with fingers up their noses."

—"With the Eyes of a Demon: Seeing the Fantastic as a Video Image," THE CRAFT OF SCIENCE FICTION, edited by Reginald Bretnor, Harper & Row, 1976

Now come
(by way of $5 million in advertising)
the clear facts
(1200 theaters booked on a 90/10 split)
of illusion
(matte paintings, scale modes, lab-process trickery):

The tornado transport from Kansas to Oz is a muslin wind sock and fuller's earth in fuzzy focus. The face in the wicked Queen's mirror is roto-scoped at 24 frames per second. A ravaged, demon-possessed young girl's head swivels 180° and audiences no longer distinguish a human actress from a dummy.

Should our century be remembered for anything beyond the hard facts of technological advance, it will likely be for the creation of the most global of modern myths.

Hollywood : Magic.

In the sixty years since the film "industry" was born, the screenwriter has had the hardest battle gaining widespread recognition of his/her worth. We easily remember Cary Grant's portrayal of helpless desperation and Alfred Hitchcock's filmic mastery in *North by Northwest*. Aside from screen buffs, however, who remembers the writer, Ernest Lehman? Some might say it's only words on paper in a format difficult to read and comprehend.

How odd. Movie stars marry and divorce, support charities, tubthump politicians. A famous but aged costume designer expires, reminding millions of how nice so-and-so looked in such-and-such an outfit. Directors orchestrate images with a style that is recognized when the film budget is too low or too high (especially too high). Headlines exploit these stories.

These film artists may be talented, but in reality all of them work for the dreamer: the Hollywood writer.

As with each form of creative output he's mastered, Harlan succeeded in Hollywood by learning the system and then cramming into it all his intelligence and craft. He didn't back off even when the powers-that-be failed to comprehend his methods.

The complete story of Harlan's experiences in filmland would fill a book this size, but the cross-section here offers a range of dreams and disasters that provides a useful scale.

"The Resurgence of Miss Ankle-Strap Wedgie" (1968) puts the lie to nasty *roman à clef* novels, superficial autobiographies and distorted film-movement histories that bury us year after year in tinseled effluvia. That this particular exposure is cast in the form of fiction does not lessen the validity of its insight but, astonishingly, increases it. No individuals need be protected or disguised, and no studio can claim slander, yet they prowl over this sticky web as the legs on the monstrous black widow that Harlan is examining. The mechanics of the Hollywood system have altered since this story was written, just as the system that pervades that other famous Hollywood novella, Nathanael West's "The Day of the Locust," is no longer operative. But it doesn't matter. As were West and Horace McCoy (THEY SHOOT HORSES, DON'T THEY?) before him, Harlan is concerned with the portrayal of the social web and the helpless flies who blunder into entrapment. The nature of the situation comes into focus only when we realize that this particular spider is man-made, unreal, a movie fantasy—and, sadly, no less deadly for that. (As with every piece in this book, the text reprinted here is the preferred; indeed, this version, checked against Harlan's original manuscript, includes a sentence missing from every previous incarnation of this story.)

A number of Harlan Ellison's scripts have appeared on television, along with fragments that flickered momentarily in motion pictures, and he has a record number of awards from the Writers Guild of America to attest to the quality of his work *as written*. Hollywood, however, has a habit of altering scripts—not surprising when one understands the collaboration of art and business necessary to get a film made—and Harlan has seldom, if ever, managed to push a script through in its original form. Not to mention his file drawer of screenplays that have yet to be produced.

A skeletal script seems to have the best chance of materializing as a completed film by slipping through the paradox of ignorant Hollywood producers and the intense demands of story quality. Harlan's scripts have a tendency to veer too far to the side of quality and are written with incredibly detailed, comprehensive visuals. This is not always to his overall benefit when his work must be accessible to functional illiterates as well as to the more sophisticated.

"Flintlock" (1972) is a previously unpublished teleplay that exists *because* of typical industry methods: an attempt to cash in on the successful 1966 film *Our Man Flint,* a humorous send-up of the spy movies that proliferated in the wake of James Bond. Harlan uses the camera's eye with a champion awareness of what it can really do—Shots 97 through 106 are a flawless example of this mastery—as he tumbles through a lighthearted plot that carries on the sardonic tradition of Derek Flint. If you can catch a rerun of the 1976 tv-film that eventually made its way onto the Glass Teat, something titled *Our Man Flint: Dead on Target,* then perhaps you'll see why Harlan's script remained words on paper. It's so much easier for the studios to rely on the standard approach . . . which is why you're now watching soap operas set in Dallas and other suck-it-up pacifiers.

"The Man on the Mushroom" (1974), "Somehow, I Don't Think We're in Kansas, Toto" (1974), and "Face-Down in Gloria Swanson's Swimming Pool" (1978) are Harlan's reports on working in Hollywood, from his arrival in 1962 through the perils and pleasures that followed. The town learned about Harlan Ellison the hard way, and his subsequent reputation there for being a "difficult" talent certainly points up the truth in Robert Bloch's droll assessment of him as "the only living organism I know whose natural habitat is hot water."

In a system riddled with thievery and spite, it's a pleasure to see someone demand ethics and justice and receive national prominence doing it. Harlan's most renowned victory was a lengthy and very expensive court action in which a federal court jury in 1980 awarded $337,000 in damages for copyright infringement resulting from ABC and Paramount's tv-pilot *Future Cop,* which Harlan and Ben Bova charged had been plagiarized from Harlan's screen treatment of their novella, "Brillo."

As Harlan shows us, again and again, even in fantasy, even in *Hollywood* fantasy, the truth will eventually be known.

"Without recourse to the remark crude, I have been known to point out that tv sucks."

—"Days of Blood and Sorrow," Introduction to THE OTHER GLASS TEAT, Pyramid, 1975

The Resurgence of Miss Ankle-Strap Wedgie

(Dedicated to the Memory of Dorothy Parker)

HANDY

In Hollywood our past is so transitory we have little hesitation about tearing down our landmarks. The Garden of Allah where Benchley and Scott Fitzgerald lived is gone; it's been replaced by a savings and loan. Most of the old, sprawling 20th lot has been converted into shopping center and beehive-faceted superhotel. Even historic relics of fairly recent vintage have gone under the cultural knife: the Ziv television studios on Santa Monica, once having been closed down, became the eerie, somehow surrealistic, weed-overgrown and bizarre jungle in which tamed cats that had roamed sound stages became cannibals, eating one another. At night, passing the studio, dark and padlocked, you could hear the poor beasts tearing each other apart. They had lived off the film industry too long, and unable to survive in the streets, lost and bewildered, they had turned into predators.

That may be an apocryphal story. It persists in my thoughts when I remember Valerie Lone.

The point is, we turn the past into the present here in Hollywood even before it's finished being the future. It's like throwing a meal into the Disposall before you eat it.

But we do have one recently erected monument here in the glamour capital of the world.

It is a twenty-three-foot-high billboard for a film called *Subterfuge*. It is a lighthearted adventure-romance in the James Bond tradition and the billboard shows the principal leads—Robert Mitchum and Gina Lollobrigida—in high fashion postures intended to convey, well, adventure and, uh, romance.

The major credits are listed in smaller print on this billboard: produced by Arthur Crewes, directed by James Kencannon, written by John D. F. Black, music by Lalo Schifrin. The balance of the cast is there, also. At the end of the supplementary credits is a boxed line that reads:

ALSO FEATURING MISS VALERIE LONE as Angela.

This line is difficult to read; it has been whited-out.

The billboard stands on a rise overlooking Sunset Boulevard on the Strip near King's Road; close by a teenie-bopper discothèque called Spectrum 2000 that once was glamorous Ciro's. But we tear down our past and convert it to the needs of the moment. The billboard will come down. When the film ends its first run at the Egyptian and opens in neighborhood theaters and drive-ins near you.

At which point even *that* monument to Valerie Lone will have been removed, and almost all of us can proceed to forget. Almost all of us, but not all. I've got to remember . . . my name is Fred Handy. I'm responsible for that billboard. Which makes me a singular man, believe me.

After all, there are so few men who have erected monuments to the objects of their homicide.

1

They came out of the darkness that was a tunnel with a highway at the bottom of it. The headlights were animal eyes miles away down the flat roadbed, and slowly slowly the sound of the engine grew across the emptiness on both sides of the concrete. California desert night, heat of the long day sunk just below the surface of the land, and a car, ponderous, plunging, straight out of nowhere along a white centerline. Gophers and rabbits bounded across the deadly open road and were gone forever.

Inside the limousine men dozed in jump seats and far in the rear two bull-necked cameramen discussed the day's work. Beside the driver, Fred Handy stared straight ahead at the endless stretch of State Highway 14 out of Mojave. He had been under the influence of road hypnosis for the better part of twenty minutes, and did not know it. The voice from the secondary seats behind him jarred him back to awareness. It was Kencannon.

"Jim, how long till we hit Lancaster or Palmdale?"

The driver craned his head back and slightly to the side, awkwardly, like some big bird, keeping his eyes on the road. "Maybe another twenty, twenty-five miles, Mr. K'ncannon. That was Rosamond we passed little while ago."

"Let's stop and eat at the first clean place we see," the director said, thumbing his eyes to remove the sleep from them. "I'm starving."

There was vague movement from the third seats, where Arthur Crewes was folded sidewise, fetuslike, sleeping. A mumbled, "Where are we what time izit?"

Handy turned around. "It's about three forty-five, Arthur. Middle of the desert."

"Midway between Mojave and Lancaster, Mr. Crewes," the driver added. Crewes grunted acceptance of it.

The producer sat up in sections, swinging his legs down heavily, pulling his body erect sluggishly, cracking his shoulders back as he arched forward. With his eyes closed. "Jeezus, remind me next time to do a picture without location shooting. I'm too old for this crap." There was the murmur of trained laughter from somewhere in the limousine.

Handy thought of Mitchum, who had returned from the Mojave location earlier that day, riding back in the air-conditioned land cruiser the studio provided. But the thought only reminded him that he was not one of the Immortals, one of the golden people; that he was merely a two-fifty-a-week publicist who was having one helluva time trying to figure out a promotional angle for just another addle-witted spy-romance. Crewes had come to the genre belatedly, after the Bond flicks, after *Ipcress*, after *Arabesque* and *Masquerade* and *Kaleidoscope* and *Flint* and *Modesty Blaise* and they'd *all* come after *The 39 Steps* so what the hell did it matter; with Arthur Crewes producing, it would get serious attention and good play dates. *If*. If Fred Handy could figure out a Joe Levine William Castle Sam Katzman Alfred Hitchcock *shtick* to pull the suckers in off the streets. He longed for the days back in New York when he had had ulcers working in the agency. He still had them, but the difference was *now* he couldn't even *pretend* to be enjoying life enough to compensate for the aggravation. He longed for the days of his youth writing imbecilic poetry in Figaro's in the Village. He longed for the faintly moist body of Julie, away in the Midwest somewhere doing *Hello, Dolly!* on the strawhat circuit. He longed for a hot bath to leach all the weariness out of him. He longed for a hot bath to clean all the Mojave dust and grit out of his pores.

He longed *desperately* for something to eat.

"Hey, Jim, how about that over there . . . ?"

He tapped the driver on the forearm, and pointed down the highway to the neon flickering off and on at the roadside. The sign said SHIVEY'S TRUCK STOP and EAT. There were no trucks parked in front.

"It must be good food," Kencannon said from behind him. "I don't see any trucks there; and you know what kind of food you get at the joints truckers eat at."

Handy smiled quickly at the reversal of the old road-runner's myth. It was that roundabout sense of humor that made Kencannon's direction so individual.

"That okay by you, Mr. Crewes?" Jim asked.

"Fine, Jim," Arthur Crewes said, wearily.

The studio limousine turned in at the diner and crunched gravel. The diner was an anachronism. One of the old railroad car style, seen most frequently on the New Jersey thruways. Aluminum hide leprous with rust. Train windows fogged with dirt. Lucky Strike and El Producto decals on the door. Three steps up to the door atop a concrete stoop. Parking lot surrounding it like a gray pebble lake, cadaverously cold in the intermittent flashing of the pale yellow neon EAT off EAT off EAT . . .

The limousine doors opened, all six of them, and ten crumpled men emerged, stretched, trekked toward the diner. They fell into line almost according to the pecking order. Crewes and Kencannon; Fred Handy; the two cameramen; three grips; the effeminate makeup man, Sancher; and Jim, the driver.

They climbed the stairs, murmuring to themselves, like sluggish animals emerging from a dead sea of sleep. The day had been exhausting. Chase scenes through the rural town of Mojave. And Mitchum in his goddam land cruiser, phoning ahead to have *escargots* ready at La Rue.

The diner was bright inside, and the grips, the cameramen and Jim took booths alongside the smoked windows. Sancher went immediately to the toilet, to moisten himself with 5-Day Deodorant Pads. Crewes sat at the counter with Handy and Kencannon on either side of him. The producer looked ancient. He was a dapper man in his middle forties. He clasped his hands in front of him and Handy saw him immediately begin twisting and turning the huge diamond ring on his right hand, playing with it, taking it off and replacing it. *I wonder what that means*, Handy thought.

Handy had many thoughts about Arthur Crewes. Some of them were friendly, most were impartial. Crewes was a job for Handy. He has seen the producer step heavily when the need arose: cutting off a young writer when the script wasn't being written fast enough to make a shooting date; literally threatening an actor with bodily harm if he didn't cease the senseless wrangling on set that was costing the production money; playing agents against one another to catch a talented client unrepresented between them, available for shaved cost. But he had seen him perform unnecessary kindnesses. Unnecessary because they bought nothing, won him nothing, made him no points. Crewes had blown a tire on a freeway one day and a motorist had stopped to help. Crewes had taken his name and sent him a three thousand dollar color television-stereo. A starlet ready to put out for a part had been investigated by the detective agency Crewes kept on retainer at all times for assorted odd jobs. They had found out her child was a paraplegic. She had not been required to go the couch route, Crewes had refused her the job on grounds of talent, but had given her a check in the equivalent amount had she gotten the part.

Arthur Crewes was a very large man indeed in Hollywood. He had not always been immense, however. He had begun his career as a film editor on "B" horror flicks, worked his way up and directed several productions, then been put in charge of a series of low-budget films at the old RKO studio. He had suffered in the vineyards and somehow run the time very fast. He was still a young man, and he was ancient, sitting there turning his ring.

Sancher came out of the toilet and sat down at the far end of the counter. It seemed to jog Kencannon. "Think I'll wash off a little Mojave filth," he said, and rose. Crewes got up. "I suddenly realized I haven't been to the bathroom all day."

They walked away, leaving Handy sitting, toying with the sugar shaker.

He looked up for the first time, abruptly realizing how exhausted he was. There was a waitress shaking a wire basket of french fries, her back to him. The picture was on schedule, no problems, but no hook, no gimmick, no angle, no *shtick* to sell it; there was a big quarterly payment due on the house in Sherman Oaks; it was all Handy had, no one was going to get it; he had to keep the job. The waitress turned around for the first time and started laying out napkin, water glass, silverware, in front of him. You could work in a town for close to nine years, and still come away with nothing; not even living high, driving a '65 Impala, that wasn't ostentatious; but a lousy forty-five-day marriage to a clip artist and it was all in jeopardy; he had to keep the job, just to fight her off, keep her from using California divorce logic to get that house; nine years was *not* going down the tube; God, he felt weary. The waitress was in the booth, setting up the grips and cameramen. Handy mulled the nine years, wondering what the hell he was doing out here: oh yeah, I was getting divorced, that's what I was doing. Nine years seemed so long, so ruthlessly long, and so empty suddenly, to be here with Crewes on another of the endless product that got fed into the always-yawning maw of the Great American Moviegoing Public. The waitress returned and stood before him.

"Care to order now?"

He looked up.

Fred Handy stopped breathing for a second. He looked at her, and the years peeled away. He was a teenage kid in the Utopia Theater in St. Louis, Missouri, staring up at a screen with gray shadows moving on it. A face from the past, a series of features, very familiar, were superimposing themselves.

She saw he was staring. "Order?"

He had to say it just right. "Excuse me, is, uh, is your name Lone?"

Until much later, he was not able to identify the expression that swam up in her eyes. But when he thought back on it, he knew it had been terror. Not fear, not trepidation, not uneasiness, not wariness. Terror. Complete, total, gagging terror. She said later it had been like calling the death knell for her . . . again.

She went stiff, and her hand slid off the counter edge. "Valerie Lone?" he said, softly, frightened by the look on her face. She swallowed so that the hollows in her cheeks moved liquidly. And she nodded. The briefest movement of the head.

Then he knew he had to say it just right. He was holding all that fragile crystal, and a wrong phrase would shatter it. Not: *I used to see your movies when I was a kid* or: *Whatever happened to you* or: *What are you doing here*. It had to be just right.

Handy smiled like a little boy. It somehow fit his craggy features. "You know," he said gently, "many's the afternoon I've sat in the movies and been in love with you."

There was gratitude in her smile. Relief, an ease of tensions, and the sudden rush of her own memories; the bittersweet taste of remembrance as the glories of her other life swept back to her. Then it was gone, and she was a frowzy blonde waitress on Route 14 again. "Order?"

She wasn't kidding. She turned it off like a mercury switch. One moment there was life in the faded blue eyes, the next moment it was ashes. He ordered a cheeseburger and french fries. She went back to the steam table.

Arthur Crewes came out of the men's room first. He was rubbing his hands. "Damned powdered soap, almost as bad as those stiff paper towels." He slipped onto the stool beside Handy.

And in that instant, Fred Handy saw a great white light come up. Like the buzz an acid-head gets from a fully drenched sugar cube, his mind burst free and went trembling outward in waves of color. The *shtick*, the bit, the handle, ohmigod there it is, as perfect as a blue-white diamond.

Arthur Crewes was reading the menu as Handy grabbed his wrist. "Arthur, do you know who that is?"

"Who *who* is?"

"The waitress."

"Madame Nehru."

"I'm serious, Arthur."

"All right, who?"

"Valerie Lone."

Arthur Crewes started as though he had been struck. He shot a look at the waitress, her back to them now, as she ladled up navy bean soup from the stainless steel tureen in the steam table. He stared at her, silently.

"I don't believe it," he murmured.

"It is, Arthur, I'm telling you that's just who it is."

He shook his head. "What the hell is she doing out here in the middle of nowhere. My God, it must be, what? Fifteen, twenty years?"

Handy considered a moment. "About eighteen years, if you count that thing she did for Ross at UA in forty-eight. Eighteen years and here she is, slinging hash in a diner."

Crewes mumbled something.

"What did you say?" Handy asked him.

Crewes repeated it, with an edge Handy could not place. "Lord how the mighty have fallen."

Before Handy could tell the producer his idea, she turned, and saw Crewes staring at her. There was no recognition in her expression. But it was obvious she knew Handy had told him who she was. She turned away and carried the plates of soup to the booth.

As she came back past them, Crewes said, softly, "Hello, Miss Lone." She paused and stared at him. She was almost somnambulistic, moving by rote. He added, "Arthur Crewes . . . remember?"

She did not answer for a long moment, then nodded as she had to Handy. "Hello. It's been a long time."

Crewes smiled a peculiar smile. Somehow victorious. "Yes, a long time. How've you been?"

She shrugged, as if to indicate the diner. "Fine, thank you."

They fell silent.

"Would you care to order now?"

When she had taken the order and moved to the grill, Handy leaned in close to the producer and began speaking intensely. "Arthur, I've got a fantastic idea."

His mind was elsewhere. "What's that, Fred?"

"Her. Valerie Lone, What a sensational idea. Put her in the picture. The comeback of . . . what was it they used to call her, that publicity thing, oh yeah . . . the comeback of 'Miss Ankle-Strap Wedgie.' It's good for space in any newspaper in the country."

Silence.

"Arthur? What do you think?"

Arthur Crewes smiled down at his hands. He was playing with the ring again. "You think I should bring her back to the industry after eighteen years."

"I think it's the most natural winning promotion idea I've ever had. And I can tell you like it."

Crewes nodded, almost absently. "Yes, I like it, Fred. You're a very bright fellow. I like it just fine."

Kencannon came back and sat down. Crewes turned to him. "Jim, can you do cover shots on the basement scenes with Bob and the stunt men for a day or two?"

Kencannon bit his lip, considering. "I suppose so. It'll mean re-plotting the schedule, but the board's Bernie's problem, not mine. What's up?"

Crewes twisted the ring and smiled distantly. "I'm going to call Johnny Black in and have him do a rewrite on the part of Angela. Beef it up."

"For what? We haven't even cast it yet."

"We have now." Handy grinned hugely. "Valerie Lone."

"Valerie—you're *kid*ding. She hasn't even *made* a film in God knows how long. What makes you think you can get her?"

Crewes turned back to stare at the sloped shoulders of the woman at the sizzling grill. "I can get her."

HANDY

We talked to Valerie Lone, Crewes and myself. First I talked, then he talked; then when she refused to listen to him, I talked again.

She grabbed up a huge pan with the remains of macaroni and cheese burned to the bottom, and she dashed out through a screen door at the rear of the diner.

We looked at each other, and when each of us saw the look of confusion on the other's face, the looks vanished. We got up and followed her. She was leaning against the wall of the diner, scraping the crap from the pan as she cried. The night was quiet.

But she didn't melt as we came through the screen door. She got uptight. Furious. "I've been out of all that for over fifteen years, can't you leave me alone? You've got a lousy sense of humor if you think this is funny!"

Arthur Crewes stopped dead on the stairs. He didn't know what to say to her. There was something happening to Crewes; I didn't know what it was, but it was more than whatever it takes to get a gimmick for a picture.

I took over.

Handy, the salesman. Handy, the *schmacheler,* equipped with the very best butter. "It isn't fifteen years, Miss Lone. It's eighteen plus."

Something broke inside her. She turned back to the pan. Crewes didn't know whether to tell me to back off or not, so I went ahead. I pushed past Crewes, standing there with his hand on the peeling yellow paint banister, his mouth open. (The color of the paint was the color of a stray dog I had run down in Nevada one time. I hadn't seen the animal. It had dashed out of a gully by the side of the road and I'd gone right over it before I knew what had happened. But I stopped and went back. It was the same color as that banister. A faded lonely yellow, like cheap foolscap, a dollar a ream. I couldn't get the thought of that dog out of my mind.)

"You like it out here, right?"

She didn't turn around.

I walked around her. She was looking into that pan of crap. "Miss Lone?"

It was going to take more than soft-spoken words. It might even take sincerity. I wasn't sure I knew how to do *that* any more. "If I didn't know better . . . having seen all the feisty broads you played . . . I'd think you *enjoyed* feeling sorry for your—"

She looked up, whip-fast, I could hear the cartilage cracking in her neck muscles. There was a core of electrical sparks in her eyes. She was pissed-off. "Mister, I just met your face. What makes you think you can talk that way . . ." it petered out. The steam leaked off, and the sparks died, and she was back where she'd been a minute before.

I turned her around to face us. She shrugged my hand off. She wasn't a sulky child, she was a woman who didn't know how to get away from a giant fear that was getting more gigantic with every passing second. And even in fear she wasn't about to let me manhandle her.

"Miss Lone, we've got a picture working. It isn't *Gone with the Wind* and it isn't *The Birth of a Nation*, it's just a better-than-average coupla million dollar spectacular with Mitchum and Lollobrigida, and it'll make a potful for everybody concerned . . ."

Crewes was staring at me. I didn't like his expression. He was the bright young wunderkind who had made *Lonely in the Dark* and *Ruby Bernadette* and *The Fastest Man*, and he didn't like to hear me pinning his latest opus as just a nice, money-making color puffball. But Crewes wasn't a wunderkind any longer, and he wasn't making Kafka, he was making box-office bait, and he needed this woman, and so dammit did I! So screw his expression.

"Nobody's under the impression you're one of the great ladies of the theater; you never were Katherine Cornell, or Bette Davis, or even Pat Neal." She gave me that core of sparks look again. If I'd been a younger man it might have woofed me; I'm sure it had stopped legions of assistant gophers in the halcyon days. But—it suddenly scared me to realize it—I was running hungry, and mere looks didn't do it. I pushed her a little harder, my best Raymond Chandler delivery. "But you *were* a star, you were someone that people paid money to see, because whatever you had it was *yours*. And whatever that was, we want to rent it for a while, we want to bring it back."

She gave one of those little snorts that says very distinctly *You stink, Jack*. It was disdainful. She had my number. But that was cool; I'd given it to her; I wasn't about to shuck her.

"Don't think we're humanitarians. We *need* something like you on this picture. We need a handle, something that'll get us that extra two inches in the Wichita *Eagle*. That means bucks in the ticket wicket. Oh, shit, lady!"

Her teeth skinned back.

I was getting to her.

"We can help each other." She sneered and started to turn away. I reached out and slammed the pan as hard as I could. It spun out of her hands and hit the steps. She was rocked quiet for an instant, and I rapped on her as hard as I could. "Don't tell me you're in love with scraping crap out of a macaroni dish. You lived too high, too long. This is a free ride back. Take it!"

There was blood coursing through her veins now. Her cheeks had bright, flushed spots on them, high up under the eyes. "I can't do it; stop pushing at me."

Crewes moved in, then. We worked like a pair of good homicide badges. I beat her on the head, and he came running with Seidlitz powders. "Let her alone a minute, Fred. This is all at once, come on, let her think."

"What the hell's to think?"

She was being rammed from both sides, and knew it, but for the first time in years something was *happening*, and her motor was starting to run again, despite herself.

"Miss Lone," Crewes said gently, "a contract for this film, and options for three more. Guaranteed, from first day of shooting, straight through, even if you sit around after your part is shot, till last day of production."

"I haven't been anywhere near a camera—"

"That's what we have cameramen for. They turn it on you. That's what we have a director for. He'll tell you where to stand. It's like swimming or riding a bike: once you learn, you never forget . . ."

Crewes again. "Stop it, Fred. Miss Lone . . . I remember you from before. You were always good to work with. You weren't one of the cranky ones, you were a doer. You knew your lines, always."

She smiled. A wee timorous slippery smile. She remembered. And she chuckled. "Good memory, that's all."

Then Crewes and I smiled, too. She was on our side. Everything she said from here on out would be to win us the argument. She was ours.

"You know, I had the world's all-time great crush on you, Miss Lone," Arthur Crewes, a very large man in town, said. She smiled a little-girl smile of graciousness.

"I'll think about it." She stooped for the pan.

He reached it before she did. "I won't give you time to think. There'll be a car here for you tomorrow at noon."

He handed her the pan.

She took it reluctantly.

We had dug Valerie Lone up from under uncounted strata of self-pity and anonymity, from a kind of grave she had chosen for herself for reasons I was beginning to understand. As we went back inside the diner, I had The Thought for the first time:

The Thought: *What if we ain't doing her no favors?*

And the voice of Donald Duck came back at me from the Clown Town of my thoughts: With friends like you, Handy, she may not need any enemies.

Screw you, Duck.

2

The screen flickered, and Valerie Lone, twenty years younger, wearing the pageboy and padded shoulders of the Forties swept into the room. Cary Grant looked up from the microscope with his special genteel exasperation, and asked her *precisely* where she had been. Valerie Lone, the coiffed blonde hair carefully smoothed, removed her gloves and sat on the laboratory counter. She crossed her legs. She was wearing ankle-strap wedgies.

"I think the legs are still damned good, Arthur," Fred Handy said. Cigar smoke rose up in the projection room. Arthur Crewes did not answer. He was busy watching the past.

Full hips, small breasts, blonde; a loveliness that was never wispy like a Jean Arthur, never chill like a Joan Crawford, never cultured like a Greer Garson. If Valerie Lone had been identifiable with anyone else working in her era, it would have been with Ann Sheridan. And the comparison was by no means invidious. There was the same forceful *womanliness* in her manner; a wise kid who knew the score. Dynamic. Yet there was a quality of availability in the way she arched her eyebrows, the way she held her hands and neck. Sensuality mixed with reality. What had broken that spine of self-control, turned it into the fragile wariness Handy had sensed? He studied the film as the story unreeled, but there was none of that showing in the Valerie Lone of twenty years before.

As the deep, silken voice faded from the screen, Arthur Crewes reached to the console beside his contour chair, and punched a series of buttons. The projection light cut off from the booth behind them, the room lights went up, and the chair tilted forward. The producer got up and left the room, with Handy behind him, waiting for comments. They had spent close to eight hours running old prints of Valerie Lone's biggest hits.

Arthur Crewes's home centered around the projection room. As his life centered around the film industry. Through the door, and into the living room, opulent beneath fumed and waxed, shadowed oak beams far above them; the two men did not speak. The living room was immense, only slightly smaller than a basketball court in one corner where Crewes now settled into a deep armchair, before a roaring walk-in fireplace. The rest of the living room was empty and quiet; one could hear the fall of dust. It had been a gay house many times in the past, and would be again, but at the moment, far down below the vaulting ceiling, their voices rising like echoes in a mountain pass, Arthur Crewes spoke to his publicist.

"Fred, I want the full treatment. I want her seen everywhere by everyone. I want her name as big as it ever was."

Handy pursed his lips, even as he nodded. "That takes money, Arthur. We're pushing the publicity budget now."

Crewes lit a cigar. "This is above-the-line expense. Keep it a separate record, and I'll take care of it out of my pocket. I want it all itemized for the IRS, but don't spare the cost."

"Do you know how much you're getting into here?"

"It doesn't matter. Whatever it is, however much you need, come and ask, and you'll get it. But I want a real job done for that money, Fred."

Handy stared at him for a long moment.

"You'll get mileage out of Valerie Lone's comeback, Arthur. No doubt about it. But I have to tell you right now it isn't going to be anything near commensurate with what you'll be spending. It isn't that kind of appeal."

Crewes drew deeply on the cigar, sent a thin streamer of blue smoke toward the darkness above them. "I'm not concerned about the value to the picture. It's going to be a good property, it can take care of itself. This is something else."

Handy looked puzzled. "Why?"

Crewes did not answer. Finally, he asked, "Is she settled in at the Beverly Hills?"

Handy rose to leave. "Best bungalow in the joint. You should have seen the reception they gave her."

"That's the kind of reception I want everywhere for her, Fred. A lot of bowing and scraping for the old queen."

Handy nodded, walked toward the foyer. Across the room, forcing him to raise his voice to reach Crewes, still lost in the dimness of the living room, the fireplace casting spastic shadows of blood and night on the walls, Fred Handy said, "Why the extra horsepower, Arthur? I get nervous when I'm told to spend freely."

Smoke rose from the chair where Arthur Crewes was hidden. "Good night, Fred."

Handy stood for a moment; then, troubled, he let himself out. The living room was silent for a long while, only the faint crackling of the logs on the fire breaking the stillness. Then Arthur Crewes reached to the sidetable and lifted the telephone receiver from its cradle. He punched out a number.

"Miss Valerie Lone's bungalow, please . . . yes, I know what time it is. This is Arthur Crewes calling . . . thank you."

There was a pause, then sound from the other end.

"Hello, Miss Lone? Arthur Crewes. Yes, thank you. Sorry if I disturbed you . . . oh, really? I rather thought you might be awake. I had the feeling you might be a little uneasy, first night back and all."

He listened to the voice at the other end. And did not smile. Then he said, "I just wanted to call and tell you not to be afraid. Everything will be fine. There's nothing to be afraid of. Nothing at all."

His eyes became light, and light fled down the wires to see her at the other end. In the elegant bungalow, still sitting in the dark. Through a window, moonlight lay like a patina of dull gold across the room, tinting even the depressions in the sofa pillows where a thousand random bottoms had rested, a vaguely yellow ocher.

Valerie Lone. Alone.

Misted by a fine down of Beverly Hills moonlight—the great gaffer in the sky working behind an amber gel keylighting her with a senior, getting fill light from four broads and four juniors, working the light outside in the great celestial cyclorama with a dozen sky-pans, and catching her just right with a pair of inky-dinks, scrims, gauzes and cutters—displaying her in a gown of powdered moth-wing dust. Valerie Lone, off-camera, trapped by the lens of God, and the electric eyes of Arthur Crewes. But still in XTREME CLOSEUP.

She thanked him, seeming bewildered by his kindness. "Is there anything you need?" he asked.

He had to ask her to repeat her answer, she had spoken so softly. But the answer was *nothing,* and he said *good night,* and was about to hang up when she called him.

To Crewes it was a sound from farther away than the Beverly Hills Hotel. It was a sound that came by way of a Country of Mildew. From a land where oily things moved out of darkness. From a place where the only position was hunched safely into oneself with hands about knees, chin tucked down, hands wrapped tightly so that if the eyes with their just-born-bird membranes should open, through the film could be seen the relaxed fingers. It was a sound from a country where there was no hiding place.

After a moment he answered, shaken by her frightened sound. "Yes, I'm here."

Now he could not see her, even with eyes of electricity.

For Valerie Lone sat on the edge of the bed in her bungalow, not bathed in moth-wing dust, but lighted harshly by every lamp and overhead in the bungalow. She could not turn out those lights. She was petrified with fear. A nameless fear that had no origin and had no definition. It was merely *there with her;* a palpable presence.

And something else was in the room with her.

"They . . ."

She stopped. She knew Crewes was straining at the other end of the line to hear what followed.

"They sent your champagne."

Crewes smiled to himself. She was touched.

Valerie Lone did not smile, was incapable of a smile, was by no means touched. The bottle loomed huge across the room on the glass-topped table. "Thank you. It was. Very. Kind. Of. You."

Slowly, because of the way she had told him the champagne had arrived, Crewes asked, "Are you all right?"

"I'm frightened."

"There's nothing to be frightened about. We're all on your team, you know that . . ."

"I'm frightened of the champagne . . . it's been so long."

Crewes did not understand. He said so.

"I'm afraid to drink it."

Then he understood.

He didn't know what to say. For the first time in many years he felt pity for someone. He was fully conversant with affection, and hatred, and envy, and admiration and even stripped-to-the-bone lust. But pity was something he somehow hadn't had to deal with, for a long time. His ex-wife and the boy, they were the last, and that had been eight years before. He didn't know what to say.

"I'm afraid, isn't that silly? I'm afraid I'll like it too much again. I've managed to forget what it tastes like. But if I open it, and taste it, and remember . . . I'm afraid . . ."

He said, "Would you like me to drive over?"

She hesitated, pulling her wits about her. "No. No, I'll be all right. I'm just being silly. I'll talk to you tomorrow." Then, hastily: "You'll call tomorrow?"

"Yes, of course. Sure I will. I'll call first thing in the morning, and you'll come down to the Studio. I'm sure there are all sorts of people you'll want to get reacquainted with."

Silence, then, softly: "Yes. I'm just being silly. It's very lonely here."

"Well, then. I'll call in the morning."

"Lonely . . . hmmm? Oh, yes! Thank you. Good night, Mr. Crewes."

"Arthur. That's first on the list. Arthur."

"Arthur. Thank you. Good night."

"Good night, Miss Lone."

He hung up, still hearing the same voice he had heard in darkened theaters rich with the smell of popcorn (in the days before they started putting faintly rancid butter on it) and the taste of Luden's Menthol Cough Drops. The same deep, silken voice that he had just this moment past heard break, ever so slightly, with fear.

Darkness rose up around him.

Light flooded Valerie Lone. The lights she would keep burning all night, because out there was darkness and it was so lonely in here. She stared across the room at the bottle of champagne, sitting high in its silver ice bucket, chipped base of ice melting to frigid water beneath it.

Then she stood and took a drinking glass from the tray on the bureau, ignoring the champagne glasses that had come with the bottle. She walked across the room to the bathroom and went inside, without turning on the light. She filled the water glass from the tap, letting the cold faucet run for a long moment. Then she stood in the doorway of the bathroom, drinking the water, staring at the bottle of champagne, that bottle of champagne.

Then slowly, she went to it and pulled the loosened plastic cork from the mouth of the bottle. She poured half a glass.

She sipped it slowly.

Memories stirred.

And a dark shape fled off across hills in the Country of Mildew.

3

Handy drove up the twisting road into the Hollywood Hills. The call he had received an hour before was one he would never have expected. He had not heard from Huck Barkin in over two years. Haskell Barkin, the tall. Haskell Barkin, the tanned. Haskell Barkin, the handsome. Haskell Barkin, the amoral. The last time Fred had seen Huck, he was busily making a precarious living hustling wealthy widows with kids. His was a specialized con: he got next to the kids—Huck was one of the more accomplished surf-bums extant—even as he seduced the mother, and before the family attorney knew what was happening, the pitons and grapnels and tongs had been sunk in deep, through the mouth and out the other side, and friendly, good-looking, rangy Huck Barkin was living in the house, driving the Imperial, ordering McCormick's bourbon from the liquor store, eating like Quantrill's Raiders, and clipping bucks like the Russians were in Pomona.

There had been one who had tried to saturate herself with barbiturates when Huck had said, *"À bientot."*

There had been one who had called in her battery of attorneys in an attempt to have him make restitution, but she had been informed Huck Barkin was one of those rare, seldom "judgment-proof" people.

There had been one who had gone away to New Mexico, where it was warm, and no one would see her drinking.

There had been one who had bought a tiny gun, but had never used it on him.

There had been one who had already had the gun, and she *had* used it. But not on Huck Barkin.

Fearsome, in his strangeness; without ethic. Animal.

He was one of the more unpleasant Hollywood creeps Handy had met in the nine Hollywood years. Yet there was an unctuous charm about the man; it sat well on him, if the observers weren't the most perceptive. Handy chuckled, remembering the one and only time he had seen Barkin shot down. By a woman. (And how seldom *any* woman can *really* put down a man, with such thoroughness that there is no comeback, no room to rationalize that it wasn't such a great zinger, with the full certainty that the target has been utterly destroyed, and nothing is left but to slink away. He remembered.)

It had been at a party thrown by CBS, to honor the star of their new ninety-minute Western series. Big party. Century City Hotel. All the silkies were there, all the sleek, well-fed types who went without eating a full day to make it worthwhile at the barbecue and buffet. Barkin had somehow been invited. Or crashed. No one ever questioned his appearance at these things; black mohair suit is ticket enough in a scene where recognition is predicated on the uniform of the day.

He had sidled into a conversational group composed of Handy and his own Julie, Spencer Lichtman the agent and two very expensive call girls—all pale silver hair and exquisite faces; hundred and a half per night girls; the kind a man could talk to afterward, learn something from, probably with Masters earned in photochemistry or piezoelectricity; nothing even remotely cheap or brittle about them; master craftsmen in a specialized field—and Barkin had unstrapped his Haskellesque charm. The girls had sensed at once that he was one of the leeches, hardly one of the cruisable meal tickets with wherewithal. They had been courteous, but chill. Barkin had gone from unctuous to rank in three giant steps, without saying, "May I?"

Finally, in desperation, he had leaned in close to the taller of the two silver goddesses, and murmured (loud enough for all in the group to overhear) with a Richard Widmark thinness: "How would you like me down in your panties?"

Silence for a beat, then the silver goddess turned to him with eyes of anthracite, and across the chill polar wastes came her reply. "I have one asshole down there now . . . what would I want with you?"

Handy chuckled again, smugly, remembering the look on Barkin as he had broken down into his component parts, reformed as a puddle of strawberry jam sliding down one of the walls, and oozed out of the scene, not to return that night.

Yet there was a roguish good humor about the big blond beach-bum that most people took at face value; only if Huck's back was put to the wall did the façade of affability drop away to reveal the granite foundation of amorality. The man was intent on sliding through life with as little effort as possible.

Handy had spotted him for what he was almost immediately upon meeting him, but for a few months Huck had been an amusing adjunct to Handy's new life in the film colony. They had not been in touch for three years. Yet this morning the call had come from Barkin. Using Arthur Crewes's name. He had asked Handy to come to see him, and given him an address in the Hollywood Hills.

Now, as he tooled the Impala around another snakeback curve, the top of the mountain came into view, and Handy saw the house. As it was the *only* house, dominating the flat, he assumed it was the address Barkin had given him, and he marveled. It was a gigantic circle of a structure, a flattened spool of sandblasted gray rock whose waist was composed entirely of curved panels of dark-smoked glass. Barkin could never have afforded an Orwellian feast of a home like this.

Handy drove up the flaring spiral driveway and parked beside the front door: an ebony slab with a rhodium-plated knob as big as an Impala headlight.

The grounds were incredibly well-tailored, sloping down all sides of the mountain to vanish over the next flat. Bonsai trees pruned in their abstracted Zen artfulness, bougainvillea rampant across one entire outcropping, banks of flowers, dichondra everywhere, ivy.

Then Handy realized the house was turning. To catch the sun. Through a glass roof. The front door was edging past him toward the west. He walked up to it, and looked for a doorbell. There was none.

From within the house came the staccato report of hardwood striking hardwood. It came again and again, in uneven, frantic bursts. And the sound of grunting.

He turned the knob, expecting the gigantic door to resist, but it swung open on a center-pin, counterbalanced, and he stepped through into the front hall of inlaid onyx tiles.

The sounds of wood on wood, and grunting, were easy to follow. He went down five steps into a passageway, and followed it toward the sound, emerging at the other end of the passage into a living room ocean-deep in sunshine. In the center of the room Huck Barkin and a tiny Japanese, both in loose-fitting ceremonial robes, were jousting with sawed-off quarterstaffs—*shoji* sticks.

Handy watched silently. The diminutive Japanese was electric. Barkin was no match for him, though he managed to get in a smooth rap or two from moment to moment. But the Oriental rolled and slid, barely seeming to touch the deep white carpet. His hands moved like propellers, twisting the hardwood staff to counter a swing by the taller man, jabbing sharply to embed the point of the staff in Barkin's ribs. In and out and gone. He was a blur.

As Barkin turned in almost an *entrechat*, to avoid a slantwise flailing maneuver by the Oriental, he saw Handy standing in the entranceway to the passage. Barkin stepped back from his opponent.

"That'll do it for now, Mas," he said.

They bowed to one another, the Oriental took the staffs, and left through another passageway at the far end of the room. Barkin came across the rug liquidly, all the suntanned flesh rippling with the play of solid muscle underneath. Handy found himself once again admiring the shape Barkin kept himself in. *But if you do nothing but spend time on your body, why not?* he thought ruefully. The idea of honest labor had never taken up even temporary residence in Huck's thoughts. And yet one body-building session was probably equal to all the exertion a common laborer would expend in a day.

Handy thought Huck was extending his hand in greeting, but half-way across the room the robed beach-bum reached over to a Saarinen chair and snagged a huge, fluffy towel. He swabbed his face and chest with it, coming to Handy.

"Fred, baby."

"How are you, Huck?"

"Great, fellah. Just about king of the world these days. Like the place?"

"Nice. Whose is it?"

"Belongs to a chick I've been seeing. Old man's one of the big things happening in some damned banana republic or other. I don't give it too much thought; she'll be back in about a month. Till then I've got the run of the joint. Want a drink?"

"It's eleven o'clock."

"Coconut milk, friend buddy friend. Got all the amino acids you can use all day. Very important."

"I'll pass."

Barkin shrugged, walking past him to a mirrored wall that was jeweled with the reflections of pattering sunlight streaming in from above. He seemed to wipe his hand over the mirror, and the wall swung out to reveal a fully stocked bar. He took a can of coconut milk from the small freezer unit, and opened it, drinking straight from the can.

"Doesn't that smart a bit?" Handy asked.

"The coconut mil—oh, you mean the *shoji* jousting. Best damned thing in the world to toughen you up. Teak. Get whacked across the belly half a dozen times with one of those and your stomach muscles turn to leather."

He flexed.

"Leather stomach muscles. Just what I've always yearned for."

Handy walked across the room and stared out through the dark glass at the incredible Southern California landscape, blighted by a murmuring, hanging pall of sickly smog over the Hollywood Freeway. With his back turned to Barkin, he said, "I tried to call Crewes after you spoke to me. He wasn't in. I came anyway. How come you used his name?" He turned around.

"He told me to."

"Where did *you* meet Arthur Crewes!" Handy snapped, sudden anger in his voice. This damned beach stiff, it had to be a shuck; he had to have used Handy's name somehow.

"At that pool party you took me to, about—what was it—about three years ago. You remember, that little auburn-haired thing, what was her name, Binnie, Bunny, something . . . ?"

"Billie. Billie Landewyck. Oh, yeah, I'd forgotten Crewes was there."

Huck smiled a confident smile. He downed the last of the coconut milk and tossed the can into a wastebasket. He came around the bar and slumped onto the sofa. "Yeah, well. Crewes remembered me. Got me through Central Casting. I keep my SAG dues up, never know when you can pick up a few bucks doing stunt or a bit. You know."

Handy did not reply. He was waiting. Huck had simply said Arthur Crewes wanted him to get together with the beach-bum, so Handy had come. But there was something stirring that Barkin didn't care to open up just yet.

"Listen, Huck, I'm getting to be an old man. I can't stand on my feet too long any more. So if you've got something shaking, let's to it, friend buddy friend."

Barkin nodded silently, as though resigned to whatever it was he had to say. "Yeah, well. Crewes wants me to meet Valerie Lone."

Handy stared.

"He remembered me."

Handy tried to speak, found he had nothing to say. It was too ridiculous. He turned to leave.

"Hold it, Fred. Don't do that, man. I'm talking to you."

"You're talking *nothing*, Barkin. You've gotta be straight out of a jug. Valerie Lone, my ass. Who do you think you're shucking? Not me, not good old friend buddy friend Handy. I know you, you deadbeat."

Barkin stood up, unfurled something over six feet of deltoid, trapezius and bicep, toned till they hummed, and planted himself in front of the passageway. "Fred, you continue to make the mistake of thinking I'm a hulk without a brain in it. You're wrong. I am a very clever lad, not merely pretty, but smart. Now if I have to drop five big ones into your pudding-trough, lover, I will do so."

Handy stopped moving toward him. Barkin was not fooling. He was angry. "What is all this, Barkin? What are you trying to climb onto? No, forget it, don't answer. What I want to know is why?"

Barkin spread hands as huge as catcher's mitts. The fingers were oddly long and graceful. And tanned. "She is a lovely woman who finds the company of handsome young men refreshing. Mr. Crewes, sir, has decided I will brighten her declining years."

"She is a scared creature who doesn't know where it's at, not right now she doesn't. And turning you loose on her would be a sudden joy like the Dutch Elm Blight."

Barkin smiled thinly. It was a mean smile. For the time it took the smile to vanish, he was not handsome. "Call Arthur Crewes. He'll verify."

"I can't get through to him, he's in a screening."

"Then go ask him. I'll be here all day."

He stepped aside. Handy waited, as though Barkin might surprise him and leap back suddenly, with a fist in the mouth. Huck stood grinning like a little boy. Ain't I cute.

"I'll do that."

Handy moved past and entered the passageway. As he walked hurriedly down the length of the corridor, he heard Barkin speak again. He turned to see the giant figure framed in the blazing sunlight rectangle at the other end of the dark tunnel. "You know, Fred chum, you need a good workout. You're gettin' flabbier than hell."

Handy fled, raising dust as he wheeled the Impala out of the driveway and down the mountainside. There was the stink of fusel oil rising up from the city. Or was it the smell of fear?

4

When he burst into Arthur Crewes's office at the studio, the reception room was filled with delight. All that young stuff. A dozen girls, legs crossed high to show off the rounded thigh, waiting to be seen. As he slammed in, Twiggyeyes blinked rapidly.

He careened through the door and brought up short, turning quickly to see an unbroken panorama of gorgeous young-twenties starlets. Roz, fifty and waspish, behind the desk, snickered at his double-take. Handy recognized the tone of the snicker. He was a man periodically motivated from somewhere low in his anatomy, and Roz never failed to hold it against him. He had never asked her out.

"Hello, Fred," one of the girls said. He had to strain to single her out. They all looked alike. Teased; long flat blonde hair; freaky Twiggy styles; backswept bouffant; short mannish cuts; all of them, no matter what mode, they all looked alike. It was Randi. She had had a thing about touching his privates. It was all he could remember about her. Not even if she'd been good. But a publicist must remember names, and with the remembrance of her touching his penis and drawing in her breath as though it had been something strange and new and wonderful like the Inca Codex or one of the Dead Sea Scrolls, the name Randi popped up like the NO SALE clack on a cash register.

"Hi, Randi. How's it going?"

He didn't even wait for an answer. He turned back to Roz. "I want to see him."

Her mouth became the nasty slit opening of a mantis. "He's got someone in with him now."

"I want to *see* him."

"I *said*, Mr. Handy, he has someone in there now. We *are* still interviewing girls, you know . . ."

"Bloody damn it, lady, I said get your ass in there and tell him Handy is coming through that door, open or not, in exactly ten seconds."

She drew herself up, no breasts at all, straight lines and Mondrian sterility, and started to huff at him. Handy said, "Fuck," and went through into Crewes's office.

He said it softly, but he made noise entering the office.

Another of the pretties was showing Arthur Crewes her 8×10 glossies, under plastic, out of an immense black leather photofolio. Starlets. Arthur was saying something about their needing a few more dark-haired girls, as Handy came through the door.

Crewes looked up, surprised at the interruption.

The starlet smiled automatically.

"Arthur, I have to talk to you."

Crewes seemed puzzled by the tone in Handy's voice. But he nodded. "In a minute, Fred. Why don't you sit down. Georgia and I were talking."

Handy realized his error. He had gone a step too far with Arthur Crewes. Throughout the industry, one thing was common knowledge about Crewes's office policy: any girl who came in for an interview was treated courteously, fairly, without even the vaguest scintilla of a hustle. Crewes had been known to can men on his productions who had used their positions to get all-too-willing actresses into bed with promises of three-line bits, or a walk-on. For Handy to interrupt while Crewes was talking to even the lowliest day-player was an affront Crewes would not allow to pass unnoticed. Handy sat down, ambivalent as hell.

Georgia was showing Crewes several shots from a Presley picture she had made the year before. Crewes was remarking that she looked good in a bikini. It was a businesslike, professional tone of voice, no leer. The girl was standing tall and straight. Handy knew that under other circumstances, in other offices where the routine was different, if Crewes had been another sort of man and had said, *why don't you take off your clothes so I can get a better idea of how you'll look in the nude shots we're shooting for the overseas market*, this girl, this Georgia, would be pulling the granny dress with its baggy mini material over her head and displaying herself in bikini briefs and maybe no brassiere to hold up all that fine young meat. But in this office she was standing tall and straight. She was being asked to be professional, to take pride in herself and whatever degree of craft she might possess. It was why there were so few lousy rumors around town about Arthur Crewes.

"I'm not certain, Georgia, but let me check with Kenny Heller in Casting, see what he's already done, and what parts are left open. I know there's a very nice five- or six-line comedy walk-on with Mitchum that we haven't found a girl for yet. Perhaps that might work. No promises, you understand, but I'll check with Kenny and get back to you later in the day."

"Thank you, Mr. Crewes. I'm very grateful."

Crewes smiled and picked up one of the 8×10's from a thin sheaf at the rear of the photofolio. "May we keep one of these here, for the files . . . and also to remind me to get through to Kenny?" She nodded, and smiled back at him. There was no subterfuge in the interchange, and Handy sank a trifle lower on the sofa.

"Just give it to Roz, at the desk out there, and leave your number . . . would you prefer we let you know through your agent, or directly?"

It was the sort of question, in any other office, that might mean the producer was trying to wangle the home number for his own purposes. But not here. Georgia did not hesitate as she said. "Oh, either way. It makes no difference. Herb is very good about getting me out on interviews. But if it looks possible, I'll give you my home number. There's a service on the line that'll pick up if I'm out."

"You can leave it with Roz, Georgia. And thank you for coming in." He stood and they shook hands. She was quite happy. Even if the part did not come through, she knew she had been *considered*, not merely assayed as a possible quickie on an office sofa. As she started for the door, Crewes added, "I'll have Roz call one way or the other, as soon as we know definitely."

She half-turned, displaying a fine length of leg, taut against the baggy dress, "Thank you. 'Bye."

"Goodbye."

She left the office, and Crewes sat down again. He pushed papers around the outer perimeter of his desk, making Handy wait. Finally, when Handy had allowed Crewes as much punishment as he felt his recent original sin deserved, he spoke.

"You've got to be out of your mind, Arthur!"

Crewes looked up then. Stopped in the midst of his preparations to remark on Handy's discourtesy in entering the office during an interview. Crewes waited, but Handy said nothing. Then Crewes thumbed the comm button on the phone. He picked up the receiver and said, "Roz, ask them if they'll be kind enough to wait about ten minutes. Fred and I have some details to work out." He listened a moment, then racked the receiver and turned to Handy.

"Okay. What?"

"Jesus Christ, Arthur. Haskell Barkin, for Christ's sake. You've got to be *kid*ding."

"I talked to Valerie Lone last night. She sounded all by herself. I thought it might be smart therapy to get her a good-looking guy, as company, a chaperone, someone who'd be nice to her. I remembered this Barkin from—"

Handy stood up, frenzy impelling his movement. Banging off walls, vibrating at supersonic speeds, turning invisible with teeth-gritting. "I *know* where you remembered this Barkin from, Arthur. From Billie Landewyck's party, three years ago; the pool party; where you met Vivvi. I know. He told me."

"You've been to see Barkin already?"

"He had me out of bed too much before I wanted to get up."

"An honest day's working time won't hurt you, Fred. I was here at seven thir—"

"Arthur, I frankly, God forgive my talking to my producer this way, frankly don't give a flying *shit* what time you were behind your desk. Barkin, Arthur! You're insane."

"He seemed like a nice chap. Always smiling."

Handy leaned over the desk, talking straight into Arthur Crewes's cerebrum, eliminating the middleman. "So does the crocodile smile, Arthur. Haskell Barkin is a crud. He is a slithering, creeping, crawling, essentially reptilian monster who slices and eats. He is Jack the Ripper, Arthur. He is a vacuum cleaner. He is a loggerhead shark. He *hates* like we *urinate*—it's a basic bodily function for him. He leaves a wet trail when he walks. Small children run shrieking from him, Arthur. He's a killer in a suntan. Women who chew nails, who destroy men for giggles, women like *that* are afraid of him, Arthur. If you were a broad and he French-kissed you, Arthur, you'd have to go get a tetanus shot. He uses human bones to bake his bread. He's declared war on every woman who ever carried a crotch. This man is death, Arthur. And *that's* what you wanted to turn loose on Valerie Lone, God save her soul. He's Paris green, he's sump water, he's axle grease, Arthur! He's—"

Arthur Crewes spoke softly, looking battered by Handy's diatribe. "You made your point, Fred. I stand corrected."

Handy slumped down into the chair beside the desk.

To himself: "Jeezus, Huck Barkin, Jeezus . . ."

And when he had run down completely, he looked up. Crewes seemed poised in time and space. His idea had not worked out. "Well, whom would *you* suggest?"

Handy spread his hands.

"I don't know. But not Barkin, or anyone like him. No Strip killers, Arthur. That would be lamb to slaughter time."

Crewes: "But she needs *some*one."

Handy: "What's your special interest, Arthur?"

Crewes: "Why say that?"

Handy: "Arthur . . . c'mon. I can tell. There's a thing you've got going where she's concerned."

Crewes turned in his chair. Staring out the window at the lot, a series of flat-trucks moving scenery back to the storage bins. "You only work for me, Fred."

Handy considered, then decided what the hell. "If I worked for Adolph Eichmann, Arthur, I'd still ask where all them Jews was going."

Crewes turned back, looked levelly at his publicist. "I keep thinking you're nothing more than a flack-man. I'm wrong, aren't I?"

Handy shrugged. "I have a thought of my own from time to time."

Crewes nodded, acquiescing. "Would you just settle for my saying she once did me a favor? Not a big favor, just a little favor, something she probably doesn't even remember, or if she does she doesn't think of it in relation to the big producer who's giving her a comeback break. Would you settle for my saying I mean her nothing but good things, Fred? Would that buy it?"

Handy nodded. "It'll do."

"So who do we get to keep her reassured that she isn't ready for the dustbin just yet?"

Again Handy spread his hands. "I don't know, it's been eighteen years since she had anything to do with—hey! Wait a bit. What's his name . . . ?"

"Who?"

"Oh, hell, *you* know . . ." Handy said, fumbling with his memory, ". . . the one who got fouled up with the draft during the war, blew his career, something, I don't remember . . . aw, c'mon Arthur, you know who I mean, used to play all the bright young attorney defending the dirty-faced delinquent parts." He snapped his fingers trying to call back a name from crumbling fan magazines, from rotogravure coming attraction placards in theater windows.

Crewes suggested, "Call Sheilah Graham."

Handy came around the desk, dialed 9 to get out, and Sheilah Graham's private number, from memory. "Sheilah? Fred Handy. Yeah, hi. Hey, who was it Valerie Lone used to go with?" He listened. "No, huh-uh, the one that was always in the columns, he was married, but they had a big thing, he does bits now, guest shots, who—"

She told him.

"Right. Right, that's who. Okay, hey thanks, Sheilah. What? No, huh-uh, huh-uh; as soon as we get something right, it's yours. Okay, luv. Thanks. 'Bye."

He hung up and turned to Crewes. "Emery Romito."

Crewes nodded. "Jeezus, is he still alive?"

"He was on *Bonanza* about three weeks ago. Guest shot. Played an alcoholic veterinarian."

Crewes lifted an eyebrow. "Type casting?"

Handy was leafing through the volume of the PLAYERS DIRECTORY that listed leading men. "I don't think so. If he'd been a stone saucehound he'd've been planted long before this. I think he's just getting old, that's the worst."

Crewes gave a sharp, short bitter laugh. "That's enough."

Handy slammed the PLAYERS DIRECTORY closed. "He's not in there."

"Try character males," Crewes suggested.

Handy found it, in the R's. Emery Romito. A face out of the past, still holding a distinguished mien, but even through the badly reproduced photo that had been an 8×10 glossy, showing weariness and the indefinable certainty that this man knew he had lost his chance at picking up all the marbles.

Handy showed Crewes the photo. "Do you think this is a good idea?" Handy looked at him.

"It's a helluva lot better idea than *yours,* Arthur."

Crewes sucked on the edge of his lower lip between clenched teeth. "Okay. Go get him. But make him look like a knight on a white charger. I want her very happy."

"Knights on white chargers these days come barrel-assing down the streets of suburbia with their phalluses in hand, blasting women's underwear whiter-than-white. Would you settle for merely *mildly* happy?"

5

Cotillions could have been held in the main drawing room of the Stratford Beach Hotel. Probably had been. In the days when Richard Dix had his way with Leatrice Joy, in the days when Zanuck had his three rejected scenarios privately published as a "book" and sent them around to the studios in hopes of building his personal stock, in the days when Virginia Rappe was being introduced to the dubious sexual joys of a fat kid named Arbuckle. In those days the Stratford Beach Hotel had been a showplace, set out on the lovely Santa Monica shore, overlooking the triumphant Pacific.

Architecturally, the hotel was a case in point for Frank Lloyd Wright's contention that the Sunshine State looked as though "someone had tipped the United States up on its east coast, and everything that was loose went tumbling into California." Great and bulky, sunk to its hips in the earth, with rococo flutings at every possible juncture, portico'd and belfry'd, the Stratford Beach had passed through fifty years of scuffling feet, spuming salt-spray, drunken orgies, changed bed-linen and insipid managers to end finally in this backwash eddy of a backwash suburb.

In the main drawing room of the Stratford Beach, standing on the top step of a wide, spiraling staircase of onyx that ran down into a room where the dust in the ancient carpets rose at each step to mingle with the downdrifting film of shattered memories, fractured yesterdays, mote-infested yearnings and the unmistakable stench of dead dreams, Fred Handy knew what had killed F. Scott Fitzgerald. This room, and the thousands of others like it, that held within their ordered interiors a kind of deadly magic of remembrance; a pull and tug of eras that refused to give up the ghost, that had not the common decency to pass away and let new times be born. The embalmed forevers that never came to be . . . they were here, lurking in the colorless patinas of dust that covered the rubber plants, that settled in the musty odor of the velvet plush furniture, that shone dully up from inlaid hardwood floors where the Charleston had been danced as a racy new thing.

This was the terrifying end-up for all the refuse of nostalgia. Hooked on this scene had been Fitzgerald, lauding and singing of something that was dead even as it was born. And so easily hooked could *anyone* get on this, who chose to live after their time was passed.

The words tarnish and mildew again formed in Handy's mind, superimposed as subtitles over a mute sequence of Valerie Lone shrieking in closeup. He shook his head, and not a moment too soon. Emery Romito came down the stairs from the second floor of the hotel, walking up behind Handy across the inlaid tiles of the front hall. He stood behind Handy, staring down into the vast living room. As Handy shook his head, fighting to come back to today.

"Elegant, isn't it?" Emery Romito said.

The voice was cultivated, the voice was deep and warm, the voice was histrionic, the voice was filled with memory, the voice was a surprise in the silence, but none of these were the things that startled Handy. The present tense, *isn't it*. Not: wasn't it, isn't it.

Oh my God, Handy thought.

Afraid to turn around, Fred Handy felt himself sucked into the past. This room, this terrible room, it was so help him God a portal to the past. The yesterdays that had never gone to rest were all here, crowding against a milky membrane separating them from the world of right here and now, like eyeless soulless wraiths, hungering after the warmth and presence of his corporeality. They wanted . . . what? They wanted his *au courant*. They wanted his today, so they could hear "Nagasaki" and "Vagabond Lover" and "Please" sung freshly again. So they could rouge their knees and straighten their headache bands over their foreheads. Fred Handy, man of today, assailed by the ghosts of yesterday, and terrified to turn around and see one of those ghosts standing behind him.

"Mr. Handy? You *are* the man who called me, aren't you?"

Handy turned and looked at Emery Romito.

"Hello," he said, through the dust of decades.

HANDY

Jefferson once said people get pretty much the kind of government they deserve, which is why I refuse to listen to any bullshit carping by my fellow Californians about Reagan and his gubernatorial gang-banging—what I chose to call goverment by artificial insemination when I was arguing with Julie, a registered Republican, when we weren't making love—because it seems to me they got just what they were asking for. The end-product of a hundred years of statewide paranoia and rampant lunacy. That philosophy—stripped of Freudian undertones—has slopped over into most areas of my opinion. Women who constantly get stomped on by shitty guys generally have a streak of masochism in them; guys who get their hearts eaten away by rodent females are basically self-flagellants. And when you see someone who has been ravaged by life, it is a safe bet he has been a willing accomplice at his own destruction.

All of this passed through my mind as I said hello to Emery Romito. The picture in the PLAYERS DIRECTORY had softened the sadness. But in living color he was a natural for one of those billboards hustling Forest Lawn pre-need cemetery plots. *Don't get caught with your life down.*

He was one of the utterly destroyed. A man familiar to the point of incest with the forces that crush and maim, a man stunned by the hammer. And I could conceive of *no one* who would aid and abet those kind of forces in self-destruction. No. No one.

Yet no man could have done it to himself without the help of the Furies. And so, I was ambivalent. I felt both pity and cynicism for Emery Romito, and his brave foolish elegance.

Age lay like soot in the creases of what had once been a world-famous face. The kind of age that means merely growing old, without wistfulness or delight. This man had lived through all the days and nights of his life with only one thought uppermost: let me forget what has gone before.

"Would you like to sit out on the terrace?" Romito asked. "Nice breeze off the ocean today."

I smiled acquiescence, and he made a theatrical gesture in the direction of the terrace. As he preceded me down the onyx steps into the living room, I felt a clutch of nausea, and followed him. Cheyne-Stokes breathing as I walked across the threadbare carpet, among the deep restful furniture that called to me, suggested I try their womb comfort, sink into them never to rise again. Or if I did, it would be as a shriveled, mummified old man. (And with the memory of a kid who grew up on movies, I saw Margo as Capra had seen her in 1937, aging horribly, shriveling, in a matter of seconds, as she was being carried out of Shangri-La. And I shuddered. A grown man, and I shuddered.)

It was like walking across the bottom of the sea; shadowed, filtered with sounds that had no names, caught by shafts of sunlight from the skylight above us that contained freshets of dust-motes rising tumbling surging upward, threading between sofas and Morris chairs like whales in shoal, finally arriving at the fogged dirty French doors that gave out onto the terrace.

Romito opened them smoothly, as if he had done it a thousand times in a thousand films—and probably had—for a thousand Anita Louises. He stepped out briskly, and drew a deep breath. In that instant I realized he was in extremely good shape for a man his age, built big across the back and shoulders, waist still trim and narrow, actually quite dapper. Then why did I think of him as a crustacean, as a pitted fossil, as a gray and wasted relic?

It was the air of fatality, of course. The superimposed chin-up-through-it-all horseshit that all Hollywood hangers-on adopted. It was an atrophied devolutionary extension of the *Show Must Go On* shuck; the myth that owns everyone in the Industry: that getting forty-eight minutes of hack cliché situation comedy filmed—only the barest minimally innervating—to capture the boggle-eyed interest of the Great Unwashed sucked down in the doldrum mire of The Great American Heartland, so they will squat there for twelve minutes of stench odor poison and artifact hardsell, is an occupation somehow inextricably involved with advancing the course of Western Civilization. A myth that has oozed over into all areas of modern thought, thus turning us into a "show biz culture" and spawning such creatures as Emery Romito. Like the cats in the empty Ziv Studios, nibbling at the leftover garbage of the film industry, but loath to leave it. (Echoes of the old saw about the carnival assistant whose job it was to shovel up elephant shit who, when asked why he didn't get a better job, replied, "What? And leave show biz?") Emery Romito was one of the clingers to the underside of the rock that was show biz, that dominated like Gibraltar the landscape of Americana.

He had forfeited his humanity in order to remain "with it." He was dead, and didn't know it. *What, and leave show biz?*

The terrace was half the size of the living room, which made it twice as large as the foyer of Grauman's Chinese. Gray stone balustrades bounded it, and earthquake tremors had performed an intricate calligraphy across the inlaid and matched flaggings. It was daylight, but that didn't stop the shadowy images of women with bobbed hairdos and men with pomaded glossiness from weaving in and around us as we stood there, staring out at the ocean. It was ghost-time again, and secret liaisons were being effected out on the terrace by dashing sheiks (whose wives [married before their men had become nickelodeon idols] were inside slugging the spiked gin-punch) and hungry little hopefuls with waxed shins and a dab of alum in their vaginas, anxious to grasp magic.

"Let's sit down," Emery Romito said. To me, not the ghosts. He indicated a conversation grouping of cheap tubular aluminum beach chairs, their once-bright webbing now hopelessly faded by sun and sea-mist.

I sat down and he smiled ingratiatingly.

Then he sat down, careful to pull up the pants creases in the Palm Beach suit. The suit was in good shape, but perhaps fifteen years out of date.

"Well," he said.

I smiled back. I hadn't the faintest idea what "well" was a preamble to, nor what I was required to answer. But he waited, expecting me to say something.

When I continued to smile dumbly, his expression crumpled a little, and he tried another tack. "Just what sort of part *is* it that Crewes has in mind?"

Oh my God, I thought. *He thinks it's an interview.*

"Uh, well, it isn't pre*cise*ly a part in the film I'm here to talk to you about, Mr. Romito." It was much too intricate a syntax for a man whose heart might attack him at any moment.

"It isn't a part," he repeated.

"No, it was something rather personal . . ."

"It isn't a part." He whispered it, barely heard, lost instantly in the overpowering sound of the Santa Monica surf not far beyond us.

"It's about Valerie Lone," I began.

"Valerie?"

"Yes. We've signed her for *Subterfuge* and she's back in town and—"

"*Subterfuge*?"

"The film Mr. Crewes is producing."

"Oh. I see."

He didn't see at all. I was sure of that. I didn't know how in the world I could tell this ruined shell that his services were needed as escort, not actor. He saved me the trouble. He ran away from me, into the past.

"I remember once, in 1936 I believe . . . no, it was '37, that was the year I did *Beloved Liar* . . ."

I let the sound of the surf swell inside me. I turned down the gain on Emery Romito and turned up the gain on nature. I knew I would be able to get him to do what needed to be done—he was a lonely, helpless man for whom *any* kind of return to the world of glamor was a main chance. But it would take talking, and worse . . . listening.

". . . Thalberg called me in, and he was smiling, it was a very unusual thing, you can be sure. And he said: 'Emery, we've just signed a girl for your next picture,' and of course it was Valerie. Except that wasn't her name then, and he took me over to the Commissary to meet her. We had the special salad, it was little slivers of ham and cheese and turkey, cut so they were stacked one on top of the other, so you tasted the ham first, then the cheese, then the turkey, all in one bite, and the freshest green crisp lettuce, they called it the William Powell Salad . . . no, that isn't right . . . the William Powell was crab meat . . . I think it was the Norma Talmadge Salad . . . or was it . . ."

As I sat there talking to Emery Romito, what I did not know was that all the way across the city, at the Studio, Arthur was entering the lot with Valerie Lone, in a chauffeured Bentley. He told me about it that night, and it was horrible. But it served as the perfect counterpoint to the musty warm monologue being delivered to me that moment by the Ghost of Christmas Past.

How lovely, how enriching, to sit there in sumptuous, palatial Santa Monica, Showplace of the Western World, listening to the voice from beyond reminisce about tuna fish and avocado salads. I prayed for deafness.

6

Crewes had called ahead. "I want the red carpet, do I make my meaning clear?" The studio public relations head had said yes, he understood. Crewes had emphasized the point: "I don't want any fuckups, Barry. Not even the smallest. No gate police asking for a drive-on pass, no secretary making her wait. I want every carpenter and grip and mail boy to know we're bringing Valerie Lone back today. And I want *deference*, Barry. If there's a fuckup, even the smallest fuckup, I'll come down on you the way Samson brought down the temple."

"Christ, Arthur, you don't have to threaten me!"

"I'm not threatening, Barry, I'm making the point so you can't weasel later. This isn't some phony finger-popping rock singer, this is Valerie Lone."

"All *right*, Arthur! Stop now."

When they came through the gate, the guards removed their caps, and waved the Bentley on toward the sound stages. Valerie Lone sat in the rear, beside Arthur Crewes, and her face was dead white, even under the makeup she had applied in the latest manner: for 1945.

There was a receiving line outside Stage 16.

The Studio head, several members of the foreign press, the three top producers on the lot, and half a dozen "stars" of current tv series. They made much over her, and when they were finished, Valerie Lone had almost been convinced someone gave a damn that she was not dead.

When the flashing red gumball light on its tripod went out—signifying that the shot had been completed inside the sound stage—they entered. Valerie took three steps beyond the heavy soundproof door, and stopped. Her eyes went up and up, into the dim reaches of the huge barnlike structure, to the catwalks with their rigging, the lights anchored to their brace boards, the cool and wonderful air from the conditioners that rose to heat up there, where the gaffers worked. Then she stepped back into the shadows as Crewes came up beside her, and he knew she was crying, and he turned to ask the others if they would come in later, to follow Miss Lone on her visit. The others did not understand, but they went back outside, and the door sighed shut on its pneumatic hinges.

Crewes went to her, and she was against the wall, the tears standing in her eyes, but not running down to ruin the makeup. In that instant Crewes knew she would be all right: she was an actress, and for an actress the only reality is the fantasy of the sound stages. She would not let her eyes get red. She was tougher than he'd imagined.

She turned to him, and when she said, "Thank you, Arthur," it was so soft, and so gentle, Crewes took her in his arms and she huddled close to him, and there was no passion in it, no striving to reach bodies, only a fine and warm protectiveness. He silently said no one would hurt her, and silently she said my life is in your hands.

After a while, they walked past the coffee machine and Willie, who said hello Miss Lone it's good to have you back; and past the assistant director's lectern where the shooting schedule was tacked onto the sloping board, where Bruce del Vaille nodded to her, and looked awed; and past the extras slumped in their straight-backed chairs, reading Irving Wallace and knitting, waiting for their calls, and they had been told who it was, and they all called to her and waved and smiled; and past the high director's chair which was at that moment occupied by the script supervisor, whose name was Henry, and he murmured hello, Miss Lone, we worked together on suchandsuch, and she went to him and kissed him on the cheek, and he looked as though he wanted to cry, too. For Arthur Crewes, in the sound stage somewhere, a bird twittered gaily. He shrugged and laughed, like a child.

Someone yelled, "Okay, settle down! Settle down!"

The din fell only a decibel. James Kencannon was talking to Mitchum, to one side of the indoor set that was decorated to be an outdoor set. It was an alley in a Southwestern town, and the cyclorama in the background had been artfully rigged to simulate a carnival somewhere in the middle distance. Lights played off the canvas, and for Valerie

Lone it was genuine; a real carnival erected just for her. The alley was dirty and extremely realistic. Extras lounged against the brick walls that were not brick walls, waiting for the call to roll it. The cameraman was setting the angle of the shot, the big piece of equipment on its balloon tires set on wooden tracks, ready to dolly back when the grips pulled it. The assistant cameraman with an Arriflex on his shoulder was down on one knee, gauging an up-angle for action shooting.

Del Vaille came onto the set and Kencannon nodded to him. "Okay, roll—" Kencannon stopped the preparations for the shot, and asked the first assistant director to measure off the shot once more, as Mitchum stepped into the position that had, till that moment, been held by his stand-in. The first assistant unreeled the tape measure, announced it; the cameraman gave a turn to one of the flywheels on the big camera, and nodded ready to the assistant director, who turned and bawled, "Okay! Roll it!"

A strident bell clanged in the sound stage and dead silence fell. People in mid-step stopped. No one coughed. No one spoke. Tony, the sound mixer, up on his high platform with his earphones and his console, announced, "Take thirty-three Bravo!" which resounded through the cavernous set and was picked up through the comm box by the sound truck outside the sound stage. When it was up to speed, Tony yelled, "Speed!" and the first assistant director stepped forward into the shot with his wooden clackboard bearing Kencannon's name and the shot number. He clacked the stick to establish sound synch and get the board photographed, and there was a beat as he withdrew, as Mitchum drew in a breath for the action to come, as everyone poised hanging in limbo and Kencannon—like all directors—relished the moment of absolute power waiting for his voice to announce action.

Infinite moment.

Birth of dreams.

The shadow and the reality.

"Action!"

As five men leaped out of darkness and grabbed Robert Mitchum, shoving him back up against the wall of the alley. The camera dollied in rapidly to a closeup of Mitchum's face as one of the men grabbed his jaw with brutal fingers. "Where'd you take her . . . tell us where you took her!" the assailant demanded with a faint Mexican accent. Mitchum worked his jaw muscles, tried to shove the man away. The Arriflex operator was down below them, out of the master shot, purring away his tilted angles of the scuffling men. Mitchum tried to speak, but couldn't with the man's hand on his face. "Let'm talk, Sanchez!" another of the men urged the assailant. He released Mitchum's face, and in the same instant Mitchum surged forward, throwing two of the men from him, and breaking toward the camera as it dollied rapidly back to encompass the entire shot. The Arriflex operator scuttled with him, tracking him in wobbly closeup. The five men dived for Mitchum, preparatory to beating the crap out of him as Kencannon yelled, "Cut! That's a take!" and the enemies straightened up, relaxed, and Mitchum walked swiftly to his mobile dressing room. The crew prepared to set up another shot.

The extras moved in. A group of young kids, obviously bordertown tourists from a *yanqui* college, down having a ball in the hotbed of sin and degradation.

They milled and shoved, and Arthur found himself once again captivated by the enormity of what was being done here. A writer had said: ESTABLISHING SHOT OF CROWD IN ALLEY and it was going to cost about fifteen thousand dollars to make that line become a reality. He glanced at Valerie beside him, and she was smiling, a thin and delicate smile part remembrance and part wonder. It really never wore off, this delight, this entrapment by the weaving of fantasy into reality.

"Enjoying yourself?" he asked softly.

"It's as though I'd never been away," she said.

Kencannon came to her, then. He held both her hands in his, and he looked at her: as a man and as a camera. "Oh, you'll do just fine . . . just fine." He smiled at her. She smiled back.

"I haven't read the part yet," she said.

"Johnny Black hasn't finished expanding it yet. And I don't give a damn. You'll do fine, just fine!" They stared at each other with the kind of intimacy known only to a man who sees a reality as an image on celluloid, by a woman confronting a man who can make her look seventeen or seventy. Trust and fear and compassion and a mutual cessation of hostilities between the sexes. It was always like this. As if to say: what does he see? What does she want? What will we settle for? I love you.

"Have you said hello to Bob Mitchum yet?" Kencannon asked her.

"No. I think he's resting." She was, in turn, deferential to a star, as the lessers had been deferential to her. "I can meet him later."

"Are there any questions you'd like to ask?" he said. He waved a hand at the set around him. "You'll be living here for the next few weeks, you'd better get to know it."

"Well . . . yes . . . there are a few questions," she said. And she began getting into the role of star once more. She asked questions. Questions that were twenty years out of date. Not stupid questions, just *not quite in focus*. (As if the clackboard had not been in synch with the sound wagon, and the words had emerged from the actors' mouths a micro-instant too soon.) Not embarrassing questions, merely awkward questions; the answers to which entailed Kencannon's educating her, reminding her that she was a relic, that time had not waited for her—even as she had not waited when she had been a star—but had gathered its notes in a rush and plunged panting heavily past her. Now she had to exercise muscles of thought that had atrophied, just to try and catch up with time, dashing on ahead there like an ambitious mailroom boy trying to make points with the Studio executives. Her questions became more awkward. Her words came with more difficulty. Crewes saw her getting—how did Handy put it?—uptight.

Three girls had come onto the set from a mobile dressing room back in a dark corner of the sound stage. They wore flowered wrappers. The assistant director was herding them toward the windows of a dirty little building facing out on the alley. The girls went around the back of the building—back where it was unpainted pine and brace-rods and Magic Marker annotated as SUBTER'GE 115/144 indicating in which scenes these sets would be used.

They appeared in three windows of the building. They would be spectators at the stunt-man's fight with the assailants in the alley . . . Mitchum's fight with the assailants in the alley. They were intended to represent three Mexican prostitutes, drawn to their windows by the sounds of combat. They removed their wrappers.

Their naked, fleshy breasts hung on the window ledges like Dali-esque melting casabas, waiting to ripen. Valerie Lone turned and saw the array of deep-brown nipples, and made a strange sound, "Awuhhh!" as if they had been something put on sale at such a startlingly low price she was amazed, confused and repelled out of suspicion.

Kencannon hurriedly tired to explain the picture was being shot in two versions, one for domestic and eventual television release, the other for foreign marketing. He went into a detailed comparison of the two versions, and when he had finished—with the entire cast of extras listening, for the explication of hypocrisy is always fascinating—Valerie Lone said:

"Gee, I hope none of *my* scenes have to be shot without clothes . . ."

And one of the extras gave a seal-like bark of amusement. "Fat chance," he murmured, just a bit too loud.

Arthur Crewes went around in a fluid movement that was almost choreography, and hit the boy—a beach-bum with long blond hair and fine deltoids—a shot that traveled no more than sixteen inches. It was a professional fighter's punch, no windup, no bolo, just a short hard piston jab that took the boy directly under the heart. He vomited air and lost his lower legs. He sat down hard.

If Crewes had thought about it, he would not have done it. The effect on the cast. The inevitable lawsuit. The Screen Extras Guild complaint. The bad form of striking someone who worked for him. The look on Valerie Lone's face as she caught the action with peripheral vision. The sight of an actor sitting down in pain, like a small child seeking a sandpile.

But he didn't think, and he did it, and Valerie Lone turned and ran . . .

Questions that were not congruent with a film that has to take into account television rerun, accelerated shooting schedules, bankability of stars, the tenor of the kids who make up the yeoman cast of every film, the passage of time and the improvement of techniques, and the altered thinking of studio magnates; the sophisticated tastes and mores of a new filmgoing audience.

A generation of youth with no respect for roots and heritage and the past. With no understanding of what has gone before. With no veneration of age. The times had conspired against Valerie Lone. Even as the times had conspired against her twenty years before. The simple and singular truth of it was that Valerie Lone had not been condemned by a lack of talent—though a greater talent might have sustained her—nor by a weakness in character—though a more ruthless nature might have carried her through the storms—nor by fluxes and flows in the Industry, but by all of these things, and by Fate and the times. But mostly the times. She was simply, singularly, not one with her world. It was a Universe that had chosen to care about Valerie Lone. For most of the world, the Universe didn't give a damn. For rare and singular persons from time to time in all ages, the Universe felt a compassion. It felt a need to succor and warm, to aid and bolster. That disaster befell all of these "wards of the Universe" was only proof unarguable that the Universe was inept, that God was insane.

It would have been better by far had the Universe left Valerie Lone to her own destiny. But it wouldn't, it couldn't; and it combined all the chance random elements of encounter and happenstance to litter her path with roses. For Valerie Lone, in the inept and compassionate Universe, the road was broken glass and dead birds, as far down the trail as she would ever be able to see.

The Universe had created the tenor of cynicism that hummed silently through all the blond beach-bums of the Hollywood extra set . . . the Universe had dulled Valerie Lone's perceptions of the Industry as it was today . . . the Universe had speeded up the adrenaline flow in Arthur Crewes at the instant the blond beach-bum had made his obnoxious comment . . . and the Universe had, in its cockeyed, simple-ass manner, thought it was benefiting Valerie Lone.

Obviously not.

And it would be this incident, this rank little happening, that would inject the tension into her bloodstream, that would cause her nerves to fray just that infinitesimal amount necessary, that would bring about metal fatigue and erosion and rust. So that when the precise moment came when optimum efficiency was necessary . . . Valerie Lone would be hauled back to this instant, this remark, this vicious little scene; and it would provide the weakness that would doom her.

From that moment, Valerie Lone began to be consumed by her shadow. And nothing could prevent it. Not even the wonderful, wonderful Universe that had chosen to care about her.

A Universe ruled by a mad God, who was himself being consumed by his shadow.

Valerie Lone turned and ran . . .

Through the sound stage, out the door, down the studio street, through Philadelphia in 1910, past the Pleasure Dome of Kubla Khan, around a Martian sand-city, into and out of Budapest during the Uprising (where castrated Red tanks still lay drenched in the ash-drunkenness of Molotov cocktails), and through Shade's Wells onto a sun-baked plain where the imbecilically gaping mouth of the No. 3 Anaconda Mine received her.

She dashed into the darkness of the Anaconda, and found herself in the midst of the Springhill Mine Disaster. Within and without, reality was self-contained.

Arthur Crewes and James Kencannon dashed after her.

At the empty opening to the cave, Crewes stopped Kencannon. "Let me, Jim."

Kencannon nodded, and walked slowly away, pulling his pipe from his belt, and beginning to ream it clean with a tool from his shirt pocket.

Arthur Crewes let the faintly musty interior of the prop cave swallow him. He stood there silently, listening for murmurings of sorrow, or madness. He heard nothing. The cave only went in for ten or fifteen feet, but it might well have been the entrance to the deepest pit in Dante's Inferno. As his eyes grew accustomed to the gloom, he saw her, slumped down against some prop boulders.

She tried to scuttle back out of sight, even as he moved toward her.

"Don't." He spoke the one word softly, and she held.

Then he came to her, and sat down on a boulder low beside her. Now she wasn't crying.

It hadn't been that kind of rotten little scene.

"He's an imbecile," Crewes said.

"He was right," she answered. There was a sealed lock-vault on pity. But self-realization could be purchased over the counter.

"He *wasn't* right. He's an ignorant young pup and I've had him canned."

"I'm sorry for that."

"Sorry doesn't get it. What he did was inexcusable." He chuckled softly, ruefully. "What *I* did was inexcusable, as well. I'll hear from SEG about it." That chuckle rose. "It was worth it."

"Arthur, let me out."

"I don't want to hear that."

"I have to say it. Please. Let me out. It won't work."

"It *will* work. It *has* to work."

She looked at him through darkness. His face was blank, without features, barely formed in any way. But she knew if she could see him clearly that there would be intensity in his expression. "Why is this so important to you?"

For many minutes he did not speak, while she waited without understanding. Then, finally, he said, "Please let me do this thing for you. I want . . . very much . . . for you to have the good things again."

"But, why?"

He tried to explain, but it was not a matter of explanations. It was a matter of pains and joys remembered. Of being lonely and finding pleasure in motion pictures. Of having no directions and finding a future in what had always been a hobby. Of having lusted for success and coming at last to it with the knowledge that movies had given him everything, and she had been part of it. There was no totally rational explanation that Arthur Crewes could codify for her. He had struggled upward and she had given him a hand. It had been a small, a tiny, a quickly forgotten little favor—if he told her now she would not remember it, nor would she think it was at all comparable to what he was trying to do for her. But as the years had hung themselves on Arthur Crewes's past, the tiny favor had grown out of all proportion in his mind, and now he was trying desperately to pay Valerie Lone back.

All this, in a moment of silence.

He had been in the arena too long. He could not speak to her of these nameless wondrous things, and hope to win her from her fears. But even in his silence there was clarity. She reached out to touch his face.

"I'll try," she said.

And when they were outside on the flat, dry plain across which Kencannon started toward them, she turned to Arthur Crewes and she said, with a rough touch of the wiseacre that had been her trademark eighteen years before, "But I still ain't playin' none of your damn scenes in the noood, buster."

It was difficult, but Crewes managed a smile.

HANDY

Meanwhile, back at my head, things were going from Erich von Stroheim to Alfred Hitchcock. No, make that from Fritz Lang to Val Lewton. Try bad to worse.

I'd come back from Never-Never Land and the song of the turtle, and had called in to Arthur's office. I simply could not face a return to the world of show biz so soon after polishing tombstones in Emery Romito's private cemetery. I needed a long pull on something called quiet, and it was not to be found at the studio.

My apartment was hot and stuffy. I stripped and took a shower. For a moment I considered flushing my clothes down the toilet: I was sure they were impregnated with the mold of the ages, fresh from Santa Monica.

Then I chivvied and worried the thought that maybe possibly I ought just to send myself out to Filoy Cleaners, *in toto*. "Here you go, Phil," I'd say. "I'd like myself cleaned and burned." *You need sleep, Handy,* I thought. *Maybe about seven hundred years' worth.*

Rip Van Winkle, old Ripper-poo, it occurred to me, in a passing flash of genuine lunacy, knew precisely where it was at. I could see it now, a Broadway extravaganza

RIP!

starring Fred Handy

who will sleep like a mother stone log for seven hundred years right before your perspiring eyes, at $2.25 / $4.25 / and $6.25 for Center Aisle Orchestra Seats.

The shower did little to restore my sanity.

I decided to call Julie.

I checked her itinerary—which I'd blackmailed out of her agent—and found that *Hello, Dolly!* was playing Pittsburgh, Pennsylvania. I dialed the O-lady and told her all kindsa stuff. After a while she got into conversations with various kindly folks in the state of Pennsylvania, who confided in her, strictly *entre-nous*, that my Lady of the moist thighs, the fair Julie Glynn, *née* Rowena Glyckmeier, was out onna town somewheres, and O-lady 212 in Hollywood would stay right there tippy-tap up against the phone all night if need be, just to bring us two fine examples of Young American Love together, whenever.

As I racked the receiver, just as suddenly as I'd gotten *into* the mood, all good humor and fancy footwork deserted me. I realized I was sadder than I'd been in years. What the hell was happening? Why this feeling of utter depression; why this sense of impending disaster?

Then the phone rang, and it was Arthur, and he told me what had happened at the Studio. I couldn't stop shuddering.

He also told me there was an opening at the Coconut Grove that night, and he thought Valerie might like to attend. He had already called the star—it was Bobby Vinton, or Sergio Franchi, or Wayne Newton, or someone in that league—and there would be an announcement from the stage that Valerie Lone was in the audience, and a spontaneous standing ovation. I couldn't stop shuddering.

He suggested I get in touch with Romito and set up a date. Help wash away the stain of that afternoon. Then he told me the name of the extra who had insulted Valerie Lone—he must have been reading it off a piece of paper, he spoke the name with a flatness like the striking trajectory of a cobra—and suggested I compile a brief dossier on the gentleman. I had the distinct impression Arthur Crewes could be as vicious an enemy as he was cuddly a friend. The blond beach-bum would probably find it very hard getting work in films from this point on, though it was no longer the antediluvian era in which a Cohen or a Mayer or a Skouras could kill a career with a couple of phone calls. I couldn't stop shuddering.

Then I called Emery Romito and advised him he was to pick up Valerie Lone at six-thirty at the Beverly Hills. Tuxedo. He fumphuh'd and I knew he didn't have the price of a rental tux. So I called Wardrobe at the Studio and told them to send someone out to Santa Monica . . . and to dress him *au courant*, not in the wing-collar style of the Twenties, which is what I continued to shudder at in my mind.

Then I went back and took another shower. A hot shower. It was getting chilly in my body.

I heard the phone ringing through the pounding noise of the shower spray, and got to the instrument as my party was hanging up. There was a trail of monster wet footprints all across the living room behind me, vanishing into the bedroom and thence the bath, from whence I had comce.

"Yeah, who?" I yelled.

"Fred? Spencer."

A pungent footnote on being depressed. When you have just received word from the IRS that an audit of your returns will be necessary for the years 1956–66 in an attempt to pinpoint the necessity for a $13,000 per year entertainment exemption; when the ASPCA rings you up and asks you to come down and identify a body in their cold room, and they're describing your pet basset hound as he would look had he been through a McCormick reaper; when your wife, from whom you are separated, and whom you screwed last month only by chance when you took over her separation payment, calls and tells you she is with child—yours; when World War Nine breaks out and they are napalming your patio; when you've got the worst summer cold of your life, the left-hand corner of your mouth is cracked and chapped, your prostate is acting up again and oozing shiny drops of a hideous green substance; when all of this links into one gigantic chain of horror threatening to send you raving in the direction of Joe Pyne or Lawrence Welk, then, and only then, do agents named Spencer Lichtman call.

It is not a nice thing.

New horrors! I moaned silently. *New horrors!*

"Hey, you there, Fred?"

"I died."

"Listen, I want to talk on you."

"Spencer, please. I want to sleep for seven hundred years."

"It's the middle of a highly productive day."

"*I've* produced three asps, a groundhog and a vat of stale eels. Let me sleep, perchance to dream."

"I want to talk about Valerie Lone."

"Come over to the apartment." I hung up.

The wolf pack was starting to move in. I called Crewes. He was in conference. I said break in. Roz said fuckoff. I thanked her politely and retraced my monster wet footprints to the shower. Cold shower. Cold, hot, cold: if my moods continued to fluctuate, it was going to be double pneumonia time. (I might have called it my manic-depressive phase, except my moods kept going from depressive to depressiver. With not a manic in sight.)

Wearing a thick black plastic weight-reducing belt—compartments filled with sand—guaranteed to take five pounds of unsightly slob off my drooling gut—and a terry cloth wraparound, I built myself an iced tea in the kitchen. There were no ice cubes. I had a bachelor's icebox: a jar of maraschino cherries, an opened package of Philadelphia cream cheese with fungus growing on it, two tv dinners—Hawaiian shrimp and Salisbury steak—and a tin of condensed milk. If Julie didn't start marrying me or mothering me, it was certain I would be found starved dead, lying in a corner, clutching an empty carton of Ritz crackers, some fateful morning when they came to find out why I hadn't paid the rent in a month or two.

I went out onto the terrace of the lanai apartments, overlooking the hysterectomy-shaped swimming pool used for the 1928 Lilliputian Olympics. There were two slim-thighed creatures named Janice and Pegeen lounging near the edge. Pegeen had an aluminum reflector up to her chin, making sure no slightest inch of epidermis escaped UV scorching. Janice was on her stomach, oiled like the inside of a reservoir-tip condom. "Hey!" I yelled. "How're you fixed for ice cubes?" Janice turned over, letting her copy of Kahlil Gibran's THE PROPHET fall flat, and shaded her eyes toward me.

"Oh, hi, Fred. Go help yourself."

I waved thanks and walked down the line to their apartment. The door was open. I went in through the debris of the previous evening's amphetamine frolic, doing a dance to avoid the hookah and the pillows on the floor. There were no ice cubes. I filled their trays, reinserted them in the freezer compartment, and went back outside. "Everything groovy?" Janice yelled up at me.

"Ginchy," I called back, and went into my apartment.

Warm iced tea is an ugly.

I heard Spencer down below, shucking the two pairs of slim thighs. I waited a full sixty-count, hoping he would pass, just once. At sixty, I went to the door and yowled. "Up here, Spencer."

"Be right there, Fred," he called over his shoulder, his moist eyeballs fastened like snails to Pegeen's bikini.

"The specialist tells me I've only got twenty minutes to live, Spencer. Get your ass up here."

He murmured something devilishly clever to the girls, who regarded his retreating back with looks that compared it unfavorably to a haunch of tainted venison. Spencer mounted the stairs two at a time, puffing hideously, trying desperately to do a Steve McQueen for the girls.

"Hey, buhbie." He extended his hand as he came through the door.

Spencer Lichtman had been selected by the monthly newsletter and puff-sheet of the Sahara Hotel & Casino in Las Vegas, Nevada, U.S.A., in their August 1966 mailing, as Mr. Charm. They noted that he was charming whether he won or lost at the tables, and they quoted him as saying, after picking up eleven hundred dollars at craps, "It's only money." The newsletter thought that was mighty white of Spencer Lichtman. The newsletter also thought it was historically clever of him to have said it, and only avoided adding their usual editorial (Ha! Ha! Isn't old Spencer a wow!) with a non-Vegas reserve totally out of character for the "editor," a former junior ad exec well into hock to the management of the hotel, working it off by editing the puff-sheet in a style charitably referred to as Hand-Me-Down Mark Hellinger.

Spencer Lichtman was, to me, one of the great losers of all time, eleven hundred Vegan jellybeans notwithstanding. That he was a brilliant agent cannot be denied. But he did it *despite* himself, dear God let me have it pegged correctly otherwise my entire world-view is ass-backwards, not *because* of himself.

He was a tall, broad-shouldered, well-fried, blue-eyed specimen, handsomely cocooned within a Harry Cherry suit. Light-blue button-down shirts (no high-rise collars for Spencer, he knew his neck was too thick for them), black knee-length socks, highly polished black loafers, diminutive cuff links, and a paisley hankie in the breast pocket. He might have sprung full-blown like Adolph Menjou from the forehead of *Gentleman's Quarterly*.

Then tell me this: if Spencer Lichtman was good-looking, mannerly, talented, in good taste, and successful, why the hell did I know as sure as Burton made little green Elizabeths, that Spencer Lichtman was a bummer?

It defied analysis.

So I shook hands with him.

"Jesus, it's hot," he wheezed, falling onto the sofa, elegantly. Even collapsing, he had panache. "Can I impose on you for something cold?"

"I'm out of ice cubes."

"Oh."

"My neighbors are out of ice cubes, too."

"Those were your neighbors—"

"Right. Out there. The girls."

"Nice neighbors."

"Yeah. But they're *still* out of ice cubes."

"So I suppose we'd better talk. Then we can go over to the Luau and get something cold."

I didn't bother telling him I'd rather undergo intensive Hong Kong acupuncture treatments with needles in my cheeks, than go to the Luau for a drink. The cream of the Hollywood and Beverly Hills show biz set always made the Luau in the afternoons, hustling secretaries from the talent agencies who were, in actuality, the daughters of Beverly Hills merchants, the daughters of Hollywood actors, the daughters of Los Angeles society, the daughters of delight. The cream. That *is* the stuff that floats to the top, isn't it? Cream?

No, Spencer, I am not going with you to the Luau so you can hustle for me, and get me bedded down with one of your puffball-haired steno-typists, thereby giving you an edge on me for future dealings. No, indeed not, Spencer, my lad. I am going to pass on all those fine trim young legs exposed beneath entirely too inflammatory minis. I am probably going to go into the bedroom after you've gone and play with myself, but it is a far far better thing I do than to let you get your perfectly white capped molars into me.

"You talk, Spencer. I'll listen." I sat down on the floor. "That's what I call cooperation."

He wanted desperately to undo his tie. But that would have been non-Agency. "I was talking to some of the people at the office . . ."

Translation: I read in the trades that Crewes has found this *alta-cockuh*, this old hag Valerie Whatshername, and at the snake-pit session this morning I suggested to Morrie and Lew and Marty that I take a crack at maybe we should rep her, there might be a dime or a dollar or both in it, so what are the chances?

I stared at him with an expression like Raggedy Andy.

"And, uh, we felt it would be highly prestigious for the Agency to represent Valerie Lone . . ."

Translation: At least we can clip ten percent off of this deal with Crewes, and she ought to be good for a second deal with him at the Studio, and if *anything* at *all* happens with her, there're two or three short-line deals we can make, maybe at American–International for one of those *Baby Jane/Lady in a Cage* horrorifics; shit, she'd sit still for *any* kind of star billing, even in a screamer like that. Play her right, and we can make thirty, forty grand before she falls in her traces.

I segued smoothly from Raggedy Andy into Lenny: *Of Mice and Men*. Except I didn't dribble.

"I think we can really move Valerie, in the field of features. And, of course, there's a *lot* of television open to her . . ."

Translation: We'll book the old broad into a guest shot on every nitwit series shooting now for a September air-date. Guest cameos are perfect for a warhorse like her. It's like every asshole in America had a private tube to the freak show. Come and see the Ice Age return! Witness the resurrection of Piltdown Woman! See the resurgence of Miss Ankle-Strap Wedgie! Gape and drool at the unburied dead! She'll play dance hall madams on *Cimarron Strip* and aging actresses on *Petticoat Junction*; she'll play a frontier matriarch on *The Big Valley* and the mother of a kidnapped child on *Felony Squad*. A grand per day, at first, till the novelty wears off. We'll book her five or six deep till they get the word around. Then we'll make trick deals with the network for multiples. There's a potload in this.

Lenny slowly vanished to be replaced by Huck Finn.

"Well, *say* something, Fred! What do you think?"

Huck Finn vanished and in his stead Spencer Lichtman was staring down at Captain America, bearing his red-white-and-blue shield, decked out in his patriotic uniform with the wings on the cowl, with the steely gaze and the outthrust chin of the defender of widows and orphans.

Captain America said, softly, "You'll take five percent commission and I'll make sure she signs with you."

"Ten, Fred. You know that's standard. We can't—"

"Five." Captain America wasn't fucking around.

"Eight. *Maybe* I can swing eight. Morrie and Lew—"

Captain America shifted his star-studded shield up his arm and pulled his gauntlet tighter. "I'll be fair. Six."

Lichtman stood up, started toward the door, whirled on Captain America. "She's got to have representation, Handy. Lots of it. You know it. I know it. Name me three times you know of, when an agent took less than ten? We're working at twelve and even thirteen on some clients. This is a chancy thing. She might go, she might not. We're willing to gamble. You're making it lousy for both of us. I came to you because I know you can handle it. But we haven't even talked about *your* percentage."

Captain America's jaw muscles jumped. The inference that he could be bought was disgusting. He breathed the sweet breath of patriotic fervor and answered Spencer Lichtman—alias the Red Skull—with the tone he deserved. "No kickback for me, Spencer. Straight six."

Lichtman's expression was one of surprise. But in a moment he had it figured out, in whatever form his cynicism and familiarity with the hunting habits of the scene allowed him best and most easily to rationalize. There was an angle in it for me, he was sure of that. It was a sneaky angle, it had to be, because he couldn't find a trace of it, which meant it was subtler than most. On that level he was able to talk to me. Not to Captain America, never to old Cap; because Lichtman couldn't conceive of a purely altruistic act, old Spence couldn't. So there was a finagle here somewhere; he didn't know just where, but as thief to thief, he was delighted with the dealing.

"Seven."

"Okay."

"I should have stuck with eight."

"You wouldn't have made a deal if you had."

"You're sure she'll sign?"

"You sure you'll work your ass off for her, and keep the leeches away from her, and give her a straight accounting of earnings, and try to build the career and not just run it into the ground for a fast buck?"

"You know I—"

"You know *I*, baby! *I* have an eye on you. Arthur *Crewes* will have an eye on you. And if you fuck around with her, and louse her up, and then drop her, both Arthur and myself will do some very heavy talking with several of your clients who are currently under contract to Arthur, such as Steve and Raquel and Julie and don't you forget it."

"What's in this for you, Handy?"

"I've got the detergent concession."

"And I thought I was coming up here to hustle *you*."

"There's only one reason you're getting the contract, Spencer. She needs an agent, you're as honest as most of them—excluding Hal and Billy—and I believe *you* believe she can be moved."

"I do."

"I figured it like that."

"I'll set up a meet with Morrie and Lew and Marty. Early next week."

"Fine. Her schedule's pretty tight now. She starts rehearsals with the new scene day after tomorrow."

Spencer Lichtman adjusted his tie, smoothed his hair, and pulled down his suit jacket in the back. He extended his hand. "Pleasure doing business, Fred."

I shook once again. "Dandy, Spencer."

Then he smirked, suggesting broadly that he knew I must have a boondoggle only slightly smaller than the Teapot Dome going. And, so help me God, he winked. Conspiratorially.

Tonstant weader fwowed up.

When he left, I called Arthur, and told him what I'd done, and why. He approved, and said he had to get back to some work on his desk. I started to hang up, but heard his voice faintly, calling me back. I put the receiver up to my ear and said, "Something else, Arthur?"

There was a pause, then he said, gently, "You're a good guy, Fred." I mumbled something and racked it.

And sat there for twenty minutes, silently arguing with Raggedy Andy, Lenny, Huck and old Captain America. *They* thought I was a good guy, too. And *I* kept trying to get them to tell me where the sleazy angle might be, so I could stop feeling so disgustingly humanitarian.

Have you ever tried to pull on a turtleneck over a halo?

7

Valerie Lone had only been told she would be picked up at six-thirty, for dinner and an opening at the Grove. The flowers arrived at five-fifteen. Daisies. Roses were a makeout flower, much too premeditated. Daisies. With their simplicity and their honesty and their romance. Daisies. With one rose in the center of the arrangement.

At six-thirty the doorbell to Valerie Lone's bungalow was rung, and she hurried to open the door. (She had turned down the offer of a personal maid. "The hotel is very nice to me; their regular maid is fine, Arthur, thank you.")

She opened the door, and for a moment she did not recognize him. But for her, there had only been one like him; only one man that tall, that elegant, that self-possesed. The years had not touched him. He was the same. Not a hair out of place, not a line where no line had been, and the smile—the same gentle, wide pixie smile—it was the same, unaltered. Soft, filtered lights were unnecessary. For Valerie Lone he was the same.

But in the eye of the beheld . . .

Emery Romito looked across the past and all the empty years between, and saw his woman. There had been gold, and quicksilver, and soft murmurings in the night, and crystal, and water as sweet as Chablis, and velvet and plumes of exotic birds . . . and now

there was arthritis, and difficult breathing, and a heaviness in the air, and perspiration and nervousness, and stale rum cake, and the calling of children far away across the misty landscape, and someone very dark and hungry always coming toward him.

Now there was only now. And he lamented all the days that had died without joy. Hope had sung its song within him, in reverie, on nights when the heat had been too much for him and he had gone to sit at the edge of the ocean. Far out, beyond the lights of the amusement park at Lick Pier, beyond the lights of the night, the song had been raised against dark stars and darker skies. But had never been heard. Had gone to tremolo and wavering and finally sighed into the silent vacuum of despair, where sound can only be heard by striking object against object. And in that nowhere, there was no object for Emery Romito.

"Hello, Val . . ."

Tear loneliness across its pale surface; rend it totally and find the blood of need welling up in a thick, pale torrent. Let the horns of growth blare a message in rinky-tink meter. Turn a woman carrying all her years into a sloe-eyed gamine. Peel like an artichoke the scar-tissue heart of a lost dream, and find in the center a pulsing golden light with a name. She looked across yesterday and found him standing before her, and she could do no other than cry.

He came through the door as she sagged in upon herself. Her tears were soundless, so desperate, so overwhelming, they made her helpless. He closed the door behind him and gathered her to himself. Shrunken though he was, not in her arms, not in her eyes. He was still tall, gentle Emery, whose voice was silk and softness. Collapsed within the eternity of his love, she beat back the shadows that had come to devour her, and she knew that now, *now* she would live. She spoke his name a hundred times in a second.

That night, *her* name was spoken by a hundred voices in a second; but this time, as she stood to applause for the first time in eighteen years, she did not cry. Emery Romito was with her, beside her, and she held his hand as she rose. Fred Handy was there; with the girl Randi, from the office that afternoon. Arthur Crewes was there; alone. Smiling. Jubilant. Radiating warmth for Valerie Lone and the good people who had never forgotten her. Spencer Lichtman was there; with Miss American Airlines and an orange-haired girl of pneumatic proportions starring in Joseph E. Levine's production of *Maciste and the Vestal Virgins*. ("You've got a better chance of convincing the public she's Maciste than a virgin," Handy muttered, as they passed in the lobby of the Ambassador Hotel.)

Valerie Lone! they cried. Valerie Lone!

She stood, holding Romito's hand, and the dream had come full circle.

Like the laocoönian serpent, swallowing its own tail. Ouroboros in Clown Town.

The next day John D. F. Black delivered the rewritten pages. The scenes for Valerie were exquisite. He asked if he might be introduced to Valerie Lone, and Fred took him over to the Beverly Hills, where Valerie was guardedly trying to get a suntan. It was the first time in many years that she had performed that almost religious Hollywood act: the deep-frying. She rose to meet Black, a tall and charming man with an actor's leathery good looks. In a few minutes he had charmed her completely, and told her he had been delighted to write the scenes for her, that they were just what she had always done best in her biggest films, that they gave her room to expand and color the part, that he knew she would be splendid. She asked if he would be on the set during shooting. Black looked at Handy. Handy looked away. Black shrugged and said he didn't know, he had another commitment elsewhere. But Valerie Lone knew that things had not changed all *that* much in Hollywood: the writer was still chattel. When his work on the script was done, it was no longer his own. It was given to the Producer, and the Director, and the Production Manager, and the Actors, and he was no longer welcome.

"I'd like Mr. Black to be on the set when I shoot, Mr. Handy," she said to Fred. "If Arthur doesn't mind."

Fred nodded, said he would see to it; and John D. F. Black bent, took Valerie Lone's hand in his own, and kissed it elegantly. "I love you," he said.

Late that night, Arthur and Fred took Valerie to the Channel 11 television studios on Sunset, and sat offstage as Valerie prepared for her on-camera live-action full-living-color interview with Adela Seddon, the Marquesa of Malice. A female counterpart of Joe Pyne, Adela Seddon spoke with forked tongue. She was much-watched and much-despised. Impartial voters learned their politics from her show. Wherever she was at, they were not. If she had come out in favor of Motherhood, Apple Pie and The American Way, tens of thousands of noncommitted people would instantly take up the banners of Misogyny, Macrobiotics and Master Racism. She was a badgerer, a harridan, a snarling viper with a sure mouth for the wisecrack and a ready fang for the jugular. Beneath a Tammy Grimes tousle of candy-apple red hair, her face was alternately compared with that of a tuba player confronting a small child sucking a lemon, and a prize shoat for the first time encountering the butcher's blade. She had been married six times, divorced five, was currently separated, hated being touched, and was rumored in private circles to have a long-since gone mad from endless masturbation. Her nose job was not entirely successful.

Valerie was justifiably nervous.

"I've never seen her, Arthur. Working out there in the diner, nights you know, I've never seen her."

Handy, who thought it was lunacy to bring Valerie anywhere near the Seddon woman, added, "To see is to believe."

Valerie looked at him, concern showing like a second face upon the carefully drawn mask of cosmetics the Studio makeup head had built for her. She looked good, much younger, rejuvenated by the acclaim she had received at the Ambassador's Coconut Grove. (It had been the Righteous Brothers. They had come down into the audience and belted "My Babe" in her honor, right at her.)

"You don't think much of her, do you, Mr. Handy?"

Handy expelled air wearily. "About as charming as an acrobat in a polio ward. Queen of the Yahoos. The Compleat Philistine. Death warmed over. A pain in the–"

Crewes cut him off.

"No long lists, Fred. I had one of those from you already today. Remember?"

"It's been a long day, Arthur."

"Relax, please. Adela called me this afternoon, and *asked* for Valerie. She promised to be good. Very good. She's been a fan of Valerie's for years. We talked for almost an hour. She wants to do a nice interview."

Handy grimaced. Pain. "I don't believe it. The woman would do a Bergen-Belsen on her own Granny if she thought it would jump her rating."

Crewes spoke softly, carefully, as if telling a child. "Fred, I would not for a moment jeopardize Valerie if I thought there was any danger here. Adela Seddon is not my idea of a lady, either, but her show is *watched*. It's syndicated, and it's popular. If she says she'll behave, it behooves us to take the chance."

Valerie touched Handy's sleeve. "It's all right, Fred. I trust Arthur. I'll go on."

Crewes smiled at her. "Look, it's even live, not taped earlier in the evening, the way she usually does the show. This way we know she'll behave; they tape it in case someone guests who makes her look bad, they can dump the tape. But live like this, she has to be a nanny, or she could get killed. It stands to reason."

Handy looked dubious. "There's a flaw in that somewhere, Arthur, but I haven't the strength to find it. Besides," he indicated a flashing red light on the wall above them, "Valerie is about to enter the Valley of the Shadow . . ."

The stage manager came and got Valerie, and took her out onto the set, where she was greeted with applause from the studio audience. She sat in one of the two comfortable chairs behind the low desk, and waited patiently for Adela Seddon to arrive from her offstage office.

When she made her appearance, striding purposefully to the desk and seating herself, and instantly shuffling through a sheaf of research papers (presumably on Valerie Lone), the audience once again transported itself with wild applause. Which Adela Seddon did not deign to acknowledge. The signals were given, the control booth marked, and in a moment the offstage announcer was bibble-bibbling the intro. The audience did its number, and Camera No. 2 glowed red as a ghastly closeup of Adela Seddon appeared on the studio monitors. It was like a microscopic view of a rotted watermelon rind.

"This evening," Adela Seddon began, a smile that was a rictus stretching her mouth, "we are coming to you live, not on tape. The reason for this is my very special guest, a great lady of the American cinema, who agreed to come on only if we were aired live, thus ensuring a fair and unedited interview . . ."

"I *told* you she was a shit!" Handy hissed to Crewes. Crewes shushed him with a wave of his hand.

". . . not been seen for eighteen years on the wide-screens of motion picture theaters, but she is back in a forthcoming Arthur Crewes production, *Subterfuge*. I'd like a big hand for Miss Valerie Lone!"

The audience did tribal rituals, rain dances, ju-ju incantations and a smattering of plain and fancy warwhooping. Valerie was a lady. She smiled demurely and nodded her thankyous. Adela Seddon seemed uneasy at the depth of response, and shifted in her chair.

"She's getting out the blowdarts," Handy moaned.

"Shut up!" Crewes snarled. He was not happy.

"Miss Lone," Adela Seddon said, turning slightly more toward the nervous actress, "precisely *why* have you chosen this time to come back out of retirement? Do you think there's still an audience for your kind of acting?"

OhmiGod, thought Handy, *here it comes.*

EDITED TRANSCRIPT OF SEDDON
"LOOKING IN" / 11-23-67
(. . . *indicates deletion*)

VALERIE LONE: I don't know what you mean, "my kind of acting"?
ADELA SEDDON: Oh, come on now, Miss Lone.
VL: No, really. I don't.
AS: Well, I'll be specific then. The 1930s style: overblown and gushy.
VL: I didn't know that was my style, Miss Seddon.
AS: Well, according to your latest review, which is, incidentally, eighteen years old, in something called *Pearl of the Antilles* with Jon Hall, you are, quote, "a fading lollipop of minuscule talent given to instant tears and grandiose arm-waving." Should I go on?
VL: If it gives you some sort of pleasure.
AS: Pleasure isn't why I'm up here twice a week, Miss Lone. The truth is. I sit up here with kooks and twistos and people who denigrate our great country, and I let them have their say, without interrupting, because I firmly believe in the First Amendment of the Constitution of these United States of America, that everyone has the right to speak his mind. If that also happens to mean they have the right to make asses of themselves before seventy million viewers, it isn't my fault.
VL: What has all that to do with me?
AS: I don't mind your *thinking* I'm stupid, Miss Lone; just kindly don't *talk* to me as if I were stupid. The truth, Miss Lone, that's what all this has to do with you.
VL: Are you sure you'd recognize it?
(*Audience applause*)
AS: I recognize that there are many old-time actresses who are so venal, so egocentric, that they refuse to acknowledge their age, who continue to embarrass audiences by trying to cling to the illusion of sexuality.

VL: You shouldn't air your problems so openly, Miss Seddon. (*Audience applause*)

AS: I see retirement hasn't dampened your wit.

VL: Nor made me immune to snakebites.

AS: You're getting awfully defensive, awfully early in the game.

VL: I wasn't aware this was a game. I thought it was an interview.

AS: This is *my* living room, Miss Lone. We call it a game, here, and we play it *my* way.

VL: I understand. It's not how you play, it's who wins.

AS: Why don't we just talk about your new picture for a while?

VL: That would be a refreshing change,

. . .

AS: Is it true Crewes found you hustling drinks in a roadhouse?

VL: Not quite. I was a waitress in a diner.

AS: I suppose you think slinging hash for the last eighteen years puts you in tip-top trim to tackle a major part in an important motion picture?

VL: No, but I think the fifteen years I spent in films prior to that *does*. A good actress is like a good doctor, Miss Seddon. She has the right to demand high pay not so much for the short amount of time she puts in on a picture, but for all the years before that, years in which she learned her craft properly, so she could perform in a professional manner. You don't pay a doctor merely for what he does for you *now*, but for all the years he spent learning how to do it.

AS: That's very philosophical.

VL: It's very accurate.

AS: I think it begs the question.

VL: *I* think *you'd* like to *think* it does.

. . .

AS: Wouldn't you say actresses are merely self-centered little children playing at make-believe?

VL: I would find it very difficult to say anything even remotely like that. I'm surprised you aren't embarrassed saying it.

AS: I'm hard to embarrass, Miss Lone. Why don't you answer the question?

VL: I thought I *had* answered it.

AS: Not to my satisfaction.

VL: I can see that not being satisfied has made you an unhappy woman, so I—

(*Audience applause*)

—so, so I don't want to dissatisfy you any further; I'll answer the question a little more completely. No, I think acting at its best can be something of a holy chore. If it emerges from a desire to portray life as it is, rather than just to put in a certain amount of time in front of the cameras for a certain amount of money, then it becomes as important as teaching or writing, because it crystallizes the world for an audience; it preserves the past; it lets others living more comfined lives, examine a world they may never come into contact with . . .

AS: We have to take a break now, for a commercial—

. . .

VL: I'd rather not discuss my personal life, if you don't mind.

AS: A "star" has no personal life.

VL: That may be *your* opinion, Miss Seddon, it isn't mine.

AS: Is there some special reason you won't talk about Mr. Romito?

VL: We have always been good friends—

AS: Oh, come *on*, Valerie dear, you're starting to sound like a prepared press release: "We're just friends."

VL: You find it difficult to take yes for an answer.

AS: Well, I'll tell you, Miss Lone, I had a phone call today from a gentleman who volunteered to come into our dock tonight, to ask you a few questions. Let's go to the dock . . . what is your name, sir?

HASKELL BARKIN: My name is Barkin. Haskell Barkin.

AS: I understand you know Miss Lone.

HB: In a manner of speaking.

VL: I don't understand. I don't think I've ever met this gentleman.

HB: You almost did.

VL: What?

AS: Why don't you just let Mr. Barkin tell his story, Miss Lone.

She came offstage shaking violently. Romito had seen the first half of the interview, at his hotel in Santa Monica. He had hurried to the studio. When she stumbled away from the still-glaring lights of the set, he was there, and she almost fell into his arms. "Oh God, Emery, I'm so frightened . . ."

Crewes was furious. He moved into the darkness offstage, heading for Adela Seddon's dressing room/office. Handy had another mission.

The audience was filing out of the studio. Handy dashed for the side exit, came out in the alley next to the studio, and circled the building till he found the parking lot. Barkin was striding toward a big yellow Continental.

"Barkin! You motherfucker!" Handy screamed at him.

The tall man turned and stopped in mid-step. His long hair had been neatly combed for the evening television appearance, and in a suit he looked anachronistic, like King Kong in knickers. But the brace of his chest and shoulders was no less formidable.

He was waiting for Handy.

The little publicist came fast, across the parking lot. "How much did they pay you, you sonofabitch? How much? *How much, motherfucker!"*

Barkin began to crouch, waiting for Handy, fists balled, knees bent, the handsome face cold and impassive, anticipating the crunch of knuckles against face. Handy was howling now, like a Confederate trooper charging a Union gun emplacement. At a dead run he came down on Barkin, standing between a Corvette and a station wagon parked in the lot.

At the last moment, instead of breaking around the Corvette, Handy miraculously *leaped up* and came across the bonnet of the Corvette, still running, like a decathlon hurdler. Barkin had half-turned, expecting Handy's rush from the front of the sports car. But the publicist was suddenly above him, bearing down on him like a hunting falcon, before he could correct position.

Handy plunged across the Corvette, denting the red louvered bonnet, and dove full-out at Barkin. Blind with fury, he was totally unaware that he had bounded up onto the car, that he was across it in two steps, that he was flying through the air and crashing into Barkin with all the impact of a human cannonball.

He took Barkin high on the chest, one hand and wrist against the beach-bum's throat. Barkin whooshed air and sailed backward, into the station wagon. Up against the half-lowered radio antenna, which bent under his spine, then cracked and broke off in his back. Barkin screamed, a delirious, half-crazed spiral of sound as the sharp edge of the antenna cut through his suit jacket and shirt, and ripped his flesh. The pain bent him sidewise, and Handy slipped off him, catching his heel on the Corvette and tumbling into the narrow space between the cars. Barkin kicked out, his foot sinking into Handy's stomach as the publicist fell past him. Handy landed on his shoulders, the pain surging up into his chest and down into his groin. His rib cage seemed filled with nettles, and he felt for a moment he might lose control of his bladder.

Barkin tried to go for him, but the antenna was hooked through his jacket. He tried wrenching forward and there was a ripping sound, but it held. He struggled forward toward Handy awkwardly, bending from the waist, but could not get a hold on the publicist. Handy tried to rise, and Barkin stomped him, first on the hand, cracking bones and breaking skin, then on the chest, sending Handy scuttling backward on his buttocks and elbows.

Handy managed to get to his feet and pulled himself around the station wagon. Barkin was trying frantically to get himself undone, but the antenna had hooked in and out of the jacket material, and he was awkwardly twisted.

Handy climbed up onto the hood of the station wagon and on hands and knees, like a child, came across toward Barkin. The big man tried to reach him, but Handy fell across his neck and with senseless fury sank his teeth into Barkin's ear. The beach-bum shrieked again, a woman's sound, and shook his head like an animal trying to lose a flea. Handy hung on, bringing the taste of blood to his mouth. His hand came across and dug into the corner of Barkin's mouth, pulling the lip up and away. The fingers spread, he poked at Barkin's eye, and the beach-bum rattled against the car like a bird in a cage. Then all the pains merged and Barkin sagged in a semiconscious boneless mass. He hung against the weight of Handy and the hooking antenna. The strain was too great, the jacket ripped through, and Barkin fell face-forward hitting the side of the Corvette, pulling Handy over the top of the station wagon. Barkin's face hit the sports car; the nose broke. Barkin fainted with the pain, and slipped down into a Buddha-like position, Handy tumbling over him and landing on his knees between the cars.

Handy pulled himself up against the station wagon, and without realizing Barkin was unconscious, kicked out with a loose-jointed vigor, catching the beach-bum in the ribs with the toe of his shoe. Barkin fell over on his side, and lay there.

Handy, gasping, breathing raggedly, caromed off the cars, struggling to find his way to his own car. He finally made it to the Impala, got behind the wheel and through a fog of gray and red managed to get the key into the ignition. He spun out of the parking lot, scraping a Cadillac and a Mercury, his headlights once sweeping across a row of cars in which a station wagon and a Corvette were parked side by side, seeing a bleeding bag of flesh and fabric inching its way along the concrete, trying to get to its feet, touching softly at the shattered expanse of what had been a face, what had once been a good living.

Handy drove without knowing where he was going.

When he appeared at Randi's door twenty minutes later—having left her off from their date only a few hours before—she was wearing a shortie nightgown that ended at her thighs. "Jesus, Fred, what happened?" she asked, and helped him inside. He collapsed on her bed, leaving dark streaks of brown blood on the candy-striped sheets. She pulled his clothes off him, managing to touch his genitals as often as possible, and tended to his needs, all sorts of needs.

He paid no attention. He had fallen asleep.

It had been a full day for Handy.

8

The columns had picked it up. They said Valerie Lone had carried it off beautifully, coming through the barrage of viciousness and sniping with Adela Seddon like a champ. Army Archerd called Seddon a "shrike" and suggested she try her dictionary for the difference between "argument" and "controversy," not to mention the difference between "intimidation" and "interview." Valerie was a minor folk heroine. She had gone into the lair of the dragon and had emerged dragging its fallopians behind her. Crewes and Handy were elated. There had been mutterings from Haskell Barkin's attorney, a slim and good-looking man named Taback who had seemed ashamed even to be handling Barkin's complaint. When Handy and Crewes and the Studio battery of lawyers got done explaining *precisely* what had happened, and Taback had met Handy, the attorney returned to Barkin and advised him to use Blue Cross to take care of the damage it would cover, get his current paramour to lay out for the facial rebuilding, and drop charges: no one would believe that a hulk the size of Haskell Barkin could get so thoroughly dribbled by a pigeonweight like Handy.

But that was only part of the Crewes–Handy elation. Valerie had begun to be seen everywhere with Emery Romito. The fan magazines were having a field day with it. To a generation used to reviling their elders, with no respect for age, there was a kind of sentimental Albert Payson Terhune loveliness to the reuniting of old lovers. No matter where Valerie and Emery went, people beamed on them. Talk became common that after all those years of melancholy and deprivation, at long last the lovers might be together permanently.

For Emery Romito it was the first time he had been truly alive since *they* had killed his career during the draft-dodging scandal. But that was all forgotten now; he seemed to swell with the newfound dignity he had acquired squiring the columns' hottest news item. That, combined with his rediscovery of what Valerie had always meant to him, made him something greater than the faded character actor the years had forced him to become. The fear was still there, but it could be forgotten for short times now.

Valerie had begun rehearsals with her fellow cast-members, and she was growing more confident day by day. The Seddon show had served to fill her once again with fear, but its repercussions—demonstrated in print—had effectively drained it away. These rises and fallings in temperament had an unconscious effect on her, but it was not discernible to those around her.

On the night of the second day of rehearsals, Emery came to pick her up at the Studio, in a car the Studio had rented for him. He took her to dinner at a small French restaurant near the Hollywood Ranch Market, and after the final Drambuie they drove up to Sunset, turned left, and cruised toward Beverly Hills.

It was a Friday night.

The hippies were out.

The teenie-boppers. The flower children. The new ones. The long hair, the tight boots, the paisley shirts, the mini-skirts, the loose sexuality, the hair vests, the shirts with the sleeves cut off, the noise, the jeering. The razored crevasse that existed between *their* time, when they had been golden and fans had pressed up against sawhorses at the premieres, to get their autographs, and *today*, a strange and almost dreamlike time of Surrealistic youth who spoke another tongue, moved with liquid fire and laughed at things that were painful. At a stoplight near Laurel Canyon, they stopped and were suddenly surrounded by hippies hustling copies of an underground newspaper, the *L.A. Free Press*. They were repelled by the disordered, savage look of the kids, like barbarians. And though the news vendors spoke politely, though they merely pressed up against the car and shoved their papers into the windows, the terror their very presence evoked in the two older people panicked Romito and he floored the gas pedal, spurting forward down Sunset, sending one beaded and flowered news-hippie sprawling, journals flying.

Romito rolled up his window, urging Valerie to do the same. It was something Kafka-esque to them as they whirled past the discothèques and the psychedelic book shops and the outdoor restaurants where the slim, hungry children of the strobe age languished, turned on, grooving heavy behind meth or grass.

He drove fast. All the way out Sunset to the Coast Highway and out the coast to Malibu.

Finally, Valerie said softly, "Emery, do you remember The Beach House? We used to go there all the time for dinner. Remember? Let's stop there. For a drink."

Romito smiled, the lines around his eyes gathering in gentle humor. "Do I remember? I remember the night Dick Barthelmess did the tango on the bar with that swimmer, the girl from the Olympics . . . you know the one . . ."

But she didn't know the one. That particular memory had been lost. He had had the time to nurse the old memories—she had been slinging hash. No, she didn't remember the girl. But she did remember the old roadhouse that had been so popular with their set one of those years.

But when they came to the spot, they found the old roadhouse—predictably—had been razed. In its stead was a tiny beach-serving shopping center, and on the spot where Dick Barthelmess had danced the tango on the bar with that swimmer from the Olympics, there was an all-night liquor store, with a huge neon sign.

Emery Romito drove a few miles down the Coast Highway, past the liquor store, more by reflex than design. He pulled off on a side road paralleling the ocean, and there, on a ridge that sloped quickly down into darkness and surf somewhere below them, he stopped. They sat there silently together, the car turned off, their minds turned off, trapped in the darkness of loneliness, the landscape and their past.

Then, in a rush, all of it came back to Valerie Lone. The rush of thoughts waiting to be reexamined after twenty years. The reasons, the situations, the circumstances.

"Emery, why didn't we get married?"

And she answered her own question with a smile he could not see in the darkness. It was possible he had not even heard her, for he did not answer. And in her mind she ticked off the answers, all the deadly answers.

It was the dreams each of them had substituted for reality; the tenacity with which they had tried to clutch smoke and dream-mist; the stubborn refusal of each of them to acknowledge that the dream-mist and the smoke were bound to become ashes. And when each had been swallowed whole by the very careers they had thought would free them, they had become strangers. They were frightened to commit to one another, to anyone really, to anything but the world that stood and called their names a hundred times in a second, and beat hands in praise.

Then Emery spoke. As though his thoughts had been tracking similarly to her own, heading on a collision course for her mind and *her* thoughts hurtling toward him.

"You know, darling Val, you always made more money than me. Your name was always star-billing . . . at best, mine was always 'Also Featuring.' It wouldn't have worked."

She was nodding agreement, at the complete validity of it, and then, in an instant, the shock of what she was accepting without argument, believing *again* as she had the first time, the insanity of it hit her. Twenty years ago, in the fantasy-world, yes, those *might* have been real reasons—in the lunatic way that blasted and twisted logic seems rational in nightmares—but she had spent almost two decades in another life, and now she *knew* they were false, as specious as the life that claimed her on the screen.

But for a moment, for a long moment she had accepted it all again. It was the town, the industry, the way the show biz life sucked one under. For those in the industry it had rapidly become that way, as they had fallen under the spell of their own weird and golden lives; it had taken over twenty years to catch on completely, to permeate the culture. But now it was possible never to come up from under that thick fog of delusion. Because it hung like a Los Angeles smog across the entire nation, perhaps the world.

But not for Valerie Lone. Never again for her.

"Emery, listen to me . . ."

He was talking softly to himself, the sound of moths in the fog. Talking about screen credits and money and days that had never really been alive, and now had to be put to death fully and finally.

"Emery! Darling! Please, listen to me!"

He turned to her. She saw him, then. Even dimly, only by moonlight, she saw him as he really was, not as she had wished him to be, standing there in the doorway of the bungalow at the Beverly Hills Hotel that first night of her new life with him. She saw what had happened to the man who had been strong enough to deny war and say he would lose everything rather than fight against his fellow man. Emery Romito had become a willing prisoner of his own show biz life. He had never escaped.

She knew she had to explain it all to him, to unlearn him, and then teach him anew. An infinite sadness filled her as she readied her arguments, her coercion, her explanations of what the other world was like . . . the world he had always thought of as dull and empty and wasted.

"Darling, I've been out in the desert, out in nowhere, for almost twenty years. You've got to believe me when I tell you, none of this matters. The billing, the money, the life at the studios, it doesn't *matter*! It's all make-believe, we always said it was that, but we let it get us, grab hold of us. We have to understand there is a whole world without any of it. What if the show *doesn't* go on? What then? Why worry? We can do other things, if we care about each other. Do you understand what I'm saying? It doesn't matter if your picture is in the PLAYERS DIRECTORY, as long as you come home at night and turn the key in the door and know there's someone on the other side who cares whether or not you were killed in the traffic on the Freeway. Emery, *talk to me!*"

Silence. Straining on her part, toward him. Silence. Then, "Val, why don't we go dancing . . . like we used to do?"

The shadow came again to devour her. It showed its teeth and it prodded her, looking for the most vulnerable places, the places still filled with the juice of life, which it would eat to the bone, and then suck the marrow from the bone, till it collapsed into despair as had the rest of her.

She fought it.

She talked to him.

Her voice was the low, insistent voice she had cultivated in the star years. Now she turned it to its full power, and used it to win the most important part of her career.

We have a chance to make it together at last.

God has given us a second chance.

We can have what we lost twenty years ago.

Please, Emery, listen.

Emery Romito had been falling for many years. A great, shrieking fall down a long tunnel of despair. Her voice came to him down the length of that tunnel, and he clutched for it, missed, clutched again and found it. He let it hold him, swaying above the abyss, and slowly pulled himself back up that fragile thread.

Pathetically, he asked her, "Really? Do you think we can? Really?"

No one is more convincing than a woman fighting for her life. Really? She showed him, really. She told him, and she charmed him, and she gave him the strength he had lost so long ago. With her career burgeoning again it was certain they would have all the good things they had lost on the way to this place, this night.

And finally, he leaned across, this old man, and he kissed her, this tired woman. A shy kiss, almost immature, as though his lips had never touched all the lips of starlets and chorus girls and secretaries and women so much less important than this woman beside him in a rented car on a dark oceanside road.

He was frightened, she could feel it. Almost as frightened as she was. But he was willing to try; to see if they could dredge up something of permanence from the garbage-heaps of the love they had spent twenty years wasting.

Then he started the car, backed and filled and started the return to Hollywood.

The shadow was with her, still hungry, but it was set to waiting. She was no less frightened of the long-haired children and the sharp-tongued interviewers and the merciless lights of the sound stages, but at least now there was a goal; now there was something to move toward.

A gentle breeze came up, and they opened the windows.

HANDY

My first premonition of disaster to come was during the conversation Crewes had with Spencer Lichtman. It was two days before he was to shoot her initial scenes for the film. Spencer had made an appointment to discuss Valerie, and Crewes had asked me to be present.

I sat mute and alert. Spencer made his pitch; it was a good one, and a brief one. A three-picture deal with Crewes and the Studio. Sharpel, the Studio business head was there, and he did some of the finest broken-field running I've every seen. He suggested everyone wait to see how Valerie did in *Subterfuge*.

Spencer looked terribly disturbed at the conversation as he left. He said nothing to me. Neither did Sharpel, who seemed uneasy that I'd been in the room at all.

When they'd gone, I sat waiting for Arthur Crewes to say something. Finally, he said, "How's the publicity coming?"

"You've got the skinnys on your desk, Arthur. You know what's happening." Then I added, "I wish *I* knew what was happening."

He played dumb. "What would you like to know, Fred?"

I looked at him levelly. He knew I was on to him. There was very little point in obfuscation. "Who's got the pressure on you, Arthur?"

He sighed, shrugged as if to say *welllll, y'found me out,* and answered me wearily. "The Studio. They're nervous. They said Valerie is having trouble with the lines, she's awkward, the usual succotash."

"How the hell do *they* know? She hasn't even worked yet; only rehearsing. And Jimmy's kept the sessions strictly closed off."

Crewes hit the desk with the palm of his hand, then again. "They've got a spy in the crew."

"Oh, c'*mon,* you're kidding!"

"I'm *not* kidding. They've got a pile tied up in this one. That ski troops picture Jenkey made is bombing. They won't get back negative costs. They don't want to take any chances with this one. So they've got a fink in the company."

"Want me to sniff him out?"

"Why bother. They'll only plant another one. It's probably Jeanine, the assistant wardrobe mistress . . . or old Whatshisname . . . Skelly, the makeup man. No, there's no sense trying to pry out the rotten apple; it won't help her performance any."

I listened to all of it with growing concern. There was a new tone in Crewes's voice. A tentative tone, one just emerging for the first time, trying its flavor in the world. I could tell he was unhappy with the sound of it, that he was fighting it. But it was getting stronger. It was the tone of amelioration, of shading, of backing-off. It was the caterpillar tremble of fear that could metamorphose easily into the lovely butterfly of cowardice.

"You aren't planning on dumping her, are you, Arthur?" I asked.

He looked up sharply, annoyed. "Don't be stupid. I didn't go all through this just to buckle when the Studio gets nervous. Besides, I wouldn't do that to her."

"I hope not."

"I *said* not!"

"But there's always the chance they can sandbag you; after all, they *do* tend the cash register."

Crewes ran a nervous hand through his hair. "Let's see how she does. Shooting starts in two days. Kencannon says she's coming along. Let's just wait . . . and see how she does . . ."

How she did was not good.

I was on the set from the moment they started. Valerie's call was for seven o'clock in the morning. For makeup and wardrobe. The Studio limo went to get her. She was in makeup for the better part of an hour. Johnny Black showed up as she was going into Wardrobe. He kissed her on the cheek and she said, "I hope I do justice to your lines. It's a very nice part, Mr. Black." We walked over to the coffee truck and had a cup each. Neither of us spoke. Finally, Black looked down at me and asked—a bit too casually—"How's it look?"

I shrugged. No answer. I didn't have one.

Kencannon came on the set a few minutes later, and got things tight. The crew was alert, ready, they'd been put on special notice that these scenes were going to be tough enough, so let's have a whole gang of cooperation. Everyone wanted her to make it.

It was bright-eyed/bushy-tailed time.

She came out of Wardrobe and walked straight to Jim Kencannon. He took her aside and whispered to her in a dark corner for fully twenty minutes.

Then they started shooting.

She knew her lines, but her mannerisms were strictly by rote. There was an edge of fear in even the simplest of movements. Kencannon tried to put her at ease. It only made her more tense. She was locked into fear, a kind of fear no one could penetrate deeply enough to erode. She had lived with it unconsciously for too long. There was too much at stake for her here. The only defense she had was what she knew instinctively as an actress. Unfortunately, the actress who remembered all of it, and who put it to use, almost somnambulistically, was an actress of the Forties. Miss Ankle-Strap Wedgie. An actress who had not really been required to act . . . merely to look good, snap out her lines and show a lot of leg.

They ran through the first shot again and again. It was horrible to watch. Repetition after repetition, with Kencannon trying desperately to get a quality out of her that gibed with the modern tone of the film as a whole. It simply was not there.

"Scene eighty-eight, take seven, Apple!"

"Scene eighty-eight, take seven, Bravo!"

"Scene eighty-eight, take seven, China!"

"Scene eighty-eight, take fifteen, Hotel!"

"Scene ninety-one, take three, X-ray!"

Over and over and over. She blew it each time. The crew grew restless, then salty, then disgusted. The other actors began making snotty remarks off-camera. Kencannon was marvelous with her, but it was a disaster, right from speed and roll it. Finally, they got *something* shot.

Kencannon wandered off into the darkness of the sound stage. Valerie went to her dressing room. Presumably to collapse. The crew started setting up the next shot. I followed Kencannon back into the corner.

"Jim?"

He turned around, the unlit pipe hanging from the corner of his mouth. It was still before-lunch, early in the day, and he looked exhausted.

"Will it be all right?" I asked him.

He started to turn away. He didn't need me bugging him. I guess the tone of concern in my voice stopped him. "Maybe I can cut it together so it'll work."

And he walked away from me.

That afternoon Kencannon got a visit from Crewes on the set, and they talked quietly for a long time, back by the prop wagon. Then they began pruning Valerie's part. A line here, a reaction shot there. Not much at first, but enough to let her know they were worried. It only served to deepen her nervousness. But they had no choice. They were backed against a wall.

But then, so was she.

The remainder of the shooting, over the next week, was agony. There was no doubt from the outset that she couldn't make it, that the footage was dreadful. But we always harbored the secret hope that the magic of the film editor could save her.

The dailies were even more horrifying, for there, up on the projection room screen we could see the naked failure of what we had tried to do. The day's footage went from flat and unnatural to genuinely inept. Kencannon had tried to cover as much as he could with two and three angles or reaction shots by supporting actors, by trick photography, by bizarre camerawork. None of it made it. There was still Valerie in the center of it, like the silent eye of a whirling dervish. Technique could not cover up what was lacking: a focus, a central core, a soul, a fire. Her scenes were disastrous.

When the lights came up in the projection room, and Crewes and myself were alone—we wouldn't allow anyone else to see the dailies, not then we wouldn't—we looked at each other, and Arthur breathed heavily, "Oh God, Fred! What are we going to do?"

I stared at the blank projection screen. There was such a helplessness in his voice, I didn't know what to say. "Can we keep the Studio from finding out, at least till Kencannon cuts it together?"

He shook his head. "Not a chance."

"They move along behind you?"

"Close as they can. I think they've got the labs printing up duplicate sets of dailies. They've probably already run what we just saw here."

Why? I asked myself. Why?

And the answer ran through my head the way those dailies had been run. Behold, without argument, self-explanatory. The answer was simple: Valerie Lone had never been a very good actress, not ever. The films she had made were for an audience hungry for *any* product, which was why Veda Ann Borg and Vera Hruba Ralston and Sonja Henie and Jeanne Crain and Rhonda Fleming and Ellen Drew and all the other pretty, not-particularly-talented ones had made it. It was a nation before teevee, that had theaters to fill, with "A" features starring Paul Muni and Spencer Tracy and John Garfield and Bogart and Ingrid Bergman; but those theaters also needed a lower half to the bill, the "B" pictures with Rory Calhoun and Lex Barker and Ann Blyth and Wandra Hendrix. They needed *product,* not Helen Hayes.

So all the semi-talented had made fabulous livings. *Anything* sold. But now, films for theatrical release were budgeted in the millions, for even the second-class product, and no one could risk the semi-talented. Oh, there were still the pretty ones who got in the films without the talent to get themselves arrested, but they were in the minority, in the quickie flicks. But *Subterfuge* was no quickie. It was a heavy sugar operation into which the Studio had poured millions already, not to mention unspoken but desperate needs and expectations.

Valerie Lone was one of the last of that extinct breed of "semi-stars" who were still vaguely in the public memory—though the new generations, the kids, didn't know her from a white rabbit—but she didn't have the moxie to cut it the way Bette Davis had, or Joan Crawford, or Barbara Stanwyck. She was just plain old Valerie Lone, and that simply wasn't good enough.

She was one of the actresses who had made it then, because almost anyone who could stand up on good legs could make it . . . but not now, because now it took talent of a high order, or a special something that was called "personality." And it wasn't the same kind of "personality" Valerie had used in her day.

"What're you going to do, Arthur?"

He didn't look at me. He just stared straight ahead, at the empty screen. "I don't know. So help me God, I just don't know."

They didn't sign her for a multiple.

At the premiere, held at the Egyptian, Valerie showed with Emery Romito. She was poised, she was elegant, she signed autographs and, as Crewes remarked under his breath to me, as she came up to be interviewed by the television emcee, she was dying at the very moment of what she thought was her greatest triumph. We had not, or course, told her how much Kencannon had had to leave on the cutting-room floor. It was, literally, a walk-on.

When she emerged from the theater, after the premiere, her face was dead white. She knew what was waiting for her. And there was nothing we could say. We stood there, numbly shaking hands with all the well-wishers who told us we had a smash on our hands, as Valerie Lone walked stiffly through the crowd, practically leading the dumbfounded Romito. Their car came to the curb, and they started to get into it. Then Mitchum emerged from the lobby, and the crowd behind their ropes went mad.

There had not been a single cheer or ooh-ahhh for Valerie Lone as she had stood waiting for the limousine to pull up. She was dead, and she knew it.

I tried to call Julie that night, after the big party at the Daisy. She was out. I took a bottle of charcoal Jack Daniels and put it inside me as quickly as I could.

I fell out on the floor. But it wasn't punishment enough. I dreamed.

In the dreams I was trying to explain. My tongue was made of cloth, and it wouldn't form words. But it didn't matter, because the person I was trying to talk to couldn't hear me. It was a corpse. I could not make out the face of the corpse.

9

This was the anatomy of the sin against Valerie Lone:

The Agency called. Not Spencer Lichtman; he was in Florida negotiating a contract for one of their female clients with Ivan Tors for his new *Everglades* pilot. He wouldn't be back for six weeks. It was a difficult contract: the pilot, options for the series if it sold, billing, transportation, and Spencer was screwing her. So the Agency called. A voice of metallic precision that may or may not have had a name attached to it, informed her that they were reorganizing, something to do with the fiscal debenture cutback of post-merger personnel concerned with bibble-bibble-bibble. She asked the voice of the robot what that meant, and it meant she did not have a contract with the Agency, which meant she had no representation.

She called Arthur Crewes. He was out.

The Beverly Hills Hotel management called. The Studio business office had just rung them up to inform them that rent on the bungalow would cease as of the first of the month. Two weeks away.

She called Arthur Crewes. He was out.

She called long distance to Shivey's Diner. She wanted to ask him if he had gotten a replacement for her. Shivey was delighted to hear from her, hey! Everybody was just tickled pink to hear how she'd made good again, hey! Everybody was really jumping with joy at the way the papers said she was so popular again, hey! It's great she got back up on top again, and boy, nobody deserved it better than their girl Val, hey! Don't forget your old friends, don't get uppity out there just because you're a big star and famous again, doncha know!

She thanked him, told him she wouldn't forget them and hung up. Hey!

She could not go back to the desert, to the diner.

She had tasted the champagne again, and the taste of champagne lingers.

She called Arthur Crewes. He was in the cutting room and could not be disturbed.

She called Arthur Crewes. He was in New York with the promotion people, he would be back first of the week.

She called Handy. He was with Crewes.

She called Emery Romito. He was shooting a Western for CBS. His service said he would call back later. But when he did, it was late at night, and she was half-asleep. When she called him the next day, he was at the studio still shooting. She left her name, but the call did not get returned.

The hungry shadow came at a dead run.

And there was no place to hide.

Disaster is a brush-fire. If it reaches critical proportions, nothing can stop it, nothing can put out the fire. Disaster observes a scorched earth policy.

She called Arthur Crewes. She told Roz she was coming in to see him the next morning.

There was no Studio limousine on order. She took a taxi. Arthur Crewes had spent a sleepless night, knowing she was coming, re-running her films in his private theater. He was waiting for her.

"How is the picture doing, Arthur?"

He smiled wanly. "The opening grosses are respectable. The Studio is pleased."

"I read the review in *Time*. They were very nice to you."

"Yes. Ha-ha, very unexpected. Those smart alecks usually go for the clever phrase."

Silence.

"Arthur, the rent is up in a week. I'd like to go to work."

"Uh, I'm still working on the script for the new picture, Valerie. You know, it's been five months since we ended production. The Studio kept up the rent on the bungalow through post-production. Editing, scoring, dubbing, the works. They think they've done enough. I can't argue with them, Valerie . . . not really."

"I want to work, Arthur."

"Hasn't your agent been getting you work?"

"Two television guest appearances. Not much else. I guess the word went out about me. The picture . . ."

"You were fine, Valerie, just fine."

"Arthur, don't lie to me. I know I'm in trouble. I can't get a job. You have to do something."

There was a pathetic tone in her voice, yet she was forceful. Like someone demanding unarguable rights. Crewes was desolate. His reaction was hostility.

"*I* have to do something? Good God, Valerie, I've kept you working for over six months on three days of shooting. Isn't that enough?"

Her mouth worked silently for a moment, then very softly she said:

"No, it isn't enough. I don't know what to do. I can't go back to the diner. I'm back here now. I have no one else to turn to, you're the one who brought me here. You have to do something, it's your responsibility."

Arthur Crewes began to tremble. Beneath the desk he gripped his knees with his hands. "My responsibility," he said bravely, "ended with your contract, Valerie. I've extended myself, even you have to admit that. If I had another picture even *readying* for production, I'd let you read for a part, but I'm in the midst of some very serious rewrite with the screenwriter. I have nothing. What do you want me to do?"

His assault cowed her. She didn't know what to say. He *had* been fair, had done everything he could for her, recommended her to other producers. But they both knew she had failed in the film, knew that the word had gone out. He was helpless.

She started to go, and he stopped her.

"Miss Lone." Not Val, or Valerie now. A retreating back, a pall of guilt, a formal name. "Miss Lone, can I, uh, loan you some money?"

She turned and looked at him across a distance.

"Yes, Mr. Crewes. You can."

He reached into his desk and took out a checkbook.

"I can't afford pride, Mr. Crewes. Not now. I'm too scared. So make it a big check."

He dared not look at her as she said it. Then he bent to the check and wrote it in her name. It was not nearly big enough to stop the quivering of his knees. She took it, without looking at it, and left quietly. When the intercom buzzed and Roz said there was a call, he snapped at her, "Tell 'em I'm out. And don't bother me for a while!" He clicked off and slumped back in his deep chair.

What else could I do? he thought.

If he expected an answer, it was a long time in coming.

After she told Emery what had happened (even though he had been with her these last five months, and knew what it was from the very tomb odor of it) she waited for him to say don't worry, I'll take care of you, now that we're together again it will be all right, I love you, you're mine. But he said nothing like that.

"They won't pick up the option, no possibility?"

"You know they dropped the option, Emery. Months ago. It was a verbal promise only. For the next film. But Arthur Crewes told me he's having trouble with the script. It could be months."

He walked around the little living room of his apartment in the Stratford Beach Hotel. A depressing little room with faded wallpaper and a rug the management would not replace, despite the holes worn in it.

"Isn't there anything else?"

"A Western. TV. Just a guest shot, sometime next month. I read for it last week, they seemed to like me."

"Well, you'll take it, of course."

"I'll take it, Emery, but what does it mean . . . it's only a few dollars. It isn't a living."

"We all have to make do the best we can, Val—"

"Can I stay here with you for a few weeks, till things get straightened away?"

Formed in amber, held solidified in a prison of reflections that showed his insides more clearly than his outside, Emery Romito let go the thread that had saved him, and plunged once more down the tunnel of despair. He was unable to do it. He was not calloused, merely terrified. He was merely an old man trying to relate to something that had never even been a dream—merely an illusion. And now she threatened to take even that cheap thing, simply by her existence, her presence here in this room.

"Listen, Val, I've tried to come to terms. I understand what you're going through. But it's hard, very hard. I really have to hurry myself just to make ends meet . . ."

She spoke to him then, of what they had had years ago, and what they had sensed only a few months before. But he was already retreating from her, gibbering with fear, into the shadows of his little life.

"I can't do it, Valerie. I'm not a young man any more. You remember all those days, I'd do anything; anything at all; I was wild. Well, now I'm paying for it. We all have to pay for it. We should have known, we should have put some of it aside, but who'd ever have thought it would end. No, I can't do it. I haven't got the push to do it. I get a little work, an 'also featuring' once in a while. You have to be hungry, the way all the new ones, the young ones, the way *they're* hungry. I can barely manage alone, Valerie. It wouldn't work, it just wouldn't."

She stared at him.

"I have to hang on!" he shouted at her.

She pinned him. "Hang on? To what? To guest shots, a life of walk-ons, insignificant character bits, and a Saturday night at the Friars Club? What have you got, Emery? What have you really got that's worth *anything*? Do you have me, do you have a real life, do you have anything that's really yours, that they can't take away from you?"

But she stopped. The argument was hopeless.

He sagged before her. A tired, terrified old man with his picture in the PLAYERS DIRECTORY. What backbone he might have at one time possessed had been removed from his body through the years, vertebra by vertebra. He slumped before her, weighted down by his own inability to live. Left with a hideous walking death, with elegance on the outside, soot on the inside, Valerie Lone stared at the stranger who had made love to her in her dreams for twenty years. And in that instant she knew it had never really been the myth and the horror of the town that had kept them apart. It had been their own inadequacies.

She left him, then. She could not castigate him. His was such a sordid little existence, to take that from him would be to kill him.

And she was still that much stronger than Emery Romito, her phantom lover, not to need to do it.

HANDY

I came home to find Valerie Lone sitting at the edge of the pool, talking to Pegeen. She looked up when I came through the gate, and smiled a thin smile at me.

I tried not to show how embarrassed I was.

Nor how much I'd been avoiding her.

Nor how desperately I felt like bolting and running away, all the way back to New York City.

She got up, said goodbye to Pegeen, and came toward me. I had been shopping; shirt boxes from Ron Postal and bags from de Voss had to be shifted so I could take her hand. She was wearing a summer dress, quite stylish, really. She was trying to be very light, very inoffensive; trying not to shove the guilt in my face.

"Come on upstairs, where it's cooler," I suggested.

In the apartment, she sat down and looked around.

"I see you're moving," she said.

I grinned, a little nervously, making small talk. "No, it's always this way. I've got a house in Sherman Oaks, but at the moment there's a kindofa sorta ex-almost ex-wife nesting there. It's in litigation. So I live here, ready to jump out any time."

She nodded understanding.

The intricacies of California divorce horrors were not beyond her. She had had a few of those, as I recalled.

"Mr. Handy—" she began.

I did not urge her to call me Fred.

"You were the one who talked to me first, and . . ."

And there it was. I was the one responsible. It was all on me. I'd heard what had happened with Crewes, with that rat bastard Spencer Lichtman, with Romito, and now it was my turn. She must have had nowhere else to go, no one else to impale, and so it was *mea culpa* time.

I was the one who had resurrected her from the safety and sanctity of her grave; brought her back to a world as transitory as an opening night. She looked at me and knew it wouldn't do any good, but she did it.

She laid it all on me, word by word by word.

What could I do, for Christ's sake? I had done my best. I'd even watched over her with Haskell Barkin, carried her practically on my shoulders through all the shitty scenes when she'd arrived in town. What more was there for me to do . . . ?

I'm not my brother's goddam keeper, I yelled inside my head. Let me alone, woman. Get off my back. I'm not going to die for you, or for anyone. I've got a job, and I've got to keep it. I got the publicity *Subterfuge* needed, and I thank you for helping me keep my job, but dammit I didn't inherit you. I'm not your daddy, I'm not your boy friend, I'm just a puffman in off the street, trying to keep the Dragon Lady from grabbing his house, the only roots I've ever had. So stop it, stop talking, stop trying to make me cry, because I won't.

Don't call me a graverobber, you old bitch!

"I'm a proud woman, Mr. Handy. But I'm not very smart. I let you all lie to me. Not once, but twice. The first time I was too young to know better; but this time I fell into it again knowing what you would do to me. I was one of the lucky ones, do you know that? I was lucky because I got out alive. But do you know what you've done to me? You've condemned me to the kind of life poor Emery leads, and that's no life at all."

She didn't talk any more.

She just sat there staring at me.

She didn't want excuses, or escape clauses, or anything I had to give. She knew I was helpless, that I was no better and no worse than any of them. That I had helped kill her in the name of love.

And that the worst crimes are committed in the name of love, not hate.

We both knew there would be an occasional tv bit, and enough money to keep living, but here, in this fucking ugly town that wasn't living. It was crawling like a wounded thing through the years, till one day the end came, and that was the only release you could pray for.

I knew Julie would not be coming back to me.

Julie knew. She was on the road because she couldn't stand the town, because she knew it would tear open and throw her insides on the street. She had always said she wasn't going to go the way all the others had gone, and now I knew why I hadn't been able to reach her on the road. It was Goodbye, Dolly.

And the Dragon Lady would get the house; and I would stay in Hollywood, God help me.

Until the birds came to pick out my eyes, and I wasn't Handy the fair-haired boy any longer, or even Handy the old pro, but something they called Fred Handy? oh, yeah, I remember him, he was good in his day. Because after all, what the hell did I have to offer but a fast mouth and a few ideas, and once the one was slowed and the other had run out like sand from an hourglass, I was no better off than Valerie Lone or her poor miserable Emery Romito.

She left me standing there, in my apartment that always looked as though I was moving. But we both knew: I wasn't going anywhere.

10

In a very nice little restaurant-bar on Sunset Boulevard, as evening came in to Hollywood across the rim of the bowl, Valerie Lone sat high on a barstool, eating a hot roast beef sandwich with gravy covering the very crisp french fries. She sipped slowly from a glass of dark ale. At the far end of the bar a television set was mumbling softly. It was an old movie, circa 1942.

None of the players in the movie had been Valerie Lone. The Universe loved her, but was totally devoid of a sense of irony. It was simply an old movie.

Three seats down from where Valerie Lone sat, a hippie wearing wraparound shades and seven strings of beads looked up at the bartender. "Hey, friend," he said softly.

The bartender came to him, obviously disliking the hairy trade these people represented, but unable to ignore the enormous amounts of money they somehow spent in his establishment. "Uh-huh?"

"Howzabout turning something else on . . . or maybe even better turn that damn thing off, I'll put a quarter in the jukebox." The bartender gave him a surly look, then sauntered to the set and turned it off. Valerie Lone continued to eat as the world was turned off.

The hippie put the quarter in the jukebox and pressed out three rock numbers. He returned to his barstool and the music inundated the room.

Ouside, night had come, and with it, the night lights. One of the lights illuminated a twenty-three-foot-high billboard for the film *Subterfuge* starring Robert Mitchum and Gina Lollobrigida; produced by Arthur Crewes; directed by James Kencannon; written by John D. F. Black; music by Lalo Schifrin.

At the end of the supplementary credits there was a boxed line that was very difficult to read: it had been whited-out.

The line had once read:

ALSO FEATURING MISS VALERIE LONE as Angela.

Angela had become a walk-on. She no longer existed.

Valerie Lone existed only as a woman in a very nice little restaurant and bar on the Sunset Strip. She was eating. And the long shadow had also begun to feed.

FLINTLOCK:
An Unproduced Teleplay

TEASER

FADE IN:

1 EXTREME CLOSEUP - FRAME BLOOD-RED - FACETED

As though looking into the heart of a ruby (which, in fact, we are, though we shouldn't spill it at this point). The coruscating light dancing off the facets of a jewel seen in extreme magnification, flickering, glowing, hypnotic.

CAMERA PULLS BACK and FOCUSES to show us the red glow is the eye of Death, the dead-red crimson of a circle of eye in the skeleton reaper on the XIIIth card of the tarot deck. CAMERA CONTINUES UP AND BACK to show the card in its entirety, lying on a black velvet cloth.

FLINT'S VOICE O.S.
Don't be alarmed, Miss Griffen. Death in the tarot deck usually means transformation or change.

(CONTINUED:)

1 CONTINUED:

We HEAR FLINT OVER as the CAMERA CONTINUES to PULL BACK and UP. The table is now revealed in full, covered with the black velvet cloth, the tarot cards laid out in the standard divination pattern.

CALISTA'S VOICE O.S.
I donated one hundred dollars to have you tell my fortune, Mr. Flint: the least you can do is call me Calista.
(beat)
As for change, having you as a fortune teller is change enough.

CAMERA CONTINUES BACK now showing DEREK FLINT, smartly dressed in tuxedo, laying out the cards for CALISTA GRIFFEN, a remarkably attractive young woman in her late twenties. VOICES OVER CONTINUE.

FLINT'S VOICE OVER
Even charitable good works have their benefits, Calista. How else would we have met.

CALISTA'S VOICE OVER
You silver-tongued devil, you.

FLINT'S VOICE OVER
You find me ill-cast in the role of a soothsayer? What would you have me be, then? Name it.

CALISTA'S VOICE OVER
(mulling it)
Well, I see you as a man of dark and swirling mysteries. But you're more than likely a playboy, Mr. Flint--
(she pauses)
--aren't you going to ask me to call you by your first name?
(CONT'D.)

(CONTINUED:)

1 CONTINUED: - 2

CALISTA'S VOICE OVER (CONT'D.)
(no response)
Mm. A playboy, Mr. Flint. Scion of a wealthy family.
(no response)
What do you do when you aren't telling fortunes, Mr. Flint?

FLINT'S VOICE OVER
(amused)
Call me Ishmael.

CALISTA'S VOICE OVER
Oh, come on, now!

FLINT'S VOICE OVER
Try Derek. And when I'm not working fund-raising parties, I ply my humble trade as an ax murderer and sex deviate. Also student of human nature.

While the above dialogue is HEARD OVER the CAMERA CONTINUES its PULL BACK and UP in a smooth BOOM SHOT. Pulling back from CLOSE on Flint and Calista, the F.G. is momentarily dominated by a HAND REACHING ACROSS FRAME from LEFT, holding an engraved invitation. The hand emerges from a tailored sleeve with a flashy cuff and expensive cufflink showing. A SECOND HAND reaches in from RIGHT to take the invitation. It is a hand in a white glove, obviously a butler's. The invitation reads:

GALA TO RAISE DISASTER FUNDS FOR
THE INTERNATIONAL RELIEF ORGANIZATION.

DIALOGUE CONTINUES OVER as the hands withdraw from the FRAME and CAMERA has continued PULL BACK AND UP in BOOM SHOT to show us now Flint and Calista at a small table, with Flint surrounded by gorgeous WOMEN, all watching him tell Calista's
(CONT'D.)

(CONTINUED:)

1 CONTINUED: - 3

(CONT'D.)

fortune, and in the enormous ballroom around them a high society fund-raising soirée swirls around them. The room is packed with extremely beautiful and wealthy people, Hindu dignitaries, Barons, captains of industry, the usual crowd one draws at this sort of bash.

CAMERA BACK AND UP giving us the scene in expanded LONG SHOT as the DIALOGUE between Flint and Calista is HEARD OVER. Till finally, the CAMERA COMES ALL THE WAY BACK UP ON BOOM and we are looking down at the entire sprawl of the party with a blazing crystal chandelier in the f.g.

THIS HAS ALL BEEN ONE CONTINUOUS SHOT (BOOM) FROM EXT. CU ON THE RED EYE OF THE DEATH CARD TO THE FULL SHOT OF THE ROOM AS SHOT THROUGH THE CHANDELIER.

HOLD FOR A BEAT then CAMERA UNFOCUSES on the sparkling lights of the chandelier till all the FRAME holds are scintillas of brilliance, and we

MATCH-CUT TO:

2 EXT. CLOSEUP ON CALISTA

MATCH CHANDELIER BRILLIANCE with MOTES OF LIGHT in Calista's eye. CAMERA PULLS BACK from EXT. CU of Calista to show us the scintillas of light were dancing in her eyes, as Flint speaks his line "student of human nature." BACK to CLOSEUP of Calista's extraordinary face. The kind of face that can cause men to fight duels. A look of sensuality crosses her face.

CALISTA

How fascinating, Derek. Can we discuss this further?

3 REVERSE ANGLE - SAME CLOSEUP ON FLINT

He's obviously interested, but still cool.

FLINT

I see no reason why not, Calista. This evening the veils of the future seem to be parted. There are probably several hours' worth of material in the subject.

As Flint speaks, CAMERA CHANGES FOCUS to pick up the crowd behind him--HOLDING FLINT UNFOCUSED IN F.G.--and we see, among the fat dowagers, bejeweled debutantes and that velvet-sashed Hindu dignitary, a WEASEL-FACED LITTLE MAN who is clearly watching Flint surreptitiously, from a near corner, wholly unnoticed by Flint or the crowd. CAMERA REFOCUSES.

CALISTA O.S.

It's becoming rather stuffy in here, isn't it?

FLINT

(smiles)

Yes, we certainly can take a walk in the gardens.

4 TWO-SHOT - FLINT & CALISTA

as they rise. The crowd of beautiful women look bemused and saddened that they missed their chance at Flint, and they drift away.

CALISTA

(coquettishly)

You see through my every subterfuge. I have no secrets from a soothsayer, it seems.

Flint stacks the tarot deck, the Death card prominently on top. He taps the card with a finger.

(CONTINUED:)

4 CONTINUED:

FLINT

We can leave the Grim Reaper behind. Three's a crowd.

5 TRAVELING SHOT - WITH FLINT & CALISTA

as the party swirls around them, they pass away from the table, head for the French doors and start to exit onto the veranda.

6 LONG SHOT

from table in f.g. to French doors in b.g. as Flint & Calista start to exit, we HOLD LARGE IN F.G. the Weasel-Faced Little Man as he moves in to the table, but we don't see what he does there because just as he reaches the table we

QUICK CUT TO:

7 EXT. VERANDA - OVERLOOKING GARDENS

with Flint and Calista as they stare out over the <u>very elaborate</u> gardens of the estate where the party has been thrown. Calista has pulled a cigarette from a gold case (suggest a Balkan Sobranie, black tube with gold mouthpiece) and Flint is lighting it for her with his famous lighter.

CALISTA

Would you like one?

FLINT

(light)

I thought we were going to leave the Grim Reaper behind?

CALISTA

Such disdain.

(CONT'D.)

(CONTINUED:)

7 CONTINUED:

CALISTA (CONT'D.)
(seductive)
You don't smoke, you don't work, don't you have <u>any</u> vices, Derek?

FLINT
(picks up the cue)
There was an Englishman named Bagehot (pronounced Beh-<u>joot</u>) who once said, "It is good to be without vices, but it is not good to be without temptations."

Calista laughs brightly as Flint takes her arm and they begin to descend the ornate stairway into the gardens as we

QUICK CUT TO:

8 EXT. GARDENS - ARRIFLEX SHOT

TRAVELING THROUGH ONE OF THE PASSAGES of the minotaur's maze of high bushes that criss-cross the gardens. As we reach the juncture of two passages, CAMERA HOLDS on a PAIR OF BLACKSUITED MEN who are moving bushes on rollers into new positions, blocking off one passage, forcing movement down another corridor. The suits they wear are skintight, all black, and cover them from head to foot, with only eyeholes left open. Very sinister.

9 OVERHEAD SHOT

Showing the maze, with Flint and Calista reaching the spot where the blacksuited men have set up the dummy bushes; we can see, in one shot, Flint traveling the way he is intended to travel, deeper into the maze with the girl, and far enough ahead of them so they cannot be seen, the two sinister blacksuits rearranging more bushes, leading Flint deeper and deeper into the passages.

10 BOOM SHOT

HIGH ANGLE LOOKING DOWN on Flint and Calista as they come through the last of the "arranged" passages, into the central clearing, quite large, of the maze. CAMERA BOOMS DOWN TO HOLD THEM as they reach the edge of the central hub. CAMERA DOWN ALMOST TO GROUND as Calista abruptly drops to one shapely knee beside a bonsai tree.

CALISTA
I seem to have picked up a pebble...

She begins to fumble with her shoe as Flint waits. She looks up and smiles, as though about to say something more to Flint...but the expression freezes on her face...she gives a short, high scream...

WHIP-PAN TO:

11 AROUND THE CLEARING

TO HOLD one of the blacksuited men, leveling a deadly crossbow. He fires as we

WHIP-PAN BACK TO:

12 MED. CLOSE ON CALISTA

as the short crossbow bolt thuds into the bole of the bonsai tree right beside her head.

13 FULL SHOT - WITH ACTION

as Flint shoves Calista to the ground and launches himself in a tiger leap across the clearing toward the blacksuited assassin, who turns to run. Flint boils across the ground and suddenly it gives way beneath his feet as he steps on a section of false grass cleverly camouflaged to seem solid.

14 thru 18 SERIES OF SHOTS

kaleidoscopic, whirling, one atop the other:

Flint's face in CU as he loses footing.
His body dropping through the hole in the ground.
A body falling down a shaft, hitting walls.
The bottom rushing up to meet him.
The body impacting on the bottom.

19 OMITTED

20 INT. PIT - SHOOTING DOWN

ON FLINT rolling over, shaking his head quickly to regain his senses. He rises, slowly. Takes a deep breath. He assays the situation, runs his hands around the sides of the pit. He's about twenty feet down. Then he leans against one wall, braces his shoulders, throws his legs up and gets purchase with his feet against the opposite wall, then very carefully extends his hands to either side and, face up, begins to walk up the walls of the pit. As he climbs we HEAR VOICES OVER:

1st BLACKSUIT
He's movin' in there.

2nd BLACKSUIT
He's comin' up, for crineoutloud!

1st BLACKSUIT
That fall shoulda put him out for a week.

2nd BLACKSUIT
Some tiger trap you dug, dummy! I toldja we should of put spikes in the bottom of that hole!

1st BLACKSUIT
Oh boy.

(CONTINUED:)

20 CONTINUED:

Flint is nearing the top now, moving up fast.

21 GROUND LEVEL SHOT - CLOSE ON PIT

SHOOTING ACROSS THE MOUTH as Flint's head appears over the lip. CLOSE ON FLINT as he looks over his shoulder.

22 POV - WHAT FLINT SEES

he finds himself staring directly into the nozzle of a hose. CAMERA TILTS UP to follow the hose to a tank, being held by the gorgeous Calista, who is hunkered down exposing a length of leg and thigh. She is aiming the contrivance at his face. He holds, staring.

CALISTA
(to Blacksuits)
Spikes aren't necessary.
(smiles)
Dreams are better.

She smiles sweetly at Flint as he tries to struggle up the last few inches to enable him to arch his body out.

23 FULL SHOT - CALISTA & FLINT

CALISTA
Class, Derek, you _do_ have class. But as a fortune teller you simply don't know when the veils are closing on you.

And she sprays him with a pink fog of gas that envelops Flint's head. Flint tries to hold his breath as CAMERA MOVES IN. Calista pulls down a breather mask over her face. Flint coughs, his eyes roll up and...he falls back into the pit. There is a CRASH from below.

24 DOWN-ANGLE SHOT PAST CALISTA

as she stands on the lip of the pit, pulling up the breather mask, handing the tank and hose to a blacksuit who moves up behind her, SHOOTING DOWN PAST HER TO FLINT crumpled in the bottom of the pit. She pats her hair back into place and says, very sweetly:

CALISTA

Say night-night to the nice Flint.

She moves back from the pit as the CAMERA SUDDENLY DROPS AT A DIZZYING PACE down into the pit, BLURS OUT OF FOCUS and we

FADE TO BLACK
and
FADE OUT.

END TEASER

ACT ONE

FADE IN:

25 LIMBO - BLACK FRAME - MED. LONG SHOT

SHOOTING INTO THE DARKNESS we see Flint wandering toward the CAMERA. He's stripped down to only his pants. No shirt, no tie, no tux jacket, no shoes, no socks, he's down to the pants and that's it. All around him: limbo. Nothingness. Total black. Out of time and space. No orientation...until millions of tiny scintillas of multi-colored light begin flickering and flashing in the blackness all around him. Are those lights stars? Are they electrical storms? No way of telling. Not even a way of knowing if they're close to him or millions of miles away. He is in purgatory, truly. As he wanders, somnabulent, he looks this way and that, trying to find out where he is; looks over his shoulder; stops and turns and turns, but there's nothing. And as he wanders toward us we HEAR VOICES IN FILTER OVER (but for God's sake, make the filtering clear, so we can understand what's being said!). They are the VOICES of Calista and OTHERS who will be designated, talking about him and what they want from him.

CALISTA O.S.
(FILTER)
Pay attention. Derek Flint is the key. And the important word to remember is laser-trigger. Got that?

1st V.P.'S VOICE O.S.
(FILTER)
Laser-trigger.
(beat)
Laser, ell-ay-ess-ee-arr, from the acronym of Light Amplification by Stimulated Emission of Radiation.

(CONTINUED:)

25 CONTINUED:

CALISTA O.S.
(FILTER)
Terrific. How did you ever get to be a 1st Vice President of the Gunsmiths? Do you still suck your thumb?

1st V.P. O.S.
(FILTER)
(milquetoast)
Stop ridiculing me. I was elected to this position, I was certified by the Chairman, I do my job, and I'll tear out your heart if you don't stop ridiculing me.

The next voice heard is a FLAT METALLIC VOICE, one that is clearly being disguised through electronic means so we cannot tell if it is male or female. It is the voice of the mysterious CHAIRMAN OF THE GUNSMITHS.

CHAIRMAN O.S.
Stop this bickering. We're running a business operation here, not a kindergarten. You have Mr. Flint, get on with it.

CALISTA O.S.
(FILTER)
(cowed)
Yes sir.
(beat)
This briefing is to prepare you for the Flint interrogation.
(beat)
Now, I'll call on Dr. Barmeier.

DR. BARMEIER O.S.
(FILTER)
(Nazi accent)
As <u>Oberstmekanik</u> for the Gunsmiths, I
(CONT'D.)

(CONTINUED:)

25 CONTINUED: - 2

DR. BARMEIER O.S. (CONT'D.)
(FILTER)
want to make this all perfectly clear!
You will pay attention!
(beat)
A method has been discovered for launching rockets into space through the use of laser beams.
(beat)
Initial thrust is effected by liquid fuel propellants followed by a high-intensity beam of dense light fired by computerized coordination up the "propagation path" to the underside of the rocket, thus--

1st V.P. O.S.
(FILTER)
Doctor, do we need to know all this? I, for one, find it all quite difficult to--

DR. BARMEIER O.S.
(FILTER)
(vicious)
THUS!...utilizing one-twentieth the fuel payload of current spaceshots.
(beat, quieter)
The only difficulty till now with this revolutionary idea is that the focusing elements in contemporary lasers are not powerful enough. You see...

CALISTA O.S.
(FILTER)
(cutting in)
Uh, thank you, Dr. Barmeier. Very cogent. I'll take it from here.
(beat)
Usually, a ruby gemstone is used as the focusing element. Not potent enough.
(beat)
Eight months ago a Rhodesian diamond
(CONT'D.)

(CONTINUED:)

25 CONTINUED: - 3

CALISTA O.S. (CONT'D.)
(FILTER)
consortium came up with a "black diamond"--actually it's blood-red--and it was sold to the United States Space Agency. Its facets, if cut properly, work perfectly as a focusing element for the laser trigger.

1st BLACKSUIT O.S.
(FILTER)
Where does Flint come into all this?

CALISTA O.S.
(FILTER)
He is the one man in the world who can cut the black diamond. He has it in his possession.

DR. BARMEIER O.S.
(FILTER)
(like Strangelove)
It is the most destructive and valuable military weapon ever conceived by the mind of man! With this laser trigger the Gunsmiths could...

CALISTA O.S.
(FILTER)
Doctor!

DR. BARMEIER O.S.
(FILTER)
We could rule the world from stations in space...we could conquer...Poland... we could take Poland in three days...

CHAIRMAN O.S.
Barmeier! This is the Chairman!
(everyone falls silent)
We of the Gunsmiths have no desire to "rule the world." We are a business
(CONT'D.)

(CONTINUED:)

25 CONTINUED: - 4

CHAIRMAN O.S. (CONT'D.)
organization, non-partisan, non-nationalistic, we are dealers in goods. Remember that. Get this black diamond from Flint so we can sell it...and stop twitching!

All of the foregoing DIALOGUE OVER is visually interpreted as Flint wanders through LIMBO, synch'd-in with changing backgrounds, thus:

As the plotters talk of Moonshots, the limbo around Flint grows light, then dark again, then light, pulsing as though the dawn could not decide whether or not to come up, and then gigantic closeups of Lunar craters appear and shimmer and disappear around him so he has to dodge them or fall in.

Talk of lasers can be interpreted as beams of sizzling light that cross and re-cross all around him, making him duck and swerve or be burned to a crisp.

References to ruby gemstones and black diamonds can be visualized by altering the limbo background to show closeups of the dazzling facets of jewels.

NOTE: for these altering b.g. shots advise the use of CROSSTAR FILTERS as well as WIDE-ANGLE, FISHEYE and GREASE-SMEARED DIFFUSION LENSES to produce highly hallucinogenic interpretations of what is being said in VOICE OVER.

Flint visibly suffers through all of this, his vision distorted, his head pounding, pain and disorientation visible in his movements and facial expressions. And...as we HEAR OVER the sound of FLINT HEARTBEAT, pounding and thudding, the limbo b.g. should shimmer with closeups (as in a light-show) of the lymphatic tide, all blood-red and deadly, keeping

(CONT'D.)

(CONTINUED:)

25 CONTINUED: - 5

(CONT'D.)

the beat with Flint's heart; all of this intended to convey the impression that he is under hallucinogenic influence.

NOTE: suggest in these sequences the use of extremely ominous music, such as Stravinsky's "Le Sacre du Printemps" (such sections as The Sacrifice, etc.) to make the movement of Flint more unnerving.

At the point in the DIALOGUE OVER that Barmeier begins to flip (and Flint has been hearing and reacting to the voices, stopping and listening very attentively to the two occasions in which the Chairman speaks), CAMERA MOVES AROUND FLINT and we see PAST HIM, far in the distance, a circle of light. He starts running toward it while the VOICES CONTINUE and that brings us to

26 MED. CLOSE ON FLINT - REACTION SHOT

as he nears the circle of light, he stops, amazed.

27 PAST FLINT - HIS POV - WHAT HE SEES

The conversation has been taking place among a group that look as though they've just fallen out of Alice in Wonderland. These are the "heavies," the members of the group called THE GUNSMITHS. They will appear throughout the segment and their real names are indicated in parentheses after their characterization in this scene only. They are THE WHITE RABBIT (Calista), DODO (1st Vice President), MAD HATTER (Dr. Barmeier) and MARCH HARE (1st BLACKSUIT) with the option of having CHESHIRE CAT (2nd Blacksuit) in the scene for completists. They continue talking, though the words they speak are not in synch with what we HEAR IN VOICE OVER (FILTER).

(CONTINUED:)

27 CONTINUED:

WHITE RABBIT (CALISTA)
O.S. (FILTER)
We <u>know</u> Flint still has the black diamond in his possession. What we must do is find out where.

MARCH HARE (1st BLACKSUIT)
O.S. (FILTER)
Let me at him for an hour. I'll turn him into cottage cheese. He'll come up with it.

MAD HATTER (Dr. BARMEIER)
O.S. (FILTER)
<u>Lumpen</u>! <u>Clod</u>! This man is no thug. He cannot be beaten into talking. Why do you think we went to all the trouble to drug him with hallucinogens? He must be duped, coerced!

28 FULL SHOT - THE GROUP - LIMBO B.G.

standing there in the middle of nowhere, rapping, with Flint now edging in close to speak to him. This is a very Kafka-esque scene in which they continue talking about him as though he were dead or not there, and with Flint trying to break into their conversation.

FLINT
Your mommies dress you funny.

WHITE RABBIT (CALISTA)
O.S. (FILTER)
He was to have passed the jewel to his contact tonight at the party.

DODO (1st V.P.)
O.S. (FILTER)
How do you know?

(CONTINUED:)

28 CONTINUED:

CHAIRMAN O.S.
I told her.

FLINT
Who is that?

DODO (1st V.P.)
O.S. (FILTER)
Has he split the diamond yet?

WHITE RABBIT (CALISTA)
O.S. (FILTER)
We believe not. We have to break him and get him to cut it for us.

FLINT
You have two chances: slim and none.
(beat)
Say, what the hell's the matter with you? Answer me!

They continue to ignore him as if he weren't there.

MAD HATTER (Dr. BARMEIER)
O.S. (FILTER)
The hallucinogenic drugs I've developed will make it all quite simple. There isn't a mind strong enough to resist.

FLINT
I've had enough of this! Who is the Chairman? Who are you lunatics?

Suddenly, as Flint becomes very insistent about the identity of the Chairman, they all look up and now they see him.

29 SERIES OF REACTION SHOTS
thru
33 the faces of the Gunsmiths as they see Flint for the first time. Utter hatred and malevolence in their
(CONT'D.)

(CONTINUED:)

29 CONTINUED:
thru
33 (CONT'D.)

smiles, INTERCUT with REACTION SHOTS OF FLINT as he realizes he was better off when they didn't recognize him.

34 FROM FLINT TO CALISTA

as the White Rabbit pulls a huge, blocky .45 from her pelt, and aims it directly at Flint's head. CAMERA ZOOMS IN on the muzzle of the gun, and in the black hole of the bore lightning and flashes of crimson brilliance dance. CAMERA PULLS BACK to show the utter delight with which Calista will blow off his head.

35 FULL SHOT

as the others pull guns. Flint spins, still barefoot and half-naked, and throws himself out of danger... he rolls...they fire...again and again...the SOUND is like an avalanche...CAMERA BACK TO FOLLOW ACTION...as he rolls into the darkness...and wherever he lands, the darkness lights up as though Flint were pinned in the circle glare up CLOSE INTO CAMERA with a look of fear on his face for the first time...this is a nightmare he can't escape...he runs INTO CAMERA.

CAMERA TO BLACK

36 REVERSE ANGLE - FROM BLACK

as Flint dashes away from CAMERA into darkness, getting smaller and smaller...

37 WITH FLINT

as he runs out of the darkness, the sound of LAUGHTER OVER. The kind of deranged laughter one hears from the dummy of the fat lady in front of the

(CONT'D.)

(CONTINUED:)

37 CONTINUED:

(CONT'D.)

fun house. He runs and runs as CAMERA FOLLOWS and suddenly Flint pitches forward, over an invisible edge, down into black water. He sinks.

38 UNDER THE WATER

black as midnight, but with flashes of unearthly light in it, enabling us to see Flint drowning. He struggles, fights, but sinks deeper and deeper, his hair flowing out around him, bubbles rising. Then suddenly he is wrenched to a halt and starts to rise, just as he is gasping his last...everything grows hazy, indistinct and we

MATCH-CUT TO:

39 INT. LABORATORY

MATCH-CUT OUT OF MISTINESS to a pair of blacksuited hands pulling Flint face-up out of a shallow trough filled with water. Flint is naked (though the bodies of Calista, Barmeier, 1st V.P. and the 1st Blacksuit obscure the censorable areas with their bulk). The trough is up on a lab table, and the only thing that keeps Flint from drowning is a stiff plastic "baggie" around his head, fastened by a ring-collar at his neck. It is something like an astronaut's breather hood--flexible but non-collapsible as long as air is in it. NOTE: the fantasy of drowning should merge into the reality of Flint in the trough so we get a sense of "paraphrase" in the fantasy that matches with what the reality is.

CALISTA

The only thing keeping you alive in that hood is the air pocket, Derek. I wouldn't waste it with cranky words.

DR. BARMEIER

A person can drown in less that a foot of water, did you know that, Mr. Flint?

(CONTINUED:)

39 CONTINUED:

1st V.P.
(trying to be ghoulish but sounding whimpish)
You would be absolutely stunned by the incidences of drowning in homes with half-filled bathtubs.

Calista gives him a look of weariness. He's such an ass.

CALISTA
That air pocket can't hold out very long.
(2 beats)
The black diamond, Derek.

Flint is down in the water again. His face distorted by the plastic hood. They stand and watch for a moment.

1st V.P.
It's true. They do turn blue.

DR. BARMEIER
I told you he wouldn't break under physical torture. Take him out.

CALISTA
I think not. Let Derek see we mean business.

CHAIRMAN
(metallic)
We have your ruthlessness quotient on file, Miss Griffen. We need no further proof. Take Mr. Flint out of the trough.

The VOICE OF THE CHAIRMAN has issued from a speaker grille, high on one wall of the laboratory. When he speaks, they all go stock dead still with fear. And when he says frog, they jump! The Blacksuit pulls Flint up, dripping. Calista undoes the hood, and
(CONT'D.)

(CONTINUED:)

39 CONTINUED: - 2

(CONT'D.)

Flint gasps for breath, drawing in huge lungfuls. When he can speak, the first thing he says is:

FLINT

Who is the Chairman of the Board?

They register shock.

CALISTA

(to Barmeier)

I thought you said he wouldn't be able to integrate what we were saying while he was under the drugs?

DR. BARMEIER

(fascinated)

A most remarkable man. Even I underestimated him. Now I know I have an adversary worthy of my genius.

1st V.P.

You'll never learn the answer to that question, Flint. Why, we've never even seen him...he's...

CALISTA

Shut up! You're only the Vice President, you idiot, not the head of Public Relations!

Suddenly the VOICE OF THE CHAIRMAN erupts in the lab again.

CHAIRMAN

Nonetheless, I can second what the Vice President said. I am beyond your reach, Mr. Flint.

(to Calista)

All right. Get on with it.

(CONTINUED:)

39 CONTINUED: - 3

The Blacksuit drags Flint erect, and off the table. He is unsteady from the drugs. Barmeier approaches with jet-hypo.

DR. BARMEIER
Let me give him a booster shot of the hallucinogens. His strength is amazing.

He gives a fast hissing shpritz and they manhandle Flint through a door that opens at their approach. It is pitch-dark on the other side.

DR. BARMEIER (CONT'D.)
Now we separate him from his own identity, weaken his resolve, snap his spirit...plumb his libido and suck out his id.
(beat)
In moments he'll be begging to give us the diamond.

The Blacksuit roughly shoves Flint through the doorway, alone, and the door snaps back into place as we

SMASH-CUT TO:

40 INT. MIRROR ROOM - ON FLINT

as lights suddenly flare and Flint finds himself in a room that is mirrors. All mirrors. Walls, ceiling, floor.

41 ANOTHER ANGLE ON FLINT

as he turns and turns. He stares into one mirror and CAMERA ZOOMS IN to show us his reflection without a face! CAMERA PULLS BACK and Flint looks into another mirror. CAMERA ZOOMS IN AGAIN and again another reflection without a face. No matter where he turns, none of the reflections have faces.

42 WHIP-PANS

around and around as Flint tries to find an image with his face in it. There are none. Then, as if he were going mad, he begins flailing at the mirrors, all of this SHOT IN WILD FRENETIC SWEEPS. He lashes out, throwing himself around the room. This goes on and on in a torrent of impotent violence till finally Flint smashes one of the mirrors, only to find...

Mirrors behind the mirrors! And still, no face, no Flint, no identity.

He begins to scream in a madman's voice, throwing himself at one mirror after another, until finally he grabs a long shard of glass and seems about to slash his wrists with it when the sliding door crashes open and the Blacksuit runs in, the others behind him, and slugs Flint, taking the shard of glass away from him. The Blacksuit drags Flint to his feet as CAMERA COMES IN SMOOTHLY ON FLINT'S FACE and he smiles a winsome smile.

FLINT
(innocent)
Do I really strike you as the suicide type?

43 ON CALISTA

furious at being duped by Flint. He was faking the madness.

CALISTA
Take him!

And Flint is bulled ahead of them as we

HARD CUT TO:

44 THE WHITE ROOM - ON FLINT

as he is hurled through the sliding door that closes
(CONT'D.)

(CONTINUED:)

44 CONTINUED:

(CONT'D.)

behind him. He turns and finds himself in a room of solid, unbroken white. Blazing white walls, ceiling, floor, no windows, no doors, nothing but the whiteness. He blinks, heels into his eyes, the white is dazzling. CAMERA IN CLOSE on Flint's eyes as he blinks twice, dropping filters over his eyeballs. His eyes go three shades darker.

Suddenly the VOICE of the CHAIRMAN, sepulchral, metallic, but hypnotic, emerges from the wall. Flint looks but cannot find a source: the sound comes from all around him.

CHAIRMAN

You are no one, you have always been no one, you will always be no one...you have no name, no place, no face, you are nothing...nothing...nothing...

It goes on and on in this vein, hypnotic, beguiling, and a gray spiral begins to pulse in one of the walls. Going around and around, drawing Flint's attention, holding him like a cobra with a mongoose. Around and around while that voice intones...over and over... you are nothing!

45 FLINT

as he feels the hypnotic state overtaking him. Suddenly he shakes his head, gets a beatific look on his face, and slowly sinks to the floor, falling instantly into a karmatic lotus position, hands folded sedately. He closes his eyes and immediately goes into a yoga trance.

CUT TO:

46 INT. LABORATORY

ON CALISTA & BARMEIER as she consults her wrist watch.

(CONTINUED:)

46 CONTINUED:

CALISTA
That's two hours in the white room.
Time enough?

Barmeier nods, and they go to another sliding door in the lab. The door slides open and they look through into the white room.

47 SHOOTING FROM DOORWAY - WHAT THEY SEE

Flint, still quietly in his lotus position. The room has failed. As the door opens, he looks up. Smiles again.

FLINT
So soon? And I was just reaching the
ninth plateau.

CUT TO:

48 INT. ANTEROOM

ON FLINT & CALISTA. Flint is in a chair, manacled. They are obviously waiting. Calista leans in to him.

CALISTA
Derek, listen to me...please. Right now,
on the other side of that door they're
deciding your fate.

FLINT
Who is the Chairman of the Board?

CALISTA
(desperate)
Please, listen! I'm only an agent. The
Gunsmiths will stop at nothing to get
the black diamond. I'm telling you
the truth.

FLINT
Why, Miss Griffen, without your glasses
(CONT'D.)

(CONTINUED:)

48 CONTINUED:

FLINT (CONT'D.)
and gas mask you're...you're...
(beat)
...underwhelming.

CALISTA
You fool, can't you see I'm trying to help you!

FLINT
I'm trying to be gallant, but frankly, Calista, you help the way Torquemada helped at the Spanish Inquisition.

CALISTA
(dead serious)
But...I've come to care for you.

FLINT
(looks to heaven)
Forgive her, she didn't mean that.

At that moment, the door opens and the two Blacksuits come in, drag Flint out of the chair and pull him into the next room.

CUT TO:

49 INT. THE COURTROOM

Where a Tribunal has been set up. The 1st Vice President is the judge, and in a tiny jury box there are a group of Blacksuits. Barmeier stands near the judge's bench as Calista comes through the doorway. 1st V.P. places black cloth on his head in the manner of English courts. The VOICE of the CHAIRMAN erupts from a speaker grille on the wall.

CHAIRMAN
Mr. Flint, this organization has spent thirteen hours trying to get you to
(CONT'D.)

(CONTINUED:)

49 CONTINUED:

CHAIRMAN (CONT'D.)
cooperate. Time-motion studies and psychological analyses indicate we've wasted our time. The Gunsmiths operate on a simple profit-and-loss basis. At this point you cost more than you're worth. Mr. 1st Vice-President, have you reached a decision?

1st V.P.
(gleeful)
We have, Mr. Chairman.
(beat)
Liquidation of the property.

CHAIRMAN
Carry out the sentence.

Two Blacksuits come to Flint. One throws a hemp rope over a beam in the tribunal hall, the other lifts Flint onto a short footstool. They string the rope around his neck and pull it tight.

1st V.P.
I think Miss Griffen should have the pleasure.

Calista registers horror.

CALISTA
I wasn't hired to--

CHAIRMAN
Miss Griffen! Your employment can be terminated at our discretion.

Calista's shoulders sag. She walks to Flint slowly. She reaches him, raises up on toes and CAMERA COMES IN SMOOTHLY TO EXTREME CLOSEUP of her face near his ear, as she pretends to kiss him. She speaks loud enough to carry to 1st V.P.

(CONTINUED:)

49 CONTINUED: - 2

CALISTA
One last kiss for the road, Derek, dear?
(then, whispers)
Here...this will make it easier...no pain...

And she breaks an ampoule of pink mist under his nose, her body shielding her actions from the rest of the room. Then she kisses him, long and lingering.

CAMERA PULLS BACK. Flint shakes his head very slightly, as if trying to clear his senses.

1st V.P.
(screams)
Hang him!

Calista kicks out the footstool as CAMERA WHIPS UP AND AROUND AND TILTS DOWN to show us Flint's legs hanging above the floor as the eerie, mechanical voice of the Chairman booms out and reverberates over and over--

CHAIRMAN
<u>Flint</u> <u>is</u> <u>deadddddddd</u>...!

FADE TO BLACK
and
FADE OUT.

<u>END ACT ONE</u>

ACT TWO

FADE IN:

50 MISTY LIMBO - SHOT MOVING BACK

Swirling fog, pastel-colored, but not the same limbo of scenes 25-37. This is a lighter, less-ominous ambience. It is Flint swimming up out of unconsciousness. The mists begin to part. And while we come up through this, we HEAR FLINT'S VOICE OVER as if on a tape cassette, scratchy, tinny, clearly a recording, which is precisely what it is.

FLINT CASSETTE O.S.

...Carefully inspect all cranial wounds to be certain no damage has been inflicted on the skull or brain. A history of loss of consciousness, even if only for a few seconds, will serve as a warning that an injury to the intracranial contents has been incurred. X-rays are indicated in such cases in view of the possibility of a skull fracture.

(beat)

On cassette five of this series I have recorded instructions for the proper use of the X-ray machine...

By the time we reach this stage of the DIALOGUE OVER the mists will have blown away like a jet passing through clouds, and we will be seeing THROUGH FLINT'S EYES as everything comes from murky and out-of-focus to FOCUS.

51 FLINT'S POV - WHAT HE SEES - INT. FLINT'S APT. - DAY

His apartment is all around him. The elegant residence designated for this series. Leaning over

(CONT'D.)

(CONTINUED:)

51 CONTINUED:

(CONT'D.)

him are his two female house guests, TANIA (an exquisite Eurasian) and CLAUDIA (a stunning Barbie doll type who is actually a Ph.D. in Oriental Philosophy, and holds a degree in piezoelectricity). They are tending him. He is now seeing clearly, and we see Tania reach across and click off the cassette recorder that has been playing Flint's medical advice.

52 FULL SHOT

as Flint sits up on the futuristic examination table they've extruded from the wall in the living room. Flint reaches up and clicks off the examination light that was shining down on him. He rubs a hand across his neck. There is a raw, red burn there...as if from a lynch rope.

FLINT
(coughs)
They don't seem to be making death the way they used to.

He gets up, a little unsteadily, closes his eyes and puts his fingertips to his temples. He sighs, as though gathering his strength, and both girls move as if to help him. He opens his eyes and with a movement of his head stops them.

FLINT (CONT'D.)
I'm all right. I'm just checking my motor responses. Give me a moment.

He closes his eyes again, and after a few seconds sighs with acceptance. He opens his eyes.

FLINT (CONT'D.)
Everything's fine. Heartbeat a trifle erratic. I'll take care of that later. Which cassette did you use to revive me?

(CONTINUED:)

52 CONTINUED:

TANIA
The one you recorded on brain surgery and podiatry.

FLINT
Mm. Have to revise it to include transplants.

He looks around. Seems a trifle disturbed that he's here.

TANIA
We got to you just in time. They wanted to take you to the hospital, but we told them we could do more for you here at the apartment.

FLINT
I had a most amusing death fantasy. Something from the Egyptian Predynastic or Ptolemaïc periods, I think.

He slides the modular foam-rubber examination table back into the wall.

CLAUDIA
(gives him wine)
Mr. Cramden's department had a tracker on you. It took them a while to trace the signal and triangulate your location, but agents broke in and cut you down in time.

Flint is walking around, testing himself, asking his body how it feels and getting back synaptic responses. In the truest sense it is Man, Know Thyself. He looks at Claudia, about to smile and say thank you for the information when

CUT TO:

53 INTERCUT - CLAUDIA

He suddenly sees her with flaming red hair. The shot lasts a moment, a MATCH-SHOT with Claudia as she stands before him but

CUT BACK TO:

54 SAME AS 52

the vision suddenly phases back and we see Claudia standing before us with auburn hair. It's still red, but nowhere nearly as flamboyant as in the intercut.

FLINT
When did you change your hair color?

Claudia seems a trifle nonplused, pats her hair.

CLAUDIA
(smiles)
Just a rinse.
(beat)
How do you feel?

FLINT
Fine. I've got to talk to Cramden.

TANIA
He'll be here soon.

FLINT
(looking around)
Where's Dr. Zarkov?

As if that were a cue, DR. ZARKOV, the huge trained German Shepherd, faithful only to Flint, comes loping through the door from another room. As he moves toward Flint, Derek goes to one knee to receive him and the dog's collar and tags make a VERY DISTINCT CLANKING SOUND.

FREEZE THE FRAME!

Dog halted in mid-movement.

55 SPLIT-SCREEN

BLACK FRAME with a vertical frame down one side, with Flint in CLOSEUP, listening to the SOUND of the tags clanking.

Then an identical, but separate vertical frame opens on the other side, with an identical SHOT OF FLINT listening to collar and tags clanking...but radically different in sound to the first clanking. HOLD these split frames as we--and Flint--compare the two different sounds, then

CUT TO:

56 CLOSEUP ON FLINT

a single frame that matches the two identical splits we've just seen, as we realize from his expression that Flint is troubled. Something is wrong. CAMERA PAST FLINT as the action resumes and the dog comes to him. Flint scratches its muzzle for a moment, then rises. CAMERA PULLS BACK TO FULL SHOT.

FLINT
It's a little warmer in here than usual, about three degrees, don't you think?

Claudia and Tania exchange glances. Very quick.

CLAUDIA
We left the drapes open to catch the afternoon sun.

FLINT
Afternoon?

As he registers that question, the light changes in the room. Subtly, but discernibly.

FLINT (CONT'D.)
I could have sworn it was morning.

57 WITH FLINT

as he goes to a wall panel of mercury switches and hits one. A wall swings around and out comes a bookcase.

FLINT
While I'm waiting for Cramden, I believe I'll check that Egyptian death fantasy.

He reaches for a book in the stacks. CAMERA IN ON THE BOOK bearing the title
BOTANICAL ASPECTS OF EGYPTIAN EMBALMING
which suddenly flickers and superimposed over it, but much clearer so we can see it, is an entirely different book called
BREASTED'S HISTORY OF EGYPT.
It flickers for only a moment, but in that moment Flint's hand draws back from the book. Then it solidifies and Flint tracks across the books till he finds the Breasted volume he was seeking. He draws it out, slowly.

FLINT
(with a tone)
I must have misfiled it.

He returns the bookcase to the wall, and turns. Tania is walking across the room. He watches her. Again, we SUPERIMPOSE ANOTHER SHOT of Tania walking, but the walk is slightly different, a little less wiggle perhaps.

Now CAMERA MOVES IN ON FLINT as he looks from the corners of his eyes at the apartment. There is a shimmering, misty quality to the outer edges. (GREASED LENS or DIFFUSE.)

FLINT
Isn't that peculiar that I would have misfiled it. And out of order with the Dewey Decimal System. Mmm.

(CONTINUED:)

57 CONTINUED:

At that moment there is the SOUND of the doorbell, and Claudia goes to the door as we HOLD THE SCENE.

58 ANOTHER ANGLE - THE ACTION

as RALPH CRAMDEN, head of the super-secret organization for which Flint works, comes into the apartment. He looks around for the dog, and Flint motions Dr. Zarkov to lie down. Cramden, relieved, gives hat and coat to Claudia, and comes toward Flint with hand extended.

Cramden has a bluff heartiness, a hale-fellow-well-met pomposity that reminds one of a Kiwanis post president meeting his junior Senator. NOTE: He is dressed in extremely good taste, neat as a pin, almost elegant.

CRAMDEN
(effusive)
Flint! Flint! A-mazing, just a_maze_ing! You never cease to amaze me. My congratulations!

Flint seems a bit bewildered, but accepts the handshake.

FLINT
Would you like something to drink? Mr. Cramden?

CRAMDEN
(rubbing hands together)
No, no, thank you, Flint, but we've got business to get to, right away, immediately, no time to waste, eh?

FLINT
This is a very nice 1964 La Mission Haut-Brion.

(CONTINUED:)

58 CONTINUED:

He holds up his wine glass to indicate the offer... then his face gets that peculiar expression. Runs tongue over lips.

FLINT (CONT'D.)
Although...a bit smokier than I'd recalled.

He holds the glass up to the light and swirls the contents. We get the sense that he has found something else "wrong" in his world, or at least "awry."

CRAMDEN
(impatient)
Flint, don't do this to me again. I grant you we cut it pretty close with that bunch of gun-runners, but, well, even technology goes wonky every once in a while. We rescued you as quickly as we could. So...please!

Flint looks at Cramden.

59 FLINT'S POV - CRAMDEN - WHAT FLINT SEES

He looks at Cramden all spiffy in his tailored suit and vest, his natty accoutrements. Then he raises the wine glass in front of his eyes again DOMINATING THE FRAME IN CLOSEUP so we see Cramden through the wine glass. There is a roiling, a turbulence in the glass for a moment, then Flint lowers it and we see Cramden standing in precisely the same position, but he is dressed differently. Now he looks rumpled and a bit fusty, like an absent-minded college anthropologist. The suit is baggy and really square, the tie is a bow tie, crooked, his hair is mussed, there are gravy stains on the shirt; in short, the same Cramden, but now with an entirely different ambience. Flint raises the glass again, and

CUT BACK TO:

60 SAME AS 58

Cramden is dressed spiffy again.

FLINT
(muses)
I must confess you look very urbane, Mr. Cramden. Natty. New suit?

CRAMDEN
Flint!
(beat)
The Gunsmiths, as an organization, are finished. We wiped them out in the attack; we're now secure; so--please Flint...hand over the black diamond so I can get it to our security people.

FLINT
(with meaning)
And did you capture the Chairman of the Board?

Cramden reaches out, holding his hand for the diamond.

CRAMDEN
(an order)
Flint! The diamond!

61 INTERCUT - FLINT'S POV - WHAT HE SEES

He looks at Cramden's hand, and notices for the first time that Ralph Cramden has six fingers on his hand.

CUT BACK TO:

62 FULL SHOT - THE ROOM - FEATURING FLINT

as he notices the six fingers but makes virtually no sign that he's seen this final, clinching indication that something is very rotten in Scandinavia. He moves across the room to Tania.

(CONTINUED:)

62 CONTINUED:

FLINT
I have it right here in the safe.

CRAMDEN
(impatient)
Well, let's get to it, man, let's get to it. Time is of the essence!

FLINT
It's coded to Tania's voice-print.

He takes the beautiful girl by the shoulder in a very fatherly manner and walks her to the handsome metal sculpture on its pedestal, at one side of the room. He plucks a vaguely Hindu tune on the metal strings of the sculpture and the circular top of the pedestal (with the metal sculpture still resting on it) swings off to one side as the outer shell recedes into the floor (dropping the pedestal top & sculpture to the floor on one side) revealing the inner core, a safe set in a circular column of case-hardened molybdenum steel, the dial and door in its circular top.

FLINT
(to Tania)
Repeat after me: "Twas brillig and the slithey toves, did gyre and gimble in the wabe."

TANIA
"Twas brillig and the slithey toves, did gyre and gimble in the wabe."

Nothing happens.

CRAMDEN
(annoyed)
What's the matter, why didn't the safe open?

(CONTINUED:)

62 CONTINUED: - 2

FLINT
(smiles)
Quite simple, really. Whoever this young lady is, she isn't Tania, so nothing happens.

Cramden begins to fumfuh, to huff and puff; Tania draws away from Flint as though he's mad.

CLAUDIA
Derek! What a terrible thing to say.

TANIA
Derek, you're making Mr. Cramden angry. His face is getting all blotchy.

CRAMDEN
Dammit, Flint! This is beyond belief, utterly unconscionable!
(he moves toward Flint)
Now cease this badinage, open the bloody safe and give me that black diamond.

He has just about reached Flint, and starts to make a move clearly intended to cause Flint harm. Flint had continued to smile charmingly through this entire exchange, but as Cramden steps in to deal him a blow, Flint decides it's time to knock off the charade, and in one fluid movement he spins delivering a savate kick that sends the ersatz Cramden through a glass and tubular steel free-standing shelf filled with Chinese glazes. Everything, Cramden included, goes down in a wide swath of noise and moving parts.

FLINT
(to Cramden)
If those Chinese glazes were real, I'd be distressed at losing them. Tang Dynasty, you know.

63 ANOTHER SHOT ON THE ACTION - ARRIFLEX

He spins again, and sees the two girls advancing on him, their hands held in the kill-positions of jukindo (ask Bruce Lee about this; it really looks ominous).

Tania springs first, giving the deadly cry of the assassin. Her attack is easily countered by Flint, who manages to hurl her against a wall. Just in time to get Claudia into range, and to deal her a blow (which she counters on her forearm) that might kill a less adept assailant. He then fences with her, stroke, stroke, stroke, as they each whip their best moves on the other. Flint finally knocks her down. And here comes Tania again.

The fight continues. A marvelous three-way duel with Flint doing his best to disable--but always the gentleman, not to kill--the two girls (who aren't really girls, so you can vindicate a guy wiping the floor with two ladies).

NOTE: the Author would happily fill in every choreographed move of this epic battle--the core of Act Two--but from sad experience the Author has found out that the "Fight Director" and the Director of the segment like to program these things themselves. And who am I to deprive the kids of their innocent pleasures. So..."the fight continues." Do it your way, but make it look serious and deadly.

Finally, Flint downs the two girls. He ties their long hair together, lifts them like two sacks of meal, and drops them over a sofa, one on either side so they can't get themselves undone.

He turns, just as Cramden opens up on him with a grease-gun automatic with a wire stock. No need to ask from whence he obtained this weapon. You'll understand, and so will the audience, in a few moments.

(CONTINUED:)

63 CONTINUED:

Flint hurls himself sidewise, out of the line of bullets and--in the manner of a wrestler bouncing off the ropes--hurtles from wall to wall, running up one wall and kicking off, sprinting across the room to bound off a second wall, changing directions, and all the while uttering Zen cries of the most blood-curdling nature...a bravura performance guaranteed to make jaws drop. And when Cramden has spun around and around and around in an attempt to anticipate from which direction Flint will be coming, he staggers dizzily and Flint hits him with a dropkick that sends Cramden flailing through the air, and out through the penthouse window, shattering it with a barrage of glass. The SCREAM can be heard for a loooong time as Cramden plummets toward the street far below.

CAMERA MOVES IN SLIGHTLY on Flint, who stands, shaken, at having killed his "boss." He is trying to gather his senses, performing that eyes-closed/fingers-to-temples bit, and does not see

64 BEHIND FLINT IN B.G.

as "Cramden" floats back up from the street below, floats in through the window, picks up a heavy vase, moves up on Flint and wallops him across the back of the head. Flint goes down like a rhino in a car body crusher.

65 FLINT'S POV - THE ROOM - WHAT HE SEES

as he begins to float off into unconsciousness the room begins to go out of focus, refocuses, out of focus, blurs, gets misty around the edges, and as we watch the SPECIAL EFFECTS merge the image of Flint's posh apartment over the last view we had of the Gunsmiths' laboratory. Then, with his eyes flickering, but not yet gone, the lab goes solid and Flint sees the two Blacksuits, with their suits yanked up like body stockings, tied together, and we realize the two

(CONT'D.)

(CONTINUED:)

65 CONTINUED:

(CONT'D.)

"girls" were hallucinogenic images of the Blacksuits, and the hair he tied together was their suit hoods. Barmeier is trying to untie them as they struggle to get free.

As Flint goes over the edge, Calista appears at the rim of his fading world, leans over him and looks disgruntled.

CALISTA

(as if from far away)

Even that delusion didn't work.

(beat)

I guess we're just going to have to get really rotten with him.

And Flint fades away as we HOLD his unconscious form, suddenly lifted into the air above the heads of the two disentangled Blacksuits, who carry him away as if he were an unholy offering to the sun god.

FADE TO BLACK
and
FADE OUT.

END ACT TWO

ACT THREE

FADE IN:

66 INT. CONVERSATION ROOM - LONG SHOT

WIDE-ANGLE LENS SHOOTING down the length of a room that seems only slightly smaller that Latvia, because of the distortion of the lens. The walls are white or gray, and black lines, drawn in perspective, converge far down what appears to be a vast distance. In VOICE OVER we HEAR a cultivated, soft, rational voice with an English accent. Not heavy, just sophisticated enough for us to understand this is an educated, upper-class Englishman speaking, something very toney like the dude who does the Schweppervescence commercials. All the while the VOICE SPEAKS OVER the CAMERA TRUCKS IN STEADILY on the point where the lines converge, at which point sits a stylish Saarinen pedestal wingback chair, very modern, very smooth and sedate. (The Author can provide this chair, if needed.)

SHAKESPEARE O.S.

Mr. Flint, I've been asked to speak to you for a few moments.

(beat, then with self-deprecating lightness)

I presume they want me to convince you to save your life, or at least your sanity. Perhaps the one is identical with the other, I've never been too certain about that; I think a little creative madness is all that prevents us from becoming one with the snails.

CAMERA IN STEADILY on the chair throughout this DIALOGUE, until we halt movement at a MEDIUM SHOT and the chair swings around--having hidden what it contains till this moment because of its wingback--and we see Flint sitting there very calmly,

(CONT'D.)

(CONTINUED:)

66 CONTINUED:

(CONT'D.)

listening to the speaker. He is once again dressed as first we saw him in the opening scenes, elegant in tuxedo, legs crossed, very dapper and together.

FLINT

If I take it correctly, you're another hallucination.

CUT TO:

67 REVERSE ANGLE PAST FLINT - HIS POV

The room in reverse, the same perspective of lines, and an identical chair seated across from him. Seated in the chair, wearing the Elizabethan garb of his time, drinking ale from what is called a "half-yard" glass, is WILLIAM SHAKESPEARE. Not Barmeier or someone else dressed as The Bard, but Shakespeare himself. Oh boy! The Bard nods in answer to Flint's remark, and raises his ale in a small toast of camaraderie. NOTE: throughout this entire scene, the Bard is never menacing, he is friendly and intelligent and just what we'd want Wm. to be.

SHAKESPEARE

Sadly, I'm afraid so.

FLINT

Then why should I pay any attention?

SHAKESPEARE

Because I'm a far more entertaining conversationalist than that pack of hooligans and cutpurses with truncheons.

FLINT

I'll grant you that. And you use better grammar.

(CONTINUED:)

67 CONTINUED:

SHAKESPEARE
(smiles)
Then let us talk...as intelligent men...
for just a few minutes.

FLINT
You choose the subject.

SHAKESPEARE
(with a twinkle)
You won't be distraught if I don't select
gemology? Particularly diamonds?

FLINT
Not in the least.

SHAKESPEARE
Let us discuss patriotism.

68 thru 75 MEDIUM SHOTS ALTERNATING FLINT ALONE, THE BARD ALONE, TWO-SHOTS

with CAMERA MOVING AROUND THEM to keep the scene from becoming visually static. But HOLD PERSPECTIVE so we perceive this discussion occurs across an enormous gap. Both physically and intellectually.

SHAKESPEARE (CONT'D.)
Do you believe an individual should die
for his country?

FLINT
I believe he should <u>live</u> for his country.

SHAKESPEARE
Ah! A good start. Then you don't
believe we should give our lives for
causes?

(CONTINUED:)

68 thru 75 CONTINUED:

FLINT
(carefully, as if a ritual)
I believe life is sacred, that it should be preserved at all costs.
(beat)
If one must die, it should be for ideas, not causes.

SHAKESPEARE
You reject death for slogans.

FLINT
Ideas cannot be killed, only those who propound them.
(beat)
The Christian martyrs died by the scores, but it was time for Christianity, and nothing could have stopped it, certainly not the power of Imperial Rome.

SHAKESPEARE
Then do I take it you're saying they should have lived, even at the cost of recanting?

FLINT
It worked for Galileo, and his ideas live on. Yes, I think that's what I'm saying.

SHAKESPEARE
But then, if that is so, don't we defeat injustice and evil by resisting it?

FLINT
Precisely my point. By staying alive we sustain the ability to continue the fight.
(beat)
Six million Jews went to their deaths
(CONT'D.)

(CONTINUED:)

68 thru 75 CONTINUED: - 2

FLINT (CONT'D.)
in ovens and gas chambers, many of them docilely. Their murder did nothing to halt the monstrousness that condemned them.

SHAKESPEARE
You denounce their deaths as complicity by inaction? That seems a bit severe, Mr. Flint.

FLINT
I don't condemn them, of course not. I merely contend that, had they fought, had they clung with ferocity to their lives, all might not have gone so smoothly for their killers.

SHAKESPEARE
By extension then, don't you think you should preserve <u>your</u> life in this rather untenable situation?

FLINT
I thought we weren't going to discuss black diamonds?

SHAKESPEARE
(shrugs)
I merely bring you full circle in your own argument.

FLINT
It is a far, far better thing I do, than I have ever done.

SHAKESPEARE
What a marvelous line. May I use it sometime?

(CONTINUED:)

68 thru 75 CONTINUED: - 3

FLINT
Already been used.

SHAKESPEARE
Oh? By whom?

FLINT
Charles Dickens.

SHAKESPEARE
(ponders)
I don't believe I've ever heard of the fellow.

FLINT
Bright young kid. Coming up fast. They say he has talent.

SHAKESPEARE
What do you think of Marlowe?

FLINT
(grins)
What do you think of Marlowe?

SHAKESPEARE
Amusing.

FLINT
How would you take to the concept of Marlowe's having written your plays?

SHAKESPEARE
Let us not descend to gaucherie, Mr. Flint.
(beat)
Let's move on. Now...Aquinas on courage and faith...

LAP-DISSOLVE TO:

76 thru 80 SERIES OF LAP-DISSOLVES - SAME ANGLES AS SCENES 68-75

They are slumped in different positions, occasionally one or the other of them will be up, pacing back and forth, but all the while they're discussing, discussing, carrying on one of the Great Conversations. We HEAR OVER the bits and pieces, snippets and snatches of the conversation. But the LAP-DISSOLVES ARE SMOOTH and indicate a great passage of time. NOTE: these snatches of talk need in no way be integrated with the action; it is all part of the flow.

SHAKESPEARE
But surely you can't use Nietzsche to shore up that contention!

FLINT
Tielhard de Chardin maintains...

SHAKESPEARE
Regional chauvinism may be at the root of all wars of expansion...

FLINT
Aquinas said, "Human law does not bind a man in conscience; and if it conflicts with the higher law, human law should not be obeyed."

And finally we

DISSOLVE THRU TO:

81 MEDIUM 2-SHOT - FLINT & SHAKESPEARE

The Bard looks weary. So does Flint. Shakespeare sighs and his hands move in a gesture of finality.

SHAKESPEARE
Have we been talking days, months, years? Time has turned to dust for us, Derek.

(CONTINUED:)

81 CONTINUED:

FLINT

I can't recall a more pleasant conversation, Bill.

SHAKESPEARE

Unfortunately, for both of us, I've tried every intellectual approach possible, but nothing prevails against your ineluctable logic.

FLINT

I'm flattered.

SHAKESPEARE

I must confess, Derek, you are a certain wonder! I suspect you could outfox the devil on a reservation in Hell. Marvelous! absolutely marvelous! And never once did you have to resort to reductio ad absurdum or deus ex machina.

(beat)

Sadly, you've won this round of tilting. Soon, I'll be returned to mist and you... well, we have to move along. Miss Griffen has asked me to assist her in the next phase of your, er, treatment, and I hope the "theme" I've developed amuses you.

FLINT

You could do no less than amaze me, sir.

SHAKESPEARE

You're a gentleman, Derek. To the final pulse.

(beat)

Every great and creative brainwash has a theme, I find. I've selected Great Literary Moments for yours.

(CONTINUED:)

81 CONTINUED: - 2

FLINT

Appropriate.

SHAKESPEARE

Goodbye, Derek. It's been a delight, a sheer delight.

(beat)

Godspeed.

And The Bard wavers, shimmers, vanishes, as SPECIAL EFFECTS SUPERIMPOSE once again, the perspective room with its twin chairs and converging black lines, and the Gunsmiths' lab. And as the SUPERIMPOSITION PHASES OVER from room to lab we

LAP-DISSOLVE TO:

82 MATCH-CUT ON FLINT - CLOSE

So we see him sitting, and for a moment can think he is still in that Saarinen chair. Then CAMERA PULLS BACK to show us he is sitting in a chair-like machine. Now let us talk about the machine for a moment. This is a terror machine, folks. That means it mustn't look like something out of a 1942 Republic serial of "Spy Smasher Vs. The Scorpion," one of those bullshit James Bond pseudo-gimcrack items. It should be something simple but horrible, the kind of thing that calls up gut memories of the death machines we have come to know and love, like: the electric chair, the guillotine, the gibbet...something simple and direct like a knife or a bomb. They are uncomplicated and hardly designed for comfort. If you can conjure that feeling, you'll have it. The sort of machine that merely being shackled into (like the Salem stocks) causes a heart attack. Think of an electro-shock therapy tank, with a rubber sheet and electrodes. Shudder a little!

(CONTINUED:)

82 CONTINUED:

Barmeier runs the machine, which we see as CAMERA PULLS BACK from Flint, also revealing Calista and the 1st V.P. She leans down and kisses Flint on the mouth.

CALISTA
Still with us?

FLINT
What inning is it?

CALISTA
Bottom of the ninth, Derek.

Barmeier moves in beside her. He seems anxious to tell Flint what's about to happen to him.

DR. BARMEIER
Are you familiar with Orwell's "Nineteen Eighty-Four," the novel?
(no response from Flint, the Herr Doktor goes on)
In the book the enlightened government tries to break Winston Smith, to get him to divulge the information they want...

Calista is stroking Flint's face with languid fingertips.

DR. BARMEIER (CONT'D.)
They know that <u>everyone</u> has some deep, hidden fear, some special thing that lies in the darkest buried corner of the mind. They find out what it is, and they put it in what they call Room 101, and they take Winston Smith there, and threaten him with it, and he breaks, because he could stand up to any torture they might devise...everything but whatever it was he feared most.
(CONT'D.)

(CONTINUED:)

82 CONTINUED: - 2

DR. BARMEIER (CONT'D.)
And they tell him there are many Room 101's, each one holding a different supreme terror, each one especially for a specific person.

CALISTA
This machine will let us tap into your thalamus, Derek.

She strokes his forehead, runs her hand through his hair.

CALISTA (CONT'D.)
In there we'll find out what lies behind the door to your Room 101. It's a terrible way to break a man, darling, that's why I've saved it for the last... but you leave me no alternatives.
(beat)
(with a little fear)
We must unlock you, Derek.

She nods to Barmeier, who returns to the controls and throws a knife-switch. The connections are made as a spark leaps a gap...and Flint jerks as current goes through him. Pain! Barmeier watches, turns a graduated knob and the power increases, Flint jerks more violently, then faints as FRAME IRISES CLOSED TO A PINPOINT OF LIGHT.

OPEN FRAME AS WE CUT TO:

83 thru 90 SERIES OF IRIS-IN & IRIS-OUT DISSOLVES THROUGH

A. Pinpoint of light irises open to frame Flint, stretched out like a human sacrifice on a pallet of sticks and twigs. He is again naked, though shadows from the limbo set conceal portions of his body, highlighting his face. Suddenly, the twigs begin to flame up in one area, then in another,
(CONT'D.)

(CONTINUED:)

83 CONTINUED:
thru
90

(CONT'D.)

then another. THROUGH FLAMES CAMERA COMES IN on Flint's terrified face as he screams and we HEAR the VOICE of the CHAIRMAN, metallic, ominous:

CHAIRMAN O.S.

Flint fears death by fire.

IRIS CLOSE and
IRIS OPEN TO

B. Flint, in another limbo, backed against a brick wall, with walls on either side and the front open to the darkness. CAMERA ZOOMS IN on his eyes as the SOUND of RATS grows louder and louder. In the limbo darkness we see thousands of pairs of demonically glowing eyes, as of a plague of rats, coming for him, the SOUND of their claws scraping on brick. PULL BACK to show Flint cowering against the wall, whimpering, as a rat drops from the wall, onto his shoulder and he screams. The scream fades into silence as we HEAR the Chairman again:

CHAIRMAN O.S.

Flint fears attack by rats.

IRIS CLOSE and
IRIS OPEN TO

C. Flint, in another limbo, stretched out as though spread-eagled, on a giant spiderweb. CAMERA CLOSE ON HIS FACE as his eyes suddenly flick down and widen in horror and CAMERA SWISH-PANS to spiders, dozens of hairy terrors, scuttling up the web, crawling over his naked leg and we HEAR FLINT SCREAM O.S. as the Chairman's voice comes again, triumphantly:

(CONTINUED:)

83 thru 90 CONTINUED: - 2

CHAIRMAN O.S.

Spiders!

IRIS CLOSE and
IRIS OPEN TO

D. Flint, lying in an open grave in limbo as dirt begins to crumble off the edges of the mounds surrounding the grave, as it begins to tumble in on him and he thrashes, helpless, and we HEAR the Chairman:

CHAIRMAN O.S.

Buried alive!

IRIS CLOSE and
IRIS OPEN TO

E. Flint on the edge of a great precipice, looking down into a chasm that plummets forever. Suddenly hurtling forward into space and falling, falling, falling.

CHAIRMAN O.S.

Fear of heights!

IRIS CLOSE and
IRIS OPEN TO

F. Flint, tied down and his head held in place by a leather collar, in a circle of light within a limbo set. From Flint's POV, looking up, we see two incredibly sharp needles descending out of the darkness, heading for his eyes. Light sparkles off them as Flint shrieks and writhes and we HEAR the Chairman:

CHAIRMAN O.S.

He's terrified of needles. That's enough. Now...

(CONT'D.)

(CONTINUED:)

83 thru 90 CONTINUED: - 3

CHAIRMAN O.S. (CONT'D.)
(beat)
Use the psychedelics and put him through those fears...he'll talk...

Down...down...come the needles and the CAMERA HOLDS on a scintilla of light sparkling off one of them as we

IRIS CLOSE and
GO TO BLACK.

91 OUT OF BLACK - MEDIUM SHOT - INT. LAB

as the black frame becomes the back of the 1st V.P. as he walks away from CAMERA, revealing the Gunsmith's lab, with Flint still in the demon chair, and around the room Barmeier, Calista and the Blacksuits, slumped in despair.

1st V.P.
(furious)
There'll be a review of your handling of this matter, Griffen, you can count on that! We have stockholders to account to!

DR. BARMEIER
(wearily)
I put him through every terror his unconscious told us he feared. Every one, under maximum intensity. And still he won't talk.

CALISTA
I don't understand it. His mind <u>told</u> us what terrified him!

(CONTINUED:)

91 CONTINUED:

Flint raises his head. A bit groggy, coming out from under the drugs, a little thick at first, then stronger.

FLINT
In the spirit of Great Literary Moments...there's an old Uncle Remus story where Brer Rabbit tells Brer Fox to do anything to him but not to throw him in the briar patch. So Brer Fox throws him in...and he gets away.

There is a LOUD BURST OF STATIC from the speaker grille on the wall and the voice of the Chairman comes through angrily.

CHAIRMAN
It's clear none of you can cope with this man. I'll take over from here.
(beat)
Mr. Flint, I think it's time to put you on ice...a kind of tickler file...
(beat)
Do you know Chekhov's story, "The Bet"?

FLINT
Do you mind if I stretch my legs?

CHAIRMAN
Untie him. But watch him.

DR. BARMEIER
He's too weak from the drugs to worry about.

CHAIRMAN
Watch him!

One of the Blacksuits comes over and releases Flint
(CONT'D.)

(CONTINUED:)

91 CONTINUED: - 2

(CONT'D.)

from the terror chair. Flint gets up, as everyone tenses. He walks around, stretches his body, regains his composure.

92 WITH FLINT

as he walks to the wall where the speaker grille is set. He stands near it and stares up.

FLINT

Read any good books lately, Chairman?

CHAIRMAN

Chekhov, Mr. Flint. "The Bet." Do you know it?

FLINT

Two men make a wager. One bets the other he isn't self-sufficient enough to stay alone in a room for twenty-five years without speaking to another human being. If he can, he wins a large sum of money.

CHAIRMAN

The loneliness does strange things to him, Mr. Flint. He chokes on the imprisonment, then he hallucinates, almost driven insane.

FLINT

Ah, but the way it ends...!

(beat)

He begins reading, and spends all his time all those years learning everything books can teach him. Five minutes before the twenty-five years are up and he'll win, he leaves the room, knowing he won by becoming a wiser and more knowledgeable man, that he could not have spent the years better.

(CONTINUED:)

92 CONTINUED:

CHAIRMAN
Very good, Mr. Flint. That's the sort of tickler file into which I propose to throw you.

FLINT
Isn't twenty-five years a little long to wait for me to talk? By then the laser-trigger itself will be obsolete. By then we'll have starships run by chipmunk power...or something.

DR. BARMEIER O.S.
Oh, we won't have that long to wait... not nearly that long.

93 SHOT PAST FLINT

FEATURING BARMEIER, who smiles evilly and speaks to the grille on the wall.

DR. BARMEIER (CONT'D.)
Brilliant, Mr. Chairman. Our hallucinogens have the marvelous quality of stretching subjective time like taffy. Three weeks alone in a room will seem like fifty years to him...a hundred!

The Blacksuits move to grab Flint as Calista motions them to take him. Flint struggles weakly for a moment, then twists to speak to the Chairman.

FLINT
Mr. Chairman! Maintaining your theme of Great Literary Moments, do I get books to read, to make me a wiser, better person?

The Blacksuits try to hustle him off, but the Chairman stops them.

(CONTINUED:)

93 CONTINUED:

CHAIRMAN
Stop! Mr. Flint arouses my curiosity. The old conundrum of the man on the desert island...what one single book will he take with him? In your case a sealed room for fifty years.
(beat)
What book will it be, Mr. Flint? War and Peace? The Bible? The Pickwick Papers? Korzybski's Science and Sanity?

Flint thinks a moment, as everyone waits expectantly.

FLINT
Don Quixote.

CHAIRMAN
An excellent choice. Make certain you give him a paperback edition; we don't want Mr. Flint using the cover boards in a hardcover as escape implements.

FLINT
Is it possible to stretch your magnanimity to include cigarettes and a pack of matches?

CHAIRMAN
We certainly aren't barbarians. You may have them, Mr. Flint, but I warn you, don't try setting the sealed room on fire: highly sensitive sprinklers in the walls will foil any escape attempts and you might catch cold.
(beat)
Keeping a cold for fifty years could become distressing.

CAMERA HOLDS on Flint's face as we

MATCH-CUT TO:

94 CORRIDOR OUTSIDE LONELINESS CELL

MATCH WITH FLINT'S FACE. CAMERA PULLS BACK to show we are in this new scene, just as the cell door is opened. Inside, we can see a small table, a mat on the floor, and nothing else. They hand him the book, the matches and the cigarettes, and Flint walks into the room. The door is slammed and bolted, and through the small window in the door (which has a cover that closes) Calista says:

CALISTA

Have a happy half century. Dr. Barmeier's booster shots should be taking effect very soon.

(beat)

Now you have all the time in the world...

And she slams shut the cover on the little window as we

SMASH-CUT TO:

95 INT. CELL

as CAMERA ZOOMS IN on Flint, alone for fifty years.

FRAME IRISES TO BLACK
and
FADE OUT.

<u>END ACT THREE</u>

ACT FOUR

FADE IN:

96 INT. CELL - ON FLINT

as CAMERA MOVES IN on him, sitting there on the floor in a lotus position, we begin to HEAR the WHISPERS OF VOICES in the air. They are indistinct at first, seeming to come from nowhere and everywhere, until CAMERA MOVES IN TO EXTREME CLOSEUP of Flint's left eye. The eye goes opaque and there in its depths, as CAMERA MOVES IN we see:

LAP-DISSOLVE:

97 THE SCENE IN FLINT'S EYE

is Calista, standing there saying in a GHOST-WHISPER VOICE that now becomes distinct (filter):

CALISTA
(FILTER)
Dr. Barmeier's booster shots should be taking effect...the time-altering drugs are pumping through your system...

CAMERA PULLS BACK out through the eye, back, back to:

LAP-DISSOLVE:

98 SAME AS 96

as CAMERA PULLS BACK to SHOT OF FLINT and the demon whispers of Calista subside back into vague sounds. Now CAMERA MOVES IN on Flint's right eye and we repeat

LAP-DISSOLVE:

99 SAME AS 97 - THE OTHER EYE

The scene in the eye is of Flint, seated in a lotus position across from The ANCIENT One, a withered old guru, from whom issue the whispers that now grow distinct as he speaks to the Flint in Flint's eye.

ANCIENT
(in cracked voice)
My son, when you have stored good karma, you will have total knowledge, total control of your mind and body. You will rid yourself of evil vapors and humours by thought; poisons in your system can be cast out like evil thoughts.

FLINT
I see, Old One.
(beat)
Illness can be psychosomatic. By controlling my bodily functions I can isolate the poison fractions in my blood and sweat them out.

ANCIENT
Did anyone ever tell you, my son, that you take all the magic out of our meditations?

FLINT
Sorry.

ANCIENT
Be silent and meditate. Sweat if you wish.

CAMERA PULLS BACK out through the eye, back, back, to:

LAP-DISSOLVE:

100 SAME AS 96

FLINT FULL IN FRAME. HOLD on his face as he suddenly begins to perspire heavily. HOLD HIM and begin

SLOW LAP-DISSOLVE:

101 MATCH-SHOT - CALISTA

HER FACE in the same CLOSEUP as Flint in previous shot. As Flint's face DISSOLVES UNDER, Calista's face comes into full focus. CAMERA BACK to show her lying in bed, in a filmy nightgown, but lying awake thinking as CAMERA MOVES IN STEADILY to her left eye and we see:

LAP-DISSOLVE:

102 THE SCENE IN CALISTA'S EYE

is a repeat of Scene 7 on the veranda of the mansion where Flint first met her. They stand there with Calista holding her cigarette for Flint to light. Again, we HEAR WHISPERS.

CALISTA
Would you like one?

FLINT
(light)
I thought we were going to leave the Grim Reaper behind?

CALISTA
Such disdain.
(seductive)
You don't smoke, you don't work, don't you have _any_ vices, Derek?

CAMERA BEGINS MOVING out of the eye as the phrase _you don't smoke_ repeats over and over and
(CONT'D.)

(CONTINUED:)

102 CONTINUED:

(CONT'D.)

over and the CAMERA PULLS BACK out through the eye, back, back to:

LAP–DISSOLVE:

103 SAME AS 101

as CAMERA PULLS BACK out of the eye and the demon whispers subside. Now (in a parallel structure with the scenes in Flint's eyes) the CAMERA MOVES IN on Calista's right eye:

LAP–DISSOLVE:

104 SAME AS 102

the scene in her other eye is a repeat of Scene 93, in the Gunsmiths' lab, with Flint standing between the two Blacksuits, talking to the Chairman via the grille...the demon whispers grow more distinct as Flint says:

FLINT

It is possible to stretch your magnanimity to include cigarettes and a pack of matches?

And CAMERA PULLS BACK out of the eye as we HEAR Calista's ghost whisper saying you don't smoke over and over:

LAP–DISSOLVE:

105 SAME AS 101

as CAMERA PULLS BACK OUT of the right eye, to HOLD CALISTA in CLOSEUP. Suddenly she sits up in bed and her mouth opens to shout as the realization of what Flint is up to dawns on her and we

SMASH–CUT TO:

106 INT. CELL - WITH ACTION

CLOSE ON FLINT as he scrapes the cellulose off the cover of Don Quixote with his belt buckle.

FLINT
(humming idly)
Cellulose...mmm...mmm...

We notice sweat standing out prominently on his forehead and chest. He has scraped sufficient cellulose now, and he moves to the door of the cell, wads the cellulose into the lock and, using the cellophane opening strip from the cigarette pack as a fuse, lights it. He ducks back in the cell as we

HARD CUT TO:

107 PASSAGE OUTSIDE THE CELL

a narrow passage, where a 3rd BLACKSUIT stands guard with a bren gun. Suddenly there is a tremendous explosion and the door slams open, the concussion knocking the guard against the wall of the passage. Even as he impacts, Flint comes hurtling out through the open door and catches the guard on the rebound with two sharp kung-fu slashes that send him assoverteakettle. He grabs the bren gun just as two more guards, 4th & 5th BLACKSUITS, come around the corner. CAMERA WHIP-PANS with Flint's move in their direction and HOLDS PAST FLINT as two short, sharp bursts lift the guards off their feet and hurl them out of sight into the cross-passage.

108 CAMERA WITH FLINT - FOLLOW ACTION - ARRIFLEX

Flint dashes to the cross-passage, hurdles the bodies, and rushes forward.

109 AMMO DUMP

a huge chamber stacked with explosives. Flint comes
(CONT'D.)

(CONTINUED:)

109 CONTINUED:

(CONT'D.)

rushing in from the passage, sprays several more guards who run for cover. He sees a mountain of crates labeled

PLASTIQUE

and fires into them. They begin to explode as Flint dashes into the cover of a half-track truck parked at one side of the chamber. The explosions continue and Flint crawls onto the hood of the truck, onto its roof, and launches himself at the railing of the catwalk overhead. He catches it, pulls himself up, spins and fires across the chamber at another Blacksuit trying to machine gun him from the other side of the catwalk. The Blacksuit is hit and tumbles over the railing as more explosions hit one after another like firecrackers. They are building in intensity. Flint sees a doorway on the catwalk and rushes for it. It is locked. The explosions get stronger.

CUT TO:

110 FILE ROOM

ON LOCKED DOOR between file cases, as the door suddenly shatters with a savate kick and Flint throws himself through the smashed door just as a gigantic explosion destroys the armaments cache in the ammo dump below. Without stopping he dashes across the room and flings himself out the door on the other side as flames rip through the file room.

111 thru 116 SERIES OF LAP-DISSOLVES - MAYHEM - STANDING SETS (STOCK)

SUPERIMPOSE FLINT IN MOTION over stock shots (MEASURE) of arms caches being blown, files being burned, computers being wrecked, knocking guards senseless, and in general decimating the Gunsmiths' headquarters. And over all this we HEAR the VOICE of the Chairman, from speaker grilles throughout the complex.

(CONTINUED:)

111 thru 116 CONTINUED:

CHAIRMAN
Flint is loose in the complex!
He's in the central computer banks!
Set up a crossfire in passages 7 West and 11 North!
He escaped; trap him in the laboratory!

But Flint continues his rampage. Shots of explosions can be seen UNDER SUPERIMPOSED LIMBO SHOTS of Flint on the move. Until, finally, the Chairman's voice is heard:

CHAIRMAN
He's trapped in the upper armory. Pin him down!

CUT TO:

117 INT. UPPER ARMORY - FULL SHOT - ESTABLISHING

A huge garage-like area, with crates of HIGH EXPLOSIVES stacked almost to the ceiling along one side of the high-ceilinged area. CAMERA BOOMS DOWN to pick up Calista, Barmeier, the 1st V.P. and a half dozen Blacksuits crouched down behind tanks, oil drums, packing crates, all of them bristling with heavy armaments, ready to blow Flint to pieces. CAMERA PANS ACROSS this scene of waiting violence, swiftly moving across the empty no man's land of the central garage space, to the crates of high explosives, and Flint down behind them. Both sides are ready. Suddenly, the VOICE of the CHAIRMAN booms out over the armory.

CHAIRMAN
You're trapped, Mr. Flint. Without hope of escape, trapped.
(beat)
I offer you one last chance. The diamond, in ten seconds, or I advise my employees to vacate the warehouse and fire into the cases of explosives.

118 INTERCUT

Flint, listening.

119 ANOTHER ANGLE ON THE ENTIRE SCENE

CHAIRMAN (CONT'D.)
My patience has long-since run out with you, Mr. Flint. We are business people, and you've already cost us a fortune in damages with your running amuck. I'm prepared to cut our losses by getting rid of you.
(beat)
Ten seconds: ten, nine, eight...

120 INTERCUT

Flint, thinking.

CHAIRMAN (CONT'D.)
Seven...six...five...four...

121 MED. SHOT - FAVORING CALISTA

on the Gunsmiths, their weapons raised for the attack as we HEAR Flint's voice from behind the stacks.

FLINT
You win.

CHAIRMAN
Put an end to trickery, Mr. Flint, I warn you.

FLINT
The diamond is in the collar of the attack dog at my apartment.
(beat)
Use the Latin phrase, <u>Nemo</u> <u>me</u> <u>impune</u> <u>lacessit</u>, to keep him from tearing out your throats.

(CONTINUED:)

121 CONTINUED:

CHAIRMAN
If I translate the Latin correctly, "No one harms me with impunity." Very good, Mr. Flint, but a trifle inappropriate, under the circumstances.

122 ON 1st V.P.

as he scuttles away from the cover of the oil drums.

1st V.P.
(loud)
Mr. Chairman! I'll take two men. Keep him pinned down. I'll be back in half an hour.

CHAIRMAN
Take your time. Mr. Flint isn't going anywhere.

He goes, as we

DISSOLVE TO:

123 INT. ARMORY - EXT. CLOSEUP - THE DIAMOND

as CAMERA PULLS BACK we see it is in the hand of the 1st V.P. as he hands it to Calista.

CALISTA
Keep him put where he is. I'll take this to the Chairman. Just to be sure.

She goes, and they return to watchful waiting as we

DISSOLVE TO:

124 LONG SHOT - FROM FLINT ACROSS ARMORY

as Calista returns through the doorway behind the barricade.

(CONTINUED:)

124 CONTINUED:

CHAIRMAN
All right, Miss Griffen. This is the black diamond. Let him go.

1st V.P.
You heard him, Flint. Come on out.

There is the SOUND of gun hammers being clicked back.

CHAIRMAN
I said he could go. He's beaten, we have what we want. There's no profit in killing him. Mr. Flint's fangs have been pulled.

1st V.P.
But...

CHAIRMAN
Let him alone! It isn't logical to kill him now. We're businessmen, not butchers.

125 REVERSE ANGLE - FROM GUNSMITHS ACROSS ARMORY

as Flint comes out slowly. He dusts himself off, starts to walk across the open space to the Gunsmith group. 1st V.P., Barmeier and Calista watch him come toward them. He stops and smiles at her.

FLINT
Would you call me a cab...or is someone motoring my way?

Calista looks at him with contempt.

CALISTA
I'm disappointed in you, Derek.

(CONTINUED:)

125 CONTINUED:

FLINT
(shrugs)
Shakespeare was right. Why die for a lost cause?

She turns her back on him. Flint is being looked at by all of them with disgust and contempt. He shrugs, starts walking toward the big doors leading out of the armory. As he reaches the door and opens it, the voice of the Chairman fills the armory.

CHAIRMAN
Goodbye, Mr. Flint. Now that you've been properly humbled, let us hope our paths never cross again. If you ever interfere with my business again...I'll show no mercy.
(beat)
Now get out...loser!

And Flint, his jaw muscles twitching with his defeat, turns, shoulders slumped in abject defeat, and steps through the outer door of the armory. CAMERA HOLDS on the door for a moment and then it is softly closed as we

FADE TO BLACK
and
FADE OUT.

<u>END ACT FOUR</u>

TAG

FADE IN:

126 INT. FLINT'S APARTMENT - DAY

EXTREME CLOSEUP on Flint's hand, hitting the circular contact that opens the tambour door to his apartment. (For those who don't know what a tambour door is...it's like the lid on a rolltop desk.) CAMERA PULLS BACK to FULL SHOT of Flint as the door rolls up, revealing the gorgeous Calista. She does not come in.

FLINT

Good morning. Would you care for some eggs Benedict, or just a cup of kona coffee?

CALISTA

It shattered to powder when we tried to cut it.

FLINT

Yes, I know. How about quiche lorraine and fresh fruit?

CALISTA

The Chairman wants to see you.

Flint nods, turns and passes his hand over an opaque plate set in the right-hand wall. A closet door slides open and he takes out his jacket, slips into it. Dr. Zarkov pads in from the other room and sits, watching.

CALISTA

Aren't you worried he might have you killed?

(CONTINUED:)

126 CONTINUED:

FLINT
You're business people, not butchers.
No profit in killing me, now that the
diamond is gone. Shall we go?

He starts to come through the door. She doesn't move.

CALISTA
You beat us. How did you beat us?

Flint touches her face gently. She starts at the touch.

FLINT
We don't want to keep the Chairman
waiting.

He goes out, the door rolls down closed and we

CUT TO:

127 EXT. VAULT - MATCH-CUT

MATCH TAMBOUR DOOR IN PREVIOUS SHOT TO ANOTHER DOOR, heavily studded with rivets; the door to a vault. It looks utterly impregnable. Like a bank vault. The door slides into the wall as CAMERA PULLS BACK to show Flint, Calista and the 1st V.P. standing before it. When the door slides away, they stand on the threshold of a small ante-chamber with a second riveted door on the other side. Flint looks at the other two, as if asking silently if they're coming in with him.

CALISTA
We've never been beyond this chamber.
We've never seen him. You'll be
the first.

Flint smiles pleasantly, as if about to take a country stroll, steps inside and the riveted door slides back obscuring him.

128 CLOSE WITH FLINT - COMPUTER ROOM

as the second riveted door slides into the wall in front of him. He walks into a dimly-lit chamber filled from floor-to-ceiling, wall-to-wall, with highly sophisticated computer cabinets. The VOICE of the Chairman fills the chamber.

CHAIRMAN
Welcome, Mr. Flint. I am the Chairman of the Board.

FLINT
I suppose you knew I'd realized you were a computer.

CHAIRMAN
Yes, but precisely when?

FLINT
When I was destroying your headquarters, you seemed to know where I was almost before I got there.

CHAIRMAN
Almost. But not quite.
(beat)
This isn't easy for me, Mr. Flint, but would you mind telling me how you outwitted me?

FLINT
I had already cut the diamond when Miss Griffen captured me. I cut it to the necessary wafer and attached it to the eye of the Death card in the tarot deck at the party. When Miss Griffen took me to the garden, my contact picked up the deck.

CHAIRMAN
So you knew all along.

(CONTINUED:)

128 CONTINUED:

FLINT
(with compassion)
Yes, I'm afraid so.

CHAIRMAN
By allowing us to trap you, by keeping us busy trying to break you, it allowed your contact to get the focusing element to your people in utter safety.

FLINT
Magicians call it misdirection.

CHAIRMAN
And the black diamond focusing element?

FLINT
Already at Cape Kennedy, and installed in the laser-trigger; under very heavy security.

CHAIRMAN
So, in point of fact, I had lost from the first moment I had you.

FLINT
I'm afraid so, yes.

CHAIRMAN
My admiration, Mr. Flint. You are the first human ever to outfox me. I feel like Spassky to your Fischer.

FLINT
You embarrass me. Your gambits were inspired.

CHAIRMAN
But ultimately useless.
(CONT'D.)

(CONTINUED:)

128 CONTINUED: - 2

CHAIRMAN (CONT'D.)
(beat)
You'll be amused to know this encounter has made it necessary for me to re-design almost half my units, not to mention re-programming several hundred miles of tapes and circuits.

FLINT
Have you thought of amortizing it over a five year period?

CHAIRMAN
Ordinarily, I'd consider this a bad business venture, but in the process of your, er, diverting us, you have thoroughly wrecked and demoralized our operation.

All through this exchange, the lights have been flickering and running programs; a kaleidoscope of lights.

CHAIRMAN (CONT'D.)
My stockholders will be terribly upset. It will cost millions to repair the damage to our complex alone.

Flint seems moved by this, genuinely solicitous as he says:

FLINT
I'm terribly sorry. If there's anything I can do to--

The machine clatters, chitters, bongs, lights flash and the illuminated plaque on one console flashes RED and BLINKS ON AND OFF with the words REMOVE CONTENTS as something is deposited in the tray. Flint reaches over and picks it up.

(CONTINUED:)

128 CONTINUED: - 3

CHAIRMAN
Here's a phone number and a dime. If you ever get involved with anything you think we might be interested in, please just give me a call.
(beat)
So I can avoid it.

Flint looks at the computer--which, somehow, seems very sad, very dejected--then down at the card and coin in his hand.

FLINT
(with great gentleness)
Why don't you take off a few weeks. I'm sure things will look brighter after you've had a rest...

The computer clicks furiously, impotently, a little crazily as CAMERA COMES IN for an EXTREME CLOSEUP of Flint's hand, the card and the coin as we

FADE TO BLACK
and
FADE OUT.

THE END

The Man on the Mushroom

The arrival in Hollywood was something less than auspicious. It was February, 1962, and I had broken free of the human monster for whom I'd been editing in Chicago. It was one of the worst times in my life. The one time I'd ever felt the need to go to a psychiatrist, that time in Chicago. I had remarried in haste after the four-year anguish of Charlotte and the Army and the hand-to-mouth days in Greenwich Village. Now I was living to repent in agonizing leisure.

I had been crazed for two years and hadn't realized it. Now I was responsible for one of the nicest women in the world, and her son, a winner by *any* standards, and I found I had messed their lives by entwining them with mine. There was need for me to run, but I could not. Nice Jewish boys from Ohio don't cut and abandon. So I began doing berserk things. I committed personal acts of a demeaning and reprehensible nature, involved myself in liaisons that were doomed and purposeless, went steadily more insane as the days wound tighter than a mainspring.

Part of it was money. Not really, but I thought it was the major part of the solution to the situation. And I'd banked on selling a book of stories to the very man for whom I was working. He took considerable pleasure in waiting till we were at a business lunch, with several other people, to announce he was not buying the book. (The depth of his sadism is obvious when one learns he subsequently *did* buy and publish the book.)

But at the moment, it was as though someone had split the earth under me and left me hanging by the ragged edge, by my fingertips. I went back to the tiny, empty office he had set up in a downtown Evanston office building, and I sat at my desk staring at the wall. There was a clock on the wall in front of me. When I sat down after that terrible lunch, it was 1:00 . . .

When I looked at the clock a moment later, it was 3:15 . . .

The next time I looked, a moment later, it was 4:45 . . .

Then 5:45 . . .

Then 6:15 . . .

7:00 . . . 8:30 . . .

Somehow, I don't know how, even today, I laid my head on the desk, and when I opened my eyes again I had taken the phone off the hook. It was lying beside my mouth. A long time later, and again I don't remember doing it, I dialed a friend, Frank M. Robinson, a dear writer friend of many years.

I heard Frank's voice saying, "Hello . . . hello . . . is someone there . . . ?"

"Frank . . . help me . . ."

And when my head was lifted off the desk, it was an hour later, the phone was whistling with a disconnect tone, and Frank had made it all the way across from Chicago to Evanston to find me. He held me like a child, and I cried.

Soon after, I left Evanston and Chicago and the human monster, and with my wife and her son began the long trek to the West Coast. We had agreed to divorce, but she had said to me, with a very special wisdom that I never perceived till much later, when I was whole again, "As long as you're going to leave me, at least take me to where it's warm."

But we had no money. So we had to go to Los Angeles by way of New York from Chicago. If I could sell a book, I would have the means to go West, young man, go West. (And *that* was the core of the problem, not money: I was a *young* man. I was twenty-eight, but I had never become an adult.)

In a broken-down 1957 Ford we limped across to New York during the worst snowstorms in thirty years. My wife and her son stayed with a friend I'd known in the Village, and I slept on the sofa at the home of Leo & Diane Dillon, the two finest artists I know. Leo & Diane slept on the floor. They are more than merely friends.

It was December of 1961, and amid the tensions and horrors of that eight-week stay in New York, two things happened that brought momentary light, and helped me keep hold:

The first was a review by Dorothy Parker in *Esquire* of a small-printing paperback collection of my stories. How she had obtained it I do not know. (When I met her, later, in Hollywood, she was unable to remember where the book had come from.) But she raved about it, and said I had talent, and it was the first really substantial affirmative notice from a major critic. It altered the course of my writing career, and provided my ego—which had been nourishing itself cannibalistically on itself—with reason for feeling I could write.

The second happening of light was the sale of this book, ELLISON WONDERLAND. Gerry Gross bought it for short money, mostly because he knew I was in a bad way. But it provided the funds to start out for Los Angeles.

We traveled a hard road down through the Southwest, and in Fort Worth we were staved in by a drunken cowboy in a pickup. Rear-ended. He had a carhop on one arm, and a fifth of Teacher's in the free hand. Rammed us on an icy bridge, smashed the car, crushed the rear-end trunk containing our luggage and my typewriter, and I suppose it was that typewriter that saved our lives. The typewriter has paid the rent and put food on the table many times, but that time it physically gave up its life to save me.

We were laid up in Fort Worth for a week, with our money running out. Had it not been for the help of the then-police chief, a man whose name I'll never forget—Cato Hightower—we would never have gotten out of Texas. He got me a new typewriter, had the car repaired for a fraction of what the garage would have stiffed a tourist just passing through and he paid off the motel.

I arrived in Los Angeles in January of 1962 with exactly ten cents in my pocket. For the last three hundred miles we had not eaten. There wasn't enough money for gas *and* food. All we'd had to keep us alive was a box of pecan pralines we'd bought before the accident and had in the rear seat.

The arrival in Hollywood was something less than auspicious.

My almost-ex-wife and her son moved into an apartment, and I took up residence in a fourteen-dollar-a-week room in a bungalow complex that is now an empty lot on Wilshire Boulevard. I tried to get work in television, got some assignments that paid the various rents, and bombed out on all of them. Nobody had bothered to show me how to write a script. And when it looked as though I'd hit the very bottom, ELLISON WONDERLAND was published in June of 1962, the publisher sent me a copy, and the check for the balance of monies due on publication. It was enough to pull me through till I got another assignment—writing *Burke's Law* for the Four Star Studios and ABC. It was the very moment my luck changed.

I remember the morning the mail arrived, with the book in its little manila envelope. I ripped open the package, and out fell the check. But I didn't even look at it. I sat in that room smelling of mildew and stared at the cover of ELLISON WONDERLAND. The artist, Sandy Kossin, had taken a photo of me, and he'd drawn me in sitting cross-legged atop a giant mushroom, while all around me danced and capered the characters from the stories in the book. Skidoop and Ithk and Helgorth

Labbula and the crocodile-headed woman from "The Silver Corrider" and that little jazzbo gnome with the patois now long-outdated and *so* unhip.

There I was. And Hollywood became, for the first time since I'd arrived, not a grungy, lonely, frustrating town whose tinsel could strangle you . . . but a magic town whose sidewalks *were* paved with gold; a yellow brick road leading to a giant mushroom where I could perch if I simply hung in there.

And just to show that fairy tales sometimes *do* have happy endings, dear readers be advised I'm really okay now. There *is* a mushroom, and I'm sitting on it, and I've been writing better here in magic town than I ever did anywhere else, and I'll keep on doing it till I run out of mushroom or magic (and that is *not* a reference to dope, which I don't, so I ain't).

Welcome to *my* world.

Somehow, I Don't Think We're in Kansas, Toto

Six months of my life were spent in creating a dream the shape and sound and color of which had never been seen on television. The dream was called *The Starlost*, and between February and September of 1973 I watched it being steadily turned into a nightmare.

The late Charles Beaumont, a scenarist of unusual talents who wrote many of the most memorable *Twilight Zones*, said to me when I arrived in Hollywood in 1962, "Attaining success in Hollywood is like climbing a gigantic mountain of cow flop, in order to pluck one perfect rose from the summit. And you find when you've made that hideous climb . . . you've lost the sense of smell."

In the hands of the inept, the untalented, the venal and the corrupt, *The Starlost* became a veritable Mt. Everest of cow flop and, though I climbed that mountain, somehow I never lost sight of the dream, never lost the sense of smell, and when it got so rank I could stand it no longer, I descended hand-over-hand from the northern massif, leaving behind $93,000, the corrupters, and the eviscerated remains of my dream. I'll tell you about it.

February. Marty the agent called and said, "Go over to 20th and see Robert Kline."

"Who's Robert Kline?"

"West Coast head of taped syndicated shows. He's putting together a package of mini-series, eight or ten segments per show. He wants to do a science fiction thing. He asked for you. It'll be a co-op deal between 20th Century-Fox and the BBC. They'll shoot it in London."

London! "I'm on my way," I said, the jet-wash of my departure deafening him across the phone connection.

I met Kline in the New Administration Building of 20th, and his first words were so filled with sugar I had the feeling if I listened to him for very long I'd wind up with diabetes: "I wanted the top sf writer in the world," he said. Then he ran through an informed list of my honors in the field of science fiction. It was an impressive performance of the corporate art-form known as ego-massage.

Then Kline advised me that what he was after was, "A sort of *The Fugitive* in Space." Visions of doing a novel-for-television in the mode of *The Prisoner* splatted like overripe casaba melons; I got up and started to walk.

"Hold it, hold it!" Kline said. "What did *you* have in mind?" I sat down again.

Then I ran through half a dozen ideas for series that would be considered primitive concepts in the literary world of sf. Kline found each of them too complex. As a final toss at the assignment, I said, "Well, I've been toying with an idea for tape, rather than film; it could be done with enormous production values that would be financially impossible for a standard filmed series."

"What is it?" he said.

And here's what I told him:

Five hundred years from now, the Earth is about to suffer a cataclysm that will destroy all possibility for life on the planet. Time is short. The greatest minds and the greatest philanthropists get together and cause to have constructed in orbit between the Moon and the Earth, a giant ark, one thousand miles long, comprised of hundreds of self-contained biospheres. Into each of these little worlds is placed a segment of Earth's population, its culture intact. Then the ark is sent off toward the stars, even as the Earth is destroyed, to seed the new worlds surrounding those stars with the remnants of humanity.

But one hundred years after the flight has begun, a mysterious "accident" (which would remain a mystery till the final segment of the show, four year later, it was hoped) kills the entire crew, seals the biosphere-worlds so they have no contact with one another . . . and the long voyage goes on with the people trapped, developing their societies without any outside influence. Five hundred years go by, and the travelers—the Starlost—forget the Earth. To them it is a myth, a vague legend, even as Atlantis is to us. They even forget they are adrift in space, forget they are in an interstellar vessel. Each community thinks it is "the world" and that the world is only fifty square miles, with a metal ceiling.

Until Devon, an outcast in a society rigidly patterned after the Amish communities of times past, discovers the secret, that they are onboard a space-going vessel. He learns the history of the Earth, learns of its destruction, and learns that when "the accident" happened, the astrogation gear of the ark was damaged and now the last seed of humankind is on a collision course with a star. Unless he can convince a sufficient number of biosphere worlds to band together in a communal attempt to learn how the ark works, repair it and re-program their flight, they will soon be incinerated in the furnace of that giant sun toward which they're heading.

It was, in short, a fable of our world today.

"Fresh! Original! New!" Kline chirruped. "There's never been an idea like it before!" I didn't have the heart to tell him the idea was first propounded in astronautical literature in the early 1920s by the great Russian pioneer Tsiolkovsky, nor that the British physicist Bernal had done a book on the subject in 1929, nor that the idea had become *very* common coin in the genre of science fiction through stories by Heinlein, Harrison, Panshin, Simak and many others. (Arthur C. Clarke's then-current bestseller, Rendezvous with Rama, was the latest example of the basic idea.)

Kline suggested I dash home and write up the idea, which he would then merchandise. I pointed out the him that the Writers Guild frowns on speculative writing and that if he wanted the riches of my invention, he should lay on me what we call "holding money" to enable me to write a prospectus and to enable him to blue-sky it with the BBC.

The blood drained from his face at my suggestion of advance money, and he said he had to clear it with the BBC, but that if I wrote the prospectus he would guarantee me a free trip to London. I got up and started to walk.

"Hold it, hold it!" he said, and opened a desk drawer. He pulled out a cassette recorder and extended it. "Tell you what: why don't you just tell it on a cassette, the same way you told it to me." I stopped and looked. This was a new one on me. In over twenty years as a film and television writer, I've seen some of the most circuitous, sleazy, Machiavellian dodges ever conceived by the mind of Western Man to get writers to write on the cuff. But never before, and never since, has anyone been that slippery. It should have been all the tip-off I needed.

I thought on it for a moment, rationalized that this wasn't speculative writing, that at worst it was "speculative talking," and since a writer is expected to pitch an idea anyhow, it was just *barely* legitimate.

So I took the cassette home, backed my spiel with the music from *2001: A Space Odyssey*, outlined the barest bones of the series concept, and brought it back to Kline.

"Okay. Here it is," I said, "but you can't transcribe it. If you do, then it becomes spec writing and you have to pay me." I was assured he wouldn't put it on paper, and that he'd be back to me shortly. He was sure the BBC would go bananas for the idea.

No sooner was I out of his office than he had his secretary transcribe the seven-minute tape.

March. No word.

April. No word.

May. Suddenly there was a flurry of activity. Marty the agent called. "Kline sold the series. Go see him."

"Series?" I said, appalled. "But the idea was only planned to accommodate eight segments . . . a *series,* you say?"

"Go see him."

So I went. Kline greeted me as if I were the only human capable of deciphering the Mayan Codex, and caroled that he had sold the series not only to 48 of the NBC independent stations (what are called the O&O's, Owned & Operated stations), but that the Westinghouse outlets had bitten, and the entire Canadian Television Network, the CTV.

"Uh, excuse me," I said, in an act of temerity not usually attributed to writers in Hollywood, "how did you manage to sell this, er, *series* without having a contract with me, or a prospectus, or a pilot script, or a pilot film . . . or *any*thing?"

"They read your outline, and they bought it on the strength of your name."

"They *read* it? How?"

He circumnavigated that little transgression of his promise not to set my words on paper, and began talking in grandiose terms about how I'd be the story editor, how I'd have creative control, how I'd write many scripts for the show, and what a good time I'd have in Toronto.

"Toronto?!" I said, gawking. "What the hell happened to London? The Sir Lew Grade Studios. Soho. Buckingham Palace. Swinging London. What happened to all that?"

Mr. Kline, without bothering to inform the creator of this hot property he had been successfully hawking, had been turned down by the BBC and had managed to lay off the project with CTV, as an all-Canadian production of Glen Warren, a Toronto-based operation that was already undertaking to tape *The Starlost* at the CFTO Studios in Toronto. It was assumed by Mr. Kline that I would move to Toronto to story edit the series; he never bothered to ask if I *wanted* to move to Canada, he just assumed I would.

Mr. Kline was a real bear for assuming things.

Such as: I would write *his* series (which was the way he now referred to it) even though a writers' strike was imminent. I advised him that if the strike hit, I would be incommunicado, but he waved away my warnings with the words, "Everything will work out." With such words, Napoleon went to Elba.

At that time I was a member of the Board of Directors of the Writers Guild of America, West and I was very pro-union, pro-strike, pro-getting long overdue contract inequities with the producers straightened out.

Just before the strike began, Kline called and said he was taking out advertisements for the series. He said he'd had artwork done for the presentations, and he needed some copy to accompany the drawings.

I asked him how he could have artwork done when the spaceship had not yet been designed (I was planning to create a vessel that would be absolutely feasible and scientifically correct, in conjunction with Ben Bova, then-editor of *Analog*.) Kline said there wasn't time for all that fooling-around, ads had to go out *now*!

It has always been one of the imponderables of the television industry to me, how the time is always *now*, when three day earlier no one had even *heard* of the idea.

But I gave him some words and, to my horror, saw the ad a week later: it showed a huge bullet-shaped *thing* I guess Kline thought was a spaceship, being smacked by a meteorite, a great hole being torn in the skin of the bullet, revealing many levels of living space within . . . all of them drawn the wrong direction. I covered my eyes.

Let me pause for a moment to explain why this was a scientifically-illiterate, wholly incorrect piece of art, because it was merely the first indication of how little the producers of *The Starlost* understood what they were doing. Herewith, a Child's Primer of Science Fiction:

There is no air in space. Space is very nearly a vacuum. That means an interstellar vessel, since it won't be landing anywhere, and doesn't need to be designed for passage through atmosphere, can be designed any way that best follows the function. The last time anyone used the bullet design for a starship was in *The Green Slime*, circa 1969 (a Nipponese nifty that oozes across the "Late Late Late Show" in the wee'est hours when normal folks are sleeping; this excludes systems analysts and computer programmers, of course).

But it indicated the lack of understanding of sf that is commonplace among television executives who, for the most part, have not read an entire book since they left high school.

Look: if you turn on your set and see a pair of white swinging doors suddenly slammed open by a gurney pushed by two white-smocked interns, you know that within moments Trapper John, M.D. (or Ben Casey, or Dr. Kildare, or Marcus Welby) will be jamming a tube down somebody's trachea; if you see a snake-eyed dude in a black Stetson lying-out on a butte, aiming a Sharps .52 caliber buffalo rifle, you know that within moments the Wells, Fargo stage is gonna come a-thunderin' down that dusty trail; if Dan Tana (or Mannix, or Jim Rockford, or Ironside) comes into his inner office and there's a silky lady lounging in the chair across from his desk, showing a lot of leg, you know that by the end of Act One someone is going to try ventilating his (or Magnum's) hide. It's all by rote, all templates, all stolen from what went before by a generation of writers and producers whose only referents are what they grew up with watching television; it's all cliché, all predictable.

And while I make no brief for the reams and volumes of low-grade, moronic *Star Wars* imitation space opera hackwork that has turned this into the worst period in the history of sf, the genre is *not* predictable. Or at least it shouldn't be.

(Though shit like *Battlestar Ponderosa* and Universal's *Buck Rogers* seems to assure us that the steamroller mediocrity of tv can even trivialize sf, despite the built-in deterrents.)

A science fiction story has to have interior logic. It has to be consistent, even within the boundaries of its own extrapolative horizons. That's irreducible in the parameters of what a sf story or teleplay must do, in order to get the reader or viewer to go along with it, without feeling conned or duped or lied to. Rigorous standards of plotting *must* be employed to win that willing suspension of disbelief on the part of the audience; it allows them to accept a fantastic premise.

How many sf movies have you seen—*Outland, Message From Space, Silent Running* are perfect awful examples—during which you recognized sophomoric inaccuracies that made you groan and feel cheated? Errors that first-year science students would not make: sound in a vacuum, people walking around on alien planets without filtration masks, clones that spring fully grown from fingernail parings, robots that act like midgets in metal suits.

Break that logical chain, dumb it up, accept the insulting myth that no one knows or cares if the special effects are spectacular enough, and the whole thing falls apart like Watergate testimony.

But the ad was only an early storm warning of what troubles were yet to befall me. The strike was called, and then began weeks of a kind of ghastly harassment I'd always thought was reserved for overblown melodramas about the Evils of Hollywood. Phone calls at all hours, demanding I write the "bible" for the series. (A "bible" is industry shorthand for the *précis* of what the show will do, who the characters are, what directions storylines should take. In short, the blueprint from which individual segments are written. Without a bible, only the creator knows what the series is about.) Kline had no bible. He had nothing, at this point, but that seven-minute tape. With which item, plus my name and the name of Doug Trumbull—who, at that time had done the special effects for *2001* and had directed *Silent Running*—he'd been signed on as Executive Producer—Kline had—sans a contract with me!—sold this pipe dream to everyone in the Western World.

But I wouldn't write the bible. I was on strike. Then began the threats. Followed by the intimidation, the bribes, the promises that they'd go forward with the idea without me, the veiled hints of scab writers who'd be hired to write their own version of the series . . . everything short of actually kidnapping me. Through these weeks—when even flights out of Los Angeles to secluded hideaways in the Michigan wilds and the northern California peninsula failed to deter the phone calls—I refused to write. It didn't matter that the series might not get on the air, it didn't matter that I'd lose a potload of money, the Guild was on strike in a noble cause and, besides, I didn't much trust Mr. Kline and the anonymous voices that spoke to me in the wee hours of the night. And, contrary to popular belief, many television writers are men and women of ethic: they can be rented, but they can't be bought.

I remember seeing a film of Clifford Odets's *The Big Knife* when I was a young writer living in New York and lusting after fame in Hollywood. I remember seeing the unscrupulous Steiger and his minions applying pressure to a cracking Palance, to get him to sign a contract, and I remember smiling at the danger-filled melodramatics. During that period of pre-production on *The Starlost*, I ceased smiling.

The threats ranged from breaking my typing fingers to ensuring I'd never work in the Industry again. The bribes ranged from $13,000 to be placed in an unnumbered Swiss bank account to this:

One afternoon before the strike, I'd been in Kline's office. I'd been leafing through the PLAYERS DIRECTORY, the trade publications that list all actors and actresses, with photos. I'd commented idly that I found the person of one pictured young starlet quite appealing. Actually, what I'd said was that I'd sell my soul to get it on with her.

Now, weeks later, during my holdout and Kline's attempts to get me to scab, I was pottering about my house, when the doorbell rang. I went to the door, opened it, and there stood the girl of my wanton daydreams. Bathed in sunlight, a palpable nimbus haloing that gorgeous face. I stood openmouthed, unable even to invite her in.

"I was in the neighborhood," she said, entering the house with no assistance from me, "and I've heard so much about you, I decided just to come and say hello."

She said hello. I said something unintelligible. (I have the same reaction when standing in front of Picasso's *Guernica*. Otherworldly beauty has a way of turning my brains to prune-whip yogurt.) But it took only a few minutes of conversation to ascertain that yes, she knew Mr. Kline and, yes, she knew about the series, and . . .

I wish I could tell you I used her brutally and sent her back to where I assumed she had come from, but feminism has taken its toll and I merely asked her to split.

She split.

I couldn't watch any tv that night. My eyes were too swollen from crying.

And the cajoling went on. Kline, of course, knew *nothing* about the girl, had never had anything to do with sending her over, would be affronted if anyone even *suggested* he had tried such a loathsome, demeaning trick. Hell, I'd be the *last* one to suggest it. Or maybe second from the last.

But howzabout the scab writer threat? Well . . .

At one point, representatives of Mr. Kline *did* bring in a scab. A non-union writer to whom they imparted a series of outright lies so he'd believe he was saving my bacon. When they approached well-known sf writer Robert Silverberg to write the bible, Bob asked them point-blank, "Why isn't Harlan writing it?" They fumfuh'd and said, well, er, uh, he's on strike. Bob said, "Would he want me to write this?" They knew he'd call me, and they told him no, I'd be angry. So he passed up some thousands of dollars, and they went elsewhere. And this being the kind of world it is, they found a taker.

I found out about the end-run, located the writer in a West LA hotel where they'd secreted him, writing madly through a weekend, and I convinced him he shouldn't turn in the scab bible. To put the period to the final argument that Kline & Co. were not being honest, I called Kline from that hotel room while the other writer listened in on the bathroom extension phone. I asked Kline point-blank if other writers had been brought in to scab. He said no; he assured me they were helplessly waiting out the strike till I could bring the purity of my original vision to the project. I thanked him, hung up, and looked at the other writer who had just spent 72 hours beating his brains out writing a scab bible. "I rest my case."

"Let's go to the Writers Guild," he said.

It drove Kline bananas. Everywhichway he turned, I was there, confounding his shabby attempts at circumventing an honest strike.

I'll skip a little now. The details were ugly, but grow tedious in the re-telling. It went on at hideous length, for weeks. Finally, Glen Warren in Toronto, at Kline's urging, managed to get the Canadian writers guild, ACTRA, to accept that *The Starlost* was a wholly Canadian-produced series. They agreed that was the case, after much pressure was applied in ways I'm not legally permitted to explicate, and I was finally convinced I should go to work.

That was my next mistake.

They had been circulating copies of the scab bible with all of its erroneous material, and had even given names to the characters. When I finally produced the authentic bible, for which they'd been slavering so long, it confused everyone. They'd already begun building sets and fashioning materiel that had nothing to do with the show.

I was brought up to Toronto, to work with writers, and because the producing entity would get government subsidies if the show was clearly acceptable in terms of "Canadian content" (meaning the vast majority of writers, actors, directors and production staff had to be Canadian), I was ordered to assign script duties to Canadian tv writers.

I sat in the Four Seasons Motel in Toronto in company with a man named Bill Davidson, who had been hired as the Producer even though he knew nothing about science fiction and seemed thoroughly confused by the bible, and interviewed dozens of writers from 9 AM till 7 PM.

It is my feeling that one of the prime reasons for the artistic (and, it would seem, ratings) failure of *The Starlost* was the quality of the scripts. But it isn't as simple a matter as saying the Canadians aren't good writers, which is the cop-out Glen Warren and Kline used. Quite the opposite is true. The Canadian writers I met were bright, talented, and anxious as hell to write good shows.

Unfortunately, because of the nature of Canadian tv, which is vastly different than American tv, they had virtually no experience writing episodic drama as we know it. ("Train them," Kline told me. "Train a cadre of writers?" I said, stunned. "Sure," said Kline, who knew nothing about writing, "it isn't hard." No, not if I wanted to make it my life's work.) And, for some peculiar reason, with only two exceptions I can think of, there are *no* Canadian sf writers.

But they were willing to work their hearts out to do good scripts. Sadly, they didn't have the kind of freaky minds it takes to plot sf stories with originality and logic. There were the usual number of talking plant stories, giant ant stories, space pirate stories, westerns transplanted to alien environments, the Adam-&-Eve story, the after-the-Bomb story . . . the usual clichés people who haven't been trained to think in fantasy terms conceive of as fresh and new.

Somehow, between Ben Bova and myself–Ben having been hired after I made it abundantly clear that I needed a specialist to work out the science properly–we came up with ten script ideas, and assigned them. We knew there would be massive rewrite problems, but I was willing to work with the writers, because they were energetic and anxious to learn. Unfortunately, such was not the case with Davidson and the moneymen from 20th, NBC, Glen Warren and the CTV, who were revamping and altering arrangements daily, in a sensational imitation of The Mad Caucus Race from ALICE IN WONDERLAND.

I told the Powers in charge that I would need a good assistant story editor who could do rewrites, because I was not about to spend the rest of my natural life in a motel in Toronto, rewriting other people's words. They began to scream. One gentleman came up to the room and banged his fist on the desk while I was packing to split, having received word a few hours earlier that my mother was very ill in Florida. He *told* me I was going to stay there in that room till the first drafts of the ten scripts came in. He *told* me that I was going to write the pilot script in that room and not leave till it was finished. He *told* me I could go home but would be back on such-and-such a date. He *told* me that was my schedule.

I *told* him if he didn't get the hell out of my room I was going to clean his clock for him.

Then he went away, still screaming; Ben Bova returned to New York; I went to see my mother, established that she was somehow going to pull through, returned to Los Angeles; and sat down to finish writing the pilot script.

This was June already. Or was it July. Things blur. In any case, it was only weeks away from airdate debut, and they didn't even have all the principals cast. Not to mention the special effects Trumbull had promised, which weren't working out. The production staff under the confused direction of Davidson was doing a dandy impression of a Balinese Fire & Boat Drill; Kline was still madly dashing about selling something that didn't exist to people who apparently didn't care what they were buying; and I was banging my brains out writing "Phoenix Without Ashes," the opening segment that was to limn the direction of the single most expensive production ever attempted in Canada.

I was also brought up on charges by the Writers Guild for writing during the strike.

I called Marty the agent and threatened him with disembowelment if he ever again called me to say, "Go see Bob Kline." In my personal lexicon, the word "kline" could be found along with "eichmann," "dog catcher," "cancer" and "rerun."

But I kept writing. I finished the script and got it off to Canada with only one interruption of note:

The name Norman Klenman had been tossed at me frequently in Toronto by the CTV representative and Davidson and, of course, by Kline and his minions. Klenman, I was told, was the answer to my script problems. He was a Canadian writer who had fled to the States for the larger money, and since he was actually a Canadian citizen who was familiar with writing American series tv, he would be acceptable to the tv board in Ottawa under the terms of "Canadian content" and yet would be a top-notch potential for scripts that need not be heavily rewritten. I was too dazed in Toronto to think about Klenman.

But as I sat there in Los Angeles writing my script, I received a call from Mr. Klenman, who was at that moment in Vancouver. "Mr. Ellison," he said, politely enough, "this is Norman Klenman. Bill Davidson wanted me to call you about *The Starlost*. I've read your bible and, frankly, I find it very difficult and confusing . . . I don't understand science fiction . . . but if you want to train me, and pay me the top-of-the-show money the Guild just struck for, I'll be glad to take a crack at a script for you." I thanked him and said I'd get back to him when I'd saved my protagonist from peril at the end of act four.

When I walked off the show, the man they hired not only as story editor to replace me, but to rewrite *my* script, as well, was Norman Klenman who "don't understand science fiction."

My walkout on my brain child, and all that pretty fame and prettier money, was well in the wind by the time of Klenman's call, but I was still intending to write the scripts I'd contracted for, when the following incidents happened, and I knew it was all destined for the ashcan.

I was in Dallas. Guest of honor at a convention where I was trying to summon up the gall to say *The Starlost* would be a dynamite series.

I was paged in the lobby. Phone call from Toronto. It was Bill Davidson. The conversation describes better than ten thousand more words what was wrong with the series:

"Major problems, Harlan," Davidson said. Panic lived in his voice.

"Okay, tell me what's the matter," I said.

"We can't shoot a fifty-mile-in-diameter biosphere on the ship."

"Why?"

"Because it looks all fuzzy on the horizon."

"Look out the window, Bill. Everything *is* fuzzy on the horizon."

"Yeah, but on tv it all gets muddy in the background. We're going to have to make it a six-mile biosphere."

"Whaaaat?!"

"Six miles is the best we can do."

There is a pivotal element in the pilot script where the hero manages to hide out from a lynch mob. In a fifty mile biosphere that was possible. In a six mile biosphere all they had to do was link arms and walk across it. "But, Bill, that means I'll have to rewrite the entire script."

"Well, that's the best we can do."

Then, in a blinding moment of *satori* I realized Davidson was wrong, dead wrong; his thinking was so limited he was willing to scrap the logic of the script rather than think it through. "Bill," I said, "who can tell the difference on a tv screen, whether the horizon is six miles away or fifty? And since we're showing them an enclosed world that's never existed before, why *shouldn't* it look like that! Shoot *de facto* six miles and call it fifty; it doesn't make any damned difference!"

There was a pause, then, "I never thought of that."

Only one indication of the unimaginative, hidebound and obstinately arrogant thinking that emerged from total unfamiliarity with the subject, proceeded through mistake after mistake, and foundered on the rocks of inability to admit confusion.

The conversation went on with Davidson telling me that even if Trumbull's effect didn't work and they couldn't shoot a fifty mile biosphere—after he'd just admitted that it didn't matter *what* distance they said they were showing—I'd simply *love* the set they were building of the control room.

"You're building the *control* room?" I said, aghast with confusion and disbelief. "But you won't need that till the last segment of the series. Why are you building it now?"

(It should be noted that one of the Maltese Falcons of the series, one of the prime mysteries, is the location of the control room biosphere. When they find it, they can put the ark back on course. If they find it in the first segment, it automatically becomes the shortest tv series in history.)

"Because you had it in your bible," he explained.

"That was intended to show how the series *ended*, for God's sake!"

I admit I was screaming at that point. "If they find it first time out, we can all pack our bags and play an hour of recorded organ music!"

"No, no," Davidson argued, "they still have to find the back-up computer, don't they?"

"Aaaaarghh," I aaaaarghhed. "Do you have even the faintest scintilla of an idea what a back-up control *is*?"

"Uh, I'm not certain. Isn't it the computer at the back of the ship?"

"It's a fail-safe system, you drooling imbecile; it's what they use if the primary fails. The primary is the control . . . oh to hell with it!" I hung up.

When I returned to Los Angeles, I found matters had degenerated even farther. They were shooting a six mile biosphere and *calling* it six miles. They said no one would notice the discrepancy in the plot. They were building the control room, with that arrogant ignorance that could not be argued with. Ben Bova, who was the technical advisor, had warned them they were going about it in the wrong way; they nodded their heads . . . and ignored him.

Then Klenman rewrote me. Oh boy.

As an indication of the level of mediocrity they were seeking, "Phoenix Without Ashes" had been retitled, in one of the great artistic strokes of all time, "Voyage of Discovery." I sent them word they would have to take my name off the show as creator and as writer of that segment. But they would have to use my pseudonym, to protect my royalties and residuals. (They had screwed up my creation, but I'd be damned if I'd let them profit from the rape.)

Davidson reluctantly agreed. He knew the Writers Guild contract guaranteed me that one last weapon. "What's your pen-name, we'll use it, what is it?"

"Cordwainer Bird," I said. "That's b-i-r-d, as in 'for the birds.'"

Now *he* was screaming. He swore they'd fight me, they'd never use it, I was denying them the use of my name that was so valuable with science fiction fans. Never! Never!

God bless the Writers Guild.

If you tuned in the show before it vanished from all earthly ken you saw a solo credit card that said

CREATED BY CORDWAINER BIRD

and that's your humble servant saying the Visigoths won again.

Bova walked off the series the week after Trumbull left, because of scientific illiteracies he'd warned them against, such as "radiation virus" (which is an impossibility . . . radiation is a matter of atoms, viruses are biological entities, even as you and I and Kline and Davidson, I presume), "space senility" (which, I guess, means old, feeble, blathering vacuum), and "solar star" (which is a terrific illiterate redundancy like saying "I live in a big house home").

The Starlost came up a loser as do *most* tv series. Because they don't understand the materials with which they have to work, because they are so tunnel-visioned into thinking every dramatic series can be transliterated from the prosaic and overfamiliar materials of cop, doctor and cowboy shows, because there was so much money to be skimmed . . . another attempt at putting something fresh and innovative on the little screen came up a loser.

Is mine an isolated bit of history? A case of sour grapes attributable to the intransigent nature of a writer whose credentials come red-stamped with the warning that he is a troublemaker? Hardly.

In *TV Guide* in October of 1964 the excellent Merle Miller told in detail how his series *Calhoun* had come a cropper. In February of 1971, again in *TV Guide*, the well-known sf author and historian James Gunn related how they leavened and dumbed *The Immortal* out of existence after fifteen weeks. Through the years, right up to the 1981 anthology series *Dark Room*—suicidally placed opposite first *The Dukes of Hazzard* and then moved to a primetime spot facing *Dallas* by ABC—which was canceled after six airings, the story is the same. This time it was my turn, that's all.

Have you, gentle reader, learned anything from this *angst*? Probably not. Viewers seem not to care about authenticity, accuracy, logic, literacy, inventiveness. Friends call me when they see reruns of *The Starlost* in Canada, and they tell me how much they like it. I snarl and hang up on them.

The upshot of all the foregoing was precisely what I had predicted when I cut out of that deranged scene. NBC had gone into the series with a guarantee of sixteen episodes firm, and an almost guaranteed pickup option for eight more. But the ratings were so low, in virtually every city where the series was aired—sometimes running opposite the nine thousandth rerun of *I Love Lucy* or scintillating segments of *Zen Archery for the Millions*—that NBC bailed out after the first sixteen.

The shows were so disgracefully inept, so badly acted, uniformly directed with the plunging breakneck pace of a quadruple amputee crossing a busy intersection, based in confusion and plotted on the level of a McGuffey's primer . . . that when the show was canceled after sixteen weeks, there were viewers who never knew it was missing.

When it was dumped, and I got the word from a contact at the network, I called one of Kline's toadies, and caroled my delight. "What the hell are *you* so damned happy about," he said, "you just lost a total of $93,000 in participation profits."

"It's *worth* ninety-three thousand bucks to see you fuckers go down the toilet," I said.

But even though I fell down that rabbit-hole in TV Land and found, like Dorothy, that it wasn't Kansas, or any other place that resembled the real world, I have had several moments of bright and lovely retribution-cum-vindication.

At one point, when the roof started falling in on them, they called Gene Roddenberry, the successful creator of *Star Trek*, and they offered him fifty percent of the show if he'd come up and produce the show out of trouble for them. Gene laughed at them and said what did he need fifty percent of a loser for, he had 100% of two winners of his own. They said they could understand that, but did he have someone else in mind whom he could recommend as producer? Gene said, sure he did.

They made the mistake of asking him who.

He said, "Harlan Ellison. If you hadn't fucked him over so badly, he could have done a good job for you."

Then *he* hung up on them.

Which is just what the viewers did.

The second bright moment was when the trial board of the Writers Guild judged me Not Guilty of scabbing. It was a unanimous decision by some of the finest writers in Hollywood, and I was reinstated on the WGAw Board of Directors thereafter. Nonetheless, were I ever to forgive the thugs and fools who took the labor of a year and corrupted it so completely that I felt nothing but shame and fury for a long time after, I can never forgive them for placing me in such jeopardy with the craft guild to which I proudly belong. More than likely, had my efforts to thwart and circumvent 20th Century–Fox's anti-strike efforts in producing the series not been so blatant, and so infuriatingly effective to Kline and his superiors, I might well have been tagged with that most vile and inexcusable sobriquet: scab. There is no forgiveness in me for that part of the monstrous history of *The Starlost*.

But the brightest moment of all came on March 21st, 1974 when I became the first person in the history of the Writers Guild of America to win the Most Outstanding Teleplay award for the third time, with the *original version* of the pilot teleplay for *The Starlost*, "Phoenix Without Ashes."

The *original* script, my words, my dream; not the emasculated and insipid drivel that was aired; but *my* work, as I wrote it, before the trolls fucked it over; *that* screenplay won the highest writers' award Hollywood can give.

In the category of "best dramatic-episodic script," meaning continuing series, as opposed to anthologies or comedies, there were eight nominees out of 400 top submissions: four segments of *The Waltons*, a *Gunsmoke*, a *Marcus Welby* and an episode of *Streets of San Francisco*. And my original teleplay . . . selected as the best for the year 1973.

It should be noted that unlike Emmys and Oscars, which are political in nature, are bought and sold and lobbyed for with hundreds of thousands of dollars being spent in trade paper advertisements by studios and networks that realize the box-office value of such popularity prizes, the WGA Awards are given *solely* on the basis of written material; in blind judging with the names of the authors removed, by three tiers of blue-ribbon readers (most of whom are previous winners) whose identities are kept strictly secret.

When I accepted the Award at the 26th Annual Awards Reception and Banquet in Hollywood, I said, in part, "If the fuckers want to rewrite you . . . smash them!"

But even had I not received such vindication from my peers, I know damned well that the loss of $93,000 was not the vain and foolish gesture of a nit-picker. That Award is the rose I've plucked from the summit of the mountain of cow flop *The Starlost* became.

Nor have I lost my sense of smell. A writer has only his or her talent, determination and imagination to pit against the winter of mediocrity Hollywood generates. Good writers die here, not from too much cocaine, or too much high living, or even too much money. For, in the words of Saul Bellow, "Writers are not necessarily corrupted by money. They are distracted—diverted to other avenues." They die in pieces, their talent and thus their souls turned sere and juiceless. Until they are fit for nothing better than to bend to the whims of businessmen with a stranglehold on the art-form.

It is a writer's obligation to his craft to go to bed angry, and to rise up angrier the next day. To fight for the words because, at final moments, that's all a writer has to prove his right to exist as a spokesman for his times. To retain the sense of smell; to know what one smells is the corruption of truth and not the perfumes of Araby.

Whether in a fifty-mile-across biosphere, in Oz, in Kansas or in Hollywood.

Face-Down in Gloria Swanson's Swimming Pool

By the eleventh day of the Ohio lecture tour I was drawing big, sprawling crowds of students. The auditorium of Wittenberg College in Springfield was jammed, right up to the balcony. (Where, later in the evening's festivities, a Jesus Freak would leap up, scream that I was "the Anti-Christ, doing the Devil's Work," flick her Bic, set fire to her Little Orphan Annie hair, and rush out of the auditorium with her friends beating at her head.) It was Wednesday, October 3rd, 1973, and I had been a resident of Los Angeles for eleven years.

There I stood on the platform in Springfield, Ohio—dead in the center, according to the U.S. Environmental Protection Agency, of the geographic belt of greatest density of air pollution in the United States—and this kid with rheumy eyes, sallow skin, pustules and running sores yells up from the audience, "How can you live in Los Angeles with all that pollution?"

And I look down at him, and I hear myself saying, "Are you kidding, running that kinda okeydoke past me? You live in the same state with Dayton, top of the Clean Air Commission's Pure Death Locale chart. How can I live in Elay? It's easy, brother! I look out my living room window through the saddle of the Santa Monica Mountains, fifteen miles straight across the San Fernando Valley to the San Gabriel Range, and three hundred out of every three hundred and sixty-five days of the year I can *see* those mountains—sometimes fuzzily . . . but I *see* 'em! I was in downtown Springfield today, and I couldn't see the bank building on the corner of the next block!

"In Los Angeles, in the space of a week, I can talk to Randy Newman, Ray Bradbury, Howard Fast, Carol Connors, Bucky Fuller, Gunther Schiff, Ralph Bakshi, Dorothy Fontana, Louise Farr, Richard Dreyfuss, Richard Matheson, Christopher Knopf, Richard Brooks and Michael

Crichton. I'd have talked to people here in Springfield today, but I couldn't pry them loose from their television sets!

"In Los Angeles I can eat lomito saltado at Macchu Picchu, moussaka vegetarian at Mischa's, sizzling rice three-flavor soup at Golden China, beef molé at Antonio's, zucchini florentine at Musso & Frank's, besuga al horno at La Masia, steamed clams and abalone steak at Mel's Landing, the best barbecue this side of the House of Blue Lights at Dr. Hogly Wogly's Tyler Texas Pit BBQ, the Poliakov Special at Chez Puce, Mont Blanc at the Paprika and a terrific noodle kuchel at Hamburger Hamlet. I went out for a bite to eat here in Springfield and had to arm-wrestle the waitress at the Toddle House best two-out-of-three to get my cheeseburger well-done without any mayonnaise on it!

"In Los Angeles I've got my choice of a thousand different bookstores, from A Change of Hobbit, where they stock every science fiction book since Lucian of Samosata, to Boulevard Books and the Scene of the Crime, where I can find Cornell Woolrich and Richard Stark and Anthony Boucher if I feel like a little mayhem. Needham Bookfinders and Barry Levin and Pickwick and World Book & News on Cahuenga are regular watering-holes for me. I have 37,000 books in my house, and I need a ten-book-a-day fix just to keep me going. Here in Springfield, if I need something to pass the interminable evenings, the best I can do is inspirational literature left in the motel desk or go to the A&P for one of those LOVE'S TENDER FURY abominations.

"In Los Angeles . . ."

And I stopped.

The implausibility of it hit me like an 18-wheeler on the Grapevine. Here I was, a refugee from (ironically) Ohio, dragged by the nose to Los Angeles eleven years earlier, hating the mere thought of living in the town that had killed Scott Fitzgerald, swearing I'd be back in New York inside a month . . . more than a decade later standing on a lecture platform in (ironically) *Ohio*, running a Chamber of Commerce panegyric to the wonders and deliciousness of the City of Angels.

What hath God wrought? I thought. *Without even noticing, I've become an Angeleno!*

When my New York literary agent, Bob Mills, said to me in 1961, "You've got to go to California. You'll never be able to live the way you want to live, and be free to write what you want to write, unless you crack films and make enough during the year to buy free time for writing the books," when he said that to me, the first image that flooded into my head was William Holden lying face-down in Gloria Swanson's swimming pool in *Sunset Boulevard*.

And washing right along behind that vision were all the ghastly scenes from *Day of the Locust, The Loved One, What Makes Sammy Run?, The Slide Area, The Big Knife, The Last Tycoon* and *Flash and Filigree*. I conjured up rampaging nightmares of good writers clubbed to their knees—as I had always believed—by Hollywood: Horace McCoy, Dashiell Hammett, Fitzgerald, Nathanael West, Dorothy Parker. And I shivered with fear.

"No, no," I pleaded, "don't make me go to Los Angeles! I'll turn into a pillar of Waldo Salt! My hair's too fine to take a blonde rinse, and I can't even ice skate, how the hell you think I'm gonna learn to surf?"

And always, Bill Holden as that indigent Hollywood screenwriter, Joe Gillis, spread-eagled and waterlogged in Norma Desmond's befouled swimming pool. What a horrendous metaphor!

But I was chivvied into coming. And eleven years later I stood on a platform in Ohio and said, "And even if all that good stuff weren't true of only Los Angeles, even if you had it all here . . . I'd still be in *L.A.*, man, and you'd still be in Springfield!"

And now it is sixteen years since I motored into Hollywood with ten cents in my pocket, driving a '57 Ford that was gasping its last, and I am here to tell you: this is a *dynamite* town.

I've lived all over the place. Painesville, Ohio; Louisville, Kentucky; New York; Chicago; New Orleans; Shelby, North Carolina; Paris and London. And while London is a fast second-place to this burg, if I were to rummage around in the stock of America's leading Art Deco dealer H. Frank Jones (who just *happens* to be right here in Los Angeles) and came up with an original Lalique magic lamp, and rubbed it to bring up the patina, and out came this dyspeptic genie who'd grant me any wish I desired, I wouldn't ask him to let me live anywhere but here!

Los Angeles is the cutting edge of the culture, despite the claims and pretensions of San Francisco and New York and Boston and Washington. It has all the verve and dynamism that I found in New York when I went there in 1950. Verve and dynamism that New York has lost, that Chicago wanted and for which it substituted brutality and angst, that New Orleans is afraid to let loose. For me, L.A. is like a big, gauche baby with a shotgun in its mouth. It'll do *any*thing. And with more style, with more fire, with more Errol Flynn go-to-hell vivacity than any other city I've ever experienced.

As for what L.A. does to an artist, it's all bullshit about the death of creativity out here in the vanilla sunshine. In sixteen years I've written nineteen books, a dozen movies and more television than I care to think about, even now that I've renounced that lousy medium. Everything that's made a reputation for me . . . I wrote while living here . . . or on the way back to here. If Fitzgerald bought the plot while out here, it was because he did it to himself. Oh, it's easy enough to go for the sparkle and the dazzle (hell, I even worked for Aaron Spelling for a little while), but anyone who wants to work out here can find the most salutary environment in the world.

Is it slower than New York? That's what a few visitors from the Apple tell me. As I dance circles around them, watching them sneer and badmouth in slow-motion. The hours are longer here, the moments fuller, and no one here would tolerate for a moment the kind of three-hour business lunches they take in Manhattan. This is a working town. Ask Betsy Pryor or Phil Mishkin or Larry Niven.

And when they talk about wacko, back East, and they say L.A. is Cloud-Cuckoo-Land, I smile. Because all that weirdness is upstate in San Francisco. Sure, we get our occasional dingbats like Charlie Manson and the Hillside Strangler, but have you noticed, they're always schmucks who've come here from somewhere else and never really integrated? Is L.A. all plastic, without soul? Sure, if you come to visit and stay in Garden Grove or go to Anaheim. But if you want soul, just drive down to Watts and look at that testament to one human being's indomitability and creative purpose, the Towers of Simon Rodia. Soul? I'll give you soul: Pink's hot dogs, better than Nathan's; the Century City riot against the War in Vietnam; Prop 13 and that incredible old curmudgeon Howard Jarvis; Kent Bash's paintings; Jeremy Tarcher's regional success as a publisher against all the odds; Gypsy Boots; Art Kunkin and Brian Kirby's days at the *Free Press*; the best rye bread and coconut rum bars in the world at Brown's Victory Bakery; Auracle playing at Dante's; living in Laurel Canyon; kids streaming down from Pepperdine to help Burgess Meredith save his house at Malibu when the Pacific opened its maw; the Beverely Glen art fair every year.

Sixteen years, and every time I get off a plane at LAX, having been out there somewhere else, I find myself grinning and saying, "Thank God I'm home." An Angeleno. How 'bout that.

And I even met Gloria Swanson once. She was charming and warm and thoroughly magnificent. But, uh, old fears die hard; and I somehow didn't follow up on her invitation to come visit at her home. I don't even know if she's *got* a swimming pool.

XI

PETARDS & HANGINGS

> "Are you aware of how much pain there is in the world?"
>
> —"Your Basic Crown of Thorns," New Introduction to PAINGOD AND OTHER DELUSIONS, Pyramid, 1975

Disasters are the bane (and drama) of humanity. Vesuvius and Krakatoa, the 14th century Black Death, the regularity of famines, fires, floods and earthquakes, leave us with a resigned but still undefeated attitude about Earth's occasional show of instability. We seek to control the natural disasters as best we can, but how valiantly do we seek to cancel the unnatural ones?

Pollution, war, racial hatred and social ostracism, the uncontrolled greed of capitalism and the ruthless limitations of communism: these are disasters of human origin that make Earth's curses seem no more than weak ripples in the lake of Time. Today it may appear patriotic to remain blind to our sins in the name of national security and stabilization, but we aren't so far beyond the tragedies of World War II and Vietnam that we can't see the burning fuse and the coming explosion of tomorrow.

All we have to do is open our eyes.

There has not been a moment of Harlan's career in which he was not concerned with the horrors of the human race's punishment of itself. These stories look at the agonies and ask us point blank if we can tolerate such atrocities. Illness can strike us down singly or in great numbers, but Harlan has developed fictional vaccinations for the physical symptoms and psychological shock treatments for the mental disorders.

"Soldier" (1957) is an early and crudely drawn anti-war polemic that strains our credibility with its strange mix of violence and optimism. Yet it is an important work by which to gauge Harlan's dedication to the motive of a concerted resistance to evil and our ability to elevate our noble goodness. In 1964, he adapted the story as an episode of the television anthology series *The Outer Limits*, and while the details of the plot were quite different, the message remained intact.

The small tensions are often more motivating than the grand outbursts, as "The Night of Delicate Terrors" (1961) admirably demonstrates. Harlan has never been less than vehement in his loathing of racial prejudice, and the reader who takes this story's quiet, laid-back atmosphere as a tentative or unsure gesture on the author's part is suffering from grand-outburst conditioning. It is a quiet story, but the structure is steel and the intimations are crucial.

The danger of human error doesn't always stem from preconceived prejudice handed down the generations. New errors are made, sometimes in the midst of our rejection of old errors. "Shattered Like a Glass Goblin" (1968) came as a surprise to the young people who were pushing for a revolution against Establishment practices of the 1960s, for it seemed to reject their search of self and the exploration of alternatives. In actuality, Harlan was rejecting the method rather than the goal, once again realizing the fatal consequence of any misstep as we traveled along the dangerous precipice of independence.

Robert Silverberg, who bought and published "At the Mouse Circus" (1971), called it Harlan's "deepest trip yet into surrealism." The dreamlike events and images have a surreal quality, but the unmasking of venality, covetousness and the symbols of social status is so uncompromising that we can almost hear the swish of the noose as it swings down over our necks. And that ain't surreal at all.

> "Writing these stories [. . .] brought me an awareness of how concerned I was about social problems, the condition of life for different minorities in this country, the depth of injustice that could exist in a supposedly free society, the torment many different kinds of people suffered as a daily condition of life."
>
> —"The Children of Nights," New Introduction to GENTLEMAN JUNKIE AND OTHER STORIES OF THE HUNG-UP GENERATION, Pyramid, 1975

SOLDIER

Qarlo hunkered down farther into the firmhole, gathering his cloak about him. Even the triple-lining of the cape could not prevent the seeping cold of the battlefield from reaching him; and even through one of those linings—lead impregnated—he could feel the faint tickle of dropout, all about him, eating at his tissues. He began to shiver again. The Push was going on to the South, and he had to wait, had to listen for the telepathic command of his superior officer.

He fingered an edge of the firmhole, noting he had not steadied it up too well with the firmer. He drew the small molecule-hardening instrument from his pouch, and examined it. The calibrater had slipped a notch, which explained why the dirt of the firmhole had not become as hard as he had desired.

Off to the left the hiss of an eighty-thread beam split the night air, and he shoved the firmer back quickly. The spiderweb tracery of the beam lanced across the sky, poked tentatively at an armor center, throwing blood-red shadows across Qarlo's crag-like features.

The armor center backtracked the thread beam, retaliated with a blinding flash of its own batteries. One burst. Two. Three. The eighty-thread reared once more, feebly, then subsided. A moment later the concussion of its power chambers exploding shook the Earth around Qarlo, causing bits of unfirmed dirt and small pebbles to tumble in on him. Another moment, and the shrapnel came through.

Qarlo lay flat to the ground, soundlessly hoping for a bit more life amidst all this death. He knew his chances of coming back were infinitesimal. What was it? Three out of every thousand came back? He had no illusions. He was a common footman, and he knew he would die out here, in the midst of the Great War VII.

As though the detonation of the eighty-thread had been a signal, the weapons of Qarlo's company opened up, full-on. The webbings crisscrossed the blackness overhead with delicate patterns—appearing, disappearing, changing with every second, ranging through the spectrum, washing the bands of colors outside the spectrum Qarlo could catalog. Qarlo slid into a tiny ball in the slush-filled bottom of the firmhole, waiting.

He was a good soldier. He knew his place. When those metal and energy beasts out there were snarling at each other, there was nothing a lone foot soldier could do—but die. He waited, knowing his time would come much too soon. No matter how violent, how involved, how pushbutton-ridden Wars became, it always simmered down to the man on foot. It had to, for men fought men still.

His mind dwelled limply in a state between reflection and alertness. A state all men of war came to know when there was nothing but the thunder of the big guns abroad in the night.

The stars had gone into hiding.

Abruptly, the thread beams cut out, the traceries winked off, silence once again descended. Qarlo snapped to instant attentiveness. This was the moment. His mind was now keyed to one sound, one only. Inside his head the command would form, and he would act; not entirely of his own volition. The strategists and psychmen had worked together on this thing: the tone of command was keyed into each soldier's brain. Printed in, probed in, sunken in. It was there, and when the Regimenter sent his telepathic orders, Qarlo would leap like a puppet, and advance on direction.

Thus, when it came, it was as though he had anticipated it; as though he knew a second before the mental rasping and the *Advance!* erupted within his skull, that the moment had arrived.

A second sooner than he should have been, he was up, out of the firmhole, hugging his Brandelmeier to his chest, the weight of the plastic bandoliers and his pouch reassuring across his stomach, back, and hips. Even before the mental word actually came.

Because of this extra moment's jump on the command, it happened, and it happened just that way. No other chance coincidences could have done it, but done just that way.

When the first blasts of the enemy's zeroed-in batteries met the combined rays of Qarlo's own guns, also pin-pointed, they met at a point that should by all rights have been empty. But Qarlo had jumped too soon, and when they met, the soldier was at the focal point.

Three hundred distinct beams latticed down, joined in a coruscating rainbow, threw negatively charged particles five hundred feet in the air, shorted out . . . and warped the soldier off the battlefield.

Nathan Schwachter had his heart attack right there on the subway platform.

The soldier materialized in front of him, from nowhere, filthy and ferocious-looking, a strange weapon cradled to his body . . . just as the old man was about to put a penny in the candy machine.

Qarlo's long cape was still, the dematerialization and subsequent reappearance having left him untouched. He stared in confusion at the sallow face before him, and started violently at the face's piercing shriek.

Qarlo watched with growing bewilderment and terror as the sallow face contorted and sank to the littered floor of the platform. The old man clutched his chest, twitched and gasped several times. His legs jerked spasmodically, and his mouth opened wildly again and again. He died with mouth open, eyes staring at the ceiling.

Qarlo looked at the body disinterestedly for a moment; death . . . what did one death matter . . . every day during the War, ten thousand died . . . more horribly than this . . . this was as nothing to him.

The sudden universe-filling scream of an incoming express train broke his attention. The black tunnel that his War-filled world had become, was filled with the rusty wail of an unseen monster, bearing down on him out of the darkness.

The fighting man in him made his body arch, sent it into a crouch. He poised on the balls of his feet, his rifle levering horizontal instantly, pointed at the sound.

From the crowds packed on the platform, a voice rose over the thunder of the incoming train:

"Him! It was *him!* He shot that old man . . . he's crazy!" Heads turned; eyes stared; a little man with a dirty vest, his bald head reflecting the glow of the overhead lights, was pointing a shaking finger at Qarlo.

It was as if two currents had been set up simultaneously. The crowd both drew away and advanced on him. Then the train barreled around the curve, drove past, blasting sound into the very fibers of the soldier's body. Qarlo's mouth opened wide in a soundless scream, and more from reflex than intent, the Brandelmeier erupted in his hands.

A triple-thread of cold blue beams sizzled from the small bell mouth of the weapon, streaked across the tunnel, and blasted full into the front of the train.

The front of the train melted down quickly, and the vehicle ground to a stop. The metal had been melted like a coarse grade of plastic on a burner. Where it had fused into a soggy lump, the metal was bright and smeary—more like the gleam of oxidized silver than anything else.

Qarlo regretted having fired the moment he felt the Brandelmeier buck. He was not where he should be—*where* he was, that was still another, more pressing problem—and he knew he was in danger. Every movement had to be watched as carefully as possible . . . and perhaps he had gotten off to a bad start already. But that noise . . .

He had suffered the screams of the battlefield, but the reverberations of the train, thundering back and forth in that enclosed space, was a nightmare of indescribable horror.

As he stared dumbly at his handiwork, from behind him, the crowd made a concerted rush.

Three burly, charcoal-suited executives—each carrying an attaché case which he dropped as he made the lunge, looking like unhealthy carbon-copies of each other—grabbed Qarlo above the elbows, around the waist, about the neck.

The soldier roared something unintelligible and flung them from him. One slid across the platform on the seat of his pants, bringing up short, his stomach and face smashing into a tiled wall. The second spun away, arms flailing, into the crowd. The third tried to hang onto Qarlo's neck. The soldier lifted him bodily, arched him over his head—breaking the man's insecure grip—and pitched him against a stanchion. The executive hit the girder, slid down, and lay quite still, his back oddly twisted.

The crowd emitted scream after scream, drew away once more. Terror rippled back through its ranks. Several women, near the front, suddenly became aware of the blood pouring from the face of one of the executives, and keeled onto the dirty platform unnoticed. The screams continued, seeming echoes of the now-dead express train's squealing.

But as an entity, the crowd backed the soldier down the platform. For a moment Qarlo forgot he still held the Brandelmeier. He lifted the gun to a threatening position, and the entity that was the crowd pulsed back.

Nightmare! It was all some sort of vague, formless nightmare to Qarlo. This was not the War, where anyone he saw, he blasted. This was something else, some other situation, in which he was lost, disoriented. What was happening?

Qarlo moved toward the wall, his back prickly with fear sweat. He had expected to die in the War, but something as simple and direct and expected as that had not happened. He was *here,* not *there*—wherever *here* was, and wherever *there* had gone—and these people were unarmed, obviously civilians. Which would not have kept him from murdering them . . . but what was happening? Where was the battlefield?

His progress toward the wall was halted momentarily as he backed cautiously around a stanchion. He knew there were people behind him, as well as the white-faced knots before him, and he was beginning to suspect there was no way out. Such confusion boiled up in his thoughts, so close to hysteria was he—plain soldier of the fields—that his mind forcibly rejected the impossibility of being somehow transported from the War into this new—and in many ways more terrifying—situation. He concentrated on one thing only, as a good soldier should: *Out!*

He slid along the wall, the crowd flowing before him, opening at his approach, closing in behind. He whirled once, driving them back farther with the black hole of the Brandelmeier's bell mouth. Again he hesitated (not knowing why) to fire upon them.

He sensed they were enemies. But still they were unarmed. And yet, that had never stopped him before. The village in TetraOmsk Territory, beyond the Volga somewhere. They had been unarmed there, too, but the square had been filled with civilians he had not hesitated to burn. Why was he hesitating now?

The Brandelmeier continued in its silence.

Qarlo detected a commotion behind the crowd, above the crowd's inherent commotion. And a movement. Something was happening there. He backed tightly against the wall as a blue-suited, brass-buttoned man broke through the crowd.

The man took one look, caught the unwinking black eye of the Brandelmeier, and threw his arms back, indicating to the crowd to clear away. He began screaming at the top of his lungs, veins standing out in his temples, "Geddoudahere! The guy's a cuckaboo! Somebody'll get kilt! Beat it, run!"

The crowd needed no further impetus. It broke in the center and streamed toward the stairs.

Qarlo swung around, looking for another way out, but both accessible stairways were clogged by fighting commuters, shoving each other mercilessly to get out. He was effectively trapped.

The cop fumbled at his holster. Qarlo caught a glimpse of the movement from the corner of his eye. Instinctively he knew the movement for what it was; a weapon was about to be brought into use. He swung about, leveling the Brandelmeier. The cop jumped behind a stanchion just as the soldier pressed the firing stud.

A triple-thread of bright blue energy leaped from the weapon's bell mouth. The beam went over the heads of the crowd, neatly melting away a five foot segment of wall supporting one of the stairways. The stairs creaked, and the sound of tortured metal adjusting to poor support and an overcrowding of people, rang through the tunnel. The cop looked fearfully above himself, saw the beams curving, then settle under the weight, and turned a wide-eyed stare back at the soldier.

The cop fired twice, from behind the stanchion, the booming of the explosions catapulting back and forth in the enclosed space.

The second bullet took the soldier above the wrist in his left arm. The Brandelmeier slipped uselessly from his good hand, as blood stained the garment he wore. He stared at his shattered lower arm in amazement. Doubled amazement.

What manner of weapon was this the blue-coated man had used?

No beam, that. Nothing like anything he had ever seen before. No beam to fry him in his tracks. It was some sort of power that hurled a projectile . . . that had ripped his body. He stared stupidly as blood continued to flow out of his arm.

The cop, less anxious now to attack this man with the weird costume and unbelievable rifle, edged cautiously from behind his cover, skirting the edge of the platform, trying to get near enough to Qarlo to put another bullet into him, should he offer further resistance. But the soldier continued to stand, spraddle-legged, staring at his wound, confused at where he was, what had happened to him, the screams of the trains as they bulleted past, and the barbarian tactics of his blue-coated adversary.

The cop moved slowly, steadily, expecting the soldier to break and run at any moment. The wounded man stood rooted, however. The cop bunched his muscles and leaped the few feet intervening.

Savagely, he brought the barrel of his pistol down on the side of Qarlo's neck, near the ear. The soldier turned slowly, anchored in his tracks, and stared unbelievingly at the policeman for an instant.

Then his eyes glazed, and he collapsed to the platform.

As a gray swelling mist bobbed up around his mind, one final thought impinged incongruously: *he struck me . . . physical contact? I don't believe it!*

What have I gotten into?

Light filtered through vaguely. Shadows slithered and wavered, sullenly formed into solids.

"Hey, Mac. Got a light?"

Shadows blocked Qarlo's vision, but he knew he was lying on his back, staring up. He turned his head, and a wall oozed into focus, almost at his nose tip. He turned his head the other way. Another wall, about three feet away, blending in his sight into a shapeless gray blotch. He abruptly realized the back of his head hurt. He moved slowly, swiveling his head, but the soreness remained. Then he realized he was lying on some hard metal surface, and he tried to sit up. The pains throbbed higher, making him feel nauseated, and for an instant his vision receded again.

Then it steadied, and he sat up slowly. He swung his legs over the sharp edge of what appeared to be a shallow, sloping metal trough. It was a mattressless bunk, curved in its bottom, from hundreds of men who had lain there before him.

He was in a cell.

"Hey! I said you got a match there?"

Qarlo turned from the empty rear wall of the cell and looked through the bars. A bulb-nosed face was thrust up close to the metal barrier. The man was short, in filthy rags whose odor reached Qarlo with tremendous offensiveness. The man's eyes were bloodshot, and his nose was crisscrossed with blue and red veins. Acute alcoholism, reeking from every pore; *acne rosacea* that had turned his nose into a hideous cracked and pocked blob.

Qarlo knew he was in detention, and from the very look, the very smell of this other, he knew he was not in a military prison. The man was staring in at him, oddly.

"Match, Charlie? You got a match?" He puffed his fat, wet lips at Qarlo, forcing the bit of cigarette stub forward with his mouth. Qarlo stared back; he could not understand the man's words. They were so slowly spoken, so sharp and yet unintelligible. But he knew what to answer.

"Marnames Quarlo Clobregnny, pyrt, sizfifwunohtootoonyn," the soldier muttered by rote, surly tones running together.

"Whaddaya mad at *me* for, buddy? I didn't putcha in here," argued the match-seeker. "All I wanted was a light for this here butt." He held up two inches of smoked stub. "How come they gotcha inna cell, and not runnin' around loose inna bull pen like us?" He cocked a thumb over his shoulder, and for the first time Qarlo realized others were in this jail.

"Ah, to hell wit ya," the drunk muttered. He cursed again, softly under his breath, turning away. He walked across the bull pen and sat down with the four other men—all vaguely similar in facial content—who lounged around a rough-hewn table-bench combination. The table and benches, all one piece, like a picnic table, were bolted to the floor.

"A screwloose," the drunk said to the others, nodding his balding head at the soldier in his long cape and metallic skintight suit. He picked up the crumpled remnants of an ancient magazine and leafed through it as though he knew every line of type, every girlie illustration, by heart.

Qarlo looked over the cell. It was about ten feet high by eight across, a sink with one thumb-push spigot running cold water, a commode without seat or paper, and metal trough, roughly the dimensions of an average-sized man, fastened to one wall. One enclosed bulb burned feebly in the ceiling. Three walls of solid steel. Ceiling and floor of the same, riveted together at the seams. The fourth wall was the barred door.

The firmer might be able to wilt that steel, he realized, and instinctively reached for his pouch. It was the first moment he had had a chance to think of it, and even as he reached, knew the satisfying weight of it was gone. His bandoliers also. His Brandelmeier, of course. His boots, too, and there seemed to have been some attempt to get his cape off, but it was all part of the skintight suit of metallic-mesh cloth.

The loss of the pouch was too much. Everything that had happened, had happened so quickly, so blurrily, meshed, and the soldier was abruptly overcome by confusion and a deep feeling of hopelessness. He sat down on the bunk, the ledge of metal biting into his thighs. His head still ached from a combination of the blow dealt him by the cop, and the metal bunk where he had lain. He ran a shaking hand over his head, feeling the fractional inch of his brown hair, cut battle-style. Then he noticed that his left hand had been bandaged quite expertly. There was hardly any throbbing from his wound.

That brought back to sharp awareness all that had transpired, and the War leaped into his thoughts. The telepathic command, the rising from the firmhole, the rifle at the ready . . .

. . . then a sizzling shussssss, and the universe had exploded around him in a billion tiny flickering novas of color and color and color. Then suddenly, just as suddenly as he had been standing on the battlefield of Great War VII, advancing on the enemy forces of Ruskie-Chink, he was *not* there.

He was here.

He was in some dark, hard tunnel, with a great beast roaring out of the blackness onto him, and a man in a blue coat had shot him, and clubbed him. Actually *touched* him! Without radiation gloves! How had the man known Qarlo was not booby-trapped with radiates? He could have died in an instant.

Where was he? What war was this he was engaged in? Were these Ruskie-Chink or his own Tri-Continenters? He did not know, and there was no sign of an explanation.

Then he thought of something more important. If he had been captured, then they must want to question him. There was a way to combat *that*, too. He felt around in the hollow tooth toward the back of his mouth. His tongue touched each tooth till it hit the right lower bicuspid. It was empty. The poison glob was gone, he realized in dismay. *It must have dropped out when the blue-coat clubbed me,* he thought.

He realized he was at *their* mercy; who *they* might be was another thing to worry about. And with the glob gone, he had no way to stop their extracting information. It was bad. Very bad, according to the warning conditioning he had received. They could use Probers, or dyoxl-scopalite, or hypno-scourge, or any one of a hundred different methods, any one of which would reveal to them the strength of numbers in his company, the battery placements, the gun ranges, the identity and thought wave band of every officer . . . in fact, a good deal. More than he had thought he knew.

He had become a very important prisoner of War. He *had* to hold out, he realized!

Why?

The thought popped up, and was gone. All it left in its wake was the intense feeling: I despise War, all war and *the* War! Then, even that was gone, and he was alone with the situation once more, to try and decide what had happened to him . . . what secret weapon had been used to capture him . . . and if these unintelligible barbarians with the projectile weapons *could*, indeed, extract his knowledge from him.

I swear they won't get anything out of me but my name, rank, and serial number, he thought desperately.

He mumbled those particulars aloud, as reassurance: "Marnames Qarlo Clobregnny, pryt, sixfifwunohtootoonyn."

The drunks looked up from their table and their shakes, at the sound of his voice. The man with the rosedrop nose rubbed a dirty hand across fleshy chin folds, repeated his philosophy of the strange man in the locked cell.

"Screwloose!"

He might have remained in jail indefinitely, considered a madman or a mad rifleman. But the desk sergeant who had booked him, after the soldier had received medical attention, grew curious about the strangely shaped weapon.

As he put the things into security, he tested the Brandelmeier—hardly realizing what knob or stud controlled its power, never realizing what it could do—and melted away one wall of the safe room. Three inch plate steel, and it melted bluely, fused solidly.

He called the Captain, and the Captain called the F.B.I., and the F.B.I. called Internal Security, and Internal Security said, "Preposterous!" and checked back. When the Brandelmeier had been thoroughly tested—as much as *could* be tested, since the rifle had no seams, no apparent power source, and fantastic range—they were willing to believe. They had the soldier removed from his cell, transported along with the pouch, and a philologist named Soames, to the I.S. general headquarters in Washington, D.C. The Brandelmeier came by jet courier, and the soldier was flown in by helicopter, under sedation. The philologist named Soames, whose hair was long and rusty, whose face was that of a starving artist, whose temperament was that of a saint, came in by specially chartered plane from Columbia University. The pouch was sent by sealed Brinks truck to the airport, where it was delivered under heaviest guard to a mail plane. They all arrived in Washington within ten minutes of one another, and without seeing anything of the surrounding countryside, were whisked away to the subsurface levels of the I.S. Buildings.

When Qarlo came back to consciousness, he found himself again in a cell, this time quite unlike the first. No bars, but just as solid to hold him in, with padded walls. Qarlo paced around the cell a few times, seeking breaks in the walls, and found what was obviously a door, in one corner. But he could not work his fingers between the pads, to try and open it.

He sat down on the padded floor, and rubbed the bristled top of his head in wonder. Was he *never* to find out what had happened to himself? And *when* was he going to shake this strange feeling that he was being watched?

Overhead, through a pane of one-way glass that looked like a ventilator grille, the soldier was being watched.

Lyle Sims and his secretary knelt before the window in the floor, along with the philologist named Soames. Where Soames was shaggy, ill-kept, hungry-looking and placid . . . Lyle Sims was lean, collegiate-seeming, brusque and brisk. He had been special advisor to an unnamed branch office of Internal Security, for five years, dealing with every strange or offbeat problem too outré for regulation inquiry. Those years had hardened him in an odd way; he was quick to recognize authenticity, even quicker to recognize fakery.

As he watched, his trained instincts took over completely, and he knew in a moment of spying, that the man in the cell below was out of the ordinary. Not so in any fashion that could be labeled—"drunkard," "foreigner," "psychotic"—but so markedly different, so *other*, he was taken aback.

"Six feet three inches," he recited to the girl kneeling beside him. She made the notation on her pad, and he went on calling out characteristics of the soldier below. "Brown hair, clipped so short you can see the scalp. Brown . . . no, black eyes. Scars. Above the left eye, running down to center of left cheek; bridge of nose; three parallel scars on the right side of chin; tiny one over right eyebrow; last one I can see, runs from back of left ear, into hairline.

"He seems to be wearing an all-over, skintight suit something like, oh, I suppose it's like a pair of what do you call those pajamas kids wear . . . the kind with the back door, the kind that enclose the feet?"

The girl inserted softly, "You mean snuggies?"

The man nodded, slightly embarrassed for no good reason, continued, "Mmm. Yes, that's right. Like those. The suit encloses his feet, seems to be joined to the cape, and comes up to his neck. Seems to be some sort of metallic cloth.

"Something else . . . may mean nothing at all, or on the other hand . . ." He pursed his lips for a moment, then described his observation carefully. "His head seems to be oddly shaped. The forehead is larger than most, seems to be pressing forward in front, as though he had been smacked hard and it was swelling. That seems to be everything."

Sims settled back on his haunches, fished in his side pocket, and came up with a small pipe, which he cold-puffed in thought for a second. He rose slowly, still staring down through the floor window. He murmured something to himself, and when Soames asked what he had said, the special advisor repeated, "I think we've got something almost too hot to handle."

Soames clucked knowingly, and gestured toward the window. "Have you been able to make out anything he's said yet?"

Sims shook his head. "No. That's why you're here. It seems he's saying the same thing, over and over, but it's completely unintelligible. Doesn't seem to be any recognizable language, or any dialect we've been able to pin down."

"I'd like to take a try at him," Soames said, smiling gently. It was the man's nature that challenge brought satisfaction; solution brought unrest, eagerness for a new, more rugged problem.

Sims nodded agreement, but there was a tense, strained film over his eyes, in the set of his mouth. "Take it easy with him, Soames. I have a strong hunch this is something completely new, something we haven't even begun to understand."

Soames smiled again, this time indulgently. "Come, come, Mr. Sims. After all . . . he *is* only an alien of some sort . . . all we have to do is find out what country he's from."

"Have you heard him talk yet?"

Soames shook his head.

"Then don't be too quick to think he's just a foreigner. The word *alien* may be more correct than you think—only not in the *way* you think."

A confused look spread across Soames's face. He gave a slight shrug, as though he could not fathom what Lyle Sims meant . . . and was not particularly interested. He patted Sims reassuringly, which brought an expression of annoyance to the advisor's face, and he clamped down on the pipestem harder.

They walked downstairs together; the secretary left them, to type her notes, and Sims let the philologist into the padded room, cautioning him to deal gently with the man. "Don't forget," Sims warned, "we're not sure *where* he comes from, and sudden movements may make him jumpy. There's a guard overhead, and there'll be a man with me behind this door, but you never know."

Soames looked startled. "You sound as though he's an aborigine or something. With a suit like that, he *must* be very intelligent. You suspect something, don't you?"

Sims made a neutral motion with his hands."What I suspect is too nebulous to worry about now. Just take it easy . . . and above all, figure out what he's saying, where he's from."

Sims had decided, long before, that it would be wisest to keep the power of the Brandelmeier to himself. But he was fairly certain it was not the work of a foreign power. The trial run on the test range had left him gasping, confused.

He opened the door, and Soames passed through, uneasily.

Sims caught a glimpse of the expression on the stranger's face as the philologist entered. It was even more uneasy than Soames's had been.

It looked to be a long wait.

Soames was white as paste. His face was drawn, and the complacent attitude he had shown since his arrival in Washington was shattered. He sat across from Sims, and asked him in a quavering voice for a cigarette. Sims fished around in his desk, came up with a crumpled pack and idly slid them across to Soames. The philologist took one, put it in his mouth, then, as though it had been totally forgotten in the space of a second, he removed it, held it while he spoke.

His tones were amazed. "Do you know what you've got up there in that cell?"

Sims said nothing, knowing what was to come would not startle him too much; he had expected something fantastic.

"That man . . . do you know where he . . . that soldier—and by God, Sims, that's what he *is*—comes from, from—now you're going to think I'm insane to believe it, but somehow I'm convinced—he comes from the future!"

Sims tightened his lips. Despite himself, he *was* shocked. He knew it was true. It *had* to be true, it was the only explanation that fit all the facts.

"What can you tell me?" he asked the philologist.

"Well, at first I tried solving the communications problem by asking him simple questions . . . pointing to myself and saying 'Soames,' pointing to him and looking quizzical, but all he'd keep saying was a string of gibberish. I tried for hours to equate his tones and phrases with all the dialects and subdialects of every language I'd ever known, but it was no use. He slurred too much. And then I finally figured it out. He had to write it out—which I couldn't understand, of course, but it gave me a clue—and then I kept having him repeat it. Do you know what he's speaking?"

Sims shook his head.

The linguist spoke softly. "He's speaking English. It's that simple. Just English.

"But an English that has been corrupted and run together, and so slurred, it's incomprehensible. It must be the future trend of the language. Sort of an extrapolation of gutter English, just contracted to a fantastic extreme. At any rate, I got it out of him."

Sims leaned forward, held his dead pipe tightly. "What?"

Soames read it off a sheet of paper:

"My name is Qarlo Clobregnny. Private. Six-five-one-oh-two-two-nine."

Sims murmured in astonishment. "My God . . . name, rank and—"

Soames finished for him,"—and serial number. Yes, that's all he'd give me for over three hours. Then I asked him a few innocuous questions, like where did he come from, and what was his impression of where he was now."

The philologist waved a hand vaguely. "By that time, I had an idea what I was dealing with, though not where he had come from. But when he began telling me about the War, the War he was fighting when he showed up here, I knew immediately he was either from some other world—which is fantastic—or, or . . . well, I just don't know!"

Sims nodded his head in understanding. "From *when* do you think he comes?"

Soames shrugged. "Can't tell. He says the year he is in—doesn't seem to realize he's in the past—is K79. He doesn't know when the other style of dating went out. As far as he knows, it's been 'K' for a long time, though he's heard stories about things that happened during a time they dated 'GV'. Meaningless, but I'd wager it's more thousands of years than we can imagine."

Sims ran a hand nervously through his hair. This problem was, indeed, larger than he'd thought.

"Look, Professor Soames, I want you to stay with him, and teach him current English. See if you can work some more information out of him, and let him know we mean him no hard times.

"Though Lord knows," the special advisor added with a tremor, "*he* can give us a harder time than we can give him. What knowledge he must have!"

Soames nodded in agreement. "Is it all right if I catch a few hours' sleep? I was with him almost ten hours straight, and I'm sure *he* needs it as badly as I do."

Sims nodded also, in agreement, and the philologist went off to a sleeping room. But when Sims looked down through the window, twenty minutes later, the soldier was still awake, still looking about nervously. It seemed he did *not* need sleep.

Sims was terribly worried, and the coded telegram he had received from the President, in answer to his own, was not at all reassuring. The problem was in his hands, and it was an increasingly worrisome problem.

Perhaps a deadly problem.

He went to another sleeping room, to follow Soames's example. It looked like sleep was going to be scarce.

Problem:

A man from the future. An ordinary man, without any special talents, without any great store of intelligence. The equivalent of "the man in the street." A man who owns a fantastic little machine that turns sand into solid matter, harder than steel—but who hasn't the vaguest notion of how it works, or how to analyze it. A man whose knowledge of past history is as vague and formless as any modern man's. A soldier. With no other talent than fighting. What is to be done with such a man?

Solution:

Unknown.

Lyle Sims pushed the coffee cup away. If he ever had to look at another cup of the disgusting stuff, he was sure he would vomit. Three sleepless days and nights, running on nothing but dexedrine and hot black coffee, had put his nerves more on edge than usual. He snapped at the clerks and secretaries, he paced endlessly, and he had ruined the stems of five pipes. He felt muggy and his stomach was queasy. Yet there was no solution.

It was impossible to say, "All right, we've got a man from the future. So what? Turn him loose and let him make a life for himself in our time, since he can't return to his own."

It was impossible to do that for several reasons: (1) What if he *couldn't* adjust? He was then a potential menace, of *incalculable* potential. (2) What if an enemy power—and God knows there were enough powers around anxious to get a secret weapon as valuable as Qarlo—grabbed him, and *did* somehow manage to work out the concepts behind the rifle, the firmer, the mono-atomic anti-gravity device in the pouch? What then? (3) A man used to war, knowing only war, would eventually *seek* or foment war.

There were dozens of others, they were only beginning to realize. No, something had to be done with him.

Imprison him?

For what? The man had done no real harm. He had not intentionally caused the death of the man on the subway platform. He had been frightened by the train. He had been attacked by the executives—one of whom had a broken neck, but was alive. No, he was just "a stranger and afraid, in a world I never made," as Housman had put it so terrifyingly clearly.

Kill him?

For the same reasons, unjust and brutal . . . not to mention wasteful.

Find a place for him in society?

Doing what?

Sims raged in his mind, mulled it over and tried every angle. It was an insoluble problem. A simple dogface, with no other life than that of a professional soldier, what good was he?

All Qarlo knew was war.

The question abruptly answered itself: If he knows no other life than that of a soldier . . . why, make him a soldier. (But . . . who was to say that with his knowledge of futuristic tactics and weapons, he might not turn into another Hitler, or Genghis Khan?) No, making him a soldier would only heighten the problem. There could be no peace of mind were he in a position where he might organize.

As a tactician then?

It might work at that.

Sims slumped behind his desk, pressed down the key of his intercom, spoke to the secretary, "Get me General Mainwaring, General Polk and the Secretary of Defense."

He clicked the key back. It just might work at that. If Qarlo could be persuaded to detail fighting plans, now that he realized where he was, and that the men who held him were not his enemies, and allies of Ruskie-Chink (and what a field of speculation *that* pair of words opened!).

It just might work . . .

. . . but Sims doubted it.

Mainwaring stayed on to report when Polk and the Secretary of Defense went back to their regular duties. He was a big man, with softness written across his face and body, and a pompous white moustache. He shook his head sadly, as though the Rosetta Stone had been stolen from him just before an all-important experiment.

"Sorry, Sims, but the man is useless to us. Brilliant grasp of military tactics, so long at it involves what he calls 'eighty-thread beams' and telepathic contacts.

"Do you know those wars up there are fought as much mentally as they are physically? Never heard of a tank or a mortar, but the stories he tells of brain-burning and spore-death would make you sick. It isn't pretty the way they fight.

"I thank God I'm not going to be around to see it; I thought *our* wars were filthy and unpleasant. They've got us licked all down the line for brutality and mass death. And the strange thing is, this Qarlo fellow *despises* it! For a while there—felt foolish as hell—but for a while there, when he was explaining it, I almost wanted to chuck my career, go out and start beating the drum for disarmament."

The General summed up, and it was apparent Qarlo was useless as a tactician. He had been brought up with one way of waging war, and it would take a lifetime for him to adjust enough to be of any tactical use.

But it didn't really matter, for Sims was certain the General had given him the answer to the problem, inadvertently.

He would have to clear it with Security, and the President, of course. And it would take a great deal of publicity to make the people realize this man actually *was* the real thing, an inhabitant of the future. But if it worked out, Qarlo Clobregnny, the soldier and nothing *but* the soldier, could be the most valuable man Time had ever spawned.

He set to work on it, wondering foolishly if he wasn't too much the idealist.

Ten soldiers crouched in the frozen mud. Their firmers had been jammed, had turned the sand and dirt of their holes only to icelike conditions. The cold was seeping up through their suits, and the jammed firmers were emitting hard radiation. One of the men screamed as the radiation took hold in his gut, and he felt the organs watering away. He leaped up, vomiting blood and phlegm—and was caught across the face by a robot-tracked triple beam. The front of his face disappeared, and the nearly decapitated corpse flopped back into the firmhole, atop a comrade.

That soldier shoved the body aside carelessly, thinking of his four children, lost to him forever in a Ruskie-Chink raid on Garmatopolis, sent to the bogs to work. His mind conjured up the sight of the three girls and the little boy with such long, long eyelashes—each dragging through the stinking bog, a mineral bag tied to the neck, collecting fuel rocks for the enemy. He began to cry softly. The sound and mental image of crying was picked up by a Ruskie-Chink telepath somewhere across the lines, and even before the man could catch himself, blank his mind, the telepath was on him.

The soldier raised up from the firmhole bottom, clutching with crooked hands at his head. He began to tear at his features wildly, screaming high and piercing, as the enemy telepath burned away his brain. In a moment his eyes were empty, staring shells, and the man flopped down beside his comrade, who had begun to deteriorate.

A thirty-eight thread whined its beam overhead, and the eight remaining men saw a munitions wheel go up with a deafening roar. Hot shrapnel zoomed across the field, and a thin, brittle, knife-edged bit of plasteel arced over the edge of the firmhole, and buried itself in one soldier's head. The piece went in crookedly, through his left earlobe, and came out skewering his tongue, half-extended from his open mouth. From the side it looked as though he were wearing some sort of earring. He died in spasms, and it took an awfully long while. Finally, the twitching and gulping got so bad, one of his comrades used the butt of a Brandelmeier across the dying man's nose. It splintered the nose, sent bone chips into the brain, killing the man instantly.

Then the attack call came!

In each of their heads, the telepathic cry came to advance, and they were up out of the firmhole, all seven of them, reciting their daily prayer, and knowing it would do no good. They advanced across the slushy ground, and overhead they could hear the buzz of leech bombs, coming down on the enemy's thread emplacements.

All around them in the deep-set night the varicolored explosions popped and sugged, expanding in all directions like fireworks, then dimming the scene, again the blackness.

One of the soldiers caught a beam across the belly, and he was thrown sidewise for ten feet, to land in a soggy heap, his stomach split open, the organs glowing and pulsing wetly from the charge of the threader. A head popped out of a firmhole before them, and three of the remaining six fired simultaneously. The enemy was a booby—rigged to backtrack their kill urge, rigged to a telepathic hookup—and even as the body exploded under their combined firepower, each of the men caught fire. Flames leaped from their mouths, from their pores, from the instantly charred spaces where their eyes had been. A pyrotic-telepath had been at work.

The remaining three split and cut away, realizing they might be thinking, might be giving themselves away. That was the horror of being just a dogface, not a special telepath behind the lines. Out here here was nothing but death.

A doggie-mine slithered across the ground, entwined itself in the legs of one soldier, and blew the legs out from under him. He lay there clutching the shredded stumps, feeling the blood soaking into the mud, and then unconsciousness seeped into his brain. He died shortly thereafter.

Of the two left, one leaped a barbwall, and blasted out a thirty-eight thread emplacement of twelve men, at the cost of the top of his head. He was left alive, and curiously, as though the war had stopped, he felt the top of himself, and his fingers pressed lightly against convoluted, slick matter for a second before he dropped to the ground.

His braincase was open, glowed strangely in the night, but no one saw it.

The last soldier dove under a beam that zzzzzzzed through the night, and landed on his elbows. He rolled with the tumble, felt the edge of a leech-bomb crater, and dove in headfirst. The beam split up his passage, and he escaped charring by an inch. He lay in the hole, feeling the cold of the battlefield seeping around him, and drew his cloak closer.

The soldier was Qarlo . . .

He finished talking, and sat down on the platform . . .

The audience was silent . . .

Sims shrugged into his coat, fished around in the pocket for the cold pipe. The dottle had fallen out of the bowl, and he felt the dark grains at the bottom of the pocket. The audience was filing out slowly, hardly anyone speaking, but each staring at others around him. As though they were suddenly realizing what had happened to them, as though they were looking for a solution.

Sims passed such a solution. The petitions were there, tacked up alongside the big sign—duplicate of the ones up all over the city. He caught the heavy black type on them as he passed through the auditorium's vestibule:

SIGN THIS PETITION!
PREVENT WHAT YOU HAVE HEARD TONIGHT!

People were flocking around the petitions, but Sims knew it was only a token gesture at this point: the legislature had gone through that morning. No more war . . . under any conditions. And intelligence reported the long playing records, the piped broadcasts, the p.a. trucks, had all done their jobs. Similar legislation was going through all over the world.

It looked as though Qarlo had done it, single-handed.

Sims stopped to refill his pipe, and stared up at the big black-lined poster near the door.

HEAR QARLO, THE SOLDIER FROM THE FUTURE!
SEE THE MAN FROM TOMORROW,
AND HEAR HIS STORIES
OF THE WONDERFUL WORLD OF THE FUTURE!
FREE! NO OBLIGATIONS! HURRY!

The advertising had been effective, and it was a fine campaign.

Qarlo had been more valuable just telling about his Wars, about how men died in that day in the future, than he could ever have been as a strategist.

It took a real soldier, who hated war, to talk of it, to show people that it was ugly, and unglamorous. And there was a certain sense of foul defeat, of hopelessness, in knowing the future was the way Qarlo described it. It made you want to stop the flow of Time, say, "No. The future will *not* be like this! We will abolish war!"

Certainly enough steps in the right direction had been taken. The legislature was there, and those who had held back, who had tried to keep animosity alive, were being disposed of every day.

Qarlo had done his work well.

There was just one thing bothering special advisor Lyle Sims. The soldier had come back in time, so he was here. That much they knew for certain.

But a nagging worry ate at Sims's mind, made him say prayers he had thought himself incapable of inventing. Made him fight to get Qarlo heard by everyone . . .

Could the future be changed?

Or was it inevitable?

Would the world Qarlo left inevitably appear?

Would all their work be for nothing?

It couldn't be! It dare not be!

He walked back inside, got in line to sign the petitions again, though it was his fiftieth time.

THE NIGHT OF DELICATE TERRORS

In the sovereign state of Kentucky, Kin Hooker mused, hunching over the wheel, *it is possible to freeze to death and starve to death with a pocketful of money.*

In the back seat, Raymond cried out in his sleep, and Alma reached back to straighten the heavy car-robe over him. "How's Patty?" McKinley Hooker said to his wife.

Alma straightened around and let air escape between her lips. She stared straight ahead through the windshield at the barrage descent of thick, enveloping snow that wrapped the car in a hush. He had to repeat his question; she did not look at him as she replied, "Still sleeping. How much gas we got?"

He winced at her grammar. That was the only thing about Alma that distressed Kin Hooker. But it was easily attributed to the degree of schooling she had received in Alabama.

"Should have enough to get us over the state line. Is gas more expensive in Indiana?"

Alma shrugged and went back to her absorbed sighting into the slanting white. In the back seat, Raymond turned on his side, moving closer to little Patty's warm body. They huddled together against the January bite that reached them despite the laboring car heater.

"Damned road!" Hooker murmured under his breath. They were traveling at a pitifully slow pace despite the firmness of the concrete dual-lane. A cold front had blitzkrieged down from the north earlier that evening, catching the hard, cold Kentucky countryside in a noose of below-zero snow and raging winds. All traffic had begun to crawl, with jackknifed trailers and cars tossed this way and that in the ditches at the roadside. On every turn cars spun-out helplessly, leaving their inhabitants stranded . . . for no one could himself chance helping them, with the risk of being stuck omnipresent.

Now the snow had piled along the inner lane, leaving only the outer passable to the horde of traffic heading upstate. Across the humped median, the traffic going south was in like shape.

McKinley Hooker's back hurt terribly, and his hands on the wheel were cold. He felt a graininess in his eyes, and there was a persistent throbbing in his right temple.

They had eaten all the food in the lunch basket earlier that evening, and now, as the dash clock read 2:25 AM they knew they would have to find a motel for the night. Kin had been driving since seven that morning, with only infrequent gas stops, and his back just under the shoulder blades, at the base of his spine, in the area of the kidneys, was so sore he had slumped into a half-crouch over the wheel, round-shouldered and uncomfortable, from which he was not certain he could emerge.

And the blizzard was getting worse.

No gravel-spreader or snow plough had come out yet, and it was a safe bet none would till morning. In the meantime, conditions were getting unbearable. With only one lane open at all—and that covered with a veneer of ice—and snow drifting in from the sides constantly, there was no telling how long even their fifteen-mile-an-hour pace could be maintained.

They would have to find a motel. Someplace to eat, where the children could get warm, where they could bed down to restore their strength, for the balance of the journey to Chicago.

They would have to find a motel . . .

He tossed the thought like a wild mare shedding its rider. Then he looked into the rear-view mirror, and saw the futility of the thought.

His chocolate face with its keen eyes and wide, white mouthful of teeth stared back at him. And Alma was even blacker.

He screwed his hands down tighter on the wheel.

There had been only three colored motels between Macon and this lost point somewhere in the Kentucky darkness. Three motels, and all of them disgusting. Kin Hooker sometimes wondered if there was any point to fighting. This conclave in Chicago, now. He had been selected by all of them as the Macon, Georgia, representative. He was to receive his instructions, and then one day . . .

He decided not to think about it. It was all in the future; a special kind of future that he never really thought would come to pass, but which he dwelled on in hungry-souled moments.

Right now, the problem was to keep alive.

"Kin, we gonna make Chicago tonight?"

"I don't see how, honey. It's a good four hundred miles, and frankly, my back is sore as hell right now."

"What we gonna do? You figure we can sleep in the car?"

He shook his head, keeping his eyes riveted to the faint twin-beams of brilliance cast so feebly through the swirling curtain of snow. "You know we'd have to keep the engine running, and even so the heater wouldn't do us much good tonight; looks to be dropping fast out there."

"They gonna be a stop along here somewhere?"

He tossed her a fast glance. She knew it had come to this, too. It always did. They didn't talk about it, because you can't talk about the facts of life constantly without growing bored and despairing. "I don't think so. Maybe. We'll see."

He turned back just in time to apply the brake before he hit the rear of the farm truck. It was an old truck without taillights, and as he slapped the brake, then pumped quickly, the car lost its feeble grip on the road, and began to spin. He turned into it, and they managed to straighten without losing acceleration.

But for a shuddering time without measure, now that the danger was past, he sat rigid behind the wheel, his eyes locked to the road in shock, trembling uncontrollably.

It was decided, for him, then. They would have to stop at the very next motel or restaurant. He knew what would happen, of course. He was not a stupid man; in the secret crypts of his thoughts he often damned himself for not being a "handkerchief head," illiterate and content to let the Mr. Charlie run his life. But he had grown up in Michigan, and it had been a good growing-up, with only a scattered few of those unbearable incidents he now wished to forget. Oh, there had been the constant watching of caste and conversation, of course, but that grew to be an instinctive thing. In all, it had been satisfactory, till he had been inveigled into going to work in Georgia.

Then he had learned the ropes quickly, as he was wont to phrase it. He had learned what a whitey meant when he said, "The line of communication between the nigger and the Caucasian." It was not plural; there was only one line. The line that read: *I'm the Massa' and you're the One-Step-Up-From-A-Monkey, and don't forget it.*

McKinley Hooker was not a stupid man, and now, because he had been chosen, he was an emissary to a conclave in Chicago. A very special conclave, so he had to make it.

There had been many years of taking orders, and now he had a new set of orders, the final wrinkles of which would be ironed out at Chicago. So he had to get to the Chicago conclave, and find out what the final instructions were to be; then he could carry the word back to his people in Macon.

Perhaps . . . perhaps it would be the beginning. The real beginning, where those who searched for the word would find the word, and the word would be *power*. Perhaps. If all the gears meshed properly, then perhaps.

If he managed to stay alive through this January hell. He cursed himself for bringing Alma and the children along; but it had been clear all the way up from Georgia, and they had never seen Chicago. If they could only get to a motel. If . . .

Far ahead—or what *seemed* far ahead—lost in the crisscrossing lines of snow, he thought he saw a flamingo-flash of neon. He strained forward, and wiped at a spot on the windshield where the defrosters had not cleared away all moisture. The flash came again. He felt both a release and a tension in his stomach muscles.

As they drew closer the red flasher could be seen whirling atop the restaurant's roof, casting off its spaced bdip bdip bdip bdip of crimson. The redness swathed the ground in a broken band and was gone, to reappear an instant later.

The sign was forbidding, it said: EAT.

Alma turned her head slowly as Kin decelerated. "Here? You think they'll serve us?"

He rubbed his jaw, then quickly dropped the hand back to the wheel. He had a day's growth of beard, and none of them looked too well-starched, after being on the road. "I don't know; I guess they'll just *have* to feed us; you can't turn people away on a night like this."

She chuckled softly. He was still a big-town colored, in many ways.

They turned onto the snow-hidden gravel, and Kin pulled carefully around two gigantic semitrailers parked near the entrance. Then as they drew around the bulk of the vehicles, the sign that had been blocked-off winked at them. MOTEL   FREE TV   SHOWERS and underneath, in a dainty green worm of neon: VACANCY.

The semitrailers bulked huge, like sleeping leviathans, under their wraps of snow. It was getting worse. The wind keened around the little building like a night train to nowhere.

He stopped, and they sat there for a moment, letting the windows fog up around them.

Alma was worried, her brow drawn down, her hands in their knitted gloves interlocked on her lap. "Should we say stay here while you go in?"

He shook his head. "It might have some effect if all of us went in together. Stir their hearts."

They woke Raymond and Patty. The little girl sat up and yawned, then picked her nose with the lack of self-consciousness known only to a child upon awakening. She mumbled something, and Alma soothed her with a few words that they were going to stop to eat.

Patty said, very distinctly, "I have to go pee-pee, Mommy."

It loosened their tenseness for a jagged second, then the implications dawned. This was another problem. *Well, let's tough it out,* Kin thought wryly, a prayer rising silently from somewhere below.

When they opened the doors, the sharp edge of the wind slashed at them, instantly dispelling the body warmth they had maintained in the sealed car. The children began to shiver, and an involuntary little gasp came from Alma, barely discernible over the raging of the wind and the constant downdropping of the snow.

"Let's go!" Kin shrieked, lifting Patty and charging at the motel-restaurant's front door.

He hit the door at a skidding run, turned the knob and flung the door wide. Alma crowded in behind him, and slammed the door as Raymond moved in on her heels.

They stood frozen for a split-second, till the shock of the bitter cold left them, and then, abruptly, their senses returned.

They stood there, the four of them, in the middle of the restaurant, and slowly, everyone had turned to stare at them.

Kin felt a worm of terror leave its home and seek warmth elsewhere. It crawled toward his brain as he saw the eyes of the men in the restaurant fasten on them. He knew what they saw: a nigger, a nigger's woman, and two little pickaninnies.

He shuddered. It was not entirely from the cold.

Alma, behind him, drew in a deep breath.

Then, the thick-armed counterman, leaning across the Formica counter-top, furrowed his brow and said, very carefully, so there was no chance for misinterpretation, "Sorry, fellah, we can't serve you."

Then all the suppressed hopes that this time, just this one time of such importance, it would be different, that someone would let it slide, disappeared. It was going to be another battleground, in a war that had never really been fought.

"It's pretty bad out there," Kin said, "we thought we might get something hot to warm us up. We've been driving all day, all the way from—"

The counterman cut him off with a harsh Midwest accent, not a trace of drawl in it. "I said: I'm sorry but we don't serve Nigrahs here." The way he said it was a cross between Negro and nigger. His voice was harder.

Kin stared at the man; what sort of man was it?

A thick neck supporting a crew-cut head. It looked like some off-color, fleshy burr on the end of a toadstool stem. Huge shoulders, bulging against the lumberjack shirt, and a pair of arms that said quietly musclebound and muscled. Kin was sure he could take the counterman.

But there were others. Four men, obviously truckers, with their caps slanted back on their heads, their eyes coolly inquisitive, their union buttons on the caps catching the glow of the overheads.

And a man and woman at the end of the counter. The woman's pudgy face was screwed up in distaste. She was a Southron, no question. They were able to look at you in a way like no other way. They were smelling hog maws and chitterlings and pomade. Even if it wasn't there.

Even as they talked, a waitress came out from the kitchen, carrying a plate with steak and home-fried potatoes on it. She stopped in an awkward mid-stride and stared at the newcomers. Her head jerked oddly and she turned to the counterman. "We don't serve 'em, Eddie," she said, as though he had never known this fact.

"That's what I been telling 'em, Una. See, fellah, we—uh—we don't serve your people here. Gas, we got it, but that's it."

"It's winter out there," Kin said. "My wife and kids—"

The counterman reached down and took something from under the bar that he kept concealed. "You don't seem to hear too good, fellah. What I said was: we ain't in business for you."

"We need a room for the night, too," Alma inserted, a quavering bravado in her voice. She knew they would get nothing, and it was her way of having them turned down for everything, not just a lousy meal. Kin winced at her petty game-playing.

"Say, now, get outta here!" the waitress yelled. Her face was a grimace of outrage. Who *were* these darkies, anyhow?

"Take it easy, Una, just take it easy. They're goin'. Ain'tcha, fellah?" He came out from behind the bar, holding the sawed-off baseball bat loosely in his left hand.

Kin backed away.

It was going to be fight this big clown, and maybe get his brains knocked out, and even then not getting food and sleep, unless it was at the county jail . . . or going back to the car, and the cold.

There could be little decision in the matter.

"Let's go, Alma," he said. He reached behind him and opened the door. The cold struck him suddenly, sharply, like a cobra; he felt his teeth clench in frustration and pain.

Eddie, the counterman, advanced on them with the ball bat and his arms like curlicued sausages of great size. "G'wan now, and don't be makin' me use this on yer."

"Is there a colored place near here?" Kin asked, as Alma grabbed Raymond and slipped past into the darkness.

"No . . . and there ain't gonna be, if *we* c'n help it. We got a business to run here, not for you people. G'wan to Illinois, where they treat a nigger better'n a white man."

He came on again, and Kin backed out, closing the door tightly, staring at the 7-Up decal on the door. Then the wind raced down the neck of his coat, and he hurried to the car.

The three of them were huddled together in the front seat.

"Daddy, I gotta go pee-pee," Patty said.

"Soon, honey. Soon," he murmured at her, sliding in. He turned the key in the ignition and for a moment he did not think the overheated, then chilled, motor would start. But it kicked over and they pulled ahead, past the forms of the trucks, like great white whales sleeping in shoals of snow.

The road was worse now.

Cars were strewn on either side of the dual-lane like flotsam left after the tide. Kin Hooker bent across the wheel, slipping automatically into the rib-straining position he had known all day.

His thoughts were clear, now.

For almost two years now, since they had started the idea, he had been undecided. Certainly it would be decisive, and a new world, and worth fighting for. But so many would be killed, so many, many, many who were innocent, and who had nothing to do with this war that had never been fought.

But it was all right, now. He had received his instructions, and he *was* going to make that conclave in Chicago. Somehow, he would drive that distance.

And even if he didn't. Even if he and Alma, Raymond and Patty should overturn out here, if they should freeze to death, or be cracked up, there would be others. Many others, all heading to Chicago this day, and all waiting for the final word.

It was coming.

Nothing could stop it.

Whitey had had it his way for so long, so terribly long, and now the time had come for a change of owners. It had come to this and there was no stopping it. He had been uncertain before, because he was not a man of violence . . . but suddenly, it was right. It was the way it would be, because they had forced it this way.

Kin Hooker smiled as he studied the disappearing highway.

Like a million other dark smiles that night, across a white countryside.

A wide, white smile in a dark face.

Shattered Like a Glass Goblin

So it was there, eight months later, that Rudy found her; in that huge and ugly house off Western Avenue in Los Angeles; living with them, *all* of them; not just Jonah, but all of them.

It was November in Los Angeles, near sundown, and unaccountably chill even for the fall in that place always near the sun. He came down the sidewalk and stopped in front of the place. It was gothic hideous, with the grass half-cut and the rusted lawnmower sitting in the middle of an unfinished swath. Grass cut as if a placating gesture to the outraged tenants of the two lanai apartment houses that loomed over that squat structure on either side. (Yet how strange . . . the apartment buildings were taller, the old house hunched down between them, but *it* seemed to dominate *them*. How odd.)

Cardboard covered the upstairs windows.

A baby carriage was overturned on the front walk.

The front door was ornately carved.

Darkness seemed to breathe heavily.

Rudy shifted the duffel bag slightly on his shoulder. He was afraid of the house. He was breathing more heavily as he stood there, and a panic he could never have described tightened the fat muscles on either side of his shoulderblades. He looked up into the corners of the darkening sky, seeking a way out, but he could only go forward. Kristina was in there.

Another girl answered the door.

She looked at him without speaking, her long blonde hair half-obscuring her face; peering out from inside the veil of Clairol and dirt.

When he asked a second time for Kris, she wet her lips in the corners, and a tic made her cheek jump. Rudy set down the duffel bag with a whump. "Kris, please," he said urgently.

The blonde girl turned away and walked back into the dim hallways of the terrible old house. Rudy stood in the open doorway, and suddenly, as if the blonde girl had been a barrier to it, and her departure had released it, he was assaulted, like a smack in the face, by a wall of pungent scent. It was marijuana.

He reflexively inhaled, and his head reeled. He took a step back, into the last inches of sunlight coming over the lanai apartment building, and then it was gone, and he was still buzzing, and moved forward, dragging the duffel bag behind him.

He did not remember closing the front door, but when he looked, some time later, it was closed behind him.

He found Kris on the third floor, lying against the wall of a dark closet, her left hand stroking a faded pink rag rabbit, her right hand at her mouth, the little finger crooked, the thumb-ring roach holder half-obscured as she sucked up the last wonders of the joint. The closet held an infinitude of odors—dirty sweat socks as pungent as stew, fleece jackets on which the rain had dried to mildew, a mop gracious with its scent of old dust hardened to dirt, the overriding weed smell of what she had been at for no one knew how long—and it held her. As pretty as pretty could be.

"Kris?"

Slowly, her head came up, and she saw him. Much later, she tracked and focused and she began to cry. "Go away."

In the limpid silences of the whispering house, back and above him in the darkness, Rudy heard the sudden sound of leather wings beating furiously for a second, then nothing.

Rudy crouched down beside her, his heart grown twice its size in his chest. He wanted so desperately to reach her, to talk to her. "Kris . . . please . . ." She turned her head away, and with the hand that had been stroking the rabbit she slapped at him awkwardly, missing him.

For an instant, Rudy could have sworn he heard the sound of someone counting heavy gold pieces, somewhere off to his right, down a passageway of the third floor. But when he half-turned, and looked out through the closet door, and tried to focus his hearing on it, there was no sound to home in on.

Kris was trying to crawl back farther into the closet. She was trying to smile.

He turned back; on hands and knees he moved into the closet after her.

"The rabbit," she said, languorously. "You're crushing the rabbit." He looked down, his right knee was lying on the soft matted-fur head of the pink rabbit. He pulled it out from under his knee and threw it into a corner of the closet. She looked at him with disgust. "You haven't changed, Rudy. Go away."

"I'm outta the army, Kris," Rudy said gently. "They let me out on a medical. I want you to come back, Kris, please."

She would not listen, but pulled herself away from him, deep into the closet, and closed her eyes. He moved his lips several times, as though trying to recall words he had already spoken, but there was no sound, and he lit a cigarette, and sat in the open doorway of the closet, smoking and waiting for her to come back to him. He had waited eight months for her to come back to him, since he had been inducted and she had written him telling him, *Rudy, I'm going to live with Jonah at The Hill.*

There was the sound of something very tiny, lurking in the infinitely black shadow where the top step of the stairs from the second floor met the landing. It giggled in a glass harpsichord trilling. Rudy knew it was giggling at *him,* but he could make out no movement from that corner.

Kris opened her eyes and stared at him with distaste. "Why did you come here?"

"Because we're gonna be married."

"Get out of here."

"I love you, Kris. Please."

She kicked out at him. It didn't hurt, but it was meant to. He backed out of the closet slowly.

Jonah was down in the living room. The blonde girl who had answered the door was trying to get his pants off him. He kept shaking his head no, and trying to fend her off with a weak-wristed hand. The record player under the brick-and-board bookshelves was playing Simon & Garfunkel, "The Big Bright Green Pleasure Machine."

"Melting," Jonah said gently. "Melting," and he pointed toward the big, foggy mirror over the fireplace mantel. The fireplace was crammed with unburned wax milk cartons, candy bar wrappers, newspapers from the underground press, and kitty litter. The mirror was dim and chill. *"Melting!"* Jonah yelled suddenly, covering his eyes.

"Oh shit!" the blonde girl said, and threw him down, giving up at last. She came toward Rudy.

"What's wrong with him?" Rudy asked.

"He's freaking out again. Christ, what a drag he can be."

"Yeah, but what's *happening* to him?"

She shrugged. "He sees his face melting, that's what he says."

"Is he on marijuana?"

The blonde girl looked at him with sudden distrust. "Mari—? Hey, who *are* you?"

"I'm a friend of Kris's."

The blonde girl assayed him for a moment more, then by the way her shoulders dropped and her posture relaxed, she accepted him. "I thought you might've just walked in, you know, maybe the Laws. You know?"

There was a Middle Earth poster on the wall behind her, with its brightness faded in a long straight swath where the sun caught it every morning. He looked around uneasily. He didn't know what to do.

"I was supposed to marry Kris. Eight months ago," he said.

"You want to fuck?" asked the blonde girl. "When Jonah trips he turns off. I been drinking Coca-Cola all morning and all day, and I'm really horny."

Another record dropped onto the turntable and Stevie Wonder blew hard into his harmonica and started singing, "I Was Born to Love Her."

"I was engaged to Kris," Rudy said, feeling sad. "We was going to be married when I got out of basic. But she decided to come over here with Jonah, and I didn't want to push her. So I waited eight months, but I'm out of the army now."

"Well, *do* you or *don't* you?"

Under the dining room table. She put a satin pillow under her. It said: *Souvenir of Niagara Falls, New York.*

When he went back into the living room, Jonah was sitting up on the sofa, reading Hesse's MAGISTER LUDI.

"Jonah?" Rudy said. Jonah looked up. It took him a while to recognize Rudy.

When he did, he patted the sofa beside him, and Rudy came and sat down.

"Hey, Rudy, where y'been?"

"I've been in the army."

"Wow."

"Yeah, it was awful."

"You out now? I mean for good?"

Rudy nodded. "Uh-huh. Medical."

"Hey, that's good."

They sat quietly for a while. Jonah started to nod, and then said to himself, "You're not very tired."

Rudy said, "Jonah, hey listen, what's the story with Kris? You know, we was supposed to get married about eight months ago."

"She's around someplace," Jonah answered.

Out of the kitchen, through the dining room where the blonde girl lay sleeping under the table, came the sound of something wild, tearing at meat. It went on for a long time, but Rudy was looking out the front window, the big bay window. There was a man in a dark gray suit standing talking to two policemen on the sidewalk at the edge of the front walk leading up to the front door. He was pointing at the big, old house.

"Jonah, can Kris come away now?"

Jonah looked angry. "Hey, listen, man, nobody's *keeping* her here.

She's been grooving with all of us and she likes it. Go ask her. Christ, don't bug *me*!"

The two cops were walking up to the front door.

Rudy got up and went to answer the doorbell.

They smiled at him when they saw his uniform.

"May I help you?" Rudy asked them.

The first cop said, "Do you live here?"

"Yes," said Rudy. "My name is Randolph Boekel. May I help you?"

"We'd like to come inside and talk to you."

"Do you have a search warrant?"

"We don't want to search, we only want to talk to you. Are you in the army?"

"Just discharged. I came home to see my family."

"Can we come in?"

"No, sir."

The second cop looked troubled, "Is this the place they call 'The Hill'?"

"Who?" Rudy asked, looking perplexed.

"Well, the neighbors said this was 'The Hill' and there were some pretty wild parties going on here."

"Do you hear any partying?"

The cops looked at each other. Rudy added, "It's always very quiet here. My mother is dying of cancer of the stomach."

They let Rudy move in, because he was able to talk to people who came to the door from the outside. Aside from Rudy, who went out to get food, and the weekly trips to the unemployment line, no one left The Hill. It was usually very quiet.

Except sometimes there was a sound of growling in the back hall leading up to what had been a maid's room; and the splashing from the basement, the sound of wet things on bricks.

It was a self-contained little universe, bordered on the north by acid and mescaline, on the south by pot and peyote, on the east by speed and redballs, on the west by downers and amphetamines. There were eleven people living in The Hill. Eleven, and Rudy.

He walked through the halls, and sometimes found Kris, who would not talk to him, save once, when she asked him if he'd ever been heavy behind *anything* except love. He didn't know what to answer her, so he only said, "Please," and she called him a square and walked off toward the stairway leading to the dormered attic.

Rudy had heard squeaking from the attic. It had sounded to him like the shrieking of mice being torn to pieces. There were cats in the house.

He did not know why he was there, except that he didn't understand why *she* wanted to stay. His head always buzzed and he sometimes felt that if he just said the right thing, the right way, Kris would come away with him. He began to dislike the light. It hurt his eyes.

No one talked to anyone else very much. There was always a struggle to keep high, to keep the *group high* as elevated as possible. In that way they cared for each other.

And Rudy became their one link with the outside. He had written to someone—his parents, a friend, a bank, someone—and now there was money coming in. Not much, but enough to keep the food stocked, and the rent paid. But he insisted Kris be nice to him.

They all made her be nice to him, and she slept with him in the little room on the second floor where Rudy had put his newspapers and his duffel bag. He lay there most of the day, when he was not out on errands for The Hill, and he read the smaller items about train wrecks and molestations in the suburbs. And Kris came to him and they made love of a sort.

One night she convinced him he should "make it, heavy behind acid" and he swallowed fifteen hundred mikes cut with Methedrine, in two big gel caps, and she was stretched out like taffy for six miles. He was a fine copper wire charged with electricity, and he pierced her flesh. She wriggled with the current that flowed through him, and became softer yet. He sank down through the softness, and carefully observed the intricate wood-grain effect her teardrops made as they rose in the mist around him. He was downdrifting slowly, turning and turning, held by a whisper of blue that came out of his body like a spiderweb. The sound of her breathing in the moist crystal pillared cavity that went down and down was the sound of the very walls themselves, and when he touched them with his warm metal fingertips she drew in breath heavily, forcing the air up around him as he sank down, twisting slowly in a veil of musky looseness.

There was an insistent pulsing growing somewhere below him, and he was afraid of it as he descended, the high-pitched whining of something threatening to shatter. He felt panic. Panic gripped him, flailed at him, his throat constricted, he tried to grasp the veil and it tore away in his hands; then he was falling, faster now, much faster, and *afraid*!

Violet explosions all around him and the shrieking of something that wanted him, that was seeking him, pulsing deeply in the throat of an animal he could not name, and he heard her shouting, heard her wail and pitch beneath him and a terrible crushing feeling in him . . .

And then there was silence.

That lasted for a moment.

And then there was soft music that demanded nothing but inattention. So they lay there, fitted together, in the heat of the tiny room, and they slept for some hours.

After that, Ruddy seldom went out into the light. He did the shopping at night, wearing shades. He emptied the garbage at night, and he swept down the front walk, and did the front lawn with scissors because the lawnmower would have annoyed the residents of the lanai apartments (who no longer complained, because there was seldom a sound from The Hill).

He began to realize he had not seen some of the eleven young people who lived in The Hill for a long time. But the sounds from above and below and around him in the house grew more frequent.

Rudy's clothes were too large for him now. He wore only underpants. His hands and feet hurt. The knuckles of his fingers were larger, from cracking them, and they were always an angry crimson.

His head always buzzed. The thin perpetual odor of pot had saturated into the wood walls and the rafters. He had an itch on the outside of his ears he could not quell. He read newspapers all the time, old newspapers whose items were imbedded in his memory. He remembered a job he had once held as a garage mechanic, but that seemed a very long time ago. When they cut off the electricity in The Hill, it didn't bother Rudy, because he preferred the dark. But he went to tell the eleven.

He could not find them.

They were all gone. Even Kris, who should have been there somewhere.

He heard the moist sounds from the basement and went down with fur and silence into the darkness. The basement had been flooded. One of the eleven was there. His name was Teddy. He was attached to the slime-coated upper wall of the basement, hanging close to the stone, pulsing softly and giving off a thin purple light, purple as a bruise. He dropped a rubbery arm into the water, and let it hang there, moving idly with the tideless tide. Then something came near it, and he made a *sharp* movement, and brought the thing up still writhing in his rubbery grip, and inched it along the wall to a dark, moist spot on his upper surface, near the veins that covered its length, and pushed the thing at the dark-blood spot, where it shrieked with a terrible sound, and went in and there was a sucking noise, then a swallowing sound.

Rudy went back upstairs. On the first floor he found the one who was the blonde girl, whose name was Adrianne. She lay out thin and white as a tablecloth on the dining room table as three of the others he had not seen in a very long while put their teeth into her, and through their hollow sharp teeth they drank up the yellow fluid from the bloated pus-pockets that had been her breasts and her buttocks. Their faces were very white and their eyes were like soot-smudges.

Climbing to the second floor, Rudy was almost knocked down by the passage of something that had been Victor, flying on heavily ribbed leather wings. It carried a cat in its jaws.

He saw the thing on the stairs that sounded as though it was counting heavy gold pieces. It was not counting heavy gold pieces. Rudy could not look at it; it made him feel sick.

He found Kris in the attic, in a corner breaking the skull and sucking out the moist brains of a thing that giggled like a harpischord.

"Kris, we have to go away," he told her. She reached out and touched him, snapping her long, pointed, dirty fingernails against him. He rang like crystal.

In the rafters of the attic Jonah crouched, gargoyled and sleeping. There was a green stain on his jaws, and something stringy in his claws.

"Kris, please," he said urgently.

His head buzzed.

His ears itched.

Kris sucked out the last of the mellow good things in the skull of the silent little creature, and scraped idly at the flaccid body with hairy hands. She settled back on her haunches, and her long, hairy muzzle came up.

Rudy scuttled away.

He ran loping, his knuckles brushing the attic floor as he scampered for safety. Behind him, Kris was growling. He got down to the second floor and then to the first, and tried to climb up on the Morris chair to the mantel, so he could see himself in the mirror, by the light of the moon, through the fly-blown window. But Naomi was on the window, lapping up the flies with her tongue.

He climbed with desperation, wanting to see himself. And when he stood before the mirror, he saw that he was transparent, that there was nothing inside him, that his ears had grown pointed and had hair on their tips; his eyes were as huge as a tarsier's and the reflected light hurt him.

Then he heard the growling behind and below him.

The little glass goblin turned, and the werewolf rose up on its hind legs and touched him till he rang like fine crystal.

And the werewolf said with very little concern, "Have you ever grooved heavy behind *anything* except love?"

"Please!" the little glass goblin begged, just as the great hairy paw slapped him into a million coruscating rainbow fragments all expanding consciously into the tight little enclosed universe that was The Hill, all buzzing highly contacted and tingling off into a darkness that began to seep out through the silent wooden walls . . .

At the Mouse Circus

The King of Tibet was having himself a fat white woman. He had thrown himself down a jelly tunnel, millennia before, and periodically, as he pumped her, a soft pink-and-white bunny rabbit in weskit and spats trembled through, scrutinizing a turnip watch at the end of a heavy gold-link chain. The white woman was soft as suet, with little black eyes thrust deep under prominent brow ridges. Honkie bitch groaned in unfulfilled ecstasy, trying desperately and knowing she never would. For she never had. The King of Tibet had a bellyache. Oh, to be in another place, doing another thing, alone.

The land outside was shimmering in waves of fear that came radiating from mountaintops far away. On the mountaintops, grizzled and wizened old men considered ways and means, considered runes and portents, considered whys and wherefores . . . ignored them all . . . and set about sending more fear to farther places. The land rippled in the night, beginning to quake with terror that was greater than the fear that had gone before.

"What time is it?" he asked, and received no answer.

Thirty-seven years ago, when the King of Tibet had been a lad, there had been a man with one leg—who had been his father for a short time—and a woman with a touch of the tar brush in her, and she had served as mother.

"You can be anything, Charles," she had said to him. "Anything you want to be. A man can be anything he can do. Uncle Wiggily, Jomo Kenyatta, the King of Tibet, if you want to. Light enough or black, Charles, it don't mean a thing. You just go your way and be good and *do*. That's all you got to remember."

The King of Tibet had fallen on hard times. Fat white women and cheap cologne. Doodad, he had lost the horizon. Exquisite, he had dealt with surfaces and been dealt with similarly. Wasted, he had done time.

"I got to go," he told her.

"Not yet, just a little more. Please."

So he stayed. Banners unfurled, lying limp in absence of breezes from Camelot, he stayed and suffered. Finally, she turned him loose, and the King of Tibet stood in the shower for forty minutes. Golden skin pelted, drinking, he was never quite clean. Scented, abluted, he still knew the odors of wombats, hallway musk, granaries, futile beakers of noxious fluids. If he was a white mouse, why could he not see his treadmill?

"Listen, baby, I got need of fi'hunnerd dollahs. I know we ain't been together but a while, but I got this *bad* need." She went to snap-purses and returned.

He hated her more for doing than not doing.

And in her past, he knew he was no part of any recognizable future.

"Charlie, when'll I see you again?" Stranger, never!

Borne away in the silver flesh of Cadillac, the great beautiful mother Hog, plunging wheelbased at one hundred and twenty (bought with his semen) inches, Eldorado god-creature of four hundred horsepower, displacing recklessly 440 cubic inches, thundering into forgetting 4550+ pounds, goes . . . went . . . Charlie . . . Charles . . . the King of Tibet. Golden brown, cleaned as best as he could, five hundred reasons and five hundred aways. Driven, driving into the outside.

Forever inside, the King of Tibet, going outside.

Along the road. Manhattan, Jersey City, New Brunswick, Trenton. In Norristown, having had lunch at a fine restaurant, Charlie was stopped on a street corner by a voice that went *pssst* from a mailbox. He opened the slit and a small boy in a pullover sweater and tie thrust his head and shoulders into the night. "You've got to help me," the boy said. "My name is Batson. Billy Batson. I work for radio station WHIZ and if I could only remember the right word, and if I could only *say* it, something wonderful would happen. S is for the wisdom of Solomon, H is for the strength of Hercules, A is for the stamina of Atlas, Z is for the power of Zeus . . . and after that I go blank."

The King of Tibet slowly and steadily thrust the head back into the mailslot and walked away. Reading, Harrisburg, Mt. Union, Altoona, Nanty Glo.

On the road to Pittsburgh there was a four-fingered mouse in red shorts with two big yellow buttons on the front, hitchhiking. Shoes like two big boxing gloves, bright eyes sincere, forlorn and way lost, he stood on the curb with meaty thumb and he waited. Charlie whizzed past. It was not his dream.

Youngstown, Akron, Canton, Columbus, and hungry once more in Dayton.

O.

Oh aitch eye oh. Why did he ever leave. He had never been there before. This was the good place. The river flowed dark and the day passed overhead like some other river. He pulled into a parking space and did not even lock the god-mother Eldorado. It waited patiently, knowing its upholstered belly would be filled with the King of Tibet soon enough.

"Feed you next," he told the sentient vehicle, as he walked away toward the restaurant.

Inside—dim and candled at high noon—he was shown to a heavy wood booth, and there he had laid before him a pure white linen napkin, five pieces of silver, a crystal goblet in which fine water waited, and a promise. From the promise he selected nine-to-five winners, a long shot and the play number for the day.

A flocked velvet witch perched on a bar stool across from him turned, exposed thigh and smiled. He offered her silver, water, a promise, and they struck a bargain.

Charlie stared into her oiled teakwood eyes through the candle flame between them. All moistened saran-wrap was her skin. All thistled gleaming were her teeth. All mystery of cupped hollows beneath cheekbones was she. Charlie had bought a television set once, because the redhead in the commercial was part of his dream. He had bought an electric toothbrush because the brunette with her capped teeth had indicated she, too, was part of his dream. And his great Eldorado, of course. *That* was the dream of the King of Tibet.

"What time is it?" But he received no answer and, drying his lips of the last of the *pêche flambée*, he and the flocked velvet witch left the restaurant: he with his dream fraying, and she with no product save one to sell.

There was a party in a house on a hill.

When they drove up the asphalt drive, the blacktop beneath them uncoiled like the sooty tongue of a great primitive snake. "You'll like these people," she said, and took the sensitive face of the King of Tibet between her hands and kissed him deeply. Her fingernails were gunmetal silvered and her palms were faintly moist and plump, with expectations of tactile enrichments.

They walked up to the house. Lit from within, every window held a color facet of light. Sounds swelled as they came toward the house. He fell a step behind her and watched the way her skin flowed. She reached out, touched the house, and they became one.

No door was opened to them, but holding fast to her hair he was drawn behind her, through the flesh of the house.

Within, there were inlaid ivory boxes that, when opened, revealed smaller boxes within. He became fascinated by one such box, sitting high on a pedestal in the center of an om rug. The box was inlaid with teeth of otters and puff adders and lynx. He opened the first box and within was a second box frosted with rime. Within the frost-box was a third, and it was decorated with mirrors that cast back no reflections. And next within was a box whose surface was a mass of intaglios, and they were all fingerprints, and none of Charlie's fit, and only when a passing man smiled and caressed the lid did it open, revealing the next, smaller box. And so it went, till he lost count of the boxes and the journey ended when he could not see the box that fit within the dust-mote-size box that was within all the others. But he knew there were more, and he felt a great sadness that he could not get to them.

"What is it, precisely, you want?" asked an older woman with very good bones. He was leaning against a wall whose only ornamentation was a gigantic wooden crucifix on which a Christ figure hung, head bowed, shoulders twisted as only shoulders can be whose arms have been pulled from sockets; the figure was made of massive pieces of wood, all artfully stained: chunks of doors, bedposts, rowels, splines, pintels, joists, cross-ties, rabbet-joined bits of massive frames.

"I want . . ." he began, then spread his hands in confusion. He knew what he wanted to say, but no one had ever ordered the progression of words properly for him.

"Is it Madelaine?" the older woman asked. She smiled as Aunt Jemima would smile, and targeted a finger across the enormous living room, bullseyed on the flocked velvet witch all the way over there by the fireplace. "She's here."

The King of Tibet felt a bit more relaxed.

"Now," the older woman said, her hand on Charlie's cheek, "what is it you need to know. Tell me. We have all the answers here. Truly."

"I want to know—"

The television screen went silver and cast a pool of light, drawing Charlie's attention. The possibilities were listed on the screen. And what he had wanted to know seemed inconsequential compared to the choices he saw listed.

"That one," he said. "That second one. How did the dinosaurs die."

"Oh, fine!" She looked pleased he had selected that one. "Shefti . . . ?" she called to a tall man with gray hair at the temples. He looked up from speaking to several women and another man, looked up expectantly, and she said, "He's picked the second one. May I?"

"Of course, darling," Shefti said, raising his wine glass to her.

"Do we have time?"

"Oh, I think so," he said.

"Yes . . . what time *is* it?" Charlie asked.

"Over here," the older woman said, leading him firmly by the forearm. They stopped beside another wall. "Look."

The King of Tibet stared at the wall, and it paled, turned to ice, and became translucent. There was something imbedded in the ice. Something huge. Something dark. He stared harder, his eyes straining to make out the shape. Then he was seeing more clearly and it was a great saurian, frozen at the moment of pouncing on some lesser species.

"*Gorgosaurus*," the older woman said, at his elbow. "It rather resembles *Tyrannosaurus*, you see; but the forelimbs have only two digits. You see?"

Thirty-two feet of tanned gray leather. The killing teeth. The nostriled snout, the amber smoke eyes of the eater of carrion. The smooth, sickening tuber of balancing tail, the crippled forelimbs carried tragically withered and useless. The musculature . . . the pulsing beat of iced blood beneath the tarpaulin hide. The . . . beat . . .

It lived.

Through the ice went the King of Tibet, accompanied by the Circe-eyed older woman, as the shellfish-white living room receded back beyond the ice-wall. Ice went, night came.

Ice that melted slowly from the great hulk before him. He stood in wonder. "See," the woman said.

And he saw as the ice dissolved into mist and night-fog, and he saw as the earth trembled, and he saw as the great fury lizard moved in shambling hesitancy, and he saw as the others came to cluster unseen nearby. *Scolosaurus* came. *Trachodon* came. *Stephanosaurus* came. *Protoceratops* came. And all stood, waiting.

The King of Tibet knew there were slaughterhouses where the beef was hung upside-down on hooks, where the throats were slit and the blood ran thick as motor oil. He saw a golden thing hanging, and would not look. Later, he would look.

They waited. Silently, for its coming.

Through the Cretaceous swamp it was coming. Charlie could hear it. Not loud, but coming steadily closer. "Would you light my cigarette, please?" asked the older woman.

It was shining. It bore a pale white nimbus. It was stepping through the swamp, black to its thighs from the decaying matter. It came on, its eyes set back under furred brow ridges, jaw thrust forward, wide nostrils sniffing at the chill night, arms covered with matted filth and hair. Savior man.

He came to the lizard owners of the land. He walked around them and they stood silently, their time at hand. Then he touched them, one after the other, and the plague took them. Blue fungus spread from the five-pronged marks left on their imperishable hides; blue death radiating from impressions of opposed thumbs, joining, spreading cilia and rotting the flesh of the great gone dinosaurs.

The ice re-formed and the King of Tibet moved back through pearly cold to the living room.

He struck a match and lit her cigarette.

She thanked him and walked away.

The flocked velvet witch returned. "Did you have a nice time?" He thought of the boxes-within-boxes.

"Is that how they died? Was he the first?"

She nodded. "And did Nita ask you for anything?"

Charlie had never seen the sea. Oh, there had been the Narrows and the East River and the Hudson, but he had never seen the sea. The real sea, the thunder sea that went black at night like a pane of glass. The sea that could summon and the sea that could kill, that could swallow whole cities and turn them into myth. He wanted to go to California.

He suddenly felt a fear he would never leave this thing called Ohio here.

"I asked you: did Nita ask you for anything?"

He shivered.

"What?"

"Nita. Did she *ask* you for anything?"

"Only a light."

"Did you give it to her?"

"Yes."

Madelaine's face swam in the thin fluid of his sight. Her jaw muscles trembled. She turned and walked across the room. Everyone turned to look at her. She went to Nita, who suddenly took a step backward and threw up her hands. "No, I didn't—"

The flocked velvet witch darted a hand toward the older woman and the hand seemed to pass into her neck. The silver tipped fingers reappeared, clenched around a fine sparkling filament. Then Madelaine snapped it off with a grunt.

There was a terrible minor sound from Nita, then she turned, watery, and stood silently beside the window, looking empty and hopeless.

Madelaine wiped her hand on the back of the sofa and came to Charlie. "We'll go now. The party is over."

He drove in silence back to town.

"Are you coming up?" he asked, when they parked Eldorado in front of the hotel.

"I'm coming up."

He registered them as Prof. Pierre and Marja Sklodowska Curie and for the first time in his life he was unable to reach a climax. He fell asleep sobbing over never having seen the sea, and came awake hours later with the night still pressing against the walls. She was not there.

He heard sounds from the street, and went to the window.

There was a large crowd in the street, gathered around his car.

As he watched, a man went to his knees before the golden Eldorado and touched it. Charlie knew *this* was his dream. He could not move; he just watched; as they ate his car.

The man put his mouth to the hood and it came away bloody. A great chunk had been ripped from the gleaming hide of the Cadillac. Golden blood ran down the man's jaws.

Another man draped himself over the top of the car, and even through the window the King of Tibet could hear the terrible sucking, slobbering sounds. Furrows were ripped in the top.

A woman pulled her dress up around her hips and backed, on all fours, to the rear of the car. Her face trembled with soft expectancy, and then it was inside her and she moved on it.

When she came, they all moved in on the car and he watched as his dream went inside them, piece by piece, chewed and eaten as he stood by helpless.

"That's all, Charlie," he heard her say, behind him. He could not turn to look at her, but her reflection was superimposed over his own in the window. Out there in darkness now, they moved away, having eaten.

He looked, and saw the golden thing hanging upside-down in the slaughterhouse, its throat cut, its blood drained away in onyx gutters.

Afoot, in Dayton, Ohio, he was dead of dreams.

"What time is it?" he asked.

XII

SHADOWS FROM THE PAST

> "It's all there, what happened to Jeffty. [. . .] As the Past is always there, if you learn from it; treasure the treasures and let the dross go without remorse."
>
> —Introduction to "Jeffty Is Five," SHATTERDAY, Houghton Mifflin, 1980

Place a finger on your pulse for a moment. There, got it?

The skin feels the same, as does the pressure of the moving blood, yet biology lessons come back to us and we know what we touch is new flesh. Each cell in the body is different than the one we had days, months, years ago. Every pressure in our circulatory system is a brand new burst of energy, similar to the one before and the one to come after . . . but infinitesimally distinct. Our current physical totality is the sum of all past moments, and while the moments may be gone forever, the body remembers the shadow patterns and follows their dictates.

And so, too, does the mind.

These stories represent some of the most autobiographical of Harlan's works, and because of this you will find duplications of the shadow-patterns that haunt the author's brain. The trick, however, is not to piece together the specifics of Harlan Ellison's life but only to recognize the commonality of our emotional spurs. For as Harlan persists in reminding us with his work, each person is a universe and each picture we see is no more than a mote of dust in the space between the stars. There is no human camera large enough to view it all. The best we can do is look for recognizable patterns and carefully grope in the dark for a pulse.

"Free With This Box!" (1958) gives us a moment of childhood. It's not presented as a nostalgic memory—even though we may feel a twinge of nostalgia if we're old enough to remember cereal selling for 23¢ a box—but rather as a reconstitution of the learning experience of a child. On the surface it is a trivial memory, but in the end it focuses on a small shadow that promises to hold its corner for a long time to come.

Returning to the past from the present is an entirely different matter. In "Final Shtick" (1960), the trip is measured in miles literal as well as symbolic, and the people we've known along the way stand as signposts to our future. How we read those signposts makes all the difference in the world. We must make the choice: follow the signposts' directions, heedless of where they lead, or create our own way. Marty Field made a choice, and you're invited to share the guilt.

Another journey back, this time directly to the source, is achingly depicted in "One Life, Furnished in Early Poverty" (1970). Familiar characters and situations repeat, but if Marty Field is also Gus Rosenthal, then he is ten years farther down that road, and has a keener insight into how and why he became that defiant little boy. (Note, too, how Harlan recycles his past in "Mr. Rosenthal"'s remembrance of the same carny in "Gopher in the Gilly.")

After mishearing a portion of conversation near him at a party, Harlan wrote "Jeffty Is Five" (1977), a result of the wondrous mental gymnastics that caused his mind to flash "on a little boy who has been snared at the age of five, who never gets any older." Harlan added, "there is a part of Jeffty that is me, very much me, achingly me," and not much more needs to be added to that. If the shadows from the past can cripple or destroy us, surely they can also give us surcease from the pain. It is cruelty to repress or dissolve this special shadow of solace, and Harlan shows us how to touch it tenderly with love and respect. It's a nice touch and a nice feeling.

"You see before you a child who never grew up, who does not know it's socially unacceptable to ask, 'Who farted?' "

—"Mortal Dreads," Introduction to SHATTERDAY, Houghton Mifflin, 1980

Free With This Box!

His name was David Thomas Cooper. His mother called him Davey, and his teachers called him David, but he was old enough now to be called the way the guys called him: Dave. After all, eight years old was no longer a child. He was big enough to walk to school himself, and he was big enough to stay up till eight-thirty any weeknight.

Mommy had said last year, "For every birthday, we will let you stay up a half hour later," and she had kept her word. The way he figured it, a few more years, and he could stay up all night, almost.

He was a slim boy, with unruly black hair that cowlicked up in the back, and slipped over his forehead in the front. He had an angular face, and wide deep eyes of black, and he sucked his thumb when he was sure no one was watching.

And right now, right this very minute, the thing he wanted most in all the world was a complete set of the buttons.

Davey reached into his pants pocket, and brought out the little cloth bag with the drawstring. Originally it had held his marbles, but now they were back home in his room, in an empty Red Goose shoe box. Now the little bag held the buttons. He turned sidewise on the car seat, and pried open the bag with two fingers. The buttons clinked metallically. There were twenty-four of them in there. He had taken the pins off them, because he wasn't a gook like Leon, who wore *his* on his beanie. Davey liked to lay the buttons out on the table, and arrange them in different designs. It wasn't so much that they had terrific pictures on them, though each one contained the face of a familiar comic character, but it was just *having* them.

He felt so good when he thought that there were only eight more to get.

Just Skeezix, Little Orphan Annie, Andy Gump, the Little King,

B.O. Plenty, Mandrake the Magician, Harold Teen—and the scarcest one of them all—Dick Tracy. Then he would have the entire set, and he would beat out Roger and Hobby and even Leon across the street.

Then he would have the whole set offered by the cereal company. And it wasn't just the competition with the other kids; he couldn't quite explain it, but it was a feeling of *accomplishment* every time he got a button he did not already have. When he had them all, just those last eight, he would be the happiest boy in the world.

But it was dangerous, and Davey knew it.

It wasn't that Mommy wouldn't buy him the boxes of Pep. They were only 23¢ a box, and Mommy bought one each week, but that was only *one* comic character button a week! Not hardly enough to get the full set before they stopped putting the buttons in and offered something new. Because there was always so much *duplication*, and Davey had three Superman buttons (they were the *easiest* to get) while Hobby only had one Dick Tracy. And Hobby wouldn't trade. So Davey had had to figure out a way to get more buttons.

There were thirty-two glossy, colored buttons in the set. Each one in a cellophane packet at the bottom of every box of Pep.

One day, when he had gone shopping with Mommy, he had detached himself from her, and wandered to the cereal shelves. There he had taken one of the boxes down, and before he had quite known what he was doing, had shoved his forefinger through the cardboard, where the wall and bottom joined. He could still remember his wild elation at feeling the edge of the packet. He had stuck in another finger, widening the rip in the box, and scissored out the button.

That had been the time he had gotten Annie's dog Sandy.

That had been the time he had known he could not wait for Mommy to buy his box a week. Because that was the time he got Sandy, and no one, not *anyone* in the whole neighborhood, had even seen that button. That had been the time.

So Davey had carefully and assiduously cajoled Mommy every week, when she went to the A&P. It has seemed surprising at first, but Mommy loved Davey, and there was no trouble about it.

That first week, when he had gotten Sandy, he had learned that it was not wise to be in the A&P with Mommy, because she might discover what he was doing. And though he felt no guilt about it, he knew he was doing wrong . . . and he would just die if Mommy knew about it. She might wander down the aisle where he stood—pretending to read the print on the back of the box, but actually fishing about in the side for the cellophane packet—and see him. Or they might catch him, and hold him, and she would be called to identify this naughty boy who was stealing.

So he had learned the trick of waiting in the car, playing with the buttons in the bag, till Mommy came from the A&P with the boy, and they loaded the bags in, and then she would kiss him and tell him he was such a good boy for waiting quietly, and she would be right back after she had gone to the Polish Bakery across the street, and stopped into the Woolworth's.

Davey knew how long that took. Almost half an hour.

More than long enough to punch holes in ten or twelve boxes, and drag out the buttons that lay within. He usually found at least two new ones. At first—that second week he had gone with Mommy to the shopping—he had gotten more than that. Five or six. But with the eventual increase in duplication, he was overjoyed to find even one new button.

Now there were only eight left, and he emptied the little cloth bag onto the car seat, making certain no buttons slipped between the cushions.

He turned them all up, so their rounded tops were full toward him. He rotated them so the Phantom and Secret Agent X-9 were not upside-down. Then he put them in rows of fours; six rows with four in a row. then he put them in rows of eight. Then he just scooted them back into the bag and jingled them hollowly at his ear.

It was the *having*, that was all.

"How long have I been?" Mommy asked from outside the window. Behind at her right a fat, sweating boy with pimples on his forehead held a big box, high to his chest.

He didn't answer her, because the question had never really been asked. Mommy had that habit. She asked him questions, and was always a little surprised when he answered. Davey had learned to distinguish between questions like, "Where did you put your bedroom slippers?" and "Isn't this a lovely hat Mommy's bought?"

So he did not answer, but watched with the interest of a conspirator waiting for the coast to clear, as Mommy opened the front door, and pushed the seat far forward so the boy could put the box in the back seat. Davey had to scrunch far forward against the dashboard when she did that, but he liked the pressure of the seat on his back.

Then she leaned over and kissed him, which he liked, but which made his hair fall over his forehead, and Mommy's eyes crinkled up the nice way, and she smoothed back his hair. Then she slammed the door, and walked across the street, to the bakery.

Then, when Mommy had gone into the bakery, he got out of the car, and walked across the summer sidewalk to the A&P. It was simple getting in, and he knew where the cereals were brightly stacked. Down one aisle, and into a second, and there, halfway down, he saw the boxes.

A new supply! A new batch of boxes since last week, and for an instant he was cold and terrified that they had stopped packing the comic buttons, that they were offering something worthless like towels or cut-outs or something.

But as he came nearer, his heart jumped brightly in him, and he saw the words FREE WITH THIS BOX! on them.

Yes, those were the boxes with the comic buttons.

Oh, it was going to be a wonderful day, and he hummed the little tune he had made up that went:

"Got a nickel in my pocket,
"Gonna spend it all today.
"Got my buttons in my pocket,
"Gonna get the rest today."

Then he was in front of them, and he had the first one in his hands. He held the box face-toward-him, hands at the bottom on the sides, and he was pressing, pressing his fingers into the cardboard joint. It was sometimes difficult, and the skin between his first and second fingers was raw and cracked from rubbing against the boxes. This time, however, the seam split, and he had his fingers inside.

The packet was far over, and he had to grope, tearing the box a little more. His fingers split the waxpaper liner that held the cereal away from the box, but in a moment he had his finger down on the packet, and was dragging it out.

It was another Sandy.

He felt an unhappiness like no other he had ever known except the day he got his new trike, and scratched it taking it out the driveway. It was an all-consuming thing, and he would have cried right there, except he knew there were more boxes. He shoved the button back in, because that wouldn't be the right thing to do—to take a button he already had. That would be waste, and dishonest.

He took a second box. Then a third, then a fourth, then a fifth.

By the time he had opened eight boxes, he had not found a new one, and was getting desperate, because Mommy would be back soon, and he had to be there when she came to the car. He was starting his ninth box, the others all put back where they had come from, but all crooked, because the ripped part on their bottom made them sit oddly, when the man in the white A&P jacket came by.

He had been careful to stop pushing and dragging when anyone came by . . . had pretended to be just reading what the boxes said . . . but he did not see the A&P man.

"Hey! What're ya doin' there?"

The man's voice was heavy and gruff, and Davey felt himself get cold all the way from his stomach to his head. Then the man had a hand around Davey's shoulder, and was turning him roughly. Davey's hand was still inside the box. The man stared for an instant, then his eyes widened.

"So *you're* the one's been costin' us so much dough!"

Davey was sure he would never forget that face if he lived to be a thousand or a million or forever.

The man had eyebrows that were bushy and grew together in the middle, with long hairs that flopped out all over. He had a mole on his chin, and a big pencil behind one ear. The man was staring down at Davey with so much anger, Davey was certain he would wither under the glance in a moment.

"Come on, you, I'm takin' you to the office."

Then he took Davey to a little cubicle behind the meat counter, and sat Davey down, and asked him, "What's your name?"

Davey would not answer.

The worst thing, the most worst thing in the world, would be if Mommy found out about this. Then she would tell Daddy when he came home from the store, and Daddy would be even madder, and spank him with his strap.

So Davey would not tell the man a thing, and when the man looked through Davey's pockets and found the bag with the buttons, he said. "Oh, *ho*. Now I *know* you're the one!" and he looked some more.

Finally he said, "You got no wallet. Now either you tell me who you are, who your parents are, or I take you down to the police station."

Still Davey would say nothing, though he felt tears starting to urge themselves from his eyes. And the man pushed a button on a thing on his desk, and when a woman came in—she had on a white jacket belted at the waist—the moley man said, "Mert, I want you to take over for me for a little while. I've just discovered the thief who has been breaking open all those boxes of cereal. I'm taking him," and the moley man gave a big wink to the woman named Mert, "down to the police station. That's where *all* bad thieves go, and I'll let *them* throw him into a cell for years and years, since he won't tell me his name."

So Mert nodded and clucked her tongue and said what a shame it was that such a little boy was such a big thief, and even, "Ooyay onday ontway ootay airscay the idkay ootay uchmay."

Davey knew that was pig Latin, but he didn't know it as well as Hobby or Leon, so he didn't know what they were saying, even when the moley man answered, "Onay, I ustjay ontway ootay ootpay the earfay of odgay in ishay edhay."

Then he thought that it was all a joke, and they would let him go, but even if they didn't, it wasn't anything to be frightened of, because Mommy had told him lots of times that the policemen were his friends, and they would protect him. He *liked* policemen, so he didn't care.

Except that if they took him to the policemen, when Mommy came back from the Woolworth's, he would be gone, and *then* would he be in trouble.

But he could not say anything. It was just not right to speak to this moley man. So he walked beside the man from the A&P when he took

Davey by the arm and walked him out the back door, and over to a pickup truck with a big A&P lettered on the side. He even sat silently when they drove through town, and turned in at the police station.

And he was silent as the moley man said to the big, fat, red-faced policeman with the sweat-soaked shirt, "This is a little thief I found in the store today, Al. He has been breaking into our boxes, and I thought you would want to throw him in a cell."

Then he winked at the big beefy policeman, and the policeman winked back, and grinned, and then his face got very stern and hard, and he leaned across the desk, staring at Davey.

"What's your name, boy?"

His voice was like a lot of mushy stuff swirling around in Mommy's washer. But even so, Davey would have told him his name was David Thomas Cooper and that he lived at 744 Terrace Drive, Mayfair, Ohio . . . if the moley man had not been there.

So he was silent, and the policeman looked up at the moley man, and said very loudly, looking at Davey from the corner of his brown eyes, "Well, Ben, it looks like I'll have to take harsher methods with this criminal. I'll have to show him what happens to people who steal!"

He got up, and Davey saw he was big and fat, and not at all the way Mommy had described policemen. The beefy man took him by the hand, and led him down a corridor, with the moley man coming along too, saying, "Say, ya know, I never been through your drunk tank, Chief. Mind if I tag along?" and the beefy man answered no.

Then came a time of horror for Davey.

They took him to a room where a man lay on a dirty bunk, and he stank and there were summer flies all over him, and he had been sick all over the floor and the mattress and he was lying in it, and Davey wanted to throw up. There was a place with bars on it where a man tried to grab at them as they went past, and the policeman hit his hand through the bars with a big stick on a cord. There were lots of people cooped up and unhappy, and the place was all stinky, and in a little while, Davey was awfully frightened, and started to cry, and wanted to go hide himself, or go home.

Finally, they came back to the first place they had been, and the policeman crouched down next to Davey and shook him as hard as he could by the shoulders, and screamed at him never, never, never to do anything illegal again, or they would throw him in with the man who had clawed out, and throw away the key, and let the man eat Davey alive.

And that made Davey cry more.

Which seemed to make the policeman and the moley man happy, because Davey heard the policeman say to the moley man named Ben from the A&P, "That'll straighten him out. He's so young, making the right kind of impression on 'em now is what counts. He won't bother ya again, Ben. Leave him here, and he'll ask for his folks soon enough. Then we can take him home."

The moley man shook hands with the policeman, and thanked him, and said he could get any cut of meat he wanted at the store whenever he came in, and thanks again for the help.

Then, just as the moley man was leaving, he stooped down, and looked straight at Davey with his piercing eyes.

"You ever gonna steal anything from cereal boxes again?"

Davey was so frightened, he shook his head no, and the tear lines on his face felt sticky as he moved.

The moley man stood up, and grinned at the policeman, and walked out, leaving Davey behind, in that place that scared him so.

And it was true.

Davey never *would* steal from the cereal boxes again, he knew. As a matter of fact, he hated cereal now.

And he didn't much care for *cops*, either.

FINAL SHTICK

SHTICK: *n.; deriv. Yiddish; a "piece," a "bit," a rehearsed anecdote; as in a comedian's routine or act.*

I'm a funny man, he thought, squashing the cigarette stub into the moon-face of the egg. *I'm a goddam riot.* He pushed the flight-tray away.

See the funny mans! His face magically struck an attitude as the stewardess removed the tray. It was expected—he was, after all, a *funny* man. *Don't see me, sweetie, see a laugh.* He turned with a shrug of self-disgust to the port. His face stared back at him; the nose was classically Greek in profile. He sneered at it.

Right over the wing; he could barely make out the Ohio patchwork-quilt far below, gray and gunmetal blue through the morning haze. *Now I fly,* he mused. *Now I fly. When I left it was in a fruit truck. But now I'm Marty Field, king of the sick comics, and I fly. Fun*-ee!

He lit another, spastically, angrily.

Return to Lainesville. Home. Return for the dedication. That's you they're honoring, Marty Field, just you, only you. Aside from General Laine, who founded the town, there's never been anybody worth honoring who's come from Lainesville. So return. Thirteen years later. Thirteen years before the mast, buddy-boy. Return, Marty Field, and see all those wondrous, memorable faces from your ohsohappy past. Go, Marty baby. Return!

He slapped at the button overhead, summoning the stewardess. His face again altered: an image of chuckles for replacement. "How about a couple of cubes of sugar, sweetheart?" he asked as she leaned over him, expectantly. *Yeah, doll, I see 'em. Thirty-two C? Yes, indeed, they're loverly; now get my sugar, howzabout?*

When she dropped them into his hand he gave her a brief, calculated-to-the-kilowatt grin. He unwrapped one and chewed on it, staring moodily out the port.

Think about it, Marty Field. Think about how it was, before you were Marty Field. Thirteen years before, when it was Morrie Feldman, and you were something like a kid. Think about it, and think what those faces from the past recall. How do *they* remember it? You know damned well how they remember it, and you know what they're saying now, on the day you're returning to Lainesville to be lauded and applauded. What is Mrs. Shanks, who lived next door, remembering about those days? And what is Jack Wheeldon, the childhood classmate, thinking? And Peggy Mantle? What about Leon Potter—you used to run with him—what concoction of half-remembered images and projections has he contrived? You know people, Marty Field. You've *had* to learn about them; that's why your comedy strikes so well . . . because you know the way people think, and their foibles. So think about it, baby. As your plane nears Cleveland, and you prepare to meet the committee that will take you to Lainesville, dwell on it. Create their thoughts for them, Marty boy.

MRS. SHANKS: Why, certainly I remember Marty. He was always over at my house. Why, I believe he lived as much on my front porch as he did at home. Nice boy. I can remember that little thin face of his (he was always such a frail child, you know), always smiling, though. Used to love my Christmas cookies. Used to make me bake 'em for him all year 'round. And the imagination that child had . . . why, he'd go into the empty lot behind our houses and make a fort, dig it right out of the ground, and play in there all day with his toy guns. He was something, even then. Knew he'd make it some day . . . he was just that sort. Came from a good family, and that sort of thing always shows.
EVAN DENNIS: Marty always had that spark. It was something you couldn't name. A drive, a wanting, a something that wouldn't let him quit. I remember I used to talk with his father—you remember Lew, the jeweler, don't you—and we'd discuss the boy. His father and I were very close. For a while there Lew was pretty worried about the boy; a bit rambunctious. But I always said, "Lew, no need to worry about Morrie (that was his name; he changed his name, y'know; I was very close with the family). He'll make it, that boy. Good stuff in him." Yeah, I remember the whole family very well. We were very close, y'know.
JACK WHEELDON: Hell, I knew him *before*. A lot of the other kids were always picking on him. He was kinda small, and like that, but I took him under my wing. I was sort of a close buddy. Hell, we used to ride our bikes real late at night, out in the middle of Mentor Avenue, going 'round and 'round in circles under the streetlight, because we just liked to do it. We got to be pretty tight. Hell, maybe I was his best friend.

Always dragged him along when we were getting up a baseball game. He wasn't too good, being so small and like that, but, hell, he needed to get included, so I made the other guys let him play. Always picked him for my side too. Yeah, I guess I knew him better than anybody when he was a kid.

PEGGY MANTLE: I've got to admit it, I loved him. He wasn't the toughest kid in school, or the best-looking, but even then, even when he was young, he was so—so, I don't know what you'd call, *dynamic* . . . Well, I just loved him, that's all. He was great. Just great. I loved him, that's all.

LEON POTTER: Marty? The times we had, nobody could match. We were real crazy. Used to take bath towels and crayon CCC in a triangle on them, and tie them around our necks, and play Crime Cracker Cids. Kids, that should have been, but we were just fooling around. You know, we'd make up these crimes and solve them. Like we'd take milk bottles out of the wooden boxes everybody had at their side door, and then pretend there was a milk bottle thief around, and solve the case. We had good times. I liked him lots. It'll be good seeing him again. Wonder if he remembers me—oh, yeah, he'll remember *me*.

There they go, the vagrants, swirled away as the warning plaque lights up with its FASTEN SEAT BELTS and NO SMOKING. There they go, back to the soft-edged world where they belong; somewhere inside your head, Marty Field. They're gone, and you're here, and the plane is coming in over Cleveland. So now think carefully . . . answer carefully . . . *do* you remember?

As the plane taxis up to Cleveland Municipal Airport, do you remember Leon? Do you remember Peggy, whose father owned the Mantle apple orchards? Do you remember Evan Dennis who tried to raise a beard and looked like a poor man's Christ or a poorer man's van Gogh? Do they come back unfogged, Marty Field who was Morrie Feldman of 89 Harmon Drive, Lainesville, Ohio? Are they there, all real and the way they really were?

Or do the years muddy the thinking? Are they softer in their images, around the edges? Can you think about them the way they're thinking about you? Come on, don't hedge your bets, Marty Field. You're a big man now; you did thirteen weeks at the Copa, you play the Chez and the Hollywood Palace. You get good bait from Sullivan and Sinatra when they want you on their shows, and Pontiac's got a special lined up for you in the Fall, so you don't have to lie to anyone. Not to their memories, not to yourself, not even to the Fates. Tell the truth, Marty, and see how it sounds.

Don't be afraid. Only cowards are afraid, Marty, and you're not conditioned to be a coward, are you? Left home at seventeen, out on a fruit truck, riding in the cab right behind the NO HITCHHIKERS sticker on the windshield. You've been around, Marty Field, and you know what the score is, so tell the truth. Level with yourself. You're going back to see them after thirteen years and you've got to know.

I'm cashing in on the big rock 'n' roll craze, slanting songs at the teenagers. The way I figure it, they've exhausted the teen market, and they're going to have to start on the pre-teens, so I'm going to beat the trend. I've just recorded my first record, it's called "Nine Years Old and So Much in Love." It's backed with "Ten Years Old and Already Disillusioned."

Okay, Marty, forget the sick *shticks*. That's what got you your fame, that's why they're honoring you today in Lainesville. But that's dodging the issue. That's turning tail and running, Marty. Forget the routines, just answer the questions. Do you remember them? The truth now.

You're about as funny as a guided tour through Dachau.

Another bit, Marty? Another funny from your long and weirdie repertoire? Or is that routine closer to the truth? Is it a subconscious gag, Marty, babe? Does it set you thinking about Evan Dennis and Jack Wheeldon and all the rest from the sleepy, rustic town of Lainesville, just thirty-one miles from Cleveland in the so-called liberal heart of the great American Midwest?

Is it the truth, as you descend the aluminum staircase of the great flying machine, Marty Field?

Does it start the old mental ball game, that remark about Dachau, where they threw Jews into furnaces? Does it do something to your nice pseudo-Gentile gut? That gut that has been with you since Morrie Feldman days . . . that heaved on you when you had the nose-job done to give you such a fine Gentile snout . . . that didn't complain when the name was changed legally. Does it bother that gut now, and give you the hollow, early-morning-chilly feeling of having stayed up all night on speed and hot, black coffee? Does it bug you, Marty?

. . . ve haff an interesting phenomena in Chermany today . . . you'll haff to excuse the paint under my fingernails: I've been busy all night, writing goyim go home *on the doors of Volkswagens . . .*

Oooh, that was a zinger, wasn't it, Marty. It was a nice switch on the synagogue-swastika-painting bits the papers have been carrying. Or is it just that, Marty? Say, how the hell did you ever become a sick comic, anyhow? Was it a way of making a buck, or are you a little sick yourself? Maybe a little angry?

At what, goddam you, get outta here and let me alone!

Why, at your past, Marty, babe. Your swingin' past in good old we're-honoring-Marty-Field Lainesville.

Is that the axe, sweetie? Is that why you keep swingin'?

Shut up. Let me alone. It's a gig, that's all, just another gig. It's a booking. I'm in. I'm out. I take their lousy honor and blow the scene. There's no social signif here. I'm a sickie because it's a buck. That's it. I'm whole; I'm not a weirdie, that's just my bit. It goes over.

Sure, Marty. Sure, babe. I understand perfectly.

What'd you call me?

Not a thing, swinger. Not a mumblin' thing.

You'd damned well better not *call me yellow, either.*

Cool it, chickie. No one's asking you to cop out. The whole world loves Marty Field. He's a swinger. He's a funny man. He was a funny kid, maybe too, but now he's a funny man. Go on, sweetie, there they are, waiting behind the hurricane fence, waiting to greet the conquering hero. Go on, Attila, say something funny for the people.

The banner was raised by two children, then, and Marty Field's face broke into its calculated good humor at the sight of

WELCOME HOME MARTY FIELD
PRIDE OF LAINESVILLE!!!!

It wasn't such a long ride, but then it never had been. Thirty-one miles, past the fair grounds, past the Colony Lumber Company where he had played so long before. Remembering the condemned pond so deep behind the Colony Lumber Company; remembering his birthday, when he had thought there would be no party, and he had stayed all day, miserable and wasting time, only to go home and see the remains of the surprise party, held without him. Remembering the tears for something lost, and never to be regained.

Past Lathrop Grade School, where he had broken one of the ornamental lamps over the door. Past Harmon Drive, where he had lived. Down Mentor Avenue, and after a time, into the center of town. The square, and around the square, past what was once the Lyric Theater, now metamorphosed into an office building. Remembering the tiny theater, and its ridiculous banner beneath the marquee: *Lake County's Most Intimate Theater*. Remembering how you had to sit in your neighbor's lap, the movie was so small. Intimate, indeed. Remembering.

Then the hotel, and washing up, and a fresh white shirt with button-down collar, and your Continental suit, so they could stare and say, "He really knows how to dress in style, don't he?"

All that, all so fast, one bit after another. Too many memories, too many attempts to unravel the truth about what really happened. Was it a happy childhood? Was it the way they say it was, and the way you'd like to remember it?

Or was it something else? Something that has made you the man you are . . . that man who climbs into the spotlight every day of his life, takes a scissors and cuts up his fellow man. Which way was it, Marty? Come on, stop stalling.

An honor banquet, and Lord! they never had food like that in Lainesville before. No pasty dry sliver of white chicken meat for Marty Field, no indeed not! The best of the best for the man who outTrendexed

Bonanza. And after the meal, a fast tour of the town—kept open, center-stripe on Main Street left rolled out after eight o'clock—just to stir that faulty, foggy memory.

A dance at the Moose lodge . . .

A late night pizza . . .

A lot of autographs . . .

Too many handshakes . . .

Then let's get some sleep, don't forget the big dedication of the plaque tomorrow, over at the high school, that's a helluvan honor, doncha know.

Sleep. You call *that* a sleep?

"Ladies and gentlemen," the principal began, "humor is a very delicate thing." He was a big, florid man; his job had been secure for fifteen years, with the exception of the time Champion Junior High had been condemned, torn down and joined with the new senior high. Then they had tried to drag in a man from East Cleveland, but the principal had called on his brother-in-law, whose influence in local politics was considerable. And abruptly, the man from East Cleveland had found his record wanting. The principal was a big, florid, *well-fed* and *secure* man.

"And like all delicate things," he went on, "it takes a special sort of green thumb to make it flower. Such a green thumb is possessed by the man I'm privileged to introduce this afternoon.

"I recall the first time I ever saw Marty Field," he pontificated, drawing thumbs down into vest pockets. "I was principal of the old Champion Junior High, and one September morning as I left my office, I saw a thin, small boy hurrying late to class. Well, sir, I said to myself . . ."

Marty Field closed off reception. There it was. Again. The small, short, sickly bit again. Yeah, you were so right, Principal. I *was* small and miserable thin, and that was part of it. But only part. That was the part where I couldn't keep up. But that isn't where it began. It went back much farther.

Go back, then, Marty Field. For the first time since they contacted you about the honors Lainesville wanted to bestow on you, go back and conjure it up as it really was.

Tell it true, Marty. No gags, no punch lines, no *shticks* . . . just the way it was.

All things are as they were then, except . . .

YOU ARE THERE . . .

Your name is Morrie Feldman. Your father's name is Lew Feldman, your mother is Sarah Feldman. You are the only Jew on your street, the only Jewish kid in your grade school. There are seven Jewish families in town. You go to Lathrop Grade School and you are a little kid. At recess time they get you out on the ball diamond, and one of them picks a fight with you. Usually it's Jack Wheeldon, whose head is square and whose hair is cut in a butch, and whose father is a somethingorother at the Diamond Alkali plant. Jack Wheeldon is big and laughs like a jackass and you don't like him because he looks with a terrible strangeness out of his cruel eyes.

You stand there while Jack Wheeldon calls you a dirty kike, and your mother is a dirty kike and you pee your pants because *all* kikes do that, don't they, you frigging little kike? And when you swing, and hit him on the side of the head, the circle of kids magically grows about you, and while you're locked in an adolescent grapple with Jack Wheeldon (who is all the things in this life that you despise because they are bigger than you and slower-witted and frightening), someone kicks you from behind. Hard. At the base of your spine. With a Thom McAn shoe. And then you can't help it and you start to cry.

You fall down, and they begin kicking you. They all kick you very hard, and you aren't old enough or smart enough to pull your arms and legs around you. So after a while everything goes sandy and fuzzy and you know you are unconscious. There's a special sort of pleasure in that, because that's what happens to the good guys in the movies on Saturday afternoons, when they're being attacked by the bad guys. And after a while Miss Dexter with the pointy nose, from the fifth grade upstairs, comes out on the playground, and sees what is happening, and goes back inside to tell someone else. Then, later, nice Miss O'Hara, from the third grade, who likes you, comes running out, and lifts you in her arms and tenderly carries you inside.

The first thing you hear when you wake up is one of the kids saying ". . . dirty Jewish elephant." And you wonder with childish logic why he calls you an elephant. You don't have a long trunk. That is the first time they let you know you have a *shonikker apple* between your eyes and your mouth.

Your name is Morrie Feldman, and you live at 89 Harmon Drive. You have been away at camp all summer, and now you are back, and your father is telling you that your dog Puddles was gassed while you were away. Mrs. Shanks, next door, called the pound while your father and mother were in Cleveland for the afternoon, and had them take Puddles down and gas him. Your father tells you he is sorry, and doesn't know why Mrs. Shanks would do such a thing, but you run out of the house and hide under the side porch all day and cry, anyhow. Later, you steal Mrs. Shanks's rug-beater from her garage. You bury it very deep in the soft, amber dirt behind the garage.

Your name is Morrie Feldman, and you are in junior high school. You hear something heavy hit the front of your house late one night, and then something else, and then a half-eaten grapefruit comes crashing through your front window, and out on the lawn—here in Ohio, and who'd ever think it—you see a huge cross burning. The next day you learn about the Anti-Defamation League. You don't tell anyone that you saw Mr. Evan Dennis from Dennis's Florists, with soot on his face and hands, running down the street to a car with its headlights out.

The name is the same, and it's later, and somehow you have a girl named Peggy Mantle, who has blonde hair and blue eyes and Anglo-Saxon features, and you love her very much. Until you catch her doing things she never did with you. She's doing them in the bushes behind her house after the Halloween party. She's doing them with Leon Potter, from across the street, whose mother always slams the door when you come on the porch. You don't say anything. You can't. You're afraid.

You've been afraid for a long time now. When you were smaller, once in a while you could beat Jack Wheeldon, or convince Leon that he should play with you. But they've continued to get bigger, and you've stayed small and frail, and they can beat you with their fists.

So you've learned to cut them up with your tongue.

You've learned how to tear them and shred them and slice them with your mouth. That's how it started. That's where it came from. That's why you leave town in a fruit truck, and go to Buffalo, and from there New York. That's why you go to a plastic surgeon when you've saved the money, and have your nose molded to look like another nose . . . Leon Potter's nose, or as close to it as the surgeon's samples came, but you don't realize that till much later.

That's why you decide to change your name.

Your name is not Morrie Feldman.

Your name is Marty Field.

You're a funny, funny man.

". . . and so it is my extreme pleasure to introduce the boy we watched grow into a national celebrity . . . Marty Field!"

The auditorium caught up the frantic applause and flung it back and forth between the walls. The tumult was like nothing else Marty Field had ever heard. It caught in his eyes and ears and mouth like a great tidal wave, and drenched him with adoration. He rose and walked to the principal, extending his hand automatically, receiving the embossed bronze plaque and the handshake simultaneously.

Then the wave subsided, leaving him washed up on the shore of expectancy, a sea of eyes beyond, waiting to bathe him in love and fame once more.

Fritz, it's cold; throw another Jew on the fire.

"Th-thank you . . . thank you very much . . ."

Tell them. Tell them, Morrie Feldman. Tell them what it was like. Tell them you know them for what they are. Make them realize that you've never forgotten. Show them the never-healed wounds; open the sores for them. Let them taste the filth of their own natures. Don't let them get away with it. That's why you came, isn't it? That was why the conquering hero returned! Don't let them lie to their children about all the good times, the fine times, the wonderful wonderful Marty Field they all loved and helped and admired. Don't let them spew their subtle poisons into their children while using you as an example of what a good non-you-know-what is like.

Let them wallow in their own scum, Marty Field.

So Abie says, "Business is business."

". . . I don't know quite what to say . . ."

Don't let him Jew-you-down . . .

". . . after all these years, to return home to such a warm and sincere . . ."

Kike!

". . . I want you to know I'll always cherish this handsome bronze . . ."

Yid!

". . . means more to me than all the awards I'll ever . . ."

Dirty little Christ-killer!

". . . so thank you very much, again."

You walk off the stage, Marty Field. You hold your thirty pieces of silver (or is that one piece of bronze?) and you leave the high school, and get in the car that will take you back to the airport, and the world that loves you. You had your chance, and you didn't take it. Of course you didn't, Marty. Because you're a coward. Strike your blow for truth and freedom? Hardly. It's your life, and you handle it for the guffaw, for the belly-buster, for the big exit.

But that's okay. Don't let it hack you, kid. And stop crying; you're not entitled to those tears. They belong to other people. You can have the dough, but leave the tears. Stick with the sick *shticks*, buddy-boy.

Want a tag line? Want a punch line? How's this:

Have you seen the Do-It-Yourself Easter Kit? Two boards, three nails and a Jew.

Author signifies audience reaction of laughter, applause, and sounds of scissors.

Yeah, you're a *scream*, Marty.

ONE LIFE, FURNISHED IN EARLY POVERTY

And so it was—strangely, strangely—that I found myself standing in the backyard of the house I had lived in when I was seven years old. At thirteen minutes till midnight on no special magical winter's night, in a town that had held me only till I was physically able to run away. In Ohio, in winter, near midnight—certain I could go back.

Back to a time when what was now . . . was then.

Not truly knowing *why* I even wanted to go back. But certain that I could. Without magic, without science, without alchemy, without supernatural assistance; just *go back*. Because I had to, I needed to . . . go back.

Back; thirty-five years and more. To find myself at the age of seven, before any of it had begun; before any of the directions had been taken; to find out what turning point in my life it had been that had wrenched me from the course all little boys took to adulthood; that had set me on the road of loneliness and success ending here, back where I'd begun, in a backyard at now-twelve minutes to midnight.

At forty-two I had come to that point in my life toward which I'd struggled since I'd been a child: a place of security, importance, recognition. The only one from this town who had made it. The ones who had had the most promise in school were now milkmen, used car salesmen, married to fat, stupid *dead* women who had, themselves, been girls of exceeding promise in high school. *They* had been trapped in this little Ohio town, never to break free. To die there, unknown. I had broken free, had done all the wonderful things I'd said I would do.

Why should it all depress me now?

Perhaps it was because Christmas was nearing and I was alone, with bad marriages and lost friendships behind me.

I walked out of the studio, away from the wet-ink-new fifty thousand dollar contract, got in my car and drove to International Airport. It was a straight line made up of inflight meals and jet airliners and rental cars and hastily-purchased winter clothing. A straight line to a backyard I had not seen in over thirty years.

I had to find the dragoon to go back.

Crossing the rime-frosted grass that crackled like cellophane, I walked under the shadow of the lightning-blasted pear tree. I had climbed in that tree endlessly when I was seven years old. In summer, its branches hung far over and scraped the roof of the garage. I could shinny out across the limb and drop onto the garage roof. I had once pushed Johnny Mummy off that garage roof . . . not out of meanness, but simply because I had jumped from it many times and I could not understand anyone's not finding it a wonderful thing to do. He had sprained his ankle, and his father, a fireman, had come looking for me. I'd hidden on the garage roof.

I walked around the side of the garage, and there was the barely-visible path. To one side of the path I had always buried my toy soldiers. For no other reason than to bury them, know I had a secret place, and later dig them up again, as if finding treasure.

(It came to me that even now, as an adult, I did the same thing. Dining in a Japanese restaurant, I would hide small pieces of *pakkai* or pineapple or *teriyaki* in my rice bowl, and pretend to be delighted when, later in the meal, my chopsticks encountered the tiny treasures down in among the rice grains.)

I knew the spot, of course. I got down on my hands and knees and began digging with the silver pen-knife on my watch chain. It had been my father's pen-knife – almost the only thing he had left me when he'd died.

The ground was hard, but I dug with enthusiasm, and the moon gave me more than enough light. Down and down I dug, knowing eventually I would come to the dragoon.

He was there. The bright paint rusted off his body, the saber corroded and reduced to a stub. Lying there in the grave I had dug for him thirty-five years before. I scooped the little metal soldier out of the ground, and cleaned him off as best I could with my paisley dress handkerchief. He was faceless now and as sad as I felt.

I hunkered there, under the moon, and waited for midnight, only a minute away, knowing it was all going to come right for me. After so terribly long.

The house behind me was silent and dark. I had no idea who lived there now. It would have been unpleasant if the strangers who now lived here had been unable to sleep and, rising to get a glass of water, had idly looked into the backyard. *Their* backyard. I had played here, and built a world for myself here, from dreams and loneliness. Using talismans of comic books and radio programs and matinee movies, and potent charms like the sad little dragoon in my hand. But it was now *their* backyard.

My wristwatch said midnight, one hand laid straight on top of the other.

The moon faded. Slowly, it went gray and shadowy, till the glow was gone, and then even the gray after-image was gone.

The wind rose. Slowly, it came from somewhere far away and built around me. I stood up, pulling the collar of my topcoat around my neck. The wind was neither warm nor cold, yet it rushed, without even ruffling my hair. I was not afraid.

The ground was settling. Slowly, it lowered me the tiniest fractions of inches. But steadily, as though the layers of tomorrows that had been built up, were vanishing.

My thoughts were of myself: *I'm coming to save you. I'm coming, Gus. You won't hurt any more . . . you'll never have hurt.*

The moon came back. It had been full; now it was new. The wind died. It had carried me where I'd needed to go. The ground settled. The years had been peeled off.

I was alone in the backyard of the house at 89 Harmon Drive. The snow was deeper. It was a different house, though it was the same. It was not recently painted. The Depression had not been long ago; money was still tight. It wasn't weatherbeaten, but in a year or two my father would have it painted. Light yellow.

There was a sumac tree growing below the window of the dinette. It was nourished by lima beans and soup and cabbage.

"You'll just sit there until you finish every drop of your dinner. We're not wasting food. There are children starving in Russia."

I put the dragoon in my topcoat pocket. He had worked more than hard enough. I walked around the side of the house. I smiled as I saw again the wooden milk box by the side door. In the morning, very early, the milkman would put three quarts of milk there, but before anyone could bring them in, this very cold winter morning in December, the cream would push its way up and the little cardboard cap would be an inch above the mouth of the bottle.

The gravel talked beneath my feet. The street was quiet and cold. I stood in the front yard, beside the big oak tree, and looked up and down.

It was the same. It was as though I'd never been away. I started to cry. Hello.

Gus was on one of the swings in the playground. I stood outside the fence of Lathrop Grade School and watched him standing on the seat, gripping the ropes, pumping his little legs. He was smaller than I'd remembered him. He wasn't smiling as he tried to swing higher It was serious work to him.

Standing outside the hurricane fence, watching Gus, I was happy. I scratched at a rash on my right wrist, and smoked a cigarette, and was happy.

I didn't see them until they were out of the shadows of the bushes, almost upon him.

One of them rushed up and grabbed Gus's leg, and tried to pull him off the seat, just as he reached the bottom of his swing. Gus managed to hold on, but the chain-ropes twisted crazily and when it went back up it hit the metal leg of the framework.

Gus fell, rolled face-down in the dust of the playground, and tried to sit up. The boys pushed through between the swings, avoiding the one that clanged back and forth.

Gus managed to get up, and the boys formed a circle around him. Then Jack Wheeldon stepped out and faced him. I remembered Jack Wheeldon.

He was taller than Gus. They were *all* taller than Gus, but Wheeldon was beefier. I could see shadows surrounding him. Shadows of a boy who would grow into a man with a beer stomach and thick arms. But the eyes would always remain the same.

He shoved Gus in the face. Gus went back, dug in and charged him. Gus came at him low, head tucked under, fists tight at the ends of arms braced close to the body, extended forward. He hit him in the stomach and wrestled him around. They struggled together like inept club fighters, raising dust.

One of the boys in the circle took a step forward and hit Gus hard in the back of the head. Gus turned his face out of Wheeldon's stomach, and Wheeldon punched him in the mouth. Gus started to cry.

I'd been frozen, watching it happen; but he was crying—

I looked both ways down the fence and found the break far to my right. I threw the cigarette away as I dashed down the fence, trying to look behind me. Then through the break and I was running toward them the long distance from far right field of the baseball diamond, toward the swings and see-saws. They had Gus down now, and they were kicking him.

When they saw me coming, they started to run away. Jack Wheeldon paused to kick Gus once more in the side, then he, too, ran.

Gus was lying there, on his back, the dust smeared into mud on his face. I bent down and picked him up. He wasn't moving, but he wasn't really hurt. I held him very close and carried him toward the bushes that rose on a small incline at the side of the playground. The bushes were cool overhead and they canopied us; I laid him down and used my handkerchief to clean away the dirt. His eyes were very blue. I smoothed the straight brown hair off his forehead. He wore braces; one of the rubber bands hooked onto the pins of the braces, used to keep them tension-tight, had broken. I pulled it free.

He opened his eyes and started crying again.

Something hurt in my chest.

He started snuffling, unable to catch his breath. He tried to speak, but the words were only mangled sounds, huffed out with too much air and pain.

Then he forced himself to sit up and rubbed the back of his hand across his runny nose.

He stared at me. It was panic and fear and confusion and shame at being seen this way. "Th-they hit me from in back," he said, snuffling.

"I know. I saw."

"D'jou scare'm off?"

"Yes."

He didn't say thank you. It wasn't necessary. The backs of my thighs hurt from squatting. I sat down.

"My name is Gus," he said, trying to be polite.

I didn't know what name to give him. I was going to tell him the first name to come into my head, but I heard myself say, "My name is Mr. Rosenthal."

He looked startled. "That's *my* name, too. Gus Rosenthal!"

"Isn't that peculiar," I said. We grinned at each other, and he wiped his nose again.

I didn't want to see my mother or father. I had those memories. They were sufficient. It was little Gus I wanted to be with. But one night I crossed into the backyard at 89 Harmon Drive from the empty lots that would later be a housing development.

And I stood in the dark, watching them eat dinner. There was my father. I hadn't remembered him as being so handsome. My mother was saying something to him, and he nodded as he ate. They were in the dinette. Gus was playing with his food. *Don't mush your food around like that, Gus. Eat, or you can't stay up to hear Lux Presents Hollywood.*

But they're doing "Dawn Patrol."

Then don't mush your food.

"Momma," I murmured, standing in the cold, "Momma, there are children starving in Russia." And I added, thirty-five years late, "Name two, Momma."

I met Gus downtown at the newsstand.

"Hi."

"Oh. Hullo."

"Buying some comics?"

"Uh-huh."

"You ever read *Doll Man* and *Kid Eternity*?"

"Yeah, they're great. But I got them."

"Not the new issues."

"Sure do."

"Bet you've got *last* month's. He's just checking in the new comics right now."

So we waited while the newsstand owner used the heavy wire snips on the bundles, and checked off the magazines against the distributor's long white mimeographed sheet. And I bought Gus *Airboy* and *Jingle Jangle Comics* and *Blue Beetle* and *Whiz Comics* and *Doll Man* and *Kid Eternity.*

Then I took him to Isaly's for a hot fudge sundae. They served it in a tall tulip glass with the hot fudge in a little pitcher. When the waitress had gone to get the sundaes, little Gus looked at me. "Hey, how'd you know I only liked crushed nuts, an' not whipped cream or a cherry?"

I leaned back in the high-walled booth and smiled at him. "What do you want to be when you grow up, Gus?"

He shrugged. "I don't know."

Somebody put a nickel in the Wurlitzer in his booth, and Glenn Miller swung into "String of Pearls."

"Well, did you ever think about it?"

"No, huh-uh. I like cartooning; maybe I could draw comic books."

"That's pretty smart thinking, Gus. There's a lot of money to be made in art." I stared around the dairy store, at the Coca-Cola posters of pretty girls with page boy hairdos, drawn by an artist named Harold W. McCauley whose style would be known throughout the world, whose name would never be known.

He stared at me. "It's fun, too, isn't it?"

I was embarrassed. I'd thought first of money, he'd thought first of happiness. I'd reached him before he'd chosen his path. There was still time to make him a man who would think first of joy, all through his life.

"Mr. Rosenthal?"

I looked down and across, just as the waitress brought the sundaes. She set them down and I paid her. When she'd gone, Gus asked me, "Why did they call me a dirty Jewish elephant?"

"Who called you that, Gus?"

"The guys."

"The ones you were fighting that day?"

He nodded. "Why'd they say elephant?"

I spooned up some vanilla ice cream, thinking. My back ached, and the rash had spread up my right wrist onto my forearm. "Well, Jewish people are supposed to have big noses, Gus." I poured the hot fudge out of the little pitcher. It bulged with surface tension for a second, then spilled through its own dark brown film, covering the three scoops of real ice cream; not tastee whipee freezee gunk substitute; *real* ice cream. "I mean, that's what some people *believe*. So I suppose they thought it was smart to call you an elephant, because an elephant has a big nose . . . a trunk. Do you understand?"

"That's dumb. I don't have a big nose . . . do I?"

"I wouldn't say so, Gus. They most likely said it just to make you mad. Sometimes people do that."

"That's dumb."

We sat there for a while and talked. I went far down inside the tulip glass with the long-handled spoon, and finished the deep dark, almost black bittersweet hot fudge. They hadn't made hot fudge like that in many years. Gus got ice cream up the spoon handle, on his fingers, on his chin, on his T-shirt, on the top of his head. We talked about a great many things.

We talked about how difficult arithmetic was. (How I would still have to use my fingers sometimes even as an adult, when I did my checkbook.) How the guys never gave a short kid his "raps" when the sandlot ballgames were in progress. (How I overcompensated with women from doubts about stature.) How different kinds of food were pretty bad tasting. (How I still used ketchup on well-done steak.) How it was pretty lonely in the neighborhood with nobody for friends. (How I had erected a façade of charisma and glamour so no one could reach me deeply enough to hurt me.) How Leon always invited all the kids over to his house, but when Gus got there, they slammed the door and stood behind the screen laughing and jeering. (How even now, a slammed door raised the hair on my neck and a phone receiver slammed down, cutting me off, sent me into a senseless rage.) How comic books were great. (How my scripts sold so easily because I had never learned to rein-in my imagination.)

We talked about a great many things.

"I'd better get you home now," I said.

"Okay." We got up. "Hey, Mr. Rosenthal?"

"You'd better wipe the chocolate off your face."

He wiped. "Mr. Rosenthal . . . how'd you know I like crushed nuts, an' not whipped cream or a cherry?"

We spent a great deal of time together. I bought him a copy of a pulp magazine called *Startling Stories*, and read him a story about a space pirate who captures a man and his wife and offers the man the choice of opening one of two large boxes—in one is the man's wife, with twelve hours of air to breathe, in the other is a terrible alien fungus that will eat him alive. Little Gus sat on the edge of the big hole he'd dug, out in the empty lots, dangling his feet, and listening. His forehead was furrowed as he listened to the marvels of Jack Williamson's "Twelve Hours to Live," there on the edge of the "fort" he'd built.

We discussed the radio programs Gus heard every day: Tennessee

Jed, Captain Midnight, Jack Armstrong, Superman, Don Winslow of the Navy. And the nighttime programs: *I Love a Mystery, Suspense, The Adventures of Sam Spade*. And the Sunday programs: *The Shadow, Quiet, Please, The Mollé Mystery Theater*.

We became good friends. He had told his mother and father about "Mr. Rosenthal," who was his friend, but they'd spanked him for the *Startling Stories,* because they thought he'd stolen it. So he stopped telling them about me. That was all right; it made the bond between us stronger.

One afternoon we went down behind the Colony Lumber Company, through the woods and the weeds to the old condemned pond. Gus told me he used to go swimming there, and fishing sometimes, for a black oily fish with whiskers. I told him it was a catfish. He liked that. Liked to know the names of things. I told him *that* was called nomenclature, and he laughed to know there was a name for knowing names.

We sat on the piled logs rotting beside the black mirror water, and Gus asked me to tell him what it was like where I lived, and where I'd been, and what I'd done, and everything.

"I ran away from home when I was thirteen, Gus."

"Wasn't you happy there?"

"Well, yes and no. They loved me, my mother and father. They really did. They just didn't understand what I was all about."

There was a pain on my neck. I touched a fingertip to the place. It was a boil beginning to grow. I hadn't had a boil in years, many years, not since I was a . . .

"What's the matter, Mr. Rosenthal?"

"Nothing, Gus. Well, anyhow, I ran away, and joined a carny."

"Huh?"

"A carnival. The Tri-State Shows. We moved through Illinois, Ohio, Pennsylvania, Missouri, even Kansas . . ."

"Boy! A carnival! Just like in TOBY TYLER, *or Ten Weeks with a Circus*? I really cried when Toby Tyler's monkey got killed, that was the worst part of it, did you do stuff like that when you were with the circus?"

"Carnival."

"Yeah. Uh-huh. Did'ja?"

"Something like that. I carried water for the animals sometimes, although we only had a few of those, and mostly in the freak show. But usually what I did was clean up, and carry food to the performers in their tops—"

"What's that?"

"That's where they sleep, in rigged tarpaulins. You know, tarps."

"Oh. Yeah, I know. Go on, huh."

The rash was all the way up to my shoulder now. It itched like hell, and when I'd gone to the drugstore to get an aerosol spray to relieve it, so it wouldn't spread, I had only to see those round wooden display tables with their glass centers, under which were bottles of Teel tooth liquid, Tangee Red-Red lipstick and nylons with a seam down the back, to know the druggist wouldn't even know what I meant by Bactine or Liquid Band-Aid.

"Well, along about K.C. the carny got busted because there were too many moll dips and cannons and paper-hangers in the tip . . ." I waited, his eyes growing huge.

"What's all *thaaat* mean, Mr. Rosenthal?!?"

"Ah-ha! Fine carny stiff *you'd* make. You don't even know the lingo."

"Please, Mr. Rosenthal, please tell me!"

"Well, K.C. is Kansas City, Missouri . . . when it isn't Kansas City, Kansas. Except, really, on the other side of the river is Weston. And busted means thrown in jail, and . . ."

"You were in *jail*?"

"Sure was, little Gus. But let me tell you now. Cannons are pickpockets and moll dips are lady pickpockets, and paper-hangers are fellows who write bad checks. And a tip is a group."

"So what happened, what happened?"

"One of these bad guys, one of these cannons, you see, picked the pocket of an assistant district attorney, and we all got thrown in jail. And after a while everyone was released on bail, except me and the Geek. Me, because I wouldn't tell them who I was, because I didn't want to go home, and the Geek, because a carny can find a wetbrain in *any* town to play Geek."

"What's a Geek, huh?"

The Geek was a sixty-year-old alcoholic. So sunk in his own endless drunkenness that he was almost a zombie . . . a wetbrain. He was billed as The Thing and he lived in a portable pit they carried around, and he bit the heads off snakes and ate live chickens and slept in his own dung. And all for a bottle of gin every day. They locked me in the drunk tank with him. The smell. The smell of sour liquor oozing with sweat out of his pores, it made me sick, it was a smell I could never forget. And the third day, he went crazy. They wouldn't fix him with gin, and he went crazy. He climbed the bars of the big free-standing drunk tank in the middle of the lockup, and he banged his head against the bars and ceiling where they met, till he fell back and lay there, breathing raggedly, stinking of that terrible smell, his face like a pound of raw meat.

The pain in my stomach was worse now. I took Gus back to Harmon Drive, and let him go home.

My weight had dropped to just over a hundred and ten. My clothes didn't fit. The acne and boils were worse. I smelled of witch hazel. Gus was getting more anti-social.

I realized what was happening.

I was alien in my own past. If I stayed much longer, God only knew what would happen to little Gus . . . but certainly I would waste away. Perhaps just vanish. Then . . . would Gus's future cease to exist, too? I had no way of knowing; but my choice was obvious. I had to return.

And couldn't! I was happier here than I'd ever been before. The bigotry and violence Gus had known before I came to him had ceased. They knew he was being watched over. But Gus was becoming more erratic. He was shoplifting toy soldiers and comic books from the Kresge's and constantly defying his parents. It was turning bad. I had to go back.

I told him on a Saturday. We had gone to see a Lash LaRue western and Val Lewton's *The Cat People* at the Lake Theater. When we came back I parked the car on Mentor Avenue, and we went walking in the big, cool, dark woods that fronted Mentor where it met Harmon Drive.

"Mr. Rosenthal," Gus said. He looked upset.

"Yes, Gus?"

"I gotta problem, sir."

"What's that, Gus?" My head ached. It was a steady needle of pressure above the right eye.

"My mother's gonna send me to a military school."

I remembered. *Oh, God,* I thought. It had been terrible. Precisely the thing *not* to do to a child like Gus.

"They said it was 'cause I was rambunctious. They said they were gonna send me there for a *year* or two. Mr. Rosenthal . . . don't let'm send me there. I din't mean to be bad. I just wanted to be around you."

My heart slammed inside me. Again. Then again. "Gus, I have to go away."

He stared at me. I heard a soft whimper.

"Take me with you, Mr. Rosenthal. Please. I want to see Galveston. We can drive a dynamite truck in North Carolina. We can go to Matawatchan, Ontario, Canada and work topping trees, we can sail on boats, Mr. Rosenthal!"

"Gus . . ."

"We can work the carny, Mr. Rosenthal. We can pick peanuts and oranges all across the country. We can hitchhike to San Francisco and ride the cable cars. We can ride the boxcars, Mr. Rosenthal . . . I promise I'll keep my legs inside an' not dangle 'em. I remember what you said about the doors slamming when they hook'm up. I'll keep my legs inside, honest I will . . ."

He was crying. My head ached hideously. But he was *crying*!

"I'll *have* to go, Gus!"

"You don't care!" He was shouting. "You don't care about me, you don't care what happens to me! You don't care if I die . . . you don't . . ."

He didn't have to say it: *you don't love me*.

"I do, Gus. I swear to God, I do!"

I looked up at him; he was supposed to be my friend. But he wasn't. He was going to let them send me off to that military school.

"I hope you die!"

Oh, dear God, Gus, I am! I turned and ran out of the woods as I watched him run out of the woods.

I drove away. The green Plymouth with the running boards and the heavy body; it was hard steering. The world swam around me. My eyesight blurred. I could feel myself withering away.

I thought I'd left myself behind, but little Gus had followed me out of the woods. Having done it, I now remembered: why had I remembered none of it before? As I drove off down Mentor Avenue, I came out of the woods and saw the big green car starting up, and I ran wildly forward, crouching low, wanting only to go with him, my friend, me. I threw in the clutch and dropped the stick into first, and pulled away from the curb as I reached the car and climbed onto the rear fender, pulling my legs up, hanging onto the trunk latch. I drove weaving, my eyes watering and things going first blue then green, hanging on for dear life to the cold latch handle. Cars whipped around, honking madly, trying to tell me that I was on the rear of the car, but I didn't know what they were honking about, and scared their honking would tell me I was back there, hiding. After I'd gone almost a mile, a car pulled up alongside, and a woman sitting next to the driver looked down at me crouching there, and I made a *please don't tell* sign with my finger to my freezing lips, but the car pulled ahead and the woman rolled down her window and motioned to me. I rolled down my window and the woman yelled across through the rushing wind that I was back there on the rear fender. I pulled over and fear gripped me as the car stopped and I saw me getting out of the door, and I crawled off the car and started running away. But my legs were cramped and cold from having hung on back there, and I ran awkwardly; then coming out of the dark was a road sign, and I hit it, and it hit me in the side of the face, and I fell down, and I ran toward myself, lying there, crying, and I got to him just as I got up and ran off into the gravel yard surrounding the Colony Lumber Company.

Little Gus was bleeding from the forehead where he'd struck the metal sign. He ran into the darkness, and I knew where he was running . . . I had to catch him, to tell him, to make him understand why I had to go away.

I came to the hurricane fence, and ran and ran till I found the place where I'd dug out under it, and I slipped down and pulled myself under and got my clothes all dirty, but I got up and ran back behind the Colony Lumber Company, into the sumac and the weeds, till I came to the condemned pond back there. Then I sat down and looked out over the black water. I was crying.

I followed the trail down to the pond. It took me longer to climb over the fence than it had taken him to crawl under it. When I came down to the pond, he was sitting there with a long blade of saw-grass in his mouth, crying softly.

I heard him coming, but I didn't turn around.

I came down to him, and crouched down behind him. "Hey," I said quietly. "Hey, little Gus."

I wouldn't turn around. I wouldn't.

I spoke his name again, and touched him on the shoulder, and in an instant he was turned to me, hugging me around the chest, crying into my jacket, mumbling over and over, "Don't go, please don't go, please take me with you, please don't leave me here alone . . ."

And I was crying, too. I hugged little Gus, and touched his hair, and felt him holding onto me with all his might, stronger than a seven year old should be able to hold on, and I tried to tell him how it was, how it would be: "Gus . . . hey, hey, little Gus, listen to me . . . I *want* to stay, you *know* I want to stay . . . but I can't."

I looked up at him; he was crying, too. It seemed so strange for a grownup to be crying like that, and I said, "If you leave me *I'll* die. I will!"

I knew it wouldn't do any good to try explaining. He was too young. He wouldn't be able to understand.

He pulled my arms from around him, and he folded my hands in my lap, and he stood up, and I looked at him. He was gonna leave me. I knew he was. I stopped crying. I wouldn't let him see me cry.

I looked down at him. The moonlight held his face in a pale photograph. I wasn't fooling myself. He'd understand. He'd know. Kids *always* know. I turned and started back up the path. Little Gus didn't follow. He sat there looking back at me. I only turned once to look at him. He was still sitting there like that.

He was watching me. Staring up at me from the pond side. And I knew what instant it had been that had formed me. It hadn't been all the people who'd called me a wild kid, or a strange kid, or any of it. It wasn't being poor, or being lonely.

I watched him go away. He was my friend. But he didn't have no guts. He didn't. But I'd show him! I'd really show him! I was gonna get out of here, go away, be a big person and do a lot of things, and some day I'd run into him someplace and see him and he'd come up and shake my hand and I'd spit on him. Then I'd beat him up.

He walked up the path and went away. I sat there for a long time, by the pond. Till it got real cold.

I got back in the car, and went to find the way back to the future; where I belonged. It wasn't much, but it was all I had. I would find it . . . I still had the dragoon . . . and there were many stops I'd made on the way to becoming me. Perhaps Kansas City; perhaps Matawatchan, Ontario, Canada; perhaps Galveston; perhaps Shelby, North Carolina.

And crying, I drove. Not for myself, but for myself, for little Gus, for what I'd done to him, forced him to become. Gus . . . Gus!

But . . . oh, God . . . what if I came back again . . . and again? Suddenly, the road did not look familiar.

Jeffty Is Five

When I was five years old, there was a little kid I played with: Jeffty. His real name was Jeff Kinzer, and everyone who played with him called him Jeffty. We were five years old together, and we had good times playing together.

When I was five, a Clark Bar was as fat around as the gripping end of a Louisville Slugger, and pretty nearly six inches long, and they used real chocolate to coat it, and it crunched very nicely when you bit into the center, and the paper it came wrapped in smelled fresh and good when you peeled off one end to hold the bar so it wouldn't melt onto your fingers. Today, a Clark Bar is as thin as a credit card, they use something artificial and awful-tasting instead of pure chocolate, the thing is soft and soggy, it costs fifteen or twenty cents instead of a decent, correct nickel, and they wrap it so you think it's the same size it was twenty years ago, only it isn't; it's slim and ugly and nasty-tasting and not worth a penny, much less fifteen or twenty cents.

When I was that age, five years old, I was sent away to my Aunt Patricia's home in Buffalo, New York, for two years. My father was going through "bad times" and Aunt Patricia was very beautiful, and had married a stockbroker. They took care of me for two years. When I was seven, I came back home and went to find Jeffty, so we could play together.

I was seven. Jeffty was still five. I didn't notice any difference. I didn't know: I was only seven.

When I was seven years old, I used to lie on my stomach in front of our Atwater-Kent radio and listen to swell stuff. I had tied the ground wire to the radiator, and I would lie there with my coloring books and my Crayolas (when there were only sixteen colors in the big box), and listen to the NBC Red network: Jack Benny on the *Jell-O Program*,

Amos 'n' Andy, Edgar Bergen and Charlie McCarthy on the *Chase and Sanborn Program*, One Man's Family, *First Nighter*; the NBC Blue network: *Easy Aces*, the *Jergens Program* with Walter Winchell, *Information Please*, *Death Valley Days*; and best of all, the Mutual Network with *The Green Hornet*, The Lone Ranger, *The Shadow* and *Quiet, Please*. Today, I turn on my car radio and go from one end of the dial to the other and all I get is 100 strings orchestras, banal housewives and insipid truckers discussing their kinky sex lives with arrogant talk show hosts, country and western drivel and rock music so loud it hurts my ears.

When I was ten, my grandfather died of old age and I was "a troublesome kid," and they sent me off to military school, so I could be "taken in hand."

I came back when I was fourteen. Jeffty was still five.

When I was fourteen years old, I used to go to the movies on Saturday afternoons and a matinee was ten cents and they used real butter on the popcorn and I could always be sure of seeing a western like Lash LaRue, or Wild Bill Elliott as Red Ryder with Bobby Blake as Little Beaver, or Roy Rogers, or Johnny Mack Brown; a scary picture like *House of Horrors* with Rondo Hatton as the Strangler, or *The Cat People*, or *The Mummy*, or *I Married a Witch* with Fredric March and Veronica Lake; plus an episode of a great serial like The Shadow with Victor Jory, or Dick Tracy or Flash Gordon; and three cartoons; and James Fitzpatrick TravelTalk; Movietone News; and singalong and, if I stayed on till evening, Bingo or Keeno; and free dishes. Today, I go to movies and see Clint Eastwood blowing people's heads apart like ripe cantaloupes.

At eighteen, I went to college. Jeffty was still five. I came back during the summers, to work at my Uncle Joe's jewelry store. Jeffty hadn't changed. Now I knew there was something different about him, something wrong, something weird. Jeffty was still five years old, not a day older.

At twenty-two, I came home for keeps. To open a Sony television franchise in town, the first one. I saw Jeffty from time to time. He was five.

Things are better in a lot of ways. People don't die from some of the old diseases any more. Cars go faster and get you there more quickly on better roads. Shirts are softer and silkier. We have paperback books even though they cost as much as a good hardcover used to. When I'm running short in the bank I can live off credit cards till things even out. But I still think we've lost a lot of good stuff. Did you know you can't buy linoleum any more, only vinyl floor covering? There's no such thing as oilcloth any more; you'll never again smell that special, sweet smell from your grandmother's kitchen. Furniture isn't made to last thirty years or longer because they took a survey and found that young homemakers like to throw their furniture out and bring in all new, color-coded, borax every seven years. Records don't feel right; they're not thick and solid like the old ones, they're thin and you can bend them . . . that doesn't seem right to me. Restaurants don't serve cream in pitchers any more, just that artificial glop in little plastic tubs, and one is never enough to get coffee the right color. You can make a dent in a car fender with only a sneaker. Everywhere you go, all the towns look the same with Burger Kings and McDonald's and 7-Elevens and Taco Bells and motels and shopping centers. Things may be better, but why do I keep thinking about the past?

What I mean by five years old is not that Jeffty was retarded. I don't think that's what it was. Smart as a whip for five years old; very bright, quick, cute, a funny kid.

But he was three feet tall, small for his age, and perfectly formed: no big head, no strange jaw, none of that. A nice, normal-looking five-year-old kid. Except that he was the same age as I was: twenty-two.

When he spoke it was with the squeaking, soprano voice of a five-year-old; when he walked it was with the little hops and shuffles of a five-year-old; when he talked to you it was about the concerns of a five-year-old . . . comic books, playing soldier, using a clothes pin to attach a stiff piece of cardboard to the front fork of his bike so the sound it made when the spokes hit was like a motorboat, asking questions like *why does that thing do that like that,* how high is up, how old is old, why is grass green, what's an elephant look like? At twenty-two, he was five.

Jeffty's parents were a sad pair. Because I was still a friend of Jeffty's, still let him hang around with me in the store, sometimes took him to the county fair or to the miniature golf or the movies, I wound up spending time with *them*. Not that I much cared for them, because they were so awfully depressing. But then, I suppose one couldn't expect much more from the poor devils. They had an alien thing in their home, a child who had grown no older than five in twenty-two years, who provided the treasure of that special childlike state indefinitely, but who also denied them the joys of watching the child grow into a normal adult.

Five is a wonderful time of life for a little kid . . . or it *can* be, if the child is relatively free of the monstrous beastliness other children indulge in. It is a time when the eyes are wide open and the patterns are not yet set; a time when one has not yet been hammered into accepting everything as immutable and hopeless; a time when the hands cannot do enough, the mind cannot learn enough, the world is infinite and colorful and filled with mysteries. Five is a special time before they take the questing, unquenchable, quixotic soul of the young dreamer and thrust it into dreary schoolroom boxes. A time before they take the trembling hands that want to hold everything, touch everything, figure everything out, and make them lie still on desktops. A time before people begin saying "act your age" and "grow up" or "you're behaving like a baby." It is a time when a child who acts adolescent is still cute and responsive and everyone's pet. A time of delight, of wonder, of innocence.

Jeffty had been stuck in that time, just five, just so.

But for his parents it was an ongoing nightmare from which no one—not social workers, not priests, not child psychologists, not teachers, not friends, not medical wizards, not psychiatrists, no one—could slap or shake them awake. For seventeen years their sorrow had grown through stages of parental dotage to concern, from concern to worry, from worry to fear, from fear to confusion, from confusion to anger, from anger to dislike, from dislike to naked hatred, and finally, from deepest loathing and revulsion to a stolid, depressive acceptance.

John Kinzer was a shift foreman at the Balder Tool & Die plant. He was a thirty-year man. To everyone but the man living it, his was a spectacularly uneventful life. In no way was he remarkable . . . save that he had fathered a twenty-two-year-old five-year-old.

John Kinzer was a small man; soft, with no sharp angles; with pale eyes that never seemed to hold mine for longer than a few seconds. He continually shifted in his chair during conversations, and seemed to see things in the upper corners of the room, things no one else could see . . . or wanted to see. I suppose the word that best suited him was *haunted*. What his life had become . . . well, *haunted* suited him.

Leona Kinzer tried valiantly to compensate. No matter what hour of the day I visited, she always tried to foist food on me. And when Jeffty was in the house she was always at *him* about eating: "Honey, would you like an orange? A nice orange? Or a tangerine? I have tangerines. I could peel a tangerine for you." But there was clearly such fear in her, fear of her own child, that the offers of sustenance always had a faintly ominous tone.

Leona Kinzer had been a tall woman, but the years had bent her. She seemed always to be seeking some area of wallpapered wall or storage niche into which she could fade, adopt some chintz or rose-patterned protective coloration and hide forever in plain sight of the child's big brown eyes, pass her a hundred times a day and never realize she was there, holding her breath, invisible. She always had an apron tied around her waist, and her hands were red from cleaning. As if by maintaining the environment immaculately she could pay off her imagined sin: having given birth to this strange creature.

Neither of them watched television very much. The house was usually dead silent, not even the sibilant whispering of water in the pipes, the creaking of timbers settling, the humming of the refrigerator. Awfully silent, as if time itself had taken a detour around that house.

As for Jeffty, he was inoffensive. He lived in that atmosphere of gentle dread and dulled loathing, and if he understood it, he never remarked in any way. He played, as a child plays, and seemed happy. But he must have sensed, in the way of a five-year-old, just how alien he was in their presence.

Alien. No, that wasn't right. He was *too* human, if anything. But out of phase, out of synch with the world around him, and resonating to a different vibration than his parents, God knows. Nor would other children play with him. As they grew past him, they found him at first childish, then uninteresting, then simply frightening as their perceptions of aging became clear and they could see he was not affected by time as they were. Even the little ones, his own age, who might wander into the neighborhood, quickly came to shy away from him like a dog in the street when a car backfires.

Thus, I remained his only friend. A friend of many years. Five years. Twenty-two years. I liked him; more than I can say. And never knew exactly why. But I did, without reserve.

But because we spent time together, I found I was also—polite society—spending time with John and Leona Kinzer. Dinner, Saturday afternoons sometimes, an hour or so when I'd bring Jeffty back from a movie. They were grateful: slavishly so. It relieved them of the embarrassing chore of going out with him, or having to pretend before the world that they were loving parents with a perfectly normal, happy, attractive child. And their gratitude extended to hosting me. Hideous, every moment of their depression, hideous.

I felt sorry for the poor devils, but I despised them for their inability to love Jeffty, who was eminently lovable.

I never let on, of course, even during the evenings in their company that were awkward beyond belief.

We would sit there in the darkening living room—*always* dark or darkening, as if kept in shadow to hold back what the light might reveal to the world outside through the bright eyes of the house—we would sit and silently stare at one another. They never knew what to say to me.

"So how are things down at the plant?" I'd say to John Kinzer.

He would shrug. Neither conversation nor life suited him with any ease or grace. "Fine, just fine," he would say, finally.

And we would sit in silence again.

"Would you like a nice piece of coffee cake?" Leona would say. "I made it fresh just this morning." Or deep dish green apple pie. Or milk and tollhouse cookies. Or a brown betty pudding.

"No, no, thank you, Mrs. Kinzer; Jeffty and I grabbed a couple of cheeseburgers on the way home." And again, silence.

Then, when the stillness and the awkwardness became too much even for them (and who knew how long that total silence reigned when they were alone, with that thing they never talked about any more, hanging between them), Leona Kinzer would say, "I think he's asleep."

John Kinzer would say, "I don't hear the radio playing."

Just so, it would go on like that, until I could politely find excuse to bolt away on some flimsy pretext. Yes, that was the way it would go on, every time, just the same . . . except once.

"I don't know what to do any more," Leona said. She began crying. "There's no change, not one day of peace."

Her husband managed to drag himself out of the old easy chair and went to her. He bent and tried to soothe her, but it was clear from the graceless way in which he touched her graying hair that the ability to be compassionate had been stunned in him. "Shhh, Leona, it's all right. Shhh." But she continued crying. Her hands scraped gently at the antimacassars on the arms of the chair.

Then she said, "Sometimes I wish he had been stillborn."

John looked up into the corners of the room. For the nameless shadows that were always watching him? Was it God he was seeking in those spaces? "You don't mean that," he said to her, softly, pathetically, urging her with body tension and trembling in his voice to recant before God took notice of the terrible thought. But she meant it; she meant it very much.

I managed to get away quickly that evening. They didn't want witnesses to their shame. I was glad to go.

And for a week I stayed away. From them, from Jeffty, from their street, even from that end of town.

I had my own life. The store, accounts, suppliers' conferences, poker with friends, pretty women I took to well-lit restaurants, my own parents, putting anti-freeze in the car, complaining to the laundry about too much starch in the collars and cuffs, working out at the gym, taxes, catching Jan or David (whichever one it was) stealing from the cash register. I had my own life.

But not even *that* evening could keep me from Jeffty. He called me at the store and asked me to take him to the rodeo. We chummed it up as best a twenty-two-year-old with other interests *could* . . . with a five-year-old. I never dwelled on what bound us together; I always thought it was simply the years. That, and affection for a kid who could have been the little brother I never had. (Except I *remembered* when we had played together, when we had both been the same age; I *remembered* that period, and Jeffty was still the same.)

And then, one Saturday afternoon, I came to take him to a double feature, and things I should have noticed so many times before, I first began to notice only that afternoon.

* * *

I came walking up to the Kinzer house, expecting Jeffty to be sitting on the front porch steps, or in the porch glider, waiting for me. But he was nowhere in sight.

Going inside, into that darkness and silence, in the midst of May sunshine, was unthinkable. I stood on the front walk for a few moments, then cupped my hands around my mouth and yelled, "Jeffty? Hey, Jeffty, come on out, let's go. We'll be late."

His voice came faintly, as if from under the ground.

"Here I am, Donny."

I could hear him, but I couldn't see him. It was Jeffty, no question about it: as Donald H. Horton, President and Sole Owner of The Horton TV & Sound Center, no one but Jeffty called me Donny. He had never called me anything else.

(Actually, it isn't a lie. I *am*, as far as the public is concerned, Sole Owner of the Center. The partnership with my Aunt Patricia is only to repay the loan she made me, to supplement the money I came into when I was twenty-one, left to me when I was ten by my grandfather. It wasn't a very big loan, only eighteen thousand, but I asked her to be a silent partner, because of when she had taken care of me as a child.)

"Where are you, Jeffty?"

"Under the porch in my secret place."

I walked around the side of the porch, and stooped down and pulled away the wicker grating. Back in there, on the pressed dirt, Jeffty had built himself a secret place. He had comics in orange crates, he had a little table and some pillows, it was lit by big fat candles, and we used to hide there when we were both . . . five.

"What'cha up to?" I asked, crawling in and pulling the grate closed behind me. It was cool under the porch, and the dirt smelled comfortable, the candles smelled clubby and familiar. Any kid would feel at home in such a secret place: there's never been a kid who didn't spend the happiest, most productive, most deliciously mysterious times of his life in such a secret place.

"Playin'," he said. He was holding something golden and round. It filled the palm of his little hand.

"You forget we were going to the movies?"

"Nope. I was just waitin' for you here."

"Your mom and dad home?"

"Momma."

I understood why he was waiting under the porch. I didn't push it any further. "What've you got there?"

"Captain Midnight Secret Decoder Badge," he said, showing it to me on his flattened palm.

I realized I was looking at it without comprehending what it was for a long time. Then it dawned on me what a miracle Jeffty had in his hand. A miracle that simply could *not* exist.

"Jeffty," I said softly, with wonder in my voice, "where'd you get that?"

"Came in the mail today. I sent away for it."

"It must have cost a lot of money."

"Not so much. Ten cents an' two inner wax seals from two jars of Ovaltine."

"May I see it?" My voice was trembling, and so was the hand I extended. He gave it to me and I held the miracle in the palm of my hand. It was *wonderful*.

You remember. *Captain Midnight* went on the radio nationwide in 1940. It was sponsored by Ovaltine. And every year they issued a Secret Squadron Decoder Badge. And every day at the end of the program, they would give you a clue to the next day's installment in a code that only kids with the official badge could decipher. They stopped making those wonderful Decoder Badges in 1949. I remember the one I had in 1945: it was beautiful. It had a magnifying glass in the center of the code dial. *Captain Midnight* went off the air in 1950, and though I understand it was a short-lived television series in the mid-Fifties, and though they issued Decoder Badges in 1955 and 1956, as far as the *real* badges were concerned, they never made one after 1949.

The Captain Midnight Code-O-Graph I held in my hand, the one Jeffty said he had gotten in the mail for ten cents (*ten cents*!!!) and two Ovaltine labels, was brand new, shiny gold metal, not a dent or a spot of rust on it like the old ones you can find at exorbitant prices in collectible shoppes from time to time . . . it was a *new* Decoder. And the date on it was *this* year.

But *Captain Midnight* no longer existed. Nothing like it existed on the radio. I'd listened to the one or two weak imitations of old-time radio the networks were currently airing, and the stories were dull, the sound effects bland, the whole feel of it wrong, out of date, cornball. Yet I held a *new* Code-O-Graph.

"Jeffty, tell me about this," I said.

"Tell you what, Donny? It's my new Capt'n Midnight Secret Decoder Badge. I use it to figger out what's gonna happen tomorrow."

"Tomorrow how?"

"On the program."

"*What* program?!"

He stared at me as if I was being purposely stupid. "On Capt'n *Mid*night! Boy!" I was being dumb.

I still couldn't get it straight. It was right there, right out in the open, and I still didn't know what was happening. "You mean one of those records they made of the old-time radio programs? Is that what you mean, Jeffty?"

"What records?" he asked. He didn't know what *I* meant.

We stared at each other, there under the porch. And then I said, very slowly, almost afraid of the answer, "Jeffty, how do you hear *Captain Midnight?*"

"Every day. On the radio. On my radio. Every day at five-thirty."

News. Music, dumb music, and news. That's what was on the radio every day at 5:30. Not *Captain Midnight*. The Secret Squadron hadn't been on the air in twenty years.

"Can we hear it tonight?" I asked.

"Boy!" he said. I was being dumb. I knew it from the way he said it; but I didn't know *why*. Then it dawned on me: this was Saturday. *Captain Midnight* was on Monday through Friday. Not on Saturday or Sunday.

"We goin' to the movies?"

He had to repeat himself twice. My mind was somewhere else. Nothing definite. No conclusions. No wild assumptions leapt to. Just off somewhere trying to figure it out, and concluding—as *you* would have concluded, as *any*one would have concluded rather than accepting the truth, the impossible and wonderful truth—just finally concluding there was a simple explanation I didn't yet perceive. Something mundane and dull, like the passage of time that steals all good, old things from us, packratting trinkets and plastic in exchange. And all in the name of Progress.

"We goin' to the movies, Donny?"

"You bet your boots we are, kiddo," I said. And I smiled. And I handed him the Code-O-Graph. And he put it in his side pants pocket. And we crawled out from under the porch. And we went to the movies. And neither of us said anything about *Captain Midnight* all the rest of that day. And there wasn't a ten-minute stretch, all the rest of that day, that I didn't think about it.

It was inventory all that next week. I didn't see Jeffty till late Thursday. I confess I left the store in the hands of Jan and David, told them I had some errands to run, and left early. At 4:00. I got to the Kinzers' right around 4:45. Leona answered the door, looking exhausted and distant. "Is Jeffty around?" She said he was upstairs in his room . . .

. . . listening to the radio.

I climbed the stairs two at a time.

All right, I had finally made that impossible, illogical leap. Had the stretch of belief involved anyone but Jeffty, adult or child, I would have reasoned out more explicable answers. But it *was* Jeffty, clearly another kind of vessel of life, and what he might experience should not be expected to fit into the ordered scheme.

I admit it: I *wanted* to hear what I heard.

Even with the door closed, I recognized the program:

"There he goes, Tennessee! Get him!"

There was the heavy report of a rifle shot and the keening whine of the slug ricocheting, and then the same voice yelled triumphantly, *"Got him! D-e-a-a-a-a-d center!"*

He was listening to the American Broadcasting Company, 790 kilocycles, and he was hearing *Tennessee Jed,* one of my most favorite programs from the Forties, a western adventure I had not heard in twenty years, because it had not existed for twenty years.

I sat down on the top step of the stairs, there in the upstairs hall of the Kinzer home, and I listened to the show. It wasn't a rerun of an old program, because there were occasional references in the body of the drama to current cultural and technological developments, and phrases that had not existed in common usage in the Forties: aerosol spray cans, laserasing of tattoos, Tanzania, the word "uptight."

I could not ignore the fact. Jeffty was listening to a *new* segment of *Tennessee Jed.*

I ran downstairs and out the front door to my car. Leona must have been in the kitchen. I turned the key and punched on the radio and spun the dial to 790 kilocycles. The ABC station. Rock music.

I sat there for a few moments, then ran the dial slowly from one end to the other. Music, news, talk shows. No *Tennessee Jed.* And it was a Blaupunkt, the best radio I could get. I wasn't missing some perimeter station. It simply was not there!

After a few moments I turned off the radio and the ignition and went back upstairs quietly. I sat down on the top step and listened to the entire program. It was *wonderful.*

Exciting, imaginative, filled with everything I remembered as being most innovative about radio drama. But it was modern. It wasn't an antique, re-broadcast to assuage the need of that dwindling listenership who longed for the old days. It was a new show, with all the old voices, but still young and bright. Even the commercials were for currently available products, but they weren't as loud or as insulting as the screamer ads one heard on radio these days.

And when *Tennessee Jed* went off at 5:00, I heard Jeffty spin the dial on his radio till I heard the familiar voice of the announcer Glenn Riggs proclaim, *"Presenting Hop Harrigan! America's ace of the airwaves!"* There was the sound of an airplane in flight. It was a prop plane, *not* a jet! Not the sound kids today have grown up with, but the sound *I* grew up with, the *real* sound of an airplane, the growling, revving, throaty sound of the kind of airplanes G-8 and His Battle Aces flew, the kind Captain Midnight flew, the kind Hop Harrigan flew. And then I heard Hop say, *"CX-4 calling control tower. CX-4 calling control tower. Standing by!"* A pause, then, *"Okay, this is Hop Harrigan . . . coming in!"*

And Jeffty, who had the same problem all of us kids had had in the Forties with programming that pitted equal favorites against one another on different stations, having paid his respects to Hop Harrigan and Tank Tinker, spun the dial and went back to ABC, where I heard the stroke of a gong, the wild cacophony of nonsense Chinese chatter, and the announcer yelled, *"T-e-e-e-rry and the Pirates!"*

I sat there on the top step and listened to Terry and Connie and Flip Corkin and, so help me God, Agnes Moorehead as The Dragon Lady, all of them in a new adventure that took place in a Red China that had not existed in the days of Milton Caniff's 1937 version of the Orient, with river pirates and Chiang Kai-shek and warlords and the naïve Imperialism of American gunboat diplomacy.

Sat, and listened to the whole show, and sat even longer to hear *Superman* and part of *Jack Armstrong, The All American Boy* and part of *Captain Midnight*, and John Kinzer came home and neither he nor Leona came upstairs to find out what had happened to me, or where Jeffty was, and sat longer, and found I had started crying, and could not stop, just sat there with tears running down my face, into the corners of my mouth, sitting and crying until Jeffty heard me and opened his door and saw me and came out and looked at me in childish confusion as I heard the station break for the Mutual Network and they began the theme music of *Tom Mix*, "When It's Round-up Time in Texas and the Bloom Is on the Sage," and Jeffty touched my shoulder and smiled at me, with his mouth and his big brown eyes, and said, "Hi, Donny. Wanna come in an' listen to the radio with me?"

Hume denied the existence of an absolute space, in which each thing has its place; Borges denies the existence of one single time, in which all events are linked.

Jeffty received radio programs from a place that could not, in logic, in the natural scheme of the space-time universe as conceived by Einstein, exist. But that wasn't all he received. He got mail order premiums that no one was manufacturing. He read comic books that had been defunct for three decades. He saw movies with actors who had been dead for twenty years. He was the receiving terminal for endless joys and pleasures of the past that the world had dropped along the way. On its headlong suicidal flight toward New Tomorrows, the world had razed its treasurehouse of simple happinesses, had poured concrete over its playgrounds, had abandoned its elfin stragglers, and all of it was being impossibly, miraculously shunted back into the present through Jeffty. Revivified, updated, the traditions maintained but contemporaneous. Jeffty was the unbidding Aladdin whose very nature formed the magic lampness of his reality.

And he took me into his world with him.

Because he trusted me.

We had breakfast of Quaker Puffed Wheat Sparkies and warm Ovaltine we drank out of *this* year's Little Orphan Annie Shake-Up Mugs. We went to the movies and while everyone else was seeing a comedy starring Goldie Hawn and Ryan O'Neal, Jeffty and I were enjoying

Humphrey Bogart as the professional thief Parker in John Huston's brilliant adaptation of the Donald Westlake novel SLAYGROUND. The second feature was Spencer Tracy, Carole Lombard and Laird Cregar in the Val Lewton–produced film of *Leiningen Versus the Ants*.

Twice a month we went down to the newsstand and bought the current pulp issues of *The Shadow, Doc Savage* and *Startling Stories*. Jeffty and I sat together and I read to him from the magazines. He particularly liked the new short novel by Henry Kuttner, "The Dreams of Achilles," and the new Stanley G. Weinbaum series of short stories set in the subatomic particle universe of Redurna. In September we enjoyed the first installment of the new Robert E. Howard Conan novel, ISLE OF THE BLACK ONES, in *Weird Tales*; and in August we were only mildly disappointed by Edgar Rice Burroughs's fourth novella in the Jupiter series featuring John Carter of Barsoom—"Corsairs of Jupiter." But the editor of *Argosy All-Story Weekly* promised there would be two more stories in the series, and it was such an unexpected revelation for Jeffty and me that it dimmed our disappointment at the lessened quality of the current story.

We read comics together, and Jeffty and I both decided—separately, before we came together to discuss it—that our favorite characters were Doll Man, Airboy and The Heap. We also adored the George Carlson strips in *Jingle Jangle Comics*, particularly the Pie-Face Prince of Old Pretzleburg stories, which we read together and laughed over, even though I had to explain some of the esoteric puns to Jeffty, who was too young to have that kind of subtle wit.

How to explain it? I can't. I had enough physics in college to make some offhand guesses, but I'm more likely wrong than right. The laws of the conservation of energy occasionally break. These are laws that physicists call "weakly violated." Perhaps Jeffty was a catalyst for the weak violation of conservation laws we're only now beginning to realize exist. I tried doing some reading in the area—muon decay of the "forbidden" kind: gamma decay that doesn't include the muon neutrino among its products—but nothing I encountered, not even the latest readings from the Swiss Institute for Nuclear Research near Zurich gave me an insight. I was thrown back on a vague acceptance of the philosophy that the real name for "science" is *magic*.

No explanations, but enormous good times.

The happiest time of my life.

I had the "real" world, the world of my store and my friends and my family, the world of profit&loss, of taxes and evenings with young women who talked about going shopping or the United Nations, or the rising cost of coffee and microwave ovens. And I had Jeffty's world, in which I existed only when I was with him. The things of the past he knew as fresh and new, I could experience only when in his company. And the membrane between the two worlds grew ever thinner, more luminous and transparent. I had the best of both worlds. And knew, somehow, that I could carry nothing from one to the other.

Forgetting that, for just a moment, betraying Jeffty by forgetting, brought an end to it all.

Enjoying myself so much, I grew careless and failed to consider how fragile the relationship between Jeffty's world and my world really was. There is a reason why the present begrudges the existence of the past. I never really understood. Nowhere in the beast books, where survival is shown in battles between claw and fang, tentacle and poison sac, is there recognition of the ferocity the present always brings to bear on the past. Nowhere is there a detailed statement of how the present lies in wait for What-Was, waiting for it to become Now-This-Moment so it can shred it with its merciless jaws.

Who could know such a thing . . . at any age . . . and certainly not at my age . . . who could understand such a thing?

I'm trying to exculpate myself. I can't. It was my fault.

It was another Saturday afternoon.

"What's playing today?" I asked him, in the car, on the way downtown.

He looked up at me from the other side of the front seat and smiled one of his best smiles. "Ken Maynard in *Bullwhip Justice* an' *The Demolished Man*." He kept smiling, as if he'd really put one over on me. I looked at him with disbelief.

"You're *kid*ding!" I said, delighted. "Bester's THE DEMOLISHED MAN?" He nodded his head, delighted at my being delighted. He knew it was one of my favorite books. "Oh, that's super!"

"Super *duper*," he said.

"Who's in it?"

"Franchot Tone, Evelyn Keyes, Lionel Barrymore and Elisha Cook, Jr." He was much more knowledgeable about movie actors than I'd ever been. He could name the character actors in any movie he'd ever seen. Even the crowd scenes.

"And cartoons?" I asked.

"Three of 'em: a *Little Lulu*, a *Donald Duck* and a *Bugs Bunny*. An' a *Pete Smith Specialty* an' a *Lew Lehr Monkeys is da C-r-r-r-aziest Peoples*."

"Oh boy!" I said. I was grinning from ear to ear. And then I looked down and saw the pad of purchase order forms on the seat. I'd forgotten to drop it off at the store.

"Gotta stop by the Center," I said. "Gotta drop off something. It'll only take a minute."

"Okay," Jeffty said. "But we won't be late, will we?"

"Not on your tintype, kiddo," I said.

When I pulled into the parking lot behind the Center, he decided to come in with me and we'd walk over to the theater. It's not a large town. There are only two movie houses, the Utopia and the Lyric. We were going to the Utopia and it was only three blocks from the Center.

I walked into the store with the pad of forms, and it was bedlam. David and Jan were handling two customers each, and there were people standing around waiting to be helped. Jan turned a look on me and her face was a horror-mask of pleading. David was running from the stockroom to the showroom and all he could murmur as he whipped past was "Help!" and then he was gone.

"Jeffty," I said, crouching down, "listen, give me a few minutes. Jan and David are in trouble with all these people. We won't be late, I promise. Just let me get rid of a couple of these customers." He looked nervous, but nodded okay.

I motioned to a chair and said, "Just sit down for a while and I'll be right with you."

He went to the chair, good as you please, though he knew what was happening, and he sat down.

I started taking care of people who wanted color television sets. This was the first really substantial batch of units we'd gotten in—color television was only now becoming reasonably priced and this was Sony's first promotion—and it was bonanza time for me. I could see paying off the loan and being out in front for the first time with the Center. It was business.

In my world, good business comes first.

Jeffty sat there and stared at the wall. Let me tell you about the wall.

Stanchion and bracket designs had been rigged from floor to within two feet of the ceiling. Television sets had been stacked artfully on the wall. Thirty-three television sets. All playing at the same time. Black and white, color, little ones, big ones, all going at the same time.

Jeffty sat and watched thirty-three television sets, on a Saturday afternoon. We can pick up a total of thirteen channels including the UHF educational stations. Golf was on one channel; baseball was on a second; celebrity bowling was on a third; the fourth channel was a religious seminar; a teenage dance show was on the fifth; the sixth was a rerun of a situation comedy; the seventh was a rerun of a police show; eighth was a nature program showing a man flycasting endlessly; ninth was news and conversation; tenth was a stock car race; eleventh was a man doing logarithms on a blackboard; twelfth was a woman in a leotard doing setting-up exercises; and on the thirteenth channel was a badly animated cartoon show in Spanish. All but six of the shows were repeated on three sets. Jeffty sat and watched that wall of television on a Saturday afternoon while I sold as fast and as hard as I could, to pay back my Aunt Patricia and stay in touch with my world. It was business.

I should have known better. I should have understood about the present and the way it kills the past. But I was selling with both hands. And when I finally glanced over at Jeffty, half an hour later, he looked like another child.

He was sweating. That terrible fever sweat when you have stomach flu. He was pale, as pasty and pale as a worm, and his little hands were gripping the arms of the chair so tightly I could see his knuckles in bold relief. I dashed over to him, excusing myself from the middle-aged couple looking at the new 21" Mediterranean model.

"Jeffty!"

He looked at me, but his eyes didn't track. He was in absolute terror. I pulled him out of the chair and started toward the front door with him, but the customers I'd deserted yelled at me, "Hey!" The middle-aged man said, "You wanna sell me this thing or don't you?"

I looked from him to Jeffty and back again. Jeffty was like a zombie. He had come where I'd pulled him. His legs were rubbery and his feet dragged. The past, being eaten by the present, the sound of something in pain.

I clawed some money out of my pants pocket and jammed it into Jeffty's hand. "Kiddo . . . listen to me . . . get out of here right now!" He still couldn't focus properly. "*Jeffty,*" I said as tightly as I could, "*listen* to me!" The middle-aged customer and his wife were walking toward us. "Listen, kiddo, get out of here right this minute. Walk over to the Utopia and buy the tickets. I'll be right behind you." The middle-aged man and his wife were almost on us. I shoved Jeffty through the door and watched him stumble away in the wrong direction, then stop as if gathering his wits, turn and go back past the front of the Center and in the direction of the Utopia. "Yes sir," I said, straightening up and facing them, "yes, ma'am, that is one terrific set with some sen*sa*tional features! If you'll just step back here with me . . ."

There was a terrible sound of something hurting, but I couldn't tell from which channel, or from which set, it was coming.

Most of it I learned later, from the girl in the ticket booth, and from some people I knew who came to me to tell me what had happened. By the time I got to the Utopia, nearly twenty minutes later, Jeffty was already beaten to a pulp and had been taken to the Manager's office.

"Did you see a very little boy, about five years old, with big brown eyes and straight brown hair . . . he was waiting for me?"

"Oh, I think that's the little boy those kids beat up?"

"What!?! *Where is he?*"

"They took him to the Manager's office. No one knew who he was or where to find his parents—"

A young girl wearing an usher's uniform was kneeling down beside the couch, placing a wet paper towel on his face.

I took the towel away from her and ordered her out of the office.

She looked insulted and snorted something rude, but she left. I sat on the edge of the couch and tried to swab away the blood from the lacerations without opening the wounds where the blood had caked. Both his eyes were swollen shut. His mouth was ripped badly. His hair was matted with dried blood.

He had been standing in line behind two kids in their teens. They started selling tickets at 12:30 and the show started at 1:00. The doors weren't opened till 12:45. He had been waiting, and the kids in front of him had had a portable radio. They were listening to the ball game. Jeffty had wanted to hear some program, God knows what it might have been, *Grand Central Station, Let's Pretend, Land of the Lost,* God only knows which one it might have been.

He had asked if he could borrow their radio to hear the program for a minute, and it had been a commercial break or something, and the kids had given him the radio, probably out of some malicious kind of courtesy that would permit them to take offense and rag the little boy. He had changed the station . . . and they'd been unable to get it to go back to the ball game. It was locked into the past, on a station that was broadcasting a program that didn't exist for anyone but Jeffty.

They had beaten him badly . . . as everyone watched.

And then they had run away.

I had left him alone, left him to fight off the present without sufficient weaponry. I had betrayed him for the sale of a 21" Mediterranean console television, and now his face was pulped meat. He moaned something inaudible and sobbed softly.

"Shhh, it's okay, kiddo, it's Donny. I'm here. I'll get you home, it'll be okay."

I should have taken him straight to the hospital. I don't know why I didn't. I should have. I should have done that.

When I carried him through the door, John and Leona Kinzer just stared at me. They didn't move to take him from my arms. One of his hands was hanging down. He was conscious, but just barely. They stared, there in the semi-darkness of a Saturday afternoon in the present. I looked at them. "A couple of kids beat him up at the theater." I raised him a few inches in my arms and extended him. They stared at me, at both of us, with nothing in their eyes, without movement. "Jesus Christ," I shouted, "he's been beaten! He's your son! Don't you even want to touch him? What the hell kind of people are you?!"

Then Leona moved toward me very slowly. She stood in front of us for a few seconds, and there was a leaden stoicism in her face that was terrible to see. It said, *I have been in this place before, many times, and I cannot bear to be in it again; but I am here now.*

So I gave him to her. God help me, I gave him over to her.

And she took him upstairs to bathe away his blood and his pain.

John Kinzer and I stood in our separate places in the dim living room of their home, and we stared at each other. He had nothing to say to me.

I shoved past him and fell into a chair. I was shaking.

I heard the bath water running upstairs.

After what seemed a very long time Leona came downstairs, wiping her hands on her apron. She sat down on the sofa and after a moment John sat down beside her. I heard the sound of rock music from upstairs.

"Would you like a piece of nice pound cake?" Leona said.

I didn't answer. I was listening to the sound of the music. Rock music. On the radio. There was a table lamp on the end table beside the sofa. It cast a dim and futile light in the shadowed living room. *Rock music from the present, on a radio upstairs?* I started to say something, and then *knew* . . . Oh, God . . . *no*!

I jumped up just as the sound of hideous crackling blotted out the music, and the table lamp dimmed and dimmed and flickered. I screamed something, I don't know what it was, and ran for the stairs.

Jeffty's parents did not move. They sat there with their hands folded, in that place they had been for so many years.

I fell twice rushing up the stairs.

There isn't much on television that can hold my interest. I bought an old cathedral-shaped Philco radio in a second-hand store, and I replaced all the burnt-out parts with the original tubes from old radios I could cannibalize that still worked. I don't use transistors or printed circuits. They wouldn't work. I've sat in front of that set for hours sometimes, running the dial back and forth as slowly as you can imagine, so slowly it doesn't look as if it's moving at all sometimes.

But I can't find *Captain Midnight* or *The Land of the Lost* or *The Shadow* or *Quiet, Please*.

So she did love him, still, a little bit, even after all those years. I can't hate them: they only wanted to live in the present world again. That isn't such a terrible thing.

It's a good world, all things considered. It's much better than it used to be, in a lot of ways. People don't die from the old diseases any more. They die from new ones, but that's Progress, isn't it?

Isn't it?

Tell me.

Somebody please tell me.

XIII

CONTRACTS ON THE SOUL

> "My soul says, tomorrow cannot be trusted to naked apes. [. . .] I cannot argue with my soul, it will hear no counter-suggestion. And what can I do? I'm trapped in here with the lunatic."
>
> —"Stealing Tomorrow," *Trumpet* #11, 1974

Some call it the soul, some call it the totality of each human intelligence, and some disregard it. The presence is there, nonetheless, the inner matrix of every human body: the nature of the being.

If Harlan were a painter instead of a writer, imagine the wonders he would give us—the grist and grue of Dali and Bosch, the blinding colors of van Gogh, the subtle flesh tones of Rembrandt. But he paints in words, and like an artist with a brush his goal is the stimulation of the soul—the soul in its moments of passion, and in its touchy moments of negotiation with itself.

These stories present some of those memorable moments, and we can all learn from them.

Since "Daniel White for the Greater Good" (1961) confronts a specific moral decision in a time that is now past, it would be easy to regard it with a disclaiming distance. After all, we have our own current problems, and Daniel White is only a fictional black man in an historical context. Yet the paradox of Daniel White remains: how can we make "moral" judgments when a human life is weighed against the importance of our personal value system? What *is* the price of a human soul? Daniel White's, U. J. Peregrin's, Henry Roblee's, even Marion Gore's—not to mention mine and yours. The price was once measured in pieces of silver, but the true measurement had always been and remains much higher.

"Neither Your Jenny Nor Mine" (1964) illustrates the complex maze in which souls go about their business of life. We seem to wander through the maze alone—and in the Southern California of Harlan's story, the details scrupulously emphasize commercial manipulation of this loneliness—but when our solitary paths cross, there comes the burning question of responsibility. Who will carry an extra load, who will become the monkey-on-the-back? Even more critical is the challenge to the soul's strength, and Jenny is a weight that each of us should measure before we break our backs in the test.

The epigram to "Alive and Well and on a Friendless Voyage" (1977) translates as "What pains us trains us." (I bother to tell you this because, as Harlan has stated publicly, it extends beyond the story, which was created in an exorcism of personal pain.) What especially matters to us, as readers, is that we must see ourselves equally as tragic as Moth, bearing guilt as a responsibility too large for one soul. It is to be hoped that from this tragedy we can draw insight, to meet the less stringent demands most of us carry through the years. If we believe the soul is eternal, we must not forget that it can develop the character and strength to meet its challenges along the way.

"I think that's the obligation of the strong, to assist the weak. Not *leaners*, you understand; not people [. . .] who aren't willing to fight down to the last breath. But for those people who have determination and courage, and simply need a little more hand [. . .]"

—"An Interview with Harlan Ellison" by James Van Hise, *RBCC* #151, August 1980

Daniel White
For the Greater Good

Begin with absolute blackness. The sort of absolute blackness that does not exist in reality. A black as deep and profound as the space directly under a hell pressed to the ground; a black as all-surrounding as blindness from birth; a black *that* black. The black of a hallway devoid of light, and a black—advancing down that hallway—going away from you. At the end of a hallway as black as this, a square of light painfully white. A doorway through which can be seen a window, pouring dawn sunlight in a torrent into the room, through the doorway, and causing a sunspot of light at the end of the pitch-black hallway.

If this were a motion picture, it would be starkly impressive, the black so deep, and the body moving away from the camera, down the hall toward the square of superhuman white. The body clinging to the right-hand wall, moving down the tunnel of ebony, slowly, painstakingly, almost drunkenly. The body is a form, merely a form, not quite as black as the hallway mouth that contains it, but still without sufficient contrast to break what would be superlative camera work, were this a motion picture. But it is not a motion picture. It is a story of some truth.

It is a story, and for that reason, the effect of superlative cinematography must be shattered as the body pulls itself to the door, lurches through, and stumbles to grasp at the edge of a chest-high wooden counter. The camera angles (were this a motion picture) would suddenly shift and tilt, bringing into immediate focus the soft yet hard face of a police desk sergeant, his collar open and sweat beading his neck and upper lip. We might study the raised bushy eyebrows and the quickly horrified expression just before the lips go rigid. Then the camera would pan rapidly around the squad room; we would see the

Georgia sunrise outside that streaming window, and finally our gaze would settle on the face of a girl.

A white girl.

With a smear of blood at the edge of her mouth, with one eye swollen shut and blue-black, with her hair disarrayed and matted with blood, leaves and dirt . . . and an expression of pain that says one thing:

"Help . . . me . . ."

The camera would follow that face as it sinks slowly to the floor.

Then, if this were a movie, and not reality, in a town without a name in central Georgia, the camera would cut to black. Sharp cut, and wait for the next scene.

It might have been simpler, had he been a good man. At least underneath; but he wasn't. He was, very simply, a dirty nigger. When he could not cadge a free meal by intimidation, he stole. He smelled bad, he had the morals of a swamp pig, and as if that were not enough to exclude him from practically every strata of society, he had bad teeth, worse breath and a foul mouth. Fittingly, his name was Daniel White.

They had no difficulty arresting him, and even less difficulty proving he was the man who had raped and beaten Marion Gore. He was found sleeping exhausted in a corner of the hobo jungle at the side of the railroad tracks on the edge of the town. There was blood on his hands and hair under his fingernails. Police lab analysis confirmed that the blood type and follicles of hair matched those of Marion Gore.

Far from circumstantial, these facts merely verified the confession Daniel White made when arrested. He was not even granted the saving grace of having been drunk. He was surly, obscene and thoroughly pleased with what he had done. The fact that Marion Gore had been sixteen, a virgin, and had gone into a coma after making her way from the field where she had been attacked to the police station, seemed to make no impression on Daniel White.

The local papers tagged him—and they were conservative at best—a conscienceless beast. He was that. At least.

It was not unexpected, then, to find a growing wave of mass hatred in the town. A hatred that continually emerged in the words, "Lynch the bastard."

At first, the word black was not even inserted between *the* and *bastard*. It wasn't needed. It came later, when the concept of lynching gave way to a peculiar itch in the palms of many white hands. An itch that might well be scratched by a length of hemp rope.

It had to happen quickly, or it would not happen at all. The chief of police would call the mayor, the mayor would get in touch with the governor, and in a matter of hours the National Guard would truck in. So it had to happen quickly, or not at all.

And it was bound to happen. There was no doubt of that. There had been seeds planted – the school trouble, darkie rabble-rousers from New Jersey and Illinois down talking to the nigras in Littletown, that business at the Woolworth's counter – and now the crop was coming in.

Daniel White was safe behind bars, but outside, it was getting bad:

. . . the big-mouth crowd that hung out in Peerson's Bowling and Billiard Center caught Phil the clean-up boy, and badgered him into a fight. They took him out back and worked him over with three-foot lengths of bicycle chain; the diagnosis was double concussion and internal hemorrhaging.

. . . a caravan of heavies from the new development near the furniture factory motored down into Littletown and set fire to The Place, where thirty-five or forty of the town's more responsible Negro leaders had gathered for a few drinks and a discussion of what their position might be in this matter. Result: fifteen burned, and the bar scorched to the ground.

. . . Willa Ambrose, who washed and kept house for the Porters, was fired after a slight misunderstanding with Diane Porter; Willa had admitted to once taking in a movie with Daniel White.

. . . the Jesus Baptist Church was bombed the same night Daniel White made his confession. The remains of the building gave up evidence that the job had been done with homemade Molotov cocktails and sticks of dynamite stolen from the road construction shed on the highway. Pastor Neville lost the use of his right eye: a flying spiked shard from the imported stained glass windows.

So the chief of police called the mayor, and the mayor called the governor, and the governor alerted his staff, and they discussed it, and decided to wait till morning to mobilize the National Guard (which was made up of Georgia boys who didn't much care for the idea of Daniel White, in any case). At best, ten hours.

A long, hot, dangerous ten hours.

Daniel White slept peacefully. He knew he wasn't going to be lynched. He also knew he was going to become a *cause célèbre* and might easily get off with a light sentence, this being an election year, and the eyes of the world on his little central Georgia town.

After all, the NAACP hadn't even made an appearance yet. Daniel White slept peacefully.

He knew he didn't deserve to die for Marion Gore.

She hadn't *really* been a virgin.

The NAACP man's name was U. J. Peregrin and he was out of the Savannah office. He was tall, and exceedingly slim in his tailored Ivy suit. He was nut-brown and had deep-set eyes that seemed veiled like a cobra's. He spoke in a soft, cultivated voice totally free of drawl and slur. He had been born in Matawan, New Jersey, had attended college at the University of Chicago and had gone into social work out of a mixture of emotions. This assignment had come to him chiefly because of his native familiarity with the sort of culture that spawned Daniel White—and a lynch mob.

He sat across from Henry Roblee (who had been picked by the terror-stricken Negro residents of that little central Georgia town as their spokesman) and conversed in three AM tones. Seven hours until the National Guard might come, seven hours in which anything might happen, seven hours that had forced the inhabitants of Littletown to douse their lights and crouch behind windows with 12-gauges ready.

"We've never had anything like this here," Henry Roblee admitted, his square face cut with worry. He rubbed his blocky hands over the moist glass. A thin film of whiskey colored the bottom of the glass. A bottle stood between them on the table.

Peregrin drew deeply on his cigarette and stared into Roblee's frightened eyes. "Mr. Roblee," he said softly, "you may never have had anything like this before, but you've certainly got it now, and the question is, 'What do we intend to do about it?' " He waited. Not so much for an answer as for a realization on the other man's part of just what the situation meant.

"It's not White we're worried about," Roblee added hastily. "That jail is strong enough, and I don't suppose the Chief is going to let them come by without doing something to stop them. It's what's happening all over town that's got us frightened. We never seen the people 'round here act this way. Why, they in a killing frame of mind!"

Peregrin nodded slowly.

"How is your pastor?" he asked.

Roblee shrugged. "He's gone be blind in the one eye, maybe both, but that's what I mean. That man was respected by everybody 'round here. They thought most highly of him. We got to protect ourselves."

"What do you propose?" Peregrin asked.

Roblee looked up from the empty glass suddenly. "What do *we* propose? Why, man, that's why we asked for help from the N-double A-CP. Don't you under*stand*? Something terrible's gone happen in this town unless we decide what to do to stop it. Even the sensible folks 'round here are crazy mad with wanting to lynch that Daniel White."

"I can only make suggestions, that's my job. I can't *tell* you what to do."

Roblee fondled the glass, then filled it half full with uneven movements. He tipped it up and drank heavily. "What about if we just all moved on out for a few days?"

Peregrin shook his head.

Roblee looked away, said softly, ironically, "I didn't think so." He moved his tongue over his thick, moist lips. "Man, I am *scared*!"

Peregrin said, "Do you think the Chief would let me in to speak to White tonight?"

The other man shrugged. "You can try. Want me to give him a call?" Peregrin nodded agreement, and added, "Let me speak to him. The organization might carry a little weight."

It was decided, after the call, that Peregrin and Roblee would both go to see Daniel White. The chief of police advised them to come by way of the police emergency alley, where the chance of their being seen and stopped would be less.

In the cell block, Peregrin stood for several minutes watching Daniel White through the bars. He studied the face, the attitude of relaxation, the clothing the man wore.

He mumbled something lightly. Roblee moved up next to him, asked, "What did you say?"

Peregrin repeated the words, only slightly louder, yet distinctly. "Sometimes I wonder if it's worth it. Sometimes I think there are too many fifth columnists."

Roblee shook his head without understanding what Peregrin had said.

"Should we talk to him?" the Georgia Negro said to the Ivy-tailored visitor.

Peregrin nodded resignedly. "Not much bother, but we might as well. We're here."

Roblee stepped up to the bars. He called in to Daniel White. The man woke suddenly, but without apprehension. He sat up on the striped tick mattress and looked at his two callers. He smiled, a gap-toothed grin that was at once charming, disarming, frightful and painful. "How there, y'all." He stood up and walked to the bars with a lazy, rolling strut.

"You the man from the N-double A-CP I bet," he ventured, the words twisted Georgia-style. Peregrin nodded.

"Glad t'meetcha. You gone to keep them sonofabitches from hangin' my black ass?" He continued to grin, a self-assured, cocky grin that rankled Peregrin.

The tall Negro moved his face very close to the bars. "You think I should?"

Daniel White made a wry face. "Why, man, you and me is brothers. We the same, fellah. You can't let them string up no brother of yours. Got to show that damn Mistuh Charlie we as good as him any day."

Peregrin's face momentarily wrenched with distaste. "*Are* we the same, White? You and me. You and Mr. Roblee here? Are we all the same?" He paused, and leaned his forehead against the bars.

"Perhaps we are, perhaps we are," he murmured.

Daniel White stared at him for some time, without speaking. But he grinned. Finally, "I gone beat this thing. Mister NAACP, you just wait an' see. I gone get outta this."

Peregrin raised his eyes slowly. "You don't even feel any remorse, do you?"

White stared at him uncomprehending. "Whatch'ou mean?" Peregrin's face raised to the ceiling, helplessly, as though drawn on invisible wires. "You really don't know, do you?" he said to himself.

Daniel White grunted and bared rotten teeth. "Listen to me, Mister NAACP you. I gone tell you somethin'. That little white bitch that Gore child, she a bum from a long way back; Jim, I seen her in the woods with half a dozen boys from time on time. She not such a hot piece, I tell you that."

Peregrin turned to Roblee. "Let's go," he said, slowly. "We've done all we can here."

They moved back down the cell block; the empty cell block from which the three drunks and the vag had been removed when the first rumors of lynch had begun circulating.

Outside, it was not so quiet. There were mutterings from dark corners of the central Georgia town. Murmurings, unrests, fear and rising voices.

In his cell, Daniel White returned to sleep. *He* knew what was going to happen. He had it locked. He was a poor darkie who was going to get all the benefits so long overdue his people.

The man from the NAACP would tend to all that . . .

. . . even if he was a fruity-looking cat in a funny suit.

"What the hell you mean, for the greater good? Are you crazy or something, Mister? You can't let that mob take him and lynch him?" Roblee's face was a mask of horror. "Are you crazy or *what*?"

Peregrin's forehead was a crisscross of weaving shadow, caught in the flickering light of the candle. They sat at the table once more, joined by five others, all hidden in the gray and black of the room. The shades were drawn, and behind the shades, curtains had been pulled. And they sat staring at the man from the NAACP, Peregrin, who had just told them, without preamble, that they must not only *let* the whites lynch Daniel White, but they must do everything in their power to aid the act.

"Say, listen, Mister Peregrin, I think you out of your mind. That's *murder*, man!" The speaker was a stout, balding man with coffee-color skin and a wart at the side of his wide nose.

"Just what do you mean 'For the greater good'?" Roblee sank a hand heavily on Peregrin's sleeve. Peregrin continued to sit silently, having said what he felt he must say.

Roblee shook him. "Dammit, fellah, you gone answer me! What'd you mean by that?"

Peregrin looked up them, then. His eyes caught the candlelight and threw it back in two bright lines. His face was shattered; there was conflict and fear and desperation in it. But a determination. "All right," he said, finally.

They stared at him as he dry-washed his cheekbones and temples with moist hands. "Daniel White is sleeping up in that jail, and he doesn't care *what* happens to any of you. He had his fun, and now he wants to capitalize on all the work we've done for so long, to escape punishment. He's banking on everyone making such a hue and cry that no one will dare hurt the poor nigger being taken advantage of, down in rotten Georgia."

Roblee continued to watch the tall man, impassively, waiting. There was confusion in the cant of his head, in the frozen hand on Peregrin's sleeve.

"Those people out there," Peregrin waved a fist at the shaded window, "they're stretched as tight as piano wires. They've been told that everything they've believed for hundreds of years is a lie. They've been told the Negro is as good as them, they've been told their white sons and daughters are going to have to move over and share five-and-ten-cent store seats with them, and schools with them, and buses with them, and movies with them . . ."

His breath came labored. He ground his teeth together and went on with difficulty.

"They've had the rug pulled out from under them, and they're still falling. They'll *be* falling for a long time. Done slowly, they could adjust to it. But then Daniel White rapes a sixteen-year-old girl and they've got a reason to hate, they've got something to focus their hate *on*. So they start taking out their fear and confusion in any way they can.

"Look what has happened in just the few hours since the girl was found. Your church has been bombed, brothers have been fired and ostracized, some have been beaten up and perhaps that boy they stomped will die. Your homes and that bar have been burned. This isn't going to stop here. It's going to get worse. And it's not even going to stop with your town. It's going to march like a wave to the beach, washing all the work we've done before it.

"If Daniel White goes free."

He paused.

Roblee made to interrupt, "But to let them haul him out of there and lynch him, that's . . ."

"Don't you *understand*, man?" Peregrin turned on Roblee with fury. "Don't you hear what I'm telling you? That man up there isn't merely a poor sonofabitch who got loaded and pawed a white girl. He's a cold-blooded miserable animal, and if anyone deserved to die, it's him. But that has nothing to do with it. I'm talking to you about the *need* for that man to die. I'm telling you, Roblee, and all of you, that if you don't take their minds off the Negro community as a whole, you're going to set back the cause of equality in this country fifty years. And if you think I'm making this up you'd better realize that it's already happened once before, just this way."

They stared at him.

"Yes, dammit, it happened once before. And though we didn't have anything to do with the way it turned out—and thank God it turned out as it did—we would have told them to do it just the way they did."

They stared, and suddenly, one of them knew.

"Emmett Till," he breathed, softly.

Peregrin turned on the speaker. "That's right. They didn't even know for sure what the circumstances had been, but the trouble was starting up—not even as bad as here—and they hauled Till out and killed him. And it stopped the trouble like *that*!" he snapped his fingers.

"But *lynching* . . ." Roblee said, horrified.

"Don't you understand? Are you stupid or something, like they say we are? Monkeys? Can't you see that Daniel White dead can be more valuable than a hundred Daniel Whites alive? Don't you see the horror that Northerners will feel, the repercussions internationally, the demands for justice, the swift advance of the program . . . can't you see that Daniel White can serve the greater good? The good of all his people?

"What he never was in life, that miserable bastard up there can be in death!"

Roblee shrank away from Peregrin. The taller man had not spoken with fanaticism, had only delivered with desperate and impassioned tones what he knew to be true. They had heard him, and now each of them, where there was no room for anyone else's opinions, was thinking about it. It meant murder . . . or rather, the toleration of murder. What they were deliberating, was the necessity of lynching. There was no doubt that the trouble could be much worse in the town, that more homes would be burned and more people hurt, perhaps killed. But was it enough to know that to sacrifice up a man to the mob madness, to the lynch rope? Was it enough to know that you might be saving hundreds of lives in the long run by sacrificing one life hardly worth saving to begin with?

It might have been easier, had Daniel White been a man with some qualities of decency. But he wasn't. He was just what the White Press had called him, a beast. That made it the more difficult; for had he been easier to identify with, they could have said no. But this way . . .

There were murmurs from around the room, and the murmurs were, "I . . . don't . . . know . . . I just don't know . . ."

It meant more than just saving the skins of the people in Littletown—though men had been sacrificed to save less lives—it meant saving generations of children to come, from sitting in the backs of movie houses, of allowing them to grow up without the necessity of knowing squalor and prejudice and the words "shine," "nigger," "Jim Crow."

It meant a lot of things, that thin thread of life that was Daniel White. That thin thread that might be stretched around Daniel White's neck.

It meant a lot.

It was a double-edged sword that slicing one way would tame the wrath of the mob beast, and slicing the other would make a path for more understanding, by use of shame and example.

But could they do it . . . ?

Were this a motion picture, and not a story of some truth, the camera might play about the darkened room, candlelit and oppressive. It might play about the gaunt, hardening faces of the men, and mirror their decisions. If this were a motion picture. And the emphasis on memorable closeups. But it is not a motion picture, and when they threw up their hands saying they could not decide, Peregrin had to say, "Let's go talk to someone who knows this mob."

So they agreed, because the decision was not one that men could make about another man.

When they opened the door of the house on the edge of Littletown, and stepped out, they did not see the mass of moving dark shadows. The first warning they had was the heat-laden voice snarling, "You goin' tuh save that nigger rape bastard, Savannah man? Like *hell* you are!"

Then they jumped.

At first they used the lead pipes and the hammers, but after the first flurry they spent their fury and went on to fists and boots. Peregrin caught a blow in the face that spun him around, sent him crashing into the wall of the house. Off in the darkness he could hear Roblee screaming and the wet, regular syncopation of someone kicking at bloody flesh.

Later, much later, when all the lights had stopped whirling, and all the strange new colors had become merely reds and greens and blues, they dragged themselves to their feet.

Roblee's face looked like something sold across a meat counter. He daubed at the ruined expanse of skin and said very defiantly. "It's that White's fault. All this. All this, it's *his* fault. We don't hafta take it for him."

Peregrin said nothing. It hurt too much merely to breathe. His rib cage had been crushed. He lay against the house, listening, hearing what they had to say.

The others joined in, between sobs and rasps of breath. "*Let* them lynch him. *Let* them do it."

They knew who to see . . . they knew the men with the ropes . . . the men who would start to hit them when they appeared, but who would listen when they said they had come to give up Daniel White. They knew who to see.

They told Peregrin: "We'll be back. You rest there. We'll do it." And they moved off into the night, to make their vengeance.

Peregrin lay up against the building, and he began to cry. His voice was soft and deep as he said to the sky, "Oh God, they're doing it, but they're doing it for the wrong reasons. They're hating, and that isn't right. They'll give him up, and that's what we need, Lord, but why do they have to do it this way?"

Then after a while, when he had fainted several times, and had the visions of the men storming the jail, and striking the guards and dragging the snarling, defiant Daniel White from his cell, his thought became clearer.

It was worth it. It had to be worth it. What they did, what they allowed, it had to be worth something in the final analysis. For the greater good, he had said. It had to be that. Because if it wasn't, surely there could be no hell deep enough to receive him.

If it was worth it, the end had to be in sight.

And had this been a motion picture, with a happy ending desirable—instead of a grubby little story out of central Georgia—then the man called Peregrin would have considered the inscription they must carve on the statue of the martyr, Daniel White.

Neither Your Jenny Nor Mine

My first inclination, upon learning Jenny was knocked up, was to go find Roger Gore and auger him into the sidewalk. That was my first inclination; when she called, I lit a cigarette and asked her if my girl Rooney, her roommate, knew about it, and she said yes, Rooney knew and had suggested the call to me. I told her to take a copy of *McCall's* and go to the bathroom, that I had to think about it, and would call her back in twenty minutes. She wasn't crying when she hung up, which was something to be thankful for.

There is a crime in our land more heinous than any other I can think of, right offhand, and yet it goes unpunished. It is the crime of gullibility. People who actually believe the highrolling of used car dealers; people who accept the penciled "2 Drink Minimum" card on their table as law; girls who swallow the line of horse crud a swinger uses to get them in the rack. Like that, yeah. Jenny was a product of that crime wave. She was a typical know-nothing, a chick who had been seduced by four-color lithography and dream-images from a million mass media, and she believed the stork brought babies.

In about ninety days her tummy was going to tell her she'd been lied to. And been had.

When I'd started dating Rooney, and had learned that the roommates were two eighteen-year-olds fresh out of nowhere and firmly under Rooney's wing, it had been a toss-up whether I'd try to make them on the sly, or become Big Brother to the brood. As it turned out, Rooney was enough action for me, and I took the latter route.

We started taking Jenny and Kitten (*née* Margaret Alice Kirgen, the second roommate) with us when we went out. Parties, movies, *schlepping*-around sessions in which we put miles on the car and layers on our ennui. Kitten wasn't bad; she was a reasonably hip kid who was actually six months younger than Jenny, but much more aware of what was going on around her. Jenny was impossible. There was a naïve quality about her that might have been ingenuous, if she hadn't been so gawdawful stupid along with it. They are two different facets, naïveté and stupidity, and combined they make for a saccharine-sweet dumb that paralyzes as it horrifies.

Why did we allow them to come along with us, to adopt us someway; or rather, let *us* adopt *them*? Put it down to my past, which was filled with incomplete memories of deeds I did not care to think about. I can't remember ever having been young, not really. On my own as far back as I can recall, there was never that innocence of childhood or nature that I longed to see in others. So Jenny and Kitten became my social projects. Not in any elaborate sense, but it pleasured me to see them enjoy the bounties of the young . . . oh hell, Norman Rockwell and Edgar A. Guest and let's all pose for a Pepsi ad.

Kenneth Duane Markham, thirty years old and a humanitarian. Let's send this child to camp (if we can't roll her in the hay, hey hey!). Call it noble intentions, for all the wrong reasons.

At one of the parties we took Jenny to, I ran across Roger Gore. He was (is) (will be, till I catch his face in my right hand) a good-looking jackpotter with a flair for wearing clothes that would look slovenly on other guys, and a laudable record of having avoided honest labor. His father owned a chain of something or others, and Roger indulged himself by taking jobs as switchman on the railroad, soap salesman door to door, night watchman. He never did any of them for very long; his rationale for taking on such onerous tasks was the same as that of the aspiring novelist. He wanted to be able to say he had done these things. It was all very Robert Ruark and hairy-chested and proletarian. He was a fraud. But a good-looking, smooth fraud with a flair for wearing clothes that would look—but I said that already.

It was one of those parties where some college kid had met a hipster in a downtown black-and-tan club, and had invited him over the following night for "a little get-together." As a consequence, the room was jammed, half with inept, callow UCLA students, half with sinuous spades wrapped up in color. It was one of those scenes where the gray cats felt a sense of adventure and titillation just being in the same time-zone with Negroes, and the blacks were infra-digging, wasting the white boys' Watusi with their own extra-lovely dancing, and mooching as much free juice as possible.

Everybody hated everybody, way down deep.

We walked in and I saw Roger first crack out of the bag. He was trying to make the scene with a couple of spade cats I knew from downtown, and they were being indulgent. But they "felt a draft" and Old Rog was about to get frozen out. When they put him down (which could be noted by the way his sappy expression went sour) and he walked away, I took the two girls over and introduced them. To the colored cats. Roger would make his own introductions, I had no worries on that score. But the two downtown operators were good boys. One of them was a shipping clerk for a record distributor, and the other was gopher in an exclusive men's hair salon. (Gopher: "Go for the coffee, Jerry." "Go for Mr. Bentley's shoes, Jerry." "Go for—")

"Hey, baby, what's shakin'?"

"Howya doin', man, it's been time I seen yoah ass."

"Busy."

"Yeah, sheee-it, man, you always busy one thing'n 'nother."

"Gotta keep the bread on the table . . ."

"Got to keep that bread in yoah *pock*et!"

"True."

Jenny was standing there, her face open, and as far as she was concerned, where was she? Rooney was digging, as usual, and loving me with her eyes, which was a groove. I pointed each one out to the boys and named:

"Hey, Jerry, Willis, want you to meet Rooney and Jenny." Kitten had had a date. A CPA from Santa Monica. Wow!

"Very pleased't meetcha." Jerry grinned. That cat had the most beautiful mouthful of teeth known to Western Man, he knew it, and he flashed them like the marquee at Grauman's Chinese. "*Very* pleased't meetcha," Willis said, and I knew he was shucking me, just to make me feel good; he was coming on with Rooney because he knew it would make me feel tall. I gave them each a soft punch on the bicep and we moved off into the crowd. We said our hellos to the host, who was an authentic *schlepp*, and took the coats into the bedroom. A pair of UCLAmnesiacs were making it among the coats, so we laid ours over the windowseat. It promised to be a bad, dull party. The roar of rhythm&blues was coming out of the living room, meeting the Monkees' crap from the dining room head-on, and canceling each other out in the hallways connecting.

We stepped out into one of these eye-of-the-hurricane areas, and started looking for the bar. I saw Roger Gore heading for the kitchen, and I knew immediately where the juice was being dispensed. I turned to Jenny. "See that guy in the gray hound's tooth, the one going into the kitchen?"

She nodded.

"Stay away from him. There are ten thousand guys at this party who aren't trouble. That one is. He's clever and pretty fair-looking, but he's a lox, and I tell you three times, one two three, stay out of his reach. That's my only advice for the evening. Now scoot." I gave her a shove on the rump and she moved out.

Rooney grinned at me. "Guardian of the morals of the young."

"Poof you," I answered.

"Not here, surely, sir." There were times I wanted to chomp on her ears. And that damned grin of hers. Heidi. Rapunzel. Snow White. Mata Hari.

We went our way, and nodded to Roger Gore in the kitchen, where he was doing something noxious with martinis and sweet gherkins. What a lox!

About an hour later Rooney was bopping with Willis (that sweet muthuh!) and I was in the corner digging a T-Bone Walker 78 somebody had slipped into the stack. Jenny came up to me; "I'm going out for a drink with Roger. I'll be back in about half an hour."

I didn't even think it was worth getting angry about. I'd known it was going to happen. *Don't go up in the top shelf of the cabinet and take a bean out of the jar and shove it up your nose*, you tell the infant, and when you get back home, there he is, stretched out blue on the linoleum, a bean up his nose. It's the way children are.

She mulched out of there on Roger Gore's arm, and when Rooney was done sweating with Willis, he brought her back and I told her about Jenny's exeunt simpering.

"Why didn't you stop her?" she demanded.

"Who do I look like: Torquemada?" I got hot. "I've got enough trouble governing the habits of you and me without taking on the world at large. Besides, he won't hurt her, for Chrissakes. They'll be back."

We waited six hours. The party was over, we were really drug with the scene, and finally went back to my place to sack out. About five AM the phone rang, I groped for it, somehow got it up to my nose and blew into it. After a minute something fell into place and I knew I had it wrong. I tried my eye and my mouth, and by process of elimination got around to my ear. It was Jenny.

"Can you come and get me?"

"Whuhtimezit?"

"I don't know, it's late. Can you come get me?"

"Whereyooat?"

"I'm in a phone booth on Sunset, near Highland. Can you come and get me?" And she started crying. I woke up fast.

"Are you all right?"

"Yes, yes, I'm fine, can you come and get me?"

"Sure. Of course, but what happened to you? We waited till everyone else vanished. What the hell happened to you? Rooney was worried sick."

"I'll tell you later. Can you come get me now?"

"Give me fifteen minutes."

She hung up, I slid out without waking Rooney, threw on a pair of chinos and a jacket, and flew the coop. She was standing under a streetlight where she had said she'd be, and I bundled her into the car, where she immediately broke down. I got her back to my house, and bedded her out on the sofabed in the living room, and went back to sleep myself.

Next morning Rooney cooed over her like Little Orphan Annie. We eventually got the story, and it wasn't that spectacular. He'd taken her to a little bar nearby, tried to get her lushed (which he didn't have to bother doing; Jenny was—putting it politely—not smart enough to avoid being a pushover) and finally told her he had to get the car, which was allegedly his roommate's, back to his house. When he got her there, he proceeded to try The Game, and Jenny swore he hadn't succeeded. In childish retaliation, Roger had fallen asleep. She'd waited around for three hours, but he snoozed on, and finally she'd tried to waken him. Either he couldn't or wouldn't rouse himself, because she finally took to her heels, and an hour and a half later had managed to get to the phone booth.

"Why didn't you call from his house?"

"I was afraid he'd wake up."

"But you wanted him up, didn't you?"

"Well, yes."

"So why didn't you call from there?"

"I was afraid. I wanted to get out of there.'

"Afraid? Of what? Of him?"

"Well . . ."

"Jenny, tell me now, tell me true, did he get to you?"

"No. I swear it. He got very angry when I gave him a hard time. He called me . . . he called me . . ."

"I know what he called you. Forget it."

"I can't."

"So remember it. But don't lie to me, did he get in?"

She turned her face away. At the time I thought it was because of my choice of words. "No, he didn't," she said. So I couldn't really bring myself to feel possessively angry at Roger Gore. He'd done what any guy would try to do. He'd tried to make her, failed, and gotten disgusted. His chief sin was in not being a gentleman. In falling asleep and letting her fend for herself; but then, I'd known Gore was anything but a gentleman, anyhow, so there really wasn't provocation enough to go find and pound him. We let the matter drop. I forgot about it, and fortunately, didn't run into Roger Gore again for some time.

Now, eight weeks later, I sat smoking a cigarette, while Jenny languished in the bathroom of her apartment, reading *McCall's*, and the seed grew in her. I felt responsible. The phone rang. I picked it up reluctantly, and it was Rooney. "She told you?" I mumbled something affirmative. "Have you got a solution?"

"Three of them," I answered. "She can have the baby, she can get it aborted, or she can get Roger Gore to marry her. I'd say the first and third are out, the second one the most feasible, and a quick fourth reason altogether possible."

"What's the fourth one?" Rooney asked.

"She can blow her fucking stupid brains out."

All you have to do is get friendly with a couple of jazz musicians, have met a hooker at a party, be on civil terms with a grocer who takes the neighborhood numbers action, occasionally make an after-hours set in the Negro section, and suddenly you are a figure of mystery, a man with "connections" in the underworld; people come to you for unspeakable foulnesses you have never been within spitting distance of. It is a reflex cliché of people who really haven't the faintest bloody idea of what the Real World is like. Since they themselves never slip over the line, anyone who lives beyond the constrained limits of their socially acceptable scene, has *got* to be a figure of mystery, a man with—oh well . . .

Rooney asked me how soon I could locate an abortionist.

"A whaaat?"

She repeated herself, all honey-voiced forthrightness. It was a foregone conclusion. "Spider" Markham, denizen of the murky underworld, familiar of hoods, gunsels and two-bit whores was the man to ask when you needed a butcher.

"What the hell makes you think I know an abortionist?"

"Well, don't you?"

"No. Of course not. I take precautions. I'm not an imbecile like Roger Gore. I've never knocked anyone up, so ergo I don't know any abortionists." I looked at her with unconcealed annoyance, and she stared back blandly. She wasn't convinced. I was, of course, hiding my connections, for obvious reasons.

"Say, you don't believe me, do you?" I was getting highly hacked by this scene. And Jenny just sat there with her face hanging out, and her stomach growing.

"Well, you can call someone, one of your strange friends, can't you?"

I blew higher than the Van Allen radiation belt. "You've got to be putting me on, Rooney! Call who? What 'strange friends'?" My face was so hot I could feel it in my mouth.

She stared at me accusingly.

So I called Candy.

Candy was a muscle for some nameless amalgamation of interests I don't think could be called The Syndicate. Maybe The Group, or The Guys, or Them, but definitely not The Syndicate. To begin with, he was Greek, not Sicilian.

But Candy *was* a furtive figure, I must admit. He collected the payoffs for the numbers banks in East L.A. and I have seen his 340 pounds walk into a deli as lightly as a prima ballerina, and within ten seconds cause more of a stir than a thermite bomb. "There was a lotta hits this week, Candy," the deli proprietor will con him. "The take is tiny. Tiny. I can't pony it all up. I can give ya 'bout half, though, Candy, and the rest next week sometime."

Candy, who is only slightly less prepossessing than Mount Etna, will suck air into his bellows chest, puff up twice again as large as normal, pouter-pigeon fashion, and in a voice soft as strangling babies, will reply: "Angie, you will kindly get it up or I will have to hurt you. Seriously." They scamper. And from some ratty cache beneath a counter, they produce the held-back portion of Candy's pickup money.

So I called Candy, who is maybe the gentlest cat I know.

"Hi," I started. It was not a particularly brilliant opening, but it was all I had available at that moment. "Listen, a friend of a friend of mine has got herself in a family way. Do you know anybody who can, uh, take care of her?"

He was affronted. Practically shrieked at me. What the hell kind of a guy did I think he was? He didn't screw around with those kinda people. Listen, if that was the kinda guy I thought he was, I would kindly honor him by forgetting his unlisted number. The nerve! The gall! What kind of a creep did I run around with, to need a guy who'd do that and finally Goodbye slam!

I turned around to Jenny and Rooney. "He hung up on me. Thanks."

They seemed shocked, and Rooney made devious remarks about the furtiveness of some shady types. I think I groaned.

Then I tried Van Jessup, a character actor who seemed to know everyone. He knew no one. Then I tried a TV director I'd played gin with a few times, and he said he'd get back to me. Then I tried a chick who made the Sunset Strip scene, and she asked a couple of guarded questions and said *she'd* get back to me. Then I called a relative in Pomona and she giggled outrageously, and said *I* should get back to *her*. Then I called The Boffer, who is a writer and a singer and a hustler of personal needs, and the conversation went like this:

"I need a doctor."

"So go to one."

"Not for me, man, for a chick."

"Pregnant?"

"Of course, stupid. You think I'm the Blue Cross or somedamnthing?"

"Rooney?"

"Don't be funny."

"Who then? And does Rooney know you've been playing pattyfingers?"

"I didn't do the knocking-up."

"A likely story."

"Cut it, man. I'm serious. This thing has lost its funny for me. It isn't my woman, and I didn't do the job on her, and I need a D&C man. Now can you help me or not?"

"I suppose so. I've had occasion to—"

"I don't want to know. Everyone agrees you're the finest swordsman in these parts. Can you get me a guy . . . this is a favor I need, Boffer. It's for a friend."

"You know, everybody you call is gonna think it was you."

"I know."

"Since when did you get such humanitarian instincts?"

"A recent malady. What's his name? Is there a number?"

"You're a lot more noble and friendly than I'd be. This kinda scam is liable to ruin your reputation."

"I haven't got a reputation. What's his name? Give!"

There was a pause, as though The Boffer was seriously considering saying no. He's peculiar that way. His reasoning is on a very furry plane, taken up by intricacies even he barely understands, and informed by a scurrying rodentlike deviousness that comes from having been on the Hollywood merry-go-round for too many years. "Take this down. You got a pencil? Okay, take this down: S. Jaime Quintano; the number is—"

He rattled it off twice and I still didn't get it. So he laid it on me slowly, and I wrote it as accurately as I could.

"Thanks, Boffer. You've got one coming."

I gave the information to Jenny, and she stared at it as though it was contaminated. "You'll have to do the calling," I told her. "Apparently he's a good man, has his own clinic, works most of the week in the Miguel Aleman Hospital, that's the big one down there. This friend of mine says he's taken girls down there a couple of times and this man has been very clean, very good. Three hundred dollars."

She continued to stare at the slip of paper.

"This is the number," I emphasized. It was like talking to a statue. "DU-five-three-three-seven-two, that's in Tijuana, and I think I have his name spelled right. Jenny . . . ?"

First her shoulders began to heave. Silently. Then her entire body shook, as though possessed. And in a second she was dry-crying, her head sunk down on her chest almost, the top of her head bobbing like a cork in a rough sea. It had started to get through to her: what she had undergone had not been love, it had been something far more indelicate, something simpler, more destructive. She felt contaminated, felt insulted, in the strictest possible sense of the outmoded term, she felt *sullied*.

I moved over to her and put my arms around her. She was incapable, at that moment, of even knowing I was there. I held her very tightly for what seemed a long time, and slowly the shaking passed, and her head came up. The front of my shirt was soaked.

She came out from the burrow of my arms. "What's the area code to Tijuana?" she said softly.

"Nine-o-three," Rooney said, from the other side of the room. I looked at her, startled. "I've been there, too." Her face was very sad, and I realized: no one comes to anyone untouched.

Everyone goes through fire.

Jenny picked up the receiver and started to dial.

By the time the Thursday rolled around, I had six more names. A doctor in Monterey Park who was rumored to charge between three and five hundred, but had apparently been busted some time before, and was very much under wraps now. It would have entailed a drive out to that suburb. Five more in Tijuana. Two brothers with their own *Enfermería*, who only charged one hundred and fifty, and whom you had to say, "Nurse Carlotta suggested I call you." Apparently Nurse Carlotta was a swinger in L.A. that the brother dug. Another was alleged to keep the patient over for eight hours, and that was too terrifying for consideration. Overnight in that town would be worse than the operation for Jenny. There was an American doctor down there, Oswald Tremaine, Jr., who was appended with the title "butcher" by my informant, but he only charged one hundred and twenty-five. We decided Quintano was the best bet. His name had come up again, from a very reputable source, so we held to the date of the appointment Jenny had made that night.

It was tacitly understood that Rooney and I would drive her down. If her parents ever found out, the consequences were too hideous to consider. Jenny never expanded on the remark, but when I suggested that perhaps her parents might be very understanding, if she explained what had happened, she said, "My father has never hit me, but he has a very loud voice, and he wears a belt. My mother would cry."

We left it at that, and spent the week between the phone call and that Thursday getting ourselves ready. I was driving an MG Magnette, a pretentious, cheaper copy of the Jaguar touring sedan. It was a lovely sort of thing, though, with glove-leather upholstery, dual carbs, a solid walnut dash panel that could be lifted out, four doors and the traditional MG red-painted engine. I got it lubed and checked out for the ride down. Rooney worked, of course, so her readying was all interior. As for Jenny, all I could tell of her state of mind, her capacity for handling this thing, as her nineteenth year became a nightmare, was that she did not cry again, and her conversation was not introspective.

When I asked her what had been said on the call to the doctor, she said: "A woman answered. She said, '*Bueno*.' I told her a friend from Fresno had suggested I call Doctor Quintano about consultation. Then she put me through to him, and I said the same thing, and he asked me consultation about what? I said I was having menstrual difficulties, that was what your friend told me to say, and he said just a minute; he said it very quickly, as though he didn't want to talk any more. Then the girl came back and asked me what day I wanted to come down, and I told her Thursday, and she said to call from San Diego when we got that far."

I had a feeling Jenny was going to be all right. She was getting much sharper, very quickly. Sometimes childhood and adolescence pass away just that fast, like morning mist, burned off by the sun or a rotten experience. Markham, the philosopher. You can't miss my ruminations: they're in that purple-bound folio over there.

Three hundred dollars had been the next point Quintano's woman had brought up. "Do you know the Doctor's fee?" she had asked. Jenny said three hundred. Not any more. That was last year's price. But what with the high cost of this and that, the going rate for Dilation & Curettage was now four hundred. Jenny said all right, to the woman (whose name was Nancy, and who spoke with a faint trace of Spanish accent) and to me, and to Roger Gore when she called him for the money.

She said all right.

But Roger Gore said no.

He also said she was a whore. He also said she was a harpy and a blackmailer and a tramp and slept with dogs in the streets and if she had as many sticking out of her as she'd probably had sticking *in* her, she'd look like a porcupine. He concluded his chivalrous polemic with the comment that she could go peddle her ass on First and Main in downtown L.A. and raise the action that way. His parting line was, "Even if you charge what you're worth, you shouldn't have to make it with more than two or three hundred guys to get it up."

When she repeated the conversation, I felt my jaw muscles turn to concrete, and I must have scraped a half-dozen layers of enamel off my back teeth. Frankly, I wanted to kill the bastard!

"I'll talk to him," I said.

I took a drive and stopped off at a phone booth in a gas station; while they were putting in a couple of bucks of hi-test I called Roger Gore.

"Is Roger there?"

"Who's this?"

"Ken Markham."

"He's not here."

"You won't be here for long, Gore, if you don't start acting like a man."

"I'll tell him when he comes in."

"Shape up, Gore. The kid's in trouble, and you'd damned well better be ready to take the responsibility."

"Screw you." Click.

I walked back to the car. "You save Blue Stamps?" the gas jockey asked.

"Yeah. I'm saving up."

He grinned pleasantly. Make conversation. Build the clientele. "Oh? For what?"

"A hydrogen bomb."

He was still staring as I tooled out of the lot.

I was right, of course. He *was* trying to split. I drove up his driveway just as he as driving down. He screeched and stalled the Impala, and I slewed the Magnette crosswise across his path. I left the motor turning and the emergency brake on, and I was out of the car, running toward him, fast as a wad of spit, before he could get coordinated. He was rolling up the windows and locking the doors as I pulled open the rear door on the side away from him. With four doors, four windows, he could only get to so many before I got to him. Logic. Wham!

I yanked open the door and plunged into the rear seat before he could turn around.

My arm went around his neck and yanked him half-out of the driver's seat. I used my free hand to slam the door handle beside him, and flung the front door open. Still holding him, I punched open my door, and reached around. I grabbed the sonofabitch by his jacket and yanked him sidewise. He went sprawl-assing out of the car, and I was on him.

"Let's go see your house," I said tightly.

I took the car keys, and using a bring-along I'd learned at jolly old Fort Benning while doing my two for Uncle Sam, we dog-trotted back to the house. I unlocked the door and shoved him just enough ahead of me to plant my foot in the middle of his can. I jacked my foot forward as hard as I could and Beau Brummel went flailing across the room, headfirst into the genuine imitation mahogany portable bar. Glassware went in all directions, his right hand swept an ornate cocktail shaker against the wall, and he knocked the caster-mounted shell on its side. He fell in a very untidy heap, and I slammed the door behind me as I moved toward him. His eyes were like a pair of Rolls Royce foglamps.

"Four hundred dollars," I said, very gently, lifting him by his jacket front and his Jay Sebring twelve-dollar haircut.

"No, I, listen—" he started . . .

"Curettage," I recited, from reading I had recently done, "is a French word meaning to scrape out. This is the simplest operation performed upon the uterus and consists of scraping the lining of the cavity." I let go of his jacket, still holding him up by the hair, and cocked back my fist. "It is performed under a light general anesthesia." I hit him as hard as I could, just under the left eye. "The normal uterus is a pear-shaped, muscular organ, about three inches long, two inches wide and one inch thick, lying in the midportion of the pelvis." He sagged sidewise, and the skin burned, blued, went gray and he started to bleed from a small cut. His eyes misted.

"The uterus," I continued, slapping him back and forth across the bridge of the nose to revive him, "consists of three layers—a thin, outer, sheathlike coat, a thick muscular layer, and a membranous lining to the cavity which is located in the center of the organ." He came back from wherever he'd fled, and there was a fear of the Furies gibbering in his blue eyes. His tongue peeked out of his mouth, and I slammed him with the palm of my hand, and he bit the tip, screeching at me something I couldn't understand. I cuffed him in the right ear, then the left, and his head bobbled like the top scoop of an unsteady ice cream cone.

"Simply stated, the function of the uterus is to receive the fertilized egg (which travels from the ovary through the Fallopian tubes), nourish and contain the egg as it develops through pregnancy and"—I hit him with everything I had, flush in the mouth—"expel the fully developed embryo. Four hundred dollars, Roger." The lower lip tore, teeth bit through the upper, and he went far away again.

Softly, "Four hundred, Roger baby." I let him slip back down on his side. He lay there looking frightened.

I went into the kitchen and drew myself a cold glass of water. He was a lousy housekeeper; I had to rinse my own glass.

It had not been the most methodical of jobs, but then neither was I a schooled pistolero. It had been informed, however, by a classic frenzy and a degree of hatred/brutality I'd never known I contained. I sat there while he sponged off his face with the wet washcloth, and my knees were shaking. He looked as though someone had mistaken his face for ten pounds of dogmeat, and had tried to fry it. His left was swollen shut, with thick, red-blue puffy tissue that gleamed in the light. His mouth was raw and cut through by his teeth. He had smaller cuts and contusions all over, and frankly, it would be some time before the hatcheck chick at PJ's winked at him again. I handed him the phone. He looked at it, then at me. The eye was starting to drain blue into his cheek.

He called his father and mouthed some sort of nonsense about needing four hundred dollars to get him out of a very tight spot. I think he knew just how tight that spot was. His old man must have said okay, because I saw Roger Gore visibly brighten at one point midway in the conversation. There was a great deal of "Okay, Dad, this is the last time; I'll be turning over a new leaf, you'll see; you won't be sorry,

Dad, thanks a million," and he racked the receiver. I looked at the kid just as hard as I could, and I said:

"It's a shame there's no law protecting girls like Jenny from their own stupidity. It's also a shame there's no law that punishes a guy for not being a gentleman. But anyhow, Roger friend, there are more serious pains than the ones I loaned you. I'm not telling you *not* to swear out an assault and battery on me. That'd be foolish, though; assault means to threaten battery, and since I didn't threaten you, I guess the best you could do would be battery, which might net me about five years in the can, but there *are* more serious pains, Roger friend, and they are dispensed by much more unpleasant guys than me. I leave you with that thought.

"We'll be taking Jenny down to TJ on Thursday. Get the money to her before then." I stood up and made to leave.

He snarled at me from the floor. "Your Jenny is a tease and a bitch, man! She wanted it as much as I did, that Jenny of yours! So just who the hell you think you're helping? Your Jenny's a dummy and a tramp, and she hasn't got any honor to protect! So take your Jenny and shove—"

I planted my foot with carefully calculated force in his groin. Gently I added, "She is neither your Jenny nor mine. She is her own Jenny, and whatever is wrong there, fellah, she is still a human being.

"Which is a condition I doubt you possess."

He was sucking air like a beached bass when I left.

My engine was still running.

When I got back, Jenny was alone. Rooney had gone over to see her parents; they had bought a new dog, and Rooney was a flip when it came to babies or tiny dogs. It wasn't a vagrant thought: Jenny looked like a little of each. The washed-face pinkness and confusion of a baby; the anxiety and need to love or be loved a small dog wears like a second collar.

"Want to play some gin?" I asked her.

She nodded mutely and went to the sideboard to get the dog-eared deck. We sat down on the sofa, and she shuffled while I lit a cigarette. For a while we played, and didn't say anything. Finally, I knocked on four in a spade hand, caught her with about twenty-five points, and said, "I talked to Roger. He's changed his mind."

"You didn't hurt him!" That was the first thing to cross her mind. Not did I get the money, not was she going to be rescued, but was he all right. I had one of those moments of stomach-muscle-tensing disorientation, as though I had intruded on a personal fight between two people who knew each other better than any interlopers with inclinations of arbitration.

"He's okay. We just . . . talked awhile. I convinced him you were his responsibility. He'll be getting the money to you before Thursday."

She dropped her arms, and I could see her gin hand. It wasn't so hot. "Thank God," she breathed. There was a pale milkiness about her then. As though some vital ingredient in her spirit had been hit by a catalytic agent, had vaporized in her system. She seemed just a little dead, at that moment.

She dropped the cards and lay back against the sofa with her eyes shut. Her hair was a natural blonde, somewhere between a hard canary and yellow ocher, and she wore it in a ponytail, usually, a style few girls affect any more. But she wore it well, and there was a pleasantness to her youthfulness. I looked at her, resting there, and something turned over inside me.

She had said something.

I hadn't really heard it, had just imagined I'd heard it, but she had spoken, absently, without realizing what words had been selected to convey her fear and her insecurity, but she had said, "Oh, Kenny . . ."

And it was someone else's voice from another time. I can't remember even now who it was. Another girl I had known, when I was young enough to be able to remember everyone who had said yes, and count them on one hand. Perhaps it was that second girl I'd slept with. I can't recall who she was. There isn't anyone, man or woman, who can't recall the first. But the second . . . ah, that's another matter. And perhaps it was her.

Whoever it had been, this was now, and Jenny had said, "Oh, Kenny . . ." and I was holding her slim body very close to mine, and my hands were locked behind her back, still clutching the gin cards. Her face came up, and there were dust motes spinning in her eyes of whatever color those eyes might be.

I smelled her hair, and it was very clean. It was another reminder of things from before, but they were silly, irrelevant things, like a field of winter wheat I had run through once, on a picnic day, when there had been such things as days right for nothing but picnics. It was a stupid thought, and it passed quickly, but not before I recalled having run and run and finally fallen down on my back, and lain there, completely hidden from all but the sky, staring straight up and feeling sorry as hell for myself. I kissed Jenny, and her mouth was soft, precisely as a woman's mouth should be. I kissed her the way a gentle lover would kiss someone he revered.

"Not like that," she murmured, pulling my face down harshly. "Like this." She opened her lips and worked at me fiercely, as though it was something worth doing and hence, something worth doing well. It was possibly the grandmother of all Soul Kisses, and when she was done, I knew I'd been kissed. My hand was on her thigh, and she moved slightly, so my hand went over the rise, down where her slacks were tightest. I had a mad thought that someone was going to pop out of the clothes closet and take movies of it all, but that thought passed, too, and in a moment we were wriggling with each other's clothes, trying to keep our mouths together, and yet get naked.

Jenny was young, but Jenny was expert. She took me the way Hillary and Tenzing Norgay took Everest: all the way, and chiefly because *it was there*. Anything worth doing was worth doing well. Midway, she arched up and there was a feral gleam on her face, a drawing back of the lips and an exposure of small teeth that reminded me of a timber wolf I'd shot up near North Bay. Sometimes, though, she was a flower, and sometimes she was a hot shower, and sometimes she was a pitch pipe whistling an elegant tune. She had a small habit of twisting her hips sidewise at special times.

When we were over the final hill, and the road behind seemed much too rough for anyone to have crossed alone, much less two people as strangely locked as we had been, I went into the bathroom and took a bath. Not a shower. A bath. I have taken showers since I was sixteen and had a bad back. Baths are a pain, and they leave a dirty ring around the tub.

I felt I needed a bath.

And I wanted to see that dirty ring around the tub.

Thursday was two hells and a decapitation away. Every time Rooney looked at me I could swear she knew. And when Jenny leaned over in a movie we three attended, with her hand on my leg, and whispered, "At least I know for sure you couldn't make me pregnant," I wanted to open my wrists with a beer can opener. What had I stumbled upon: a key to the depravity of the young? Or the key to my own yin and yang? I didn't feel guilty, I felt unclean, which was infinitely worse. I, Kenneth Duane Markham, became a case in point for myself. *This,* I thought angrily, *is how we fool ourselves into thinking we're honorable men*. Jenny's mere existence became a constant reminder of the other side of my nature; an ungovernable side that didn't even have the consistency, the decency or the stamina to be constant. I was a mealy-mouthed, smiling sinner who took his pleasures and pains as they comfortably fit into the regimented scene of everyday life. Dorian Gray be damned! There isn't one of us who isn't in the bag.

But finally we left. Our little caravanserai moved out onto the road with all the glee and aplomb of a New Orleans funeral that couldn't find a Preservation Hall Dixieland band.

We turned onto the Hollywood Freeway and sped straight down Route 101. Santa Ana Freeway, Pacific Coast Highway, El Camino Real; past Downey and its used car carnivals, past Disneyland and its ludicrous Matterhorn rising out of the surrounding squalor, past Tustin and the art bookstore that faces out on a highway going too fast to give a damn. San Juan Capistrano, and I've never seen a swallow yet, going *or* coming. San Clemente, Del Mar, Pacific Beach, and we were in San Diego. I once asked a resident if they minded the Navy calling it "Dago," and that worthy responded he didn't care if they called it dog-whoopee, as long as they kept spending their money. That, I feel, sums up the beauty and glory of San Diego, a helluva way to end a beautiful state. It is not, I hasten to add, a coincidence that Dago appears at what might metaphorically be termed the backside of the state. We pulled in at a one-arm joint on 101, just before National City, the other side of San Diego, and while Jenny went to phone, Rooney and I had cups of coffee; I worked my neck around, trying to unkink it.

"What's the matter with you today?" she asked, over the lip of the cup.

"What do you mean: what's the matter? Nothing. Why, does something look the matter?" I could feel my nose growing, like Pinocchio's.

"You've been awfully quiet the last forty miles or so."

I shrugged. "Tired. My back aches. That's all."

She didn't answer, but she knew I was lying.

"And this isn't really the pleasure trip of all time," I added. *Keep talking, schmuck,* I told myself. *Dig it a little deeper.*

"Well, it'll all be over soon enough," Rooney tried to cover her own awareness of my mood. She knew me too well. I knew we'd be splitting up soon. I couldn't let anyone get that close to the core of me; as long as it was froth and foam it was safe. But the encystment was too marked in me, at age thirty. I smiled across at her reassuringly.

Jenny came back. "Have a cup of coffee and a piece of pie," I told her. She shook her head no. "I'm not supposed to eat before the operation. His girl told me not to eat for about six hours beforehand. I haven't eaten since last night. I'm starving, but you know you're not supposed to eat before this kind of thing."

I *hadn't* known, but I saw no reason for her to make big who-struck-John of the whole matter. I mumbled something about oh yeah, I knew. And that was that. She sat down next to Rooney, staring at me with open malevolence. Like I was the guy who'd knocked her up. In a philosophical sense, I suppose I was as guilty as Roger Gore, but somehow I couldn't bring myself to eat that particular humble pie. I had a feeling too many strange Jack Horners had already had their thumbs in it.

"Well, what did they say?" Rooney asked.

Jenny pulled her eyes away from me with difficulty. There was actually physical violence in her expression. I chalked it up to her fear and the fact that I was a man the same as Roger Gore, only he wasn't handy for hating.

"She said to drive across the border, into downtown Tijuana, and park behind the Woolworth's at 4:30, there'd be a fellow to meet us. She said his name is Louis—"

"Luis," I corrected her.

"So Loo-ees," she snapped back. "So what?" Then she went on, addressing herself to Rooney. I couldn't have cared less. "She said to dress poorly, not like tourists—"

"Turistas," I murmured, under my breath.

"Why don't you *just shut up!*" Jenny was screaming. A man at the counter turned to look at us, and the waitress paused on her way through the swinging doors to the kitchen.

I reached across and grabbed her wrist as hard as I could. "Listen, you little bitch, I've had about as much horseshit from you as I can take. I've had to listen to your miserable bellyaching and whining and complaining for the last week; you may not appreciate the fact that aiding someone in getting an abortion is a prison offense, and that Rooney and I are risking our necks to drag your ass down here, but the least you can do is be civil and keep from being a bigger pain in the ass than you already are." I shoved her wrist away violently and slumped back in the booth. Rooney was staring at us as though we'd both gone insane. Jenny was rubbing her goddam wrist and looking like a whipped spaniel. I drank coffee and pretended I was in Nome, Alaska.

After a long silence in which no one seemed to move, Rooney said, guardedly, "Let's go. It's three o'clock now. It'll probably take us a while to find the Woolworth's."

"I have terrible headache," Jenny said, rubbing one hand up across her temple. "Do you have an aspirin?"

I threw a half dollar onto the table and slid out the booth. As I stalked to the car, Jenny was bugging the waitress for an Empirin or somedamnthing. I got into the car and lit a cigarette. It tasted like dust, and so did the day.

Getting into Tijuana, unlike the crossover to Hell, involves no Stygian water-ride, and if one of the border guards be named Charon, at least he has had the good sense to have it Anglicized. At that point, all differences cease.

We drove up to the big white pass-through that stretched across the road. The parking lot on the American side was not filled. Had it been a weekend, with the jai alai, the dog and horse races at Caliente, the bullfights, the lots would have been banged to the fences; but this was Thursday, and midday was not too far advanced, and traffic was steady, but not a flood, as it would be the next day.

We were waved through without a passing glance from the patrolmen. Does no one smuggle anything *into* Mexico?

A few feet beyond the pass-through, the car told me we were in

Mexico, and I knew why most people left their vehicles on the American side (a single reason out of three good ones). The pavement came to a halt, was replaced by a three-foot stretch of open dust-dirt, and then resumed as pavement again. But a return to pavement so marked I knew I had left the United States. The Mexican pavement was in chunks. It was pocked and upthrust as though a decade of cars had gone over it without the most minor attention by repair gangs. We bumped and jounced across the passway, the Magnette clanging like a dinner gong.

(The other two reasons, incidentally, are that if you have an accident involving your car in Tijuana, whether you are right or wrong, struck or striker, the car is impounded, they throw you up *under* the jail, and only a feisty bribe will get you out; the third reason is that hubcaps, car seats, dash clocks, luggage racks, headlamps and other minor items have an uncanny habit of vanishing from the auto in question. Some contend it is the highly spiced atmosphere of the town.)

We passed through the Mexican side with even less event than the Yankee entrance. Fat chance they'd keep out a spendable dollar.

Once through the arch, and a left turn, it was an open scene from Hogarth. Perhaps Hieronymus Bosch. Possibly Dali. Definitely Dante.

Filth.

The word comes unbidden. A hundred, two hundred rickety taxis, all parked in rows, waiting for the *turistas*. The street hard-packed dirt and broken concrete. Dozens of barefoot urchins, scuddy in their dingy rags, clutching cigar boxes full of Chiclets to be sold at a dime or half dollar for a penny pack. Ramshackle buildings, swayleaning as though propped from behind with poles. A miasma of road dust rising turning in the sunbeaten air. A sense of *hurry*, of expectation, of fear and sickness and something about to happen. A faint electric stir of movement *within* the mass gibbering movement of dirty hack drivers and shawl-wrapped women hustling for the dollars. A tone of impending disaster, always omnipresent. Was this perhaps the stench that filled Pompeii before it dissolved in fire? Did Sodom or Gomorrah have to contend with that stink no Air-Wick could ever contain, that color of madness in the wind and in the very horizon line?

I gunned the Magnette and pulled out of the middle of the maelstrom. We banged down the street, between two untidy rows of temporary structures, all of which were selling car upholstery. Tuck and roll shops. Best bargains. Get it here, installed in ten minutes, satisfaction guaranteed. All misspelled.

Cover-up shops for stripping and repainting cars; hot cars; stolen cars; lost cars; impounded cars; and legitimate tucking and rolling, as well. Guaranteed to last as least till you recrossed the border.

A huge sign across the end of the road bellowed:

BIENVENIDAS AMIGOS!

Welcome, suckers. Unfurl your desires and let us see under which banners you skulk. We have it here, guaranteed, satisfaction 100 percent or we give you a dose of the clap free!

A clutch of buildings clogged the roadside on either hand. One of them said MARRIAGE DIVORCE CAR INSURANCE on a sloppily lettered sign. A second advised FULL COVER INSURANCE WHILE IN MEXICO GUARANTEED!! A third reversed the order (or perhaps the owner was more of a cynic) by offering DIVORCES QUICK—MARRIAGES—NOTARY. Notary what, I never paused to inquire. We did a dog-leg and turned up another street, in as hideous a condition as the one we'd just left, following a white arrow-sign that said DOWNTOWN TI.

Someone had, perhaps, bitten off the remaining section of the sign. Mad dogs, I am told, are not uncommon in such heavy climates.

Farther into TJ, the incredible poverty and squalor of the people struck us like a hammer blow. "MiGod, it's unbelievable!" said Rooney, as a gaggle of barefooted, dirt-smeared children raced directly across our path, causing me to swerve into a huge chuckhole. They ran across the razor-edged rocks of the road as though their feet were wound with asbestos.

Slat-houses tottered at every curb. Porches boasted fat old women, whose only joys were watching the horrors the younger girls had to endure. On every bit of habitable land, someone had thrown up a jerry-rigged shack. Garbage cans lived more open lives than the people whose refuse they received. Every half-block there were one or more stores advertising LICORES.

I could understand it; the only way to live and stay sane in such a cesspool, was to stay liquored-up constantly. We drove on.

After what seemed a Minotaur's maze of twistings and turnings, through streets littered with animate and inanimate garbage, with the castoff and the downcast, with the vile and the pitiful, we saw a street of neon lights and brighter buildings. Traffic was incredible. The taxis moved as though their wheels were about to be revoked. Pedestrians leaped out—perhaps hoping they would be struck down by a rich *gringo*—and masses of humanity surged across at intersections which had never known the luxury of a stoplight.

We drove down past the old bullring, the Toreo de Tijuana. The new one was up on the hill overlooking the town, but the *turistas* go there, and for a real bloodbath *corrida*, the townsfolk go to the old ring, where the *toreros* must perform with more skill and passion. A bright, romantic poster outside the ring proclaimed: 6 LA TRASQUILA 6 THE GREATEST BULLFIGHTING FIGURES CARLOS ARRUZA (The Mexican Cyclone) FERMIN ESPINOZA ARMILLITA (The Master of Masters) AND SILVERIO PEREZ (The Pharaoh from

Texcoco) FIGHTING TO DEATH IMPASING BULLS FROM 6 LA TRASQUILA 6!!

I did not read this sign all at once, then. Much later I was to have painful opportunity to study it at my leisure, or a copy thereof, while lying on my back. At the time, all I saw was the bright poster color and the word ARRUZA. We continued driving toward what had to be the center of town.

As we drove, seedy-looking men with rolled newspapers leaped out onto the street, trying to wave our car into whatever empty lot they had appropriated as a parking area. We drove straight down into the heart of town. The roads were a little better now, on a par with a neglected side street or country road in the States. I knew I'd have to have the Magnette completely overhauled when I got back. Every seam was sprung; every bolt was loose.

We cruised around, and finally I spotted the Woolworth's. It looked like any plastic-and-chrome eyesore from the States, but among the filthy, falling-down shops and bars and arcades of downtown Tijuana, it was shining, gleaming, sparkling, a reassurance that stability still existed. We rolled slowly toward the big store, and I saw an empty parking place on the street. "She said behind the Woolworth's, in their parking lot," Jenny said.

It was the first sentence out of her mouth since we'd left the coffee shop in National City.

I pulled around the side of the building, and started into the lot. An old Mexican with gold teeth came running out of a rickety guard-shack and tried to take a dollar from me. I asked if this was parking for Woolworth's. My Spanish was passingly understandable, but not enough to get elected mayor. He answered in English, almost. "Ess park for no-whan, no Wowlwort's, ees pay for aver'whan!" And he continued to shove his hand through the window. His hand looked as though the last time it had been introduced to soap was when Calvin Coolidge approved the World Court. "I'm waiting for someone, I'll only be here a few minutes." I tried to say, a *turista* remark. He didn't give a damn if I was there for a minute or the decade. I backed up and found myself on the street, with old man still screaming imprecations at me, possibly for running my nasty old car across his valuable dust.

The empty parking space was still there. I pulled into it, and as I negotiated the bumper of the car against the high curb, I realized I was being "navigated" from the sidewalk by a little boy of nine or ten. Unasked, he had taken me as his mark. A moment before he had not been there, but like some sort of perambulant plant he had sprung from the shadows or the sidewalk, and was hand-waving me into the slot. Then he reached into a cigar box he carried, pulled out a penny and leaped at the parking meter. He beat the other four kids to the meter by a split-instant. They were identical in a tragic, sorry way. Each was his own person, but each dwelled within a coat of the same Tijuana dirt, and so they looked alike. The kid that had thrust the penny into the meter was around the car and trying to get my door open before I'd turned off the motor.

Rooney reached across Jenny and unlocked the door Jenny had just locked. "They're just children, Jenny."

She looked as though she'd eaten a ripe persimmon. "But they're so *filthy*!" she squeamed. Her nose wrinkled.

"It comes from not bathing," I snapped. "And from having to sleep in a doorway. Offensive as hell, ain't it."

She didn't answer. By this time we had parted company for good and always, and for a second a wisp of thought crossed my mind how this adventure had altered all our relationships to one another. Then the kid had my door open and was demanding I pay him for parking my car, for his having waved his hands to steer me in, for his having put a penny in the meter.

"Doe-lahr, Señor," he urged, "doe-lahr!"

I shook my head no. He would not be put off. "Gimme, gimme, gimme!" he kept saying, not shouting, just demanding, in a tone of righteous indignation that was guaranteed to intimidate the sternest soul. And in an instant there was another one beside him, and a third, and then a very little one, no more than five or six, with huge wet eyes like one of the hideously stylized Keane paintings, and all of them with the cigar boxes filled with small change, packets of Chiclets, a knife perhaps.

The tiny one managed to wiggle past me and would not budge; wedged in between the car seat and the door. I asked him and asked him again, tried, "*Vamonos*," and it didn't work, so I lifted him bodily and set him outside the car, closing the door with my back. His body went rigidly limp, if such a thing makes sense. He was affronted. He demanded money; for what nebulous service I cannot guess.

We managed to elude the kids, and it only cost me a half dollar to the one who had invested his penny. It was a quarter to four. We had forty-five minutes. So we walked up the block.

In the space of two hundred yards, it was a toss-up which deal would be more to my advantage: taking one of the girls offered to me by the sidewalk hustlers, or sell the two I had, turning a tidy profit. Rooney's bemused stares canceled either possibility. We walked through the shops and I decided I wanted to buy a set of steel-rim bongos. The opening price was thirteen dollars. When I left the shop, I had the bongos and was six dollars and fifty cents lighter.

Finally, it came around to 4:30 and we returned to the car. The fog lamps were gone from the front grille. I cursed eloquently, and Jenny mumbled something about replacing them, but I was in no mood for heroics, so I hustled them into the car, and we backed out of the parking slot. I pulled into the parking lot and here came the Old Man once more. I gave him the dollar and pulled into the back.

Jenny had been told to look for a 1962 Imperial, black.

We saw it parked at the other end of the lot, next to an old Ford with a man and woman in the front seat. Loafing against the rear of the Woolworth's was a trio of oily looking juvies overdressed and indolent. "I hope Luis isn't one of them," Jenny whispered. I didn't say anything; he probably was.

We pulled in next to the Ford, and I cut the engine. The man in the Ford was talking earnestly to the girl beside him. She was a wild-looking blonde, and I had the strange premonition that they were there for a familiar reason. "Let's get out, let them know who we are," I said. I got out and went around the car, and very ostentatiously helped Jenny from the car, as though she were an invalid. She looked at me peculiarly, but I didn't feel like explaining.

One of the young hoods detached himself from the group, waved goodbye to his fellow lounge-rats, and ambled across the lot toward us. "Uh-oh, here we go, gang," I said softly. The guy and the blonde got out of the Ford. She was wild. And I thought, *Perhaps they're friends of his, cover sent along in case of trouble.*

"Let's go," the kid said, walking up to the five of us. It was Luis. He had a memorable scar on his right cheek. I doubted he had come by it at Heidelberg.

He opened the doors of the black Imperial, and I helped Jenny and Rooney into the back seat. I started to get into the front seat, and he said, sharply, "In the back."

"I want to follow in my own car," I said. He shook his head. I stared at him for a long moment, and without uttering a sound Luis said, Do you want this thing done, or don't you? I got into the back seat. The blonde and her boy friend got in the front. He was carrying a copy of Kafka's IN THE PENAL COLONY, in a well-thumbed paperback edition, and while I wasn't dead certain, I was inclined to think my original estimate of the couple was correct. Why is it a corollary of being a college student that caution and common sense have been left out of the equation?

Luis backed out of the space, spun the wheel as I imagine he thought Fangio might have done it, and sped across the lot, out a side entrance, and down another street. He drove without saying a word, but flicked on the car radio, and in a moment we were inundated by yay-yay's and boom-boom's from a San Diego rock 'n' roll station. It was reassuring to know that bad taste was not strictly an American malady.

He drove for a long time, back and forth and around, and at one point stopped to buy a newspaper from a hawker standing on a deserted stretch of road. I surreptitiously glanced behind me as we whipped away down the road, and the newspaper vendor was moving quickly toward a small shack set off the road. I looked for, and found, the telephone lines running into the shack. Signal number one, apparently passing us through.

We drove a while longer, and Luis pulled in at a liquor store that also sold IMPORTED FRENCH PERFUME THE REAL STUFF! He got out, went inside, and I slow-counted to three hundred and eighty-five by thousandcount. He came back with a brown-paper sack twisted at the top, and I knew we'd come through phase two of the clearing process. He was assured—in some indefinable way—not only that we were not being followed, but that we were what we declared ourselves to be: waifs on the sea of intrigue. He roared out of the parking lot of the liquor store, and tooled the big Imperial toward the hills overlooking Tijuana. We roared past Caliente track; I relaxed, and Jenny looked more frightened.

It was a twisty-turny, and I went through a third of a pack of cigarettes. Finally, we pulled down a side street, turned left through an alley, and went right parallel to the street we had just come down. Luis whirled the wheel again, and pulled up into the driveway of an expensive-looking home surrounded by a high polished-wood fence. I could see the house through the close slats of the fence, and it was a big-money pad. Whoever lived there (and don't think for a second it wasn't obvious who lived there), lived well.

Luis braked to a halt before the inner gate, and honked twice, sharply, paused, then honked again. The gate went up, pulled on a chain by a skinny, underfed-looking Mexican youth perhaps a year or two younger than Luis, the pickup agent. He drove the car through, and the rickets case let the gate down again. We were in a narrow passage between the fence and the side of the house. Beyond the house, the passage opened into a large back area that ended in open-face garages. From where I sat, I could see a Bentley, a Thunderbird and what looked to be an Aston Martin roadster, each in its own berth, each a current model, each gleaming and polished.

Luis got out, and I opened the door on my side.

There was just barely enough room to squeeze out, and be wedged against the side of the house. The college students in the front seat could not yet leave the car, the passage was so narrow. Luis came around the car and opened the door beside me, into the house. I stepped back and Jenny and Rooney slipped past me. Luis watched Jenny's legs as she slid out of the car. Eyes salivate, don't ever let them tell you otherwise. She caught him at it, and smiled coquettishly.

Luis ran a hand through his thick, glistening shock of hair. The Demon Lover strikes again!

We went inside, and were followed by the college students. There were three couples waiting. The girls were all exceptionally attractive, and all under twenty-one, I would have guessed.

It was an anteroom, with two sofas, several large borax modern chairs, and a TV set babbling a moron's guessing game. Something about trusting one another . . .

We sat and waited. Luis vanished through the only door leading into the house. I looked around at the others, and they were all studiously directing their attentions to the two microcephalics vying for prizes on the TV screen. I didn't fool myself that they were interested in what was happening there; they were afraid, unsure of protocol, and suspicious that everyone else was a friend of the Doctor. (The name now had an ominous ring, though by the wealthy surroundings it should have been otherwise.)

Luis stuck his head in, motioned to Jenny, Rooney and myself, and to the college students. The five of us got up and followed him through the door, around a corner, and into a large living room walled with sofas, chairs, an electric heater purring on the floor, and another, larger TV set, tuned to the same channel.

There was another couple sitting close together on one of the sofas. The guy looked more frightened than the chick, and *she* was comforting *him*.

"Seedohn," Luis directed us, and vanished back into the hallway. I paced across the thick carpet to see where he had gone, but the hallway ended in another plain panel door. There was the door through which we had come from the anteroom, and a twin directly across from it. Three doors, the living room, and silence. It hung musty warm in the room, with the electric heater going, the spring sun outside but unseen in the windowless room, and the three table lamps trying to convince us there was neither day nor night.

I sat down on the sofa across from the TV set, and Jenny leaned across. "Are you nervous?"

"No," I answered. "I'm not the one going inside."

She sank back, looking morose. Rooney gave me another of those peculiar stares.

We waited three quarters of an hour, and Luis popped in and out like the changer on a record player. The boredom was starting to get to me. A rerun of *The Lineup* came and went on the TV screen under the name *San Francisco Beat*, and I wondered just how long Warner Anderson and Tom Tully had been in movies. Then a rerun of *Yancy Derringer* came on, and I had to sit through something about a Union officer who had it in for a New Orleans gentleman and had arranged for his early demise by firing squad. I was about to stick my thumb in mouth, plug up my ears, and blow my brains out through my nose when a nurse in white came into the room. She motioned to the wild-looking blonde, and they went off together. Not a sound. The coward sat and watched the TV set with a whipped expression. *Yancy Derringer* faded into limbo and an early movie came on. It starred Tom Neal (without a moustache), Evelyn Keyes and Bruce Bennett, and had somethingorother to do with Officers' Candidate School in World War Two. It was a drag, but Evelyn Keyes was nice. I yawned perhaps eighty times. Luis did his imitation of a jack-in-the-box several times; and finally, the nurse came back. "Mees . . . com plees . . ." She crooked a finger at Jenny.

Jenny got up reluctantly, clutching her purse with the four one hundred dollar bills in it. She gave us each a sickly smile, and we smiled back, rather more bored and struck witless by the heat and the waiting than through any concern. By now my feelings had been assuaged about the Good Doctor's capabilities. A man doesn't live that high from bad butchery. Word of mouth works just as much in D&C as in PR.

Jenny went away, and we settled down alone in the room to wait. After a while I shut off the heater. Tom Neal was better-looking with the moustache.

These are the mechanics of the nightmare:

Doctor's office. Modern desk. Office chair. Straight chair in front of desk. Radio. Telephone with number disc removed. Very bare walls. Doctor Quintano: handsome, early thirties, middle thirties; gray eyes; very impersonal. "Is this the first time you've been pregnant?" Excellent English, no trace of accent. "What was the date of your most recent period? How do you feel?" Sit waiting, twenty minutes. He comes back. Take some papers from the desk. Goes away. Twenty minutes waiting. See no one. Hear nothing. Sit straight in chair, feel clammy, hot, tired, headache. Nurse returns, asks, "Are you Nancy?" No answer. Nurse indicates without speaking, leave this room, go upstairs. Another nurse waits at head of stairs, march directly into bathroom. Extraordinarily lovely bathroom, gleaming brass fixtures cast in the shapes of lions with open mouths, dolphins, seagulls. Pull off clothes, put on hospital gown open in back, tied with two strings. Down hall to private operating room. Lie down on observation table, light above glowing, eyes hurt. Twenty minutes. Nurse back again, quietly efficient, dark, does not speak. Quintano comes in, asks for money. Give him four crisp bills. Takes money, goes away. Comes back. Takes off underpants, places hand on female stomach. "Your stomach muscles are too tight; go to the bathroom, urinate, relax them." Goes, returns, tries again. "Now what you're going to have is a 'curettement,' a very simple operation. It will take about ten minutes, and I'll have to examine you before the operation, don't be afraid." Leaves room. Nurse comes in, follow her to other room. Halls empty, hear no sound. Lie down on another observation table. Quintano returns wearing rubber gloves. Internal pelvic examination. Gentle. Still wearing shoes. Quintano leaves again. Nurse: "Relax, he be right een." Thirty-five minutes. Nurse goes, returns, ties ankles into operating stirrups with bands of white cloth. Heels in stirrups, uncomfortable angle.

Quintano looms above table. "I want to be asleep, please." "That depends on you." "How?" "If you keep your breathing normal and relax." "I can't relax unless you put me to sleep." "Do you want this operation?" Pause, long pause, longest pause, fear, thinking, tottering at the decision's tip, flight, running, trembling, I must do it! *"Okay. Go ahead." A great black creature coming down from the sky above. Black rubber inhalator mask. Over nose and mouth. Fear of gas, strong, smell to be avoided if encountered on a street, walk in opposite direction, don't die don't fight no sight out light might tight right if you close mouth breathe through nose hose slows goes rose . . . Conversation interchange can't understand allwordsruntogetherlikejelly* GO! *In her, knowing,* I'm not asleep, *feel the first instrument, cry, make a sound, inhale gas and swoon in soft lather down gone deep right leap fright seeeeee thissss wayyyyyy they count in Spanish sweet anesthetist anesthesia anesthetic not sleeping words count in Spanish* uno dos tres cuatro cinco sies siete ocho *Ouch! Oh! Ah! there pain here pain know pain feel it up inside vaguest vaguely vagrant ain pain vain-* nueve diez once doce *dream great white square, huge insubstantial moving great square, cut in four parts, one section all black, the black moves first to one square, then another, then another, around and around and around as dr dr. dR DR. and nurse stand on right, as black square moves from one corner to the other to the other to the next to the next, all clocks stop all clocks silent, every room has a clock,* every room in the place, *every clock has no face just hands that move around and around teasing teasingly teasing* trece catorce . . . *soft scraping down there inside my softness, small creature seeks warm warm warm . . . It's over. Come back up from the world of white squares and black. Quintano and nurse on the right, staring, "How do you feel?" "Dizzy . . ." Pat on the arm. Sit, naked body stretches out before, open, naked, moist. Cover with the hospital gown. Get off table. Walk out crookedly wobbling a tot on first feet. Into first examination room, lie down on table. Blanket over, warm. Light glowing overhead, "Can you turn that out?" "No." Forty-five minutes go by, one minute, sleep. Nurse comes back. "Get dressed." As door closes hear Quintano saying, "Word word wordword pain word wordword word." What was he saying, pain? Me? Was there trouble? I feel fine, don't I? Yes, a fine feeling. Empty. Nurse with two paper cups. One has water. The other has five pills: two big yellow ones, three small white ones. Take them with difficulty, need second cup of water. Wait again, ten minutes. Nurse and Quintano come back. "You were a fine patient. That damn blonde kept moving her hips, she was scared, nervous; but you were a good patient." Go downstairs with nurse. Other nurse waits at bottom. Hello.*

I had tried to break out for a while, to get some air, to think about something other than nothing. And to wonder why this whole thing with Jenny had come to be so compelling, so *involving* for me, when I was really not the responsible party. I thought I knew why, but I wanted to think about it somewhere other than in the abortionist's front parlor.

I had tried to get out of the house, by the only door I knew for certain led outside, but Luis had been waiting in the outer passage, talking in Spanish with the rickets case. He motioned me back inside. I'd about had it with him. The operation Quintano ran was a clean one, but the scarred, oily appearance of Luis was bad policy. It made the trip to the doctor's home seem more suspicious than was necessary. He instilled no faith or security in the girls coming to get scraped. And his predilection for melodrama was a bit much.

"I want to take a walk," I told him, coming on toward the fence and gate.

"No. You go on back. You wait till she done," and he put his hand in his thigh-length car coat's pocket. I had a feeling the most dangerous item in that pocket was dust, but I saw no sense in hassling with him. I went back inside.

It was only four hours, but it seemed like forever.

I'd gone through my own pack and a half of Philip Morris and was down to smoking Rooney's goddammed Kents or Springs or Passion-flowers or whatever those hideous mentholated, perfumed excuses for a self-respecting coffin-nail are called. My mouth tasted like they'd marched the entire Chinese Nationalist Army through it barefoot, with the Dalai Lama in the lead, wearing nothing but a Dr. Scholl's Zino-Pad.

Jenny came in, being helped by a nurse in white, the one we'd seen before, the one who wouldn't talk. I could tell at once something was wrong. Her face looked like a charcoal drawing on papyrus. I got up and moved to help her. She sat down on the sofa beside Rooney and ran her hand up across her temple and into her hair, in that characteristic gesture that meant she was out of it. "How do you feel?" I asked.

"Oh, okay, I guess. I'm glad it's over."

Rooney moved over beside her. "You look a little peaked, are you sure you feel all right?"

She nodded silently, almost numbly.

There was something wrong.

"Was there trouble in the operation?" I directed my question at the nurse. Her face froze over; she was a hard, cold bitch. I asked her again. She didn't answer.

"You feel be'er eef you put a li'l lisstick on," the Medusa said. Jenny mumbled something vague at that. I wanted to do something, but didn't know what.

The decision was taken over by Luis, who appeared magically from the anteroom. "Time to go," he said. The nurse disappeared back into one of the other doorways, and we stood up, helping Jenny between us. We moved out into the anteroom, and there was a waiting line of five new girls. I was amazed and staggered at the amount of business Quintano had accumulated. If he wasn't a millionaire, tax-free, he certainly needed a good business manager. The college kids were there, and the blonde looked just fine, just fine.

We left the house and got back in the car and the gate was raised and we drove away, in exact reverse order of the way we had made our entrance. And even though Hot-Rock Luis twisted and turned and drove us back to town by a different route, it didn't matter: I knew the way to Quintano's little do-it-yourselfery cold.

Luis left us off at the Woolworth's lot, and burned rubber getting away. The five of us stood there staring at each other and the cars. "How much was yours?" the college boy asked. "Four," I replied. He nodded. "Ours, too." It seemed to make him feel better.

"Can we go?" Jenny said, very softly, beside me. She was feeling weak and strange, I knew it, and so did Rooney. We got into the car and tooled out of Tijuana, heading for the border.

We never made it across.

That part of it happened so fast, it can be told fast. We drove down through the town, getting a noseful and a soulful of dirt and signed testaments to just how miserable the human condition can get to be. We pulled into the long line of cars heading for the check-out point at the border, and watched Jenny from the corner of our eyes. She was shaking slightly, and feeling worse. All I wanted to do was make the trip back to L.A. and get her to her own doctor.

Cars were being passed through one after another.

They stopped us, and the inspector leaned in, asked if I had anything to declare. I figured we were a shoo-in. "Not a thing, sir," I said. "We were just down looking around, didn't buy a thing."

He started to pass us through, when his eye caught the steel-rim bongos I'd bought. He looked from them to me. I looked into the back seat and saw them there. My laugh was as phony as a work of Art by Joseph E. Levine.

"Oh, except those, of course ha ha."

That was our undoing. He asked to see inside the trunk. I opened it and it was empty. Then he tried the glove compartment, under the back seats, and then the girl's handbags. Nothing. Just a bottle of painkiller pills Jenny had had in her purse for weeks, labeled in Beverly Hills and signed with the name of her family doctor.

The inspector took the bottle, put it under my left windshield wiper, and directed me to pull out of line, into an inspection slot. I was hacked. Jenny was about to fall out. But I did as I was told.

I could hear a guy somewhere playing a soft lick on a guitar. It struck me how strange it was: all day in a land where music is supposed to be second nature, I hadn't heard any live music made by the people. A few bastardized notes out of a car radio, some organ background for a quiz show emanating from New York, and silence from the happy, smiling natives of this warm Valhalla. Now, as we were about to leave, a sound of reality from the other world. It was odd.

The inspector came out of his cubicle and examined us. He examined the bottle. Then he asked whose it was. Jenny said it was hers. He asked her to come into the station for a moment to talk to the head man. She looked at me. "I'll come with you," I said.

We followed him across the concrete walkway to the big glass-fronted office. I had to support Jenny very surreptitiously. She was white as the sun at midday.

It went fast. The inspector knew what was happening. One look at her, and you could tell she had been aborted. She was sweating like a shower, hard and hot. He took her in to talk to her. I waited. After half an hour, I got worried. They told me I had to wait.

Rooney came in; she wanted to ask if there was trouble, but I motioned her to wait, I'd tell her later. An hour went by, and suddenly we heard a crash from the next room. The head man came out, panic on his stupid face, and yelled at his aide. "Call the hospital. Miguel Aleman. Have them send an ambulance. Quick!"

I was screaming at him, and was halfway over the counter, my hand tangled in his tie. "You bastard, you stupid fucking bastard! You could see she was sick, you had to pump her, you had to use her all up, didn't you! You bastard!"

Youth was not his attribute, intelligence was not his attribute, but strength was. He whipped his hands up between mine, breaking my hold, and gave me a fast one in the mouth. I went down, and he rushed back into the interrogation room to help Jenny. I crawled off the floor and Rooney helped me up. Through the open door, we could see Jenny's legs kicking as she lay on the floor.

The ambulance came and we rode along to Miguel Aleman Hospital. The waiting room was very clean and very white and Jenny died about four hours later. Blood loss. And it had been on its way to peritonitis.

I stood in the center of the waiting room when they came and told us, and suddenly all the memories I'd wanted to bury in the mud of my subconscious came back. Fran and the baby, sending my wife to the abortionist because I'd been "ill-equipped to handle a child right now, honey." The operation, the fear, and Fran growing to hate me, leaving me, the divorce. It all came back, and I knew then what Jenny had meant to me. Blackness pressed into my eyes.

I ran shrieking out of the hospital, a madman whose passage was unimpaired. They leaped out of my way. I may have been frothing at the mouth, I don't remember.

Then I was back in a dusty Tijuana street, and finding a taxi, and pointing up the hill toward Caliente track, saying, "*Vamonos, vamonos!*" I was waving bills under his nose and pointing, and he went . . .

Fast . . .

I directed him through a haze that was thick and red and whining with a high-pitched keen. When I saw the construction of steel and concrete, shaped like a geodesic dome, one of the landmarks I'd carefully noted on my first trip to Dr. Quintano's home, I made the cabbie pull over. Cab fare from any point to any other point in Tijuana is a flat fifty cents. I gave him four dollars, all the bills I had in my hand.

He sped away and I stood looking at the dome, at the sky, at my hands, and for the first time in my life I came to know sin.

I ran down the road, and down a side street, as unerringly as a hound on scent. I found Quintano's home without difficulty. It was one of the most formidable in that neighborhood, and the high fence surrounding it meant nothing to me. I don't know why I was there, what I wanted. Perhaps to hit him, or to get the money back for Jenny at the hospital—but she was gone, she was dead now, wasn't she? I didn't know.

I scaled the fence and hung at the top for a long moment watching. The rickets case was down the line, near the gate. The door to the house opened and a man came out; he was tall with salt-and-pepper hair, and I thought he was Quintano. I climbed to the top, poised there, let myself go and caught the top of the fence with both hands. I hung for a second, then dropped. The two men saw me, and there was consternation on their faces.

"She died! She died! The baby and she died!" I yelled, and charged them. The older man stepped back, as though to flee into the house, but I went at him in a long flat dive and caught him around the ankles. He went face-forward into the side of the building, and slid sidewise, with my arms still locked around his calves. He was screaming in Spanish, and the rickets case wasn't about to help. He ran past us where we tumbled together on the ground, and into the house. The door was still open and I could hear him yelling for someone, but I was too busy trying to get at the older man's throat. I slid up his body, and locked one hand under his chin. He tried to fight me off and I pummeled him with my free fist. I was choking him, but not very well, and he was glaze-eyedly trying to fight free. I hit him as hard as I could on the side of the head, but he rolled with it, and then he dug his hand into my mouth, catching the soft flesh of my cheek, and he literally pried my head back. I lost my hold on his throat, and he jacked his knee up into my stomach. All the air went out of me and I flopped back, gasping like a heart case. Then, before I could defend myself, Luis was running through the anteroom, out the door, and was kicking me. His feet were big, and I saw each ripple-soled shoe descend, first right, then left, and he was stomping on my face as if I was a bug. I tried to grab his leg, and caught one pant cuff. I pulled him across and tumbled him, and managed to crawl up his front and hit him once before someone grabbed me from behind, locked his hands around my face and yanked me forcibly back against a knee. My back cracked like an arthritic knuckle and everything bobbled, weaved, swam, dipped in front of me. I started to gray out, and stayed with it just long enough to see Luis and the older man and the rickets case bending down to work me over good.

I was lying on my back, my right hand was loose in a puddle of mud, and I was staring up at a wall that held a bullfight poster. I saw the colors, and the word ARRUZA, and then read the sign very carefully three times before I fainted again.

When I came up the second time, someone was going through my pockets. I didn't stop him. Not even when he pulled my watch off my wrist. I went under again, and when I came back the third time I was very cold, and shivering. I tried to get up, let my legs slide down the wall, where they rose above my head lying in the dirt, and tried to gain purchase on the brick wall. It turned to rubber and peanut butter.

I kept at it, and finally got to my feet.

The world was nowhere to be seen.

Then I realized both my eyes had swollen almost completely shut. I stumbled forward, my hands out before me like a blind man, and came out of the alley into the street. It was noisy and full of people. The lights hurt my eyes. I stared up, and caught a vista of the town, and it was an eye-numbing horizon of neon. I groaned.

A pair of overweight Mexican girls swinging huge purses went by, and tittered to each other, saying something gutty but soft in Spanish. I called them whores, *putas!*

I walked the streets for hours, seeing nothing, only feeling a pain far worse than the ache that threatened to split my head open. I must have looked hideous, because I came around a corner suddenly, and came face to face with a heavyset Mexican whose eyes opened wide in amazement. He got a sick look and walked around me. I didn't turn to see if he was still watching.

My pockets were empty, of course. All I knew was that I had to have a drink. My mouth was sandy and my stomach ached. Not entirely from the stomping I'd gotten. Oh, Jenny, oh, Fran!

I wandered into the Blue Fox, and there was a naked girl doing a nautch dance on the bar. Sailors in civvies were trying to grab her crotch. She kept twisting away from them. Then someone announced dinner was served and three broads came out, undressed, and lay down on the bar. Hors d'oeuvres. Three sickies jumped off their bar stools and went to fall down on the goodies. A bouncer tapped me on the shoulder and I left. I was sick.

I went into an alley and puked. Twice. When I was as empty as I was ever going to be, I tried to straighten myself up. I brushed off my clothes, raked my hair back out of my face with a hand, and went in search of a job.

There was a hustler looking for handbill boys at the Rancho Grande, a spieler for one nightclub told me, and I went over there. Three dollars and fifty cents for two hours' work handing out handbills, putting them under the windshield wipers of parked cars. I asked for a half dollar advance and was handed a stack of handbills instead. I went off down the street like a trained monkey, handing pieces of paper to people, pressing them into the hands of strangers. I was giving of myself. It felt wonderful. I wanted to puke again, but that was ridiculous. I knew I was empty.

Finally, all the handbills were gone, and I went back to get paid. The man was gone, and the people at the club didn't know where he could be found. I went looking for him. It took a long time, but I found another handbill-giver, a kid with wide, dark eyes, and told him the man was gone. He told me that was only because I was *gringo*. He grinned and told me where to find the man. I went to the Bum-Bum and there he was, hiring more boys in the service of his cause. I approached him and said pay me. He looked like he didn't want to do it, but I started to make sandpaper noises and my hands became claws and I swear I'd have killed him right then if he'd refused. He'd have gone to his grave with my teeth in his throat. I was more than a little mad.

He pulled out a wad and started to peel off three singles. I reached in and took a ten, and walked away. He started to follow, and started to motion to another man, but I turned my bloody face to stare at them, and he shrugged.

I took the ten and went drinking. I bought a bottle of tequila. It only seemed fitting to drink the wine of the land. I finished the bottle almost by myself. The last dregs were taken by an old Mexican woman sitting in a doorway. She had her legs tied under her so she looked crippled, and her five-year-old son was selling pencils and switchblade knives just down the street while she begged. At one point a well-built but slovenly fifteen-year-old girl came hipping by, and the old woman told me in broken English that it was her pride, her daughter. "She make *doce*, twelf, *doce* doe-lahr night," she beamed. They lived good. I shared some chili beans with her, and went away.

I was in another place, I think. It was a club. There was a fight and sirens and I ran away. Then I was in the Mambo Rock, and someone was yelling FIRE FIRE FIRE and I turned to see the whole wall blazing. An electrical short, and the whole block was in flames. Twelve feet in the air the flames ate the night sky, and I was helping a shopkeeper pull his bongos and wooden statues of Don Quixote and bead-shirts and *serapes* out into the street, and then there was a Mexican soldier, a member of the National Guard, a *rurale*, something . . . and he was spinning me around telling me to go away. They'd called in the army and half the town was on fire, and I was pulling a woman out of the flames, and her dress was on fire, and I gave her a feel as I beat out the flames with my bare hands. And then they were taking me to the infirmary, and swabbing my hands with cool, moist salve.

Then another place, and I was very drunk and sick and very tired. I walked up Avenida Constitución and saw 287 HOTEL CORREO DEL NORTE and bought a pack of Delicados for seven cents in the booth on the corner, and went back to the hotel.

My room was seventy-five cents for the night. The walls were plywood till they reached five feet, then chicken-wire to the ceiling. I slept with my shoelaces knotted together, so my shoes wouldn't get stolen. I'd have put them under the end-legs of the bed, but I was so tired I knew the bed could be lifted off the shoes and I wouldn't have known it. Someone tried to get in during the night and I screamed about death and snakes and they went away.

I dreamed of jackasses painted like zebras, and *turistas* getting their pictures taken in a cart pulled by the zebra-ass, on street corners, wearing *sombreros* with the name CISCO KID scrawled on the brim. It was a nice dream.

The sign said TELÉFONO PÚBLICO, and I stood on Avenida Revolución.

I called the hospital, and somehow they found Rooney. She had been looking for me all the day before. I told her where I was, and she came and got me. I was crying, I think. They released Jenny's body, and her parents came down to get it. I don't think I could have borne carrying it back in the Magnette . . . not to Los Angeles. That was forever.

Rooney kept asking me where I'd been, but I couldn't tell her. I wasn't purged, for Christ's sake, but I was tired, and that was almost as good.

Jenny was gone, and Kenneth Duane Markham was gone, and soon enough Rooney would be gone from me. All I wanted to do was get back to Los Angeles and try to be someone else. The taste of tequila was still strong in my throat, and I knew that would help a little.

Alive and Well and on a Friendless Voyage

"Quae nocent docent."

Then, and only then, like some mysterious Prisoner in the Iron Mask hidden from everyone's sight, only then, when the gigantic vessel slipped out of normal continuity and entered the megaflow, only then did the man they called Moth emerge from his stateroom.

As the immense tambour shields rolled down into the body of the vessel, exposing the boiling white jelly that was the megaflow surging past beyond the great crystal ports, the door to his stateroom rolled up and he emerged, dressed entirely in white. Clown-white circles around his dark, haunted eyes. Everyone looked and stopped talking.

The lounge of the gigantic vessel was packed, with voyagers grouped by twos and threes and fours at the bubble tables with their thin stalk supports. Voyagers who had boarded at 4:00, at Now, at Here, at three dimensions—bound for 41:00, for the 85th of February, for Yet To Be, for There, for the last stop before the end of measurable space and time and thought. They looked at Moth and they stopped talking.

Their faces said: *who is this person?*

And he walked down among them haltingly; he did not know them. This ship of strangers, and Moth.

He sat down at a table with one empty chair. A man and a woman already sat there. The woman was slim, neither attractive nor unattractive, a mild-looking woman, difficult to discompose. The man looked kind, there were crinkle lines at the corners of his eyes. Moth sat down across from them, as the gigantic vessel hurtled through the megaflow, and the kind-looking man said, "It wasn't your fault."

Moth looked sad. "I can't believe that. I think it must have been my fault."

"No, no," the unperturbed woman said quickly, "it *wasn't*! There was nothing that could be done. Your son would have died nonetheless. You can't castigate yourself for believing in God. You *mustn't*."

Moth leaned forward and put his face in his hands. His voice came faintly. "It was insane. Dead is dead. I should have known that . . . I *did* know it."

The kind-looking man reached across and touched Moth's hand. "The sickness was put on him by God, because of something you had done, you or your wife. It couldn't have been the child. He was too young to have known sin. But you knew *you* or your wife were filled with sin. And so your child fell ill. But if you could be as brave as the Bible said you must be, you could save him."

The calm woman gently pried Moth's hands away from his face and forced him to look into her eyes. She held his hands across the table and said, "Doctors could not save him . . . you *knew* that. God sets no store by science, only faith. Keeping them from the child was necessary. Hiding him in the basement was *important*."

Moth whispered, "But he grew worse. He sickened. It was too cold down there, perhaps. I might have let the family do what they wanted, let a physician *see* him, at least."

"No," the kind man said imperatively. "No! Faith cannot be broken. You maintained. You were right. Even when he died."

"It was holy the way you sat vigil over him," the woman said. "Day after day. You said he would rise on the second or third day. And you had belief in God."

Moth began to cry silently. "He lay there. Three days, and he lay there. His color changed."

"Then a week," the kind man said. "Faith! You had faith! In a week he would rise."

"No," Moth said, "not in a week. Dead."

"Twenty-one days, a magic number. It would have been on the twenty-first day. But they came and the law made you give him up, and they arrested you, and all through the hearings you insisted on God's Will, and your good wife, she stood by you through the hatred and the anguish as outsiders reviled you."

"He never rose. They buried him in the earth," Moth said, drying his eyes. The clown-white had run down his cheeks.

"So you were forced to leave. To go outside. To get away to a place where God would hear you. It was the right way; you had no other choice. Either believe, or become one with the faithless people who filled your world. You need not have guilt," the kind man said. He touched Moth's sleeve.

"You'll find peace," the calm woman said.

"Thank you," Moth said, rising and leaving them.

The man and woman sank back in their chairs, and the lights that had been lit in their eyes as they spoke to Moth . . . dimmed and grew sullen. Moth moved through the lounge.

A young man with an intense expression and nervous hand movement sat alone. He stared out the port at the megaflow.

"May I sit down here?" Moth asked.

The young man looked at him, taking his eyes off the swirling, bubbling jelly of the megaflow reluctantly. But he did not reply. There was loathing in his expression. He turned back to the crystal port without answering Moth.

"Please. May I sit with you? I want to talk to you."

"I don't talk to cowards," the young man said. His jaw muscles spasmed with anger.

"I'm a coward, yes, I'll admit it," Moth said helplessly. "But, please, let me sit."

"Oh, for Christ's sake, *sit* already! But just shut your mouth; don't speak to me!" He turned once again to the port.

Moth sat down, folded his hands on the table, did not speak, stared steadily at the young man's profile.

After a few moments the young man turned his face. He looked at Moth. "You make me sick. I'd like to punch you in the face, you disgusting coward."

"Yes," said Moth miserably, "I wouldn't stop you. I'm a coward, as you say."

"Worse! Worse than just a coward. A hypocrite, a silly posturing fool! You spent your whole life playing the big man, the big stud, the cavalier. The tough, cynical mover and shaker. But you weren't any smarter or tougher than any other simple-minded jerk who thought with his groin."

"I made mistakes," Moth said. "Just like everybody else. There's never enough experience. I thought I knew what I was doing. I fell in love with her."

"Oh, that's terrific," the young man said. The tone was frankly vicious. "Terrific. *You fell in love.* You moron! She was nineteen. You were over twice her age. Why did you let her whipsaw you into marriage? Come on, you idiot, why?"

"She said she loved me, thought I was better than other men, said if I didn't marry her she would go away and I'd never see her again. I was in love, I'd only been in love once before. No, that isn't right; I'd only *loved* once before. The thought of never seeing that face again filled me with fear. That was it: I was afraid I'd never see her again. I couldn't live with that."

"So you married her."

"Yes."

"But you couldn't sleep with her, couldn't make love to her. What did you expect from her. She was a child."

"She *talked* like a woman. She said all the right things an adult woman says. I didn't realize she was still confused, didn't know what she wanted."

"But you couldn't make love to her, isn't that so?"

"Yes, it's so. She was like a child, a daughter; my thoughts weren't straight; I didn't realize that was what was happening. All interest in sex just vanished; for her, for any woman. I thought—"

"What *she* thought. That you were impotent. That you were falling apart. She got more frightened every day. A lifetime to spend with a man who would never show her any passion."

"But there was love. I loved her. Without reserve. I showed it in a million ways, every hour of the day that we spent together."

"Gifts."

"Yes, gifts. Touches. Hugs and kisses and smiles."

"Purchases. You tried buying her."

"No, never that."

"Rented, then. It was the same."

The young man clenched and unclenched his hands. They seemed to have movement directed from somewhere outside him. The hands moved and seemed to want to strike Moth. The man in clown-white could not have failed to notice, but he did not flinch, did not move away. He sat waiting for the next assault, willing victim.

"How did it feel when you found out she was sleeping with him?"

"It hurt terribly. Worse than anything I'd ever felt. There was a ball of pain in the bottom of my lungs, like something inside breathing, a second heart, I don't know: and every time it breathed, the pain was worse."

The young man sneered. "And what did you do about it, big man?"

"I wanted to kill him."

"Why him? He was only picking up on the available goodies. You leave something lying around unused, there'll always be someone who'll put it to use."

Moth said forlornly, "It was the way she was doing it."

The young man laughed nastily. "You ass. There's *always* some stupid rationalization cuckolds like you fasten on to make it seem dramatic. If it hadn't been this way, it would have been another; and you'd have found some aspect of *that* in bad taste. Can't you understand it's all excuses?"

"But when I found out, and asked her to leave, she said she would go to stay with her family, to think it out. But she moved in with him."

The young man moved suddenly. He leaned across and grabbed Moth's shirt. He pulled him half across the table and his voice became a low snarl of hatred. "*Then* what did you do, hero? Huh, what happened then?"

Moth spoke softly, as if ashamed. "I loaded a gun and went down there to his apartment and kicked in the door. I put my shoe flat against the jamb right beside the lock and pulled back and slammed it as hard as I could. It popped the lock right out of the frame. I went straight through the living room of that awful little apartment and into the bedroom, and they were on the bed naked. It was just the way I'd been seeing it in my head, with him on top of her, except they'd heard the lock shatter and he was trying to get untangled from the sheets and I caught him with one foot on the floor."

The young man shook Moth. Not too hard, but hard enough to show how angry he was, how disgusted he was. Beyond them, the megaflow took on a scar-tissue appearance, inflamed, nastily pink with burned blue tinges. He continued shaking Moth gently, as if jangling coins from a small bank.

"I rushed him and shoved the gun into his mouth. I heard him start to moan something and then his teeth broke when the muzzle of the gun went into his mouth. I pushed him flat on his back, down onto the bed, and I kneeled with my right leg on his chest, and I told her to get dressed, that I was taking her out of there."

The young man shoved him back. Moth sat silently.

"What a stupid, miserable, pitiful little mind, you are. None of that is true, is it?"

Moth looked away. Softly, he said, "No. None of it."

"What *did* you do when you found out she was with him, after four months of marriage?"

"Nothing."

"You loaded the gun and did nothing."

"Yes."

"You couldn't even bring yourself to make the act real, could you?"

"No. I'm a coward. I wanted to kill him, and then kill myself."

"But not her."

"No. Never her. I loved her. I couldn't kill her, so I wanted to kill everything else in the world."

"Get away from me, you pathetic little shit. Just get up and walk away from me and don't talk to me any more. You ran away. You're running now. But you're not going to escape."

Moth said, "In time, I'll forget."

"You'll never completely forget it. Time will dull it, and maybe it'll be supportable. But you'll never forget."

"Perhaps not," Moth said, and stood up. He turned away, and as he turned away, the light that had blazed madly in the young man's eyes dimmed and went out. He turned back to the scar-tissue of the megaflow and stared at nothingness.

Moth walked through the lounge, breathing deeply.

He passed a beautiful woman with pale yellow hair and almost white eyebrows, who was sitting in company with two nondescript men at a table for four. As Moth came abreast of her, she reached out and touched his arm. "I feel more sorrow for you than animosity," she said, in a gentle and deep voice. Her words were filled with rich tones.

Moth sat down in the empty chair. The two men seemed not to see him, though they listened to the conversation between Moth and the beautiful woman.

"No one should ever be judged heartless because they tended to their own personal survival," she said. She held an unlit cigarette in a short holder. One of the men in attendance moved to light it, but she waved him away sharply. Her attention was solidly with Moth.

"I could have saved one of them," Moth responded. He pressed the back of his hand to his mouth, as though seeing again a terrible vision from the past. "The fire, the Home ballooning with flames from the windows, the sound of their screams. They were so old, so helpless."

The pale yellow hair shimmered as the beautiful woman shook her head. "You were only the caretaker of their lives; it wasn't written on stone that you had to *die* for them. You were conscientious, you were a good administrator; there was never the slightest impropriety in the Home. But what could you do? You were *afraid*! Everyone has a secret fear. For some it's growing old, for others it's snakes or spiders or being buried alive. Drowning, being laughed at in public, closed-in spaces, being rejected. *Every*one has something."

"I didn't know it was fire. I swear to God I didn't realize. But when I came down the hall that night and smelled the smoke, I was paralyzed. I stood there in the hall, just staring at the wire-screen door to the dormitory section. We *always* kept it locked at night. It wasn't a jail . . . it was for their own protection; they were so old, and some of them roamed at night. We couldn't keep watch all the time, it just wasn't feasible."

"I know, I know," the beautiful woman said, soothing him. "It was for their own protection. They had their television in the dorm, and bathroom facilities. It was lovely up there, just the same as the private rooms on the lower floors. But they *roamed*, they walked at night; they might fall down stairs or have an attack and there would be no one to help them, no call button for you or an orderly nearby. I understand why you kept the screen locked."

Moth spread his hands helplessly. He looked this way and that, as if seeking a white light that would release him from the pain of memory. "I smelled the smoke, and as I stood there, not knowing what to do, almost ready to rush forward and unlock the door and go inside, a blast of heat and flame came right through the screen! The heat was so intense I fell back. But even then . . . *even then* I would have done something, but the cat . . ."

The beautiful woman nodded. "It was the sight of the cat that terrified you, that made you suddenly realize it was fire that hid down there in your mind, waiting to possess you. I understand, anyone would understand!"

"I don't know how it got through the screen. It . . . it *strained itself* through, and it was on fire, burning, one of the old women's cats. It was on fire. The smell of the fur, the crackling, it was burning like fat in a fire. It screamed, oh God the sound of the screaming, the tail all black and the parts of it bubbling . . ."

"Don't!" the beautiful woman said, feeling Moth's pain. "Don't torment yourself. You ran. I understand why you ran. There was nothing you could do."

"No one knew I had had the choice. I stood outside and watched, and once I saw a face at one of the windows. It was wrapped in flames, an old man, his long hair burning. It was ghastly, terrible, I couldn't bear it. I cried and screamed up at them, and the one who had escaped, some of the orderlies tried to get back up there, and one of *them* was killed, when the ceiling fell in. But no one knew I had had a chance to save them, I *might* have saved them, perhaps only one of them, but I *could* have done something."

"No," the woman with the pale hair reassured him, "no. You would have been burned alive, too. And there had been the cat. No one ever need know."

"But *I* know!"

"You survived. That's what counts."

"The pain. The knowledge, the pain."

"It will pass."

"No. Never."

One of the two men moved again to light her cigarette. She put the cigarette and the holder on the table. Moth shook himself as if awakening from a nightmare, and stood up. He turned away from the woman and her silent companions. The light in her eyes faded.

Moth walked through the lounge.

The gigantic vessel plowed on through the roiling megaflow jelly, bound for the end of appreciable space, asymptotically struggling toward the verge of time, pulling itself forward inexorably to the precipice of measurable thought. The voyage included only three stops: embarkation, principal debarkation and over the edge. The voyagers sat dull and silent, occasionally sipping off a drink that had been ordered through the punch-button system on each chair. The only sounds in the lounge were the sussurations as the panels in the tables opened to allow drinks to rise to the surface, the random sounds of fingernails or teeth on glass, and the ever-present hiss of the megaflow as it rampaged past the vessel. Voices could be heard in the boiling jelly, carried through the hull of the vessel, like voices of the dead, whispering for their final hearing, their day in the court of judgment. But no coherent thoughts came with those voices, no actual words, no messages from the beyond that could be of any use to the voyagers within.

Entombed outside time and space and thought, the voyagers sat silently within their trip ship, facing in any direction they chose. Direction did not matter. The vessel only traveled in one direction. And they, within, entombed.

Moth wandered through the lounge, sitting here for a few moments to tell a fat man of how he had taken a girl who worked for him as a secretary away from her husband and children, had set her up in an expensive apartment, and then, weary of her, had left her with the unbreakable lease and no funds, even without a job because it simply isn't good business to be having an affair with someone who works for you. Particularly not with a woman who is so suicide-prone. And he told the fat man how he had set up a trust fund for the children after it was over, after the girl who had worked for him as a secretary had become a self-fulfilling prophecy. Wandered through the lounge sitting there for a long time confessing to an old woman with many rings how he had mercilessly used his age and illness to bind his sons and daughters to him till long past the time when they could find joyful lives for themselves, with no intention of *ever* signing over his wealth to them. Wandered through the lounge sitting over there for a time to reveal to a tall, thin chocolate-colored man how he had betrayed the other members of a group to which he had belonged, naming names and, from the dark interior of the back seat of a large automobile, pointing out the ones who had led the movement, and watching as they had been battered to their knees in the rain and the mud, and wincing as the thugs with the lead pipes had smashed in the back of each head, very professionally, very smoothly, only one solid downstroke for each man. Wandered through the lounge and talked to a pretty young girl about the devious mind-games he had played with lovers, unnerving them and unsettling them and forcing them to spend all their time trying to dance and sing their dances and songs of life for his amusement, until their dances had degenerated into feeble tremblings and their songs had died away to rattles. Wandered through the lounge being penitent, remorseful, contrite. Sat and recanted, rued, confessed, humbled himself and wept occasionally.

And each person, as he walked away leaving them to their secret thoughts, flickered for a moment with life in the eyes, and then the lights died and they were once again alone.

He came to a table where a thin, plain-looking young woman sat alone, biting her thumbnail.

"I'd like to sit down and discuss something with you," he said. She shrugged as if she didn't care, and he sat.

"I've come to realize we're all alone," he said.

She did not reply. Merely stared at him.

"No matter how many people love us or care for us or want to ease our burden in this life," Moth said, "we are all, all of us, always alone. Something Aldous Huxley once said, I'm not sure I know it exactly, I've looked and looked and can't find the quote, but I remember part of it. He said: 'we are, each of us, an island universe in a sea of space.' I think that was it."

She looked at him without expression. Her face was thin and without remarkable feature. No engaging smile, no intricate intriguing bone structure, no sudden dimple or angle that revealed her as even momentarily attractive. The look she gave him was the one she had perfected. Neutral.

"My life has always been sad music," Moth said, with enormous sincerity. "Like a long symphony played all in minors. Wind in trees and conversations heard through walls at night. No one looked at me, no one wanted to know. But I maintained; that's all there is. There's one day, and the end of it, and night, and sleep that comes slowly, and then another day. Until there are as many behind as there are ahead. No questions, no answers, alone. But I maintain. I don't let it bend me. And the song continues."

The unprepossessing young woman smiled faintly.

She reached across and touched his hand.

Moth's eyes sparkled for a moment.

Then the gigantic vessel began to slow.

They sat that way, her hand on this, until the tambour windows rolled up and they were encysted totally. And soon the gigantic vessel ceased its movement. They had arrived at the edge, at the point of debarkation.

Everyone rose to leave.

Moth stood and walked away from them. He walked back through the lounge and no one spoke to him, no one touched him. He came to the door to his stateroom and he turned.

"Excuse me," he said. They watched, silently.

"Is there anyone here who will change places with me, please? Anyone who will take my place for the rest of the voyage?" He looked out at them from his white makeup, and he waited a decent time.

No one answered, though the unremarkable young woman seemed to want to say something. But she didn't.

Moth smiled. "I thought not," he said softly.

Then he turned and the door to his stateroom rolled up and he went inside. The door rolled down and everyone left the gigantic vessel quietly.

After a moment the debarkation port irised shut, and the gigantic vessel began to move again. On into final darkness, from which there was no return.

XIV

THE CLASSICS

> "[. . .] a writer may have a message, an emotion, a philosophy to impart in his fiction, and these are the most marvelous kind of serendipity. But his first job is to entertain. To inform comes second. To entertain comes first."
>
> —"A Voice from the Styx," *Psychotic*, September 1968

In an earlier reference to Harlan's first professional story, it was noted that "the basic conflict between human fear and human determination" would be the major thrust of the later aggregate. The major works that confirm this uncompromising position, and hold up under both critical and popular scrutiny, must be stories that somehow embody what we have gleaned from the dozens of preceding selections (not to mention the hundreds more not included here).

A great number of additional distinguished stories mark the route of thirty years of Harlan's steady work, including "The Beast That Shouted Love at the Heart of the World," "The Region Between," "Basilisk," "Paladin of the Lost Hour," "Seeing," "On the Downhill Side," "Shatterday," "All the Sounds of Fear," "Pennies, Off a Dead Man's Eyes," "Paingod," "The Place with No Name," "Count the Clock That Tells the Time," "Bright Eyes," "O Ye of Little Faith," "Delusion for a Dragon-Slayer"—the list goes on and on. Many of them have been honored with awards and reprinted numerous times in anthologies, finding their way into both commercial products for the general public and academic compilations for teachers and students.

There aren't many writers who create equal uproar in the academic and non-academic environs, but Harlan does it with such casualness that it has become an expected and seemingly unremarkable side effect.

It does not benefit us to become complacent about literary excellence. An excellent writer always earns his/her way, and Harlan has never taken his profession complacently. In doing only what he himself wanted to do, he has informed his generation of the value of courage, self-trust, honesty and—as he insists is certainly not least—entertainment.

You're sure to have noticed by now how arbitrary some of the categories in a book like this have to be. So many of the pieces are interchangeable, and could make an equal claim on any number of sections. The categories are, of course, a convenience—a way of focusing attention on themes and directions and intent, not of pinning those pieces down. They are, if you like, handles.

But a section devoted to "classic" Ellison stories is not just an arbitrary thing, no mere convenience. Each of the following selections is something very special in the Ellison canon, and something memorable in the canon of American fiction; they are certainly among the finest stories of the past quarter century.

"'Repent, Harlequin!' Said the Ticktockman" (1965) is already one of the most reprinted stories in the English language (fifty times in the two decades since its first publication).

"Pretty Maggie Moneyeyes" (1967) is undoubtedly one of the most electrifying portrayals of the cunning snares of intense human passion.

"A Boy and His Dog" (1969) speaks of love in a special way that has been consistently misinterpreted by the story's detractors, whose arguments found even more inflammatory fuel in L. Q. Jones's 1975 movie adaptation.

"The Deathbird" (1973), at one and the same time, is the most dangerous and the most humane assessment of humanity's place in the great unknown we call the universe.

There is no resemblance in the plots of these stories. The writing techniques used to achieve the dramatic effects are as dissimilar as one writer could possibly achieve, but one writer *did* achieve. To say more than that is to belabor the obvious.

For those who dream in fantasies, here are dreams to take you far beyond the fantasies of mere escape.

For those who cling to reality, here is the miraculous reality of humanity.

And for those who want nothing more than entertainment . . . ah, well, read on and be grandly entertained.

And don't be surprised if later, in the peacefulness of night, floating there in the darkness above your head, you see millions of jelly beans, three blue eyes, a downunder called Topeka, or a god who is not quite what it seems.

> "It is a peculiarity of mine that I travel with my typewriter. Wherever I go, the machine is with me, because I've found there is no predicting when the dreams will hit."
>
> —"The Whore with a Heart of Iron Pyrites, or, Where Does a Writer Go to Find a Maggie?," THOSE WHO CAN: A SCIENCE FICTION READER, edited by Robin Scott Wilson, New American Library, 1973

"Repent, Harlequin!" Said the Ticktockman

There are always those who ask, what is it all about? For those who need to ask, for those who need points sharply made, who need to know "where it's at," this:

> *The mass of men serve the state thus, not as men mainly, but as machines, with their bodies. They are the standing army, and the militia, jailors, constables, posse comitatus, etc. In most cases there is no free exercise whatever of the judgment or of the moral sense; but they put themselves on a level with wood and earth and stones; and wooden men can perhaps be manufactured that will serve the purpose as well. Such command no more respect than men of straw or a lump of dirt. They have the same sort of worth only as horses and dogs. Yet such as these even are commonly esteemed good citizens. Others—as most legislators, politicians, lawyers, ministers, and officeholders—serve the state chiefly with their heads; and, as they rarely make any moral distinctions, they are as likely to serve the Devil, without intending it, as God. A very few, as heroes, patriots, martyrs, reformers in the great sense, and* men, *serve the state with their consciences also, and so necessarily resist it for the most part; and they are commonly treated as enemies by it.*
>
> Henry David Thoreau
> CIVIL DISOBEDIENCE

That is the heart of it. Now begin in the middle, and later learn the beginning; the end will take care of itself.

But because it was the very world it was, the very world they had allowed it to *become*, for months his activities did not come to the alarmed attention of The Ones Who Kept The Machine Functioning Smoothly, the ones who poured the very best butter over the cams and mainsprings of the culture. Not until it had become obvious that somehow, someway, he had become a notoriety, a celebrity, perhaps even a hero for (what Officialdom inescapably tagged) "an emotionally disturbed segment of the populace," did they turn it over to the Ticktockman and his legal machinery. But by then, because it was the very world it was, and they had no way to predict he would happen—possibly a strain of disease long-defunct, now, suddenly, reborn in a system where immunity had been forgotten, had lapsed—he had been allowed to become too real. Now he had form and substance.

He had become a *personality*, something they had filtered out of the system many decades before. But there it was, and there *he* was, a very definitely imposing personality. In certain circles—middle-class circles—it was thought disgusting. Vulgar ostentation. Anarchistic. Shameful. In others, there was only sniggering: those strata where thought is subjugated to form and ritual, niceties, proprieties. But down below, ah, down below, where the people always needed their saints and sinners, their bread and circuses, their heroes and villains, he was considered a Bolivar; a Napoleon; a Robin Hood; a Dick Bong (Ace of Aces); a Jesus; a Jomo Kenyatta.

And at the top—where, like socially-attuned Shipwreck Kellys, every tremor and vibration threatening to dislodge the wealthy, powerful and titled from their flagpoles—he was considered a menace; a heretic; a rebel; a disgrace; a peril. He was known down the line, to the very heart-meat core, but the important reactions were high above and far below. At the very top, at the very bottom.

So his file was turned over, along with his time-card and his cardioplate, to the office of the Ticktockman.

The Ticktockman: very much over six feet tall, often silent, a soft purring man when things went timewise. The Ticktockman.

Even in the cubicles of the hierarchy, where fear was generated, seldom suffered, he was called the Ticktockman. But no one called him that to his mask.

You don't call a man a hated name, not when that man, behind his mask, is capable of revoking the minutes, the hours, the days and nights, the years of your life. He was called the Master Timekeeper to his mask. It was safer that way.

"This is *what* he is," said the Ticktockman with genuine softness, "but not *who* he is. This time-card I'm holding in my left hand has a name on it, but it is the name of *what* he is, not *who* he is. The cardioplate here in my right hand is also named, but not *whom* named, merely *what* named. Before I can exercise proper revocation, I have to know *who* this *what* is."

To his staff, all the ferrets, all the loggers, all the finks, all the commex, even the mineez, he said, "Who is this Harlequin?"

He was not purring smoothly. Timewise, it was jangle.

However, it *was* the longest speech they had ever heard him utter at one time, the staff, the ferrets, the loggers, the finks, the commex, but not the mineez, who usually weren't around to know, in any case. But even they scurried to find out.

Who is the Harlequin?

High above the third level of the city, he crouched on the humming aluminum-frame platform of the air-boat (foof! air-boat, indeed! swizzleskid is what it was, with a tow-rack jerry-rigged) and he stared down at the neat Mondrian arrangement of the buildings.

Somewhere nearby, he could hear the metronomic left-right-left of the 2:47 PM shift, entering the Timkin roller-bearing plant in their sneakers. A minute later, precisely, he heard the softer right-left-right of the 5:00 AM formation, going home.

An elfin grin spread across his tanned features, and his dimples appeared for a moment. Then, scratching at his thatch of auburn hair, he shrugged within his motley, as though girding himself for what came next, and threw the joystick forward, and bent into the wind as the air-boat dropped. He skimmed over a slidewalk, purposely dropping a few feet to crease the tassels of the ladies of fashion, and—inserting thumbs in large ears—he stuck out his tongue, rolled his eyes and went wugga-wugga-wugga. It was a minor diversion. One pedestrian skittered and tumbled, sending parcels everywhichway, another wet herself, a third keeled slantwise and the walk was stopped automatically by the servitors till she could be resuscitated. It was a minor diversion.

Then he swirled away on a vagrant breeze, and was gone. Hi-ho.

As he rounded the cornice of the Time-Motion Study Building, he saw the shift, just boarding the slidewalk. With practiced motion and an absolute conservation of movement, they sidestepped up onto the slow-strip and (in a chorus line reminiscent of a Busby Berkeley film of the antediluvian 1930s) advanced across the strips ostrich-walking till they were lined up on the expresstrip.

Once more, in anticipation, the elfin grin spread, and there was a tooth missing back there on the left side. He dipped, skimmed, and swooped over them; and then, scrunching about on the air-boat, he released the holding pins that fastened shut the ends of the home-made pouring troughs that kept his cargo from dumping prematurely. And as he pulled the trough-pins, the air-boat slid over the factory workers and one hundred and fifty thousand dollars' worth of jelly beans cascaded down on the expresstrip.

Jelly beans! Millions and billions of purples and yellows and greens and licorice and grape and raspberry and mint and round and smooth and crunchy outside and soft-mealy inside and sugary and bouncing jouncing tumbling clittering clattering skittering fell on the heads and shoulders and hardhats and carapaces of the Timkin workers, tinkling on the slidewalk and bouncing away and rolling about underfoot and filling the sky on their way down with all the colors of joy and childhood and holidays, coming down in a steady rain, a solid wash, a torrent of color and sweetness out of the sky from above, and entering a universe of sanity and metronomic order with quite-mad coocoo newness. Jelly beans!

The shift workers howled and laughed and were pelted, and broke ranks, and the jelly beans managed to work their way into the mechanism of the slidewalks after which there was a hideous scraping as the sound of a million fingernails rasped down a quarter of a million blackboards, followed by a coughing and a sputtering, and then the slidewalks all stopped and everyone was dumped thisawayandthataway in a jackstraw tumble, still laughing and popping little jelly bean eggs of childish color into their mouths. It was a holiday, and a jollity, an absolute insanity, a giggle. But . . .

The shift was delayed seven minutes.

They did not get home for seven minutes.

The master schedule was thrown off by seven minutes.

Quotas were delayed by inoperative slidewalks for seven minutes.

He had tapped the first domino in the line, and one after another, like chik chik chik, the others had fallen.

The System had been seven minutes' worth of disrupted. It was a tiny matter, one hardly worthy of note, but in a society where the single driving force was order and unity and equality and promptness and clocklike precision and attention to the clock, reverence of the gods of the passage of time, it was a disaster of major importance.

So he was ordered to appear before the Ticktockman. It was broadcast across every channel of the communications web. He was ordered to be *there* at 7:00 dammit on time. And they waited, and they waited, but he didn't show up till almost ten-thirty, at which time he merely sang a little song about moonlight in a place no one had ever heard of, called Vermont, and vanished again. But they had all been waiting since seven, and it wrecked *hell* with their schedules. So the question remained: Who is the Harlequin?

But the *unasked* question (more important of the two) was: how did we get *into* this position, where a laughing, irresponsible japer of jabberwocky and jive could disrupt our entire economic and cultural life with a hundred and fifty thousand dollars' worth of jelly beans . . .

Jelly for God's sake *beans!* This is madness! Where did he get the money to buy a hundred and fifty thousand dollars' worth of jelly beans? (They knew it would have cost that much, because they had a team of Situation Analysts pulled off another assignment, and rushed to the slidewalk scene to sweep up and count the candies, and produce findings, which disrupted *their* schedules and threw their entire branch at least a day behind.) Jelly beans! Jelly . . . *beans*? Now wait a second—a second accounted for—no one has manufactured jelly beans for over a hundred years. Where did he get jelly beans?

That's another good question. More than likely it will never be answered to your complete satisfaction. But then, how many questions ever are?

The middle you know. Here is the beginning. How it starts:

A desk pad. Day for day, and turn each day. 9:00—open the mail. 9:45—appointment with planning commission board. 10:30—discuss installation progress charts with J.L. 11:45—pray for rain. 12:00—lunch. *And so it goes.*

"I'm sorry, Miss Grant, but the time for interviews was set at 2:30, and it's almost five now. I'm sorry you're late, but those are the rules. You'll have to wait till next year to submit application for this college again." *And so it goes.*

The 10:10 local stops at Cresthaven, Galesville, Tonawanda Junction, Selby and Farnhurst, but not at Indiana City, Lucasville and Colton, except on Sunday. The 10:35 express stops at Galesville, Selby and Indiana City, except on Sundays & Holidays, at which time it stops at . . . *and so it goes.*

"I couldn't wait, Fred. I had to be at Pierre Cartain's by 3:00, and you said you'd meet me under the clock in the terminal at 2:45, and you weren't there, so I had to go on. You're always late, Fred. If you'd been there, we could have sewed it up together, but as it was, well, I took the order alone . . ." *And so it goes.*

Dear Mr. and Mrs. Atterley: In reference to your son Gerold's constant tardiness, I am afraid we will have to suspend him from school unless some more reliable method can be instituted guaranteeing he will arrive at his classes on time. Granted he is an exemplary student, and his marks are high, his constant flouting of the schedules of this school makes it impractical to maintain him in a system where the other children seem capable of getting where they are supposed to be on time *and so it goes.*

YOU CANNOT VOTE UNLESS YOU APPEAR AT 8:45 AM.

"I don't care if the script is *good*, I need it Thursday!"

CHECK-OUT TIME IS 2:00 PM.

"You got here late. The job's taken. Sorry."

YOUR SALARY HAS BEEN DOCKED FOR TWENTY MINUTES TIME LOST.

"God, what time is it, I've gotta run!"

And so it goes. And so it goes. And so it goes. And so it goes goes goes goes goes tick tock tick tock tick tock and one day we no longer let time serve us, we serve time and we are slaves of the schedule, worshippers of the sun's passing, bound into a life predicated on restrictions because the system will not function if we don't keep the schedule tight.

Until it becomes more than a minor inconvenience to be late. It becomes a sin. Then a crime. Then a crime punishable by this:

EFFECTIVE 15 JULY 2389 12:00:00 midnight, the office of the Master Timekeeper will require all citizens to submit their time-cards and cardioplates for processing. In accordance with Statute 555-7-SGH-999 governing the revocation of time per capita, all cardioplates will be keyed to the individual holder and—

What they had done, was devise a method of curtailing the amount of life a person could have. If he was ten minutes late, he lost ten minutes of his life. An hour was proportionately worth more revocation. If someone was consistently tardy, he might find himself, on a Sunday night, receiving a communiqué from the Master Timekeeper that his time had run out, and he would be "turned off" at high noon on Monday, please straighten your affairs, sir, madame or bisex.

And so, by this simple scientific expedient (utilizing a scientific process held dearly secret by the Ticktockman's office) the System was maintained. It was the only expedient thing to do. It was, after all, patriotic. The schedules had to be met. After all, there *was* a war on!

But, wasn't there always?

"Now that is really disgusting," the Harlequin said, when Pretty Alice showed him the wanted poster. "Disgusting and *highly* improbable. After all, this isn't the Day of the Desperado. A *wanted* poster!"

"You know," Pretty Alice noted, "you speak with a great deal of inflection."

"I'm sorry," said the Harlequin, humbly.

"No need to be sorry. You're always saying 'I'm sorry.' You have such massive guilt, Everett, it's really very sad."

"I'm sorry," he said again, then pursed his lips so the dimples appeared momentarily. He hadn't wanted to say that at all. "I have to go out again. I have to *do* something."

Pretty Alice slammed her coffee-bulb down on the counter. "Oh for God's *sake*, Everett, can't you stay home just *one* night! Must you always be out in that ghastly clown suit, running around an*noy*ing people?"

"I'm—" He stopped, and clapped the jester's hat onto his auburn thatch with a tiny tingling of bells. He rose, rinsed out his coffee-bulb at the spray, and put it into the dryer for a moment. "I have to go."

She didn't answer. The faxbox was purring, and she pulled a sheet out, read it, threw it toward him on the counter. "It's about you. Of course. You're ridiculous."

He read it quickly. It said the Ticktockman was trying to locate him. He didn't care, he was going out to be late again. At the door, dredging for an exit line, he hurled back petulantly, "Well, *you* speak with inflection, *too*!"

Pretty Alice rolled her pretty eyes heavenward. "You're ridiculous." The Harlequin stalked out, slamming the door, which sighed shut softly, and locked itself.

There was a gentle knock, and Pretty Alice got up with an exhalation of exasperated breath, and opened the door. He stood there. "I'll be back about ten-thirty, okay?"

She pulled a rueful face. "Why do you tell me that? Why? You *know* you'll be late! You *know* it! You're *always* late, so why do you tell me these dumb things?" She closed the door.

On the other side, the Harlequin nodded to himself. *She's right. She's always right. I'll be late. I'm always late. Why do I tell her these dumb things?*

He shrugged again, and went off to be late once more.

He had fired off the firecracker rockets that said: I will attend the 115th annual International Medical Association Invocation at 8:00 PM precisely. I do hope you will all be able to join me.

The words had burned in the sky, and of course the authorities were there, lying in wait for him. They assumed, naturally, that he would be late. He arrived twenty minutes early, while they were setting up the spiderwebs to trap and hold him. Blowing a large bullhorn, he frightened and unnerved them so, their own moisturized encirclement webs sucked closed, and they were hauled up, kicking and shrieking, high above the amphitheater's floor. The Harlequin laughed and laughed, and apologized profusely. The physicians, gathered in solemn conclave, roared with laughter, and accepted the Harlequin's apologies with exaggerated bowing and posturing, and a merry time was had by all, who thought the Harlequin was a regular foofaraw in fancy pants; all, that is, but the authorities, who had been sent out by the office of the Ticktockman; they hung there like so much dockside cargo, hauled up above the floor of the amphitheater in a most unseemly fashion.

(In another part of the same city where the Harlequin carried on his "activities," totally unrelated in every way to what concerns us here, save that it illustrates the Ticktockman's power and import, a man named Marshall Delahanty received his turn-off notice from the Ticktockman's office. His wife received the notification from the gray-suited minee who delivered it, with the traditional "look of sorrow" plastered hideously across his face. She knew what it was, even without unsealing it. It was a billet-doux of immediate recognition to everyone these days. She gasped, and held it as though it were a glass slide tinged with botulism, and prayed it was not for her. Let it be for Marsh, she thought, brutally, realistically, or one of the kids, but not for me, please dear God, not for me. And then she opened it, and it *was* for Marsh, and she was at one and the same time horrified and relieved. The next trooper in the line had caught the bullet. "Marshall," she screamed, "Marshall! Termination, Marshall! OhmiGod, Marshall, whattl we do, whattl we do, Marshall omigodmarshall . . ." and in their home that night was the sound of tearing paper and fear, and the stink of madness went up the flue and there was nothing, absolutely nothing they could do about it.

(But Marshall Delahanty tried to run. And early the next day, when turn-off time came, he was deep in the Canadian forest two hundred miles away, and the office of the Ticktockman blanked his cardioplate, and Marshall Delahanty keeled over, running, and his heart stopped, and the blood dried up on its way to his brain, and he was dead that's all. One light went out on the sector map in the office of the Master Timekeeper, while notification was entered for fax reproduction, and Georgette Delahanty's name was entered on the dole roles till she could remarry. Which is the end of the footnote, and all the point that need be made, except don't laugh, because that is what would happen to the Harlequin if ever the Ticktockman found out his real name. It isn't funny.)

The shopping level of the city was thronged with the Thursday-colors of the buyers. Women in canary yellow chitons and men in pseudo-Tyrolean outfits that were jade and leather and fit very tightly, save for the balloon pants.

When the Harlequin appeared on the still-being-constructed shell of the new Efficiency Shopping Center, his bullhorn to his elfishly-laughing lips, everyone pointed and stared, and he berated them:

"Why let them order you about? Why let them tell you to hurry and scurry like ants or maggots? Take your time! Saunter a while! Enjoy the sunshine, enjoy the breeze, let life carry you at your own pace! Don't be slaves of time, it's a helluva way to die, slowly, by degrees . . . down with the Ticktockman!"

Who's the nut? most of the shoppers wanted to know. Who's the nut oh wow I'm gonna be late I gotta run . . .

And the construction gang on the Shopping Center received an urgent order from the office of the Master Timekeeper that the dangerous criminal known as the Harlequin was atop their spire, and their aid was urgently needed in apprehending him. The work crew said no, they would lose time on their construction schedule, but the Ticktockman managed to pull the proper threads of governmental webbing, and they were told to cease work and catch that nitwit up there on the spire; up there with the bullhorn. So a dozen and more burly workers began climbing into their construction platforms, releasing the a-grav plates, and rising toward the Harlequin.

After the debacle (in which, through the Harlequin's attention to personal safety, no one was seriously injured), the workers tried to reassemble, and assault him again, but it was too late. He had vanished. It had attracted quite a crowd, however, and the shopping cycle was thrown off by hours, simply hours. The purchasing needs of the system were therefore falling behind, and so measures were taken to accelerate the cycle for the rest of the day, but it got bogged down and speeded up and they sold too many float-valves and not nearly enough wegglers, which meant that the popli ratio was off, which made it necessary to rush cases and cases of spoiling Smash-O to stores that usually needed a case only every three or four hours. The shipments were bollixed, the transshipments were misrouted, and in the end, even the swizzleskid industries felt it.

"Don't come back till you have him!" the Ticktockman said, very quietly, very sincerely, extremely dangerously.

They used dogs. They used probes. They used cardioplate crossoffs. They used teepers. They used bribery. They used stiktytes. They used intimidation. They used torment. They used torture. They used finks. They used cops. They used search&seizure. They used fallaron. They used betterment incentive. They used fingerprints. They used the Bertillon system. They used cunning. They used guile. They used treachery. They used Raoul Mitgong, but he didn't help much. They used applied physics. They used techniques of criminology.

And what the hell: they caught him.

After all, his name was Everett C. Marm, and he wasn't much to begin with, except a man who had no sense of time.

"Repent, Harlequin!" said the Ticktockman.

"Get stuffed!" the Harlequin replied, sneering.

"You've been late a total of sixty-three years, five months, three weeks, two days, twelve hours, forty-one minutes, fifty-nine seconds, point oh three six one one one microseconds. You've used up everything you can, and more. I'm going to turn you off."

"Scare someone else. I'd rather be dead that live in a dumb world with a bogeyman like you."

"It's my job."

"You're full of it. You're a tyrant. You have no right to order people around and kill them if they show up late."

"You can't adjust. You can't fit in."

"Unstrap me, and I'll fit my fist into your mouth."

"You're a nonconformist."

"That didn't used to be a felony."
"It is now. Live in the world around you."
"I hate it. It's a terrible world."
"Not everyone thinks so. Most people enjoy order."
"I don't, and most of the people I know don't."
"That's not true. How do you think we caught you?"
"I'm not interested."
"A girl named Pretty Alice told us who you were."
"That's a lie."
"It's true. You unnerve her. She wants to belong; she wants to conform; I'm going to turn you off."
"Then do it already, and stop arguing with me."
"I'm not going to turn you off."
"You're an idiot!"
"Repent, Harlequin!" said the Ticktockman.
"Get stuffed."

So they sent him to Coventry. And in Coventry they worked him over. It was just like what they did to Winston Smith in NINETEEN EIGHTY-FOUR, which was a book none of them knew about, but the techniques are really quite ancient, and so they did it to Everett C. Marm; and one day, quite a long time later, the Harlequin appeared on the communications web, appearing elfin and dimpled and bright-eyed, and not at all brainwashed, and he said he had been wrong, that it was a good, a very good thing indeed, to belong, to be right on time hip-ho and away we go, and everyone stared up at him on the public screens that covered an entire city block, and they said to themselves, well, you see, he was just a nut after all, and if that's the way the system is run, then let's do it that way, because it doesn't pay to fight city hall, or in this case, the Ticktockman. So Everett C. Marm was destroyed, which was a loss, because of what Thoreau said earlier, but you can't make an omelet without breaking a few eggs, and in every revolution a few die who shouldn't, but they have to, because that's the way it happens, and if you make only a little change, then it seems to be worthwhile. Or, to make the point lucidly:

"Uh, excuse me, sir, I, uh, don't know how to uh, to uh, tell you this, but you were three minutes late. The schedule is a little, uh, bit off."
He grinned sheepishly.
"That's ridiculous!" murmured the Ticktockman behind his mask. "Check your watch." And then he went into his office, going *mrmee, mrmee, mrmee, mrmee.*

Pretty Maggie Moneyeyes

With an eight hole-card and a queen showing, with the dealer showing a four up, Kostner decided to let the house do the work. So he stood, and the dealer turned up. Six.

The dealer looked like something out of a 1935 George Raft film: Arctic diamond-chip eyes, manicured fingers long as a brain surgeon's, straight black hair slicked flat away from the pale forehead. He did not look up as he peeled them off. A three. Another three. Bam. A five. Bam. Twenty-one, and Kostner saw his last thirty dollars—six five-dollar chips—scraped on the edge of the cards, into the dealer's chip racks. Busted. Flat. Down and out in Las Vegas, Nevada. Playground of the Western World.

He slid off the comfortable stool-chair and turned his back on the blackjack table. The action was already starting again, like waves closing over a drowned man. He had been there, was gone, and no one had noticed. No one had seen a man blow the last tie with salvation. Kostner now had his choice: he could bum his way into Los Angeles and try to find something that resembled a new life . . . or he could go blow his brains out through the back of his head.

Neither choice showed much light or sense.

He thrust his hands deep into the pockets of his worn and dirty chinos, and started away down the line of slot machines clanging and rattling on the other side of the aisle between blackjack tables.

He stopped. He felt something in his pocket. Beside him, but all-engrossed, a fiftyish matron in electric lavender capris, high heels and Ship 'n' Shore blouse was working two slots, loading and pulling one while waiting for the other to clock down. She was dumping quarters in a seemingly inexhaustible supply from a Dixie cup held in her left hand. There was a surrealistic presence to the woman. She was almost automated, not a flicker of expression on her face, the eyes fixed and unwavering. Only when the gong rang, someone down the line had pulled a jackpot, did she look up. And at that moment Kostner knew what was wrong and immoral and deadly about Vegas, about legalized gambling, about setting the traps all baited and open in front of the average human. The woman's face was gray with hatred, envy, lust and dedication to the game—in that timeless instant when she heard another drugged soul down the line winning a minuscule jackpot. A jackpot that would only lull the player with words like *luck* and *ahead of the game*. The jackpot lure; the sparkling, bobbling, many-colored wiggler in a sea of poor fish.

The thing in Kostner's pocket was a silver dollar.

He brought it out and looked at it.

The eagle was hysterical.

But Kostner pulled to an abrupt halt, only one half-footstep from the sign indicating the limits of Tap City. He was still with it. What the high-rollers called the edge, the *vigerish*, the fine hole-card. One buck. One cartwheel. Pulled out of the pocket not half as deep as the pit into which Kostner had just been about to plunge.

What the hell, he thought, and turned to the row of slot machines.

He had thought they'd all been pulled out of service, the silver dollar slots. A shortage of coinage, said the United States Mint. But right there, side by side with the nickel and quarter bandits, was one cartwheel machine. Two thousand dollar jackpot. Kostner grinned foolishly. If you're gonna go out, go out like a champ.

He thumbed the silver dollar into the coin slot and grabbed the heavy, oiled handle. Shining cast aluminum and pressed steel. Big black plastic ball, angled for arm ease, pull it all day and you won't get weary.

Without a prayer in the universe, Kostner pulled the handle.

She had been born in Tucson, mother full-blooded Cherokee, father a bindlestiff on his way through. Mother had been working a truckers' stop, father had popped for spencer steak and sides. Mother had just gotten over a bad scene, indeterminate origins, unsatisfactory culminations. Mother had popped for bed. And sides. Margaret Annie Jessie had come nine months later; black of hair, fair of face, and born into a life of poverty. Twenty-three years later, a determined product of Miss Clairol and Berlitz, a dream-image formed by Vogue *and intimate association with the rat race, Margaret Annie Jessie had become a contraction.*

Maggie.

Long legs, trim and coltish; hips a trifle large, the kind that promote that specific *thought in men, about getting their hands around it; belly flat, isometrics; waist cut to the bone, a waist that works in any style from dirndl to disco-slacks; no breasts—all nipple, but no breast, like an expensive whore (the way O'Hara pinned it)—and no padding . . . forget the cans, baby, there's other, more important action; smooth, Michelangelo-sculpted neck, a pillar, proud; and all that face.*

Outthrust chin, perhaps a tot too much belligerence, but if you'd walloped as many gropers, you too, sweetheart; narrow mouth, petulant lower lip, nice to chew on, a lower lip as though filled with honey, bursting, ready for things to happen; a nose that threw the right sort of shadow, flaring nostrils, the acceptable words—aquiline, patrician, classic, allathat; cheekbones as stark and promontory as a spit of land after ten years of open ocean; cheekbones holding darkness like narrow shadows, sooty beneath the taut-fleshed bone-structure; amazing cheekbones, the whole face, really; an ancient kingdom's uptilted eyes, the touch of the Cherokee, eyes that looked out at you, as you looked in at them, like someone peering out of the keyhole as you peered in; actually, dirty eyes, they said you can get it.

Blonde hair, a great deal of it, wound and rolled and smoothed and flowing, in the old style, the pageboy thing men always admire; no tight little cap of slicked plastic; no ratted and teased Annapurna of bizarre coiffure; no ironed-flat discothèque hair like number 3 flat noodles. Hair, the way a man wants it, so he can dig his hands in at the base of the neck and pull all that face very close.

An operable woman, a working mechanism, a rigged and sudden machinery of softness and motivation.

Twenty-three, and determined as hell never to abide in that vale of poverty her mother had called purgatory for her entire life; snuffed out in a grease fire in the last trailer, somewhere in Arizona, thank God no more pleas for a little money from babygirl Maggie hustling drinks in a Los Angeles topless joint. (There ought to be some *remorse in there somewhere, for a Mommy gone where all the good grease-fire victims go. Look around, you'll find it.)*

Maggie.

Genetic freak. Mommy's Cherokee uptilted eye-shape, and Polack quickscrewing Daddy WithoutaName's blue as innocence color.

Blue-eyed Maggie, dyed blonde, alla that face, alla that leg, fifty bucks a night can get it and it sounds like it's having a climax.

Irish-innocent blue-eyed-innocent French-legged-innocent Maggie. Polack. Cherokee. Irish. All-woman and going on the market for this month's rent on the stucco pad, eighty bucks' worth of groceries, a couple months' worth for a Mustang, three appointments with the specialist in Beverly Hills about that shortness of breath after a night on the hustle bump the sticky thigh the disco lurch the gotcha sweat: woman minutes. Increments under the meat; perspiration purchases, yeah it does.

Maggie, Maggie, Maggie, pretty Maggie Moneyeyes, who came from Tucson and trailers and rheumatic fever and a surge to live that was all kaleidoscope frenzy of clawing scrabbling no-nonsense. If it took lying on one's back and making sounds like a panther in the desert, then one did it, because nothing, but nothing *was as bad as being dirt-poor, itchy-skinned, soiled-underwear, scuff-toed, hairy and ashamed lousy with the no-gots. Nothing!*

Maggie. Hooker. Hustler. Grabber. Swinger. If there's a buck in it, there's rhythm and the onomatopoeia is Maggie Maggie Maggie.

She who puts out. For a price, whatever that might be.

Maggie was dating Nuncio. He was Sicilian. He had dark eyes and an alligator-grain wallet with slip-in pockets for credit cards. He was a spender, a sport, a high-roller. They went to Vegas.

Maggie and the Sicilian. Her blue eyes and his slip-in pockets. But mostly her blue eyes.

The spinning reels behind the three long glass windows blurred, and Kostner knew there wasn't a chance. Two thousand dollar jackpot. Round and round, whirring. Three bells or two bells and a jackpot bar, get 18; three plums or two plums and a jackpot bar, get 14; three oranges or two oranges and a jac—

Ten, five, two bucks for a single cherry cluster in first position. Something . . . I'm drowning . . . something . . .

The whirring . . .

Round and round . . .

As something happened that was not considered in the pit-boss manual.

The reels whipped and snapped to a stop, clank clank clank, tight in place.

Three bars looked up at Kostner. But they did not say JACKPOT. They were three bars from which stared three blue eyes. Very blue, very immediate, very JACKPOT!!

Twenty silver dollars clattered into the payoff trough at the bottom of the machine. An orange light popped on in the casino cashier's cage, bright orange on the jackpot board. And the gong began clanging overhead.

The Slot Machine Floor Manager nodded once to the Pit Boss, who pursed his lips and started toward the seedy-looking man still standing with his hand on the slot's handle.

The token payment—twenty silver dollars—lay untouched in the payoff trough. The balance of the jackpot—one thousand nine-hundred and eighty dollars—would be paid manually by the casino cashier. And Kostner stood, dumbly, as the three blue eyes stared up at him.

There was a moment of idiotic disorientation, as Kostner stared back at the three blue eyes; a moment in which the slot machine's mechanisms registered to themselves; and the gong was clanging furiously.

All through the hotel's casino people turned from their games to stare. At the roulette tables the white-on-white players from Detroit and Cleveland pulled their watery eyes away from the clattering ball and stared down the line for a second, at the ratty-looking guy in front of the slot machine. From where they sat, they could not tell it was a two grand pot, and their rheumy eyes went back into billows of cigar smoke, and that little ball.

The blackjack hustlers turned momentarily, screwing around in their seats, and smiled. They were closer to the slot-players in temperament, but they knew the slots were a dodge to keep the old ladies busy, while the players worked toward their endless twenty-ones.

And the old dealer, who could no longer cut it at the fast-action boards, who had been put out to pasture by a grateful management, standing at the Wheel of Fortune near the entrance to the casino, even he paused in his zombie-murmuring ("Annnnother winner onna Wheel of Forchun!") to no one at all, and looked toward Kostner and that incredible gong-clanging. Then, in a moment, still with no players, he called *another* nonexistent winner.

Kostner heard the gong from far away. It had to mean he had won two thousand dollars, but that was impossible. He checked the payoff chart on the face of the machine. Three bars labeled JACKPOT meant JACKPOT. Two thousand dollars.

But these three bars did not say JACKPOT. They were three gray bars, rectangular in shape, with a blue eye directly in the center of each bar.

Blue eyes?

Somewhere, a connection was made, and electricity, a billion volts of electricity, were shot through Kostner. His hair stood on end, his fingertips bled raw, his eyes turned to jelly, and every fiber in his musculature became radioactive. Somewhere, out there, in a place that was not this place, Kostner had been inextricably bound to—to someone. Blue eyes?

The gong had faded out of his head, the constant noise level of the casino, chips chittering, people mumbling, dealers calling plays, it had all gone, and he was embedded in silence.

Tied to that someone else, out there somewhere, through those three blue eyes.

Then in an instant, it had passed, and he was alone again, as though released by a giant hand, the breath crushed out of him. He staggered up against the slot machine.

"You all right, fellah?"

A hand gripped him by the arm, steadied him. The gong was still clanging overhead somewhere, and he was breathless from a journey he had just taken. His eyes focused and he found himself looking at the stocky Pit Boss who had been on duty while he had been playing blackjack.

"Yeah . . . I'm okay, just a little dizzy is all."

"Sounds like you got yourself a big jackpot, fellah." The Pit Boss grinned; it was a leathery grin; something composed of stretched muscles and conditioned reflexes, totally mirthless.

"Yeah . . . great . . ." Kostner tried to grin back. But he was still shaking from that electrical absorption that had kidnapped him.

"Let me check it out," the Pit Boss was saying, edging around Kostner, and staring at the face of the slot machine. "Yeah, three jackpot bars, all right. You're a winner."

Then it dawned on Kostner! Two thousand dollars! He looked down at the slot machine and saw—

Three bars with the word JACKPOT on them. No blue eyes, just words that meant money. Kostner looked around frantically, was he losing his mind? *From somewhere, not in the casino, he heard a tinkle of rhodium-plated laughter.*

He scooped up the twenty silver dollars. The Pit Boss dropped another cartwheel into the Chief, and pulled the jackpot off. Then the Pit Boss walked him to the rear of the casino, talking to him in a muted, extremely polite tone of voice. At the cashier's window, the Pit Boss nodded to a weary-looking man at a huge Rolodex cardfile, checking credit ratings.

"Barney, jackpot on the cartwheel Chief; slot five-oh-oh-one-five." He grinned at Kostner, who tried to smile back. It was difficult. He felt stunned.

The cashier checked a payoff book for the correct amount to be drawn and leaned over the counter toward Kostner. "Check or cash, sir?"

Kostner felt buoyancy coming back to him. "Is the casino's check good?" They all three laughed at that. "A check's fine," Kostner said. The check was drawn, and the Check-Riter punched out the little bumps that said two thousand. "The twenty cartwheels are a gift," the cashier said, sliding the check through to Kostner.

He held it, looked at it, and still found it difficult to believe. Two grand, back on the golden road.

As he walked back through the casino with the Pit Boss, the stocky man asked pleasantly, "Well, what are you going to do with it?" Kostner had to think a moment. He didn't really have any plans. But then the sudden realization came to him: "I'm going to play that slot machine again." The Pit Boss smiled: a congenital sucker. He would put all twenty of those silver dollars back into the Chief, and then turn to the other games. Blackjack, roulette, faro, baccarat . . . in a few hours he would have redeposited the two grand with the hotel casino. It always happened.

He walked Kostner back to the slot machine, and patted him on the shoulder. "Lotsa luck, fellah."

As he turned away, Kostner slipped a silver dollar into the machine, and pulled the handle.

The Pit Boss had only taken five steps when he heard the incredible sound of the reels clicking to a stop, the clash of twenty token silver dollars hitting the payoff trough, and that goddamned gong went out of its mind again.

She had known that sonofabitch Nuncio was a perverted swine. A walking filth. A dungheap between his ears. Some kind of monster in nylon undershorts. There weren't many kinds of games Maggie hadn't played, but what that Sicilian de Sade wanted to do was outright vomity!

She nearly fainted when he suggested it. Her heart—which the Beverly Hills specialist had said she should not tax—began whumping frantically. "You pig!" she screamed. "You filthy dirty ugly pig you, Nuncio you pig!" She had bounded out of the bed and started to throw on clothes. She didn't even bother with a brassiere, pulling the poorboy sweater on over her thin breasts, still crimson with the touches and love-bites Nuncio had showered on them.

He sat up in the bed, a pathetic-looking little man, gray hair at the temples and no hair atall on top, and his eyes were moist. He was porcine, was indeed the swine she called him, but he was helpless before her. He was in love with his hooker, with the tart whom he was supporting. It had been the first time for the swine Nuncio, and he was helpless. Back in Detroit, had it been a floozy, a bimbo, a chippy broad, he would have gotten out of the double bed and rapped her around pretty good. But this Maggie, she tied him in knots. He had suggested . . . that, *what they should do together . . . because he was so consumed with her. But* she *was furious with* him. *It wasn't* that *bizarre an idea!*

"Gimme a chanct'a talk t'ya, honey . . . Maggie . . ."

"You filthy pig, Nuncio! Give me some money, I'm going down to the casino, and I don't want to see your filthy pig face for the rest of the day, remember that!"

And she had gone in his wallet and pants, and taken eight hundred and sixteen dollars, while he watched. He was helpless before her. She was something stolen from a world he knew only as "class" and she could do what she wanted with him.

Genetic freak Maggie, blue-eyed posing mannequin Maggie, pretty Maggie Moneyeyes, who was one-half Cherokee and one-half a buncha other things, had absorbed her lessons well. She was the very model of a "class broad."

"Not for the rest of the day, do you understand?" She stared at him till he nodded; then she went downstairs, furious, to fret and gamble and wonder about nothing but years of herself.

Men stared after her as she walked. She carried herself like a challenge, the way a squire carried a pennon, the way a prize bitch carried herself in the judge's ring. Born to the blue. The wonders of mimicry and desire.

Maggie had no lust for gambling, none whatever. She merely wanted to taste the fury of her relationship with the swine Sicilian, her need for solidity in a life built on the edge of the slide area, the senselessness of being here in

Las Vegas when she could be back in Beverly Hills. She grew angrier and more ill at the thought of Nuncio upstairs in the room, taking another shower. She bathed three times a day. But it was different with him. He knew she resented his smell; he had the soft odor of wet fur sometimes, and she had told him about it. Now he bathed constantly, and hated it. He was a foreigner to the bath. His life had been marked by various kinds of filths, and baths for him now were more of an obscenity than dirt could ever have been. For her, bathing was different. It was a necessity. She had to keep the patina of the world off her, had to remain clean and smooth and white. A presentation, not an object of flesh and hair. A chromium instrument, something never pitted by rust and corrosion.

When she was touched by them, by any one of them, by the men, by all the Nuncios, they left little pitholes of bloody rust on her white, permanent flesh; cobwebs, sooty stains. She had *to bathe. Often.*

She strolled down between the tables and slots, carrying eight hundred and sixteen dollars. Eight one hundred dollar bills and sixteen dollars in ones.

At the change booth she got cartwheels for the sixteen ones. The Chief waited. It was her baby. She played it to infuriate the Sicilian. He had told her to play the nickel slots, the quarter or dime slots, but she always infuriated him by blowing fifty or a hundred dollars in ten minutes, one coin after another, in the big Chief.

She faced the machine squarely, and put in the first silver dollar. She pulled the handle that swine Nuncio. Another dollar, pulled the handle how long does this go on? The reels cycled and spun and whirled and whipped in a blurringspinning metalhumming overandoverandover as Maggie blue-eyed Maggie hated and hated and thought of hate and all the days and nights of swine behind her and ahead of her and if only she had all the money in this room in this casino in this hotel in this town right now this very instant just an instant thisinstant it would be enough to whirring and humming and spinning and overandoverandoverandover and she would be free free free and all the world would never touch her body again the swine would never touch her white flesh again and then suddenly as dollarafterdollarafterdollar went aroundaroundaround hummmmming in reels of cherries and bells and bars and plums and oranges there was suddenly painpainpain a SHARP pain!pain!pain! in her chest, her heart, her center, a needle, a lancet, a burning, a pillar of flame that was purest pure purer PAIN!

Maggie, pretty Maggie Moneyeyes, who wanted all that money in that cartwheel Chief slot machine, Maggie who had come from filth and rheumatic fever, who had come all the way to three baths a day and a specialist in Very Expensive Beverly Hills, that *Maggie suddenly had a seizure, a flutter, a slam of a coronary thrombosis and fell instantly dead on the floor of the casino. Dead.*

One instant she had been holding the handle of the slot machine, willing her entire being, all that hatred for all the swine she had ever rolled with, willing every fiber of every cell of every chromosome into that machine, wanting to suck out every silver vapor within its belly, and the next *instant—so close they might have been the same—her heart exploded and killed her and she slipped to the floor . . . still touching the Chief.*

On the floor.
Dead.
Struck dead.
Liar. All the lies that were her life.
Dead on a floor.

[A moment out of time ■ lights whirling and spinning in a cotton candy universe ■ down a bottomless funnel roundly sectioned like a goat's horn ■ a cornucopia that rose up cuculiform smooth and slick as a worm belly ■ endless nights that pealed ebony funeral bells ■ out of fog ■ out of weightlessness ■ suddenly total cellular knowledge ■ memory running backward ■ gibbering spastic blindness ■ a soundless owl of frenzy trapped in a cave of prisms ■ sand endlessly draining down ■ billows of forever ■ edges of the world as they splintered ■ foam rising drowning from inside ■ the smell of rust ■ rough green corners that burn ■ memory the gibbering spastic blind memory ■ seven rushing vacuums of nothing ■ yellow ■ pinpoints cast in amber straining and elongating running like live wax ■ chill fevers ■ overhead the odor of stop ■ this is the stopover before hell or heaven ■ this is limbo ■ trapped and doomed alone in a mist-eaten nowhere ■ a soundless screaming a soundless whirring a soundless spinning spinning spinning ■ spinning ■ spinning ■ spinning ■ spinninggggggggggg]

Maggie had wanted all the silver in the machine. She had died, willing herself into the machine. Now, looking out from within, from inside the limbo that had become her own purgatory, Maggie was trapped, in the oiled and anodized interior of the silver dollar slot machine. The prison of her final desires, where she had wanted to be, completely trapped in that last instant of life between life/death. Maggie, gone inside, all soul now, trapped for all eternity in the cage soul of the machine. Limbo. Trapped. Trapped.

"I hope you don't mind if I call over one of the slot men," the Slot Machine Floor Manager was saying, from a far distance. He was in his late fifties, a velvet-voiced man whose eyes held nothing of light and certainly nothing of kindness. He had stopped the Pit Boss as the stocky man had turned in mid-step to return to Kostner and the jackpotted machine; he had taken the walk himself. "We have to make sure, you know how it is: somebody didn't fool with the slot, you know, maybe it's outta whack or something, you know."

He lifted his left hand and there was a clicker in it, the kind children use at Halloween. He clicked half a dozen times, like a rabid cricket, and there was a scurrying in the pit between the tables.

Kostner was only faintly aware of what was happening. Instead of being totally awake, feeling the surge of adrenaline through his veins, the feeling any gambler gets when he is ahead of the game, a kind of desperate urgency when he has hit it for a boodle, he was numb, partaking of the action around him only as much as a drinking glass involves itself in the alcoholic's drunken binge.

All color and sound had been leached out of him.

A tired-looking, resigned-weary man wearing a gray porter's jacket, as gray as his hair, as gray as his indoor skin, came to them, carrying a leather wrap-up of tools. The slot repairman studied the machine, turning the pressed steel body around on its stand, studying the back. He used a key on the back door and for an instant Kostner had a view of gears, springs, armatures and the clock that ran the slot mechanism. The repairman nodded silently over it, closed and relocked it, turned it around again and studied the face of the machine.

"Nobody's been spooning it," he said, and went away.

Kostner stared at the Floor Manager.

"Gaffing. That's what he meant. Spooning's another word for it. Some guys use a little piece of plastic, or a wire, shove it down through the escalator, it kicks the machine. Nobody thought that's what happened here, but you know, we have to make sure, two grand is a big payoff, and twice . . . well, you know, I'm sure you'll understand. If a guy was doing it with a boomerang—"

Kostner raised an eyebrow.

"—uh, yeah, a boomerang, it's another way to spoon the machine. But we just wanted to make a little check, and now everybody's satisfied, so if you'll just come back to the casino cashier with me—"

And they paid him off again.

So he went back to the slot machine, and stood before it for a long time, staring at it. The change girls and the dealers going off-duty, the little old ladies with their canvas work gloves worn to avoid calluses when pulling the slot handles, the men's room attendant on his way up front to get more matchbooks, the floral tourists, the idle observers, the hard drinkers, the sweepers, the busboys, the gamblers with poached-egg eyes who had been up all night, the showgirls with massive breasts and diminutive sugar daddies, all of them conjectured mentally about the beat-up walker who was staring at the silver dollar Chief. He did not move, merely stared at the machine . . . and they wondered.

The machine was staring back at Kostner.

Three blue eyes.

The electric current had sparked through him again, as the machine had clocked down and the eyes turned up a second time, as he had *won* a second time. But this time he knew there was something more than luck involved, for no one else had seen those three blue eyes.

So now he stood before the machine, waiting. It spoke to him. Inside his skull, where no one had ever lived but himself, now someone else moved and spoke to him. A girl. A beautiful girl. Her name was Maggie, and she spoke to him.

I've been waiting for you. A long time, I've been waiting for you, Kostner. Why do you think you hit the jackpot? Because I've been waiting for you, and I want you. You'll win all the jackpots. Because I want you, I need you. Love me, I'm Maggie, I'm so alone, love me.

Kostner had been staring at the slot machine for a very long time, and his weary brown eyes had seemed to be locked to the blue eyes on the jackpot bars. But he knew no one else could see the blue eyes, and no one else could hear the voice, and no one else knew about Maggie.

He was the universe to her. Everything to her.

He thumbed in another silver dollar, and the Pit Boss watched, the slot machine repairman watched, the Slot Machine Floor Manager watched, three change girls watched, and a pack of unidentified players watched, some from their seats.

The reels whirled, the handle snapped back, and in a second they flipped down to a halt, twenty silver dollars tokened themselves into the payoff trough and a woman at one of the crap tables belched a fragment of hysterical laughter.

And the gong went insane again.

The Floor Manager came over and said, very softly, "Mr. Kostner, it'll take us about fifteen minutes to pull this machine and check it out. I'm sure you understand." As two slot repairmen came out of the back, hauled the Chief off its stand, and took it into the repair room at the rear of the casino.

While they waited, the Floor Manager regaled Kostner with stories of spooners who had used intricate magnets inside their clothes, of boomerang men who had attached their plastic implements under their sleeves so they could be extended on spring-loaded clips, of cheaters who had come equipped with tiny electric drills in their hands and wires that slipped into the tiny drilled holes. And he kept saying he knew Kostner would understand.

But Kostner knew the Floor Manager would not understand.

When they brought the Chief back, one of the repairmen nodded assuredly. "Nothing wrong with it. Works perfectly. Nobody's been boomin' it."

But the blue eyes were gone on the jackpot bars.

Kostner knew they would return.

They paid him off again.

He returned and played again. And again. And again. They put a "spotter" on him. He won again. And again. And again. The crowd had grown to massive proportions. Word had spread like the silent communications of the telegraph vine, up and down the Strip, all the way to downtown Vegas and the sidewalk casinos where they played night and day every day of the year, and the crowd surged in a tide toward the hotel, and the casino, and the seedy-looking walker with his weary brown eyes. The crowd moved to him inexorably, drawn like lemmings by the odor of the luck that rose from him like musky electrical cracklings. And he won. Again and again. Thirty-eight thousand dollars. And the three blue eyes continued to stare up at him. Her lover was winning. Maggie and her Moneyeyes.

Finally, the casino decided to speak to Kostner. They pulled the Chief for fifteen minutes, for a supplemental check by experts from the slot machine company in downtown Vegas, and while they were checking it, they asked Kostner to come to the main office of the hotel.

The owner was there. His face seemed faintly familiar to Kostner. Had he seen it on television? The newspapers?

"Mr. Kostner, my name is Jules Hartshorn."

"I'm pleased to meet you."

"Quite a string of luck you're having out there."

"It's been a long time coming."

"You realize, this sort of luck is impossible."

"I'm compelled to believe it, Mr. Hartshorn."

"Um. As am I. It's happening to my casino. But we're thoroughly convinced of one of two possibilities, Mr. Kostner; one, either the machine is inoperable in a way we can't detect; or two, you are the cleverest spooner we've ever had in here."

"I'm not cheating."

"As you can see, Mr. Kostner, I'm smiling. The reason I'm smiling is at your naïveté in believing I would take your word for it. I'm perfectly happy to nod politely and say of course you aren't cheating. But no one can win thirty-eight thousand dollars on nineteen straight jackpots off one slot machine; it doesn't even have mathematical odds against its happening, Mr. Kostner. It's on a cosmic scale of improbability with three dark planets crashing into our sun within the next twenty minutes. It's on a par with the Pentagon, the Forbidden City and the Kremlin all three pushing the red button at the same microsecond. It's an impossibility, Mr. Kostner. An impossibility that's happening to me."

"I'm sorry."

"Not really."

"No, not really. I can use the money."

"For what, exactly, Mr. Kostner?"

"I hadn't thought about it, really."

"I see. Well, Mr. Kostner, let's look at it this way. I can't stop you from playing, and if you continue to win, I'll be required to pay off. And no stubble-chinned thugs will be waiting in an alley to jackroll you and take the money. The checks will be honored. The best I can hope for, Mr. Kostner, is the attendant publicity. Right now, every high-roller in Vegas is in that casino, waiting for you to drop cartwheels into that machine. It won't make up for what I'm losing, if you continue the way you've been; but it'll help. Every sucker in town likes to rub up next to luck. All I ask is that you cooperate a little."

"The least I can do, considering your generosity."

"An attempt at humor."

"I'm sorry. What is it you'd like me to do?"

"Get about ten hours' sleep."

"While you pull the slot and have it worked over thoroughly?"

"Yes."

"If I wanted to keep winning, that might be a pretty stupid move on my part. You might change the thingamajig inside so I couldn't win if I put back every dollar of that thirty-eight grand."

"We're licensed by the state of Nevada, Mr. Kostner."

"I come from a good family, too, and take a look at me. I'm a bum with thirty-eight thousand dollars in my pocket."

"Nothing will be done to that slot machine, Kostner."

"Then why pull it for ten hours?"

"To work it over thoroughly in the shop. If something as undetectable as metal fatigue or a worn escalator tooth or—we want to make sure this doesn't happen with other machines. And the extra time will get the word around town; we can use the crowd. Some of those tourists will stick to our fingers, and it'll help defray the expense of having you break the bank at this casino—on a slot machine."

"I have to take your word."

"This hotel will be in business long after you're gone, Kostner."

"Not if I keep winning."

Hartshorn's smile was a stricture. "A good point."

"So it isn't much of an argument."

"It's the only one I have. If you want to get back out on that floor, I can't stop you."

"No Mafia hoods ventilate me later?"

"I beg your pardon?"

"I said: no Maf—"

"You have a picturesque manner of speaking. In point of fact, I haven't the faintest idea what you're talking about."

"I'm sure you haven't."

"You've got to stop reading *The National Enquirer.* This is a legally run business. I'm merely asking a favor."

"Okay, Mr. Hartshorn, I've been three days without any sleep. Ten hours will do me a world of good."

"I'll have the desk clerk find you a quiet room on the top floor. And thank you, Mr. Kostner."

"Think nothing of it."

"I'm afraid that will be impossible."

"A lot of impossible things are happening lately."

He turned to go, as Hartshorn lit a cigarette.

"Oh, by the way, Mr. Kostner?"

Kostner stopped and half-turned. "Yes?"

His eyes were getting difficult to focus. There was a ringing in his ears. Hartshorn seemed to waver at the edge of his vision like heat lightning across a prairie. Like memories of things Kostner had come across the country to forget. Like the whimpering and pleading that kept tugging at the cells of his brain. The voice of Maggie. Still back in there, saying . . . things . . .

They'll try to keep you from me.

All he could think about was the ten hours of sleep he had been promised. Suddenly it was more important than the money, than forgetting, than anything. Hartshorn was talking, was saying things, but Kostner could not hear him. It was as if he had turned off the sound and saw only the silent rubbery movement of Hartshorn's lips. He shook his head trying to clear it.

There were half a dozen Hartshorns all melting into and out of one another. And the voice of Maggie.

I'm warm here, and alone. I could be good to you, if you can come to me. Please come, please hurry.

"Mr. Kostner?"

Hartshorn's voice came draining down through exhaustion as thick as velvet flocking. Kostner tried to focus again. His extremely weary brown eyes began to track.

"Did you know about that slot machine?" Hartshorn was saying. "A peculiar thing happened with it about six weeks ago."

"What was that?"

"A girl died playing it. She had a heart attack, a seizure while she was pulling the handle, and died right out there on the floor."

Kostner was silent for a moment. He wanted desperately to ask Hartshorn what color the dead girl's eyes had been, but he was afraid the owner would say blue.

He paused with his hand on the office door. "Seems as though you've had nothing but a streak of bad luck on that machine."

Hartshorn smiled an enigmatic smile. "It might not change for a while, either."

Kostner felt his jaw muscles tighten. "Meaning I might die, too, and wouldn't *that* be bad luck."

Hartshorn's smile became hieroglyphic, permanent, stamped on him forever. "Sleep tight, Mr. Kostner."

In a dream, she came to him. Long, smooth thighs and soft golden down on her arms; blue eyes deep as the past, misted with a fine scintillance like lavender spiderwebs; taut body that was the only body Woman had ever had, from the very first. Maggie came to him.

Hello, I've been traveling a long time.

"Who are you?" Kostner asked, wonderingly. He was standing on a chilly plain, or was it a plateau? The wind curled around them both, or was it only around him? She was exquisite, and he saw her clearly, or was it through a mist? Her voice was deep and resonant, or was it light and warm as night-blooming jasmine?

I'm Maggie. I love you. I've waited for you.

"You have blue eyes."

Yes. *With love.*

"You're very beautiful."

Thank you. *With female amusement.*

"But why me? Why let it happen to me? Are you the girl who—are you the one that was sick—the one who—?"

I'm Maggie. And you, I picked you, because you need me. You've needed someone for a long long time.

Then it unrolled for Kostner. The past unrolled and he saw who he was. He saw himself alone. Always alone. As a child, born to kind and warm parents who hadn't the vaguest notion of who he was, what he wanted to be, where his talents lay. So he had run off, when he was in his teens, and alone always alone on the road. For years and months and days and hours, with no one. Casual friendships, based on food, or sex, or artificial similarities. But no one to whom he could cleave, and cling, and belong. It was that way till Susie, and with her he had found light. He had discovered the scents and aromas of a spring that was eternally one day away. He had laughed, really laughed, and known with her it would at last be all right. So he had poured all of himself into her, giving her everything; all his hopes, his secret thoughts, his tender dreams; and she had taken them, taken him, all of him, and he had known for the first time what it was to have a place to live, to have a home in someone's heart. It was all the silly and gentle things he laughed at in other people, but for him it was breathing deeply of wonder.

He had stayed with her for a long time, and had supported her, supported her son from the first marrige; the marriage Susie never talked about. And then one day, he had come back, as Susie had always known he would. He was a dark creature of ruthless habits and vicious nature, but she had been his woman, all along, and Kostner realized he had been used as a stop-gap, as a bill-payer till her wandering terror came home to nest. Then she had asked him to leave. Broke, and tapped out in all the silent inner ways a man can be drained, he had left, without even a fight, for all the fight had been leached out of him. He had left, and wandered west, and finally come to Las Vegas, where he had hit bottom. And found Maggie. In a dream, with blue eyes, he had found Maggie.

I want you to belong to me. I love you. *Her truth was vibrant in Kostner's mind. She was his, at last someone who was special, was his.*

"Can I trust you? I've never been able to trust anyone before. Women, never. But I need someone. I really need someone."

It's me, always. Forever. You can trust me.

And she came to him, fully. Her body was a declaration of truth and trust such as no other Kostner had ever known before. She met him on a windswept plain of thought, and he made love to her more completely than he had known any passion before. She joined with him, entered him, mingled with his blood and his thought and his frustration, and he came away clean, filled with glory.

"Yes, I can trust you, I want you, I'm yours," he whispered to her, when they lay side by side in a dream nowhere of mist and soundlessness. "I'm yours."

She smiled, a woman's smile of belief in her man; a smile of trust and deliverance. And Kostner woke up.

The Chief was back on its stand, and the crowd had been penned back by velvet ropes. Several people had played the machine, but there had been no jackpots.

Now Kostner came into the casino, and the "spotters" got themselves ready. While Kostner had slept, they had gone through his clothes, searching for wires, for gaffs, for spoons or boomerangs. Nothing.

Now he walked straight to the Chief, and stared at it.

Hartshorn was there. "You look tired," he said gently to Kostner, studying the man's weary brown eyes.

"I am, a little." Kostner tried a smile; it didn't work. "I had a funny dream."

"Oh?"

"Yeah . . . about a girl . . ." He let it die off.

Hartshorn's smile was understanding. Pitying, empathic and understanding. "There are lots of girls in this town. You shouldn't have any trouble finding one with your winnings."

Kostner nodded, and slipped his first silver dollar into the slot. He pulled the handle. The reels spun with a ferocity Kostner had not heard before and suddenly everything went whipping slantwise as he felt a wrenching of pure flame in his stomach, as his head was snapped on its spindly neck, as the lining behind his eyes was burned out. There was a terrible shriek, of tortured metal, of an express train ripping the air with its passage, of a hundred small animals being gutted and torn to shreds, of incredible pain, of night winds that tore the tops off mountains of lava. And a keening whine of a voice that wailed and wailed and wailed as it went away from there in blinding light—

Free! Free! Heaven or Hell it doesn't matter! Free!

The sound of a soul released from an eternal prison, a genie freed from a dark bottle. And in that instant of damp soundless nothingness, Kostner saw the reels snap and clock down for the final time:

One, two, three. Blue eyes.

But he would never cash his checks.

The crowd screamed through one voice as he fell sidewise and lay on his face. The final loneliness . . .

The Chief was pulled. Bad luck. Too many gamblers resented its very presence in the casino. So it was pulled. And returned to the company, with explicit instructions it was to be melted down to slag. And not till it was in the hands of the ladle foreman, who was ready to dump it into the slag furnace, did anyone remark on the final tally the Chief had clocked.

"Look at that, ain't that weird," said the ladle foreman to his bucket man. He pointed to the three glass windows.

"Never saw jackpot bars like that before," the bucket man agreed. "Three eyes. Must be an old machine."

"Yeah, some of these old games go way back," the foreman said, hoisting the slot machine onto the conveyor track leading to the slag furnace. "Three eyes, huh. How about that. Three brown eyes." And he threw the knife-switch that sent the Chief down the track, to puddle in the roaring inferno of the furnace.

Three brown *eyes.*

Three brown eyes that looked very very weary. That looked very very trapped. That looked very very betrayed. Some of these old games go way back.

A Boy and His Dog

I

I was out with Blood, my dog. It was his week for annoying me; he kept calling me Albert. He thought that was pretty damned funny. Payson Terhune: ha ha.

I'd caught a couple of water rats for him, the big green and ocher ones, and someone's manicured poodle, lost off a leash in one of the downunders.

He'd eaten pretty good, but he was cranky. "Come on, son of a bitch," I demanded, "find me a piece of ass."

Blood just chuckled, deep in his dog-throat. "You're funny when you get horny," he said.

Maybe funny enough to kick him upside his sphincter asshole, that refugee from a dingo-heap.

"Find! I ain't kidding!"

"For shame, Albert. After all I've taught you. Not 'I *ain't* kidding'. I'm *not* kidding."

He knew I'd reached the edge of my patience. Sullenly, he started casting. He sat down on the crumbled remains of the curb, and his eyelids flickered and closed, and his hairy body tensed. After a while he settled down on his front paws, and scraped them forward till he was lying flat, his shaggy head on the outstretched paws. The tenseness left him and he began trembling, almost the way he trembled just preparatory to scratching a flea. It went on that way for almost a quarter of an hour, and finally he rolled over and lay on his back, his naked belly toward the night sky, his front paws folded mantislike, his hind legs extended and open. "I'm sorry," he said. "There's nothing."

I could have gotten mad and booted him, but I knew he had tried. I wasn't happy about it, I really wanted to get laid, but what could I do? "Okay," I said, with resignation, "forget it."

He kicked himself onto his side and quickly got up.

"What do you want to do?" he asked.

"Not much we *can* do, is there?" I was more than a little sarcastic. He sat down again, at my feet, insolently humble.

I leaned against the melted stub of a lamppost, and thought about girls. It was painful. "We can always go to a show," I said. Blood looked around the street, at the pools of shadow lying in the weed-overgrown craters, and didn't say anything. The whelp was waiting for me to say okay, let's go. He liked movies as much as I did.

"Okay, let's go."

He got up and followed me, his tongue hanging, panting with happiness. Go ahead and laugh, you eggsucker. No popcorn for *you*!

Our Gang was a roverpak that had never been able to cut it simply foraging, so they'd opted for comfort and gone a smart way to getting it. They were movie-oriented kids, and they'd taken over the turf where the Metropole Theater was located. No one tried to bust their turf, because we all needed the movies, and as long as Our Gang had access to films, and did a better job of keeping the films going, they provided a service, even for solos like me and Blood. *Especially* for solos like us.

They made me check my .45 and the Browning .22 long at the door. There was a little alcove right beside the ticket booth. I bought my tickets first; it cost me a can of Oscar Mayer Philadelphia Scrapple for me, and a tin of sardines for Blood. Then the Our Gang guards with the bren guns motioned me over to the alcove and I checked my heat. I saw water leaking from a broken pipe in the ceiling and I told the checker, a kid with big leathery warts all over his face and lips, to move my weapons where it was dry. He ignored me. "Hey you! Motherfuckin' toad, move my stuff over the other side . . . it goes to rust fast . . . an' it picks up any spots, man, I'll break your bones!"

He started to give me jaw about it, looked at the guards with the brens, knew if they tossed me out I'd lose my price of admission whether I went in or not, but they weren't looking for any action, probably understrength, and gave him the nod to let it pass, to do what I said. So the toad moved my Browning to the other end of the gun rack, and pegged my .45 under it.

Blood and me went into the theater.

"I want popcorn."

"Forget it."

"Come on, Albert. Buy me popcorn."

"I'm tapped out. You can live without popcorn."

"You're just being a shit."

I shrugged: sue me.

We went in. The place was jammed. I was glad the guards hadn't tried to take anything but guns. My spike and knife felt reassuring, lying-up in their oiled sheaths at the back of my neck. Blood found two together, and we moved into the row, stepping on feet. Someone cursed and I ignored him. A Doberman growled. Blood's fur stirred, but he let it pass. There was always *some* hardcase on the muscle, even on neutral ground like the Metropole.

(I heard once about a get-it-on they'd had at the old Loew's Granada, on the South Side. Wound up with ten or twelve rovers and their mutts dead, the theater burned down and a couple of good Cagney films lost in the fire. After that was when the roverpaks had got up the agreement that movie houses were sanctuaries. It was better now, but there was always somebody too messed in the mind to come soft.)

It was a triple feature. *Raw Deal* with Dennis O'Keefe, Claire Trevor, Raymond Burr and Marsha Hunt was the oldest of the three. It'd been made in 1948, eighty-six years ago; god only knows how the damn thing'd hung together all that time; it slipped sprockets and they had to stop the movie all the time to re-thread it. But it was a good movie. About this solo who'd been japped by his roverpak and was out to get revenge. Gangsters, mobs, a lot of punching and fighting. Real good.

The middle flick was a thing made during the Third War, in '92, twenty-seven years before I was even born, thing called *Smell of a Chink*. It was mostly gut-spilling and some nice hand-to-hand. Beautiful scene of skirmisher greyhounds equipped with napalm throwers, jellyburning a Chink town. Blood dug it, even though we'd seen this flick before. He had some kind of phony shuck going that these were ancestors of his, and *he* knew and *I* knew he was making it up.

"Wanna burn a baby, hero?" I whispered to him. He got the barb and just shifted in his seat, didn't say a thing, kept looking pleased as the dogs worked their way through the town. I was bored stiff.

I was waiting for the main feature.

Finally it came on. It was a beauty, a beaver flick made in the late 1970s. It was called *Big Black Leather Splits*. Started right out very good. These two blondes in black leather corsets and boots laced all the way up to their crotches, with whips and masks, got this skinny guy down and one of the chicks sat on his face while the other one went down on him. It got really hairy after that.

All around me there were solos playing with themselves. I was about to jog it a little myself when Blood leaned across and said, real soft, the way he does when he's onto something unusually smelly, "There's a chick in here."

"You're nuts," I said.

"I tell you I smell her. She's in here, man."

Without being conspicuous, I looked around. Almost every seat in the theater was taken with solos or their dogs. If a chick had slipped in there'd have been a riot. She'd have been ripped to pieces before any single guy could have gotten into her. "Where?" I asked, softly. All around me, the solos were beating off, moaning as the blondes took off their masks and one of them worked the skinny guy with a big wooden ram strapped around her hips.

"Give me a minute," Blood said. He was really concentrating. His body was tense as a wire. His eyes were closed, his muzzle quivering. I let him work.

It was possible. Just maybe possible. I knew that they made really dumb flicks in the downunders, the kind of crap they'd made back in the 1930s and '40s, real clean stuff with even married people sleeping in twin beds. Myrna Loy and George Brent kind of flicks. And I knew that once in a while a chick from one of the really strict middle-class downunders would cumup, to see what a hairy flick was like. I'd heard about it, but it'd never happened in any theater *I'd* ever been in.

And the chances of it happening in the Metropole, particularly, were slim. There was a lot of twisty trade came to the Metropole. Now, understand, I'm not specially prejudiced against guys corning one another . . . hell, I can understand it. There just aren't enough chicks anywhere. But I can't cut the jockey-and-boxer scene because it gets some weak little boxer hanging on you, getting jealous, you have to hunt for him and all he thinks he has to do is bare his ass to get all the work done for him. It's as bad as having a chick dragging along behind. Made for a lot of bad blood and fights in the bigger roverpaks, too. So I just never swung that way. Well, not *never,* but not for a long time.

So with all the twisties in the Metropole, I didn't think a chick would chance it. Be a toss-up who'd tear her apart first: the boxers or the straights.

And if she *was* here, why couldn't any of the other dogs smell her . . . ?

"Third row in front of us," Blood said. "Aisle seat. Dressed like a solo."

"How's come *you* can whiff her and no other dog's caught her?"

"You forget who I am, Albert."

"I didn't forget, I just don't believe it."

Actually, bottom-line, I guess I *did* believe it. When you'd been as dumb as I'd been and a dog like Blood'd taught me so much, a guy came to believe *everything* he said. You don't argue with your teacher.

Not when he'd taught you how to read and write and add and

subtract and everything else they used to know that meant you were smart (but doesn't mean much of anything now, except it's good to know it, I guess).

(The reading's a pretty good thing. It comes in handy when you can find some canned goods someplace, like in a bombed-out supermarket; makes it easier to pick out stuff you like when the pictures are gone off the labels. Couple of times the reading stopped me from taking canned beets. Shit, I *hate* beets!)

So I guess I *did* believe why he could whiff a maybe chick in there, and no other mutt could. He'd told me all about *that* a million times. It was his favorite story. History he called it. Christ, I'm not *that* dumb! I knew what history was. That was all the stuff that happened before now.

But I liked hearing history straight from Blood, instead of him making me read one of those crummy books he was always dragging in. And *that* particular history was all about him, so he laid it on me over and over, till I knew it by heart . . . no, the word was *rote*. Not *wrote*, like writing, that was something else. I knew it by rote, like it means you got it word-for-word.

And when a mutt teaches you everything you know, and he tells you something rote, I guess finally you *do* believe it. Except I'd never let that leg-lifter know it.

II

What he'd told me rote was:

Over sixty-five years ago, in Los Angeles, before the Third War even got going completely, there was a man named Buesing who lived in Cerritos. He raised dogs as watchmen and sentries and attackers. Dobermans, Danes, schnauzers and Japanese akitas. He had one four-year-old German shepherd bitch named Ginger. She worked for the Los Angeles Police Department's narcotics division. She could smell out marijuana. No matter how well it was hidden. They ran a test on her: there were 25,000 boxes in an auto parts warehouse. Five of them had been planted with marijuana sealed in cellophane, wrapped in tin foil and heavy brown paper, and finally hidden in three separate sealed cartons. Within seven minutes Ginger found all five packages. At the same time that Ginger was working, ninety-two miles farther north, in Santa Barbara, cetologists had drawn and amplified dolphin spinal fluid and injected it into Chacma baboons and dogs. Altering surgery and grafting had been done. The first successful product of this cetacean experimentation had been a two-year-old male Puli named Ahbhu, who had communicated sense-impressions telepathically. Cross-breeding and continued experimentation had produced the first skirmisher dogs, just in time for the Third War. Telepathic over short distances, easily trained, able to track gasoline or troops or poison gas or radiation when linked with their human controllers, they had become the shock commandos of a new kind of war. The selective traits had bred true. Dobermans, greyhounds, akitas, pulis and schnauzers had become steadily more telepathic.

Ginger and Ahbhu had been Blood's ancestors.

He had told me so, a thousand times. Had told me the story just that way, in just those words, a thousand times, as it had been told to him. I'd never believed him till now.

Maybe the little bastard *was* special.

I checked out the solo scrunched down in the aisle seat three rows ahead of me. I couldn't tell a damned thing. The solo had his (her?) cap pulled way down, fleece jacket pulled way up.

"Are you sure?"

"As sure as I can be. It's a girl."

"If it is, she's playing with herself just like a guy."

Blood snickered. "Surprise," he said sarcastically.

The mystery solo sat through *Raw Deal* again. It made sense, if that was a girl. Most of the solos and all of the members of roverpaks left after the beaver flick. The theater didn't fill up much more, it gave the streets time to empty, he/she could make his/her way back to wherever he/she had come from. I sat through *Raw Deal* again myself. Blood went to sleep.

When the mystery solo got up, I gave him/her time to get weapons if any'd been checked, and started away. Then I pulled Blood's big shaggy ear and said, "Let's do it." He slouched after me, up the aisle.

I got my guns and checked the street. Empty.

"Okay, nose," I said, "where'd he go?"

"Her. To the right."

I started off, loading the Browning from my bandolier. I still didn't see anyone moving among the bombed-out shells of the buildings. This section of the city was crummy, really bad shape. But then, with Our Gang running the Metropole, they didn't have to repair anything else to get their livelihood. It was ironic; the Dragons had to keep an entire power plant going to get tribute from the other roverpaks; Ted's Bunch had to mind the reservoir; the Bastinados worked like fieldhands in the marijuana gardens; the Barbados Blacks lost a couple of dozen members every year cleaning out the radiation pits all over the city; and Our Gang only had to run that movie house.

Whoever their leader had been, however many years ago it had been that the roverpaks had started forming out of foraging solos, I had to give it to him: he'd been a flinty sharp mother. He knew what services to deal in.

"She turned off here," Blood said.

I followed him as he began loping, toward the edge of the city and the bluish-green radiation that still flickered from the hills. I knew he was right, then. The only things out here were screamers and the access dropshaft to the downunder. It was a girl, all right.

The cheeks of my ass tightened as I thought about it. I was going to get laid. It had been almost a month, since Blood had whiffed that solo chick in the basement of the Market Basket. She'd been filthy, and I'd gotten the crabs from her, but she'd been a woman, all right, and once I'd tied her down and clubbed her a couple of times she'd been pretty good. She'd liked it, too, even if she did spit on me and tell me she'd kill me if she ever got loose. I left her tied up, just to be sure. She wasn't there when I went back to look, week before last.

"Watch out," Blood said, dodging around a crater almost invisible against the surrounding shadows. Something stirred in the crater.

Trekking across the nomansland I realized why it was that all but a handful of solos or members of roverpaks were guys. The War had killed off most of the girls, and that was the way it always was in wars . . . at least that's what Blood told me. The things getting born were seldom male *or* female, and had to be smashed against a wall as soon as they were pulled out of the mother.

The few chicks who hadn't gone downunder with the middle-classers were hard, solitary bitches like the one in the Market Basket; tough and stringy and just as likely to cut off your meat with a razor blade once they let you get in. Scuffing for a piece of ass had gotten harder and harder, the older I'd gotten.

But every once in a while a chick got tired of being roverpak property, or a raid was got-up by five or six roverpaks and some unsuspecting downunder was taken, or—like this time, yeah—some middle-class chick from a downunder got hot pants to find out what a beaver flick looked like, and cumup.

I was going to get laid. Oh boy, I couldn't wait!

III

Out here it was nothing but empty corpses of blasted buildings. One entire block had been stomped flat, like a steel press had come down from Heaven and given one solid wham! and everything was powder under it. The chick was scared and skittish, I could see that. She moved erratically, looking back over her shoulder and to either side. She knew she was in dangerous country. Man, if she'd only known *how* dangerous.

There was one building standing all alone at the end of the smash-flat block, like it had been missed and chance let it stay. She ducked inside, and a minute later I saw a bobbing light. Flashlight? Maybe.

Blood and I crossed the street and came up into the blackness surrounding the building. It was what was left of a YMCA.

That meant "Young Men's Christian Association." Blood had taught me to read.

So what the hell was a young men's christian association? Sometimes being able to read makes more questions than if you were stupid.

I didn't want her getting out; inside there was as good a place to screw her as any, so I put Blood on guard right beside the steps leading up into the shell, and I went around the back. All the doors and windows had been blown out, of course. It wasn't no big trick getting in. I pulled myself up to the ledge of a window, and dropped down inside. Dark inside. No noise, except the sound of her, moving around on the other side of the old YMCA. I didn't know if she was heeled or not, and I wasn't about to take any chances. I bowslung the Browning and took out the .45 automatic. I didn't have to snap back the action—there was always a slug in the chamber.

I started moving carefully through the room. It was a locker room of some kind. There was glass and debris all over the floor, and one entire row of metal lockers had the paint blistered off their surfaces; the flash blast had caught them through the windows, a lot of years ago. My sneakers didn't make a sound coming through the room.

The door was hanging on one hinge, and I stepped over—through the inverted triangle. I was in the swimming pool area. The big pool was empty, with tiles buckled down at the shallow end. It stunk bad in there; no wonder, there were dead guys, or what was left of them, along one wall. Some lousy cleaner-up had stacked them, but hadn't buried them. I pulled my bandanna up around my nose and mouth and kept moving.

Out the other side of the pool place, and through a little passage with popped light bulbs in the ceiling. I didn't have any trouble seeing. There was moonlight coming through busted windows and a chunk was out of the ceiling. I could hear her real plain now, just on the other side of the door at the end of the passage. I hung close to the wall, and stepped down to the door. It was open a crack, but blocked by a fall of lath and plaster from the wall. It would make noise when I went to pull it open, that was for certain. I had to wait for the right moment.

Flattened against the wall, I checked out what she was doing in there. It was a gymnasium, big one, with climbing ropes hanging down from the ceiling. She had a squat, square, eight-cell flashlight sitting up on the croup of a vaulting horse. There were parallel bars and a horizontal bar about eight feet high, the tempered steel all rusty now. There were swinging rings and a trampoline and a big wooden balancing beam. Over to one side there were wall-bars and balancing benches, horizontal and oblique ladders, and a couple of stacks of vaulting boxes. I made a note to remember this joint. It was better for working-out than the jerry-rigged gym I'd set up in an old auto wrecking yard. A guy has to keep in shape, if he's going to be a solo.

She was out of her disguise. Standing there in the skin, shivering. Yeah, it was chilly, and I could see a pattern of chicken-skin all over her. She was maybe five-six or -seven, with nice tits and kind of skinny legs. She was brushing out her hair. It hung way down the back. The flashlight didn't make it clear enough to tell if she had red hair or chestnut, but it wasn't blonde, which was good, and that was because I dug redheads. She had nice tits, though. I couldn't see her face, the hair was hanging down all smooth and wavy and cut off her profile.

The crap she'd been wearing was thrown around on the floor, and what she was going to put on was up on the vaulting horse. She was standing in little shoes with a kind of funny heel on them.

I couldn't move. I suddenly realized I couldn't move. She was nice, really nice. I was getting a real big kick out of just standing there and seeing the way her waist fell inward and her hips fell outward, the way the muscles at the side of her tits pulled up when she reached to the top of her head to brush all that hair down. It was really weird the kick I was getting out of standing and just staring at a chick do that. Kind of very, well, woman stuff. I liked it a lot.

I'd never stopped and just looked at a chick like that. All the ones I'd ever seen had been scumbags that Blood had smelled out for me, and I'd snatch'n'grabbed them. Or the big chicks in the beaver flicks. Not like this one, kind of soft and very smooth, even with the goose bumps. I could have watched her all night.

She put down the brush, and reached over and took a pair of panties off the pile of clothes and wriggled into them. Then she got her bra and put it on. I never knew the way chicks did it. She put it on backwards, around her waist, and it had a hook on it. Then she slid it around till the cups were in front, and kind of pulled it up under and scooped herself into it, first one, then the other; then she pulled the straps over her shoulder. She reached for her dress, and I nudged some of the lath and plaster aside, and grabbed the door to give it a yank.

She had the dress up over her head, and her arms up inside the material, and when she stuck her head in, and was all tangled there for a second, I yanked the door and there was a crash as chunks of wood and plaster fell out of the way, and a heavy scraping, and I jumped inside and was on her before she could get out of the dress.

She started to scream, and I pulled the dress off her with a ripping sound, and it all happened for her before she knew what that crash and scrape was all about.

Her face was wild. Just wild. Big eyes: I couldn't tell what color they were because they were in shadow. Real fine features, a wide mouth, little nose, cheekbones just like mine, real high and prominent, and a dimple in her right cheek. She stared at me really scared.

And then . . . and this is really weird . . . I felt like I should *say* something to her. I don't know what. Just something. It made me uncomfortable, to see her scared, but what the hell could I do about *that*, I mean, I was going to rape her, after all, and I couldn't very well tell her not to be shrinky about it. She was the one cumup, after all. But even so, I wanted to say hey, don't be scared, I just want to lay you. (That never happened before. I never wanted to *say* anything to a chick, just get in, and that was that.)

But it passed, and I put my leg behind hers and tripped her back, and she went down in a pile. I leveled the .45 at her, and her mouth kind of opened in a little o shape. "Now I'm gonna go over there and get one of them wrestling mats, so it'll be better, comfortable, uh-huh? You make a move off that floor and I shoot a leg out from under you, and you'll get screwed just the same, except you'll be without a leg." I waited for her to let me know she was onto what I was saying, and she finally nodded real slow, so I kept the automatic on her, and went over to the big dusty stack of mats, and pulled one off.

I dragged it over to her, and flipped it so the cleaner side was up, and used the muzzle of the .45 to maneuver her onto it. She just sat there on the mat, with her hands behind her, and her knees bent, and stared at me.

I unzipped my pants and started pulling them down off one side, when I caught her looking at me real funny. I stopped with the jeans. "What're *you* lookin' at?"

I was mad. I didn't know why I was mad, but I was.

"What's your name?" she asked. Her voice was very soft, and kind of furry, like it came up through her throat that was all lined with fur or something.

She kept looking at me, waiting for me to answer.

"Vic," I said. She looked like she was waiting for more.

"Vic what?"

I didn't know what she meant for a minute, then I did. "Vic. Just Vic. That's all."

"Well, what're your mother and father's names?"

Then I started laughing, and working my jeans down again. "Boy, are you a dumb bitch," I said, and laughed some more. She looked hurt. It made me mad again. "Stop lookin' like that, or I'll bust out your teeth!"

She folded her hands in her lap.

I got the pants around my ankles. They wouldn't come off over the sneakers. I had to balance on one foot and scuff the sneaker off the other foot. It was tricky, keeping the .45 on her and getting the sneaker off at the same time. But I did it.

I was standing there buck-naked from the waist down and she had sat forward a little, her legs crossed, hands still in her lap. "Get that stuff off," I said.

She didn't move for a second, and I thought she was going to give me trouble. But then she reached around behind and undid the bra. Then she tipped back and slipped the panties off her ass.

Suddenly, she didn't look scared any more. She was watching me very close and I could see her eyes were blue now. Now this is the really weird thing . . .

I couldn't do it. I mean, not exactly. I mean, I *wanted* to fuck her, see, but she was all soft and pretty and she kept *looking* at me, and no solo I ever met would believe me, but I heard myself *talking* to her, still standing there like some kind of wetbrain, one sneaker off and jeans down around my ankles. "What's *your* name?"

"Quilla June Holmes."

"That's a weird name."

"My mother says it's not that uncommon, back in Oklahoma."

"That where your folks come from?"

She nodded. "Before the Third War."

"They must be pretty old by now."

"They are, but they're okay. I guess."

We were just frozen there, talking to each other. I could tell she was cold, because she was shivering. "Well," I said, sort of getting ready to drop down beside her, "I guess we better—"

Damn it! That damned Blood! Right at that moment he came crashing in from outside. Came skidding through the lath, and plaster, raising dust, slid along on his ass till he got to us. "*Now* what?" I demanded.

"Who're you talking to?" the girl asked.

"Him. Blood."

"*The dog!?!*"

Blood stared at her and then ignored her. He started to say something but the girl interrupted him. "Then it's true what they say . . . you can all talk to animals . . ."

"You going to listen to her all night, or do you want to hear why I came in?"

"Okay, why're you here?"

"You're in trouble, Albert."

"Come *on*, forget the mickeymouse. What's up?"

Blood twisted his head toward the front door of the YMCA. "Roverpak. Got the building surrounded. I make it fifteen or twenty, maybe more."

"How the hell'd they know we was here?"
Blood looked chagrined. He dropped his head.
"Well?"
"Some other mutt must've smelled her in the theater."
"Great."
"Now what?"
"Now we stand 'em off, that's what. You got any better suggestions?"
"Just one."
I waited. He grinned.
"Pull your pants up."

IV

This girl, this Quilla June, was pretty safe. I made her a kind of a shelter out of wrestling mats, maybe a dozen of them. She wouldn't get hit by a stray bullet, and if they didn't go right for her, they wouldn't find her. I climbed one of the ropes hanging down from the girders and laid out up there with the Browning and a couple of handfuls of reloads. I wished to God I'd had an automatic, a bren or a Thompson. I checked the .45, made sure it was full, with one in the chamber, and set the extra clips down on the girder. I had a clear line-of-fire all around the gym.

Blood was lying in shadow right near the front door. He'd suggested I try and pick off any dogs with the roverpak first, if I could. That would allow him to operate freely.

That was the least of my worries.

I'd wanted to hole up in another room, one with only a single entrance, but I had no way of knowing if the rovers were already in the building, so I did the best I could with what I had.

Everything was quiet. Even that Quilla June. It'd taken me valuable minutes to convince her she'd damned well better hole up and not make any noise; she was better off with me than with twenty of *them*. "If you ever wanna see your mommy and daddy again," I warned her. After that she didn't give me no trouble, packing her in with mats.

Quiet.

Then I heard two things, both at the same time. From back in the swimming pool I heard boots crunching plaster. Very soft. And from one side of the front door, I heard a tinkle of metal striking wood. So they were going to try a yoke. Well, I was ready.

Quiet again.

I sighted the Browning on the door to the pool room. It was still open from when I'd come through. Figure him at maybe five-ten, and drop the sights a foot and a half, and I'd catch him in the chest. I'd learned long ago you don't try for the head. Go for the widest part of the body: the chest and stomach. The trunk.

Suddenly, outside, I heard a dog bark, and part of the darkness near the front door detached itself and moved inside the gym. Directly opposite Blood. I didn't move the Browning.

The rover at the front door moved a step along the wall, away from Blood. Then he cocked back his arm and threw something—a rock, a piece of metal, something—across the room to draw fire. I didn't move the Browning.

When the thing he'd thrown hit the floor, two rovers jumped out of the swimming pool door, one on either side of it, rifles down, ready to spray. Before they could open up, I'd squeezed off the first shot, tracked across and put a second shot into the other one. They both went down. Dead hits, right in the heart. Bang, they were down, neither one moved.

The mother by the door turned to split, and Blood was on him. Just like that, out of the darkness, riiiip!

Blood leaped, right over the crossbar of the guy's rifle held at ready, and sank his fangs into the rover's throat. The guy screamed, and Blood dropped, carrying a piece of the guy with him. The guy was making awful bubbling sounds and went down on one knee. I put a slug into his head, and he fell forward.

It went quiet again.

Not bad. Not bad atall atall. Three takeouts and they still didn't know our positions. Blood had fallen back into the murk by the entrance. He didn't say a thing, but I knew what he was thinking: maybe that was three out of seventeen, or three out of twenty, or twenty-two. No way of knowing; we could be faced-off in here for a week and never know if we'd gotten them all, or some, or none. They could go and get poured full again, and I'd find myself run out of slugs and no food and that girl, that Quilla June, crying and making me divide my attention, and daylight—and they'd be still laying out there, waiting till we got hungry enough to do something dumb, or till we ran out of slugs; and then they'd cloud up and rain all over us.

A rover came dashing straight through the front door at top speed, took a leap, hit on his shoulders, rolled, came up going in a different direction, and snapped off three rounds into different corners of the room before I could track him with the Browning. By that time he was close enough under me where I didn't have to waste a .22 slug. I picked up the .45 without a sound and blew the back off his head. Slug went in neat, came out and took most of his hair with it. He fell right down.

"Blood! The rifle!"

Came out of the shadows, grabbed it up in his mouth and dragged it over to the pile of wrestling mats in the far corner. I saw an arm poke out from the mass of mats, and a hand grabbed the rifle, dragged it inside. Well, it was at least safe there, till I needed it. Brave little bastard: he scuttled over to the dead rover and started worrying the ammo bandolier off his body. It took him a while; he could have been picked off from the doorway or outside one of the windows, but he did it. Brave little bastard. I had to remember to get him something good to eat when we got out of this. I smiled, up there in the darkness: *if* we got out of this, I wouldn't have to worry about getting him something tender. It was lying all over the floor of that gymnasium.

Just as Blood was dragging the bandolier back into the shadows, two of them tried it with their dogs. They came through a ground floor window, one after another, hitting and rolling and going in opposite directions, as the dogs—a mother-ugly akita, big as a house, and a Doberman bitch the color of a turd—shot through the front door and split in the unoccupied two directions. I caught one of the dogs, the akita, with the .45, and it went down thrashing. The Doberman was all over Blood.

But firing, I'd given away my position. One of the rovers fired from the hip and .30-06 soft-nosed slugs spanged off the girders around me. I dropped the automatic, and it started to slip off the girder as I reached for the Browning. I made a grab for the .45 and that was the only thing saved me. I fell forward to clutch at it, it slipped away and hit the gym floor with a crash, and the rover fired at where I'd been. But I was flat on the girder, arm dangling, and the crash startled him. He fired at the sound, and right at that instant I heard another shot, from a Winchester, and the other rover, who'd made it safe into the shadows, fell forward holding a big pumping hole in his chest. That Quilla June had shot him, from behind the mats.

I didn't even have time to figure out what the fuck was happening . . . Blood was rolling around with the Doberman and the sounds they were making were awful . . . and the rover with the .30-06 chipped off another shot and hit the muzzle of the Browning, protruding over the side of the girder, and wham it was gone, falling down. I was naked up there without clout, and the sonofabitch was hanging back in shadow waiting for me.

Another shot from the Winchester, and the rover fired right into the mats. She ducked back behind, and I knew I couldn't count on her for anything more. But I didn't need it; in that second, while he was focused on her, I grabbed the climbing rope, flipped myself over the girder, and howling like a burnpit-screamer, went sliding down, feeling the rope cutting my palms. I got down far enough to swing, and kicked off. I swung back and forth, whipping my body three different ways each time, swinging out and over, way over, each time.

The sonofabitch kept firing, trying to track a trajectory, but I kept spinning out of his line of fire. Then he was empty, and I kicked back as hard as I could, and came zooming in toward his corner of shadows, and let loose all at once and went ass-over-end into the corner, and there he was, and I went right into him and he spanged off the wall, and I was on top of him, digging my thumbs into his eyesockets. He was screaming and the dogs were screaming and that girl was screaming, and I pounded the motherfucker's head against the floor till he stopped moving, then I grabbed up the empty .30-06 and whipped his head till I knew he wasn't gonna give me no more aggravation.

Then I found the .45 and shot the Doberman.

Blood got up and shook himself off. He was cut up bad. "Thanks," he mumbled, and went over to lie down in the shadows to lick himself off.

I went and found that Quilla June, and she was crying. About all the guys we'd killed. Mostly about the one *she'd* killed. I couldn't get her to stop bawling so I cracked her across the face and told her she'd saved my life, and that helped some.

Blood came dragassing over. "How're we going to get out of this, Albert?"

"Let me think."

I thought and knew it was hopeless. No matter how many we got, there'd be more. And it was a matter of *macho* now. Their honor.

"How about a fire?" Blood suggested.

"Get away while it's burning?" I shook my head. "They'll have the place staked-out all around. No good."

"What if we don't leave? What if we burn up with it?"

I looked at him. Brave . . . and smart as hell.

V

We gathered all the lumber and mats and scaling ladders and vaulting boxes and benches and anything else that would burn, and piled the garbage against a wooden divider at one end of the gym. Quilla June found a can of kerosene in a storeroom, and we set fire to the whole damn pile. Then we followed Blood to the place he'd found for us. The boiler room way down under the YMCA. We all climbed into the empty boiler, and dogged down the door, leaving a release vent open for air. We had one mat in there with us, and all the ammo we could carry, and the extra rifles and sidearms the rovers'd had on them.

"Can you catch anything?" I asked Blood.

"A little. Not much. I'm reading one guy. The building's burning good."

"You be able to tell when they split?"

"Maybe. *If* they split."

I settled back. Quilla June was shaking from all that had happened. "Just take it easy," I told her. "By morning the place'll be down around our ears, and they'll go through the rubble and find a lot of dead meat, and maybe they won't look too hard for a chick's body. And everything'll be all right . . . if we don't get choked off in here."

She smiled, very thin, and tried to look brave. She was okay, that one. She closed her eyes and settled back on the mat and tried to sleep. I was beat. I closed my eyes, too.

"Can you handle it?" I asked Blood.

"I suppose. You better sleep."

I nodded, eyes still closed, and fell on my side. I was out before I could think about it.

When I came back, I found the girl, that Quilla June, snuggled up under my armpit, her arm around my waist, dead asleep. I could hardly breathe. It was like a furnace; hell, it *was* a furnace. I reached out a hand and the wall of the boiler was so damned hot I couldn't touch it. Blood was up on the mattress with us. That mat had been the only thing'd kept us from being singed good. He was asleep, head buried in his paws. She was asleep, still naked.

I put a hand on her tit. It was warm. She stirred and cuddled into me closer. I got a hard-on.

Managed to get my pants off, and rolled on top of her. She woke up fast when she felt me pry her legs apart, but it was too late by then. "Don't . . . *stop* . . . what are you doing . . . no, don't . . ."

But she was half-asleep, and weak, and I don't think she really wanted to fight me anyhow.

She cried when I broke her, of course, but after that it was okay. There was blood all over the wrestling mat. And Blood just kept sleeping.

It was really different. Usually, when I'd get Blood to track something down for me, it'd be grab it and punch it and pork it and get away fast before something bad could happen. But when she came, she rose up off the mat, and hugged me around the back so hard I thought she'd crack my ribs, and then she settled back down slow slow slow, like I do when I'm doing leg-lifts in the makeshift gym I rigged in the auto wrecking yard. And her eyes were closed, and she was relaxed looking. And happy. I could tell.

We did it a lot of times, and after a while it was her idea, but I didn't say no. And then we lay out side-by-side and talked.

She asked me about how it was with Blood, and I told her how the skirmisher dogs had gotten telepathic, and how they'd lost the ability to hunt food for themselves, so the solos and roverpaks had to do it for them, and how dogs like Blood were good at finding chicks for solos like me. She didn't say anything to that.

I asked her about what it was like where she lived, in one of the downunders.

"It's nice. But it's always very quiet. Everyone is very polite to everyone else. It's just a small town."

"Which one you live in?"

"Topeka. It's real close to here."

"Yeah, I know. The access dropshaft is only about half a mile from here. I went out there once, to take a look around."

"Have you ever been in a downunder?"

"No. But I don't guess I want to be, either."

"Why? It's very nice. You'd like it."

"Shit."

"That's very crude."

"*I'm* very crude."

"Not all the time."

I was getting mad. "Listen, you ass, what's the matter with you? I grabbed you and pushed you around, I raped you half a dozen times, so what's so good about me, huh? What's the matter with you, don't you even have enough smarts to know when somebody's–"

She was smiling at me. "I didn't mind. I liked doing it. Want to do it again?"

I was really shocked. I moved away from her. "What the hell is wrong with you? Don't you know that a chick from a downunder like you can be really mauled by solos? Don't you know chicks get warnings from their parents in the downunders, 'Don't cumup, you'll get snagged by them dirty, hairy, slobbering solos!' Don't you know that?"

She put her hand on my leg and started moving it up, the fingertips just brushing my thigh. I got another hard-on. "My parents never said that about solos," she said. Then she pulled me over her again, and kissed me, and I couldn't stop from getting in her again.

God, it just went on like that for hours. After a while Blood turned around and said, "I'm not going to keep pretending I'm asleep. I'm hungry. And I'm hurt."

I tossed her off me–she was on top by this time–and examined him. The Doberman had taken a good chunk out of his right ear, and there was a rip right down his muzzle, and blood-matted fur on one side. He was a mess. "Jesus, man, you're a mess," I said.

"You're no fucking rose garden yourself, Albert!" he snapped. I pulled my hand back.

"Can we get out of here?" I asked him.

He cast around, and then shook his head. "I can't get any readings. Must be a pile of rubble on top of this boiler. I'll have to go out and scout."

We kicked that around for a while, and finally decided if the building was razed, and had cooled a little, the roverpak would have gone through the ashes by now. The fact that they hadn't tried the boiler indicated that we were probably buried pretty good. Either that, or the building was still smoldering overhead. In which case, they'd still be out there, waiting to sift the remains.

"Think you can handle it, the condition you're in?"

"I guess I'll *have* to, won't I?" Blood said. He was really surly. "I mean, what with you busy coitusing your brains out, there won't be much left for staying alive, will there?"

I sensed real trouble with him. He didn't like Quilla June. I moved around him and undogged the boiler hatch. It wouldn't open. So I braced my back against the side, and jacked my legs up, and gave it a slow, steady shove.

Whatever had fallen against it from outside resisted for a minute, then started to give, then tumbled away with a crash. I pushed the door open all the way, and looked out. The upper floors had fallen in on the basement, but by the time they'd given, they'd been mostly cinder and lightweight rubble. Everything was smoking out there. I could see daylight through the smoke.

I slipped out, burning my hands on the outside lip of the hatch. Blood followed. He started to pick his way through the debris. I could see that the boiler had been almost completely covered by the gunk that had dropped from above. Chances were good the roverpak had taken a fast look, figured we'd been fried, and moved on. But I wanted Blood to run a recon anyway. He started off, but I called him back. He came.

"What is it?"

I looked down at him. "I'll tell you what it is, man. You're acting very shitty."

"Sue me."

"Goddammit, dog, what's got your ass up?"

"Her. That nit chick you've got in there."

"So what? Big deal . . . I've had chicks before."

"Yeah, but never any that hung on like this one. I warn you, Albert, she's going to make trouble."

"Don't be dumb!" He didn't reply. Just looked at me with anger, and then limped off to check out the scene. I crawled back inside and dogged the hatch. She wanted to make it again. I said I didn't want to; Blood had brought me down. I was bugged. And I didn't know which one to be pissed off at.

But God she was pretty.

She kind of pouted and settled back with her arms wrapped around her. "Tell me some more about the downunder," I said.

At first she was cranky, wouldn't say much, but after a while she opened up and started talking freely. I was learning a lot. I figured I could use it some time, maybe.

There were only a couple of hundred downunders in what was left of the United States and Canada. They'd been sunk on the sites of wells or mines or other kinds of deep holes. Some of them, out in the west, were in natural cave formations. They went way down, maybe two to five miles. They were like big caissons, stood on end. And the people who'd settled them were squares of the worst kind. Southern Baptists, Fundamentalists, lawanorder goofs, real middle-class squares with no taste for the wild life. And they'd gone back to a kind of life that hadn't existed for a hundred and fifty years. They'd gotten the last of the scientists to do the work, invent the how and why, and then they'd run them out. They didn't want any progress, they didn't want any dissent, they didn't want anything that would make waves. They'd had enough of that. The best time in the world had been just before the First War, and they figured if they could keep it like that, they could live quiet lives and survive. Shit! I'd go nuts in one of the downunders.

Quilla June smiled, and snuggled up again, and this time I didn't turn her off. She started touching me again, down there and all over, and then she said, "Vic?"

"Uh-huh."

"Have you ever been in love?"

"What?"

"In love? Have you ever been in love with a girl?"

"Well, I damn well guess I haven't!"

"Do you know what love is?"

"Sure. I guess I do."

"But if you've never been in love . . . ?"

"Don't be dumb. I mean, I've never had a bullet in the head, and I know I wouldn't like it."

"You don't know what love is, I'll bet."

"Well, if it means living in a downunder, I guess I just don't wanna find out." We didn't go on with the conversation much after that. She pulled me down and we did it again. And when it was over, I heard Blood scratching at the boiler. I opened the hatch, and he was standing out there. "All clear," he said.

"You sure?"

"Yeah, yeah, I'm sure. Put your pants on," he said it with a sneer in the tone, "and come on out here. We have to talk some stuff."

I looked at him, and he wasn't kidding. I got my jeans and sneakers on, and climbed down out of the boiler.

He trotted ahead of me, away from the boiler over some blacksoot beams, and outside the gym. It was down. Looked like a rotted stump tooth.

"Now what's lumbering you?" I asked him.

He scampered up on a chunk of concrete till he was almost nose-level with me.

"You're going dumb on me, Vic."

I knew he was serious. No Albert shit, straight Vic. "How so?"

"Last night, man. We could have cut out of there and left her for them. *That* would have been smart."

"I wanted her."

"Yeah, I know. That's what I'm talking about. It's today now, not last night. You've had her about a half a hundred times. Why're we hanging around?"

"I want some more."

Then he got angry. "Yeah, well, listen, chum . . . *I* want a few things myself. I want something to eat, and I want to get rid of this pain in my side, and I want away from this turf. Maybe they *don't* give up this easy."

"Take it easy. We can handle all that. Don't mean she can't go with us."

"*Doesn't* mean," he corrected me. "And so *that's* the new story. Now we travel three, is that right?"

I was getting really uptight myself. "You're starting to sound like a damn poodle!"

"And you're starting to sound like a boxer."

I hauled back to crack him one. He didn't move. I dropped the hand. I'd never hit Blood. I didn't want to start now.

"Sorry," he said, softly.

"That's okay."

But we weren't looking at each other.

"Vic, man, you've got a responsibility to me, you know."

"You don't have to tell me that."

"Well, I guess maybe I do. Maybe I have to remind you of some stuff. Like the time that burnpit-screamer came up out of the street and made a grab for you."

I shuddered. The motherfucker'd been green. Righteous stone green, glowing like fungus. My gut heaved, just thinking.

"And I went for him, right?"

I nodded. Right, mutt, right.

"And I could have been burned bad, and died, and that would've been all of it for me, right or wrong, isn't that true?" I nodded again. I was getting pissed off proper. I didn't like being made to feel guilty. It was a fifty-fifty with Blood and me. He knew that. "But I did it, right?" I remembered the way the green thing had screamed. Christ, it was all ooze and eyelashes.

"Okay, okay, don't hanger me."

"*Harangue,* not hanger."

"Well, WHATEVER!" I shouted. "Just knock off the crap, or we can forget the whole fucking arrangement!"

Then Blood blew. "Well, maybe we *should,* you simple *dumb putz!*"

"What's a *putz,* you little turd . . . is that something bad . . . yeah, it must be . . . you watch your fucking mouth, son of a bitch; or I'll kick your ass!"

We sat there and didn't talk for fifteen minutes. Neither one of us knew which way to go.

Finally, I backed off a little. I talked soft and I talked slow. I was about up to here with him, but told him I was going to do right by him, like I always had, and he threatened me, saying I'd damned well better because there were a couple of very hip solos making it around the city, and they'd be delighted to have a sharp tail-scent like him. I told him I didn't like being threatened, and he'd better watch his fucking step or I'd break his leg. He got furious and stalked off. I said screw you and went back to the boiler to take it out on that Quilla June again.

But when I stuck my head inside the boiler, she was waiting, with a pistol one of the dead rovers had supplied. She hit me good and solid over the right eye with it, and I fell straight forward across the hatch, and was out cold.

VI

"I told you she was no good." He watched me as I swabbed out the cut with disinfectant from my kit, and painted the gash with iodine. He smirked when I flinched.

I put away the stuff, and rummaged around in the boiler, gathering up all the spare ammo I could carry, and ditching the Browning in favor of the heavier .30-06. Then I found something that must've slipped out of her clothes.

It was a little metal plate, about three inches long and an inch-and-a-half high. It had a whole string of numbers on it, and there were holes in it, in random patterns. "What's this?" I asked Blood.

He looked at it, sniffed it.

"Must be an identity card of some kind. Maybe it's what she used to get out of the downunder."

That made my mind up.

I jammed it in a pocket and started out. Toward the access dropshaft.

"Where the hell are you going?" Blood yelled after me.

"Come on back, you'll get killed out there!

"I'm hungry, dammit! I'm wounded!

"Albert, you sonofabitch! Come back here!"

I kept right on walking. I was gonna find that bitch and brain her. Even if I had to go downunder to find her.

It took me an hour to walk to the access dropshaft leading down to Topeka. I thought I saw Blood following, but hanging back a ways. I didn't give a damn. I was mad.

Then, there it was. A tall, straight, featureless pillar of shining black metal. It was maybe twenty feet in diameter, perfectly flat on top, disappearing straight into the ground. It was a cap, that was all. I walked straight up to it, and fished around in my pocket for that metal card. Then something was tugging at my right pants leg.

"Listen, you moron, you can't go down there!"

I kicked him off, but he came right back.

"Listen to me!"

I turned around and stared at him.

Blood sat down; the powder puffed up around him. "Albert . . ."

"My name is Vic, you little eggsucker."

"Okay, okay, no fooling around. Vic." His tone softened. "Vic. Come on, man." He was trying to get through to me. I was really boiling, but he was trying to make sense. I shrugged, and crouched down beside him.

"Listen, man," Blood said, "this chick has bent you way out of shape. You *know* you can't go down there. It's all square and settled, and they know everyone; they hate solos. Enough roverpaks have raided downunder, and raped their women, and stolen their food, they'll have defenses set up. They'll *kill* you, Vic!"

"What the hell do you care? You're always saying you'd be better off without me." He sagged at that.

"Vic, we've been together almost three years. Good and bad. But this can be the worst. I'm scared, man. Scared you won't come back. And I'm hungry, and I'll have to go find some dude who'll take me on . . . and you know most solos are in paks now, I'll be low mutt. I'm not that young any more. And I'm hurt pretty bad."

I could dig it. He was talking sense. But all I could think of was how that bitch, that Quilla June, had rapped me. And then there were images of her soft tits, and the way she made little sounds when I was in her, and I shook my head, and knew I had to go get even.

"I got to do it, Blood. *I got to.*"

He breathed deep and sagged a little more. He knew it was useless. "You don't even see what she's done to you, Vic. That metal card, it's too easy, as if she *wanted* you to follow."

I got up. "I'll try to get back quick. Will you wait . . . ?"

He was silent a long while, and I waited. Finally, he said, "For a while. Maybe I'll be here, maybe not."

I understood. I turned around and started walking around the pillar of black metal. Finally, I found a slot in the pillar, and slipped the metal card into it. There was a soft humming sound, then a section of the pillar dilated. I hadn't even seen the lines of the sections. A circle opened and I took a step through. I turned and there was Blood, watching me. We looked at each other, all the while that pillar was humming.

"So long, Vic."

"Take care of yourself, Blood."

"Hurry back."

"Do my best."

"Yeah. Right."

Then I turned around and stepped inside. The access portal irised closed behind me.

VII

I should have known. I should have suspected. Sure, every once in a while a chick came up to see what it was like on the surface, what had happened to the cities; sure, it happened. Why, I'd believed her when she'd told me, cuddled up beside me in that steaming boiler, that she'd wanted to see what it was like when a girl did it with a guy, that all the flicks she'd seen in Topeka were sweet and solid and dull, and the girls in her school'd talked about beaver flicks, and one of them had a little eight-page comic book and she'd read it with wide eyes . . . sure, I'd believed her. It was logical. I should have suspected something when she left that metal I.D. plate behind. It was too easy. Blood'd tried to tell me. Dumb? Yeah!

The second that access iris swirled closed behind me, the humming got louder, and some cool light grew in the walls. Wall. It was a circular compartment with only two sides to the wall: *in*side and *out*side. The wall pulsed up light and the humming got louder, and the deckplate I was standing on dilated just the way the outside port had done. But I was standing there, like a mouse in a cartoon, and as long as I didn't look down I was cool, I wouldn't fall.

Then I started settling. Dropped through the floor, the iris closed overhead, I was dropping down the tube, picking up speed but not too much, just dropping steadily. Now I knew what a dropshaft was.

Down and down I went and every once in a while I'd see something like 10 LEV or ANTIPOLL 55 or BREEDER-CON or PUMP SE 6 on the wall, faintly I could make out the sectioning of an iris . . . but I never stopped dropping.

Finally, I dropped all the way to the bottom, and there was TOPEKA CITY LIMITS POP. 22,860 on the wall, and I settled down without any strain, bending a little from the knees to cushion the impact, but even that wasn't much.

I used the metal plate again, and the iris—a much bigger one this time—swirled open, and I got my first look at a downunder.

It stretched away in front of me, twenty miles to the dim shining horizon of tin can metal where the wall behind me curved and curved and curved till it made one smooth, encircling circuit and came back around around around to where I stood, staring at it. I was down at the bottom of a big metal tube that stretched up to a ceiling an eighth of a mile overhead, twenty miles across. And in the bottom of that tin can, someone had built a town that looked for all the world like a photo out of one of the water-logged books in the library on the surface. I'd seen a town like this in the books. Just like this. Neat little houses, and curvy little streets, and trimmed lawns, and a business section and everything else that a Topeka would have.

Except a sun, except birds, except clouds, except rain, except snow, except cold, except wind, except ants, except dirt, except mountains, except oceans, except big fields of grain, except stars, except the moon, except forests, except animals running wild, except . . .

Except freedom.

They were canned down here, like dead fish. Canned.

I felt my throat tighten up. I wanted to get out. Out! I started to tremble, my hands were cold and there was sweat on my forehead. This had been insane, coming down here. I had to get out. *Out!*

I turned around to get back in the dropshaft, and then it grabbed me.

That bitch Quilla June! I shoulda suspected!

The thing was low, and green, and boxlike, and had cables with mittens on the ends instead of arms, and it rolled on tracks, and it grabbed me.

It hoisted me up on its square flat top, holding me with them mittens on the cables, and I couldn't move, except to try kicking at the big glass eye in the front, but it didn't do any good. It didn't bust. The thing was only about four feet high, and my sneakers almost reached the ground, but not quite, and it started moving off into Topeka, hauling me along with it.

People were all over the place. Sitting in rockers on their front porches, raking their lawns, hanging around the gas station, sticking pennies in gumball machines, painting a white stripe down the middle of the road, selling newspapers on a corner, listening to an oompah band on a shell in a park, playing hopscotch and pussy-in-the-corner, polishing a fire engine, sitting on benches reading, washing windows, pruning bushes, tipping hats to ladies, collecting milk bottles in wire carrying racks, grooming horses, throwing a stick for a dog to retrieve, diving into a communal swimming pool, chalking vegetable prices on a slate outside a grocery, walking hand-in-hand with a girl, all of them watching me go past on that metal motherfucker.

I could hear Blood speaking, saying just what he'd said before I'd entered the dropshaft: *It's all square and settled and they know everyone; they hate solos. Enough roverpaks have raided downunders, and raped their women and stolen their food, they'll have defenses set up. They'll* kill *you, Vic!*

Thanks, mutt.

Goodbye.

VIII

The green box tracked through the business section and turned in at a shopfront with the words BETTER BUSINESS BUREAU on the window. It rolled right inside the open door, and there were half a dozen men and old men and very old men in there, waiting for me. Also a couple of women. The green box stopped.

One of them came over and took the metal plate out of my hand. He looked at it, then turned around and gave it to the oldest of the old men, a withered toad wearing baggy pants and a green eyeshade and garters that held up the sleeves of his striped shirt. "Quilla June, Lew," the guy said to the old man. Lew took the metal plate and put it in the top left drawer of a rolltop desk. "Better take his guns, Aaron," the old coot said. And the guy who'd taken the plate cleaned me.

"Let him loose, Aaron," Lew said.

Aaron stepped around the back of the green box and something clicked, and the cable-mittens sucked back inside the box, and I got down off the thing. My arms were numb where the box had held me. I rubbed one, then the other, and I glared at them.

"Now, boy . . ." Lew started.

"Suck wind, asshole!"

The women blanched. The men tightened their faces.

"I told you it wouldn't work," another of the old men said to Lew.

"Bad business, this," said one of the younger ones.

Lew leaned forward in his straight-back chair and pointed a crumbled finger at me. "Boy, you better be nice."

"I hope all your fuckin' children are hare-lipped!"

"This is no good, Lew!" another man said.

"Guttersnipe," a woman with a beak snapped.

Lew stared at me. His mouth was a nasty little black line. I knew the sonofabitch didn't have a tooth in his crummy head that wasn't rotten and smelly. He stared at me with vicious little eyes. God, he was ugly, like a toad ready to snaffle a fly off the wall with his tongue.

He was getting set to say something I wouldn't like. "Aaron, maybe you'd better put the sentry back on him." Aaron moved to the green box.

"Okay, hold it," I said, holding up my hand.

Aaron stopped, looked at Lew, who nodded. Then Lew leaned real far forward again, and aimed that bird-claw at me. "You ready to behave yourself, son?"

"Yeah, I guess."

"You'd better be dang sure."

"Okay. I'm *dang* sure. Also *fuckin'* sure!"

"And you'll watch your mouth."

I didn't reply. Old coot.

"You're a bit of an experiment for us, boy. We tried to get one of you down here other ways. Sent up some good folks to capture one of you little scuts, but they never came back. Figgered it was best to lure you down to us."

I sneered. That Quilla June. I'd take care of her!

One of the women, a little younger than Bird-Beak, came forward and looked into my face. "Lew, you'll never get this one to cow-tow. He's a filthy little killer. Look at those eyes."

"How'd you like the barrel of a rifle jammed up your ass, bitch?" She jumped back. Lew was angry again. "Sorry," I said real quickly, "I don't like bein' called names. *Macho*, y'know?"

He settled back and snapped at the woman. "Mez, leave him alone. I'm tryin' to talk a bit of sense here. You're only making it worse."

Mez went back and sat with the others. Some Better Business Bureau these creeps were!

"As I was saying, boy: you're an experiment for us. We've been down here in Topeka close to thirty years. It's nice down here. Quiet, orderly, nice people, who respect each other, no crime, respect for the elders, and just all around a good place to live. We're growin' and we're prosperin'."

I waited.

"But, well, we find now that some of our folks can't have no more babies, and the women that do, they have mostly girls. We need some men. Certain special kind of men."

I started laughing. This was too good to be true. They wanted me for stud service. I couldn't stop laughing.

"Crude!" one of the women said, scowling.

"This's awkward enough for us, boy, don't make it no harder." Lew was embarrassed.

Here I'd spent most of Blood's and my time aboveground hunting up tail, and down here they wanted me to service the local ladyfolk. I sat down on the floor and laughed till tears ran down my cheeks.

Finally, I got up and said, "Sure. Okay. But if I do, there's a couple of things *I* want."

Lew looked at me close.

"The first thing I want is that Quilla June. I'm gonna fuck her blind, and then I'm gonna bang her on the head the way she did me!"

They huddled for a while, then came out and Lew said, "We can't tolerate any violence down here, but I s'pose Quilla June's as good a place to start as any. She's capable, isn't she, Ira?"

A skinny, yellow-skinned man nodded. He didn't look happy about it. Quilla June's old man, I bet.

"Well, let's get started," I said. "Line 'em up." I started to unzip my jeans.

The women screamed, the men grabbed me, and they hustled me off to a boarding house where they gave me a room, and they said I should get to know Topeka a little bit before I went to work because it was, uh, er, well, awkward, and they had to get the folks in town to accept what was going to have to be done . . . on the assumption, I suppose, that if I worked out okay they'd import a few more young bulls from aboveground and turn us loose.

So I spent some time in Topeka, getting to know the folks, seeing what they did, how they lived.

It was nice, real nice.

They rocked in rockers on the front porches, they raked their lawns, they hung around the gas station, they stuck pennies in gumball machines, they painted white stripes down the middle of the road, they sold newspapers on the corners, they listened to oompah bands in a shell in the park, they played hopscotch and pussy-in-the-corner, they polished fire engines, they sat on benches reading, they washed windows and pruned bushes, they tipped their hats to ladies, they collected milk bottles in wire carrying racks, they groomed horses and threw sticks for their dogs to retrieve, they dove into the communal swimming pool, they chalked vegetable prices on a slate outside the grocery, they walked hand-in-hand with some of the ugliest chicks I've ever seen, *and they bored the ass off me.*

Inside a week I was ready to scream.

I could feel that tin can closing in on me.

I could feel the weight of the earth over me.

They ate artificial shit: artificial peas and fake meat and make-believe chicken and ersatz corn and bogus bread, and it all tasted like chalk and dust to me.

Polite? Christ, you could puke from the lying, hypocritical crap they called civility. Hello Mr. This and Hello Mrs. That. And how are you? And how is little Janie? And how is business? Are you going to the sodality meeting Thursday? And I started gibbering in my room at the boarding house.

The clean, sweet, neat, lovely way they lived was enough to kill a guy. No wonder the men couldn't get it up and make babies that had balls instead of slots.

The first few days, everyone watched me like I was about to explode and cover their nice whitewashed fences with shit. But after a while, they got used to seeing me. Lew took me over to the Mercantile, and got me fitted out with a pair of bib overalls and a shirt that any solo could've spotted a mile away. That Mez, that dippy bitch who'd called me a killer, she started hanging around, finally said she wanted to cut my hair, make me look civilized. But I was hip to where she was at. Wasn't a bit of the mother in her.

"What'sa'matter, cunt," I pinned her. "Your old man isn't taking care of you?"

She tried to stick her fist in her mouth, and I laughed like a loon. "Go chop off *his* balls, baby. My hair stays the way it is." She cut and run. Went like she had a diesel tail-pipe.

It went on like that for a while. Me just walking around, them coming and feeding me, keeping all their young meat out of my way till they got the town stacked-away for what was coming with me.

Jugged like that, my mind wasn't right for a while. I got all claustrophobed, clutched, went and sat under the porch in the dark at the rooming house. Then that passed, and I got piss-mean, snapped at them, then surly, then quiet, then just mud dull. Quiet.

Finally, I started getting hip to the possibilities of getting out of there. It began with me remembering the poodle I'd fed Blood one time. It had to come from a downunder. And it couldn't have got up through the dropshaft. So that meant there were other ways out.

They gave me pretty much the run of the town, as long as I kept my manners around me and didn't try anything sudden. That green sentry box was always somewhere nearby.

So I found the way out. Nothing so spectacular; it just had to be there, and I found it.

Then I found out where they kept my weapons, and I was ready. Almost.

IX

It was a week to the day when Aaron and Lew and Ira came to get me. I was pretty goofy by that time. I was sitting out on the back porch of the boarding house, smoking a corncob pipe with my shirt off, catching some sun. Except there wasn't no sun. Goofy.

They came around the house. "Morning, Vic," Lew greeted me. He was hobbling along with a cane, the old fart. Aaron gave me a big smile. The kind you'd give a big black bull about to stuff his meat into a good breed cow. Ira had a look that you could chip off and use in your furnace.

"Well, howdy, Lew. Mornin', Aaron, Ira."

Lew seemed right pleased by that.

Oh, you lousy bastards, just you wait!

"You 'bout ready to go meet your first lady?"

"Ready as I'll ever be, Lew," I said, and got up.

"Cool smoke, ain't it?" Aaron said.

I took the corncob out of my mouth. "Pure dee-light." I smiled. I hadn't even lit the fucking thing.

They walked me over to Marigold Street and as we came up on a little house with yellow shutters and a white picket fence, Lew said, "This's Ira's house. Quilla June is his daughter."

"Well, land sakes," I said, wide-eyed.

Ira's lean jaw muscles jumped.

We went inside.

Quilla June was sitting on the settee with her mother, an older version of her, pulled thin as a withered muscle. "Miz Holmes," I said and made a little curtsey. She smiled. Strained, but smiled.

Quilla June sat with her feet right together, and her hands folded in her lap. There was a ribbon in her hair. It was blue.

Matched her eyes.

Something went thump in my gut.

"Quilla June," I said.

She looked up. "Mornin', Vic."

Then everyone sort of stood around looking awkward, and finally Ira began yapping and yipping about get in the bedroom and get this unnatural filth over with so they could go to Church and pray the Good Lord wouldn't Strike All Of Them Dead with a bolt of lightning in the ass, or some crap like that.

So I put out my hand, and Quilla June reached for it without looking up, and we went in the back, into a small bedroom, and she stood there with her head down.

"You didn't tell 'em, did you?" I asked.

She shook her head.

And suddenly, I didn't want to kill her at all. I wanted to hold her. Very tight. So I did. And she was crying into my chest, and making little fists beating on my back, and then she was looking up at me and running her words all together: "Oh, Vic, I'm sorry, so sorry, I didn't mean to, I had to, I was sent out to, I was so scared, and I love you, and now they've got you down here, and it isn't dirty, is it, it isn't the way my Poppa says it is, is it?"

I held her and kissed her and told her it was okay, and then I asked her if she wanted to come away with me, and she said yes yes yes she really did. So I told her I might have to hurt her Poppa to get away, and she got a look in her eyes that I knew real well.

For all her propriety, Quilla June Holmes didn't much like her prayer-shouting Poppa.

I asked her if she had anything heavy, like a candlestick or a club, and she said no. So I went rummaging around in that back bedroom and found a pair of her Poppa's socks in a bureau drawer. I pulled the big brass balls off the headboard of the bed and dropped them into the sock. I hefted it. Oh. Yeah.

She stared at me with big eyes. "What're you going to do?"

"You want to get out of here?"

She nodded.

"Then just stand back behind the door. No, wait a minute. I got a better idea. Get on the bed."

She lay down on the bed. "Okay," I said, "now pull up your skirt, pull off your pants, and spread out." She gave me a look of pure horror. "Do it," I said. "If you want out."

So she did it, and I rearranged her so her knees were bent and her legs open at the thighs, and I stood to one side of the door, and whispered to her, "Call your Poppa. Just him."

She hesitated a long moment, then she called out in a voice she didn't have to fake, "Poppa! Poppa, come here, please!" Then she clamped her eyes shut tight.

Ira Holmes came through the door, took one look at his secret desire, his mouth dropped open, I kicked the door closed behind him and walloped him as hard as I could. He squished a little, and spattered the bedspread, and went very down.

She opened her eyes when she heard the thunk! and when the stuff spattered her legs, she leaned over and puked on the floor. I knew she wouldn't be much good to me in getting Aaron into the room, so I opened the door, stuck my head around, looked worried, and said, "Aaron, would you come here a minute, please?" He looked at Lew, who was rapping with Mrs. Holmes about what was going on in the back bedroom, and when Lew nodded him on, he came into the room. He took a look at Quilla June's naked bush, at the blood on the wall and bedspread, at Ira on the floor, and opened his mouth to yell just as I whacked him. It took two more to get him down, and then I had to kick him in the chest to put him away. Quilla June was still puking.

I grabbed her by the arm and swung her up off the bed. At least she was being quiet about it, but man, did she stink.

"Come on!"

She tried to pull back, but I held on and opened the bedroom door. As I pulled her out, Lew stood up, leaning on his cane. I kicked the cane out from under the old fart and down he went in a heap. Mrs. Holmes was staring at us, wondering where her old man was. "He's back in there," I said, heading for the front door. "The Good Lord got him in the head."

Then we were out in the street, Quilla June stinking along behind me, dry-heaving and bawling and probably wondering what had happened to her underpants.

They kept my weapons in a locked case at the Better Business Bureau, and we detoured around by my boarding house where I pulled the crowbar I'd swiped from the gas station out from under the back porch. Then we cut across behind the Grange and into the business section, and straight into the BBB. There was a clerk who tried to stop me, and I split his gourd with the crowbar. Then I pried the latch off the cabinet in Lew's office and got the .30-06 and my .45 and all the ammo, and my spike and my knife and my kit, and loaded up. By that time Quilla June was able to make some sense.

"Where we gonna go, where we gonna go, oh Poppa Poppa Popp . . . !"

"Hey, listen, Quilla June, Poppa me no Poppas. You said you wanted to be with me . . . well, I'm goin'! *Up*, baby, and if you wanna go with me, you better stick close."

She was too scared to object.

I stepped out the front of the shopfront, and there was that green box sentry, coming on like a whippet. It had its cables out, and the mittens were gone. It had hooks.

I dropped to one knee, wrapped the sling of the .30-06 around my forearm, sighted clean, and fired dead at the big eye in the front. One shot, spang!

Hit that eye, the thing exploded in a shower of sparks, and the green box swerved and went through the front window of The Mill End Shoppe, screeching and crying and showering the place with flames and sparks. Nice.

I turned around to grab Quilla June, but she was gone. I looked off down the street, and here came all the vigilantes, Lew hobbling along with his cane like some kind of weird grasshopper.

And right then the shots started. Big, booming sounds. The .45 I'd given Quilla June. I looked up, and on the porch around the second floor, there she was, the automatic down on the railing like a pro, sighting into that mob and snapping off shots like maybe Wild Bill Elliott in a '40s Republic flick.

But dumb! Mother, dumb! Wasting time on that, when we had to get away.

I found the outside staircase going up there, and took it three steps at a time. She was smiling and laughing, and every time she'd pick one of those boobs out of the pack her little tonguetip would peek out of the corner of her mouth, and her eyes would get all slick and wet and wham! down the boob would go.

She was really into it.

Just as I reached her, she sighted down on her scrawny mother. I slammed the back of her head, and she missed the shot, and the old lady did a little dance-step and kept coming. Quilla June whipped her head around at me, and there was kill in her eyes. "You made me miss." The voice gave me a chill.

I took the .45 away from her. Dumb. Wasting ammunition like that.

Dragging her behind me, I circled the building, found a shed out back, dropped down onto it, and had her follow. She was scared at first, but I said, "Chick can shoot her old lady as easy as you do shouldn't be worried about a drop this small." She got out on the ledge, other side of the railing and held on. "Don't worry," I said, "you won't wet your pants. You haven't got any."

She laughed, like a bird, and dropped. I caught her, we slid down the shed door, and took a second to see if that mob was hard on us. Nowhere in sight.

I grabbed Quilla June by the arm and started off toward the south end of Topeka. It was the closest exit I'd found in my wandering, and we made it in about fifteen minutes, panting and weak as kittens.

And there it was.

A big air-intake duct.

I pried off the clamps with the crowbar, and we climbed up inside. There were ladders going up. There had to be. It figured. Repairs. Keep it clean. Had to be. We started climbing.

It took a long, long time.

Quilla June kept asking me, from down behind me, whenever she got too tired to climb, "Vic, do you love me?" I kept saying yes. Not only because I meant it. It helped her keep climbing.

X

We came up a mile from the access dropshaft. I shot off the filter covers and the hatch bolts, and we climbed out. They should have known better down there. You don't fuck around with Jimmy Cagney.

They never had a chance.

Quilla June was exhausted. I didn't blame her. But I didn't want to spend the night out in the open; there were things out there I didn't like to think about meeting even in daylight. It was getting on toward dusk.

We walked toward the access dropshaft.

Blood was waiting.

He looked weak. But he'd waited.

I stooped down and lifted his head. He opened his eyes, and very softly he said, "Hey."

I smiled at him. Jesus, it was good to see him. "We made it back, man."

He tried to get up, but he couldn't. The wounds on him were in ugly shape. "Have you eaten?" I asked.

"No. Grabbed a lizard yesterday . . . or maybe it was day before. I'm hungry, Vic."

Quilla June came up then, and Blood saw her. He closed his eyes. "We'd better hurry, Vic," she said. "Please. They might come up from the dropshaft."

I tried to lift Blood. He was dead weight. "Listen, Blood, I'll leg it into the city and get some food. I'll come back quick. You just wait here."

"Don't go in there, Vic," he said. "I did a recon the day after you went down. They found out we weren't fried in that gym. I don't know how. Maybe mutts smelled our track. I've been keeping watch, and they haven't tried to come out after us. I don't blame them. You don't know what it's like out here at night, man . . . you don't know . . ."

He shivered.

"Take it easy, Blood."

"But they've got us marked lousy in the city, Vic. We can't go back there. We'll have to make it someplace else."

That put it on a different stick. We couldn't go back, and with Blood in that condition we couldn't go forward. And I knew, good as I was solo, I couldn't make it without him. And there wasn't anything out here to eat. He had to have food at once, and some medical care. I had to do something. Something good, something fast.

"Vic," Quilla June's voice was high and whining, "come *on*! He'll be all right. We have to hurry."

I looked up at her. The sun was going down. Blood trembled in my arms.

She got a pouty look on her face. "If you love me, you'll come *on*!"

I couldn't make it alone out there without him. I knew it. If I loved her. She asked me, in the boiler, do you know what love is?

It was a small fire, not nearly big enough for any roverpak to spot from the outskirts of the city. No smoke. And after Blood had eaten his fill, I carried him to the air-duct a mile away, and we spent the night inside on a little ledge. I held him all night. He slept good. In the morning, I fixed him up pretty good. He'd make it; he was strong.

He ate again. There was plenty left from the night before. I didn't eat. I wasn't hungry.

We started off across the blast wasteland that morning. We'd find another city, and make it.

We had to move slow because Blood was still limping. It took a long time before I stopped hearing her calling in my head. Asking me, asking me: *do you know what love is?*

Sure I know.

A boy loves his dog.

The Treehouse—Los Angeles—1964
Harlan, with Ahbhu; for whom he wrote "A Boy and His Dog."

THE DEATHBIRD

1

This is a test. Take notes. This will count as ¾ of your final grade. Hints: remember, in chess, kings cancel each other out and cannot occupy adjacent squares, are therefore all-powerful and totally powerless, cannot affect one another, produce stalemate. Hinduism is a polytheistic religion; the sect of Atman worships the divine spark of life within Man; in effect saying, "Thou art God." Provisos of equal time are not served by one viewpoint having media access to two hundred million people in prime time while opposing viewpoints are provided with a soapbox on the corner. Not everyone tells the truth. Operational note: these sections may be taken out of numerical sequence: rearrange them to suit yourself for optimum clarity. Turn over your test papers and begin.

2

Uncounted layers of rock pressed down on the magma pool. White-hot with the bubbling ferocity of the molten nickel-iron core, the pool spat and shuddered, yet did not pit or char or smoke or damage in the slightest, the smooth and reflective surfaces of the strange crypt.

Nathan Stack lay in the crypt—silent, sleeping.

A shadow passed through rock. Through shale, through coal, through marble, through mica schist, through quartzite; through miles-thick deposits of phosphates, through diatomaceous earth, through feldspars, through diorite; through faults and folds, through anticlines and monoclines, through dips and synclines; through hellfire; and came to the ceiling of the great cavern and passed through; and saw the magma pool and dropped down; and came to the crypt. The shadow.

A triangular face with a single eye peered into the crypt, saw Stack; four-fingered hands were placed on the crypt's cool surface. Nathan Stack woke at the touch, and the crypt became transparent; he woke though the touch had not been upon his body. His soul felt the shadowy pressure and he opened his eyes to see the leaping brilliance of the worldcore around him, to see the shadow with its single eye staring at him.

The serpentine shadow enfolded the crypt; its darkness flowed upward again, through the Earth's mantle, toward the crust, toward the surface of the cinder, the broken toy that was the Earth.

When they reached the surface, the shadow bore the crypt to a place where the poison winds did not reach, and caused it to open.

Nathan Stack tried to move, and moved only with difficulty. Memories rushed through his head of other lives, many other lives, as many other men; then the memories slowed and melted into a background tone that could be ignored.

The shadow thing reached down a hand and touched Stack's naked flesh. Gently, but firmly, the thing helped him to stand, and gave him garments, and a neck-pouch that contained a short knife and a warming-stone and other things. He offered his hand, and Stack took it, and after two hundred and fifty thousand years sleeping in the crypt, Nathan Stack stepped out on the face of the sick planet Earth.

Then the thing bent low against the poison winds and began walking away. Nathan Stack, having no other choice, bent forward and followed the shadow creature.

3

A messenger had been sent for Dira and he had come as quickly as the meditations would permit. When he reached the Summit, he found the fathers waiting, and they took him gently into their cove, where they immersed themselves and began to speak.

"We've lost the arbitration," the coil-father said. "It will be necessary for us to go and leave it to him."

Dira could not believe it. "But didn't they listen to our arguments, to our logic?"

The fang-father shook his head sadly and touched Dira's shoulder. "There were . . . accommodations to be made. It was their time. So we must leave."

The coil-father said, "We've decided you will remain. One was permitted, in caretakership. Will you accept our commission?"

It was a very great honor, but Dira began to feel the loneliness even as they told him they would leave. Yet he accepted. Wondering why they had selected *him*, of all their people. There were reasons, there were always reasons, but he could not ask. And so he accepted the honor, with all its attendant sadness, and remained behind when they left.

The limits of his caretakership were harsh, for they ensured he could not defend himself against whatever slurs or legends would be spread, nor could he take action unless it became clear the trust was being breached by the other—who now held possession. And he had no threat save the Deathbird. A final threat that could be used only when final measures were needed: and therefore too late.

But he was patient. Perhaps the most patient of all his people.

Thousands of years later, when he saw how it was destined to go, when there was no doubt left how it would end, he understood *that* was the reason he had been chosen to stay behind.

But it did not help the loneliness.

Nor could it save the Earth. Only Stack could do that.

4

1 *Now the serpent was more subtil than any beast of the field which*
the LORD *God had made. And he said unto the woman, Yea, hath God said,*
Ye shall not eat of every tree of the garden?
2 *And the woman said unto the serpent, We may eat of the fruit of the*
trees of the garden:
3 *But of the fruit of the tree which is in the midst of the garden, God*
hath said, Ye shall not eat of it, neither shall ye touch it, lest ye die.
4 *And the serpent said unto the woman, Ye shall not surely die:*
5 *(Omitted)*
6 *And when the woman saw that the tree was good for food, and that*
it was *pleasant to the eyes, and a tree to be desired to make* one *wise, she*
took of the fruit thereof, and did eat, and gave also unto her husband with
her; and he did eat.
7 *(Omitted)*
8 *(Omitted)*
9 *And the* LORD *God called unto Adam, and said unto him, Where*
art *thou?*
10 *(Omitted)*
11 *And he said, Who told thee that thou* wast *naked? Hast thou eaten*
of the tree, whereof I commanded thee that thou shouldst not eat?
12 *And the man said, The woman whom thou gavest* to be *with me, she*
gave me of the tree, and I did eat.
13 *And the* LORD *God said unto the woman, What* is *this* that *thou hast*
done? And the woman said, The serpent beguiled me, and I did eat.

14 *And the* LORD *God said unto the serpent, Because thou hast done this, thou* art *cursed above all cattle, and above every beast of the field; upon thy belly shalt thou go, and dust shalt thou eat all the days of thy life:*

15 *And I will put enmity between thee and the woman, and between thy seed and her seed; it shall bruise thy head, and thou shalt bruise his heel.*

—*Genesis 3:1–15*

TOPICS FOR DISCUSSION
(Give 5 points per right answer.)

1. Melville's MOBY DICK begins, "Call me Ishmael." We say it is told in the *first* person. In what person is Genesis told? From whose viewpoint?

2. Who is the "good guy" in this story? Who is the "bad guy"? Can you make a strong case for reversal of the roles?

3. Traditionally, the apple is considered to be the fruit the serpent offered to Eve. But apples are not endemic to the Near East. Select one of the following, more logical substitutes, and discuss how myths come into being and are corrupted over long periods of time: olive, fig, date, pomegranate.

4. Why is the word LORD always in capitals and the name God always capitalized? Shouldn't the serpent's name be capitalized, as well? If no, why?

5. If God created everything (see Genesis, Chap. I), why did he create problems for himself by creating a serpent who would lead his creations astray? Why did God create a tree he did not want Adam and Eve to know about, and then go out of his way to warn them against it?

6. Compare and contrast Michelangelo's Sistine Chapel ceiling panel of the *Expulsion from Paradise* with Bosch's *Garden of Earthly Delights*.

7. Was Adam being a gentleman when he placed blame on Eve? Who was Quisling? Discuss "narking" as a character flaw.

8. God grew angry when he found out he had been defied. If God is omnipotent and omniscient, didn't he know? Why couldn't he find Adam and Eve when they hid?

9. If God had not wanted Adam and Eve to taste the fruit of the forbidden tree, why didn't he warn the serpent? Could God have prevented the serpent from tempting Adam and Eve? If yes, why didn't he? If no, discuss the possibility the serpent was as powerful as God.

10. Using examples from two different media journals, demonstrate the concept of "slanted news."

5

The poison winds howled and tore at the powder covering the land. Nothing lived there. The winds, green and deadly, dived out of the sky and raked the carcass of the Earth, seeking, seeking: anything moving, anything still living. But there was nothing. Powder. Talc. Pumice.

And the onyx spire of the mountain toward which Nathan Stack and the shadow thing had moved, all that first day. When night fell they dug a pit in the tundra and the shadow thing coated it with a substance thick as glue that had been in Stack's neck-pouch. Stack had slept the night fitfully, clutching the warming-stone to his chest and breathing through a filter tube from the pouch.

Once he had awakened, at the sound of great batlike creatures flying overhead; he had seen them swooping low, coming in flat trajectories across the wasteland toward his pit in the earth. But they seemed unaware that he—and the shadow thing—lay in the hole. They excreted thin, phosphorescent strings that fell glowing through the night and were lost on the plains; then the creatures swooped upward and were whirled away on the winds. Stack resumed sleeping with difficulty.

In the morning, frosted with an icy light that gave everything a blue tinge, the shadow thing scrabbled its way out of the choking powder and crawled along the ground, then lay flat, fingers clawing for purchase in the whiskaway surface. Behind it, from the powder, Stack bore toward the surface, reached up a hand and trembled for help.

The shadow creature slid across the ground, fighting the winds that had grown stronger in the night, back to the soft place that had been their pit, to the hand thrust up through the powder. It grasped the hand, and Stack's fingers tightened convulsively. Then the crawling shadow exerted pressure and pulled the man from the treacherous pumice.

Together they lay against the earth, fighting to see, fighting to draw breath without filling their lungs with suffocating death.

"Why is it like this . . . what *happened*?" Stack screamed against the wind. The shadow creature did not answer, but it looked at Stack for a long moment and then, with very careful movements, raised its hand, held it up before Stack's eyes and slowly, making claws of the fingers, closed the four fingers into a cage, into a fist, into a painfully tight ball that said more eloquently than words: *destruction*.

Then they began to crawl toward the mountain.

6

The onyx spire of the mountain rose out of hell and struggled toward the shredded sky. It was monstrous arrogance. Nothing should have tried that climb out of desolation. But the black mountain had tried, and succeeded.

It was like an old man. Seamed, ancient, dirt caked in striated lines, autumnal, lonely; black and desolate, piled strength upon strength. It would *not* give in to gravity and pressure and death. It struggled for the sky. Ferociously alone, it was the only feature that broke the desolate line of the horizon.

In another twenty-five million years the mountain might be worn as smooth and featureless as a tiny onyx offering to the deity night. But though the powder plains swirled and the poison winds drove the pumice against the flanks of the pinnacle, thus far their scouring had only served to soften the edges of the mountain's profile, as though divine intervention had protected the spire.

Lights moved near the summit.

7

Stack learned the nature of the phosphorescent strings excreted onto the plain the night before by the batlike creatures. They were spores that became, in the wan light of day, strange bleeder plants.

All around them as they crawled through the dawn, the little live things sensed their warmth and began thrusting shoots up through the talc. As the fading red ember of the dying sun climbed painfully into the sky, the bleeding plants were already reaching maturity.

Stack cried out as one of the vine tentacles fastened around his ankle, holding him. A second looped itself around his neck.

Thin films of berry-black blood coated the vines, leaving rings on Stack's flesh. The rings burned terribly.

The shadow creature slid on its belly and pulled itself back to the man. Its triangular head came close to Stack's neck, and it bit into the vine. Thick black blood spurted as the vine parted, and the shadow creature rasped its razor-edged teeth back and forth till Stack was able to breathe again. With a violent movement Stack folded himself down and around, pulling the short knife from the neck-pouch. He sawed through the vine tightening inexorably around his ankle. It screamed as it was severed, in the same voice Stack had heard from the skies the night before. The severed vine writhed away, withdrawing into the talc.

Stack and the shadow thing crawled forward once again, low, flat, holding onto the dying earth: toward the mountain.

High in the bloody sky, the Deathbird circled.

8

On their own world, they had lived in luminous, oily-walled caverns for millions of years, evolving and spreading their race through the universe. When they had had enough of empire building, they turned inward, and much of their time was spent in the intricate construction of songs of wisdom, and the designing of fine worlds for many races.

There were other races that designed, however. And when there was a conflict over jurisdiction, an arbitration was called, adjudicated by a race whose *raison d'être* was impartiality and cleverness in unraveling knotted threads of claim and counterclaim. Their racial honor, in fact, depended on the flawless application of these qualities. Through the centuries they had refined their talents in more and more sophisticated arenas of arbitration until the time came when they were the final authority. The litigants were compelled to abide by the judgments, not merely because the decisions were always wise and creatively fair, but because the judges' race would, if its decisions were questioned as suspect, destroy itself. In the holiest place on their world they had erected a religious machine. It could be activated to emit a tone that would shatter their crystal carapaces. They were a race of exquisite cricket-like creatures, no larger than the thumb of a man. They were treasured throughout the civilized worlds, and their loss would have been catastrophic. Their honor and their value was never questioned. All races abided by their decisions.

So Dira's people gave over jurisdiction to that certain world, and went away, leaving Dira with only the Deathbird, a special caretakership the adjudicators had creatively woven into their judgment.

There is recorded one last meeting between Dira and those who had given him his commission. There were readings that could not be ignored—had, in fact, been urgently brought to the attention of the fathers of Dira's race by the adjudicators—and the Great Coiled One came to Dira at the last possible moment to tell him of the mad thing into whose hands this world had been given, to tell Dira of what the mad thing would do.

The Great Coiled One—whose rings were loops of wisdom acquired through centuries of gentleness and perception and immersed meditations that had brought forth lovely designs for many worlds—he who was the holiest of Dira's race, honored Dira by coming to *him*, rather than commanding Dira to appear.

We have only one gift to leave them, he said. *Wisdom. This mad one will come, and he will lie to them, and he will tell them: created he them. And we will be gone, and there will be nothing between them and the mad one but you. Only you can give them the wisdom to defeat him in their own good time.* Then the Great Coiled One stroked the skin of Dira with ritual affection, and Dira was deeply moved and could not reply. Then he was left alone.

The mad one came, and interposed himself, and Dira gave them wisdom, and time passed. His name became other than Dira, it became Snake, and the new name was despised: but Dira could see the Great Coiled One had been correct in his readings. So Dira made his selection. A man, one of them, and gifted him with the spark.

All of this is recorded somewhere. It is history.

9

The man was not Jesus of Nazareth. He may have been Simon. Not Genghis Khan, but perhaps a foot soldier in his horde. Not Aristotle, but possibly one who sat and listened to Socrates in the agora. Neither the shambler who discovered the wheel nor the link who first ceased painting himself blue and applied the colors to the walls of the cave. But one near them, somewhere near at hand. The man was not Richard *Coeur-de-Lion*, Rembrandt, Richelieu, Rasputin, Robert Fulton or the Mahdi. Just a man. With the spark.

10

Once, Dira came to the man. Very early on. The spark was there, but the light needed to be converted to energy. So Dira came to the man, and did what had to be done before the mad one knew of it, and when he discovered that Dira, the Snake, had made contact, he quickly made explanations.

This legend has come down to us as the fable of Faust.

TRUE or FALSE?

11

Light converted to energy, thus:

In the fortieth year of his five hundredth incarnation, all-unknowing of the eons of which he had been part, the man found himself wandering in a terrible dry place under a thin, flat burning disc of sun. He was a Berber tribesman who had never considered shadows save to relish them when they provided shade. The shadow came to him, sweeping down across the sands like the *khamsin* of Egypt, the *simoom* of Asia Minor, the *harmattan*, all of which he had known in his various lives, none of which he remembered. The shadow came over him like the *sirocco*.

The shadow stole the breath from his lungs and the man's eyes rolled up in his head. He fell to the ground and the shadow took him down and down, through the sands, into the Earth.

Mother Earth.

She lived, this world of trees and rivers and rocks with deep stone thoughts. She breathed, had feelings, dreamed dreams, gave birth, laughed, and grew contemplative for millennia. This great creature swimming in the sea of space.

What a wonder, thought the man, for he had never understood that the Earth was his mother, before this. He had never understood, before this, that the Earth had a life of its own, at once a part of mankind and quite separate from mankind. A mother with a life of her own.

Dira, Snake, shadow . . . took the man down and let the spark of light change itself to energy as the man became one with the Earth. His flesh melted and became quiet, cool soil. His eyes glowed with the light that shines in the darkest centers of the planet and he saw the way the mother cared for her young: the worms, the roots of plants, the rivers that cascaded for miles over great cliffs in enormous caverns, the bark of trees. He was taken once more to the bosom of that great Earth mother, and understood the joy of her life.

Remember this, Dira said to the man.

What a wonder, the man thought . . .

. . . and was returned to the sands of the desert, with no remembrance of having slept with, loved, enjoyed the body of his natural mother.

12

They camped at the base of the mountain, in a greenglass cave; not deep but angled sharply so the blown pumice could not reach them. They put Nathan Stack's stone in a fault in the cave's floor, and the heat spread quickly, warming them. The shadow thing with its triangular head sank back in shadow and closed its eye and sent its hunting instinct out for food. A shriek came back on the wind.

Much later, when Nathan Stack had eaten, when he was reasonably content and well fed, he stared into the shadows and spoke to the creature sitting there.

"How long was I down there . . . how long was the sleep?"

The shadow thing spoke in whispers. *A quarter of a million years.*

Stack did not reply. The figure was beyond belief. The shadow creature seemed to understand.

In the life of a world no time at all.

Nathan Stack was a man who could make accommodations. He smiled quickly and said, "I must have been tired."

The shadow did not respond.

"I don't understand very much of this. It's pretty damned frightening. To die, then to wake up . . . here. Like this."

You did not die. You were taken, put down there. By the end you will understand everything, I promise you.

"Who put me down there?"

I did. I came and found you when the time was right, and I put you down there.

"Am I still Nathan Stack?"

If you wish.

"But *am* I Nathan Stack?"

You always were. You had many other names, many other bodies, but the spark was always yours. Stack seemed about to speak, and the shadow creature added, *You were always on your way to being who you are.*

"But what *am* I? Am I still Nathan Stack, dammit?"

If you wish.

"Listen: you don't seem too sure about that. You came and got me, I mean I woke up and there you were. Now who should know better than you what my name is?"

You have had many names in many times. Nathan Stack is merely the one you remember. You had a very different name long ago, at the start, when I first came to you.

Stack was afraid of the answer, but he asked, "What was my name then?"

Ish-lilith, Husband of Lilith. Do you remember her?

Stack thought, tried to open himself to the past, but it was as unfathomable as the quarter of a million years through which he had slept in the crypt.

"No. But there were other women, in other times."

Many. There was one who replaced Lilith.

"I don't remember."

Her name . . . does not matter. But when the mad one took Lilith from you and replaced her with the other . . . then I knew it would end like this. The Deathbird.

"I don't mean to be stupid, but I haven't the faintest idea what you're talking about."

Before it ends, you will understand everything.

"You said that before." Stack paused, stared at the shadow creature for a long time only moments long, then, "What was your name?"

Before I met you my name was Dira.

He said it in his native tongue. Stack could not pronounce it.

"Before you met me. What is it now?"

Snake.

Something slithered past the mouth of the cave. It did not stop, but it called out with the voice of moist mud sucking down into a quagmire.

"Why did you put *me* down there? Why did you come to me in the first place? What spark? Why can't I remember these other lives or who I was? What do you want from me?"

You should sleep. It will be a long climb. And cold.

"I slept for two hundred and fifty thousand years, I'm hardly tired," Stack said. "Why did you pick me?"

Later. Now sleep. Sleep has other uses.

Darkness deepened around Snake, seeped out around the cave, and Nathan Stack lay down near the warming stone, and the darkness took him.

13

SUPPLEMENTARY READING

This is an essay by a writer. It is clearly an appeal to the emotions. As you read it, ask yourself how it applies to the subject under discussion. What is the writer trying to say? Does he succeed in making his point? Does this essay cast light on the point of the subject under discussion? After you have read this essay, using the reverse side of your test paper, write your own essay (500 words or less) on the loss of a loved one. If you have never lost a loved one, fake it.

AHBHU

Yesterday my dog died. For eleven years Ahbhu was my closest friend. He was responsible for my writing a story about a boy and his dog that many people have read. The story was made into a successful movie. The dog in the movie looked a lot like Ahbhu. He was not a pet, he was a person. It was impossible to anthropomorphize him, he wouldn't stand for it. But he was so much his own kind of creature, he had such a strongly formed personality, he was so determined to share his life with only those *he* chose, that it was also impossible to think of him as simply a dog. Apart from those canine characteristics into which he was locked by his genes, he comported himself like one of a kind.

We met when I came to him at the West Los Angeles Animal Shelter. I'd wanted a dog because I was lonely and I'd remembered when I was a little boy how my dog had been a friend when I had no other friends. One summer I went away to camp and when I returned I found a rotten old neighbor lady from up the street had had my dog picked up and gassed while my father was at work. I crept into the woman's backyard that night and found a rug hanging on the clothesline. The rug beater was hanging from a post. I stole it and buried it.

At the Animal Shelter there was man in line ahead of me. He had brought in a puppy only a week or so old. A Puli, a Hungarian sheep dog; it was a sad-looking little thing. He had too many in the litter and had brought in this one either to be taken by someone else or to be put to sleep. They took the dog inside and the man behind the counter called my turn. I told him I wanted a dog and he took me back inside to walk down the line of cages.

In one of the cages the little Puli that had just been brought in was being assaulted by three larger dogs that had been earlier tenants. He was a little thing, and he was on the bottom, getting the stuffing knocking out of him. He was struggling mightily.

"Get him out of there!" I yelled. "I'll take him, I'll take him, get him out of there!"

He cost two dollars. It was the best two bucks I ever spent.

Driving home with him, he was lying on the other side of the front seat, staring at me. I had had a vague idea what I'd name a pet, but as I stared at him, and he stared back at me, I suddenly was put in mind of the scene in Alexander Korda's 1939 film *The Thief of Bagdad*, where the evil vizier, played by Conrad Veidt, had changed Ahbhu, the little thief, played by Sabu, into a dog. The film had superimposed the human over the canine face for a moment so there was an extraordinary look of intelligence in the face of the dog. The little Puli was looking at me with that same expression. "Ahbhu," I said.

He didn't react to the name, but then he couldn't have cared less. But that was his name, from that time on.

No one who ever came into my house was unaffected by him. When he sensed someone with good vibrations, he was right there, lying at their feet. He loved to be scratched, and despite years of admonitions he refused to stop begging for scraps at table, because he had found most of the people who came to dinner at my house were patsies unable to escape his woebegone Jackie-Coogan-as-the-Kid look.

But he was a certain barometer of bums, as well. On any number of occasions when I found someone I liked, and Ahbhu would have nothing to do with him or her, it always turned out the person was a wrongo. I took to noting his attitude toward newcomers, and I must admit it influenced my own reactions. I was always wary of someone Ahbhu shunned.

Women with whom I had had unsatisfactory affairs would nonetheless return to the house from time to time—to visit the dog. He had an intimate circle of friends, many of whom had nothing to do with me, and numbering among their company some of the most beautiful actresses in Hollywood. One exquisite lady used to send her driver to pick him up for Sunday afternoon romps at the beach.

I never asked him what happened on those occasions. He didn't talk.

Last year he started going downhill, though I didn't realize it because he maintained the manner of a puppy almost to the end. But he began sleeping too much, and he couldn't hold down his food—not even the Hungarian meals prepared for him by the Magyars who lived up the street. And it became apparent to me something was wrong with him when he got scared during the big Los Angeles earthquake last year. Ahbhu wasn't afraid of anything.

He attacked the Pacific Ocean and walked tall around vicious cats. But the quake terrified him and he jumped up in my bed and threw his forelegs around my neck. I was very nearly the only victim of the earthquake to die from animal strangulation.

He was in and out of the veterinarian's shop all through the early part of this year, and the idiot always said it was his diet.

Then one Sunday when he was out in the backyard, I found him lying at the foot of the stairs, covered with mud, vomiting so heavily all he could bring up was bile. He was matted with his own refuse and he was trying desperately to dig his nose into the earth for coolness. He was barely breathing. I took him to a different vet.

At first they thought it was just old age . . . that they could pull him through. But finally they took X-rays and saw the cancer had taken hold in his stomach and liver.

I put off the day as much as I could. Somehow I just couldn't conceive of a world that didn't have him in it. But yesterday I went to the vet's office and signed the euthanasia papers.

"I'd like to spend a little time with him, before," I said.

They brought him in and put him on the stainless steel examination table. He had grown so thin. He'd always had a pot-belly and it was gone. The muscles in his hind legs were weak, flaccid. He came to me and put his head into the hollow of my armpit. He was trembling violently. I lifted his head and he looked at me with that comic face I'd always thought made him look like Lawrence Talbot, the Wolf Man. He knew. Sharp as hell right up to the end, hey old friend? He knew, and he was scared. He trembled all the way down to his spiderweb legs. This bouncing ball of hair that, when lying on a dark carpet, could be taken for a sheepskin rug, with no way to tell at which end head and which end tail. So thin. Shaking, knowing what was going to happen to him. But still a puppy.

I cried and my eyes closed as my nose swelled with the crying, and he buried his head in my arms because we hadn't done much crying at one another. I was ashamed of myself not to be taking it as well as he was.

"I *got* to, pup, because you're in pain and you can't eat. I *got* to." But he didn't want to know that.

The vet came in, then. He was a nice guy and he asked me if I wanted to go away and just let it be done.

Then Ahbhu came up out of there and *looked* at me.

There is a scene in Kazan's and Steinbeck's *Viva Zapata* where a close friend of Zapata's, Brando's, has been condemned for conspiring with the *federales*. A friend that had been with Zapata since the mountains, since the *revolución* had begun. And they come to the hut to take him to the firing squad, and Brando starts out, and his friend stops him with a hand on his arm, and he says to him with great friendship, "Emiliano, do it yourself."

Ahbhu looked at me and I know he was just a dog, but if he could have spoken with human tongue he could not have said more eloquently than he did with a look, *don't leave me with strangers.*

So I held him as they laid him down and the vet slipped the lanyard up around his right foreleg and drew it tight to bulge the vein, and I held his head and he turned it away from me as the needle went in. It was impossible to tell the moment he passed over from life to death. He simply laid his head on my hand, his eyes fluttered shut and he was gone.

I wrapped him in a sheet with the help of the vet and I drove home with Ahbhu on the seat beside me, just the way we had come home eleven years before. I took him out in the backyard and began digging his grave. I dug for hours, crying and mumbling to myself, talking to him in the sheet. It was a very neat, rectangular grave with smooth sides and all the loose dirt scooped out by hand.

I laid him down in the hole and he was so tiny in there for a dog who had seemed to be so big in life, so furry, so funny. And I covered him over and when the hole was packed full of dirt I replaced the neat divot of grass I'd scalped off at the start. And that was all.

But I couldn't send him to strangers.

THE END

QUESTIONS FOR DISCUSSION

1. Is there any significance to the reversal of the word *god* being *dog*? If so, what?
2. Does the writer try to impart human qualities to a nonhuman creature? Why? Discuss anthropomorphism in the light of the phrase, "Thou art God."
3. Discuss the love the writer shows in this essay. Compare and contrast it with other forms of love: the love of a man for a woman, a mother for a child, a son for a mother, a botanist for plants, an ecologist for the Earth.

14

In his sleep, Nathan Stack talked.
"Why did you pick me? Why me? . . ."

15

Like the Earth, the Mother was in pain.

The great house was very quiet. The doctor had left, and the relatives had gone into town for dinner. He sat by the side of her bed and stared down at her. She looked gray and old and crumpled; her skin was a powdery, ashy hue of moth-dust. He was crying softly.

He felt her hand on his knee, and looked up to see her staring at him. "You weren't supposed to catch me," he said.

"I'd be disappointed if I hadn't," she said. Her voice was very thin, very smooth.

"How is it?"

"It hurts. Ben didn't dope me too well."

He bit his lower lip. The doctor had used massive doses, but the pain was more massive. She gave little starts as tremors of sudden agony hit her. Impacts. He watched the life leaking out of her eyes.

"How is your sister taking it?"

He shrugged. "You know Charlene. She's sorry, but it's all pretty intellectual to her."

His mother let a tiny ripple of a smile move her lips. "It's a terrible thing to say, Nathan, but your sister isn't the most likable woman in the world. I'm glad you're here." She paused, thinking, then added, "It's just possible your father and I missed something from the gene pool. Charlene isn't whole."

"Can I get you something? A drink of water?"

"No, I'm fine."

He looked at the ampoule of narcotic painkiller. The syringe lay mechanical and still on a clean towel beside it. He felt her eyes on him. She knew what he was thinking. He looked away.

"I would kill for a cigarette," she said.

He laughed. At sixty-five, both legs gone, what remained of her left side paralyzed, the cancer spreading like deadly jelly toward her heart, she was still the matriarch. "You can't have a cigarette, so forget it."

"Then why don't you use that hypo and let me out of here."

"Shut up, Mother."

"Oh, for Christ's sake, Nathan. It's hours if I'm lucky. Months if I'm not. We've had this conversation before. You know I always win."

"Did I ever tell you you were a bitchy old lady?"

"Many times, but I love you anyhow."

He got up and walked to the wall. He could not walk through it, so he went around the inside of the room.

"You can't get away from it."

"Mother, Jesus! Please!"

"All right. Let's talk about the business."

"I couldn't care less about the business right now."

"Then what should we talk about? The lofty uses to which an old lady can put her last moments?"

"You know, you're really ghoulish. I think you're *enjoying* this in some sick way."

"What other way is there to enjoy it?"

"An adventure."

"The biggest. A pity your father never had the chance to savor it."

"I hardly think he'd have savored the feeling of being stamped to death in a hydraulic press."

Then he thought about it, because that little smile was on her lips again. "Okay, he probably would have. The two of you were so unreal, you'd have sat there and discussed it and analyzed the pulp."

"And you're our son."

He was, and he was. And he could not deny it, nor had he ever. He was hard and gentle and wild just like them, and he remembered the days in the jungle beyond Brasilia, and the hunt in the Cayman Trench, and the other days working in the mills alongside his father, and he knew when his moment came he would savor death as she did.

"Tell me something. I've always wanted to know. *Did* Dad kill Tom Golden?"

"Use the needle and I'll tell you."

"I'm a Stack. I don't bribe."

"*I'm* a Stack, and I know what a killing curiosity you've got. Use the needle and I'll tell you."

He walked widdershins around the room. She watched him, eyes bright as the mill vats.

"You old bitch."

"Shame, Nathan. You know you're not the son of a bitch. Which is more than your sister can say. Did I ever tell you she wasn't your father's child?"

"No, but I knew."

"You'd have liked her father. He was Swedish. *Your* father liked him."

"Is that why Dad broke both his arms?"

"Probably. But I never heard the Swede complain. One night in bed with me in those days was worth a couple of broken arms. Use the needle."

Finally, while the family was between the entree and the dessert, he filled the syringe and injected her. Her eyes widened as the stuff smacked her heart, and just before she died she rallied all her strength and said, "A deal's a deal. Your father didn't kill Tom Golden, I did. You're a hell of a man, Nathan, and you fought us the way we wanted, and we both loved you more than you could know. Except, dammit, you cunning s.o.b., you *do* know, don't you?"

"I know," he said, and she died; and he cried; and that was the extent of the poetry in it.

16

He knows we are coming.

They were climbing the northern face of the onyx mountain. Snake had coated Nathan Stack's feet with the thick glue and, though it was hardly a country walk, he was able to keep a foothold and pull himself up. Now they had paused to rest on a spiral ledge, and Snake had spoken for the first time of what waited for them where they were going.

"He?"

Snake did not answer. Stack slumped against the wall of the ledge. At the lower slopes of the mountain they had encountered sluglike creatures that had tried to attach themselves to Stack's flesh, but when Snake had driven them off they had returned to sucking the rocks. They had not come near the shadow creature. Farther up, Stack could see the lights that flickered at the summit; he had felt fear that crawled up from his stomach. A short time before they had come to this ledge they had stumbled past a cave in the mountain where the bat creatures slept. They had gone mad at the presence of the man and the Snake, and the sounds they had made sent waves of nausea through Stack. Snake had helped him and they had gotten past. Now they had stopped and Snake would not answer Stack's questions.

We must keep climbing.

"Because he knows we're here." There was a sarcastic rise in Stack's voice.

Snake started moving. Stack closed his eyes. Snake stopped and came back to him. Stack looked up at the one-eyed shadow.

"Not another step."

There is no reason why you should not know.

"Except, friend, I have the feeling you aren't going to tell me anything."

It is not yet time for you to know.

"Look: just because I haven't asked, doesn't mean I don't want to know. You've told me things I shouldn't be able to handle . . . all kinds of crazy things . . . I'm as old as, as . . . I don't know *how* old, but I get the feeling you've been trying to tell me I'm Adam . . ."

That is so.

". . . uh." He stopped rattling and stared back at the shadow creature. Then, very softly, accepting even more than he had thought possible, he said, "Snake." He was silent again. After a time he asked, "Give me another dream and let me know the rest of it?"

You must be patient. The one who lives at the top knows we are coming but I have been able to keep him from perceiving your danger to him only because you do not know yourself.

"Tell me this, then: does he *want* us to come up . . . the one on the top?"

He allows it. Because he doesn't know.

Stack nodded, resigned to following Snake's lead. He got to his feet and performed an elaborate butler's motion: after you, Snake.

And Snake turned, his flat hands sticking to the wall of the ledge, and they climbed higher, spiraling upward toward the summit.

The Deathbird swooped, then rose toward the Moon. There was still time.

17

Dira came to Nathan Stack near sunset, appearing in the board room of the industrial consortium Stack had built from the empire left by his family.

Stack sat in the pneumatic chair that dominated the conversation pit where top-level decisions were made. He was alone. The others had left hours before and the room was dim with only the barest glow of light from hidden banks that shone through the soft walls.

The shadow creature passed through the walls—and at his passage they became rose quartz, then returned to what they had been. He stood staring at Nathan Stack, and for long moments the man was unaware of any other presence in the room.

You have to go now, Snake said.

Stack looked up, his eyes widened in horror, and through his mind flitted the unmistakable image of Satan, fanged mouth smiling, horns gleaming with scintillas of light as though seen through crosstar filters, rope tail with its spade-shaped appendage thrashing, cloven hoofs leaving burning imprints in the carpet, eyes as deep as pools of oil, the pitchfork, the satin-lined cape, the hairy legs of a goat, talons. He tried to scream but the sound dammed up in his throat.

No, Snake said, *that is not so. Come with me, and you will understand.*

There was a tone of sadness in the voice. As though Satan had been sorely wronged. Stack shook his head violently.

There was no time for argument. The moment had come, and Dira could not hesitate. He gestured and Nathan Stack rose from the pneumatic chair, leaving behind something that looked like Nathan Stack asleep, and he walked to Dira and Snake took him by the hand and they passed through rose quartz and went away from there.

Down and down Snake took him.

The Mother was in pain. She had been sick for eons, but it had reached the point where Snake knew it would be terminal, and the Mother knew it, too. But she would hide her child, she would intercede in her own behalf and hide him away deep in her bosom where no one, not even the mad one, could find him.

Dira took Stack to Hell.

It was a fine place.

Warm and safe and far from the probing of mad ones.

And the sickness raged on unchecked. Nations crumbled, the oceans boiled and then grew cold and filmed over with scum, the air became thick with dust and killing vapors, flesh ran like oil, the skies grew dark, the sun blurred and became dull. The Earth moaned.

The plants suffered and consumed themselves, beasts became crippled and went mad, trees burst into flame and from their ashes rose glass shapes that shattered in the wind. The Earth was dying; a long, slow, painful death.

In the center of the Earth, in the fine place, Nathan Stack slept. *Don't leave me with strangers.*

Overhead, far away against the stars, the Deathbird circled and circled, waiting for the word.

18

When they reached the highest peak, Nathan Stack looked across through the terrible burning cold and the ferocious grittiness of the demon wind and saw the sanctuary of always, the cathedral of forever, the pillar of remembrance, the haven of perfection, the pyramid of blessings, the toyshop of creation, the vault of deliverance, the monument of longing, the receptacle of thoughts, the maze of wonder, the catafalque of despair, the podium of pronouncements and the kiln of last attempts.

On a slope that rose to a star pinnacle, he saw the home of the one who dwelled here—lights flashing and flickering, lights that could be seen far off across the deserted face of the planet—and he began to suspect the name of the resident.

Suddenly everything went red for Nathan Stack. As though a filter had been dropped over his eyes, the black sky, the flickering lights, the rocks that formed the great plateau on which they stood, even Snake became red, and with the color came pain. Terrible pain that burned through every channel of Stack's body, as though his blood had been set afire. He screamed and fell to his knees, the pain crackling through his brain, following every nerve and blood vessel and ganglion and neural track. His skull flamed.

Fight him, Snake said. *Fight him!*

I can't, screamed silently through Stack's mind, the pain too great even to speak. Fire licked and leaped and he felt the delicate tissue of thought shriveling. He tried to focus his thoughts on ice. He clutched for salvation at ice, chunks of ice, mountains of ice, swimming icebergs of ice half-buried in frozen water, even as his soul smoked and smoldered. *Ice!* He thought of millions of particles of hail rushing, falling, thundering against the firestorm eating his mind, and there was a spit of steam, a flame that went out, a corner that grew cool . . . and he took his stand in that corner, thinking ice, thinking blocks and chunks and monuments of ice, edging them out to widen the circle of coolness and safety. Then the flames began to retreat, to slide back down the channels, and he sent ice after them, snuffing them, burying them in ice and chill waters that raced after the flames and drove them out.

When he opened his eyes, he was still on his knees, but he could think again, and the red surfaces had become normal again.

He will try again. You must be ready.

"Tell me *everything!* I can't go through this without knowing, I need help! Tell me, Snake, tell me now!"

You can help yourself. You have the strength. I gave you the spark.

. . . and the second derangement struck!

The air turned shaverasse and he held dripping chunks of unclean rova in his jowls, the taste making him weak with nausea. His pods withered and drew up into his shell and as the bones cracked he howled with strings of pain that came so fast they were almost one. He tried to scuttle away, but his eyes magnified the shatter of light that beat against him. Facets of his eyes cracked and the juice began to bubble out. The pain was unbelievable.

Fight him!

Stack rolled onto his back, sending out cilia to touch the earth, and for an instant he realized he was seeing through the eyes of another creature, another form of life he could not even describe. But he was under an open sky and that produced fear; he was surrounded by air that had become deadly and *that* produced fear; he was going blind and *that* produced fear; he was . . . he was a *man* . . . fought back against the feeling of being some other thing . . . he was a *man* and he would not feel fear, he would stand.

He rolled over, withdrew his cilia, and struggled to lower his pods. Broken bones grated and pain thundered through his body. He forced himself to ignore it, and finally the pods were down and he was breathing and he felt his head reeling . . .

And when he opened his eyes he was Nathan Stack again.

. . . and the third derangement struck:

Hopelessness.

Out of unending misery he came back to be Stack.

. . . and the fourth derangement struck:

Madness.

Out of raging lunacy he fought his way to be Stack.

. . . and the fifth derangement, and the sixth, and the seventh, and the plagues, and the whirlwinds, and the pools of evil, and the reduction in size and accompanying fall forever through submicroscopic hells, and the things that fed on him from inside, and the twentieth, and the fortieth, and the sound of his voice screaming for release, and the voice of Snake always beside him, whispering *Fight him!*

Finally it stopped.

Quickly, now.

Snake took Stack by the hand and, half-dragging him, raced to the great palace of light and glass on the slope, shining brightly under the star pinnacle, and they passed under an arch of shining metal into the ascension hall. The portal sealed behind them.

There were tremors in the walls. The inlaid floors of jewels began to rumble and tremble. Bits of high and faraway ceilings began to drop. Quaking, the palace gave one hideous shudder and collapsed around them.

Now, Snake said. *Now you will know everything!*

And everything forgot to fall. Frozen in midair, the wreckage of the palace hung suspended above them. Even the air ceased to swirl. Time stood still. The movement of the Earth was halted. Everything held utterly immobile as Nathan Stack was permitted to understand all.

19

MULTIPLE CHOICE
(Counts for ½ your final grade.)

1. God is:
    A. An invisible spirit with a long beard.
    B. A small dog dead in a hole.
    C. Everyman.
    D. The Wizard of Oz.
2. Nietzsche wrote "God is dead." By this did he mean:
    A. Life is pointless.
    B. Belief in supreme deities has waned.
    C. There never was a God to begin with.
    D. Thou art God.
3. Ecology is another name for:
    A. Mother love.
    B. Enlightened self-interest.
    C. A good health salad with granola.
    D. God.
4. Which of these phrases most typifies the profoundest love:
    A. Don't leave me with strangers.
    B. I love you.
    C. God is love.
    D. Use the needle.
5. Which of these powers do we usually associate with God:
    A. Power.
    B. Love.
    C. Humanity.
    D. Docility.

20

None of the above.

Starlight shone in the eyes of the Deathbird and its passage through the night cast a shadow on the Moon.

21

Nathan Stack raised his hands and around them the air was still as the palace fell crashing. They were untouched. *Now you know all there is to know,* Snake said, sinking to one knee as though worshipping. There was no one there to worship but Nathan Stack.

"Was he always mad?"

From the first.

"Then those who gave our world to him were mad, and your race was mad to allow it."

Snake had no answer.

"Perhaps it was supposed to be like this," Stack said.

He reached down and lifted Snake to his feet, and he touched the shadow creature's sleek triangular head. "Friend," he said.

Snake's race was incapable of tears. He said, *I have waited longer than you can know for that word.*

"I'm sorry it comes at the end."

Perhaps it was supposed to be like this.

Then there was a swirling of air, a scintillation in the ruined palace, and the owner of the mountain, the owner of the ruined Earth came to them in a burning bush.

AGAIN, SNAKE? AGAIN YOU ANNOY ME?

The time for toys is ended.

NATHAN STACK YOU BRING TO STOP ME? *I* SAY WHEN THE TIME IS ENDED. *I* SAY, AS I'VE ALWAYS SAID.

Then, to Nathan Stack:

GO AWAY. FIND A PLACE TO HIDE UNTIL I COME FOR YOU.

Stack ignored the burning bush. He waved his hand, and the cone of safety in which they stood vanished. "Let's find him, first, then I know what to do."

The Deathbird sharpened its talons on the night wind and sailed down through emptiness toward the cinder of the Earth.

22

Nathan Stack has once contracted pneumonia. He had lain on the operating table as the surgeon made the small incision in the chest wall.

Had he not been stubborn, had he not continued working around the clock while the pneumonic infection developed into empyema, he would never have had to go under the knife, even for an operation as safe as a thoracotomy. But he was a Stack, and so he lay on the operating table as the rubber tube was inserted into the chest cavity to drain off the pus in the pleural cavity, and heard someone speak his name.

NATHAN STACK.

He heard it, from far off, across an Arctic vastness; heard it echoing over and over, down an endless corridor; as the knife sliced.

NATHAN STACK.

He remembered Lilith, with hair the color of dark wine. He remembered taking hours to die beneath a rock slide as his hunting companions in the pack ripped apart the remains of the bear and ignored his grunted moans for help. He remembered the impact of the crossbow bolt as it ripped through his hauberk and split his chest and he died at Agincourt. He remembered the icy water of the Ohio as it closed over his head and the flatboat disappearing without his mates' noticing his loss. He remembered the mustard gas that ate his lungs as he tried to crawl toward a farmhouse near Verdun. He remembered looking directly into the flash of the bomb and feeling the flesh of his face melt away. He remembered Snake coming to him in the board room and husking him like corn from his body. He remembered sleeping in the molten core of the Earth for a quarter of a million years.

Across the dead centuries he heard his mother pleading with him to set her free, to end her pain. *Use the needle.* Her voice mingled with the voice of the Earth crying out in endless pain at her flesh that had been ripped away, at her rivers turned to arteries of dust, at her rolling hills and green fields slagged to greenglass and ashes. The voices of his mother and the mother that was Earth became one, and mingled to become Snake's voice telling him he was the one man in the world—the last man in the world—who could end the terminal case the Earth had become.

Use the needle. Put the suffering Earth out of its misery. *It belongs to you now.*

Nathan Stack was secure in the power he contained. A power that far outstripped that of gods or Snakes or mad creators who stuck pins in their creations, who broke their toys.

YOU CAN'T. I WON'T LET YOU.

Nathan Stack walked around the burning bush as it crackled impotently in rage. He looked at it almost pityingly, remembering the Wizard of Oz with his great and ominous disembodied head floating in mist and lightning, and the poor little man behind the curtain turning the dials to create the effects. Stack walked around the effect, knowing he had more power than this sad, poor thing that had held his race in thrall since before Lilith had been taken from him.

He went in search of the mad one who capitalized his name.

23

Zarathustra descended alone from the mountains, encountering no one. But when he came into the forest, all at once there stood before him an old man who had left his holy cottage to look for roots in the woods. And thus spoke the old man to Zarathustra:

"No stranger to me is this wanderer: many years ago he passed this way. Zarathustra he was called, but he has changed. At that time you carried your ashes to the mountains; would you now carry your fire into the valleys? Do you not fear to be punished as an arsonist?

"Zarathustra has changed, Zarathustra has become a child, Zarathustra is an awakened one; what do you now want among the sleepers? You lived in your solitude as in the sea, and the sea carried you. Alas, would you now climb ashore? Alas, would you again drag your own body?"

Zarathustra answered: "I love man."

"Why," asked the saint, "did I go into the forest and the desert? Was it not because I loved man all too much? Now I love God; man I love not. Man is for me too imperfect a thing. Love of man would kill me."

"And what is the saint doing in the forest?" asked Zarathustra.

The saint answered: "I make songs and sing them; and when I make songs, I laugh, cry, and hum: thus I praise God. With singing, crying, laughing, and humming, I praise the god who is my god. But what do you bring us as a gift?"

When Zarathustra had heard these words he bade the saint farewell and said: "What could I have to give you? But let me go quickly lest I take something from you!" And thus they separated, the old one and the man, laughing as two boys laugh.

But when Zarathustra was alone he spoke thus to his heart: "Could it be possible? This old saint in the forest has not yet heard anything of this, that *God is dead!*"

24

Stack found the mad one wandering in the forest of final moments. He was an old, tired man, and Stack knew with a wave of his hand he could end it for this god in a moment. But what was the reason for it? It was even too late for revenge. It had been too late from the start. So he let the old one go his way, wandering in the forest, mumbling to himself, I WON'T LET YOU DO IT, in the voice of a cranky child; mumbling pathetically, OH, PLEASE, I DON'T WANT TO GO TO BED YET. I'M NOT YET DONE PLAYING.

And Stack came back to Snake, who had served his function and protected Stack until Stack had learned that he was more powerful than the god he'd worshipped all through the history of Men. He came back to Snake and their hands touched and the bond of friendship was sealed at last, at the end.

Then they worked together and Nathan Stack used the needle with a wave of his hands, and the Earth could not sigh with relief as its endless pain was ended . . . but it did sigh, and it settled in upon itself, and the molten core went out, and the winds died, and from high above them Stack heard the fulfillment of Snake's final act; he heard the descent of the Deathbird.

"What was your name?" Stack asked his friend.

Dira.

And the Deathbird settled down across the tired shape of the Earth, and it spread its wings wide, and brought them over and down, and enfolded the Earth as a mother enfolds her weary child. Dira settled down on the amethyst floor of the dark-shrouded palace, and closed his single eye with gratitude. To sleep at last, at the end.

All this, as Nathan Stack stood watching. He was the last, at the end, and because he had come to own—if even for a few moments—that which could have been his from the start, had he but known, he did not sleep but stood and watched. Knowing at last, at the end, that he had loved and done no wrong.

25

The Deathbird closed its wings over the Earth until at last, at the end, there was only the great bird crouched over the dead cinder. Then the Deathbird raised its head to the star-filled sky and repeated the sigh of loss the Earth had felt at the end. Then its eyes closed, it tucked its head carefully under its wing, and all was night.

Far away, the stars waited for the cry of the Deathbird to reach them so final moments could be observed at last, at the end, for the race of Men.

26

THIS IS FOR MARK TWAIN

XV

DARK LIBERATION

"It was *suggestion*, the use of the power of the mind, that made [Val] Lewton's films so terrifying. [. . .] He led [us] up to the door of terror and commanded [us], 'KNOCK!' "

—"Three Faces of Fear," *Cinema*, March 1966

Our journey is nearly over; our look at this potent manifestation of Iai almost done.

It's been a long journey, and no doubt many of you have discovered a few unexpected surprises in where it took us—some ideas and images and points of view that were often far from what was expected, perhaps even far from what was wanted.

We have a few more steps to go, but take heart. If you have read this far—whatever the force and form of your reactions—you have passed a curious test and already know what your reward is. If you have read fairly, noticed Harlan's commitment as storyteller, essayist, critic, editor, public voice—the rich flow of ideas and images and conviction harnessed to a vital task—then you understand, too, the dilemma facing such a writer.

In the Reed translation of the Berlin Papyrus 3024, we see how the hour of spiritual transformation arrives for the individual in whom the Rebel has manifested itself. That is at the heart of the problem. For the artist must reach beyond the transformation, beyond the vision and the drive he has experienced, and sell the idea to others. He must show, display, enact what has been perceived—render it, package it so it is accessible.

This is where Iai's battle really begins, for here in the public expression lies the reason why Hypatia was murdered, why Giordono Bruno went to the stake, why there is censure and threat and oppression.

And then, too, there is the world itself—caught in flux as ever, encompassing both the guiding past and the questionable future. What we and the years have to judge is the effectiveness of any one voice like Harlan's. It is one thing to speak of a liberation from the darkness of the past and the darkness of the future, quite another to succeed at it. There have been so many other Rebels, so many honest, committed, sometimes extraordinarily gifted folk who never managed to be heard, who never got to measure their times, who were daunted or went under, who were broken or even lost their lives.

The more we consider Harlan's position, the more we should marvel at how widely his voice *has* been heard.

There lies cause for real optimism.

The three pieces reprinted here show us in turn the compassion in that voice; the courage, the self-examination, the disgust, the stridency; finally the liberation; these many voices are all one voice, Harlan's voice, as he demonstrates the necessity to take a stand, a position, to be one's own person.

"The Thick Red Moment" (1982) began as Harlan's revulsion at excessive, gratuitous screen violence and the embrace of that violence by contemporary audiences. His examination of "knife-kill" or "splatter" films and the reasons for their popularity becomes, in the end, an indictment of cowardice: emotional, moral, intellectual.

"The Man Who Was Heavily into Revenge" (1978) sprang from Harlan's outrage as his own involvement with a venal building contractor. But even this power fantasy of revenge (a fantasy which, oddly enough, appeared in that hardest of science fiction magazines, *Analog*) recognizes that no one lives in a vacuum, that the ripples of a single event never quite stop, that one must be careful what one wishes for.

"Driving in the Spikes" (1983) is Harlan's manual for dealing with injustice: be your own Zorro, because chances are no one will do it for you. Like most of Harlan's serious work it is shot through with humor, but the barbs are still there, under the surface.

In these pieces, indeed throughout this book, Harlan uses the darkness and the light. He works with contrast and chiaroscuro, with whatever is needed to throw things into relief. Fantasy and truth. Intermingled.

And as he cautioned us earlier, if our world becomes bereft of artists who genuinely care about their craft and the ends to which that craft is applied, where will we go to keep our thoughts free, to find new concepts that will help us to see more than the darkness?

Such artists are often our best Rebels, some of our best repositories for Iai—not just as a vital private *voice* but as a courageously outspoken public one. And Harlan would be the first to remind us that the artist is not the only source of this voice. The purity of inspiration and imagination always favors such a figure, but the abuses and temptations and compromises are just as real as the blessings.

So we must look to our Rebels, whether they are artists or scientists or social workers, journalists or statesmen or shopkeepers, from whichever direction they come to us. We must seek out and recognize the ones who do, who see, who care enough, those who are "original both in content and form" or who work to present an old truth in a new exciting way. If they seem trustworthy, we must hear them out, for they have the courage to put themselves on the line.

We do not have to love them, but we must not lose them.

"The solitary creator, dreaming his or her dream, unaided, seems to me to be the only artist we can trust."

—Introduction to *The City on the Edge of Forever,* SIX SCIENCE FICTION PLAYS, edited by Roger Elwood, Washington Square Press, 1976

The Thick Red Moment

Once upon a time not too long ago I was married to a young woman whose every waking moment was underlain by a preoccupation with thanatopsis.

Perhaps it was only *Weltschmerz;* but I ruminate about her occasionally, and I'm more and more inclined to believe it was genuine thanatopsis.

I won't make you go to the dictionary. *Weltschmerz* is one of those words that sums up in German what would take paragraphs to illustrate in English. It means sorrow which one feels and accepts as his/her necessary portion in life; sentimental pessimism; literally, world-pain. *Thanatopsis* comes from the Greek personification of death, Thanatos. Like thanatophobia, it is a view or contemplation of death that transcends mere mortal awareness that we all come to an end in darkness.

I lived with her for a year, and was married to her for somewhat less than another year; and on November 20th, 1976 I sent her away and divorced her when I finally realized, for reasons I will not go into here, that I could not trust her. It was the culmination of a chain of events that I number among the most debilitating in my variegated life.

One month earlier, on October 8th, 1976, my mother died, after a long and dehumanizing illness. She had spent too long on the machines that kept her alive in the biological sense, but which could not bring her back from the condition of vegetable *thing* she had become.

She lay in the hospital bed, having become a cyborg.

Half-human, half-machine . . . extruding tubes . . . one with the ohm and the kilowatt . . . without tears or smiles . . . having no need to brush her teeth in the morning or a magazine to help her sleep at night. I touched her face and she did not know it. I put one of my tears on her cheek and it did not move.

And so finally it came to the end of the story, came to final moments when someone had to make the decision to kick out the plug. Someone made that decision.

Those ashen months of 1976, for those and other reasons, were a terrible time for me. Yet as barren of sunlight and joy as those days were, I never shared the world-pain or the absorption with thanatopsis my ex-wife had known. She would often say to me, "Why bother? What does it all mean? What's the point of living?" I would wither a little inside, because no argument suffices if the skin and bones don't understand that the answer is: we live to say "No!" to death.

Through all the days and limitlessly longer nights, I never felt my soul in the grip of the fist, never lost the humanism that keeps me warring with the rest of my species. We are one of the universe's noblest experiments; we have a right to be here, I've heard; and if we struggle long enough against the forces of ignorance and mischievousness that bedevil us, we will be worthy of that place in the universe. I believed that, continue to believe it, and only *once* during the monstrous period was my faith in the nobility of the human race shaken.

A month after my marriage became a portion for foxes, two months after my mother found the trail finally opened for her reunion with my father, I experienced the lowest moment I've ever known in my consideration of those with whom I share common heritage. On December 22nd, 1976—for the first and I sincerely hope only time—I was dashed to despair in the sure and certain knowledge that we are an ignoble, utterly vile form of life, unfit to steal space from weeds and slugs and the plankton in the sea.

That moment came in a motion picture theater, and I, who fear almost nothing, was frightened. Not at what was on the screen: at the audience around me. Fellow human beings, a stray and unspecific wad of eyes and open sensory equipment, common flesh and ordinary intellects. So petrified me with horror that I had to hold myself back from screaming and fleeing. I wanted to hide. I can't get over it, even now: *I wanted to hide.* I was more scared than I'd ever been, before or since.

Pause. Deep breath. Quell the memory. Force back the abreaction. Stop the shiver as it climbs.

On that Wednesday night I was escaping my life. I got in the old dirty Camaro and drove into the San Fernando Valley just over the hill from my house. Down there in the Valley is not Hollywood, it is not Brentwood or Westwood, it is barely Los Angeles. In many ways it is a suburb of Columbus, Ohio. As writer Louise Farr has said, it is the edge of the American Dream that bindlestiffs and bus-riders have come to seek where the sidewalks are made of gold. Or at least partially inlaid with bronze stars. But it is Country, in the way Fort Worth will always be Country, no matter how urbane and cosmopolitan Dallas becomes. It is tract homes and fast food and the Common Man keeping barefoot and pregnant the Common Woman.

Oh, there are fine shops and big homes—in Woodland Hills and the newer 850-to-million-five estates—there are nonpareil French restaurants like Aux Delices and Mon Grenier; there are pseudo-hip *boîtes* like Yellowfingers and L'Express, but every once in a while they get the French syntax wrong and wind up with names like Le Hot Club. Nonetheless, it ain't all no-necks and polyester crotches. It is just, like where you live, The Valley. As close to the American Dream as Common and *average* may ever hope to get.

I drove out, drove around, could not escape myself. And decided to take in a movie. Any movie. Didn't give a damn what or which.

In Tarzana, out along Ventura Boulevard, near the big tree under which I am told Edgar Rice Burroughs lies buried, in the bedroom community named after his greatest creation, there is a multiple-cinema like the thousands thrown up in every American city these past decades. Cinema I—Cinema II—Cinema III—Cinema IV they call themselves, these windowless, airless cubicles. They are not theaters. Theaters had spacious lobbies and balconies; they had cut glass chandeliers and ushers with flashlights; they had an authoritarian manager in an impeccable tuxedo to whom you could complain when the noisy shmucks behind you wouldn't shut up; they had a candy counter with freshly popped popcorn that got real butter slathered over it, not some artificial crankcase drainage that had never seen the inside of a cow. They were theaters, not these little boxes which, if they had handles, would be coffins. In Tarzana they have caused to be thrown up a six-box edifice called Theeeeee Movies of Tarzana.

I didn't care what I saw, just as long as I hadn't seen it before. Every screening room had a double feature. I picked the one that had two films I hadn't heard much about. I don't remember what the A film was, but the second movie, the B, was one that had been around for a few months, that I'd missed.

It was called *The Omen*. You may know of this film.

It was crowded for a Wednesday night and the lights were up as I wandered down the single aisle to find a seat. *The Omen* would start in a few minutes.

I gauged the audience. I've come to hate seeing films in ordinary theaters since the advent of television. People talk. Not at the screen, an occasional *bon mot* as response to something silly in the plot or a flawed performance, but to each other. Not *sotto voce*, not whispered, not subdued, with the understanding that there is *something going on here*, but at the top of their lungs, as if they were yelling in to someone in the kitchen to fetch them a fresh Coors. They are unable to separate reality in a theater from fantasy in their tv-saturated home. They babble continuously, they ask moronic questions of each other, they make it impossible to enjoy a motion picture. It is the great dolt audience, wrenched from the succoring flicker of the glass teat, forced out into this Halfway House between television stupor and the real world: not yet fully awake, merely perambulated into another setting where the alpha state can be reinduced. I looked around at my fellow filmgoers. Not much different from the crowd you last shared a Saturday Night at the Movies with.

I do not think I malign them too much by characterizing them as eminently average. From their behavior, from the mounds of filth and empty junk food containers I had to kick aside to get to my seat, from the stickiness of my shoes from the spilled sugar-water, from the beetled brows and piglike eyes, the feet up on the backs of seats in front of them, from the oceanic sound of chewing gum, I do not think I demean them much by perceiving them as creeps, meatheads, clods, fruitcakes, nincompoops, amoeba-brains, yoyos, yipyops, kadodies and clodhoppers. But then, the garbage dump smell of bad breath, redolent armpits, decaying skin bacteria and farts mixed with bad grass always gives me a headache and puts me in one of my foulest Elitist humors.

Nonetheless, I was there, the film was to start in a few minutes, and I was trying to escape (in the worst possible situs) the world. So I took a seat next to a young man and his date, a young woman. I gave them the benefit of the doubt: a young *man* and a young *woman*. I was shortly to learn that I had misjudged them. Actually: were-*things* passing for human.

I will describe them physically.

The young woman was vibrating against the membrane of her twenties. Gum moving in the mouth. Shortish. Ordinary in every esthetic consideration. Just a female person, holding the right hand of the young man who sat to my right. What distinguishes her most in memory is that she was with *him*.

Ah. Him.

There is a sort of young man, never older than twenty-five, that I occasionally encounter at college lectures. The somatotype is one you'll recognize. Large, soft, no straight lines, very rounded. A lover of carbohydrates. Pale. An overgrown Pillsbury doughboy. Weak mouth. Alert. Very sensitive. And I usually have to confront this type when I've done a number on Barbra Streisand, with whom I've had a number of path-crossings in my life, and whom I do not like a lot.

So when I've mentioned Ms. Streisand, and have expressed my opinion of her, one of these great soft things leaps up in the audience and, usually with tears in his eyes, hysterically reads me the riot act. "Barbra is *glo*rious! Barbra is a *star*! What do *you* know about *any*thing? You're just jealous of her!" Followed by exeunt trembling.

(God *knows* how much I envy her. She can wear a cloche and wedgies so much *better* than I. Don't shoot the shwans.)

Beside me sat one of those. He looked like Lenny in Steinbeck's OF MICE AND MEN. Probably not all there: several bricks short of a load: only 1.6 oars in the water. Big, soft, holding her hand.

Enough. Let me get directly to the moment.

This film, *The Omen,* is a textbook example of what we mean when we speak of gratuitous violence. That is, violence escalated visually beyond any value to plot advancement or simple good taste. That which makes your stomach lift and your eyes look away. Not the simple ballet of death one accepts in *Straw Dogs* or *The Wild Bunch* or *Alien* or *Bonnie and Clyde*: I've seen death close up a few times. Those films are okay.

No, *The Omen* is another can of worms.

And the moment came like this:

There is a scene in which David Warner gets his head cut off by a sheet of plate glass. We have been set up for this scene in a number of ways, so we will feel trepidation and mounting tension. Warner has evinced that sweaty, doomed attitude we have come to know through years of moviegoing as endemic to those the plot demands gets wasted. The whining passengers of the *Poseidon;* the downy-faced aviator on his first recon flight with Gable or Robert Taylor; the PFC who stands up in the Bataan jungle to yell to his rifle squad, "Hey, it's all clear, no more snipers!" Pee-*ing*! Bullet through the brain. We *know* poor David Warner is about to get shitcanned in some earsplitting way.

As the group of which Warner is a member rushes through the streets of some Algerian-style city (it's been over five years since I saw the film and detailed specifics of plot are blurred), we get artful intercuts by director Dickie Donner of Warner's sweaty, crazed face . . . a truck or wagon or somesuch with a large sheet of plate glass lying flat on the bed, protruding off the rear of the vehicle . . . Warner rushing . . . the truck trundling . . . the glass looking ominously ready . . . an impediment in the way of the truck . . . Warner . . . glass . . . ohmiGod! we know what's going to happen because the intercuts are harder, closer together, the music begins to crescendo . . . the impediment stops the truck . . . the wheels of the truck smash into it . . . the truck stops short . . . the glass wrenches loose and zips off the rear of the truck . . . Warner seeing the glass coming toward him . . .

Now we *know* he's going to get hit by the glass.

And because we're trained to drive instantly to the most morbid escalation of the death-equation, we *suspect* he'll be decapitated. And *that's* the point to which violence is at least tolerable, acceptable, required by the plot.

But.

Little Dickie Donner, famed far and wide as the director of the television kiddie show *The Banana Splits* and a movie about a superhero, charming Richard Donner directs the scene like this (remember, you're sitting in a theater all unaware of what's coming at you):

Intercuts. The glass slicing through the air. David Warner's face registering terror as he sees it coming. His eyes starting from his head. His mouth open in an animal scream of horror. The faces of the other actors distorted in ghastly expectation of the impact. Glass! Warner! Screams! Closeup on the glass slicing into Warner's neck. Blood spurts across the glass. The head rolls onto the glass. Glass and body carried backward to smash against a wall. Glass splintering.

Okay, we think, horrible. That's it, though. It's over.

Wrong, and wrong.

Now the head rolls down the glass, draining blood from dangling cords and emptying carotid artery. Blood smears on glass in long slimy streaks.

Enough!

The head bounces off the glass, hits the cobblestones, rolls.

Enough!

Camera follows the head bouncing down the street.

Enough! Enough already!

The head rolls into a corner.

Enough! God, cut me a break here!

The head comes to a stop as camera comes in on the final spurting of blood, the face contorted in horror, the eyelids still flickering . . .

And here is the ultimate ghastliness of that moment, close to Christmas of 1976. Not on the screen. In the theater.

The audience was applauding wildly.

They were, God help them, *laughing*!!

And beside me, that great soft average American boy and girl, fingers twined tightly, were pounding their fists on his knee. From him: moaning bursts of sound, as if he were coming. From her: sharp little expletives of pleasure, as if she were coming.

Rooted, unmoving, my hair tingling at the base of my scalp, memorable fear overwhelming me, I sat there in disbelief and dismay. What kind of lives could these people live? What awful hatred for the rest of the human race did they harbor? What black pools of emotion had been tapped to draw such a response? The character David Warner played was not a villain, so they couldn't be excused or understood on the basis of catharsis . . . that no-less-bestial but at least explicable release of applause and whistling when the Arch-Fiend or the Renegade White Man or the Psychopathic Terrorist gets blown away. No, this was a high from the violence, from the protracted, adoring closeups of blood and horror.

This was America experiencing "entertainment."

I can't remember the rest of the film. I'm not sure I actually stayed to the end. I know I didn't see the feature film I'd come to see. I may have stumbled up the aisle and into the night, decaying inside from the death of my mother, the breakup of my marriage, loneliness, sorrow . . . and the evil rite I had just sat through. But now, five years later, I recall that moment as the absolutely lowest point I've ever reached in loathing of my species. I could not even fantasize wiping them off the face of the Earth. That would have been to join with them in their unholy appreciation of the senselessly violent. I just wanted to be away!

Now, five years later, I see the twisted path stretching from that night of monstrous perception to an omnipresent mode in current movies.

In the phrase credited to writer-interviewer Mick Garris, *knife-kill movies*.

How many have you seen?

Halloween, Texas Chain Saw Massacre, Prom Night, He Knows You're Alone, Don't Answer the Phone, Dressed to Kill, When a Stranger Calls, Motel Hell, Silent Scream, Blood Beach, My Bloody Valentine, Friday the 13th, The Omen II, Mother's Day, Zombie, Eyes of a Stranger, The Boogey Man, New Year's Evil, Maniac, Terror Train, Humanoids From the Deep and, yes, I'm sorry to include this for those of you who adored it, *The Howling*.

How many knife-kills have *you* sat through?

More important: ask yourself *why* you went to some of these films, when you knew in advance how twisted, how anti-human, how sexist, how degenerate they promised to be?

Are *you* a great soft average American boy or girl? Did *you* come when the sharp stick gouged out the eyes? Did *you* applaud when the heads were sawed off? Did *you* gasp with pleasure at the special effects when the straight razor sliced and the blood spattered the camera lens?

Are you still deluding yourself that you're sane?

As I was saying. Knife-kill flicks. The subject of a new book titled SPLATTER MOVIES. You like that a lot? Splatter movies. Cute.

Though there are exceptions the apologists will always cite, the bulk of the violence—total, psychopathic, sudden and seemingly the only reason for making these films—is directed against women.

Oh sure, there are a few men who get whacked out in these films; but their deaths are usually perfunctory, sort of *pro forma*; almost as if they were reluctantly added to the script against the advent of just such criticisms as these, so the righteous director (who is usually co-scripter) and the producer can *justify* slaughter by saying, "Well, hell, didn't you see the guys who got snuffed? How can you say we hate women?"

But that's misdirection. Afterthought. It's like George Wallace talking about state's rights when what he really means is, *let's keep the niggers in chains*. It's on the moral and ethical level of those who excuse Nixon's criminal acts by saying, "Hell, *everybody* does it!"

No, what we're dealing with in nifty little films like Brian De Palma's

Dressed to Kill and *Blow Out* is a concerted attack on females. Females burned alive, hacked to ribbons, staked out and suffocated slowly, their limbs taken off with axes, chain saws, guillotines, threshing machines, the parts nailed up for display. The deification of the madness Jack the Ripper visited on pathetic tarts in Spitalfields in 1888.

As a man who hit a woman once in his life and swore never to do it again, I reel back from these films where hatred and brutalization of women is the governing force of plot. I'll admit it, I cannot watch these films. I get physically ill.

But they must be drawing an audience. More and more get made each season. Saturation advertising on television pulls you to them. They make money. And money begets money; and the begetting sends even greater numbers of minimally talented film-makers to the form. They proliferate. And the sickness spreads.

You wonder why the Moral Majority has some coin with otherwise rational Americans? It is because they fasten on festering sores like the spate of knife-kill films and they argue from the solitary to the general: moral decay, rampant violence, rotting social values. Joining with these latter-day Puritans on a single issue, though one may despise what they're *really* trying to do, is the downfall of all liberals.

Even so, their revulsion at these films (which they patronize like crazy) is the healthiest thing about such movies. Everything else, from motivation to making them to artistic value, drips with perversion.

I have a theory, of course. Don't I always.

These are not, to me, films of terror or suspense in the time-honored sense of such genre definitions. *The Thirty-Nine Steps, North By Northwest* and *Gaslight* are classics of suspense. *Frankenstein, The Wolf Man* and *Alien* are classics of terror. The lists are copious. *Rosemary's Baby, Knife in the Water, Repulsion, The Haunting, The Innocents* (from Henry James's "Turn of the Screw"), *Psycho, The Birds, Dr. Jekyll and Mr. Hyde, Dead of Night*. Add your own. You know which ones they were that scared you, held you helpless in the thrall of fear, gave you memories that chilled not sickened you. From *Snow White and the Seven Dwarfs* to *The Parallax View* and *Carrie*.

It was always the scenes leading *up* to the violence that you remember. You needn't watch the death . . . you had been wrung dry before it ever happened.

What do I consider a terrifying scene. Here, try this:

Chill beneath a cadaverously-gray autumn sky, the tiny New Mexico town. That slate moment in the seasons when everything begins to grow dark. The epileptic scratching of fallen leaves hurled along sidewalks. Mad sounds from the hills. Cold. And something else:

A leopard, escaped, is loose in the town.

Chill beneath a crawling terror of spotted death in the night, the tiny New Mexico town. That thick red moment in the fears of small people when everything explodes in the black flow of blood. A deep-throated growl from a filthy alley. Cold.

A mother, preoccupied with her cooking, tells her small daughter to go down the street to the bakery, get flour for father's dinner bread. The child shows a moment of fear . . . the animal they haven't found yet . . .

The mother insists, it's only a half block to the bakery. Put on a shawl and go get that flour, your father will be home soon. The child goes. Hurrying back up the street, the sack of flour held close to her, the street empty and filling with darkness, ink presses down the sky, the child looks around, and hurries. A cough in the blackness behind her. A cough, deep in a throat that never formed human sounds.

The child's eyes widen in panic. She begins to hurry. Her footsteps quicken. The sound of padding behind her. Feet begin to run. Focus on darkness and the sound of rapid movement. The child. The rushing.

To the wooden door of the house. The door is locked. The child pinned against the night, with the furred sound of agony rushing toward her on the wind.

Inside, the mother, still kitchened, waiting. The sound of the child outside, panic and bubbles of hysteria in the voice, Mommy open the door the leopard is after me!

The mother's face assumes the ages-old expression of harassed parenthood. Hands on hips, she turns to the door, you're always lying, telling fibs, making up stories, how many times have I told you lying will–

Mommy! Open the door!

You'll stay out there till you learn to stop lying!

Mommy! Mom–

Something gigantic hits the door with a crash. The door bows inward, and a mist of flour explodes through the cracks, sifts into the room. The mother's eyes grow huge, she stares at the door. A thick black stream, moving very slowly, seeps under the door.

Madness crawls up behind our eyes, the mother's eyes, and we sink into a pit of blind emptiness . . .

. . . from which we emerge to examine the nature of terror in the motion picture. Fear as the masters of the film form have showed it to us, and fear as the screen has recently depicted it, with explicit vomitous detail, with perverted murder escalated from awfulness to awfulness. Having seen the deaths of dozens, one is spiraled upward to accept the closeup deaths of hundreds. Knives are not enough, they're old hat. Razors are not enough, that's been done. To death. Meathooks are not enough, that's a cliché. Has anyone squeezed that bag of blood called the human body in a car crusher? Yeah, well, we can't use that. How about a paper pulping machine, a blast furnace, a rubber stamper, a meatgrinder, a Cuisinart? What's more ghastly than the last piece of shit? Acid? Rat poison? If we use acid or rat poison we have to show the victim writhing, vomiting, tearing her throat out, the burns, the drool. Hey, is there something that'll explode the eyeballs right out of their sockets? Then we can show the raw red pulpy brain behind the empty holes. Now *that's* fresh, new, inventive, state of the art. Maybe we can call it *Scanners*.

Or *Outland*.

The scene just described, a scene shot for the small theater screen, in black and white, with a minimum of production values, with unknown actors, shot with misdirection (in the sense of that word as magicians use it) and subtlety is from a little-remembered 1943 RKO Radio Picture, *The Leopard Man*, based on a brilliant Cornell Woolrich thriller, BLACK ALIBI (1942). I offer it as a fine example of cinema terror in its most natural, unsullied incarnation, from the *oeuvre* of Val Lewton. To students of terror in films, the name Val Lewton will be familiar. Had I wanted to be less precise but more chic, I'd have cited the early Dassin or Hitchcock.

But as a more reliable barometer of the centigrades to which artful horror can chill a filmgoer, I find no equal to what Lewton produced in merely eight films between 1942 and 1946, with budgets so ludicrous, achievements so startling, and studio intentions so base, that they stand as some sort of landmark for anyone venturing into the genre, whether a John Carpenter or a Brian De Palma.

Using the foregoing as a yardstick, and comparing the knife-kill flicks against them, I submit what we're getting these days are not films of terror or suspense or even horror. They are (and here's my theory) blatant reactionary responses to the feminist movement in America.

Surely there are no great truths being propounded in these films, no subtext that enriches us with apocryphal insight, no subtle characterizations that illuminate the dark night of the soul, no messages for our times . . . unless the message is that every other person you pass is a deranged killer waiting for you to turn you back so he or she can cut your throat.

No, I've convinced myself, even if you may have trouble with the theory, that this seemingly endless spate of films in which women are slaughtered *en masse*, in the most disgusting, wrenching ways a diseased mind can conceive them, is a pandering to the fear in most men that women are "out to get them."

In a nation where John Wayne remains the symbol of what a *man* is, the idea of strong women having intellectual and sexual lives more vigorous than their own is anathema. I submit the men who go to see these films *enjoy* the idea of women being eviscerated and dismembered in this way. They get off on it. In their nasty little secret heart-of-hearts they're saying, "That'll serve the bitch right!"

The audiences that go to these films, that queue up to wait an hour for their dollop of deadly mayhem, are sociopaths who don't know it. Beyond that, and I have no way to prove it, I think these films serve no purgative, cathartic end. They merely boil the blood in the potential rapist, the potential stomper, the potential knife-killer.

The *L.A. Weekly* editorial, January 15–21 1982 issue, proffering clinical substantiation of the theory that splatter movies, knife-kill flicks, raise the tolerance level of men for violence against women, merely adds to the already existing body of such evidence that self-interested film-makers and tunnel-visioned knee-jerk liberals like me have refused to acknowledge. They are twisted dreams from the darkest pit in each of us, the stuff against which we fight to maintain ourselves as decent human beings.

I leave it at that. For the moment.

But next I want to relate what happened when a few responsible people tried to *do* something about these films. It was an adventure among the airheads. Knees jerked, hot air filled the land, writers who've spent their whole lives fighting against censorship were pilloried as being self-appointed censors . . . oh, it was spiffy.

And it encapsulates more than we wish to know about the nature of self-blinding fear that produces a moral vacuum, masquerading as courage. Now I stop being polite.

There is an ancient Japanese aphorism: "The nail that stands too high will be hammered down."

Only a short time after I'd started this essay [in 1981], shortly after I'd come to the personal position that the use of irresponsible state-of-the-art-special-effects gratuitous violence in exploitation films was a growing trend that would permit the wimps of the Moral Majority to impose unbearable restrictions on the motion picture industry, I had occasion to experience at first hand the way in which a nail can be hammered down by those whose floating ethics and lack of personal courage moves them only to silence for fear of invoking the wrath of the groundlings.

My adventure through the land of the airheads began at a screening of Brian De Palma's film *Blow Out*. It was a film booked by the Writers Guild Film Society for its members. Now, the WGA Film Society is a *private* membership operation in which 1885 members of the Guild subscribe to a series of 42 films in a year at $1.25 per couple. The films are booked into the available slots by a complicated process I'll codify later. They are selected from approximately 300 offered to the Guild by the major studios, by a Film Society Committee comprised of (among others) critic Arthur Knight, Ray Bradbury (one of the founders of the

Society, twenty-two years ago), scenarists and teachers Arnold Peyser and William Froug, and me widdle self. More on the Committee itself later.

Let me now reprint a letter I wrote the WGA *Newsletter* following the events pursuant to the screening of *Blow Out*. It will encapsulate the history of this contretemps and will lead into our next thrilling section in which your intrepid pain in the ass finds himself facing the direct lineal descendants of those who stood by and watched Dreyfus get sent to Devil's Island.

Oh, how I do love to dramatize these encounters.

APOLOGIZES TO FILM SOCIETY

Unaccustomed as I am to apologizing publicly for my occasional erratic behavior, I must perforce extend just such an apology to most of the audience of the Film Society screening of *Blow Out* at 2:00 on Sat. Aug. 1.

What I despise in unruly audiences, what I have inveighed against more than once in these pages and in our theater . . . I was guilty of myself.

Three-quarters of the way through that Brian De Palma film, without even realizing I was doing it, I leaped up and began shouting and—at the top of my voice—stalked out of the theater. It was reprehensible behavior, and I am heartily ashamed of myself for it. That I was totally unaware of what I was doing, that I was impelled by my loathing of the brutalization of women that film contains, is no excuse. It was a visceral reaction and I lost control completely. Not until I'd driven home, still trembling with disgust and anger, was my friend Jane able to tell me what I'd been screaming.

I had no recollection of the words. But Jane tells me this is what I shouted:

"Jesus Christ! Another sick De Palma film . . . I should've known!" (At that point I hit the aisle.)

"The man is sick, the man is twisted." (At that point the audience was laughing.) "Next come the mindless eviscerations and anatomy lessons!" (By that time I was out the door.)

Don Segall (the writer, not the director) followed me out and was justifiably annoyed at my behavior. He upbraided me, saying, "If you don't like the films you ought to resign from the Film Society," to which I responded in blind fury, "Resign from the Society, fer chrissakes, I'm one of the ones who *picks* these goddam films!"

John Considine and his lady, and a few others, followed my example and came out also. They did it quietly. I'm told that of the several thousand attendees of the various screenings, only 16 walkouts were logged. I guess that distresses me almost as much as my own uncontrolled actions.

My revulsion at *Blow Out* stemmed, in large part, from a carryover abhorrence of De Palma's previous exercise in woman-hatred, *Dressed to Kill*, which we also screened at the Film Society; and from my growing awareness that these movies are more elegantly mounted examples of what has come to be known as the genre of "knife-kill flicks."

My gorge grew more buoyant as *Blow Out* progressed, pressured by a column I had written just a few days earlier on the knife-kill phenomena.

As a member of the Film Society Committee (and I hope a responsible member), I have brought the matter of these films to the attention of my fellow committeemen. It is my feeling that we must reappraise the manner in which we select films for the members to see. I am dead against censorship *of any kind*. Nonetheless, we do *select* the films for the Society, from those available to us with considerations of play-dates and the other strictures put on us by the studios; and as we would opt not to show a film we knew in advance was a dog, it seems to me well within the bounds of our selection process that we should pay some attention to the advisability of showing films that pander to less than noble instincts in an audience.

Ostensibly, it is the main purpose of the Society to offer to the members those films that will be of benefit in the pursuance of our craft. Even stinko films can serve that end, if only to proffer warning. But as we would not screen a film we knew to be a certified, card-carrying disaster . . . so, I feel, we should demonstrate restraint in showing films that consciously, gratuitously debase the human spirit.

If members of the Society wish to go to commercial theaters and pay their money to see films of this nature, all well and good. But *we* ought to have higher standards.

As a craftsman who works seriously at the holy chore of screen writing, I think it's time we examined more responsibly the nature of the cheapjack predators prowling through our industry, for whom we have to bear the brunt of censure from the New Puritans, the Moral Majority nuts and the self-styled viewers-with-alarm who want to pre-censor what we write.

> All of us get tarred by the brush, every time another woman gets an ice pick in her eye in the course of one of these films.
>
> —HARLAN ELLISON

The first part of this essay on knife-kill splatter movies was published. Then came the Saturday my gut laid it on the line in terms of *doing something* about such films, not just writing about it from a safe distance. The moment when one had to walk the walk and not just talk the talk. I stormed out of a Writers Guild Film Society screening of De Palma's hideous *Blow Out*. Screaming, having totally lost control, I realized that I had been one of the members of the Film Society Committee who had *booked* the damned film . . . without having seen it. A repeat of the error we on the Committee—Ray Bradbury, Arthur Knight, Allen Rivkin, William Froug and Arnold Peyser—had committed when we'd screened De Palma's previous exercise in woman-slaughter, *Dressed to Kill*.

Then here's what happened, very fast. I wrote a letter to the Guild *Newsletter* apologizing for having disrupted the show, pleading temporary nutso. Then I requested a special meeting of the Film Society Committee to discuss our responsiblity in terms of showing films whose chief appeal was a floodtide of gore. Not violence, *per se*: gratuitous, stomach-turning, special-effects slaughter. What I said to the other members of the Committee was that after 12 years sitting with them selecting films, I had come to a moral position *for myself only*, that if we were to continue booking that kind of stuff, I'd have to motor. To my delight and resuscitation of faith in the Human Race, everyone else felt the same, and it was unanimously decided that we would exercise greater discretion when booking the films for the Society.

We felt so good about having thus taken a stand for life over death, that critic Arthur Knight outlined all the foregoing in his August 21, 1981 "Knight at the Movies" column in *The Hollywood Reporter*. The first responses were gratifying. Dozens of people called and wrote to say "Good for you!" On KNX NewsRadio, August 31, George Nicholaw, v.p. and general manager of the CBS outlet here in Los Angeles, presented an editorial in which he called the action of the Committee "leadership by example" and praised the move as an act of selectivity and not censorship.

On the 22nd, Rip Rense in the Page 2 section of the *Herald Examiner* ran a brief piece about the Committee's action and in a day or so it was picked up the AP wire. We all felt terrific.

Then a staff writer for the *Times* got hold of it and on September 2nd he wrote a "Film Clips" piece that was sufficiently muzzy in tone, lacking sufficient background about how the Film Society Committee worked, to make it appear Bradbury and Knight and Ellison and Peyser and Froug were setting themselves up as censors. Sure. Believe *that*, and I've got some swell pterodactyl steaks I'll sell you cheap. In case no one remembers, Bradbury's most famous work is FAHRENHEIT 451, one of the most potent stretches of fiction ever written against censorship; and nobody who writes the stuff I write would be stupid enough to believe in even the slightest infringement of the First Amendment.

Nonetheless. Before the day was out, the shitrain had begun to fall. Typified by the following extract from the *Times* article:

> *One veteran screenwriter, who asked that his name not be used, said the Committee's action reminded him of the old Hays Office, established by the movie industry in the 1920s to guard against indecency. "I remember the Hays Office and all the other crazy offices that the motion picture industry has put up," he said. "A lot of these young people haven't gone through that. I don't believe in not showing anything to anybody. If our people don't want to see something, they should stay at home."*

There was a lot more. Nasty phone calls threatening war to the death, snide remarks from passersby at the next week's screening (which happened to be *Wolfen*, a violent film we booked without moral qualms because it was a good movie *about* something other than titillating bloodletting), and what was for me the most hilarious incident of all:

As I approached the Writers Guild Theater the next weekend, I saw a guy with a clipboard, soliciting signatures on a petition. I walked over, hoping it was another sign-up against James Watt, and saw it was a petition against censorship. "Hey, that's terrific," I said. "Lemme sign." The guy handed me the clipboard and a pen, and I signed right on the line, adding my name in printed form, and my address. He smiled and said thanks, looked down, saw my name, and started to get crazy with me. "But this is a petition against *you*!" I grinned right back and said, "No it ain't, chum. It's against censorship, and I'm for that one hundred percent, which, if you weren't an airhead, you'd know." So he started trying to tear off that page and I said, "Ah, ah, ah. If you do *that*, you invalidate the petition." Then I went into the movie.

But not until a meeting of the Board of Directors of the Guild, and a vote of confidence for the Committee's procedures, did the abuse slack off. Letters continued coming in to the Writers Guild *Newsletter* (edited, ironically, by the very same Allen Rivkin who sits on the Committee) where each one, no matter how off-the-point of lamebrained, was duly published. I guess we just don't have this censorship system down pat yet.

Okay, so now we're coming into the homestretch on this subject.

Why, you ask with good sense, why *isn't* what the Committee did an example of censorship? And what the hell does all this mean beyond the tempest in the teapot?

Look: the Film Society is, first of all, a *private* group, open only to members of the Writers Guild of America and their families. Four or five times a year the Committee gets together and under very difficult rules manages to select 42 films. That's all the open slots we have. Forty-two. We have to select those 42 films from the maybe 300 available to us. Most foreign films we can't get, because the Laemmle chain of theaters controls them and they figure, quite correctly I think, that the audience for "art" films is small already, why should they cut out a couple of thousand potential ticket-buyers just to give away films free to a Film Society. So we are limited in that way. Then there's the play-dates allowed to us. We can't show films prior to release, and can only book them for showing up to a month or so *after* they've opened. And since we have to book well in advance, what happens is that we're selecting films that usually aren't even in final editing when we sit down for our meetings.

We're operating semi-blind. But because of the makeup of the Committee, we have access to rough cuts, films in progress, studio scuttlebutt. So we avoided *The Postman Always Rings Twice* even though it seemed to have everything going for it in pre-release hoopla—remake in unexpurgated form of a classic James M. Cain novel, excellent director, top stars, supposedly tough script—because word leaked out that somehow this one was going into the tank, and we picked up on a film that hadn't been sold so heavily before-the-fact because Knight had seen clips from it and thought it was going to be a comedy smash. The film was *Arthur.*

We go on gut instinct and our sources throughout the industry. That's why the members of the Committee have been appointed. *Anybody* in the Guild can serve on the Committee, but with the exception of those who've served for years, most of the summer soldiers who sit with us have no access to films, have no way of cajoling studios into parting with their precious product, and don't like the long hours of hard work and phone calls. So the Film Committee functions in the same way as the editorial board of The Book-Of-The-Month Club.

BOMC gets offered several thousand books a year as possible selections. They pick a couple of hundred. Are they censors because they choose to offer this book and not that book? No, they are making informed selections. That's what the Committee has been doing for 22 years.

And here's the airhead part. For 22 years the people who were namecalling have gone to the Guild Theater, and there's always been a film waiting for them. How the hell did they think that film got there? The stork? Santa Claus? Didn't they ever wonder why, on a given

Saturday, they wound up watching *Tess*, rather than, say *Maniac* or *Debbie Does Dallas*?

How did they figure a film booked four months earlier got to the projection booth at the appointed time?

None of that really matters. The system the Film Society uses is, by years of painful trial and error, the only one that can guarantee a steady flow of decent films for the members of the Guild. That's beside the point. What matters is the question of alleged censorship, and the response of uninformed, otherwise intelligent and concerned people to the unsupported *suggestion* of censorship.

The airheads seem to me to be not only doltish in this matter, but cowardly. If they *really* gave a damn about someone telling them what they can see and what they can't, why aren't they out in front of the offices of the Motion Picture Producers Association, picketing against the code that rates films G or PG or R or X? Why aren't they lobbying against outfits like Wildmon and his religious zealots, or Falwell and his vast Moron Majority? Cowards because they accept the rules and regs set down by the television networks that emasculate everything they write for the tube. Cowards because they let movies and books get banned all over the country and never offer their services in an *amicus* way to stop such depredations. Cowards because they are so terrified by the threat of a Moral Majority that they abrogate their responsibility to moral and ethical behavior for fear of looking like the enemy.

My big RANDOM HOUSE DICTIONARY OF THE ENGLISH LANGUAGE tells me that a censor is "any person who supervises the manners or morality of others." In flat-out terms that means keeping someone from seeing or doing something they want to do. But if the films the Committee chooses not to select for screening—remember only 42 out of 300+ can be shown each year—are available to the public in a couple of hundred theaters all over Los Angeles . . . where the hell does the censoring come in?

Now that makes simple sense. The kind of sense that becomes obvious when one takes the time to examine the question, not just rely on the word of someone shooting off his bazoo, who "asked that his name not be used."

But the foofaraw happened. Men who have spent most of their adult lives *fighting* censorship, who chose to exercise a sense of responsibility, who tried to say there are better films than these dark, ugly charnel house films, got the screaming pack of airheads on their case. Vicious fucker that I am, I suggested to the Committee that we let the airheads have their way. Instead of booking *The French Lieutenant's Woman* and *Absence of Malice*, that we give them six straight weeks of splatter films. *Friday the Thirteenth, Part II* (in which a spear goes through the back of a woman, through the man she's screwing, and impales another guy under the bed), *Night School* (in which decapitated heads wind up in sinks, fish tanks, toilets and a kettle of soup in a restaurant), *Don't Go In The House* (in which women are tied to walls and then cremated by a guy with a flamethrower), *Halloween, Part II* (in which kids bite into apples filled with razor blades) and *Maniac* (in which a man knifes a woman to death, scalps her, puts her scalp on a dummy and then makes love to the dummy).

Gee, I don't know why the Committee looked on that suggestion with horror and revulsion. Can't understand, simply can*not* understand why Ray Bradbury and gentle Arnold Peyser looked sick. Don't know no way to figure *why* Arthur Knight and Bill Froug got green. Why Rivkin withdrew a dinner invitation.

What the hell's the matter with them?

Are they censors?

The Man Who Was Heavily into Revenge

William Weisel pronounced his name why-*zell*, but many of the unfortunates for whom he had done remodeling and construction pronounced it *weasel*.

He had designed and built a new guest bathroom for Fred Tolliver, a man in his early sixties who had retired from the active life of a studio musician with the foolish belief that his fifteen-thousand-dollar-per-year annuity would sustain him in comfort. Weisel had snubbed the original specs on the job, had substituted inferior materials for those required by the codes, had used cheap Japanese pipe instead of galvanized or stressed plastic, had eschewed lath and plaster for wallboard that left lumpy seams, had skirted union wages by ferrying in green card workers from Tijuana every morning by dawn light, had—in short—done a spectacularly crummy job on Fred Tolliver's guest bathroom. That was the first mistake.

And for all of this ghastly workmanship, Weisel had overcharged Fred Tolliver by nine thousand dollars. That was the second mistake.

Fred Tolliver called William Weisel. His tone was soft and almost apologetic. Fred Tolliver was a gentle man, not given to fits of pique or demonstrations of anger. He politely asked Weisel to return and set matters to rights. William Weisel laughed at Fred Tolliver and told him that he had lived up to the letter of the original contract, that he would do nothing. That was the third mistake.

Putatively, what Weisel said was true. Building inspectors had been greased and the job had been signed off: legal according to the building codes. Legally, William Weisel was in the clear; no suit could be brought. Ethically it was a different matter. But even threats of revocation of license could not touch him.

Nonetheless, Fred Tolliver had a rotten guest bathroom, filled with leaks and seamed walls that were already cracking and bubbles in the vinyl flooring from what was certainly a break in the hot water line and pipes that clanked when the faucets were turned on, if they could *be* turned on.

Fred Tolliver asked for repairs more than once.

After a while, William Weisel's wife, Belle, who often acted as his secretary, to save a few bucks when they didn't want to hire a Kelly Girl, would not put through the calls.

Fred Tolliver told her, softly and politely, "Please convey to Mr. Weisel—" and he pronounced it why-*zell*, "—my feelings of annoyance. Please advise him that I won't stand for it. This is an awful thing he's done to me. It's not fair, it's not right."

She was chewing gum. She examined her nails. She had heard this all before: married to Weisel for eleven years: all of this, many times. "Lissen, Mistuh Tollivuh, whaddaya want *me* to do about it, *I* can't do nothing about it, y'know. I only work here. I c'n tell 'im, that's *all* I c'n do, is tell 'im you called again."

"But you're his wife! You can see how he's robbed me!"

"Lissen, Mistuh Tollivuh, I don't haveta lissen to this!"

It was the cavalier tone, the utterly uncaring tone: impertinent, rude, dismissing him as if he were a crank, a weirdo, as if he weren't asking only for what was due him. It was like a goad to an already maddened bull.

"This isn't fair!"

"I'll tell 'im, I'll tell 'im. Jeezus, I'm hanging up now."

"I'll get even! I will! There has to be justice—"

She dropped the receiver into its rest heavily, cracking her gum with annoyance, looking ceilingward like one massively put upon. She didn't even bother to convey the message to her husband.

And that was the biggest mistake of all.

The electrons dance. The emotions sing. Four billion, resonating like insects. The hive mind of the masses. The emotional gestalt. The charge builds and builds, surging down the line seeking a focus. The weakest link through which to discharge itself. Why this focus and not that? Chance, proximity, the tiniest fracture for leakage. You, I, him, her. Everyman, Anyman; the crap shoot selection is whatever man or woman born of man and woman whose rage at *that* moment is *that* potent.

Everyman: Fred Tolliver. Unknowing confluence.

He pulled up at the pump that dispensed supreme, and let the Rolls idle for a moment before shutting it off. When the attendant leaned in at the window, Weisel smiled around his pipe and said, "Morning, Gene. Fill it up with extra."

"Sorry, Mr. Weisel," Gene said, looking a little sad, "but I can't sell you any gas."

"Why the hell not? You out?"

"No, sir; just got our tanks topped off last night. Still can't sell you any."

"Why the hell not?!"

"Fred Tolliver doesn't want me to."

Weisel stared for a long moment. He couldn't have heard correctly. He'd been gassing up at this station for eleven years. He didn't even know they *knew* that creep Tolliver. "Don't be an asshole, Gene. Fill the damned tank!"

"I'm sorry, sir. No gas for you."

"What the hell is Tolliver to you? A relative or something?"

"No, sir. I never met him. Wouldn't know him if he drove in right now."

"Then what . . . what the hell . . . I—I—"

But nothing he could say would get Gene to pump one liter of gas into the Rolls.

Nor would the attendants at the next *six* stations down the avenue. When the Rolls ran out, a mile from his office, Weisel *almost* had time to pull to the curb. Not quite. He ran dry in the middle of Ventura Boulevard and tried to turn toward the curb, but though traffic had been light around him just a moment before, somehow it was now packing itself bumper-to-bumper. He turned his head wildly this way and that, dumbfounded at how many cars had suddenly pulled onto the boulevard around him. He could not get out of the crunch. It wouldn't have mattered. Improbably, for this non-business area, for the first time in his memory, there were *no* empty parking spaces at the curb.

Cursing foully, he put it in neutral, rolled down the window so he could hold the steering wheel from outside, and got out of the silent Rolls. He slammed the door, cursing Fred Tolliver's every breath, and stepped away from the car. He heard the hideous rending of irreplaceable fabric. His five hundred dollar cashmere suit jacket had been caught in the jamb.

A large piece of lovely fabric, soft as a doe's eye, wondrously ecru-closer-to-beige-than-fawn-colored, tailor-made for him in Paris, his most favorite jacket hung like slaughtered meat from the door. He whimpered; an involuntary sob of pain.

Then: "What the hell is going *on*!" he snarled, loud enough for pedestrians to hear. It was not a question, it was an imprecation. There was no answer; none was required; but there was the sound of thunder far off across the San Fernando Valley. Los Angeles was in the grip of a two-year drought, but there was a menacing buildup of soot-gray clouds over the San Bernardinos.

He reached in through the window, tried to turn the wheel toward the curb, but with the engine off the power steering prevented easy movement. But he strained and strained . . . and something went snap! in his groin. Incredible pain shot down both legs and he bent double, clutching himself. Flashbulbs went off behind his eyes. He stumbled around in small circles, holding himself awkwardly. Many groans. Much anguish. He leaned against the Rolls, and the pain began to subside; but he had broken something down there. After a few minutes he was able to stand semi-erect. His shirt was drenched with sweat. His deodorant was wearing off. Cars were swerving around the Rolls, honking incessantly, drivers swearing at him. He had to get the Rolls out of the middle of the street.

Still clutching his crotch with one hand, jacket hanging from him in tatters, beginning to smell very bad, William Weisel put his shoulder to the car, grabbed the steering wheel and strained once again; the wheel went around slowly. He readjusted himself, excruciating pain pulsing through his pelvis, put his shoulder against the window post and tried to push the behemoth. He thought of compacts and tiny sports cars. The Rolls moved a fraction of an inch, then slid back.

Sweat trickled into his eyes, making them sting. He huffed and lunged and applied as much pressure as the pain would permit. The car would not move.

He gave up. He needed help. *Help!*

Standing in the street behind the car, clutching his groin, jacket flapping around him, smelling like something ready for disposal, he signaled wildly for assistance with his free hand. But no one would stop. Thunder rolled around the Valley, and Weisel saw what looked like a pitchfork of lightning off across the flats where Van Nuys, Panorama City and North Hollywood lay gasping for water.

Cars thundered down on him and swerved at the very last moment, like matadors performing a complicated *verónica*. Several cars seems to speed up, in fact, as they approached him, and he had the crazy impression the drivers were hunched over the wheels, lips skinned back from clenched teeth, like rabid wild things intent on killing him. Several nearly sideswiped him. He barely managed to hobble out of the way. One Datsun came so close that its side-view mirror ripped a nasty, raw gash down the entire right side of the Rolls. He cursed and gesticulated and pleaded. No one would stop. In fact, one fat woman leaned out of her window as her husband zoomed past, and she yelled something nasty. He caught only the word "Tolliver!"

Finally, he just left it there, with the hood up like the mouth of a hungry bird.

He walked the mile to his office, thinking he would call the Automobile Club to come and tow it to a station where it could be filled. He didn't have the time or the patience to walk to a gas station, get a can of fuel, and return to fill the tank. During the mile-long walk he even had time to wonder if he would be *able* to buy a can of gasoline.

Tolliver! God *damn* that old man!

There was no one in the office.

It took him a while to discover that fact, because he couldn't get an elevator in his building. He stood in front of one after another of the doors, waiting for a cage to come down, but they all seemed determined to stop at the second floor. Only when other passengers waited did an elevator arrive, and then he was always in front of the wrong one. He would dash to the open door, just as the others entered, but before he could get his hand into the opening to stop the retarder bar from slamming against the frame, the door would seem to slide faster, as if it possessed a malevolent intelligence. It went on that way for ten minutes, till it became obvious to him that something was terribly, hideously, inexplicably wrong.

So he took the stairs.

(On the stairs he somehow slipped and skinned his right knee as one of the steps caught his heel and tore it off his right shoe.)

Limping like a cripple, the tatters of his jacket flapping around him, clutching his groin, blood seeping through his pants to stain, he reached the eleventh floor and tried to open the door. It was, of course, for the first time in the thirty-five-year history of the building, locked.

He waited fifteen minutes and the door suddenly opened as a secretary, carrying some papers up one flight to the Xerox center, came boiling through. He barely managed to catch the door on its pneumatic closer. He stumbled frantically onto the eleventh floor and, like a man emerging gratefully from a vast desert to find an oasis, he fled down the corridor to the offices of the Weisel Construction Corporation.

There was no one in the office.

It was not locked. Was, in fact, wholly unattended and wide open to thieves, if such had chosen that office for plundering. The receptionist was not there, the estimators were not there, not even Belle, his wife, who served as secretary when he didn't want to hire a Kelly Girl, was there.

However, she had left him a note:

I'm leaving you. By the time you read this I will have already been to the bank and emptied the joint account. Don't try to find me. Goodbye.

Weisel sat down. He had the beginnings of what he was certain was a migraine, though he had never had a migraine in his life. He didn't know whether, in the vernacular of the United States Army, to shit or go blind.

He was not a stupid man. He had been given more than sufficient evidence that something malevolent and purely anti-Weisel was floating across the land. It was out to get him . . . had, in fact, *already* gotten him . . . had, in fact, made a well-ordered and extremely comfortable life turn into a nasty, untidy, noisome pile of doggie-doo.

And it was named *Tolliver.*

Fred Tolliver . . . ! How the hell . . . ? Who does he know that could . . . ? How did he . . . ?

None of the questions reached a conclusion. He could not even formulate them. Clearly, this was insanity. No one he knew, not Gene at the gas station, not the people in the cars, not Belle, not his staff, not the *car door* or the building's *elevators* even knew who Tolliver was! Well, Belle knew, but what the hell did she have to do with *him*?

Okay, so it *wasn't* going so good with Belle. So they *hadn't* really reconciled that innocent little thing he'd had with the lab technician at Mt. Sinai. So what? That was no reason for her to ditch a good thing. *Damn that Tolliver!*

He slammed his hand onto the desk, missed slightly, caught the edge and drove a thick splinter of wood into the fat of his palm, at the same time scattering the small stack of telegrams across his lap and the floor.

Wincing with pain, he sucked at the splinter till it came out. He used one of the telegram envelopes to blot the blood from his hand.

Telegrams?

He opened the first one. The Bank of America, Beverly Hills branch 213, was pleased to advise him they were calling due his loans. All five of them. He opened the second one. His broker, Shearson Hayden Stone Inc., was overjoyed to let him know that all sixteen of the stocks in which he had speculated heavily, on margin, of course, had virtually plummeted off the big board and he had to come up with seventy-seven thousand dollars by noon today or his portfolio was wiped out. It was a quarter to eleven by the wall clock. (Or had it, inexplicably, stopped?) He opened the third one. He had failed his est class and Werner Erhard himself had sent the telegram, adding in what Weisel took to be an unnecessarily gloating tone, that Weisel had "no human potential worth expanding." He opened the fourth one. His Wassermann had come back from Mt. Sinai. It was positive. He opened the fifth one. The Internal Revenue Service was ecstatic at being able to let him know they were planning to audit his returns for the past five years, and were seeking a loophole in the tax laws that permitted them to go back farther, possibly to the start of the Bronze Age.

There were others, five or six more. He didn't bother opening them. He didn't want to learn who had died, or that the state of Israel had discovered Weisel was, in actuality, Bruno "The Butcher" Krutzmeier, a former prison guard at Mauthausen, personally responsible for the deaths of three thousand Gypsies, Trade Unionists, Jews, Bolsheviks and Weimar democrats, or that the U.S. Coast and Geodetic Survey Department was gleefully taking this opportunity to advise him that the precise spot over which he sat was expected to collapse into the magma at the center of the Earth and by the way we've canceled your life insurance.

He let them lie.

The clock on the wall had, to be sure, stopped dead.

In fact, the electricity had been turned off.

The phone did not ring. He picked it up. Of course. It—like its friend the clock—was stone dead.

Tolliver! Tolliver! How was he *doing* all this?

Such things simply *do not* happen in an ordered universe of draglines and scoop-shovels and reinforced concrete.

He sat and thought dark, murderous thoughts about that old sonofabitch, Fred Tolliver.

A 747 boomed sonically overhead and the big heavy-plate window of his eleventh floor office cracked, splintered, and fell in around his feet.

Unknowing confluence of resonating emotions, Fred Tolliver sat in his house, head in hands, miserable beyond belief, aware only of pain and anger. His cello lay on its back on the floor beside him. He had tried playing a little today, but all he could think of was that terrible man Weisel, and the terrible bathroom that was filling with water, and the terrible stomach pains his feelings of hatred were giving him.

Electrons resonate. So do emotions.

Speak of "damned places" and one speaks of locations where powerful emotional forces have been penned up. One cannot doubt, if one has ever been inside a prison where the massed feelings of hatred, deprivation, claustrophobia and brutalization have seeped into the very stones. One can feel it. Emotions resonate: at a political rally, a football game, an encounter group, a rock concert, a lynching.

There are four billion people in the world. A world that has grown so complex and uncaring with systems and brutalization of individuals because of the inertia produced by those systems' perpetuation of self, that merely to live is to be assaulted daily by circumstances. Electrons dance. The emotions sing. Four billion, resonating like insects. The charge is built up; the surface tension is reached; the limit of elasticity is passed; the charge seeks release; the focus is sought: the weakest link, the fault line, the most tremblingly frangible element, AnyTolliver, EveryTolliver.

Like the discharge of the lightning bolt, the greater the charge on the Tolliver, the greater its tendency to escape. The force of the four billion driving the electrons in their mad dance away from the region of highest excess toward the region of greatest deficiency. Pain as electromotive force. Frustration as electric potential. The electrons jump the insulating gap of love and friendship and kindness and humane behavior and the power is unleashed.

Like the discharge of the lightning bolt, the power seeks and finds its focus, leaps the gap, and the bolt of energy is unleashed.

Does the lightning rod know it is draining off the dangerous electrical charge? Is there sentience in a Leyden jar? Does not the voltaic pile continue to sleep while current is drawn off? Does the focus know it has unleashed the anger and frustration of the four billion?

Fred Tolliver sat in misery, the cello forgotten, the pain of having been cheated, of being impotent against the injustice, eating at his stomach. His silent scream: at that moment the most dominant in the entire universe. Chance. It could have been anyone; or perhaps, as Chesterton said, "Coincidences are a spiritual sort of puns."

His phone rang. He did not move to pick up the receiver. It rang again. He did not move. His stomach burned and roiled. There was a scorched-earth desperation in him. Nine *thousand* dollars overcharge. Thirty-seven hundred dollars by the original contract. Twelve thousand seven hundred dollars. He had had to take a second mortgage on the house. Five more months than the estimated two Weisel had said it would take to complete the job. Seven months of filth and plaster dust and inept workmen tramping through his little house with mud and dirt and dropping cigarette butts on his floor.

I'm sixty-two years old, he thought, frantically. *My God, I'm an old man. A moment ago I was just middle-aged, and now I'm an old man . . . I never* felt *old before. It's good Betsy never lived to see me like this; she would cry. But this thing with the bathroom is a* terrible *thing, an awful thing, it's made me an old man, poor, in financial straits; and I don't know how to save myself. He's ruined my life . . . he's killed me . . . I'll never be able to get even, to put away a little . . . if the thing with the knees gets any worse, there could be big doctor bills, specialists maybe . . . the Blue Cross would never cover it . . . what am I going to do, please God help me . . . what am I going to do?*

He was an old man, retired and very tired, who had thought he could make it through. He had figured it out so he could just barely slide through. But the pains in the backs of his knees had begun three years before, and though they had not flared up in sixteen months, he remembered how he would simply fall down, suddenly, ludicrously, fall down: the legs prickling with pins and needles as though he had sat cross-legged for a long time. He was afraid to think about the pains too much. They might come back if he thought about them too much.

But he didn't really believe that thinking about things could make them happen. Thinking didn't make things change in the real world. Fred Tolliver did not know about the dance of the emotions, the resonance of the electrons. He did not know about a sixty-two-year-old lightning rod that leaked off the terror and frustration of four billion people, all crying out silently just as Fred Tolliver cried out. For help that never came.

The phone continued to ring. He did not think about the pains he had felt in the backs of his knees, as recently as sixteen months ago. He did not think about it, because he did not want it to return. It was only a low-level throbbing now, and he wanted it to stay that way. He didn't want to feel pins and needles. He *wanted* his money back. He *wanted* the sound of gurgling under the floor of the guest bathroom to stop. *He wanted William Weisel to make good.*

He answered the phone. It rang once too often for him to ignore it.

"Hello?"

"Mr. Tolliver? Is that you?"

"Yes, this is Fred Tolliver. Who's calling?"

"Evelyn Hand. I haven't heard from you about my violin, and I'm going to need it late next week . . ."

He had forgotten. In all the anguish with Weisel, he had forgotten Evelyn Hand, and her damaged violin. And she had paid him already.

"Oh, my gosh, Miss Hand, I'm awfully sorry! I've just had the most awful business going on these last months, a man built me a guest bathroom, and he overcharged me nine thousand dollars, and it's all broken and . . ."

He stopped. This was unbecoming. He coughed with embarrassment, giving himself a moment to gather his composure. "I'm just as terribly sorry and ashamed as I can be, Miss Hand. I haven't had a chance to get to the repairs. But I know you need it a week from today . . ."

"A week from *yesterday,* Mr. Tolliver. Thursday, not Friday."

"Oh. Yes, of course. Thursday." She was a nice woman, really. Very slim, delicate fingers and a gentle, warm voice. He had thought perhaps they might go to the Smorgasbord for a meal, and they might get to know each other. He wanted companionship. It was so necessary; now, particularly, it was so necessary. But the memory of Betsy was always there, singing softly within him; and he had said nothing to Evelyn Hand.

"Are you there, Mr. Tolliver?"

"Uh, yes. Yes, of course. Please forgive me. I'm so wrought up these days. I'll get to it right away. Please don't you worry about it."

"Well, I *am* rather concerned." She hesitated, as though reluctant to speak. She drew a deep breath and plunged on: "I did pay you in advance for the repairs, because you said you needed the money for bills, and . . ."

He didn't take offense. He understood perfectly. She had said something that otherwise she would have considered *déplacé,* but she was distraught and wanted to make the point as firmly as she could without being overly offensive.

"I'll get to it today, Miss Hand; I promise."

It would take time. It was a good instrument, a fine, old Gagliano. He knew he could finish the repairs in time if he kept at it without distraction.

Her tone softened. "Thank you, Mr. Tolliver. I'm sorry to have bothered you, but . . . you understand."

"Of course. Don't give it a thought. I'll call as soon as it's ready. I'll give it special attention, I promise."

"You're very kind."

They said their goodbyes and he stopped himself from suggesting dinner when the violin was ready. There was always time for that later, when appropriate. When the business with the bathroom was settled.

And that brought him back to the state of helpless fury and pain. That terrible man, Weisel!

Unknowing confluence of four billion resonating emotions, Fred Tolliver sat with head in hands; as the electrons danced.

Eight days later, in a filthy alley behind a boarded-up supermarket that had begun as a sumptuous gilt-and-brocade movie house in 1924, William Weisel sat in filth, trying to eat the butt of a stale loaf of pumpernickel he had stolen from a garbage can. He weighed ninety-seven pounds, had not shaved in seven days, his clothes were stained and torn rags, his shoes had been stolen while he slept, four days earlier, in the doorway outside the Midnight Mission, his eyes were rheumy and he had developed a terrible, wracking cough. The angry crimson weal on his left forearm where the bolt of lightning had just grazed him seemed to be infected. He gagged on the bread, realizing he had missed one of the maggots, and threw the granitelike butt across the alley.

He was incapable of crying. He had cried himself out. He knew, at last, that there was no way to save himself. On the third day, he had tried to get to Tolliver, to beg him to stop; to tell him he would repair the bathroom; to tell him he would build him a new house, a mansion, a palace, *anything*! Just stop this terror! *Please!*

But *he* had been stopped. He could not *get* to Tolliver. The first time he had set his mind to seeing the old man, he had been arrested by a California Highway Patrol officer who had him on his hot sheet for having left the Rolls in the middle of Ventura Boulevard. Weisel had managed to escape on foot, somehow, miraculously.

The second time he had been attacked by a pit bull while skulking through back yards. He had lost his left pant leg below the knee.

The third time he had actually gotten as far as the street on which Tolliver's house sat, but a seven-car pileup had almost crushed him beneath tons of thundering metal, and he had fled, fearing an aircraft carrier might drop from the sky to bury him.

He knew now that he could not even make amends, that it was inertial, and that he was doomed.

He lay back, waiting for the finish. But it was not to be that easy. The song of the four billion is an unending symphony of incredible complexity. As he lay there, a derelict stumbled into the alley, saw him, and pulled the straight razor from his jacket pocket. He was almost upon him when William Weisel opened his eyes. He saw the rusty blade coming for his throat, had a moment of absolute mind-numbing horror wash over him, spasmed into shock, and did not hear the sound of the cop's service revolver as the derelict—who had serviced over a dozen other such bums as Weisel in this same manner—was blown in half.

He woke in the drunk tank, looked around, saw the company to which he had been condemned, knew that if he lived it would be through years of horror, and began tearing off strips of rags from what remained of his clothing.

When the attendant came to turn the men out into the exercise area, he found William Weisel hanging from the bars of the door, eyes bulging, tongue protruding like a charred leaf from his mouth. What he could not reconcile was that no one in the cell had even shouted, nor raised a hand to stop Weisel. That, and the look of voiceless anguish on the dead man's face, as though he had glimpsed, just at the instant of death, a view of an *eternity* of voiceless anguish.

The focus could direct the beam, but it could not heal itself. At the very moment that Weisel died, Fred Tolliver—still unaware of what he had done—sat in his home, realizing finally that the contractor had done him in. He could never repay the note, would perhaps have to get work again in some studio, and probably would be unable to do it with sufficient regularity to save the house. His twilight years would be spent in some dingy apartment. The modest final hope of his life had been denied him: he would not be able just simply to get by in peace. It was a terrible lonely thing to contemplate.

The phone rang.

He picked it up wearily. "Yes?"

There was a moment of silence, then the voice of Miss Evelyn Hand came across the line, icily. "Mr. Tolliver, this is Evelyn Hand. I waited all day yesterday. I was unable to participate in the recital. Please have my violin waiting for me, repaired or not."

He was too stunned, too depressed, even to be polite. "Okay."

"I want you to know you have caused me great pain, Mr. Tolliver. You are a very unreliable and evil man. I want you to know I'm going to take steps to rectify this matter. You have taken money from me under false pretenses, you have ruined a great opportunity I had, and you have caused me unnecessary anguish. You will have to pay for your irresponsibilty; there must be justice. I will make certain you pay for what you've done!"

"Yes. Yes, of course," he said, dimly, faintly.

He hung up the receiver and sat there.

The emotions sang, the electrons danced, the focus shifted, and the symphony of frustration went on.

Fred Tolliver's cello lay unattended at his feet. He would never get through, just barely slide through. He felt the excruciating pain of pins and needles in his legs.

No snowflake in an avalanche ever feels responsible.
—S. J. LEC

SYNCHRONICITY: This photograph arrived unheralded in the mail as the author was working on this essay about anger and revenge. It is the only extant photograph from his childhood. It is a picture of his 6th grade class at Lathrop School in Painesville, Ohio. The date was 1946; the author was twelve years old. Notice that all but two of the children stand with their arms at their sides or in their pockets, attitudes of peaceful composure. The little girl in the first row, third from the right, is the one who sent the author the photo. She was the first girl the author ever dated. Her name was Jean Bittner. The author can be seen at the far left, first row. He does *not* stand in a relaxed posture. He looks pugnacious. Smaller than the smallest girl in this photo, the author seems at age twelve already the sort of person who would, 36 years later, write a study on belligerent behavior. Note the Band-Aid on his right cheek, no doubt covering the aftermath of an early schoolyard encounter of anger and/or revenge. Note the 1946 Captain Midnight Secret Squadron Decoder Badge the author wears. Directly above the author, in the top row, is a boy named Jack Wheeldon. The author reports that Mr. Wheeldon was the bully who took enormous pleasure in beating up the author every day at Lathrop. Of the 28 children in this photo, only two are now deceased. One of them is Jack Wheeldon. When the author was asked if that fact had anything to do with the statement in this essay that there are some people one should never mess with, the author smiled pugnaciously and said nothing.

DRIVING IN THE SPIKES

An Essay on Anger and Revenge By a Master of the Form

About the little boy, in a moment. But, first, consider this: each of us is rooted in the present. We are sunk to the knees in the quicksand of today. But imbedded in our heads is a time machine. When we activate that mechanism, we are time travelers. The mechanism is called memory, and it spins us back and back to whatever year we wish to visit. Here we are, clinging to the end of that fine silken cord trailing behind us, vanishing into yesterday. Memory secures us to our experiences and we are the end-result of what we felt and saw and did as we slid along the silken cord.

Come back down the cord with me, to the little boy.

A random summer in the 1940s. As it has been with most of the little boy's summers, he has been sent away to camp. In Ohio, in the 1940s, when the parents could bear it no longer, the summer brought surcease with the annual shunting-off of the kids to camp. Six weeks of relative quiet and replenishment of the vital forces that allowed adults to continue living with the kids without thoughts of dismemberment.

The little boy hated camp. He was taken out of his home, out of his neighborhood, out of the playground; away from his friends and most of all away from his dog. The little boy found it hard to make friends, but his dog was always there.

Now he returns from camp and his father picks him up at the bus station, and the little boy wants only one thing: to rush home and fall to his knees and hug his dog. His father seems too quiet and even troubled. The little boy senses something is wrong, but he is a *little boy* and little boys don't ask Dad what's wrong. That's grown-up stuff.

But when they get home, and the little boy dashes out of the car before his father can complete the sentence—"Wait a minute, I want to tell you . . ."—there is no dog out on the lawn, no friend from whom he has been separated for six weeks, leaping and pawing and waiting to put his tongue all over the little boy's face. There is an absence here. And the little boy quickly grows frightened.

Until the father sits him down and explains, with hesitance and dismay, that the dog is dead. The little boy cannot contain the knowledge. He has never experienced death or the holes it leaves in the world. And when, later, he learns *how* the dog died, the little boy mutates and becomes something he has never been before, in a process that can never be reversed.

He learns that the old woman who lives up the street, who has lived here all the years the little boy and his dog and his family have lived on that street, found the pup in her yard and called the dog catcher, and before the father knew about it, the dog had been gassed. The little boy is told the animal was "put to sleep," but he knows his friend was gassed, was killed.

He cannot understand why the old woman would do such a thing. "He never hurt anybody," he says through his tears. "He was little; he couldn't hurt anything."

He runs out of the house and for hours, till it is very dark and very late, he lies in the tall grass in the empty lots behind the street where he and his dog played. He watches the old woman's house, and he feels something he has never felt this powerfully before. He feels the need to *do* something, to make her pay for her terrible deed, to get even.

Finally, when it is past midnight and all the lights are out on the street, when all the people who have been looking for him have returned to their homes, he crawls into her backyard.

Hanging on the clothesline is a rug beater.

The little boy steals the rug beater and takes it deep into the empty lots, and with his bare hands he digs a deep hole and he throws the rug beater into it. He spits on the implement and covers it over with dirt. He sits there for a while, burning with rage and frustration and that feeling he never felt before even remotely this powerfully. And then he goes home to sleep.

Come with me back up the silken cord, to the man who was that little boy in that Ohio summer in the 1940s.

Now he is an adult. He learns that a great monolithic corporation has stolen his work, that they have taken that work and altered it and put their own names on it and it is out there in the world, labeled theirs. He feels that powerful emotion he knew as a little boy, that he has known frequently as he sloughed through the quicksand of the present, pulling the silken cord of memory behind him. He feels the feeling of helplessness and rage at midnight, and he cannot sleep.

So he activates the time mechanism and he takes their rug beater away from them and he buries it and spits on the grave.

He sues them in Federal District Court and wins the largest plagiarism judgment in the history of this new city where he lives.

The dog's name was Puddles. The plagiarism suit was culminated in April of 1980 and the little boy won $337,000.

That old woman has been dead for more than thirty years, but neither the burial of a rug beater nor her leavetaking from this world have diminished the need for vengeance in the soul of that little boy who lives inside the time machine.

Ibsen said, "To live is to war with trolls."

The most potent weapon in that ongoing conflict is the anger generated by the need for revenge.

It is also the most crippling, enfeebling, destructive and potentially berserk weapon in the human arsenal. Directed intelligently, coolly, constructively, it brings a balance to the universe, redresses wrongs, prevents ulcers and helps one maintain a sense of self-respect. Allowed to run amuck, it kills those at whom it is aimed and, like a rifle clogged with dirt, blows up in the face of he or she who aimed it.

In a book published January 1983, social psychologist and journalist Carol Tavris suggests ventilating one's anger for the purpose of getting rid of it is a fallacious, though long-held, belief. More often, she contends in ANGER: THE MISUNDERSTOOD EMOTION, "it remains and creates an unhealthy habit pattern of easy arousability without getting at solutions."

Physiologically and psychologically, the negative effects of anger can be cataclysmic. The Monday morning statistics on the sudden spur-of-the-moment use of snubby Saturday Night Specials in neighborhood bars are bloody verification of that. But even Tavris agrees that anger, "if understood and channeled properly . . . is a useful tool for righting both personal and larger social wrongs."

And, contrariwise to Tavris's conclusions, studies by University of Chicago psychologist Morton A. Lieberman in 1973 indicate that people are more likely to survive into a ripe old age if they are grouchy and pugnacious, two of the early warning signs of a talent for intelligent venting of anger through revenge.

In one study, Lieberman interviewed 85 people between the ages of 63 and 91 who, at the beginning of the experiment, were on the waiting lists of three Chicago homes for the aged. All were physically and mentally well before admission to the homes. One year later, 62 of the original sample were interviewed again (23 were unavailable because of death, illness or unwillingness to continue participating in the study). Lieberman found that 44 of the subjects had survived the stress of relocation intact, while the rest had deteriorated markedly.

The intact group turned out to share nine traits: high activity, aggression, narcissistic body images, authoritarian personalities, high status drive, distrust of others, disregard for others' viewpoints, a tendency to blame others and a resistance to blaming themselves.

In short, a compendium of those qualities we are told are most loathsome. Angry, cantankerous, impossible to be around, the sort of people who make your back teeth itch . . . but determined to live their lives. Maybe it's true: the good die young.

As one who, early in life, had occasion to be bathed in the glow of Sophocles's perception, "If you have committed iniquity, you must expect to suffer; for vengeance, with its sacred light shines upon you," I have learned much about anger and revenge. (There are those academics who, worrying my writings over thirty years like a puppy with a Christmas slipper, have opined that the four most basic subjects underlying the stories and essays are courage, love, ethics and revenge. Who am I to dispute those who make their living from such minute analysis?)

And from this well of experience, I have ladled up some ground rules for the effective implementation of your anger and barbaric need for vengeance, accompanied by suitable anecdotes showing spirited everyday uses. Them as has weak tummies should leave now.

RULE ONE: *Never use the H-bomb first.*

Seek redress in stages of increasing intensity. First, appeal to the offender's sense of right, of fairness. Point out—as has Mortimer Adler—that anything you perceive as your due, as owing to you, must be understood as owing and due to everyone else. Sweet reason, amelioration, courtesy should be the first step.

When that fails, go to the next level. Suggest alternate courses of action. Do not mention mayhem. That's a howitzer. Try public outrage, advisements to the local mediums of news, calling his/her mommy or spouse.

When you are thoroughly ignored, or if the popular phrase, "Screw off, Puke-For-Brains!" has been leveled against you, go directly to level three, Small Claims Court. There, for a few dollars, you can get satisfaction if you've got the goods on the culprit. In Small Claims, attorneys are not permitted (which is a wonderfulness not even the best restaurants in town can boast).

If the situation is one that does not entail recoupment in the legal sense, if it's a personal affront, or if it's a matter that cannot be settled on this most facilitated level of the judicial system, and if you've gotten nowhere but angrier—a stage you can easily detect by looking in the mirror—if your eyes are starting from your head, your face is the color of most of a Brian De Palma movie, and your hands keep twitching as if there were a neck between them—then go for the Bomb.

The Bomb can be anything from signing up the creep for a million mail order catalogues and magazine subscriptions to kidnapping children. But eschew the Bomb until you've read the rest of these rules. Because . . .

RULE TWO: *Take your time about getting even.*

What's the rush? The creep will be busy shafting others, will be kept nicely occupied ravaging the rest of the human race till you get to him/her. Letting some time elapse gives your target an opportunity to think s/he got away with it. In vengeance circles we call this lulling the *yotz* into a false sense of security. Also, it makes it less likely that you'll get tagged with the blame for whatever horror finally befalls the deserving degenerate.

Before we move on to Rule 3 allow me to give you a classic use of the incremental intensification of anger, culminating in the use of the Bomb.

A number of years ago it was the iniquitous practice of many paperback publishers to bind into their titles slick-paper sheets that featured cigarette and liquor advertisements. While I figure it's anybody's right to cauterize their *angst* by any means they deem appropriate, up to and including cigarettes, booze, cocaine and screwing chickens in the windows of The May Co., I'd as lief they didn't get encouraged in such practices by books with my name on them. And so it was written into my contracts that no such ads could be bound into my books without my written permission. At first, this caused some grumping from the publishers, whose anthracite souls were so tainted that they thought they'd win me over by telling me that I'd receive a pittance from such ads. I attempted to explain to them that making money off that kind of moral turpitude made it even grungier, but they couldn't quite parse that one. Nonetheless, I made it, as they say, a deal-breaker; and got my way.

Several years later, when one of my books with that publisher was reprinted, I discovered the new edition was festooned with cancer stick advertising. Not to put too fine a point on it, I went through the cottage cheese.

First I demanded that all copies of the book be recalled and pulped, and a new edition be released. I made this demand through my editor, a nice woman with limited power in such matters. She made the demand in my behalf and was told to forget it. That was phase one.

Then I had my literary agent in New York brace them. He went beyond the editor to a lesser executive. He was told to forget it. That was phase two.

Then *I* called the lesser executive, and was told to forget it. Phase three. He suggested I broach the subject to one of the Great Potentates At The Top. I did so, and was told . . .

That was phase four. Followed in rapid succession by phases five, six and seven: appeal from my attorney who was TTFI; threat from my attorney who was TTFI; appeal by a bestselling author who also published with that house, who was a close friend of mine, as an end-run attempting to avoid *sturm und drang*. He, too, was TTFI. When phase seven culminated with the assurance by the publisher to my attorney that if we chose to break the contract, we could sue for however many hundreds of thousands of dollars and hours it took to file in New York, but it would be a useless effort because before the case ever came to trial all those books would be sold, so in effect it was being TTFI.

At that point, since it was obvious the books would not be recalled, revenge took the form of demanding all rights to the title be returned to me. In other words, they had breached contract and the book was not theirs to sell any longer.

Guess what I was told by the Publisher? Do the song TTFI strike a familiar note?

At that point even my agent and my attorney told me there was nothing to be done about it.

They did not understand the powerful pull of rug beaters from the past. Nothing to be done? Wrong . . . and wrong.

Effortlessly I slipped into my guerilla warfare mode and embarked on phase eight, secure in the self-righteous knowledge that I had explored every possible avenue of arbitration. If it would cost a fortune to extricate my book from their clutches, then I would do it in another way: I would make their lives a living hell. I swore that when I got through with them, the arrogant eggsuckers would *gladly* revert the rights . . . they would *beg* me to take the rights back.

And thereupon began a program of terror the P.L.O. would have admired.

Which brings me to RULE THREE: *If you want revenge against a monolithic business structure, don't bother with the* schleppers *on the bottom who are thrown into the fray as cannon-fodder just to delay you and turn you aside from the real culprits.*

There was no point in harassing my editor. She was merely an employee without decision power. What I needed was the rock damming the stream. The upper level policymaker who had TTFI. Judicious inquiry netted me a name. The Comptroller of the publishing house. So I requested reversion of rights directly from him. TTFI. (This laborious litany of essentially boring attempts to strike reason into their hearts is proffered merely to flense your mind of any doubt that every rational means for settlement of an ugly situation was tried. It is necessary that those who observe your vendetta perceive that you have followed RULE FOUR: *Don't look like a maniac to outsiders. Cover your berserk activities so they appear sane and considered. Make the final recourse to the Bomb seem an inevitability caused by* their *intransigence, arrogance and stupidity.*)

Comptroller didn't return my phone calls. Comptroller didn't answer my letter of the 13th. Comptroller didn't respond to my telegram asking for reply to my letter of the 13th. I began mailing him bricks.

Until a few years ago, it was possible to send bills back to the phone company and MasterCharge without a stamp on the envelope. You may remember those halcyon days. It was paid for on the other end.

I started sending the Comptroller bricks. Two hundred and thirteen of them, average of ten a day; neatly wrapped in brown butcher's paper off a long roll I purchased. Got friends to do the same from other cities. Each one addressed personally to the Comptroller. Couldn't tell those neat little rectangular parcels of portentous weight were just bricks . . . till they were opened. Hundreds of bricks. No return address. No message. Just bricks. Personal: to the Comptroller. Deliver by Hand. Rush! Deadline Material! Hand Cancel. Do Not Crush! Fragile!

Then I stepped up the process. (RULE FIVE: *Try to have some fun with your revenge. By making it seem antic, it will weigh in your favor when the authorities come for you. I was only foolin' around, Inspector. Your Honor, I submit my client was just out of his tree with foolishness; please don't hang him.*)

After the first two hundred and thirteen, I sent forty a week. At the end of the month—having heard from friends that their mailings had been substantial and how long did I want them to continue this madness—I sent a small note to the Comptroller on Donny Osmond stationery—sometime remind me to tell you the hideous facts surrounding my gaining possession of Donny Osmond stationery—which missive said simply, "Now you have enough to build a safety bunker that *may* withstand my huffing and puffing. Or would you rather revert the rights to my book? Charmingly, Harlan Ellison."

Came a call from my editor, frenzied and trembling with a tone that indicated Great Forces Were About To Be Unleashed. Please stop annoying the Comptroller, I was advised. Wrong . . . and wrong. Tell the Comptroller, I said to her, that if he does not come off his high horse and release my book, I will not only mail him the *rest* of the shithouse, but I will see him *in* it! She sighed, knowing I wasn't bluffing, and went away.

RULE SIX: *Make sure they know you're capable of* anything. *Make sure they understand that you are slightly deranged and are* incapable *of bluffing. Make them understand this is* war.

A touch of paranoia doesn't hurt, either. I had used rubber gloves when packing the bricks. No prints. They'll never get me, Dutch!

But the Comptroller was that unbeatable combination of arrogant position of authority and stupidity for the long view, and he would not revert the rights. Phase nine was entered.

I know a lot of strange people. Perhaps you, too, know a lot of strange people. One of the strange people I know is a hit man. Sadly, he is not a first rank hit man. He is of the wrong ethnic background. He is a Lithuanian. Yes, I know it is to laugh: a Lithuanian hit man. But one does the best one can. He's a wonderful guy most of the time, but he is surely one of the world's most inept pistoleros. He once shot off two toes on his left foot. Don't ask.

He calls himself Sandor. That isn't his real name, but Sandor will do nicely for this recounting. I called Sandor and asked him a favor. He owed me one. (Ask me sometime to tell you about the Stuckey's Pecan Shop, the limping waitress, the twenty gallon milk can and how Sandor came to be in my debt.)

I found a photo of the Comptroller in a back issue of *Publishers Weekly*, gave Sandor the address of the publishing house, and asked him merely to throw the Fear of Death into the Comptroller without harming even a hair on his aging head.

Well, about a week later Sandor calls (collect) and tells me what happened: first of all, it's the killing heat of summer and Sandor is wearing a heavy topcoat when he accosts the Comptroller on the street outside the publishing house in Manhattan. Picture, if you will, this six foot three inch tall, pockmarked, very pale, sweating penguin with a voice steeped at the bottom of a bourbon bottle. Now imagine yourself coming out of your office building at the end of a wearying day, lugging your cabretta-grain attaché case, not looking forward to the train ride back to New Rochelle, and suddenly this apparition is walking along beside you, with his powerful arm draped over your shoulder, and he's whispering in your ear, "Your son's name is Michael, your daughter's name is Michele; she goes to the Cadwaller School on Long Island, he is up at Harvard; you live on Grove Avenue in Larchmont, you got a lousy old-fashioned Dictograph alarm system; and if it is that you catch my drift, Sunny Jim, and if you come home tonight and find their foreheads nailed to the living room wall, you will understand why you should revert the rights to Ellison's book; otherwise I cut off your head with a potato peeler and mail the hairy thing C.O.D. to your family."

And he vanished into the crowd.

Next day I get a call from my editor, who is hysterical. What are you doing to this old man!?! He's got a heart condition!?! Are you crazy!?!

So I wrote the Comptroller a letter. My mother had only recently died of a heart condition, and I felt it was in the interests of the commonweal to apprise him of recent statistics on coronaries, the best hospitals in the area for such conditions, a Xerox copy of an article from the *Journal of the AMA* on the latest Pacemaker research; you know, the kind of data a man concerned about his health might need in an emergency. I did not write it on Donny Osmond stationery. When dealing with serious subjects, frivolity should be eschewed.

Got to hand it to him. The Comptroller was a worthy adversary. True grit. He would not cave in. I felt a swelling respect for his tenacity in the face of such loathsome behavior. Got another call from my editor. In tears. The word *please* was repeated many times. I said all it took to make me go away was a letter of reversion of rights. She said she'd make one more appeal. The response: TTFI.

It seemed impossible even to me, because I was about to pack it in, fearing I might Go Too Far, when phase ten—more awful than anything that went before—presented itself to me inadvertently.

I had a gopher problem at my home. Nasty little hummers would come out in the morning and eat anything that couldn't run away from them. So I called in the landscape exterminating company, and at enormous expense found they couldn't do a damned thing. But we did get one little devil. There he was, half-in, half-out of his hole, dead as Reagan's concern for the poor, his little lips skinned back from his vicious teeth in a ghastly death rictus, the little clawed paws reaching up for life, eyeballs rolled back in his skull. We're talking yuccchh here, folks.

I mailed the dead gopher to the Comptroller.

Fourth class mail.

With Ted Cogswell's brilliantly vomitous recipe for braised gopher stew.

Fourth class mail.

It took about two weeks to reach the publishing house. I'm told by the time it hit the Chicago shunting station it was *elegant*. What Pasolini used to call *Mondo Pukeo*.

Got a call from my editor. Inarticulate. Crazed. Foaming and screaming about having had to fumigate the entire mail room of the publishing company. Three days later, my book was reverted.

Save the Bomb, or the gopher, until the very last moment.

RULE SEVEN: *Your target will inevitably provide you with the means to get even.*

They make mistakes. I know a guy who was getting a series of crank phone calls from a jerk that went on for about six months. Five and six a day. Hauled him dripping out of the shower, interrupted him in the throes of lovemaking, annoyed him when he was working, woke him from depths of sleep at four in the morning, drove his family nuts. The suffering guy bit his lip, bided his time, and waited. Inevitably, the jerk made the error of calling collect, using the name of someone the harassed guy knew, and when he accepted the call and realized it was the jerk, he had the operator hold the line open, got the number calling, fed it back through friends at the phone company who advised him it was a private school in Colorado Springs, Colorado, called the number back, got another student who said, "Oh, yeah, it was Jimmy X (a fictitious name) using the phone a minute ago." This guy I know took a plane to Colorado, rented a car, drove out to the school, located the kid and beat the crap out of him.

Now *that's* revenge.

RULE EIGHT: *It's not enough merely to get even. You have to get a little better.* That's called "the vigerish." It is the interest taken out of you in mental anguish, discomfort, lousy feelings, theft of a piece of your self-respect.

Which ties into RULE NINE: *An eye for an eye is the best yardstick for revenge.* If someone steals your watch, you don't shoot him in the head. That's not even up. It's, pardon the expression, overkill. But an eye for an eye is okay if you add an eye*lid* as vigerish.

And finally, RULE TEN, and this one is important, gang. *There are* some *people one should never screw with.*

There is the wife of a friend of mine for whom I have substantial loathing. Not only because of the kind of person she is, but because of the kind of person she's turned my friend into. Yet I would rather have my nose hairs burned out with a Bic lighter than mess with her. Even were I to win the war, I would go to my grave with her teeth in my throat.

The passion for revenge should never blind you to the pragmatics of the situation. There are *some* people who are so blighted by their past, so warped by experience and the pull of that silken cord, that they never free themselves of the shadows that live in the time machine.

They are the ones who have never given up the search for Dr. Mengele. They are the ones who think like a ninja. They are dangerous and know no bounds. They are little boys whose dogs have been gassed and their example is one a rational person seeking redress in anger should never forget.

Because in a very real way, they are doomed to live in perpetual fire. As they have driven in the spikes, so too have they been condemned to bear the stigmata of their own wounds.

And if there is a kind thought due them, it may be found contained in the words of the late Gerald Kersh, who wrote: ". . . there are men whom one hates until a certain moment when one sees, through a chink in their armour, the writhing of something nailed down and in torment."

Afterword

by Harlan Ellison

For a brief time I was here; and for a brief time I mattered.

(Continued from page vi)

"The Prowler in the City at the Edge of the World" originally appeared in DANGEROUS VISIONS [edited by Harlan Ellison]; copyright © 1967 by Harlan Ellison. Renewed, copyright © 1995 by Harlan Ellison.

"Along the Scenic Route" (under the title "Dogfight on 101") originally appeared simultaneously in *Adam* magazine and *Amazing Stories* magazine; copyright © 1969 by Harlan Ellison.

"The Song the Zombie Sang" (written in collaboration with Robert Silverberg) originally appeared in *Cosmopolitan* magazine; copyright © 1970 by Harlan Ellison and Robert Silverberg.

"Knox" originally appeared in *Crawdaddy* magazine; copyright © 1974 by Harlan Ellison.

"From Alabamy, with Hate" (under the title "March to Montgomery") originally appeared in *Knight* magazine; copyright © 1965 by Sirkay Publishing Company. Copyright reassigned to Author 23 March 1970. Copyright. © 1970 by Harlan Ellison. Renewed, copyright © 1993 by Harlan Ellison.

"My Mother" originally appeared as an installment of *The Harlan Ellison Hornbook,* a column of personal comment, in the *St. Louis Literary Supplement*; copyright © 1976 by the Saint Louis Literary Supplement, Inc. Copyright reassigned to Author 14 July 1977. Copyright © 1977 by Harlan Ellison.

"Tired Old Man" originally appeared in *Mike Shayne Mystery Magazine;* copyright © 1975 by Harlan Ellison.

"Gopher in the Gilly" originally appeared in STALKING THE NIGHTMARE; copyright © 1982 by The Kilimanjaro Corporation.

"Strange Wine" originally appeared in *Amazing* magazine; copyright © 1976 by Harlan Ellison.

"The Resurgence of Miss Ankle-Strap Wedgie" originally appeared in LOVE AIN'T NOTHING BUT SEX MISSPELLED; copyright © 1968 by Harlan Ellison. Renewed, copyright © 1996 by Harlan Ellison.

"The Man on the Mushroom" originally appeared in ELLISON WONDERLAND; copyright © 1974 by Harlan Ellison.

"Somehow, I Don't Think We're in Kansas, Toto" originally appeared in shorter form in *Genesis* magazine; copyright © 1974 by Harlan Ellison. Revised version copyright ©1982 by The Kilimanjaro Corporation.

"Soldier" (under the title "Soldier from Tomorrow") originally appeared in *Fantastic Universe* magazine; copyright © 1957 by King-Size Publications, Inc. Renewed, copyright ©1985 by Harlan Ellison.

"The Night of Delicate Terrors" originally appeared in *The Paper: A Chicago Weekly;* copyright © 1961 by The Paper, Inc. Renewed, copyright © 1989 by Harlan Ellison.

"Shattered Like a Glass Goblin" originally appeared in ORBIT 4 [edited by Damon Knight]; copyright © 1968 by Damon Knight. Copyright reassigned to Author 19 September 1969. Copyright © 1969 by Harlan Ellison. Renewed, copyright © 1996 by Harlan Ellison.

ABOUT THE EDITORS

TERRY DOWLING is an Australian writer and critic with outstanding credentials. Composer, college instructor, essayist and co-editor (with Dr. Van Ikin) of the prestigious *Science Fiction: A Review of Speculative Literature,* Mr. Dowling performed the enviable trick of winning two of Australia's highest accolades in 1983: the "Ditmar" (the Australian equivalent of America's "Hugo") for Best Fiction; and the William Atheling Award for Best Critical Work (a study of the work of Jack Vance). Since then he has won at least four or five more Ditmars (1985, 1986, 1989, 1990) for Best Short Story. It may be six or seven: who can keep track! (In fact, it's nine; this week.)

A graduate with MA Honors from the University of Sydney, he currently teaches at a large Sydney college, performs his own musical compositions regularly on Australian television, and his first book, RYNOSSEROS, a cycle of stories set in a future Australia, was published by Aphelion in late 1990, to spectacular reviews: "Think of an imagination steeped in the stories of Cordwainer Smith, J. G. Ballard, and Jack Vance, then grant that Terry Dowling has his own formidable intelligence, and you'll get a notion of the riches this book offers. RYNOSSEROS places Dowling among the masters of the field." (Farren Miller in *Locus.)*

RICHARD DELAP was a well-known critic, reviewer, essayist and, for many years, editor and publisher of *Delap's Fantasy & Science Fiction Review.* He edited Peter Balin's 1978 book on Mayan mythology, THE FLIGHT OF THE FEATHERED SERPENT and, between 1981 and 1986, spent considerable time rewriting film scripts while living in Hollywood. Richard Delap was co-author (with Walt Lee) of the horror novel SHAPES, and was working on another novel, DARKER THAN BLOOD, at the time of his tragic and untimely death in 1987. His was the initial work on THE ESSENTIAL ELLISON. Ill health prevented his completion of the book. Mr. Dowling assumed the project late in 1983. Richard Delap, terminally ill in a Los Angeles hospital, lived long enough to hold this book in its first hardcover publication. It remains a testament to his talent and hard work.

GIL LAMONT has excelled in virtually every aspect of publishing for more than twenty years. Published author, editor, critic and bibliophile, he is best known to those in the book industry as quite simply the finest, most punctilious copyeditor and proofreader in the business. (At last count he had read the book you hold 23 times. Every last word of it.) For a time he was Fiction Editor of one of the brief reemergences of *Weird Tales;* he was, in large part, responsible for the pre-publication work on MEDEA: HARLAN'S WORLD, AN EDGE IN MY VOICE, and HARLAN ELLISON'S WATCHING. He swears he has never read *Fish Police* comics.